Home Sweet Home Front

by

Richard Veit

WingSpan Press
Livermore, California

Published in the United States and the United Kingdom
by WingSpan Press, Livermore, CA

The WingSpan name, logo and colophon are the trademarks of WingSpan Publishing.

www.wingspanpress.com

Second edition 2020

Printed in the United States of America

Publisher's Cataloging-in-Publication Data

Veit, Richard.
Home sweet home front / Richard Veit.
p. cm.
ISBN: 978-1-59594-692-8 (hardcover)
ISBN: 978-1-59594-501-3 (pbk.)
ISBN: 978-1-59594-848-9 (e-book)
1. World War, 1939-1945—Fiction. 2. Coming of age—Fiction.
3. Families—Texas—Fiction. 4. Texas—Fiction.   I. Title.
PS3622.E427 H66 2013
813—dc23

2013944557

1 2 3 4 5 6 7 8 9 10

ACKNOWLEDGMENTS

Richard Veit wishes to express gratitude to the men and women of the Allied forces, who placed their lives on the line against the Axis foe during World War II. Among this heroic generation were Mr. Veit's father, Richard Earl Veit, his uncle, Wesley Arthur Veit, and his wife Patti's uncles, James Philip Haston and Robert Weldon Haston. The author would also like to thank two friends and literary mentors, American playwright Horton Foote and English screenwriter John Finch, for their invaluable influence and encouragement. Further appreciation goes to Baylor University and the city of Waco, Texas, without whose historical settings—in time and place—this book's honest depiction of the American home front would have been impossible to achieve.

Home Sweet Home Front

Wesley Franklin Brower fell in love with radio the instant he set foot in the lobby of KWXN. The first thing that seized his attention was a metal paperweight lying on the front desk—an RCA microphone with the vertical letters "CBS" affixed to each side. "Five Star Jones" could be heard from a pair of loudspeakers overhead. Behind the desk, the wall was paneled in rich hardwood and bedecked with framed publicity photographs of Eddie Cantor, Al Jolson, Cecil B. DeMille (autographed), and Burns and Allen.

Even the receptionist was elegant, a pretty brunette who spoke to him with what seemed to be genuine respect. "Yes, sir. How may I help you?" she asked. Her lovely smile made him go weak in the knees.

"I'm delivering a package for Superior Office Supply," Wesley said. "My dad told me to bring it over here on my way back to school." Then, to explain his apparent truancy, he added, "I've been home for lunch."

"Oh, you have, have you? Well, thank you ever so much, Mr. ...?"

"I'm Wesley Brower ... but my friends call me Wes."

"Well, thank you ever so much, Mr. Wesley Brower. I'm sure we were needing this package very badly."

"Yes, ma'am. It's just a letter opener, a pencil sharpener, and a couple of ink wells."

She smiled at him again, and despite intense effort, he could feel his face beginning to redden. A moment later, when she returned to her telephone duties, he noticed the nameplate on the desk: "Miss Elkins."

As Wesley walked toward the doorway, repeating her name over and over to himself, he was impressed by the way the people around him were dressed. A distinguished gentleman with gray hair was talking to two younger men. All were attired in expensive-looking, pin-striped, black or charcoal suits, and their shoes gleamed like polished mirrors. To an excitable, nine-year-old mind, these men seemed to be shady figures from the underworld, but in actuality they were probably salesmen.

Wesley Brower was nearly sixteen when he again found himself standing in the lobby of the radio station. That was in October of 1942. Sadly, Miss Elkins was no longer there, and a portly woman of about sixty now occupied the front desk. But she was friendly and helpful, which made his ordeal just that much easier. He had come looking for a job.

Elaine Overmire directed Wesley to a small table, where he was required to fill out the application form. In the square for age, he stretched the truth to "16," reasoning that his birthday was only four weeks away, and certainly nothing would turn up before then. Sorrow stabbed at him when he reached a line requesting "Parent or Guardian's Name (if applicant is under 21)," for Harold Brower, the boy's father, had died suddenly of heart failure four years earlier.

Wesley was sitting at his desk in school when the news came. Mrs. Taylor was called to the door, where the principal stood, surveying the class. She said something to Mr. Jamieson, who closed his eyes and nodded his head. A moment later, Wesley sensed that the principal looked directly at him, although from his vantage point across the room he could not really be sure. When Mrs. Taylor approached his desk and quietly asked him to report to the principal's office, something in her tone of voice made him shudder with fear.

The office door was open when he arrived, so Wesley took a hesitant step inside. Mr. Jamieson was standing with his back toward him, but he turned around when he heard the boy enter. "Have a seat, Wesley." He motioned to the children's chair near his desk. Mr. Jamieson made no eye contact, and Wesley noticed that the principal's hands were shaking as he spoke.

"I'm afraid I have some bad news for you, son."

Wesley thought at once of his loved ones—Mommy, Daddy, Steve, Lizzie, Grandma Coleman, Uncle Matt. Mr. Jamieson cleared his throat and finally looked straight at the boy.

"It's your daddy, Wesley. Your momma's brother called and said they found him unconscious at work. He was gone before they could even get him to the hospital." The principal put a strong hand on the boy's shoulder. "I'm sorry, son. You're excused to go home, of course. Your Uncle Matthew will pick you up in a few minutes. You just wait here, and I'll go retrieve your books and jacket."

Wesley appreciated not having to go back to the classroom, and he never forgot this small act of kindness on the principal's part. Mr. Jamieson sat with him in his office until Uncle Matt arrived to take him home.

"Mr. Brower, if you'll come with me, they'd like you to do a mike test while you're here." Mrs. Overmire, application in hand, opened a door leading to a long hallway and waited for Wesley to follow.

"Now ...?" Wesley asked. He was stunned by the suddenness of the employment process.

"If you don't mind. We prefer to attach an evaluation to the application form, if we possibly can."

Wesley stood up and did as he was told. It did not take a keen observer of the human condition to see that this teenager was suffering from acute stage fright. "Don't worry," whispered the receptionist. "It's pretty straightforward. You'll do fine."

The announcing booth was just slightly larger than a broom closet—perhaps five feet by seven feet. It was heavily padded, with thick acoustic insulation on walls and ceiling. Near the window, at eye level, hung an RCA 44-BX microphone on a short metal boom. What appeared to be an ordinary music stand stood directly beneath the microphone.

"Give me a voice level, please," came instructions over the speaker.

Wesley was unsure what to do. "I ... uh ... don't understand."

"Just say 'Mary had a little lamb. Its fleece was white as snow.' We need to set a mike level on the pot."

Wesley took a deep breath and quoted the nursery rhyme.

"That's fine. Hollis will be bringing you some copy to read," the same disembodied voice said. "Stand a little closer to the mike, please."

The door opened, and an elderly man, presumably "Hollis," handed Wesley some United Press news copy. "Read this when the red light comes on," he said. "We'll give you a couple of minutes to look it over." The door closed with an airtight *thump*.

Off in the distance, across a darkened studio, Wesley could see three or four men lounging around a smoke-filled control room. Hollis disappeared into the darkness and then emerged to join the others. There was absolute silence. Wesley looked down at the two jagged sheets of yellow newsprint, which he felt sure would either make or break his radio career. He scanned the words, hoping to find no "solipsisms" or "pokladnas."

After an intense five minutes, during which Wesley scrutinized his script so many times that he could nearly repeat it from memory, a more resonant—almost Wellesian—voice came over the booth's loudspeaker: "Have you had enough time to look over the copy?" Wesley's mouth went dry. Years of faithful listening left no doubt whatsoever that he was now in the rarefied presence of Marshall McFall, the Dean of Central Texas Announcers.

Wesley cleared his throat and mumbled something to the effect of, "Yes, sir. I guess I think I have." Then he looked up, waiting for the executioner to throw the switch. The red light came on. His mike was open. He began reciting.

HERE ARE THE LATEST NEWS HEADLINES FROM THE UNITED PRESS ...

GERMAN AND RUSSIAN REPORTS TODAY INDICATED THAT WINTER IS BEGINNING TO CLOSE DOWN ON THE LONG RUSSIAN FRONT ... FROM THE APPROACHES TO THE CAUCASUS OIL COUNTRY TO THE BATTLEGROUNDS OF LENINGRAD AND THE FAR NORTH.

THE NAVY ANNOUNCED TODAY THAT AN ENEMY SUBMARINE HAD TORPEDOED BUT FAILED TO SINK A MEDIUM-SIZED UNITED STATES MERCHANT VESSEL OFF THE PACIFIC COAST. THE ATTACK OCCURRED SEVERAL DAYS AGO AND SURVIVORS HAVE LANDED AT A WEST COAST PORT.

CHIEF FRED S. WALLACE OF THE AGRICULTURAL ADJUSTMENT AGENCY SAID TODAY THAT ALTHOUGH 1942 SET AGRICULTURAL PRODUCTION RECORDS, MORE IS NEEDED FOR NEXT YEAR AND ... QUOTE ... "WE SHOULD EXAMINE OURSELVES TO SEE IF WE ARE DOING ALL WE CAN TO WIN THIS WAR."

THE WAR DEPARTMENT TODAY ASKED CONGRESS FOR IMMEDIATE ENACTMENT OF LEGISLATION TO REDUCE THE DRAFT AGE TO EIGHTEEN, IN LINE WITH PRESIDENT ROOSEVELT'S ENDORSEMENT OF THAT PROPOSAL IN HIS RADIO ADDRESS LAST NIGHT.

AND ...

BRITISH FOUR-MOTORED BOMBING PLANES ATTACKED INDUSTRIAL AREAS OF NORTHERN GERMANY DURING THE NIGHT, AT THE COST OF ONLY TWO PLANES. GERMANY, ADMITTING DAMAGE TO NORTHERN AND EASTERN GERMANY BY INCENDIARY BOMBS, SAID SEVERAL PLANES WERE SHOT DOWN.

Wesley stopped reading and breathlessly watched for the red light to go dark. Though he had flubbed "incendiary" and momentarily stumbled over "immediate enactment," overall he was quite pleased with himself. In fact, he wished he could keep the news copy as a souvenir, but he decided that might not seem "professional." When the door finally opened, he handed the copy to Hollis, who escorted him back to the lobby.

Mrs. Overmire was busy on the telephone, so Wesley waved goodbye to her as he walked by. She did not notice him and continued reading off a set of figures from the station's rate card. "Pepper Young's Family" was on the air, and Wesley listened while viewing the revised collection of framed photographs on the wall behind her desk: Major Edward Bowes, Fred Allen, Cecil B. DeMille (autographed), and Kate Smith. Then he wandered out to where he had left his bicycle for the two-mile ride home.

Hollis returned to the studio, tossed the United Press wire copy into the wastebasket, and lit up another cigarette.

◆   ◆   ◆

"Portia Faces Life," said National Broadcasting Company announcer George A. Putnam, "a story reflecting the courage, spirit, and integrity of American women everywhere ..."

It was 4:15 on a Tuesday afternoon, and Nora Brower was in the kitchen, pressing her family's laundry. She always positioned her ironing board near the table radio, so the Frigidaire's cycling motor would not disturb her enjoyment of the daytime serials. These were her only escape from an otherwise spartan routine of housework and doing her bit for the war effort. Monthly stipends from the administrator of Superior Office Supply enabled her to manage the home while still keeping food on the table. Like frugal women across the nation, she lived by the wartime slogan of "Use it up, wear it out, make it do, or do without."

Nora never had to change the dial from 820 kilocycles during the four-o'clock hour because WBAP in Fort Worth and WFAA in Dallas carried a succession of her NBC favorites on that uniquely apportioned frequency. "When a Girl Marries" had just ended, and today's installments of "Just Plain Bill" and "Front Page Farrell" were yet to come. Her younger son, Wesley, was already upstairs, tackling his homework, but Nora knew that within fifteen minutes he would be sprawled in front of the Philco radio/phonograph cabinet for "Superman" on WACO. Dinner tonight would be baked chicken with store-bought sweet corn and homegrown black-eyed peas.

The other two children, Elizabeth and Steve, were also home—she talking to her best friend, Susan Keeley, on the telephone, and he lifting his barbells. Nora could hear the weights striking the floor above her, despite the layers of rugged gymnasium matting that Steve borrowed from Coach Harry Stiteler.

Stephen Collins Brower was the athlete in the family, a strapping 180-pound fullback who seemed destined for Baylor University's gridiron squad until the war intervened. Now he was anxious to enlist in the Navy, though his mother first made him promise to complete his senior year at Waco High School. Steve had turned seventeen on July Fourth, a patriotic birthday he shared with nineteenth-century composer Stephen Collins Foster, in whose honor his music-loving father named him.

Elizabeth Ivy Brower, on the other hand, was the namesake of her maternal grandmother, Ivy Elizabeth (Hahn) Coleman. Though she went by "Beth" at school, her relatives and close friends continued to call her "Lizzie." She was fourteen, two years younger than the middle child, Wesley, and an active leader in neighborhood scrap drives. Her enthusiasm was positively contagious. During the fall, the team that she captained managed to collect the highest volume of discarded metal among all eighth graders citywide. Elizabeth played the piano for her Sunday school department and the flute in the North Junior High School band.

Over the sound of "Portia Faces Life," Nora heard footsteps running down the stairway and glanced over her shoulder to see who it was. Elizabeth entered the kitchen with a conspiratorial gleam in her eye. "Mother, do you know what Susan saw in today's newspaper? You'll never guess!"

"I'm sure I don't know," Nora said. "I saw the paper after breakfast, but I didn't notice anything out of the ordinary." She resumed ironing.

"Not this morning's paper. The *Times-Herald*."

"I give up, Lizzie. Tell me."

"Marsha Dent is getting married ... on Friday, week."

Nora looked up, still moving the iron. "No! Our little Marsha at the USO?"

"That's what Susan told me. Her mother saw it in the paper and showed it to her."

"But she's only sixteen. Are you sure there isn't some mistake?"

Elizabeth flashed a mischievous smile and made certain no one else was within earshot. "That's just it, Mother. There *was* some kind of mistake, and that's why she has to get married."

Her mother looked embarrassed. "Lizzie!"

"Well, can you explain it otherwise? She doesn't have a boyfriend. Susan says Marsha wasn't even dating anyone ... at least from school. Just dancing with those Army guys from the airfield."

"Doesn't the newspaper say who the bridegroom is?"

Elizabeth took a step closer to the ironing board. "No, it doesn't, and that's what's so mysterious about this whole thing. It just says 'Marsha Dent of this city announces her wedding plans for December 4 at Austin Avenue Methodist.' Susan was so upset she was nearly crying."

"Are they close friends?"

"I guess so. Of course, Susan's just in the eighth grade like me, but they must know each other from church."

"I thought Susan went to First Baptist."

"She does, and so does Marsha Dent. But for some reason the wedding's going to be at Austin Avenue Methodist."

The 4:30 station break caught Nora's ear, and Elizabeth apologized for interrupting her mother's listening.

"Oh, don't worry about that. Portia can get along fine without me." Nora examined the white blouse she was ironing. "Listen, if it'll make you and Susan feel better, I'll give Mabel Johns a call after dinner. She knows the Dents."

"Can't you do it now?"

"No, not now. I'm busy and so is Mabel, I'm sure." She folded the blouse. "You know, this just shocks the daylights out of me ... if what you say is true. I didn't think Marsha was that kind of girl."

"I don't know—those uniforms can do awfully funny things to a girl," Elizabeth said. She giggled when her startled mother looked up at her.

Nora shook her head. "And I don't want you hanging around that USO unless I'm right there with you."

"Yes, ma'am. You sure don't have to worry about that."

Tssssssshhhhhhhh. The water in the pot of black-eyed peas had bubbled over and was dripping into the gas burner.

"Oh, dear. Turn that down for me, will you, Lizzie? Just let it simmer."

While Elizabeth took care of that minor emergency, Nora unplugged the iron and laid it upright on the kitchen counter. She folded the legs of the ironing board, turned it on its side, and carried it, cradled in both arms, toward the utility closet. Then she remembered something and stopped short. "Oh, Lizzie, would you ask Wes to go buy some coffee for me? Maxwell House. We're all out, and I don't want to have to run to the store in the morning. Moek's doesn't open until 8:30."

"Can't we have it delivered?"

Nora put the ironing board away and brushed some loose strands of hair from her eyes. "Now, I'm not going to have poor Russell Mimms trek all the way over here with a one-pound package of coffee—not with two able-bodied young men in the house. Steve will be all sweaty from his exercising, so Wes can do it after 'Superman' finishes." She walked over to her ration box. "He'll need to take a coffee coupon with him—number 27—and there's a half-dollar lying next to the toaster." She handed the coupon to her daughter and heard the heavy tread of her older son's footsteps coming down the stairs.

Steve, breathless and with a towel draped around his neck, came into the kitchen to get some ice water from the refrigerator. He was sweating profusely, and the accompanying odor contorted the faces of his mother and sister.

"You're dripping all over the floor!" Elizabeth squealed.

Steve swallowed a mouthful of water and smiled at her. "You should have seen me before I dried off."

Elizabeth held her nose with her right hand, grasped the coin beside the coupon in her left, and hurried from the room.

"Honestly, Steve, you really should take a shower before you come down here," Nora said.

He emptied his glass and began pouring another. "Couldn't wait, Mom. Too thirsty."

"Who do you play on Friday?"

He raised an index finger, as if to scold his mother. "*Whom.*"

Nora laughed. "All right, 'whom' do you play this Friday?" She shook her head and walked over to the gas range. "You know, 'Mr. Clifton Fadiman,' you're getting too smart for your own good." She stirred the black-eyed peas.

"Sorry. I just happened to have a good English teacher last year. It's been drilled into me." He reached into the cupboard for some potato chips. "Our game is against Bryan High. Their coach used to play for Baylor." Steve stuffed a few chips into his mouth and continued talking with his mouth full. "Name's Pete Jones. Ever hear of him?"

"I don't think so. Why?"

"He was the captain of Baylor's team in 1928—back when they played on campus instead of at Muny Stadium. You remember Carroll Field?"

"I've heard of Carroll Field, but that's about all," she said. "I never saw it."

"It stood where they're constructing that new student union building now—there and Minglewood Bowl, I guess." He took the towel from his neck and wiped the perspiration off his face. "The game's going to be on radio."

"Is it really? What time?"

"At 7:55 on WACO—but they won't be carrying the half-hour from 8:30 to 9:00."

"That's silly. Why not?"

"I guess they don't have any choice," Steve said. He munched a fresh mouthful of chips. "Someone at school said the station has to carry 'Spotlight Bands' and 'Gracie Fields,' or the Blue Network might cancel their contract."

"Well, I think a radio station's first loyalty should be to its community."

"Hah! That's not the way the real world operates." He patted the top of his mother's head. "Don't worry. I'll make sure that I don't score unless we're on the air."

◆　　　◆　　　◆

As the Christmas season approached in 1942, Wesley had abandoned all hope of securing a position with the radio station, so he took on a morning newspaper route instead. Though by nature an early riser, within four days he reached the conclusion that crawling out of bed at 4:15 was beyond the pale of reasonable behavior. Still, he persisted.

One thing he did like about throwing the *News-Tribune* was the sense of solitude it afforded him—particularly during the early stretches of his delivery routine, prior to 5:30, when the streets were nearly deserted. For blocks at a time, he would not see another human being, and except for an occasional dog bark, the early-morning silence would only be broken by the sound of his bicycle tires rotating against the pavement. The cold air felt good on his face, and it was a pleasant sensation to exhale in short puffs, allowing his condensed breath to hang like miniature clouds around him.

He never failed to see Frank Jackey, the Pure Milk man, who had been a welcome visitor to the Brower household long before Wesley was born. Now the pair would wave hello as they passed each other, which usually occurred on either Homan or Lyle, just as Wesley was beginning his return trip home. Mr. Jackey drove standing up, with the doors wide open, and Wesley envied his freedom. While most motorists were restricted to three gallons of gasoline a week, deliverymen—with "C" stickers on their windshields—sailed far above such petty concerns. As effortlessly as gods, they simply filled up their fuel tanks and signed company vouchers before leaving the motor pool each morning.

Even in the short time that he had been a paperboy, Wesley noticed a marked increase in the number of homes displaying Son in Service flags in their front windows. Each of these vertical banners consisted of a small star on a white field, bordered in red and suspended from above by a heavy gold cord. So far, every such star that Wesley saw was blue in color, emblematic of a family member serving in the military. He had never yet encountered a gold star, which signified that a father, husband, brother, or son had been killed in the war. He knew there were some around—the Jacksons on Maple, the McDuffs on North Sixteenth, the Bellamys on Grim—but they were not on his route.

One Monday after school, as Wesley walked home from his friend Morton Wilson's house, he could see his mother talking with the postman, Mr. Bill Johnston, who had just handed her the afternoon mail. The wind was out of the northwest and bitterly cold, so it pummeled Wesley directly in the face with every step he took. Despite the protection of his heavy coat and gloves, he felt chilled to the bone. When his mother and Mr. Johnston turned to greet him, so benumbed were his facial muscles that all he could manage in response were some slurred syllables of incoherent grunting. It was embarrassing, but even he had to laugh at his inability to produce normal human speech.

"Why don't you go inside?" his mother said. "I was just hanging this wreath when the mail came. I'll heat up some soup for you."

Still red-faced and laughing, Wesley opened the front door and tossed a nod of goodbye in the direction of Mr. Johnston. Once the door closed behind him, it felt wonderfully warm in the house. He took off his gloves, then his coat and scarf, and only his feet remained cold. As Wesley changed out of his school clothes, he heard the front door slamming shut and his mother clanging a saucepan in the kitchen.

"Campbell's chicken noodle," he shouted.

"Okay," came Nora's shout in reply. "Hurry on down. I have something important to tell you."

Wesley descended the stairs three steps at a time, keeping a loose grip on the handrail just in case he stumbled. He could hear a Sterling Drugs commercial on the kitchen radio, so he knew either "Lorenzo Jones" or "Young Widder Brown" must be on NBC. A glance at the electric wall clock told him the former must be just ending.

"Get yourself some crackers and sit down, Wes," Nora said. "I'll have it ready for you in a jiffy."

He took a cardboard box of saltine crackers from the pantry and laid it on the kitchen table, where he settled in a chair facing his mother. "You wanted to tell me something?" He began eating a cracker.

"You got a telephone call today from the radio station."

"No kidding? From KWXN?" A smile beamed across his face.

"I guess so. The Columbia station."

"I'd about given up on them. Did they say what they wanted?"

Nora laid a steaming bowl of chicken noodle soup in front of Wesley. So scalding was it that she needed a pair of hot pads to transport the bowl over to the table. "No, he didn't say, but I'll bet he wants to offer you a job. You're supposed to call him back as soon as you can."

"Who was it? Anyone you'd ever heard of?"

"No." She picked up a slip of paper from the counter and read it. "Mr. Roger Devlin at 2-8-6-7. His voice sounded very official."

"Do you think I should call him now?"

"No, you go ahead and finish your soup first. He said he'd be there until five."

"But it's too hot to eat. Besides, I'd rather call before Steve and Lizzie get home."

"Well, Lizzie's staying over at Frieda's house for dinner, so you don't have to worry about her. I'm not sure when Steve will be home. He's getting some training in civilian defense—he and a couple of his friends. You know, Billy Paul's father is an air raid warden."

Wesley heard the familiar voice of George Ansbro on the radio: "Now it's time for 'Young Widder Brown'." The boy blew on a spoonful of soup to cool it down, but to no immediate avail. "'Young Widder Brown'," the announcer continued, "the story of the age-old conflict between a mother's duty and a woman's heart."

◆　　◆　　◆

It would be untruthful to say that Wesley was overwhelmed by the magnificence of KWXN's newsroom. In fact, he was downright disappointed. No doubt this was more a function of his own unreasonable expectations than any intrinsic shortcomings of the room itself. Wesley simply was anticipating too much from the number two station in a small market.

The only radio newsroom that he could remember seeing was a breathtaking photograph of WGN's facility in Chicago—snapped on an incredibly busy news day (or was it staged by the *Chicago Tribune* photographer?)—with cigar-chomping reporters frantically hunting and pecking the latest fast-breaking stories, pageboys trampling each other to carry communiqués from desk to desk, and an assemblage of wall clocks proclaiming the precise times in such exotic places as Manila, Cairo, and Rio de Janeiro.

KWXN's newsroom consisted of six desks, with typewriters and candlestick telephones, and a single teletype machine. The clock showed Central War Time.

Wesley labored under no delusions as to how he had landed the weekend news reporter's job, for his announcing voice, though passable, was still untrained and immature. He had not yet learned to project from the diaphragm, a failing that, despite his most careful articulation, conspicuously betrayed the tender years of inexperience.

No, it was just that KWXN, in common with most business establishments of the day, had found itself seriously short of manpower. Three full-time announcers had enlisted, one was drafted, and two weekenders had quit—one to resume his studies and possibly avoid conscription, and the other to accept a customary forty-eight-hour position at the Bluebonnet Ordnance Plant in McGregor.

Wesley's job in radio was to gather, write, and present a total of five evening newscasts—three on Saturday and two on Sunday—each of which was five minutes in duration (four minutes if sponsored). For the first weekend, December 19 and 20, he tagged along after his predecessor, Myron Burgess, who had suddenly felt drawn to increase his study load at Baylor University and thus would be leaving the station's employ at mid-week.

Myron showed Wesley how to check the county and city law enforcement blotters (or, in the parlance, "SO" and "PD"), as well as the myriad other regular stops that might turn up leads for public consumption. "You'll need about ninety seconds' worth of local stuff," he explained. "The rest is just 'rip and read' from UP."

The teenager soon learned that Myron Burgess's driving habits were eccentric, to say the least. He parked the news unit wherever it happened to coast to a stop after he turned off the ignition. He used the rear-view mirror as a vanity for in-transit mustache trimming. He backed up like a contortionist, with the door ajar and his head nearly resting on the running board. And on well-lit streets he doused his headlights, "… in case we come under enemy attack." He seemed blissfully ignorant of the thirty-five-miles-per-hour nationwide speed limit.

Wesley would never forget his first actual newscast, which he delivered at 10:55 P.M. on Sunday, December 20, 1942. Myron Burgess was in the booth with him—ostensibly for moral support, though he clearly seemed more concerned with the relative merits of Chesterfields and Old Golds than with Wesley's maiden voyage through the ether. The lead stories that night were the Russian Army's winter offensive in the Don Valley and the record-shattering cold wave that had New England in its grip. Locally, the headliner was the opening of Providence Hospital's *Ask for the Moon*, a three-act comedy at Sacred Heart Academy to raise money for the purchase of war bonds.

Wesley's family stayed up to hear the two Sunday evening broadcasts, and his mother even greeted him when he returned home at 12:40. Particularly at night, it worried her whenever Wesley drove. He had secured his driver's license only five weeks earlier—on November 17, three days after his sixteenth birthday—so he was a relative novice behind the wheel. With a sense of relief, Nora turned on the outside light after detecting the sound of their 1938 Chevrolet crackling the gravel driveway. Then, hearing him fumbling with his keys, she opened the back door to give him a warm hug and a kiss. "I only wish your father could have been here," she said. "He would have been the proudest man in Waco."

After setting his alarm clock for 4:15, Wesley went directly to bed. Still, sleep deprivation caused him to toss that morning's edition of the *News-Tribune* in a disoriented stupor. Only the cold rain managed to keep him awake as he pedaled along his route.

◆　　◆　　◆

"Let's try 'My Bonnie Boy' again," Walter Merkens said to the junior high band. "From bar forty-three, please, the 'Poco allegro' section." Then the band director appended some words of inspiration, which he hoped might evoke greater intensity and commitment from his young woodwind, brass, and percussion players. "Ralph Vaughan Williams," he said, careful to pronounce the first name in the British fashion (rhyming it with "safe"), "is probably England's greatest living composer, so let's do him honor by the way that we play. Keep in mind, boys and girls, that he and his countrymen have survived the terrible Blitz, so it's the least we can do, as Americans, to let the music of Britain breathe amongst us in these times of sacrifice."

One of the boys, no doubt Haywood Sanders, chose that awkward moment to cough, and a round of quiet titters passed through the ranks. Mr. Merkens ignored the affront. "The *English Folk Song Suite*, of which we are playing the second movement, was written twenty years ago, but just this year Gordon Jacob arranged it for full orchestra. So you may be hearing it some Sunday afternoon on one of the networks." He stared directly at a clarinetist. "Ramona, you came in a whole beat too early the last time we played it straight through. Uh-huh, you know what I'm talking about—at bar twenty-two, where it's marked 'Cantabile.' I can't be holding your hand on this. You need to count those rests very carefully."

Humiliated in front of her classmates, Ramona Eccles fought back tears and avoided looking at her betrayer. She fixed her gaze on the stand that she shared with Penny Plum, then reached over and penciled in a notation on the score. "Concho!" she whispered to herself.

Following rehearsal, as the woodwinds were disassembling their instruments and gathering up their music, Ramona noticed her friend, Sylvia Baines, talking with two other flutists. "Syl," she said, "what do you think of our new bandleader now?" Her voice was too loud for the sensitive message it carried.

Sylvia glanced around before answering. "Not much. He seems to be kind of a ... twerp ... don't you think?" Ramona laughed her approval. The other girls, Christine McElroy and Elizabeth Brower, were amused but said nothing.

"He's always picking on me," Ramona told the two bystanders, "even when I play something perfectly. And it's always 'Ramona' whenever somebody squeaks in the clarinets."

"I liked Mr. Bell better," Christine said, and Elizabeth nodded in agreement.

The band hall was nearly empty now. Besides the four girls, there was just a janitor sliding the music stands to the back of the stage.

Ramona spoke more softly now, as if to reveal some classified information. "I guess you know why Mr. Merkens can stay, while Mr. Bell is off fighting for his country. My dad says Walter Merkens is a CO ... a conscientious objector." She waited for the enormity of the disclosure to sink in. "He's too yellow to fight. He's a pansy ... a coward."

The janitor turned off some of the lights. "You girls had better be going," he told them. "Time to shut down."

"Yes, sir," they said, and they walked together down the corridor to their lockers.

Sylvia was the first to speak. "It really irritates me to see someone like Mr. Merkens taking it easy ... while our boys are dying all over the world. Mike Lightsey was in the Philippines when it fell, you know. And the Boyers lost a son at Pearl Harbor."

"Mr. and Mrs. Fischer already have three sons in the service," Christine added, "and Billy Fischer's going to join the Marines when school's out in June."

"So's my brother, Steve," Elizabeth said. "The Navy. He wants to serve on a destroyer."

"How old's your other brother?" Sylvia asked.

"Wes? He's just sixteen. He's got another couple years to wait."

Ramona knew better. "You can join up when you're seventeen now. They just can't draft you."

"Wow!" Sylvia said. "You might have two blue stars hanging in your window by next year at this time."

Elizabeth shook her head. "Mother would never let Wes enlist until he finished high school. He's only a sophomore."

◆   ◆   ◆

Whenever the weather permitted, Wesley would ride his bicycle to KWXN on weekends. The Browers' family automobile—a dark green 1938 Chevrolet two-door coupe—had a common "A" sticker on its windshield, which meant that governmental rationing allotted only three gallons of gasoline for the fuel tank every week. At seven miles per gallon, this did not permit any frivolous driving. Too, the automobile's tires were becoming dangerously shy of tread. Purchased as original equipment from a Chevy showroom in October of 1937, the tires were long overdue for replacement—at the very time when war conditions had created a global rubber shortage.

Truth to tell, Wesley's bicycle tires were also rather bald, and now that he was delivering the *News-Tribune* six mornings a week, their mileage was accumulating quickly. New twenty-four-inch tires were unavailable, except on the black market, and such coveted items almost never appeared in the used classified ads. Someday, he thought, if he could just secure more work hours at the radio station, he would quit his newspaper job for good. In the meantime, it was a matter of restricted usage and the occasional patching of flats.

One Sunday afternoon in late April, as Wesley pedaled up Sanger Avenue toward the radio station, he heard an automobile horn impatiently honking behind him. He waved for the vehicle to pass, but it stayed right where it was—about ten feet away, directly to the rear of his bicycle. It was still shadowing him when he turned onto Colcord, so he jumped the curb and turned around quickly to spot who was driving. The automobile pulled to a stop alongside him, obliging Wesley to lean downward in order to see the driver's face.

It was a girl, about his own age, but no one he recognized from school. She was smiling and motioning for him to come over to the window. Almost as a reflex, Wesley smiled back and laid his bicycle on the sidewalk. He heard her say, "Hello again!" as he approached the car, and the cheerful familiarity in her voice was confusing. He hesitated a moment before speaking.

"I don't ... Am I supposed to know you from somewhere?" he asked.

She turned off the engine. "Don't you remember me? I'm Sandy ... from church. Sandra Whittsel."

"No. I'm sorry. I ..." His mind raced, but he could not place this girl at all. "Are you sure it was Columbus Avenue Baptist?"

"That's right," she said. "I saw you in the hallway this morning. You're the radio announcer!"

Dazed and flattered, Wesley tried not to seem overly boastful. "Well, yes," he said with a grin, "I guess I am." The automobile's passenger window was down, so he rested his forearms on its waist-high lower frame and studied the girl's face. This he did in profile, for she reacted to his probing look by quickly averting her eyes toward the dashboard—a quality of shyness that he found intriguing. It did cross his mind, however, to wonder why a girl who was capable of tailing a strange bicyclist for several blocks suddenly would feel compelled to withdraw from a direct encounter.

From what he could see of them, her eyes were dark brown with long lashes, and they complemented well her pretty, turned-up nose. Her hair was dark brown, really closer to black, and trimmed short in the stylish fashion of a pageboy. He could not assess her mouth very distinctly because of the way she was sitting—with her right elbow resting upon her leg and her right hand partially obstructing his view—but her complexion was creamy and without any discernible blemish. She was slender and quite petite, in fact barely able to see over the top of the steering wheel.

"Where do you go to school?" Wesley asked. "I haven't seen you around."

Sandy turned partially toward him but still did not make eye contact. "I start sometime next week," she said. "We just moved here from Georgia."

"At Waco High? Gee, that's swell. Maybe you'll be in some of my classes."

"I hope so." She looked directly at him for an instant and smiled.

Wesley's heart was beating faster, and a euphoric feeling swept through him. Yet he surprised himself with how confident he remained, in the presence of such a lovely young girl. It was really quite easy, he discovered, when the object of his attention was so shy and so obviously impressed with his standing as a Radio Announcer.

"My daddy's in the Army," Sandy said after an awkward moment of silence. "At Blackland Air Field. He's a flight instructor."

"That's what I'd like to do someday," Wesley heard himself say. "Fly a fighter plane. You know, my brother's going to join the Navy in a couple of months, after school's out. But me ... I've always preferred the Army." An automobile raced by, and Wesley waved at his school chum, Ron Casper. Ron had no driver's license yet, but that did not keep him from running short errands for his mother.

"Well, I'd better let you go," Sandy said. "It was nice seeing you again."

"Same here."

"Are you going to be at church tonight?"

"Can't. I've got two newscasts to do."

"What station are you on?"

"KWXN—1170 kilocycles. I just do Saturday and Sunday nights right now ... because of school, you know."

"I'd like to hear you sometime. Maybe next Saturday."

Wesley fought back a smile. "I guess I'll be seeing you around. I think you'll really like it at Waco High. Just hope you don't get Mrs. Symes for English."

"Okay. Thanks for the warning! 'Bye."

"'Bye," he said. She started the automobile—a 1937 Pontiac Silver Streak—and Wesley stepped back as she placed it in gear and slowly drove off. He noticed that there was a military sticker on the rear bumper.

Wesley's bicycle lay on the sidewalk, but now he wished he had walked to work today. He wanted time to think.

◆　　◆　　◆

Almost without exception, Nora Brower did her main grocery shopping on Thursday mornings, following that up with the purchase of some perishable goods on the ensuing Monday. She traded at Moek Grocery, a small neighborhood store on Colcord, not far from the Twenty-fifth Street Theatre. Hermann and Gertrude Moek were German immigrants who settled in San Antonio in 1911, just two summers after their marriage in Dresden's historic Frauenkirche. By the time the United States entered the World War in the spring of 1917, Hermann Moek was a twenty-nine-year-old dry goods salesman who could speak fluent English with only the barest trace of his Teutonic roots. Still, because of his "Boche" background and the fact that his parents continued to correspond with him from Kempten, he was suspected of lukewarm Americanism. The couple moved to Waco, with their son and daughter, four months after the Armistice.

Moek Grocery offered a remarkable variety of food items for a store of such modest physical dimensions. The exterior of this rectangular, wood-framed structure was deceiving. Once inside, the uninitiated customer was struck immediately by how much larger it had suddenly become—a function of Hermann Moek's clever shelving that stretched from floor to ceiling on the outer walls and snaked like a Victorian maze within. The store was not self-serve, like the new Piggly Wiggly markets. A grocer shopped for each customer and then consolidated the merchandise into boxes near the ornate cash register, which stood atop a side counter.

Nora contended she could find dozens of products at Moek's that one might seek in vain at much larger stores. She also liked the friendly service, the competitive prices, and the proximity of the store to the Brower home. Stock boy Russell Mimms could deliver right to her door within ten minutes, except at peak business hours. Most of all, Nora liked chatting with Gertrude, a semi-weekly visit that more than exhausted the fifteen to twenty minutes it took for Hermann to fulfill the Brower grocery list. Hermann never begrudged his wife this time of relaxation with clientele because she kept their home spotless and orderly, as well as maintaining the store's fine inventory of fresh fruits and vegetables, some of which she grew in the Moeks' own victory garden.

Gertrude Moek was from Dresden, about three hundred miles northeast of her husband's native Kempten. Like Hermann, she too was short and plump. In contrast to him, however, Gertrude still had one foot in the Old World, whereas he was thoroughly Americanized ("Whatcha fellas need today, huh?"). Nora Brower used to wonder why this would be, until one day she came right out and asked her friend to explain the odd disparity. Far from being offended by Nora's bluntness, Gertrude found it endearing that anyone should actually wish to hear her theory on linguistics.

"I can only t'ink of two reasons why d'at might be," she said. "One ... Hermann was studying English all his life, from d'e age of eight. Me, I'm too stupit to go to college. And two ... during d'e last war, it was very dangerous to talk wit' d'e German accent. Oh, yes! 'Specially for d'e man. Germans was d'e enemy, you know." She put her hand on Nora's arm and made sure her husband was not within hearing range. "Old Hermann ... he had d'e Deutsch scared right out of him!"

What Gertrude's analysis failed to note was that Hermann Moek was a natural polyglot. He was reared in dairy country, near the Swiss and Italian borders, and he could speak French, Italian, and German with graceful facility by the time he was four. In school, he assimilated English like water through a funnel, though it was not until his move to the United States that he managed to fight off the last vestiges of a foreign accent. He exuded that special patriotic fervor peculiar to a naturalized immigrant.

Hermann and Gertrude Moek had a daughter and a son. Anneliese lived with her husband and three (soon to be four) children in Boerne, Texas, not far from Lampasas. Conrad, though, was an expatriate. In 1934, at the age of twenty-one, he journeyed to his ancestors' fatherland for the first time and stayed. His parents had not heard from him in several years, and they seldom brought up his name in conversation.

◆　　◆　　◆

Stephen Brower analyzed his reflection in a full-length mirror that was attached to the back of the closet door in his parents' bedroom. With his sister and mother doing their thrice-weekly work at the United Service Organizations canteen on Washington Avenue and his brother away at the public library, he thought this might be a good opportunity to try on his cap and gown without the constructive criticism that normally accompanied such vulnerable moments. The cap seemed a bit snug, but the gown fitted perfectly, barely dusting the tops of his dress shoes. Graduation was now only one month off.

His father's clothes still filled one entire side of the closet, and he wondered why his mother had never bothered to sell them or give them away. Steve ran his right hand across the long rack of suits, dress shirts, and neckties, and he noticed that eight pairs of men's shoes were neatly arranged on the floor. His practical mind refused to admit the possibility that his mother simply could not bear to part with them, but that may well have been the case. Were there not still a half-dozen ashtrays scattered about the house, even though none of Harold Brower's survivors had acquired his taste for cigarettes?

Steve thought he heard the front door open, so he snatched off the cap and gown and carried them to his own room. He tossed them in an unceremonious heap on his bed and began rereading a letter he had received that afternoon from Cynthia Mills. "That you, Wes?" he shouted toward the doorway.

"No, it's us," came his mother's reply from below.

"It is *we*," Steve said, but he got no reaction from the inside joke.

"Come on down. We want you to hear something."

Steve took one final look at the bottom of the letter: "Love always, C—." Like it or not, that Cynthia was getting to him, even though he had no burning desire to ever see her again. Strange. She claimed to be living in Joplin, Missouri, but the envelope was postmarked "McAlester, Okla." He laid the letter on his nightstand and went downstairs.

His sister, Elizabeth, was crouched by the Philco radio/phonograph, holding some record albums in her hands. "Listen to this." She placed a disc on the turntable. "Mrs. Huddleston donated a bunch of English recordings to the USO."

Their mother, Nora, was seated on the sofa, digging through a large grocery sack of recordings, and she added a few words of explanation. "Mrs. Huddleston's brother brought them over with him from England last year. His home in Coventry was damaged by the Nazi bombs, so he had been staying with his son in London."

Steve sat down on the arm of one of the easy chairs to listen. As Elizabeth placed the needle on the spinning disc, she paraphrased Mrs. Huddleston's ironic commentary. "Her brother makes it through the Blitz, sails across the Atlantic through all those U-boats ... and then dies of the *measles* in Elm Mott, Texas!"

A few seconds of pops and crackles could be heard, but soon the extraneous noise subsided, and the music began. Steve recognized the song as one he had heard a couple of times at Sheila Marshall's senior party.

"There'll be blue birds over/The White Cliffs of Dover/Tomorrow, just you wait and see./There'll be love and laughter/And happy ever after/Tomorrow, when the world is free ..."

"It's Vera Lynn," Elizabeth said. "They call her 'The Forces' Sweetheart' over there."

"Mrs. Huddleston told me that of all the singers, she was her brother's particular favorite," Nora said. "There are several of her recordings in this sack."

They also listened to "We'll Meet Again" and "When the Lights Go on Again." Steve—no great lover of music—had to admit that he liked what he heard. "And exactly how long do you plan on keeping this government property?" he asked his mother.

"We'll have to take them back with us on Saturday," she said. "Mrs. Huddleston just wanted us to hear them before they went into the general collection."

Music! For a moment, Nora recalled how frustrated her husband had become when he tried to teach young Stevie and Wes the clarinet. Of the three children, only Elizabeth would ever embrace that muse. She gravitated toward the piano but was also quite proficient on her father's single-reed instrument—that is, until Kenneth Bell switched her over to the flute because of what he perceived to be her "natural transverse embouchure."

After the three Vera Lynn sides, Elizabeth put on the nostalgic "A Nightingale Sang in Berkeley Square" by Elsie Carlisle and "There's a Boy Coming Home on Leave" by Bebe Daniels and Ben Lyon.

Deanna Durbin's Brunswick release of "Beneath the Lights of Home" was playing when Wesley came in the front door with a stack of schoolbooks under his left arm. "What're we having here ... a platter party?" he asked over the music.

"Shhhh!" Elizabeth said.

Wesley put his right index finger over his lips and looked suitably apologetic. He tiptoed across the room to the sofa, where he kissed his mother and sat down with the paper sack between them. Idle curiosity compelled him to shuffle through the shellac discs that remained inside it.

"They're for the USO," Nora whispered to him.

Wesley nodded his head and suddenly became serious. "Were these Pop's?" He leaned forward to lay his textbooks on the coffee table.

"No, Mrs. Huddleston's brother's."

He nodded again and listened to the record.

"Deanna Durbin was only nineteen years old when she sang this," Elizabeth said. "She's a Canadian actress and vocalist, but the record came from England."

"... Let me live my memory/Once again I long to be/Beneath the lights of home."

When the song ended, there was a brief silence, and then Steve spoke up. "Wes, I'm going to need your help after dinner."

Wesley noticed that his brother seemed preoccupied. "Sure thing," he said. "What gives?"

"Just a little moving project, that's all. Shouldn't take longer than about a half-hour." Steve forced a smile. "It's for the war effort." On the phonograph, Bertha Willmott started singing "Bless 'em All."

Wesley glanced at his mother and sister, then back at Steve.

"You'll get no promotion/This side of the ocean/So cheer up, my lads/Bless 'em all."

Excusing herself, Nora made her way slowly toward the kitchen, and Elizabeth gathered up the discs.

"Oh, no, don't stop," Nora said to her. "I'm enjoying the music." But her voice sounded hollow and tired.

After her mother left the room, Elizabeth looked again at the record album she was holding and ran her hand across its tattered cover. There was some lettering in the upper right-hand corner, "Harry Wickham," apparently made with a rubber stamp. "I'll be in to help in a few minutes, Mother," she called to the kitchen.

Steve lowered his head, as if an errant stitch of carpet had caught his attention.

◆   ◆   ◆

"Help me move these boxes downstairs," Steve said to his brother after dinner. "I can't budge them by myself." He and Wesley were standing in the doorway of Steve's bedroom, which did not appear to be as cluttered as it normally was.

Wesley swallowed hard. "Your barbells?"

"Well, be honest—don't you think I'd slow everybody down if I carried them around in my seabag?"

Wesley sat on the edge of the bed. "So you're really going through with this, huh?"

"Sure I am. What made you think I wasn't?"

"I don't know. You just haven't said anything about it lately."

Steve shook his head. "You know how Mom is. It upsets her to even think about one of her chicks finally leaving the nest. The tough part will be getting her to sign that parental permission form. I won't be eighteen until July."

Wesley smiled. "She'll do it, though, just the same."

Steve walked over to the corner of the room, where the metal bar was leaning with its collars still intact. "I'd give them to you, but I know you'd never use them." He laid the bar down next to the boxes.

"You haven't already enlisted, have you?"

"No, but some of the guys have—Mike, Pete, both Swansons ... Jim first and then his brother the very next day. They'll all be leaving as soon as graduation is over. Five or six on the football team have already signed up. I'll be going downtown on Monday, week—just for a physical, you know—and it's anybody's guess when they'll decide to take me. Like I say, I'm underage, so I'll need to get Mom's okay first."

"Well, I'm proud of you." Wesley offered his hand. "We all are."

Embarrassed, Steve shook his brother's hand. "Hey, I'm no hero. I'd be drafted anyhow."

"Yeah, but you've been talking about this ever since the war started."

"Talk is cheap. At least this way I get my choice of services."

"Navy?"

"That's right. I just hope they don't put me on one of those subs."

"Tell them you like to sleep with the windows open."

Steve laughed. "You know, I don't even like to get on an elevator. Are you that way?"

"No," Wesley said. Despite living in the same house for sixteen years—in the same room for the first six—it struck Wesley how little he really knew about his own brother.

Steve walked over to the desk. "You want my slide rule for trigonometry next year?" he asked. "You're going to need it."

"Maybe I'll just borrow it from you until you get back."

"Take it." Steve placed it firmly in the palm of his brother's hand. "I don't plan on being an engineer. Here, take my microscope, too ... and my radio."

Wesley shook his head. "No, I couldn't do that."

Steve saw that Wesley meant what he said, so he backed down. "Okay. They'll be here if you need them." He looked out his window to the street below. "The Army's sending a scrap truck over here at 7:30. We'd better be getting this stuff downstairs."

Wesley kicked one of the boxes. "How much do you think they weigh?"

"I can tell you *exactly* how much they weigh. Each box ..." He did some quick mental calculations. "Each box weighs one hundred and eighty ... ninety ... ninety-five pounds. One ninety-five. Times two is three hundred ninety in all."

"That'll make a lot of shells," Wesley said.

"And one of those shells could save my life someday." He feigned a punch to Wesley's stomach. "Come on, let's get this over with. Remember to lift with your legs, not your back."

◆　　　◆　　　◆

Only a few weeks of school remained when the new pupil arrived in class on a Friday afternoon. Wesley's algebra teacher, Mrs. Krenek, ushered the girl to one of two vacant seats at the rear of the room. That situated her right next to Rollie Barnes, Waco High's starting first baseman in just his sophomore year and a standout guard on the varsity basketball team.

"Boys and girls, listen, please." Everyone turned around to hear the teacher's announcement. "This is Sandra Whittsel. She comes from Georgia. Was it Savannah, dear?"

"Yes, ma'am."

"And her daddy's in the United States Army Air Corps. Please make her feel at home."

Wesley tried to get a good look at her, but Ruth McAllister's ample girth and flowing hair effectively prevented that. He had not seen the new girl since their chance meeting on Sanger Avenue almost a week earlier, and he was curious to confirm his first impression of her. At the conclusion of class, he hurried toward the door, only to watch the newcomer being escorted toward the sophomore lockers by Mary Jean Lowe, Miss Lowe's friend Annie Heitmueller, and Rollie Barnes.

Julius Dunnam stopped him a couple of minutes later, just before the bell rang for English. "That new girl's a looker, don't you think?" he asked.

Wesley shrugged his shoulders. "Not too bad. 'Course I was way up at the front of the room, so I can't say for sure. I think her old man's a flight instructor."

"I wonder if they've already found a place to stay."

"Oh, lay off, Casanova," Wesley told him. He shook his head and grinned.

Two days passed, and church came and went—uneventfully, from a social perspective. Not only was the new girl nowhere to be found, but clumsy Howard Forsch spilled orange juice all over the refreshment table at Sunday school, saturating the crotch of Wesley's new slacks. Maybe it was a good thing she was not there after all.

That night, Wesley's mother and sister were slated to work at the USO, so Nora decided to drop him off at the radio station en route. Wesley rode in the back seat, and Elizabeth sat up front, alongside her mother. The girl's flute case was there too, just in case the director thought some live entertainment might brighten the fly-boys' spirits.

Whenever she was in an automobile, Elizabeth would preside over the dashboard radio, adjusting its dial every few seconds until she located a song she wanted to hear. Perry Como was singing "On the Island of Catalina" with the Ted Weems Orchestra, so she allowed it to play.

> *On the island of Catalina,*
> *I fell in love at a single glance.*
> *On the island of Catalina,*
> *A paradise for our romance . . .*

Nora glanced in the rear-view mirror. "Are you sure someone can bring you home?" she asked. "That's a long walk after midnight, and there's supposed to be some bad weather on the way."

"Dave said he could take me," Wesley said. "He lives over on Colcord."

For we had music an' moonlight to guide us,
And the peaceful Pacific beside us ...
On the island of Catalina,
I fell in love with you!

Keeping her eyes on the road, Nora turned her head slightly toward the front-seat passenger. "Oh, honey, I forgot to tell you ... Mr. Merkens called about an hour ago, while you were still upstairs dressing."

Elizabeth stared blankly at her. "Mr. Merkens?"

"Uh-huh. Didn't you hear the telephone ring?"

"What in the world could *he* possibly want?"

Nora let the clutch out, waiting momentarily for a streetcar to pass. The conductor rang its bell.

"Oh, Lord," Elizabeth said with a sigh, "you don't suppose he'll make our quintet play *Pomp and Circumstance* a thousand times at graduation."

"No, I hardly think so. You can call him back when we get to the USO." Nora pointed to her purse. "I wrote his number on a slip of paper."

Wesley spoke up. "I hear Walter Merkens is on his way out."

"What?" Elizabeth shifted in her seat to look squarely at her brother. "Where did you hear that?"

"There's a rumor going around."

"Tell me."

Nora pulled the automobile into the KWXN parking lot and brought it to a stop with the engine idling. Wesley opened the door to get out.

"Tell me!" Elizabeth said. "Don't say something like that and then just walk away."

"I need to go punch in," Wesley told her. He slammed the door.

Elizabeth rolled her window all the way down. "Wes!"

"It sounds like Merkens is up to his neck in hot water. Someone accused him of being a Nazi, and the school board is digging into it." He waved to his mother. "I'll be home by 12:30."

"Okay, dear. Don't forget to set your alarm."

◆   ◆   ◆

The Washington Avenue USO was almost as serene as a library when Nora and Elizabeth walked inside. A pair of GIs sat in a corner, smoking and pensively listening to a collection of jazz discs. Five or six other soldiers were scattered at various tables, reading. Two non-coms from the recruiting depot were playing a halfhearted game of pool. And one young private sat with misty eyes as he penned a letter back home on the supplied stationery. Nora went directly to the food counter to arrange a tray of doughnuts and pastries. There was no evident shortage of sugar in the military.

By now, Elizabeth had found the telephone number in her mother's purse and called Walter Merkens. She expected her band director to answer and was momentarily flustered to hear a woman instead.

"Uh ... may I speak with Mr. Merkens please?" the girl finally asked.

The voice on the other end of the line inquired who was calling.

"Oh, I'm sorry. Elizabeth Brower ... but I go by Beth at school. I'm in his junior high band. Yes, ma'am ... Thank you."

An unlikely bank-shot at the pool table brought some loud derision just as Madeleine Givens came into the room and hobbled toward the kitchen entrance. She had been injured in an automobile accident on Labor Day and still noticeably favored her left leg—something the doctor told her she would probably always do. Initially a volunteer, Mrs. Givens accepted a full-time USO position when Marsha Dent hastily married and accompanied her dashing young corporal to aerial gunnery school in Las Vegas.

Madeleine was a statuesque brunette in her lower thirties, married and the mother of two young children. She was not blessed with delicate features—Dominick, the deliveryman, called her "that horse face" behind her back—but the Army boys did not seem to mind. She was as lonely as they were, with her husband serving in England and the twins living in Riesel at her in-laws' farmhouse.

Nora looked up from her pastry tray. "Hello, Madeleine. Would you mind taking this punch bowl over to the rec room? Stella tells me there's going to be a hot time in the old town tonight."

"Oh?" Madeleine laid down her purse and took off her gloves.

"Some big brass are dropping in to give us the once over, and they're bringing a couple dozen gals from Baylor with them—something Pat Neff cooked up to help rally the troops. The Army was all for it, of course."

"Do you think I'll have time to stock the cigarettes?"

"I guess so. They'll be driving up in a deuce-and-a-half, so you'll hear them coming from a mile away."

Four youthful cadets entered the room, and one of them whistled at Elizabeth, who was hurrying over to the kitchen.

"Mother," she said, "it's worse than you could imagine."

Nora wiped the pastry icing off her hands. "What is it?" Her daughter's face was pale.

"Mr. Merkens wants me to tell him everything I know about Ramona Eccles and her older brother." She was short of breath. "Wes was right, Mother. Mr. Merkens is in huge trouble. There's even going to be a public hearing on Thursday night."

"But why would Mr. Merkens want to talk with you?"

"Beats me. I don't even know Ramona all that well. I sit near her in band, but so do a lot of other girls—and guys too. I think maybe he's trying to gather as much information as he can before he's put on trial."

"Well, a hearing is hardly a trial," her mother said.

Just then, one of the newly arrived cadets approached Elizabeth. "Say, girlie, how's about a dance?"

Nora bristled for a moment, but the young man had an endearing innocence that disarmed her protective nature. "My daughter's only fourteen," she told him. "And besides that, she doesn't dance with the soldiers. You'll have to wait until eight, just like everyone else."

"I'm sorry, miss," the cadet said. "I didn't know she was your ... I didn't know the rules around here." He retreated, with an apple tart and cup of coffee in hand, to the safety of his buddies across the room. They burst out laughing at their humbled comrade, who licked some sticky icing from his fingers.

"Shut up, and gimme a smoke," he said.

◆　　◆　　◆

Vertical red streaks appeared on the yellow paper, a telltale sign that the UP roll was in need of changing. Wesley had delayed tackling this little chore as long as he dared, but now the situation was becoming critical. Taking a deep breath, he switched off the teletype machine and opened the glass cover. This was his lifeline. If, for some reason, he were unable to get the machine running again, he would have no fresh copy to read on the 11:55 newscast.

He removed the old roll and inserted a new one, careful that its end-flap was facing upward at the front. Gingerly, he leaned the glass into position and reached for the power switch. The machine jumped back into action with a reassuring hum, and he gave a sigh of relief.

Twenty-five minutes later, after he had rewritten the local news and confirmed his ride home with engineer Dave Flint, Wesley was stunned to discover that the dreaded teletype machine had been "free falling" for the better part of a half-hour. He looked through the glass cover and could see that nothing was printing. In a panic, he pulled forward the dozen or more feet of "exposed" paper, coiled haphazardly behind the wooden casing. It, too, was blank. Somehow, in his inexperienced fumbling, he had managed to leave the paper atop the typing assembly instead of threading it behind the ink ribbon.

There was no time to lose—seventeen minutes to his newscast. Wesley discarded the wasted paper and attempted to install the end-flap properly. His fingers shook. With just under sixteen minutes to go, the machine whirred back to life, producing a steady flow of readable script. Wesley leaned against the wooden sound case and waited impatiently for the World News Round-Up to appear.

The stock market report ... thirteen minutes to news time. Sports headlines ... eleven minutes. Wesley paced the floor. Agricultural news ... nine and a half minutes. Then an interminable pause, and he walked over to the machine to gaze helplessly at the idling motor. He began pacing the floor again. Finally, a mere six and a half minutes before airtime, the typing resumed. He rushed over to have a look, but the words were chilling: Fort Worth Livestock Report.

Conceding defeat in his race with the clock, Wesley ran to the announcer's booth, fished his previous hour's news copy from the metal tray, sorted the pages in logical sequence, and placed them on the table next to the mike stand. Old news is better than dead air, he reasoned, but he also knew that the station manager could see no excuse for a stale newscast. Not in wartime.

What were his options? The inspiration struck him that a late-breaking item from Wall Street might freshen the pot a bit, so he raced back to the teletype machine to select a likely passage. What he saw almost brought tears of joy to his eyes. There before him crept the letters he had been longing to see: HERE IS THE LATEST NEWS FROM THE UNITED PRESS.

Four and a quarter minutes to news time. Granted, it would be "rip and read," but at least now there might be enough copy to fill his allotted time—particularly with a few local items added to the mix and a sixty-second Monnig's commercial inserted at mid-break. With less than one minute to spare, the UP World News Round-Up was virtually complete, so he tore the paper along the glass cover and tucked it under his arm.

Wesley hurried around the corner and slammed the announcing booth door, hastily separating the individual stories with the use of a straightedge ruler. Through the soundproof window in front of him, he saw Dave Flint sitting at the control panel. Overhead, he could hear the final strains of the regular Sunday night feature of transcribed dance-band music.

"Thirty seconds," Dave said over the intercom. His right hand rested on the turntable pot.

"... *next week at this same time, when again we bring you the sentimental sounds of rhythm in the air ...*"

"Wes, somebody called you a few minutes ago to say she'd be listening to your newscast."

"... *with Marty Fellows and His Orchestra. Until then, this is your ...*"

Wesley nodded his head and cleared his throat. It was unlike his mother to call the radio station at such an hour.

"... *saying goodbye until we meet again.*"

Dave opened the mike and cued him.

"Good evening. This is Wesley Brower with the 11:55 edition of KWXN news, brought to you by Monnig's, the Friendly Store, downtown at 604 Austin Avenue.

"President Roosevelt tonight congratulated General Dwight D. Eisenhower for the brilliant Allied victory in Tunisia and said the unprecedented degree of Allied cooperation involved 'makes a pattern for the ultimate defeat of the Axis.'

"United States air forces struck at Palermo, Sicily, today with more than four hundred planes ... the heaviest raid ever launched from Africa and one of the biggest daylight attacks of the war, dropping a weight of bombs five times greater than on any previous Mediterranean raid.

"In news from the Pacific Theater, massive bombing raids around the Solomon Islands battered three Japanese destroyers and four enemy bases. One destroyer suffered a direct hit. Dauntless dive bombers, torpedo bombers, and heavy bombing planes all joined in the widespread assaults that hit shipping and shore installations yesterday."

When Wesley began reading the generic commercial for Monnig's Department Store—by now so familiar to him that it had become somewhat mechanical—his thoughts drifted briefly to the telephone message that Dave had received. He hoped nothing was wrong at home.

The newscast continued. "British and Indian forces in western Burma have withdrawn from Buthidaung, one of the last Allied footholds in the Japanese-occupied colony. Field Marshall Sir Archibald Wavell's forces probably will have to await the end of the monsoon season before starting a new offensive. The 10th US Air Force has announced that its four-motored Liberator bombers dropped thirty thousand pounds of bombs yesterday on the railroad yards at Rangoon.

"Waco will find out Monday night at eight o'clock what an air raid is really like in 'Action Overhead,' a bombing exhibition at Municipal Stadium. A small, white house, which has been constructed at the stadium, will be ripped apart by a high-explosive bomb, while from attics, roofs, and windows of nearby structures will come the white glare of burning magnesium as fire bombs find their mark. The planes, the bombs, and the fires will be real, but the planes will be friendly raiders from a nearby airfield. The bombs will be planted in advance and detonated by experts of the chemical warfare service, and the fires will be brought under control by the officers and men putting on the demonstration for the Office of Civilian Defense. Preceding 'Action Overhead,' the Waco Civilian Defense Council will present a musical program by the Waco High School Band.

"Mother's Day was observed today with a USO breakfast for mothers of men and women in the armed services whose children were not here in Waco for the occasion ... and also for soldiers or sailors, stationed locally, who were unable to return to their own homes for the day. An estimated five hundred mothers and soldiers gathered in the USO lobby and were escorted to the dining room on the second floor.

"Finally in the news, don't forget to pile that scrap metal and rubber in front of your house before daybreak this morning. Trucks from Waco and Blackland Army Air Fields will start making their rounds at dawn, picking up as much scrap as they can on this, the first day of the drive. The process will continue through the week for as long as necessary, until all of the stacks have been removed."

Without exception, seven days a week, KWXN sign-off came precisely at midnight, so Wesley stretched the news closing slightly so as to allow the second hand of the network slave-clock to reach the "12." Then Dave Flint played a recording of "The Star-Spangled Banner" before shutting down the transmitter and bringing the broadcast day to an end.

All that remained now were the mundane cleanup chores. Dave slipped the sixteen-inch transcription of "Marty Fellows and His Orchestra" back into its cardboard sleeve and returned it to the play shelf. He did the same with the national anthem. Wesley, meanwhile, went to the newsroom to file the copy from his two broadcasts. He also did a quick rewrite of the few local stories that would still be usable in the morning.

It was not until a quarter past twelve, after they had locked the front door to the station and were already halfway to Dave's automobile, that the telephone message again crossed Wesley's mind. He stopped walking. "Say, did my mother want me to call her back before we left?"

"What do you mean?"

"My mother. Wasn't I supposed to call her back?"

Dave stared at him blankly.

"You got a phone call for me before the news ..."

"Oh!" Dave shook his head. "No, that wasn't your mother. Some girl called to wish you luck."

◆   ◆   ◆

Most Monday mornings, before she turned her attention to the weekly wash, Nora made it a point to pay a short visit to Hermann and Gertrude Moek. Mr. Moek was a stickler for punctuality, so the store was always open by 8:30 sharp. That is what puzzled Nora so much when she reached Colcord Avenue and noticed that, from a distance at least, Moek Grocery appeared to be totally dark.

The streets were still wet from a round of early-morning thunderstorms, so she was careful not to step in the areas of standing water. More than an inch and a half of rain fell during the night, and several of the surrounding counties sustained some serious wind damage. Powerful claps of thunder woke her up between two and three o'clock, and she closed all the bedroom windows to keep the blowing rain from coming inside. Much to her relief, the showers were well on their way to east Texas when Wesley set out on his bicycle to throw the *News-Tribune*.

As Nora walked closer to the grocery store, she could see a white piece of paper fluttering on its front screen door. The masking tape on one corner of the paper had come loose, so she pressed it back down with her thumb. The notice read, CLOSED UNTIL SATURDAY. DEATH IN FAMILY. There were no lights on inside.

Upon arriving back home, Nora called the Moeks on the telephone but received no answer. Perhaps they had to go out of town for the funeral. A new CBS serial, "This Life Is Mine," was on the radio by the time she began her washing, but she could not enjoy it. Gnawing concern for Hermann and Gertrude would not go away. She decided to call Mabel Johns.

"Yes, 3-6-5-9, please," she told the operator. The family cat, Valentino, jumped into the wicker laundry basket and curled up for a nap. "Scat!" Nora said, but the cat did not move.

"Hello, Mabel. This is Nora. I hope I'm not interrupting your washday."

"That's all right, dear. I can use the break."

"What do you know about Hermann and Trudy Moek? The store is closed up tight, and a sign on the front door says there's been a death in the family."

"Oh, my goodness! I haven't the faintest idea," Mabel said. "I saw them at church yesterday morning."

"I thought they went to the Evangelical and Reformed Church."

"They do, but Hermann wanted to visit ours because the E and R was having a guest preacher. That's what Trudy told me."

Nora reached for her yardstick and rapped sharply on the side of the basket to coax the cat to more appropriate quarters. "Well, I haven't seen them since Thursday," she said, "but they seemed perfectly fine then."

"I tell you what, dear. Rather than just speculate, let me ask Virginia or Mildred. I'm sure one of them will know." Mabel was one of those ladies who took it upon themselves to get to the bottom of things—even when it was none of their business. This, however, was a rare instance that might transform her inherent nosiness into a virtue.

♦   ♦   ♦

Rollie Barnes was starting to get on Wesley's nerves. To begin with, he was a math whiz, and he made sure everyone else was aware of it. Even Mrs. Krenek had to be on guard, just to stay one step ahead of him. Not a week went by when his graceful mastery did not make the rest of the class look foolish by comparison.

He was also unfairly tall—six foot two and growing like a bamboo shoot. He was a southpaw guard who had the ball-handling ability of Wyoming's Kenny Sailors, the competitive speed of Brooklyn's Pete Reiser, and the boyish good looks of Hollywood's Robert Walker. He smiled, and the girls swarmed around him, falling all over themselves to catch his eye. It was downright embarrassing.

At school parties, while most of the other sophomores were content with simply being seen—wandering around the finger sandwiches or chatting on the periphery of the upperclassmen—Rollie seemed to feel perfectly at home on the dance floor. Of course, he had an advantage, being on the varsity basketball and baseball teams.

If Wesley looked over his right shoulder and leaned forward a few inches, he couldn't help but see him now, absurdly grinning as he whispered in conversation with his neighbors. Wesley didn't mind if Mrs. Krenek reprimanded Mary Jean Lowe for talking in class, but it really peeved him that the new girl, Sandra Whittsel, was being placed in such a compromising position. As for Rollie himself, he was much too smooth to get caught. Besides, he was the teacher's pet.

"Mr. Brower, turn around and answer number sixteen on the board, please."

The teacher frowned as Wesley made his way slowly to the front of the room and picked up a piece of chalk.

Given that y = 3, find the value of x in the following equation: 4xy - 15 = 69.

From the length of the entire room, he could feel two pretty, brown eyes burning a hole in the back of his neck.

Meanwhile, over to his right, Mrs. Krenek leaned against the edge of her desk and prompted him. "What is the first step?"

"Substituting the 3 for y?"

"All right. That's not the way I would do it, but it will certainly work. What does that give you?"

"4x times 3 minus 15 equals 69." He wrote the new equation as he talked. "That makes 12x minus 15 equals 69. Or 12x equals 84, so x equals, uh ... 7?"

"Good. It might be a bit easier to wait until you've justified both sides of the equation before you introduce the 3. Try it that way."

Wesley swallowed hard. "Say again, ma'am?"

A few students snickered, and Wesley could feel his face turning hot. He kept his eyes on the teacher.

"Try moving the 15 to the right side of the equals sign," she said.

He turned back to the chalkboard and confronted the original problem. "4xy equals, uh ... 84." He wrote down the revised equation and took a deep breath. "So xy equals 21." Then he smiled and felt his confidence restored. "And y equals 3, so x must be 7."

"Fine. You may be seated."

Wesley returned to his desk, stealing a quick glance at the back of the classroom. The girl was not even looking. Her math book was open, and her index finger was moving across the page. She sure did seem studious.

Twenty minutes later, when class was excused, Wesley hurried past the teacher's desk and out the left door. A bottleneck of bodies clogged the door to the right, so he was in the hallway, already waiting, when the people from the back of the room finally exited.

Rollie Barnes was nearly a foot taller than anyone else in the hallway, so he was easy to spot as he ambled toward the chemistry lab. But the new girl was not in sight. Lost among the crowd, she had disappeared without a trace. Wesley paused for a moment, took one last look, and could not believe his eyes. She was avoiding him, that much was clear. Reluctantly, he went the other direction for English.

The day dragged on, and Wesley felt terribly sleepy, as he always did around this time on Monday afternoons. He was walking in a daze, just before the bell for last period was about to ring, when Mr. Howell stopped him at the bottom of the stairway. "Is Steve going to enlist?"

"Yes, sir, he leaves right after graduation."

"Well, tell him we'll be praying for him."

"I'll do that. Thank you, sir."

"He was a hard runner. I enjoyed working with him very much. Never gave us coaches a bit of trouble."

"He'll appreciate that."

"Tell him Coach Stiteler feels the same way."

"Thank you, sir. I will."

They shook hands, and Mr. Howell left for the practice field. Morning PE classes had been held indoors, but perhaps the grounds had dried out enough by now. In the distance behind him, Wesley heard someone calling. "Wes! Wait up." It was a boy's voice, and he turned to see who it was.

Rollie Barnes came jogging toward him. "Wes," he said, "I think you need to know something."

This was the last person in the world Wesley expected to see. "Hi, Rollie," he said. There was not much enthusiasm in his voice.

"You know ... that new girl, Sandy Whittsel? She really likes you ... a lot."

Wesley could not take a breath. He studied Rollie's eyes to see whether he was serious.

"Honest, Wes. She really does."

"I've only talked to her once in my entire life."

"She says you're her announcer."

"Her announcer?" He had to laugh. "I just do the weekend news."

"That doesn't matter to her. She's really got it bad for you."

Wesley rubbed the back of his neck. "Gosh, I hardly even know the girl."

"I just thought you should know," Rollie said.

"Thanks for telling me. Does she know you're here?"

"No, of course not. She's afraid to talk to you, so I'm clearing the way."

There was an awkward silence, as Wesley could not think of anything to say.

Rollie sighed with a smile. "Now I wish I'd gotten into radio instead of basketball. She's a honey."

Wesley took the long way home that afternoon, giving himself some time to think. Two angry mockingbirds squawked as they chased a crow overhead. Several piles of scrap metal baked in the sun along Jefferson Avenue. Some children laughed and shouted on a backyard slide. Rounding the curve on Ninth, a streetcar's wheels made a steely sound, electrical sparks floating down to the pavement like snowflakes. There was a tiny pebble trapped in his right shoe, but he did not bother to stop. A basset hound barked at him on Morrow, but an elderly lady clapped her hands and told the dog to hush.

You know, that Rollie Barnes really is a swell guy.

A vision of Sandy flashed through his mind. Her hair was dark brown, and so were her eyes. She was not more than five feet tall, barely able to see over the top of the steering wheel.

Wesley went to bed at the regular time, a quarter to ten, setting his alarm clock for 4:15.

"Good night, Wes," his mother said as she peeked into the darkened room.

"Good night. I'll try not to wake you up when I leave."

"Did you hear the bombardment over at Muny Stadium?" she asked.

"No, I guess we're too far away."

"I thought I heard it once when I locked the garage door, but I couldn't really be sure."

Wesley tried to stifle a yawn. "Was the sky lit up?"

"Not that I could tell," she said. "Too many trees in the way."

"The radio said there were about thirteen thousand people there."

"Didn't you want to go?"

"No, I'm kind of beat from last night. Besides, we're running low on gas."

Valentino, the cat, was rubbing against her legs as Nora turned to leave. "Well, good night, son. See you after your route."

"Good night."

His window was open, and the streetlight below filtered through the blowing curtains. Lying on his back under a sheet, he could hear the distant sound of a train whistle. The neighbors' dog heard it, too, and howled in reply. The pillow under his head seemed flat and uncomfortable, so he shook it with both hands and folded it in half. Still restless an hour later, he rolled over from his right side to his left. A tree limb was brushing its leaves against the roof of the house, so it must have gotten a little windier outside. He heard the clock bong once downstairs. Could it really be one o'clock, or was that just a half-hour chime? Which half-hour? He picked up his flashlight to look at the alarm clock on the nightstand but thought better of it. Was Steve asleep? Lizzie? The room seemed a bit cool now, so he reached to the floor and pulled up a blanket to cover his legs. Had he remembered to set the alarm? Yes, he was sure that he had. He rolled onto his back and watched the tree's shadow dance on the ceiling. Valentino hopped onto the bed, purring loudly and curling up between his ankles. Now Wesley felt pinned to the mattress, hating to disturb the cat's slumber. Sometimes he wished he were a cat, to fall straight asleep like that. The crickets certainly were active tonight. Even from the second floor they seemed loud.

String-tied stacks of Tuesday's *Waco News-Tribune* were already being tossed from distribution trucks to curbside when the boy finally surrendered to his wakefulness, relaxed a bit, and fell into a peaceful, if abbreviated, sleep.

◆   ◆   ◆

So many times in the past two days had Mabel Johns asked the operator to connect her with the Moek telephone that she was shocked when somebody finally answered. It was late Wednesday morning.

"Is this ... the Moek residence?" she said.

"Yes, it is. Who is speaking, please?"

"Hermann, is that you?"

"That's right."

"Hermann, this is Mabel Johns ... from over on Fort Avenue."

"Oh, yes. Hello, Miz Johns."

"May I speak with Trudy?"

"She's outside in the garden right now, Miz Johns." His voice sounded weary. "Would you like for me to have her call you back?"

Mabel was unsure what to do. "Well, no, please don't bother her now. I'm calling because we've all been very concerned about the notice on your store."

"Yes, that was our boy, Conrad. He died in North Africa about two weeks ago. The Red Cross let us know."

"I'm sorry to hear that," Mabel said. She sensed that she was in politically thorny territory. "I'm sure he was a fine young man."

"Thank you."

"May we come see Trudy?"

"Certainly."

That very afternoon, Mabel and Nora paid a visit to the Moek home. Hermann opened the screen door for the ladies and asked them to follow him to the living room. "Trudy is taking this rather hard," he said.

The room was dim, with the curtains drawn and a single lamp burning atop the end table. Once the ladies' eyes became accustomed to the darkness, they could see that Gertrude was seated at one end of the sofa with her elbows on her knees and her head cradled in both hands. She was sobbing quietly.

"Trudy," Hermann said, almost whispering. "Miz Johns and Miz Brower are here to pay you a visit." He motioned for the ladies to sit alongside her and then excused himself from the room, closing the door behind him.

"Trudy," Nora said, "Mabel Johns and I are here to see you and to offer our prayers and condolences. We were terribly sad to hear about your son's death." There was no indication that Gertrude heard a single word. "We both want to tell you how very sorry we are."

"Yes," Mabel said. "I never knew Conrad, but Nora says he was a fine boy."

Gertrude moved her hands away from her face, but she continued to gaze down at the floor. Finally, she spoke. "He was a good boy, yes. You remember him, Nora? He was a good boy."

"Yes, I remember Conrad when he was just a youngster—only about six or seven, I think. Later on, he used to pack my groceries sometimes. And I remember when he learned to drive the delivery truck."

Nora thought she detected a smile as Gertrude looked up at her. "Ah, he always did love d'e trucks—real ones and also d'e toys. You know, we still have all his little toys. D'ey're in a wood box—what you call it?"

"A cedar chest?" Mabel said. "A hope chest?"

Gertrude nodded her head. "Yes, a cedar chest in d'e attic." No longer crying, she used her apron to wipe away the tears from her cheeks. "His letters are in d'ere too."

Hermann opened the door from the kitchen. "Pardon me, ladies," he said. "Trudy, would you be all right if I checked on the store? There's some stock that needs to be tended to, and we open up again tomorrow."

"Oh, sure, sure. Don't worry about me. D'at will be fine."

Hermann took a step back into the kitchen and closed the door.

"Do you have many letters from Conrad?" Nora asked. "You said he wasn't much of a writer."

"No, none in d'e last few years, d'at's true. But we wrote letters to him many times, so he knew all about us here in Texas. He's born in San Antonio, you know, so he's an American boy."

Mabel averted her eyes and noticed a painting of the Alamo hanging above the upright piano.

Gertrude leaned forward. "Miz Johns, I'm 'shamed to say d'at he fought on d'e German side, but Conrad was not a Nazi. Please ... you must believe d'at."

Mabel reached across Nora's lap and squeezed Gertrude's hand in her own. "Oh, I know that, dear. I believe you."

"And Conrad always hated Hitler," Nora added, "right from the very start. He went to Germany at a very difficult time."

"Oh, yes," Gertrude said to Mabel. "I showed Nora d'e last letter he wrote to us—just a year before d'e Nazis attacked Poland. He was afraid d'at d'e letter might be seen by d'e censors, and he would be shot. He was more American d'an lots of boys in d'e service over here."

Mabel chose not to follow that dangerous line of argument. "I believe you, Trudy. I really do."

Gertrude continued to look at her for a moment. Then, satisfied that her point was made, she let the subject drop.

Nora began to stand up. "Well, we don't want to tire you out, dear."

"No, not at all. I'm happy d'at you came by to visit." Gertrude struggled to her feet, pushing heavily on the armrest for support, and Mabel also took the opportunity to rise.

"It was very kind of bot' of you to come by," Gertrude said. "How is your family, Nora?"

"Fine. I think we're all fine. Steve graduates in two weeks."

"Does he really? D'at's hard to believe. You know, I remember when he was a little boy too."

"I know you do. His first trip away from home was a ride to Moek Grocery in his perambulator."

The ladies laughed, but Gertrude suddenly became quite serious and took Nora's hand in both of her own. "I only t'ank God d'at your son was not at Bizerta like my Conrad. D'at's where he's buried now, my baby boy."

◆　　◆　　◆

Robert Brister, Superintendent of Public Schools, was the first to speak. He walked over to the big, oakwood lectern and, summoning the merest hint of a smile, formally greeted the three hundred or so citizens who awaited the grim proceedings. Pressed into duty as a makeshift hearing room was the Waco High School cafeteria, which only six hours earlier had echoed with the cheerful sounds of the tenth-grade lunch crowd. North Junior High School did not have a room large enough to accommodate such a turnout.

A half-dozen members of the school board sat shoulder-to-shoulder behind a large, rectangular table. Directly in front of them, on the opposite side of a similarly shaped but much smaller table, was the troubled music teacher and director of the junior high band, Walter Merkens. No charges had been filed, but late word had it that allegations were taking on a more scandalous tone. Accordingly, the hearing was already well in progress before two harried janitors were able to import a sufficient number of additional chairs from the gymnasium.

Wesley Brower was there, and so were his brother and sister. While Elizabeth felt that she had a personal stake in the matter—being a member of the junior high band and also a friend of one of the accusers—Steve, like many of the high school kids, was present more out of curiosity than any deep-seated emotional interest. Once inside the cafeteria, he made his way directly to the back of the room, where several of his noisy football chums had begun to congregate. "Cynthia Mills is back in town," one of them said. "She might even show up tonight." She never did, but Steve spent the rest of the evening scanning the audience for the blonde-haired beauty who still refused to admit that she stole his thirty-dollar class ring to wear around her neck on a silver chain.

Elizabeth found a spot about ten rows from the front and saved an adjacent chair for her best friend, Susan Keeley, who arrived shortly thereafter, out of breath. "Hi, Lizzie," she said. "Sorry I'm late. I had to hitch a ride from a couple of wild boys over at Woolworth's."

"What were you doing there at this time of day?"

"It's a long story. George Smith works at Woolworth's, you know, and his dad's car had a flat tire right there on Austin Avenue. Mom and I were eating at the Elite Café across the street—she has to work tonight—and we could see George and Brian Duffy out the window, changing the tire. Mom was on her way to Aerl's, way out by the Texas Theatre on Fifteenth, so she asked if I would mind riding back to school with those boys."

Lots of people were still chatting when Mr. Brister began introducing the board members, so the principal, Douglas Johnson, stepped forward and shushed the crowd.

"Sorry to disappoint you," Elizabeth whispered, "but George and Brian are not wild boys. Whoever told you that?"

"No one. They just seem that way to me."

"Well, you're imagining things. I don't know about George, but Brian's father is a policeman, and I doubt whether he's been in trouble in his entire life."

"They could have done something wild, you know. It was only those two and me, all alone in the car."

Susan was not a member of the band, but four or five of her closest friends were. As the self-appointed junior high gossip, she wanted to be there, just in case the evening brought with it some of the promised spicy revelations.

"Mr. Goddard, if you please," the superintendent said.

"Thank you, Mr. Brister. I would like to begin this session by reading the written statements of two of our band musicians, who, for obvious reasons, shall remain nameless. Bear in mind that this is an informal public discussion, not a legal proceeding."

On the very first row, along with three other eighth-grade girls and one eleventh-grade boy, sat Ramona Eccles. She wore a white chiffon dress with a large, red bow tied in front and a matching one adding a touch of color to her Shirley Temple coiffure. Perhaps her appearance could best be described as schoolgirlish. Flutist Sylvia Baines was alongside her and so were fellow clarinetist Linda Poetchen, flutist Rebecca Vandergriff, and Ramona's brother, Vincent Eccles, whose instrument of choice was the trombone.

As school board president Raymond Goddard started to read from the typewritten allegations, a large woman, with her emaciated husband in tow, seated herself directly in front of Wesley. This being a cafeteria rather than a proper auditorium, the audience did not enjoy the usual benefits of a sloping floor—much less an elevated stage—so Wesley's view was obscured by the human equivalent of a total eclipse. The visual element removed, he quickly lost interest in the droning, faceless voices and whatever drama may have been enacting itself across the room.

One central notion he did manage to glean from the discussion was that some of the female students were claiming that Mr. Merkens had approached them, more than once, in a manner they judged to be too friendly or casual. Another point of contention was the band director's ambiguous status with the Selective Service System. As far as Wesley could tell, the words "slacker" or "draft dodger" never actually emerged, but they floated conspicuously enough near the surface.

"Yes, sir, I have registered with my draft board, in accordance with federal law."

"Mr. Dyson?"

"He has indeed, Mr. Goddard," Wilbert Dyson said. Besides serving on the school board, Mr. Dyson was a local Selective Service administrator.

"Why has his number not been called?"

"He was rejected for medical reasons and is now categorized as 4-F."

"Can you tell us the specific reason for his rejection?"

"Yes, sir. He suffers from a herniated ulcer."

"Is this a permanent condition?"

"It is chronic, yes, sir."

Wesley noticed that the woman in front of him was doing something with her pudgy arms, possibly crocheting, and her husband was fast asleep with his nose in the air. Between their heads, when he leaned slightly to the right, Wesley could see that his sister and Susan Keeley were busy writing notes back and forth to each other, covering their mouths to stifle the giggles. Two varsity football players got up from their seats and walked to the back of the cafeteria, where they joined several of their teammates. Steve was standing among them, though he did not seem to be paying much attention to the other players.

"But it has not yet been determined that these charges have any substance to them," President Goddard told the panel.

"True enough, but we must take them seriously, just the same," board member Charley Branch said. "For instance, can Mr. Merkens explain what he was doing in the darkened band hall with one of his female students?"

"When was this, sir?" the chairman asked.

"A week ago last Friday."

Raymond Goddard turned to the accused. "Mr. Merkens?"

"How should I know? I probably just switched the lights off and walked out of the room with the girl. Is there a law against that?"

"She alleges that you took her by the arm and then kissed her on the cheek," Mr. Branch said.

"That's a lie! Who is this girl?"

"We're not at liberty to say."

"Don't I have the right to clear my name?"

"Yes, you do, Mr. Merkens," Charley Branch said, "by answering the question."

"I did answer it. I categorically deny any such behavior, and I can produce as many character witnesses as I need to testify in my own behalf."

"Now, now, now. No witnesses are needed," the school board chairman said. "You're not on trial here."

"Well, you could have fooled me ..."

Mr. Branch's face reddened. "Don't use that tone of voice with us!"

Wesley heard only the final part of this heated exchange, but he could feel a ripple of tension in the air. He glanced over at Elizabeth and Susan. Both were now paying rapt attention, and so was the couple in front of him.

"We're not going to allow this discussion to deteriorate into a shouting match," Raymond Goddard said. "Mr. Merkens contends he does not recall the incident in question ... and I, for one, believe him. There are some vindictive sentiments at work here, and we cannot let them influence our good judgment."

It was 9:40 before the hearing finally came to a close. After consulting briefly with the school board, Mr. Brister announced that Walter Merkens would be permitted to finish the school year on the North Junior High payroll, but that his future at the institution was unclear.

As for Ramona Eccles, she smiled with admiration at her brother as they exited the cafeteria together. Just as Vincent had promised, Mr. Merkens was nothing more than a dead leaf, helplessly clinging to a tree until the next gentle breeze.

◆   ◆   ◆

More and more service flags were appearing in the windows of houses along Wesley Brower's paper route. He noticed that the Malcolms and the Seiferts now had blue stars on display, as did the Walkers on Eleventh and the Boatwrights on Trice. The Arthur Smith home had three blue stars in its front window, the most he had ever seen.

According to an article in the newspaper, the John Norris family at Fifteenth and Jefferson had no fewer than four sons in the armed services, plus a son-in-law and a grandson, but they were not on Wesley's route. His mother told him that poor Arizona Norris broke her arm when she fell while picking flowers. That did not stop her from attending the Mother's Day breakfast at the USO, assisted by Army Private Mitchell Norris and Marine Corporal Burton Norris.

Over on Barron Avenue, pretty Millicent Hainey—still the very image of a blushing bride—proudly displayed a blue service star for her husband of seven years, Captain Bruce Hainey, who now served as an officer in the Marines. Among all of Wesley's customers, Mrs. Hainey was his favorite. On a typical collection day, she chatted amiably with him for ten or fifteen minutes. Then, after paying her *News-Tribune* fee, without fail she purchased from him some war stamps or even a bond. She would stand at the doorway waving a flirtatious goodbye, and his giddy infatuation would turn to heartache. He knew beyond doubt that Captain Hainey would be the happiest man in the world when he was finally able to return home to his wife.

None of Wesley's subscribers had lost a boy to the war, but he knew all along that it was only a matter of time. The sun was already peeking over the horizon one Wednesday in the middle of May when he noticed something unusual about the Patman home. Curious, he climbed off his bicycle, leaning it against the decorative lamppost at the curb. As he walked up the stepping-stones toward the front door, he became aware of luminous sunlight shining on a service flag that was somehow different—more beautiful—than any others he had seen. It was of white fabric, bordered in red and hanging from a gold cord. But in the middle was a gold star. Almost fearful, he carefully placed a newspaper on the porch and retreated to his bicycle. Then, peddling up the street, he stared with fascination at the gold service star once again.

He asked his mother about the Patmans when he came home from school that afternoon.

"Yes, that's right. Madeleine Givens told me that poor Kendall was killed in a training exercise somewhere in England. I don't know anything more about it than that."

"Golly, that's terrible," Wesley said.

"Do you remember him? He used to work at the Elite Café—the new one on the Circle—bussing tables. I'm sure you've seen him."

"I don't know. Maybe."

Wesley dreaded collecting from Jean Patman the next time her payment came due. He had not been confronted with death in such a personal way since his own father's passing five years earlier, and he was not sure that he would be able to gather the right words and in the proper manner. He rehearsed an appropriate sentence or two just before ringing the door chimes. It was Thomas Patman who answered, not his wife.

"Come in, son," he said. "Wait here, and I'll be right with you."

The entry room had a hardwood floor, and a grandfather clock ticked at the opposite end. Otherwise, the room was bare except for a small telephone table, a coat rack, and an umbrella stand that advertised some restaurant in New Orleans.

Mr. Patman returned with a few coins and counted them out for Wesley. "Mrs. Patman is away today, visiting her parents and brother, but I'll tell her you came by."

"Thank you, sir." Wesley started to leave, but as Mr. Patman was shutting the door, the boy turned to him. "I was sorry to hear about your son."

Thomas Patman closed his eyes and nodded his head. "Thank you, young man," was all he said. He looked to be at peace.

"My brother will be joining up next week," Wesley told him.

"Is that so?" Mr. Patman looked directly into his eyes and managed a weary smile. "Good for him, my boy. I wish him well. What's your brother's name?"

"Steve ... Steve Brower."

"You go to Waco High?"

"Yes, sir."

"Well, let me hear how Steve's doing occasionally, okay? I work over at Beard and Stone Electric, not too far from the high school."

"I will, sir. Goodbye."

Wesley tried his best to visualize Kendall Patman, but he could not remember him at all.

◆ ◆ ◆

The Sunday night baccalaureate services inside Waco Hall exhibited an unmistakable military bearing. Even the guest speaker, Waco High graduate Leslie Rogers, was in uniform. Now a chaplain in the US Army, he was stationed locally at Blackland Army Air Field. He spoke of the sacred mission that his generation was entrusted to fulfill. With the Holy Spirit guiding their every step, his fellow WHS graduates—now scattered throughout the world as brothers in arms—would steadfastly persevere in their Christian pilgrimage.

As in high schools everywhere and in every era, very little actual learning occurred during the final week of classes, particularly among the seniors. But in all other respects, wartime had a profound impact on academic life at Waco High School. Some of the male students had enlisted and were already at their basic training or duty stations, and a large percentage of those who stayed in school were planning to join the armed services immediately after the Thursday night commencement ceremonies. Many of the boys who withdrew early had designated proxies—close family members or friends—to represent them at the exercises. If such provisions had not been made, as in the case of Randall Huggett and others already seeing action on the front lines, the degree would be presented *in absentia*.

Graduation parties for the remaining Class of 1943 members were either subdued or non-existent, depending upon the senior's gender and immediate plans. Still, Elizabeth Brower decided to organize a small celebration in honor of her older brother, and her mother agreed to assist.

Nora was scrubbing the stovetop, where her wooden spoon had left a stubborn tomato-paste residue. "What time is commencement—eight o'clock?" she asked.

"No, 8:15," Elizabeth told her. "So we could probably start around 10:30. Is that too late?"

Nora rinsed the scouring pad and tossed it onto the counter. "I don't think so. I'm afraid Steve won't be getting much sleep that night anyway." She walked over to the kitchen table and sat in a chair.

Elizabeth thought she could see wrinkles in her mother's face that were not there before. She pulled a chair next to Nora's and sat down, patting her gently on the shoulder. "I don't think any of us will." She was shocked at how fast her mother was aging. Perhaps it was the dim ceiling light, but gray hairs suddenly seemed to outnumber the black, and she appeared unusually tired and frail.

"Mother, I'll handle all the arrangements," Elizabeth said. "You have enough to worry about without taking on another project. Besides, Susan and her mother said they'd help out."

"No, Lizzie, that's all right. I want to stay busy, really."

Elizabeth hesitated before speaking. "I need to ask you about Thursday. Will Steve be spending the night here or over at Max Gent's? Some of the boys are going over to the recruiting station from there—awfully early in the morning."

Nora turned to look at her daughter. "Well, if I have anything to say about it, Steve will be right here with us. That's the first I've heard about the Gents."

"Good. I'm sure he would have mentioned it to you."

Nora stood up and walked over to her ration box. "Listen, Lizzie, I still have stamp 12, and it doesn't expire until the end of the month. Do me a favor and go over to Moek's tomorrow morning and buy us some sugar. I'll bake Steve a cake for the party."

"Is it okay if Mrs. Keeley brings one too? She was wanting to."

"Of course, dear. That would be fine." Nora smiled at her daughter, amazed at how fast she was growing up, right before her very eyes.

♦   ♦   ♦

The grandstand at Municipal Stadium began filling shortly after seven o'clock, and most of the high school band—minus the seniors, of course—arrived to tune their instruments about a half-hour later. Nora drove the family car, with Steve in the front passenger seat and Wesley and Elizabeth in back. It was ninety-one degrees, so the windows were down, and Steve's graduation gown was folded neatly beside him with the mortarboard on top of it. The family rode along in silence, mixed emotions muting what normally would be a joyous occasion.

When the automobile came to a stop in the dusty, gravel parking lot, Steve opened his door and put on the cap and gown. "How do I look?" he asked.

"Just like Kay Kyser," Wesley told him.

Steve grinned at his brother. "That's right—you're wrong!"

"Honestly, son, you're as handsome as any movie star," his mother said. She motioned for him to come nearer. "Here, let me take a snapshot."

Steve stood next to the automobile and posed for Nora's Brownie with what he saw as an elegance worthy of Ronald Colman.

"Hey, Steve!" Teddy Gaunce shouted from across the lot. Teddy was an all-district end on the football team who, like Steve, was planning to enlist the following day. He ran up to the Browers' Chevrolet and shook hands with Steve and Wesley, nodding greetings to Elizabeth and Nora. "A few of the guys are going to get together after the hoopla," he said. "Want to come along?"

"No, thanks, Tee Gee. I've got a little send-off arranged for me at home."

Teddy was slapping Steve's arm but looking at Elizabeth when he added, "Well, if you change your mind ..." The girl smiled back at him, then glanced at her mother.

"I'll see you out there in the jury box in a few minutes," Steve said. He steered his pal toward the grassy field.

"All right. Let's get this over with," Teddy told him. "And then we can start killing us some Japs." He stole one final glimpse of Elizabeth before departing.

Music director Lyle Skinner led the Waco High School Band in the traditional Elgarian processional, as the senior class filed onto the field in alphabetical order and took their seats—just as they had done the night before at rehearsal. Nora could see her son, uncharacteristically serious, seated between homely Catherine Brookens and his childhood friend, Dennis Buckley. It was Buckley whose father worked at the *Waco News-Tribune* and secured for Wesley a job delivering newspapers.

Dusk was falling when Reverend Earl Lightfoot voiced the invocation, and the Browers' own pastor, Hubbard Hoyt Hargrove of Columbus Avenue Baptist Church, followed with the benediction. The senior class stood as one, hands over their hearts, and sang "The Star-Spangled Banner" under the direction of choir teacher Elden Werner. Salutatorian Norma Cimo spoke briefly, as did valedictorian Patricia Mistretta, and then it was time for Superintendent Robert Brister to deliver the main address. "In case you were wondering," he told the audience, "the diplomas were signed by our principal, Mr. Howard Torrance, before he left Waco to become a lieutenant in the US Navy. By the way, I'm sure you'll all want to join me in expressing our gratitude to Mrs. Butler for handling this difficult job in his absence." There was a warm round of applause for Marian Butler, a widowed teacher who was thrust into the role of high school principal upon the enlistment of Mr. Torrance.

Catherine Brookens was in the process of shaking hands with School Board President Raymond Goddard when Steve heard his name called: "Stephen Collins Brower." Solemnly, he walked over to accept the diploma. He saw his mother in the audience, and it struck him hard that this was a watershed moment. When he awoke tomorrow, his life would never be—even remotely—quite the same again.

Returning to his seat with sheepskin in hand, he winked at Teddy Gaunce and was caught by the subtle beauty of Marianne Green's profile. He found it difficult to take his eyes off her for the rest of the evening, and he wondered how in the world he had overlooked such a pretty young lady throughout their four years of high school together. He had never so much as said hello to her, and he felt a sudden emptiness inside.

Goodbye. It was all he could do to keep from crying.

♦　　♦　　♦

While walking from Sunday school to the sanctuary with a couple of his church friends, Wesley thought he could see Sandra Whittsel down the hallway. It was always difficult to spot her among a crowd because she was so petite in stature. He decided to orchestrate a chance meeting, so he said an abrupt farewell to Duane and Alex and hurried into the sanctuary, entering on the organ side. Not wishing to call attention to himself by breaking into an outright run, he moved in the style of an Olympic walker—careful to keep one heel on the floor at all times.

As he was halfway across the sanctuary, drawing even with the altar, he saw Sandy enter from the piano side. But the opportunity to intercept her alone was soon gone. She greeted a deacon, walked to a pew near the back, and sat next to a tanned gentleman in an Army uniform. A dark-haired woman, who had been talking with an elderly couple on the aisle, joined them a few seconds later.

Sighing, Wesley stopped short, reversed his field, and trudged toward the Brower family's customary pew on the opposite side of the room. His mother was already there, fanning herself with the order of worship, but as of yet he detected no sign of Elizabeth. There was a flash of lightning outside, followed quickly by a startling clap of thunder. Fortunately, the church's source of electricity was not lost. Raindrops could be heard pelting against the stained-glass windows.

Now that he thought of it, Wesley had not seen Sandy at Sunday school a single time since she enrolled at Waco High over three weeks ago, and only once had he noticed her at a morning service. Maybe the Whittsels had been visiting other churches, something newcomers to town were often known to do until they settled upon a fellowship that made them feel welcome and comfortable. In that case, it could be that Sandy's attendance this morning augured well for the future.

Later that same day, while his mother was in the kitchen preparing dinner, Wesley picked up the telephone. "Yes, operator," he said, "I need a new listing for Whittsel ... W-H-I-T-T-S-E-L ... No, two 'T's and one 'L' ... Duncan Whittsel on Gorman." The thunderstorm had passed, but rain was still dripping from the eaves. He looked at his wristwatch—1:20. Elizabeth was next door, helping Mrs. Bloom with her canning. He hoped his mother could not hear his conversation. When the operator returned to the line, Wesley scribbled the information on a scrap of paper. "1-8-0-2 ... No, ma'am, I'll try it later on. Thank you."

The palms of his hands were sweaty when, just after 1:30, he finally worked up enough courage to place the call. This time a different operator answered, and he asked her to connect him with 1802. "Yes, *sir*," the woman told him. Her emphasis on the latter word was an innocuous nuance, to be sure, but it served to bolster his confidence. And yet, when he heard the number begin to ring, this newfound *élan* just as suddenly deserted him. For an instant, he even considered hanging up the receiver. What did Sandy sound like? He couldn't even remember her voice. The ringing stopped.

"Major Whittsel speaking."

Wesley choked out, "May I speak to your daughter, sir?" He cleared his throat. "Who is this, please?"

"Wesley Brower, sir. I saw her at church this morning." Not an eloquent opening, but it would have to do.

"Just a minute. I'll see if she can come to the telephone."

Wesley became short of breath, and there was a pounding sensation in his throat. The next voice he heard would be hers. He waited for nearly two minutes.

"I'm sorry, but I can't find her anywhere," the major told him.

Wesley felt equal measures of disappointment and relief. "That's all right, sir. I'll try again later." He resolved then and there to call her again that night—but in the relative seclusion of the newsroom.

His mother beckoned him from the kitchen. "Time to eat, Wes. Would you go next door and ask Lizzie to come home?"

"Sure, Mom," he said. The fried chicken and corn casserole smelled wonderful, causing his stomach to growl in anticipation.

No more than ten minutes passed before the three of them were sitting down to eat, and it proved to be a rather tense meal. Steve's empty chair brought a poignancy to dinnertime that struck Wesley harder than he expected. His mother was very quiet, and Elizabeth seemed anxious to compensate by launching into one chatty subject after another.

"Mother, I heard that Deborah Epps and her husband—what's his name, Nicholas?—are moving to Los Angeles. I think they're both in aircraft construction now ..."

"I saw the funniest picture this morning. Audrey Adderley brought it, and it showed a cow standing on top of some thatched-roof house, back in the old west. I don't think it was here in Texas ..."

"Wes, did you know that Walter Merkens resigned? Of course, no one was really surprised ..."

"Carroll Livengood says there's going to be another blackout sometime this summer, but he wasn't sure when. Willis just laughed at him and said an air raid is becoming less and less likely ..."

"Mother, do you know of any rooms for a whole family anywhere? There are at least five couples who moved here this past week, and our Sunday school leader says they're desperate ..."

"Linda Tate and her sister listen to the New York Philharmonic on Sundays. She said that's what they do every week. Did you know they like that kind of music? They seem more like 'Barn Dance' girls to me, but that just goes to show you ..."

Through it all, Wesley's thoughts drifted back to Sandra Whittsel. Yes, he would definitely talk to her that very night, probably after winding up his newscast at eleven o'clock. He imagined several different scenarios, rehearsing spontaneous responses to each. If she was flattered: "I'm about to go on the air, but I have a moment or two before the red light comes on." If she was confused: "You know—the radio announcer ... algebra ... a friend of Rollie Barnes." If she was annoyed: "Sorry to bother you, but my mother is collecting for the paper drive." And, of course, if she was not at home: "Thank you, sir or ma'am. No, I'll just see her tomorrow at school." It never hurt to be prepared.

◆　　◆　　◆

One thing was obvious the moment Wesley arrived at the radio station and began clearing the UP wire—there was no shortage of news to announce that night.

The US Navy was reporting that Attu Island in the Aleutians had fallen into Allied hands after nineteen days of fierce resistance by Japanese troops. British and Canadian aircraft had devastated Wuppertal, home of the Farben Chemical Works, dropping more than 1,500 tons of bombs. British planes, flying dawn patrols over the Atlantic, had sunk five Axis U-boats in the past ten days. And, on the eastern front, the Russians claimed to have shot down 2,069 German planes, during the month of May alone, in heavy fighting around Kuban and Leningrad. Locally, there had been crowded Memorial Day services in most of the churches that morning—despite the heavy rain—and the area's gold star mothers were honored in posthumous tribute to their fallen sons.

Wesley edited his 10:55 newscast in short order, earning himself the luxury of enjoying nearly twenty minutes of leisure time before going on the air. He yawned, stretched his arms, and leaned back in his chair. He was reading over his news copy while listening to the station's CBS programming—music from the Woody Herman Orchestra—when the telephone rang.

"Newsroom," he said.

"Wesley Brower?"

"Yes ..." He froze.

"Wes, this is Sandy Whittsel."

"Sandy."

"My dad said you called me today."

"I did, yes." She had a pretty voice. He remembered it now.

"Well?"

"Huh?"

She laughed. "Why did you call me this afternoon?"

"No reason, really, just to say hello."

"Oh? Well, hello." She sounded like she was smiling.

"But you weren't there," he said. "I was thinking of calling you back tonight."

"I was afraid you might, so that's why I called you instead. My dad goes to bed at 9:30 sharp, and I didn't want the telephone to wake him."

Wesley laid his news copy on the desk. "Your father goes to bed at 9:30?"

"Yes, he does, just like clockwork. But of course he calls it 2130."

That was intimidating. "Gosh, he talks that way at home?"

Sandy ignored the comment. "He works at Blackland Field, you know, and reveille is at 5:30. He has to start teaching right after PT."

Wesley found it difficult to feel much sympathy for Major Whittsel's hours. "Gee, I get up at 4:15 to deliver my papers, and I don't usually get into bed much before eleven."

"Well, you're not forty-one years old, either," she said.

"No, I'm not ... or I wouldn't still be going to Waco High."

She did not hear his joke. "And besides, Wes, you can always catch up on your sleep in math class."

He detected someone else talking on the line. "Who's that?"

"Oh, my mom wants me to hang up now. I told her I would just be a minute. You've got a newscast to announce."

"Yes, I do," he said, "but I think I'm ready for it."

"Are you on right after Woody Herman?"

"We have to fill for about ten minutes. I think Dave has some organ interludes or something."

"Well, goodbye. I'm glad we could talk." There was a silence, so she added, "I just couldn't figure out why you called today."

Wesley did not want to leave her with a brusque goodbye, but he could think of nothing more creative than just that. Then inspiration struck. "Hey, maybe I can show you around the radio station sometime."

"Wow, sure. That would be nice," she said. "Well, goodbye."

"Goodbye ... Sandy."

He had trouble falling asleep when he returned home after midnight, but it was the most delicious bout of insomnia that he had ever suffered.

◆　　◆　　◆

As the legal owner of her late husband's company, Superior Office Supply, Nora Brower received a percentage of the firm's monthly profits. With unbroken regularity, a voucher arrived in the mail on the first, followed by a check on the fifth. For some time now, she had noticed that her bank deposits were gradually dwindling with each passing month.

The postman was not yet out of sight when Nora decided to walk downtown and investigate. She tucked the voucher in her purse, put on her gloves and hat, and opened the front door, only pausing long enough to assure Elizabeth that she did not suspect her administrator, Wayne Espy, of dishonest conduct. On the contrary, he had been integrity personified for more than twelve years, ever since early 1931 when Harold Brower, in his declining health, named him his right-hand man.

A tiny bell tinkled when the shop door swung open. The room was dingy and stuffy, and it smelled of ink. As her eyes adjusted to the dim lighting, Nora could see that the manager was stacking some boxes of stencils on upper shelves near the rear.

"Well, Mrs. B.," he said. "Nice to see you." He wiped his forehead and stepped down from the ladder. After the usual pleasantries—and her apologies for being such an infrequent visitor—they retired to the back room and fortified themselves with steaming cups of coffee.

"Wayne," she asked, "are we in danger of going under?"

"No, certainly not," he told her. "It's just a normal downturn in the business cycle. We'll need to tighten our belts a bit for the duration, but I think it's already stabilizing."

"So you think there's nothing to fear?"

"Definitely not ... no, no. Scissors, paper clips, staples, hole punchers ... they're all in short supply. This current batch of typing paper is pretty shoddy—look at the quality—and it's hard to sell. Who wants to buy it in large quantities when something better will turn up when the war's over? Our competitors are having the same problems we are. Just ask Neil Burns over at Liberty. I saw him at Rotary yesterday, and he told me as much."

"Well, I'm sorry to hear that. I don't wish ill to anyone ..."

Espy nodded his head. "I understand perfectly."

"... but at least it means there's an equal slump for everybody in town, and not just us," she added.

"Precisely. Rubber stamps are down, of course—the Japs have seen to that—and I haven't been able to order a typewriter in more than a year. We'll make it, ma'am. Don't you worry about that."

Nora frowned. "You wouldn't be painting me a rosy picture, would you, Wayne?"

"Rosy?" he said. "No, ma'am. It's hardly that."

"But if we were in danger, you'd tell me."

"Oh, yes, ma'am. We're doing as well as can be expected. We're more than holding our own."

She returned home within the hour—small, brown sack in hand—and Elizabeth was right there at the front door to meet her.

"Mr. Espy gave me some note cards," Nora told her daughter. "They're imperfects, cut crooked, but I think the staff can use them in the church office."

Elizabeth smiled but then turned to hurry away. "Mother, Wes and I have something to discuss with you. Wait in the kitchen, and I'll go get him."

"Oh, dear. What now?" Nora removed her hat and gloves and watched the girl disappear from view around the corner.

"Nothing so terribly awful," Elizabeth shouted. She ran up the stairs.

Wesley and his sister both seemed to be in chipper spirits when they joined their mother at the kitchen table.

"Now, what is this great mystery of yours?" Nora asked. She was seated at the kitchen table and in the process of filling the salt and pepper shakers. Wesley thought they already seemed quite full.

"Brace yourself, Mother," Elizabeth said, "and don't say no until you've heard the whole story,"

"I promise." Nora closed her eyes and pretended to grimace. "Hit me with it."

Elizabeth pointed to her brother. "Wes, you go first."

"Me! Why me?"

"Because you're older. It's the law."

Wesley sighed. "Okay." He took a deep breath and looked at his mother. "We've decided—both of us—to quit school and get jobs."

Nora stood up and walked to the pantry. "You'll do nothing of the sort."

"But, Mother!" Elizabeth said.

"Absolutely not." Nora turned to face them. "I'll not have my children drop out of school—war or no war—and I do not wish to discuss the matter any further."

"But you yourself said we could use the extra dough," Elizabeth said. "We only want to help."

"Well, I appreciate that, I really do, but quitting school is out of the question. Do you understand me?"

"Yes, Mother." Elizabeth seated herself at the table and pouted.

Nora eyed her son. "Wes?"

"Yes, ma'am. I understand."

Elizabeth spoke up. "But could I at least try to make some money by getting a part-time job?"

"I think that would be fine, dear, but with all your volunteer work, how in the world could you possibly find the time?"

"That's why I offered to quit school for a while."

"Lizzie ..."

"Well, I could find something this summer and then cut back on the hours when school starts. That wouldn't leave me much time for scrap drives and the USO, but maybe the war will have ended by then."

Nora walked over to the table and sat down again. "There's something I've been wanting to tell both of you for a couple of weeks now, and this is as good a time as any."

Wesley swallowed hard, noticing how serious she had become.

"I'm thinking of renting out Steve's bedroom for the duration. There's a terrible housing shortage right now, and the government says it's our patriotic duty. Besides, we surely could use the income. How do you two feel about that?"

"I'm all for it," Elizabeth said. "If he happens to be a cute Army boy, that is."

Nora giggled. "How touching."

Wesley was not so sure. "What would we do with all of Steve's things? That's still his room, you know."

Nora nodded her head. "Everything would have to go into storage, except for the furniture, which the boarder could use. I think we could ask for twenty dollars a month. That seems reasonable."

"Do you suppose anyone would pay that much for a single room?" Elizabeth asked.

"Certainly, and the person would be free to eat with us whenever he or she chooses."

Wesley's eyes widened. "She?"

"Yes, he or she. Whoever applies."

"Oh, don't get all excited, lover boy!" Elizabeth told him. "I wouldn't expect Veronica Lake to show up on our doorstep."

◆　　◆　　◆

Less than a week passed before a brief classified ad was running in both Waco newspapers. In the meantime, Nora removed most vestiges of Steve's belongings and had Wesley carry them in boxes up to the attic.

"Does Steve know you're doing this?" he asked.

"Yes, I'm sure he does by now. I wrote to him three or four days ago that we might have to rent his room, and I think he'll be all for it."

"I guess so. It's only temporary."

Four people came by to enquire about the room on the very first day that the ad appeared. The first two were civilians, one a bachelor who walked with a noticeable limp and was unable to climb the stairway without great difficulty, and the other an elderly man who had moved to town to be near his twin daughters, both of whom were mothers with husbands in the armed services. The men were extremely pleasant, but Nora made no secret of the fact that she preferred to rent the room to a serviceman or war worker. She told these first two applicants exactly that, and they said they fully understood.

The next person who responded to the advertisement seemed to fit the bill nicely. He was a polite gentleman in his late forties or early fifties who had secured a job at the Bluebonnet Ordnance Plant, which occupied about eighteen thousand acres of land just to the southwest of McGregor. As a result of its new industry, the population of McGregor had tripled in three months to more than six thousand, and housing was at a premium. Many workers, including this Milford Bandy, turned to nearby Waco in desperation. He said he would check back in the morning, after he had the opportunity to follow up on two Coryell County leads.

Fourth among the candidates for lodging was Edward Neal, Elizabeth's personal favorite. Wesley classified him as a playboy, but Elizabeth saw him through different eyes. He was slight of stature but very muscular, and his hairy forearms might well have belonged to someone under Longfellow's spreading chestnut tree. Why he was not in the military was anybody's guess, and no one ventured to ask. And yet he possessed a self-assured dignity of bearing that attracted Elizabeth's interest at once. He also had a disarming smile and perfectly aligned white teeth that looked like they might glow in the dark.

It should be said, too, that Mr. Neal was very much taken by Miss Brower's comeliness, even helping her up the stairway to view the room when she was quite capable of traversing the steps unassisted. Somehow, this considerate attitude did not escape Nora's notice, though it manifested itself behind her back as they climbed to the second floor.

"And what do you do for a living, if I may ask?" she said when he expressed the desire to sign a six-month lease, paid in advance.

"Well, I used to be a rodeo cowboy out in the Los Angeles area, but since things got hot overseas I've decided to settle down and help with the war effort."

Nora studied his face, to no avail. "That's funny," she told him. "It seems like most people are going to California for the war industries ... and here you are, leaving LA to find work in Texas."

He flashed his smile. "I'm a country boy at heart—from Salinas—and I've always wanted to see what Texas is all about."

"Well, I'm afraid you'll be disappointed. In times like these, I guess Texas is pretty much like anywhere else."

"I already like what I see," the cowboy said. He was careful to avoid looking at the third party in Steve's bedroom.

There were loud footsteps coming up the stairs. "Superman" was over, and Wesley was curious to scrutinize this latest potential boarder. He joined the others under the pretense of raising the window shade. "I wanted to see if the Ables' dog was running loose again. Sorry to interrupt."

"Wes, this is Edward Neal," his mother said.

"How do you do?" Wesley asked.

The stranger's handshake nearly cracked his knuckles, so he flexed his fingers at his side when Neal turned back to Nora.

"Mr. Neal is a rodeo star," Elizabeth told her brother.

"Well, hardly," Neal said, "and I've got the bruises to prove it. No, I was what you call a five-second bronc rider, and that just won't generate many earnings. But I thank the lady all the same."

Elizabeth blushed, and Nora stepped between them. "We're really looking for a war worker to stay here," she informed the cowboy. "To help with the war effort … like you said."

He took her hint cheerfully and allowed that, in any case, far north Waco was really where he preferred to live. "The traffic is not so congested, and I could stable a horse up there."

After he had left, Nora declared to her children, "We'll give it just two more days. Then I'll call Mr. Bandy to see whether he's still interested. Could be that McGregor and Gatesville are all booked up."

Only Elizabeth seemed sorry to see Mr. Neal go, and she tucked the slip of paper he gave her into the skirt pocket of her dress.

◆　　◆　　◆

Weekends were not an accurate representation of what life was really like at KWXN. Wesley learned this lesson anew each time he rode his bicycle over to the station on a weekday to pick up his paycheck—and witnessed an entirely divergent universe unfolding before his eyes.

For one thing, there were the salesmen: vociferous, backslapping, chain-smoking, pin-striped, thin-mustached, shiny-shoed, wire-bespectacled, slick boys who spent their time making cold calls on wary, tightfisted merchants entrenched in the various shops around town. The radio station served as this intrepid cadre's sanctuary from the combative rigors of direct sales, so they felt perfectly entitled to relax for a moment and tell a dirty joke or two before reentering the fray.

Also nowhere to be seen on weekends were the pretty office girls, most of them single or divorced, thrown into the exciting machinations of the workaday world by circumstances beyond their control. They kept very much to themselves, leaving little doubt that they were both unavailable and disinterested in establishing lasting personal relationships. Exactly why this should be remained a puzzle to the naïve college men who performed servile duties around the station and were the office pool's main source of social contact. These poor hopefuls could never quite grasp the fact that their dream girls did not actually see them at all but were looking straight through to the wider circle of doctors and lawyers outside—those who had it in their power to rescue them someday from such a mundane existence.

Most impressive of all, of course, was the backstage world of on-air talent, about two dozen men and women, along with their supportive technicians, whose sole purpose in life was to rise each morning, Monday through Friday, and convey to their unseen listeners the sort of news, tunes, comedy, and drama that would engage as many fickle ears as possible for just long enough to be reflected in the Hooper ratings.

Wesley always made it a point to take a self-guided tour of the control room on his paydays. No one seemed to acknowledge him with so much as a condescending wave of the hand, but neither did they ask security to forcibly remove him from the premises. In due time, he felt like he was accepted as one of their own—a legitimate, if shadowy, presence. It could be that everyone in the room merely assumed he was someone else's friend and never thought to demand an explanation as to why he was there.

Seated before the console on a typical weekday afternoon were technical director Sol Glickman, his soundman Dickie Waterhouse, and one of the sponsors, someone like Anthony Potter of Nash-Robinson & Co. or perhaps Ron Gibbs of the Raleigh Hotel. Behind the soundproof glass, rehearsing for the next day's "Behold Tomorrow" serial, were people such as Douglas Pierson ("Anson Gabriel"), Neddy Wright ("Bud Hanson"), and Phyllis Sherry ("Jeannie Gabriel"). Sound-effects man Rodney DeBonaventura was surrounded by his beloved noisemaking paraphernalia.

Viewing it all from a respectable distance was announcer Marshall McFall, still just twenty-six but blessed with the patriarchal *basso cantante* of an Ezio Pinza. He had his heart set on the larger markets, preferably Detroit or Chicago, but so far had progressed only the hundred-odd miles from Brownwood to Waco. To his credit, he was generous in his acceptance of public foibles, such as when someone disturbed his meal to request an autograph. Indeed, so tolerant was he that there were times when he had himself paged at crowded restaurants to see the heads turn his way.

Wesley admired Marshall McFall to the point of idolatry, something that he shared with most everyone who did not know him well. He was a legend of the airwaves. Just put a script in front of him, and he could do no wrong. Once, when they happened to pass each other in the hallway, Wesley thought of actually saying hello to the august Voice of KWXN, but he reconsidered at the last possible moment and feigned a cough instead, accidentally ejecting his chewing gum in the process. It rolled against the wall with an almost inaudible *thwack*, and he was pleased to see that McFall had already begun studying his fingernails by then.

The only backstage person with whom Wesley had struck up an acquaintance was the script girl, Monica Dillon Whaley, a relative newcomer to radio whose job it was to retype the copy and then mimeograph enough revisions for all the studio talent to hold before them as they stood at the microphones. She worked closely with the writers of both of KWXN's daytime serials, but except in dire emergencies, such as unavoidable last-second revisions, she lacked the authority to make literary suggestions of her own. That was the exclusive realm of Marcus and Betty Hoskins for "West of the Brazos" and the "Behold Tomorrow" troika of Gerald Byrd, Ethel Coody, and Harvey Samuelson.

But creative writing was not Monica Whaley's ambition anyway. She was a Baylor University graduate who married the geology TA in her senior year and, following Herbert Whaley's induction into the Marine Corps, became stranded in Waco. Three months after the wedding, and utterly shattering her idyllic visions of building a home overlooking the blue Pacific, her parents and sister were all killed in an automobile accident not a quarter-mile from their sprawling but peacock-infested house near the Arboretum and Botanic Garden in Arcadia. Understandably, after such a trauma, that locale was no longer home to her, and she resigned herself to waiting out the war as best she could.

Unmindful of her piteous history, Wesley blundered in their first encounter by mentioning that her manner of speech did not sound particularly Texan to him. She happened to be chatting with her friends in the business office while old Mrs. Allen leafed through the checks in search of the name "Wesley Brower."

"Well, maybe that's because I'm from California. I don't think we have accents out there." One of the other girls snickered at this.

Wesley saw the large diamond ring on Monica's left hand. "Is your husband in the service?"

"Yes, he is."

Mrs. Allen could not find his check and began shuffling through the stack again.

"My brother is training in California right now," Wesley told Monica. "He joined the Navy right after graduation. Did you grow up anywhere near San Diego?"

"Nope. Farther north—LA County."

"Do your folks still live out there?" he asked. Mrs. Allen looked up from her searching.

"No," Monica said. She stood there in silence, twisting her wedding ring.

Wesley could sense that something had gone wrong. Was it something he said? Becky Headrick saved the moment by offering to help locate the missing paycheck.

"Oh, it's probably about to bite my finger off," Mrs. Allen said.

Wesley watched with bewilderment as Monica Whaley excused herself from the room and walked down the hall to continuity.

◆　　◆　　◆

It was a renter's market, no doubt about it.

During the next two days, eleven people came to call on Nora Brower in response to the newspaper ad. A twelfth, Milford Bandy, returned to notify her that he had found suitable accommodations with a Crawford farming couple and would not be needing the room after all. As he was leaving, Nora thanked him for his courtesy and wished him well at his new job in McGregor. He gave her the "thumbs up" sign and recited the Bluebonnet slogan, "No duds."

Some of the applicants were military personnel, including one Army corporal who brought his wife and eight-month-old daughter along with him. Steve's old room was simply too small for the young family, and they had no choice but to scratch the Brower address off their dwindling list of possibilities. Half a dozen of the others were civilians, caught in the housing squeeze that plagued Waco and all urban centers across the nation. Nora figured that she owed it to the boys in uniform to earmark this rental space for someone directly involved in a war industry.

That left out a young lady named Mary Bond, whose husband had deserted her—and their one-year marriage—when he went AWOL from the 4th Fighter Group to elope with an English woman at Debden, Essex. British military authorities later apprehended the bigamist, and a court of law summarily annulled the illicit union. Nora explained her patriotic rental philosophy to the woman and even offered to allow her to stay at no charge until the room was rented, but Mrs. Bond, overcome with frustration and grief, would accept no such charity. With tears streaming from her eyes, she fled down the stairs and into the Waco night with nowhere to go. Nora felt terrible about the incident and immediately dispatched her son to retrieve the woman, who she feared may have become mentally unstable. Returning empty-handed, Wesley reported the matter to the police, but evidently Mary Bond was able to elude them as well. Her name never appeared in the newspaper, so Nora comforted herself with the thought that perhaps daylight had granted this desperate creature some promise and a sense of renewal.

For the Browers, that same daylight ushered in a nineteen-year-old woman who would enter their lives as a mere boarder and then, over the course of time, become a member of the family.

Hannah Deborah Lane was a North Carolinian through and through, hailing from the community of Mount Airy, just south of the Virginia line. The daughter of an old-style, fire-and-brimstone preacher, she had the singular misfortune of choosing an era of global conflict to transfer her educational pursuits from the world's second-largest Baptist institution, Wake Forest College, to the world's largest, Baylor University. Why she would select such an inauspicious juncture to adjust her sights eleven hundred miles to the west was something that no one could answer sensibly, least of all Hannah herself.

Not that it caused her any great concern. Questioned about it by a Baylor counselor on the day of her arrival in Waco, she looked at him with scorn. "I just felt called. Can you think of a better reason?"

"No, ma'am," he said. "What are you, a preacher's kid or something?"

Also of small moment to her was the sobering notion that Wake Forest was a humble town north of provincial Raleigh, while Waco was a substantial city south of cosmopolitan Dallas. This prospect, purely statistical, held no particular terror for her, and neither did the nightmarish train trip—six and a half days of false hopes and excruciating delays—accompanied by a steamer trunk of China hardwood that was heavy enough to make a stevedore shudder under the strain. To facilitate its handling, the good Reverend Lane had constructed for her a special cart with roller-skate wheels, but that contrivance had become useless by the time she reached Gastonia, and she donated it to the scrap-metal drive.

More often than she could count, the train was shunted off to the siding to allow hundred-car shipments of *matériel* to pass. Her train's glacial progress was interrupted at every conceivable stopping point along the way—at ramshackle stations of all descriptions, the names of which were familiar to no one beyond a fifty-mile radius. Men in uniform took precedence over civilians, of course, so in a number of instances she was left standing on the platform as the train she thought was hers chugged away without her.

"Another one will be along in a couple of hours," a disinterested stationmaster would tell her.

"I'm in no hurry," she would reply.

On what turned out to be her final grueling day of westward travel, Hannah was consigned to a rattling Missouri-Kansas-Texas (M-K-T, or "Katy" for short) Railroad coach that smelled of vomit or dead crickets—she could not decide which. As it drew near the outskirts of Waco, she craned her neck to see where on earth she would be spending the balance of her collegiate years. Having done no preliminary research beyond a cursory glance at the university bulletin, she was taken by surprise when the city's skyline came into view through the open window. The twenty-two-story Amicable Life Insurance Building stood like a sentinel as the train passed over the Brazos River Bridge from East Waco to the downtown area. When the Katy came to a lurching stop at Waco's passenger depot, Hannah stood up and leaned out the window, squinting her eyes while attempting to block the sun with her right hand. Though several nearer structures stood between her and the Amicable Building, the skyscraper's upper-story brickwork and flagpole remained clearly visible above them.

"Son, you'll have to get off now," the conductor told her.

Turning to confront him, she saw that everyone else had already detrained. "Do I really look like a boy to you, pops?" she asked.

He shifted his tobacco to the other cheek. "Sorry, miss. But you still need to get off now."

Had she been bluntly honest with herself, Hannah would have conceded that the conductor's *faux pas* was understandable. From the rear, her build was not all that much different from a boy's, and her traveling duds resembled something that a sandlot ballplayer might sport. Her father's plaid, flannel shirt and suspenders, complemented by heavy denim trousers with a hole the size of a four-bit piece in the right knee did nothing to resolve her androgynous appearance. Neither did her closely cropped blonde hair, highlighted by a thousand miles' worth of railway soot.

The conductor picked up a folded newspaper from one of the seats and tucked it under his arm. He spit through the open half of the nearest window, all but a small portion of the purplish-brown juice finding its proper target.

"Pardon me, but are you going to throw that paper away?" Hannah asked.

"It won't do you no good," he said. "Someone must've bought it in Longview. You can buy a *Times-Herald* from that ragamuffin over there by the baggage carts."

She winked. "Much obliged."

The conductor smiled and looked at her afresh.

◆　◆　◆

Nora's friend, Mabel Johns, had come calling, and it was she who answered the door when Hannah Lane pounded the brass knocker.

"Mrs. Brower?" the young woman said.

"No, miss. She's busy in the kitchen. Is there something I can help you with?"

Hannah looked past her to the entryway. She could hear a radio playing loudly. "I'm here to rent the room. Would you please tell the mistress of the house that I'm here?"

Mabel frowned and excused herself. She uttered an audible "Hrumph!" as she disappeared from view.

Hannah was scrubbed and passably attired in a rumpled, print housedress. Before leaving the passenger depot, she asked the conductor to see to it that the porter contact the engineer to request that the stationmaster instruct the ticket agent to permit her to store her wooden trunk in an inconspicuous corner of the depot, safely behind the customer service counter. Then she washed her face in the public rest room and changed clothes in the privacy of a toilet stall. She arrived at the Brower residence on foot in the late afternoon, having taken care along the way to seek each shady overhang so as not to soil her clean clothing. She was keenly aware that housing was at a premium.

Nora accompanied Mabel to the front door and, after bidding her friend goodbye, turned to the visitor and smiled. "Yes, miss," she said. "I'm Mrs. Brower."

Hannah grinned at her prospective landlady. "Well, as I told the maid, I'm here to see about renting your room, the one that's advertised in the paper." Odd, the lady seemed to be amused by that.

"Won't you come in, Miss ...?" Nora said.

"Oh, sorry. I'm Hannah Lane." She walked into the entry room, and Nora shut the door.

From where they stood, Hannah could see a service flag in the living room window, something she had failed to notice as she came up the walkway outside. "Is your son in the Army?" she asked. Realizing that she had neglected to remove her chewing gum, she closed her mouth and tried not to pop too loudly.

"Navy. He's still at boot camp. In fact, it's his room that we're renting." Nora studied this latest applicant for a moment. "Are you from around here? You don't sound like you're from Texas."

"Nope, North Carolina. I'll be going to Baylor in the fall."

"I see. Well, I need to tell you that we're only renting to someone in war work. What are your plans for the summer?"

"I don't really know. The Good Lord sent me here, and I'm willing to do anything He wants of me."

"Including war work?"

"Sure." Hannah saw a cat sleeping on the stairway. It raised its head and yawned.

"I don't want to be too discouraging," Nora told the applicant, "but my daughter's been looking for work for about a week now. Waco's not an industrial city, so it's not too easy to find."

The girl shrugged her shoulders. "My daddy's a friend of Pat Neff. Maybe he can help me land a job. I'll take anything."

Nora was impressed. "How does your daddy know Pat Neff?"

"From the SBC, I guess. Pat Neff's the president of the convention, you know. And I think he and my daddy might have gone to college together or something."

"No, I hardly think so," Nora said. "Your daddy would be much too young for that."

"He used to be governor, didn't he?"

"Pat Neff? Yes, he did ... back in the twenties."

"And now he's president of Baylor University—my new college—so maybe he would be willing to help me find a job."

"Well, don't expect him to wait in the car while you're applying."

Ignoring the flippant remark, Hannah said, "Mrs. Brower, if you rent me this room, I'll have a war job by Monday, week—with or without the help of Pat Neff."

"So you're really serious about contacting him?" Nora asked. Her skepticism was melting away.

Hannah nodded her head. "Sure, if I have to. Like my daddy always says, every man in the world puts his pants on one leg at a time—except for Harry Houdini. 'Course, he's a very busy man, President Neff, so I'll just bother him if all else fails—like an ace up my sleeve. I've already gotten permission to live off campus."

As they went upstairs, Hannah stooped to pet the cat. "Are you mommy's little kitty?" she said in baby talk. Valentino rolled over on his side and, with claws retracted, playfully batted her hand.

It took Hannah only a minute to assess the room. "This would suit my needs perfectly, ma'am," she said. "Would that be twenty dollars before the month or after?"

"In advance. Tomorrow's the tenth of June, so we'll make the payment due on the tenth of each month, if that's all right with you. There's no lease to sign—I wouldn't even know how to draw one up. Just give me the rent money whenever it's due, and we won't have any trouble. Cash only, though. I can't accept checks."

The girl's eyes strayed to some sports trophies lining the top of the bookshelf. "That sounds fine to me, Mrs. Brower."

"But listen carefully, uh ... Hannah, is it?"

"Yes, ma'am, Hannah Lane."

"If you haven't secured a job in some sort of war industry within a reasonable amount of time—let's say the next ten days—we'll have no choice but to contact someone else on our waiting list."

"Yes, ma'am, I understand. What about meals?"

"You're welcome to eat whenever we do at no extra charge. It's just as easy to cook for four as it is for three."

Across the room, standing on the dresser, was a framed snapshot of two children and their parents, posing for the camera in front of a mammoth redwood. Hannah walked over to get a closer look. "That your family?"

"Yes ... Well, of course, my husband's gone now, but those are a couple of my children. Lizzie hadn't arrived yet."

Nora's hair was coal black in the photo, but her smile had not changed in the slightest. "What are their names?" Hannah asked.

"That's Stephen, and that's Wesley. Steve's in the Navy now, and Wes will be a junior at Waco High School next year."

"They're nice-looking boys," the girl said. "I take it, Steve's the athlete?"

Nora was at a loss for an answer, so Hannah pointed to the bookshelf.

"Oh, yes, those are Steve's trophies. He was a tailback for the varsity."

The clock downstairs began striking five. "Say, Mrs. Brower, I really need to get my things."

"Before you go, I should tell you that there's a rest room down the hall—first door on the right. Please make yourself feel at home."

"Thank you."

"Oh, no visitors of either sex are allowed upstairs. And no loud music after nine o'clock—my son has to get up early to deliver newspapers. Anything you'd like to ask?"

"No, ma'am. I've got twenty dollars in my trunk, and I'll pay you as soon as I retrieve it from the train station. I'm on foot, so it'll be a while."

Nora was shocked. "You walked all this way? Dear me!"

"Yep, I can walk forever—always could." Her dress was clinging to her, so she was eager to sink into a tub of bathwater.

"Wes should be home any minute now. He has enough gasoline to get you to the train station and back. How big's the trunk?"

Hannah laughed. "How big's the car?"

Nora motioned for her new boarder to come with her down the stairs. "We'll wait for him in the living room," she said. "Shall we be expecting you for dinner, then?"

"Yes, ma'am. I'm starved."

The cat raced past them to the bottom of the stairway.

Hannah inhaled the wonderful smells from the kitchen. "This'll be real nice, Mrs. Brower," she said. "I think you'll enjoy having me here."

◆   ◆   ◆

It was an innocent, off-hand remark by Madeleine Givens that led fourteen-year-old Elizabeth on a successful quest for the first paying job of her life.

Sixty or seventy soldiers were in the USO that night, and Madeleine was dancing with a coarse-mouthed PFC from Omaha. Her left leg was causing particularly intense pain, so she was anxious to take two aspirin and leave the jitterbugging to others.

Elizabeth was across the room, chatting with some V-5 naval reserve officers. These natty young men, mostly college-educated and well behaved, were stationed for their training at Baylor University's Burleson Hall, which, being home for the Navy's V-1, V-7, and V-12 units as well, naturally acquired the campus sobriquet of "USS Burleson."

Even from a distance, Elizabeth could see Madeleine's discomfort—less graceful than usual and biting her lower lip with the smallest exertion—so she walked over to the dance floor and offered to relieve her post. As a general rule, Elizabeth was too young to dance with the soldiers, but she made an exception to assist her co-worker.

"Thanks, kid. I won't forget you for this," Madeleine said. She lit a cigarette and limped toward the kitchen.

"Jeez, did I do that?" the private asked. "I didn't step on her foot more than once or twice." He took Elizabeth into his arms and hardly missed a beat.

"She was hurt in a car wreck a year ago, and the leg's still giving her some trouble."

"She's got nice stems, though. I've got to give her that much."

"I'm sure she'd be thrilled."

When it was Elizabeth's turn to have a break, she decided to join Madeleine in the library section. She found her sitting at a table, all alone, leafing through a *Life* magazine. She was teary eyed, so Elizabeth said nothing when she took a seat beside her.

After a time, Madeleine laid the magazine down and began crying softly to herself. "Lizzie, I don't know what to do," she said. "I'm about at the end of my rope."

"Your leg giving you a lot of pain?"

"No, it's not that at all."

"Is there anything I can do to help?"

"No, Lizzie, you've been swell." She stifled a sob.

A lanky GI two tables away looked up at them, but when he saw that Elizabeth noticed him, he returned to his book in embarrassment.

"What, then?"

Madeleine wiped the tears away with the back of her hand. "I'm just so ... lonely," she said. "Kind of silly, isn't it? Here I am, sitting in the USO with hundreds of good-looking men all around, and I feel like I'm the last person on earth."

"No, I don't think it's silly at all," Elizabeth said. She rotated the magazine around to glance at the cover: Alfred Eisenstaedt's photo showed a soldier telling his wife farewell. "But things will get better—you'll see. The war can't last forever."

Madeleine lit another cigarette and slid the ashtray in front of herself. "Maybe this is the wrong place to work. Maybe I need to go somewhere else."

"You mean leave Waco?"

"No, this is my home. I mean work somewhere that there's not so many men sizing up my figure."

Elizabeth looked toward the dance floor. "Did that PFC do something he shouldn't have?"

"No, he was all right ... well, a little fresh maybe, but no worse than the others."

"Could the twins come live with you?"

Madeleine shook her head. "Harland would have none of that. He's from out in the country, you know, and he wants his children to grow up on the farm. Besides, I've got to be at work during the day."

"Couldn't you quit your job and live with his parents, or would that open a new front in the war?"

"Oh, no, nothing like that," Madeleine said. "We get along fine, believe it or not. It's just that I feel I should be doing something to help the guys in uniform. I hope there's someone in England who's paying a little attention to Harland."

"You trust him, huh?"

"Sure. Why shouldn't I? And he knows I'll always be faithful to him. In fact, he's the one who suggested I come to work here."

Elizabeth smiled. "You're a lucky girl, Mad."

"I know, and I feel better now. Thanks for listening."

"I'm in the market for a job myself."

"Aren't you a little young?"

"Mother says it's all right with her, as long as I stay in school."

"What kind of work are you looking for?"

"I haven't the foggiest."

"Pat Lamb works across the street at the filling station. Maybe she could get a job for you."

Elizabeth chuckled at that notion. "Pumping gasoline? A girl? I couldn't do that."

"Why not?"

"Well, it's just not very feminine, that's all. And what do I know about cars?"

"Pat says all she does is clean the windshield and check under the hood. And pump gasoline, of course, and sometimes air up the tires. They don't do any mechanical work."

"Gee, I don't know."

"Mr. Downer owns it—Ralph Downer. But tell him you're older than you really are."

◆　　◆　　◆

Wesley thought payday would be a good chance to show Sandra Whittsel where he worked, but his carefully calculated, visionary plans did not go as smoothly as he might have wished—and worse yet, much of the blame could not be assigned to anyone but himself.

Although it was Wesley's own suggestion to meet Sandy in front of the high school building at 2:15, he was the one who failed to arrive at the appointed time.

Sandy waited in the oak trees' shadows for a good fifteen minutes before she slowly began to walk north on Eighth Street, presuming that he would follow his usual route to the radio station and catch up with her along the way.

Wesley overtook the girl as she was crossing Barron. "Sorry I'm late!" he shouted from behind. "My mother wanted me to meet the new boarder." He was out of breath.

Sandy turned to him and smiled. "That's okay. I think it's very sweet of you to walk with me instead of riding your bike." He had expected her to be angry with him, but instead she just giggled and fluttered her skirt. "I have a bicycle too, you know, but I was afraid my hem would get snagged in the sprocket."

They began to stroll along together, not saying a word. Sandy looked stylish in her "going to church" clothes, a knee-length yellow dress with white collar and trim. Her hat was white, and its wide brim was embellished with concentric yellow circles. White gloves completed the enchanting ensemble, and Wesley suddenly regretted the appearance of his nondescript sport shirt and trousers.

As they neared the KWXN studios, Sandy gazed up at him and finally spoke. "This is exciting. I've never been to anything like this before." Her eyes shone a lovely dark brown beneath the shadow of her hat, and Wesley could not help but smile. Though he was not especially tall for his age, he supposed that, allowing for the hat differential, the top of her head would not even reach his shoulders. He felt warm inside, protective of her and—he had to confess—more than a little self-satisfied.

"Hi, Myra," he said to the receptionist when they arrived.

"Hiya, Wes. Must be payday."

"Yup."

"Who's your friend?"

"This is Sandra Whittsel. She goes to school with me." Sandy removed her hat and nodded a silent greeting.

Myra nodded back. "How do you do, Sandra?"

"And Sandy," the boy added, "this is Myra Culp. She's our receptionist."

"So I guessed, sitting at the front desk and all. How do you do, Mrs. Culp?"

"*Miss* Culp," the receptionist said, "but Wes has been after me for years to change that."

Wesley shook his head. "Don't listen to her. She's man crazy, like most of the women around this place."

A patriotic CBS program, "Green Valley, U.S.A.," could be heard over the lobby's dual speakers. Emboldened by a sudden rush of confidence, Wesley took Sandy's hand and led her away. "Well, see you later," he said over his shoulder.

"'Bye," Myra shouted as the two teenagers disappeared around the corner.

Sandy did not remove her hand from Wesley's, so he continued to hold it until they were about to enter bookkeeping. The hand felt tiny and fragile to him, and the glove was of a downy soft cotton.

Once he had pocketed his biweekly paycheck, Wesley glanced at the hall clock—five minutes before three—and ushered Sandy down the corridor toward the main studio. It was nearly time for "Behold Tomorrow."

Cautious from past experience, he was hesitant to invite her inside the control room before the program was actually under way. Sometimes the final few minutes before airtime brought with them the eruption of salty language and, on occasion, an obscene gesture and appropriate response. Of course, this could happen at any given moment in such a stressful workplace, but it was most likely to flare up beneath the grave pressure of the opening cue.

Wesley decided to risk it. He swung the heavy door open for Sandy and followed her into the room, motioning for her to stand at the rear wall. The pair received a few glances from the technical crew, but otherwise their presence went virtually unnoticed. He whispered to her, "That's Marshall McFall in the booth." Sandy saw a handsome young man standing behind a microphone, but the name meant nothing to her.

"Sixty seconds," director Hugh Kenton said into the intercom. "Doug, did Monica give you that final revision? ... Take a look at page nine. Has Dr. Rawlinson's line been removed? ... Good."

Wesley looked down at the girl, who glanced up and smiled.

Mustache twitching, Kenton resumed his last-minute instructions. "Everyone, blue page eleven is an insert. I'll let you know whether we'll be using it—depending on our time coming out of commercial. Thirty seconds."

Sound-effects man Rodney DeBonaventura calmly sauntered over to his table of goodies, chatting with Douglas Pierson as he sat down and perused the opening page. The thirty-second adjacency was coming to an end.

"Stand by. Five seconds ... four ... three ... two ... one. Cue the organ."

Helen Tichman began playing the signature tune, "This Day of Days"—known in more cultured circles as Chopin's Nocturne in E major, Opus 10, No. 3—and soundman Dickie Waterhouse potted her down slightly at the designated entrance.

"Cue Marshall."

"Yes, Williams Drug Company ... the friendly stores ... presents 'Behold Tomorrow,' heard each day at this time as a courtesy of Williams Drug Company's three Waco locations ... at 501 Franklin Avenue in the Professional Building, at the southeast corner of Ninth and Austin, and at 423 Austin Avenue, the Old Corner Drug Store across from the Amicable Life Insurance Building. And now ... 'Behold Tomorrow'."

"Organ music down and out."

"As we left you yesterday, Jeannie Gabriel was informed by her lawyers, most notably Travis Earnshaw, that there was a definite possibility that Odom Cashley could legally evict her parents from the spacious mansion where they had lived for more than forty years. It was the home where Jeannie herself was born, and she was determined to have Bud Hanson spy on the desperately injured con artist by posing as a surgeon who had drifted over to the wrong side of the law."

"Stand by ... Mikes."

"We pick up our story as Anson Gabriel talks to his lovely bride in the train station, where he has just returned from a business trip to Chicago ... Listen."

"Sound. Establish the trains ... louder ... Now down. Cue Phyllis."

"Darling, I've missed you so. It's wonderful to see you again. Did all go well on the trip?"

"Everything except we lost the entire Colson project to Witherwax, that's all! Here, let me grab my bags."

"Oh, honey, what went wrong?"

"Somebody's been sabotaging the whole blasted affair ... that's pretty clear to me now. I thought so all along, but now I know for sure."

"Well, let's get a cup of coffee. That'll settle you down."

"The only thing that will settle me down is to see Kramer, Hennessy, and the whole bunch of them behind bars. Come on, I'm bushed."

Wesley cocked his head slightly, so he could steal a peek at Sandy. She seemed to be enthralled, absorbing everything around her. When she sensed his glance, she looked up and tapped him on the arm. "Who does the baby crying on the show? My mother says you can hear it sometimes."

He leaned down and whispered, "Beverly Jaynes, in the purple dress. She does all the children's voices."

During the final moments of "Behold Tomorrow," just as Marshall McFall began to recite his closing comments, all studio microphones were muted. This enabled Monica Whaley to wander to and fro, placing fresh copy on each of the six music stands. "West of the Brazos" would air at precisely 3:15.

Rodney DeBonaventura made good use of the interim to reposition his equipment, particularly his favorite sets of horse's hooves—coconut shells, wooden cups, plungers—all of which he used, some more than others, depending upon the stated weather and terrain. His arsenal of firearms, seldom called for in the preceding romantic drama, was prominently heard in the western and thus shifted front and center. Buckley Sledge's famous whip, actually two wooden blocks, also was accorded a place of honor on the sound-effects table.

While DeBonaventura was fussing over his self-styled "junk," cast members who had speaking roles in only the first of KWXN's two afternoon dramas hurried from the studio, taking the welcome opportunity to light up cigarettes and guffaw at each other's still-resonating flubs on "Behold Tomorrow." Four-letter words were bandied about, mixed company or not, and the women were nearly as guilty as the men in this respect. Nothing was considered sacrosanct in studio gossip except for the sponsors and their products, which were inviolable. In private conversation, once removed from the strictures of eavesdropping salesmen and control-room tours, the more cynical among them would deprecate the shows themselves as "Behold the Brazos" and "West of Tomorrow."

◆　　◆　　◆

SOUND: Horses galloping, two gunshots

ANNOUNCER: Before the days of streetcars and automobiles and airplanes, Waco, Texas, was often referred to as "Six-Shooter Junction." Come with us now as we relive those exciting days of gunslingers and lawmen, when civilization pushed back the frontiers of Texas and established a settlement "West of the Brazos."

Thus, without the slightest variation, opened each and every segment of KWXN's second daytime serial, a western with artistic aspirations that attempted to sidestep the usual cowpoke clichés in favor of human emotion. The program's creators, Marcus Hoskins and his wife, Betty Hillier Hoskins, reasoned from the very inception that it would be foolhardy to target the genre's natural audience when, for roughly three quarters of the year, most school kids were not yet at home to enjoy it. So the writers turned the problematic 3:15 time slot to their own advantage.

"Mikes ... Cue Phyllis."

"That's one thing I'll never understand, Jason ... why someone would go to the trouble of coming all the way out here from the east, and then just pack up and move out with the first sign of a setback."

"Aw, they never really had their hearts in it, Ev. You could see it in Buff's eyes. They had no business being here in the first place."

"It makes me shudder to think that we could have lost everything by investing in their store. Some folks did, you know."

"Kellen and Violet Scoggins, to name a couple."

"No!"

"Yep, they threw it all away on the whim of pocketing a quick buck ... everything they'd lived for since before the war ended."

"Is there anything we can do to help them?"

"Take them some food. Keep the predators away from their livestock. Pray."

A dozen minutes later, as Marshall McFall was intoning the close, Wesley nudged Sandy's arm and motioned for her to follow him. They exited the control room and wound their way along the brightly lit corridor to an office marked "NEWS."

"This is where I work on weekends," Wesley said. He opened the door and looked inside. "Hi, Grant. Mind if I show someone around?"

Five people were there, two of them typing and the others lounging with their feet on the desks. It was evidently a slow news day, and acrid smoke filled the air.

"Say, this is the kind of tour I don't mind at all," Grant Tollefson said. He grinned while admiring the girl's prettiness. Sandy was very demure in her summery outfit, her arms hanging casually in front of her, grasping the brim of her hat in both hands.

When she smiled back at the flattering reporter, Wesley was struck by something he had never noticed before, the coyness of her response. In that terrible instant, fleeting but haunting too, he could not quite decide whether her captivating shyness was ingenuous or manufactured by design.

The topic of the day seemed to be last night's capture of two of the seven German fugitives who had escaped from the prisoner-of-war unit at Camp Hood the week before. Ludwig Jung and Harald Stalleicken were apprehended about twenty miles west of Austin as they attempted to hitchhike their way to Mexico.

One of the newsmen took his feet off the desk and straightened his maroon-colored necktie. "I don't know if I'd have the guts to take them like that postmaster did."

"Well, you never really know until it happens to you," another reporter said. He paused long enough to swallow a sip of coffee. "Do we have any details on this Roscoe Faubion? I thought he was working at a filling station."

"Right, but he was also the postmaster out there in Cedar Park."

"Some school teacher turned in the report," Grant said. "I guess those dumb Krauts were trying to act like Americans, just walking along Highway 29 and hoping to thumb a ride. I hate to think what would've happened to that teacher if she'd stopped."

The man with the coffee cup laid it down and unfolded a newspaper. "It says here they dressed in their fatigue uniforms. They had some canned milk and some bread to eat—and a map of Mexico."

"Did they cause any trouble?" Wesley asked.

"Nope," Grant told him. "They surrendered without so much as a whimper. They're locked up in the Travis County jail right now." Then he smiled at Sandy and added, "They say they don't want to return to Germany until after the war—and I really can't say as I blame them."

Ten minutes later, as Wesley passed through the front lobby with Sandy at his side, he waved a goodbye to Myra Culp. "See you in a couple of weeks," he told her.

"Bye-bye," Myra said. Then she told his pretty friend, "Come back and see us, Sandra."

"That would be nice," Sandy said with a smile.

Wesley opened the door for the girl and watched as she carefully arranged her hat to keep the sunlight out of her eyes.

♦　　♦　　♦

She certainly does seem much older, Nora thought. Gertrude was helping another customer while Nora waited by the cash register, only about ten feet away. Mrs. Moek's eyes were listless, she had lost so much weight that her face appeared skeletal, and her disorderly shock of hair was now entirely gray. In contrast, Hermann, who was several years her senior, had returned to work a scant six days after learning of their son's death, and he seemed the very picture of health. For Gertrude, the healing process was much more protracted, perhaps even dangerously so.

As the other customer made her way toward the front door, carrying a small box of groceries, Gertrude turned to Nora with tears welling in her eyes and, without saying a word, walked over to embrace her in an affectionate bear hug.

"Hello, Trudy," Nora said. "How are you feeling?"

Gertrude took a step back and wiped the tears away with her sleeve. "Oh, I'm getting a little better each day," she said. "I've had a dreadful time of it, d'ough.

No one can imagine what it's like to lose a child like d'at. But I'm sure he is wit' d'e Lord. My Conrad was a good boy, you know, and d'at gives me comfort."

"We've been praying for you all along."

"T'ank you."

Nora surveyed the store. "Where is Hermann?"

Gertrude chuckled and walked behind the counter to pour Nora a cup of coffee. "Oh, d'at man," she said. "He'll be d'e deat' of me yet. Do you know what he's doing now? He's gotten it into his head d'at we need to have a soda fountain in d'e store. How're we going to make money wit' a soda fountain in d'is little store?"

"Well, it could be that he just wants to keep busy."

Gertrude laid Nora's cup on the counter and stirred in a few drops of cream. "D'at's part of it, I'm sure, but I also t'ink he's determined to compete wit' d'e others—like Sout'western and Williams."

Nora sampled the coffee, which was just the right temperature to drink. "And don't forget Goldstein's."

"Yeah, and Goldstein's too. He's taking all kinds of measurements to see if we can add on another room in d'e back. I t'ink it's a bad idea, 'specially wit' all d'e war shortages. Now, you tell me, where does he t'ink we're going to get all d'e sugar we need to run a soda fountain?"

"Maybe he thinks the war will end soon, and he's just planning for the future."

Gertrude began gathering the products that Nora routinely purchased. "God willing," she said. "I hope you're right." She reached for a package of sugar on the back shelf. "Do you have your stamp 13?"

Nora rummaged through her purse. "Yes, it's in here somewhere. Do I need to buy it now?"

"No, d'e stamp's good t'rough August 15. You want to wait until next week on d'at?"

"Well, I guess I'll have to," Nora told her. "Where in the world ...? Is it in book 1?"

"D'at's right."

"Here's a stamp 24 for the coffee. We're using more of that than we should, now that Wes has developed a taste for it."

"Maxwell House?"

"Yes, please."

"And how is your Steve doing? Have you heard from him lately?"

"No, I send a few lines to him nearly every day, but he only gets around to writing a couple times a week, if that. He's not what you would call a prolific writer."

Gertrude walked around the counter to the cereal section. "What did he have to say? Is he doing well?"

"Oh, yes," Nora said. She picked up some cans of soup and laid them near the cash register. "He's in San Diego right now for boot camp, and I think that lasts for about eight weeks. Then he'll be assigned to a training school somewhere."

Two customers entered the store, to the jingling of a small bell above the screen door. Gertrude called to them, "Hello, Priscilla. Hello, Mrs. Thomas."

"Hi, Mrs. Moek," Priscilla Drake said. "Is it too early to buy a couple of roasting chickens from you?"

"Give Hermann about ten minutes, will you? He's out back, but I'll get him for you."

"Thank you, Mrs. Moek."

Gertrude studied the two women. "Excuse me for asking," she said, "but are you mutter and daughter?"

"Yes, we are," Priscilla said with a puzzled look. "I thought you knew that."

Gertrude laughed. "No. I just never did make d'e connection, I guess. Maybe I've never seen you in here toget'er before." She walked toward the rear of the store.

After laying a loaf of bread on the counter, Nora glanced at her wristwatch and wondered what calamities would befall Dr. Bob that day on "Bachelor's Children." Janet and Ruth Ann were no more exasperating than real kids, she thought, and she shook her head in amusement. Mrs. Thomas and Priscilla nodded a greeting as they passed her in the aisle to await Hermann Moek's assistance at the meat counter.

Nora looked up when the bell jingled above the door again, and in came her daughter. Elizabeth glanced around the store and then rushed toward her. "Oh, good, Mother. I was hoping you were still here," she said. "I wanted you to be the first to know."

"My goodness. What is it?"

"I finally landed a job this morning! Do you believe that? I start on Saturday."

"That's wonderful, dear. Doing what?"

"Before I tell you, you've got to swear that you won't get mad."

Nora gave Elizabeth a suspicious look. "Sounds like trouble coming."

"Mother ..."

"Okay, what'll you be doing, working in a bar or one of those burlesque shows?"

Elizabeth laughed. "No, it's a perfectly respectable job. Promise me you won't get mad."

"All right, I promise. Apparently, it's too late for me to do anything about it anyway."

Hermann entered the store through the rear door, with Gertrude following behind. He greeted the ladies at the meat counter and began washing his hands in the porcelain sink. "Hello, Mrs. Thomas ... Mrs. Drake."

Elizabeth drew out the suspense of her announcement, something she always enjoyed doing whenever there was exciting news to reveal.

"Well?" Nora said.

"Mother, beginning Saturday morning at nine o'clock, I will be working at the Service Refining Company."

"That's a filling station. What sort of job is that for a girl?"

"You said you wouldn't get mad."

"I'm not mad. I'm just trying to figure out why, with all the jobs in the world, my daughter would decide to become a ... grease monkey. What do you know about cars?"

"Nothing. But Madeleine says I don't need to."

"Madeleine?"

"Madeleine says Pat Lamb works over at the Park Lot Service Station, across from the USO, and all she does is pump gasoline, wash windshields, and check the dipsticks. Mr. Downer and the boys do all the repair work."

"Well, I think this is just plain silly."

"I asked Mr. Downer for a job, but he's already got Pat Lamb and Kathleen Cook working for him, so he said I should check with Hoyle Harkins at Eleventh and Washington. He needs me."

"Does he know you're only fourteen?"

A guilty look flashed across Elizabeth's face. "Not exactly."

"Well, exactly how old does he think you are, then?"

"Sixteen. But Madeleine said it would be all right to fib about my age. I'll be fifteen in less than three months, so that's not such a big lie."

Nora shook her head. "Listen, honey, I'm proud of you for wanting to get a job—Lord knows, we can use the extra money—but I am very disappointed that you've resorted to deceit to do it."

"I didn't have any choice. No one is going to hire a fourteen-year-old. It was either lying about my age or baby-sitting for ten cents an hour."

"War or no war, I hate to think that we have to compromise our ethics to get by. The black-market crooks are no worse than we are."

Elizabeth was unswayed by her mother's logic. "But that's where you're wrong. Don't you see? They're hurting the war effort, and I'm trying my best to help."

Nora conceded the point with a smile. "Lizzie, dear, you have the makings of a good lawyer."

◆   ◆   ◆

The war was a ravenous consumer of a whole litany of commodities beyond the essential front-line component of military explosives. Canvas goods of every description were vital weapons in the battle against the Axis, and the city of Waco, Texas, suddenly found itself the recipient of a windfall prosperity that would have been unthinkable before the outbreak of hostilities at the beginning of the decade. By the end of the first full year of America's participation as a belligerent, Waco had become the armed forces' leading manufacturer of tents, mattresses, cots, and barracks bags—virtually anything that was fabricated from such fibrous goods as hemp, cotton, and flax.

Nine major defense plants arose in the city, and of their many thousands of workers, no fewer than three out of every five were women. One who joined their ranks on the morning of Friday, June 18, 1943, was Hannah Lane. She awoke to her alarm clock at 6:30, washed, dressed, and was out of the Brower house, walking south in the warm sunlight, before an hour had elapsed. She ate an apple along the way and tossed its core into the waves of foot-tall grass that covered a vacant lot near

Twelfth and Morrow. She never could see the reason to "properly" dispose of food remnants when they might be so valued by hungry populations of birds and ants.

Her destination was Third and Jackson, alongside the same Katy train tracks that had brought her to Waco a mere nine days earlier. It seemed more like nine years of stupor to her, what with all the walking, knocking on doors, tedious application forms, and unsympathetic rejections by a parade of unctuous personnel managers.

As she crossed Mary Avenue and then the Saint Louis & Southwestern Railway tracks, she could already see the imposing structures of the Crawford-Austin Manufacturing Company, occupying both sides of Third Street at the crossroads of Jackson Avenue. Waving proudly near the American flag was the coveted Army-Navy "E" pennant, presented to company president Wilbur Crawford some ten months back in stirring ceremonies at Municipal Stadium, an event carried live by KWXN's chief rival, radio station WACO. Emblematic of "Excellence in War Products Production," the "E" Award was received by only twenty-two businesses in the entire nation, so industry giant Crawford-Austin was among elite company.

Hannah saw at once that Crawford-Austin took a different approach to employee relations. She sensed a decidedly more respectful attitude than had been apparent in the hiring rooms of the other firms on her list. Here the people actually seemed happy to be at their jobs, and an almost tactile feeling of teamwork permeated the air. An impressive gallery of oversized photographs lined the walls, attesting to the rich heritage with which the present contingent of employees was entrusted.

When Hannah accepted an application form from the lady at the personnel desk, she glanced at the walls and asked, "Gosh, how many people work here?"

"More than five thousand now," came the reply. The lady, Mrs. Deacon, beamed with pride as she said it. "Of course, they're not all here. This is just the display room and some administrative offices. Our big plant is down Jackson at Sixth Street, on the northwest corner. You've probably seen it."

"Maybe I did, coming in on the train."

"Then, too, we've got the smaller building across the street, which houses our subsidiaries. Here, take this." Mrs. Deacon handed Hannah a pencil. "Waco Tent and Awning Company specializes in gigantic tents for circuses, revivals, and county fairs, that sort of thing," she said. "It's been retooled for the Army now because that's where most of the orders are. Our other division, the Douglas Company, manufactures beds and bedding supplies, but now it's mostly making Army cots and fireproof mattresses for the boys."

Hannah was a bit overwhelmed by the magnitude of the Crawford-Austin operations. To her way of thinking, its work force of five thousand employees was like an autonomous city, larger than the entire population of Mount Airy. As if sensing her unease, the personnel secretary simplified matters. "But don't worry about memorizing our divisions," she said. "If you're looking for war work, you'll be at the plant on Sixth. They do shift work, and most people like it over there."

The applicant hesitated before speaking. "I plan to go to college in the fall. Can I cut back my hours to part-time in September?"

"That would be up to your supervisor. They don't like doing that—it's a drain on production—but it's possible they can arrange something. You might have to settle for the graveyard shift and go to class when you get off work."

"I can handle it," Hannah said. "My daddy's counting on my getting a Baylor degree, and I don't want to let him down."

Mrs. Deacon shuffled some papers. "I understand," she said. "Fill out these forms, and then I'll take you in for a short interview with our personnel counselor, Mr. Tubbs."

"Yes, ma'am." Hannah sat in the nearest chair and placed a magazine on her lap to serve as a writing surface.

"Oh, and a word to the wise," Mrs. Deacon told her. "You might have better luck if you take that chewing gum out of your mouth. This isn't Wrigley's."

Hannah popped her gum one last time before wadding it back into the wrapper for later use.

◆　　◆　　◆

Dear Mom,

Boot camp is nearly half over for me, and I am looking forward to getting some training for an actual job. I wrote to you earlier about our trip aboard the troop train from S.A. to S.D., so I won't bore you with that again now. Suffice it to say that it was pretty uneventful, though I got to see a lot of desert along the way. How some folks can say this is beautiful is beyond me.

The toughest things so far are the obstacle course and the hand-to-hand combat. We learned some jujitsu, but not really enough to help us against a Jap opponent. Our size, though, counts for something.

We do our marching in formation, using some old wooden rifles that look like something Pershing's men might have carried. I was in pretty good shape all along, thanks to Coach Stiteler, so I haven't had any problems. His two-a-days were as bad as any boot camp, so I'm glad I already had that behind me.

Some of the guys could not swim when they got here, but the Navy changed that real fast. They made us float on our backs, kicking our legs, for a minimum of 50 yards. If you could cover that distance, then you qualified. One recruit from northern California could not do it without sinking to the bottom. He would have drowned, except that there were two instructors to fish him out. Eventually, they tied ropes to him and pulled him along from the side. Once he got enough confidence to do it unaided, he was fine—and now he's one of the better swimmers in our crowd.

The worst experience was going into a small cabin with gas masks on, whereupon the instructors remove your mask and prevent you from leaving long enough for the tear-gas (or whatever it was) to sink in. It's a terrible feeling, affecting the eyes and throat, and lots of guys panicked and ran toward the exit like they were nuts. The non-coms would trip them or block their way. It's all for a good reason, though, and you really come to appreciate your mask that way! Nothing tasted as delicious as breathing fresh air again after leaving the gas chamber.

We've done a lot of marching and bivouacking, though I don't see when we'll ever get a chance to use that aboard ship. Well, I guess maybe if we were shipwrecked and stranded on a deserted isle. Personally, I would ask some beautiful native girl to fix something for me to eat—perhaps bring me some grapes while I relax in a hammock.

There could be some furlough time coming to us in a couple of weeks, so you might be seeing me before I'm assigned to my next duty station. Fix an apple pie if you can locate enough sugar, OK? I'd like to get into fire control or become a radio operator, but I suppose that just depends on what's available.

One word of warning—I've taken up the tobacco habit. Not cigarettes, nothing as commonplace as that. No, a friend of mine from Arizona, Bobby Revueltas, has introduced me to the fine art of pipe smoking. Of course, it doesn't work too well in the field, but it gives the barracks a nice aroma. My favorite is vanilla maple, a Virginia-grade tobacco that's blended with natural cavendish and dark, sun-cured pipe tobaccos from Brazil. Ahhh!

Good-bye for now. I'll keep you posted as to the time off for good behavior. Give my love to Lizzie and Wes—and Uncle Matt too. He's sent two letters to me, but I haven't written him back because I don't have his address. Looks like he's still living in Harlingen, judging from the postmark, but he didn't include a return address.

Go Tigers!

Love, S—

Steve's words were still fresh in her mind when Nora heard John Milton Kennedy proclaim to radio listeners from coast to coast, "Lux presents Hollywood," and Robert Armbruster's title music signified that it was eight o'clock, Central War Time. How comforting it was to soak in these familiar sounds. Somehow, it made her feel that all was right with the world whenever Louis Silvers gave the downbeat and the CBS Orchestra launched into its twenty-six-second opening theme.

Announcer Kennedy continued, "The 'Lux Radio Theatre' brings you Ronald Colman in *In Which We Serve*, with Edna Best. Ladies and gentlemen, your producer, Mr. Cecil B. DeMille." Then came the revered voice of one of the world's great movie directors, who himself might have enjoyed a fine announcing career, had he not already been rather busy presiding over such screen hits as *The Sign of the Cross*, *This Day and Age*, *The Crusades*, *The Plainsman*, *The Buccaneer*, and *Union Pacific*—not to mention a dazzling array of silent-era classics like the Biblical epics *The Ten Commandments* and *The King of Kings*.

"Greetings from Hollywood, ladies and gentlemen," he said. "The slim, gray shape of a destroyer is a thing of beauty as it knifes through the sea ... and a thing of power and fury with its guns ablaze. But look below the steel shell, and you'll find a heart and a personality, intimately known to the captain on the bridge and to the men who are proud to be called destroyer sailors."

It was a rare Monday when Nora missed the "Lux Radio Theatre." The myriad household chores were normally complete by that time of evening, so she could settle, guilt-free, into one of the living room's overstuffed chairs—with a piping hot cup of coffee sitting within easy reach on the end table. And the radio receiver inside the Philco cabinet emitted a softly glowing light of its own that made her listening experience that much more cozy.

Choosing from among all the available nighttime programs, she would have to classify this long-running dramatic anthology as her favorite. Its production values were such that, against all odds, sometimes the sixty-minute radio version actually proved to be superior to the full-length film on which it was based. One such instance was Thornton Wilder's *Our Town*, which actually preceded the theatrical release of the film by several weeks—and with virtually the same cast too—though, alas, without Aaron Copland's affecting musical score.

Not so with *In Which We Serve*. While she had not seen the motion picture yet, she read somewhere that Noël Coward's screen portrayal of Captain Kinross was superb—as were his efforts as producer, director, and screenwriter. He even composed the music.

But her high expectations led to disappointment in the radio drama, which seemed a bit lackluster and poorly edited. Perhaps too much of the original had wound up on the radio adapter's cutting-room floor, or perhaps too many characters were retained, at the cost of making them all seem two-dimensional. Certainly the fault did not belong to Ronald Colman, who read his lines flawlessly and with genuine emotion.

Prior to John Milton Kennedy's recitation of the closing credits, Mr. DeMille stepped forward to say, "Our sponsors, the makers of Lux Toilet Soap, join me in inviting you to be with us again next Monday night when the 'Lux Radio Theatre' presents Barbara Stanwyck, Joseph Cotten, and Chester Morris in *The Great Man's Lady*. This is Cecil B. DeMille saying good night to you ... from ... Hollywood."

By the time the "Lady Esther Screen Guild Theater" came on the air, Nora was already in the kitchen, her mind preoccupied as she rinsed out her coffee cup. The thought of her son clinging to a life raft terrified her, and after hearing *In Which We Serve*, she hoped Steve would not be assigned to destroyer duty. Surely a carrier was more difficult to sink.

She heard a key being slipped into the front door and then a slight squeaking noise when it opened. Valentino stood up and stretched while looking between the table legs to see who was there.

"It's just me," Hannah Lane called.

"Oh, hello, dear," Nora said. She was busy wiping a drop of spilled gravy off the countertop with a dishrag. "Come in here if you have a minute."

The new boarder wore coveralls, and a dark brown bandana was tied around her hair. Her face was grimy. "Well, tell me how it went," Nora said. "Coffee?"

"Yes, please—black."

They sat at the kitchen table, and Hannah described her first day on the job—just a half-day, really, following all the red tape and orientation that the federal bureaucracy saw fit to impose. She ended up working the first four hours of the swing shift but was told to report back the following morning at 7:30 to begin a normal eight-hour stint. From then on, she would work whenever needed—day, swing, or graveyard—as dictated by the posted schedule.

"I must be some dish," she said, "to judge from a couple of wolves that I met today. Either that, or they must really be desperate."

Nora smiled and pointed out the obvious. "You've got to remember that those men don't come into contact with many eligible young women such as yourself. Most of the females working there are either married or middle-aged—or both."

"Well, the men at Crawford-Austin aren't exactly movie stars themselves," Hannah said. "At least any that I saw. A few of them were the leering type." She took a sip of coffee.

"That comes with the territory these days, I'm afraid. You know, beneath all that grease and grit is a very pretty girl, and you're just going to have to get used to it."

"I nearly kicked one of them below the belt," Hannah said. She blew on her coffee to cool it off. "I can't even remember his name, and I hope I never cross paths with him again."

"Oh, he'll be back," Nora said with a grin.

"What gets into them anyway? He was nothing special to look at, unless you're in the market for a gray-haired playboy with Coke-bottle eyeglasses. He's probably a slacker or 4-F anyway. Of all the gall."

Later that night, as Nora was preparing for bed, she thought back to when she was twenty. Times had changed considerably since then, of course, but not so human nature. Idly combing her long hair for the prescribed one hundred strokes, she suspected that Hannah Lane may have been less disturbed by the behavior of these male workers than she was by their quality.

◆　　　◆　　　◆

The town of Childress lay some 265 miles to the northwest of Waco, not far from where the 100th meridian intersected the meandering Red River to form the southeastern extremity of the Texas panhandle. A couple of miles west of the city limits was Childress Army Air Field, a 2500-acre complex that produced over one tenth of the nation's wartime bombardiers. CAAF opened for cadet training in February of 1943 and graduated its first class of precision bombardiers and dead-reckoning navigators in May.

A few weeks later, on Independence Day, Waco's pair of military installations became targets for the most recent class of Childress aviators, and the US Army encouraged male prospects between the ages of seventeen and twenty-seven to attend afternoon bombing demonstrations at both bases. Though Wesley would not be seventeen for another four months, he accepted Sandy's invitation to accompany her father to Blackland Army Air Field.

Major Whittsel honked the automobile horn at 12:40, and Wesley bounded down the stairway at top speed. "Goodbye," he shouted as he ran out the door. "Can't keep the Army waiting." His mother was in the kitchen, having changed into her work dress and apron after returning from church. It was Steve's eighteenth birthday, and his absence on the special occasion caused her spirits to sink.

"Have a good time," she called out, "and don't forget to say please and thank you." She felt guilty about feeding her younger son such a quick, improvised meal.

Waiting in the Pontiac at curbside, Sandy's father was in his flight uniform, and he received Wesley with a perfunctory "Glad you could come."

"Thank you, sir," Wesley said. He nodded at Sandy, who smiled back.

Major Duncan Whittsel was a careful driver, implicitly obeying the "victory speed" and grumbling indecipherable oaths to passing motorists who chose to squander the nation's finite oil and rubber supply by exceeding the thirty-five-miles-per-hour limit. Wesley thought it was a fortunate thing that a machine gun was not mounted on the dashboard of Major Whittsel's car.

Sandy sat between them in the front seat, which was agreeable to Wesley. It would have been awkward, had her father driven them chauffeur-style, and more than that, Wesley would have disliked feeling two steely eyes gazing at him in the rear-view mirror. He glanced at Sandy's hands, folded in her lap, and a pleasant sensation came over him when he recalled that this was the same automobile in which she trailed his bicycle up Sanger Avenue those three months ago.

When they arrived at Blackland Army Air Field, in the China Spring area outside of town, one of the two guards at the main gate greeted the major with a snappy salute and waved his automobile through. They parked in a spot marked "Maj. Whittsel" and from there proceeded to walk to the exhibition sector. On the way, returning an occasional salute, Sandy's father appeared to be quite affable, but he said not a word. He took leave of them by issuing what sounded like a command: "I'll meet you by the car at 1730 hours."

Visitors on the flight line were invited to view the basic and twin-engine airplanes that were used in Blackland's teaching programs. The doors to the instrument training section were also open, enabling the curious to inspect, first-hand, the little Link Trainers. Around 1:30, crowds filed into the post theater to watch the feature *Target for Tonight*, along with scratchy prints of the instructional films *How to Take Off* and, of course, its sequel, *How to Land*.

Then, emerging from the theater before their eyes had become fully adjusted to the bright sunlight, Sandy and Wesley glanced up in time to see seven aircraft flying in V formation overhead. "I think one of those is Daddy," Sandy shouted over the engine noise. She was squinting, with both hands shading her eyes.

Wesley smiled, impressed by how tightly they flew, and he shouted back, "Do you know which one is his?"

"Nope. It's probably the lead plane, but I can't say for sure." Sandy looked adorable in her kelly green Sunday dress, and Wesley wished he had not changed into such informal attire after church. Maybe he should have asked her what she was planning to wear.

Twenty training planes roared away from the base at two o'clock, destined for a strafing mission at Waco Army Air Field, which was located about ten miles to the east. Six or seven minutes later, their opening volley was answered by a group of WAAF pursuit aircraft, which attacked Blackland with dummy ammunition.

By the time the Army band began to play, the sweltering temperature had risen into the middle nineties, so the crowd was more than willing to follow their ears to the relative shade of post operations headquarters, where a brief pops concert was staged. Wesley thought the musicians sounded terrific.

"My sister played the flute in her junior high band," he said, in between selections. "Do you play any instruments?"

"Gosh, no," Sandy said. "Whatever gave you that idea?"

"Don't they have a good music program in Savannah?"

"Oh, yes, I suppose so. It's just that no one in my family is the least bit musical. Mommy was in some theatrical plays when she was younger, but she certainly didn't sing."

"Don't you like to listen to music?"

"Sure. I like Bob Eberle and the Andrews Sisters—like everybody else—and some of Glenn Miller's music is nice."

"What about your parents?" Wesley asked.

"I guess Mommy likes the Dorsey brothers the best, and some of that Spike Jones stuff. 'Der Fuehrer's Face' is a scream. Daddy doesn't talk about music much, but I think he's a fan of Benny Goodman—and, of course, any kind of marches. He's absolutely nuts over John Philip Sousa. Does that surprise you?"

Wesley grinned. "Not really, no."

Soon after the concert, visitors to Blackland Army Air Field congregated near the landing areas to view the aerial bombing demonstration. Several one-hundred-foot silhouettes of enemy ships had been constructed between the concrete runways, and squadrons of AT-11s, finally arriving from Childress, were instructed to bomb the targets from an altitude of four thousand feet. This scale would roughly simulate an attack on eight-hundred-foot vessels from a more normal bombing height of thirty-two thousand feet.

Upon hearing the planes' approach, Wesley, Sandy, and the rest of the crowd stared upward and watched as scores of hundred-pounders rained from the skies. First appearing as tiny dots in the air, the robin's-egg-blue bombs grew in size until, twelve to fifteen seconds after leaving the bomb bays, they crashed to the ground, splintering the targets beyond recognition in short order. Hundred-pounders of the regular training variety were used, with white powder substituted for explosives, and the bombardiers' accuracy was signaled by puffs of white smoke upon impact.

When it was all over, and retreat was being sounded by the post bands at HQ, Wesley followed Sandy back to the parked car. Major Whittsel was awaiting them, and he shocked Wesley with his friendliness.

"What do you think of our boys now?" he asked them both.

"They put on a grand show, sir," Wesley said. He hoped not to embarrass himself with anything he might say, but he need not have worried. The major was in such good humor that any remark was accepted as gleaming pearls of wisdom. For her part, Sandy did not seem at all surprised, having long since grown accustomed to her father's mood fluctuations within the stern military bearing.

"Did you fellas see the Link Trainers?" the major asked. "Aren't those little guys something?" He climbed into the car and started its engine.

Wesley opened the other door, allowing Sandy to enter and then seating himself by the passenger window. "Yes, sir, they sure are," he said.

Traffic was heavier than it had been earlier, with hundreds of visitors—mainly prospective recruits and their families—departing toward the BAAF gate.

"The Army has contracted for thousands of them now, you know," Major Whittsel said. "We can operate that C-3 model for about four cents an hour, and no one's ever been killed in one of them yet—"

"—because it never leaves the ground," Sandy added. Clearly, she had heard her father's familiar sentence many times before.

"That's right," he said, proud as a new papa, "and, Wesley, the flight simulation is uncanny. It turns, tilts, and bounces—just like the real thing. Its inventor, Edwin Link, was an organ builder by trade, so he incorporated all sorts of air-pump valves and bellows to make his trainer move in response to the controls."

"I'd like to try it out sometime," Wesley said. "Is that how you learned to fly?"

The major laughed. "No, I learned IFR the hard way—on the job. They didn't have the Blue Box in my day."

"Daddy's from the Old School," his daughter said.

"We use those Link Trainers for teaching IFR—that's Instrument Flight Rules—so a pilot can learn how to use radio range for determining his plane's position in bad weather and also his let-down to a field for landing. The instructor sits at that desk outside, and he makes it seem like the plane is flying through a thunderstorm. Of course, we're in constant radio contact with the trainee, and we ask him to climb, turn, and descend, all the while reacting to the changing weather conditions."

"How can he tell if he's done a good job?" Wesley asked.

"We can follow his course at the desk, with a remote bug tracing the plane's movements in red ink. Then, later on, the pilot can review his decisions by referring to the ink line on the paper. It's really pretty nifty. We call it the Pilot Maker."

A guard at the main gate glanced at the major's bumper sticker and then saluted as he waved him by.

"The worst part is how hot it gets inside the trainer, especially during the summer here in Texas. The Link has a lot of nice features, but refrigeration is not one of them."

As they neared Herring Avenue, an automobile sped by them, going at least fifty miles per hour, and the major's eyes flared with contempt. He shook his head, counted silently to ten, and lit a cigarette.

"Wesley," he said, "is it all right if we stop to get some gasoline before we drop you off? The tank's about empty."

"Oh, yes, sir. Please do," came the reply. It was then that Wesley first saw the "C" sticker on the car's windshield. How he coveted that red sticker with the bold "C" in white! But this was a mileage ration sticker, reserved for drivers who performed essential activities, such as governmental or Red Cross workers, physicians, ministers, scrap agents, telegram delivery couriers, and—in Major Whittsel's case—members of the armed services. The Browers' automobile had the much more common black square with the white "A," a gasoline ration sticker that entitled the family to just three gallons of fuel per week.

"It'll only take a few minutes," Major Whittsel said. "I think I know a station that's open on Sundays."

At least that left out the Service Refining Company. Wesley shuddered at the thought of having his own sister suddenly appear on the scene in a set of greasy coveralls, performing men's work for a regal officer of the United States Army Air Forces and his lovely daughter. He even dreaded the thought of talking about it.

Fortunately, the major brought up another matter. "Say, Wesley, doesn't your mother work at the USO here in town?"

"Yes, sir, and my sister too. They're both volunteers."

"Well, the reason I ask is because I have a mechanic in my outfit who might like to visit there sometime. He's kind of shy, and I'm sure he wouldn't go over there unless I ordered him to."

"Yes, sir. It's a nice place. Plenty of stuff to read and eat."

"And girls too," the major said. He smiled through a puff of smoke.

The change of subject proved to be only a brief reprieve. As they sat in the automobile, waiting for the attendant to finish pumping the gasoline, Sandy asked Wesley the abhorrent question about Elizabeth, whom she had never met. "Doesn't your sister work at a filling station?"

Wesley swallowed hard. "Yes, for the past couple of weeks now—over on Washington. But she works at the USO mostly." He flipped through the recruiting materials from Blackland.

"How does she like it?" Sandy asked. "I mean the filling station. Does she get lots of ribbing from the men?"

A brochure slid off his lap, and he bent down to retrieve it from the floorboard. "Oh, sure," he said.

When he sat back up straight, he noticed that there was mischief in Sandy's eyes.

"Well?" she asked.

"Well, what?"

"What do the customers say?"

"I think one of them asked Elizabeth if it was about time to change the air in his tires."

Sandy and her father both laughed. "Change the air in his tires, huh?" the major said. "I'll try to remember that for the next time I pull into a filling station."

Wesley glanced to his left, and he could see that Sandy was still amused at his discomfort. "Actually," he said, "my sister wouldn't even be there except for the manpower shortage. It's not the money, so much. She's just trying to do her bit for the war effort."

Major Whittsel took another drag on his cigarette and blew a smoke ring. "Sandy tells me you're doing the daytime news on the radio now."

"Yes, sir. Well, whenever one of the regular announcers is on vacation. During school, I just do the weekend news at night."

Wesley heard a voice to his right, where a gentleman in a Continental Oil Company uniform was wiping the windshield. "Check under the hood?" the attendant asked. He was a thin black man with graying hair.

"Yes, please," the major said.

The man gazed at all three of them. "You folks been out to the bombing show?"

"That's right," Sandy's father told him. "And from the looks of it, some birds wanted to try out those maneuvers on my car."

The attendant chuckled and said, "They did that. Yes, sir, they did do that."

◆　　◆　　◆

Waco was not such a bad place to be assigned. Danny Rignold glanced at the storefronts as he kicked a small stone along the sidewalk of Eighth Street. There was the Raleigh Barber Shop, a Yellow Cab station, even a Safeway grocery store. He could have been sent to any of a dozen flying schools in the region: Enid, Lubbock, Maxwell, Bowman, Williams—the list went on and on. At least Blackland was in the south, where he felt comfortable with the customs and manner of speaking.

An errant kick made the stone roll off the curb and into the gutter. Across the street was Frank Trapolina's shoe repair shop and, after the auto park, the savory smells of Charlie Lugo's Mexican restaurant.

Private Daniel Arthur Rignold was about five hundred miles away from his family's town of Kosciusko, Mississippi, but he was not as homesick as he had feared. The Army kept him plenty busy, which certainly helped, and the fact that he was the platoon champion at mail call also served to keep his spirits high. Just yesterday he received a letter from his mother, one from his sister, and still another from a neighborhood acquaintance whom he hardly knew. He suspected that the church asked its members to write to a mailing list to boost servicemen's morale. He carried the envelopes with him now, buttoned inside his fatigues—not strictly regulation, but he was off duty until reveille beckoned him to morning formation.

When he crossed to the north side of Washington Avenue, Danny happened to notice his reflection in the window of Central City Commercial College, better known locally as Four-C business school. His khaki uniform looked sharp, from what he could tell in the glass, but he was not able to pause for long because he thought he could distinguish some people sitting at desks inside, and he did not want to appear to be posing.

Farther along the block stood an auto repair shop and a real estate office. Across Washington was the Masonic Temple, and he made a mental note to mention this in his next letter to his father. He spotted two NCOs approaching him on the sidewalk, and Danny nodded to them as they passed. Once, as a raw recruit, he had mistaken a captain's bars for the two chevrons of a corporal, drawing a frown but no verbal reprimand from the offended officer. He knew that it would only make matters worse to chase after the captain and apologize to his face.

Danny walked past the Frank B. Jones Printing Company and halted for a moment on the northwest corner of Seventh and Washington. Directly across the street was the Park Lot Service Station, and on his left was the entrance to the United Service Organizations. Waco's USO was a much larger establishment than he had expected—a full third of a city block long and two stories tall. A couple of days ago, he overheard someone in the mess hall say that a soldier could record his voice and then mail it back home for his folks to play on whatever conventional turntable they might have. He was determined to give it a try.

An elderly lady said hello to Danny as he passed through the doorway and gazed around the room. About forty GIs were there—as well as a handful of Navy men—lounging in the chairs, writing letters at the tables, and listening to phonograph records. A grandmotherly worker was wrapping a package for a baby-faced private to send home to his girlfriend. Another volunteer was sewing a unit insignia on the sleeve of a cadet. Several non-coms were visiting with some young ladies around the refreshment table, taking turns fishing goodies out of the cookie jar.

Danny noticed that a middle-aged woman in the library section would occasionally glance at him as she reshelved a musty supply of books. He blushed, realizing that he must have appeared to be lost. Quickly he sat down on a sofa and pretended to straighten the knot of his necktie. The lady wheeled the rickety book cart over to him. "May I help you find something?" she asked.

"Not really. This is my first time here, so I'm just lookin' around," he said.

"Well, we're glad to have you, private. Would you like for me to give you the grand tour of the place?"

"No, thanks. I could use a cup of coffee though."

She pointed toward the back wall. "Right over there, on the other side of the pool table. There are also some finger sandwiches and potato chips—and don't forget to get some cake for dessert."

"Thank you, ma'am," Danny said. He walked toward the refreshments.

A cute girl, probably of high school age, was ladling some strawberry punch into paper cups, and she smiled at him as he reached for a ceramic mug near the coffee dispenser. An older lady, perhaps thirty-five, was scrubbing the entire length of the counter with a white dishrag. She moved along with a noticeable limp.

Private Rignold brought his cake and coffee over to a table near some phonographs, so he could listen to the music. He unfastened the bottom two buttons of his shirt and removed the envelopes. Seeing as how the middle-aged woman with the book cart was still nearby, he asked her where he could find some stationery.

The lady called to the girl at the refreshment table, "Lizzie, would you bring this gentleman something to write on?"

"Yes, Mother," the young worker said. She wiped her hands with a towel and walked toward Danny, picking up a few sheets of writing paper as she passed the supply shelf.

"Do you have a pencil or pen?" the girl asked him.

"Yes, ma'am," he said.

She giggled at his formality. "Goodness. Do I look old enough to be called that?"

"No, ma'am," he said with a laugh.

She handed him the USO stationery. "You're from the south, aren't you? We get soldiers from all over the country here."

"Yes, miss. I live in Kosciusko, Mississippi."

"Never heard of it."

"But I'm really from the Hattiesburg area—a little town called Petal."

"Never heard of that either."

"Not many people have." He smiled at her and took a sip of coffee.

"What's your name, airman?" the teenager asked. Her manner of speech, far beyond her years, imitated that of full-timer Madeleine Givens and one or two of the brasher volunteers.

"Oh, I'm no airman—at least in the sense of flyin'," Danny said. Picking up the fork, he sampled the tempting dessert, a small square of white cake with plain vanilla frosting. It was a delight to taste the unfamiliar sweetness of real sugar in his mouth. "Gosh, that's good," he said.

The girl looked at his hands. There was evidence of grease under the fingernails. "Then what do you do in the Army?" she asked. It was her job to engage in small talk and make the servicemen feel welcome.

"Well, I'm just a ground-gripper right now, but I do hope to go to gunnery school one of these days."

"You're on a ground crew?"

"Yes, miss. I help to service those washin' machines over at Blackland Field."

"Washing machines!"

"You bet." He laughed at her gullibility. "That's what we call the trainin' planes the cadets fly."

"I didn't know the Army had such a good sense of humor," she said.

"Yep. See, the fliers who can't make the grade are washed out. Get it?"

"How clever."

"And the engines are coffee grinders. That's what we call 'em." He savored another bite of cake.

The girl took a step forward. "So, what's your name, ground-gripper?" They shook hands.

"The name's Danny Rignold. R-I-G-N-O-L-D. We pronounce the 'g,' but the French don't."

"Well, very nice to meet you, Danny. I'll let you write your letter." She began walking away.

Danny jumped to his feet. "Say, miss, I need to ask you somethin' ... before you go."

"Yes?" She turned toward him but was looking down at the carpet.

"I heard someone say that soldiers can use their own voices to make records and then mail them to the folks back home."

"Yes, that's right. I'll get my mother to show you how."

"Is she the only one who knows?" Danny asked. He leaned forward with a conspiratorial whisper. "What is it, some sort of classified information?"

"Hardly. It's just that I haven't been trained on that equipment yet." She glanced up at him and then headed toward the library section.

"Wait!" he said. "You haven't even told me your name."

The girl stopped. "Elizabeth." She stared at him for a moment and then added, "I'll see if I can find her."

"Thank you, Elizabeth," he said. His voice was suddenly quiet. "Maybe I'll see you around."

Elizabeth looked away. "Yes, maybe," she said. "I go by 'Lizzie' for short."

Nora Brower escorted Danny to the back room, cautioning him to put his thoughts into words beforehand. "You only have a fraction over two minutes, so you can't dilly-dally around. Some of the fellas write down their messages, but others like to just wing it. That's up to you."

"Yes, ma'am."

The mysterious machine actually turned out to be little more than a glorified Dictaphone, but Nora assured the young man that the quality was surprisingly good. "We could record at 16 rpm, but we choose to use 78 instead because that way everyone can play it at home."

Danny hoped that the volunteer would leave while he spoke into the recording device, but that turned out to be impossible. "Just pretend that I'm not here," Nora said. "I hear a dozen of these little chats each day, so there's no need to feel self-conscious about it. Just no off-color wisecracks is all we ask. The censor will not allow it."

"I'll try to keep that to a minimum," he said. "And who's the censor?"

Nora smiled. "You're looking at her."

"Jeez. Then I really *will* be on my best behavior."

Nora inserted a disc into the recording unit. "Seriously, though, Private ..."

"Rignold."

"... Private Rignold. No obscenities, no troop movement information, no speculation on future duty stations. Those will not fly."

"Understood." He cleared his throat.

"Take the chewing gum out of your mouth, please," the woman said. Danny stuck the gum on the fingernail of his left thumb.

"Oh, splendid," she said, perhaps with a touch of sarcasm. She sounded for all the world like his ninth-grade teacher, old Mrs. Weems. "All set?"

"Yes, ma'am. Just tell me when."

Nora pressed a button and then pointed to the soldier.

"Mom, Dad, this is Danny. You know where I am, so I won't go into that. Besides, the censor won't permit me to say." He winked at the recording lady. "I'm doin' fine nowadays, helpin' to keep a whole trainin' school's worth of fly-boys in the air. I've graduated to twin-engine models from those eggbeaters I worked on at my earlier assignment, so of course the horsepower and aerial performance standards are much higher. Eventually, I'm hopin' to go on to even bigger and better duties, maybe show those Krauts and Japs a trick or two before I'm finished. My bosses in the hangar are Sergeant Hillenbrand and Sergeant Tooker, and I suppose they're all right. One of the lifers—I won't mention his name—is a class-A jerk who must have been a con artist in civvy life. He's a real apple-polisher who always seems to come out smellin' like a rose. The officers are easier to deal with and actually take some interest in the welfare of their troops. One of them gave me direct orders to check out the USO, which is where I'm makin' this record. The Army food is not too bad, but it sure is hard to fall asleep in the barracks—what with all that snorin' constantly goin' on. Is everythin' okay back home? I hope Melanie has heard from Cap by now. I'm sure he is doin' fine and gettin' into tip-top shape. Please remind Cappy-Boy that I told him not to eat so much dessert the week before he left for boot camp or he wouldn't fit into any of Uncle Sam's uniforms. I guess it's almost time for the Whippets to begin their practices. I certainly do hope they play better than last year. I met a guy from Poplar Creek the other day. Who'da thought that two small-town boys from central Miss would wind up in the same outfit? Did you ever get the icebox door fixed? Dad swears he doesn't know how it happened, but I'll bet you it was those Ducey kids. Sis lets them come in for Kool-Aid, you know. The temperatures here have been just like home, with highs in the middle nineties for the most part. Can't complain, though—remember how humid it is in Natchez this time of year? Well, the recordin' lady is lookin' at her watch and frownin', so I'd better close now. Say hi to Rosalind for me—or maybe you can just let her hear this record. I don't know how many times you can listen before it wears out. All my love, Danny."

Nora pressed a button to stop the electronic apparatus from spinning, then pulled a lever to release the record from its housing. Habitually, she offered to let the serviceman listen to his voice-letter, but like most of her clients, he declined the invitation. "Write down your mailing address on the label, please," she told him, placing a square-shaped mailer on the desk next to the machine. The envelope contained a cardboard insert for rigidity.

"Yes, ma'am." Danny returned the chewing gum to his mouth. Then, realizing that he had left his writing utensil on the table across the room, he asked the lady, "May I ...?" A pencil was resting atop her ear, and she handed it to him.

He began addressing the envelope. "I want you to know that I really appreciate your help, ma'am. You've been swell." His handwriting was swift and wretched. "Say thanks to your daughter too. She's a livin' doll."

"Very well, private. That's what we're here for," Nora said with a courteous smile. But her face darkened when she added, "Do you mind if I ask how old you are?"

"Why, no. Why should I care about that?"

"Some people are sensitive about such things, that's all."

He erased the three numerals of his address and rewrote them for legibility. "Thanks for the use of your pencil." He handed it back to her.

"Certainly, private."

"I'm twenty-two," Danny said.

"That so? I've got a son who's eighteen and in the Navy, and then another who's sixteen. You've met Elizabeth, who is fourteen years old."

He nearly swallowed his gum. "Fourteen! She's younger than my baby sister."

"She'll be fifteen in September."

"Golly, I hope she didn't think I was—"

"Lizzie is used to that by now," Nora said. Then, with a weary sigh, she added, "I'm sure you're no better or worse than the others."

"You seem awfully defensive about this, ma'am, if you don't mind my sayin' so."

The woman's face softened. "I'm sorry, private. I don't mean to take it out on you. Lizzie has a job now, and she's been hearing lots of wolf whistles from men who are old enough to be her father."

Danny grinned. "Well, I never learned how to whistle."

Nora smiled in return. "You seem like a nice boy, private. Come again whenever you have some free time."

"I'll do that, ma'am," he said. On his way to the table where his stationery still lay, he turned back to Nora. "What about the postage?"

"No charge."

◆　　◆　　◆

During her first couple of weeks at Crawford-Austin, Hannah Lane worked irregular hours—rotating haphazardly among the three shifts, filling in for absentees whenever needed. Then work-force attrition simplified the matter, at least for the balance of the summer, as the names of two people in her section were struck from the graveyard roster.

One man with accumulated seniority requested and received a day-shift position when an elderly tent-pole worker retired to a part-time role. And one seamstress was forced to request an extended leave when her pregnancy became too pronounced for comfort. While Hannah was neither a woodcraftsman nor an accomplished seamstress, some juggling of tasks landed her an apprenticeship in the fabled "loom room," from which, as local lore had it, there was no escape.

In point of fact, she found the experience to be rather interesting, if repetitious. Her supervisor was a cadaverous shadow of a man named Mr. Hinckley—*Paul* Hinckley, she thought, but she never learned his first name. Unfit for military service, Mr. Hinckley threw himself headfirst into war production, and the effort consumed his every waking moment. He had not missed a single hour of duty since March of 1942, often working without pay on his weekly day off.

A confirmed bachelor, Mr. Hinckley was essentially sexless. Indelicate humor and rude jokes about anyone from Errol Flynn to Eleanor Roosevelt struck a hollow chord with him, and earthy newcomers soon learned that he would not countenance their rowdiness, no matter how playfully intended. And yet so genuine was his work ethic that he earned the respect of everyone around him. Though his spindly appearance made him an easy target for office wags, somehow such attempts at cheap humor always missed their mark—producing at best a round of nervous chuckles that left the raconteur feeling more shame than comedic satisfaction.

Whenever their work hours coincided, Hannah would ride home with Bernadette Reid Fetters, who lived on Herring Avenue with her older sister and brother-in-law, along with their three children. Bee was, like Hannah, a member of First Baptist Church. She was a graduate of Baylor University, where she studied English Literature under the tutelage of Allie Webb and Luther Weeks Courtney, not to mention the venerable A. Joseph Armstrong himself. Precisely six months before the attack on Pearl Harbor, Bee's teaching aspirations were dashed, voluntarily, when she married her college sweetheart, a medical student by the name of T. R. "Ronnie" Fetters. Actually, as she was fond of saying, they "went to different colleges together." They had met at a Baylor football game in Austin less than a year before, when his Texas Longhorns shut out the Bears, 13-0. So gracious was he in victory that he won her heart sometime between the final gun and their slow walk to the Texas Memorial Stadium exit tunnel, and the ensuing hundred-mile courtship soon developed into love and a marriage proposal. Ronnie was away now, serving as a hospital corpsman in the US Navy. Before leaving for military duty, he taught Bee to drive his light blue 1939 DeSoto, and he assured her that the tires had more than enough tread for the duration of the war.

It was 8:20 in the morning when the automobile pulled up to the Brower house, and Bee was having terrible difficulty staying awake. The unruly playing of her nieces and nephew had kept her from sleeping properly the day before, and it was only the admirably strong coffee inside the commissary pot that prevented her from dozing off at her post in the packing room. Twice on the way home, Hannah had to nudge her in the ribcage to bring her out of her dazed state. Finally, Bee cranked open the wing window to provide a steady flow of air on her face, and that seemed to help.

Hannah arrived just in time for breakfast—at least she hoped she was not too late. Before waving goodbye to her sleepy friend, she advised Bee to ask for a set of earplugs to help maintain her health during the summer months, when the children were not in school. These protective inserts were readily available from the shop foreman, and Bee agreed to request a pair. Of more immediate concern to Hannah was the question of whether Bee would be able to coax the DeSoto safely to her sister's house today. With worry in every step, Hannah traversed the length of the walkway before she finally saw the automobile pull away from the curb and continue down the street on a relatively stable course.

"Hannah's here," Wesley shouted when he heard the front door close. He was busy manning the toaster.

"I'll be right there," his mother shouted back. She was in the downstairs bathroom, gathering linens for the morning wash.

Hannah entered the kitchen and said, "Sorry I'm late, Wes. My ride was in no condition to be driving."

"Drunk?"

She smirked. "Of course not. Bee Fetters—drinking?"

"Well, I didn't know who brought you home. I thought maybe it was one of your boyfriends."

"Oh, sure," Hannah said. "Which one?"

Wesley carried a plate of hot toast over to the table. He had stirred a batch of yellow margarine the night before, and he brought that with him too.

At this particular moment, Hannah could not have been happier. Lazily surveying the kitchen, a wave of euphoria swept over her. Funny how something as simple as the aroma of fresh coffee could bring back memories of home. The same could be said for the sound of a radio show. "The Breakfast Club," a Blue Network staple for as long as she could remember, was playing softly on the table radio, and host Don McNeill's kindly approach always brought a homey feeling to the morning meal, just like back in Mount Airy.

Wesley seated himself at the breakfast table. "You still want me to take you over to Baylor this afternoon?" He picked up a piece of toast and began spreading margarine on it. A dollop of strawberry jam was in a dish nearby.

Nora came into the kitchen and said to Hannah, "Goodness, child—sit down. Lord knows you've earned it, working all night like that."

"Yes, ma'am, but I need to wash my hands first." Hannah removed her chewing gum and tossed it into the garbage sack beneath the sink. Her tattered coveralls and short blonde hair made her look, every inch, like a teenage boy, a thought that was not lost on Wesley. He laughed to himself and shook his head.

Hannah sensed his amusement. "Excuse me, but did I say something funny?" She struggled to maintain a straight face.

"Oh, it's nothing you said. You just don't look very feminine in those dungarees, that's all. And the black stuff all over your nose and chin doesn't exactly help."

Hannah wiped her nose with the sleeve of her blouse. "Well, maybe that's because I'm not *trying* to look like a lady just now. Don't you know there's a war on?"

"Hey, I'm just trying to help," Wesley said. "You certainly don't want to wind up being a spinster, do you?"

Nora intervened. "Now, Wes, that's enough of such talk. Leave poor Miss Hannah alone. There'll be plenty of time for Cupid to work his magic after the war." She reached into the kitchen cabinet for some cups.

The sound of footsteps was heard coming down the stairway, and Elizabeth, her hair still in curlers, made a tardy appearance in the kitchen. "Mother, may I borrow your silver necklace—the one with the little teardrops?" she asked. Then she noticed the others. "Oh, hi, Hannah. You like your job?"

"So far, yeah. How about you?"

"Not bad, but I'm only getting ten or twelve hours a week." She whisked a stray strand of hair out of her eyes. "And school hasn't even started yet, so they can't use that as an excuse."

Nora poured some coffee for herself. "The necklace is in my blue jewelry box," she told her daughter, "but don't forget to put it back when you're finished." She saw that there was nothing on the boarder's plate. "Eat up, Hannah. We've got some biscuits and gravy. I'm afraid we've run out of meat rations for sausage, so I had to concoct something. And there's orange juice and coffee to drink. Wes doesn't care for my experiments, so he's having toast and jam."

Hannah spooned some of the simulated sausage gravy over a biscuit and dipped her finger into it, placing the sample on the tip of her tongue. "This is wonderful, Mrs. Brower." She began to get up for some coffee, but Nora motioned for her to remain seated.

"Thanks for the vote of confidence, dear," Nora said. She laid a steaming cup of the brew in front of her. "Of course, you've been working all night long, so anything would taste good to you."

"No, really. It's swell," Hannah said. She gave Wesley an elbow when he rolled his eyes.

Once Elizabeth and Nora joined the others at the table, Hannah paused for a moment to offer the blessing, and then it was time to enjoy a homemade meal that she had been anticipating for her final two or three hours on the production line. Though improvised with the drippings of bacon and pork chops, the "sausage" gravy made for hearty eating over biscuits, just what Hannah's famished appetite was craving. She consciously forced herself to eat slowly, so as not to appear indecently ravenous at the table.

"You never did answer my question," Wesley told her.

Hannah held up a finger to indicate that she did not wish to talk with a mouthful of food. After swallowing, she said, "All I recall hearing from you were some rude comments about my looks."

Nora laughed while she stirred the coagulating gravy, but Wesley brushed off Hannah's remark. "Do you still want me to take you over to Baylor today?" he asked.

"Oh, my gosh. I almost forgot," Hannah said. "My days and nights are all mixed up—what with these crazy work shifts. Is this still Monday?"

"Still Monday."

"Then yes, if you can spare the time and gasoline. But first let me get a few hours of sleep."

"Okay, will do," he said. "How long will it take at Baylor? I need to be at the radio station from 3:30 to six."

"Less than an hour, I think."

Wesley nodded his head, and Hannah smiled in appreciation.

"I didn't know you had to do the news today," Nora said.

"Yes, ma'am. Marshall McFall is on vacation for another week, and Grant Tollefson won't be back at the station until Thursday. That just leaves me for the afternoon slot."

♦   ♦   ♦

Hannah Lane was well aware that seldom, if ever, would she be able to rely on the Browers' automobile as her means of transportation to and from the Baylor University campus. Gasoline and rubber were much too precious for that, and besides, she had no desire to be beholden to anyone. Still, inasmuch as Wesley had offered to chauffeur her to registration, she was happy to accept. The fall quarter would open on September 15, and from then on she planned to make it a strict habit to ride the streetcar to her classes.

Being a transferring undergraduate, Hannah was required to take a psychological test prior to admission, just like any incoming freshman. She would arrange for that today, in addition to paying her miscellaneous fees. According to the college bulletin, this would amount to about thirty dollars. Already mailed to the Baylor registrar were her high school records, along with transcripts from her two years at Wake Forest College. Safely tucked in a ragged envelope addressed to "Rev. S. D. Lane, Calvary Bapt. Church, Mt. Airy, No. Car." was her prized free-tuition voucher, without which she could not afford to attend a private institution such as Baylor. It was a long-standing custom that all ministerial students—as well as ministers' sons and daughters—could enjoy the benefits of a tuition waiver, provided the Head of the Department of Bible had validated their vouchers.

Well before Hannah ever considered traveling west to attend Baylor University, she was convinced that she wanted to join the Southern Baptist ministry in some capacity. This would not be as a preacher, of course—"wrong plumbing," she liked to quip—but perhaps as a minister of children or possibly pursuing missionary work of some sort, even if it meant relocating overseas. Now, with civilian travel abroad effectively out of the question, she had her sights set on becoming a minister of education, hopefully somewhere in the southeast.

Baylor's summer quarter was going strong, so the campus was far from deserted. Still, enrollment only amounted to about a third of the regular-session total, so there was less traffic than normal. Indeed, Wesley was fortunate enough to park the 1938 Chevrolet in a choice spot—at the curb in the shade of a large pecan tree. As he turned off the engine, he noticed several coeds passing by on their way to the New Women's Dormitory. Looking around further, he was struck by the fact that most of the people he saw were women. Had he access to university statistics, he would have known why. Reflecting the perilous times, of the seven hundred students enrolled during the summer term, nearly two thirds were female. And soon to join them was this pert North Carolinian, now sitting just an arm's length away.

Wesley opened his door to allow a breeze to blow through the car. "Don't forget to meet me back here in an hour and a half," he told her. "There won't be anyone to do the four-o'clock news if I'm late to work."

Hannah was searching for something in her purse, but she nodded her head. "Don't worry. I'll be here," she said. "Want a stick of gum?"

"Sure."

She handed him the chewing gum and asked what he would do to keep himself occupied while she was gone.

"I'll probably go over to the bookstore for a while. I need to buy Sandy Whittsel a get-well card."

"Oh?" Hannah looked concerned.

"She has the mumps."

Hannah put a stick of gum in her mouth. "Why don't you just tell her in person?"

"Because I've never had the mumps," Wesley said. He unwrapped his gum and chewed. It tasted cool and refreshing to him—Wrigley's Spearmint.

Hannah studied the boy's face, and the corners of her mouth rose slightly. Finally she asked, "Does this Sandy go to high school with you?"

Wesley squirmed in his seat. "She was new this year."

Now Hannah smiled broadly. "You sweet on her?"

"Naw, not really," he said. "I used to be. Who told you that?"

"Just a wild guess. Is she a Christian?"

Wesley glanced at her and then began rubbing a spot of dust off the dashboard. "I guess so. Her family goes to my church sometimes."

Her face became earnest. "No, I wasn't asking if she goes to church. I mean, is she saved? Those are two entirely different things."

He reached down to make sure the parking brake was secure. "Golly, how should I know if she's saved? It's never come up in conversation."

Hannah leaned forward, almost confrontational. "My daddy always told me never to be embarrassed about asking that question."

Wesley was still looking at the floorboard. "Well, my gosh, isn't that sort of a personal matter?" he asked.

"Not at all! You want her to go to hell?"

"Of course not," he said, but when he turned to look directly at her, the annoyance melted into curiosity. "Is your daddy a minister or something?"

Hannah seemed amused. "Sure. I thought you knew that. I told your mama about him."

"You don't seem like a preacher's kid to me."

She sat back in her seat, the zeal ebbing from her eyes. "Thanks. I'll take that as a compliment."

Wesley grinned and allowed his eyes to linger on her for a second or two longer than he feared was appropriate. He motioned to her hand. "Here, I'll get rid of that." He stuffed her empty gum wrapper and his own into the Chevy's ashtray.

"I collect the foil," she said, "so remind me to get it from you later. It's amazing how fast it mounts up."

"For the war effort?"

"Yep."

"Say, you want me to show you where the bookstore is?" he asked. "I know my way around Baylor pretty well."

Hannah did not seem to notice his interest in her. "No, thanks. I've already studied the map." She closed her eyes, visualizing the layout of the campus.

"The bookstore," she said, "happens to be on the other side of Old Main—between the Science Building and the Band Hall." She opened her eyes and smiled, pleased with herself. "Anyway, if I don't get started right away, there won't be any four-o'clock newscast on that station of yours."

He glanced at his wristwatch and nodded. A moment later, standing on opposite sides of the automobile, they waved goodbye to each other.

"See you at three," Hannah said. She was shading her eyes from the sun, which was almost directly overhead. Wesley was enchanted anew by her squinting smile, and his heart was beating fast when he turned to walk toward the bookstore. Suddenly, any and all thoughts of Sandra Whittsel were far from his mind.

He stood behind a tree and watched Hannah's trim figure slowly disappear from view.

◆　　◆　　◆

Hannah Lane's first stop was the Admissions Office, where she verified that her transcripts and high school records were on file. She also signed the mandatory "no hazing" pledge and vowed not to "join or have any part in any organization whatever, named or unnamed, not approved by the Faculty." Then she searched, in vain, for an athletic ticket booth or application window. Reverend Lane, perhaps hoping for a good excuse to visit his daughter during the school year, had asked Hannah to check on the price of tickets for the homecoming football game.

"Haven't you heard?" the registrar's student assistant said. "There won't be a homecoming game this year. In fact, there won't even be a season."

Hannah was confused. "How could there not be a season?"

"The Bears aren't playing in '43. Too many of them are in the service," the student told her.

A cynic might say this was a blessing in disguise. The previous season had begun promisingly, with the Baylor Bears jumping out to a 6-1 record. But then they stumbled badly, getting blanked by Texas, Tulsa, and Rice, and only managing a 6-6 tie with lowly Southern Methodist. No, though the rest of the Southwest Conference would be playing in 1943, Baylor would not be taking part.

Her final task was to have the tuition waiver signed, so she walked over to the Department of Bible and knocked on the office door of the revered Josiah Blake Tidwell. He stood briefly when she entered the room, then seated himself behind a noble oakwood desk, accepted the voucher from her with a smile, and signed it at once. Though Dr. Tidwell had never met Hannah's father, Pat Neff notified him beforehand that "a most excellent gentleman's daughter" would be calling on his office sometime toward the end of July. Indeed, President Neff spoke so highly of Reverend Samuel Lane's evangelical work with the Southern Baptist Convention that Dr. Tidwell was predisposed to offer Miss Lane a departmental position as student worker—that is, if she discovered that, despite the tuition waiver, expenses would be tight.

Hannah graciously declined the offer. "Sorry, sir," she said, "but I want to keep my war-work job during the school year."

The Bible Department founder and patriarch raised his eyebrows. "War work?"

"Yes, sir."

He nodded his head but said nothing, lips curling as he pondered the young lady's determination. Hannah, after enduring an uneasy moment of silence, felt compelled to elaborate. "I'm on the payroll of Crawford-Austin," she said, "an apprentice in the tentworks section."

"And do you think that will interfere with your educational pursuits?"

"Well, if that happens, I guess I'll just have to choose between them."

Again he nodded, and Hannah saw a wistful look come across his face. Then she watched, puzzled, as he slowly stood and turned his back, ostensibly browsing the books on the wooden shelf along the wall. Windows to either side of the shelving provided a lovely view of the campus, and a summer breeze was rustling the long, white curtains.

Nearing the age of seventy-three, Dr. Tidwell was none too steady on his feet, and he stumbled slightly as he returned to his chair. "Commendable," he said. "In this day and age, that is certainly commendable."

Hannah was at a loss for words, wondering exactly what the old man meant.

"I'm referring to your war work," he told her. "Don't neglect your war work. There'll be time enough for studies once this conflict is won."

"Yes, sir," Hannah said. But then, hearing her gum make a slight popping sound, she froze in embarrassment. Here she was, casually chatting with one of the south's truly historical figures, and she had forgotten to remove the chewing gum from her mouth.

She wanted to leave quickly, but the signed voucher was still lying on the desk, and Dr. Tidwell seemed to be in no particular hurry to return it. He glanced at Hannah with a bemused look and said, "Promise me this. If you take Old Testament History—that's Bible 113—you'll sign up for the J. B. Tidwell course. I would be honored to teach your father's daughter."

"Yes, sir," she said. He handed her the tuition waiver, and she thanked him and turned to leave.

"One more thing, Miss Lane." She stopped.

"If you take Old Testament History, and you happen to sign up for the J. B. Tidwell course, you'll please leave your chewing gum in the dormitory, where it properly belongs."

♦ ♦ ♦

A transient just stepping off the bus in Waco on July 23, 1943, might well have wondered what all the commotion was two blocks away, in front of the Walgreen Drug Company at the corner of Sixth and Austin. To the locals, though, this was a weekly phenomenon. Every Friday in July, wives of cadets from both Blackland Army Air Field and Waco Army Air Field promoted sales of war bonds and stamps in a fund-raising effort that they hoped would net $100,000 in McLennan County alone.

Nationwide, the goal was a hefty $130,000,000, which also happened to be the price tag for completion of the USS *Shangri-La*, an Essex-class aircraft carrier now being constructed at the Norfolk Navy Yard in Portsmouth, Virginia. Her keel had been laid six months earlier, on January 15, and should the necessary funding be secured, the ship was expected to be launched within the first couple of months of 1944.

The fact that Mrs. James Harold Doolittle was the ship's sponsor added luster to the project, and her enthusiasm was boundless—fueled in equal parts by a healthy dose of patriotism and conjugal love. The very name of the "mystery ship" had its origins in her husband's B-25 bombing raid on Tokyo, just four months after Pearl Harbor was attacked. Jimmy Doolittle's daring mission, on April 18, 1942, was the first time in history that medium bombers of the US Army had taken off from an aircraft carrier to strike the enemy. So novel was the concept that when President Roosevelt answered reporters' questions at a press conference, he deliberately sidestepped any suggestion that a carrier was involved. The planes, came his evasive reply, had departed on their eight-hundred-mile bombing run from a secret base in "Shangri-La." Thus would the tranquil paradise of *Lost Horizon* soon find a non-fictional namesake in a 27,000-ton warship—and legitimately too, with the full blessings of author James Hilton.

One of the most tireless helpers at the war-bonds booth—and, for that matter, at the *Shangri-La* auction the night before—was Elizabeth Brower, whose summer was devoted as much to scrap drives and charity work as it was to her own part-time job pumping gasoline for the Service Refining Company. Something had to give, and it was her music that suffered the most. For the past ten weeks, her flute practice had dwindled to almost nothing, to such an extent that she actually feared for her embouchure when band reconvened in September.

Elizabeth heard a child's voice say, "A dollar's worth of stamps, please." She looked down to see a youngster who could not have been older than six. He laid four quarters on the counter top.

"Yes, sir, coming right up," Elizabeth told him. With a wink in her eye, she peeled off ten stamps and handed them to the lad for insertion into his gradually thickening book. A proud lady behind him, obviously the boy's mother, smiled back and nodded her head in thanks.

As Elizabeth was watching the tyke walk away, an elderly woman in the booth tapped her on the shoulder. "Would you get a deposit ready, Lizzie?" she asked. "It's nearly three o'clock."

"Sure, Mrs. Fine." Bending at her knees, Elizabeth noticed that there was a bundle of coin wrappers on the shelf below the counter, right next to the cloth bank bag. She began sorting her currency.

Along with Elizabeth, there were eleven cadet wives and two other volunteers staffing the booth, and except for a lull just before and after lunchtime, business had been brisk for most of the day. Claude Stewart, head of the retailers' committee that sponsored the bond drive, made a brief appearance and posed for some publicity photos by a newspaper cameraman. As manager of the Texas Consolidated Theatres, Inc., Stewart was one of the city's business leaders. His conglomerate operated fully half of Waco's motion picture theaters: The Waco, The Orpheum, The Strand, The Rivoli, and The Texas. Also on hand for several hours, pitching in with the others, was Alma Nichols, chairman of the Women's Committee for War Bond and Stamp Sales. Her husband, Robert, was a buyer for the Clayton Anderson Cotton Company, over on Third Street.

Elizabeth was kneeling to count out a stack of one-dollar bills when someone from above said her name. She stared up at the toothy grin of Edward Neal. "Why didn't you say you were married, Lizzie Brower? That would have saved me a trip downtown."

Instinctively, she played for time. "Do I know you?" she asked.

He chuckled. "You certainly do, *Mistress* Brower, and I've been wondering why you haven't given my buddy a call. I gave you his telephone number."

Elizabeth shook her head slightly. "Sorry, but I'm awfully busy right now." She resumed her counting.

The former rodeo cowboy leaned over the counter. "What's your new name," he asked, "now that you're hitched to a flying cadet?"

She looked up at him for a moment, his white teeth gleaming at her in a friendly smile. Something about his unrelenting nature frightened her to the core. "I don't know what you're talking about, mister," the girl said. "You must have me confused with somebody else." Rising, she took a step away from the counter.

Neal, too, stepped back, pointing to a waist-high banner that was thumbtacked to the front of the booth. "It says here that you ladies are 'cadet wives ... the women behind the men'."

Elizabeth laughed nervously. "Some of us are just volunteers from the community. I'm only helping out."

He removed his white cowboy hat, placed it over his heart, and took a step forward. "And how long will you be helping out, Lizzie Brower? I bought a new car about a week ago, and it's parked behind the Kinney Shoe Store over there. It's a grey Olds—only about forty thousand miles on it—and I'd be honored to take you for a spin whenever you can get away."

Elizabeth could not manage a reply, but one of the Army wives, Wanda Kiel, came to her rescue. "Is there anything the matter?" the woman asked.

Neal greeted the intruder with a nod. "Good afternoon."

"Mrs. Kiel," Elizabeth said with a quivering voice, "I don't know who this man is, but he's keeping me from doing my work."

Neal put his hat back on and apologized. "Ma'am," he said, "this is a simple case of mistaken identity. Lizzie here has forgotten who I am. We met a few weeks back, and I was just offering to take her home when she got off work. I'll leave right now, if I am disrupting anything."

"Maybe you should," Mrs. Kiel said. She motioned for two uniformed onlookers to approach. The stern-faced GIs walked purposefully toward the man in the cowboy hat, and he turned to go. "Well, excuse me for wanting to help out," Neal said. He lit a cigarette and tossed the extinguished match in the general direction of the soldiers.

Once he had disappeared around the corner of Walgreen's, Elizabeth seated herself on a stool to collect her thoughts.

"Don't let him worry you, Lizzie. We've got plenty of security men around here," Wanda Kiel said. She fanned the teenager with a small cardboard placard. "And a couple of the officers are carrying their side arms too," she added, "because of all the money we're taking in."

◆   ◆   ◆

Being summer, it was already nearing daybreak by the time Wesley finished throwing his newspapers. Mr. Ochmann was backing out of his driveway, and just across the street, the milkman had stopped in front of the Rylander home. A stray mama dog cowered as she trotted along the sidewalk, keeping a wary eye on the bicyclist. Wesley could not think properly on a morning such as this. He much preferred the fall and winter months, when he could navigate the residential district in darkness throughout.

The moment he turned onto Eleventh Street, a jolt of adrenalin shot through his body like an electric shock. Off in the distance—leaning against the street sign at the intersection of Morrow Avenue, directly in front of the Graves Apartments— was a serviceman carrying what appeared to be a duffle bag. Wesley hesitated, then picked up speed as he neared the strangely familiar apparition.

When he finally drew within earshot, he heard the man in uniform say to him, "Wesley Brower, I presume." The sailor tossed his seabag to the ground.

Wesley jumped off his bike and allowed it to career onto the grass, its pedal cutting a divot in the turf and the front wheel idly spinning in the air. "Steve!" He ran toward his brother. "Is it really you?" He approached with hand extended, but Steve embraced him instead, and they patted each other on the back. Then they stood a couple of paces apart and looked at each other.

"You son of a son of a gun!" Steve said. Now he offered a handshake, which Wesley accepted with ardor.

"What are you doing here?" Wesley asked. "Why didn't you write?"

"Well, I hinted that I might be getting a furlough after basic, so it won't be a complete surprise to Mom."

"Yes, it will. She hasn't planned anything."

"Good," Steve said. "That's just the way I want it to be."

"How long can you stay?"

"Two weeks—unless I'm called away."

Wesley looked down at the seabag, now lying in some weeds at the edge of the sidewalk. "Does the Navy have your telephone number?"

"Sure. Do you think they can win this war without me?"

Wesley smiled and shook his head in disbelief. "Why are you showing up at such a weird hour?"

"I got a ride from some farmer in Cleburne. Good thing I did, too, or I'd still be standing out there with the cattle and buzzards."

"He was on his way to Waco?"

"Nope, but he offered to take me down here—wouldn't take 'no' for an answer."

"Gosh, all the way from Cleburne?" Wesley asked. A wave of emotion swept over him.

"Just south of there, yeah. He said he had unlimited gasoline, so he was glad to help out."

"Does he have a son in the service or something?"

"Didn't say. I don't think so. Anyway, he said he always gets up around four." Steve lifted his seabag again, and the brothers began walking toward the contorted bicycle.

"How'd you get to Cleburne?" Wesley asked.

"Caught a plane to Fort Worth and then hitchhiked down from there."

"Have you gotten any sleep?"

"Only two hours, but I'm not complaining. Waco looks great to me."

"Better than San Diego?"

Steve was serious. "Yep, it really does."

When the brothers reached home—Wesley coasting his bicycle and Steve walking with the seabag over his shoulder—Eileen Bloom stared in amazement, as if reaching down for the newspaper had frozen her in that posture. "Stephen? Is that you?"

"Yes, ma'am. How are you, Mrs. Bloom?"

She stood up. "Welcome home, boy. Does Nora know you're here?"

"Nope. I thought I'd surprise her."

Mrs. Bloom's cocker spaniel peeked out the open front door and came running at top speed, barking and growling.

"McGonnigle, stop that!" the dog's master said. "Don't you recognize your next-door neighbor?" McGonnigle stopped barking but remained on full alert with teeth bared.

Steve tossed his seabag to the grass, and McGonnigle relaxed at once. No longer threatened by the large, menacing object, he sniffed to make certain it was inanimate, and then, with tail wagging, slithered over to the sailor to be petted.

Mrs. Bloom shook her head. "What a ferocious watchdog I've got there. Be careful, or he'll love you to death."

Removing his cap, Steve squatted down to shower the spaniel with affection.

"At least he minds," Wesley said. "He stopped barking on your command."

"When he wants to, yes." Mrs. Bloom stomped her foot on the grass. "Mackie, don't lick his hand. Bad dog."

A slight movement caught Wesley's eye, and he glanced at the front window of his house. Someone was pulling the curtain back, probably to investigate the barking commotion. The blue-starred flag swayed against the glass. "Oops, I think the jig is up," Wesley said.

"Well, nice to have you home," Mrs. Bloom told Steve. "God bless you, boy." Turning to leave, she clapped her hands, instructing McGonnigle to follow her.

Steve put his cap back on and picked up the seabag. He had taken no more than two steps toward the house when the door opened, and Nora appeared. Tears were streaming down her cheeks, and she was biting her lower lip, unable to say a word.

"Hi, Mom," Steve said. "Popeye's back in town."

Nora wiped away her tears with the bathrobe sleeve and, taking a step onto the front porch, opened her arms. "Come here, son," she said. Steve obeyed with a good-natured smile, laying down the bag while his mother hugged him for what seemed to him like two or three minutes. At one point, she was nearly suffocating him, so he shifted just far enough to extricate his nose and mouth from the embrace.

Finally he struggled free and stood at arm's length. "Golly, Mom," he said, "I've only been gone for eight weeks." He brushed her tears from the collar and shoulder of his uniform.

"I don't care. You're my boy, and I've missed you. We all have."

Wesley nodded his agreement.

"Don't feel too sorry for me. Soaking up the sun in California is not exactly tough duty. There were even some Hollywood starlets out there to keep us entertained."

"Really? Who?" Wesley asked.

Steve grinned. "Gee, I never did think to ask them their names."

"Sure, right."

"Come on in, boys," Nora said. "I'm on display for the whole neighborhood, standing out here in my nightgown and robe."

"Old Man Cox is probably enjoying the floor show," Steve told her.

Wesley picked up his brother's seabag and carried it into the house. Steve followed, with cap in hand.

"It's so good to see you again," Nora said as she closed the door behind them.

"I wonder if you can put up with me for two whole weeks."

"We'll give it a good try," she said. "I can promise you that."

◆　　　◆　　　◆

An hour and a half later, just as the Browers were about to sit down to a mouth-watering breakfast of fluffy pancakes and eggs, a light blue DeSoto pulled up to the curb, its brakes squeaking as it rolled to a halt. The driver, Bee Fetters, waved goodbye to her passenger and departed for her sister's house on Herring Avenue. The fuel gauge warned her that she would need to swing by the Humble station on the way home.

Hannah limped up the walkway to the front door, knowing that her landlady would have a meal prepared and waiting for her the moment she entered the house. A pleasant aroma enveloped her in the entry room. "Hi, Mrs. B.," she shouted. "Sorry I'm late."

When Hannah entered the kitchen, she said, "Some delivery guy boxed in Bee's car, and luckily we got him to move his truck. Otherwise, I guess we'd still be there." She stopped short when a sailor stood up at the breakfast table.

"Hannah, dear," Nora said, "this is Wesley's older brother, Stephen." Still standing, the sailor nodded politely, and Hannah responded in kind. "He's home on leave from the Navy—just dropped in from out of the blue this morning, with no warning whatsoever."

"I know how much you like surprises," Steve said with a wink.

Hannah smiled—but at Nora, not her son. After working a full shift at the plant, she knew she must look a mess.

Nora continued with the introductions. "And Steve, this is Hannah Lane, the Baylor student I wrote you about who's renting the room."

"Nice to meet you, Hannah."

"Same here."

Pancakes and scrambled eggs were all it took to make Steve feel very much at home. The moment he settled into his regular seat at the table and began eating his mother's cooking, boot camp and San Diego seemed a lifetime away. He sensed that it was unwise to allow himself to return entirely to a civilian mentality, but for now, enjoying the most basic of creature comforts was pleasure enough. Clover honey took the place of maple syrup, but otherwise the meal was just as he had savored it in his mind for the past two months. These were real eggs, too, not the powdered kind.

Wesley and Elizabeth sat directly across from each other, as usual, so Hannah had no choice but to pull up a chair at the end of the table between them. Actually, of course, she could have moved to the other end, between Nora and her older son, but she was too exhausted to bother conversing with a stranger. The sailor now occupied the place at the table where she herself normally sat, but no doubt that was his accustomed chair. After saying grace, Hannah consumed three hefty pancakes, which were accompanied by a glass of chilled orange juice. Then, while the others were still eating, she excused herself to go upstairs, where a warm bath and cool sheets awaited her. She hoped that the throbbing in her right knee, resulting from a collision with the stretching machine, would not keep her awake. She dreaded seeing the nasty bruise that it surely left.

When Steve's mother began washing breakfast dishes to the sound of KGKO's "Music While You Work," the sailor indulged in a leisurely walking tour of the house, renewing acquaintances with artifacts that had seemed commonplace before military service removed them from his life. His parents' wedding photograph still stood next to the San Francisco ashtray on the end table. Four issues of *The Daisy Chain*, his Waco High School yearbook, lay in a stack atop the bookshelf, idly gathering dust. Never had he so much as opened them, once the obligatory autograph foray was completed each spring. A reproduction of the Albert Bierstadt painting *Sundown at Yosemite* dominated the wall directly across from the sofa, just like it always had, for as long as he could remember.

Valentino was busy clawing his scratching post, which—as befitted a spoiled feline—occupied the center of the living room. When Steve squatted to pet him, he was careful to stay clear of the cat's tummy, a ticklish area that had led to more than a few blood-drawing scratches over the past five years.

Wesley asked his older brother where he would be sleeping, and Steve stood up with a puzzled look on his face. "Jeez, I haven't given it any thought. In my dreams, I've always pictured myself back in my own room, but obviously that's out of the question now."

"Obviously," Wesley said. "What do you think of Hannah, the new boarder?"

"Oh, she's okay." Steve laid himself full-length on the sofa. "Not very friendly, is she?"

"You have to get to know her."

"Yeah, maybe so."

"Her dad's a preacher back east."

Steve looked surprised. "Baptist?"

"I guess so. I don't know if she's ever told me."

"Well, she's going to Baylor, isn't she?"

Wesley shrugged his shoulders. "That doesn't mean anything. There are probably some Buddhists there too. Everyone who goes to Baylor isn't a Baptist."

Nora came into the living room, wiping her hands on her apron. Observing her supine son brought a halfhearted look of disapproval. She dragged his feet off the sofa and sat down next to him. "Wes laid your bag in his room for now," she said. "We'll have to give the sleeping arrangements some thought. You know, I really didn't expect you for another week or so."

Steve kicked off his shoes and swung his legs across his mother's lap. "Ahhhh, this is the life."

"Don't get too comfortable just yet," Nora said.

With a knowing glance, Wesley said, "Uh-oh!"

Steve gazed at his brother for an explanation, but Wesley made him wait until he had settled himself, cross-legged, on the carpet. Then he told Steve, "I think Mom wants to show you off to some hens."

"Wesley!" Nora said with a frown. "You don't even know what you're talking about."

"Don't I?"

Nora stared at Steve, who by now had closed his eyes with his hands behind his head. "Well, Wes is right about one thing," she said. "Sometime in the next couple of days, after you've gotten situated, I'd like for you to come with me down to the USO. Madeleine Givens has been asking about you, and you haven't seen Bunny Hope in ages."

Steve opened his drowsy eyes and focused them on his mother. "Is old 'Bunny Hop' still around? I thought she got married and moved up north."

Nora straightened the magazines on the coffee table. "We don't talk about that anymore. She's gone through so much since she retired."

Wesley added, "Her husband had two kids in Nevada that she didn't know anything about." He leaned forward, elbows on his legs and hands under his chin, and whispered dramatically. "He had a hidden past."

Nora laughed. "Now, Wes, don't make it even worse than it really was. He wasn't breaking the law or anything. He was legally divorced at the time. But Bunny resented the fact that he never said a word about his children—or even told her that he'd been married before."

Wesley looked at his brother. "Say, why do you call her 'Bunny Hop' anyway?"

Steve began to answer, but Nora interrupted. "Because the boys around here are just terrible, that's why," she said. "It all started when some school mail was misaddressed to her that way—I think it was spelled 'H-O-P-P'—and it caught on. That was way back when she first came to Waco."

"Did you have her in fifth grade?" Wesley asked.

"Fourth," Steve said. "She was still a fourth-grade teacher back then."

"I had Mrs. Powers in fourth."

Nora cleared her throat. "I also want you to say hello to Mabel Johns ... and Celia Kessler."

Steve sat up with a grimace. "Oh, Mom, not her."

"Now, Celia may be a talker—don't I know!—but she's genuinely interested in how you're doing, and I think we owe her the courtesy of a visit. She'll be home this afternoon, if you want to get it over with."

"I'd rather take boot camp all over again than go see Miz Kessler."

"Stephen ..."

"When do you need the car, Mom?" Wesley asked.

Nora looked at him. "Why? Do you work today?"

"At 3:30."

"Well, I'm afraid you'll just have to ride your bike this time. I only have one more gallon left for the month."

"Yes, ma'am."

"I'll do the driving today, Mom," Steve said, "and when we get inside the house, we can tell Miz Kessler that we left the engine running."

◆   ◆   ◆

The Service Refining Company, a modest establishment at the northeast corner of Eleventh and Washington, was not nearly as profitable an operation as it had been in the heyday of the automobile—before the war broke out—but somehow it still managed to generate enough revenue to pay its handful of employees and put bread on the table of Hoyle and Lucille Harkins and their two children.

Although the Harkins residence was a good eight blocks away from the family's filling station, that did not stop Hoyle Harkins from walking to work whenever the weather permitted. As manager of one of the two local SRC stations—the other being in East Waco, at the intersection of Renick and Dallas—theoretically there was nothing to stop him from diverting as much gasoline into his own automobile's fuel tank as it could consume. Harkins was patriotic enough to resist that temptation.

One fair, late-summer morning found him strolling down Twelfth Street. He heard a distant roar and instinctively searched the skies for its source. A moment later, a half-dozen twin-engine trainers from Blackland flew overhead, provoking hundreds of startled grackles to flee from their resting perches. Those same trees offered Harkins some welcome islands of shade, but the sultry combination of temperature and humidity caused him to perspire nonetheless. That was inescapable on a day such as this, with southerly winds too light to bring much relief from the central Texas heat.

As was his normal routine, he headed left when he reached Barron, where the Risher Apartments stood, and made his way to Eleventh Street. An automobile drove by, and when it stopped at the intersection, Harkins noticed that one of its taillights was not functioning. Vehicles everywhere were in disrepair, which was all that was keeping him in business. It certainly was not the pumps, which he now entrusted to female employees instead of his two qualified mechanics.

Funny, he thought, how the public naïvely accepted the perceived fuel shortage. What few Americans realized was that gasoline rationing was not implemented to force motorists to conserve fuel. The primary objective was to extend the life expectancy of the family automobile's tire tread. In other words, the actual shortage was not gasoline but rubber, a commodity that had plummeted into desperately short supply with the Japanese conquest of Malaya and the Dutch East Indies.

Dinah Reidelhuber and Elizabeth Brower already had two hours on the time clock when Harkins made his appearance at 9:30. "There's the boss," Dinah said. She wiped her brow and looked away.

"Did he see the sign?" Elizabeth asked.

"I don't think so. He's going into the office."

Someone during the night had gotten too close to the curb and dented the framework of the advertising placard, a two-by-three-foot depiction of a warship's port hole, a sailor, and the words "If You Talk Too Much, This Man May Die." One of the mechanics could repair the damage with little effort, but it was just the sort of vexation that would cause Mr. Harkins to fall into a bad humor for the rest of the day. It was best if he did not see it until after Louis or Butch had a chance to straighten the frame in their workbench vise.

Business was slow, so the girls were hosing down the oil-stained pavement near the pumps. Young Bradley Gann failed to do so the night before, but he did leave a note of excuse ("Cant wash down—leffed cause mother sick") that seemed plausible enough. Bradley had dropped out of Waco High the year before, but he was only sixteen, so not yet eligible for military service. His home life was execrable, reputedly infested by an abusive father whose new wife was a dope fiend. His biological mother lived across town in a motel room that she rented on monthly terms.

"Are you still interested in that airman?" Elizabeth asked Dinah. She had to shout over the sound of splashing water and her co-worker's push broom.

"Sure am." Dinah's gums extended down so far that they made her long teeth protrude through her lips, habitually impelling her to cover her mouth with a hand whenever she smiled. "He's gonna take me to the movies on Saturday after he's off duty."

Elizabeth aimed her hose to loosen a patch of dry mud, sending it flowing into the gutter along with the rainbow-colored stream of oily water. "What's your fella's name?"

"Gregory."

"Is he from Texas?"

Dinah nodded. "Brownwood."

"He's lucky to be so close to home. My brother was sent all the way out to San Diego."

"Navy?"

"Uh-huh. He's home on leave now—for two weeks. Maybe you'll see him. He said he'd drop by the station one of these days."

Elizabeth noticed that Hoyle Harkins was standing in the office doorway, motioning to get her attention. She lowered her hose to minimize the sound of rushing water. "Yes, Mr. Harkins?" she shouted. Dinah stopped sweeping.

"Ask Dinah if she punched in this morning."

Shading her eyes from the sun, Dinah said, "Yes, Mr. Harkins, I'm sure I did."

"Well, your time card isn't in the rack."

Dinah leaned her broom against a gasoline pump and walked toward the office.

A 1940 Ford pulled into the station and stopped to avoid running over the hose. "Go ahead, mister. That won't hurt it," Elizabeth said. The automobile continued forward and parked next to a pump.

"I don't need any gasoline, missy," the driver said. He was a bespectacled man who appeared to be in his middle sixties. "Would you please take a look at my tires?"

"Yes, sir." Elizabeth turned off the water, removed a tire gauge from her white coveralls, and knelt down to check the air pressure. A couple minutes later, she told the man, "Your left-rear tire is a little low, but the others are okay." He nodded acknowledgement, so she extended the compressed-air hose to bring the underinflated tire up to standard.

"Want me to get your windshield?"

"No, thanks, not today. Here." He handed Elizabeth a fifty-cent piece.

"Oh, there's no charge for air," she said.

"Take it. I'm Ben Reich—used to work for Superior, back when dinosaurs still roamed the earth. You're Harold Brower's girl, aren't you?"

"Yes, sir."

"I haven't been back to Waco in a dozen years or more. I was here once after Wayne Espy took over handling the store. I remember your daddy took me out to lunch at the Purple Cow."

Dinah came walking back to retrieve her broom.

"Did you ever find your time card?" Elizabeth asked. She slipped the coin into her breast pocket.

"Finally. I must have laid it on the map case when the telephone rang."

Elizabeth introduced Dinah to Ben Reich, who politely touched the brim of his hat and then reached down to start his engine. "I'd better let you gals get back to work. I was in town and just wanted to stop in and say hello."

Elizabeth smiled and said, "How did you know I was working here?"

"Your momma told me. I'm about ready to head back to Stephenville, and I didn't want to leave town without paying my respects to the Browers. Your daddy was awfully nice to me."

"What brought you to town?"

"A funeral."

Elizabeth took a step back to allow the automobile to turn toward the exit onto Washington Avenue. "Goodbye, Mr. Reich," she said.

Ben Reich waved his hand and said, "Goodbye, Lizzie Brower. I delivered something to your mother for you to have." The automobile pulled onto the street, turned left at the intersection, and then disappeared from view down Eleventh.

"What do you suppose he meant by that?" Elizabeth asked. Dinah shrugged and resumed sweeping.

A twist of the wrist brought Elizabeth's hose back to life, and she focused a stream of water on an oblong spot of congealed motor oil. She was concentrating intently on that target when a 2½-ton Army truck, unable to make it back to base, came sputtering into the garage for servicing. Its tires splashed the girls' pants legs with brackish water as it passed by.

They eyed each other and laughed, both probably thinking the same thing: "No sense trying to keep white coveralls clean."

♦   ♦   ♦

One of the people Steve most wanted to see during his brief stay in Waco was his good friend, Teddy Gaunce. A talented blocker and receiver on the Waco High football team, Teddy had tried to enlist the day after graduation, but his troublesome right knee caused him to be rejected before he was five minutes into the preliminary medical examination. "You're 4-F, son," the dispassionate Army physician told him, and he dismissed the applicant with a few sheets of paperwork for processing. A later attempt to pass the physical also failed, despite the fact that he submitted a signed affidavit from his own family doctor. No one could say he did not try.

Steve wrote to Teddy once from San Diego but never received a reply. That did not surprise him, as his pal was not the kind to hold a pen with any regularity. Though possessing above-average intelligence, during his high school days he was consigned to remedial English and mathematics, popularly designated as the "dumbbell" classes. He simply did not expend enough effort to reach his academic potential, and his grades suffered accordingly. His father, streetcar conductor Nolan Gaunce, was much the same in that respect, causing Renata Gaunce to harangue her stoic husband with the accusatory disclaimer, "Well, that apple did not fall far from the tree."

Teddy was exactly where Mrs. Gaunce told Steve he might be—drinking coffee at the soda fountain of the Williams "Old Corner" Drug Store, adjacent to the Amicable skyscraper. Steve wanted to sneak up behind him, but Teddy saw him through the window and was already standing when the sailor entered. "Admiral!" he shouted and held out his hand.

Steve rushed forward to shake it. "Tee Gee," he said, "how's the world treating you?" He was surprised to find that Teddy was not alone in the booth.

"Oh, can't complain," Teddy said. "I guess you know I was rejected for service."

Steve became serious. "Yeah, my mother told me the final verdict in one of her letters. That's a rough break."

"I'm getting used to it by now. I thought for sure I'd be accepted that second time. I don't think my knee's as bad as they say, and neither does Doctor Kruysen."

Steve looked at the girl who was sitting across the table from Teddy's coffee cup. Teddy glanced at her, too, and apologized. "Oh, sorry. Steve, I'd like for you to meet Agnes Matteson." She smiled. "Aggie, this is a football buddy of mine, Steve Brower."

Agnes had long brown hair—just this side of blonde—but instead of arranging it straight down her back, she curled it around the neck, allowing it to drape forward over the left shoulder. It was just eccentric enough to be intriguing. "So you're wearing another uniform these days," she said.

Steve nodded his head. "Uncle Sam's."

"That sure beats Uncle Harry's, doesn't it?" Teddy said, and the two men laughed.

Agnes was confused, and she was not one to miss out on a joke. "I don't get it," she said to Teddy.

"Harry *Stiteler*," he told her, but the blank stare remained. "*Coach* Stiteler," he added, shaking his head in frustration. "Jeez, it's never gonna seem funny if I have to paint you a picture."

Humiliated in front of a good-looking stranger, Agnes reached for her coffee cup and blew the steam away. "You're right about that," she said. "It sure wasn't very funny." Steve gave a shallow chuckle, unsure whether she was kidding.

Teddy turned to his pal. "You'll have to excuse her. She's from Oglesby."

The girl's face flashed red, and Agnes pointed a finger at Teddy. "Thaddeus Gaunce," she said, "I am getting sick and tired of that particular snotty comment of yours. If I ever hear you say it again, so help me, we're through."

Teddy raised his hands in pseudo defense. "Well, my God," he said, "Pardon me for breathing Your Majesty's air."

Agnes balled up her cloth napkin and angrily threw it at Teddy. It glanced off his forehead and landed on the floor behind him.

Steve took a step back, thoroughly embarrassed. "Maybe I'd better let you two talk this out," he said. By the time he finished his sentence, Agnes had slid across the seat and was storming toward the exit. She turned long enough to toss a dime onto the floor.

"Here, big spender," she shouted. "I wouldn't want you to waste your daddy's allowance on me." The coin rolled to a stop near Teddy's feet, and he kicked it violently amidst the tables and chairs. Two startled couples sitting near the door tried to remain casual, but their conversation came to an abrupt halt. "Excuse us," Agnes told them. Then she slammed the door as she left.

After motioning for Steve to sit across from him, Teddy seated himself heavily in the booth, descending as if all the strength had left his legs. He gazed at the tabletop with a faraway look in his eyes. "That girl's gonna drive me crazy."

Steve thought better of saying anything, choosing instead to wipe up a bit of coffee that had spilled when Agnes bolted from her seat.

Though Teddy's face betrayed no emotion, his hands were shaking slightly as he turned his attention back to the coffee cup in front of him. "You want something to eat or some java?" he asked. "My treat."

"No, but thanks anyway," Steve said. He stared at his friend, who yawned and began idly folding his napkin into geometric patterns. "Say, Tee Gee, I hope I wasn't the cause of that little squabble of yours."

For the first time, Teddy's eyes acknowledged that there was someone else seated in the booth. He looked directly at the sailor. "Naw, she's always like that. She'll get over it. We have a date for Friday, and I'll bet you a steak she'll be there."

"How long have you known each other?"

"Aggie? Six weeks, I guess. We've never gotten along—right from the very start."

Puzzled, Steve rubbed his chin. "Then why do you keep on dating?"

Teddy laughed. "Why do you think?"

Steve nodded his head but said nothing.

"Hey," Teddy told him, "maybe I can fix you up with her cousin. She's a doll."

Steve was amused. "Is she anything like Agnes?"

"Shorter temper."

"No, thanks, pal."

◆　　◆　　◆

There was no bicycle rack outside KWXN, so Wesley leaned his Hiawatha Arrow against a tree. Experience had taught him that the tripod kickstand did not work well on bumpy ground such as this.

The moment he walked around the corner and came in view of the windowed entrance, he could tell that something was wrong. Nearly two dozen people were standing in the lobby, talking in small groups, when he pulled the glass door open.

"What's going on?" he asked Monica Whaley. The script girl was standing near the wood-paneled wall, talking with some of her office cronies.

Becky Headrick walked away when Wesley arrived, and he thought he could see tears in her eyes.

"Larry Underwood was killed this morning," Monica told him.

Wesley was shocked, of course, but not shattered by the news. He nodded his head sadly, just as he might upon learning of the sudden death of any casual acquaintance or perhaps a Hollywood celebrity, but he felt no acute sense of personal loss. He had spoken with the station's news director only once, at a going-away party for Clyde Ash—now Corporal Ash of the US Army—and it was not a happy conversation. Indeed, it was this same Lawrence Underwood who decided, on the spot, that Wesley was not vocally equipped to join the weekend announcing team, except in the late-night hours or on a substitute basis. Wesley had no choice but to bite his tongue and accept the directive with as much composure as he could summon.

"How did it happen?" he asked Monica.

"He crashed his car into a ditch or culvert on North Twelfth Street."

"Whereabouts?"

"Up by Trice or Proctor, I think."

"It was the Barron Branch Creek Bridge," Louise Thatcher said. "They think he just lost control."

Wesley turned to Louise. "When was it? Was he on his way to work?"

"No. The police got the report around five o'clock—that's according to Grant Tollefson. He said Larry was going way over the speed limit."

Wesley knew the area well. The bridge was between Cumberland and Brook, almost as far north as Herring. "Do they know why he was going so fast?"

Louise lowered her voice a bit. "He'd been up all night at a friend's house. He was in no condition to come to work—let me put it that way."

"Who said that—Grant?"

"Yeah."

"Was there anyone else in the car?"

"No, thank God. Just Larry. He'd taken his daughter over to his ex-wife's house a few hours earlier."

"I didn't know he was a drinker."

Louise laughed. "You really didn't know him very well, did you?"

Wesley could hear someone sobbing in the newsroom, and he wagged a finger in that direction.

"Rachel Warren," Monica said. "Evidently, they were very close."

Louise looked toward the newsroom with raised eyebrows. "I would guess so."

"Who's Rachel—someone new?" Wesley asked.

Monica answered, almost inaudibly, "An intern." She seemed embarrassed to use the word.

Louise shook her head in disapproval. "Only eighteen," she said. "In fact, she just turned eighteen about a month ago." Then, after a moment of reflection, she added, "Larry must have been around forty, I guess. He told me he was too old for the draft."

Wesley decided to avoid the newsroom for the time being, reasoning that he would not have to clear the United Press wire for another hour or so. Instead, he wandered back to the control room, fully expecting it to be relatively quiet during the morning block of network programming.

Oddly, no one was anywhere to be found, not even soundman Dickie Waterhouse. A coffee cup was sitting above his console, though, and Wesley thought he detected the last vestiges of steam rising from its surface. Probably Dickie had slipped away once an appropriate level was established for "This Is My Life" from the Columbia System. There was no reason for local personnel to ride the gain for national transmissions. Someone at the other end, presumably in New York City, would be seeing to that.

Actress Betty Winkler's voice could be heard as Eden Channing, struggling valiantly to remain faithful to her fiancé while Paul served his country overseas. Fending off the persistent advances of stateside suitor Bob Hastings, she continued to meet "our changing world with two conflicting points of view."

Through the soundproof window, Wesley could see Neddy Wright preparing for that afternoon's appearance as Bud Hanson. So engrossed was Neddy in reviewing his "Behold Tomorrow" script that the ashes of his Chesterfield had grown to alarming proportions. Four spent cigarette butts already lay crushed in the ashtray to his left, a blue-glass replica lifeboat, balancing precariously on the narrow base of a music stand.

Neddy motioned toward the lone figure in the control room, and Wesley responded by opening the door into the studio. "Did you want to tell me something?" he asked.

The near-sighted actor had no idea who was speaking. "Who are you?"

"Wesley Brower. I'm in the News Department."

"Is Monica Whaley anywhere around?" He moved his right hand slightly, and the ashes fell onto the floor.

"I saw her in the lobby when I came in."

"Well, I have a question about the copy, and those blasted writers never seem to show up for work until around noon."

"Jerry Byrd's up front too," Wesley told him.

Neddy discounted that revelation. "Christ, he seems to know less about the script than I do," he said with a smirk. "Hey, kid, are you going up there anytime soon?"

"Yeah, I need to clear the wire for 10:15."

"Do me a favor and tell Monica that I need to see her right away," Neddy said. He was poring over the script again. "I'd go myself, but I don't want to get caught in all that hen cackle about Larry."

"Give me a few minutes, and then I'll do it. I'm sort of waiting for that new girl to leave the newsroom. I think she's having a nervous breakdown."

Neddy turned the page and looked up. "Oh? Who's that?"

"Rachel something."

He returned to his script. "Never heard of her."

Dickie Waterhouse came back into the control room and began lounging with his cup of coffee. It looked to Wesley like the soundman was in the process of leafing through a comic book.

Neddy lit another cigarette, and Wesley interrupted his reading. "Say, Neddy, I was going to ask Mr. Glickman something, but he's nowhere around."

"Sol doesn't come in until 12:30, kid. He's on the late shift because of the dramas."

"Okay, I'll check back later," Wesley said.

He was about to close the door when he heard a shout. "Hey, you! Don't forget to send Monica back here."

Wesley nodded his head and smiled. Then he waved to Dickie as he passed through the control room. The soundman, not knowing Wesley from Wendell Willkie, gestured a halfhearted greeting by wiggling a couple of fingers. The exploits of fighter pilot Terry Lee were far more interesting to him at the moment.

When Wesley arrived in the lobby, he was surprised to see that most of the mingling people had dispersed. Among the missing was Monica, but receptionist Myra Culp informed him that the script girl and Louise Thatcher had taken Rachel Warren back to her dormitory at Baylor University.

"Rachel was really upset about poor Larry," Myra told him. Then she turned to one of the salesmen loitering nearby. "Do you think there was more to it than meets the eye?"

Calvin Trent chewed on his cigar butt. "Beats me. Who's Rachel?"

"A news intern. You've seen her ... pretty, dishwater blonde."

He leaned forward and whispered, "That little girl with the big ...?"

Myra giggled. "That's her."

"Always smoking?"

"Yep."

Wesley tapped her desk with the knuckles of one hand. "Say, Myra, when Monica comes back, would you send her to the studio? Neddy needs to see her right away."

"Sure, Wes," she said. "Anything important?"

"Some problem with the script."

The salesman waved to Myra and aimlessly walked toward the front door.

"Uh, I saw Gerald Byrd in here a few minutes ago," Myra said. "Can he help?"

Wesley shook his head. "Not according to Neddy. Just let Monica know, will you? I'll be in the newsroom if you need me."

"Right-o," Myra said over the ring of the telephone. "At 3:15, Monday through Friday," she told the caller. "You're welcome."

Good intentions aside, Myra never gave the message to Monica, so Monica never addressed Neddy's concerns. Consequently, there was a gaping hole in the plot that no doubt confused attentive listeners and even had chief writer Ethel Coody scratching her head. Mrs. Coody vented her anger on Monica, who complained to members of the "Behold Tomorrow" cast, one of whom alleged right to her face that he had asked "some newsboy" to send her to the studio and rectify the textual glitch.

"Oh, wonderful," Monica said. "So now Ethel has stuck a fishhook up my nose just because you decided to go through some third party instead of telling me yourself."

Neddy was steaming. "Don't give me that bull. Any script girl worth her salt should be available for consultation around the clock, and not running an ambulance service to Baylor." Word had circulated that she was absent from the station for upwards of an hour.

Monica bit her tongue and glared at the accuser. Fine thanks she got for being a Good Samaritan.

◆   ◆   ◆

Against her better judgment—and despite the fact that she was profoundly ill-suited for the assignment—Elizabeth Brower agreed to become a matchmaker. Madeleine Givens approached her with the disclosure that one of the USO's occasional visitors, Private Daniel Rignold, was having difficulty mixing with the female staff. "Look at him over there," Madeleine said. Danny was sitting by himself at a table, swaying with the phonograph music but otherwise not participating in the benign revelry that took place on a typical weekend at Seventh and Washington. A deck of playing cards and a couple of magazines lay in front of him.

Elizabeth had a bemused look on her face. "What am I supposed to do about him? You know, Mother said she doesn't want me to become too chummy with any one soldier."

Madeleine giggled. "No, nothing like that, Lizzie. In fact, your mother is the one who brought this to my attention. I gather that Private Rignold is one of her favorites, and she just wants to make sure he has a good time. Find someone he might like, and pair him up with her—someone who'll give him a few laughs and maybe a dance or two."

They glanced at their unsuspecting prey once more but then quickly turned away when his eyes wandered in their direction. Madeleine lit a cigarette. "Do you know this fellow, Rignold?" She blew smoke out of the corner of her mouth, straight up into the air.

"I've met him, yes."

"Well, he's your new project. I've got Marcus Hanner and Craig Umbedacht and one or two others. My big success is Andy Chapman. I'll have him engaged before this war is over."

Danny had begun dealing the cards to himself.

"Oh, Lord—solitaire," Madeleine whispered. "You've got your work cut out for you."

"It seems like he's friendly enough. Maybe he's just bashful around girls."

"Could be." Madeleine gave him the once-over. "I don't see anything else wrong with him. He's rather nice looking."

Elizabeth nodded her head in agreement. From this distance, he resembled a younger William Holden, around the time of *Golden Boy*. "You know," she said, "it might be kind of fun at that."

Madeleine stole another peek. "Have anyone in mind? He doesn't seem to be particularly taken with any of the usuals."

Elizabeth thought for a moment. "Maybe he has a girl back home."

"Where's he from?"

"Alabama or Mississippi, I think."

Madeleine took another drag on her cigarette, and she exhaled smoke when she said, "Too bad I'm such an old married woman."

Just then, a couple of naval reservists from Baylor passed by on their way to the refreshments. "Help yourselves, men," Madeleine told them. When she turned back to Elizabeth, a scheming look was in her eyes. "You never answered my question, Lizzie. Do you have anyone in mind for Private Rignold?"

"Not really. Most of the people I know are just my age."

"That pretty redhead is out of his league, don't you think?"

"Definitely not his type," Elizabeth said.

"What about Nancy Flynn? She's got a nice figure."

"Nancy Flynn?" Elizabeth spoke the name so loudly that several soldiers looked her way. She lowered her voice and added, "I don't think she's right for Danny at all. From what little I've seen of him, he's a respectable boy."

"And Nancy's not respectable?"

"Hardly. Did you see the dress she was wearing on Sunday night?"

"No."

"Cut down to here. The GIs were swarming around her like bees."

For the rest of the evening, Elizabeth ruminated over how to force Danny Rignold to have a good time in the service of his country. Her plan was to introduce him to an attractive someone at Saturday night's BAAF/WAAF dance. Getting him there would be no problem. She could simply ask Wesley to ask Sandra Whittsel to ask her father to order Danny to attend.

The key, she knew, would be to find a suitable girl—and she had just three days in which to do it.

◆　　　◆　　　◆

Steve's furlough was nearly half over when he received an urgent telephone call at home from Viola Hastings, whose name he recognized as one of the Waco High School cafeteria ladies.

"My daughter would absolutely kill me if she knew that I called," the lady told him after introducing herself.

"Your daughter?" Steve was very much at a loss for words, not wanting to seem disrespectful, of course, but wondering what a middle-aged woman from his past might have in mind. "Look, I'm kind of baffled by this, Mrs. Hastings," he said. "Do I know your daughter from school or something?"

"No, Beverly went to Bruceville. We live in Eddy, you know."

Steve waited for an explanation, but the other end of the line was silent, so he had no choice but to speak up again. "I get the impression that I'm supposed to be aware of your daughter, but I'm totally in the dark."

Viola laughed nervously. "All right, here goes. This is rather awkward for me, so please excuse the way I'm acting."

"Well, we could do it by charades," he said, "but I can't see your hands over the telephone."

Her voice seemed to relax a bit. "Stephen, my Beverly has a cousin who says she has a terrible crush on you, and I was wondering whether you would go out with her one time while you're still here in Waco."

Steve felt like an escaping prisoner, caught in the searchlight. "Gee, I don't think that'll be possible," he said. "I may be on some troop train a week from today."

"It's a lot to ask, Lord knows, but it would really be a dream come true for her."

He changed the subject, giving himself a moment to think. "How did you happen to know I was home from the service?"

"I saw Beth at the filling station, and we got to talking about you."

"Beth?"

"Your sister."

Steve chuckled. "Oh, Lizzie!" He had forgotten that Elizabeth went by the name of Beth at school. "Who's the cousin? Do I know her?"

"Her name's Donna Gorsey. She's a year younger than you are." There was a pause, as Viola cleared her throat. "Donna's in the high school band—and the glee club too, I think. She'll be a senior at Waco High this year."

Steve heard a key rattling in the front-door lock, so he lowered his voice. "Say, I don't want to be rude, Mrs. Hastings, but I've never gone out on a blind date before, and I really don't think that I ..."

"I understand completely, Stephen, and I'm awfully embarrassed to be calling. I wouldn't be asking you this except that I'm sure you and Donna would get along great."

"Well, maybe so, but it's just that—" Nora entered the house and, noticing that Steve was on the telephone, quickly proceeded to the kitchen, where she laid a small sack of vegetables in the refrigerator. Then, not wishing to eavesdrop any more than necessary, she walked into the living room to give her son some privacy.

Steve spoke more quietly now. "Listen, Mrs. Hastings ... If you don't mind, give me a little while to think about this, okay? I've got a lot of arrangements to take care of before I leave again, so I really can't say for sure."

"Oh, certainly, Stephen. Take as long as you like. The last thing I want to do is disrupt your time at home."

Immediately after his conversation with Viola Hastings, Steve went into the living room, scratching his head.

"Who was that on the telephone, dear?" Nora asked.

"Oh, the aunt of some high school girl. She's trying to arrange a blind date, and she wants me to be her guinea pig."

"You don't know the girl at all?"

"No, but she seems to know me well enough."

"The football star, huh?"

He laughed. "Yeah, I guess."

"So it's not really a blind date for her."

"Nope."

"Are you going to go?"

"Not unless it's in the next couple of days. You know, I just don't have enough time to—" He stopped in mid-sentence, but a darkness crossed Nora's face. Up until now, he had been careful to avoid the subject of leaving.

"Well, do what you want, son," she said. "Will you be needing the car, then?"

"No, probably not. I doubt that I'll go, but I told the lady I'd call her back. She gave me her telephone number."

"Who is it?"

"The lady who called?" Nora nodded her head and began walking away. Steve sat on the sofa and reached for his pipe and tobacco, which were lying on the end table. "Her name's Hastings—Mrs. Hastings. I can't recall the first name." His mother did not answer, and he turned just in time to see her disappear into the kitchen.

A thought crossed his mind, and he said to himself, "Donna Gorsey." After laying the pipe and tobacco pouch on the coffee table, he made his way over to the bookshelf. Then he pulled down his most recent issue of *The Daisy Chain* and searched through the organization pictures. It would almost make it easier if she was as homely as sin.

Steve turned the page and spotted a group photo of the Junior Band. The caption identified one of its members as Donna Gorsey, so he used his index finger to count heads from left to right. There she was—a girl seated with the others, holding what appeared to be a clarinet. Then he browsed through the book until he came to the Intermediate Girls' Glee Club. Sure enough, there again was a listing for her, and he could see at once that she was the same person.

Donna Gorsey was certainly no beauty queen, but to someone squinting hard enough, she did bear a vague resemblance to the current Miss America, Jo-Carroll Dennison. Steve smiled, recalling the day the so-called "Texas Tornado" addressed a small crowd in Fort Worth—back when she was still touring the state as Miss Texas. Then, after her national triumph at the Warner Theater in Atlantic City in September of 1942, he happened to see a newspaper photo of the talent competition. And there was this same Jo-Carroll Dennison from Tyler, now dressed in a cowgirl outfit and singing "Deep in the Heart of Texas."

In all honesty, Donna Gorsey would probably not even be a serious contender for Miss Waco—and yet she was much prettier than he had any right to expect, given the curious circumstances of an aunt trying to line up a date for her.

Steve closed the yearbook and returned to the sofa. The timing was just not good, and he decided then and there to call back this Mrs. Hastings with his regrets. If he and his blind date turned out to have nothing in common but the flimsy coincidence of their alma mater, the whole experiment would have been nothing more than a waste of precious time at home, with who knows how many intervening months or years before he would see his family again. On the other hand, if he and the girl somehow hit it off, as her aunt suspected they might, then one single date would stand for next to nothing—no real test of time, merely a source of frustration and heartache for them both. Most of all, he had no desire to spend three hours squinting at a stranger, trying to imagine that she was Jo-Carroll Dennison.

That settled, he flirted with the notion of giving Cynthia Mills a call, but he had no idea how to reach her. According to her most recent letter—one of only two that she had ever sent to him—the enigmatic Cynthia continued to live in Joplin, Missouri, but someone on his football team insisted that this was just her father's business address. Actually, that informant revealed, she was working as a night-shift waitress somewhere in Oklahoma.

Complicating matters even further was the fact that Steve's mother was still badgering him to confront Miss Mills about the whereabouts of his valuable class ring. "Don't let that tart walk off with your possessions like that," she would say.

"But I don't know for a fact that she has it."

"Oh, don't be so gullible. I wouldn't believe half of what she tells you."

He could not argue with that. What he could not admit to his mother was that the girl's untrustworthiness only enhanced her allure. Cynthia Mills was exciting, and he was not the only one who felt that way.

◆　　◆　　◆

Elizabeth was busy navigating a push broom late on Saturday night, occasionally glancing over her shoulder while she cleaned up a swath of cake, chips, and cookie crumbs that surrounded the USO's refreshment table. Technically, the dance still had another hour to go, but most of the attractive young ladies from the Girls' Service Organization had already departed, so the soirée was downshifting into low gear. Even the cockiest soldiers—those the staff called "lounge lizards"—were beginning to lose interest in the affair, and only the most pathetic among them still entertained the desperate fantasy of discovering some racy new dance partner.

Far across the room from the half-dozen swaying partners and the small combo, the jukebox quietly played "I've Heard That Song Before." Featuring trumpeter Harry James and His Orchestra, along with vocalist Helen Forrest, this record had been one of the biggest sellers of the previous year, and it still held great appeal for those in uniform.

It was nearly 11:15 when Danny Rignold's prospective date finally opened the front door, removed her hat, and ventured a few halting steps into the room. Spotting Elizabeth Brower at the refreshment table, she advanced more confidently but still seemed to be either nervous or confused.

"Sorry I'm so late, but I had to walk," she said.

Elizabeth was startled. "You walked all the way from home?"

"Sure. Why not?"

"Well, it's just not safe at this time of night."

She shrugged and began taking off her gloves. "Oh, I'm used to walking. Besides, I don't think there's a thief alive who can keep up with me." She wiped a few defiant strands of blonde hair from her eyes and looked across the room. "What do you want me to do first?"

Guilt swept over Elizabeth, and what had once seemed like a brilliantly conceived plan suddenly soured into the meanest form of subterfuge. Here stood Hannah Lane, willing to do her part for the war effort, only to be blindsided by a sophomoric ruse that would rob her of what little leisure time she could call her own.

When the Harry James record finished playing, Danny stood up and appeared ready to leave. He nodded politely to the custodian, Mitchell Bishop, who was beginning to straighten chairs and pick up the twenty or so empty drinking cups that had collected on wooden tables. One of the cups had overturned during the evening's festivities, and a small puddle of Coca-Cola gleamed no more than an inch away from a stack of *Life* magazines.

"Let's go help Mitchell clean up," Elizabeth said, and Hannah followed her over to the rec room like an obedient child. Peeking through the kitchen doorway, Madeleine Givens shook her head in amusement. She was wearing an apron, and her hands were covered with flour. A stool behind the taller of two supply carts afforded her a tolerable view of the romantic drama, so she made herself comfortable and lit up a cigarette.

"Hi, Danny," Elizabeth said. "Leaving so soon?"

Danny looked at the two young ladies. "Yeah. Mornin' chow is at 6:30, and I need to help service a couple of trainers right after that."

"Danny's a mechanic," Elizabeth told Hannah, who nodded her head but said nothing.

Elizabeth noticed that there were bandages around two of Danny's fingers. "What happened to your hand?" she asked.

"Oh, just a burn—nothin' severe." He wiggled his fingers self-consciously. "Got too close to a hot engine, that's all. Fortunately, I'm right-handed."

Hannah had turned away and was helping Mitchell straighten the tables. Five of the smaller ones—no more than card tables really—were off to one side of the room, probably shoved there by a couple of the GIs to create a makeshift dance floor.

"Hannah, Danny's from Mississippi," Elizabeth said. "What's the town called?"

"Kosciusko."

Hannah did not appear to be listening very intently, so Elizabeth took the liberty of repeating the name. "He's from Kahs ... Kahsk ... What is it?"

"Kahs-ee-US-ko." Danny drawled as he pronounced it again, slowly articulating each syllable. "Named after a Revolutionary War hero from Poland."

Elizabeth's face lit up with a smile. "Hannah's from the south too. From North Carolina—north of Charlotte."

"*Way* north of Charlotte," Hannah said. "All the way across the state." Taking her cue from Mitchell Bishop, she continued to move the heavy, straight-legged tables and then hoist chairs upside-down upon them, presumably to make way for the Hoover cleaner.

Danny stepped forward to offer his assistance. "Here, let me help you with that." He took the chair she was holding and stowed it on a table.

"Thanks," she said. There was no particular warmth in her voice, and she bent over to pick up some napkins that littered the floor. Elizabeth frowned, disappointed that Hannah's interest was impersonal at best. As for Danny, he was so used to hard work that he thought nothing of muscling a few tables back into place. This chance encounter was going nowhere.

"Mitchell, would you come here for a minute?" Madeleine asked. She was trying to push a supply cart back to the kitchen, but her game leg was giving her trouble. "And bring Lizzie with you, if she's free."

Mitchell tossed his washrag onto a tabletop. "Yes, ma'am." Elizabeth suppressed a smile and followed him to the back of the room.

Watching the others leave, Hannah turned to Danny. "Want a piece of gum?" she asked.

"Sure, I guess so." The gum freshened his mouth after all the strong coffee he had been drinking, and he winked thanks to Hannah, slipping the crumpled wrapper into his pocket.

"Listen, I'll take that foil—unless, of course, you collect it too."

He glanced at the girl, wondering if she was teasing. Seeing that she was not, he reached into his pocket and produced the wrapper. "Here. Be my guest," Danny said. He handed it to her with a shrug. It seemed awfully peculiar to him to place so much importance in a negligible piece of metallic foil. Just how far did this girl really think it would go toward winning the war?

Hannah tucked the shiny foil into her purse. "Where do you go to church, soldier?"

The question caught Danny off guard, and his face reddened. "Oh, I haven't been to church in years," he said. "Wait—I take that back. I did go to a weddin' back in June. That was in a church—someplace downtown. Presbyterian, I think."

Hannah was aghast. "Okay, then what denomination does your family belong to back home?"

"You mean ... what religion?"

"Of course, what religion? It's a simple question." Her eyes were deadly serious.

Danny looked toward the kitchen. Where in God's name was Lizzie? This new girl made him feel uncomfortable, and he was anxious to flee from The Inquisition. What he did not realize was that Elizabeth and Madeleine were observing the entire scene from afar, while Mitchell rolled the supply cart back into the kitchen.

"Listen, whatever your name is ..." Danny said.

"The name's Hannah. Lizzie told you that, didn't she?" Hannah knelt down to flatten a rug that had curled underneath itself.

He blushed anew. "Well, sure, but—"

"I recall hearing that your name is Danny." She was still peering at the floor. "I don't have a particularly keen memory, but it's just common courtesy to pay attention when you're introduced to someone."

"Excuse me, but I've got better things to do than listen to this," he said. "Chrissakes, my sergeant can chew me out, if that's what I want."

Hannah squinted in anger. "I'll thank you not to take the Lord's name in vain, Private ... Mechanic."

Danny shook his head. "Say, miss, I've got to run. Real nice meetin' you." He picked up his cap and started to leave.

"Look me up again, Danny, once you've made your peace with the Lord—and decided it was worth your effort to remember my name, that is."

Danny turned and pointed an index finger at her. "Hey, I didn't look you up. Whatever gave you that idea? All I'm tryin' to do is have a little relaxation—not easy around here—and my commandin' officer practically ordered me to do that. I wouldn't even be in this hellhole except for the war."

Hannah gathered some party debris and sauntered away.

But Private Danny Rignold was not finished with her quite yet. "Who do you think you are, Billy Sunday?" he shouted in the general direction of the kitchen. "Jeez, if you're a such a God-fearin' Christian, then that's the last thing I want to be." He put his cap on and fumed toward the exit, pausing when he heard the sound of running footsteps.

It was Elizabeth Brower, hot in pursuit. "Danny, wait!" She narrowly avoided a pair of soldiers who failed to notice that she was on a collision course with them. "Danny, please don't go."

He considered for a moment but then continued toward the door.

"Danny," she said when she caught up with him, "it was all my fault, not hers. I planned the whole thing, and I apologize for being such a dunderhead."

He motioned toward the rear of the room. "You don't pick your friends very carefully, do you?"

"Hannah's our boarder. She lives at our house," Elizabeth said. "Please forgive me."

Danny shook his head and stormed the other direction.

Elizabeth glanced around in time to see that Hannah—apparently quite unaffected by the quarrel—was on her way to the kitchen, carrying a tray of cups and spoons. Before Elizabeth could turn back to Danny, he was already far out the door, so she ran along the sidewalk to catch up.

"Danny, won't you even accept my apology?" she called to him. When the soldier knelt long enough to retie his shoelace, she said, "Forget Hannah Lane. I don't want you to be mad at me or the USO. I was just trying to introduce you to someone you might like. It was a stupid idea—or at least a bad choice."

Danny had to smile at that. "How well do you know that friend of yours?"

"I told you. She's just a boarder at our house."

"And you really thought I would like her?"

"Yeah, I guess I did. Maybe I don't know her as well as I thought."

"She's nothin' but a ..." He paused, searching for the right euphemism. "She's a downright shrew."

Elizabeth almost burst out laughing. "A *shrew?*" she asked. "What's a shrew?"

In spite of himself, Danny smiled too. "Haven't you ever read any Shakespeare?"

"Just a funny play—I forget which one. We had to read it in school."

Danny nodded his head. "Probably *As You Like It.*"

"That's it," she said.

He turned to look at the sparse traffic on Washington Avenue.

Elizabeth, though, was still amused by the English lesson. "What in the world does Shakespeare have to do with Hannah Lane?"

Danny thought he would leave it at that. "I'll let you figure it out," he said.

With his shoe now in good order, he stood up and began crossing Seventh Street.

"How are you going to get to the air field?" Elizabeth asked.

"Hitchhike," he said over his shoulder. "People are happy to pick up a man in uniform."

Elizabeth watched him until he was nearly to the Barbecue Garden Restaurant. "I'm sorry!" she shouted to him, and she thought she saw him shrug.

A gray Oldsmobile pulled up to the curb. Its driver leaned over to the passenger window and said, "Howdy there, pretty Miss Brower."

Elizabeth froze. "What are *you* doing here?" She turned to go back inside.

"Wait, Lizzie. Don't be in such a big hurry." He slid over to the passenger door and opened it, partially blocking her path to the USO. When she sidestepped the automobile door, he jumped to his feet and smiled. Edward Neal was shorter than she remembered, but he had a powerful build with a slim waist and muscular forearms. "All I'm trying to do is apologize for the way I acted—at that bond drive or whatever it was. I'd been drinking a little at the time." The automobile's engine was still running.

Elizabeth took a quick step to her left, but Neal was very light on his feet and managed to position himself directly between her and the USO doorway. He was not overtly confrontational, but nonetheless Elizabeth felt a sudden rush of adrenalin, and her heart began pounding in panic. Neal's persistent smile, on the other hand, suggested that he was treating the encounter as nothing more than a diverting game of cat and mouse.

In desperation, Elizabeth tried to sound as threatening as possible. "Please let me by or ... so help me, I'll scream!"

It was the wrong approach. Neal was upon her in a flash, placing his hand over her mouth and jumping behind her like a panther, dragging her toward the open automobile door. Her eyes were red in terror.

"Now, you settle down, Miss Brower," he whispered in her ear. "I don't want the whole Army after me." She tried to kick him, but he was much too nimble. "Listen to me, Lizzie. All I want to do is take you for a ride in my new car. What's so horrible about that?"

She continued to struggle, but her frantic effort was no match for a rodeo cowboy's strength. He shoved her violently inside the automobile and slammed the door. Then, in a single motion, he ran around to the driver's side, climbed in, and closed the door with a deafening thud.

Elizabeth was dazed momentarily, having struck her head on the roofline of the Oldsmobile, so Neal was able to snatch her trembling hand from the door handle and seize her left wrist, pulling the girl away from any hope of escape. A burning sensation shot through her arm, and she cried out in pain. She closed her eyes tightly, praying to God that the nightmare would end.

Neal depressed the clutch and shifted into first gear. As the vehicle lurched forward, a hand secured his collar so tightly that his eyes began to bulge in shock, and he gagged for a moment until the top button of his shirt ripped free.

He stepped on the gas pedal but was unable to avoid the automobile parked in front of him, its bumper crushing his right fender and shattering the headlight.

Out of the corner of his eye, he glimpsed the khaki blur of a uniform, and before he could react, two hands grasped him around the throat. With a powerful thrust of his forearm, he broke free and threw open the door, clipping his attacker on the right hip and knocking him momentarily to the pavement. He jumped from the automobile and took a swing at the soldier, hitting him squarely in the stomach.

Terrified, Elizabeth managed to open the passenger door and stumble from the automobile. As she wobbled to her feet, she screamed for help and staggered toward the brightly lit first floor of the USO. Behind her, she could hear the fierce scuffle and then the sound of Edward Neal's gray Oldsmobile, still drivable despite the collision, speeding away into the night. She doubled over in pain and, shakily swaying on hands and knees, vomited onto the sidewalk. Footsteps of a dozen or more servicemen came running to her rescue from the entryway. She could see the pants legs of their uniforms.

"Are you hurt, miss?"

She could not answer. Still looking down, she shook her head and began to cry uncontrollably.

"Send for the medic," came a voice from over in the darkness of the street. "This one's hurt bad."

◆　　◆　　◆

Steve took the news especially hard, but there was little time to do anything substantive about it. He was due to report back in three days, and Edward Neal was unlikely to show himself in public until excitement over the whole matter finally subsided. Nora notified the police, in person, but was frustrated when they accorded the incident little more interest than a sparring match at the local gym.

"Listen, officer, my daughter has a badly sprained wrist—nearly broken—and an inch-long scab where she was conked on the head. She could have been kidnapped and who knows what else."

"We'll look into it," the grumpy desk sergeant told her. He brushed some eraser dust from the blotter in front of him. "We have our hands full just now with the war, you know."

Private Danny Rignold was hospitalized for four days—for overnight observation at Providence Hospital and then in the base infirmary—but his injuries proved to be not as serious as had been feared from the initial cursory examination. There was a mild concussion, one lost tooth and another one cracked, a contusion on his right hip, a broken nose, one eye swollen shut, and a badly bruised hand—suffered when he landed his only solid blow of the fracas, a roundhouse left hook to the side of Edward Neal's head.

Steve drove his mother and sister to the infirmary after Sunday night services, and the three were joined by Hannah Lane, who that evening accompanied them to Columbus Avenue instead of her home church of First Baptist. Wesley was working at the radio station, so he was unable to partake in any visitation.

Though Nora felt duty-bound to fulfill her three-hour commitment to the Red Cross—her name appeared on the rotation list one Sunday night out of every four—she was pleased to accept Daisy Mohr's kind offer to trade shifts.

"That Daisy," she said to Hannah in the automobile. "She's an angel on earth. I wish I were even half the Christian lady she is."

Hannah nodded her head and smiled. "I'd like to meet her someday."

Steve turned his head slightly but kept his eyes on the road. "You talking about Miz Mohr?" He chuckled to himself. "She's a gem—no doubt about it. She used to take care of me in the church nursery all those years. Wes too, I guess."

"And me," Elizabeth added.

"Daisy's one of the church secretaries," Nora said, "just working part-time for the pastor." She smiled, a faraway look in her eyes. "One time, when my husband was deathly ill, Daisy took him back and forth to the office each day for nearly three weeks so he could keep up with the books. That was before I learned to drive, and the boys were much too young. She wouldn't accept any gasoline money and, in fact, gave him a ten-dollar bill for Christmas. It was in an unmarked white envelope, but I'm sure it came from her. He found it in his suit coat pocket on Christmas Eve."

In the flickering darkness, Nora thought she saw tears begin to well up in Hannah's eyes, so she decided it was best to change the subject. "I have never heard the youth choir sound as wonderful as they did tonight," she said. "What about you, Lizzie?"

"No, ma'am."

Steve switched on the radio to catch the last part of "Summer Theater," but the wartime speed limit still made it seem like a lengthy trip.

Elizabeth entered the hospital bay first, leaving the others to chat among themselves in the corridor, about midway between the chaplain's office and the nurses' station. "I won't be long," she told them.

Danny was lying on his back in bed, and at first Elizabeth failed to recognize him. All of the patients were about the same age, of course, and the twenty-four beds were virtually identical, with diagnostic charts hanging from their metal frames. She glanced from side to side as she made her way through the room.

Then she heard a quiet voice behind her. "Lizzie?"

She turned in the direction of the sound and found herself staring at a pugilist who had lost a fifteen-round TKO. The top of the man's head was wrapped in a white gauze, an adhesive bandage completely obscured his flattened nose, one eye was dark purple and swollen shut, the right corner of his mouth was covered with dried blood, and his left hand was grotesquely oversized and the somber color of wet sand. With effort, he managed a smile.

Elizabeth took a halting step toward him. "Danny?" she asked.

He nodded his head.

"Oh, Danny!" She drew closer in a circuitous fashion, seemingly studying his bruises from every conceivable angle. Then, when she finally arrived at the bedside, she took his battered hand between her own gloved hands and patted it gently. "Does it hurt awfully bad?"

"Not as much as earlier," he said. "I think maybe they've got me on drugs."

Elizabeth sat on the edge of the bed. "My poor Danny!"

"Gee, don't ..."

"It's all my fault. None of this would've happened if it hadn't been for me."

Reluctantly, fearing that the scene might appear improper, he withdrew his hand from her grasp and laid it at his side. "Don't be a goose," he said. "You're not to blame."

She leaned forward and softly traced her finger along the bridge of his nose. "Is it broken?"

"So they say." He tried to grin.

"I've never had a broken bone. Does it throb all the time?"

"Only when I sneeze. But I guess this is more of a cartilage than a bone. Haven't you taken anatomy?"

Elizabeth could not help but grinning. "No, silly," she said. "I'm not even in high school yet."

Danny's smile faded a bit, and he looked toward the foot of the bed, wiggling his toes under the blanket. "Sorry. You seem a little older."

"No need to apologize," she said. When his eye met hers, she did not turn away. "You may have saved my life last night."

"Oh, I doubt that. I just saw some headlights and happened to turn around."

"He forced me into his car, and he was about to drive off with me. I'd say what you did was pretty brave. You did a courageous thing."

"Aw, not really," Danny said. "He's probably just some hooligan. There's a lot of them around these days. Slackers, most of them. Packs a mean punch, though—I can vouch for that." He rubbed his jaw and pretended to grimace.

Elizabeth smiled again. "Just the same, I'll never forget what you did."

Danny said nothing but seemed pleased by the comment. Then he took a deep breath and tentatively exhaled, a twinge of pain emanating from his ribcage. He struggled to sit up in bed, and she helped to position the pillow behind him. Even this exertion seemed to drain his energy, so Elizabeth resolved to usher the others in and out as quickly as possible.

"I'll be back in a minute," she whispered. "There are a couple of people who want to see you." She stood up and walked toward the door.

"Wait," Danny said. "What about you? That goon didn't hurt you, did he?"

"No. Just a bump on the head—didn't duck fast enough when he shoved me into the car. And my wrist is kind of sore."

Danny sighed and seemed to be studying her face. "Sorry I didn't ask about you right away," he said. "Jeez, you must think I'm really a selfish jerk."

"Hardly. I owe you more than I could ever hope to repay."

"It's just that you seemed perfectly normal to me, walkin' in here like that." He thought for an instant and then added, "In fact, you looked downright swell."

She waved a gloved hand, almost gaily, before leaving the room.

Three or four minutes elapsed, and Danny took a sip of water from a cup on the nightstand. His head was aching, and the dry scabbing on his lower lip cracked as he attempted to drink. At one point, he nearly lost his grip on the cup, sloshing a few drops of water onto the white sheet. So swollen was his left hand that it was difficult to hold anything securely, and the superficial burns he suffered the morning before only aggravated the discomfort.

When Elizabeth reappeared in the doorway, she escorted her mother toward Danny's bed. Steve and Hannah followed behind them, about five steps back. As the four visitors passed by a middle-aged nurse, she stopped them for a moment, whispering something to Nora, who nodded in agreement. Danny cleared his throat and had a short coughing spell. He reached for his cup of water, drank, and the paroxysm subsided almost at once.

"Are you all right?" Elizabeth asked. She took the cup from him and laid it on the table. "Poor dear. As if you haven't already gone through enough."

"It's nothin' to worry about—just a little cough." Despite his impaired depth perception, he noticed that her mother's hand was extended toward him.

"You're a remarkable young man, Danny Rignold," Nora said. She shook his hand warmly. "Lord knows what might have happened if you hadn't come to Lizzie's rescue."

"Well, no, I'm not ..." As he spoke, Danny was scanning the faces of two strangers standing at the foot of the bed.

"Oh, this is my older brother, Stephen," Elizabeth said.

He stepped forward and shook Danny's hand. "Call me Steve."

Danny nodded a greeting. "You on leave, sailor?"

"Furlough—two weeks. I report back the day after tomorrow."

Elizabeth urged the boarder to come closer. "And you've already met Hannah Lane," she said.

Hannah approached the side of the bed as if at gunpoint, and it suddenly dawned on Danny that this was the girl in the USO. Same short blonde hair, same boyish build, same cow-masticating-her-cud chewing gum. "Well, by golly, it's Billy Sunday," he said.

She scowled at him. "That's high praise indeed. And you mock the Lord at your own peril."

"I ain't mockin' no one. I just think you're a hypocrite."

Hannah stepped toward the bed, fire in her eyes, and shouted, "Who're you calling a hypocrite?"

Elizabeth rushed between them, and Hannah backed off without a further word, wiping a tuft of stray hair from her forehead and glaring out the window curtains.

"Hey, what gives?" Steve asked his sister. He looked from Hannah to Danny and back again. "What's with her?"

Elizabeth shook her head. "They just haven't hit it off too well, that's all."

Steve laughed. "Well, you could've fooled me. And here I thought they were Ginger Rogers and Fred Astaire."

Nora reached behind Danny's head and began to fluff his pillow. She could see Steve in the corner of her eye. "Oh, there was a little misunderstanding last night—nothing more than that. Everything will work out fine."

The same nurse who had spoken to them earlier interrupted the conversation with a directive that Danny be allowed to rest. She cast a frown at Hannah as she spoke.

"Sorry, nurse," Nora said. "We won't be a minute."

The nurse looked sternly at her and returned to her rounds.

"Listen, pal," Steve said to the patient, "we're indebted to you and wish you a swift recovery."

"It was the least I could do," Danny said. He wiggled the fingers on his left hand. "I'm afraid I didn't make a very good showin' of myself."

Steve pointed toward his sister and whispered, "Hogwash! Can you look at her and tell me that? She's safe, and we have no one to thank but you."

The two men shook hands again. "Good luck, sailor," Danny said. "Kill a few Japs for me, will you?"

"I'll try. And you watch over my sister while I'm gone."

Elizabeth leaned across the bed and kissed Danny on the cheek.

Danny smiled until he happened to spot Hannah walking away. "Hey, Hannah Lane," he called after her, "thanks for comin'." She turned around, still confrontational. "Really," he said. "I mean it."

Her face softened a bit, but all she said was, "God bless."

◆　　◆　　◆

Early on Tuesday morning, while the sun was still an orange ball on the horizon, Steve boarded a northbound Texas Electric Railway car, allowing himself plenty of time for the trip to the Dallas Interurban Terminal on Houston Street. From there, he would transfer by taxi to Union Station and catch the departing 1:35 train for Fort Worth, Weatherford, and points west.

The past two weeks had been both joyful and bittersweet, and he made a conscious effort to marshal his defenses against the onslaught of heartache that was sure to strike. It was a familiar struggle—a secret one that had plagued him all his life—whether leaving for summer camp or simply for his annual fishing weekend with Everett and Freddie Collier before the resumption of school.

Without warning, the train began to move, and he swallowed hard while waving out the window to his mother and brother. The sun's rays, reflecting at such a low angle off the depot glass, impaired his visibility, so he leaned forward into the shade of the window post. Nora was no more than fifty feet away, wiping her eyes with a handkerchief while waving fitfully with the other hand. At her left stood Wesley, all smiles, beaming as if his older brother had just scored the winning touchdown against Notre Dame.

Steve thought he heard Coach Stiteler's voice, but it was just a sergeant's in a seat across the aisle. By the time he turned back to the window, his family was no longer in sight. He craned his neck, savoring the last view of Waco that he would have for many months, perhaps even years. Possibly forever.

When the train crossed over the bridge and reached the east bank of the Brazos, Steve sat back in his seat and closed his eyes—fighting to concentrate on wartime duties, endeavoring above all else to clear his mind of sentimental thoughts.

But still they came.

Elizabeth, due at work by seven o'clock that morning, had said her goodbyes to him at home, and yet he could see her clearly now, as the interurban rumbled down its tracks. She stood in the kitchen, young and fragile—just a kid, really. He prayed to God that her recent scare would leave no ill effects.

And then there was old Mrs. Moek at the grocery store, handing him a small sheet of wax paper that was folded around an assortment of hard candies. "Oh, Mutter," her husband said, "Stephen's a full-grown man now. Don't embarrass him like this in front of the customers. Besides, soldiers can get as much candy as they want—can't you, Steve? Not like us, stateside!" A half-dozen bystanders, caught in this little drama, laughed good-naturedly and went about their business.

Even the female boarder, Hannah Lane, had wished him luck. The night before, when she arrived home from Crawford-Austin at precisely 12:30—the clock chimed once as she entered the house—she saw that Steve and his mother were chatting over coffee in the living room. "Don't get up. Wait here a minute," Hannah said. She disappeared upstairs for a brief while and returned with a tiny book in hand. "This is a New Testament. Keep it with you while you're away, and it will bring you peace." Steve did not have the heart to tell her that every serviceman received one just like it at the reception center. She laid it on the table beside him.

The train shook, and Steve opened his eyes to survey the scene around him. It seemed that fully half the people aboard were wearing military uniforms. Most were Army, but there were a good many sailors too. Three of them—each dressed, like him, in summer fatigues with a white cap—were seated near the front of the car. Above them was a familiar placard from the Office of Defense Transportation: "Is Your Trip Necessary? Needless Travel Interferes with the War Effort."

He looked upward to his right and saw a full-color poster, showing a sailor with a seabag over his shoulder. At the bottom of the poster, emblazoned on a blood-red background, were some cautionary words in stark white: "If you tell where he's going ... he may never get there."

Steve pulled out his pipe and began filling it with tobacco. Then he tapped the soldier in front of him on the shoulder. "Say, do you mind if I smoke?" he asked.

"Be my guest ..." the GI said with a shrug. The young lady next to him peeked over the top of her chair back and added, "That is, if it's not a cigar!" Steve held up his pipe for her to see, and she nodded her head playfully.

Although currents of air blew in from the slightly lowered windows, still his pipe smoke drifted lazily throughout much of that section of the car, giving the ride a more comfortable, homey feel. Being an electric conveyance, instead of steam or diesel, the interurban rolled along rather quietly, save for an occasional screech of metal-on-metal, and the general serenity gave him a chance to think. He tried to picture what was in store for him at his next training station. He wanted sea duty—that much he knew—but beyond that it would be "Navy's choice." In a perverse way, the very ambiguity of his immediate future somehow made the military experience more palatable, more like an adventure. That was a healthy attitude to adopt, he decided then and there.

A short distance past Hillsboro, as the dry grassland rushed by at a mile a minute, he allowed his thoughts to drift back to the evening before, when his mother sat across the living room from him, silently mending a nickel-sized hole that had developed in his seabag. The telephone rang, disturbing Valentino a mere thirty seconds after Steve had finally managed to coax the cat into curling up on his lap. On the line was H. H. Hargrove, who said, "God be with you, Stephen. Your name is on my prayer list, and it will remain so for the duration." Steve thanked the pastor and agreed to write home regularly.

Whenever the interurban tracks happened to curve slightly to the east, the entire car became bathed in sunlight. Illuminated dust particles, suspended in the air, floated about in such profusion that it seemed a wonder anybody could breathe. Above the lulling sound of the wheels, he heard the couple in front of him, kidding one another and whispering their private jokes. Through the narrow opening between chairs, he could see that their heads were resting against each other, and it made him a little envious.

As so often before, he thought of Cynthia Mills—blonde, impetuous, and a bit of a tease. Would he ever see her again? And the photos of Donna Gorsey crossed his mind—sitting among the others, not daring to look into the lens, and yet favoring the yearbook cameraman with a bashful smile. For some unaccountable reason, the peppery Agnes Matteson came to mind. Steve could still see Teddy Gaunce's spirited friend, the long hair curling forward over her shoulder.

He puffed his pipe, savoring the sweet aroma, and then consulted his wristwatch. Even past Dallas, where he would transfer at Union Station, there was a long trip ahead of him. Looking down into the rumpled brown sack that lay at his feet, he could not help but laugh. Never had he gone on a trip, no matter how transitory, without carrying—compliments of his mother—a brown sack full of sandwiches and an apple. Evidently, military service was no exception.

Steve reached into the sack for the morning newspaper, which he had purchased from a vendor at the passenger depot. He unfolded it and scanned the headlines: "Final Battle for Messina Bridgehead Nears: Yankees, British Cut Deeply into Last Axis Lines," "Mighty Force of Bombers Swarm Toward Germany: One of Largest Fleets of RAF's Night Raiders Ever," "Ship Named for Grandfather of Waco Barrister: Liberty Freighter Will Slide Down the Ways Today, Bearing the Name of R. M. Williamson, Known to History As the Patrick Henry of Texas."

When he returned the newspaper to the sack, Mrs. Moek's gift scattered about, so he blindly fished along the bottom for a piece of candy—hoping for a red one, either raspberry or strawberry. But his hand came into contact with something flat and leathery, buried under the wrapped sandwiches. Curious, he picked up the sack and laid it on his lap. After shifting the sandwiches to one side, he could see one corner of the mysterious object. Pulling it from the sack, he saw that it was a tiny book, the New Testament that Hannah had shown him but then "forgotten" to give. Steve idly leafed forward through the book until his eyes came upon the frontispiece and title page. There he noticed a handwritten inscription: "Dear Stephen, please keep this NT with you at all times. It will protect you and bring you back to us safely. Write to me if you have some spare time. Hannah Lane."

◆　　◆　　◆

That Sunday was Wesley's worst on-air presentation in recent memory, and he was glad that his brother was not around to hear it. Though he blamed his sub-par announcing on the typewriter ribbon, which badly needed changing, the real cause was a distraction on the other side of the soundproof glass. There in the control room, pacing and looking impatiently at his pocket watch, was Hugh Kenton, director of the station's two daytime serials. Kenton was virtually never to be seen in these environs at such an advanced hour—five minutes before midnight— especially on a weekend.

While Wesley was flubbing his way through a local story on McLennan County housing prices, Kenton even went so far as to hold up a piece of paper with the words DON'T LEAVE–I NEED TO TALK TO YOU scrawled on it. Wesley nodded and tried to refocus his attention on the copy in front of him. A minute later, when he happened to catch the eye of board operator Dave Flint, he was met with an apologetic shrug. Wesley surmised that the studio director's presence had unnerved Dave too.

Kenton threw open the news-booth door the instant the red light went out. He was holding a small stack of papers in one hand. "Brower, listen," he said. "You need to help us with a major problem. Tell me you can be back at the station by nine in the morning."

"I guess so. Why?"

"Benny Randall jumped ship—Uncle Sam grabbed him for service." He paused, waiting for a reaction from Wesley, but all he got was a blank stare.

"Jeez, man," he said, "don't you ever listen to your own station?"

Wesley just stood there, looking thoroughly embarrassed. "Not very often. I'm still in school, you know."

Kenton removed his eyeglasses and began wiping them with a handkerchief. "Sorry, Brower. It's just that we're in a tight spot here, and you've been mentioned as our ticket out of trouble."

"Me?"

"Benny plays Kip Hanson on 'Behold Tomorrow'—at least he *did* until Friday. Now he's leaving, and we've got no one to play the part. Monica Whaley's our script girl, and she recommended you."

Wesley felt his knees growing weak. "Why me?" he asked. "I don't know anything about ... acting."

Kenton put his glasses back on. "Three reasons. First, you have some on-air experience, reading the news—for whatever that's worth. Second, Monica thinks you could handle it. And third, to be honest with you, there's no way we can find anyone else by tomorrow at three."

"Tomorrow!"

Kenton extended his hands, palms forward, indicating that he was powerless. "We've got a show to produce, and a sponsor's not gonna pay for fifteen minutes of dead air."

"But tomorrow?"

Kenton nodded his head sympathetically.

Wesley turned away and suddenly longed to be Dave Flint on the other side of the glass. There he sat, methodically signing off the station and then heading for home.

"Is this person on the show every day?" Wesley asked.

"Kip Hanson? Well, I talked with one of the writers about it yesterday. Her name's Ethel Coody—you'll meet them all—and she said that Kip's character is being developed into a slightly bigger role. In other words, she can't write him out of the next few scripts."

Wesley leaned against the wall of the news booth, eyes fixed on the floor and saying nothing. He rubbed his chin nervously.

Kenton smiled. "Really, Brower, it's not that big of a deal. We'll have you into the role in no time. What do you say?"

Wesley raised his eyebrows, mired in worry. "Gosh, I don't know."

"I've already checked it out with Grant Tollefson," Kenton said, "and he tells me they can spare you."

Wesley looked up. "Why Grant?"

"He's taking over for Larry Underwood."

Wesley was shocked. "Grant Tollefson's the news director now?"

"Yep. I thought you knew. The old man appointed him sometime last week."

Mention of Grant Tollefson's name evoked unsettling memories of Sandra Whittsel. Wesley had not thought about her very much over the past few weeks, but now that all changed. With a sudden burst of bravado, he took a deep breath and said, "Sure, Mr. Kenton, I'll take the job."

"'Hugh'."

"Okay ... Hugh." Already he could feel his confidence draining away, and he was sorry that he blurted out his acceptance.

"Here's the script, Wes—you don't mind if I call you that, do you? Show up around nine in the morning, and we'll give you some pointers. You're not in tomorrow's show very much, but then things pick up on Tuesday."

Wesley cleared his throat. "Who is this Kip Hanson supposed to be?"

"All right, I'll give you the low-down. Kip is Bud Hanson's nephew, see? Bennie played him a bit older than you are—but just be a high school kid, and that'll be fine. As I say, he's only been a shadowy figure until now."

Wesley thought of something that might derail the whole idea. "But if I stay in this role, what happens when school starts again?"

"When's that?"

"September thirteenth."

Kenton frowned. "We'll cross that bridge when we come to it."

"Who plays my uncle?"

"That's Neddy Wright."

"Uh-oh."

"Something the matter?"

Wesley gave a tense laugh. "It's just that I think he may still be a little sore at me."

Kenton shook his head. "Well, I'm not a member of his fan club either. Just remember—you're not working for Neddy Wright. When you're on 'Behold Tomorrow,' you're working for the Williams Drug Company."

"The friendly stores," Wesley said.

Kenton smiled. "That's right, the friendly stores, with three Waco locations to—"

A sudden silence made the director stop short. Years of experience had taught him to say nothing once an open mike had muted the speakers. Instinctively, he glanced at the control room. The national anthem had ended, and Dave Flint was busy shutting down the transmitter.

"Listen, Brower," Kenton said, "I've got to run. Try to get some sleep tonight."

"Yes, sir."

"See you at nine—sharp."

"Do I need to bring anything? What do I wear?"

"This isn't the movies, son. Wear whatever you want." Kenton looked amused, and the tips of his mustache curved up when he added, "You're an actor now, so just about all you'll need are your vocal cords." Then he thought for a moment. "Oh, and bring this copy of the script with you. Paper doesn't grow on trees."

Wesley was only half listening, so he was taken by surprise when Kenton began chuckling at his own witticism.

◆　　◆　　◆

A condemned man taking his last walk to Old Sparky could not have felt more jittery than Wesley did when he slowly dismounted his bicycle and plodded toward the entrance of KWXN. The anxiety of reading his first newscast was still vivid in his memory, but that ordeal was a piece of cake compared to becoming a radio actor. Who was this Kip Hanson character anyway, and how was a virtual novice supposed to make him come alive in people's homes simply through voice inflection and emotional wizardry? He envied the other cast members who, with years of performance behind them, lounged around smoking their cigarettes until deigning to glance over their scripts a few seconds before airtime.

The first person he saw upon entering the lobby was Hugh Kenton, who sat cross-legged on the sofa and puffed smoke rings from a fine, twenty-five-cent cigar.

Now that Elaine Overmire had resigned to care for her two grandchildren, Myra Culp was KWXN's morning and afternoon receptionist, leaving her evenings free to gossip on the telephone, just as she had been doing at work all along. But as ill fortune would have it, Myra had deserted her desk for the moment, so Wesley was thrust immediately into his new assignment, with no luxury of casual small talk. He laid his script on the coffee table, amidst the scattered magazines.

"Well, if it isn't Kip Hanson!" the director said. There was something affected in his cheerfulness.

Wesley put his hands in his trouser pockets. "Hello, Mr. Kenton."

"'Hugh'," Kenton said. "Remember?" Leaning forward with his right leg still crossed over the left, he offered his hand.

Wesley laughed nervously. "Oh, sure ... Hugh." He drew his right hand out of its pocket, and Kenton's confident handshake nearly crushed his finger joints.

"Did you look over the script last night?"

"Yes, Mr. Kenton."

The director rolled his eyes and sighed. "Just call me 'Hugh,' son, and we'll get along fine."

Wesley nodded his agreement. Suddenly, when the exertion of pedaling to work finally made itself felt, the room seemed oppressively muggy to him, and drops of perspiration tickled his back as they rolled in a rivulet down to the waistband of his underwear. He hoped the beads of sweat that dotted his face were not too noticeable.

"It looks like only a couple of the cast are here on time," Kenton said. He glanced at the wall clock above the receptionist's desk. "Jeez, I guess that's about par for the course." He stood, stretched his arms as if awakening on a lazy Saturday morning, and then shifted gears—walking purposefully down the corridor, trailing a plume of cigar smoke behind him. Wesley gulped and tried to catch up with him, but the director was already well past the newsroom when he said over his shoulder, "Didn't you forget something, son?" Kenton did not bother to slow his pace, but Wesley stopped dead in his tracks.

"Yes, sir," he said, and he ran back to the lobby. By now, Myra Culp was returning to her desk, and she shouted hello to him as he circled the coffee table and rushed toward the studio with a stack of mimeographed papers fluttering under his arm.

Studio A was empty except for a couple of microphones on stands, five or six chairs, some sound-effects paraphernalia, two rectangular tables, and the janitor's mop and bucket. Phyllis Sherry was there, too, and so was Neddy Wright. They sat next to the sound table, each of them eating a glazed doughnut. "Hey, Hugh, want one?" Neddy asked.

"No, thanks, and neither should you. Terrible for your voice."

"We've got coffee to wash them down," Phyllis said while chewing.

Kenton gave the actress a piercing look. "And it doesn't exactly do wonders for your figure, either."

"Hey, this is radio. Who's to know?"

Kenton shook his head in disgust and changed the subject. "Are we on war time or what?" he said. "When I say nine o'clock sharp, people around here think I mean sometime before ten."

Neddy and Phyllis both shrugged their shoulders, and Kenton apologized. "I shouldn't be preaching to you. You're the only two who got here on time—you and Kip Hanson here." He motioned with his cigar-laden hand. "Gang, this is Wesley Brower. Benny's gone off to war, you know, and this is his replacement."

Wesley nodded shyly but did not step forward to shake hands.

"Welcome aboard," Phyllis said. She pulled a napkin from the doughnut box and wiped the side of her mouth, careful not to smear the bright-red lipstick.

Neddy studied Wesley's face for a moment. "Are you from the newsroom?"

"That's right, he's one of our weekend announcers," Kenton said. He stepped in front of the newcomer. "I'm sure you'll agree that we're lucky to get someone with on-air experience."

"I'm still waiting for Monica to show up, Brower. You left me high and dry, and old lady Coody was not amused."

"Sorry. I told Myra, but I guess she—"

"Drop it, Wes," Kenton told him. "There's no need for you to justify yourself in his eyes. Neddy should have fetched her himself if it was so blasted important to him."

Neddy glowered at the director, who stared him down while continuing to speak. "I trust you both got scripts last week. I gave one to Wes here. Monica has a couple of minor changes to pass along, but those won't be ready until after lunch. They'll be green sheets, so be looking for them." Neddy finally abandoned the visual confrontation, so Kenton relaxed and sat on the corner of the other table, cigar in mouth and hands folded in his lap. He was beginning to speak again when Phyllis said, "How is Jeannie ... Oh, I beg your pardon."

"Go ahead. Ladies first." Kenton took the cigar out of his mouth and smoothed down his mustache with the fingers of his other hand.

"I was just going to ask how Jeannie is supposed to know about the stolen papers when she's never even been to Anson's new office."

"She's been there now—presumably over the weekend—and the audience will just have to deduce that."

"Well, it didn't make any sense to me. Will the listeners know what's going on?"

"Trust Jerry. He's way ahead of us on this. I think he's already working on *next* Tuesday's show."

Neddy was shocked. "A week from tomorrow?"

"Yep."

"What's gotten into him all of a sudden? Have all the bars closed or something?"

Phyllis winced at this uncaring remark. "Hey, lay off the rabbit punches, if you don't mind."

"It's no secret, Phyl," Neddy said. "Jerry's been Centennial's best customer since Calvin Coolidge was President."

Kenton stood up and crushed the remains of his cigar in the ashtray. "Look, Neddy. Jerry's little ... libation problem is of no concern to us, so long as he keeps producing quality material. And I think he's doing just that, he and Ethel. No thanks to Harvey lately, but that's another story entirely."

Wesley had no idea what the others were talking about, and he felt distinctly like an outsider. He cleared his throat nervously, and three pairs of eyes looked at him as if their owners had forgotten he was in the room.

Kenton cleared his own throat, but very loudly, almost comically. "Well, Wes, what say you do a little reading for us, huh?" The director motioned for Phyllis to hand him his master copy of the script, and returning to his tabletop perch, he began flipping through it. "Try ... uh ..." He considered one passage, then went to another. "Have a go at page eleven here, right after the cop asks you if you've seen your uncle lately."

"Do you want me to sit or stand?"

Kenton shook his head and gave a weary smile. "I don't care if you do cartwheels, Brower. Just read a few lines for us, if you don't mind."

Wesley held the script at arm's length and scanned the copy, stopping when his eyes came to COP: *Have you seen Bud Hanson? I understand you're his nephew.* The pages were shaking badly in his right hand, but he began reading just the same.

"No, officer, I haven't seen my uncle in a month or more," Wesley announced. He was aghast at how quivery his voice sounded, but he thought it best to forge ahead. "Why?" he continued. "Is he in some sort of trouble?"

In a perfunctory monotone, Kenton provided the other lines, his voice devoid of all expression: "Could be, but you can help him out by answering a few questions for me."

"What sort of questions?" Wesley read. "I hardly even know my uncle. We're not very close."

"Clam up, punk, and quit wasting my time with rubbish like that. We happen to know you're almost like a son to him."

"Sorry, sir, but you must have me mixed up with somebody else. I've only been in town for about a year—less than that—and I don't think I've seen my uncle more than a dozen times. Like I say, we're ..."

"Okay, Brower, that's plenty." Kenton's baritone was back to normal.

Wesley's voice trailed off, "... not very close," and he glanced with wounded ego at the other cast members.

Neddy slapped his knee. "Oh, that's terrific. Jeez-Louise, close your eyes, and Paul Muni is right here with us."

"Shut up, Wright," Kenton said, and there was no mistaking his tone. Neddy looked up in shock, and Phyllis turned her head away. Kenton nodded toward the newcomer. "Wes here was just putting some life into his reading. Don't you think Kip Hanson would be kind of nervous talking with a cop about his uncle? It's called 'acting,' Neddy. You ought to try it sometime."

Neddy aimed an index finger at Kenton. "I don't have to sit here and take that from you," he said.

"No, you don't. You can pack up your things right now and walk out of here. We've still got nearly six hours to airtime, and believe me, I've got the old man's ear in matters of dissension. We'll either find someone to take over or else write Bud out of the script for today. That'll buy us some time to find your replacement."

Neddy scowled at Wesley and, with a loud "Sheesh," wadded up his script and threw it against the back wall of the studio. As it whizzed by, the projectile came within inches of hitting Phyllis in the head, so she stood up and scrambled away from her incensed colleague.

Kenton took a couple of steps toward Neddy and said, in a controlled, surprisingly conversational tone, "Frankly, I don't much care if you leave or stay. That's up to you." He gestured toward the wall. "But if you stay, then that's the script you're going to use. It's your decision, and you need to make it right now." Though growling incomprehensible oaths, Neddy was quick to capitulate.

The five remaining cast members did not arrive until just after 9:30, a tardiness that was interpreted by Kenton as slothful apathy, even though each of those so maligned surely would have been able to fabricate a perfectly plausible excuse if called to account by management. Only Beverly Jaynes felt compelled to offer any explanation, and hers was a rather lame narrative about a streetcar conductor who was more interested in filling out his logbook than he was in observing the motorman's unwritten code of punctuality.

Kenton took Wesley to lunch that day, a ritual that he had maintained, with rare exceptions, ever since he began recruiting dramatic talent for KWXN in 1937. Invariably, his proselytes were treated to a meal at the Purple Cow Sandwich Shop, several blocks south of the radio station at Eighth and Austin—just a stone's throw from the Greyhound Bus Terminal and next door to the Raleigh Hotel.

While awaiting their food, the discussion turned to the first script reading, and Wesley volunteered the fact that his faltering studio delivery had precious little to do with any perceived acting ability. No, he confessed, it was not Kip Hanson who was nervous but Wesley Brower.

Kenton waved off the comment. "Good, then you've got real promise, son. Tap into those genuine emotions, and let them spill over into your character. That's something very difficult to conjure up when you don't really feel it."

Wesley nodded his head, desperately wanting to believe the director but never quite escaping the nagging suspicion that Kenton's impromptu remarks were, in actuality, little more than a battle-tested stratagem to put a fledgling thespian at ease. It was just blind luck that Kip's quivering voice under police interrogation happened to be in character, and Wesley was ashamed to accept bravos for his effort. He watched with admiration as the director lay an unlit cigar on the table, almost as if it were an additional eating utensil, and he marveled at how easy radio veterans like Kenton made it all seem.

◆　　◆　　◆

Nora was beside herself with frustration. This was the third flat tire she had suffered since school ended back in May. The rubber tread's alarming thinness made all four tires—five, counting the pathetic spare—prime candidates for blowouts, and yet any thought of replacement was out of the question. Supplies had dwindled to abysmal levels, and the onerous waiting lists were demoralizing to all but the most stubborn of optimists.

It was nearly 2:30, and Nora was a good two miles away from home, waiting impatiently for young Bradley Gann to appear on the scene. Her automobile was pulled over to the side of the road, but Herring Avenue carried a relatively high volume of traffic, even during these depressed times of vehicle attrition. For safety's sake, Bradley probably would have to push the automobile onto a side street before attempting to remove the tire.

Four times a truck had approached, and in each case Nora presumed it was Bradley at the wheel of an SRC vehicle. The Service Refining Company had a pair of tow trucks, one for the East Waco shop and one to handle the needs of the Eleventh and Washington location. Once she even flagged the driver down, only to discover that it was a delivery truck for the Empire Seed Company. He offered to change the tire for her—saving a damsel in distress, as he jokingly put it—but she declined with thanks, explaining that help was already on the way. Less than a block after the *thump-a-thump-a-thump* noise began, she had stopped outside a Piggly Wiggly Store in the 1500 block and called Elizabeth at work.

By the time Bradley Gann arrived, it was seventeen minutes before three. He squeaked the truck to a halt and jumped down from the cab. "Sorry, Miz Brower, but I been workin' on a lube job."

"That's all right, Bradley. Thanks for coming. Did Lizzie tell you what I needed you for?"

"No, ma'am," Bradley said. He appraised the tilting car. "But I see it's a blowout."

"Can you change the tire for me?"

"Sure. That's what I do, mostly. You got a spare?"

She nodded her head. "Would you be able to take this one back to the station and patch it?"

"Well, you know, I'm just a grease boy, Miz Brower," he said, "but I think I might could. Ol' Butch, he's the one that usually does that."

"Then maybe you'd better ask Butch to do it for me. Would you mind?"

"No, ma'am, but I'm pretty sure I could do it." When he grinned, there were two separate half-inch gaps in his teeth. "Lord knows, I've watched him enough times."

Nora shook her head. "No. Just ask Butch to do it for me, will you?"

Bradley's brow furrowed in thought. "What if he's not around?"

"Does Louis Panufnik still work there?"

"Sure does."

"Then ask him."

The light returned to Bradley's eyes, and he beamed a smile. "Oh, yeah, sure. I kin ask Loo-ie to do it."

"Do we need to move the car away from the road?"

"Naw, we're okay here."

To Nora's amazement, Bradley replaced the flat with machinelike authority. "Sometimes I do as many as thirty of these a week," he told her. "All over town. I kin do it in my sleep."

As he was slinging the deflated tire into the truck's flatbed, he paused for a moment and reflected sadly, "You know, you've got bad tires—some of the worst ones I've seen. I don't know how many more times we kin fix 'em."

"Thank you, Bradley. I'm painfully aware of that." Nora reached inside the automobile for her purse. "I'm almost embarrassed to let people see them. Isn't that silly?" She giggled at the thought.

But Bradley was not amused. "These kin be dangerous, Miz Brower. I wouldn't go over the speed limit with 'em, that's for sure."

"Does the station have any retreads for sale?"

"Hah! Are you kiddin'?"

"Well, do you have a standby list? You said yourself that these could be dangerous."

"Not anymore, ma'am," he said. "We used to, but not anymore. Some stations do, 'specially over in East Waco, but I don't know where they get the tires."

Nora flashed him a knowing glance. "I'm not interested in those. I'd rather walk."

Bradley started to climb into the truck but stopped. "Oh, that'll be four bits, Miz Brower. I kin't charge you for the patchin' job 'til you come pick up the tire."

She fumbled through her coin purse and handed Bradley a half-dollar. "Thank you ever so much for your help. Here's an extra quarter for your troubles."

He nodded his head in appreciation. "Thank you, ma'am. Watch out for nails on the way home. Remember, you don't have no spare."

It was four minutes to three when Nora started the engine. Quickly she switched on the radio and tuned it to KWXN. She sighed in disappointment but tried to remain philosophical. Ever since Wesley's surprise announcement at the breakfast table, she had planned to hear the Monday edition of "Behold Tomorrow" in style—on the living room console. Now the automobile's dashboard would have to suffice.

◆　　◆　　◆

Even though Nora was not there to hear it, her Philco radio/phonograph would be carrying the start of Wesley's debut on "Behold Tomorrow" nonetheless. At two minutes before three o'clock, a boyish young woman with tousled blonde hair came bounding down the stairs and switched the set on, giving the vacuum tubes plenty of time to warm up before the broadcast began. Hannah was scheduled to work the swing shift that day, but she calculated that this should give her more than enough time to report to Crawford-Austin before the whistle blew.

Her athletic dash from stairway to living room startled Valentino, who had been curled up with his back resting against the overstuffed arm of the sofa. He scampered into the hallway and turned to gaze at the intruder, his fur bristled in fright.

"Oh, kitty, I'm sorry," Hannah said in her baby voice. "I didn't know you were there." Valentino relaxed his guard and proudly strolled toward his food dish, in no mood to grant cheerful forgiveness to the disturber of his sleep. Hannah walked over to the dining cat and repeated her apology—"I'm sorry, kitty"—but when she leaned down and began stroking his fur, Valentino did not deign to acknowledge that she was even there.

The adjacency that day was a thirty-second commercial for Cogdell's, an automotive supply store at Ninth and Austin that lately had been stocking more hardware and household appliances—at least for the duration. A deep-throated announcer gave the time and call letters, and then, at precisely three o'clock, Central War Time, the signature organ tune notified listeners that "Behold Tomorrow" was on the air.

"Yes, Williams Drug Company ... the friendly stores ... presents 'Behold Tomorrow,' heard each day at this time as a courtesy of Williams Drug Company's three Waco locations—at 501 Franklin Avenue in the Professional Building, at the southeast corner of Ninth and Austin, and at 423 Austin Avenue, the Old Corner Drug Store across from the Amicable Life Insurance Building. And now ... 'Behold Tomorrow.'

"As we left you on Friday, Bud Hanson was fleeing from the law after bungling his attempt to convince the gravely wounded Ned Cashley that he had come over to his side of the racketeering scheme. Meanwhile, Jeannie Gabriel remained unaware of this perilous turn of events ... and, as she drove to her parents' mansion, her chief attorney, Travis Earnshaw, was trying desperately to intercept the car, knowing full well that a gang of thugs awaited her arrival. We join Jeannie Gabriel as she calmly turns the corner onto Grand Peninsula Boulevard and an appointment with doom. Listen."

After adjusting the volume knob to a more comfortable level, Hannah settled herself on the sofa and awaited the appearance of Wesley Brower, but his character seemed to be out of the story entirely. It was not until well into the quarter-hour—after the scene changed to a secluded alley, where faint sounds of automobile traffic could be detected—that the script finally began to suggest that Kip Hanson could not be far away.

An urgent clatter in the front door's keyhole jarred Hannah from her concentration, and she noticed that the cat's ears were alert with curiosity. Nora rushed in, slamming the door behind her. "Well, I had a flat tire ... again! Is he on yet?" she asked. Nora tossed her purse onto the easy chair and stood not more than five feet away from the radio console.

"No, ma'am, but Wes said there's going to be a policeman with him, and I think I just heard a siren."

Staring at the dim light on the console, Nora backed over to the easy chair and sat down. Annoyed by an object poking her in the ribs, she reached behind her and laid the purse on the floor.

"Shhhh! You hear that, Kip?"

"Yeah."

"Someone's coming. Hurry! Put that stuff away, and head over to Connie Barcus's place. I'll meet you there at 9:30. Tell him I sent you."

"Okay."

The man's voice was receding as he ran away. "Don't let me down, kid. That Odom doesn't mess around."

There was a frantic rustling of paper, which stopped suddenly with the unmistakable sound of approaching footsteps. They seemed to advance nearer and nearer as crickets maintained their steady chorus of chirping. Then the noise of shoe soles on pavement came to an abrupt halt when someone bumped against a metallic trash can, causing its lid to strike the ground with an ear-splitting rattle.

"All right. Who's there? Don't try to hide. I can see you in my flashlight."

There was nothing but silence for a couple of seconds.

"I see you. Come out with your hands up."

"Don't shoot, officer. I didn't know you were a cop."

"Lean over, and put your hands on the wall. Spread your legs."

"But officer, I wasn't doing nothing wrong."

"Then why are you hiding from the police? Okay, you can turn around."

"Like I say, I didn't know you were a cop. All I saw was a flashlight shining down the alley, and I got scared."

"And I suppose you didn't hear the siren?"

"Sure I did, but how was I supposed to know it was a cop carrying the flashlight?"

"Let me see some identification."

"I don't have any."

"What's your name?"

"Kip Hanson."

"Yep, I thought that's who you might be."

There was uneasy quiet for a moment, broken only by the policeman's measured footsteps, presumably as he circled around to position himself directly in front of the boy.

"Have you seen Bud Hanson? I understand you're his nephew."

"No, officer, I haven't seen my uncle in a month or more. Why? Is he in some sort of trouble?"

"Could be, but you can help him out by answering a few questions for me."

"What sort of questions? I hardly even know my uncle. We're not very close."

"Clam up, punk, and quit wasting my time with rubbish like that. We happen to know you're almost like a son to him."

"Sorry, sir, but you must have me mixed up with somebody else. I've only been in town for about a year ... less than that ... and I don't think I've seen my uncle more than a dozen times. Like I say, we're not very close."

"You know someone named Odom Cashley?"

"Nope."

"We'll just see about that. You're coming with me."

"Hey, you're hurting my arm."

"Come on, you."

"Where you taking me?"

"We're going downtown. You ever been in jail before?"

"Jail!"

"Unless you feel like talking now."

"Nope, I don't have nothing to say. Listen, officer, can't I even tell my mom?"

"Sure can. You can call her from PD."

"PD?"

"The police station."

"That would be PS."

"Oh, a wise guy, huh? Come along, sonny boy."

"Hey, quit hurting my arm."

When the dramatic organ music came up, a full-voiced announcer closed the program and invited listeners to patronize the Williams Drug Company, "proud sponsor of 'Behold Tomorrow,' heard each weekday at three o'clock on this station."

Nora was reserved in her praise. "I thought he did fine," she told Hannah, "although he may have sounded a little nervous."

"Well, who wouldn't be—in that situation? I think Wesley did swell, Mrs. B., broadcasting all over central Texas like that. Anyway, his character ..."

"Kip Hanson."

"Kip Hanson was being questioned by the police, so maybe he was supposed to sound nervous. I'm sure that's what it was."

The telephone rang, and Nora walked into the entryway to answer it. Hannah, still sitting on the sofa, could not help overhearing the conversation.

"Yes, dear, I did ... Uh-huh, I thought he sounded fine, very professional ..." Nora laughed. "Well, he's hardly that, Mabel, but we're mighty proud of him just the same ... Yes, every day, from what I understand ... I'm not sure. Maybe the teachers can make an allowance for that. First he needs to see whether he wants to stay in the role, and if the radio station wants to keep him ... For the duration, I suppose. He went into the service, you know."

When Nora returned to the living room, she sat down next to Hannah. "That was Mabel Johns, as you might have gathered. I told her this morning that Wes would be on, but I'm not sure she believed me at first."

"What did she think of the broadcast?" Hannah asked.

"She was pleasantly surprised, it sounded like. I have always thought Mabel was a little jealous of my two boys. You know, her Davey has never really amounted to anything—just bouncing from one job to another. I think he's working as a meat cutter's assistant over in Bryan. Nothing wrong with that, of course, but poor Davey never stays with any job for longer than a couple of months or so—usually a lot less than that."

"Who went into the service?" Hannah asked.

Nora looked puzzled.

"You mentioned to Miz Johns that someone went into the service. Were you talking about Stephen?"

Nora shook her head. "No, dear, that was the boy—well, really a man—who used to play the part of Kip on the radio program. I forget his name."

"Did he give Wesley some pointers?"

"No, as I understand it, he ... Oh, Benny was his name, I think. Anyway, he got drafted and was not able to give any notice at all. He just took off and left a message with the receptionist."

"And Wesley stepped in?"

"Yes, and I don't know if he'd ever even heard the show before."

"That's tough."

Nora stood up and walked toward the kitchen. "Yes, it is, and I think he did fine ... just fine."

Hannah began petting the cat, which had rubbed his side against her leg. "I do too, Mrs. B.," she said over her shoulder.

Amidst the clatter of pots and pans, Nora repeated her earlier comment—but now very quietly, almost to herself. "He did sound a little nervous, though."

◆　　◆　　◆

Lieutenant Colonel Duncan Whittsel, still feeling a novel sense of pride in his silver oak leaves, was greeted at the door by his wife and daughter, both of whom wore serious faces. "What's this, a welcoming committee?" he asked, hoping they would respond with smiles.

"Honey, your brother called from Macon. Your father died."

"Good Lord," he said. "When did this happen?" His face went ashen, and he laid his cap atop the hat rack.

"Sometime late this morning. I tried to telephone you over and over at work, but every single time the secretary said you were tied up in meetings."

"Yeah—Battalion. Is Barry with Mom now?"

Charlotte nodded her head. "He called from your parents' house."

Colonel Whittsel walked away. "My God, and he seemed so healthy!" When he turned around, he noticed that his daughter was crying, so he put his arm around her shoulder. He faced Charlotte, but his eyes were gazing at the floor. "Was it a heart attack?"

"The doctor thinks so—or a massive stroke."

"Good Lord. I just can't believe it. I talked with him on Tuesday, and he seemed perfectly fine. Not a pain in his body."

"How old was he?"

Colonel Whittsel looked at his wife. "Just, uh ... sixty-two. He was born in 'eighty-one ... June. He was barely sixty-two."

Sandy spoke up, her voice almost a whisper. "Will we be going to Georgia to be with Gram?"

"Yes, Kitten, I'm sure we will. When does your school start up again?"

"Not until the thirteenth."

"Then that gives us more than a week." He rubbed his chin and planned out loud. "I'll put in for a flight tomorrow. It'll be military, but not too uncomfortable. We'll need to take Digger to a kennel."

Sandy wiped both eyes with the backs of her hands. "Daddy, can I see Wesley Brower before we go?"

"Who?" He seemed annoyed at the thought.

"Wesley Brower—the boy we took to Blackland for Independence Day."

"No, there won't be any time for that."

"But he's on a radio show now—an actor."

Shaking his head, Colonel Whittsel gave an exasperated sigh. "No," he said, "You can see this boy whenever we return to Waco." His look was stern and decisive.

"Yes, sir," Sandy said, and she was careful not to frown. Past experience had taught her that it was futile to argue.

Charlotte gently squeezed her daughter's hands, which were still wet with tears. "Do as your father says, sweetie. This is no time for socializing with the boys."

"Yes, ma'am."

Charlotte gave the colonel a belated kiss and, being a good Army wife, facilitated his next move. "Honey," she said, "if you need to make a phone call, I'll have dinner ready for around 6:15."

"Yeah, I think I should call HQ right away—planes are at a premium just now." He walked toward his study but came back to add, "I'd better give Barry a call too. I don't want him to feel like he's isolated with all the condolences and funeral details. Better make it 1830 hours."

Charlotte never could master the concept of speaking in military time, so her husband long ago dropped his demand that she try. But that did not stop him from using it himself.

◆　　◆　　◆

For the first time in nine months, Wesley slept in on a Saturday. With three weeks of acting experience under his belt and the exciting prospect of nearly half-time status at KWXN—even during the school year—he had telephoned the *Waco News-Tribune* four days earlier to inform the circulation manager that Friday would be his last day on the job.

"We usually like to have at least two weeks' notice," the manager said. There was a touch of anger in his voice, but once it became clear that Wesley's determination was unlikely to waver, the older man's tone mellowed noticeably, and he even wished the teenager well.

"No kidding?" he asked. "You're going to be acting on radio?"

"Yes, sir. I already have been—since August sixteenth."

"What's the name of the show? Maybe I'll try to catch it sometime."

"It's called 'Behold Tomorrow.' Have you heard of it?"

"I don't think so."

"It's probably on when you're working—weekdays at three."

"Well, maybe I'll ask my wife to give it a listen." There was a pause, and the hectic sounds of the circulation office could be heard. "Okay," the manager said to someone else, "we'll get you a Thursday issue. Sure, I do—south of Dutton." Then he was back on the line. "Well, good luck to you, Brower. I'll stop dropping papers at your place after Friday, and you can come by and pick up your last paycheck on Friday, week."

Now the boy could focus his extra-curricular attention solely on radio—and even get some additional sleep in the bargain. The only drawback that he could detect was the chronic case of nervousness that had become his constant companion.

As his bedroom brightened with the rising sun, Wesley rolled over beneath the sheet and looked at the ticking clock on his nightstand—7:45. He had grand designs for the day, but this was a little too early in the morning to place such an important telephone call. On the dresser top across the room lay Monday's script, replete with Kip Hanson's name on most of the pages. In a supine position, with hands behind his head, he stared at the ceiling, wondering when those fluttering butterflies would finally leave his stomach. Involuntarily, the discouraging notion struck him that maybe he was not destined for life in front of a microphone after all. Wakeful beyond the point of return, he arose from bed to clear his mind.

Nora was away from home, rolling bandages at the Red Cross, so breakfast that day consisted of a quick bowl of Post Toasties corn flakes. He remembered his mother telling him that this prepared breakfast food was known as "Elijah's Manna" until some religious groups accused old C. W. Post of sacrilege. "Your grandfather called it 'Elijah's Manna' all his life," Nora said, "even though the name was changed way back in the early years of this century." She shook her head in amusement. "He could be pretty stubborn, I can tell you."

The toilet flushed upstairs. Probably it was Elizabeth, as this was about the time she usually got up on Saturdays, but it could have been Hannah as well. Wesley was never really sure what the boarder's hours were because there did not seem to be any discernible pattern to her work schedule. As for his own job, the immediate future looked rosy indeed. Just the day before, he had received his radio paycheck, and he was pleased to discover that it was nearly three times as large as his customary biweekly wages before he joined the ranks of "dramatic talent." Now he was anxious to deposit the check into his savings account—preferably that very morning, as the bank would remain open until noon.

But it was a girl, rather than money, that occupied center stage in his thoughts. Wesley had not been consciously avoiding Sandra Whittsel, but neither had he spoken with her for nearly a month, except for an inconsequential chance encounter with her family while passing through the turnstile of Katy Park. Somehow, her flirtatious newsroom demeanor with Grant Tollefson continued to gnaw at him, forcibly removing her from the pedestal he had constructed in his imagination and planting an element of doubt in their relationship that he found impossible to ignore. Yet he well knew that she would be aware of his fledgling career in acting by now, and it was only natural that he seek to bask in the reflected glory of his local fame.

The footsteps on the wooden stairway proved to belong to Elizabeth, and she greeted Wesley with a verbal grunt as she came into the kitchen, carrying a book the size of *War and Peace* or *The Count of Monte Cristo*.

"Hi, Lizzie," he said with his mouth full.

"Fix me a bowl of cereal, will you? I've got to be over at the bus depot by nine." She laid her book on the table.

"Why should I? You never do it for me."

"Just do it, Wes. I don't have time to stand here and argue. I promised Mother that I would clean these window sills, and I forgot to last night."

Wesley stood up and walked over to the counter. "What're you reading?" he asked.

"*Gone With the Wind*." She found a dust cloth in the drawer and began wiping the sill.

"Whose is it, the library's?"

"Nope. It belongs to one of Mother's friends. The lady's finished with it and thought I would like it. Her name is Mrs. Peplow."

"Do you?"

"Do I what?" She turned back to look at her brother.

"Do you like the book?"

Elizabeth rolled her eyes. "Of course I do, dopey. It's only the Great American Novel, that's all."

"Who says, your English teacher?" He poured some milk over the Rice Krispies.

"Lots of people. Have you ever read it?"

"No, but I've seen the picture."

"Well, it's way better than the picture," she said. "They have to leave out so much in a four-hour movie. I hope to meet Margaret Mitchell someday."

Wesley laid the bowl next to Elizabeth's book and sat down. "Why do you need to go to the bus depot?"

"Ramona Eccles is coming home from camp."

"I thought you hated her—for what she did to your band director."

"No, she's all right. I think her brother put her up to it."

"Why would he do that?" Wesley finished his breakfast and carried his empty bowl over to the sink.

"I don't know. Just didn't like him, I guess."

"But Vince will be a senior this year. Why would he care about some junior high teacher?"

"How should I know?" Elizabeth asked. "Ramona told me it was his idea, and I believe her."

Wesley glanced at the kitchen clock. "You'd better be going. How do you plan to get downtown?"

"Susan Keeley's mother is picking me up at quarter 'til. Then we're all going over to Susan's house to listen to an opera."

"On the radio?"

"No, Mrs. Keeley's brother is a singer in Chicago, and he's on some records— just a small role, but I think it's on Victor."

"I sure didn't think you liked opera."

She tossed her dust cloth onto the linoleum floor. "I don't know much about it, except for a few famous arias," she said, "but I'm willing to give it a try."

When she sat down and immediately opened *Gone With the Wind* at the bookmark, Wesley took this as a signal to end their conversation. He was well aware that his sister liked to read at meals, even if for only a page or two, so he went into the living room to await his chance to be alone.

Elizabeth's ride to the bus depot was five minutes late, but there was still ample time to get there before the motor coach did. Wesley watched the Keeleys' automobile back out of the driveway and then disappear from view down the street. He already had the telephone receiver in his hand when Hannah suddenly disrupted his plans by trotting down the stairs.

"Sorry. Did I scare you?" she asked.

"Well, I was about to make a call, but it can wait." He laid the receiver down.

"Is it private? Just say the word, and I'll make myself scarce."

"No, it's nothing special," he said with a frown. "Why are you home anyway? I thought you'd be at work."

"Swing shift. I didn't get in until after one." Hannah started to walk toward the kitchen but then stopped. "I get the distinct impression that I'm interrupting something here. I'm very good at sensing things like that." She studied Wesley's face, and he blushed. "It's Sandy, isn't it?" Hannah said, and she poked her finger at his stomach.

Wesley retreated a step, laughing. "What makes you think that?"

"I can read you like a book. For an actor, you really are a lousy liar."

"I'm just ticklish, that's all," he said.

She flashed him a pretty smile and shook her head.

Impulsively, surprising even himself, he blurted out, "Did you know you slept on your hair wrong?" and he reached over to brush an errant blonde curl from her eyes.

Hannah did not pull away but stood silent, giving him a questioning look. Then her face brightened, and she said in an impish voice, "Yes, I'm a very sound sleeper, and I've got the sad-sack coiffure to prove it."

Grasping for the right words to say, Wesley offered what may have sounded like a patronizing comment, "Well, it seems just fine to me," but he was genuinely sincere. Her hair, indeed, was as soft to the touch as a kitten's, and he felt a tingling sensation down his spine. Averting his eyes, he began to walk away, but Hannah stopped him by placing a hand on his shoulder. "Listen," she said, "I've got to be upstairs for about fifteen minutes—maybe twenty—so go ahead and use the telephone."

"Okay, but I don't know if the store is open this early on Saturday."

She considered for a moment and then began ascending the stairs. "Yeah, some of those stores keep funny hours," she said, but the playful tone in her voice made it clear that she was not so easily fooled. He heard her shout down the stairs, "And I promise to put on a record to muffle your talk."

The fact that Wesley had not spoken with Sandy in more than three weeks made the task before him more difficult than it really should have been. When she asked why the long silence between them, as she was sure to do, he had to have a convincing explanation at hand. Telling her that he was very busy these days, though true enough, would not count for much. He decided to avoid any mention of the cozy familiarity she displayed toward Grant Tollefson and the other news reporters, opting instead for the desperate stratagem of blaming their imposed separation on her recent bout with the mumps.

"Hello. 1-8-0-2, please," he told the operator.

"Yes, sir. One moment, please," came the response.

Wesley peeked around the corner, surveying as much of the staircase as the telephone cord would permit, to make certain that Hannah was not within hearing range. It always made him self-conscious to talk on the telephone with others around, and the uneasiness was intensified when the person on the other end of the line happened to be a pretty girl.

"I'm sorry, sir, but there is no answer."

He swallowed hard in disappointment. "Thank you, operator." It was difficult steeling his courage to make such a call, and now he would have to go through it all over again. He went into his father's modest study and seated himself at the battered, roll-top desk, trying to collect his thoughts. Like Harold Brower before him, Wesley had adopted this humble, twelve-by-sixteen-foot retreat as his sanctuary from all the anxieties of the world. Somehow, it gave him an inner peace to view the mementos from a generation ago, particularly the State Fair ashtray and the framed one-dollar bill. The latter had graced the wall of Superior Office Supply for years, but Nora brought it home with her husband's other belongings shortly after his sudden death.

Wesley took a deep breath and tried, with limited success, to picture the loveliness of Sandra Whittsel. Funny how his mental image of her would always grow hazy whenever he encountered that boarding student from North Carolina. The same thing had happened when he drove Hannah down to the Baylor campus for registration. It was pure nonsense, he knew, because the boarder would only be with them for either the duration of the war or her graduation from college, whichever came first. Furthermore, he estimated that, as a transferring junior, Hannah must be a good four years older than he was.

He decided to ride his bicycle over to the Whittsel house, a substantial commitment on such a steamy day in late summer. He yelled up to Hannah that he was leaving, but she did not reply, so he bounded up the stairs to tell her in person. She was lying facedown on the bed, propped up by her elbows and flipping through a large catalogue—probably Sears, Roebuck and Company or Montgomery Ward—and listening to some music on her portable record player.

"I'm going downtown," he said, "just in case Mom wonders where I am."

A gospel quartet was singing "When I Survey the Wondrous Cross," and she hurried across the room to turn down the volume. "Sorry. I have a tendency to play music too loud. I like it that way, but Daddy said it will ruin my ears."

Wesley nodded his head. "Would you tell Mom that I've gone downtown on my bike?"

"Sure. So I guess that store was open after all, huh?" But she sensed that the boy was not even listening to her little joke. Her eyes swept across the room and spotted a brassiere and panties, draped carelessly across the back of the chair. "Oops," Hannah said. She collected the unmentionables and tossed them in the top drawer of the dresser. "Well, now you know all my secrets. Wouldn't your brother have a fit if he saw what's become of his room?"

"I doubt that," Wesley said, and the tingling sensation returned.

The Whittsel family resided about two miles away, southwest of the Browers in an affluent district known as the Village of Castle Heights. This incorporated area, just outside the Waco city limits, was named after the historic Cottonland Castle, a Victorian stone edifice at the corner of Thirty-third Street and Austin Avenue. Though many of their neighbors' homes could rightfully be described as mansions, the Whittsels themselves inhabited a rather less opulent structure than that. And yet it, too, was quite comfortable, as befitted a high-ranking Army officer whose wife was fond of entertaining. Their living quarters stood two stories tall, with three bedrooms and over two thousand square feet of floor space, and the fenced backyard was spacious enough for the family dog to roam to his heart's content. Certainly Duncan Whittsel had been very fortunate indeed to secure such fine accommodations in Waco's glutted housing market.

Wesley leaned his bicycle against a pecan tree and then walked across the paved, circular driveway to the front porch. He pressed the doorbell button and immediately heard the first four notes of Westminster chimes. There was no human response, and it seemed a bit pointless to ring again, considering how deep-throated the tubular bells were that had announced his presence the first time. Shielding his eyes from his own reflection, he peeked through the front window into the living room. All was dark and deserted, but he could see that the furniture remained in place. He wandered around to the back of the residence, dry grass crackling underfoot, and noticed a brick-oven barbecue pit and a padlocked tool shed. A doghouse was there too—Sandy often talked about "Digger O'Dell"— but Wesley saw no evidence of the collie himself. Now he became worried.

When he heard the faint sound of a door slamming, he returned to the front yard. There he came upon a neighbor from the next house over, a thin woman of about fifty. She was kneeling down, turning on a sprinkler to water her flower bed. Unaware of his presence, she coughed loudly several times, indicative of a heavy smoker, and then pulled a few scraggly weeds before arising to go back inside.

"Excuse me ..." Wesley said over the waist-high hedge that separated them.

"Yes?" The neighbor was curt and unsmiling.

"Do you know where the Whittsels are?"

"They've gone back to Georgia," was all the lady would say. She volunteered no further information and left him without so much as a civil nod of the head.

◆   ◆   ◆

Three days before Elizabeth's fifteenth birthday, Marshal Pietro Badoglio—the man who ousted Mussolini—announced to the world that Italy had severed its ties with the Axis and was pulling out of the war. This paved the way for an Allied invasion force to land on the shores of Salerno, uneventfully at first but then encountering tenacious resistance from the entrenched German troops.

On that same day, September 8, 1943, US destroyers were busy shelling the Japanese stronghold of Lae in New Guinea from their positions in the Bismarck Sea. This action would be a decisive factor in rendering nearby Salamaua vulnerable to an assault by the Australian 5th Division.

Though Elizabeth knew little about naval warfare, she could sense her mother's anxiety whenever news reports carried accounts of an Allied offensive overseas. Seaman Second Class Stephen Brower had written with reasonable frequency until the first of the month. Then the letters stopped coming altogether, and Nora began suspecting that perhaps her son had shipped out before the scheduled completion of his advanced schooling. Now every naval encounter worldwide took on a personal dimension that left her feeling drained and weary of heart.

Elizabeth tried to assuage her fears. "Mother, the Navy can't just throw someone into battle without notifying his family first."

"Certainly they can, dear. It probably happens all the time."

"But Steve doesn't even have a specialty yet—you heard him say so yourself. How can they send him overseas?"

Nora's frown turned a bit more hopeful, and she wiped the spoon rest with a dishrag. "Well, maybe you're right." The dried gravy was a stubborn foe, so she reached for a scouring pad instead.

"Sure," Elizabeth said. "Why get so upset over nothing? Maybe we'll get a letter in the afternoon mail."

But when Nora spotted the postman coming up the walkway a couple of hours later, her optimism was dashed by the nearly imperceptible shaking of Mr. Johnston's head, even before the door was fully opened. There was no letter from Steve, just the light bill and a birthday card for Elizabeth from Uncle Matt.

At least the latter was some consolation. It had been four years since Nora's older brother moved his family to Harlingen, and she missed him terribly. Though fully half a decade separated the siblings in age, theirs had been an unusually close relationship. To this day, she cherished a deep affection for the introverted side of the man, whereas most everyone else knew him only from his public persona.

Actually, personae—plural—would be a better way to put it, for no one short of a professional vaudevillian could perform celebrity impersonations better than Matthew Coleman. Always the center of the party at any family or community gathering, his uncanny ability to distill and recreate the essence of speech and character brought roars of approval from acquaintances but proved to be an unmarketable commodity on anything but a purely amateur level, particularly in middle-class suburbia, where he chose to hang out his shingle. Not that it mattered an iota to Uncle Matt—far from it. He was perfectly satisfied to pursue the mundane comforts of a certified public accountant.

His was only one of a dozen birthday greetings that Elizabeth received that week. Susan Keeley remembered the occasion, as did three other school chums, Rachel Wassermann, Muriel Josey, and pretty Jennie Loggins. As usual, Aunt Dee's was the first to appear—more than a week ago—and those from that lady's sister, daughter, and two sons were not far behind. Hers was a very punctual side of the family. Madeleine Givens came through too, although resorting to USO stationery in lieu of a proper card. There was even a short note from Elizabeth's grandmother, eighty-three-year-old Marguerite Brower, illegibly scrawled on nursing home stationery and mailed from Amarillo. It was eloquent testimony to the diligence of the US Post Office that this envelope ever found its destination.

One boy from school, Dudley Rollins, chose that evening to call on Elizabeth, notifying her by telephone just a couple of hours before his arrival. She had been aware for some time that Dud (as he was known by his peers) had a crush on her, ever since he volunteered to serve as a captain in the citywide paper drive a couple of weeks prior to the close of the spring term of classes. Anyone who was even remotely acquainted with him knew that this was not in keeping with his torpid character, so Elizabeth became suspicious at once. And now Dudley was coming to pay his respects in her own home, a distasteful ordeal that she had no way of circumventing.

Fortunately, prayer meeting would curtail his efforts, and Elizabeth's mother told her as much. "Just talk with him for a half-hour or so, and then I'll come in from the kitchen and announce that it's almost time to leave for church."

"Oh, Mother, I'll just die if I have to be with him for that long. What'll we talk about?"

"Is he in the band?"

"No."

"Choir?"

"No."

"Sports?

"Not anymore."

"What about war work? Is he involved in that?"

"Yes, but I don't know if his heart is really in it."

"How so?"

Elizabeth forced a sad smile. "Let me put it this way—he's got ulterior motives."

Nora nodded her head. "Well, you're far too young for any boy to get seriously interested in you. How old is this Dudley anyway?

"He's already sixteen."

"Sixteen! And he's just now going into the ninth grade?"

"Uh-huh. His parents held him back in the first or second grade—maybe both."

"Do you know why?"

"Illness, he says—rheumatic fever or something. But I'll bet he just couldn't learn his ABCs."

"Oh, wonderful," Nora said. She glanced at the wall clock. "Well, you mustn't be discourteous to a visitor, so you'll need to chat with him for a short while in the living room. That's the least you can do when a boy comes to call."

"Can I turn on the radio?"

"That would be very rude."

"But, Mother, we don't have a thing in common."

"Nonsense. Talk about school. Talk about ... mutual friends. Talk about the weather."

Elizabeth rolled her eyes. "Oh, sure, the weather."

"He seemed very polite on the telephone."

"I'll give him that much—he is polite. But he also happens to be very dull and boring."

"All right, then. Do you want me to stay in there with you?"

"Mother, you wouldn't!"

"Then it's settled. I'll rescue you at 6:15."

When the doorbell rang, Nora was surprised to find, standing on the porch and nervously clutching a bouquet of flowers, one of the handsomest young men she had ever seen.

"Mrs. Brower?" he said. His hand trembled as he offered her the bouquet. "Would you give these to Beth please?"

Nora recalled that her Lizzie was now using the more mature Christian name at school. "Certainly," she said, "but wouldn't you rather give them to her yourself?" He swallowed hard, weighing the options, and finally nodded his head. "Then come on in, Dudley. Don't be shy. She won't bite you. Lizzie is right inside that room over there." When she pointed her finger in the direction of the living room, the suitor followed it obediently, and Nora went to the kitchen. The laces on one of the boy's shoes had come untied, but he dared not stoop to repair the damage.

"Here," he said to the object of his affection, who suddenly decided it might seem a bit arrogant to remain seated. Arising, Elizabeth accepted the flowers with thanks, held them to her nose for the obligatory olfactory appraisal, and then laid them carefully on the coffee table in front of her. They sat down, she on the sofa and he in Harold Brower's old easy chair.

"Well!" Elizabeth said. She stared directly at Dudley and waited in vain for him to return the eye contact. "Are you looking forward to school?"

He cleared his throat. "No, not really. My sister says high school is a lot tougher than junior high."

"Oh? My brother doesn't seem to mind it, and he's no Einstein."

"Isn't he an actor?"

"Einstein? No, he's a very famous scientist."

Dudley managed a weak smile. "You know what I mean ... your brother," he said. "Isn't he an actor on the radio?"

Elizabeth giggled. "Yes, he's Kip Hanson on 'Behold Tomorrow.' Have you ever heard it?"

"I listened today, right before I called you, but I didn't hear any Kip Hanson."

"Well, he was on there. He's the kid who's always in trouble with the law."

"Maybe I was in the bathroom when he was on," Dudley said, and instantly he regretted the intimate blunder. To his relief, Elizabeth let the remark pass without perceptible notice, but then an even greater discomfort overcame him. The room went quiet.

It was only after an agonizing quarter of a minute that Elizabeth finally broke the silence by taking a deep breath and asking, "What grade is your sister in?"

"She'll be a senior. She's a year older than your brother."

That aroused Elizabeth's curiosity. "How do you know how old my brother is?"

Caught off guard by this line of questioning, Dudley fumbled for a graceful explanation. "I saw his picture in the ... uh ... the yearbook, *The Daisy Chain*," he said. "I was looking for someone else in the 'B's."

Again there was an awkward lull, and Dudley Rollins fidgeted with his shirt collar. Desperately scanning the room for a topic of conversation, he spotted Valentino, peacefully sleeping next to the sewing table. "Is that your cat?" he asked.

"No, we rent him by the month."

At first Dudley was not really sure how to react, and Elizabeth's deadpan expression betrayed nothing. Then, after letting him squirm for another moment, she broke into a smile, and he laughed at himself out of sheer embarrassment. "I'm such a dunce sometimes." He bent over to tie his shoelace.

"Do you ever listen to music?" she asked him.

"Not much. My mother says I have a cauliflower ear."

Elizabeth tried to keep a straight face. "A cauliflower ear? That's what you get from boxing, not listening to the radio."

He sat up. "Then what's it called when you're not very musical?"

"A tin ear?"

"That's it!"

"Well, just because you aren't able to carry a tune doesn't mean you can't enjoy listening to music."

He shrugged his shoulders. "I don't know Bing Crosby from Dinah Shore."

When she looked across the room, something faintly memorable attracted her attention, and she leaped to her feet. "Egad! Mother will absolutely kill me." Dudley strained to see what it was. Behind the French provincial legs of the radio/phonograph console—and effectively hidden from view by the tattered remains of an old Waco Cubs poster—sat a half-recalled brown paper sack. Elizabeth walked over to the console and, fearing the worst, picked up the shopworn container, struggling under the heavy load.

"What is it?" Dudley asked. He, too, was now standing.

She peeked inside and grimaced. "It's a whole sack full of records that someone was kind enough to donate to the USO—and I was the one who was supposed to take them down there. Mother will just kill me."

"When were you supposed to take them?"

"Several weeks ago. They're not doing the servicemen any good here in our living room."

Dudley sat back down, silent again and idly straightening a small pile of magazines on the end table. He gazed at the cover of one of them, an issue of *Woman's Day* showing a July Fourth celebration, complete with festive bunting around a bandstand.

Elizabeth gave him a sly look and nodded toward the sack. "Hey, do you want to hear them?" she asked.

His eyes widened. "All of them?"

"Of course! You may not leave this room until we hear both sides of every last one of them."

"Golly ..." Then he saw that she was not serious. "But what about your mother?"

"Well, we'll just have to take that chance. I don't think she remembered them either." If nothing else, at least this would help to pass the time.

Elizabeth laid the sack on the coffee table and removed a handful of discs. "These are mostly British songs, but there's some American stuff in here too." She sorted through the records and placed to one side a few that she thought Dudley might like to hear. Before long, the table was covered with leaning stacks of ten-inch discs—bearing such labels as Decca, EMI/Columbia, His Master's Voice, Victor, Cameo, Odeon, Parlophone, Pathé, and Brunswick.

"Do you like Vera Lynn?"

"I don't know."

Elizabeth placed an old Rex recording of "It's Love Again" on the turntable. After a jazzy introduction by Charlie Kunz and his Casani Club Orchestra, the distinctive voice of a very young Vera Lynn, not yet twenty years old, rose above the scratchy surface noise. "She's known as 'The Forces' Sweetheart' in England," Elizabeth told him, and Dudley had to admit that he liked the song.

Casting a wary eye toward the kitchen, Elizabeth turned down the volume slightly and played some of the others. They heard Al Bowlly croon "It's a Lovely Day Tomorrow," a novelty hit by Bud Flanagan and Chesney Allen called "We're Gonna Hang Out the Washing on the Siegfried Line," a Regal record by Joe Loss and His Band of "The Blackout Stroll," Arthur Askey's "Get in Your Shelter," the Gracie Fields rendition of "Sing As We Go," and Sidney Burchall's stirring "There'll Always Be an England."

Dudley's favorites seemed to be the Vera Lynn tunes, especially "The White Cliffs of Dover" and "When the Lights Go on Again." Although he liked "We'll Meet Again" well enough, he was not terribly fond of the organ accompaniment. "It sounds like one of those women's programs on the radio," he said. "My mother's always listening to those."

"Oh? Then she's probably heard of Kip Hanson."

Dudley cocked his head. "Who?"

Elizabeth sighed. "Kip Hanson on 'Behold Tomorrow.' On the radio ..."

He smiled blankly.

"I swear, Dudley Rollins, your memory isn't as long as an inchworm."

When Nora came into the living room a minute or two past the arranged time of 6:15, she gazed at the stacks of shellac on the coffee table. "Would those, by any chance, be the records that Mrs. Huddleston gave to the USO?" she asked.

Elizabeth pleaded guilty. "Yes, ma'am, I'm afraid they would."

Nora pointed an accusing finger at her daughter. "Look here, young lady— I want you to take those records over to the club just as soon as possible. Do you work tomorrow?"

"No, ma'am, not there. I'll be over at the filling station."

"Is Dinah picking you up?"

"Yes, ma'am."

"Well, ask her if she'll take you by there long enough to drop off the records. They can wait until tomorrow, but no longer. Do you hear me?"

"Yes, ma'am."

"That's a disgrace," Nora said, and she acknowledged the boy's presence with a quick smile. "Lizzie, it's time to get ready for prayer meeting. And you can ask Dudley if he'd like to come along with us."

Elizabeth went pale.

"No, ma'am," he said. "I'm not much of a churchgoer, I guess."

"Well, suit yourself, but I think you'd enjoy it."

"Excuse me, Dud, but I've got to get changed for church," Elizabeth said. She stood up and took a couple of steps toward the stairway. "It was awfully nice of you to visit."

"Yes, Dudley, thank you so much for coming," Nora added. Then she turned toward her daughter. "Aren't you going to thank him for the flowers, Lizzie?"

"I already did, Mother. But thanks again, Dud."

"You're welcome, Beth. See you at school?"

"Sure. See you at school." Elizabeth disappeared around the corner, and her footsteps could be heard as she ran up the stairs.

Nora showed the young man to the front door, and they shook hands. "How did you get here?" she asked.

"Oh, I walked. It's really not very far."

She smiled. "Well, goodbye, Dudley. Listen now, if you ever change your mind about going to church with us, the offer still stands."

Dudley nodded his head nervously and, as he was walking out the door, turned back to say, "Thanks for having me, Mrs. Brower ... and please say hello to Kip for me."

Chuckling to herself, Nora waved goodbye and did not bother to correct him.

◆　　◆　　◆

Wesley had learned through the backstage grapevine that it was Gerald Byrd who decided to expand the Kip Hanson role on "Behold Tomorrow." Ethel Coody needed to approve the notion, of course, but it was her staff writer's idea right from the start. Jerry reasoned that the use of a teenager to advance the plot might shift the perspective away from the gangster element while still retaining the underworld imagery. "He's got to be knowledgeable in the ways of the mob and yet engage our sympathy at the same time," he said. "Let's use Bud Hanson's nephew to be the liaison between the two worlds." Mrs. Coody concurred, and Harvey Samuelson chomped down on his cigar butt to indicate that he was in tacit agreement. The untimely loss of Benny Randall to the military was a blow to their plans, but Hugh Kenton's eleventh-hour replacement had proven himself satisfactory.

Back in August, when Wesley took on the responsibility of portraying Kip Hanson, he did so with the understanding that station management would later consult with the administrative personnel at Waco High to secure his continued availability during the school year. But three and a half weeks later, a mere four days before the resumption of classes, he discovered that no such consultation had ever taken place. Almost in a state of shock, Wesley asked the director, "Is it true that I'm not clear to stay with the show?"

"Technically, no, you're not," Kenton said. He gestured for the boy to come inside his office, crushed a cigarette in the pewter ashtray, and immediately reached again for his pack of Camels. He seemed to reserve his fine cigars for more leisurely times, when he was not so keyed up with stress.

Wesley waited in vain for an explanation. "So, am I being fired?"

Kenton gave a reassuring laugh. "Absolutely not. We're very pleased with your progress so far. It's just that nobody has gotten around to arranging all this with your school. You've got to understand that this is a very busy place, and sometimes we tend to overlook the formalities."

"Is that all it is, then?"

"Yep, just a formality. We've done this several times in the past. Do you remember Connie Teakell?"

"No."

"Ah, she was a doll," Kenton said. "Just a senior at Waco High, but with the voice of an angel. I think she's in Detroit now, working for the network."

"Was she on the air here?"

"Oh, yes, she certainly was—for nearly a year. She was on 'West of the Brazos' right from the beginning. In fact, she created the role of Marjorie Fallon. We sure did hate to lose her, but she had bigger fish to fry." Leaning back in his chair, he stared wistfully at the ceiling. "Her beauty is lost on radio. She should be in pictures."

"What does this have to do with me?"

Kenton seemed mildly startled, as if he had forgotten Wesley was in the office. "Sorry, kid," he said with a grin. "It's just that Connie needed permission from the high school to work for us, sort of like you do. Only that was in the fall, so she couldn't even start without it. At least you've got a leg up."

"School begins on Monday."

"Jeez! Monday? Are you sure?"

"Isn't that the thirteenth?"

Kenton moved his coffee cup to expose September on the desktop blotter. "I thought you started on the fifteenth."

"No. Baylor does, but not Waco High."

"Well, then we don't have much time, do we? I'll call over there today. Is Mr. Torrance still in charge?"

"He's in the Navy now."

Kenton frowned and opened his address book. "I'll just call the superintendent, Mr. Brister. He's always come through for us whenever we needed some help like this." He picked up the telephone. "Hello, operator. Give me 1-6-2, please."

Wesley retreated a step. "Do you want me to leave?"

"No, have a seat." With cigarette in hand, Kenton motioned to a furnishing beside the desk. It was a royal-blue director's chair that appeared to be a gag gift from someone. The white lettering on its canvas back read, "Big Shot."

"Robert Brister, please." Kenton took a long drag on his cigarette and exhaled a vertical stream of smoke. Then he covered the mouthpiece with his hand. "What grade are you in, son?"

"I'll be going into eleventh."

A voice in the earpiece turned Kenton's head. "Mr. Brister?" he said. "This is Hugh Kenton, over at KWXN Radio." He laid his burning cigarette in the ashtray. "Yes, that's right. I've talked with you a couple times on the telephone, and I met you at Kiwanis a few Tuesdays ago, over at the Raleigh. Adolph Rose introduced us." He looked at Wesley and made an OK sign with his hand. "Say, Mr. Brister, we have a problem that I hope you can help us solve."

After five minutes of negotiation, it turned out that the superintendent was unable to come to Hugh Kenton's rescue personally, but he promised to instruct the interim principal at the high school, Marian Butler, to see to it that Wesley Brower's radio career was undisturbed. "I've heard 'Behold Tomorrow' two or three times in the office," Robert Brister said, "and Ruby listens to it religiously at home. I had no idea one of our pupils was on the show."

Kenton glanced at Wesley. "Yes, he's been with us for about a month now. Rest assured that we'll try to have him miss as little school as possible. Many thanks, and say hello to Harry Stiteler for me. I hope it's a good season. So long."

Hanging up the telephone, Kenton removed his eyeglasses and, rightfully pleased with himself, touched an index finger to his tongue. Wesley nodded his thanks and stood up to leave. "Hold on a minute, Wes," the director said. He moistened the clouded lens, wiped the glass clean in a circular motion, and dried it with the handkerchief from his suit coat pocket. Then, spectacles back in place, he picked up a sheet of paper from his desktop and told the boy, "I received an application from one of your classmates in the morning mail ..."

Wesley gave a puzzled look.

"... and she used you as a reference."

Adrenalin raced through the young actor, a bracing mixture of joy and trepidation. He tried his best to appear dispassionate.

"You and Grant Tollefson," Kenton added, and Wesley felt as if he had been clubbed in the kidney with a baseball bat. He stared at the carpet and awaited the inevitable.

"Does the name Sandra Whittsel mean anything to you?"

Wesley cleared his throat. "Yes, sir. She's a friend of mine."

"Close?"

"Not really. In fact, I thought she'd moved back east."

"She must know Grant pretty well. She's even listed his apartment number, 6-B."

"I don't know anything about that."

"Can you recommend her? Not that we have any openings just now."

"She comes from a good family, if that's what you mean. Her father's an Army officer. Over at Blackland."

Kenton nodded his head. "Light colonel, it says here."

Wesley seemed doubtful. "I'm pretty sure he's just a major."

"Oh? Well, promotions come quickly during a war." The wall clock chimed four times. "Is she a pretty girl?" the director asked.

Wesley fumbled for an answer. "Sandy? Sure, I guess you'd say she's pretty. Why?"

"No reason. She just didn't include a snapshot like she's supposed to. Usually that means they're real dogs."

Wesley relaxed. "No, she's certainly no dog. I promise you that."

"Good. We've got enough of them in the offices."

◆　　　◆　　　◆

On Monday, their first day of classes, Wesley rode his bicycle to Waco High while his mother dropped Elizabeth off in the family automobile. This was common practice for an incoming freshman who lived beyond reasonable walking distance—or whose parents could not come to grips with the idea that their baby boy or girl had attained the requisite age of enrolling in high school.

The first familiar face Wesley saw was that of Morton Wilson, a tough kid in his grammar school days who had become an upright student-citizen by the time he reached the eighth grade. Now he was a junior, like Wesley, and his personality seemed to be taking on a whole new dimension.

Being a non-athlete himself, Morton's once tepid interest in the world of professional baseball had instead become so pronounced that it threatened to subvert his entire vocabulary. "Did you see what Rudy York (or Bobby Doerr or Harry "the Hat" Walker or George Case or Ducky Medwick) did yesterday?" was a common topic of conversation whenever he entered a room, and there happened to be a boy or two standing around.

Wesley was not particularly knowledgeable about the national game, but he was fond enough of the likable Morton Wilson to feign a keen interest and even occasionally contribute a manly barb or guffaw when the opportunity presented itself: "Arky Vaughn? Hah! He can't hold a candle to Marty Marion—especially going to his right, into the hole." That simple, rehearsed observation won him a friend for life.

Morton was already at the bicycle rack that Monday morning when Wesley came pedaling up on his Hiawatha Arrow. "Hi, Mort," he said. "What's going on?"

The other boy continued to kneel. "I think I might've picked up a nail or a tack."

Wesley hopped off his own bicycle and placed its front wheel in the rack. "Is it flat?"

"No, but it's getting that way." Morton slowly turned the wheel and examined the surface. "There it is!" He spat on the suspected hole, and sure enough, bubbles appeared. "You got an air pump?"

Wesley pretended to search his shirt pocket. "Not on me," he said. "Coach does. Ask him after school."

A few minutes later, on their way to first-period homeroom, Morton seemed his new self once again, and he asked, "Hey, did you see what the Browns did yesterday?"

"No, I was studying."

Morton squinted his eyes suspiciously. "You study for the first day of school?"

"Oh, sure. Doesn't everyone?" Wesley waved at Leo Blair across the hallway. "No, goofy, for the radio show. I need to know my lines."

Morton stopped dead in his tracks. "You're on the radio?"

"Yeah."

"In a show?"

"In a show."

"No fooling? What's it called?"

"'Behold Tomorrow'."

"I thought you just read the news."

"Not anymore."

"Let me get this straight," Morton said. "You're an actor on the radio?"

"If you don't believe me, listen at three o'clock."

"Today?"

"Any weekday at three."

Morton opened the classroom door. "How can you be on some radio show when school isn't even over by three?"

"I have special permission from Waco High."

"Oh, sure. And I'm Johnny Vander Meer."

The tardy bell was about to ring, so the boys hurried to their seats.

"The Browns took two from Chicago yesterday at Sportsman's Park," Morton said. Then, as the bell sounded, he whispered, "Milt Byrnes went six-for-seven with a homer. Can you believe that?"

Wesley flashed him a proper look of incredulity.

Their homeroom teacher, Miss Grace Altimore, went to the blackboard to write her name in flowing, cursive letters, and Wesley took advantage of her brief inattention to quickly survey the room. Sandra Whittsel did not appear to be in the class, but it stood to reason that he would see her in trigonometry. Mrs. Klein taught math to all of the juniors except for those few who, because of a scheduling conflict with their choir unit, found themselves in second-period PE with the underclassmen.

Sure enough, when he arrived upstairs an hour later and opened the classroom door, there sat Sandy about halfway back, chatting amiably with two other girls and looking as enchanting as ever. He sneaked up behind her and dropped the three books he was carrying with a thud on the vacant desk to her right. Turning to investigate, her alarm became a winning smile, and Wesley's heart was melted anew.

"Hello, Wes," she said.

"Hey there, Sandy." He tried to remain as casual as possible, but that was not easy. "I was afraid you moved back to Savannah."

Sandy laughed. "Gracious, no. Whatever gave you that idea?"

When Mrs. Klein entered the premises, the clamorous sound of a roomful of spirited teenagers became more subdued by half.

"I came by your house the Saturday before last, and everything was locked up tight," Wesley whispered. "Even your dog was gone."

Keeping an eye on the teacher, Sandy whispered out of the corner of her mouth. "My grandfather died, and we had to go back home for the funeral."

Wesley acknowledged the remark with a nod, noting that she still considered Georgia to be home. "Are you over the mumps now?" he asked.

The tardy bell was ringing as Sandy told him, "Of course I am, Dr. Kildare. How long do you think they last?"

Matronly Beatrice Klein, her gray hair tightly wrapped in a bun atop her head, scanned the classroom from one side to the other, smiling through the windows of her pince-nez eyeglasses. These old-fashioned spectacles—oval and rimless with a dainty gold chain that reeled itself automatically into a button-sized holder pinned to the bodice of her dress—endowed the teacher with a quaint, *fin-de-siècle* aura that was fully in keeping with her doctrinaire personality. Born in the early days of Reconstruction, during Abraham Lincoln's tragically unfulfilled second term in office and more than a year before President Andrew Johnson would pass the flame to U. S. Grant, she was a living relic of the past. Fortunately for two entire generations of students at Waco High School, Mrs. Klein was also a fine teacher of mathematics, though the dignified lady's nineteenth-century methods were derided with arrogant cynicism by her more progressive colleagues in the faculty lounge.

Following trigonometry period, in which—to no one's great shock—Rollie Barnes outshone his classmates with facile aplomb, Sandy began talking with Rollie's best friend, Norman Gunst. In fact, they exited the room together, leaving Wesley to trail behind her into the hallway. Then, as if in answer to prayer, Norman went one way and she the other, so Wesley was able to catch up with her from the rear. Her tiny frame never failed to surprise him, the top of her head barely reaching his shoulders.

"Say, Hugh Kenton mentioned your name the other day," he said to her.

"Who?" Sandy asked. She continued walking to the next class.

"Mr. Kenton, from the radio station."

Her footsteps came to an abrupt halt, and she smiled shyly. "Gee, I hope you don't think I'm trying to horn in on your territory."

"Oh, no, not at all." Her pretty smile was contagious.

"This is kind of awkward," she told him. "I never dreamed that he would come right out and mention it to you. I just did it on a whim."

"Well, Mr. Kenton said I was listed as one of your references—me and Grant Tollefson." The name made Sandy blush, but Wesley persisted. "Mr. Kenton asked a few questions about you, but he said there were no openings."

"Good. I don't know what I'd do if he actually hired me—probably just die of microphone aversion, I guess."

"I'm sure you'd be fine," Wesley said, more as a polite reflex than firm conviction.

"Honestly? You think so?"

"Oh, sure. There's really nothing to it, once you've learned your lines and gotten used to the studio and all the equipment." He gazed at the floor, realizing that his inherent civility was beginning to sound a lot more like self-serving braggadocio.

Sandy nodded her head. "Thanks anyway for talking with him about me. Maybe someday I'll work up the courage to go down there and apply in person."

Wesley sensed that she was waiting for an invitation, but he hesitated for a moment, and the opportunity was lost.

"Well, I've got to run to class ... government," Sandy said. She gave a quick wave of the hand as she disappeared down the busy corridor.

Probably just as well, Wesley thought. The prospect of Sandra Whittsel horning in on his territory—to borrow her words—was not a pleasant one. No good could come of it, and he felt his ambivalence slowly leaning towards jealousy. Certainly he would no longer be "her actor," and the specter of the station's predatory males made him shiver with foreboding.

Yes, just as well there were no openings. That was not the life for her.

◆　　◆　　◆

Daily chapel attendance at Baylor University was mandatory. The Cullen F. Thomas Chimes would ring out from the tower of Pat Neff Hall, calling the student body to assemble in the commodious auditorium of Waco Hall. The consequences of chronic absenteeism from chapel were severe. Each of the first three unexcused absences drew a penalty of three deficiency marks, and additional absences were assessed at the rate of five such marks apiece. When the total reached twenty-four— that is, when six absences were amassed—the student was placed on probation. Any further misstep meant indefinite suspension from the university.

Though sobering enough on paper, in actual practice these disciplinary measures meant little or nothing to Hannah Lane, who found herself looking forward to the hour-long reprieves from classwork and had no intention of, as Dean of Women Sadie Crawley put it, "playing hooky." The heady mixture of prayer, homily, and joyful music was a constant balm to Hannah's spirit, despite the shocking display of apathy that met her eye without too much effort. Two boys in her row to the left were particularly bothersome, loudly rattling *The Lariat* whenever the opportunity arose. She later learned that the miscreants were a pair of business majors—one from Dallas and the other from Midland—who were, according to local wag Dayton Creech, intent upon pursuing their "ATD" degrees: Avoiding the Draft.

Dayton was not your typical Bible major. He smoked, he drank, and he chased women—though, to his credit, he never tainted the reputations of any Baylor girls. Hannah met him on the first day of classes, on a sultry Wednesday afternoon, when he happened to claim the desk between her and the open, street-level window. With the prevailing summer winds creating a swirling vacuum, the stale odor of tobacco lazily transferred itself from his wrinkled, white dress shirt to her defenseless nostrils and lungs. She was even reduced to a fit of coughing, which elicited his genuine concern until he realized that this was just her way of suggesting that he please refrain from such lapses of decorum in the future.

Despite his perfunctory apology—"Well, pardon me for living!"—she persisted in glaring at a nearly empty pack of Luckies that was visible through the fabric of his shirt pocket. Finally, he could endure the scrutiny no longer and, with cavalier irony, offered her a smoke. Hannah's scowl told him this was not a wise affront, and he backed off at once with a sheepish grin. In truth, it was not so much the cigarettes that offended her as his utter disregard for propriety, bringing them with him to a session in Old Testament History. That she could not abide.

Their teacher for this class was Woodson Armes, a youngish Instructor in Bible, not yet thirty years old, who was married and living with his wife and child on the corner of Eighth and Bagby, just a block from campus. Like all others on the Bible Department faculty, he too was a Baylor graduate (Class of 1936). Besides Mr. Armes, Hannah also planned to eventually study with Associate Professor Benjamin Herring (Class of 1923) and, of course, the Slaughter Professor of Bible himself, Dr. J. B. Tidwell (Class of 1903).

By the time Woodson Armes entered the classroom, Dayton Creech had forgotten completely about his altercation with the acerbic coed to his immediate right. Instead, he was happily involved in fantasizing over his left shoulder, viewing with more than mild interest a well-endowed young lady as she ran to class across the freshly mown grass.

"Perhaps Mr. Creech would like to take a seat away from the distractions of his window," Mr. Armes said. There was not a hint of levity in his voice, and Dayton dutifully relocated to a vacant desk across the room. "Mr. Creech has already etched his name on the seating chart. You others will have until Friday to decide where to sit."

Once beyond his brusque entry and the usual first-day administrative paperwork, Mr. Armes proved to be quite an engaging speaker, and the hour ended with a fascinating overview of Old Testament times—sweeping, in a single, majestic arc, all the way from The Creation to the Divided Kingdoms of Israel and Judea.

When class was dismissed, after the issuance of a lengthy reading assignment and the bald threat of a pop quiz, Hannah left the room and came face-to-face in the hallway with a contrite Dayton Creech. "Sorry about what happened in there," he said. "I guess we didn't get off to a very good start."

Hannah could smell liquor on his breath. "How did Mr. Armes know your name?" she asked. "Have you had him before for something?"

He shook his head. "I guess Dr. Tidwell warned him about me."

"So you're not a freshman?"

Dayton laughed so loudly that several other students turned to watch. "Do I really look like a freshman to you? I've been here for five years already."

"And you're a Bible major?"

"I am now—by process of elimination."

Hannah reached into her purse for a stick of gum. "Here, chew this on the way to your next class," she said. "You never know—it may just save your career as a budding preacher."

Dayton wiped his mouth with the back of his hand. "Is it that bad?"

"It's that bad. What do you have, a pocket flask or something?"

He smiled, and for the first time she noticed how bloodshot his eyes were—and how prominent his ears.

"Creecher the Preacher, that's me."

Hannah failed to appreciate any humor in the sentiment. "Don't mock the church," she told him.

His smile vanished, as if he had been slapped in the face. "What did you say?"

"I said don't make fun of the church. That'll send you to hell faster than most anything else you can do." She looked him straight in the eye.

"Really? And who are you, the Pope?"

"My daddy's a pastor, and I'll not have you talking against him."

"I don't even know your daddy," he said. Then, in a purposefully naughty tone of voice, he added, "But I'd certainly like to meet him someday ... under more pleasant circumstances."

"Oh, please. I just ate."

Dayton brushed the comment aside and became serious, taking a step backward and viewing her as if for the first time. "You seem older than the other Baylor girls."

Hannah laughed. "Is that supposed to be a compliment?"

"Yes. It is."

She started to walk away. "Don't forget to chew your gum," she said. "And you'd better do it now if you have a two-o'clock."

He glanced at his wristwatch. "Gosh, in four minutes." He tore the wrapper off the gum. "Hey, what's your name anyway?"

"Hannah Lane. See you tomorrow, Mr. Creech—from across the room."

"The name's Dayton."

"Let me have that wrapper, unless you save them yourself."

◆   ◆   ◆

The informal arrangement with Waco High School was simple and all-inclusive. Wesley Brower would be available for any "Behold Tomorrow" activities whatsoever. Beyond the actual broadcast performances, this understanding also covered rehearsals for any scenes that required his participation, cast meetings with the writing staff, and even the occasional daytime public appearance as Kip Hanson.

Fortunately for KWXN, interim principal Marian Butler was a long-time fan of the show, though her schedule no longer permitted her to listen with any regularity. Also pledging his support was superintendent Robert Brister, who—being an administrator himself—was fully sympathetic to the practical dilemma that faced director Hugh Kenton on a daily basis.

But it was not a one-way street. For his part, Wesley was expected to make up all classwork that he missed while pursuing his extra-curricular livelihood, and no special concessions were granted with regard to any study time he may have lost. Further, Mrs. Butler encouraged Wesley's English teacher to require that he submit a twenty-page term paper, describing in exhaustive detail what was involved in the production of a radio drama.

Within a week of Wesley's assumption of the Kip Hanson role, that regrettable imbroglio with Neddy Wright had been forgotten. Kip was, after all, Bud Hanson's only nephew, and the two actors worked closely in nearly every episode of the show. In one instance—an encounter with dead air that solidified their mutual respect—the novice managed to save the veteran from an embarrassing pratfall.

It occurred when Monica Whaley improperly collated a last-minute script insertion, somehow omitting page twelve from Neddy's final compilation. When the latent calamity finally chose to manifest itself on the air, at precisely 3:09:24, the resultant disruption of dialogue caught Wesley's attention at once, just in time for him to witness his colleague being reduced to a dire state of panic. In desperation, Neddy made the universal "cut" gesture—index finger to the throat—but Hugh Kenton had his head buried in the script at that critical moment and failed to notice Neddy's silent cry for help. Instinctively, Wesley carried his own script over to Neddy's microphone, and utilizing shared copy, the scene was finished with hardly a missing beat. The dreadful moment was so fleeting that no one, including director Kenton, seemed to detect the flaw. Neddy, however, was quick to bring it to Monica's attention—before "West of the Brazos" was in its second minute—shutting her door behind him and then using words that janitor Moses Dobbs, who happened to be sweeping in an adjacent room, would not even repeat when questioned by the office gossips.

Almost imperceptibly, a taste of local fame began to drift Wesley's way, though radio—being strictly an auditory medium—was not well suited to shine a spotlight on any fledgling actor's public image. Whatever recognition he received was attributable more to incidental verbal pollination from his family and friends than to the hypnotic lure of broadcasting. Illustrative of this odd phenomenon was the fact that most of his peers at Waco High gradually became aware of Wesley's "stage life," despite the fact that very few of them (unless confined to bed by illness) had ever actually heard him portray Kip Hanson on the radio. Yet he could meander down the sidewalk of Austin Avenue on a busy Saturday afternoon in perfect anonymity.

It was the job of KWXN's promotional staff to speed the process along, and they squandered little time before launching their next push. "Can you come with us to Goldstein-Migel on Thursday night?" Claudia Talley asked. "We want to let some of the cast greet their fans—in the flesh, so to speak."

"I guess so," Wesley said. He was flattered, of course, but also more than a little unnerved. "What do I have to do?"

"Just be yourself—until we call you together to read through a brief sketch."

"In character?"

"Only in the sketch. Otherwise, just be friendly and polite to everyone. Some of them will want your autograph. Most will just want to gawk."

"What time?"

"Be here at the station by seven. We'll go in Doug Pierson's car and be back around nine o'clock—no later than that."

"How many of us are going?"

"Just you, Doug, Phyllis, and Neddy. Maybe Bev too—people love to watch her do that crying baby bit. Of course, I'll be there to do the introductions, and we'll take along a prop or two for authenticity. Harvey's cooking up a script right now."

♦   ♦   ♦

Douglas Pierson's automobile was a dark blue 1940 Buick Special, boasting such a spacious interior that all six of the cast and staff fit quite comfortably, with room to spare, for the ten-minute drive to Sixth and Austin. Being a newcomer to celebrity pampering, Wesley was astonished by the reception that awaited them. To begin with, Goldstein-Migel's secretary and chief buyer, Monte Lawrence, had seen to it that a choice parking space was reserved for the radio personalities at the front entrance of the store. There to greet them was a very proper doorman, attired in the finest Park Avenue livery. A red carpet extended from curbside to the glass doors, and a few starry-eyed fans, possibly choreographed by store management, waved American flags as the entourage made its way toward the entrance. Once inside, the doorman graciously deferred to a pair of attractive salesladies, handpicked by vice president Louey Migel himself, and it was they who escorted the distinguished artistes to a makeshift stage, erected between two display cases in the millinery department.

The radio station's promotional lady, Claudia Talley, was the first to speak, expressing her troupe's thanks for the outpouring of hospitality and apologizing for the lack of voice amplification. A large crowd had turned out for the affair, and those in back were having difficulty hearing what was said. Situated among the spectators—later estimated by the *News-Tribune* at "upwards of two hundred people"—were Wesley's mother and sister. Nora even brought her Brownie camera along to capture the occasion on film for her photo album.

A "Behold Tomorrow" skit opened the program, but not until the show's signature tune, "This Day of Days," was played—badly, in the Chopin original— on an upright piano by an elderly Goldstein-Migel employee. Then the cast read through their lines with as much emotion as they could muster in such an unsuitable setting. What Harvey Samuelson had done was to concoct what he called a "radio sampler," assembling brief scenes from several different episodes of the show and patching them together with the barest of connective tissue. In this way, each of the characters was placed in a representative context that catered to the fans' natural craving for the familiar. Wesley's role in the sketch was rather small, calling for Kip to wangle ninety-five dollars from the Gabriel bank account ("for my mother's trip to St. Paul") and argue with his Uncle Bud about whether reputed thug Marvin Hennessy was entitled to view the casino's floor plan.

Though dramatic involvement was minimal and sound effects practically non-existent, the live audience seemed to savor every perceived nuance of the presentation. Prolonged applause drew from the cast a round of deep bows and two subsequent curtain calls. Then the honored guests were ushered to their individual tables for a session of informal visitation.

Wesley's receiving line was considerably shorter than any of the others, owing to the fact that, until recently, Kip Hanson had remained a peripheral character. Now, with an expanded role to play, here was Kip making public appearances alongside such established favorites as Anson and Jeannie Gabriel, shady lawyer Quinton McFadden, and Uncle Bud. In many respects, it was a satisfying experience to be hailed as a minor celebrity. But Wesley soon discovered, both to his pleasure and discomfort, that Waco's daytime serial fans were by no means a monolithic group.

A young mother carrying a baby in her arms smiled and told him she never missed the show, quickly adding that she disliked the gangster element that was beginning to take over the story line. Though he had no say in such matters, Wesley felt duty-bound, as a bona fide representative of the station, to offer his apologies. Another young housewife was too star-struck to say much of anything, motioning for him to autograph her church bulletin, the only piece of paper she had handy. An elderly couple—she leaning on her husband's shoulder and he on his walking stick—professed how much they appreciated the program. "We listen every day," the wife said with a kindly, toothless smile, "right after our nap and before I start fixin' supper." One lady in her lower fifties informed Wesley that he sounded just like Walter Tetley—Leroy on "The Great Gildersleeve"—a well-intentioned remark that nonetheless wounded his ego for some time to come.

Despite his relatively brief tenure in the role, Wesley was greeted by a thin but steady stream of "Behold Tomorrow" fans, some more knowledgeable than others. Only once, during a painfully discomfiting four-minute stretch, was there no one at all standing across the table from him. As insecure as he may have felt when chatting with a parade of total strangers, far worse was the opposite extreme, suffering the humiliation of being passed over by that same roomful of onlookers. Strange, too, was the palpable uneasiness that a live audience could bring—in stark contrast to the isolated world of the soundstage, with its cold, impersonal microphones. Though undeniably gratifying at times, he was not so sure that he wanted to subject himself to a public affair like this one ever again.

Toward the end of the evening, while Claudia Talley was packing up the scripts and props, and the receiving lines were dwindling to almost nothing, Wesley's mother and sister decided it was a good time to visit his table. They waited patiently nearby as his last admirer, a plump teenager with pigtails and glasses, reluctantly turned to leave. "Well, 'bye," she said. "See you tomorrow." The girl grinned as she pulled her purse strap over her shoulder and lumbered away.

"Who was that?" Nora asked when the young lady was out of hearing range.

"Grace O'Reilly," Wesley said. "I think she has a crush on me—now that I'm running in such fast company."

"I've never heard you mention her before."

"Gosh, no. I'm sure I haven't. She's never even spoken to me until now." He stood up, laughing. "She even had to tell me her name. That's kind of embarrassing when you've gone to school with someone for ten years."

Elizabeth smiled nervously, looking over her shoulder at the exit. She did not seem herself tonight.

"We're real proud of you, son," Nora said. "I had no idea you were such a celebrity."

Wesley shook his head. "Well, Doug and Phyllis maybe, but not me."

"Lots of people wanted to talk with you."

"They sure did," Elizabeth added.

Wesley dismissed the notion. "Most of them were probably just trying to be nice," he said. "I think they felt sorry for me for having such a short line."

Nora touched the tip of his nose with her index finger. "Next thing you know, I'll be buying you some dark glasses, just like a movie star."

"Sure, Mom. Oh, sure."

Claudia motioned to the cast that it was time to leave for the return trip to the radio station, so Wesley walked over to excuse himself. Nora followed, camera in hand. "Wes will be going home with us, Miss Talley," she said. "Tomorrow's a school day, you know, and he still has some studying to do." First, though, Douglas Pierson and the others consented to pose for a few group shots, so Nora snapped a half-dozen pictures for her scrapbook.

During this impromptu photo session—while there were fewer than thirty of the most diehard fans still in the store—Elizabeth worked up her courage to take a few halting steps toward the glass exit door. She was relieved to see that no gray Oldsmobile was parked at the curb. Earlier in the evening, with perhaps two hundred people milling around, she suddenly froze upon glimpsing a nightmarish face. He managed to disappear into the crowd, if indeed he had been there at all.

As she departed from Goldstein-Migel, walking a step or two behind her mother and brother, Elizabeth began to tremble, actually fearing for her own sanity. Had her eyes played tricks on her? Could a traumatic experience cause a person to see apparitions, as if in a dream? She swallowed hard and kept her thoughts to herself. For all she knew, Edward Neal was a thousand miles away.

Or he was just outside, on the dark streets of Waco.

◆　　◆　　◆

Private Danny Rignold's health was back to normal by the middle of September, so he resumed his duties at Blackland and vowed to stay clear of women and the USO until further notice. His mild concussion left no lasting effects, his broken nose healed itself with scarcely a trace of asymmetry, and the Army repaired his teeth at no charge to his own bank account. Though a missing cuspid and cracked incisor very likely would have meant rejection at his initial exam in Jackson, once a mechanic was trained and on the flight line, such cosmetic issues were of little concern to Uncle Sam.

His former commanding officer had been promoted to lieutenant colonel, so now Danny reported to Major Wallace Dukes, a hidebound disciplinarian who went strictly by the book. Major Dukes was sent to central Texas from the 3rd Air Force in Tampa, Florida, and he had no love for high temperatures, high humidity, or high spirits, all of which Waco seemed to have in abundance.

"If any of my men so much as hiccup from booze while they're working for me, I promise you they'll be shipped off to Thule before they can spit out their name, rank, and serial number. Understood?"

As with a single voice, his forty-five-member ground crew said, "Yes, sir."

The officer leaned forward and repeated, more loudly still, "Understood?"

"Yes, sir!" the men shouted, and their response caused windows in the ramshackle classroom to rattle.

"Very well. Don't make me prove to you how serious I am about this." He looked from eye to eye, staring down each person in his turn. When he came to the end of the room, he turned his attention to the rosewood baton in his hand. Danny could hear the wall clock ticking.

"Dismissed."

The soldiers jumped to their feet and filed from the room without speaking.

Once outside, Grover Szekely turned to Danny. "Holy moly," he said. "Who does this guy think he is? Ain't no one who can stop an entire air wing from relaxing in the local bars. It's human nature."

"Just don't show up for work smellin' like a night club, I guess."

Chet Bevins said, "I'll bet the major has bent his elbow over a cold one on occasion. Otherwise, he'd be our chaplain."

The three men walked together to the Kansan hangar. As of this point in the war, all of the Beech AT-10 Wichitas—not to mention the old Curtiss AT-9 Jeeps—had been replaced by this newer Beech model. The Kansan AT-11 was a military version of the Beechcraft Model 18 commercial transport, complete with a transparent nose, bomb bay, and mounts for flexible gunnery training. It housed three students and a crew of two. The AT-11 was powered by two 450-horsepower, 9-cylinder radial, air-cooled Pratt and Whitney engines, providing a maximum speed of 215 miles per hour.

Student pilots were required to complete a lengthy series of combat training missions, taking continuous evasive action within a ten-mile radius of the designated target. Simulating an actual bombing run, the final approach had to be straight and level—and accomplished within the allotted time frame of sixty seconds. Trainees' hundred-pounders were practice bombs filled with sand, and the interior racks could accommodate ten per mission. Scuttlebutt was rampant that by month's end Blackland training sessions would introduce the fabled Norden bombsight, with student bombardiers adopting a compatible C-1 automatic pilot system to guide the aircraft throughout its bombing run.

Danny respected Wallace Dukes for the officer that he was, but that contrasted sharply with the bond he had forged with the major's predecessor—a relationship that, were it not for the immutable constraints of a military setting, might have been described as friendship.

By now, Colonel Whittsel was working out of HQ, and his contact with former subordinates was severed. Danny had seen him just twice since the officer's promotion—both times from afar—and he wondered how anyone with a love of flying in his blood could reconcile this seemingly vapid reassignment to a tactical ground position, whatever the practical benefits of a raise in salary and rating. But Duncan Whittsel, unquestionably the possessor of a keen military mind, was also a dedicated family man, and that, Danny figured, probably went a long way toward explaining his stoic acceptance of the new mission. What Danny Rignold had no way of knowing was that the ambitious side of Colonel Whittsel's complex character had advised him to bide his time like a good soldier, to serve his country as best he could, and to rest assured that glory was promised to those who wait.

Though just five weeks had elapsed since Danny defended the honor of that girl outside the USO, it now felt to him like an entirely different lifetime. He could no longer even remember the girl's name, though her pretty face was still fresh in his memory.

"Hey, Mike," he shouted to a corporal who was kneeling in front of the three-tiered tool cabinet. "You got a sweetheart here in Texas?" The sound of power tools in the hangar was almost deafening.

"Naw," Michael Tobin said. He cradled a grease gun in one hand while deftly lighting a match with the other. "These Waco gals is too highfalutin for my taste in females. Cindy writes about once't a week, and that's plenty good enough for me." Signs above said NO SMOKING, but no one—including the officers—paid them any heed.

"You got a picture of her?"

"Don't need one. I've got her up here." The corporal pointed to his right temple. As natural as an extra appendage, the cigarette rested comfortably between his index and middle fingers.

Danny nearly lost his footing on a slick patch of grease, so he wiped it up with a rag. "Well, I'm tryin' my best to swear them off, but I guess I'm not havin' much luck."

"Swear off women? Why don't you just stop breathing for a while?"

Danny kicked a footstool in place and climbed upon it. Then, pulling out a clean rag, he wiped the aircraft's Plexiglas nose dome. "You know, I'm beginnin' to think you may be right about that." He expectorated on the glass and continued wiping. "Have you aired her up yet?"

"Nope," Michael said. "There's the hose."

Danny hopped down from the stool and checked his jumpsuit pocket.

"Here," Michael said with a smile. "I swiped it when you wasn't looking." He tossed the pressure gauge to Danny, who casually caught it in mid-air and knelt next to the starboard tire.

"Colonel Whittsel has a dandy-lookin' daughter," Danny said, "but she's awfully young."

"Be careful, pal. You're really asking for trouble there."

Danny stood up, grinned, and took a step toward the corporal. "You know her?"

"Sandra? Sure, doesn't everyone?"

The smile disappeared. "What do you mean by that?"

Michael smirked and turned away.

"Wait, Mike. You can't just say somethin' like that and then let it drop. What do you know about Whittsel's daughter?"

Corporal Tobin shrugged his shoulders. "Nothing that ain't common knowledge. Where you been, boy?"

Danny shook his head in disbelief. "We must be talkin' about two different people. Sandra's just a high school kid—couldn't be more than sixteen."

Michael put a toothpick in his mouth. "What of it? Don't you know there's a war on?" He walked back toward the tool chest. "Hey, you seen the lug wrench?"

"Forget the lug wrench for a minute," Danny said. He pursued the conversation in a harsh tone across the hangar floor. "Describe this girl for me. I don't think you even know Sandra Whittsel. Either that, or you're gettin' her mixed up with someone else."

Michael shook his head and smiled. "She's a pert little brunette with dark brown eyes and a nifty figure—kinda thin but with plenty of curves in the right places. Not more than four-eleven, I'd say. She only comes up to about the bottom of my shirt pocket. What more do you want to know?"

Danny's voice grew unsteady. "What else can you *tell* me?"

Michael picked his teeth through a broad grin. "That depends. How intimate do you want me to get?"

"Forget it. I don't believe any of this." Seething, Danny walked back to the trainer. Both of his fists were tightly clenched, and his right hand still clutched the tire gauge. "Like I said, I don't think you even know Sandra Whittsel."

"Don't I?" Corporal Tobin asked. "You want me to describe her in every lurid detail?"

With that, Danny tossed the metal gauge aside and, in a flash, was upon Michael with arms flailing. His first blow struck the corporal directly in the nose, drawing a flow of blood. But Michael fought back, doubling Danny over with a solid punch to the mid-section and pinning the smaller private to the floor. A crowd gathered and, in short order, had the combatants separated.

Even then, Danny managed to break free momentarily—just long enough to take one final wild swing, which missed his target completely but struck one of the peacemakers on the side of the head. Freddie Biscoff grimaced with pain but kept his composure, helping to secure Danny's arms behind his back. "Okay, that's enough," Sergeant Hermie Tooker said. He was the highest-ranking man present. "You hotheads want to put on the gloves?"

Michael wiped the blood from his upper lip with an oily rag. "Naw," he said. "Listen, sarge, it weren't his fault. I was egging him on."

The sergeant turned to Danny. "Izzat so?" He did not answer, still struggling to get away, so Tooker said, "Take him outside for a while, and let him simmer down. The rest of you, get back to work."

Some of the men dragged Danny away, and Sergeant Tooker approached Corporal Tobin again. "You say you were responsible for this?"

"Yeah, sarge. He has some dame trouble, and I was teasing him about her, that's all. Don't report this—it was really nothing."

"He's only been back with us for a couple of days, and already he's in trouble. You think he's fit to work?"

Michael nodded his head. "No doubt about it, sarge. He's a good one. I was just spouting off at the mouth. I didn't think he'd take it personal."

Less than ten minutes later, Danny returned to the hangar under his own power and picked up an oil funnel, resuming his duties without so much as a word. Michael walked over to him and extended his hand. "Sorry, pal," he said. "It was my fault, and I told the sergeant so."

Danny shook his hand but did not look him in the eye.

"I was just ribbing you," Michael added. "I didn't think you'd go crazy about this Whittsel girl. Hey, you two got something cooking?"

Danny closed his eyes. "Jeez, I've never even met her—just seen her a couple of times."

That drew laughter from Michael. "Me too," he said. "I was just feeding you a line about her. As far as I know, she's one Georgia peach that's never been picked."

"Well, at least that's good to know."

Suddenly, Michael became serious, and he squinted in thought. "What difference does it make to you anyway, seeing as how you don't even know her?" Getting no more response than a shrug of the shoulders, Michael said, "If you don't mind my asking ..."

Finally, after a lengthy sigh, Danny spoke up. "I don't know, exactly. Maybe I'm nuts. All I ever seem to get out of it is beat up—this and that USO deal."

Michael's nose was still throbbing, so he rubbed it gently with the back of his hand. "Naw, I wouldn't say you're nuts. In fact, you're probably the only sane guy in our outfit." He noticed that Sergeant Tooker was watching them. "Well, I think maybe you do put them on a pedestal a little too much ... girls."

At 4:30, when the ground crew was about to fall out for chow, Corporal Biscoff cornered Michael. "Hey, what's the story on this Rignold clown?" he asked. "Why'd he fly off the handle like that?"

Michael was bending over to square up the tool cabinet. "What's it to you, Freddie? I don't remember calling for no shrink."

"Look, Jack Benny, I've got a knot on the side of my head that says it's my business."

Michael stood up just in time to see Danny leave the hangar. "If you want my opinion," he told the corporal, "Rignold's problem is nothing that a hot date wouldn't fix."

"Yeah?" Biscoff seemed amused.

"Yeah, the poor sap's got it bad—a genuine basket case of southern manners. What's it called? I can't think of the word."

"What's what called?"

"Manners. Like in the days of old England. Damsels in distress, that sort of thing."

"Chivalry?"

"Yeah, Rignold's got a bad case of southern chivalry. Sort of like the crabs, only a lot more painful."

Biscoff grinned. "What makes you think that's it? Did he tell you?"

"Naw, he can't see it himself, and he wouldn't admit it if he could. Somehow he's got the idea that it's his sacred job to protect every pretty girl in the world from northern wolves like us."

"Speak for yourself. I'm from Arizona."

"You know what I mean, Biscuit," Michael said. He glanced toward the hangar door. "All he needs is a steady girl."

Biscoff shook his head. "Join the crowd."

"Hey, I know girls like that don't exactly fall from the sky here in Waco. But in Danny's case, I think even a frisky one-nighter might do it."

"Yeah?" Biscoff said with a leer. "Well, you just leave that to me, Mikey boy. Now you're in my territory." He touched the sore spot on his head and winced. "You know, when it comes to matchmaking, I'm about the best there is. Besides, I owe him one."

Michael was suspicious. "What've you got in mind?" he asked. There was a trace of fear in his voice.

"Not sure exactly, but when this is all over, I promise you he'll know for a fact that all pretty women are not angels."

Michael laughed nervously. "You got someone in mind?"

"Nope," Biscoff said. "But there's a whole city full of possibilities, if you get my drift."

◆ ◆ ◆

On the third Tuesday in September, the postman, Mr. Bill Johnston, tried to conceal his excitement as he made his way up the sidewalk toward the Brower home. He even went so far as to pause for a few minutes, remove the leather pouch from his shoulder, and sit on the porch steps while he decided how to present the news to Nora. The temperature was still quite summerlike, so he took off his eyeglasses and wiped his brow with a handkerchief.

Mrs. Brower was no ordinary customer to him. For nearly seventeen years now, the two had greeted one another up to eleven times a week, exchanging pleasantries and catching up on the neighborhood gossip. He knew her before Wesley and Elizabeth were even born. A further connection dated from the early thirties, when Mr. Johnston was a loyal member of Harold Brower's bowling team, the "Ten Scores." They had adopted that rather strained play on words as their official name because each of the four duffers was determined—in vain, as it turned out—to break the magical two hundred mark.

After returning the handkerchief to his pocket and the eyeglasses to the bridge of his nose, Mr. Johnston cocked his head slightly and noticed a subtle rustling of the lace curtains. It was time to resume his duties anyway, so he chose this moment to stagger to his feet and harness the strap of the postal pouch over his shoulder. His thin, gray mustache twitched as he opened the mailbox, but he was careful not to stare directly at the concealed onlooker.

Finally, when he could stand it no longer, he broke into a broad grin. Though no one had knocked, Nora swung open the wooden door and said, "Bless you, Mr. Johnston! It's come!"

It had indeed. After nearly four weeks, an envelope arrived from Seaman Second Class Stephen Brower. Nora tore into it and proceeded to read while the postman waited patiently for the summary that was certain to follow. "He's still in the States," she said, "but he's pretty sure that he'll be sailing in the fall." She looked up at Mr. Johnston. "He can't give any details, of course, but he could tell me that much."

The postman nodded his head. "Lots of my letters are pretty chewed up by the censor." It was endearing to Nora how Mr. Johnston referred to the pieces of mail as though they were his very own. "Yep, one three-page letter that I got looked like someone was cutting out paper dolls."

"What do you do, hold them up to the light?"

He chuckled with embarrassment. "Well ..."

"Listen to this, Mr. Johnston. Stephen says he's gotten himself a girlfriend, a waitress named Bonita." Nora's excitement turned to a frown. "That sounds like a Mexican name, doesn't it?"

"What of it? Some of those Mexican girls are mighty pretty, Mrs. B. In fact, that's what the word means."

Nora glanced up from the letter. "What word?" she asked.

Mr. Johnston shook his head with a smile. "Bonita. The word 'bonita' means 'pretty' in Spanish. You can look it up, if you don't believe me."

"Well, maybe so, but just the same," Nora said. She scanned the back side of the paper. "He's passed all of his swimming tests—even in full gear. Stephen always was a good swimmer, you know."

"Yes, ma'am."

Nora refolded the letter and slid it back into the envelope. "I just can't tell you how much this means to me, Mr. Johnston. Thank you so much for helping me to get through all of these weeks."

"Gee, Mrs. Brower, all I did was deliver the mail."

"It's not that. You were so kind when nothing arrived. That's what I really appreciate more than anything else." Her eyes were tearing up. "Won't you come inside for some coffee and toast?"

"No, but thanks. I need to be moving on, or Mrs. Gooch is going to call the Postmaster General."

"I guess I don't know her."

"She lives over on Lyle. Nice lady, but she spits nails whenever her mail is late."

Nora was sorry that Elizabeth and Wesley were at school because she wanted desperately to share the recent correspondence with someone. She sat at the kitchen table and reread Steve's missive in its entirety. When she came to the bottom of the front side, she wondered again what her son meant by "I can't tell you anything about my MOS because that's a matter of national security, ha ha."

Nora needed to buy some flour for baking, so she decided to bring the letter along with her to Moek Grocery. Gertrude beamed the moment she saw what was in her friend's hand—almost as if the letter had come from her own son. "Well, praise d'e Lord!" she said. "Now you can sleep at night again. Bless you. I know how you must feel."

No longer was Nora the least bit hesitant to discuss the war with her. Over the healing passage of time, Gertrude had become more of a flag-waving patriot than most native-born Americans. Her husband, too, was just short of ostentatious in his display of the red, white, and blue. Hermann hung a small US flag above each aisle and at the end of each section of shelving in the store, and he pinned a tiny, hand-painted, metallic replica of Old Glory on his grocer's apron—to the left of center, directly over his heart.

For some inexplicable reason, Gertrude Moek could not read English when it was handwritten, though she had no trouble with printed type. Perhaps it had something to do with the properties of cursive script, how they varied from person to person, depending upon the individual's character traits. That being the case, Nora read Steve's writing aloud to her. Halfway through, Hermann cautioned her to speak a bit more softly. "Loose lips sink ships," he said. The grocer placed an index finger over his mouth in the universal "Shhhh" gesture.

Gertrude rolled her eyes. "Look, Hermann. Nobody else is in d'e store but Russell! Who's gonna hear?"

She was right. The store was totally empty except for the three of them and the stock boy.

"Still," Hermann said, "it's dangerous to make the assumption that no one is hiding behind a shelf—or possibly doing a sound recording or listening over a radio transmitter somewhere."

This struck Gertrude as quite funny. "Oh, sure, and I suppose Hitler's hearing everyt'ing d'at Nora says over his wireless receiver."

"Well, maybe not Hitler, but it's conceivable that useful information could be spread by an innocent third party. Just be careful, that's all." Hermann made a slow retreat to the meat counter.

"Oh, Lord," Gertrude said. "Next t'ing you know, d'e Kaiser'll be coming in here, wearing d'at spiked helmet of his."

Nora smiled at the remark but conceded that Hermann had a valid point. "No, he's right, Trudy. It's a bad policy to take a chance like that, and I'm sorry for being such a blabbermouth." She refolded the paper. "And me, of all people—with a son in the service." She glanced at Russell Mimms, who was intent on boxing a delivery order. He certainly appeared harmless enough, and Hermann once told her, "Poor boy. He can't hear thunder."

Gertrude, though, remained unconvinced of the international implications of ordinary conversation. "Honestly, sometimes d'at husband of mine t'inks he's Eliot Ness."

The two women went to the back of the store—the stock area, where deliveries were processed—and it was there that Nora, in a more restrained voice, finished reading the letter to Gertrude. She asked whether her friend had any idea what MOS meant, but she did not. "Lord, all d'at alphabet stuff—I can't keep it straight. I t'ink it started with Roosevelt." When Hermann came back there to move a pallet of canned fruit up front, Gertrude stopped discussing Steve's correspondence and said, "Hush! D'at man looks like a German spy for sure." Hermann gave an exasperated sigh but held his tongue.

The newly installed soda fountain looked fresh and gleaming as the women walked by it a moment later, but business so far was disappointing. "Have you done any advertising?" Nora asked.

"Are you kidding?" Gertrude said. "We can't afford to. I don't know how he hopes to compete wit' d'e big druggists like Sout'western."

"No."

"I guess we just need to hope and pray d'at, by some miracle, word of mout' helps us out of d'is mess."

"Maybe it will, Trudy."

"And of course we'll be listed under soda fountains in d'e new city directory and phone book."

The small bell above the screen door jingled, and Gertrude looked toward the front of the store. "Hello, Miss Coletti. You're one of our first customers all day."

"Is that so?" she asked. "I guess maybe Tuesday mornings aren't your busiest times of the week." The girl was now obscured from view as she sorted through the packages of pasta on the second aisle.

Giulia Coletti was beautiful. Not just pretty or attractive, but achingly, angelically beautiful. Her straight, black hair flowed unaffectedly to within a couple inches of her pert waistline, and those limpid, raven-colored eyes were sure to melt the heart of any male bold enough to gaze into them. So enchanting was she that—even as far back as three years earlier, when still an approachable freshman—precious few boys in the high school ever dared to ask her out on dates, fearing the rejection that would surely come from someone as desirable as she.

"Can I help you wit' anyt'ing?" Gertrude shouted over the shelf tops.

"No, ma'am," Giulia said. "I'm just reading the labels. Archie's mother is coming for dinner tonight, and I want everything to turn out right."

Gertrude grinned at Nora and said to the younger customer, "So d'en I guess you're fixing your famous spaghetti?"

"Yes, ma'am."

"She could open an eye-talian restaurant, d'at girl," Gertrude whispered, and Nora nodded her head.

"But I can't take much credit for it." Giulia's voice suddenly grew louder as she approached the counter. "Mamma makes the sauce for me, so it's really her recipe. Anyone can boil spaghetti pasta." She nodded at Nora, who smiled a greeting.

"So Archie's mom is back in town?" Gertrude asked. She carried the package of pasta over to the cash register, and the girl followed with a dollar bill in hand.

"You know, I don't t'ink I've seen her all summer long. I heard she moved to Dallas, to care for her sister."

"Yes, ma'am—but it was Tyler. Her sister's broken hip has healed very well."

Gertrude turned to Nora and said, "Bess Clarke used to buy a pot roast from me every Saturday, come rain or shine."

What the weather had to do with it was not clear, but Giulia laughed nervously and handed Gertrude the money. "Mrs. Clarke is not very fond of Italian food, but that's what Mamma told me to fix."

Gertrude gave Giulia her change and placed the package of pasta in a small sack. "Have you heard from Archie lately?"

"Yes, ma'am, yesterday. He's somewhere in Australia, but he hasn't seen any action yet."

"T'ank God."

Giulia's face turned earnest when she looked at Nora. "You're Mrs. Brower, aren't you?"

"Yes, I am."

Gertrude threw up her arms. "Oh, I'm so terribly sorry. I t'ought you two already knew each other." Her face flamed red in embarrassment.

"That's all right, Trudy," Nora said. "I know who Miss Coletti is, but we've never been formally introduced."

"I'm going to tell you a little secret, Mrs. Brower," Giulia said. "I had quite a crush on your son, Stephen, when I was a sophomore, and he was a junior."

Nora's eyes widened in surprise, but she said nothing.

"He was in my chemistry class, but Janice Poston wouldn't trade lab partners with me."

Nora looked at Gertrude and then back to the girl. "Did Steve know this?"

"I'm sure he didn't. At least, he never spoke to me about it, and I was too shy to just walk up to him and start talking."

There was a sadness in Giulia's face that touched Nora deeply. Without thinking, she asked, "Well, why don't you write to him? I can give you his address."

Giulia blushed. "I'm afraid that wouldn't be an appropriate thing to do. Archie and I are nearly engaged."

Nora apologized, but Giulia would have none of it. "No, ma'am, I'm the one who should be sorry," she said. "I was just being nostalgic or something—talking about Steve like that. I don't know what comes over me sometimes."

"It's d'e war, child," Gertrude said. "It's making us all a little bit screwball d'ese days."

"Yes, ma'am, I suppose so. Still, you must think I'm a real ninny."

"Nonsense," Nora said. "It can be very difficult having loved ones so far away." She stared at the girl's melancholy face. "Why aren't you in school, dear? It's not even noon yet."

"I've had to drop out—just for the time being, you know. I work for a few hours and take care of my mother for the rest of the day."

"Then I think you're a wonderful daughter," Nora said. "That's a very unselfish thing to do, and you'll have a gold star on your crown in heaven for it."

Gertrude thought of something and tapped Giulia on the arm. "Don't go away yet," she whispered. She walked behind the counter, produced three cinnamon stick candies, and slipped them into the girl's paper sack. "I hope Mrs. Clarke enjoys d'e dinner."

Giulia smiled. "Thank you, Mrs. Moek. That's sweet of you."

"Not at all, child. God bless you."

When Giulia looked once again at Nora, the sadness returned to her eyes. "You can mention my name to Steve, if you want to," she said. "I'd be curious to know whether he remembers me."

"I'll do that, dear. I write to him every few days."

Giulia tucked her purse under one arm and folded the top of the sack.

"How's your mother feeling?" Gertrude asked.

"Not too bad, Mrs. Moek. I guess she'll never really get much better than she is now. She's always in quite a bit of pain."

"I'm sorry to hear d'at. Is d'ere anyt'ing we can do for her?"

"No, I'm afraid not, but thanks ever so much for offering. That'll mean a lot to her."

"Say hello to her for us," Gertrude said. "And Mrs. Clarke too."

"I will."

Giulia began to leave but then hesitated, turning back to the ladies. She spoke haltingly, in a quiet, weary voice that seemed drained of all emotion. "I shouldn't be telling you this, but I don't think Archie and I will ever get married." Nora and Gertrude were shocked by the frankness of her remark.

Tears welled up in the girl's eyes, and she glanced around, making certain that no one else was listening. "I'm afraid that Archie will never return from the war," she said.

Gertrude took her hand. "Now, please don't talk like d'at. It serves no purpose."

"You don't understand." The girl looked upward and crossed herself, stifling a sob. "God forgive me ..."

"What is it, dear?" Nora asked.

Giulia swallowed hard, and her watery eyes glistened. When she closed them, a single teardrop rolled down each cheek. "I'm even more afraid," she said, "that Archie Clarke will return, and that I'll spend the rest of my life married to someone I don't really love."

◆　　◆　　◆

Mail call on the last Tuesday in September brought a tantalizing surprise to Danny Rignold. Not only did he receive his thrice-weekly letter from Kosciusko, but also a short note from someone whose name he did not even recognize.

Confused, Danny glanced suspiciously at his crew buddies for a moment—wary, from painful experience, of a prank—and then retreated to the latrine, where, in relative privacy, he turned the envelope over to verify that he was indeed its intended recipient. "Private Daniel Rignold," stated the first line of his military address, in black ink of almost calligraphic artistry. The postmark was "Waco, Tex."

Removing the envelope's contents, he held the folded paper up to his nose and breathed deeply the floral perfume. When he permitted his eyes a cursory glimpse of the body of the letter, nothing in it made any sense to him. It was scripted with elegant penmanship on Colonial Hotel stationery and signed "Admiringly, Nadine Cobb." He studied it more closely, but to little avail. A case of mistaken identity, he presumed, so he walked to the barracks and tucked the mysterious piece of correspondence away in his metal locker until he could decide what to do about it.

And yet such a fragrant, personally addressed document was impossible to ignore for long. Once he was off duty the next day, he rushed to the barracks ahead of the others. Heart beating in throat, he went directly to his locker and proceeded to unfold the note in such haste that his shaking fingers tore about a half-inch of the brittle paper along its crease. He sat on his bed, took a deep breath, and allowed his eyes to wander anew across this cryptic message from an unknown admirer. Perhaps, in the twenty-four-hour interim, the perfumed words had crystallized into perfect coherence, and he would think back in amusement at how obtuse his mind had been upon first encounter.

"Dear Private Rignold," he read silently to himself, lips moving as he pronounced the words, "You are one of eight soldiers I have been asked to contact, giving you a 'friendly face' during your stay in Waco. Please write to me if you have the time, or feel free to visit me in Room 221 at the above address. The Waco Chamber of Commerce extends its thanks for your service to our country. Enclosed you will find an embossed snapshot to demonstrate the authenticity of this letter. Admiringly, Nadine Cobb."

But there was no snapshot to be found in the envelope, nor had one fallen to the floor. He was sure that he would have noticed a picture at once—from feel, if nothing else—had one been tucked into the envelope. It was frustrating to be told of a photograph and then have it turn up missing, whether from her carelessness or his own clumsy handling. What did this Nadine look like? His curiosity was aroused, and he toyed with the idea of paying her a visit. She extended an invitation, in writing, so no one could rightfully accuse him of being fresh.

The next morning, while servicing a Beech Kansan for afternoon maneuver drills, Danny decided to counsel with his friend, Michael Tobin, about how he should deal with this baffling affair. That proved to be useless. The corporal was no help at all and seemed every bit as perplexed as he was.

"So you've never received one of these letters?" Danny asked.

"Nope, but I kinda wish I had."

"You're not on any sort of mailin' list like this?"

"Not that I know of." Michael saw Sergeant Tooker from a distance, so he picked up an oilcan and began lubricating the landing-gear bearings.

"Do you think I should go?" Danny asked.

"Why not? If she's a turkey, you can always walk out. Give her a try. Chrissakes, there's no commitment in a letter of welcome from the Chamber of Commerce."

Danny laughed. "Maybe you're right, but what if she's not really who she says she is? What if it's some con artist tryin' to roll me for my cash?"

"Don't take any. A thief's not gonna go to all that trouble to roll no private. They're out for bigger fish than that. What does she want with a private's lousy six bits of pocket change?" With his oily rag, Michael wiped a streak of dried blood from the back of his right hand. He had dinged it while trying to force a stubborn screw to release its grip from the engine cowling. Suddenly, a thought popped into his head. "Say," he said, "you want me to tag along? Could be she's got a girlfriend."

"Do you mind? This is beginning to smell like a set-up to me, and it might not hurt to have someone else around."

"Sure, I'm game."

"Thanks. It's swell of you to do this for me."

Michael recoiled from the thought. "Listen, Hortense, I'm not doing it for you." He licked the back of his injured hand and spat onto the hangar floor. "In fact, I'm not even going unless she's got a gorgeous sister or girlfriend to keep me company. You got that straight?"

"Sure, Mike. I'll drop her a note. How about Sunday morning?"

"But won't your sweet Nadine be in church?"

Danny started to reply but saw that his friend was ribbing him. He shook his head and shoved a step stool toward the port aileron.

That night, just before lights out, Private Danny Rignold addressed a short note to Miss Nadine Cobb, Rm. 221, Colonial Hotel, 120 No. 6th, City. He informed her that he would be coming to her room around 9:30 on Sunday morning, if that was acceptable. After his name, "Dan R.," he added a postscript: "Will it be O.K. if I bring an Army pal along? If that is all right with you, he might want someone nice to talk to, so could you ask a friend to be there too? By the way, there was not a photograph in your letter to me."

Nor was there a photograph accompanying Nadine's next letter to Danny, assuring him that Sunday morning at 9:30 would be just fine with her. Yes, she would indeed try to get someone nice to keep his friend company.

◆　　◆　　◆

The pair hitchhiked from the Army post to downtown Waco, riding with a young man who seemed to be about their age. He was nattily dressed, probably for church, but there was an unmistakable smell of bourbon whiskey on his breath that spoiled the illusion. A Bible sat beside him on the front seat, and the two GIs rode in back, taxi-style. Upon their arrival at Sixth and Austin, Danny and Michael thanked the young man and offered to pay him a quarter apiece, but he refused to accept any compensation. "I'm always glad to help our men in uniform." He touched the brim of his hat and added, "I intend to join up one day myself."

As the automobile drove off, the two soldiers began walking along Sixth Street, enjoying a pleasant breeze of about sixty-eight degrees. They passed the nine-story

Liberty Building on their right and then Stringfellow's Barber Shop. When they came to the Orpheum Theatre, they stopped for a moment to gaze at the NOW PLAYING poster: *Hers to Hold* with Deanna Durbin and Joseph Cotten. A banner pasted atop it read, "Hear Deanna Sing 'Begin the Beguine,' 'Say a Pray'r for the Boys over There,' and others!"

The lobby of the Colonial Hotel was ill lit and entirely deserted except for a disheveled clerk behind the counter. He eyed the soldiers suspiciously as they nodded to him and made their way toward the stairwell. "May I help you with something?" he said, tardily, as the men trudged up the steps. He did not attempt to follow them.

They stopped outside room 221 and took stock of themselves. Danny moistened his fingers with saliva and flattened the stubborn cowlick above his left eye. Michael seemed more concerned with his gig line, carefully aligning shirt buttons, belt buckle, and fly zipper, much as he would at morning formation. When Danny rapped with his knuckles on the wooden door, the men could hear a female voice coming from inside the room: "Are they here already? Tell them I'm only half dressed." They looked at each other and grinned.

A deadbolt lock slid to one side, and the brass doorknob below it made a quarter-turn. Slowly opening, the door to room 221 creaked on its hinges, much like the sound-effects prop for a scary radio program. A tall, thin woman of about thirty stood there, staring blindly at them through her very unstylish pair of eyeglasses. She wore what appeared to be a nurse's uniform, though it was not government issue. The hallway was so dark that she blinked in an effort to determine who was standing before her. "Private Rignold?" she asked.

"Yo," Danny said with a raised hand. He thought the playful approach might be a good icebreaker.

"Well, come on in," the woman said. She seemed disinterested, perhaps even chilly. The two soldiers stepped inside, looking around the sparsely furnished room.

"Are you Nadine?" Danny asked.

"Nope. She'll be here in a minute. She's cookin' somethin', I think."

The men glanced at each other, for there was no smell of food in the air.

"My name's Ann-Rae Jansek," the woman said. Instead of offering her hand, she reached forward to close the door, bringing forth another raucous complaint from its unlubricated hinges.

"Jeez, 'Inner Sanctum'!" Michael said with a laugh.

Ann-Rae remained unsmiling. "Who's your comedian friend?" she asked Danny.

"That's Corporal Tobin, but you can call him Mike if you want to."

"How do you do, Corporal Tobin?" she said, still looking at Danny. Then she shook her head and sighed. "Let me go see what's keepin' her."

When Ann-Rae disappeared from view, Michael grabbed Danny by the collar and whispered, "What're you trying to pull on me?"

Danny used a forearm to break free from his grip. "Hey, I had nothin' to do with this," he whispered. "I don't even know these girls. I just asked Nadine to bring along a friend, that's all."

The men stopped talking when they heard the sound of footsteps. Ann-Rae came back into the room, followed by a much younger woman—maybe not even twenty. She was a little overweight and a lot unkempt, her low-cut blouse hanging loosely when she stooped to pick up a pillow from the floor. She tossed it onto the threadbare sofa, flashing a familiar smile at the soldiers. "Hello, fellas," she said. "I'm Nadine Cobb. I guess you've already met Ann-Rae."

Nadine's eye make-up was grossly excessive, but despite this and other faults, there was no denying the fact that she possessed the prurient ability to capture and hold a soldier's interest.

"So this is the Chamber of Commerce," Michael said.

Nadine laughed heartily and feigned a blush. "Nope, it's in there." She nodded toward the back room.

Danny swallowed hard and looked at the exit door.

"Say, which one of you is my date?" Nadine asked with a smile, and she glanced from one soldier to the other.

"Oh, sorry," Danny said. "That would be me."

She took a step toward him. "You're kinda cute, Dan R.," she said, "but then so's your friend."

Ann-Rae seemed bored with the introductions and was now seated on the sofa, entertaining herself by shuffling a deck of playing cards at the coffee table.

Nadine turned to Michael and asked, "How'd you get the second stripe?"

"Ma'am?"

She pointed at his shirt sleeve.

"Just time of service," he said.

"Oh, what a shame. And here I thought you were a war hero." She circled behind him and locked the deadbolt.

Danny shook his head. "Say, I think you misunderstood why we're—"

Nadine put an index finger over her lips and went, "Shhhh." Then she walked over to him, not stopping until they were standing chest to chest. She looked into his eyes and said with a mischievous grin, "Don't you like me, Dan R.?" She was swaying back and forth, as if dancing without the use of her arms.

"Well, sure. I didn't mean—"

"Shhhh." She continued her dance and then made a kissing sound with her lips. "I'm glad you like me. That'll make this a lot more fun."

Michael's attention was now drawn elsewhere. He stared at the ceiling, sensing the droning sound of approach. Sure enough, a squadron of heavy bombers flew directly overhead, shaking the windows and walls of the hotel.

When the rumble finally diminished, Ann-Rae cleared her throat and said to no one in particular, "Well, I don't know about anybody else in here, but all this foreplay is startin' to make me nauseous." The two guests looked at her, but she remained driven to shuffle the cards, never so much as glancing up.

Nadine glowered at her companion for an instant but quickly recovered, turning back to Danny with a sportive smile. "My roomie's just jealous," she said, "because I always get first dibs on servicing the men who wander into our lives." Her speech was casual, as if reading that afternoon's baseball scores. She cackled lustily before adding, "Ann-Rae there couldn't care less about men because she's got a complex. She's a fallen angel, you know."

Danny was still looking at Nadine, but he could hear the sound of shuffling cards. "She's a nurse?" he asked.

"Oh, yeah. She's a nurse all right. She's gonna save the world."

Michael walked across the room, leaned over, and gently removed Ann-Rae's eyeglasses, laying them on the table in front of her. "She wouldn't be half bad looking if she'd just get rid of those." Ann-Rae turned to stone, halfway through a shuffle, and gazed at the corporal. "In fact, I think she's kind of pretty," he said. She looked down at the table, devoid of expression.

"Then you must need those glasses even more than she does," Nadine said. She strolled over to Ann-Rae and, without hesitation, flicked open the top button of her nurse's uniform. Ann-Rae did not bother to refasten it. She sat, motionless, and her jaw muscles quivered from gnashing teeth.

Nadine took two self-assured steps toward Michael. "Corporal," she said, "that poor girl can't see if you're a man or woman without the specs." She inhaled deeply through her nose, chest heaving. "Me? I've got the eyes of a hawk."

Suddenly, Michael noticed that his pal was edging his way toward the door. "Hey, where do you think you're going?" he asked, and his voice was full of annoyance.

Nadine hurried over to Danny and took him by the hand. "Don't be a killjoy, soldier. We can't have a party without you."

Danny shook his head. "No, this is not exactly what I had in mind."

Michael fell into a chair, laughing. "What did you think we were going to do in this dive—fold bandages for the Red Cross?"

Nadine ushered Danny away from the exit, pursing her lips as she said in baby talk, "... while listening to the Mormon Tabernacle Choir on the ray-dee-oh?"

Even Ann-Rae was enlivened. Indeed, she became almost giddy, convulsed in giggles like a New Year's reveler who had too much to drink. "Let's have a little merry-makin'," she shouted drunkenly, though not a drop of alcohol was flowing through her veins. She started to stand up, smoothing her white dress at the hips, but then a profound darkness came over her, and she fell back to the sofa. Angrily, she snatched her eyeglasses from the table and flung them at Michael, who ducked just in time. The errant missile gouged out a chunk of wallpaper where it struck. Then, as if all rage were spent with that single motion of violence, Ann-Rae buried her face in her hands and began sobbing.

Nadine smiled calmly at Michael. "Ann-Rae gets kinda loopy sometimes," she said.

He glanced across the room at the crumpled eyeglasses. "Jeez, you don't say."

"She don't mean anything by it. Her boyfriend jilted her a few months back, and she takes it out on anyone who wears pants."

"Thanks for the warning."

Danny had seen enough. He marched straight to the door, unlocked the deadbolt, and waved at Nadine. "Well, it's been great fun, ladies, but I really need to be goin'."

Shaking her head, she conjured up a cherubic smile. "No, you're not going anywhere, sweetie. Way down in your heart, you know you're not."

"Watch me," he said. "Mike, you comin' with me?"

Nadine turned her gaze to the corporal. "Now, don't you go running off too. I promise to make it worth your time. And Ann-Rae will come around ... you'll see."

Michael grinned sheepishly at her and then said to the private, "You go ahead, buddy. I may stick around a while."

"Suit yourself." Danny took one final look around the room and left. He traversed the stairs two steps at a time and did not notice the clerk's puzzled expression when he passed by him at the front desk.

Four days later, Corporal Michael Tobin was on sick call, the unwitting victim of his own stratagem. He had forgotten all about that brief hangar conversation, some sixteen days earlier, when Freddie Biscoff offered to play matchmaker for the chivalrous Mississippian. Now, lying on his back, he had plenty of time to recall exactly what was said. Wasn't it he himself who suggested that "a frisky one-nighter" might be just what was needed?

A shout of "I'll get you for this, Biscoff!" echoed through the infirmary, as the amused medic gave Michael a generous dollop of permethrin cream rinse to apply to his infested groin.

◆　　◆　　◆

Venturing a full load of college classes while concurrently working a forty-eight-hour week was more than Hannah could manage, and sure enough, within a few months' time, the strain began to take a physical toll. On the second Tuesday in October, she was reduced to bed, and the doctor diagnosed her sudden debility as nothing more than "exhaustion, plain and simple." He shook his head and winked at Nora, who was standing at the foot of the bed. "See to it that she rests for at least three days, Mrs. Brower."

"Yes, Doctor."

He turned back to Hannah. "You're going to have to slow down, young lady, or this could develop into something quite a bit more serious. How much sleep have you been getting?"

Hannah coughed quietly and then again more loudly. "Oh, about five hours, I suppose."

"Well, that's not enough. I realize that you're working nights some, so try to catch a nap whenever possible. What are your hours?"

"At work?"

"Yes."

"Usually four to midnight, but sometimes my boss needs me from midnight to eight."

"And then you go directly to your classes at Baylor?"

"Yes, sir."

The doctor frowned. "I can't very well tell you to quit your war work, Miss Lane, so my advice for you is to get as many late classes at Baylor as possible—beginning next quarter—and then catch a couple hours' nap on days when you haven't worked the graveyard shift the night before."

"Yes, sir." She coughed again, very deeply.

"If you can't manage that, then you may have to put your studies on hold for the duration." He looked at her sternly. "Do you understand?"

"Yes, sir."

"Good. Now, I'm going to write you a prescription for some cough medicine, and Mrs. Brower here can pick up some sleeping pills for you to use on days when you need to get some afternoon shut-eye." He spoke while scribbling the drug information on a slip of paper. "Use them sparingly, but don't be afraid of them. They're gentle to your system but strong enough to help you feel drowsy ..."—he looked at Nora—"... assuming that it stays relatively quiet around here."

Nora nodded her head. "Well, thank you, Doctor. I'll see to it that Hannah is well cared for."

"I know you will." The doctor handed Nora the prescription, latched his black valise, flashed a friendly smile to each of the ladies, and walked toward the stairway.

"Hello, kitty cat," he said to Valentino. The cat rubbed against his pants leg.

Nora followed the doctor out of Hannah's bedroom. "Now you'll have to get a brush, I'm afraid," she told him. "Our cat really does shed his fur at this time of the year."

"Can't say as I blame him," the doctor said, and Nora laughed.

Before the room was darkened and she tried to sleep, Hannah jotted down a short list of telephone numbers for her landlady to call. One dealt with her job and the others with school. She had missed four classes that day, her first absences from Baylor.

Soon after dinner, even prior to washing the dishes, Nora dutifully called Mr. Hinckley at Crawford-Austin Manufacturing Company and informed him that Hannah would be unable to work for at least the next three days.

The supervisor did not seem very sympathetic. "She's supposed to be here at midnight," he said.

"Yes, Mr. Hinckley, that's right. But the doctor has ordered her to bed."

Mr. Hinckley sighed into the mouthpiece. "Very well, seeing as how it's doctor's orders. Is Miss Lane the Baylor student we have working for us?"

"Yes, sir," Nora said. She could hear the jarring noises of heavy equipment in the background.

"Well, tell her that we may have to reconsider her desire to ride two horses if this happens again."

"Yes, sir, I'll tell her."

Nora also called the campus number of Dayton Creech, but he was not there, and it was his roommate who answered. He assured her that Dayton would have no idea which chapters of the textbook Mr. Armes had assigned. In fact, he snickered, Dayton might have been hoping that Hannah could tell him. Nora called an alternate number on Hannah's list, and sure enough, that source was more reliable.

Within a couple of days, Hannah was back on her feet again, caught up on her college coursework, and determined to follow her doctor's counsel to the letter. In order to foster a regimen of afternoon napping—a concept entirely foreign to her nature—she even paid for the installation of blackout curtains on her bedroom windows.

The following Monday, she returned to Crawford-Austin feeling contrite, only to find that her supervisor, Mr. Hinckley, had suddenly reversed his stance and was now supportive of his young employee's educational goals. "Stay in school, Miss Lane, by all means. If you can tackle both pursuits at the same time—and manage to stay healthy, of course—then more power to you. We're pleased to have you in our corps of workers."

Hannah was dumbfounded but smiled her thanks. So abrupt was her supervisor's change in attitude that she could not escape the feeling that someone had intervened in her behalf, a suspicion that was probably well-founded. Though she was in no position to fathom the labyrinthine sequence of events that led to her reinstatement, it is likely that the origin could be traced back to a telephone in the pastor's study at her home in Mount Airy, North Carolina. Her father, by his own admission, was a rather good friend of Baylor President Pat Neff, who happened to mention her predicament to one of the university's patriarchs, Dr. Josiah Blake Tidwell. He, in turn, broached the subject of female education with Crawford-Austin Vice President Raymond Goddard, who then discussed Miss Lane's favorable employment status with her immediate supervisor.

In any case, Mr. Hinckley, an unimpeachable soldier of the home front himself, never again brought into question Hannah's value to the company or to the war effort. And so it came to be that, through no effort of her own—save for a solid work ethic that complemented perfectly her supervisor's idealized vision of the arsenal of democracy—Hannah Lane won an unfailing advocate who would stand behind her like a sentinel for the duration.

◆　　◆　　◆

By definition, touch football is not a violent sport, but that did not prevent Wesley Brower from fracturing his wrist one day during physical education class at school. It happened on a third-and-ten pass play with his squad on the lean end of a 28-0 shellacking.

Never very athletic, Wesley nonetheless was considered by his peers to be a valuable team member because of his compensatory tenacity. When he and defender Warren Ducey both went up for a long, desperation heave from quarterback "Midge" Myers, he snagged the ball with his left hand but fell awkwardly on his right.

First indications were positive. "It's just a sprain," Coach Tolar said with great certainty. "If you can move it, it's just a sprain." But an intramural athletic teacher is not a qualified physician, and his cheery dismissal of the injury proved to be misguided.

This became clear by one o'clock when Wesley's right arm swelled alarmingly and began to throb with a pain that showed no signs of subsiding. The school nurse asked the assistant principal to drive him to Hillcrest Memorial Hospital to have the wrist examined by a doctor, and the results confirmed Wesley's fears. Nora was summoned at once, and she gave permission for medical procedures to commence.

So it was that Wesley spent the next six weeks in an itchy plaster cast that immobilized his right hand and compelled him to eat and write with his ungainly south paw. Suddenly, driving the family automobile became a difficult proposition, as did such everyday tasks as brushing his teeth, tying his shoes, and buttoning his shirts. Even playing the phonograph became a struggle, causing him to inflict a nasty scratch to the entry grooves of a Connie Boswell record. Tying a Windsor knot on Sunday mornings was out of the question, and not one female in the household was able to offer any assistance. Then his fortunes changed for the better. Just four days after sustaining the injury, Wesley was surprised to receive, by special delivery, a mysterious package from his Uncle Matt in Harlingen. Tearing the tissue paper away, he found inside the flat box a polychromatic "clip-on" necktie, short on fashion appeal but long on practicality. To be perfectly honest, the tie was little more than a vaudevillian prop—a quick-change accouterment for use in the illegitimate theater—but it served Wesley well in his time of need.

Sufferers of broken bones have always worn their casts as badges of honor, and Wesley was no exception. Despite the relentless inconvenience of carrying around a nine-inch shard of pottery on his right arm, he was flattered by all the attention it brought. Very nearly two dozen schoolmates autographed the surface of his white plaster wrist, and the family's boarder, Hannah Lane, drew for him an artistic silhouette of a B-17 Flying Fortress. Sandra Whittsel's ornately feminine signature was on the underside of the cast, about where a watchband might be, and Wesley found himself gazing at it several times each day. Was that a tiny heart dotting the "i"? A magnifying glass confirmed that it was, but assigning a deeper meaning to the flourish was a futile exercise in wishful thinking. For all he knew, she may have signed her name that way for anyone.

Radio being strictly an auditory medium, Wesley's physical setback caused him remarkably few complications at work. Indeed, during his month and a half of incapacitation, he missed not a single performance of "Behold Tomorrow," and his character continued to develop in stature and complexity until, with the welcome onset of cooler weather, Kip Hanson had become almost as indispensable to the story line as Bud, the Gabriels, and Quinton McFadden.

Hugh Kenton was delighted when he learned that Wesley was willing to remain working, despite the obvious discomfort. With a sigh of relief, the director smiled and said to staff writer Harvey Samuelson, "This boy is a real trouper!" Samuelson was unimpressed, shrugging his shoulders and chewing an unlit cigar butt, all the while admiring the shapely posterior of Monica Whaley as she bent over to lay the latest script revisions on Studio A's conference table. "Christ, it's his job, isn't it?" was all he said. He looked unwell, and it was a common feeling among those who knew him best that Harvey Samuelson would soon be retiring to his farm in Rosenthal. How that would affect the daytime serial was anybody's guess.

Nothing had come of Sandy's application for employment at KWXN, and Wesley assumed that it had been just a lark. She possessed no theater experience whatsoever, and her diction was only fair, the pronounced southern accent surely disqualifying her from all but the most specialized roles. That is why he was so shocked by what he saw late one afternoon, as he was exiting the studio for home. Deep, rumbling laughter—what might be expected to emanate from the *basso profondo* in an opera buffa—drew his attention to the announcing booth. There, alongside the garrulous Marshall McFall, stood someone who, from the back at least, closely resembled Sandra Whittsel. Wesley cautiously approached the booth, just out of curiosity, but then changed his mind and began to leave.

It was McFall's stentorian voice, insistent but not unfriendly, that brought him up short. "Brower, come here for a second, will you?" McFall was propping the door open with what appeared to be an unabridged dictionary.

Wesley swallowed hard and tried to act casual. "Sure," he said, and he took a few steps toward the booth. "You need me for something?" He pretended not to notice the girl.

"You're probably wondering what we're doing in here," McFall told him. There was a touch of amusement in his carefully trained voice.

"Not really," Wesley said.

"How's the arm?"

"Better, I guess."

At this point, the girl turned around, and Wesley acknowledged the familiar face with a nod. Sandy, however, did not make eye contact. "Hello, Wes," she said to the wall's soundproof insulation. Her nervous smile was not very convincing.

"Hi, Sandy." Wesley cleared his throat and, after casting a glance at McFall, asked the girl, "What brings you to the radio station?"

Sandy finally looked up at him and started to explain, but just as her lips were pursing to form the first word, McFall intervened with a glib narrative that flowed from his tongue almost as effortlessly as the truth.

"This is a bit embarrassing," he said with a modest blush. "You see, Miss Whittsel here is working on a series of radio spots—public service announcements—for the Army. Her father is an officer in the Air Corps. A lieutenant colonel, I believe ..."

"Yes, that's right," Sandy added.

"I remember," Wesley said. He looked at her, but again there was no bipartisan visual contact.

McFall smiled confidently, and his straight, white teeth fairly gleamed. "Anyway, Miss Whittsel here needed someone to coach her in public speaking— projecting from the diaphragm, you know, Brower." He reached out playfully, as if to pat Wesley in the abdomen, but Wesley avoided the hand by pushing it away and retreating a step. He was in no mood for games.

McFall's facial expression darkened, but his voice did not waver in the slightest or even become harsh. "Frankly," he said, "I don't think it's any of your business what Sandy is doing here." He pulled a cigarette from his shirt pocket, lit up, and took a long drag.

"No, it's not. So why are you both so anxious to explain to me why you were in that booth together?"

Sandy's face reddened, and she struggled for the right words to defend her honor. McFall, though, stepped between the two and, glowering down at Wesley, issued an incontrovertible statement. "Listen, Brower. There is no reason for her to feel any sort of obligation to justify her actions to you. She wasn't doing anything improper, and even if she was, I don't see that it would be any concern of yours." He scowled through his own cigarette smoke. "When you stop to think about it, Mr. Kip Hanson, do you really believe a glass booth is where I'd try to pull off an amorous conquest?"

Sandy eased McFall aside with the back of her hand. "I'm truly sorry, Wes. We were just afraid you wouldn't understand. If I look guilty of something, it's only because I thought you might jump to the wrong conclusions."

That changed everything. Sandy appeared so feminine and vulnerable, standing there beside the athletic Marshall McFall, that Wesley had no choice but to accept her plea at face value. All anger evaporated with the melting of his heart, and involuntarily he found himself breaking into a grin.

"Sure, I believe you," he said. Suddenly Wesley became oblivious to the pair of clenched fists just five feet away from his chin. He stood there, as docile as a puppy, helplessly admiring Sandy's turned-up nose and the contours of her crisp, white blouse.

McFall shattered this euphoric spell when his resonant voice intoned, "So get lost, Brower. Miss Whittsel and I have a lesson to do, and we haven't got all day to play nursemaid to your infantile whining." Clearly, the only place Mr. McFall wanted to bury the hatchet was in Mr. Brower's back.

Wesley focused on the announcer's shadow-chiseled face for a moment and decided against escalating the affray any further. "See you tomorrow at school," he said to the girl.

She responded with a comely smile. "Okay. See you."

Firing a parting glare at his adversary, Wesley turned to walk away.

McFall's cigarette tilted up and down as he added, "And don't interrupt us again—if you know what's good for you." By now, the announcer had become overtly confrontational, hands on hips and edging slowly forward.

"Hey, you called me over here, not the other way around," Wesley shouted over his shoulder. "I was just trying to go home."

McFall scoffed at such reasonable logic, casting one final pronouncement: "Fine. That's where you need to be. Go home, and play in your sandbox."

Then Marshall McFall, Dean of Central Texas Announcers, nudged the heavy dictionary aside with his foot, and the door thudded shut. He placed his right arm around Sandy's shoulders and flipped through the pages of US Army radio copy with his left.

"Now, where were we?" he asked.

Sandy smiled up at him. "You'll have to remind me."

◆　　◆　　◆

Her normal ride from work, Bee Fetters, was on the swing shift through the end of October, so Hannah was driven home instead by Sophie Carden, a very homely, very unmarried misanthrope who spoke nary a word before stopping in front of the Brower house with a perfunctory "See ya later."

"Thanks for the lift, Sophie," Hannah said. She slammed the passenger door, but Sophie's automobile was back in motion by then, and Hannah almost fell to the sidewalk when her left foot was struck by the running board. As the vehicle disappeared from view, Hannah vowed to find alternate transportation in the future.

It was nearly five o'clock on a Wednesday afternoon, and Wesley was already home from the radio station. Nora was away, working at the USO, so she had deputized him to supervise the gas range and oven, occasionally stirring the vegetables and viewing the chicken-and-rice casserole.

After Hannah shut the front door behind her, she took a moment to enjoy the savory aroma. Hearing the console radio in the distance, she turned to see Wesley sitting in the living room. He was listening to WACO's "Dick Tracy," as was his habit each afternoon at this time. When she laid her baseball-style work cap on the entry table, she saw Wesley stand up, so she was not surprised when he joined her in the kitchen. Hannah walked over to the counter and poured some coffee into a ceramic mug marked "BGCT, Abilene, 1941."

"Hi, Wes. Want some?" she asked.

"No. That's pretty old stuff. Mom made it this morning." Noticing the girl's bewilderment, he told her, "I warmed it up for you."

"What's the occasion?" She took a sip.

"Nothing. I just didn't want it to go to waste."

Hannah winced when she swallowed. "How very kind of you ... I think."

"Can't say I didn't warn you." Wesley chuckled at the boarder's wide-eyed response. "It probably tastes like something Lizzie brought home from the filling station, huh?"

"Well, it's not quite *that* bad." Hannah laid the mug down.

"Your boss phoned a few minutes ago."

"Mr. Hinckley?"

"He was wondering if you could work twelve hours tomorrow to make up for the time you missed today."

She seemed chagrined. "He knows I have classes until eleven. Did he say which shift?"

"Nope. He wants you to call him back sometime before five o'clock to let him know."

As she hurried over to the telephone, Wesley blurted out, "You got some mail today."

Hannah stopped, receiver in hand. "What of it?" she asked. Something in his tone of voice arrested her attention.

"Oh, nothing important," he said, betraying no particular emotion.

Hannah studied his face for a moment and then, curiosity getting the better of her, replaced the receiver and walked over to the stack of mail, which was lying neatly on the counter. "You're acting very peculiar, Wesley Brower," she said. "You haven't gotten into Valentino's catnip, have you?"

Wesley took a seat at the kitchen table. "I've already sorted the mail, and yours is on top." He drummed his fingers on the table, awaiting her next move.

Hannah had no choice but to proceed. There was a letter from her father, but certainly that was not unusual. Reverend Samuel Lane wrote to her on nearly a daily basis—with the exception of Saturdays, which were reserved for studying through his sermon notes. There was also a *Baptist Standard*—late this week—and her bank statement. With growing suspicion, she squinted at Wesley. "All right, smart boy, what's up?"

"You didn't see it?" His face was all innocence as he looked out the window.

Hannah gave a loud sigh. "Okay, you've had your childish fun." She took another sip of strong coffee.

Wesley whistled softly to himself but said nothing, still tapping his fingers.

Hannah decided that she would not give him the satisfaction of seeing her squirm. "I'm sure you enjoy playing this little boy's game, but I've really got to call my boss." She laid the mail down and returned to the telephone. Wesley did not seem to care.

"Terry and the Pirates" was already coming on the radio, so she hoped it was not too late to catch Mr. Hinckley. His secretary answered, and Hannah was able to leave a message with her, indicating that she was more than willing to work a split Thursday shift, to catch up on her weekly hours.

"I'm sure that will be fine," Miss Hagen said. "We're kind of short-handed in the back, but Mr. Hinckley says we can work around your class schedule for the time being—at least until another big contract gets dropped on us from on high."

By the time Hannah finished her telephone conversation, Wesley had returned to the living room, where he lounged on the sofa in his stocking feet. The pillow at his side properly elevated his encumbered right arm. From the kitchen, Hannah confronted him again about the mysterious piece of mail, but the radio show was too loud, and he did not seem to hear. She sifted through the entire stack of mail, piece by piece, but came across nothing of unusual interest. Grumbling to herself, she left the three envelopes addressed to "Hannah Lane" on top and went up to her room. Two could play this game, so she would be just as stubborn as Wesley was prankish.

After taking a quick bath and changing clothes, Hannah came downstairs and saw that her landlady had returned from the USO. Nora was standing in the kitchen, stirring each steaming pot in turn and placing a tray of yeast rolls in the oven, alongside the lazily bubbling casserole. "Hello, dear," she said, upon spotting Hannah in the doorway. "Come on in and visit for a while. Dinner won't be ready until around six, but you can have leftover finger sandwiches for an appetizer if you want some." She pointed toward a covered pan that rested at the corner of the breakfast table.

Hannah smiled and entered the kitchen, stealing a peek at Wesley in the living room. "No, thanks, Mrs. B.," she said. "I can hold out until six."

Nora frowned at the sandwiches. "They're from the USO, and I just feel terrible about them because it was all my fault." Her apron was coming loose, so she reached back to tie the strings more securely. "Not very many of our soldier boys showed up, so we had an overabundance of food."

"Why was that?" Hannah asked, and she lifted the wax paper for a glimpse.

"The parade. I had forgotten all about it."

Hannah straightened up and looked puzzled. "What parade?"

"You know, promoting that movie."

Hannah still seemed confused, so Nora called to the living room. "Wes, come in here for a minute, if you don't mind." To Hannah she whispered, "The news is on now, so I can tear him away from that silly radio. 'Jack Armstrong' is on next, and then 'Captain Midnight,' so we'd better snag him while we can." Hannah laughed, choosing to ignore the fact that Wesley's mother was every bit as obsessive about her daytime serials.

"What, Mom?" Wesley said. He was scratching the palm of his partially casted right hand.

"Tell Hannah about that big parade downtown."

Wesley stared at the stovetop. "Yeah, it will really be something."

Hannah and Nora waited patiently, but Wesley appeared to be more interested in the progress of dinner than in any civic events. "Actually, it started about a half-hour ago," Nora said to the boarder. "Wes, tell Hannah what you know about the parade. It has something to do with that new Ronald Reagan picture, doesn't it?"

"Yes, ma'am. George Murphy's in it too, and Joan Leslie—a musical by Irving Berlin called *This Is the Army*."

"And Kate Smith sings 'God Bless America'," Nora said.

"Tickets are really steep," Wesley added. "Up to eleven dollars."

Hannah was stunned. "Eleven dollars for a movie?"

"Well, it's a Technicolor film, and they're trying to raise money for Army Relief," Wesley told her. "You can get in for a buck if you don't mind sitting in the very back." His attention wandered to the covered pan, and he asked his mother, "Do you mind if I try those finger sandwiches? I heard you telling Hannah about them."

Nora placed the vegetable pot's lid on a hot pad and turned to her son. "Go ahead, but don't spoil your dinner. Just have a couple—no more than that."

"Yes, ma'am." He raised the wax paper with his hampered right hand and took two pimento cheese sandwiches with his left, laying them on a napkin and then seating himself at the table.

His mother continued to watch him. "Do you have any homework? It'll still be a little while before we eat."

"No, ma'am. I did most of it during study hall." He took a bite of sandwich.

"Most of it?"

"I still have some trigonometry to do, but only about ten problems. Besides, 'Jack Armstrong' will be on in a just a minute."

Nora frowned at him.

"Please let me listen, Mom. I'll wrap up my trig right after dinner—I promise." He finished one sandwich and began the other.

"Oh, very well," Nora said. She wiped the perspiration from her brow with the back of a hand. "Hannah, dear, do you like turnips? I forgot to ask."

"Yes, ma'am," she said. "There's not much on God's green earth that I don't like eating. Maybe you've noticed I'm not exactly shy around the dinner table."

"You do have a healthy appetite, that's true. It's a wonder it doesn't all go to your waistline like it does mine."

On the two-week-old Blue Network—freshly independent from NBC—a fifteen-minute news report had ended, and "Jack Armstrong, the All-American Boy" was about to come on the air. Wesley swallowed his last bite and walked toward the living room. "Can I have another couple of sandwiches, Mom?" he asked. "They're not very filling. You know, there's not even any crust on them."

"Sorry, but that will just have to hold you until dinnertime."

"Gee whiz, a guy could starve to death around here." He returned to a comfortable spot on the sofa.

As Nora leaned over to open the oven door, it dawned on her that Hannah was still standing near the pantry, so she invited her to sit down at the table. "Please do, dear. Lord knows, I could use the company. I'm stuck here most days all alone in this big house."

"Thanks for the offer, but I'd better not. I've got some homework of my own to do—and I've put it off long enough."

"Oh?"

Hannah nodded her head. "I hate to admit it, but by the time I get off work, good ol' Baylor is just about the last thing on my mind. It'll be a wonder if I pass any of my classes."

"Now, I happen to know that's not true," Nora said. "Your father dropped me a note—only yesterday—to say how proud he is of the way you've been doing at college."

Hannah smiled. "Well, he may be just the slightest bit biased." She excused herself and began walking toward the stairway. "Whatever homework I can get done now will be just that much less I'll need to do tonight."

"Did you ever find the letter that came for you?" Wesley shouted from the living room.

"For me?" his mother asked.

"No, for Hannah," came the reply.

"Hannah, dear, don't go yet. Wes says there's some mail here for you."

Hannah rolled her eyes. "Yes, we've been through all that, Mrs. B. It seems that your darling son is playing a trick on me or something."

Nora laid her bread knife down and took a few steps toward the living room. "Wesley Brower, is Hannah telling the truth?" She stomped her foot in jest. "Listen, son, don't give her any trouble, or you'll be having nothing *but* turnips for dinner."

"But she did get something, Mom," he said. "Of course, I may have accidentally gotten one letter out of order when I sorted the mail."

Hannah smirked and began searching through the entire stack. On top were three pieces of mail she had already seen—the letter from home, a *Baptist Standard*, and her bank statement—and she carefully laid those to one side. Then she leafed through the remainder of the stack until she came to the very last item at the bottom. Reading its return address, her face went pale, and she stared at her landlady in shock. Nora quickly turned aside so as not to embarrass her.

"I never thought he would actually write," the boarder said.

There was fear in Nora's eyes. "Is there something wrong?"

"It's a letter from Steve," Hannah told her. "Your Steve." Her voice was thin, almost apologetic. "I never thought he would write to me. Honest, Mrs. B., I hardly even know the boy."

Unsure how to react, Nora said nothing for the time being, choosing instead to wipe the counter with a dishrag. Finally, though, she looked at the girl and forced a smile. "Well, dear, it's a free country, after all. I guess he can write to you if he wants."

Hannah peered again at the unopened envelope. "I guess."

◆　◆　◆

Mayor Charles Williams, who succeeded Hubert Johnson at city hall after the April election, proclaimed Wednesday, October 27, 1943, to be "Army Emergency Day" in Waco, and he encouraged everyone to observe the civic decree. Mayor Williams and his fellow city commissioners organized a military parade of mammoth proportions, designating Ralph Buchanan—owner of Buchanan's, the "Laundry of Personal Service," on South Eleventh Street—as parade marshal and publicity spokesman.

No one from the Brower household attended the event except for Elizabeth, who was there, largely against her will, in the company of her lovesick schoolmate, Dudley Rollins. He asked her to go with him when they happened to meet in the hallway about an hour before school ended for the day. Then again, maybe the encounter was not entirely by chance, for his sixth-period class was on a different floor than hers.

When the final bell rang, Elizabeth went to the school office to call her mother at the USO, leaving a message with the reliable Lurline Papke. Then she and Dudley walked two blocks south and secured a fine vantage point on the north side of Austin Avenue, in front of Nicosia's School of Beauty Culture. The parade route would stretch all the way from Twelfth Street to Third Street, then detour down to Franklin and cut back to Eighth Street, where it would disband in the shadow of the Federal Building. This would take it directly past the Waco Theatre, where the premiere screening of *This Is the Army* was scheduled to begin at 8:30.

From where they were standing, Elizabeth and Dudley could see the parade starting to form in the near distance, just a block or so away, about even with the Coca-Cola Bottling Company. There were artillery and infantry units, marching bands, and military vehicles of all descriptions. A cavalry platoon from Camp Hood would bring up the rear. Far in the opposite direction, three blocks away and nearly obscured from their sight, a reviewing stand had been erected for various high-ranking Army officers and local dignitaries.

As the parade would not commence until five o'clock, the two Waco High School freshmen were compelled to somehow find enough small talk to help the hour to pass. This they were unable to do—despite delving into such arcane territory as the Rollins predilection for Postum over coffee and a recitation of the Brower garbage pick-up days—and it seemed to both of them that time was standing still. A fleeting incertitude about her own abilities as a conversationalist raced through Elizabeth's head until she concluded, upon further reflection, that no such faltering speech ever occurred with anyone but the handsome youth who now stood beside her.

She had no way of knowing that Dudley was experiencing many of the same doubts and frustrations, but in his case the cause was as painfully clear and tangible as life itself. He was smitten by his own idealized concept of the charms of young womanhood, and his fantasy vision's physical proximity—so near that he could hear and even feel her breath—brought on a bad case of nerves and rendered him virtually tongue-tied.

After a quarter-hour of inconsequential discourse, Elizabeth finally came to the realization that self-enforced dialogue was only serving to make matters worse. Accordingly, she scanned the crowd, hoping to find a familiar face, but she recognized no one who might serve as deliverer from her social dilemma.

As luck would have it, Dudley had chosen that very morning to tuck his new pack of spotter cards in his shirt pocket, and it was these fifty-two tiny conversation pieces that saved the day. He shuffled the deck, chose a card at random, and asked Elizabeth to identify the depicted aircraft. She thought back to when she and Wesley had competed in the Civil Air Patrol's citywide spotter contest, not more than six months after the Pearl Harbor attack. Much to Wesley's dismay, his younger sister actually did better than he, though neither was proficient enough to win a war bond.

Dudley was holding the jack of hearts, his thumb careful to obscure the aircraft's name, and Elizabeth took a moment to examine the silhouette. It was obviously a fighter. "P-47?" she guessed.

"Nope," Dudley told her. "It's British."

She laughed and said, "I give up."

"Try."

"I forget. It's been ages since I learned the names."

"It's made by Hawker."

"Typhoon?"

Dudley was startled. "You're right. How did you know that?"

"That's the way I learned it—the Hawker Typhoon."

His face lit up, beaming with delight, and Elizabeth, too, could not help but smile. The boy's wide-mouth grin was infectious, so handsome were his features and so utterly guileless his disposition.

"Okay, give me a shot," Dudley said. He handed her the stack, and she noticed that the backs looked just like those to be found in any deck. The little cardboard box read, "Uncle Sam—by the makers of Bicycle playing cards."

Elizabeth revealed the ace of diamonds, and Dudley studied the airplane's shape.

"It's a heavy bomber," he said.

"Right ..."

But then his confidence slipped a notch, and his voice wavered as he guessed, "Heinkel?"

"No."

"Really?" He scratched his head. "Well, it's a Kraut plane, isn't it?"

"Yes."

"Focke-Wulf?"

She nodded her head. "And the model?"

Now he was back on track. "FW-200."

By the time the parade finally showed signs of coming to life, nearly every aircraft in the pack had been successfully identified. Elizabeth closed their little contest with a flourish, correctly naming an obscure Italian transport, the SM-79, manufactured by Savoia-Marchetti. Dudley simply could not get over the fact that a girl could more than hold her own in such a traditionally masculine pursuit as warfare. It was positively unnatural.

The parade was one of the largest ever to pass through central Texas, offering an imposing display of heavy weaponry and marching troops from all three major installations in the area. Most impressive of all was the lumbering M-10 tank destroyer, called "Li'l Butch," with its virtually impenetrable armor and a three-inch M-7 gun that was fully capable of reducing an Axis tank to flaming metallic rubble in a matter of seconds. Butch's twin-diesel General Motors engine could produce a respectable speed of twenty-five miles per hour on flat terrain. When the vagaries of desert warfare necessitated greater speed or a broad expanse of land to be crossed, the M-10's twenty-four-wheeler recovery truck was called into action, hoisting Butch aboard its trailer by means of a series of cables and winches.

Butch was a mainstay in the arsenal of Camp Hood's Company B—hence its popular name. Likewise, a smaller tank destroyer, "Alum," was a product of Company A. Also thundering along the parade route were heavy-duty trucks with the sobriquets of "Hi-Babe," "Hangover," and "Hopalong," all of which rolled forth under the aegis of Headquarters Company.

Sequestered behind a sturdy glass pane—for public viewing both before and after the parade—was the Army's top-secret bazooka, an innocuous-looking olive drab stovepipe with a wooden pistol handle and a top-mounted box of sophisticated electronics. Alongside, distinguished by a coat of red paint, lay its lethal, tank-piercing rocket projectile.

Shepherding all of this equipment from Camp Hood were fifty officers and enlisted men and a group of twenty WACs. Additional equipment and marching units from Waco Army Air Field and Blackland Army Air Field passed in review, each of them drawing applause from the onlookers, who stood transfixed amidst the rustling American flags.

Among the most unusual entrants, ludicrously non-military in bearing, were the junk cars, destined for the scrap heaps and eventual conversion into war *matériel.* This odd Karem Shrine patrol consisted of more than a dozen so-called "jalopies," each one of them colorfully decorated and given an illusory street worthiness by the powered assistance of a fleet of wrecker trucks. At parade's end, the Junior Chamber of Commerce would take possession of the jalopies and then sell them through sealed bids, with all financial gain benefiting the Army Emergency Relief Funds of the three military installations.

After the parade's final assemblage—a contingent of mounted troops—had passed by the throngs, a detail from the Waco Sanitation Department drew a round of good-natured cheers, and members of the crowd slowly dispersed. The more curious among them wandered over to the Austin Avenue military exhibit, where many of the vehicles and weapons that had paraded by were now available for closer inspection. War bonds were offered for sale, as were the remaining tickets for that night's premiere screening of *This Is the Army*, which would follow a stage show composed of talent from Camp Hood, Waco Army Air Field, and Blackland Army Air Field.

Elizabeth claimed to have strict orders to return home immediately after the parade, though this was stretching the truth a bit. The girl had only left a message at the USO, never talking directly to her mother at all, so the edict was more of a fanciful expediency than an actual command.

Dudley was too gullible to take much notice of the affront, and he asked her to go with him to the following night's guest appearance at Waco Hall of famed composer Sigmund Romberg. Now fifty-six years old but still at the height of his powers, Romberg would play the piano and also conduct a fifty-piece orchestra and four vocalists in excerpts from his own operettas like *The Student Prince*, *Maytime*, *The Desert Song*, *Blossom Time*, and *The New Moon*.

Elizabeth expressed her regrets, protesting that she had never heard of Sigmund Romberg. This, even the acutely unmusical Dudley Rollins found difficult to believe. "You'd recognize the tunes," he said. "Maybe you just don't know his name."

Meanwhile, what of the parade and movie that the Karem Temple had been promoting for the past two weeks? Almost to a man, city leaders deemed the occasion an unqualified success. According to William Quebe, recorder of Waco Lodge No. 92 on Seventh Street, the Army Day events—movie receipts, jalopy auction, and war bond sales—combined for a net revenue, above federal tax, of precisely $2,441.35 for the emergency relief funds. And scrap-metal proceeds would drive the total even higher.

◆   ◆   ◆

On Friday morning, in the privacy of her room, Hannah Lane reread the letter from Stephen Brower over and over again, trying to discover the hidden meanings behind it. Had she appraised his wording objectively, on its intrinsic merits, she would have concluded that nothing more was involved than a dutiful response to her own request that he write to her whenever he got the chance. But a young woman's mind, particularly within the context of wartime separation, was prone to conjure up all manner of secret motives. Neither were they always proven to be misguided. Frowning, she folded up the letter, determined to put such idle speculation out of her head.

She rode to Baylor on the streetcar, and its gently rocking motion made her feel pleasantly drowsy en route, except at those jarring moments when the motorman, for whatever reason, was compelled to clang his bell. By the time the electric coach finally snaked its way to the corner of Fifth Street and Speight, there were well over a dozen students aboard, nearly all of them females whose rental homes were apparently too remote from campus for convenient access on foot.

Hannah was sitting in her logic class, Philosophy 202, when a disturbing thought returned to her. Earlier, she had considered and rejected this very same prospect, but now, suddenly and unannounced, it burst forth with renewed energy. What if Steve was interested in establishing a serious relationship with her? As before, she tried to brush it aside, rightly assuming that such a silly notion was something an elementary schoolgirl might entertain—and even then only if she happened to have mutual feelings toward the boy. Here, that simply was not the case. She barely knew Mrs. Brower's oldest child, being on much more familiar terms with both Wesley and Elizabeth. True, she had a deep concern for Steve's health and safety, and she prayed for him nightly. But that was nothing more than she would do for anyone in the military during such perilous times. How dare he be so presumptuous as to court her through the mails!

Her mind was wandering as Dr. Hall wrote a sentence on the chalkboard, but nonetheless, almost mechanically, she transcribed the statement verbatim into her notebook. When the professor asked the class a question, Hannah felt a jolt of adrenalin shoot through her, and she came to her senses. Fortunately, he called upon someone else to address the issue, and she resolved at once to pay strict attention to the teacher, who spoke with great authority and a wisdom born of many decades in the classroom.

Professor of Philosophy Arthur Jackson Hall was a theologian whose intellectual acuity belied the fact that he was fast approaching the Biblical age of three score and ten. Indeed, back when he earned his Bachelor of Arts and Master of Arts degrees from Richmond College, President William McKinley was in the White House, and the nation was engaged in the Spanish-American War. He also held Bachelor of Divinity and Master of Theology degrees from the Upland, Pennsylvania, campus of Crozer Theological Seminary—which had served as a Union hospital a mere forty years before he enrolled—as well as a PhD from the University of Chicago.

There was no seating chart in Dr. Hall's class, and Hannah never seemed to find herself next to the same person two days in a row. Consequently, she knew none of the other students in the room by name. It so happened that on the first class day after her receipt of Steve's letter, a young man of ruddy complexion and grotesquely yellowed, chipped teeth was sitting immediately to her right. He began a conversation with her in the few minutes before the teacher arrived—nothing of a probing nature, just the sort of trivial prattle in which acquaintances are likely to engage while passing some time prior to the beginning of a session or event.

But one thing this young man, Ralph Goins, said captured Hannah's interest at once, and she made a mental note to question him about it after class was over.

With the panic of unpreparedness still fresh in her mind, she disdained all thought of Stephen Brower and became especially attentive for the balance of that course period. When Dr. Hall asked for someone to please explain how a scientific methodology could be employed to analyze the workings of human deliberation, yet without sacrificing the precepts of free will, it was Hannah who held her hand high and volunteered to elucidate this abstruse concept in readily comprehensible terms. Her ensuing discourse surprised even herself, raising a few eyebrows in class and extracting from the normally laconic teacher a grudging word of praise.

Rejecting even a negligible possibility that the sin of pride could manifest itself within someone as righteous as she, Hannah Lane paused long enough in her musings to proclaim inwardly, "This is what I am intended to be, and puerile thoughts of the opposite sex will only serve to compromise my scholarly potential and usefulness to the Lord."

The class was excused by Dr. Hall, who admonished his students to read chapter four of the textbook prior to their next meeting. He also reminded them of Monday's test, adding that they would have plenty of time for study over the weekend.

"Is it a comprehensive test?" Brian Rowlett asked from his seat up front.

Arthur Jackson Hall smiled sarcastically. "Yes, Mr. Rowlett," he said. "Seeing as how this is our first test of the quarter, I would say there is a great likelihood that it will be comprehensive." The rest of the class laughed and packed up to leave.

In the same instant that Ralph Goins slid his rickety wooden chair back from the desk to stand up, Hannah stopped him long enough to pose a question. "What did you mean when you said that your big brother was 'in transit'? Is he shipping out for overseas?"

Still seated, Ralph wore a serious expression that caused Hannah to feel an empathetic sadness. "Yeah, that's what we gather from his letters," he said. "Stu's in the Navy—a radioman."

"So's a friend of mine. In the Navy, I mean. I don't know what his job is, though."

"I can't get in," Ralph told her. "I tried, but they wouldn't accept me."

Though Hannah did not solicit an explanation, Ralph seemed very anxious to tell her why he was spending the war in relative safety, confined to the sidelines. Probably he ventured this information as a preemptive measure, to forestall any suspicion that he might be a slacker.

"What difference do someone's teeth make anyway? I'm not going to be sent out there to *bite* the Japs."

"I guess that's just Navy regulations," she said, and he acknowledged her truism with a shrug. Without thinking, Hannah glanced at his mouth, which he quickly covered with the back of his left hand—a reflex action learned through years of derision. It was then that she noticed the wedding band.

"Are you married?" she asked, happy to change the subject to something less humiliating to him.

"For going on two years," he said. He was looking away from her now, neatly stacking two textbooks on top of his red Big Chief tablet. "And she's a terrific gal."

"Does she go to Baylor too?"

"No, Laurie's a school teacher—at Sanger Avenue Elementary. She graduated from Texas State College for Women last summer and went right to work in September."

He stood up to leave, explaining that he had another class across campus, so Hannah chatted with him while they walked to the door. "When someone ships out, like your brother, how long are they generally gone?"

Ralph looked at her as if she were daft. "Maybe until the war's over—no guarantees. They try to rotate the men home every twelve months or so, but whether that actually happens is anybody's guess."

Her downcast look made him ask, "You have a sweetheart overseas?"

She giggled in embarrassment, nervously winding a blonde bang around her finger. "Good heavens, no," she said, "but I live with a family that has a son who's headed for action. He's the Navy boy I was telling you about. Maybe you know him ... Stephen Brower? He was a high school football star around here."

"Nope. I'm from Decatur. It's a little town north of Fort Worth."

"What's your brother's name? I'll add him to my prayer list."

"Stuart Goins." Not being a Bible major or preacher's kid himself, Ralph was taken aback by her candor, and it made him a bit circumspect.

"Golly, look at me," Hannah said. "Here I am, getting your brother's name, and I don't even know yours."

"I'm Ralph Goins. And you?"

She looked at him with lovely blue eyes, although to be cruelly honest, her appearance otherwise was not very feminine. "Hannah Lane," she said. "My daddy's a Baptist preacher in Mount Airy, North Carolina. Have you ever heard of it?"

"No, but then I've never been east of the Mississippi River. Neither had Stu until about a year ago."

"What church do you and your wife attend?"

Ralph swallowed hard. "None right now. Well, we've gone to Edgefield a couple of times—over on River Street, just off campus."

"I know where it is, sure." Hannah leaned closer to him and whispered, "Nice church, but kind of small."

He nodded his head and turned to walk away.

"Say, I'd like to invite you and your wife to visit First Baptist sometime. You'd probably like it there."

"I don't know. Maybe someday," he said.

"How about this Sunday? You can be my guests."

"No, I don't think so. Maybe some other time."

"Well, Godspeed," Hannah told him. She offered her hand in Christian friendship.

"Sure, same to you," Ralph said. He shook hands and hurried on to his next class, carrying with him the firm determination, beginning tomorrow, to sit as far away from this proselytizing influence as was practicable. Sociology majors had no need for Bible-thumping—and besides, Philosophy 202 was nothing more than an elective for him.

Hannah mouthed a silent prayer and, with a sigh, began walking toward the streetcar stop. Already in her young life, she was accustomed to flustered reactions to her outspokenness, such that by now they merely caused her grief rather than personal resentment. She lamented the spiritual confusion of fellow travelers Ralph and Laurie Goins, but their apathy would not dissuade her from fervently praying for the well-being of his older brother, Stuart.

Steve, too, would remain firmly in her prayers. This was the very least she could do, realizing that the Brower family, with whom she had grown very close, would not be seeing him again for as long as a year, maybe more—possibly for the duration of the war. She also decided not to write to him, knowing full well that any such notes of wartime encouragement could be misinterpreted as the emergence of romantic interest. Hannah Lane had no desire to become some half-remembered serviceman's "girl back home."

◆　　　◆　　　◆

It was while Elizabeth was airing up a customer's tires that a sense of *déjà vu* suddenly swept over her. She felt certain that she had lived through this moment before and that the incident from her past had something to do with the elderly gentleman now relaxing in his maroon Dictator coupe. Upon further reflection, she realized that she had never seen this man prior to today, nor for that matter had she ever laid eyes on his six-cylinder 1937 Studebaker.

The odd sensation was quite disconcerting to her, and Elizabeth remained in a contemplative state as she slipped the tire gauge back into the pocket of her oil-stained coveralls. Not until the man offered her a small tip in gratitude did a plausible explanation finally come to her. Several weeks earlier, a different white-haired driver had said that he used to work for her father at Superior Office Supply. That enigmatic gentleman announced that he left something for her at the Brower home. What was that other man's name? She was unable to recall, having never given him a further thought.

A few minutes later, when Dinah Reidelhuber had finished counting change from the Nehi beverage machine, Elizabeth approached her with that same question. Dinah could only answer with a question of her own: "What man?"

"Don't you remember? Kind of distinguished looking. I think he wore glasses."

"How old was he?"

"Sixty-five, I guess—maybe even older. I introduced him to you."

"You did?"

Elizabeth nodded her head. "He was driving a Ford."

"Well, if you introduced him, then you must have known his name."

"I did at the time, sure, but that was a few weeks back."

Dinah deliberated for a moment but could not recollect the stranger's name or even picture the trivial affair. When the telephone bell sounded, she dismissed the matter from her mind and walked toward the office to answer the call.

Just before 6:30, as dusk was taking hold, Nora Brower pulled the Chevrolet to a squeaking stop near the servicing bays and waited for her daughter to get off duty. The weather was cloudy and considerably cooler than it had been of late—normal for the first week in November—with the temperature dropping slowly through the lower sixties.

On school days, Elizabeth was only able to work three-hour shifts, and even then she was forced to sacrifice her extra-curricular activities to do so. This she did willingly, convinced that her modest income was more important to the family than marching at halftime in Municipal Stadium. For a short while, she tried to manage both endeavors, but her boss, Hoyle Harkins, made no secret of the fact that he was having difficulty securing enough hours from his hired help to operate the station on an efficient basis. Band director Lyle Skinner was disappointed to lose one of his better flutists, but he understood the reasons for her decision. "As long as this war continues," he said, "we must learn to be flexible."

During the drive home, even before the filling station had disappeared entirely from Nora's side-view mirror, Elizabeth brought up the matter of the puzzling visitor. "Did a man come to see you a few weeks ago?" she asked. "He said he used to work for Daddy."

Nora looked uneasy at the suggestion and shook her head. "I'll tell you about him someday, but not just yet."

"What was his name? I've been trying to think of it for more than an hour now."

"Oh, I can tell you that much, I suppose. Benjamin Reich—a dear man who came to pay his respects to the family, for all your father did for him." Elizabeth waited for more information, but none was forthcoming.

"What does this Mr. Reich do for a living?" she asked.

"I don't want to tell you any more about him until the time is right," Nora said. "You'll understand why."

Elizabeth knew better than to probe any further, so there was silence in the automobile. She reached for the radio and tuned to her favorite station for recorded music. Regrettably, she arrived at that particular frequency just in time to hear only the final measures of "All or Nothing at All" by Harry James and His Orchestra, with a vocal by Frank Sinatra. The girl sighed. "Why is it that I always catch the last few seconds of the best songs?"

"That does seem to happen an awful lot, doesn't it?" her mother said.

A commercial came on, so Elizabeth peevishly dialed to WACO for the closing minutes of "10-2-4 Ranch," a syndicated program sponsored by Dr. Pepper and featuring cowboy star Dick Foran. "This will have to do," she said.

Nora could not help but smiling. Her daughter's personality was really very similar to hers in many respects, but in none more so than her irritability at the vagaries of radio programming. Unlike her daughter, however, Nora could remember back to a more innocent day when radio did not yet exist.

Throughout Nora's own childhood, her mother regularly did the household chores with no aural companionship whatsoever, unless she went to the extreme of placing a three-minute disc on the wind-up Victrola. How spoiled today's children had become—and all within the span of a single generation.

About the time Nora steered the automobile onto Herring Avenue, a baffling thought came to her. She looked straight ahead and tried to remain as casual as possible. "Lizzie, how did you come to know about Benjamin Reich?"

Elizabeth stared at her mother, intrigued anew. "He dropped by the filling station on his way back home."

Nora nodded her head. "Mr. Reich moved to Stephenville from Kansas City after he retired. He was in town for Edwin Drescher's funeral—just for the day—and he told me he hadn't been to Waco in many years. That's kind of sad, considering he was born right here."

On the radio, "10-2-4 Ranch" was drawing to a close with a tune by the Sons of the Pioneers, and Elizabeth turned the sound down a bit. "Did he leave you something for me?" she asked.

"Mr. Reich?"

"Uh-huh."

Nora hesitated a moment before answering. "Why do you ask such a thing?"

"I just thought he said something about leaving a gift with you, that's all."

Nora cleared her throat. "A gift? No, I don't believe so. Not a gift, *per se.*" Then, with eyes trained on her driving, she added, "Listen, Lizzie, I told you earlier that I'd let you know all about Benjamin Reich one of these days, but this is hardly the time or the place."

Elizabeth studied her mother's profile. "Well, you certainly are making this Mr. Reich seem awfully mysterious. What is he, a foreign agent?"

Nora laughed at the suggestion. "No, certainly not," she said. "Now, please, let's change the subject. You'll understand why later on."

♦   ♦   ♦

Whenever possible, in the days that followed their disagreeable encounter a week earlier, Wesley avoided coming across Marshall McFall in the lobby or hallways of KWXN. Occasionally, of course, they saw one another in the studio—there was no question of withdrawing from the daily concerns of the workplace—but beyond that, the two were content to ignore each other in a mutual bond of contempt.

Sandra Whittsel, too, was stricken from Wesley's short list of friendships to be cultivated. He resented her unbecoming dalliance in the announcing booth, and—swallowing the bitter pill of disappointment—he began constructing in his heart a firm conviction that this former object of his desire suffered from a serious character flaw that rendered her unworthy of any further devotion. By such a margin did he underestimate the power of her dark brown eyes, winsome smile, and comely figure.

After school one day, as members of the junior varsity football team jogged past him to the practice field, he was struck by how thin and undeveloped his own arms were in relation to theirs. Flexing his left biceps muscle produced hardly a ripple atop the sinewy fibers that stretched between his shoulder and elbow. Suddenly repulsed by his spindly self, he resolved then and there to begin lifting the pair of dumbbells that Steve had left behind upon enlisting in the Navy. Strange to say, he already felt somewhat stronger, just thinking of it, and for the rest of the afternoon and evening he swaggered with renewed confidence, anticipating the day when he might shear the buttons off the front of his shirt simply by inhaling to the fullest capacity of his massive chest. Yes, he would begin his weightlifting regimen immediately, once the cast was removed from his atrophying right arm.

English period was unbearable that year, and not only because Sandy was in the same room. His teacher, Miss Constance Simonek, was excellent, but she required far too much reading for his taste. Hardly a night went by when the class was not expected to read a chapter or more in some novel. One brazen girl, Hope Kopperl, took the teacher to task right in front of everyone. "Why do we have to read Booth Tarkington when we're trying to learn English composition?" she asked.

A hush fell over the classroom as Miss Simonek walked over to Hope's desk and countered with a query of her own. "In your opinion, is Mr. Tarkington well-read, or was he simply born with the ability to write? Tell me what you think."

Poor Hope did not answer, so Miss Simonek gave her a reassuring smile. "Speak up, Miss Kopperl. Don't be timid."

"Well, I know what you want me to say."

"Tell me what you think, Miss Kopperl, not what you think I want you to say."

"Some authors are called 'born writers,' so I've heard," she said with an impudent smile.

The teacher raised her eyebrows in thought, careful not to reject the student's statement out of hand. "True enough, but that is a misnomer. No one can develop a proficient vocabulary—let alone write a decent work of literature—without first immersing oneself in reading. I think you will find this to be true in all cases. There are no exceptions, not even Hemingway, who writes in such a natural style."

Miss Simonek walked back to her desk and then turned to face the class. "I'm speaking to everyone now, so listen carefully. I want to explain that we are reading *Penrod* because we can never truly master a writing style unless we first surround ourselves with the great literature of the past. My brother paid visits to Mr. Booth Tarkington at his spring cottage in Indianapolis, Indiana, on two separate occasions—and both times he came away with a clear appreciation for why this great author has become one of our literary masters, the only man to win the Pulitzer Prize for the Novel twice. In a word, Mr. Tarkington is a voracious ... Miss Kopperl?"

The girl frowned. "... reader."

Miss Simonek nodded her head. "He is a voracious *reader*. Despite his failing eyesight, he is still a voracious reader. All four walls of his study, from floor to ceiling, are brimming with the great classics—and many of the better contemporary titles too."

Wesley was about forty pages behind in his traversal through *Penrod*, so he promised himself to be caught up by the end of the weekend. Not that he wanted to become a famous author like Tarkington—he was blessed with no special flair for writing—but because the daily discipline of reading seemed to be so important to his teacher. Such passion did she display for reading that surely there must be more to it than meets the eye ... so to speak. Besides, this Booth Tarkington fellow made much more sense to him than whoever wrote *Beowulf*.

And so it was that Wesley Brower found himself under a reading lamp in the living room, dutifully appreciating the value of a thirty-year-old literary classic ...

> His eyes fell slowly and inimically from the brow of Whittier to the braid of reddish hair belonging to Victorine Riordan, the little octoroon girl who sat directly in front of him. Victorine's back was as familiar to Penrod as the necktie of Oliver Wendell Holmes. So was her gayly coloured plaid waist. He hated the waist as he hated Victorine herself, without knowing why. Enforced companionship in large quantities and on an equal basis between the sexes appears to sterilize the affections, and schoolroom romances are few.

... when there came a knock on the front door.

"You want me to get it?" Wesley shouted to his mother, but there was no response. Presumably, she was upstairs, drawing a comb through her graying hair, something she always made it a habit to do prior to retiring for the night.

"Coming," Wesley said. Valentino was lying on the bottom step of the stairs, and the cat reached with one of his paws, its claws momentarily retracted, to tap the human on the leg as he passed. Wesley played with him for four or five seconds with his right hand—partially armored by the cast against inadvertent scratches—before continuing on his way. When the door opened, Valentino scrambled to his feet and fled to safety.

Standing beneath the porch light was Sandra Whittsel, motionless but with tears streaming down her cheeks. She was insulated from the chilly breeze by a man's overcoat, which she held tightly around her but did not bother to button.

Bewildered by this mystifying sight, so shocking and unexpected, Wesley could not think what to do. "Are you all right?" he asked.

Sandy shook her head but was unable to give an intelligible answer through her stifled sobs. Wesley tried to motion her inside where it was warmer, but she would not budge. Even when he took her hand and gently pulled her toward the doorway, her feet remained firmly planted. Wesley stood on the porch, staring and helpless, then reached back to silently close the door.

"I ... can't ... come ... in," she finally said, forcibly emitting each word over the sound of a moaning whimper.

"Why not? It's awfully cold out here."

"I ... just can't. Please ... don't go back inside."

He knelt on one knee, so now he was looking up into her tearful, reddened eyes. "Can you tell me what's wrong?"

She shook her head and bit her lower lip. When she shut her eyes, a few teardrops fell freely to the porch, and one of them landed in a tiny, warm splash on the back of his left hand.

"I need to talk to you ... to someone." She spoke more loudly than intended, for the crying spasms had robbed her voice of any possible control of dynamics.

Wesley glanced over his shoulder at the house. "My sister is upstairs, and so is my mother. They'll hear us out here for sure—even more than if we went inside."

Sandy took a deep breath. "Then let's go for a walk."

"At a quarter to ten?"

Sandy implored him with a nod of her head, eyes closed, lips pursed to hold back another sob.

Wesley stood up and turned to go into the house. "Just let me grab a sweater."

"No." She stopped him with a hand to his upper arm. "It's a big coat. Share it with me."

They began strolling down the sidewalk, she slowly regaining her composure. Not until they turned the corner of the block was a word uttered between them.

It was Sandy who spoke first. "Thank you for letting me talk to you." There was just the hint of a smile.

Wesley nodded assurance but did not reply. In the cramped space that the anonymous overcoat afforded, his left arm was pinned against Sandy's side, and their walking motion at times caused him to brush against her right breast. He felt embarrassed, but as Sandy did not seem to notice, he decided not to apologize and thereby call attention to his encroachment.

As they neared the Anderson "mansion"—so christened by the neighborhood children because it was by far the largest house in their miniature realm of experience—they came to a halt, and Sandy pulled the overcoat tightly around them. She began crying again, this time with a bit more restraint. "I've done a ... terrible thing," she said, "and I want you to know that I have never done anything like this before."

Wesley remained silent, sensing that it was best to let her speak without interruption. Besides, the moment was so awkward for him that he had no idea what to say or how to comfort her in this time of need.

"I let a boy see me ... more of me than he should."

Wesley swallowed hard. "All of you?" he asked.

"No, of course not." She stared at the dimly lit mansion. "What kind of girl do you think I am?"

"Well, not that kind."

Then she looked up at him, directly into his eyes, and their faces were no more than ten inches apart. "Just my underwear, from the waist up."

Again he swallowed, trying to keep that sweet vision from overtaking his thoughts. His right wrist was beginning to itch under the cast. "Why?" he asked. "Why did you do it?"

Sandy could not speak. She shook her head in confusion, and her eyes teared up as before.

"Let's walk," Wesley said. He hoped that might help to console her.

The Carver kids—two boys and their younger sister—were playing basketball outside, a floodlight attached to the corner of their house providing barely enough illumination to make the netless hoop visible against the backboard. Wesley hid his head from detection with the right shoulder of the woolen coat.

"Thanks for talking with me," Sandy said again.

"Sure." He wanted to scratch the itching wrist but dared not.

"I guess you're wondering who it was."

Wesley pretended it was of little or no interest to him, but his alert silence spoke volumes.

Sandy began to cry again, but now quite softly and without the uncontrollable sobbing that gripped her on the front porch. "Maybe I should let you go home," she said, and Wesley had the awful feeling that he was being dismissed from her confidence.

They stopped walking for a moment, beneath a swarm of moths flying around a street lamp. "Did I say something wrong?" he asked.

Sandy sighed and let her eyes wander across the neighborhood. "No. It's just that you don't seem very interested in what I have to say."

They resumed their stroll, even more slowly than before. Several dogs could be heard barking in the distance, and a rattling automobile—one headlight out of commission—drove by at a speed well below the wartime limit.

"Oh, I'm interested all right," Wesley said. His dry throat struggled with the words.

She looked up at him and smiled, as a single teardrop ran down her cheek. Even in the dim light of the antiquated street lamp, her pretty face made Wesley's heart ache with longing.

"It was Marshall McFall, wasn't it?" he said.

Sandy chose not to answer directly, instead giving a barely perceptible nod of her head.

A rush of anger shot through Wesley's body—whether due to resentment or jealousy. "Did he force you to do it?"

She shook her head.

Wesley wiped his nose with the back of his right fingers, and the overcoat almost fell from his shoulder. He caught it with his other hand and positioned it more securely in place. "Then why did you do it?"

Sandy tried to smile, but it would not come. "I don't know. I guess I just wanted him to like me."

Had she slapped him violently in the face, Wesley could not have felt more violated. He said nothing for a moment, still grappling with the shock of Sandy's admission. The annoying itch beneath his cast showed no signs of subsiding, so he reached over and allowed the fingernails of his left hand to bring some temporary relief to the mending wrist. In so doing, his eyes fell upon Sandy's ornate signature, but this time, instead of the usual euphoric pleasure, there was only a feeling of emptiness and loss.

Sandy brushed some tears away with the back of her sleeve and said, "I just want you to understand that what I did was totally out of character for me, and I feel bad about it."

Wesley nodded his head with reassurance and took a deep breath. He kicked a pebble aside and stepped over a small puddle of water that lay near a lawn sprinkler. "Tell me what happened."

She began crying again, and her speech was punctuated by loud sniffles. "We were sitting on his divan, and he gave me a glass of wine. Later, after he put his arm around me, he gave me another glass."

The rage was starting to build again inside Wesley, and his left hand clenched in a fist.

Sandy stopped walking and gazed across the street at a sea of leaves blowing in the chilly wind. "I could see how he was staring at me," she said, "and I guess I just wanted him to see me as something more than a child."

Wesley gave her an impish grin. "Well, that's one way to prove it, I suppose."

She looked directly at him, smiling in spite of herself. Glancing down at her blouse, she grumbled, "Sometimes I wonder."

"Did you take your shirt all the way off?"

She shook her head. "He just undid the top three or four buttons." Then, with a deep sigh, she added, "But I didn't try very hard to stop him."

Wesley thought for a moment and said, "Well, maybe it was the wine."

"Maybe so. I don't know for sure."

"How did you end up at my house?" he asked. A dog was barking and snarling behind a chain-link fence, so they resumed their walk.

"I just got scared, and the wine made me start to cry. He was very nice about it and said he understood. When I stood up, I buttoned my blouse and told him I had to leave. He asked where would I go. I said I didn't know, but I knew I had to leave. He made me take his coat to keep me warm."

Wesley was not so impressed by Marshall McFall's magnanimity. "And he just let you go walking out into the night?"

"He offered to drive me home, but I didn't think that was a very good idea."

"Do your parents know where you've been?"

Sandy frowned. "I told my mother that I was going to church and then to a movie with Amanda Mullins."

"You told her you were going to *church?*"

She looked down at the sidewalk. "I feel ashamed to tell you this, but I wanted to be at his apartment more than anywhere else in the world ... no matter what happened once I got there. I had never done anything like this in my whole life, and I was determined to see how far I could go. I guess I disappointed him."

"I'm sure you did," Wesley said with a smirk. "So, what now?"

The girl's jaw was quivering. "Can you take me home, please? I hate to ask you to do this for me, but I really have no other way."

He stopped walking again and slipped the overcoat off his shoulders. Sandy immediately wrapped it around herself, as her teeth were beginning to chatter from the cold. Her face seemed pathetic in the dimness of the nearest street lamp, now about fifty feet ahead. Shiny streaks of dried teardrops matted her cheeks, and her sorrowful eyes appeared reddened and puffy. And yet, even in her anguish she was lovely to behold, and Wesley could feel his resistance waning with every breath. There was really no question of fighting it. He held firm for a fleeting moment but then surrendered. "Okay, but we'll need to be awfully quiet," he said. "I'll tell my mother that Amanda's car broke down and I had to give you a ride."

She smiled up at him. "I'll never forget you for this ... for being so wonderful." Rising on her tiptoes, she kissed him gently on the cheek, and a delicious waft of perfume lingered around him for a second or two.

Momentary elation consumed him as he savored the touch of Sandy's lips, but it proved to be a hollow kind of joy, soon washed away by a much more formidable wave of desolation and longing.

"And, Wesley, whatever you do, I beg of you not to mention what I did to a single soul. If my father ever heard about this, he would disown me."

Wesley nodded agreement but added, "Maybe you're not giving him enough credit."

"My father?" She smiled, struggling against her tears.

"How do you know he wouldn't be sympathetic about it? You didn't rob a bank or something."

"Oh, I know all right," she said. "He hasn't spoken to my older brother for over three years."

Wesley was astonished. "I didn't even know you had a brother."

"He's in the Army, somewhere in Europe now, but he hasn't written home since he enlisted. My father and brother had an awful fight when we were still living in Savannah. I'm just glad I was over at my grandmother's that weekend and didn't hear it."

"What was it about? I mean ... the fight."

"Allan admitted to Daddy that his girlfriend was expecting a baby, and that he was probably the father."

"Probably?"

Sandy hesitated. "Well, that he was the father." Emotion gripped her throat, and she nearly choked on the words. There was a long silence, as she tried in vain to regain her composure.

By now, the nighttime chill had become quite penetrating, and yet Wesley could not bring himself to ask her to share the warmth of the overcoat again. She looked so lonely and forlorn in the rumpled garment. Its impressive length dwarfed Sandy's tiny stature, making her seem a mere child playing "dress up" in her parents' evening clothes. He could feel a protective instinct at work that pained him with bittersweet yearning.

"Anyway, Daddy threw him out of the house," she finally managed to say. "I may be his 'baby girl,' but I'm sure he would do the same with me." An instant later, her face was pressed against Wesley's chest, and she was crying freely, moistening the front of his shirt with warm tears. His arms drifted around her, and he patted her gently on the back, trying to provide as much compassion as he could. From the corner of his eye, he could see a neighbor lady in the nearest house pull aside her window curtain to learn the nature of the sobbing sound.

"Come on," he whispered. "Let me get you home."

In the days that followed, Wesley Brower tried to sort out the unmistakable sense of loss in his heart. Did he grieve because Sandy was not the girl he thought she was? Or was it because she was more attracted to this arrogant braggart than to himself? He saw cruel irony in her recent fling with impropriety, realizing that—if only he were honest enough to admit it—his personal stake in the whole affair amounted to nothing more than driving her getaway car. Even Sandy's perfume, so beguiling at the time, had been lovingly selected from her toiletry cabinet for the enticement of the Dean of Central Texas Announcers and not for him.

$$\bullet \qquad \bullet \qquad \bullet$$

Armistice Day of 1943 was observed at Columbus Avenue Baptist Church on November 7, it being Pastor H. H. Hargrove's annual practice to honor his congregation's World War veterans on the Sunday prior to the holiday's actual calendar date. During his words of greeting, he would ask all servicemen, both past and present, to stand and receive acknowledgment from the entire membership.

Assistant Pastor James L. Tucker, in his role as director of music, thought that a patriotic air might lend an appropriate dignity to the moment, so he asked Elizabeth Brower and staff organist Harry Lee Spencer to perform a flute-keyboard setting of "Columbia, Gem of the Ocean." That particular Sunday would also mark the end of a weeklong revival, with the concomitant overflow crowds, so he felt it doubly imperative that the morning service be made a truly memorable occasion. With that in mind, he arranged for the colors to be posted by an honor guard from Baylor University's Army Specialized Training Program.

Miss Brower's participation in the ceremony, while musically flattering, caused her more anxiety than would have been the case a mere five months earlier. Now that she was working at the filling station nearly twenty hours a week, playing in the Waco High School Band was simply out of the question, and her musicianship had suffered as a result. No one was more keenly aware of this deficiency than she, for her initial attempts at preparation seemed to be producing rather paltry results.

Elizabeth decided that this particular adaptation of the tune—with its florid embellishments in the third stanza—was too advanced for an intermediate player such as herself. She apprised the organist of her doubts, but to no avail. Harry Lee Spencer merely chuckled and told her, "Well, it will seem a lot less difficult for you after a couple weeks of practice." That was easy for him to say, she thought, what with all his talent and experience. How nice it must be to get up on Sunday mornings with not a care in the world, seating oneself at the organ console, and then doing nothing more than the regular routine, blissfully unaware of the judgmental ears of twelve hundred music critics.

But as she watched the dreaded day approach, Elizabeth noticed that an amazing thing was happening. This respected musician's faith in her was having a positive effect on her own confidence. Like a stormy sky giving way to sunlight, those two weeks of relentless effort were beginning to resuscitate her former flutist self. On Wednesday she rehearsed with the organist, and by Saturday night she felt as ready as she would ever be. Perhaps she should have joined the Waco High Band after all. Maybe she still could.

As expected, the church was filled to capacity for the morning service. It was the final day of revival and also the day before many in the church—including the pastor and his wife, Frank B. Bryan's widow, evangelist Graves Darby and his wife, and the assistant pastor and his wife—would be leaving for the state Baptist General Convention in Dallas. A good portion of those gathered, it is fair to assume, were looking forward to hearing Dr. Hargrove's stirring message on "The All-Sufficient Source." This, as was noted in the bulletin, would follow directly after a flute solo by Beth Brower: "Columbia, Gem of the Ocean, Arr."

When veterans of the Great War stood, there was a respectful hush in the sanctuary. The majority of them were now in their upper forties, some older than that, and gray hair was to be seen on many of the men's temples. This is what most struck Nora as she turned to smile at the honorees. She had selected a pew near the front of the church, not far from the organ, because that is where Elizabeth's music stand was positioned. Following a prayer of peace, the pastor invited his congregation to acknowledge the heroes among them, and the room resounded in applause. As she clapped, Nora's eyes swept across the room, and she was pleasantly surprised to see how many of the veterans she recognized. Oddly enough, one of the men at the rear of the church seemed to be smiling directly back at her, and she studied his face more carefully. She was astonished for a second or two, but then decided no, it could not possibly be.

The applause having died down, these war veterans were now free to seat themselves once again, and Nora noticed a subtle nod from Harry Lee Spencer for "his flutist" to come forward. As she watched Elizabeth position herself behind the music stand, nervously opening the score and wetting her mouthpiece, Nora closed her eyes and offered a few words of silent prayer.

She opened them just in time to see the organist begin his introduction, thankfully at a slow tempo, and then watched as Elizabeth joined the musical presentation with the oh-so-familiar patriotic strains. It sounded fine, too, not excessively breathy and with a full, round tone. As she listened, Nora recalled that her daughter had told her this was the centennial year of "Columbia, Gem of the Ocean," first sung in Philadelphia around 1843. History was not Elizabeth's strong suit, but that is what the organist imparted when he gave her the music to study.

The piece thankfully concluded, Elizabeth picked up her sheet music and carried it, with her trusty silver flute, back to where her mother was sitting. Nora smiled in approval and slid her Bible far enough for Elizabeth to sit alongside. The girl's sigh of relief was heard only by those nearby. Her hands were damp with perspiration, so she dried them on her skirt before taking a hymnal from the pew rack. So overjoyed was she to have the musical ordeal behind her that, to her shame, she heard very little of the sermon.

Several people came up to Elizabeth after the service was over, expressing their admiration for the way she played. "You need to be in the Waco Symphony," one elegantly dressed woman said. Her hair was a soft gray in color. "And I intend to tell Max Reiter about you."

Elizabeth shook her head modestly and smiled. "I hardly think they would want me."

"Oh, yes they would," the lady said. "You play beautifully."

"Well, thank you."

Nora was beaming with pride. "Yes, thank you very much, Mrs. Stallworth."

Another woman gave the young flutist a valuable gift for her efforts—a completed book of savings stamps—and Elizabeth was shocked at her generosity. Once the lady had walked away, Nora identified her as Bertie Spencer, wife of the organist.

A very elderly man, dressed in the old-fashioned style of string tie and high-neck collar, watch chain descending into his vest pocket, approached Elizabeth and teased her with the breezy words, "I want you to play at my funeral, darlin'." She blushed at first but then saw that he was not serious. "Do you know 'Time on My Hands'?" he asked with a twinkle in his eye.

Nora patted him on the shoulder. "Mr. Gates, you never could keep a straight face." The old man was still chuckling as he walked away, leaning heavily on his walking stick with every alternate step.

"Hello, Nora-Fedora," came a familiar voice behind mother and daughter. They turned to see Matthew Coleman, grinning from ear to ear.

"Matty!" Nora shouted, and she ran to throw her arms around big brother. After bear-hugging him, she took a step away and said, "So it *was* you standing back there."

"Yep, I plead guilty." He squeezed Elizabeth with his powerful right arm and said, "Hello, sugar." She smiled up at him.

"Why didn't you let us know you were coming to Waco?" Nora asked. "Where's Babs?"

"Couldn't make it this time. She's over at Aunt Polly's in Weslaco."

"You drove up here all by yourself? That must have cost you a year's rations."

"Don't tell anyone, but one of my clients is an oilman from Houston."

Nora was aghast and lowered her voice to a whisper. "You're in the black market?"

Matthew laughed. "No, sweetie, nothing as dramatic as that, I'm afraid. Actually, I'm here on business, and Jackie Helms—that's this fellow's name—paid my way. No gas shortage, no questions asked."

She shook her head and mirthfully struck him on the upper arm. "Well, do you always make it a habit of dropping in on folks unannounced?"

"Just those who are sure to turn bright red with embarrassment," he said, "and you're one of 'em." It was true. Nora's face was scarlet, and tears had come into her eyes.

"You haven't changed a bit, Matty. You still haven't grown up."

"Nope. Don't plan to, neither." He grinned at Elizabeth. "Mighty pretty playing, young lady."

"Thank you," the girl said.

"You sure don't take after your mama in that respect," he added. "I remember her piano lessons. Played the same song and nothing else for five or six years and never did get it right. What was the name of that selection?"

"The 'Largo' from *Xerxes*," she told him.

"By Handel or Haydn, one of them," Matthew said.

"Handel." Nora's face contorted into a grimace, as if recalling a painful memory. She turned to Elizabeth. "And your uncle's right, you know. I never was able to play that little piece properly. It used to drive my poor piano teacher batty."

Matthew looked at Elizabeth too. "Do you still play in the band?"

"No, sir. I have a job now, and that takes most of my free time."

"Is that so?" He stroked his chin in gentle dissent. "But it's not an 'either/or' proposition. Listen, missy, you can make big money playing music."

Nora frowned at her brother. "Now, don't you put foolish notions into her head," she said.

"But it's true. My college roommate paid for his whole education by playing the piano in clubs around Austin."

"Sure. And you saw what happened to him."

"That was years later, and it certainly wasn't music that did him in."

He raised his index finger to make a point, so Nora quickly changed the subject. "How long are you in town, Matty? I hope you're planning on staying with us."

"Nope. I've found other accommodations this time around. I know you've got a lodger, so I convinced old Mr. Helms to foot the bill for three nights at the Raleigh. He's a personal friend of Fred Smith, you know, so the rates aren't bad."

"Well, can you at least come to dinner with us?"

"Only if you promise to make some of your fried okra," he said.

Nora nodded her head in agreement. She could see Wesley across the room, walking toward them with a quizzical expression on his face. He and his friend, Morton Wilson, had been sitting with the Tower family, whose younger son, Reid, died of leukemia the previous winter. This weekly arrangement was the idea of the boys' Sunday school teacher, Joey Banks, who reasoned that Christian fellowship from someone roughly Reid's own age might comfort the parents in their time of grief. There was a sign-up sheet, and today was Wesley's and Morton's turn to, as Joey put it, "supply" as provisional sons. The Towers' older son, Horace—whom everyone called "Hog" because of his broad forehead and muscular build—was away at war and had been since February of 1942, along with the earliest influx of enlistees following the attack on Pearl Harbor.

"Wes, do you remember who this is?" Nora asked.

Wesley smiled and held out his left hand. "Sure, I do. Uncle Matt."

In response, Matthew offered his own left hand but then pulled it away as if in terror. "Son, haven't you learned that it's bad luck to shake with your left? That's the tool of the devil."

Wesley knew that his uncle was rarely serious in a public setting, so he laughed and extended his right hand as far as the sling would permit. This Matthew gladly shook. "How many autographs do you have on that thing?"

"Twenty-three, as of yesterday."

"Let's make it an even two dozen," Matthew told him. He pulled a writing instrument from the shirt pocket beneath his suit coat. Finally locating one of the few remaining blank spots on the cast, he signed "Matthew G. Coleman" in large, cursive letters, adding the words, "Quit slacking, Southpaw!"

Wesley was fascinated. "What is that?" he asked. His eyes followed his uncle's right hand.

Matthew feigned surprise and said, "Oh, this?" He opened his lapel and again produced the object of Wesley's interest. "It's a Biro pen." He handed it to the boy. "One of the accountants in our firm received it as a gift—all the way from Argentina."

Wesley turned the metallic object over and noticed the word "Eterpen."

"Here, try it out," Matthew said, and he offered his worship bulletin as a writing surface.

Wesley drew some loops with his left hand. "That's amazing."

"They say it'll write for a whole year without refilling."

"How does it work?"

"There's a tiny ball bearing in its tip—see?—and that applies the ink. It's quick-drying ink too. Watch." Matthew rubbed his index finger across Wesley's scribbling, and the ink did not smear.

"Wow!" Wesley said. With great reluctance, he handed the pen back to his uncle. "Are those for sale?"

"Nope, not yet. Some British pilots are using them in combat—high altitude stuff—but the general public won't be able to get them until the war's over. This one here's what they call a prototype—an experimental model."

Nora interrupted. "Well, if you two children are finished playing with your toy, maybe we should think about going home. I've got a chicken to bake, and I'd like to eat around two. Matty, does that suit you?"

Matthew patted his abdomen. "Sure does. You could probably hear my stomach growling from way up here in front."

She giggled. "Goodness! And I thought there was a dump truck going by."

That got Matthew's creative juices flowing. "You shouldn't say things like that, Mr. Benny," he said in his best Eddie Anderson voice. "Why not, Rochester?" came Jack Benny's response. "Because a dump truck sounds a lot better than your Maxwell, and people are starting to talk." The impersonations were accurate, dead center, masterful. "Well!" Jack said, looking off with indignation. "He's right, Mr. Benny," Dennis Day said. "The animal control squad just came and shot it, to put it out of its misery." And Rochester added, "It's still lying there at the curb, right where I parked it."

Matthew Coleman's theatrics did not reach much of an audience. The church was nearly empty by now, and the custodian was starting his rounds, pacing up the middle aisle in search of discarded worship bulletins and other debris to consign to his tattered sack. He waved shyly at Nora, who wiggled her fingers in reply.

"Come on. I'll walk you all out to the car," Matthew said. He stepped toward the rear exit.

But Nora did not follow him. "Where's your car?" she asked.

"Across the street, in front of my old chiropractor's house."

"Well, we're over here on the side, by the Catholic church."

"See you in a little while then," he said. "Wes, you want to ride with me?"

"Yes, sir." Wesley looked at his mother, who nodded her assent.

"What about you, princess?" Matthew asked. "I've got a new radio."

Elizabeth squinched her eyes. "Just as long as there's no flute music playing on it."

♦　　　♦　　　♦

That first Sunday in November was a rare instance when everybody in the extended Brower household, with the given exception of elder son Stephen, sat down together to partake in the Sabbath dinner. Steve, of course, was away in the service—at Pearl Harbor, as best the others could deduce from his expurgated letters. Somehow, his reference to a "hula dance" had evaded the censor's scissors, probably because of the sailor's illegible penmanship.

But everyone else was present at the table, including Nora's older brother, Matthew Coleman—up from Harlingen on a business trip—and the family's boarder, Hannah Lane. As the shift rotation fell that particular weekend, Hannah was excused from work for the entire day, something that had occurred on a Sunday only two times in the past five months, ever since she began her war work for Crawford-Austin Manufacturing Company in the middle of June. She was determined to make the most of her day off, studying for two imminent tests at Baylor University and catching up on her personal correspondence. Pastor Samuel Lane, her father in Mount Airy, North Carolina, had been ill for the past several days, so she was anxious to inquire about the status of his health.

It fell to Matthew, as presiding male at the table, to pronounce the blessing. He did so in a rich baritone that touched Nora's heart with a pang of regret that he had not entered the ministry, something he actually considered doing while still a teenager. Oddly enough, it was a Baptist preacher who talked him out of it. On a wintry Sunday evening in Fort Worth, Reverend Wendell Flowers, interim pastor of his church near campus, frankly advised the young man to abandon all desire to lead a congregation to Christ if he was unwilling to withdraw from the alcohol habit that had ensnared him since enrolling at TCU. While Matthew did not drink another bottle of beer after being espied at that fateful, off-campus party, neither did he ever again seriously ponder the notion of going to seminary— despite the personal entreaty of Southwestern President Lee Rutland Scarborough, who wrote him encouraging letters on two separate occasions.

Nora sat next to her brother, on the ovenward side of the table, so she could provide a steady supply of hot rolls during the meal. Hannah was across from her, with Elizabeth alongside. Wesley, being the "fifth wheel," was stationed at one cramped end of the table, between his sister and uncle. He constantly reminded himself to be vigilant not to knock his precariously positioned water glass onto his uncle's lap. The plaster cast was a clumsy dinner guest.

Just as the baked chicken breasts and thighs were being passed around, followed in close order by the steaming bowl of mashed potatoes and its accompanying gravy boat, the telephone rang, and Wesley jumped up to answer it.

Nora frowned. "Oh, dear, tell whoever it is that we just sat down to eat."

Matthew shook his head in disgust. "You know, we've stopped answering the phone when we're eating. It'd gotten to the point that we felt like adding a place-setting at the table just for the telephone." Elizabeth giggled, covering her mouth as she chewed.

"Honestly," Nora said. "You'd think people would have more consideration than to call at this hour on a Sunday afternoon." She surveyed the table in search of something more pleasant to occupy her thoughts, and her brother's plate caught her eye. "Matty, that okra came right out of our very own victory garden, so please help us eat it up."

"With pleasure." He transported another forkful into his mouth. The delicacy was breaded and then deep fried with diced potatoes and onions, just the way their mother used to make it back home in Belton. "So, tell me," he said through a mouthful of food, "how long have you been in the farming business?"

Nora shook her head. "The children started the garden about a year and a half ago—all three of them—but it seems like I've inherited most of the harvesting chores since then."

"Yes, indeed. Funny how that works," Matthew said. He winked at his niece. "Well, don't feel too bad. Bucky and Georgina are the same way." After stirring a level teaspoon of precious sugar into his iced tea, he noticed the cat's sudden appearance. "Can I give him a bite of chicken, Sis?"

"Oh, no," Nora said, "we don't give him table scraps—never have. The veterinarian told us he'll live longer that way."

"But he won't die with a smile on his face like our feline will. Babs has her spoiled rotten."

"What's her name?" Elizabeth asked.

"Bucky named her Priscilla Longhair when she was just a kitten, but we usually call her Prissy for short. She's white as snow."

Elizabeth smiled. "Mother named our cat after some old movie star."

"Some old movie star?" Nora said. "I'll have you know, young lady, that Rudolph Valentino was a combination of Clark Gable and Errol Flynn, if you can imagine anything so wonderful. He was the original matinée idol."

Matthew laughed. "According to lovelorn females between the ages of ten and fifty anyway." He became serious when Wesley returned to the dining room wearing a solemn expression.

"That was Mrs. Johns on the telephone," the boy said. He glanced at his mother. "She said one of your friend's sons died."

Nora wiped her mouth and laid the napkin down on her untouched knife and spoon. "Is she still on the line?" She scooted her chair back to stand.

"No. She said she was sorry to call during dinnertime, but she thought you should know."

"Well, did she say who it was?" Nora braced herself for the sad news.

"Someone named Tommy. I told her you'd call her back."

"Tommy Frost? Not Linda Frost's boy!"

Wesley nodded his head and sat down. "That was it. Tommy Frost."

"Are you sure?"

"Yes, ma'am."

Wesley's uncle cleared his throat and asked him, "Was he in the service, son?"

"Search me. I've never even heard of him."

Nora's face had turned pale. "Sure you have. He used to fix your bicycle spokes and broken chains. He lived over on Gorman, near the kennel. You were always afraid to ride past the barking dogs."

The thought embarrassed him, and he looked at his uncle and then quickly away. "That was when I was a baby. You make it sound like I'm still afraid of them."

"You were only five or six, I think. Oh, dear Lord—Tommy Frost." Nora took a swallow of water, and her hand was shaking so much that her wedding ring clinked rhythmically against the glass. "He was just one grade ahead of ... He joined the Navy, not even a year ago."

"Do you think we should take her some food?" Elizabeth asked.

"No, dear. It's much too early for that. Besides, we don't even know for sure that it's true." She turned to Wesley, who was spreading white margarine on a puffy yeast roll. "Are you positive that's what Mrs. Johns said?"

"Yes, ma'am. She said it twice. I just couldn't remember the last name."

"Dear me. Poor Linda," she said, and her eyes were inflamed with emotion. "Maybe I should call Mabel now, just to double-check."

Suddenly, Hannah spoke up, but very quietly. "Why don't you let me go see her?" she asked.

Nora looked surprised. "What in the world for, child? Do you know Linda Frost?"

"No, ma'am, but I knew her son."

Nora laughed nervously. "You must be mistaken, dear. He was in the service long before you ever came to Texas."

"I think I knew him."

"Tommy Frost? A tall, lanky boy with red hair?"

"Yes, ma'am."

Nora was at a loss for words, shaking her head in confusion. "I don't understand," she said. "Where did you know Tommy Frost? Back in North Carolina?"

"No, ma'am. I was his serviceman's pen pal at church. I wrote to him at least three times a month." Hannah's jaw was beginning to tremble, and her voice became hollow. "I almost felt like he was a personal friend. He even sent me a picture of his unit in San Diego, his training outfit."

"San Diego ..." Nora whispered, and she turned to look at Wesley.

Matthew leaned forward and said, "Well, if you two ladies don't mind me butting in with my big mouth, I'd like to stress that the first thing you need to do—both of you—is be one hundred percent sure that this Tommy fellow is really deceased. Don't do anything until you've established that fact beyond a shadow of a doubt. Call the Red Cross. Call his church pastor. Call the War Department. My secretary's sister-in-law got a letter of condolence from some danged busybody who mixed up the names, and it nearly terrified her to death."

"Yes, he's right," Nora said to her boarder. "Let's all just try to enjoy our Sunday dinner, and I'll call Mabel after we're finished. I want to find out where she heard about poor Tommy."

But she did not call Mabel Johns that afternoon. Soon after Wesley and Elizabeth cleared the table, Nora was busy washing the dishes when the telephone rang again. It was Madeleine Givens, calling from the USO to say that a Reverend Paulson had notified her of the death of Tommy Frost—killed in the Solomons during naval action in support of American troops landing at Bougainville. Sad to say, this was reliable confirmation, for Isaac Paulson was pastor of First Lutheran Church, where the Frost family had been members since moving to Waco from Wichita Falls in 1929.

Nora did not remember ever hearing Steve mention the young man's name, so she was not absolutely certain that they knew one other. Tommy was not involved in athletics, and it was conceivable that the two never even met. Still, his death hit Nora very hard, causing her to become uncharacteristically quiet and pensive for the next couple of days. She would bring solace to Linda Frost, yes, just as she hoped others would do for her if—God forbid—the unthinkable happened to the Brower family.

Thomas Peter Frost. Born December 23, 1923, died November 2, 1943. Graduated from Waco High School. Employed by R. T. Dennis & Co., Inc. Enlisted in United States Navy. Killed by enemy fire in Solomon Islands. War Bonds in lieu of flowers.

◆　　◆　　◆

When Wesley returned to work on Monday afternoon, the radio station was abuzz with exciting news. Three managerial personnel had been invited by the Columbia Broadcasting System to attend the network's winter meetings, which were to take place the following February in Los Angeles. It seemed to him an odd time for KWXN to receive its first CBS-West beckoning, what with wartime travel restrictions and all, but he had noticed—with something akin to pride— that the broadcasting industry always seemed to be exempt from such mundane considerations as the present global conflict.

Evidently, owner Brantley B. Wollach and station manager Clive Ramey would be making the trip, and so would director Hugh Kenton, who was being groomed for lower management after six years of loyal service in the control room. Myra Culp, the receptionist, was a wealth of information on the subject, and Wesley discovered from her that the three men would be gone for a period of two weeks, traveling by rail on Pullman sleepers, in the company of similar CBS operatives from both the Austin and Dallas/Fort Worth markets. There was a chance that they could meet some of the top stars in radio—people like Judy Canova, Lionel Barrymore, and Kate Smith.

"Who would direct our local shows while Mr. Kenton is gone?" Wesley asked.

Myra lowered her voice to a confidential volume. "Don't tell anyone," she said, "but I think Marshall McFall is interested."

Wesley was astonished. "Marshall McFall—a director?" He said it much louder than he intended, drawing some stares from a departing group of fifth graders across the lobby. "What about Hatch?" he whispered. Wesley had a point. Hatch Priggett was Hugh Kenton's assistant and therefore the logical choice to handle the directing chores in his absence.

"All I can tell you is the scuttlebutt, and I've heard that Kenton thinks it's about time Marshall McFall tries out his angel's wings on the other side of the mike." Clearly, there was no love lost between her and the announcer, whom she sometimes derided as "Young Orson." In truth, McFall, at twenty-six, was only a couple of years behind the august Mr. Welles.

"Well, that should be a fun experience," Wesley said.

There was a tone of irony in his voice, which did not escape Myra's notice. She took a sip of coffee, then squinted her eyes and smiled. "You got a rift going with Marshall?"

"I guess you could say that."

"Well, what gives?"

Wesley shrugged his shoulders and glanced away. "Oh, nothing really. He just got kind of fresh with a girl I know."

"That pretty little thing you brought in here with you?"

A look of surprise came across his face, and he paused for a moment before answering. "Yeah, Sandy Whittsel. I forgot you met each other."

"She was lovely," Myra said. "I don't blame you for being upset."

Wesley sensed that the conversation had taken a wrong turn, so he scrambled to clarify one issue before it, too, became grist for the station's rumor mill. "Uh, Sandy's not my girlfriend or anything." His manner was too defensive by half for such an astute observer as Myra Culp.

"No, I understand," she said with a wink. "You just wanted your school chum to see the radio station." She leaned back in her chair, cradling the cup of coffee in both hands.

"That's right. I gave her a tour of the studio." Wesley wished the telephone would ring, but of course it did not.

"So, how does Marshall McFall figure into all of this?" the receptionist asked.

"Well, I just don't appreciate the way he's been trying to take advantage of her innocence."

Best efforts to the contrary, he now had Myra Culp's undivided attention. "What happened?" She could scarcely conceal her delight.

Wesley glanced around the lobby and lowered his voice again. "I caught them together in the announcing booth, but that wasn't the half of it."

"Here at the radio station? She doesn't work here, does she?"

"Not yet," he said, "but if he had his way, I'm sure she would."

"Has she applied for a job?"

"Yeah, only I don't think they'd ever really consider hiring her. She doesn't have any experience at all."

"Neither did you, as I recall."

"But I wanted to be an announcer. They're not going to hire some girl for that."

"Just how fresh did he get?" Myra asked. She laid her coffee cup on the desk and took a pack of Chesterfields from her purse.

"Fresh enough to make her cry. I think she's afraid of him now."

Myra bent forward and smiled. "He got fresh with her in the announcing booth? With all those glass windows?"

"No, I'm talking about something else that happened a couple of weeks later—just last Wednesday night."

Her eyes widened. "I wonder what he did. Do you know?"

He sensed that a white lie was in order. "No, and I don't really care."

The receptionist flicked her lighter and took a shallow drag of the cigarette, barely inhaling at all. Its tip glowed red for just an instant.

Wesley felt that he had already divulged far too much for comfort, so he was happy to sight the portly figure of Michael Dill, evidently conversing with some of the girls in traffic. "Mickey," he shouted down the hallway. With a quick nod, he excused himself from Myra Culp and improvised a credible question for the loitering salesman.

Myra watched him walk away and made a mental note to explore more fully this matter of Marshall McFall and pretty Sandy What's-Her-Name. Just then the telephone's insistent ring diverted her thoughts momentarily, and Wesley's unaccountable failure to pass by the front desk on his way to the studio caused her to forget the intriguing affair for the time being.

That afternoon's installment of "Behold Tomorrow" had only a small part for Kip Hanson. In fact, a single line was all that Wesley had to prepare: "I don't think he can do anything about it ... not without getting a green light from the boys uptown."

Secretly, he enjoyed days such as this. Though professionally unfulfilling, they provided him an occasional release from the chronic anxiety that plagued neophytes to the announcing trade. It was, after all, a stressful calling to open one's mouth in front of a microphone for all of central Texas to hear. While Wesley would never admit his uneasiness to anybody else, as many times as he had been on the air—about an hour and a quarter per week for nearly eleven months—he still continued to suffer badly from what was commonly known in the trade as "mike fright." He was careful to conceal his weakness from others, choosing instead to regard those around him with envy, wondering how long his private case of jitters would persist. Nobody else was similarly afflicted—either that or they, too, were hiding their shame.

Just before three o'clock, as the cast members were gathering around their microphone stands, Hugh Kenton was on hands and knees in the studio, securing a dangerously entangling cable to the floor with cellulose tape. Waiting close-by with script in hand, Neddy Wright asked him whether the rumors were true, that the show would be without its regular director for two full weeks in February.

Kenton did not look up from his task. "That remains to be seen," he said. "I hope so, but nothing's for sure yet."

Phyllis Sherry frowned. "Well, that's a nice thing to say!"

"You know what I mean," the director told her. He lopped off a piece of tape with his penknife. "It'll be an exciting trip. And anyway, Hatch can handle things perfectly well if I'm gone."

So Myra was wrong after all, thought Wesley with relief. He would not be delivered into Marshall McFall's vengeful hands while the Waco triumvirate was out on the west coast, cavorting amidst the swaying palm trees of southern California.

♦   ♦   ♦

Even in wartime, planet Earth continues to rotate steadily on its clockwork axis, such that islands dotting the western Pacific Ocean witness the arrival of each new day a full seventeen hours before it is introduced to the American heartland. So it was that November 11 of 1943 had come and gone from that war-ravaged area by the time citizens of Waco, Texas, were awakening to greet the first sunlight of Armistice Day.

In any case, the special occasion held little significance for US forces laying siege to the volcanic graveyards of East New Britain and Bougainville. A cynic among them might have bellyached that the word "armistice" was no longer in his vocabulary. If indeed a truce had been declared in and around the Bismarck Archipelago, it was bitterly clear that no one had bothered to tell the belligerents.

During fierce naval action on that day, an American carrier-borne attack on the mammoth base at Rabaul produced seventy aircraft kills, along with the disablement of two Japanese destroyers and a light cruiser. Two distinct task forces, under Admirals Frederick Sherman and Alfred Montgomery, launched the surprise strikes, spearheaded by nearly two hundred planes from the decks of five carriers. Meanwhile, off to the east in the Solomon Islands, the US 3rd Marine Division was pushing back the Japanese 23rd Regiment on Bougainville.

In faraway McLennan County, Texas, sunrise would not occur until 7:55, Central War Time, so inhabitants of the late Harold Brower's two-story dwelling arose before daylight. It was fair outside but only thirty-six degrees Fahrenheit, and the full moon provided a ghostly illumination. Nora was in the kitchen, preparing a breakfast of toast and scrambled eggs (from powder) for Elizabeth and herself. Wesley liked to alternate between hot cereal and cold cereal, and today was a cooked cereal day for him. He had enjoyed Ralston Hot Cereal for as long as he could remember, even before he became an official Tom Mix Straight Shooter, pestering his mother for box-top offers from the T-Bar-M Ranch. Hannah was already away at

Baylor, having ridden to campus early with owlish Clinton Harris, the class genius with whom she planned to study for their Old Testament History exam.

As was Wesley's daily custom upon arriving downstairs, he went directly to the front door and retrieved the *News-Tribune* from the walkway. It galled him that the "replacement" paperboy could throw his product with much greater accuracy, in any weather conditions, than he himself had been able to manage on the most windless of mornings. He laid the newspaper on the breakfast table and seated himself near the kitchen radio, which was tuned to "News of the World" on Dallas station KRLD. "The Texas Rangers" would be coming on at 7:15.

"I sure wish we got out of school on Armistice Day," he said, and his sister nodded in agreement. Elizabeth was standing by the table, transferring homework sheets from her geography textbook into a file folder.

"We used to when I was in high school—my last three years," their mother said. "But of course that was when the Great War was still fresh on people's minds." She fluffed the eggs in the frying pan. "How soon they forget."

"Are you going to the parade today?" Wesley asked. "Mort's mother will be riding a horse in it."

Nora could not help but laugh. "Mrs. Wilson will be riding their horse in a parade?" She turned to see if her son was serious.

"Yes, ma'am. Someone in the Longhorn Club asked her to ride with them. There's a horse show this afternoon, and they wanted her to ride Molly in the pre-show parade."

"Somehow I just can't picture that—Hazel Wilson riding in the Armistice Day parade. What time does it start?"

Wesley unfolded the newspaper and found the answer staring at him from the front page. "Eleven o'clock, it says." His eyes skimmed down the article. "The horse show starts at two—in that arena over by the circle."

Nora's expression grew darker, as if a half-forgotten thought had resurfaced in her mind. "I heard that poor Linda Frost will also be in the parade," she said, "riding in one of the automobiles with the other gold star mothers. Dear me, it's hard to believe that Tommy's really gone."

Elizabeth tried to nudge the topic in another direction. "Florence Jurgen is riding a horse in the parade too," she said to her brother, "and she's the youngest one invited."

Wesley had a blank look. "Who?"

"Florence Jurgen, the tall girl who plays basketball. You've seen her. She got permission to skip school for two hours today."

Nora sighed. "Tommy Frost would have been twenty years old next month. I remember that he was born just a couple days before Christmas, so they always celebrated his birthday in June."

Elizabeth spoke up again. "Did you see yesterday's paper, Mother?" she asked. "Some lady in Waco heard her son talking on coast-to-coast radio."

"Yes, and wasn't that a marvelous thing?" Nora had her back to her daughter, spooning the eggs onto two plates. Golden-brown slices of toast, already spread with margarine, warmed themselves face-up on the edge of the stovetop.

This new topic of conversation captured Wesley's attention. "What's that about radio?" he asked. On the hot pad in front of him sat a bowl of cooked cereal, but he possessed enough table etiquette not to start eating alone.

"Someone heard her son's voice over the radio," Elizabeth said, "from out in California. Did you know the lady, Mother?"

Nora brought the plates of eggs and toast over to the table, along with a knife for spreading the orange marmalade. "No, I didn't recognize the name. Yesterday's paper is still on the counter, I think."

Elizabeth found the Wednesday paper and flipped through it until she located the news report on page six. "Here it is," she said.

"Let's say our prayer first," Nora told her, and she took her seat with the others. Together the family paused, with eyes closed, to recite a nursery rhyme that sufficed for saying grace whenever the boarder or guests were not present:

Thank you for the world so sweet;
Thank you for the food we eat.
Thank you for the birds that sing;
Thank you, God, for everything.
For Jesus's sake, amen.

"It's a real short article," Elizabeth said as her mother and brother commenced eating. Glancing at Wesley, she read it aloud: "While Mrs. P. O. Adams, 1308 North Fifteenth Street, was listening to the radio program 'Breakfast at Sardi's' Tuesday morning over the Blue Network through station WACO, she heard her son, Art Adams, Seaman First Class, who was one of the servicemen interviewed on the program. Seaman Adams has recently completed a training course at San Diego and was spending his furlough in Hollywood, where the program originated."

"You know, the Blue Network isn't owned by NBC anymore," Wesley told his sister.

But Nora's thoughts were elsewhere. "Wasn't that a wonderful surprise for her?" she said.

Elizabeth smiled, and Wesley nodded his head. Both knew full well what their mother was thinking. Steve's most recent letter had arrived home five days ago— six, if the postman were to bring nothing with the morning delivery.

Nora's spoon circled rhythmically in stirring her coffee. "I would give anything to hear Steve's voice now."

"Maybe he'll send you one of those records that they have at the USO," Wesley told her.

"No, I hardly think so."

"He might," Elizabeth said. "I'll bet most of the posts have them."

Nora had a far-off look in her eyes, watching the birds hop about in the leafless hackberry tree nearest the rear window. "But this was different. This was live, from all the way out in California." The wind had picked up, and some twigs were tapping a gentle rhythm on the corner of the house.

Wesley, rolling a hot mouthful of cereal around his mouth to keep his tongue from burning, managed to say, "Well, Steve could go to Sardi's sometime." His mother only shook her head, so he added, "It's possible, you know."

Though Nora found the youngsters' innocence endearing, she was honest enough with herself to temper their optimism. "I wish you were right, children, but he's not exactly on a vacation trip, you know. Mr. Moek told me he'd guess that Steve would be shipping out about now. Maybe he's already gone. I don't know when he'll ever get another furlough—maybe not until after this war is over."

Wesley nodded his understanding, but Elizabeth's eyes filled with tears. She looked down at her plate, hoping nobody had noticed. This was an unhappy breakfast for both of the Brower children, and for once it came as a relief to leave the house for school. Thoughts of Steve remained with them through much of the morning, until distractions in the daily routine finally guided their attention to other, less personal concerns.

Elizabeth was in civics class and Wesley in Latin when, at 10:39, the fire alarm began to clang. Such training was a common enough occurrence, so evacuation of the schoolrooms was swift and orderly. By an odd coincidence, however, just as the pupils had filed from the building and lined up with their teachers outside the rear entrance, a trio of heavy bombers roared overhead and caused some in the student ranks to fear that the two events—fire drill and fly over—were somehow related. One startled freshman in Elizabeth's class even screamed for an instant, before quelling the mental gaffe by throwing both hands over her mouth.

Back inside, Ramona Eccles teased her mercilessly until Mrs. Alammin, from far across the room, saw the callous behavior and snuffed it out with a single, frosty glare.

◆　　◆　　◆

She felt silly, a grown woman behaving like a grammar-school girl. This was the second time that Giulia Coletti had made the walk over to the corner mailbox to post her letter. She looked around, hoping that nobody was in close enough proximity to notice her childish indecision. It was more than a week now since she had gotten Stephen Brower's FPO address from his mother, and she still had not worked up sufficient courage to drop the tiny envelope into that ominous collection box.

This was not a moment to be taken lightly. Once the note had left her fingers, sliding down the metal chute into irretrievable darkness, her life might be changed forever. Surely it would be wise to reread the letter just one more time, maybe tone it down a smidgen, dilute her feelings to the point of noncommittal chattiness. "Stephen," she would write, "you probably don't remember me, but ..."

A bit ashamed of herself, Giulia turned to walk home, purposefully tearing open the envelope so she would not be tempted to do something rash at such a significant crossroads in her young life. No, if she ever mailed this letter, she wanted it to be legitimized by clear-headed action and not cheapened by an impulsive whim.

She would rewrite, craft, and finely hone the message, such that it could be taken either of two ways—patriotic if he felt nothing for her or had forgotten her entirely, flirtatious if he harbored even the least bit of latent affection for that timid brunette in chemistry class.

Upon returning home, she lay on her bed and opened the rejected draft, scanning it for perhaps the twentieth traversal. By now, the words seemed meaningless to her. So many times had she attempted to digest the content that her mind had masticated it into an amorphous pulp. Too obvious, she thought, and then, a moment later, too ambiguous. She sensed the need to remove herself for a while and then resume the task when her creative juices were flowing more freely. But her interest in the sailor lately had become a fixation, and she felt unable to think of anything else.

Bringing further complication to this already difficult process was a framed photograph of her putative intended—Sergeant Archie Clarke—watching her every move from an unnerving distance of less than twelve feet. She felt like a deceitful wretch under his accusative eye, but somehow it seemed more honest this way than to rest the photograph face down on the dresser. At least she was communing with Steve forthrightly, and whatever happened was meant to be.

"Giulia," came a call from her mother's bedroom.

"Yes, Mamma."

"Come in here for a moment, will you?" Her mother had a painful back ailment—diagnosed by doctors as a degenerative vertebrae condition—that made it difficult for her to walk, so she often summoned Giulia by the pragmatic means of shouting across the modest length of their house.

"What is it, Mamma?" Giulia asked when she arrived in her mother's room.

Paolina Coletti was lying on her back, atop a heating pad, and the door to her closet was open with the light on. "Promise me that you'll never get old, 'Bina."

"I promise, Mamma," Giulia said with a giggle. "Should I go out and throw myself off a bridge?"

Her mother frowned. "You know good and well what I mean. Look at me. I'm a pathetic sight."

"I'm sorry. It just sounded funny the way you put it."

"Would you mind finding my olive blouse?" Paolina pointed to the closet. "I looked through all my tops three times—until I finally had to lie down."

"Your good blouse? Where are you planning to go?" One by one, Giulia began hunting through a forest of garments suspended on coat hangers from a long wooden rod. "I don't think you've worn most of this stuff in fifteen years," she said. "It smells like mothballs in here."

"When you find it, would you please iron it for me, dear?"

"Yes, Mamma, but you still haven't told me where you're going."

"That's because it's none of your business," came the reply.

Giulia stepped from the closet and peered at her mother to see if she was serious. "Well, you don't have to get nasty about it. I'm just interested in your welfare."

Her mother laughed. "Can't you tell when I'm teasing?"

"Not when you're down in your back. You can get pretty spiteful when you're like this." She reentered the closet to continue her search.

"It's really no secret," Paolina said. "I'm going to help Mrs. Reimann at a war-bond booth."

"Oh?"

"At one of the movie houses—I forget which one. She's going to pick me up at 1:30."

"Aren't we going to mass tonight?"

"I'll be home by six. One of the other workers can't be there, so Mrs. Reimann asked me to help out."

"Ta-duh!" Giulia said in triumph. She held the greenish blouse in front of her face and then raised it like a theater curtain. "It was caught between two other tops, and the hangers were tangled."

"Thank you, sweetie. I guess I never would have found it."

"Well, maybe not before the war ended anyway." Giulia laid the blouse on the edge of the bed. "Will Mrs. Brower be there today?"

"Who's Mrs. Brower? Do I know her?"

"Sure, you do, Mamma. Don't be so silly. She's the sister of Matthew Coleman—the man who used to do those skits for us at the bazaar. She owns Superior Office Supply."

Paolina looked suspiciously at her daughter. "That football player's mother?"

Giulia smoothed the blouse with the palm of her hand. "I think so."

"No, I don't suppose she'll be there, but I can't say for sure. Why do you ask?"

"No reason. I was just wondering who the other workers would be."

"I haven't seen Mrs. Brower in a couple of years. What was her first name?"

"Nora." Giulia said it far too readily. She looked at her mother, who nodded her head but said nothing. Giulia picked up the blouse and turned away. "I'll have this ready for you in a jiffy."

"And don't forget to unplug the iron when you're finished."

"I won't." She left the room, and her thoughts returned to that stubborn letter that would not allow itself to be written.

Giulia ironed the delicate blouse with fastidious care, but her mind was focused squarely on Stephen Brower. In her romantically idealized vision, he was tall, strong, and handsome, infallible and of exemplary character. Odd that she should see him so clearly now, given that in real life they had been but passing acquaintances in the lab, lunchroom, and hallway. She sighed with a self-deprecating smile.

Just after noon, Giulia placed her weekly telephone call to East Waco, where her father had been living ever since the estrangement. She spoke to him with a chilly detachment in her voice, and surely he could detect that something was troubling her. Later, as Giulia prepared lunch for her mother and herself, all she could think of was her Waco High schoolmate, now away in the Navy. Never before had she felt like this about anyone, and her obsession took the girl completely by surprise. There was nothing like this in her frame of reference. It was almost frightening, as if her mental faculties were out of control.

When Paolina Coletti and her friend, Frances Reimann, left for their war-bond duties downtown, Giulia found herself alone in the house at last, and she again sat down to write the long-postponed letter. Much to her despair, it was then that her mind became a fuzzy blur. Her conception of Stephen Brower dissipated into a wispy abstraction, and as hard as she tried, even on the verge of tears, the words simply would not come. "Dear Lord," she thought, "what is the matter with me?" After forty-five minutes of intense effort and four false starts, she succumbed to a sense of resignation, adopting the philosophical attitude that such a flighty affection for a Protestant boy clearly was not the will of God.

But Giulia Coletti, by nature, was possessed of a far more cheerful spirit than that, and her deference to such a defeatist notion did not persist for long. Early the next evening, while sunset was turning to dusk, she felt satisfied with what she had written. She marched to the mailbox and, without any hesitation, dropped the envelope inside, enjoying the pleasant finality of the handled door's loud metal clap. She had no second thoughts whatsoever, never once bothering to look back over her shoulder as she returned home.

Just as she had hoped, the finished product was a bit patriotic and a bit flirtatious, a benignly noncommittal communiqué from "Yours truly, Giulia Coletti, Mrs. Chesky's Chemistry Lab—remember? 'Bye."

◆   ◆   ◆

KWXN management treated Thanksgiving as just another workday for the news department and on-air personnel. The same could be said for engineers and production folks, if they happened to be associated with either of the two serials that the station transmitted on a daily basis. More fortunate when it came to paid holidays were the office staff, the salesmen, and it goes without saying, management itself.

And yet Wesley knew that he had little cause for complaint, inasmuch as he was embarking upon a four-day respite from Waco High attendance. By contrast, Baylor University students received only Thanksgiving Day off, while resuming their classes on Friday. That inconsistency came as a disappointment to Hannah, who naturally presumed that Baylor observed a schedule similar to that of the local public schools.

The Brower family's holiday meal would be a little earlier than customary this year. Nora was aware that Wesley needed to head for the radio station by two o'clock, so she planned to have the turkey dinner ready to serve shortly after one. Elizabeth, too, like her brother, needed to eat and run, for her afternoon included a six-hour stint of volunteer service at the USO.

The other youthful resident of the household, Hannah Lane, could not be there at all to partake in the traditional feast. Thanksgiving meant valuable production time for a vital war contractor like Crawford-Austin, and Hannah was slated to work the day shift. On the brighter side, there would be plenty of leftovers to be heated up when the boarder returned home at a quarter past four. No doubt she would be famished by then, especially with all of the flavorful delicacies preying on her mind throughout the day.

While Elizabeth was setting the table and then helping her mother to transport dish after savory dish over from the stove, Wesley had been granted the privilege of lounging in front of the Philco console. The dial was tuned to 1080 kilocycles, KRLD in Dallas, for CBS's long-running serial, "Young Doctor Malone," a melodramatic saga of Jerry and Ann of Three Oaks. This was not one of Wesley's favorite programs—he preferred many a juvenile action show—but it was the best thing on at one o'clock, when he normally was in school, and it certainly did beat doing women's work. Whenever his sister and mother were bustling around the kitchen, he only seemed to get in their way.

Slightly more than a half-hour later, after the lavish meal was consumed in what seemed like a flurry, Nora excused Wesley from drying the dishes because she knew this was about the only time of the year when he had college football on his mind. For most American males, eating far too much food was a well-established routine at Thanksgiving, and so was listening to gridiron action on the radio. In the Lone Star State, this annual indulgence meant the Texas-Texas A&M game. Tuning in would be the true sports enthusiasts, of course, but also a good number of otherwise halfhearted fans, such as Wesley Brower. In normal times, he casually followed the exploits of the Baylor Bears, but now that the hometown team was "hibernating" for the duration of the war, he shifted his allegiance a hundred miles south and rooted for the Longhorns instead.

Unfortunately for him, kickoff in College Station would not occur until two o'clock, the very time he would be getting ready to leave for work, so during the interim Wesley tuned the dial to 1490 kc, hoping to pick up KNOW in Austin for the quarter-hour "Gridiron Warm-Up." Although providing a marginal signal at best for Waco listeners, that station was his only choice for pre-game coverage until 1:45, which was when San Antonio's WOAI, a clear-channel station at 1200 kc, would conclude its broadcast of "The Light of the World" and begin carrying an audio feed from the Kyle Field press box. Wesley was able to improve the reception of both stations somewhat by connecting an external antenna, but the signal still faded in and out virtually at will. Happily, game time itself posed no such problem for Wacoans, thanks to a reliably strong signal from WBAP (Fort Worth) and WFAA (Dallas) on their shared frequency of 820 kc, and that is how he heard the first few minutes of the game on the Chevy's dashboard radio. Indeed, he was listening when Ralph Park scampered around right end for a six-yard Texas touchdown just three minutes into the contest, giving the Longhorns an early 7-0 lead.

Football was nowhere to be heard in the Coletti home, across town in the southern reaches of Waco, as Paolina and her daughter enjoyed a quiet, uneventful Thanksgiving dinner together. Giulia was off work for the holiday, so she relaxed, played the piano a bit, and invested some time reading a fairly recent best seller called *Our Hearts Were Young and Gay* by Cornelia Otis Skinner and Emily Kimbrough. This being a family occasion, she also made it a point to telephone her father in East Waco.

Only a few short blocks from the Brower home stood that of the Moeks, who, though immigrants, observed Thanksgiving in quite a similar fashion to most other Americans. Gertrude was a marvelous cook, and this Germanic couple certainly had the stout physiques to prove it. Today she was fixing enough food for two additional adults and three hungry youngsters. Their daughter, Anneliese, was there from Boerne with her husband, Ross Lipphardt, and their four children. This was the first time that Grandpa and Grandma had ever seen five-month-old Sherry, who was born in Temple at the end of June.

When Anneliese offered to help with the food preparation, her mother politely told her, "You just take care of d'e kids, Liesel. D'at in itself is more work d'an one person should have." Truth be told, this is precisely the way Gertrude preferred to cook—by herself, with no interference or meddlesome assistance from anyone, even her own daughter. And all the while that she labored in the kitchen, the radio was Gertrude's constant companion. There was the dramatic "Judy Jordan, MD," followed by a game show called "Ladies Be Seated" (with hosts Ed East and his wife, Polly), and then two popular serials, "Judy and Jane" (already with eleven years under its belt) and the upstart "A Woman of America" (still in its maiden season).

Her husband, Hermann, was an avid fan of every major sport, but he followed college football perhaps closest of all—and particularly the variable fortunes of Texas A&M. Ross Lipphardt was an Aggie himself, holding a degree in mechanical engineering, so that left little doubt as to what the men would be doing on their Thanksgiving afternoon. But Gertrude put her foot down about one thing: there would be absolutely no listening to the football broadcast until the meal was finished. Never did two grown men eat so much food so fast.

At the completion of dessert, Hermann was finally granted command of the airwaves, with him and his son-in-law loudly cheering for the youthful Aggies' aerial attack to upset the veteran Longhorns' vaunted ground game. They joined the broadcast in progress, with Texas holding a slim 7-0 lead midway through the first quarter, but then the Longhorns jumped to a 13-0 lead when Jim Callahan tallied on a one-yard plunge before ten minutes had elapsed. The Aggies fought back and trimmed the lead to 13-7 late in the first quarter when Abilene's speedy Red Burditt raced for a twenty-eight-yard touchdown on the old hidden-ball trick. A&M tied the game early in the second quarter as Babe Hallmark shot over left tackle for a broken-field, thirty-four-yard sprint to the end zone. Not to be outdone, the Longhorns pulled ahead at the half, 20-13, on Ralph Park's twenty-yard run and then a drop-kicked extra point by former water boy Billy Andrews.

The second half settled into a defensive struggle until Park returned Bing Turner's punt for an apparent fifty-three-yard Texas touchdown. This turn of events discouraged Hermann and Ross momentarily, but their spirits soared again when they learned that the touchdown had been nullified by a roughing-the-kicker penalty. It was to be a temporary reprieve. Not long thereafter, A&M hearts were broken for good by the game's turning point when Ralph Ellsworth intercepted a Hallmark pass on the Texas six-yard-line, just as the Aggies were threatening to even the score. The Longhorns hit pay dirt again with three minutes remaining when

Callahan powered in from the one-yard-line for an insurance tally that stood up at the final gun. And thus, by a score of 27-13, did Coach Dana Bible's Longhorns secure their second consecutive Southwest Conference title and an invitation to the Cotton Bowl on January 1.

Aggie fans like Hermann Moek and Ross Lipphardt had to be content with the knowledge that their inexperienced team, under Homer Norton's leadership, did far better in the 1943 season than anybody thought possible, with a very respectable record of 7-2-1.

◆ ◆ ◆

While the Browers, the Colettis, the Moeks, and other local residents were enjoying a bountiful Thanksgiving, blessed to live in a nation securely protected from enemy attack, they did so without the grievous knowledge that their hometown had lost its most celebrated naval war hero on the previous morning. Though this dreadful event occurred far out in the Pacific Ocean, more than six thousand miles from Waco, Texas, it would prove to have a lasting impact on the city.

On November 24, 1943, the day before Thanksgiving, reveille sounded at 0430 aboard the Casablanca-class escort carrier *Liscome Bay* (CVE-56), and her crew of 863 reported to general quarters at 0505. It was the beginning of the fifth day of Operation Galvanic, a US naval and air offensive to liberate Makin in the Gilbert Islands. This particular "baby flattop" carried twenty-eight torpedo bombers and fighters from Air Support Group 52.3, commanded by Rear Admiral Henry Maston Mullinnix.

USS Liscome Bay was a relatively young vessel, launched from the Kaiser Shipbuilding Company in Vancouver, Washington, just seven months earlier, on April 19. She engaged in training operations off the west coast before departing San Diego for Hawaii on October 21. When she left Pearl Harbor three weeks later, on November 10, it was as part of Task Force 52, Northern Attack Force, under Rear Admiral Richard K. Turner. She would perform commendably in what was to be her first and only battle mission.

For three grueling days, beginning at dawn on November 20, carrier-launched planes flew 2,278 sorties, pounding the heavily fortified island with thousands of bombs and destroying Japanese gun emplacements, shore installations, air bases, and troop concentrations in support of an invasion by Major General Ralph C. Smith's 27th Infantry Division.

On November 23, the silent depths off Makin were visited by Japanese Kaidai VI-class submarine *I-175*, superintended by Commander Sunao Tabata, following a hasty journey from Truk naval base in the Caroline Islands. *Liscome Bay* and her two sister ships, *Coral Sea* and *Corregidor*, were steaming about twenty miles southwest of Butaritari Island. Radar from battleship *New Mexico* detected the intruder's presence, but the submarine managed to dive to safety.

The next day, as flight crews aboard *Liscome Bay* were preparing their aircraft for daybreak launchings, *I-175* fired four torpedoes at the carrier. One struck the flattop's starboard side near the engine room, producing a deadly explosion. Soon the aircraft bomb magazine went up, and—fed by aviation fuel—the ship's interior became engulfed in flames. Some 200,000 pounds of bombs detonated *en masse*, raising a fireball of smoke that towered at least a thousand feet in the air.

At 0533, twenty-three minutes after the initial blast, the disintegrating escort carrier *Liscome Bay* listed to starboard and sank, taking with her Admiral Mullinnix, Captain Irving Day Wiltsie, fifty-three other officers, and 591 enlisted men. Only 272 of her crew were rescued. Five of the doomed ship's twenty-eight Grumman F4F Wildcat fighters were already airborne and managed to escape destruction, landing on the decks of carriers *Lexington* and *Yorktown*.

Among those officially listed as missing was Doris Miller, who had distinguished himself by conspicuous bravery during the Japanese attack on Pearl Harbor. It was there that Mess Attendant Second Class Doris Miller became one of the first American heroes of the war, carrying wounded sailors to safety and firing a .50-caliber Browning anti-aircraft machine gun in defense of the battleship *West Virginia*. Five and a half months later, on May 27, 1942, this former star fullback at Waco's Moore High School stood at attention in his dress whites on the deck of the aircraft carrier *Enterprise* and received the Navy Cross from Admiral Chester W. Nimitz, Commander-in-Chief of the Pacific Fleet.

But even the most honorably earned glory can be fleeting in wartime. On Tuesday, December 7, 1943, less than two weeks after the demise of *Liscome Bay*, the Navy Department notified Connery and Henrietta Miller that their son, Ship's Cook Third Class Doris Miller, was missing in action. In a poignant irony of war, the dreaded word had come to the family farm in Speegleville precisely two years to the day after the young man's heroism under fire at Pearl Harbor.

Liscome Bay was sunk on November 24, and by naval convention, the term "presumed dead" could not be applied until a further year and a day had elapsed beyond that date. The grieving couple, like thousands of other families with blue and gold stars hanging in their windows, were obliged to endure a lengthy wait before their desperate hopes were finally dashed by legal closure.

◆　　◆　　◆

By and large, Hannah Lane had always judged her male contemporaries to be a silly breed. Much to her disgust, she found many of the boys at her high school in Mount Airy to be dimwits when it came to intellectual matters. There were some good athletes, sure, but she could not recall a single boy who took any interest whatsoever in geography or politics. Mickey Torgelson could not name the Vice President of the United States, and Lee Garvey thought Anschluss was a town in Germany. On the other hand, that same Lee Garvey's older sister, who now lived with her husband and infant daughter in Boone, had been valedictorian of her senior class. What better demonstration could there be of the superiority of the female brain?

Hannah also loathed the predatory instinct that seemed endemic to the male of the human species. Boys were always so aggressive and lustful, she observed, hardly ever exerting much effort to fight off the temptations of youth. Abigail Mirer was humiliated and had to drop out of high school to raise a baby, but was Patrick Watt not half to blame? Instead, he continued on his merry way, while she was saddled with a life-altering responsibility long before she was ready. The last Hannah heard, Abby was still living with her mother and baby girl, unable to return to school or interest a suitable young man to act as surrogate provider. It was a pity that Mr. Mirer was deceased, not only because he was a dear friend of the church, but also because a well-aimed shotgun might have forced Patrick to avow his role in the ill-considered affair.

That is what surprised Hannah most about her own conduct now, and why it felt so shameful. Seldom had she torn into a letter with such anticipation—and certainly never one from a boy. When she spotted the return address of "Mt. Airy, No. Car." and noticed that "W. Oak St." was scribbled right above it, there was no denying the fact that she felt an unwelcome twinge of excitement.

Hannah knew full well that this was a note from Alvin Reeder, whom she had not seen since the day they graduated from high school. Having no evidence to the contrary, she had assumed that he went to live in California. Alvin was forever talking about the fabled natural wonders of the Golden State. Once, when they were underclassmen, he cornered her in the school cafeteria. "Do you know that California has the highest and lowest points in the United States?" he said. "And they're only about a hundred miles apart? That's where I'm going to live."

She laughed so hard that she nearly dropped her tray. "Oh, really? You're going to live in Death Valley?"

He looked askance at her. "Of course not, you dolt. I'm going to live in Los Angeles—whenever I get out of this prison, that is."

Alvin was not a good student and professed to have little, if any, use for education. Yet, in truth, he was endowed with all the mental aptitude necessary to make something of himself, if only he would apply his natural gifts and abandon the phony cynicism that made him a "character" in the eyes of his peers.

Why would Alvin Reeder be writing to her after all these years? As Hannah unfolded the letter, her eyes swept impatiently across the cursive penmanship, picking up a few stray words here and there: "grandfather died" ... "I saw lots of" ... "remember her?" ... "collegiate" ... "to Texas" ... "nose in the air." Hearing the radio come on downstairs, she walked over to her bedroom door, closed it, and then lay on her back with the letter held at arm's length above her. It began with a surprisingly warm "Dearest Hannah." Almost as a reflex action, she flipped the paper over to see how it was signed: "All my love, Alvin." He was always way too confident with girls—presumptuous might be another word for it—and despite her initial excitement, Hannah could feel a familiar indignation beginning to boil near the surface. Opening a fresh stick of chewing gum, she read the letter to herself, with as open a mind as she could manage.

Dearest Hannah,

I'm sure you're saying to yourself (like Jane Ace), "You could knock me over with a fender." Yes, this is your old nemesis, haunting you again—and right when you had completely forgotten that I even existed. No real reason for me to write, Han, except to say that I might be seeing you one of these days. (More about that later ...)

A couple of months after we received those good-for-nothing sheepskins, my grandfather died, and my parents took me and my sister to Memphis for the funeral. I had never been west of the Mississippi before, so we crossed over into Arkansas for a few minutes just so I can proudly announce to the world that I'm no longer a pantywaist Easterner. 'Course, West Memphis ain't exactly Los Angeles, but it's a quarter of the way there. While we were traveling through Tennessee, I saw lots of Army convoys, and that was a long time before Pearl Harbor was hit.

Maybe you're wondering why I'm still at home instead of fighting for the honor of Uncle Sam like Bert and Howie and rest of our bunch. "Slacker!" you're probably saying—under your breath of course. Nope, that's not it at all. My doctor contacted the draft board to let them know my hearing's not what it should be. I'm nearly deaf in my right ear, which is why the teachers always sat me on the right side of the room. All except for that battle-ax, Mrs. Cripe—remember her?

I worked for a year and a half at the Snappy Lunch—some waiting on tables, but mostly back in the kitchen—until old man Roberson had enough of me, I guess, and canned me. I never did find out why, but I was ready to quit anyway, so it didn't break my heart.

Now I'm employed by—are you sitting down?—a Bible company. Please wipe that smirk off your face, Miss Holier Than Thou!!! I'm peddling King James all over the Piedmont—particularly in the Fayetteville area, but as far west as Asheville, up to Roanoke, and south to Myrtle Beach. "They really need the Lord bad down there," my boss says. Does he know something I don't?

As you'll recall, I never was exactly collegiate material like you are. But we had some good times, didn't we? Remember the litter of puppies that we found in my dad's rumble seat? You kept one of them for a pet, didn't you, or was that Eileen?

I said I might be visiting you. That's right, my business could be sending me to central Texas (well, Dallas anyway) for some managerial training. Heck (see, I cleaned up my language), I might even become regional sales manager down there one of these years. If I come to Waco, promise you won't ignore me with your nose in the air again, like you did at Monty's graduation party. Don't pretend you didn't see me, Han. I was heartbroken at the time. (tee hee!)

Write me back whenever your professors give you five minutes of spare time. I'll say hello to your father the next time I see him.

All my love, Alvin

Shaking her head, Hannah refolded the letter and placed it back in the envelope. It was nice to hear from her school acquaintance again, but word of his proposed visit unnerved her. Alvin was on the arrogant side and not to be fully trusted. Moreover, he suffered from wanderlust, never satisfied with where he happened to be. It seemed odd that their paths should ever cross again, especially after the passage of so many years—and at a neutral site to boot, a thousand miles away from their hometown. She eased her mind by recalling that Alvin was also prone to bluster, so it was every bit as possible that this letter, arriving at her boarding house from out of the blue, was nothing more than the handwritten equivalent of hot air.

Hannah laid the letter beside her on the bed spread. She was never very fond of Alvin Reeder, but something about his personality aroused her interest. Perhaps it was because they were such opposites. Perhaps it was because, deep down, they were so very much alike.

◆　　　◆　　　◆

Festive decorations always went up on the Monday prior to the beginning of December, and this year—the third Christmas of the war for Americans—would be no different. Madeleine Givens opened the door to the USO's musty storeroom, fumbled for the light switch, and then dragged four heavy boxes of ornaments, wreaths, tinsel, and nativity scenes into the dining hall for sorting. Her left leg was not giving her much trouble this morning, so she felt no need to ask for help. It was just a few minutes past eight o'clock, and nobody else but the custodian, Mitchell Bishop, was around at such an early hour. He tipped his cap and said, "Hello, Miss Madeleine."

"Good morning, Mitchell. How's your wife doing these days?"

"Oh, much better, thanks." He stared at the boxes. "What you up to with them?"

"It's that time of year again. I hope to have this place looking like Radio City Music Hall before I'm finished."

"Well, that I gotta see!"

Madeleine picked up a tiny manger and brushed across its surface with her forefinger. "Would you mind bringing me a wet cloth? I can't lay the stuff out like this. Where does all that dust come from?"

Mitchell shook his head. "I don't know. That room's usually kept closed, you know." His mouth curled into a smile. "But I guess dust don't need no door to come through."

"No, indeed. You sure are right about that." Madeleine blew on a plastic wreath, and her breath raised a chalky cloud. "Maybe I should just squirt the whole business off with a garden hose. What do you think?"

"I'll do it for you, Miss Madeleine. Yes, ma'am, I'll just go out back—won't take but about fifteen minutes. 'Course they won't be dry for a couple hours after that."

"That's okay, Mitchell. I would hate to put them out like this—looking like we dragged them across the Sahara Desert."

"Yes, ma'am." He chuckled at her remark and went to fetch the hose.

The first GI did not show up until nearly nine o'clock that day, and after that, four others arrived in short order. Madeleine offered them pastries and hot coffee. One of the men, a tow-headed private from Minnesota, had stayed up all night on guard duty, so the caffeine was a godsend for him. He thanked Madeleine and asked how much he owed her.

"Are you serious, soldier? You boys are welcome here anytime, but leave your money in the barracks."

He nodded in appreciation, holding the cup under his nose and inhaling the aroma. "I hope it's strong."

"Should be," she said. "I always add an extra scoop for you early birds."

It took most of the day to hang, drape, and position the motley assortment of Christmas decorations. When she had completed the task, Madeleine was surprised to see that she had gone through an entire pack of cigarettes in the process.

It was by now well past 4:30, and the USO facility, freshly adorned in its holiday finery, was filled with servicemen of all descriptions. Four GIs were playing ping-pong, and their competitive shrieks punctuated the noise level with high-decibel spikes, causing the passive readers to despair of making much headway in such an inhospitable climate. Two college girls, surrounded by a platoon from WAAF, pretended to be shocked by the airmen's flattering advances, but the coeds' playful retorts gave them away. Across the room, with their backs to the revelry, sat two forlorn V-5 reservists, determinedly leafing through maritime studies while their minds wandered to topics far afield.

After putting in a full day's work, Madeleine looked forward to a simple evening at home. Indeed, she was about ready to head out the door, into a pleasantly cool late November afternoon of fifty-three degrees. Her plans were to take a restful bath, fix herself a bite to eat—probably fried Spam, which she liked very much—and then relax in front of the radio. This was the night for "The Great Gildersleeve" and "Information Please." And, of course, "Lum and Abner" would be on the Blue Network at 7:15. But an unforeseen problem had arisen, one that was so uncharacteristic of the person involved that it caught Madeleine completely off guard.

Thumbtacked to a cork bulletin board in the back room was the weekly "Schedule of Volunteers," which clearly showed this to be young Miss Brower's designated Monday, but Elizabeth had not yet reported for duty. The pendulum clock in the rec room testified that she was nearly fifteen minutes overdue.

Impatient in her absence, Emma Bright and her sister-in-law, Hilda May Bright, were handling the refreshments, and they were none too pleased to be kept waiting. Their husbands, twins Raymond and Reece Bright, respectively, were no doubt halfway home from McGregor by now and would be expecting hot meals to be placed in front of them the moment they arrived.

"Can't you do anything about this, Mrs. Givens?" Hilda May said. She seemed quite cross.

Usually one person could manage the refreshments, but not today. And Mitchell Bishop had left an hour earlier, so he would not be able to help serve. With a sigh, Madeleine laid down her purse and removed her gloves. "I suppose I can stand in for one of you. Oran will be here at five, for whatever that's worth."

"We both need to be going," Emma said. "Our husbands are in a car pool."

"Well, we can't spare both of you ladies. Can't you see that?" It was true—hungry and thirsty servicemen were lined up four deep at the refreshment table. "I'm sure Lizzie will be here in a minute or two. Just give her a little while longer." Madeleine took off her coat and tossed it over a chair.

Ten minutes went by, and still no Elizabeth. In desperation, Madeleine limped to the back room to double-check the schedule. There it was: "LIZZIE B," scrawled in capital letters under "Mon., Nov. 29." She dialed the Brower home from Roswell Patterson's office, letting the telephone ring repeatedly, but the call went unanswered. How strange, she thought. Why would nobody be home at such an hour? Then it occurred to her that this was Nora's turn at the Red Cross. She further surmised that Nora's son might still be at work. The teenage boy was reputed to be something of a radio actor, though she herself had never heard him on the air.

Madeleine hurried back to the rec room, just in time to see her two workers walking out the main door. She was about to call to them—"Hilda May! Emma! Where do you think you're going?"—when her peripheral vision caught sight of an elderly gentleman and a high school girl calmly pouring coffee and punch for the uniformed guests. It was five o'clock. Oran Dickinson was precisely on time, and Elizabeth Brower was precisely a half-hour late.

"Hello, Mr. Dickinson," Madeleine said, and the old man smiled a greeting in return. Then she fixed her attention on the younger volunteer. "Miss Brower, weren't you supposed to be here at 4:30?"

"Yes, ma'am," came the shamefaced reply, "and I feel terrible about it." Elizabeth ladled some punch into a cup. "I have a good excuse," she said, "but I can't tell you about it right now, not in front of everyone like this. Honest, I'm awfully sorry."

Madeleine's annoyance subsided a bit—this was, after all, an unpaid volunteer—and she reached for her gloves. "That's all right. I'm sure you had a valid reason." She watched as a nearly unbroken line of soldiers continued to file into the room. "You can tell me about it tomorrow, whenever you get the chance."

"But I don't work again until Friday."

"Very well." Madeleine picked up her purse and began to walk away. "Oh, don't let Oran forget to unplug the coffee pot again. He nearly burned the place down a couple of months ago."

"Okay, you can count on me."

Madeleine looked her squarely in the eye. "Yes," she said. "I suppose so ..."

When Elizabeth was relieved of duty at nine o'clock, she rode home with Wesley, but they did not say a word to each other until he turned the corner onto Homan Avenue.

The doctor had removed Wesley's cumbersome plaster cast that very morning, so he was better able to use his newly liberated right arm to shift gears. He glanced at his sister. "You're still mad at me, aren't you?" he asked.

She did not respond, choosing instead to stare straight ahead.

"I couldn't help it, see? I don't know why you won't believe me."

Elizabeth squirmed in her seat, but her only utterance was a loud sigh.

One thing about the wartime speed limit: an automobile's heater was able to warm the interior air to a comfortable temperature well before the end of the briefest jaunt. Outside, though, it was hovering just above the forty-degree mark, heading for a low of twenty-nine.

"Listen, Lizzie, I couldn't just walk up to Sandy and tell her that I didn't want to meet her cousin. You were my only hope—my alibi." Even in the darkness, he could see that her lips were tightened in anger. "Look, if it makes any difference, I really appreciate what you tried to do for me, and I feel bad about everything that happened."

Elizabeth turned her head away, watching through the passenger window as the houses slowly drifted past. She was not the sort to forgive such affronts very quickly.

Wesley looked at her but could not see for certain whether she was crying. He cleared his throat, about to say something further, but instead swallowed the words unspoken. His sister was so maddeningly stubborn that telling her he was sorry never produced any effect whatsoever. No, now that he thought about it, he was through apologizing.

Spitefully, he shook his head and began whistling to himself an unidentifiable ditty of some sort. At this, Elizabeth's hands gripped her purse in a stranglehold, a predictable sight that inspired his whistling to become all the more rudely atonal. Soon she was fuming, and Wesley could contain himself no longer. He broke out laughing, chuckling quietly at first but then progressing to a series of loud guffaws, keeping one hand on the steering wheel while wiping away tears of mirth with the other.

Elizabeth gazed at him with an icy contempt.

"I can't help it," he said. "You just looked so silly standing there, swooning at the crooners' songs with all those other bobby-soxers!" He shook his head. "I'll never forget the expression on your face ... when you finally realized who it was that crashed Loretta Pridgeon's party in his zoot suit."

Wesley's captive audience of one, whose memory of the recent humiliation was quite fresh in her mind, saw no humor at all in what he said. She reached over and switched on the radio, at a volume considerably above the customary listening level. "The Screen Guild Theater" happened to be on CBS at the time, and announcer Truman Bradley was in the process of revealing the wonders of Lady Esther Cosmetics. That night's presentation, the delightful *Theodora Goes Wild*, with Cary Grant and Irene Dunne, suited Elizabeth's needs perfectly. A comedy's antics might not muzzle her brother's laughter, but it was sure to discourage that loathsome whistling.

When the Brower siblings finally arrived home, Wesley steered the automobile into the garage and cut off the engine, silencing the radio as well. He was still chuckling occasionally, but not to such an extent that his sister was unable to ignore it. As she reached for the door handle, Wesley asked her, "Do you want me to tell Mrs. Givens why you were late? She'll find out from Mom anyhow."

Elizabeth's response fell short of true conviviality, but at least she no longer brandished a pair of daggers in her eyes. "No, that won't be necessary. I'll explain everything to her on Friday."

"Everything?"

She surrendered a grudging smile. "No, not everything. I'll keep my end of the bargain, if you'll keep yours." She started to get out again, but he stopped her.

"Whatever you do, don't tell anyone that I saw them looking for me at the radio station. If Sandy ever found out, she'd never speak to me again."

"And what makes you think she didn't notice you leaving? Your bike isn't invisible, you know."

"I'm sure she didn't. I rode down the back alley."

Elizabeth opened the passenger door and stepped out. The cat was busy smelling one of the rear tires. "Hello, 'Tino," she said. "What are you doing out so late tonight?" He rubbed against her leg, so she stooped down to pet him.

"I'm going to tell Sandy that I was with you and your friends after I got off work," Wesley said. "That's the truth. I won't be lying."

Elizabeth frowned. "Technically."

When Wesley pulled the garage door closed, he paused long enough to secure it with a padlock—an unusual overnight procedure that all motorists were encouraged to follow, at least for the duration. The government had made it abundantly clear that there would be no new automotive products until after the war.

"Well, you do have to admit that I was the life of the party," Wesley said as they approached the back door of the house.

"Only if you count unwelcome visitors. You ruined everyone's afternoon, that's all. And you made me lie about you in front of my friends and the entire USO."

"My hands were tied. I had to avoid Sandy until she dragged her cousin to the movies. You've never seen Bernice like I have."

"She can't be all that bad. Sandy is a very pretty girl."

"Sure she is, but Bernice comes from the ugly side of the family."

Wesley held the door open for his sister, who whispered, "You know, it wouldn't have killed you to meet her. That would have been the courteous thing to do—instead of making me lie for you like I did."

Wesley whispered back, "I keep telling you, it wasn't a lie. I did want to go to that platter party—to save my own skin—and I was there with you until almost five o'clock."

"And you made me late for work, just so you wouldn't have to help entertain Sandy's cousin."

"What if one of my friends had seen me sitting next to that albatross?"

"You didn't seem to care what *my* friends thought. It may interest you to know that having you show up in that ridiculous costume ..."

"We had a studio audience today."

"... was pretty embarrassing for me. You looked like some kind of a hoodlum."

"I didn't have any choice. Besides, no harm done. Sandy's cousin will be back in Georgia by the weekend."

"How can you be so sure? It would serve you right to have her stay around for a while."

"Nope. Her father's got duty on Monday morning."

"Marianne is going to make you pay for the Sinatra record you sat on."

"That was an accident."

Elizabeth gave him a dubious look.

"Really," he added. "I thought the record jacket was empty. I like Sinatra all right."

"Well, you didn't look like you were too sad about it at the time."

"How was I to know that Marianne Grimes is in love with Frankie?"

"Are you serious? All of my friends are in love with Frankie. I'm the only one who isn't."

"Oh, sure," Wesley said. "So now who's lying?"

◆　　　◆　　　◆

It happened that classes for Baylor University's winter quarter ended earlier the same day, but junior transfer student Hannah Lane found precious little chance to enjoy any sense of relief. Soon after her last session was over, she reported to Crawford-Austin for the four-to-midnight shift. Worse yet, four days of final exams would begin the very next morning. In desperation, she placed two textbooks in her locker at work, hoping to study during the thirty minutes of accrued break time.

Though her supervisor, Mr. Hinckley, was aware of her predicament—and by no means unsympathetic—his first concern remained as it should have been: the war effort. He commiserated with Hannah but was unwilling to offer any special concessions. Faced with a formidable quota of military supplies to produce for the government, he had no choice but to attach a relatively low priority to personal issues of a less than life-threatening nature.

That night, Hannah was assigned a place next to Rowena Downing on the production line, which was fine with her. She always enjoyed chatting with Rowena because it made the repetitive tedium of her job just that much more tolerable. The lady presented herself to the world as a stereotypical grandmother figure, but under that amiable veneer prowled a crusty misanthrope whose blunt commentary on issues of the day left no one in the bureaucracy verbally unscathed, from President Roosevelt down to the humblest block warden.

Mr. Hinckley would suffer no profanity in the workplace, and yet it was not often that Rowena Downing sensed the need to descend to that level of communication anyway. She may have spit tobacco into a paper cup, but seldom did vulgarity escape her lips. So keenly developed was her euphemistic vocabulary that she could relate the vilest sentiment in words that, arranged in a slightly different sequence, might serve just as effectively in the pulpit. Her sarcastic insights—for Hannah at least—made the shift go ever so much faster.

There were those who would not agree. One such detractor was Horton Stokes, an outspoken farmer who came to the big city to lend his hand to wartime production. He was long since retired from planting and harvesting, his two sons having relieved him of that burden more than six years earlier, and his wife was but a distant memory now. Eloise Stokes had passed away in bed during the influenza pandemic of 1918, just three weeks short of the Armistice. One fifth of a million Americans succumbed to the disease in that terrible month of October alone. "She died peacefully, in her sleep," Dr. Shinnick told him, but Horton knew better. He could hear his wife gasping for each breath, as a suffocating fluid filled her air passages with bloody froth. When Eloise was rendered silent and Horton was finally invited into the contagious bedroom, the doctor had yet to wipe away all the evidence, which even in death continued to trickle from her nose and mouth.

It was not uncommon for Horton Stokes and Rowena Downing—sworn enemies despite the supposed wisdom of advancing years—to find themselves in close proximity with each other on the same assembly line, and indeed that was the case on this particular Monday night. But it was a novelty for Hannah Lane to be stationed on the battlefield of their personal combat zone. Once Horton clocked in at six o'clock, only she stood between the pair, and it would be just a slight exaggeration to say that, in so doing, she may very well have saved both of their lives from meeting violent ends.

"Oh, swell, this is gonna be a fun evenin'," Horton said when he spotted the stocky spinster next to Hannah. "I spend half my time fixin' other people's shoddy work." Though he spoke quite loudly over the whirring hum of machinery, the embarrassed Baylor coed looked down at her tent flap, pretending not to hear.

Rowena hardly flinched at his opening salvo. "Who asked that rube to take his ass-cart to town?" she said to Hannah. "This war would be over a lot sooner if we didn't have old fogeys and snot-nosed kids masquerading as a work force."

Horton glowered. "Spit it out, Mrs. Downin'. The juice is runnin' down your shirtfront again."

Rowena did just that and then used a yellowed rag to wipe the excess from her chin. For good measure, she also blew her nose into it, inserting her index finger well up a nostril.

"That's disgustin'," Horton said. "Some of my pigs have more pride than that."

"Is that right? Well, maybe if you washed your armpits once'ta month, this place wouldn't smell like the locker room at Crosley Field."

"Oh? You been in there?"

"I've not had the pleasure, but I have been to Cincy all right," she said. "And I do know enough to gag on putrid sweat when I smell it, if that's what you mean."

"Hrmph. Try breathing your own stench sometime, you miserable strumpet."

Hannah glanced around for Mr. Hinckley. She felt sure that he would bring a swift end to this sort of behavior, which appeared to be escalating toward fisticuffs. Oddly enough, though, he did not seem much concerned, at one point walking within ten feet of the altercation without saying a word.

Rowena, for her part, barely took note of the supervisor's presence, pointing a crooked finger at Horton Stokes. "Listen," she said, "why don't you do our boys in uniform a big favor and just go back home and dig in your victory garden?"

Horton's eyes narrowed. "At least I've got some kinfolk fightin' on our side. Not like some of you immigrant shirkers—nothin' but a bunch o' shiftless vagabonds is what you are."

Rowena calmly inspected a canvas swatch. "That's a laugh!" she said. "My family could have bought yours for slaves, right off the boat from Glasgow. You're just lucky that your skin was white."

That is how it went, nearly incessantly, for most of the evening. Only three or four times did the bickering subside, and that was when one principal returned to a neutral corner while the other answered nature's call.

After two hours of work, Hannah was entitled to a ten-minute break, and she tried her best to study in the employees' lounge. Then she walked back to the assembly room, earnestly chewing her Dubble Bubble gum. This treat was a scarce commodity in the war, a much-prized gift from Elizabeth Brower, who had received it as an enlisted man's come-on at the USO. Hannah's path took her directly past the office of Mr. Hinckley, and she noticed that he was relaxing outside his opened door, drinking a Nehi root beer. "Hello, Miss Lane," he said. "Getting an earful tonight?"

"Yes, sir. Plenty." She brushed a strand of blonde curls from her eye. "Sooner or later, they're going to kill each other. Maybe that would shut them up." Hannah had not planned to bring the issue to her supervisor's attention—no squealer was she—but since he asked ...

"I'm afraid there's a long and rather colorful history behind them," he said, and to Hannah's surprise, there was more affection in his voice than rancor. Mr. Hinckley tipped the glass bottle vertically, even tapping it to drain every last molecule of flavor. Then he took a handkerchief and wiped residual moisture from his black mustache. "They're quite a team, aren't they?"

"I'll say."

"Sorry to put you in their line of fire, but it wouldn't do to have them side by side. I tried that one time, and ... well, it didn't pan out too well."

"Then why do you ...?" She stopped.

"Why do I put up with all their nonsense? I don't know, really." He leaned on the wooden railing beside the steps leading up to his office. "Sometimes I think they're a detriment, but then I look at the production figures."

"They seem to get their work done."

He laughed. "They do more than that. In three separate months this year, Mrs. Downing and Mr. Stokes were better than any other two people in the whole division. Not only that, but they seem to make other workers' productivity go up as well."

Hannah was puzzled. "How could they do that?"

"Beats me. Maybe they provide a perverse sort of entertainment for the others. I'm not sure." He rubbed the back of his neck and reflected on the matter. "Either that or people just get so blamed tired of hearing them nagging at each other that they close their ears and concentrate better on their own jobs. I don't know which."

Hannah popped a large bubble. "I guess I could start wearing earplugs to work."

"Whatever it takes," Mr. Hinckley said.

Counting the allotted half-hour dinnertime and her ten-minute work breaks, Hannah was able to browse over most of the textbook material for Tuesday's two final examinations. One test, Old Testament History, simply covered the last third of the quarter, but the other, Philosophy, was cumulative and more reason for worry. She did not feel adequately prepared for either, but that could not be helped. As her father had written to her earlier in the week, "The Good Lord will not give you more than you both can handle."

By the time she arrived back at the boarding house, it was nearly 12:30 in the morning. She waved goodbye to her ride, Bee Fetters, unlocked the front door, and went directly upstairs, knowing full well that she would have, at best, a little under five hours of sleep. The weather was quite mild for almost December, so she opened one of the windows to let in some fresh air. She felt exhausted and hoped that—on this of all nights—sleep would be quick in coming. She also realized that such thoughts were, more often than not, counterproductive.

Hannah's mind wandered as she lay on her back in bed, trying without much success to remain focused on her prayers. She switched off the table lamp and closed her eyes. "Dear Lord, thank you for the many blessings ..." The following Monday would be registration for Baylor's winter quarter, after her long weekend of stitching canvas for the troops. "Please bless Daddy and Grandma Lynch and ..." How great it was going to feel to march right into that registration line at her own convenience! "Bless our men overseas ..." She had received from Baylor University a special card—one of the perquisites of wartime employment—authorizing her to register at any time during that day. "Bless Stephen Brower and everybody in the Brower family ..." Full-time students had to register at a prescribed time. "Please forgive me for where I have failed ..." And so there was a chance that some of their classes might already be full by then. "In Jesus Christ's name, I pray. Amen."

The clock on her nightstand was ticking loudly, its alarm set for 5:30. This, she estimated before falling asleep, would allow her just enough time to scan through her class notes prior to catching the southbound streetcar for campus.

◆　　◆　　◆

A holly wreath was hanging on the wall above Myra Culp's head as Wesley entered the radio station. Two salesmen stood next to her desk, discussing the price and relative merits of Havana cigars, all the while taking aim at her already overloaded ashtray to deposit their charred tobacco residue. The thick smoke made Wesley cough, inspiring one of the grinning salesmen to exhale toward him through his yellowed teeth. Both men laughed heartily, but the boy only smiled in return.

Myra shook her head. "Don't mind them. They're just being even more obnoxious than usual today."

"Hey, that's not easy to do," the other salesman said. They laughed again, and one of them patted Wesley on the back as they walked toward their offices.

From the overhead speakers came the sound of "Joy to the World," reminding Wesley to tell the receptionist, "Merry Christmas."

"And Merry Christmas to you, Wes. It won't be very long now."

He nodded toward the wall. "Something new?"

"Yep. We just use the same nail year after year. The boss doesn't like me to pound things into his wood paneling."

"It looks nice."

"Thanks. I think so too. Funny how just one little decoration like that can brighten up this whole dingy room."

"Aren't you going to hang some mistletoe?" he asked.

"I don't dare. Not with all the men in this building. I'd never get any work done."

Wesley chuckled. "Well, don't look at me!"

"Oh, no, you're an absolute gentleman, I'm sorry to say. Unlike some others around here that I could mention."

He glanced up at the clock. "I guess I'd better be hitting the studio. Lots of lines today."

"Wait, Wes. Before you go ..."

He detected a serious tone in her voice. "Yeah?"

"I need to warn you about something. You know, before you go barging into a ... a situation."

He took a step back toward the desk. There was no sign of levity in her eyes.

"Sit down, Wes," she said. "Just for a minute." Then she lowered her voice so the two of them would not be overheard. "I think you should be aware of a change."

Laughing uneasily, Wesley took a seat in the wooden chair that one of the salesmen had dragged over to her desk. "What's this all about?" he asked. "Did the station go out of business or something?"

"No, nothing as catastrophic as that."

"Well?"

"I thought you should know that your girlfriend, Sandra Whittsel, is now employed by KWXN Broadcasting Company."

Wesley raised his eyebrows in surprise. "She's working here? They gave her a job?"

"Grant Tollefson hired her as a news reporter."

"A girl reporter?"

"A girl reporter. Becky Headrick told me that Marshall McFall was in on the decision."

He swallowed hard. "Marshall recommended her?"

"I suppose so, but I think Grant already knew Miss Whittsel anyhow."

Wesley nodded his head and stood up. "Yeah, he did."

Myra reached into her purse for a cigarette. "I heard about that argument you had with Marshall ..."

He shrugged his shoulders, pleading ignorance. "All I told you was that I saw them together in the announcing booth."

"Come on, Wes. Everybody knows about the ruckus by now." She lit up her Chesterfield and brought it to life with a small puff.

"Oh, they do, huh?"

"The whole station knows. I'm surprised it hasn't been on the news."

"Swell."

"What is it between you two?"

"Marshall and me?"

"No, you and Sandra Whittsel. Are you still sweet on her? If so, maybe I can help."

He smiled, embarrassed at the suggestion. "No, we're just school friends."

Unconvinced, she squinted her eyes. "Wes ..."

"Well, sure, I think she's a pretty girl, but there's no more to it than that. Besides, she's not what I thought she was."

"Just let me know if there is anything I can do," she said. No reaction. "Promise?"

"All right. But really, she's just another girl to me."

Myra flicked her cigarette over the ashtray. "Look, I know lots of secrets about everyone at the station—all the inside dope." She smiled up at him. "You can't work at this front desk for four years without learning something."

◆　　　◆　　　◆

There were only five shopping days left until Christmas, but Nora Brower still had not purchased Wesley and Elizabeth anything nice for the occasion. She could not seem to get organized this year. Maybe it was because of outside demands—her volunteerism at the Red Cross and USO—or maybe it was simply the psychological strain of having a son away in the military. In any case, she hoped to accomplish some productive shopping that very afternoon. Her weekly laundry chores remained, but all she had to do otherwise was run one brief errand for the war effort.

She was carrying a small grocery box, but this time it was destined not for home but in precisely the opposite direction—back to the store. In it were several tin cans filled with cooking fat, and she was careful to keep them upright, as the foil wrapped tightly around their severed tops provided anything but a leakproof seal. Butchers across the country had been empowered by the Office of Price Administration to give customers four cents in cash and two red ration points for every pound of used fats that were turned in to their meat markets. The War Department processed these fats into glycerin, a necessary ingredient in the manufacture of gunpowder, medicines, and other battlefield essentials. In a very real sense, America's housewives formed a massive army of home-front munitions workers.

As Nora approached Moek Grocery on Colcord Avenue, she could see Hermann unlocking the wooden door and then reaching up to release the metal latch on the outside screen door. He let its overhead spring slam the screen shut with a soft thud. Nora waved to him, but he was already turning around, wiping his hands on the front of his apron before heading back to the soda fountain.

"And hello to you, too, Mr. Moek," she said upon entering the store.

"Oh, I'm sorry, Nora. My mind was a million miles away. Trudy's not here yet. I couldn't get her to wake up this morning."

"She never has liked Mondays."

"I don't like them very much myself, but here I am, just the same. You can't earn a living by lying in bed all day."

"You are one stern taskmaster, Hermann."

He stooped down to straighten the shelf of condensed soups. "You may not agree with me," he said over his shoulder, "but I think there should be a national law against having husbands and wives working together. That would save a lot of marriages."

"Oh, I don't know about that. As I recall, Harold and I got along fine, even during business hours."

"Well, you're the exception then. Trudy and I don't see eye to eye on anything here at the store."

"The soda fountain?"

Hermann pointed his finger at her. "Bingo! She accuses me of having it for a hobby—just for the fun of it. She claims that the fountain is more trouble than it's worth." He started to walk toward the rear of the store but halted. "You got some grease there, have you?"

"'Fill a tin, and turn it in,' as they say." Nora handed him the carton. "Just a few pounds, I'm afraid."

"Every drop helps." He carried the box over to the meat counter and put each can, one after the other, on the scales. Taking a pencil from over his ear, he jotted down the weights in a column. "That comes to seven and a quarter pounds in all—fourteen red ration points and twenty-nine cents. Will you be buying any meat or butter today?"

"No. In fact, I need to hurry home now and do a week's worth of laundry. Have you finished your Christmas shopping?"

"Yes, I have." Hermann glanced toward the rear of the store and lowered his voice. "I bought Trudy a necklace with a silver cross."

"You didn't! She'll love it."

"Yes, I think she will. I was in Fort Worth for two days last month and picked it up on Main Street."

She smiled. "Right off the street, Hermann?"

He was confused momentarily, until he saw that Nora was kidding. "Perhaps I should say that I bought it from a jewelry shop on Main Street."

"Yes, she might appreciate it more that way."

"And how about you? Are you ready for Christmas?"

"I plan to go shopping this afternoon. I don't have a thing in the world for Wes and Lizzie. Well, just some doo-dads, but nothing more than that."

"Go over to Monnig's. They've got just about everything there."

"I'll do that," she said. "Well, tell Trudy hello for me."

Hermann nodded his head. "Yes, she should be along shortly." He moved the slimy cans to one side and wiped his hands on the apron. "Would you like some breakfast? I'm serving eggs and bacon now, straight from the grill."

"No, thank you, I've already eaten. It sounds wonderful, though. Real eggs?"

"Yes, ma'am. Best breakfast in town, and just thirty-five cents—with toast, coffee, and juice."

"I'll keep that in mind. How's business?"

Hermann's face darkened. "You mean at the fountain?"

Nora nodded her head.

"Well, don't tell Mrs. Moek I said so, but I've been a little disappointed." He forced a smile. "You know, it takes time for something like this to catch on with the customers."

◆　　◆　　◆

The piny-fragrant Christmas tree had some additional gifts when the Brower family congregated around it just before daybreak on Saturday. Hannah had crept downstairs during the night and placed small packages for each of the others.

"Oh, you didn't have to do that, dear," Nora said. "It's our pleasure having you live here with us."

Hannah was wearing a flannel bathrobe over her bedclothes, casual garb that made this young college lady more closely resemble a graceless boy of thirteen or fourteen. She wiped her runny nose with the back of her hand, completing the picture.

Nora was already fully dressed for the day. She had arisen at 6:30 to stuff the turkey and to begin simmering the black-eyed peas and butter beans. The rolls were readying themselves too, rising of their own accord on the warm stovetop. Christmas music could be heard playing on the kitchen radio, and its nostalgic strains reached clear into the living room, instilling a homey feeling that even the crackling fireplace was unable to provide all by itself.

Actually, this family gathering was not quite as early in the morning as one might have assumed from how persistently night-like it remained outside. The nationwide time system turned all accustomed concepts upside down, creating exceedingly dark mornings during the winter months. The Seventy-seventh Congress had approved the adoption of War Time on January 20, 1942, "to promote the national security and defense by establishing daylight saving time."

> Be it enacted by the Senate and House of Representatives of the
> United States of America in Congress assembled, that beginning at 2
> o'clock antemeridian of the twentieth day after the date of enactment of
> this Act, the standard time of each zone ... shall be advanced one hour.
> This Act shall cease to be in effect six months after the termination of

the present war or at such earlier date as the Congress shall by concurrent resolution designate.

The clocks had remained advanced by one hour ever since February 9 of 1942—for twenty-two and a half months now—meaning that sunrise on this Christmas Day in central Texas would not occur until 8:28 A.M.

Wesley and Hannah were the only people in the little group who were drinking coffee. Nora, busy preparing breakfast and Christmas dinner, had already consumed two cups, and that was her self-imposed limit for any given morning. Lately, she had come to feel it caused her nerves to become jittery if she surpassed that amount of caffeine within a span of a few hours.

"How much rain did we get yesterday, Wes?" she called from the kitchen.

Wesley was sitting on the sofa, reading the *News-Tribune*. He glanced down at the bottom-left of the front page. "Sixty-five hundredths of an inch."

"Oh, it seemed like much more than that, don't you think?"

"That's just the official total, Mom, from out at Blackland. It seems like they always get less than we do."

The radio was playing "Silent Night," and Nora listened to it with sadness. She did not know where her firstborn child was serving. She was not even certain whether Steve was still training in this country or perhaps steaming abroad on a warship. But surely he would have told her if he were headed overseas, unless of course the censor did now allow it. That hopeful belief brought her some comfort.

"Are you sure you don't need for me to help with anything?" Elizabeth shouted.

Nora snapped out of her reverie and answered, "No, everything's under control in here. I've been doing this for nearly thirty years now, and I'm finally getting the knack of it." She began rattling through the muffin tins. One of them, even when properly greased, always seemed to cause the rolls to stick.

"At least it's not as cold outside as it was yesterday," Wesley said.

Nora was unable to hear over the clanking noise. "I'm sorry, dear. What did you say?" She stood up with the desired tray in hand.

"It's not as cold as yesterday."

"The man on the radio says it's thirty-three," she said. "But it's not supposed to get too much warmer than that all day long. Only about forty, I think."

That year's Christmas tree stood about six feet tall, and a tarnished metal star with red and green points graced its very tip. There were no candles or electric lights, only ornaments and tinsel, but it was a pretty tree, just the same. Many colorful packages were scattered around it, though clearly fewer than in recent memory. A green tree skirt, fashioned of some sort of felt, filled in the empty spaces, so the area did not look bare at all.

Elizabeth picked up one of the newly arrived packages and shook it close to her ear. "They're really nothing," Hannah said.

"Gee, you sure did a swell job wrapping those empty boxes," Wesley said from his spot on the sofa.

Hannah laughed. "Well, you know, it's the thought that counts." Playfully, she snatched the package from Elizabeth's hand and placed it back on the stack.

Later in the morning, with most of her cooking chores accomplished, Nora finally made her way to the living room, and packages were opened. She watched with amusement as Wesley tore the wrapping paper off the gift from her—a small, hand-painted metal replica of a B-17E.

"Don't you think I'm a little old for this?" he asked. Then, when she did not reply, he answered his own question. "Neither do I. Thanks, Mom." He held the tiny bomber up and peered at it from every angle. "Where'd you find something made of metal? This should really be in the scrap drive."

"You've done more than your share of salvaging already," she told him. "This is a collector's item. I found it in a craft store over on Bosque. If you want to know the truth, I don't think the owner really wanted to part with it."

"May I, Mother?" Elizabeth asked. She was holding a bulky package with her name on it. The gift was surprisingly light for its size.

"Yes, dear," Nora said, "but you're going to be disappointed. It's not really what I was trying to find for you."

It was a padded storage box for her phonograph discs, complete with a spring-release clasp and wooden carrying handle. "Oh, I love it. Thank you, Mother. Now I won't have to worry about my records so much when I take them over to Loretta's."

"As long as nobody sits on them," Wesley said. Elizabeth deflected the touchy subject with a glare.

When all the gifts had been opened, members of the Brower family and their wartime boarder sat down to a plentiful Christmas dinner of turkey and dressing, giblet gravy, hot rolls, and savory vegetables. The dining room grew quiet, and Nora asked Wesley, as the presiding male at the table, to say grace. Instantly, he became paralyzed with fear. For some reason, perhaps unknown even to him, voicing a public prayer made him unconscionably tense, a weakness dating all the way back to his earliest days of Sunday school. Wesley had no choice but to decline his mother's invitation, mumbling a plea he once heard an elderly deacon say during an evening service: "Beg to be excused."

Nora raised her eyebrows in surprise but then looked quickly away from her son. How could a young man who spoke daily to literally thousands of radio listeners become so petrified at the thought of uttering a few syllables amongst his closest relatives? Sensing his embarrassment, she smiled at the boy. "All right, dear. The Lord hears our silent prayers as well."

After an awkward moment, as Wesley stared down at his empty plate, Hannah offered to serve in his stead, and she exhibited all the facile confidence of a minister's daughter. She concluded her blessing with the invocation, "... and please be with Stephen Brower, as he embarks upon this dangerous mission—fighting against the enemies of freedom and for a world that is receptive to the spreading of your precious Word. In the powerful name of our Lord Jesus Christ, I pray. Amen."

"Amen," Nora said with the others. Her eyes shimmered with tears when she reopened them, but nonetheless she began passing bowls of steaming food clockwise around the table. Steve was still stateside, she convinced herself, but even that knowledge did not much soften her sense of motherly anguish. Never before had her elder son been missing from home on Christmas Day.

The meal was nearly finished, and Elizabeth had gotten up to dish out the desserts—pecan pie and pumpkin pie—when there came the sound of an urgent knocking on the front door.

"I'll get it," Wesley said with a loud sigh, and he scooted his chair back from the table. Truth be known, his mouth was watering for a small slice of each pie. Such sweets were a true rarity these days, representing the entire remainder of that month's sugar ration. Who would be visiting at such an hour on Christmas?

When he opened the door, his blood ran cold. Standing there with a solemn look on his face was a boy wearing a Western Union uniform. Though he was probably just a couple of years Wesley's senior, the boy appeared to be much older. There were lines in his face that bespoke the burdens of experience. Out near the street, his bicycle lay on its side where he had carelessly let it come to rest. "Telegram, sir," he said. "Is your mother at home?"

Wesley glanced over his shoulder toward the kitchen. "No. I'll take it."

"Sign here," the boy said. He consulted his wristwatch.

Wesley wrote his name on the log sheet, and the boy tipped his cap and left, exhibiting no hint of a smile or even the faintest cordiality. His daily routine had long since beaten that out of him, leaving behind only a stony façade.

With the telegram tucked into his bathrobe pocket, Wesley shut the door and walked into his father's study, seating himself at the roll-top desk.

"Who was it, Wes?" Nora called from the table.

"No one important," he shouted back. "Just a friend of mine." He noticed that his hands were trembling.

"What did he want? Doesn't he know it's Christmas?"

"Yes, Mom. He was wondering if I could come over to his house later on."

Wesley took a calming breath and placed the unopened telegram inside one of the desk's smallest wooden drawers, labeled INVENTORY. He would read it later, as time permitted, in private. He was not quite sure whether he delayed in reading it because of his mother's feelings or his own.

"Who did you say it was, dear?" his mother asked when he sat himself down at the table. There were small slices of pumpkin pie and pecan pie in front of him.

"Gee, that looks great. Thanks." He returned the cloth napkin to his lap.

"Who was that at the door? I didn't hear what you said."

He took a bite of pecan pie and spoke with his mouth full. "I didn't say ... but it was Mort."

"Morton Wilson?" She seemed surprised.

He stopped chewing and nodded his head, his lips now tense with guilt.

"That's funny," Nora said. "Hazel told me they would be visiting her husband's family in Teague today." She looked toward Elizabeth. "I hope nothing's wrong."

"Oh, I'm sure there's nothing wrong, Mom," Wesley said. "Mort didn't seem upset or anything, and I would have been able to tell."

"Well, maybe so, but just the same."

"Mort probably stayed home with his older sister. She's married, and her husband's away in the service."

Nora did not seem to hear what he said. "I wonder if they ran out of their gasoline allowance. That's a long drive."

Later, after the dishes were cleared, Hannah and her landlady sat down at the table for a cup of coffee. "I shouldn't be drinking this, you know," Nora told her. "I've already had my two cups."

"But that was hours ago, Mrs. B.," Hannah said. "Anyway, it won't affect you much on a full stomach."

Nora laughed. "Well, I certainly do have that."

Elizabeth could hear them chatting from her chair near the Christmas tree. She looked up and smiled at her mother and then returned her attention to the lovely silver bracelet that her uncle had sent from Harlingen. When Wesley abruptly arose from his seat on the sofa, she watched him disappear into their father's study. Now that she thought of it, he had seemed awfully nervous at the dinner table— not at all himself—and that business about Morton seemed contrived. Elizabeth decided to investigate and found her brother sitting in front of the roll-top desk, head down as if in prayer.

"Who was that at the door earlier?" she asked.

Startled, he looked up and his mouth began to form the name "Mort."

She interrupted. "Really, Wes. Who was there? You're not a very good liar."

It was no use. She could see right through him, and he knew it. Wesley sighed and slowly reached for the inventory drawer. "We got a telegram," he whispered, "but I'm afraid to open it."

Elizabeth gulped. "A telegram? I didn't even know they delivered on Christmas." She took two steps over to the bookshelf and leaned against it on unsteady legs.

He nodded his head. "Of course, that doesn't necessarily mean something terrible has happened. There's really no reason to suspect the worst."

"Who sent it?"

"There's no return address ... just Western Union."

"Well, don't you think you should let Mother open it?" she asked.

"I don't know. She couldn't take it if it's ..." He motioned with his hand, acknowledging their unsaid fear.

"But he's not even finished with his training yet, is he?" she whispered.

"I don't think so, but troop movements are very hush-hush. Besides, training can be just as dangerous as fighting the enemy."

"Did you try holding it up to the light?" she asked.

"Of course not. That's too sneaky."

"No sneakier than hiding the telegram from her."

He conceded the point. "Maybe so."

Elizabeth glanced over her shoulder and then looked her brother in the eye. "Here. Give it to me." She removed the lampshade and switched on the light bulb, holding the envelope at arm's length in front of it. She squinted her eyes, shook her head with a frown, and then turned the envelope over. "It's hard to see because it's folded onto itself. I can make out the name 'Steve,' but nothing else."

"So it is about Steve."

"I'm afraid so." She bit her lower lip. "Here, you try."

He took the envelope but said, "Make sure Mom and Hannah are still in the kitchen."

Elizabeth left the room far enough to hear their voices. When she came back, she whispered, "They're still talking."

Wesley set about to work, but as intently as he concentrated, he too could decipher nothing beyond the mere mention of his brother's name.

"What do you think we should do?" Elizabeth asked. "We can't just hide a telegram forever."

He pursed his lips. "We'll need to let her open it. I was just trying to figure out what it said, to make it easier on her."

"Do you want to wait until tomorrow? I'd hate to give her bad news on Christmas."

Suddenly, a smile lit up Wesley's face. "Hey," he said, "wouldn't the War Department write 'Stephen' instead of 'Steve'?"

Elizabeth thought for a moment and then ventured a smile of her own. "Sure, they would," she said aloud. "I think you're right. In fact, I know you are!"

On Christmas Day of 1943, the very best gift of all had been delivered not down some sooty chimney by a mythical, pot-bellied Santa Claus but on the front porch of the Brower home by a pimple-faced Western Union boy who had no idea what joy he was holding in his outstretched hand.

REMEMBER ALL WIRES NOT BAD NEWS. STILL HERE FOR MORE TRAINING. DOING FINE. MERRY CHRISTMAS AND LOVE TO ALL=
 STEVE.

◆ ◆ ◆

It seemed incongruous for Sandra Whittsel to be at the radio station, rubbing elbows with Wesley's thrice-familiar comrades. And yet there she was, standing outside the newsroom door, talking with two veteran reporters, Abel Carlin and Eugene Dettweiler. Wesley crowded against the corner of the wall, so that only one of his eyes was visible at the far end of the hallway. He could hear their voices but not clearly distinguish any words they were saying. As best he could surmise, it was a round of "shop talk." Eugene held a legal pad, and he was showing the trainee what was written upon it, pointing with the green brush of his typewriter eraser.

Even from such a distance, Sandy was enchanting. She wore a tan-colored sweater top, covered by an unbuttoned brown woolen coat that came nearly to her knees. There was a red and gold scarf draped around her neck. Her dark brown skirt had thin yellow stripes that ran vertically, and its hemline was a bit shorter than most, barely reaching mid-calf.

Abel said something funny, and all three of them laughed. When Sandy glanced down the hallway, Wesley stepped backward slightly to avoid detection. He had glimpsed her smile, and it sent a pain of sorrow to his throat. A louder voice was heard, and in response, the three reporters—still giggling among themselves—disappeared into the newsroom. Wesley wandered toward Studio A in a daze, wide-eyed like some desperately wounded animal. His energy sapped by gloom, he felt no inclination to compete for the girl's attention. Just who did she think she was?

Sandy's arrival was not the only change that the new year brought. There was also a replacement for Becky Headrick in bookkeeping. Over the holidays, Becky moved with her two daughters to the San Francisco area, joining her husband, Frank, who was now employed at Henry J. Kaiser's Richmond Shipyard Number Three.

Assuming the vacated post at KWXN was Anita Grier, a scrawny waif of a twenty-year-old who looked more like she was fourteen. Wesley knew she must be older than her appearance suggested because he had never once seen her at Waco High School. Besides that, she smelled of alcohol and smoked incessantly. Then, too, her indelicate vocabulary denoted someone with considerable experience in the ways of the world.

Wesley met the new employee when he turned in his first biweekly time card for 1944. Taken aback, he studied the unfamiliar face. "Hello, miss. Would you give this to Becky?"

"Becky's gone. I'm Anita." There was no denying that the undernourished, fragile body detracted from her looks, but her face was pretty enough.

Confused, Wesley stared at her through the cigarette smoke. "You mean, just for today?" He handed the girl his time card.

"Nope. I guess she's gone for good." A shred of tobacco had found its way to the tip of her tongue, so she flicked it away with a dry spit. She studied the card. "What's your name anyway?"

His face brightened. "Wesley," he told her. Maybe she was interested in becoming better acquainted. There was no ring on her left hand.

"I mean the last name," she said. "I can't read your hieroglyphics."

He swallowed. "Oh, sorry, miss. It's Brower." He glanced down at his fingernails, hoping to cover his embarrassment with aloofness.

"B-R-O-W-E-R?"

"Yes, ma'am."

"Thanks, Mr. Brower. We'll take care of it." She had already returned to another task, sorting a stack of December pay vouchers.

Wesley started to walk away but then turned around. "Your name's Anita?" he asked.

She laid her cigarette in the ashtray and looked annoyed. "Say, has anybody ever told you that you have an amazing memory?"

Wesley let the sarcasm pass without comment. "Try me on your last name," he said. The smoke from her cigarette wafted gently upward in a curlicue pattern. "Give me five guesses."

Anita shrugged her shoulders. "If that's your childish idea of a good time. Fire away." She began alphabetizing the vouchers.

"Lamarr?"

She smiled. "Not even close."

"Lake?" he asked.

"No, but I'll take her hair."

"Durbin?"

"Nope." She retrieved the cigarette.

Wesley studied her intently. It was not a movie-star face, granted, but the eyes were unusually large and as green as jade. "Uh ... Grable?"

"Hardly, but you're getting warmer. Unless I counted wrong, you're down to your final ..."

"Grier?"

Anita's jaw dropped, and she nearly fumbled the cigarette. "What did you say?"

"Grier? G-R-I-E-R."

She looked sideways at him and scanned the top of her desk. A smile crept onto her face. "Who told you my name?"

"No one—just a lucky guess. Maybe I was thinking of Greer Garson or something." He smiled and walked from the room, leaving her to puzzle for the rest of the day over his baffling clairvoyance.

On the way home from work, she mailed her electric bill in the post office at Eighth and Austin, never once considering where that particular piece of correspondence was lying just a couple of hours earlier. Its return address, barely peeking from beneath her purse, was clearly legible—even when read upside-down.

Wesley acted that day's script with a vision of Anita Grier in the back of his mind, and the thought evoked a warm feeling that he had not experienced in many months. He would show that egotistical Sandra Whittsel a thing or two. There were lots more female fish in the sea.

◆   ◆   ◆

Nearly seven weeks had passed since Giulia Coletti posted her note to Stephen Brower, and though she checked the mailbox on a twice-daily basis, no reply had yet arrived. Surely the sailor possessed enough courtesy to manage that simple task. How much effort does it require to scribble a few lines, fold a sheet of paper into thirds, and lick a gum-sealed envelope? Even the postage would be free of charge for a serviceman. Utterly inexcusable, she thought.

Then again, could not an equally convincing argument be made that it was she who stood guilty of condemning him without a fair trial? There were many plausible explanations for his exasperating silence, and she recited them to herself. Had he never received her letter? Had she sent it to the wrong address? Had it been misdirected by postal authorities? Had the mail-carrying vessel been torpedoed to the bottom? Worst of all, had he been badly injured or killed in action?

Her imagination also offered some more convoluted scenarios that, selfish or not, were every bit as painful to accept. Had he recognized her musings for the drivel they were, wadded them up, and kicked the paper ball into the sea? Was he aware of her Catholic upbringing and shying away from a "Romanist" entanglement? Or did he perhaps have a steady girl back home, someone whose surpassing charms left no room in his heart for written responses to a hopeful chorus of lesser admirers?

Whatever the reason, it would be a mistake to assume that Giulia Coletti was desperate for attention from the opposite sex. She received more than her fair share of compliments and flirtations. Her classic beauty, creamy olive complexion, and shapely figure saw to that. However, the authors of these futile advances always left much to be desired, and Giulia was nothing if not selective. This created something of a paradox, for it was the most attractive potential suitors who stayed away from her. Anyone as beautiful as she, they instinctively realized, was bound to be unapproachable. Could they not secure more modest liaisons without risking almost certain rejection? Giulia had no other choice but to stand in the wings, wearing her sad but lovely smile, while many in the graduating class of 1944 were already making plans for their nuptials.

The only exception to the uneventfulness in Giulia's love life was her intended, Archie Clarke. It had been his singular fortune—for good or ill—to catch her in a moment of weakness, at a catechism celebration for her nephew that was organized by her own mother, Paolina. To his credit, Archie knew breathtaking comeliness when he saw it. Before the afternoon was over, he had backed the bashful lass into a corner with insistent offers of finger sandwiches and cups of punch. Not a very accomplished judge of character, he brushed aside her gentle rebuffs as nothing more than playful entrapment.

Archie jumped into the nascent relationship with both feet, courting Miss Coletti nearly every day for the next two months, until he received notice in the mail that his draft number had been called. And then, when all seemed lost, he had the foresight to monopolize Giulia in his absence by exacting from her a railway-platform commitment. No doubt the tumultuous, dramatic setting that surrounded her on that Sunday morning was influential as well. The impressionable teenage girl must have felt like she was in a movie—the uniforms, the embraces, the tearful goodbyes, the bittersweet waves of the hand. Even the chilly dawn was in black and white. Whatever the cause, Giulia blurted a declaration of affection that she would come to regret. A sense of shame began to gnaw at her before his train had disappeared from view into the sunrise.

The relationship's defect was simple enough to identify. Archie's love for Giulia was genuine, but she herself was not ready to become serious. While she stopped short of actually breaking off their "understanding," neither did she fan the flames of encouragement. Inevitably, his letters—consistently passionate though they remained—gradually acquired for her the aura of just so many words from a good friend ... a casual acquaintance ... a total stranger.

The fact that this one-sided, long-distance romance stubbornly refused to wither and die was a testament to the relentless campaigning of Bess Clarke, the soldier's well-intentioned mother and proxy. Giulia had first met her some eighteen months earlier, about three weeks before Archie reported for military service. It was not a positive first impression. Mrs. Clarke was crouching down in the backyard, pulling weeds from the flower bed and stuffing them into a battered trash can. She was wearing work gloves, and the strong twisting motion of her hands never failed to extract every last root of the defenseless vegetation.

"Mother, I'd like for you to meet someone," Archie said. "This is Giulia, the girl I've been telling you about."

Mrs. Clarke was chagrined. She climbed to her feet and—momentarily forgetting the soiled gloves—began to make certain that her hair was in place. Grunting, she shook her head in annoyance at herself and removed the gloves, unceremoniously tossing them to the ground and offering her right hand to the girl. The voice, however, was regal. "How do you do, Giulia?" she said with the equanimity of a duchess. One had to be quick to notice her fleeting scowl, but Archie's well-practiced eye—on the receiving end—was up to the challenge. "Would it have been difficult to grant me some advance warning that we were to have company today?" She gave her son a tight-lipped smile.

"I don't have to be at work until two," he told her, "so I just thought we would stop by and say hello."

"Well, I'm glad you did—both of you. I'll have lunch ready in a jiffy." Through her tiny, wire-rimmed eyeglasses, she looked directly at Giulia. "You do like liverwurst sandwiches, don't you?"

Giulia glanced at Archie, who came to her rescue.

"Mother, that sounds fine, but we really can't stay. We're going over to Kenneth's house for a while, and then we're all going out to eat."

"Where?"

"I don't know. Uptown somewhere."

His mother returned to her squatting position. "Well, of course, if you'd rather." Archie took Giulia by the hand, and they effected a quick, if graceless, exit.

◆   ◆   ◆

Some of the southern boys at Blackland Army Air Field had never witnessed such a majestic sight before, except of course in periodicals, movies, picture books, and newsreels. On the thirteenth day of 1944, they awoke to a substantial dusting of snow, and the frozen precipitation continued to drift to the ground throughout much of the next twenty-four hours. By the following morning, a three-inch blanket of white covered the base, necessitating the curtailment of most outdoor drills and training. It was Waco's first heavy snowfall in four years.

While Danny Rignold was making his way to PT on that bitterly cold Friday— with temperatures hovering in the lower twenties—one of his boots slipped out from under him, and he nearly took a header onto the parade grounds. Only the sidewalk's metal guardrail saved him from injury and even deeper humiliation.

As it was, he still felt embarrassed about retrieving his disengaged cap from the bushes. Sergeant Koenig turned his head away with a dismissive glower, and it was several days before others in his platoon would let him forgot about the mishap. Danny should have known better than to disregard the slipperiness, for he was one of the winterized veterans. Kosciusko averaged about an inch and a quarter of snowfall every January.

For a few minutes after noon chow, as was his habit, Danny flipped through a newspaper in the day room. He read that impromptu snowball fights had erupted all across the city on Thursday, some of them involving the normally staid professors at Baylor. And it seems that local radio personality Mary Holliday Spillman had presented her morning program over WACO while nursing a badly sprained wrist, suffered when she slipped on the icy front porch as she attempted to pick up her home-delivered copy of the *News-Tribune*.

It was a day relegated to routine maintenance, with all basic flight-training missions grounded, and only the most experienced of student aviators were asked to take to the air. Corporal Freddie Biscoff—sounding like an itinerant carnival barker—was soliciting bets on Saturday's Texas-Texas A&M basketball game in Austin, and he cornered Danny when no NCOs were snooping around. "Four bits a square," he told him. Biscoff unfolded the dog-eared pool grid, so his next patsy might see which numbers were yet to be tapped.

"Too rich for me," Danny said.

"It's worth fifty bucks to the winner."

"And ninety-nine losers are out a half-dollar each."

Biscoff put his arm around Danny's shoulder. "Hey, pal, you're looking at it all wrong. You're never going to win anything with an attitude like that."

Danny laughed. "I've never won anythin' in my life, Biscuit, and I don't plan to start now."

Biscoff crossed himself. "Mother of God! I'll personally bless the squares you pick—if that'll make you feel any better about your chances."

"That would sink my ship for sure. What makes you think you've got the Good Lord's attention more than any of the other saps around here?"

"Because I'm holding the purse strings, see? There's a cool forty-two fifty in my locker, plus four bucks in my shirt, and I've got a feeling that whole bundle of cash has your name written all over it—plus another three and a half that's yet to be collected. But you can't win if you're not in."

"Nope. Sorry."

Biscoff sighed and shook his head. "Don't say I didn't give you an ample opportunity," he said. "I've got a good feeling about this." He turned to leave.

Danny felt a tug of curiosity as Biscoff refolded the paper. "Just let me see how it's set up. That won't cost me anythin', will it?"

Biscoff licked his lips. "No," he said. "Let's just say you're examining the merchandise. No obligation. No salesman will call." He looked around the hangar and then walked over to the tool chest, which he decided to use as a tabletop. Danny followed behind, silently berating himself as a sucker.

"Seven and five is a good combination," Biscoff said. "So's nine and two."

Danny glanced at the suggested squares. "What are you tryin' to pull? This isn't football, so no score's any better than any others."

"Don't you believe in lucky numbers?"

"Not much. Besides, if these are so great, why didn't you take them yourself?"

Biscoff was not listening. "Five and zero's a good tandem, and one and four ain't so bad either."

Danny looked at the grid more closely and jingled the coins in his pocket. "I've got a quarter, two dimes, and five pennies to my name. Give me six and four."

Biscoff broke into a broad grin. "You won't regret it, Danny Boy. I've got a good feeling about your chances." He accepted the coins with humility, depositing them into his bulging shirt pocket with the other wagers.

"How much do you have ridin' on the game?" Danny asked.

"Six squares. You saw my name, didn't you?"

"In other words, you have six times the chance to win as I do."

"That's true, but I can only net forty-seven bucks to your forty-nine fifty."

Danny marveled at the corporal's unassailable logic, but all he could see was a shiny Franklin half-dollar, sprouting wings and flying away forever.

That afternoon, clandestine cigarettes dangling from their lips as they worked, ground-crew mechanics lingered upon the timely subject of prop-less aviation. Just the previous week, Bell Aircraft Corporation informed the public of yet another encouraging flight by an experimental jet-propelled fighter, successfully realized—with derby on his head and cigar in his mouth—by civilian test pilot Robert Stanley. The formerly top-secret XP-59A Airacomet's historic first mission had taken place on October 1, 1942, high above Muroc Dry Lake in California's Mojave Desert, and a year and a third of intensive experimentation ensued. Although the four-hundred-miles-per-hour prototype could overtake a formation of speedy P-38s, at least one first-generation aviator remained unpersuaded. From his home in Dayton, Ohio, seventy-two-year-old Orville Wright assured reporters that jet propulsion would never compete with the conventional type of thrust. "Its greatest advantage," he said, "is the fact it produces a great amount of power for a few seconds." Consequently, the Father of Flight foresaw a very limited application by the Army Air Forces.

Before retiring for the night, Danny dashed off a quick letter to his parents in Mississippi. He wanted to tell them of his exciting brush with fame sixteen days earlier. While on a week's KP duty in the BAAF hospital's mess hall, he was able to meet a contingent of visiting screen celebrities. Fred MacMurray was there, fresh from filming the yet-to-be-released *And the Angels Sing* and *Double Indemnity*. Though claiming to be ten years out of practice, MacMurray borrowed an instrument from one of the base musicians and gallantly attempted a saxophone solo. Also performing for the men was young *femme fatale* Ann Savage, fast becoming one of Hollywood's most familiar faces in such low-budget features as *Passport to Suez* and the Blondie and Dagwood comedy, *Footlight Glamour*. Gamely disdaining a touch of the flu, she frolicked through a comedy skit with her handpicked "leading man" for the occasion, Corporal Marvin Williams. Another ambassador spreading cheer among the troops was bespectacled musician and actor Pinky Tomlin, recently appearing on screen in *Here Comes Elmer*, with such audience favorites as Dale Evans and the Nat "King" Cole Trio. He delighted the crowd with a stream of ad-libbed service jokes and accompanied himself on the guitar while singing some of his own compositions—including, of course, "The Object of My Affection." Rounding out the quartet of luminaries was actor Tom Conway, who had played an uncredited role in the Oscar-winning *Mrs. Miniver* and was now starring as Tom Lawrence in RKO's immensely popular Falcon series. Born Thomas Sanders, he was the older brother of highly regarded British actor George Sanders. At Blackland, Conway joined Tomlin in a few bouncy songs and then came through with a flurry of one-liners that, he assured the hospital patients, would have them all "in stitches."

Frigid weather relaxed its grip on central Texas by Sunday morning, so Private Rignold decided to stroll over to the base library. There he consulted the *News-Tribune* sports page, only to find that it ran true to his low expectations. In college basketball action the night before, the sharpshooting Longhorns had set a Southwest Conference scoring record in mauling the Aggies, 77-40. Danny had not won the fifty-dollar prize, but (he was later pleased to learn) neither did Corporal Freddie Biscoff, who had, in fact, squandered three dollars on his own racket. The winner turned out to be a lifer, Staff Sergeant Arlen Doppler.

This was just as well, thought Danny, as it is always a good idea to keep the company cook happy.

◆   ◆   ◆

A sinking feeling came over her the moment Hannah passed by the band hall and circled around the bookstore building to its entrance. She could not have chosen a worse time to buy an examination blue book, but she went inside nonetheless. The Baylor Book Store's limited floor space was teeming with servicemen of all descriptions: Navy V-5 trainees, active-duty recruits and recruiters, and cadets from the Army Specialized Training Program.

The ASTP boys outnumbered all others by a wide margin on this particular day, and quite a few were—for reasons known only to themselves and perhaps their superiors—arrogant in the extreme. One young man, blocking the aisle with his outstretched arms, greeted her with an unctuous "Hi, cutie" and then a wolf whistle. Heads turned.

"The name's not 'Cutie,' boy scout." Chewing her bubble gum noisily, Hannah waited for him to step aside.

Undeterred, the cadet tried a more subtle approach. "Aw, come on, beautiful. Be nice to the guys in khaki."

One of his friends said, "Maybe she just doesn't like that color, Zim. Maybe it's nothin' personal against you."

"We're all the same color underneath," another added, and a few bystanders snickered.

Hannah ignored the comment and tried to venture past, but a short, dumpy cadet stepped forward to obstruct her way. "Excuse me, miss," he said, "but can you tell me where they keep the foot powder? All of that marching, you know."

"I really wouldn't know. Do I look like I work here?" She took another step forward, but he held fast, defying her with a smile. "Please let me by," she said.

"Who's stopping you?"

The aisle was blocked. Worse yet, she could sense that a few servicemen had closed in behind her. Hannah's alarm turned to anger. "Get out of my way, fats," she said. This drew shouts of amusement from the others.

"There's plenty of room to get by," the cadet told her. "'Course it might be a wee bit cozy."

She chewed her gum furiously. "Hey, I pay good money to go to this university, soldier. I'm not on the government gravy-train like you are."

"Oh, sure, this is a reg'lar vacation, boys. Listen to that."

One rawboned serviceman, tall and brainy-looking, was the lone voice of reason in the standoff. "Say, fellas, give her a break," he said. "She's a nice enough gal. She doesn't need this kind of treatment."

Hannah acknowledged him without so much as a glance. "Well, thank you, kind sir."

But her pudgy adversary was in no mood to commiserate. "Judas Christ! We were only trying to have a little fun with—"

Before he could finish the sentence Hannah lashed out with the back of her hand and struck him squarely on the mouth. Her eyes flashed blood red, and so, one second later, did the corner of his swelling lower lip.

"Don't ever talk about my Savior that way," she told him, "or, so help me, I'll kick your private parts so hard that you'll be bent over for an hour." She meant it, too, and the injured soldier backed away.

"Jeez, these Baylor girls are about as sweet as ..." He watched her pass by. "They should wear jack-boots instead o' pumps." He forced a laugh, and a few of his compatriots joined in, but otherwise the surrender was unconditional.

As she pivoted to stomp toward the exit, the middle finger of Hannah's right hand was throbbing—its knuckle bruised from solid contact with one or more teeth—and she kneaded it with the fingers of her other hand. Behind her came the sound of more laughter among the ASTP cadets, but she could not have cared less.

"Did he hurt you, miss?" someone to her right said, and she recognized the voice. It was the courtly peacemaker. His eyeglasses were sliding down the bridge of his nose, so he repositioned them.

Hannah was still seething. "No, I hurt myself. He was just standing there like a baboon, and I slugged him. He deserved it."

"Maybe General Patton could use you to slap the cowards."

She glared at him, but then her face softened. "Oh, sure."

"I'll ask Ike about it—the next time I see him. He's kind of busy these days."

"You do that." She reached for the door handle to leave.

"Say, didn't you come in here to buy something?" the soldier asked.

She shook her wounded hand and chuckled. "I guess I did."

"Official escort," the soldier said. He offered his arm, but she declined. "Look, miss, I feel responsible for this. Just let me walk you over to where you need to be."

"That's not necessary," Hannah said. She marched directly toward the crowd of uniforms while the tall soldier watched in awe.

"Hey, fellas, step aside," one of the young men said, and the Red Sea parted. Even her chunky foe deferred.

Later, at the cash register, the lanky ASTP cadet stepped in line behind her with a pencil to purchase. "My name's Winton Groat," he said. "What's yours?"

"How do you do?"

He frowned. "Well, I know it's not 'Cutie.' We've already established that much." Hannah's expression did not change.

"Five cents," the cashier said to her.

"Are you going to make me guess it by process of elimination, then? That may take a while."

"Suit yourself," Hannah said. She took a nickel from her purse.

The soldier sighed. "What's your problem? Do you hate men or something?"

"All I want to do is buy this blue book, mister."

"Groat."

"Okay, Mr. Groat."

"You've got me all wrong, miss. I'm a college grad. I'm not one of them." He nodded toward the others. "Most of them are troglodytes, and I apologize for the way they behaved."

Hannah rolled her eyes. "Listen, you seem to be a nice boy. But just because you were my hero over there doesn't mean I want to get friendly."

He paid for his pencil and laughed. "I'm not asking you to marry me. I just wanted to know your name."

"What for?"

"Just to be friendly."

"How many times do I have to tell you? I don't want to get friendly." She blew a small bubble and popped it.

"All right then, just to be courteous. Do you like that word better?"

"As a matter of fact, I do."

Groat smiled and opened the door for her. "You know, I was a psychology major in college ..."

"Congratulations."

"... at Princeton. Have you heard of it?"

"Seems to me I have." She gave a wide yawn, scanning the wintry campus.

The soldier, meanwhile, was staring intently at her. "I like to learn what makes people tick. It's kind of my hobby."

"How fascinating."

Groat stopped walking and pointed at her. "I'd say you're definitely on the defensive about something, and now I'm curious to find out why."

"Nothing mysterious about it ... *doctor*. That's just the way I am." She brushed away her unruly blonde curls.

"Oh, I'm not a Doctor of Psychology, I'm afraid—or even a Master, for that matter." He pushed his sliding eyeglasses back in place. "I'm just plain old 'Bachelor' Groat, in both senses of the word."

Her eyes wandered. Three squirrels were nearby, one sitting on its haunches while eating a nut and the others fervently digging in the dormant lawn.

The soldier studied Hannah's profile for a moment, waiting for her to return the glance. When she did not, he finally said, "Well, maybe I'll see you around."

Expressionless, she massaged her bruised finger. "That's possible, I guess, but I don't plan to come to the bookstore again when it's so crowded with uniforms."

Winton Groat shook his head with a frown, paused for a second or two, and then walked away without saying another word. He kicked angrily at a rock-hard pecan shell. It skidded across the yellow-brown grass, narrowly missing a startled coed before striking loudly against the side bricks of Old Main.

◆　　◆　　◆

"Wes, come in here for a minute, will you?" It was Hugh Kenton, speaking over the intercom.

Wesley laid down his half-eaten green apple and obeyed the summons. When he peeked into the control room, he could see that it was deserted except for the director and janitor Moses Dobbs. Kenton was sitting at the console, attempting to clean the contact of a noisy mike pot. He was still wearing his hat, so he must have come inside just a moment before. "Have a seat," Kenton said, and then, puzzled, he glanced up at the wall clock. "Say, aren't you a little bit early today?"

Wesley sat down in soundman Dickie Waterhouse's chair. "Gilly Miller brought me part of the way in his truck."

The director looked at his young actor in surprise. "That crate of junk? I didn't even know it was roadworthy."

"Barely," Wesley said. "He passed me near school, so we put my bike in the flatbed."

"You're a better man than I am, Gunga Din!"

Wesley smiled at the *bon mot*, though he did not really know why. He was unacquainted with the writings of Kipling, words so familiar to an earlier generation.

Kenton stroked his mustache with his left hand and screwed the VU knob back in place with his right. He enjoyed tinkering with the station's electronics but was always careful to do so when there was no engineer in sight. Dave Flint was downtown at the moment, on a junket to purchase some new resistors.

"What are you doing in the last two weeks of February, son?"

Wesley stared blankly. "I don't know. Working here and going to school, I guess."

Kenton acknowledged the comment with a nod and cleared his throat. But no utterance was forthcoming. Wesley squirmed in his seat. He could sense that it was nearly time to read over the day's script, and besides that, the meat of his apple was surely turning brown by now.

"Have you ever been to California?"

Wesley thought he had misheard the question. "Sir?" he said.

"Have you ever been to California?" Kenton leaned forward, pretending to study the console.

Wesley thought for a second. "We went to Sequoia once, when I was a little kid."

"How would you like to go to Hollywood?" the director asked.

Wesley's eyes widened, and he was at a loss for words. "I don't understand," he finally said.

Moses Dobbs stopped sweeping and stared at the boy, whose open mouth seemed frozen in shock. Clearly, Kenton was relishing the moment, though he made every attempt to minimize his smile and keep the discussion on a professional plane.

"Do you think your mother would let you go west—on business—for two weeks next month?"

"I'm pretty sure she would," Wesley said. "But what about school?"

"You just let me deal with your school. Your principal has been very supportive all along. It's your mother that we need to convince."

Wesley looked at Dobbs, who quickly averted his eyes with a smile.

"Why me?" the boy asked.

"Mr. Wollach's not able to go to the CBS meeting, so it will just be Clive Ramey and I. He told me to suggest someone else to tag along, and I thought of you."

"But why me? Why not Marshall ... or Hatch Priggett?"

"Simple. Hatch needs to sit in for me. You know, the serials don't run themselves. As for McFall, I don't want him chasing starlets all over Hollywood on company time."

A worried look came to Wesley's face. "But what about Kip Hanson? Can somebody else play him while I'm gone."

"Won't need to," Kenton said. "I've asked the writers for a contingency script, to have Kip disappear for a couple of weeks. Held hostage or some nonsense like that. We've already established that angle with the Baltimore underworld anyway—the Cashley brothers and what have you—so they can just build on that." He noticed two cast members arriving in the studio. "Of course, if you can't go, then we'll just stick with the regular story line."

"Oh, I'll be able to go all right, Hugh. Don't worry about my mother." Never before had Wesley addressed the director by his first name—except, of course, when Kenton demanded it—and the familiarity felt good to him, as if he had achieved membership in an exclusive club.

That night, as Nora was sitting in an easy chair, listening to "Duffy's Tavern" and mending one of her late husband's socks for Wesley to wear, Elizabeth came downstairs with a paper for her to sign. "Mother," she said, "can you read this over for Mrs. Archer's class? It's about the war-bonds booth at Saturday's dance."

"I didn't think you were going."

"I'm not. At least I don't think so. I haven't been asked."

"Those boys in the ninth grade must be plain crazy. A pretty girl like you."

Elizabeth stifled a grin. "Oh, Mother ..." She took a seat on the sofa.

Nora looked up from her knitting. "Well, I mean it. There's not another girl in that entire school who's as pretty as you are. The idea that you're going to be sitting at home while—"

"Honestly, that would not be the end of the world—now, would it? Besides, there's not a boy in my class I care anything for ... in that sort of way."

"So, if you're not going, why do I need to sign this?" Nora asked.

"That's to let me work in the booth."

"Why do you need my permission?"

"Search me. I think it must be so the parents will know where their children are. Everyone is either going to be dancing or working in the booth."

"Is Dudley Rollins going? He was a very nice boy."

"He's the reason I'll be working in the booth. I know for a fact that he was going to ask me to the dance."

"Oh, really? Are you a fortune teller?"

"No, but I have a whole network of spies. All of us girls do."

Nora gave a wry smile. "Okay, I'll sign."

Elizabeth handed her the sheet of paper and a pen, pointing to where the signature should go. "I'll be working at the filling station all day Saturday, but I get off at six."

"Will that give you enough time?"

"I don't have to get all fixed up just to sell war bonds. That's another reason why I don't want to go to the dance."

Her mother handed back the paper and pen. "Well, I still think you should show more interest in the boys, dear," she said. "That poor Dudley seemed to be carrying quite a torch for you."

"Hah! Dudley Rollins is a nice boy—I'll give him that much. But he's so ... predictable. You may not have noticed, but he is one very dull person."

"Now hush. I would hate for Dudley to know you feel that way about him. That's a terrible thing to say."

"It's the truth. That's what I think about him."

"You don't need to say it out loud."

"There's no one here but you and me."

Just then Wesley stepped around the corner and into the living room. "And Kip Hanson makes three," he said.

Elizabeth's eyes became poisonous darts. "Wesley Franklin Brower! How long have you been listening to our private conversation?"

"Not long. Just long enough to hear you dragging your boyfriend's good name through the mud."

"He's not my boyfriend, and you know it. I wouldn't talk that way about my boyfriend—if I had one." Wesley could see that Elizabeth's face was reddening with rage. "And I resent you sneaking around," she said, "prying into a discussion that is, frankly, none of your business."

"Well, pardon me, madame, but I happen to live here too."

Nora laid the knitting on her lap. "Please stop that, the both of you. Wes, I do think you could be a little more considerate about eavesdropping on your sister."

"Yes, ma'am, but I wasn't sneaking around like she says. I was coming down here anyway." Wesley glared at Elizabeth, who stuck out her tongue at him. He ignored the petulant gesture and turned to his mother. "I need to ask you something important."

"You don't mind if I sit in on this, do you?" Elizabeth asked.

"As a matter of fact, I do. Mom, will you kindly make her disappear?"

"Now you know how *she* feels," Nora said. "The shoe's on the other foot."

Wesley frowned at his mother. "I told you that I was coming down here anyway. It just so happened that I reached the bottom of the stairs right when Lizzie was busy assassinating the character of her boyfriend."

"He's not my boyfriend!"

"All right, then," he said, "her friend who happens to be a boy."

Ed Gardner's razor-tongued Archie was bringing "Duffy's Tavern" to a close on NBC, and "Burns and Allen" was about to start on CBS. Nora, with her knitting still in one hand, walked over to the console. The loudspeaker whined as she dialed the tuning knob from WACO to KWXN. A public service announcement began, itemizing the benefits of food conservation. This was a meatless Tuesday.

"Don't worry, Mother," Elizabeth said. "I'll leave you two in peace. I can't think of anything Wes could say that would possibly interest me."

Nora gently scolded her. "Now, sweetie, don't behave that way. It makes me sad to see the two of you at each other's throats like this." She sat down and resumed her knitting. "And Wes, much of this is your doing—the way you're constantly teasing Lizzie from morning until night."

He winked at his sister. "That's because I love her so much."

"Oh, I think I'm going to be ill," Elizabeth said. She proudly marched from the room and up the stairs.

Nora chuckled and again laid her knitting aside. "And what is it, young man, that is so important for you to tell me?"

He looked toward the stairway and cleared his throat. "Mom, can I go to California for a couple of weeks? The radio station will pay for it."

Nora raised her eyebrows. "California! You certainly may not." The knitting slid from her lap and onto the floor.

"But, Mom, it's company business. I have to go."

"You'll do no such thing. Your schooling is more important to me than any radio station."

"What if I told you that Mrs. Butler is all for the idea?"

"I would be very surprised," Nora said with a suspicious look. She reached down to retrieve the knitting. "So she's approved this little vacation of yours?"

"Not exactly, but Mr. Kenton is going to talk with her about it." Wesley sat down on the sofa, near his mother, right where Elizabeth had been just a minute earlier. "He's pretty sure that Mrs. Butler will give me the go-ahead. She's a big fan of 'Behold Tomorrow'—at least she used to be, before Mr. Torrance went into the Navy. I don't think she has much time to listen anymore."

Nora sat back in her chair and sighed. "I'll make this deal with you. If I can talk with Marian Butler, and if she can convince me that this is in your best interest, then I'll give my permission. How many people are going?"

"Just two others—Mr. Kenton and Mr. Ramey."

"Who's he?"

"Clive Ramey is the station manager. He's one of the people who hired me."

"Are they going by train?"

"Sure, we'll be going by train. How else would we get out to California?" Wesley scooted forward, on the edge of the sofa cushion. "See, it's the big network conference. They have it every year, and this is the first time that KWXN has been invited. Anyway, Mr. Wollach can't come, so they've got an extra seat."

"Why did they select you?"

"Don't know exactly, but I can't pass up the chance. Wouldn't you want to do this, if you were in my shoes?"

"Not if it interfered with my studies," she said. That was a fib, of course, but perhaps justified in this context. "Please make an appointment with Mrs. Butler, and we'll see what she has to say about it."

The Felix Mills Orchestra played George M. Cohen's "The Love Nest," and announcer Bill Goodwin began revealing the wonders of Swan Soap. It was time for George and Gracie.

◆　　◆　　◆

As seems to happen rather often in life, Steve's letter to Giulia arrived at precisely the moment when she was least expecting it. So many weeks had elapsed since her brash decision to contact him that all realistic hope of a reply had vanished, along with any tender esteem that she had once hidden in her heart. Miss Coletti, who was by nature an optimistic young woman, had descended into a spell of the doldrums—but more closely resembling scorn than outright depression. Her mother voiced the unsolicited opinion that Giulia was only "going through a phase."

All of this came to a gleeful halt with the reception, in the Wednesday afternoon mail, of a simple four-by-five-inch envelope from a military box somewhere in the United States. Giulia saw the return address, shuddered, and immediately tore into the enclosure with the nearest sharp object she could locate on such short notice, a serrated dinner knife that rested upon the kitchen counter. Traces of dried gravy were clinging to the frayed edges of the paper when she reached inside. She was virtually alone, her mother having retired to bed in search of relief from her chronic spasms of back pain.

Giulia's heart was pounding as she gazed upon the hand-scrawled words, a brief note that represented her first-ever piece of correspondence from a serviceman other than Archie Clarke. Needless to say, she instantly forgave Stephen Brower for the flaw of procrastination in his character.

> Thanks for the letter of Nov. 20. Sure, I remember you. I sat near you in chemistry lab. (Couldn't you feel my eyes staring at you during class?!!) Promise not to spread it around, but I even asked Mrs. Chesky if I could change places with your partner—I forget his name, Brian something, huh? My sidekick, Janice Poston, didn't know a Bunsen burner from a salt shaker. She's probably married to a bank president by now! Sorry it took so long for me to write, but we've been real busy here for the past few weeks. Also, I'm not the best letter writer—just ask my Mom. What to say? I guess the censor won't scissor away a vague remark like we'll be shipping out "sometime soon." That could mean anything, you know, and it should be common knowledge that we're not being trained to mop decks stateside for the rest of our lives. Please drop me another note whenever you can. I'll try to look you up if I'm ever home on leave. Maybe we can go get a cone at Joe's. It would be nice to see some of the old gang again, but I'm sure most of them are probably fighting for their country by now. Except for Gavin Morrissey, of course. When's he getting out? He never did look good in horizontal stripes. Well, at least he's serving!
> Imaginary kisses from a homesick swab,
> Steve Brower

Giulia seemed to be floating on air as she raced from the kitchen to her own room and fell headlong upon the bed. She rolled onto her back and read the letter over and over again. Each time she came to the phrases, "... if I could change places ..." and "... I'll try to look you up ..." she felt a warm rush of excitement. But it was the "imaginary kisses" that brought the most wonderful sensation of giddiness, almost as if she had been whirling in circles like a playful grade-schooler intent on becoming dizzy. She now knew that Steve had to be about the most wonderful boy in the world—to write back, from the brink of deployment, to someone with whom he had hardly spoken a dozen words in all his life. And Mrs. Brower, too, for it was she who suggested that her son might enjoy receiving a note from a fellow Waco High Tiger.

A pleasant thought was taking shape in Giulia's mind: Steve must have mentioned her to his mother at one time or another. Why else would Mrs. Brower have suggested that she write? That would have been a most presumptuous course of action, if done entirely of a mother's own free will. Giulia also began wondering whether it was simply an accident that Mrs. Brower happened to be in Moek Grocery that fateful September morning. Perhaps it had been by feminine design. Mothers were known to venture extreme measures for the good of their offspring. Then again, maybe it was pre-ordained. God, too, was intimately concerned with the well-being of His children.

Whatever the reason, whosever the guiding hand, Giulia gave thanks for being in the right place at the right time. How funny life was! She might never have written to her secret love, had she not been compelled to purchase a trivial sack of spaghetti for the dining pleasure of her "future mother-in-law," Mrs. Bess Clarke. She shivered at that vexing thought. When would she finally work up the courage to break off her understanding with Archie? It was unfair to string him along like this. But she sensed how devastating it might be for a serviceman to receive a "Dear John" letter—half a world away, presumably in Australia—with no inkling that there was anything awry.

Once she had savored Steve's congenial note, it required all of Giulia's self-control to refrain from writing back that very moment. She wanted to "strike while the iron was hot"—as her estranged father would say—but she was also mindful that unwanted consequences might accrue from appearing too anxious, especially when Steve himself had admitted to procrastinating for several weeks before finally marshaling the energy to respond.

She smiled, kissed the envelope, and laid it on her dresser top. Then, heeding her better instincts, she marched straight to the living room, seated herself at the upright piano, and leafed through the music arrayed before her. Finding nothing of interest, she opened the piano bench's lid and searched among the sheet music folios for something that might engage her mind. Amidst the inconsequential Tin Pan Alley ditties lay a genuine diamond in the rough, "The Rosary," and she swallowed hard when the title caught her eye.

Gently placing it upon the piano rack, Giulia began sight-reading, in a slow tempo and hushed dynamic, with reverence normally reserved for a sacred hymn. She was conscious of the words as she played:

> *The hours I spent with thee, dear heart,*
> *Are as a string of pearls to me;*
> *I count them over, every one apart,*
> *My Rosary, my Rosary.*
>
> *Each hour a pearl, each pearl a prayer,*
> *To still a heart in absence wrung;*
> *I tell each bead unto the end,*
> *And there a cross is hung.*
>
> *O memories that bless and burn!*
> *O barren gain and bitter loss!*
> *I kiss each bead, and strive at last to learn*
> *To kiss the cross;*
> *Sweetheart! to kiss the cross.*

When Paolina appeared at the doorway, drawn near by the seldom-heard sound of her daughter's pianism, Giulia lifted her fingers from the keys.

"Sorry, Mamma," the girl said. "You probably couldn't even recognize it." She brushed at her right cheek with the back of a hand and giggled. "It's hard to read the notes with these silly tears in my eyes."

Paolina stepped closer and put a hand on Giulia's shoulder. "It sounded very pretty, dear. You know, I bought that piece of music in Dallas—at the State Fair a long time ago. It was one of my favorite tunes back then, but I haven't heard it in years. What made you play it now?"

"Just the title, I guess." Giulia looked down, embarrassed by her crying. "Would you like to hear something in particular?" she asked. "I'm a little out of practice, but I'll try."

Her mother was not listening. "I bought that at the Texas State Fair," she said again. "President Taft was there that day, and the crowds were just huge."

"You saw a President of the United States—in person?" Giulia was agog.

Paolina smiled, pleased at her daughter's interest. "Yes, and I heard him speak too—from a distance. I really couldn't tell what he was saying very well, but he received a grand ovation. I do remember that."

"You went there with Grandpa and Grandma Spano?"

"Yes, and my father was simply beside himself—to think that I wanted to listen to what President Taft had to say. He hated Republicans so much."

"But you got to see a President of the United States."

"I saw him, and I also saw Woodrow Wilson at the fair a couple of years later."

Giulia turned toward her mother, dangling both legs over the side of the piano bench. "You've seen two Presidents? Most people have never even seen one."

"Well, to be perfectly honest about it, President Wilson was still Governor of New Jersey at the time. Does that count?"

"Sure it does. How come you've never told me this?"

Paolina was amused at her daughter's astonished look. "You never asked," she said. "Besides, how often does the name William Howard Taft come up in conversation these days?"

When Giulia glanced at the wall clock, she jumped off the bench as if someone had set fire to it. "Oh, dear! Papà will be absolutely furious with me. I promised to bring the pictures over to him by four, and I've got a long walk to catch the streetcar."

Paolina's face darkened. "I wouldn't be in too big a hurry, if I were you," she said. "He's not punctual himself, so I don't think he really expects it in others."

"Just the same, he wanted to show someone my junior pictures from last year."

"Who's that?"

"I don't know. He didn't say. All I know is that he wanted them before four o'clock, and here I sit, noodling around on the piano at a quarter to five." By now, she was running across the room to the sewing table. Frantically searching, she shouted, "Oh, where did you put them?"

Paolina sighed, stacking the sheet music and returning it beneath the bench lid. "I really wouldn't hurry, dear. He's probably over at Birges Lee's by now. He burns up most of his 'A' sticker driving back and forth to that place."

Giulia looked up and flashed her mother a glare. "Don't say that. He hasn't been to a package store in years."

"The pictures are on the end table. I was showing them to Cora." Paolina turned to walk away, nearly stumbling on the ottoman. "And, for your information, yes, he has, I'm ashamed to say. Your father has no control over his problem, and he never will. I happen to know that he sits around with the boys—Jack Mellecker, Gifford Sammons, and that sort—nearly every afternoon. You can't paint a zebra's stripes white."

Giulia ran over to the end table, picked up the envelope of proofs, and without stopping, raced to the front door. "I'll be back by six, at the very latest, so don't bother putting my dinner in the oven."

"Archie's mother will be joining us, dear," her mother said.

Giulia's hand fell from the doorknob. Grinding her teeth, she turned and walked back to the living room. "No, not tonight, Mamma. No!"

Paolina seemed shocked and even a little hurt by the negative response. "Well, I'd have thought you'd be delighted. We haven't had her over for more than three months now." She watched as Giulia walked slowly to the sofa and sat down, tossing the envelope onto the coffee table.

"I am not up to this," the girl whispered. "I cannot see that woman tonight." Elbows on knees, she cradled her chin between the palms of both hands.

"Well, then you'll just have to snap out of it, young lady," her mother said, "because I'll not change the plans now—not after she's been planning on it for all these days."

When Giulia looked up, her beautiful eyes were red and teary. "Please tell her I'm sick, Mamma. Please."

"I'll do nothing of the sort."

"Tell her I'm sick. Tell her I'm out of town. Tell her anything that'll make her not come. Tell her I'm *dead*."

"Giulia Marcellina!" Paolina crossed herself. "What if Archie saw you acting like this?"

"What if he did? Maybe that would be the best thing." She bit her lip, instantly sorry for what she had said, and glanced fearfully at her mother.

Paolina leaned on the chair back to steady her balance. "I cannot believe my ears. Do you have any idea what you're saying? Archie Clarke is away, risking his life for us, and you have the audacity to talk like this. It's a sin!"

Giulia buried her face in her hands and began sobbing.

Paolina took a couple of steps toward the sofa, but then she stopped, taking a deep breath and waiting patiently.

Once Giulia regained her composure, she looked up at her mother. "Please ask her not to come. I just can't bear to see that woman."

"Tell me what's wrong, honey. There's more to it than just Mrs. Bess Clarke, isn't there?"

Giulia was silent for quite a long time, but then she sighed and wiped the tears from her eyes. "I'm just tired, I guess." She could not bring herself to divulge the truth, nor would her mother understand if she did. She retrieved the envelope of pictures, stood up, and began walking slowly to the front door. Halfway there, she halted and turned around. "I'm sorry for the way I acted, Mamma. I'll be home by six."

Paolina smiled. "Oh, think nothing of it, dear. That's a forgivable sin, but you're a sweet girl to apologize, just the same. The war makes us all say things we don't really mean."

Giulia nodded her head, opened the door, and heard her mother say, "I still don't think he'll be there. This is when he's out with the boys—come hell or high water. He gets thirsty about this time of day."

◆   ◆   ◆

A bell dinged inside the cluttered office, startling Elizabeth from her lazy reverie, and she immediately jumped to her feet to answer the call for assistance. That is precisely what Mr. Harkins taught her to do right from the very start—the quick response, not the loafing—and by now she responded instinctively to the sound. "Pavlov's dog" was how Dinah Reidelhuber characterized it, though she herself was no less guilty of salivating on command than the other employees of Service Refining Company. At the moment, Dinah was fifty feet away from the office, squirting down the driveway entrance at the fullest extension of the hose. Bradley Gann was there too, using the station's dilapidated push broom to loosen dried remnants of what appeared to be two squashed tomatoes.

Elizabeth was running point this afternoon. As such, it was her duty to greet the public and, unless mechanical servicing was required, to take care of whatever basic needs might arise. Business had been very slow for the past hour, so *sitting* point might have been a better way to describe her day. As she approached the automobile—a sleek 1939 Ford—the passenger side was nearer to her, so she put one foot on the running board, glanced at the "A" window sticker, and stooped slightly to smile toward the driver. "Yes, ma'am," she said. The lady was quite old, in her upper sixties perhaps, and there was a toy poodle lounging alongside her on the front seat. It lurched forward, snarling through its exposed teeth, but was restrained before inflicting any injury upon the filling station attendant.

"Rosie!" the woman shouted. She caught hold of the dog's collar and forcibly held the surly canine down, at arm's length, on the passenger seat. "Excuse me, miss. She's usually so well behaved."

Elizabeth reminded herself that the customer is always right. "Think nothing of it, ma'am. She was only trying to protect you."

The lady frowned at her feisty bodyguard. "I suppose so, but she doesn't act that way with anyone else besides the milkman."

"Maybe he wears a cap like this."

The lady thought for a moment. "He does, as a matter of fact. Yes, he does, and I'm sure that's what upset poor Rosie so much."

Elizabeth splashed some soapy water on the windshield and began wiping in wide, circular motions with a clean rag. "Do you need some gasoline, ma'am?" she asked the driver.

"Forty cents worth of high-test, please, and be sure to check under the hood."

"Yes, ma'am." The dog was watching Elizabeth's every move through the glass, and a low, growling noise could be heard. Just out of curiosity, the attendant removed her cap and held it close to the windshield. Sure enough, Rosie lunged forward, yapping wildly at what she perceived to be an aggressor. "Yes, ma'am, I think that's it," Elizabeth said. To further confirm her suspicions, she ventured back, hatless, to the driver's side window. Now the dog paid her no mind whatsoever, choosing instead to vent her anger on the SRC headgear.

The cash register's drawer was sticking again, so Elizabeth had to smack hard with the fleshy lower part of her hand to free it. She could hear a loudly clanking tire tool and the muffled sound of laughter coming from the garage bay next door. The office's pin-up calendar rustled in the breeze. That risqué adornment was mechanic Dave Rummage's idea—approved only with serious misgivings by Hoyle Harkins, who judged the beaming model to be just modest enough to bear the scrutiny of women and young people who came inside to pay their bills.

When Elizabeth walked back to the refueled automobile with her customer's sixty cents in change, the lady told her to keep the dime. Elizabeth nodded thanks and slipped the coin into her breast pocket. Though it was entirely possible to earn six bits in tips on a good day, this quiet Friday would fall well short of that.

"Are you a Waco High School student?" the elderly driver asked.

The sound of heavy aircraft could be heard. Elizabeth looked up, but nothing was in sight. "Yes, ma'am," she said. "I'm a freshman."

"How will the Tigers do next year?"

"I don't really know. I'm not much of a football fan, I'm afraid." The sound was getting louder.

"That's quite all right. There are other things in life besides sports."

"I suppose."

Four massive cargo planes came into view, flying rather low for a residential district, and their ear-splitting roar drowned out any attempt at conversation.

When the noise subsided a bit, Elizabeth grinned with pride. "My older brother played football at Waco High last year—a fullback, I think. I heard he was pretty good too."

"He graduated?"

"Yes, ma'am. He's in the Navy now."

"So's my grandson. He joined up at the end of '42."

"What's his name?"

"Ervin Lucas. Do you know him?"

"No, but my brother probably does. Did he play football?"

The lady shook her head. "Tennis. Ervin loves tennis. Always has, for as long as I can remember." She swiveled the ignition switch clockwise for an instant, and the engine came back to life. "Thank you, miss. Did I give you your tip?"

Elizabeth patted her pocket. "Yes, ma'am."

"Buy a war stamp with it, and you'll be rewarded many times over," the lady said. "Who knows? That very dime may someday save your brother's life, or my Ervin's. Stranger things have happened."

Elizabeth smiled and waved as the automobile pulled onto Washington Avenue. Rosie, the poodle, was now on her hind legs, gathering in the sights and scents that lay ahead. Going unnoticed, more than a full block away in the other direction, was the slow movement of a gray Oldsmobile, which departed from its position at the curb and then turned left onto Tenth Street. There was nothing particularly suspicious about the driver, now that his binoculars were away from view, resting on the floorboard beside him.

Traffic was light, and the weather was unusually warm for early February: sixty-eight degrees at 4:30, according to the latest weather report on the radio. It felt more like early fall than the dead of winter.

◆　　◆　　◆

Wesley Brower and Sandra Whittsel shared the same English class, but he found surprisingly few occasions to speak with her. How ironic, now that they were fellow KWXN employees as well as classmates, that the two should drift further apart from each other instead of closer together. That is not to say that Wesley went out of his way to avoid her, but neither did he find excuses for their paths to cross, as he had done during his sophomore year. Indeed, it was Sandy who initiated their most protracted encounter in several weeks, "blindsiding" him before class one day. She would have described it that way, of course, but the fact remains that Wesley had no time whatsoever to cultivate disinterest on such short notice.

He was poring over his study notes for *The Great Gatsby*, which referred him to page 209 and one of his favorite passages in the novel, Fitzgerald's witty exchange between Nick Carraway and Jordan Baker:

> *"You're a rotten driver," I protested. "Either you ought to be more careful, or you oughtn't to drive at all."*
>
> *"I am careful."*
>
> *"No, you're not."*
>
> *"Well, other people are," she said lightly.*
>
> *"What's that got to do with it?"*
>
> *"They'll keep out of my way," she insisted. "It takes two to make an accident."*

Wesley could not help but smile. In that respect, and that one alone, Jordan Baker reminded him a little of his Aunt Barbara. Before Uncle Matt finally came to his senses and forbade her from ever climbing behind a steering wheel again, she was known far and wide as Cameron County's most—

That was when he felt a light tapping on his shoulder, and there, effectively numbing his thought process, stood Sandy. She had not approached to within ten feet of him for a month or more, and yet now she glowed with delight as if they were the chummiest of friends.

"Hello, Wes," she said. "Long time, no talk."

Wesley nodded his head. "Yeah. It has been." He stared at her pretty face and blushed, at a loss for words. Her dancing eyes seemed the darkest of brown, almost black, and the corners of her mouth turned up in a charming way that made his heart race.

"Is that all you have to say for yourself?" she asked. "No greeting for an old friend?"

He swallowed hard, trying to exude more *élan* than was really his at the moment. "Hi, Sandy." Looking down, he closed the book and cleared his throat. "Are you ready for the test?"

"What test?"

"On *Gatsby*."

"The test is tomorrow, silly. Don't tell me you studied all of that for nothing."

Wesley sat up straight and grimaced at her. "Are you serious?"

"Cross my heart."

"Well, at least I'll be ready. I just hope I don't forget it all by then."

"Tomorrow is an awfully long way off all right," she said. "Okay, pop quiz: who is Meyer Wolfsheim?"

He stared at her in disbelief. No doubt about it, Sandy sure did seem friendly all of a sudden. "The gangster?"

"Good boy."

"He fixed the 1919 World Series—the Black Sox scandal."

"According to F. Scott Fitzgerald, that is. Daddy says it wasn't actually so."

"Oh? Was he there?" Wesley felt some of his old confidence returning.

"Daddy's a student of history, if that's what you mean. Most officers are."

Something was askew, he thought. This rapprochement was progressing far too smoothly for comfort.

Miss Simonek came into the room, quietly shut the door behind her, and walked toward her desk. There were still a couple of minutes before the bell would signal the beginning of class.

When Sandy smiled at him, Wesley felt his facial muscles respond in kind.

"How come your book is so thick?" she whispered. "Mine is kind of skinny compared to that one."

"This came from the public library. It's got *The Last Tycoon* in there, too, plus some short stories."

The girl was impressed. "Have you read those too?"

"No. We're just going to be tested on *Gatsby*, aren't we?"

"But what if Miss Simonek asks us to *compare and contrast* the others?"

Wesley's blood ran cold, but just for an instant—until he saw that she was teasing. Those three dreaded words have always struck fear in a student.

Sandy was drumming her fingertips on the desktop, not even an inch away from his right hand. "Maybe we can study together sometime. I've heard that's good for retention."

He moved his hand ever so slightly away. "Sure, sometime. Why not? For retention."

The bell was about to ring, so Sandy started walking toward her own desk. But then she stopped and turned around. "What did you make on *Penrod?*"

"Eighty-six."

Sandy sat down, pointed to herself, and whispered, "Ninety-one."

The next fifty minutes passed as uneventfully as any English class Wesley could recall—facilitated by the fact that his mind was drifting to things other than composition and American literature. Standing behind her desk, Miss Constance Simonek droned on about Gatsby's flawed perception of the socialite who had caught his eye: "There must have been moments even that afternoon when Daisy tumbled short of his dreams—not through her own fault, but because of the colossal vitality of his illusion."

Wesley listened but did not hear. For much of the time, his eyes wandered to the right side of the classroom, slightly toward the front. Sandy was attentive to the teacher, and not once did she so much as cast him a glance over her left shoulder. Even so, he half expected her to approach him after class, and she did not disappoint.

"I hear you're going to California," she said.

He was still seated, gathering his books together. "Who told you that?"

"I have my sources."

"Do your sources resent not going?"

Sandy looked hurt. "What do you mean by that?" Her skirt happened to brush against his right hand.

Wesley persisted. "Is your source mad at me for taking his place?" He stood up, surprised at himself for speaking so frankly.

"I don't even know what you're talking about," Sandy said. She truly did look bewildered.

"Has your source ever mentioned my name in the announcing booth?" He picked up the books.

"Look, Wesley Brower, if you're insinuating that Marshall and I—"

"Oh, so it's 'Marshall' now." He smiled, having won the point.

Anger crossed Sandy's face, but only in passing. She quickly recovered her friendly manner and steered the conversation in a different direction. "While you're there—in California—would you do me a favor?"

Wesley glanced down, became lost in her lovely eyes, and was compelled to nod his head in the affirmative. "Sure. What do you want me to do?"

Sandy placed her tiny hand on his shoulder and, rising on tiptoes, whispered into his ear. "Bring back the autograph of a movie star for me."

He was confused. "A movie star?"

"That's right," she said. "I don't care which one. Just someone I've heard of."

Though flattered by the implication of stature, Wesley was unsure that this was a promise he could fulfill. "What makes you think we'll be seeing any movie stars out there? Hollywood's a big place, and besides, we're in the radio business, not pictures. There's a difference, you know. We probably won't even be going near a movie studio."

Unfazed, she continued her request. "Someone like Clark Gable or William Holden would be fine."

Wesley laughed. "Clark Gable or William Holden? We'll be lucky to see Chill Wills."

"Be serious, Wes. Can't you see that this is very important to me?"

"Okay, I'll try, but I can't promise anything."

"And be sure to have him sign it, 'To Sandra Whittsel,' so people can see that he really wrote it to me."

"But he didn't. He doesn't even know you exist."

"No one will know the difference."

Wesley studied her trusting face and felt emboldened. He determined then and there to carry out her request, no matter how unreasonable it might seem from a distance of thirteen hundred miles. Yes, he would surprise her with a genuine autograph, and she would see that he was indeed a force to be reckoned with, someone with clout.

A bit of clarification was in order. "Why 'he'?" Wesley asked. "Does it have to be an actor? What if the only star I meet is Lana Turner?"

"Nope, no good. It has to be an actor, not an actress."

"So I'll tell her, 'No thanks, Lana, but if you happen to bump into Clark, please send him over here'."

Sandy laughed. "Or Bill Holden."

"Oh, sure. Same thing for Bill."

When the bell rang, the two walked out the door together but then went their separate ways. Wesley still could not believe what a dramatic change for the better had come over Sandra Whittsel, and these shifting fortunes encouraged him enough to roll the dice for even more. "Hey, want to go to the movies tonight?" he shouted to her. "There's a premiere of a new John Wayne picture at the Waco Theatre. I'll pay."

Walking backward, Sandy shook her head. "Gee, I'd like to, but I'd better not."

Wesley concocted a smile, but his voice wavered. "It's *The Fighting Seabees*, and there's gonna be an Army stage show too."

"No. Sorry." She turned and skipped away.

Watching her disappear around the stairwell corner, Wesley felt a gnawing sense of betrayal. Why was she toying with him like this? First she's as friendly as can be, and then she gives him the brush-off.

In the brief half-minute that it took him to get to his next class, jogging to the end of the hall with a few other stragglers, he analyzed his relationship with Miss Whittsel. It was the casual way she turned him down that really festered. Scarcely could she have been more chipper had she won the Irish Sweepstakes.

◆   ◆   ◆

The telephone rang six or seven times before Hannah Lane finally picked up its receiver. This was her normal practice. She was only a guest in the Brower house, so she felt awkward about answering calls without first giving the resident family ample opportunity to do so.

"Hello, Beth. This is Mr. Skinner," came a voice on the other end of the line.

"No, sir, this isn't Elizabeth," Hannah said. "I suppose she's at work, but I don't know for sure."

"Oh, I'm sorry. For a second you sounded like her, just when you answered the phone."

"Yes, sir. Would you like for me to have her call you?"

"Please do, at school. This is Lyle Skinner, Beth's band director at Waco High—well, used to be. I'll be here until around 6:30 today."

A key rattled in the front door, and Hannah said, "Don't hang up, sir. Maybe that's Lizzie now."

But it was Mrs. Brower, not her daughter. "Hello, Hannah, dear," Nora said. She turned to hang her sweater on the wooden rack. "I've just been over at the Hellers ... Oh, I beg your pardon. I didn't know you were on the telephone."

Hannah smiled a greeting at her but spoke into the mouthpiece. "No, sir. It's her mother instead. Would you like to talk with Mrs. Brower?" She nodded her head at his response and covered the mouthpiece with her hand. "It's Lizzie's band director at school," she whispered. When Nora reached for the handset, Hannah gave it to her and then stepped into the living room.

"Hello, Mr. Skinner. This is Lizzie's mother. ... Certainly I do. How have you been? ... She's at work right now, pumping gasoline. Isn't that a silly job for a girl? ... No, not very much lately. She did play once at church, a couple of months ago. ... I'm not sure. I'll have to ask her. ... Oh, I'm sorry to hear that. There's always something, isn't there? ... Well, I'll tell you what she says, and I'm fairly confident she can help out. ... Tomorrow night, Monday night, and Tuesday night. Yes, sir. ... Does she already know the pieces? ... Oh, goodness. Well, go ahead and pencil her name in, just the same. ... Seven o'clock should be fine. Just an hour? ... Uh-huh. She's always willing to pitch in. You know my Lizzie! ... Oh, yes: 'Beth.' I still haven't gotten used to that, I'm afraid."

When she had hung up the telephone, Nora found Hannah standing at the bookshelves in the living room, idly flipping through the *National Cyclopedia of American Biography*. "Homework?"

"No, ma'am," Hannah said. "I need to speak with you for a minute."

"Oh? Is there something wrong, dear?"

Hannah closed the book and slipped it back into its place on the shelf. "I'm not sure, Mrs. B.," she said.

"Here, let me put on some coffee for us, and then we can have some girl talk. How does that sound?"

"Yes, please. That would be nice."

A few minutes later, the two ladies were seated next to each other on the sofa. The coffee was a bit too hot to drink, but somehow it seemed comforting to have the aromatic liquid so close at hand. This was not going to be an easy thing for Hannah to discuss, so she needed all the reassurance she could muster.

"Have you heard from Steve lately?" she asked.

Nora was puzzled. "Yes, he writes to us once or twice a week—sometimes more regularly than others. Why do you ask?"

"Because I've gotten myself in an awful jam, and I'm hoping maybe he can get me out of it."

Studying Hannah's face, Nora sensed a social dilemma of some sort. "Boy troubles?"

Hannah nodded her head.

"But Steve's way out on the west coast—as far as I can tell—and maybe even ready to be shipped overseas. How can he possibly help you?"

"I don't need him here. Just a few letters should work wonders."

Nora shrugged her shoulders. "I'm sure I don't understand what you're talking about. Is Steve the problem?"

Hannah giggled. "Hardly. I wish it were that simple."

"Why don't you just come right out and say what you mean?" Nora said. She blew on her scalding coffee and managed a tiny sip. "I think you'll find that I'm a pretty good listener."

"I need Steve as an alibi, if that makes any sense."

"An alibi?"

"Yes, ma'am. I'm hoping that maybe Steve can throw someone off my scent. I'll be in a terrible bind if he can't."

"Who's this 'someone'? A Baylor student?"

"Nope, an old friend from back home—Alvin Reeder. He says he'll be coming to Waco next week."

"To see you?"

"He didn't actually come right out and say that in his letter, but I can read between the lines. He's written three letters to me since Christmas, and he always signs them 'All my love'."

"Oh, dear. Where did he get that idea?"

"About loving me?"

"Yes. Did you give him any cause to think that?"

"None at all. I haven't even seen him since high school graduation."

"But you did date him in North Carolina?"

Hannah shook her head. "No, he's just a friend."

Nora took another sip, then laid her cup back down on the coffee table. "Well, he's coming halfway across the country for some reason. He wouldn't do that on a lark."

"He has a sales meeting in Dallas, and then he's planning to catch the interurban down to Waco."

"What does he sell?"

"Bibles."

Nora raised her eyebrows, favorably impressed. "He can't be too bad of a person. Why don't you want to see him?"

Hannah stood up and walked toward the dormant fireplace, which lay empty except for its discolored iron grate and some scattered, ashen residue. "I don't know, really." She thought for a moment, as if considering the matter for the first time.

"Alvin's a nice enough boy, I suppose, but I just don't have any ... romantic interest in him, that's all."

"I still don't understand how my Stephen fits into the picture," Nora said. She waited until Hannah turned toward her again before adding, "You don't have a romantic interest in *him*, do you?"

Hannah was stunned by how forthrightly her landlady put such a private matter. "Of course not," she told her. "I don't have an interest in any boy at the moment, and I hardly even know your son. He did write to me once—because I asked him to—but I never wrote him back."

Nora grimaced with embarrassment. "I'm sorry, dear. I had no right to ask such a thing. I'm just trying to sort this out—and offer some friendly advice." She began making lazy circles with her index finger inside the coffee cup's handle. "I'm certainly no Solomon in matters such as this, but maybe I can help."

Hannah walked back toward Nora's chair and, casting all caution aside, voiced an odd request. "May I have permission to read some of the letters Steve wrote to you—just the ones you choose—sometime before Alvin Reeder shows up?"

"Whatever in the world for?" Nora's finger stopped playing with the cup handle.

"I plan to chatter about my Navy 'beau' until I'm blue in the face," Hannah told her, "but I need to know what I'm talking about to make it sound authentic."

A broad smile came across Nora's face. "Well, aren't you a clever girl!" she said.

Hannah smiled too. "My daddy says I'm Machiavellian."

"Oh? And what exactly does that mean? Sneaky?"

"Pretty much."

Nora thought for a moment and then nodded her head. "All right, dear. I'll look through the letters tonight."

"A small picture for my purse would be a nice touch too."

♦   ♦   ♦

Only two days remained before the train would be pulling out of Waco's passenger station, bound for Fort Worth and, ultimately, the great Los Angeles basin. Wesley was scheduled to work both days, though it was on the first of these, a Monday, that his character, Kip Hanson, was due to be abducted. This shocking incident would serve to explain the boy's absence from the microphone for an indefinite period of time. No doubt KWXN would receive many telephone calls from concerned listeners—fearing for the safety of the character—but at least the "Behold Tomorrow" story line would remain intact.

To Sol Glickman, Dickie Waterhouse, and the other control room regulars, it seemed bizarre for Hugh Kenton to be so passively involved in the serial, but they all understood that now it was Hatch Priggett's turn to take the reins. Kenton merely looked over his substitute's shoulder, making certain that he had a firm grasp of the stressful responsibility. He need not have worried, for Priggett was, despite his relative youthfulness, nearly Kenton's equal at the controls. Only twice did he need coaching during the entire Monday show, and both times it was for the same mental lapse: failing to give the "stand by" for voice-over narration leading up to a musical bridge. Kenton could live with that, having done precisely the same thing just six months earlier—and that after being with the show ever since its inception. Mostly he just stood there, nodding approval and smoking his cigar.

Very little had changed for the cast in the studio, as the director's voice was rarely audible to them anyway, once the program was on the air. Whenever a microphone was open, the loudspeakers automatically muted, so Priggett's high—almost female—voice was only heard by Wesley and his colleagues during one rather lengthy stretch of narration and, of course, on the two occasions when musical bridges amounted to more than just momentary "stingers." Otherwise, it was business as usual from the perspective of the studio.

What was out of the ordinary for Wesley was the sight of Sandra Whittsel's lovely visage, barely perceptible through the shadows and reflections of the control room window. Yes, it was Sandy all right, and he was pleased to notice that she ventured nowhere near the announcer's booth, where Marshall McFall, on this day at least, was too busy to pay her anything but the scantest of attention. To the best of Wesley's knowledge, Sandy had never observed a "Behold Tomorrow" performance before—at least not since that time last June when, as a lowly weekend news announcer, he escorted her on a tour of "his" radio station.

(Sound effects of a switchblade)

"You try something like that, Odom, and I'll carve your insides like I'm cleaning a trout," Neddy Wright read (as Bud Hanson).

"In case you hadn't noticed, knives don't scare me much," Grover Millich read (as Odom Cashley). "Especially when there's a rod pointed at the back of your skull."

"You think I'm going to fall for that?"

"He's not fooling," Ray Leftwich read (as Red Dykes), "and this silencer's no louder than popping open a bottle of champagne."

(Music stinger)

"All right, you've got the drop on me ... for now. But the Governor knows where I am, and he's my ticket out of here."

"The ... Governor?" Millich read.

"His chauffeur's parked at the curb, with the engine running. I'm sure his boss would love to see both of you fry."

"Uncle Bud?" Wesley Brower read (as Kip Hanson).

"Grab him, Red!"

(Sound effects of a scuffle)

"Run, Kip!"

(Sound effects of a punch to the jaw, then running feet)

"Don't worry about him, Red. Grab the kid!"

(Sound of a struggle)

"Get your hands off me, you big ape!" Wesley read.

(Sound of a scream of pain)

"Hey, the kid bit me."

"Take it easy, Red. Don't rough him up too much. He's worth a few grand to us ... easy."

"What about Bud? Now he knows where we are."

"We'll have to use the fire escape. Quick! Tie the kid's hands behind him, and bring him down. I'll keep us covered."

"But how can he get down all those steps with no hands? We're seven flights up."

"That's your job, Red. And if he falls, so help me, you'll be joining him as a bloody pulp on the pavement."

Thus was Kip Hanson written out of the story line of "Behold Tomorrow." Yet the character would remain fresh in people's minds, as Ethel Coody and the other writers saw to it that oblique mention of his name continued to turn up in dialogue on a regular basis. They calculated, with the wisdom born of experience, that audience anxiety over his condition and whereabouts was really not such a terrible thing.

Kip's voice would be heard on the Tuesday program as well, but only in a flashback sequence, a painful recollection by the boy's mother, Dolores Hanson, of what he had said to her in a fit of anger the last time they saw each other. She was just getting off work from the seedy Black Garter nightclub, where the over-aged chorus dancer was now reduced to hustling tips as a cocktail waitress. His thoughtless remarks cut her deeply, inasmuch as the steel of truth makes the sharpest blade of all.

Sales manager Lee Graffen maintained that the poor lady's emotional agony could very well translate into valuable Hooper points when a new rating book hits the Waco market.

♦　　♦　　♦

Mr. Lindeman appeared to be in his lower fifties, but Giulia Coletti knew for a fact that he was only forty-three. The office staff had treated him to a birthday lunch back in October, and his secretary, Cornelia Pollard, revealed his true age to everyone at the table. She meant it as a compliment, of course, insisting that no one would believe he was really that old. In the interest of propriety, Giulia quietly drank a swallow of lemonade and kept any contrary thoughts to herself.

Butler Lindeman was not particularly stern, as bosses go, but neither did he permit unwarranted conversation in the workplace—unless, that is, he himself was involved in the discussion. In such cases, quite often it would happen that Giulia was another participant, and sometimes it was just the two of them. Her desk faced his glass-enclosed office, so naturally his eyes wandered in her direction more than anywhere else. She thought little of it, and the wedding band on his left hand brought assurance that his motives were purely sociable.

Giulia had been employed at Rawley Flooring for five months, working half-days on a rotating schedule that gave her ample time to care for the needs of her mother. It was an entry-level job that required no education beyond the tenth grade. She entertained the hope of a more rewarding assignment someday, but for now she was satisfied. Besides, the other girls in the office were very friendly, and she maintained a good rapport with most of the salesmen, especially those who delighted in flirtatious teasing and pulling the usual deskside pranks. Mutt Sawyer was probably her favorite in this respect, though his newlywed son, Bobby, lagged not too far behind. Bobby's bride, Patrice, also worked at Rawley—that is where the couple met—but her position was direct selling to the public, and the showroom was an entirely separate operation in all but name.

Business at Rawley Flooring had been quite slow through the final quarter of 1943, and there was even some talk of company layoffs. But Lindeman, being well grounded in the cyclical vagaries of ebb and flow commerce, was not unduly alarmed. "Rumors! Nothing but rumors," he announced at the first sales meeting of the new year. "Since when did people suddenly decide that they would rather live on dirt floors? Folks, it just ain't gonna happen." And he was right. January figures indicated that a slight downturn in the commercial sector was more than offset by significant profits in residential sales. February prospects were better yet. Clearly, even in the face of wartime shortages, American breadwinners would do everything possible to provide their families with the basic necessities of physical comfort. Rawley's sales force indulged in a collective sigh of relief—and none more enthusiastically than Marlon "Mutt" Sawyer.

With over nineteen years of sales experience, Mutt had achieved considerably more seniority than anyone else on the Rawley Flooring staff. He was a pot-bellied, jovial man with a triple chin. Though still two months short of his forty-seventh birthday, his full head of hair had already turned completely white. Early in the war—when air attack was thought to be imminent—he served faithfully as a block warden, and it was his daily custom to wear a tiny stars-and-stripes pin on the lapel of his suit coat. There were some in the community who sniffed at such a display of patriotism, seeing as how his military-age son was safely cloistered between two oceans, but surely those misguided souls were unaware that young Bobby suffered from bronchial asthma, not a debilitating case but pronounced enough for MEPS examiners to rule him ineligible for military duty. Being only human, Bobby resented the questioning looks and occasional catcalls, but he tried his best to ignore them. "What can I do?" he told his father. "I can't very well hang a 4-F sign around my neck." One insolent waitress came right out and called him a slacker, refusing to serve any of the people at his table. Among them was his mortified fiancée, Patrice Youngens, whose roommate, Angie Black, had to be restrained from striking the waitress with a napkin rack. They had their meal but left no tip.

The middle Tuesday in February dawned dry and seasonably cool, with a morning low of thirty-six degrees. Mutt struggled to get into his massive winter coat as he waddled toward the exit, heading for a routine service call on a local contractor. He needed an order form, so he stopped at Giulia's desk on his way to the parking lot. "Hi, beautiful," he said. "Haven't seen you for ages."

She looked up at him and smiled. "It hasn't even been twenty-four hours yet, Mr. Sawyer."

"Really? Every moment away from you seems like an eternity."

"Oh, I'm sure it does," she said. "You dumped your car's ashtray in my waste basket just yesterday. Don't you remember? It made a mess on the carpet."

"Was that only yesterday? My, my." Mutt took a sales form from the stack on her desk and then, squinting and twitching his nose, snatched a handkerchief from his coat pocket and heartily sneezed into it, one-handed. "Say, how's your 'mamma mia' doing these days?" He wiped the excess moisture from his nose and then proceeded to wad up the soiled handkerchief and stuff it into the back pocket of his slacks.

"She's feeling pretty well, thank you," Giulia told him. "Some days are better than others." She stole a look at Lindeman's office.

"Aren't they for us all?" Mutt said. "I think I'm starting to get arthritis in my left knee—or maybe it's just my old football injury coming back to haunt me."

"Did you play at Waco High?"

Amused, he laid the sales form back on her desk. "Hah! My coach made Paul Tyson seem like a greenhorn. Have you ever heard of Amos Alonzo Stagg?"

"I think so."

"He's at C-O-P now, but I was a Maroon under him at Chicago during the glory years ... a blocking back. I hurt my knee in practice—not too bad, really, but it still flares up every once in a while."

"Were you a good player?"

"Better than average, if I do say so myself. In fact, that's where I got my name. The guys started calling me 'Bulldog' because of my line plunges, and somehow that got shortened to 'Mutt.' It's funny how those things get started." He rubbed his left knee, wincing in pain.

"Did you ever play professional football?"

"Nope. I only played college ball for two years, so I never even had the chance to be a starter. Then the war came—the first war—and that was it for my aspirations to ..."

Giulia glanced again at Lindeman's office and loudly cleared her throat.

Mutt responded at once to the signal. "Indian on the warpath?" he asked.

"Fast approaching," she whispered.

He winked at her, retrieved his paperwork, and hurried toward the door.

"Excuse me, Miss Coletti," Lindeman said as he neared her desk. He turned to watch Mutt Sawyer leave and shook his head.

"Yes, sir?"

"Miss Coletti, I need for you to go with me to the air field tomorrow morning—Blackland. Mrs. Pollard will be attending a funeral, so there's no other choice."

"But, sir, I just work in the afternoon tomorrow."

"Can you switch?"

"I guess so. I'll have to let my mother know, that's all."

"Please do, if you don't mind. There's really no one else who can break away from the office on such short notice."

"Of course, sir."

He smiled, and the business-like demeanor slipped from his face like a plaster mask. Suddenly, he became as nervous as a schoolboy, and Giulia was sure she could see beads of perspiration beginning to form at the hairline of his forehead. "We'll probably be gone for about two hours," he added. "I need to give Uncle Sam an estimate on some durable surfacing for a mess hall and three latrines."

Giulia looked away, embarrassed.

"Oh, you won't have to go with me into the latrines or any place like that. Mrs. Pollard calculates bids with me all the time, and she usually just waits in the main reception building when I'm in one of the male-only areas. The latrines are off-limits to women anyway—obviously—so don't worry about that."

"But I don't know anything about construction bids."

"Just bring a notepad, and you'll do swell. I'll walk you through it, every step of the way."

"Yes, sir. All right."

"And then maybe we can grab an early lunch on our way back to the office—strictly business, so I'll pay."

Giulia's pretty eyes widened as she searched for the right words. Finally she said, "I'm not ... I don't think that would be a good ... idea, Mr. Lindeman."

He showed the palms of both hands. "Strictly business, Miss Coletti, but really, if you'd feel uncomfortable about it ..." He smiled with confidence, waiting patiently for her consent.

Deep in thought, the girl looked down at her desktop and nervously began winding the telephone cord around her index finger. A moment later, Lindeman's smile vanished without a trace when Giulia told him, "Sorry, sir, but I just don't feel right about it. I don't think it would be proper."

To his credit, Lindeman did not press the issue. Instead, he took it like a man, clapped his hands together one time, and said, "Well, then, shall we say 9:30 tomorrow morning?"

She nodded her head.

"I'll change the schedule for you, and maybe I can get Beverly to cover during the afternoon."

"Yes, sir, that'll be fine. And I'll let my mother know."

He smiled and began walking away, but then he turned back to the desk. "Say, I trust that you don't think I was out of line with that little invitation of mine. I really didn't mean anything by it."

Giulia blushed and shook her head. "That's okay, Mr. Lindeman. I'm sure you didn't. Thanks for the invitation, but it just wouldn't look right. I hope you understand."

Butler Lindeman understood perfectly well, and he slowly retreated to the sanctity of his fishbowl office. A photograph of his attractive wife hung on the wall, right below the autographed pictures of shortstop Billy Jurges and pitcher Cliff Melton.

He had been a Giants fan for as long as he could remember.

◆　　◆　　◆

Elizabeth had played her flute only sparingly since dropping out of the school band program to accommodate her job at Service Refining Company. She and the church organist played "Columbia, Gem of the Ocean" just before Armistice Day, and she was part of an ad hoc wind quintet one Sunday morning in December, but beyond those two occasions, her flute had remained tucked away in its case, neglected and forgotten.

That all changed on the evening of February 10 when Elizabeth received a summons from band director Lyle Skinner, asking her to perform at a Victory Concert with the senior band and mixed chorus a mere five days later. No one practiced harder than Elizabeth did at the three rehearsals, which took place across Ninth Street in the old Baker residence, converted two years earlier into the Waco High School Band House. And yet she still felt musically insecure when she arrived at the WHS gymnasium on Tuesday night.

This was to be the final event of the school's Miss Liberty Belle Contest, staged in conjunction with the Fourth War Loan Drive. When the campaign opened, each room elected its own Miss Liberty Belle representative, and then each floor selected two nominees from that list of names, resulting in a pool of eight finalists. The aspirants—none of whom freshman Elizabeth Brower knew personally—were Mary Gene Wemple and Grace Hoffman (third floor), Jo Ann Muckleroy and Peggy Sue Bryant (second floor), Yvonne Ferguson and Martha Wood (first floor), and Nina Allison and Jackie Lee Taylor (basement).

By design, what began as little more than a popularity contest ended up being a highly successful war-bond drive. The student body cast their "votes" each Tuesday at a homeroom period by means of purchasing war stamps and bonds, with balloting calculated on a graduated scale of face value. Each 10¢ stamp, for instance, earned one vote for the purchaser's candidate of choice. Likewise, each 25¢ stamp was worth two votes, each 50¢ stamp four votes, and each $1 stamp eight votes. Larger transactions brought correspondingly inflated returns: a $25 bond was worth two hundred votes, a $50 bond five hundred votes, and a $100 bond eight hundred votes.

A large audience filled the Waco High School gymnasium—indeed, far more people than might attend a typical Tiger varsity basketball game. In addition to the customary bleacher seating, there were a couple hundred folding chairs arranged on the gym floor. Mr. Skinner had his band in place fifteen minutes before the start of the program, and never before had Elizabeth performed before such a massive crowd at school. The palms of her hands grew moist with perspiration under the strain, and her dry mouth felt like it was stuffed with cotton balls. On the spot, she vowed to practice the flute more often, so this stage fright would not be repeated, at least not with such awful intensity.

Speech teacher Jim Bob Healer was master of ceremonies, and true to his dictates in the classroom, he wasted little time before introducing Lyle Skinner, who rose to take a bow. The musical portion of the program consisted of a series of four patriotic compositions, three of them with choir. For Elizabeth, as a freshman among seniors, it was a nice feeling to have the choral forces cover whatever instrumental flubs there may have been. Besides, there were two other flutes in the band, so she did not feel especially conspicuous once the performance began. On a couple of dangerous notes that lay in the very highest register, she even played tacitly, simply moving her fingers but not blowing across the mouthpiece.

After the final selection, the choir received an appreciative round of applause, and then, as prompted by Mr. Skinner, members of the band stood, by section, and bowed. When Elizabeth and the other musicians took their seats, the stage was set for the culmination of the evening's festivities: appealing for generous contributions to the Fourth Liberty Loan. Admission to the concert was free of charge, but teachers Elmus Mohundro and Arnel Palmer manned a fund-raising stamp-and-bond booth in the foyer of the building.

McLennan County, unlike most of the nation, was significantly behind in its giving—in fact, a full twenty-two percent shy of its $7.8 million goal, with just two weeks remaining in the drive. Bond leaders even placed a full-page ad in the *Waco News-Tribune*, shaming readers into opening their wallets. "We have FAILED to meet our 4th loan quota," the ad said. "The people of Waco and McLennan County have FAILED to heed their conscience! Surely the conscience of every patriotic American will not let him FAIL to BUY BONDS to the LIMIT!" Purchases of E, F, and G bonds would be counted through leap day, February 29, and it was from these three issues that the shortfall had to be eradicated.

Featured speakers at the Victory Concert, sensibly chosen to touch the heartstrings—and purse strings—of the audience, were a group of disabled soldiers from the local branch of the US Army's McClosky General Hospital of Temple. These patients were bussed to Waco High School from their recuperative quarters at the far edge of town, out by the traffic circle on the northwest corner of Circle Road and Robinsonville Road. Their pleas were personal, genuine, motivational.

Almost lost in the shuffle was the single aspect of the drive that was perhaps foremost on the students' minds—the contest itself. At long last, once the votes were tallied, a pretty brunette from the first floor, Martha Wood, was proclaimed Miss Liberty Belle for 1944.

With flute case in hand, Elizabeth went searching through the crowd for her mother. En route, she happened to encounter a vaguely familiar face near the gymnasium's center court. "Has Wes already left for California?" the attractive young lady asked.

Elizabeth nodded her head. "Yesterday morning." Desperately, she tried to recall the girl's name, but it would not come to her. She had seen her with Wesley a couple of times, and yet she could not remember where or when. The girl had very dark hair and only stood about five feet tall.

"When you write to him, would you please tell him I said hello?"

"Okay, I sure will," Elizabeth said, but there was not much conviction in her voice.

The girl beamed. "He promised to bring back a movie star's autograph for me, with a personal inscription."

Elizabeth giggled. "He did?"

"Uh-huh. Somebody really famous, he said."

She seems awfully sure of herself, thought Elizabeth, and Wesley must know her rather well to make such an outlandish offer.

"Well, goodbye," the girl said. She quickly turned to go.

"'Bye."

Elizabeth spotted her mother in the crowd and hurried over to her. "Mother, who was that girl I was talking to?" she asked.

"What girl?"

"Short, very cute, black hair—a friend of Wes's."

Nora considered the description for a moment. "Sounds like that colonel's daughter."

"What's her name?"

"I can't remember. He hardly ever mentions her anymore, so I just assumed they had a falling out."

"Well, from the looks of it, I think she's fallen back in."

◆   ◆   ◆

The German 14th Army, commanded by fifty-four-year-old General Eberhard von Mackensen, launched Operation Fischfang on February 16, 1944. This major offensive was designed to strike the US 45th Division at the Italian coastal town of Anzio and drive the Americans into the sea. Following a devastating artillery barrage, coupled with air support from the Luftwaffe, German Panzers began pouring through the bleeding gap, and Allied forces were nearly severed in two. It was not until the next day, when a counterattack by Allied aircraft dropped over a thousand tons of bombs, that the German advance was finally slowed. Two days after that, the British 1st Division and the US 45th, accompanied by powerful air and naval bombardment, bludgeoned Operation Fischfang to death in a pitched battle at Carroceto Creek.

Sixty miles to the east, a siege of the historic abbey at Monte Cassino was in full progress, as waves of B-17s, B-25s, and B-26s filled the skies, dropping thousands of tons of bombs on German defensive positions within its centuries-old walls. "If we have to choose between destroying a famous building and sacrificing our own men," General Dwight D. Eisenhower said, "then our men's lives count infinitely more, and the buildings must go." President Roosevelt agreed, stating that bombing and shelling the ancient Benedictine monastery was justified because the Germans had violated its holiness by converting it into a fortress, thereby posing a choice between sparing the abbey and forfeiting countless American lives.

It was precisely while these two dramatic battles were raging on the Italian mainland that a leisurely Pullman train was winding its way through the mountain and desert regions of the western United States, destined for the Pacific. On board were hundreds of American soldiers—bound for various duty stations and embarkation points up and down the coastline. There were also three special sleepers, chartered for businessmen and a handful of California legislators. More than half of the passengers occupying the civilian cars were broadcasters in transit to their annual convention in Los Angeles.

Snow covered the plains southeast of Denver, and on the remote horizon loomed the Rocky Mountains, with some of the range's majestic peaks rising as high as twelve thousand feet into the frigid morning air. Waco passenger Wesley Brower was seated next to the train's window, taking it all in with the wide-eyed enthusiasm of a child. It suddenly occurred to him that no one else was paying the Colorado scenery any mind whatsoever. Most were reading, talking, smoking, napping, or playing cards, oblivious to the glorious panorama that transfixed his gaze. The explanation was simple. He was the youngest of the broadcasters and perhaps the only member of this group who had never before seen such an impressive snow-blanketed landscape in person. Too, the other travelers were trapped in the busy world of broadcast administration and, it might be assumed, had grown a bit jaded to the pristine beauties that God's natural wildlands had to offer.

"Hungry, Wes?" The voice came from behind him, and when he turned, there in the aisle was station manager Clive Ramey. Hugh Kenton stood alongside him, chatting for the moment with a rather debonair executive from the Dallas contingent. The seated man's tie pin resembled a tiny microphone, which bore some call letters—perhaps WFAA or KRLD—but Wesley could not read them from that distance, and he was not inclined to approach much closer to such an intimidating dignitary.

"Yes, sir," Wesley shouted back, over the metallic whining of the train wheels.

Ramey nodded his acknowledgement. "We'll be stopping in Denver in about an hour and a half," he said, "but the conductor told me we'll get our shot at the dining car beforehand—now that the soldier boys are well fed, of course."

That comment raised the eyebrows of a wiry recruiting sergeant who happened to be passing through, but the non-com relaxed when he saw that Ramey intended no disrespect or sarcasm.

Wesley could hear Kenton tell his Dallas acquaintance, "Not if I have anything to say about it. Our market's a lot more sensitive to such things than what you boys have in the big cities. We'd be swallowed whole by our competition, believe you me ..."—Kenton gestured wildly with his right hand, sending a shower of cigar ashes to the floor—"... and my boss would be sitting there on the commode, pondering what happened. Nope, we'll stick with the status quo, thank you, at least for the foreseeable future. Things could change, but I don't think so."

"Well, if you ever have second thoughts about it ..." the Dallasite said. He wore the unctuous grin of a born salesman.

The dining compartment was five cars forward, and Wesley noticed that every person in between was wearing a military uniform. A group of six nurses was the sole exception, but even they were surely attached to an Army or Navy unit of some sort. Loitering in each of the vestibules between cars were two or three servicemen, staring at the countryside, letting the cold air blow in their faces, and it was a wonder that their cigarettes were not extinguished by the rushing wind.

The food was sparse but surprisingly flavorful for railroad fare: a grilled chicken breast, succotash, mashed potatoes with poultry gravy, and a thin slice of pumpkin pie. After a single bite of dessert, Kenton disparaged it as "cinnamon-nutmeg custard glued to a cardboard triangle," so Wesley inherited most of the director's pie as well. It tasted good to him, especially during these spartan times of sugar shortage. He wondered aloud what kind of dessert the Union Pacific would have provided, had the soldiers not been aboard.

Kenton continued to pick his teeth. "Probably just crust."

"Artificially colored crust," Ramey said. That was an allusion to the unappetizing pallor of wartime oleomargarine.

"Hubba hubba!" someone shouted from across the dining car, and Wesley noticed one of the nurses walking through. Many of the male heads turned to admire her appearance. She smiled prettily in response.

"What a dish," Ramey whispered. "I'd probably get some nurse who looked like Benjamin Franklin."

Kenton laughed and then, out of deference to the teenager present, promptly changed the subject. "Well," he said, "I guess old Baylor's on the air by now, don't you think, Clive?"

"I don't know. What is today?"

"February 17 ... Thursday," Wesley said. He wanted to keep up his end of the conversation.

Ramey thought for a moment. "Then they've been on the air for two days." He chuckled to himself. "They carried a chapel service on Tuesday—at least, that was the plan—some evangelist from Memphis."

Kenton, though, remained serious. "What's their power?" With thumb and index finger, he smoothed down his mustache.

"Fifty thousand watts, but the tower's down in Corpus. It covers the coast, all the way from Brownsville to Gulfport."

Kenton seemed impressed.

"What's the station called?" Wesley asked.

Ramey's eyes were on his Union Pacific pocket timetable. "KWBU—for 'Waco, Baylor University'." He had an irksome way of talking to his menial subordinates without actually looking at them. "They're at 1010 on the dial. No competition to us, I wouldn't think."

"I wonder what Baylor hopes to get out of it," Kenton said.

Ramey shook his head. "Lord only knows. Publicity, I guess. They won't be raking in much money from sponsors—not with their programming."

Kenton leaned forward. "Such as?"

"Something called 'Campus Serenade' and 'Youth Problem Bureau.' Those are the only two I can recall."

"Who's the PD?"

"Ralph Matthews."

"I don't think I know him."

Ramey nodded toward the far corner of the car. "The owners are right over there."

Kenton and Wesley both turned to look, and Kenton said, "No, those are the Century Broadcasting bunch, from Dallas."

"That's who owns it. Baylor controls half of the capital stock, but Century's in charge of the money clip. They're the real owner-operators."

Wesley finished the last bite of pumpkin pie and laid down his fork. By now, some in the dining compartment were beginning to return to the chartered cars, so the KWXN triumvirate did likewise.

"Say, Hugh," Ramey whispered, "point me to the nearest little boy's room. I'm about to wee-wee down my pants leg if I don't find something fast."

"Don't make a spectacle of yourself, Clive," the director said, "not in front of all these big-city folks. They already think we're frontier hicks as it is."

Ramey winked. "You noticed that too, huh?"

Kenton pointed the way, and the other two followed behind, the station manager in such physical distress that he was nearly hopping on one foot.

"Blasted coffee," he said.

◆　　◆　　◆

"What sort of boy is Stephen Brower?" Giulia asked. She had intended to pose the question as naturally as possible, but somehow it came out sounding clumsily abrupt.

"Steve? He's a nice boy. Why?" There was a look of suspicion in Tina Wolff's eyes.

"No reason. It's just that Francine told me you dated him a few times before you moved away."

The two girls were sitting in the break room of Rawley Flooring, and they were due back at their desks in less than five minutes.

"No, just once," Tina said. "And it wasn't a real date anyway."

"Well, Francine said it was."

Tina frowned. "What does she know about it? She just likes to gossip."

"Maybe so, but that doesn't necessarily mean that everything she says is ..."

"A lie?"

"That doesn't mean that every single thing she says is untrue."

Tina chuckled. "You're too kind."

Giulia was ten and a half months younger than her friend. They first met each other as Rawley employees but later were surprised to learn that they had been underclassmen together at Waco High School during Giulia's freshman year. In the summer of 1941, Tina's father, Burton Wolff, moved the family to Corsicana, so Tina was compelled to change schools and finish her education there.

"Where did you go on that famous date of yours?" Giulia asked. She grinned with anticipation.

"I already told you—it wasn't a date. We were just sophomores, so Steve wasn't even old enough to drive."

"Where did you go?"

"You're going to be disappointed."

"Shoot."

"Okay, he walked over to my house—in the rain, no less—and my dad drove us to a movie at the Orpheum."

Giulia looked at her in disbelief.

"There," Tina said. "Are you satisfied?"

"That's it?"

"It was all very innocent. There was no torrid love affair or anything of that sort. Steve didn't kiss me, and the only hand he shook was my dad's."

"What picture did you see? Do you remember?"

"Sure. It was *Spring Parade*, with Deanna Durbin and Robert Cummings."

"Did your dad sit right there with you in the movie house?"

Tina laughed. "No, thank God. That would have been too embarrassing. He drove away and then picked us up when the picture was over."

"Steve didn't try anything in the dark, did he?"

"Nope. He was a perfect gentleman."

"Hmm." Giulia glanced at the wall clock and began to stand, but Tina stopped her with a question.

"Why are you so interested in Stephen Brower all of a sudden?"

Giulia shook her head. "I never said I was interested in him. I just happened to see Mrs. Brower at Moek's one day, and the subject of her son came up. He's away in the service, you know."

Tina giggled. "Well, hurrah for him! What do you plan to do, send him a fruitcake?"

Now Giulia did stand, and she began to walk away. "Very funny," she said, "but all I really wanted was to find out what kind of boy he is."

Tina tossed her sandwich paper into the wastebasket and hurried after her friend. "Don't get so huffy. I was only teasing you."

"I'm not huffy. It's just that Mr. Lindeman watches me like a hawk, and I really need to get back to my desk."

"He watches all of the young girls like a hawk, sweetie, so don't feel too bad about that. Last week his elbow brushed against Holly's breast, and she turned all colors of red."

Giulia halted in her tracks. "No!"

"He apologized, of course," Tina added, "but I'm not so sure it was an accident."

Giulia was skeptical, offering a doubtful "Oh, come on."

"Think about it," Tina said. "If things like this were accidents, wouldn't they happen to everyone equally—and not just to the pretty ones like Holly?" She stopped when she reached her office door.

"Well, look who's spreading gossip now," Giulia said. She began walking again, faster.

"Hey, it's not gossip if it's true. Holly told me this herself."

Stepping backward now, Giulia cupped her hands and whispered loudly, "If you want my opinion, I think she probably enjoyed it."

Giulia saw Lindeman twice during the course of the next hour, and—perhaps due to the power of suggestion—both times she thought he leaned over her desk just a little farther than was strictly necessary to point out minor irregularities in the job orders. She pulled away from his perceived advances, feigning clerical tasks in the file cabinet behind her.

Not until she was safely home, preparing a noonday meal for her mother and herself, did she recognize how paranoid she had become, and she felt an unmistakable twinge of shame. Maybe she should give Mr. Lindeman the benefit of the doubt. Surely he had not mutated, virtually overnight, into some sort of predatory brute. More likely it was she herself who had changed, conditioned by the ugly rumors that Tina was repeating.

But it was at her own peril that she entertained such charitable thoughts. An indiscriminately trusting spirit, if applied to scoundrels, is no better than any other character flaw. Unlike most winsome young ladies, Giulia Coletti was utterly naïve when it came to the seductiveness of her own beauty, and she accorded gentlemen with a good deal more self-control than they actually possessed.

♦   ♦   ♦

Hugh Kenton and Clive Ramey both expressed satisfaction with their historic lodgings, and Wesley, though he had no real perspective on which to base such an opinion, was quick to agree.

Except for about a dozen representatives from El Paso and the panhandle, the entire Texas contingent of Columbia broadcasters was housed in the Roosevelt Hotel, an elegant, twelve-story tower that, in its seventeen years of operation, had already established itself as a Hollywood landmark and tourist attraction. Located on Hollywood Boulevard, almost directly across the street from the even more famous Grauman's Chinese Theater—which it predated by exactly three days—the Roosevelt Hotel was within a long walking distance of most of the convention's activities. A few of the smaller meetings would take place inside the hotel itself, while nearly all of the others were in the network's west coast headquarters at Columbia Square on Sunset Boulevard.

Named in honor of FDR's distant cousin and twenty-sixth President of the United States, the Roosevelt Hotel had been home to the Motion Picture Academy of Arts and Sciences from 1927 through 1935, and it was inside the hotel's famed Blossom Room that Douglas Fairbanks presided over the very first Academy Awards ceremonies—then called Merit Awards—on May 16, 1929. That same year, a young bandleader, vocalist, saxophonist, and radio personality named Rudy Vallee chose to stay at the Roosevelt Hotel when he arrived in Hollywood to make his first feature film, *The Vagabond Lover.*

Though not planned as such, the 1944 network convention happened to dovetail with a visit to the CBS microphones by the reigning musical personality in the world. Fans of Jascha Heifetz and Arturo Toscanini might squabble with such a statement, but among the general public, there was no question where the true artistic hegemony lay—squarely at the feet of a twenty-eight-year-old Hoboken native who first decided to become an entertainer after hearing Bing Crosby on the radio. Given the erratic permutations of America's popular music industry, the young crooner's rise to fame was spectacularly swift and sure. On September 8, 1935, the national broadcast of "Major Bowes and the Original Amateur Hour" presented a vocal group called the "Hoboken Four," a male quartet that earlier had auditioned under the sobriquet of "Frank Sinatra and the Three Flashes." Presumably, this less-than-prescient revision of their name was suggested by the cagily benevolent major himself, who nonetheless would, with some justification, place "Frankie" at the very top of his short list of major discoveries. Just for the record, the other Flashes—fated to be lost to history when their standard-bearer ventured out on his own—were Jimmy Petro, Fred Tamburro, and Patty Prince.

It was on the first weekday of the convention that Ralph Hedges, of local Columbia affiliate KNX, drove two KRLD executives and the three Waco guests down Hollywood Boulevard on an improvised sightseeing tour. They had ninety minutes in between meetings, and Hedges, in this unaccustomed role of docent, was the perfect guide for out-of-towners. In terms of public attractions, he knew them all—the shops, the theaters, the restaurants, the hotels, the studios, and of course the radio stations.

His automobile, unconventional in that it had no clutch flanking the brake pedal, was a pale yellow, eight-cylinder, 1940 Oldsmobile Custom Cruiser four-door sedan with Hydra-Matic drive, a model notable for possessing the first truly reliable automatic transmission. He was proud of it—that much was clear from the serene way he lounged in stop-and-go traffic, with left elbow protruding out the window and right hand casually maneuvering the steering wheel. Such a four-year-old vehicle, in light of wartime production mandates, was considered to be relatively new. And the tires still had plenty of tread.

"Look at that mob, will you?" Hedges said. He turned the Olds south onto Vine Street, and the three Wacoans craned their necks to see. Wesley, as the junior member of this little group, was sandwiched between Kenton and Ramey in the back seat, affording him no unobstructed view in any direction. The two Dallasites were up front with the driver, long-limbed Alton Rence being an old friend of Hedges.

By leaning down slightly, Wesley could detect a mass of people on the sidewalk ahead. Though partially obscured by the rear-view mirror, they appeared to be queued up, four or five abreast, waiting for some event to begin. "That's the Vine Street Playhouse," Hedges told the others. He braked for a bus that suddenly pulled in front of him. "Frank Sinatra's on the 'Lux Radio Theatre' tonight, and those people are all waiting to see their hero in person."

"What're the chances of us getting in to see it?" Will Connover asked. He was the other Dallas rep.

"Not a prayer," Hedges said with a laugh. "The theater holds less than two thousand, and they'll probably turn away three times that many before the opening curtain."

That evening's presentation was *Wake Up and Live*, loosely based on Dorothea Brande's novel about a shy singer who suffers from mike fright, only to achieve radio stardom quite by accident. Among the tunes to be heard were "Embraceable You," "I've Heard That Song Before," "Dancing in the Dark," and of course the title song itself. Jack Haley (with the dubbed assistance of Buddy Clark's singing voice) played the part of Eddie Kane in the 1937 movie version, opposite Alice Faye, but the radio adaptation would spotlight the talents of Frank Sinatra—in his first dramatic role—and Marilyn Maxwell.

As the automobile neared the theater, Wesley could see a KNX sign on the far corner of the building and a CBS sign at the closer end. Over the entrance, a large "Lux Radio Theatre" banner was fluttering in the breeze.

"Is this where you work, Ralph?" one of the Dallas men asked.

"No, we're over on Sunset Boulevard, between Gower and El Centro," Hedges told him. "Thank God I don't have to deal with this chaos every Monday afternoon."

Though it was still a good two and a half hours before airtime, the line of noisy people already stretched well past Mike Lyman's restaurant and on up the street. Most of those standing in line seemed to be women, but there were several men in uniform scattered among them.

"Say, I can get you into the theater next week, if any of you would be interested in going," Hedges said. "I don't know what's playing, but it sure won't be as crowded as something with Mr. Sinatra in it."

Wesley looked at Kenton and nodded his head, but it was Ramey who voiced the collective response. "We may just take you up on that."

The evening hours brought some welcome solitude. With Kenton and Ramey away, attending a "watering hole" conclave at Sardi's, underage Wesley was left alone at the Roosevelt Hotel, and he decided to take advantage of this unexpected leisure time by listening to Sinatra's appearance over the KNX airwaves. The hotel did not furnish radios in any of its rooms, but a few table models were available, just for the asking, from the reservations clerk behind the front desk.

"Oh, no, sir," the telephone attendant said. "There is no need for you to come down to the lobby. I will be happy to have someone bring the radio up to you." Wesley felt very important, as if someone had just paid for his dinner with a commanding wink toward the waiter. Not five minutes later, there came a rapping at his door, and the radio was laid in place atop the nightstand.

"Sometimes the reception is not very good inside these rooms," the bellboy told him, "but I can bring you a wire aerial if that will help." They warmed up the set and listened. The tuner whined as it made its way toward 1070 kHz, but once there, the station came in tolerably well, aside from a persistent trace of static hum. The bellboy, who was only a year or so older than Wesley himself, tipped his cap, accepted a dime for his troubles, and left.

Wesley was intimately familiar with the "Lux Radio Theatre," a weekly program that, for as far back as his memory served, had always been an eight-o'clock fixture in the Brower household. But here on the west coast it originated at six o'clock, and Wesley thought it odd to be hearing it at such an early hour. It was also a strange sensation to realize that the radio show he was listening to was being created, live, in this very neighborhood. The actors, sound-effects men, announcers, and musicians were all performing so close-by that—had he possessed a stage pass and enough athletic stamina—he could have jogged a dozen blocks to the east and begun viewing the actual performance from the wings even before the curtain went up for the second act. How ironic, then, that the signal reception was so inferior to that in his central Texas living room, almost thirteen hundred miles away.

Supine on his hotel bed, hands behind his head, Wesley heard announcer John Milton Kennedy introduce that night's show ("Lux presents Hollywood ..."), and then titular producer Cecil B. DeMille—in the reassuring, grandfatherly fashion that made him a welcome visitor in homes across America—warmly painted a word picture to set the scene for Act I.

"Greetings from Hollywood, ladies and gentlemen," he said. "There's a pot of gold at the end of the Hollywood rainbow for the right answer to the question, 'What makes a star?' Nobody has found out yet, and I don't think they ever will. No two stars are alike, but each has a certain indefinable power—a power that draws people like a magnet draws bits of metal. I've watched that power at work for fifty years—in a lovely face, in a pair of dancing feet, in a voice. And it has come again this year in the voice of Frank Sinatra. When a star is born overnight, there are always the cynics who say, 'He won't last.' But he will last if that mysterious power is there. And it is my belief that, in Frank's case, it is there. For his first appearance in the dramatic end of radio, we have picked the delightful comedy that made a hit on the screen for 20th Century-Fox. It's *Wake Up and Live*, and assisting Frank to wake up and live is a quartet of people from the screen and radio: Bob Crosby, Jimmy Gleason, Marilyn Maxwell, and James Dunn."

And delightful it was. Though Curtis Kenyon's story line was contrived from opening curtain to final fade, the disarming performers swept all before them. Sinatra's portrayal of shy crooner Eddie Kane was ineptly likable, and even his flubbed line near the beginning of Act III somehow seemed endearing and altogether in character. It was clear for everyone to hear that, in the personage of young Frank Sinatra, the indefinable power was there indeed.

◆   ◆   ◆

"Someone's here to see you," Melba Kyle shouted over the deafening noise of the automated weaving looms.

"Big Melba" was a thirtyish matron whose cherubic features reminded some of the older Crawford-Austin employees of a female Roscoe Arbuckle. Hannah Lane, by virtue of her tender years, was not among them. Having never seen the late Fatty on the screen, she associated his famous name with nothing more than a series of sensational murder trials, sordid details of which occasionally crept into dinner-table discussions back home. Uncle Vernon was quite fond of speculating into the demise of Virginia Rappe and then chuckling at the flustered discomfort of his younger brother, the Good Reverend Sam.

Hannah removed the cotton wads from her ears and, pointing to herself, shouted over the din of the machinery, "To see me?" A power loom was operating just a few feet away, making normal conversation impossible.

"Yes, ma'am," Melba told her. She did so with misplaced deference, being almost ten years the other's senior. Her bovine stare was kindly but devoid of intellect.

"Thank you, Melba," Hannah shouted. "Do you know who it is?"

Melba shook her head. "No, ma'am. They never did say that part."

"Tell them I'll come up front in about ten minutes. I can't leave until my break time."

Melba took one oafish step backward, nearly toppling a coat tree that stood dangerously close to the flywheel and other moving parts. "Yes, ma'am. I'll tell them that."

Acting crew chief Rowena Downing angrily jumped to her feet and spewed a stream of yellow-brown tobacco juice into her paper cup. "Well, don't just stand there looking at it," she screamed. "Drag that menace over to the wall, will you? Them jackets could get all tangled up in the gears and kill somebody."

"And maybe even stop production," Robert Ducey added. Instantly proud of his snappy rejoinder, he looked around for approbation, but the only response from anyone on the line was Rowena's frigid glare. "Grim bunch," he said. Meanwhile, poor Melba did as she was told, nearly in tears.

Hannah finished perforating the canvas flap "on her plate," and she stretched it laterally against the sidewall panel, making certain that the two pieces would wed properly. Satisfied with that, she draped her materials over the work surface and gave Rowena a questioning look. The acting crew chief excused her with a nod of the head, so Hannah removed her protective gloves and began walking down the corridor toward the lobby area. Away from the pleasant warmth of the machinery, this drafty old building could become quite chilly, so she hesitated just long enough to deposit her chewing gum in a dented, paint-stained receptacle that stood against the wall.

"Oh, hello, Miss Lane," Annabelle Swift said at the front desk. "You have a visitor."

The only other person in the lobby was a smiling, stoop-shouldered, elderly woman with thick eyeglasses. Hannah approached her until the receptionist added, "No, I'm sorry. There's a *man* waiting for you. I guess he must have gone to the washroom for a minute." The old lady chuckled at the mistaken identity.

Rattled by the momentary awkwardness, Annabelle introduced the pair. "Miss Lane, this is Mrs. Rodgers, Bynum Fowler's grandmother."

Hannah shook the woman's hand. "How do you do?" Her eyes drifted to the GENTLEMEN sign, and she wondered who, any second now, would be opening the door beneath it.

"You know Bynum, don't you?" Annabelle asked her.

"No, I don't think so."

"Well, it's very nice to meet you anyhow," the old lady said with a playful wink. "Bynum's a wonderful boy, and I'm sure you would like him."

Hannah smiled. "Yes, I'm sure I would. He's got a sweet grandmother."

"Why, thank you, dear. I certainly do wish he would meet someone like you. Are you already spoken for?" Mrs. Rodgers, it seemed, had reached that advanced age when a *faux pas* was considered to be quaint.

Hannah laughed. "No, praise the Lord. I should say not." She swept some errant strands of hair from her eyes and smiled at the old woman.

"Are you a Waco High girl, or are you already out of school? I'm not very good at guessing ages."

"I go to Baylor."

Mrs. Rodgers's eyes lit up. "Oh? Are you Baptist, then?"

"Yes, ma'am, I am. My daddy's a preacher back home."

"Oh, he is? Here in Texas?"

Hannah shook her head. "North Carolina."

"Well, I didn't think you sounded quite like a Texan, dear. I've been to Greensboro before. Are you from near there?"

"No, ma'am—way up near the Virginia border."

Mrs. Rodgers opened her purse. "Here, let me give you Bynum's telephone number, Miss Lane. He's awful lonely, you know—now that his father and brother are both in the service. I'm sure he would enjoy meeting a nice, Christian girl like you." She wrote the number on a slip of paper. "He lives with his mother in Bellmead."

The hinges of the rest room door squeaked as a young man with a black, neatly trimmed beard came striding toward the desk. He carried a valise and abounded in confidence. That much was clear to see.

"Hannah, dear!" the mysterious figure said. It was not Alvin Reeder, thought Hannah, so who in the world could it be? Certainly not anyone else from Mount Airy. Was it a Baylor student? As he advanced ever closer, she detected a hazily recalled mannerism, something in the athletic way he carried himself, with his calf muscles fairly skipping him along. Yes, by gosh, it was too Alvin Reeder, but his face had changed so much in the intervening years that she hardly recognized him.

Hannah greeted the guest with a perfunctory "Hello, Alvin," but she was cordial enough to hold out her hand.

"Oh, we can do better than that," Alvin said. He took hold of her shoulders and landed a platonic kiss on her cheek.

Mrs. Rodgers looked away, thoroughly embarrassed, and Annabelle sat back in her chair, mouth opened wide in a state of shock.

Normally, Hannah's reflex action would have been to slap the fresh visitor across his face, but she fought the urge and instead resorted to a more cerebral approach, one that might pay higher dividends in the long run. Pulling away from him, she calmly told Mrs. Rodgers, "Well, I'm sure glad Bynum wasn't here to see that!"

Had Hannah begun speaking to her in tongues, the old lady could not have been more uncomprehending than she was now. She said nothing in response, and her befuddled eyes cowered behind the thick spectacles like two darting guppies in an aquarium.

Hannah turned back to Alvin with the friendliest of smiles. "Bynum is my protector," she told him. "I mean here at work, you know—now that Steve is away in the service."

Alvin looked at the elderly lady and nodded.

"Oh, I'm sorry," Hannah said. "This is Mrs. Roberts, Bynum's grandmother."

"Nice to meet you, Mrs. Roberts."

"Actually, it's Rodgers," the lady told him.

"Sorry ... Mrs. Rodgers," Alvin said. The receptionist seemed to be viewing all of this with more than just passing curiosity.

Alvin turned back to Hannah and, cocking his head slightly to the right, said under his breath, "Can we talk for a few minutes? How long do you have?"

Hannah looked at the wall clock. "I only have six minutes left on my break, and my boss keeps tabs on us with a stopwatch."

Placing a gentle hand on her back, he ushered her along. "Where could we go to talk?"

"The break room, I guess. Can't go far."

"I'll follow you. Show the way."

Before they started walking down the corridor, Alvin politely tipped his hat to the receptionist and the old lady. Annabelle Swift nodded her head and smiled. Mrs. Rodgers, though, was a still life, gazing without movement through her thick eyeglasses and aimlessly clutching the undelivered slip of paper in one hand.

The first thing Hannah did after opening the door was to find a spot far away from anyone else. About a half-dozen other workers were in the break room, but they were engaged in what sounded like a heated discussion of President Roosevelt's handling of the war. With valise in hand, Alvin followed Hannah to the remotest table available. He pulled out a chair for her and then, instead of sitting across the table, he settled into the seat next to hers. "It's been a long day. I've been up since 4:30."

"I got up at six," Hannah told him. She placed a piece of chewing gum in her mouth. "I try to write to Steve at least twice a week, and the early morning seems to be the best time for that."

Alvin loosened his necktie a bit. "It sure is nice being away from work for a couple of weeks. You'd really be amazed how rude some so-called Christians can be when you try to sell them a new Bible." He took a pack of cigarettes from his shirt pocket.

"Well, maybe they don't mean to be that way at all," Hannah said. "It could be they just don't need another Bible. I wouldn't take it too personally."

"That's what this training session is all about—up in Dallas—overcoming the fear of rejection. It's a rough way to earn a living, but I'm turning into a pretty good salesman, if I do say so myself. I even grew a beard to make me seem a little older." It was true. His facial hair was neatly trimmed and looked quite sophisticated for such a young man.

"I hope Steve hasn't gone and done something like that. I'm not partial to beards."

Alvin laughed good-naturedly and puffed his cigarette. "Oh? Can they wear beards in the service?"

"I think the Navy can, but I hope Steve hasn't done anything as foolish as that—or getting a tattoo, for goodness sakes. He's already started smoking a pipe."

"Don Haygood joined the Navy, you know."

"Who?"

"Tubby. You remember Tubby, don't you? The boxer?"

"Sure, but I didn't know his name was really Don."

"He joined up after his brother was killed by the Germans," Alvin said.

"I don't think Steve is overseas yet. It's hard to tell because he really can't say very much in his letters. They're pretty vague."

"Luther Haygood got killed in Sicily—fighting against the Hermann Goering Panzer Division, so I hear. They had a memorial service at your daddy's church."

"I thank God every day that Steve's in the Navy instead of a foot soldier."

Alvin scratched the hair along his jaw line and looked annoyed. "Who is this Steve you keep talking about? Someone you met at Baylor?"

Hannah beamed, reaching inside her purse. "He's the most wonderful boy in the world. Here's his picture." She handed Alvin a wallet-sized military photo. "He's the son of my landlady."

Alvin glanced at the picture and then, holding it between the index and middle fingers of his left hand, returned it to Hannah without comment.

She admired the photo anew, as if seeing it for the first time. "I hope maybe he can come back home on furlough before he's sent overseas."

"I tried to get in, but my bad ear wouldn't pass the physical," Alvin told her. He blew smoke toward the noisy table of workers.

"You seem to hear okay."

"I think so too, but the doctors sure didn't see it that way. I went to two of them, and both of them rejected me."

"Can't you try again?"

He laughed. "There's no appeal in the military. No, I'll just try to do my bit here at home—bonds, scrap drives, spotting, that sort of thing."

Hannah seemed almost amused. "Golly, do we still need spotters? I haven't heard that word in a couple of years. If the Japs wanted to bomb us, they would have done it by now."

"Sure, you feel real safe here in Texas, but it's a different story on the east coast."

"Well, I think the Germans have all they can handle—without flying all the way across the Atlantic to bomb poor Mount Airy."

Alvin began to argue the point but then relaxed with a smile. "Maybe you're right. You always were a pragmatist."

Glancing at the wall clock, Hannah said, "Well ..." and scooted her chair away from the table.

Alvin acted quickly, as if he had been rehearsing for days. In a single, graceful motion, he crushed his half-smoked cigarette in the ashtray, pivoted his chair toward hers, and placed his right hand atop Hannah's left. "May I see you after you get off work?" he asked.

She snatched her hand away—more out of surprise than revulsion—and rose to her feet. "I don't think that would be a very good idea ... in the circumstances." Viewing the other employees in the room, Hannah was pleased to see that no one was paying Alvin and her the slightest attention. "Listen," she told him, "I've really got to get back to work."

Alvin stood, too, and there was a touch of indignation in his voice as he whispered, "Do you mean to tell me that I came a hundred miles for just a six-minute visit?"

"I'm sorry," was all Hannah would say. Then she turned to leave.

"What time do you punch out?" His jaw muscles were hard at work.

"One thirty." She walked backward toward the door. "But I'll be jumping right on a streetcar. I've got a class at two. I'm awfully sorry."

Alvin sat on the edge of the table. "Look, Hannah," he said. "I'll be going back to North Carolina on Saturday, and I may not see you again for years—until you're out of college."

"Sorry." She smiled compassionately and shook her head.

"Then I'll walk you to the streetcar—if that's all of your precious time you can give me." He looked away, at the public service posters lining the wall: "Make Haste Safely," "Good Tools Deserve Good Care," "Keep Those Supplies Coming," "Work, to Keep 'Em Firing." He waited for a reasonable few seconds but heard no sound of a door opening. With a smug grin, he turned toward the exit, confident of what he would see. Sure enough, there stood Hannah Lane, perhaps contrite, her hand poised on the doorknob.

"Well, what do you say?" he asked.

"Sorry, but Bynum's already going to do that," she said. "I told you he's my protector while Steve is away."

It was all Alvin could do to hold his temper. "Yes, you did tell me that, didn't you? I stand corrected."

"But do write to me about what's going on back home," Hannah added. "My daddy's letters aren't very newsy—except about the old folks in his congregation."

Alvin's face brightened at once, sensing that there was still hope. "Swell," he said. He half expected her to come closer, but instead she opened the door and began to leave.

"God bless," Hannah told him. "It was awfully nice of you to travel so far to see me."

When she shut the door behind her, Alvin slapped his thigh and chuckled to himself. This little visit turned out better than the dreary impasse he anticipated. He stood up and blew a kiss to a recruiting poster of Uncle Sam. Then, taking his valise in hand, he swaggered over to the table of Crawford-Austin employees. "Say, would anyone be interested in purchasing a finely crafted new Bible? I represent the Piedmont Publishing Company of Washington, North Carolina."

♦　　♦　　♦

As he and nearly a hundred other CBS guests made their way down the short hallway that stretched from the front entrance to the auditorium itself, Wesley Brower felt quite pampered from all the special consideration. Accorded "VIP" status by attendants at the Vine Street Playhouse, the visiting contingent of network employees was waved past a lengthy line of locals, many of whom had been waiting outside, free tickets in hand, for up to three hours. Had he paused long enough as he walked by, he would have detected more than a few resentful scowls and even a nasty comment or two—sour words to the effect of "Who do they think they are?"

He followed Clive Ramey and Hugh Kenton in single file, and behind the Wacoans were similar groups from San Antonio, Houston, Lubbock, and Amarillo. A pleasant feeling of *déjà vu* struck Wesley when he rounded the corner and first gazed upon the auditorium proper, with its elevated stage and inclined seating. It was not so much the physical configuration of the hall as it was the exalted ambience of the place. This was just how he felt when he and his father emerged from the shadows of the grandstand into the bright sunlight of Sportsman's Park in Saint Louis, way back when he was only eight. There, warming up before him—with echoing *plops* in their mitts—were the likes of Terry Moore, Pepper Martin, and Frankie Frisch, and down the other line, Jim Bottomley, the newly acquired Kiki Cuyler, and catcher Ernie Lombardi, with that famous schnoz amplifying a friendly smile.

The seats of the auditorium were totally empty, but not for long. Now the line of conventioneers began filing in, led by a page—dressed in blue slacks, a white, long-sleeved shirt, and red necktie—who positioned them, in orderly fashion, to fill much of the first three rows. Wesley wound up slightly left of center in the second row, and from there he made a quick head count, estimating that there were ninety-one broadcasting reps in their party. He wondered, amazed, why anyone would opt not to attend such a grand event, and yet most of the passes had gone unclaimed.

He consciously studied the stage area, allowing his eyes to move slowly from left to right and back again, soaking in as much of this magical view as he could. Some two dozen ordinary-looking folding chairs were arrayed, side by side, just in front of a curtain. At center stage was a hanging microphone, down each side of which ran the distinctive CBS logo. Beneath the microphone, reaching up to within a foot and a half of it, stood a shiny, oddly shaped contraption constructed of metal railing. This, he was to learn later, was a sturdy stand (nicknamed "Oscar") that was designed for nervous performers to lean on, if they so chose, while delivering their lines. Two other microphones stood on upright stands, evenly spaced along the stage. To the far left, next to the proscenium, was a card table with its own microphone, and to the far right was the control booth. Barely visible through a rectangular opening in the curtain was someone shuffling sheets of paper about, perhaps turning pages on a music stand.

All the while, those hundreds of people who had waited so patiently along Hollywood Boulevard were being ushered to their seats inside the performance hall. Wesley glanced at his wristwatch and saw that it was just past 5:30. By now, the auditorium had grown quite loud, with the idle chatter of nearly two thousand onlookers, and there was a thrilling aura of expectancy in the air.

For some reason, a wad of fossilized chewing gum caught Wesley's eye, and the odious matter seemed to him very much out of place in such a rarefied setting. But there it was, clinging to the back of the chair directly in his line of sight to the stage. Inasmuch as the Vine Street Playhouse had been used for no activity besides the "Lux Radio Theatre" since May 13, 1940—when the program moved there from the much smaller (965-seat) Music Box Theatre—it must have been a fellow radio enthusiast who stuck this gum on the chair in an unthinking moment. To Wesley, such a repulsive act was like violating the sanctity of some hallowed landmark—Independence Hall perhaps, or Lincoln's Tomb.

The crowd hushed when a distinguished gentleman approached the microphone at center stage. He introduced himself as John Milton Kennedy, and Wesley recognized the name as the program's announcer, the first voice heard each week: "Lux presents Hollywood." Kennedy was not a true warm-up artist—someone like the waggish Bill Goodwin on that other CBS powerhouse, "The Burns and Allen Show"—but he had an urbane charm all his own that held the audience's attention simply by the musicality in his voice. This being a live show, he explained that no extraneous noise could be tolerated, except of course for "oohs and ahs" when the stars were announced and applause whenever so prompted.

Kennedy turned to his left and introduced from the wings, one by one, the supporting actors in the all-male cast who would help to bring that evening's production of *Guadalcanal Diary* to life: Gary Brockner, Norman Field, Charlie Lung, Charles Seel, Bob Young, Ken Hodge, Howard McNear, Tom Holland, Paul Zuremba, Eddie Marr, John McIntire, Ed Emerson, and Herbert Rawlinson. Each actor, after acknowledging the crowd's enthusiastic clapping with a smile, nod, or wave, took a seat at the rear of the stage.

In show business fashion, Kennedy had saved the biggest stars for last, but then, with dramatic flair, he announced each of their names individually and highlighted a few professional credits. Here came Richard Jaeckel (who would be playing the part of "Chicken"), Lloyd Nolan (as "Hook"), William Bendix (as "Taxi"), and lastly, Preston Foster (in the pivotal role of "Father Donnelly").

Though each round of applause seemed to out-crescendo the one before it, there was still ample room for the warmest ovation of all. Turning again to his left, Kennedy held out an arm to welcome the final on-air dignitary, and his manner of speech became even more dramatic than before. "And now, ladies and gentlemen, here is your producer of the 'Lux Radio Theatre,' Mr. Cecil B. DeMille!" The mere mention of his name brought down the house, and the famous *auteur* strode on stage with more alacrity than Wesley would have imagined from a legendary figure whose days in the motion picture industry dated back to pre-historic times—when Hollywood was little more than a peaceful, unassuming grove of orange trees. After taking a bow, Mr. DeMille seated himself at a card table, stage right, and took advantage of the remaining minutes by thumbing through the script to that night's show. He seemed to Wesley incredibly relaxed for someone whose voice would soon be heard from coast to coast over a network radio hook-up.

When the name of Louis Silvers was called, the venerable orchestra conductor did not join the others on stage but waved to the Vine Street Playhouse crowd from behind the curtain, framed by a rectangular "window" that was designed to give him visual contact with the director. Though surely few, if any, in the audience were aware of it, Silvers had quite an impressive list of movie credentials. With the Columbia Studio Music Department, he helped win an Academy Award for its scoring of the 1934 film, *One Night of Love*, and seven years before that, he supervised music for the very first talking picture of all, Al Jolson's *The Jazz Singer*.

The introduction of director Fred MacKaye finally brought the announcer's pre-curtain duties to an end, so now it was the director himself who stepped up to the microphone. He welcomed the audience and issued a verbal set of last-minute instructions regarding proper on-air etiquette. He also explained that everything the crowd heard would be live, including sound effects, music from the orchestra backstage, and commercial announcements during both of the intermissions. It was four minutes to six when he gave a quick wave and then disappeared from view into the wings, stage left, where the control booth was situated behind a long panel of soundproof glass.

The house lights dimmed a bit, but the stage remained fully lit. Wesley looked around to see the capacity crowd behind him, amazed at how unearthly quiet this group of two thousand spectators had become, each one of them anticipating that special moment when the on-air sign would finally illuminate. As the second hand on the network-synchronized wall clock was edging toward the twelve, John Milton Kennedy returned to the microphone and glanced at Mr. DeMille. The producer, sitting behind his card table at stage right, smiled back with a nod. Seated to his left, the long line of performers awaited their cues, some shifting nervously in their chairs, others moving their lips as they silently read through tricky passages of dialogue in preparation for the show. Kennedy peered at the control booth and watched the technical director counting down with his fingers. All across the nation—at that very instant—announcers at hundreds of radio outlets were delivering their local station identifications, but the Vine Street Playhouse audience only heard a single disembodied voice: "This is KNX, Los Angeles, ten-seventy kilohertz. The time is six o'clock." Then came the cue.

♦   ♦   ♦

"Lux presents Hollywood," John Milton Kennedy proclaimed into the hanging microphone. A downbeat from conductor Louis Silvers launched the gifted orchestra—boasting some of the entertainment industry's very finest session musicians—into Robert Armbruster's stately and instantly recognizable theme tune, which was potted under after its initial strain. "The 'Lux Radio Theatre' brings you *Guadalcanal Diary* with Richard Jaeckel," the announcer continued with a glimpse to his right. "Ladies and gentlemen, your producer, Mr. Cecil B. DeMille."

Thus, for the 428th time in its brilliant decade of weekly presentations, did the "Lux Radio Theatre" return to the airwaves—from coast to coast and, via shortwave and the subsequent dissemination of AFRS transcription discs, to thousands of American servicemen overseas. By unanimous acclamation, this was the most celebrated of all the "prestige dramas" that radio had to offer.

"Greetings from Hollywood, ladies and gentlemen," Mr. DeMille recited into his table microphone. There was a calm certitude in his voice that, in these horrifying days of carnage, seemed trustworthy, humane, and reassuring. "The war correspondent Richard Tregaskis wrote the story in *Guadalcanal Diary* just as he saw it happen. From that book, 20th Century-Fox made one of the really great motion pictures of the war, and tonight we bring it to you with the same stars you saw on the screen. We raise the curtain on the first act of *Guadalcanal Diary*, starring Lloyd Nolan as Hook, William Bendix as Taxi, and Preston Foster as Father Donnelly, with Richard Jaeckel as Chicken."

But this was radio—theater of the imagination—and the rising curtain to which Mr. DeMille alluded was merely a figurative one. The only true curtain was hanging behind the actors rather than in front of them, a pragmatic measure to isolate the audience from distracting activities backstage. During the course of the next forty-seven minutes, listeners at home "viewed" the brutal story of *Guadalcanal Diary* in full color, amidst the most panoramic of settings. An idyllic South Pacific paradise was reduced to a fiery hell on earth. And yet no bullets were ever fired, no Marines lay mortally wounded, no Jap snipers were felled from palm trees by Yank sharpshooters.

It was not quite so easy for at least one Vine Street Playhouse observer to suspend disbelief. Even before the end of the first act, Wesley Brower found himself paying more attention to the production values than to the unfolding drama on stage. Perhaps this was because he, too, was a member of the noble alliance of radio performers. "Behold Tomorrow" was a far cry from the "Lux Radio Theatre," but the basic concept remained true to form. Undeniably, there was a certain visual fascination in the logistics involved—namely, the movement of cast and crew. Each supporting actor took his place at one of the floor microphones and then immediately returned to his seat after reading that particular passage of dialogue. Stars, on the other hand, never ventured very far away from the hanging microphone. They were usually within arm's length of "Oscar" and sometimes even grasped its metal rails for support while declaiming their lines.

Despite the tension and challenges of live broadcasting—essentially performing a high-wire act without a net, with the entire nation tuned in—all went astonishingly well for such a complex production, at least as far as Wesley could determine from his seat in the auditorium. William Bendix stumbled badly over the word "kimonos" a couple of minutes into the second act, but he quickly righted himself and remained fully in character. Otherwise, there were no conspicuous flaws. Wesley suspected that a large number of microphones, in addition to the orchestra's, must have been positioned backstage. Except for the scripted dialogue, no sound sources whatsoever were apparent to the eye. Intermission commercials were voiced away from the scrutiny of the audience, as were the explosive sound effects of warfare, the lapping of ocean waves, choral-singing camaraderie among the troops, and a hefty portion of the leathernecks' background murmuring during crowd scenes.

The show's smooth efficacy would not have taken Wesley by such surprise had he been aware of the intense preparation that went into this and every other "Lux Radio Theatre" presentation. On Thursday afternoon, this same supporting cast of *Guadalcanal Diary* had met in the Vine Street Playhouse for a first reading of the script. In addition to director Fred MacKaye, sound-effects artist Charlie Forsyth was also there for the initial two-hour session, and so was sound engineer Ed Whittaker. Another two-hour rehearsal took place the next day, again with stand-ins reading for the stars. Then, later that afternoon, the principal actors joined the entire ensemble for a run-through that demanded two and a half hours.

Saturday was a day of rest, but the full cast, including stars, participated in a two-hour rehearsal beginning at 10:30 on Sunday morning. Even when the cast broke for lunch, Louis Silvers continued to drill his orchestral musicians for an additional hour. Sunday afternoon meant a full dress rehearsal, timed down to the second and simulating an actual broadcast. Only servicemen were permitted in the audience, and this rehearsal was recorded on disc for the artistic benefit of director and cast. Nor was the actual broadcast regimen as effortless as it might have appeared to the uninitiated among that Monday audience. The cast and crew that Wesley witnessed on stage had reported for duty at 3:30 that afternoon, embarking upon a final rehearsal session that lasted until one hour before curtain time.

The "Lux Radio Theatre" was the most meticulously crafted of all programs on the network airwaves—and it showed.

◆　◆　◆

After Mr. DeMille conducted "curtain call" interviews with William Bendix, Preston Foster, and Lloyd Nolan, no actors—not even the principal players—arose to leave the stage until the hour's final words were spoken into the CBS microphone: "This is your announcer, John M. Kennedy, reminding you to tune in again next Monday night to hear Bette Davis, Herbert Marshall, and Vincent Price in ... *The Letter.*" Then, with the on-air sign extinguished, the performance area sprang back to life, with the stars exiting to a warm round of applause, followed at once by the supporting cast. When the stage was totally clear, the house lights came back up, signaling the audience to stand and migrate toward the exits. Theater crew appeared out of the wings and began wandering about, gathering cables and removing the cast's chairs from view. Orchestra members could be heard backstage, noisily gathering their belongings and returning instruments to their cases.

Clive Ramey patted one of the Houston executives on the shoulder and began chatting with him, so there was little that Wesley and Hugh Kenton could do but wait. Wesley gazed at the Vine Street Playhouse stage one final time and felt sad that this exciting hour had come to an end. Moments earlier, nearly two dozen of radio's top stars and character actors were working their magic, bringing the

"Lux Radio Theatre" to millions of listeners in homes across the nation. And now, only a few minutes past seven, the crowd was filing its way out, as if nothing of significance had ever happened here, as if casually meandering from some neighborhood movie house. It was at this sobering moment that Wesley, with a cold shudder, remembered his pledge to Sandra Whittsel.

"Say, Hugh," he asked, "do you think it might be possible to get an autograph?"

"Here at the theater?"

"Yes, sir. Maybe William Bendix or Preston Foster? It has to be a man."

Kenton, who was wiping his eyeglasses with a handkerchief, shook his head. "Your chances are slim and none. Lux is very protective of its stars."

"That's what I was afraid of."

"Well, you should've done it earlier, son. There were some pretty big names at the banquet—Jimmy Durante, André Kostelanetz, Dick Powell."

"I didn't think about it until a minute ago." Using the narrow end of his comb as a chisel blade, Wesley whacked the chewing gum off the seat in front of him, leaving a telltale stain in its place.

"Are you one of those autograph hounds?" Kenton asked him.

"No, not really. This isn't for me. Someone asked me to get one for her while I'm out here in Hollywood."

Kenton put his eyeglasses back on. "Oh? Someone I know?" Then, with a hand cupping his mouth, he whispered, "A lady friend, perhaps?"

"Gee, no. Not a girl," Wesley told him. "It's just my mother. She asked me to get her an autograph. One of the big stars, if I can."

"She collects them, does she?"

"I guess so. She has two or three that my father got. One's a picture of Wiley Post sitting on top of the *Winnie Mae*."

Kenton was impressed. "Oh? Where'd your father meet Wiley Post?"

"He never said."

"You know, I once met Will Rogers in Kansas City. Did I ever tell you about that?"

"No, sir."

Though the hall was emptying fast, Clive Ramey continued talking to the Houston executive—as if he had all the time in the world and their agreeable ride, Ralph Hedges, were not standing in the lobby, idly cooling his heels. Kenton consulted his pocket watch and said to Wesley, "Well, if I happen to run into any stars, I'll have one of them inscribe something for your mother. What's her first name?" He pulled out a business card and flipped it over to the blank side.

"Uh ... Nora," Wesley said. He cleared his throat. "But I don't think she'd want it made out to her."

"Nonsense." Kenton jotted down her name. "It makes it more personal that way. I'll try to keep my eyes peeled for a celebrity. We've still got another day."

But that opportunity never did come. The network convention was breaking up, stars were dispersing in all directions, and the Wacoans' final hours, most of Tuesday morning, were spent preparing for the return trip home. With time ebbing away, Wesley even considered the desperate measure of forging a famous actor's autograph on a hotel napkin, but he soon abandoned that notion. Sandy was just crafty enough to locate a library book of celebrity signatures or some other source of graphological evidence. Comparing her new treasure with the reprinted facsimile would shed a glaring light on his scheme, however well intended it may have been. Better to endure his punishment like an honest man.

◆　　◆　　◆

The train paused to take on passengers in the town of Alhambra, about fifteen miles due east of Hollywood. Wesley looked out the Pullman window and was struck by how many civilians inhabited this sleepy suburb. It seemed to him positively unnatural for a railway station to have a minority of servicemen among its customers. Such a scene would never occur in central Texas, of that he was certain. Just then, a dozen or more GIs, led by an adolescent-looking second lieutenant, came into view as they rounded the corner onto the platform. So much for his fleeting vision of peacetime.

"Want some cake, Wes?" Kenton had returned to the passenger coach from what he liked to call the "mess hall."

"Sure, what kind?"

"I couldn't tell. Low sugar, I think."

Wesley laughed. "Sounds good to me. Whereabouts?"

"We're having a little get-together in the dining car—just for another twenty minutes or so, until they ring the chimes. There's some cherry punch too."

Wesley happened to stand up just as the train began to move again, and he was nearly thrown to the floor. Fortunately, he was able to grab hold of a cushioned seat to prevent himself from falling. "What's the occasion?" he asked.

"Clive's fifteenth birthday."

Wesley thought he had misunderstood. "What are you talking about?"

"This is Clive Ramey's fifteenth birthday," Kenton said again, and he remained perfectly serious.

Wesley smiled warily—leery of being the target of some silly prank.

"Put on your thinking cap, Wes. What's today's date?"

Wesley shook his head. "I've lost track."

"Here." Kenton tossed him his folded copy of the *Los Angeles Times*.

Wesley opened it to see the date and immediately relaxed his guard. "So Mr. Ramey only celebrates his birthday every leap year," he said.

"And I can tell you, he's gotten a lot of mileage out of that little joke, teasing the office girls."

As it turned out, the cake was rather tasty for wartime fare, but that was more than could be said for the accompanying beverage. Cherry punch it may have been, but it had a bitter edge to it that made Wesley abandon his cup after just three shallow sips. Though he himself was a total stranger to the flavor of alcohol, he had smelled enough second-hand stench on the breaths of others to wonder whether some mischievous soul had spiked the punch bowl. Considering the rowdy clientele aboard, that conclusion was entirely plausible, and the curious behavior of even the more staid representatives suggested that his suspicions were accurate. An operations manager from some tiny station in Ogden sat with head down, snoring peacefully, his red punch spilled directly below the point where a Union Pacific cup had slipped out of his hand. In the farthest corner of the car stood four of the Topeka broadcasters, sanguine-faced and bubbling over with spirit, singing "Mairzy Doats." But the most raucous celebrant of all was Clive Ramey himself, the birthday boy, who was whooping it up with a few of his Denver and Oklahoma City acquaintances from radio years gone by. They were pitching CBS lapel pins into a metal bucket for high stakes—quarters, halves, and even silver dollars—and one teetotaling man with a pencil-thin mustache and pockmarked complexion was the big winner, emptying the coin pouches of his wobbly competitors.

Wesley decided to leave the revelry and walk forward, to venture as near to the engine cars as permissible. Based on his earlier observations from rounding numerous curves, he estimated that he was well over a dozen coaches back. He wondered what sights might greet him ahead, each coach a different world unto itself.

The first car he passed through was populated, for the most part, by men in business suits and a smattering of women in chic dresses. Only about ten GIs were scattered among them. From that point on, however, he saw nothing but military uniforms—Army, Navy, and Marines, even four Coast Guardsmen being transported inland. The rattling of these service coaches seemed to him far noisier than the civilian ones behind, but of course that was not the case. It was just that there were so few human noises to mask the din of clattering metal. Most of the young servicemen lounged very still in their seats, speaking little, pensively watching the scenery go by, perhaps trying to visualize what the near future might hold. Initially, he felt a bit sorry for them as he wandered by, but then he discovered something strange. Few, if any, of them appeared to be unduly sorrowful or dejected. They possessed a seriousness of purpose, and that, he sensed, was worthy of his admiration and respect.

On Wesley's way back to the civilian coaches, he saw that the dining car was much more subdued than it had been just a few minutes earlier. The birthday well-wishers—most of whom did not know Clive Ramey from Alf Landon—had long since departed, and the tables now sported linen cloths and neatly placed stainless-steel utensils. So capable were the Union Pacific crewmen that the carpeted floor showed no ill effects from the party. Even the tiniest remnants of spilled punch and cake crumbs had vanished altogether from sight. Soon a porter would ring the one-o'clock luncheon chimes, the steward would appear with his waiters, and the mealtime process would begin again.

There was a genuine orderliness to railway operations, a rhythm of commerce and transit that hummed along year after year unchanged, comforting in its predictability. Wesley was fascinated to see that sliding doors opened miraculously by the simple expedient of placing a dime in the attendant's hand and uttering a carefree "Thank you, George." Less flattering was the knowledge that both courtesy and efficiency became noticeably compromised if travelers were, for whatever reason, too thrifty with their tips. Wesley had left home with a five-dollar roll of dimes in his suitcase, but by now only about ten of the coins remained for him to dispense.

The route back to Waco was precisely the same as the trip west had been, only in reverse. Although booking the Southern Pacific would have been much more direct for most of the Texans, especially those from Houston and San Antonio, the New York office of CBS—which was, after all, picking up the tab—wanted to group as many of its representatives together as possible, so a more northerly path was chosen instead. This meant that the eastbound Union Pacific would pass through, in sequence, such locales as San Bernardino, Las Vegas, Salt Lake City, Cheyenne, and Denver. Then those continuing on would transfer to the Santa Fe line, with further stops in Pueblo, Dodge City, Wichita, Oklahoma City, and either Fort Worth or Dallas, merging again at Cleburne on their way down to Waco, Temple, and points south.

Their Union Pacific train was passing through southwestern Utah when Wesley overheard a snippet of distant conversation that made him prick up his ears for more. He laid his *Saturday Evening Post* down and roamed forward in the lounge car, sitting in a vacant seat just two rows behind his source of information.

"Three cars back?"

"Yep, I'm sure that's who it is."

"You're crazy!"

"Well, go see for yourself, if you don't believe me."

"You've been watching too many movies."

"He's even got his hair combed the same way."

"Why would he do that if he's not on the set?"

"How should I know? Maybe he's making a public appearance."

"Why would he just happen to be on this train?"

"It left from Hollywood, didn't it? What's so strange about that?"

Word spreads fast in the confined space of a railway coach, so Wesley was not alone in making a pilgrimage to view the train's most renowned passenger. Nearly a dozen other people—each one of them an otherwise dignified radio executive—burst through the rattling vestibule, as star-struck as teenage girls, to judge for themselves the veracity of this preposterous rumor.

Even from Wesley's vantage point of about seventy feet, almost a whole car length away, it was quite obvious where the celebrity had chosen to seat himself for his "anonymous" journey east. The far right corner of the coach was crowded with onlookers, most of them shuffling their feet, craning their necks, and jockeying for position, all the while laughing at a virtually endless profusion of witty repartee. Wesley stepped closer and managed to catch a glimpse of the famous cowlicks, still identifiable after filming. Amidst the loudmouthed chatter, he could not hear the star's voice until he had pushed his way forward to within twenty feet or so.

"All right, but just once more, fellas, see? I've gotta catch a siesta or I'll be no good to anybody." Then the man took a deep breath and shouted, "Blonnnnnndie!" which brought a gale of laughter to the day coach.

And, with that, most of the satisfied fans began to return to their respective places on the train, finally leaving the beleaguered actor in peace. This was Wesley's chance, and he realized that it was either now or never. Snatching an envelope from his shirt pocket, he mustered enough hollow courage to ask, "Would you mind signing an autograph, sir—for my mother?"

The familiar-looking man was only too happy to do so. "Sure, kid."

Wesley handed him the envelope and a pencil. "Her name is Sandra."

"Sandra, huh?" He scribbled a few words. "Okay. How's that?" He gave the envelope and writing utensil back to Wesley and then, without waiting for an answer, turned to a traveling companion seated next to him. "What time do you think we'll get to Salt Lake?" he asked. His agent put on some eyeglasses and reached for a train schedule.

Wesley hurried back to his own seat before looking at the prized envelope. The inscription on it read, in bold, black script, "Best wishes to my friend, Sandra—Dagwood Bumstead, a.k.a. Arthur Lake." Yes, that would do very nicely.

◆　　◆　　◆

Bess Clarke had gotten into the habit of reading to Giulia all of her son's letters from abroad, usually within twenty-four hours of their delivery. It was plain to see that the young lady was terribly worried about Archie, and Mrs. Clarke thought it best to allay any groundless fears the poor girl might have. After all, it was not uncommon for imagined misfortunes of war to prey on the minds of young women back home, possibly even leading to such infirmities as eating disorders and, in the most extreme cases, clinical depression. She was not about to allow her future daughter-in-law to endure unnecessary mental anguish during the indefinite period of Archie's absence.

And so it was that Bess Clarke was in the Coletti home on a drizzly Friday afternoon in March. The woman of the house, Paolina Coletti, was resting in bed, and Mrs. Clarke was alone with Giulia in the living room. They were seated at opposite ends of the well-worn sofa, the fabric of which was a reddish-brown floral pattern—an archaic style that had been in vogue from the late twenties through the thirties. Mrs. Clarke was surprised to notice that the middle cushion, the one between them, was marred by three or four ugly cigarette burns. That seemed odd because there were no ashtrays to be found anywhere in the room. The radio was airing NBC's "Stella Dallas," but neither she nor Giulia was paying much attention to it.

The girl was preoccupied with something—of that Mrs. Clarke was sure. Never before had she seen Giulia so fidgety. Perhaps it was only war nerves, but whatever the cause, the moment she pulled her son's letter from the envelope, the girl stood up and proceeded to walk into the kitchen to get a glass of water. "Are you as thirsty as I am, Mrs. Clarke?" she asked from afar. "It must have been that fish I had for lunch. That's how they breathe, you know."

Archie's mother failed to detect any humor in the statement. "No, thank you," she said. "Come sit down next to me, and listen to what Archie wrote. He mentions your name a couple of times."

"I can hear you fine, Mrs. Clarke. Go ahead and start without me," Giulia told her. She began rattling some plates, cups, and silverware, evidently putting them away after removing them from the sink, where they had been draining. "Really, it's okay. I need to clean up a little in here anyway."

"Oh? May I help you with something, dear?"

"No, ma'am. That's not necessary."

Nonetheless, Mrs. Clarke arose from the sofa and joined Giulia in the kitchen, making herself comfortable on a chair next to the breakfast table. "I'll only be a few minutes," she said, "and then I've got to be running along." She unfolded a yellow sheet of paper and, after adjusting her wire-rimmed spectacles, began to read aloud from a paragraph that made reference to the girl.

> I miss you all very much, especially you and Aunt Hennie—and of course Giulia. Please give her a big hug for me, but don't bother with any kisses just now. I'll give her enough of those whenever I finally do get home from this war. According to everything I hear, it won't be very long before it's over. The Germans are on the run, and the Jap navy is being routed at every turn. Maybe I'll see some action, and maybe I won't. I haven't heard from Giulia in a long time, but I'm sure it's just the mail system. I haven't gotten anything from you in a couple of weeks either.

Mrs. Clarke looked up at Giulia. "That really concerns me because I write at least three letters to Archie every week. I suppose he'll get a whole bundle of them at once."

"I guess it's a miracle that *any* mail gets through to the boys," Giulia said. She reached high over her head to set some cereal bowls on the cabinet shelf.

Mrs. Clarke laid Archie's letter on the table and took a deep breath. "Have you written to him lately?" she asked.

Turning around, Giulia seemed stung by the innocent comment. "Not lately. I just haven't had much time, what with my job and mother and all. You know how it is."

Mrs. Clarke nodded her head. "Oh, I understand perfectly, dear. We're all so busy these days, it's hard to know whether we're coming or going."

"Yes, ma'am."

Archie's mother stood up and appeared ready to leave. Instead, she took a couple of steps toward Giulia and stopped no more than five feet away from her. "Is everything all right between you and Archie? You seem awfully distant today." The girl's pretty complexion went pale, but Mrs. Clarke persisted. "Is there something you need to tell me?"

"No, I don't think so." Giulia pulled two saucers from beneath a frying pan. "I just need to sort some things out."

"Write him a short letter, won't you, dear? He must feel terribly deserted, way off in Australia like that," Mrs. Clarke said.

Giulia turned her head toward the woman but stared at the floor. "All right, Mrs. Clarke, I will." A movement caught her eye, and she looked up to see her mother.

"Is this meeting open to anyone?" Paolina asked. A bit out of breath, she was bent forward at the waist, leaning heavily on a walking cane.

Mrs. Clarke frowned and said, "Oh, I'm sorry, Paolina. I guess we were being too loud. Giulia was putting the dishes away, and I'm afraid I was shouting to her from the living room."

"Nonsense," Paolina told her. "Please sit down. I've been awake ever since you rang the doorbell. Only it's taken me this long to finally make it in here." She seated herself in a chair next to Mrs. Clarke's.

Although Giulia welcomed the intrusion, her words were apologetic. "I could have helped you, Mamma, but I thought you were asleep."

"Oh, it's time I got up anyhow. You know what the doctor says about bed sores." She smiled at Mrs. Clarke and offered to make some coffee.

"No, thanks, dear. I can't stay. I just wanted Giulia to hear what Archie wrote."

"How is he doing?"

"Fine, as far as I can tell," Mrs. Clarke said. "I'm pretty sure his unit's still there in Australia, but of course the censor won't let him come right out and say so. He's very safe, for now at least."

Paolina seemed worried. "There's a lot of fighting going on, really not too far away from there."

"Well, if there is, Archie's never mentioned it."

"You've heard of Rabaul—the Solomon Islands."

Mrs. Clarke swallowed hard. "Yes."

"That's just north of Australia."

"Goodness!"

"Now, Mamma, don't go frightening Mrs. Clarke," Giulia said. "I'm sure Archie is safe enough in Australia."

"All I'm saying is, we shouldn't hide from the truth. There's a lot of fighting going on in New Britain right now, and that could mean Archie will be seeing some action—sooner instead of later."

"Oh, pay no attention to her, Mrs. Clarke. Sometimes Mamma thinks she's General MacArthur. Those are Marines on the islands, and Archie's in the Army. Besides, New Britain is hundreds of miles from Australia, maybe even a thousand."

Mrs. Clarke sighed in relief. "I hope you're right, dear."

Paolina patted Mrs. Clarke on the back of the hand. "Say, did you happen to read that article on Babe Ruth in today's paper? It mentions New Britain."

"I don't think so."

"Do you know where the newspaper is?" she asked her daughter.

Giulia spotted that morning's *News-Tribune* on the counter, lying next to the breadbox, and she brought it to her mother.

"Listen to this," Paolina said. She turned to one of the back pages.

Cape Gloucester, New Britain–Associated Press:

This will be news to The Babe, but Staff Sergeant Jeremiah A. O'Leary, a Marine Corps combat correspondent, reports that Japs, evidently eager to display their impoverished English vocabulary, charged Marine lines here shouting the strange battle cry, "To hell with Babe Ruth!" The charge was scored as an error–thirty Japs were struck out for good. In New York, Babe Ruth replied, "I hope every Jap that mentions my name gets shot. And to hell with all Japs anyway."

"Isn't that a funny story?"

Mrs. Clarke forced a smile but then became very solemn again. "I pray to God every day that Archie doesn't get mixed up in that kind of fighting–hand-to-hand combat, in the caves."

"If it makes you feel any better, Mrs. Clarke," Giulia said, "I think it's the Marines who do that sort of thing–on the islands, anyway." She folded her dish towel over the cupboard rack to dry.

Mrs. Clarke looked at Giulia's pretty face and suddenly felt the harsh sting of resentment. This girl did not appear to be the slightest bit concerned about her own fiancé's well-being. Here was Sergeant Archie Clarke, perhaps locked in mortal conflict at that very minute, and all Giulia could think to say was how safe he surely was, no doubt sunning himself in the backwaters of the Pacific Theater.

◆　　　◆　　　◆

Much to Wesley's surprise, his return to the halls of Waco High School on Monday morning bore a striking resemblance to a hero's welcome. Fellow students (and even a few teachers) treated him like a celebrity that day, hanging on to his every word as he enumerated the various Hollywood stars he saw–at conference sessions, on stage, aboard the train. His speech teacher allotted a full thirty minutes of class time for him to present an impromptu narrative on his adventures out west, and for his efforts, she granted him an "A" grade to replace the test score that he had missed while absent from class. "A trip like that," she said, "can be just as much of a learning experience as school."

Because of all the attention he was drawing from others, there was no time to visit with Sandra Whittsel before English period. Instead, he contented himself with savoring the vision of her jet-black hair and frilly white blouse. Sandy spoke only two words to Miss Simonek that hour–"No, ma'am"–and yet to Wesley they were a sublime chord of music. He could not even remember what the question had been, nor did it matter. During the weeks away, he had tried to distance himself from any romantic thoughts whatsoever, but Sandy's melodious Georgian drawl captivated him anew, and suddenly he dreaded the prospect of conversing with her face-to-face. When class was over, he lingered at his desk, obliging her to leave the room with several of her friends.

"Hiya, Wes," Morton Wilson said in the hallway. "Was California fun?"

"Uh-huh. In fact, I might decide to live out there someday."

"Not me. I'm going to live somewhere that has a baseball team."

Wesley grinned. "They have baseball out there."

"Oh, sure—Pacific Coast League ball. But I'm talking about the majors."

"Well, California's got just about everything else."

"Lots of shipyards and aircraft factories," Morton said. He had recently written a term paper on Henry J. Kaiser.

"I guess so. We were in Hollywood the whole time."

"See anyone famous?"

"Some."

Morton punched Wesley on the arm. "Hey, my dad saw Tris Speaker a couple of weeks ago—at a store in Fairfield. He played for Cleveland and the Boston Red Sox, but he's retired now and in the Hall of Fame. You've heard of Tris Speaker, haven't you?"

"Yes."

"He was known as the Gray Eagle when he was a player—a great outfielder, just as good as Cobb. You know, he's from right over here in Hubbard."

"Did your dad get an autograph for you?"

"No. He said a bunch of old codgers were surrounding Speaker almost the whole time he was there, so he couldn't get close enough. He never got to say a word to him."

During the next period, history class, Mr. Sherrod was unaware that there was a radio script hidden beneath Wesley's textbook. The boy glanced at his lines over and over again, feeling more ill at ease about this show than he had been for his dramatic debut, way back in the middle of August. Today, listeners all over central Texas would be hearing Kip Hanson on the airwaves for the first time in nearly three weeks, and the young actor felt frightfully unprepared. Maybe in the heat of battle, with the prompting voices of Bud Hanson, Jeannie Gabriel, and the Cashley brothers all about him, suddenly he would be swept into a theatrical rhythm and again able to capture the role's essential character. He entered the radio station with that affirmative vision in mind, desperately hoping for the best.

But such an easy breakthrough was not meant to be. No sooner had Wesley swung open the hardwood door to Studio A than he sensed that a fundamental change had come over the place during the time he was away in California. The difference was more subtle than alarming—not something he could actually put his finger on, nothing so tangible as mike stands, ashtrays, tables, or chairs. His eyes scanned the room. Hugh Kenton was not yet there, nor for that matter were Phyllis Sherry and Beverly Jaynes, but he waved cheerfully to Douglas Pierson and nodded to Grover Millich and Ray Leftwich. Across the studio, Neddy Wright could be seen chatting with sound-effects man Rodney DeBonaventura. Two writers were in the control room, and significantly, so was one of the commercial sponsors, someone Wesley had not laid his eyes upon since long before Christmas. What was up?

Wesley was still carrying that day's script under his arm. It had been waiting for him at home when he arrived back in Waco, so he had the entire weekend to look it over, as well as that clandestine refresher stint during history class. And yet, unaccountably, he felt like the proverbial elephant that sat down to play the piano at Carnegie Hall. In short, the daytime serial had become to him just a blur of empty words, jumbled in his mind by the yawning gap of thirteen missing installments. With all the plot advances, how was he expected to pick right up where he had left off, especially when two new characters had been introduced to the mix during his absence from the microphone? But time waited for no one. There would be a brief rehearsal at 2:35, and then, at precisely three o'clock, "Behold Tomorrow" would be back on the air with a full complement of characters. Ready or not, Kip Hanson would be released from bondage and set free to join the convoluted plot machinations that kept KWXN's audience returning daily for more.

Glancing toward the control room, Wesley noticed that announcer Marshall McFall occupied the adjacent booth, busily shuffling through some commercial copy while smoking what little remained of his cigarette. He took one final drag, tossing the butt downward and grinding it into the floor with the sole of his shoe. Then Wesley watched McFall nod to the sponsor and smile. How nice to be so sure of oneself, confident in the extreme.

"All set to go back to Baltimore, son?" Hugh Kenton asked. Wesley was never so glad to see anyone in his life.

"Yes, sir."

The director was referring to the serial's imaginary setting. "I think there's something you should know before we start," Kenton told him, and he motioned for Wesley to follow him to the far corner of the studio. He sat in a chair and pulled another one closer with his foot. "Sit."

Wesley was aware that the rehearsal would begin in just ten minutes, so this meeting could not be very long.

"Listen, you've been held hostage by the Cashley boys for quite a while now—two and half actual weeks, but from the audience's perspective, who really knows? Let's say it's been a week, or maybe a little bit more than that. They've kept you alive by bringing you food and water, but they've also roughed you up some. It's in the bowels of an abandoned warehouse—seedy part of town. Today, as you know from the script, is when you finally escape." Kenton grinned. "You *have* read the script, haven't you?"

Wesley laughed. "Yes, sir."

"Okay, here's what's been happening—just the stuff you need to know about. Your Uncle Bud's in the slammer, but he doesn't try to clear himself because of what the Cashleys might do to you as revenge. Anson Gabriel is having a spat with his wife over the missing bracelet, and Jeannie's brother sides with him. Of course, she sees this as a slap in the face—family disloyalty—but David badmouths her childhood and accuses Jeannie of being a spoiled brat. Questions?"

"It says I'm supposed to act 'nonplussed' on page six."

"That's just our writers trying to show us how terribly smart they are. Act a little nervous or confused there, and that'll hit the target. Anything else?"

Wesley turned to a page where he had circled two names. "Who are Florence Billings and Sally Holt?"

Kenton looked away, tapping a fingernail on his metal cigarette lighter. "Well, Florence Billings is the maid in the Sutcliffe household—you know, for Frank and Doris." He glanced at Wesley, but only for an instant. "Sally Holt, the box-office girl, is mentioned but doesn't have any lines today. She was in a few episodes while we were gone, but she's not in this one, so don't worry too much about her."

The rehearsal went very poorly—and not just for Wesley—but the performance, as sometimes happens, came together wonderfully well. Even the difficult role of a teenager being held for ransom somehow came across with conviction and style, and Wesley's palms were sweaty when the quarter-hour drew to a close. The program came within seven seconds of a "perfect landing," as Hugh Kenton liked to call it. All Marshall McFall had to do was stretch his presentation imperceptibly, and "West of the Brazos" began with the second hand straight up, dead on, worthy of a hard break. It was almost a shame that they were not trying to meet the network. Save the bull's eye for later.

Wesley felt jubilant—like some cast party celebrant following a smash premiere—but, to his disappointment, everyone else seemed to take it all in stride, just another day at the office. The rest of the troupe, after all, had been there right along, and this show was not so very different from what had taken place while he was away from the microphone.

His brief euphoria came to a crushing halt, not even five minutes later, when he overheard Myra Culp telling someone at the front desk, "Well, if it isn't Sally Holt."

◆　　◆　　◆

Danny Rignold stood in silence for a long moment, holding his cap to one side. And then he whispered, "Hi, miss. Elizabeth said that I might find you here."

It was just after two o'clock on a Tuesday afternoon, and Hannah Lane was in the Browning Room of Baylor University's Carroll Library—a secluded place for reading, purportedly one of the few tranquil study spaces on campus.

Glancing up from her textbook, she recognized the visitor at once but did not smile. "Hello, private."

"Look again," Danny said. He turned a shoulder toward her.

"When did that happen?" she asked.

"A couple weeks ago. Must be doin' somethin' right."

She was chewing some gum, and none too quietly. "Danny, isn't it?"

"That's right," he said, "but then you always were good at names, weren't you?"

Hannah bristled at the comment but let it pass. The soldier's nose, she noticed, seemed to have healed with no lasting ill effects from the fight. "How are you feeling, corporal?" she asked.

"Great. They took good care of me."

The attending student worker, a rather pretty young lady of about twenty, shushed them.

Hannah leaned closer to the soldier and whispered, "You're a hero to Elizabeth, you know."

Danny laughed. "I don't know why. All I did was stick out my jaw."

Hannah remained serious. "I respect you for what you did that night. I don't think I ever told you so."

"It was no big thing, really," he said. "Say, whatever happened to that other guy anyhow?"

"Don't know. I guess he got away."

"Do you mind if I use this chair?" Danny asked.

"Okay, but tone it down before she throws a fit." The student worker was still eyeing them with contempt.

"What're you readin'?" he whispered.

She showed him the book's cover, *The Selected Poems of Robert Browning*, and he looked around. The room was filled with Browningiana of all descriptions—the largest such collection in the world—and in the adjacent portrait gallery, twenty-five likenesses of the poet were on display. "Dumb question," he said.

Hannah smiled. "Not really. This has been my regular study place ever since I started at Baylor." She laid her book facedown on the table. "I just happen to be taking a class in Browning this quarter—English 247."

"Do you like it?"

She pondered for a moment before answering. "It's not too bad, but I think an English major would get more out of it than I am. Professor Armstrong is a world authority on the Brownings. Way over my head, I'm afraid."

By now, the student worker had reached her limits. She cleared her throat loudly and gave another stern look.

"Let's get out of here," Danny whispered. "I don't think she appreciates our conversation very much."

Hannah shook her head. "I've got a test tomorrow."

"Can't you study tonight?"

"Nope. I'm on the swing shift."

He frowned but accepted her answer as perfectly valid. What bothered him was how quickly she picked up her book and resumed reading, as if he were no longer there. Either her power of concentration was phenomenal, he thought, or she was trying to get rid of him. A minute elapsed, and out of morbid curiosity, he decided to see just how long she would continue to ignore him. Two minutes went by, then three and four, and all the while she gave him not so much as a nodding glance. On the positive side, this brusque dismissal presented him with a great opportunity to take a closer look at her from point-blank range.

She was not very pretty, viewed with a coldly objective eye, but her paucity of make-up may have accounted for some of that, at least when compared to other women of her age. And yet there was no denying that her pert lips, slightly turned up at the corners, her fair complexion, and those disorganized blonde curls all conspired to lend an unassuming charm to her appearance. Most endearing of all was her lack of pretension. She was the embodiment of tomboyishness—a scrappy softball infielder perhaps—and with all the supple athleticism that image might suggest.

Finally he whispered, "Would it make any difference if I told you I have a theological question?"

"You?" She laughed aloud.

Danny laughed, too, but then hushed her with a gesture of his hands. "I'm serious."

"Well, pardon me," she whispered, "but you don't *look* very serious."

"Your reaction was funny, that's all."

Hannah closed her poetry book and stood up. "All right. I'll walk you to the exit," she said. "I've really got to study."

A few minutes later, when they reached the Carroll Library steps, two coeds were entering, so Danny held the door open for them. Both looked with interest at the GI as they passed. Outside, it was quite a pleasant day for late March—about sixty-six degrees. An earlier rain had left the streets wet.

"So, what's this all about?" Hannah asked. She was visibly skeptical.

"You really don't believe me, do you?"

"Can you blame me? Here I am, studying for a test, and some soldier goes over the fence and clear across town to find me in a college library. What am I to think?"

He shook his head. "Listen, I'm not tryin' to pick you up, if that's what you're implyin'. And I'm sure as ... heck ... not AWOL. This is my day off—and half of tomorrow too. You know, the Army isn't as simple as civilian life. We don't get weekends."

"And who does? Some of us civilians don't have it so cushy either."

"I realize that," Danny said. Down the street, he could see the university's six-year-old brick gymnasium—the Rena Marrs McLean Physical Education Building—alongside the tennis courts. Dozens of students were coming through the building's five exits, so a class or two must have let out a few minutes earlier. Danny smiled at the girl. "Hey, could I have a piece of that gum you're chewin'?" He quickly added, "Well, not that exact piece."

Hannah rolled her eyes. "I assumed that's what you meant." She pulled out a pack of Beech-Nut Peppermint gum from her purse and gave him a stick.

Danny peeled off the foil. "Do you still save this stuff?"

"Yes, please." She tucked both thin sheets into her purse for salvage. "You have exactly two minutes, corporal."

"Yes, sir, ma'am," he said with mock deference. "I'll make it fast."

Just then, a foursome of cadets walked between them into the library, so Danny and Hannah stepped away from the entrance. He watched them go by, slightly envious, and asked, "Are those musical instruments they're carryin'?"

"They're in the ASTP Band," she said.

"The Army has a band stationed here?"

"It's the only band on campus these days. All the Baylor boys are off in the service."

Danny turned his head, catching a glimpse of the musicians' shiny shoes as they ascended the stairway. "Talk about a cushy job."

Hannah edged a few steps toward the entrance and waited. "What was it you wanted to ask me? I really need to get back to my Browning."

He took a deep breath. "Okay, here it is. Would you mind—and don't be readin' anythin' sinister into this—would you mind if I tagged along with you to church on Sunday mornin'?"

Hannah cast him a suspicious look. "To church?" she asked. "And what caused this miraculous transfiguration?"

"Oh, I've never really been all that horrible," he said. "I'm a rather sweet human bein', once you get to know me better. Ask my mother."

"I'll take your word for it."

A streetcar clanged to a stop at Fifth and Speight, and eight or nine students stepped off, some heading to the corner Piggly Wiggly, others walking north toward Burleson Quadrangle.

Hannah was curious. "Why church, all of a sudden?"

"Let's just say I've had a change of heart."

"I can accept that," she said. "But why me? I hardly even know you."

"It's just that none of my pals attend church, so I thought maybe you'd ..."

"You're sure that's all?"

"That's all—scout's honor." He raised three fingers and smiled. "Honestly, my motives are as pure as the driven snow."

He certainly did seem sincere enough.

"But, as I recall, you're a Catholic," she said.

"What of it?"

"I go to First Baptist. Won't that make you feel uncomfortable?"

"Catholics are Christians, too," he said.

Hannah nodded her head. "Actually, we do have quite a few GIs and sailors of other denominations. One of them even teaches a Sunday school class—a Lutheran soldier from Missouri."

"Do I take that as a 'yes,' then?"

"I suppose so. I certainly wouldn't want to stand in the way of your salvation."

"What time should I meet you?"

"I always ride to church with a friend. She picks me up around 9:30."

He grinned. "Jeez, what do you Baptists do, spend the whole day there?"

"We have Sunday school at 9:45, and that's part of the deal, like it or not." Then her expression darkened. "By the way," she told him, "don't ever say 'Jeez.' That's just short for 'Jesus,' and it's cursing to use His name in vain."

"Sorry. I guess that's my first lesson. And here it is, only Tuesday."

From her purse, Hannah retrieved a folded piece of newsprint—an advertisement, clipped from the local paper. "Dr. Dawson will be speaking on ... 'Stars That Do Not Wane'," she read. "I don't know what that'll be about."

He tried to keep a straight face. "You carry the sermon topic around with you?"

But she remained absolutely serious. "Sure. I'm not ashamed of it. Why should I be?"

Danny knew a precarious line of questioning when he heard one, so he quickly shifted the topic to logistics. "I s'pose you'll have to tell me where you live," he said.

Hannah shook her head. "I don't think that would be such a good idea, in the circumstances. Just meet us at the USO, the one on Washington." She opened the library door.

"Because I wear a uniform."

"That's right."

Danny sighed. "You still don't trust me, do you?"

"Not much." She hurried back inside.

"Well, at least you're honest about it," he shouted, but by then she was already gone.

◆　　◆　　◆

Valentino, the cat, was in the habit of spending his springtime afternoons near the front window, stretched out on an ottoman that stood just high enough for him to keep one eye focused on activities around the neighborhood. Usually it was he who was first aware of the postman's arrival, but—being feline rather than canine—he never made the slightest effort to alert others in the house. And so, the mail delivery on Friday, the last day of March in 1944, went unnoticed until Elizabeth happened to see an oversized envelope protruding from the metal box when she came home from school at a quarter to four. Her mother must be off somewhere, she thought, no doubt doing charity work uptown or maybe making one of her irregular visits to the family business.

Against all odds, Nora's trusty manager, Wayne Espy, had maintained Superior Office Supply at a profit level less than five percent shy of its prewar norms. Just as he had assured her, the markets for most of their smaller, mass-quantity products had proven to be remarkably insulated from the cataclysmic events overseas. Only the sales figures for more expensive apparatuses—typewriters, adding machines, cash registers, and the like—had suffered any critical decline, and that, for the duration, was out of management's control. Shortages in the steel and rubber sectors had driven prices higher than local businesses were willing to pay, and the law of supply and demand was not something Mr. Espy or anyone else on this side of the black market was likely to reverse.

When Elizabeth unlocked the front door, she was startled to discover that perhaps she was not alone in the house. A dim light emanated from upstairs, so she tiptoed in that direction to investigate. It could not be her mother—of that she was sure. Her mother would never leave the afternoon mail unchecked for so long. Certain that her brother was still at the radio station, Elizabeth could only presume it to be the Baylor student who boarded with them. However, there was no answer when she called out Hannah's name. With growing concern, she looked around, from room to empty room.

As she turned off the bathroom light, there came a loud pop, and for an instant she thought maybe the bulb had exploded. But no, the noise seemed to originate outdoors. She hurried down the stairs just in time to see Valentino scurrying for cover beneath the sewing table. She heard another pop, only now it sounded much closer. Cautiously, not knowing what she might find, Elizabeth crept toward one of the rear windows and pulled the curtain aside to peer through it. The next pop was very near indeed, almost ear-piercing in its intensity, and she noticed something fly a few feet into the air and land on the grass. Another pop caused the adjacent object to leap upward and then fall to the ground.

She went to the breakfast window and looked outside. There, with his back to her, stood Wesley, firing some sort of rifle at a squadron of toy soldiers. She stomped to the back door and flung it open. "What do you think you're doing, dopey? You nearly scared me to death!"

"Target practice." He squeezed off another round.

"Where did you get that thing?"

"At work. Neddy Wright's selling it, and he said I could bring it home and try it out."

Elizabeth was unimpressed. "Why in the world would you want that?"

"It's a Daisy air rifle, and Neddy's only asking four dollars for it."

"Is that cheap?"

"I think so," Wesley said. He cradled it on his arms for her to see. "This is a Buzz Barton model, only about ten years old, and it shoots real straight. Want to try it?"

"I don't like guns."

"It's not a gun. It's a rifle."

"What's the difference?"

Wesley did not deem that question worthy of an answer. Instead, he rubbed his hand across the smooth wood and told her, "Just one little nick on the stock, but otherwise it's in great shape."

"What are you doing home so early?"

"Neddy needs to have an answer by five o'clock, so he drove me home to let me try out the rifle."

"I saw a light on upstairs and thought we had burglars."

"Sorry, but I was in a hurry to give it the once-over," he said.

"And now you have to go all the way back to the radio station?"

Wesley nodded his head. "Before five, or he'll be gone. I was kind of hoping Mom could take me. My bike's still there."

Twenty minutes later, Elizabeth was changing clothes in her bedroom when she heard the sound of gravel crackling beneath the tires of the family Chevrolet. From the upstairs window, she watched Wesley flag down his mother and then, after leaning Neddy's rifle against the garage, run into the house for his money. A minute later, he hopped into the automobile for his second trip of the day to the radio station. Dinner would be a little late that night, Elizabeth knew, and the startling pop of an air rifle would be with them all spring and summer long—until chilly weather forced her brother inside. Boys are so silly about guns.

It was 5:15 when Wesley returned home on his bicycle. He ran into the house with his air rifle in hand and switched on the radio console to "Hop Harrigan." By then, Nora had already changed from her Red Cross uniform into a housedress and was busy in the kitchen. She had performed volunteer duty for three hours that afternoon at the surgical dressing center, which was housed in the Texas Power & Light Building at 912 Austin Avenue. In addition to her one scheduled Sunday each month, Nora did further war work for the Red Cross on an "as needed" basis—preparing box loads of gauze dressings and other surgical supplies for shipment to the troops overseas—under the able leadership of such patriotic ladies as Lillian Herrick, Lorraine Scharmacher, Celeste Harper, and Nell Spencer Berkeley. Celeste's husband, Alf Harper, was the office manager of National Cash Register Company and, coincidentally, a former business acquaintance of the late Harold Brower.

When the family finally sat down to dinner, Nora was surprised to see that Elizabeth was not wearing her usual apparel. "Why so dressed up, Lizzie?" she asked.

"I'm not all that dressed up, Mother. This is one of my regular school dresses."

Wesley grinned. "Isn't that perfume I smell?"

Elizabeth rolled her eyes but did not reply.

"It's Friday night," Nora said, "so I was just wondering if you had something planned."

"Dudley Rollins did want to go see *The Sullivans* with me tonight, but I don't know if we will or not. It opened a couple of days ago—at the Waco—and some of my friends said it's very sad."

"Well, of course it is, dear, losing five boys to the war like that," Nora said, and her voice cracked slightly. "I can't even begin to imagine how their parents were able to cope with such a tragedy."

Elizabeth's eyes were watering, but she forced a smile. "Laura Prestridge broke into tears just telling me about it."

"It's a true story too. That makes it even sadder." Nora spoke these words very quietly, hardly above a whisper, and her chin appeared to be trembling. "Dear God in heaven, how awful it must be to lose *one* boy! Like poor Lottie McDuff. And Mr. and Mrs. Bellamy. And of course the Naegles."

Wesley cleared his throat and glared at Elizabeth, who heeded the cue.

"Or we might go see *Whistling in Brooklyn*," she said. "Red Skelton's in that one, so it should be funny."

"It has Leo Durocher and some of his ballplayers, too," Wesley added. He was pleased to see that the brighter tone had a heartening effect on his mother. "They filmed the picture at Ebbets Field, or at least some of it."

Nora looked at both of them and smiled.

"My friend Mort's going, just to watch the Dodger parts," Wesley said. "He's never been to a big league ball game, but his father's promised to take him to a Cardinals game as soon as the war's over."

The girl felt terrible about introducing such painful thoughts, and she privately vowed to be more careful in the future. When she was clearing the table, she noticed that her mother stood at the counter, absently shuffling through some papers. "What is it, Mother?" she asked. "You look like an old prospector over there."

"I was trying to find today's mail. Didn't we get anything?"

"Oh!" Elizabeth laid down her dinner plates and frantically began to comb through the kitchen. "Yes, we did." She remembered removing some letters from the mailbox, but after that she had no recollection at all. She must have laid the mail down when she went to investigate that mysterious light.

"Don't worry about it, dear," Nora said. "It couldn't have gone far."

"Let me go to the front door, and I'll retrace my steps."

As it turned out, the stack of mail was lying, undisturbed, on the counter in the upstairs bathroom. Elizabeth quickly flipped through it and spotted nothing unusual—only about five pieces. She brought it to her mother in the living room and resumed clearing off the table. "What's the large envelope?" she asked.

"Some recipes from Mabel Johns. That pound cake you liked so much and a couple of casseroles."

One piece of mail had gone unnoticed by Elizabeth because it was precisely the same size as another, less significant, one on top of it. Nora gasped. "Here's a letter from Steve!"

Elizabeth laid down the vegetable bowl she was holding and came running. "Wes," she shouted, "there's a letter from Steve!"

Nora had opened the letter by the time Wesley bounded down the stairs, and she began reading aloud:

> I hope everything is fine with all of you. Me—I couldn't be better, eating that swell Navy chow and healthy as a dog. I won't keep you in suspense any longer—I'll be coming home soon. Should be there on or around April 15th. Can only stay for one week, but that's 7 days of being spoiled, so I'm looking plenty forward to it. My love to you all, Steve.

What he purposefully failed to mention, more for his mother's peace of mind than appeasing the censor, was that this was to be an embarkation leave. His months of intensive instruction—at four separate duty stations because of a change in "right arm rate" from gunner's mate to fire controlman—were finally at an end. So, too, were the uneventful patrols in coastal waters and that problematic, and ultimately abortive, shakedown cruise to Pearl. His next assignment, Steve knew, would be a different matter altogether, placing him in a combat situation for the very first time. He was already aware of his new ship posting, *USS Jeffers*, but that, of course, he was not at liberty to discuss in public. Still undisclosed to him were his impending destination, the British Isles, and the staggering magnitude of naval action that he could expect to encounter soon thereafter on a three-mile stretch of beach called Utah.

◆　　◆　　◆

Lillie Cockerham's shiny Studebaker had Austin Avenue virtually to itself on the morning of Palm Sunday, April 2. It was about 9:35, and a cool-front shower was moving into the Waco area, amounting so far to just a sprinkle and not the heavy thunderstorms that weathermen were hinting at in their oblique, wartime fashion.

It was fortunate that Lillie switched on her windshield wipers when she did. A police car was sitting near the intersection of Fourteenth Street, partially obscured by a delivery truck that was parked in front of the shop of Wolfe, the Florist. Lillie managed to notice the policeman just in time to apply her brakes and decelerate beneath the legal speed limit. Never in her life as a licensed driver—amounting to four years, now, behind the wheel—had she gotten as much as a minor traffic ticket, moving or stationary, so she glanced with trepidation in the rear-view mirror to confirm that she had avoided the long arm of the law.

"Is he coming after you?" Hannah asked. She leaned her head out the passenger window to steal a glance back, then quickly rolled up her window to keep moisture from dampening the automobile's interior.

"No, thank goodness. I was going about forty-five when I spotted him."

The girls were attired in brightly colored spring dresses. Their Bibles, stacked one upon the other, lay between them on the seat.

Hannah pointed to the left. "Turn at Seventh," she said. "It's on the corner at Washington."

Lillie had never been to Waco's USO, and she was not all that familiar with the city streets. She came to Baylor University from the Dallas area, where her father, Lester Cockerham, was a successful attorney. The 1942 Studebaker was her high school graduation gift.

When they turned left onto Washington and came to a halt, Hannah said, "Just leave the engine running." She expected Danny to join them the instant they stopped.

But he did not appear. No one was waiting inside the door or even watching for them at a window. A whole minute passed, and gasoline was far too precious to waste on an idling engine. "Turn it off. Let me go see what's keeping him." She went into the USO and asked the volunteer worker, a white-haired woman of about seventy, if she knew Corporal Danny Rignold.

"No. I'm sorry, but I don't," she said.

"We're supposed to pick him up here for church."

The lady glanced around the club but saw no one who seemed to be waiting for a ride. "Maybe he's in the washroom."

"Would you mind checking? Sunday school starts in just a few minutes."

"Certainly, miss." The elderly lady walked back to the rear of the building and knocked on the rest room door. No one answered, so she opened the door a bit, just far enough to call out, "Is there a Corporal ..."

"Rignold," Hannah said.

"Is there a Corporal Rignold in here?" No reply.

"Thank you anyway, ma'am," Hannah said as pleasantly as possible. Then she turned on her heels and marched straight out of the USO.

Still seething, she slammed the automobile door. "Well, he stood us up," she told Lillie, "exactly like I thought he would. Some change of heart he had."

"Maybe he had duty."

"Oh, sure—pillow duty. Come on, let's go."

Lillie shifted the automobile into gear and began driving west on Washington Avenue. Just as the Masonic Temple came into view on the left, Hannah saw through her window a frantic soldier in uniform, slightly disheveled and waving his arms crazily as he ran along the sidewalk in front of Southwest Body Works. She rolled down the glass and heard, "Hannah!"

Lillie pulled over to the curb and stopped. Into the back seat jumped Danny, breathing heavily from the exertion. "Sorry, gals," he told them. "I could only thumb as far as the river ... a fisherman."

Hannah shook her head and said, "You're a mess." His hair was sweaty and in disarray, his shirt was no longer tucked in, and his tie was hanging over one shoulder. She added, "It's a good thing, for your sake, that we're not Army officers."

Danny grimaced. "You're tellin' me!"

As the automobile began moving, Hannah frowned again at his appearance and then nodded toward the driver. "Danny, this is Lillie Cockerham, my friend from Baylor. Lillie, this is Corporal Daniel Rignold."

Lillie glanced in the mirror at her rumpled passenger. "A real pleasure," she said. Her voice dripped with irony, and he could only smile back, sheepishly.

"I'm not always such a sad sack," he said. Lillie's eyes had returned to the task of driving, so he hurried to straighten his tie and run a comb through his hair.

"Danny works at Blackland," Hannah told her friend.

"Is that so?" Lillie asked. "What do you do there, corporal?"

"Aircraft maintenance—ground crew. You know, keepin' the boys flyin'." Through the window to his right, he noticed a sign for the Academy of the Sacred Heart, and it brought back memories of his own schooling. Sister Mary Margaret was his favorite teacher, though she disciplined the youngster more than once by a painful slap to the back of his hand with her wooden ruler.

Lillie was accustomed to taking Ninth Street from Hannah's boarding house to church, and so—being a creature of habit—that is where she turned left to head toward Webster. The air temperature was dropping, good for comfort's sake. Otherwise it would have become quite stuffy with all windows rolled up because of the precipitation. Now the rain was beginning to come down considerably harder.

"Nice car," Danny said.

Lillie smiled into the mirror. "Thanks."

"It's a '42 President, isn't it?"

"That's right."

"Skyway."

"Uh-huh. A Land Cruiser," she told him. The pride in her voice bordered on arrogance.

"This is the last car Studebaker made," he said. "They're in the airplane engine business now—Wright Cyclones for B-17s. Military trucks, too, and those M-29 Weasels."

Lillie shrugged her shoulders. This was all news to her. "How come you know so much about cars?"

"I was an auto mechanic before my number came up."

Hannah grinned. "So if you're going to break down, now's a good time to do it."

Danny ran the palm of his hand over the luxurious upholstery. "Gosh, what did you do, rob a bank or somethin'?"

Clearly basking in the plaudits, Lillie gave a quick wink to her Baylor friend.

The corporal added, "I mean, this must have set you back plenty."

"Actually, it didn't cost me a single penny," Lillie told him. "My daddy bought it for me." She looked at the soldier's reflection, and he seemed awestruck.

"Her daddy's a big lawyer in Dallas," Hannah said.

The Palm Sunday crowd at First Baptist Church was a bit larger than usual, so Lillie had to park her Studebaker in the muddy lot across the street. From there, the girls each walked under an umbrella, but Danny made do with his garrison cap. He followed them to their Sunday school class, located in one of the education rooms upstairs, and nervously took a seat.

A cynic might well have doubted Corporal Daniel Rignold's motives for returning to the fold after so many years of wandering unchurched, but who other than the Lord Almighty can judge the sincerity of a person's walk in faith? Though Danny peeked at young Lillie Cockerham three times during the opening prayer, such a negligible human failing does not necessarily mean that his heart was unreceptive to the Word of God.

◆   ◆   ◆

Sure, it galled him. Wesley did not think it fair for someone, whether male or female, to be granted an acting job simply as a favor for a friend who happened to be on the staff. Everyone knew that Miss Sandra Whittsel was a rank amateur, with no stage experience whatsoever. By all rights, the role should have been delegated not by social connection but in the arena of performance, by competitive audition. What made him even angrier was how gracefully she made the transition from cub news reporter to nascent darling of the airwaves.

At first, the role of Sally Holt was intended to be no more than a stereotypical *ingénue*—the sassy-mouthed box-office girl at a Baltimore movie theater—but by the middle of March, writers Gerald Byrd, Ethel Coody, and Harvey Samuelson had given her a dramatic presence far beyond what even they had foreseen a mere four weeks earlier.

It all happened quite by accident. Harvey Samuelson needed to stretch one script by just under two minutes—and without doing violence to the main story line. His solution was to contrive a farcical interlude that brought mobster Ned Cashley to a movie palace in broad daylight, compelling him to look over his shoulder while trying in vain to pry some vital information from the obtuse female behind the box-office window. What was the identity of that mysterious customer who snatched a seemingly innocuous package from the lobby and then left Baltimore with ten thousand dollars in stolen currency? The scene advanced the plot not one whit, but it did supply some welcome comic relief to an otherwise unsmiling episode that dealt entirely with the ruthlessness of rival syndicate bosses.

Ethel Coody saw potential in the new character, so right away the writers began devising subplots with the cleverly dimwitted Sally Holt in the spotlight. When these, too, held the stage well, the girl began to turn up in some rather pivotal scenes, at times even driving the action forward on the strength of her own inveigling personality. Before long, Sally's patently ambitious motives were successful in elevating her economic, if not moral, standing to that of sweetheart of the mob. She became a series fixture.

Wesley was in California when Sandy first stepped in front of the "Behold Tomorrow" microphone, so he had no way of knowing for sure how she happened to win the role. He had his suspicions, of course, and in time he was able to piece together the chronology of events that led to her quick ascension to the status of local celebrity.

It seemed that Harvey Samuelson consulted someone on the production staff—probably assistant director Hatch Priggett—for advice on casting the soon-to-be-introduced role. Being a company man and the nephew of one of KWXN's minority owners, Priggett suggested that Samuelson propose the name of someone already on the station's payroll. "Try Grant," he said. "He's always got some good talent under his wing." News director Grant Tollefson did indeed have some likely candidates, and one in particular had caught his eye. But Tollefson, for whatever reason, did not wish to be seen as the decision maker in this instance, so he adroitly guided the ad hoc search committee (by now comprised of Samuelson, Ethel Coody, and Brenda Ramey, wife of the station manager) in the direction of universally revered announcer Marshall McFall. "After all, he's been with the show almost from the very start," Tollefson said. Thus was the choice left up to that impartial voice of reason.

From Wesley Brower's perspective, it made for some increasingly awkward moments. The first time he and Sandy were in the studio together as fellow cast members, they happened to be assigned to separate microphones, numbers one and three. This placed them a good twenty feet apart, which was just fine with him. Otherwise, he probably could not have read his lines without stumbling. She looked so attractive in her tight blouse that it was all he could do to keep his eyes on the script. Sandy, meantime, did not even seem to notice that he was in the same room. Whenever she glanced away from her script, it was not at him but toward the announcer's booth, where Marshall McFall could be seen eating a mid-afternoon sandwich and paying her no mind whatsoever.

On the first Friday of April, the inevitable finally occurred. Script girl Monica Whaley distributed among the cast a Wednesday episode of "Behold Tomorrow" that promised to bring Wesley and Sandy into much closer contact with each other. Wesley had realized all along that this day would almost surely arrive, but that expectation did not prepare him for the shocking sight of almost three full pages of double-spaced dialogue between Sally Holt and Kip Hanson. So confused were his emotions that, by the time this preliminary script was unveiled, he could not say with any certainty whether its prospect induced more anticipation or dread.

One thing that could be said for sure was that the following week's Tuesday show failed to focus his attention on the drama at hand—and not because of any intrinsic defect in the script. He managed to struggle through his few lines without any egregious flubs, but he would never remember this as being one of his better performances. In broadcasting parlance, he "sleepwalked" through the scene, bringing to the microphone no special insight into his character's suddenly quirky behavior. Sally Holt was not in the episode at all, so he could not rightfully blame his poor effort on Sandy's unsettling presence. The real problem was that his creative energies were consumed in trying to imagine what might happen at that day's full-cast rehearsal, scheduled to begin soon after the conclusion of "West of the Brazos."

Sometimes Wesley relaxed by watching the other serial from the control room, but he could ill afford to risk that indulgence today. What he needed was to refresh his lines over a cup of strong coffee in the staff lounge—his normal routine whenever the script load was particularly heavy. This approach had served him well in the past, and he saw no reason to tinker with success. A quick run-through would polish up the rough edges quite nicely. After all, he had been in possession of the script for more than the usual three days, so it was not as though he were going blindly into the rehearsal.

Everything changed the moment he emerged from the studio. Waiting for him on the other side of the heavy wooden door was Sandra Whittsel, who held her script high. "Let's read through it together, Wes. Do you mind?"

A rush of excitement shot through him. "No, that's fine." Wesley assumed that she would follow him toward the lounge, but instead she headed the opposite direction. He turned around with a perplexed look on his face.

"We can use my car," she told him. "Daddy let me borrow it today."

"Do you ... really think we should?"

Sandy smiled prettily, amused at his sudden case of anxiety. "Come on. Don't be shy." Her black hair matched the color of her skirt, and she wore a turquoise sweater that was very flattering to her petite figure.

"I'm not shy," Wesley said. "I just planned on having some coffee—to help me study."

She was already walking away. "Bring it with you," she said over her shoulder. "Just don't spill any on the new seat covers."

When he arrived at her Pontiac with coffee in hand, she was sitting in the driver's seat with her script propped up against the steering wheel. Wesley opened the passenger door and sat down, flipping through his script to page seven.

"Scoot over toward me," Sandy said. "We can share my copy. It's better for interaction between two characters that way. You do want to interact, don't you?"

He laughed nervously. "Well, whatever helps the show." He slid a body width to his left and craned his neck to see the copy. Her knit sweater was now less than a foot away.

"Are you comfortable?" Sandy asked. The boy's posture seemed rather odd.

"Oh, sure." He took a sip of the coffee. Actually, these were the worst possible conditions for familiarizing himself with such a dizzying multitude of lines—what amounted to a short duo-drama. And having her so close-by was no help either. He glanced in fascination at her black skirt, which revealed about half the length of her calf.

Very quietly, she said, "Would you like to see some more?"

Wesley gulped and stared at her, unable to answer. Sandy's eyes were still on the script.

"Well?" she said.

He took a deep breath and whispered, "Are you serious?"

Sandy looked up at him and smirked. "I'm serious about my acting, if that's what you mean. That's your cue." She pointed at the script, right where it read, "SALLY (quietly): Would you like to see some more?"

His face reddened, and he slid two inches closer to his acting partner, careful not to spill the coffee. In a shallow, halting voice, he recited, "Only if it's not some more of that funny money. My uncle's tired of playing the palsy."

For a moment, all Sandy could do was stare at him in disbelief. Then she said, "Oh, that was swell—just swell."

"Sorry. I guess I need to read it over some more."

"That might help, yes. And, by the way, it's 'My uncle's tired of playing the *patsy*'."

"What did I say?"

"Palsy."

"I think maybe I'm too far away from the copy."

"Then move over here," she said. "I promise you I won't bite."

When he crept a few inches nearer, Sandy took his left hand and guided it around her shoulders, so he had no choice but to nestle against her.

"Is that better?" she asked.

Wesley had to agree that it was. "Gee, I'll say." He cleared his throat and added, "I mean, I can see fine now." But better vision did not improve his reading any, and Sandy brusquely informed him that she feared for the integrity of tomorrow's program.

"We'll do fine," he said. "There's still a whole day before the show."

Sandy, though, was not so sure. She gazed into his eyes and forced a brave smile. "Please don't let me down, Wes. I can't do this without you."

Intoxicated by the fragrance of her hair and the soft curves of her sweater, he did the only thing he could do in the circumstances. He pledged to study this particular script with such diligence that, by airtime, he would be able to quote all of his lines from memory. Notwithstanding that this was a hollow boast when it came to radio, he still felt honorable for giving the trusting young lady some measure of assurance. By the time their reading session was drawing to a close, he had worked up the courage to squeeze her upper arm with his left hand. But he did it so gently that he was not even sure she had noticed. Her head leaned against his, so perhaps she had.

◆　　　◆　　　◆

The first familiar face that Stephen Brower laid eyes upon when he returned on leave for the final time was not one of his own family members but that of a fellow Waco High Tiger whom he had not seen since graduation nearly a year earlier. As he walked, seabag over one shoulder, from the train to the passenger depot's waiting area, he bumped into Billy Fischer—literally. More accurately, it was his bag that inadvertently struck Billy in the back, nearly throwing him to the platform.

"Christ, sailor! Watch where you're slingin' that thing," the civilian shouted. He caught himself with one hand before straightening back up. When he saw who his assailant was, Billy patted him on his unencumbered arm. "Steve Brower! Is that you? Don't you even recognize me?"

"Billy Eff! What're you doing here?" Steve stood his seabag on end, and the friends shook hands.

"My youngest brother's comin' home on furlough—Burton."

"Hey, if I'd known that was you, I would have slammed you a lot harder."

"What've you got in that duffel sack anyway, bowlin' balls?"

Steve jabbed at it like a punching bag. "Just dirty clothes, you pantywaist. I thought you could take a hit better than that."

Billy laughed. "Coach Stiteler's not makin' me run wind sprints these days, so I'm a little out of shape." A group of four nuns passed by, and Billy tipped his hat, greeting them with, "Sisters." They smiled back and nodded. Suddenly, Steve's pal became quite somber, and his voice weakened. "You're probably wonderin' why I'm not wearin' a uniform by now."

"Well, that did cross my mind. I heard you were in the Marines."

"Just long enough to get rejected," Billy said. "Heart murmur."

"Anything serious?"

"Yeah, the doctor says I'll only live 'til I'm ninety-five. Two of my brothers are in the Marines, though. And Gary's in the Seabees."

"You had physicals for football, didn't you?"

"Not so much that they'd find anythin'."

Steve chuckled. "Isn't that the truth."

Three trainers were flying over the downtown area, off to the northeast, just beyond the Amicable Building. They were not very close but still loud enough to interrupt the conversation. After they had passed, apparently banking to follow the river toward Whitney, Steve brought up the name of a mutual friend. "You know, Teddy didn't get in either."

That was hardly news to Billy, who scowled at the mere mention of his name. "Yeah, I see him every once in a while," he said. "He's workin' over at Geyser now, haulin' around those hundred-pound blocks of ice. Doesn't limp or nothin'."

Steve acknowledged the remark without comment, not quite certain whether Billy's spite was directed at the military doctors or Teddy Gaunce.

Billy broke the ensuing silence by patting his empty shirt pocket. "Say, I'd offer you a cigarette, but they're gettin' kind of scarce for us in civvies."

"That's okay. I don't smoke," Steve said. "Well, a pipe every now and then, but that's about it."

Billy sensed some irony there. "I hear the Army's got more cigarettes than they can possibly—"

Steve stopped him in mid-sentence with a phony cough. He had spotted his mother and brother, but they, having just arrived, had not yet seen him. "Hey, run interference for me, will you? I want to sneak up on them if I can." He pointed the pair out with a nod of the head and slung the heavy seabag over his right shoulder.

Billy grinned and said, "Follow me." He eyed the unsuspecting targets of their prank and at once began walking toward the breezeway. Steve tailed him through the small crowd of people, head down, close behind.

When they were only about ten feet away, Steve dropped his bag to the ground, raised his head, and shouted, "Taxi!" Instantly, Nora's eyes flooded with tears, and she ran to embrace her son in a bear hug. Wesley was more restrained, waiting patiently for his mother to release her grip before shaking Steve's hand.

After a couple of minutes, the sailor finally introduced his high school chum, who was standing there, awkwardly witnessing the reunion. "Mom, Wes, this is Billy Fischer. He played guard on our football team."

"How do you do?" Billy said. He looked toward the train tracks and excused himself. "Well, I really need to be goin'. Burton will be gettin' here any minute." He turned to Steve and shook his hand again. "Enjoy your time at home," he said. "Give me a call if you need somethin'."

"Thanks, Billy. Great to see you again. Stay out of trouble, okay?"

"I'll try." His face was sad, and an emptiness seemed to hang over him like a cloud. When he walked away, he did so in a methodical, shuffling manner, hardly lifting his feet from the pavement.

Nora motioned for her younger son to carry the seabag. "We would have been here sooner," she said to Steve, "but Wes just got off work."

The sailor socked his brother on the arm. "Well, at least you're gainfully employed." Wesley grinned at him and hoisted the bag aloft.

A quarter of an hour later, reveling in the familiar sight of home for the first time in eight months, Steve trotted directly to the living room and threw himself headlong onto the sofa, not even bothering to remove his shoes. Nora simply smiled and looked the other way. She said to Wesley, "Put that bag in your room, dear. He'll use your bed, and you can sleep on the cot."

"The returning hero," Steve said with a laugh, and Wesley dragged the bag upstairs.

"Wes was thrilled to hear you were coming home on leave," Nora said. "I wouldn't tell you this in front of him, of course, but I don't know when I've ever seen him so excited."

Steve brushed away the comment with a self-effacing chuckle. "I'm just a two-bit swabbie."

"Well, he really looks up to you. He always has, you know."

"Is he still doing that radio show?"

Nora smiled proudly. "Oh, yes. Wes is quite a celebrity around here."

"No fooling? Giving autographs and all that stuff?"

"Well, not much of that. This is radio—not the movies—so nobody recognizes him on the street like they would a picture star."

Valentino, the cat, jumped onto the sofa and soon curled up between Steve's legs. "Say, how about a cup of coffee, Mom? And you know what? I'm just going to lie here until you bring it to me."

"My pleasure. I've dreamed about this day for months."

That afternoon, during his reacquaintance tour of the house, Steve asked his mother if he could take a quick look at his old bedroom. The door was shut, so he thought it best to inquire first.

"Certainly, dear. I'm sure Hannah wouldn't mind. She's at work now and won't be home for hours."

"Is that the boarder?"

"Hannah Lane, yes. I thought you knew that."

"Maybe so. It sounds familiar." He opened the door and glanced inside. Everything was all frilly and feminine, scarcely resembling the bedroom he inhabited for so many years.

"Oh, I'm sure you knew Hannah's name, dear. You wrote a letter to her, didn't you?"

He looked embarrassed. "I guess I did, but that was months ago. She gave me a Bible when I first joined up, and I just wrote her back to say thanks."

"Did you ever hear from her again?"

"No, but that Coletti girl wrote to me a couple of times."

Nora nodded her head with interest. "Oh, she did?"

"I don't remember much about her, except that she was in my chemistry class—a year behind me."

"That's right. She was a junior when you were a senior."

Steve stared at his mother. "What do you know about her?"

"I told her I didn't think you'd mind if she wrote to you." Nora waited for her son to respond, but he said nothing. "Do you?" she asked.

"Do I what?"

"Do you mind that she wrote to you?"

Steve laughed. "No. Actually, it's kind of nice to get letters from a girl back home. Especially a pretty one like her. I may even look her up while I'm here. Do you think she'd mind?"

"Goodness, no. I think that would be very kind of you."

His suspicions were growing. "Do I sense a personal stake in this? You're not playing Cupid again, are you?"

"What do you mean, 'again'?"

"I seem to recall a certain blind date with Luella Ricks two years ago."

Nora giggled. "Now, don't bring up poor Luella again. That was a favor for her mother, and you know it." She watched Steve close the bedroom door. "Giulia

Coletti is just a very lovely young lady, that's all," she said. "I'm no matchmaker, believe me. What you do with the girls is your own business."

"Thank you."

"I don't like meddling women, especially when it comes to matters of the heart."

Steve gave her a sly look. "You wouldn't happen to know where this Giulia Coletti lives, would you?"

"Yes, she lives with her mother on Gurley Lane, out near Baylor."

"Anything else I should know about her?"

"Like what?"

"Well, for starters, is she serious about anyone?"

"Giulia? I don't think so." Nora considered for a moment before adding, "She does have a fiancé in the service—Archie Clarke."

Steve's jaw dropped. "Nothing serious, huh? Just a fiancé."

"No, you don't understand. She doesn't love him."

"And they're engaged to be married?" he asked.

Nora realized this was a rhetorical question, so she chose not to respond.

"If you don't mind my saying so," Steve told her, "this Giulia sounds kind of unpatriotic, stringing a serviceman along like that. How would you feel if she did something like that to me?"

"It's really not her fault. Archie's mother keeps pushing them together, and Giulia hasn't the nerve to cross her."

"She never said any of this in her letters to me. I would have thought being engaged to someone else might have seemed important enough to mention."

Nora sighed. "Archie may think of himself as being engaged, but Giulia certainly doesn't. Please go see her while you're home, dear. She's really a lovely girl."

"I wonder what this Archie Clarke fellow would think about my butting in."

Nora smiled. "All's fair ..."

Steve put his hands on her shoulders and said, "I can't believe my own sainted mother is condoning such a thing. That is a devious side of you I haven't seen."

Dinner would be about an hour late that night, but with Elizabeth still at the filling station, perhaps this delay would be for the better. Euphoria tugged at Nora's heartstrings. She felt very blessed indeed, standing at the kitchen range and seeing Steve and Wesley sprawled on the floor in the living room, listening to "Captain Midnight" on the radio console as in bygone days. It was wonderful to have her boys together again, and when their younger sister got off work at seven, the family would be complete, almost like before the war.

♦ ♦ ♦

But it was a tragic fact that the Brower family could never be truly whole again, and the biggest surprise of Steve's final leave from the service was how hard his father's absence hit him during the week at home. Harold Brower had been gone for six years now, and Steve, to his shame, had given memories of his late father scant attention over the last three or four. High school was simply too busy—what with classes, athletics, and girls—to give much thought to anything else. Thus did he attempt to rationalize his selfish neglect, but even he could not swallow that line of reasoning without having it taste like bitter medicine.

He felt the urge to make up for lost time, spending more than two hours of his first full day at home by sifting through his father's study and trying to recreate in his mind their warm, familial relationship as best he could. He ran his hand over the lacquered surface of the roll-top desk, he leaned back in the worn, leather chair, he feather-dusted the detailed metal replica of Lindy's Spirit of St. Louis, he slowly polished by hand the souvenir "Big D" ashtray from the State Fairgrounds, he flipped through the card catalogue of business contacts—civic leaders like Congressman Poage and Madison Cooper—and he winked a smile at the framed dollar bill that was now honorably retired from commerce.

Then, of course, there were the books. He browsed through a wide assortment of arcane titles on spines, some yellowed and tattered but others in pristine condition, still waiting in vain to be read. Lovingly collected over the years, they tended toward the historical—whether documentarian or biographical—with nary a work of fiction in sight: Teddy Roosevelt, Amelia Earhart, Lindbergh, Pershing, Bonaparte, the Black Sox Scandal, hits of Tin-Pan Alley, Thayer's *Life of Beethoven*, theoretical writings by Frederick Jackson Turner, a program from the 1932 Olympic Games, and a first-edition copy of *Stephen Foster: America's Troubadour* with a personalized autograph ("Thanks, Harold, for your interest in SCF, the love of whose music we share so passionately") by author John Tasker Howard.

When Steve took Carl Sandburg's *Abraham Lincoln: The Prairie Years* down from the shelf, it occurred to him that this day was an important anniversary in American history. It was precisely seventy-nine years ago that President Lincoln died from an assassin's bullet. For some reason, the date of April 15 had stuck in his memory—perhaps because it came a mere six days after General Lee's surrender of his Army of Northern Virginia in the village of Appomattox Courthouse. Steve recalled chatting with an elderly northerner in the town of Perry, near Marlin, a man who claimed to have been walking down Tenth Street in Washington on that fateful evening when the President was shot. Just a teenager then, he watched with his friends as the grievously wounded President was carried to his deathbed in Petersen's Boarding House, directly across the street from Ford's Theatre. To Steve, it was a spellbinding conversation. How could it possibly be that ancient history such as Lincoln's assassination was so intimately connected to the present—an eyewitness account—over the modest span of a solitary person's lifetime?

Almost certainly, the sturdy roll-top desk had been explored many times over by others before him, but it fell to Steve to uncover a buried treasure that would have meant little to anyone else. Behind a drawer marked SPECIAL lay a secret passage to the past. Why he happened to detach the sliding drawer from its guide rails, he had no idea, but its removal exposed to the careful eye a tiny keyhole.

An identically tiny but heretofore unidentified key had rattled in the ORDERS drawer two rows above, so he retrieved it at once to see whether it would mate with the mysterious lock. *Click!* The wooden facing pulled forward, permitting the lid to be raised just enough to free from confinement whatever contents had been secluded within. It was a paper product of some sort, lying facedown, undisturbed for all these many years.

When he turned it over and realized what he was holding, Steve was nearly overcome with emotion, and his trembling hands reverently laid the folded cardstock upon the writing surface of the desk. Even after a decade and a half, the picture still looked as familiar to him as if he had drawn it only yesterday. He walked over to the study door and softly closed it, wishing to be alone with his thoughts.

Scrawled with a red crayon were the words "happy birtday daddy." The accompanying illustration, multi-colored and childishly amorphous, depicted Harold Brower himself. Hardly recognizable to the finite limits of the adult eye, it had seemed a perfect likeness to its creator. He remembered it coming alive on the paper, drawn with love, shimmering with a soul and lifeblood of its own. Now the eyeglasses and bow tie remained clearly distinguishable, but all other characteristics had withered over the process of Steve's aging. The colors and lines had grown smeared together, one upon another, no longer as sharp as a fine rotogravure photograph. Something changed during the intervening years, and he was fearful of reflecting too honestly upon his childhood and the fragile beauty of lost innocence. His father had no such fears, glimpsing the truth and holding it close to his heart, placing it in a hidden sanctuary where no cynical human being—devoid of deeper understanding—might tarnish it with insensitive remarks.

Steve wept openly as he folded the birthday card and returned it to its final resting place in the desk. The tiny key went into a sacred corner of his wallet, there to accompany him wherever in the world he might be.

♦   ♦   ♦

By the afternoon of his fourth day of leave, Stephen Brower had grown quite restless—not tired of being spoiled with home life, to be sure, but fretful about his lack of female companionship. He decided to ride a streetcar to Giulia's neighborhood, then show up at the Coletti house, unsolicited and unannounced. In the event that Miss Coletti was not there, he would simply return home, with nothing gained but little lost by the effort. His mother, who seemed to know a surprising amount about the girl, informed him that Giulia had dropped out of high school to care for the increasing needs of Mrs. Coletti. The father was estranged from her—not an amicable parting—and now lived across the river in East Waco. Giulia worked mornings at a flooring company, Nora recalled, so the best time to catch her at home was sometime after lunch.

When he arrived on Gurley Lane, Steve double-checked the street address before approaching what he viewed as an exceedingly humble residence that was much in need of some yard work. He rang the doorbell and waited. No response. He tried it again, but still no one answered. Finally, as he was turning to leave, the door opened, and a middle-aged woman said, "Yes? May I help you?"

Steve smiled. "Is Giulia Coletti here?"

"No, I'm sorry. She's at work," the lady said. She was leaning heavily on a walking stick. "Who may I say called?"

Though Steve did not want to divulge his name, he also did not want to appear to be a suspicious prowler, so he went ahead and told her.

"Then you must be Matthew Coleman's nephew."

Steve was shocked. "Yes, ma'am, I am. How do you know him?"

"He used to perform for our church bazaars—funny skits and impersonations, that sort of stuff. He was really marvelous."

"That's Uncle Matt, all right," Steve said.

Paolina looked the sailor over carefully, from white cap to bell-bottoms. "You played football for Waco High, didn't you?"

"Yes, ma'am."

"Were you pretty good?"

He laughed. "Not too bad, I guess."

She nodded her head, satisfied with the reply. "Well, I'll tell Giulia you came by to see her."

"Thank you, ma'am." He proceeded down the footpath and heard the door shut behind him. Just for a moment, he wondered whether he should have asked the lady where her daughter worked, but he decided it was probably better that he had not. Besides, his own mother seemed to know everything else about Giulia. Maybe she knew who the girl's employer was too.

When Steve arrived back home, his mother was nowhere to be found. Frustrated, he went out the front door and glanced at the neighbors' yards. No one was there. Then he walked around the side of the house and saw that the family automobile was still parked in the garage. She could not have gone far, but he was too impatient to wait for her return. Who else, with the exception of Mrs. Coletti, would know where Giulia was working?

Steve wandered up to his brother's room and lay on the bed, thinking. It was probably silly to go chasing after a girl whom he hardly even knew. She was so young anyway. Maybe Marianne Green was still in town. At least she was his own age. Or Frances Lightsey, another good prospect. Or Nancy Fontana. He started to go downstairs for the telephone directory, but a faint noise made him stop and listen. It came from his old bedroom—he was sure of that. Tiptoeing closer, he put his ear to the door and waited. The same soft sound: *plunk!* Someone was inside the room. Was his mother cleaning in there? If so, why would she go to the trouble of closing the door?

He knocked, and it was the boarder who answered. She had a dazed look on her face, startled to see him standing there. Hannah was wearing shorts and a loose-fitting, pullover shirt, not very feminine. In fact, at first glance Steve thought she was a boy, until he recognized who it was. "Hello, miss. Sorry to bother you, but have you seen my mother?"

"You're Stephen Brower." Hannah focused her bleary eyes on him and swallowed. She wore no make-up, and her hair was a mess.

"That's right, but call me Steve. It's been a while."

"Pardon the way I look. I just woke up and was sorting through some phonograph records. The last thing I expected to see was a sailor at my door."

He grinned at her and winked. "I would imagine so. I mean, being a good Baptist and all."

Hannah ignored the remark. "To answer your question, I saw your mother this morning, but that was hours ago. I got off work at eight, and she was in the kitchen. I've been working lots of graveyard shifts lately."

Suddenly, Steve felt quite awkward. The girl was in her sleeping attire, evidently with no undergarment beneath the pink top. Not that there was much to show.

"Listen, I've got to go," he said. "If you happen to see my mother, would you please tell her I need to get some information from her?"

"Yes, sir."

"Call me Steve." He turned away, and Hannah began to close the door. "Oh, say ..." Steve said. He stopped the door with his hand. "And thanks again for the Bible."

Hannah smiled. "It was only the New Testament. I just thought it might be a handy size."

"Well, I appreciate it."

She nodded her head and then clicked the door shut without another word.

It was a very long hour before Nora Brower finally returned home, and Steve spent most of that time pacing the living room floor. He was a bit miffed when she opened the front door with a small box of groceries in her arms. "Where have you been?" he asked. "I've been looking all over for you."

She looked hurt. "Didn't I tell you I was going to Moek's? I do that every Monday, but I couldn't go this morning because of all the extra wash."

Steve grimaced. "I'm sorry. You did tell me that." He took the box from her arms and carried it to the kitchen.

"What did you need me for?" Nora asked. She began putting some tin cans in the pantry.

"You remember that Coletti girl you wanted me to go see?"

"Yes—Giulia. She's really a lovely girl."

Steve was amused. "I think we've established that by now, yes."

"Well, she is. Giulia's prettier than most movie stars."

"I know, I know." He tried not to laugh at his mother's foibles because she always had his best interests at heart. "Do you happen to know where this Giulia works? She wasn't home, and her mother told me she was still at work."

"Oh, dear. No, I don't. A flooring company somewhere—downtown, I suppose. Why didn't you ask Mrs. Coletti?"

"I felt funny doing that, and anyway, I thought maybe you would know."

"Do you think it would be proper to call on her at work?"

"Probably not," he said, "but I really don't have very much choice in the matter. I'll be leaving in three days, and that's not very long to arrange my whole life."

Nora nodded her head in silence, suddenly glum. She began rummaging around in the pantry.

Steve tried to change the subject. "How're the Moeks doing these days?" He walked to the entryway, still talking. "I think I've only seen them once since graduation—at the very end of my first leave. She gave me some hard candy to take with me."

"They're fine, both of them. They ask about you almost every time I'm there."

Steve returned with the telephone directory in his hands. "I've always liked them. Too bad about their son."

"Hermann opened a lunch counter, you know, and I think business has been pretty good, considering."

Steve was only half listening to what she said. "Maybe I'll drop in and give Giulia a try." His eyes were browsing through the business section.

"You know, Trudy was on a radio show last week—won five dollars for answering a question."

That got his attention, and he looked at his mother. "How in the world did Mrs. Moek get on a radio show?"

"She just happened to be at Levine's when a reporter came up to her with a microphone. He asked her what the capital of Nevada was, and she knew it."

He laughed. "No fooling?"

"She owns a couple of silver dollars with 'CC' mint marks on them, so she just guessed that maybe Carson City was the capital."

"Five dollars! Well, good for her." He pointed to a page in the directory. "Does McLendon Hardware sound familiar—for the Coletti girl?"

"I've heard of it, but I don't think she works there."

"What about Nash, Robinson, and Company?"

"No, I'm sure it wasn't a big outfit like that."

"Rawley Flooring?"

"Could be, dear, but I don't even know if I've heard where she works."

"Well, it's got to be one of those three. Cecil Farrow is just a contractor."

◆   ◆   ◆

It was one of the slowest afternoons that Giulia could remember. The telephone had rung only about five times since she arrived at work—and here it was, almost three o'clock. Butler Lindeman seemed unusually interested in what she was doing that day, so she tried to appear as busy as possible. Fortunately, Bobby Sawyer turned in a work order, so that gave her something to do for the next twenty minutes or so. She transferred Bobby's handwritten information, in duplicate, onto a Form D-2, with the aid of some worn-out carbon paper that kept curling up against the typewriter platen.

Two retail customers came in, so she directed them to the public showroom around the corner. This happened with regularity because, for reasons lost to company lore, the six-by-four-foot sign to Rawley Flooring was situated directly above the entrance to the company's wholesale division. In due course, that needed to be fixed, but it was a project that would have to wait. There were far more urgent matters confronting wartime business than signage.

At 3:05, a disgruntled civilian client, who was vaguely familiar to Giulia but whose name she could not recall, demanded to see upper management at once, so she laid down the work order long enough to escort him to Lindeman's office. That should keep the boss occupied for a while, she thought.

"Thank you, Giulia," Lindeman told her. He was visibly annoyed at having to deal with an unpleasant task with no prior warning.

Ten minutes later, when a young sailor appeared at her desk, Giulia sized him up as yet another misdirected customer. "Yes, sir?" she asked.

"I'd like to speak to Miss Coletti, please," he said.

She gazed at him more closely and whispered, "Steve?"

He nodded his head and removed the Navy cap. "Hello, Giulia. Sorry to pop in on you like this, but I didn't want to leave town without seeing you."

"No, I'm glad you did," she said to him. But this was an automatic response, and she did not really mean it. He had taken her off guard, and she must look a fright. Her hair was probably a wind-blown disaster, having been subjected to the effects of an open window in Lauren's automobile, and she wondered whether her blouse properly matched the skirt. Besides, the whole situation was begging for trouble. Though Lindeman's head was turned the other way as he thumbed through some pattern samples with the client, it was only a matter of time before he growled for her to return to her duties and stop the fraternization.

"Can you talk for a few minutes?" Steve asked. "I dropped by your house earlier, and your mother said you were still here."

She decided to be honest with him. "I just can't. I feel terrible about it, but Mr. Lindeman will blow his stack if he sees me talking with you."

Steve noticed that she was staring with grave apprehension at the other office, as if a cannonball might be hurtling toward her from that direction at any moment. "Is one of them Mr. Lindeman?"

Giulia nodded her head. "He's got thinning hair. The one with glasses."

"He doesn't look so ferocious to me. Anyway, how does he know I'm not here on business?"

"Oh, he'll know all right. He's very good at that." Then a mischievous gleam came to her eye, and she said, "I suppose you'll just have to buy something—to make your visit official. How about a couple thousand square feet of economical flooring?"

Her smile was contagious, so much so that Steve was rendered speechless, drinking in her physical attributes at close range. Never before had he witnessed such a stunning beauty in person—and only rarely on the movie screen. Giulia Coletti had been very pretty in chemistry class, no question about it, but that was when she was a girl of fifteen. Now, scarcely more than a year later, she was developing into a lovely young woman whose unassuming charms were the equal of any pageant winner on earth.

Lindeman looked her way and was certain to have detected that Giulia was no longer alone. "Quick," Steve said, "hand me a catalogue or something to flip through. Maybe that'll keep him happy."

But Giulia did not move. "He's smarter than that. Might as well face the music. It won't be the first time."

Steve stared again at the boss, who by now had settled back down and appeared to be putting the finishing touches on a problematic sale. He did not seem like much of an ogre, so Steve tried his best to remain open-minded. "Maybe he's only watching out for the company's interests," he said. "Your Mr. Lindeman might have a boss breathing down his neck too."

Giulia shook her head. "No, I'm afraid there's more to it than that."

"How so?"

"I think he kind of likes me."

It was all Steve could do to keep from laughing. "Him? He's got to be over fifty."

"And he's married, too," she added.

Now the sailor did laugh. "I hope his wife never sees him sitting on your lap."

Giulia remained serious and pretended to search through the middle drawer of her desk. Moving her mouth as little as possible, she whispered, "Listen, I really need to finish up this report. Can you wait for me to go on break—at 3:30?"

He glanced at the wall clock. "I'll be outside."

Giulia started to smile, but she could feel Butler Lindeman peering at her, so she maintained a straight face and gestured with her eyes for the visitor to leave.

Steve exited through the front door and then ambled down the sidewalk, placidly smoking his pipe until, after fifteen minutes or so, the girl finally appeared at the wholesale entrance.

"Sorry," she said as he approached her, "but my boss is very strict about talking to anyone who's not here on business."

Steve shook his head, unpersuaded. "From what I can see, your boss pays more attention to you than he does to the business."

Giulia blushed. "Well, maybe so."

The aroma of Steve's tobacco was wonderful but also a bit intimidating to her. Suddenly, she saw herself as little more than a child, standing there next to this worldly young man in a uniform who was smoking his pipe. It made him seem much older than he really was and more sophisticated.

Giulia pointed to a sleek automobile, parked well away from the others. "That's Mr. Lindeman's car over there—the green Ford." It was a 1942 Super Deluxe convertible, the latest model on the road.

"Which one is yours?" Steve asked.

"I don't have a car."

"How do you get to the office?"

"Lauren Fite picks me up on her lunch hour whenever I'm working afternoons. She has to go home anyway to take care of her dogs. I ride with her for my morning shifts, too, both ways. I'd sure like to return the favor someday, but I can't."

"Why not? Maybe you can save up to buy a used car."

"I don't have my license yet."

That surprised the sailor. "How old are you?" he asked.

"Sixteen and a half. What about you?"

"I'll be nineteen in July—on Independence Day."

"Right on July Fourth?"

"Uh-huh."

"I don't think I know anyone else who was born exactly on a holiday."

He puffed his pipe and smiled. "Yes, dear commoner, people all over the country celebrate my birthday."

"That'll make it easy to remember," Giulia said. And the instant it left her mouth, she regretted the presumptuous comment.

Fortunately, Steve did not seem to hear it, thanks perhaps to a school bus, filled with boisterous children, that happened to be passing by on the street just then.

Giulia motioned with her hand, so the two of them began strolling away from the building's entrance.

"How come you haven't gotten your driver's license yet?" he asked. "You're old enough for one."

"Nothing very mysterious about that. My mother never did learn to drive, so we don't even own a car."

"I'd be happy to show you how," Steve said. He realized how empty that must have sounded. "Well, you know what I mean. If I were going to be here."

"When do you have to go back?"

"Early Friday. I need to be in Dallas by noon."

Giulia frowned. "Did you know that Mrs. Chesky's son and son-in-law are both in the service? Todd's been in the Marines since before Pearl Harbor. You knew him, didn't you?"

"I knew who he was, but I never met him."

"Mrs. Chesky's daughter is worried sick, of course, like most war wives. I think her husband flies bombing missions over Germany."

"I'll keep my feet at sea level, thank you. Not so much glamour as the fly-boys, but a lot less likely to be taken prisoner."

"What's your job?"

"In the Navy?"

"Yes, on the ship."

"I trained for fire control at the Great Lakes Naval Station, north of Chicago."

"You're a fireman?"

"No," he said with a laugh. "Well, as a matter of fact, everyone's a fireman if it comes down to that. But my main job is to help aim the big guns. That's what fire control means."

"That sounds exciting."

"Can be, at times. It's awfully loud, I can tell you that."

"Well, I'm sure you're a good shot," she said, and he smiled at her innocence.

"Pretty fair, I guess. It's mostly just knowing how to read the gauges, plugging in the enemy's direction, speed, and range, that sort of thing."

Giulia's pace of walking gradually slowed to a halt. "I'm awfully sorry," she said, "but I need to get back to my desk. Ten minutes is all we're allowed."

Only now did he notice how surprisingly tall she was. The top of her head came up to his eyes, which probably made her around five foot nine. She was well proportioned, perhaps a bit on the slender side.

Steve offered to walk her back to the door, but she declined. "Maybe you'd better not, if it's all the same to you. There are lots of nosy workers in there, and they'll be watching every move I make."

He grinned at her. "What kind of moves do you plan to make?"

"I just don't want people to think that I go around picking up sailors."

"Hanging around the wharves and so forth?"

She giggled. "Something like that."

Steve sighed, and there was a moment of uneasy silence. Giulia looked at him, puzzled, as if wondering what should come next.

"I guess this is goodbye then," he said.

"I guess." Giulia turned her head away. "Do you mind if I write to you every once in a while?"

"Not at all. I'd like that."

She nodded at him and began walking backward, retreating toward the entrance. "Well, goodbye then," she said. "May God bless you and keep you safe." She half expected him to follow her and was disappointed that he did not. Instead, Steve stayed put, smiling as if amused.

"Goodbye, Giulia," he shouted from where he stood, and she gave him a cheerful wave before disappearing through the doorway of Rawley Flooring.

◆　　◆　　◆

Late the next morning, a Tuesday, Stephen Brower paid a visit to Hermann and Gertrude Moek at their grocery store. When he opened the front door, he saw Hermann, bent at the knees and waist, inventorying some cans of tuna fish on the bottom shelf of the seafood section. Steve took the other aisle and hurried to the back of the store.

"May I help you?" Hermann said. He had heard the small bell jingle and the screen door slam shut, so he knew that someone had come inside. He stood up to search for the unseen customer. Again he called, "May I help you?"

Steve could tell that the voice was coming closer. When he judged that Hermann was near, he stepped snappily around the end of the aisle, his version of a dramatic entrance, and broke into a broad grin. "Hello, Mr. Moek."

"Well, Stephen Brower!" the grocer said. "Good to see you, son. Your mother said you were in town." Placing his pencil over one ear, he shook hands with the sailor and called to his wife. "Trudy, come see who's here. It's young Stephen, Nora's boy." There was no response. "Trudy," he said, even more loudly, "come here!"

Finally, a half-minute after uttering from afar, "I'll be right d'ere," she emerged from the cool storage room, pushing a cart that carried two boxes of lettuce heads. "Hello, Stephen!" she said. "Praise d'e Lord d'at you're safe." She scampered over to him and hugged his neck.

"Thank you, Mrs. Moek. It's nice to be back."

"How long have you been in the Navy now?" Hermann asked.

"About eight months—basic training and then specialized."

"Good for you, son. We're all proud of you."

"D'en I guess you'll be seeing some action soon," Gertrude said.

Steve shook his head, apologetically, and said nothing.

"Now, Trudy," Hermann told her, "you know very well that Steve's not free to talk about such things. When Uncle Sam needs him over there, I'm sure he'll send for him."

Gertrude's face went scarlet. "I'm sorry, Stephen," she said. "I'm just d'e nosy type. I wasn't trying to steal any military secrets."

"I know you weren't. No offense taken."

"Say, would you like anything to eat, my boy?" Hermann asked. "I'll cook whatever you want, and it's on the house for our favorite serviceman."

"No, I couldn't do that, Mr. Moek. But I'll *buy* a grilled cheese sandwich from you and also some hashed brown potatoes and a fountain Coca-Cola. My mother says your new lunch counter is the best in town."

Hermann laughed. "Oh, I hardly think so, but I appreciate the sentiment, just the same." Then, winking, he told his wife, "We'll just put it on his account." She acknowledged the ploy with a knowing smile.

"So, how's business been?" Steve asked.

"Not too bad, really," the grocer said. He glanced around the empty store and frowned. "But of course some days are better than others. This morning we could have driven a tank through the place and not injured anybody."

Two other people came into the store while Steve was eating his lunch. One was an elderly man, possibly as old as eighty, who purchased some oatmeal and cinnamon. The other was a rather tall woman with graying hair, tied back in a bun, and wearing wire-rimmed spectacles whose lenses were scarcely larger than her eyes.

Steve looked up from his sandwich when he heard Gertrude greet the lady as "Mrs. Clarke." He had heard that particular name in connection with Giulia Coletti, but of course it was fairly common, so this might be no more than a coincidence. The hashed brown potatoes were delicious—savory to the palate but not too greasy—and Hermann spooned an additional portion of them on Steve's plate the moment he consumed the last mouthful.

"Another sandwich, son?"

"No, thanks, Mr. Moek."

"How about a hamburger steak ... with grilled onions and green peppers? It won't cost you any ration points."

"That's awfully tempting, but I'd better not."

Hermann gave the sailor a puckish raise of the eyebrows. "Dessert? I think Trudy made a lemon meringue pie."

That Steve could not refuse. "Golly ..."

"There's plenty of sugar around for the boys in uniform."

"Okay, sure. Why not?"

The generous serving of pie stood four and a half inches tall, a good third of which was a stratum of chilled, agreeably tart, lemon filling. Steve relished each bite, allowing the light topping to melt in his mouth and enjoying the cool sensation of citrus fruit upon the tongue. "This is swell, Mr. Moek," he said.

Smiling with pride, Hermann wiped his hands on the white apron. "I thought that might be a nice change from Navy food."

Steve swallowed the last morsel and licked his lips. "Yes, sir, it is. Our Navy chow's plenty good, but it doesn't compare to what you can get during peacetime on Main Street, USA." He swiveled back and forth on the tall stool, simply relaxing while he savored Coca-Cola through a straw.

By this time, the aged gentleman had left the store, but the woman, with sack in hand, approached the lunch counter and seated herself at the far end. She ordered a hot turkey sandwich, open-faced in brown gravy, with mashed potatoes, cabbage, and a cup of tea.

"Hello, sailor," the woman said. She adjusted her eyeglasses.

"Hello."

"Are you home on leave?"

"Yes, ma'am, for another few days."

"I know your parents must be thrilled to have you here."

"Yes, ma'am. My mother's spoiling me—every minute of every hour."

"Well, that's what she's supposed to do," the lady told him.

Steve nodded his head and grinned.

"My son's in the Army. Overseas ... in Australia."

"Is that so?"

"He's very good about writing, I must admit. I usually hear from him about twice'ta week, on average. I hope you do the same for your mother."

"I'm afraid not. And I've been stateside, so it would've been a lot easier for me."

"Archie's been abroad for a couple years now—with just three furloughs in all that time. I think that's a sin, don't you?"

Steve shrugged his shoulders, choosing not to answer. He had reached the bottom of his beverage, so his main concern now was trying to avoid making a loutish noise as he took his final sips. Gertrude was sweeping the wooden floor with a broom, very slowly so as not to raise dust for the diners. The postman came inside, placed a stack of mail on the front counter, waved to no one in particular, and silently departed.

"He's engaged to be married," the lady said.

Steve stared at her and said, "I beg your pardon?" He had begun to stand, but—thinking it rude to simply walk away during a conversation—he sat back down on his stool.

"My son's engaged to be married," she told him. Using a knife and fork, the woman was cutting her sandwich into tiny bites, all the while sliding her cabbage away from the spreading pool of gravy.

Steve was polite enough to feign interest in her story. "Oh, yes?" he asked. "Will they wait until after the war?"

"That's the plan," she said, "but you know how young people are these days."

He acknowledged the comment with a smile, but an instinct had surfaced that made him want to extricate himself from this situation. Too many aspects of her narrative were sounding familiar.

"He's engaged to a wonderful girl," the woman added, "and very pretty too."

"That's nice." Steve was relieved to see the grocer's portly form.

Hermann picked up the sailor's plates, glass, and silverware and started to carry them back to the kitchen for washing. "Are you sure you won't have another piece of pie ... on the house?" he asked.

"No, sir. I've really got to be running."

Hermann thought of something else, and he raised an index finger. "Don't go yet. I'll be right back."

Steve glanced again at the lady. Hot tea was steaming up her eyeglasses, so she took them off and laid them next to her plate. Retrieving his cap, Steve arose and said to her, "I enjoyed talking with you, ma'am. Best of luck to your son."

"Well, aren't you a nice young man? Best wishes to you too, sailor," she said. Then, after putting her eyeglasses back on, she reached into her purse and produced a ragged photo that evidently had been pawed by the hands of countless viewers. A round-faced sergeant was standing in front of a dusty jeep, with a Quonset hut visible in the background. "That's my Archie."

Hermann returned from the kitchen with a throw pillow in his hands, proudly holding it out for Steve to see. The pillow was white with red trim, and displayed across its length were the letters "Stephen Collins Brower, U.S.N." in an attractive script of navy blue. "This is a surprise for your mother," he told the sailor. "Mrs. Moek made it herself—in your honor."

Steve did not quite know how to respond, so he simply nodded his head in gratitude.

"We lost our boy in the fighting, you know, and we grieve for him every day," Hermann said, hardly above a whisper. "It was not Conrad's fault that he was on the wrong side. They would've shot him for cowardice if he refused to go."

"Yes, sir. I'm sure that's true."

Dramatically, Hermann put his right hand over his heart. "Conrad was no Nazi, Stephen. You've got to believe me."

"No, sir. I'm sure he wasn't."

Steve stole a peek at the woman. It was embarrassing to have the grocer speak so frankly to him about Conrad in front of a perfect stranger, particularly one whose son was in uniform. And indeed, the lady did appear to be awfully shaken by what she heard. Suddenly she was frowning, unfriendly, and anxious to leave. Was it Hermann's reference to the Nazis that caused her to become so upset?

Then it dawned on Steve that this customer was far from unknown to the Moeks. Had Gertrude not addressed her by name? He also suspected that, even from the far end of the counter, she was able to see the pillow quite clearly through her eyeglasses—and to read what was embroidered upon it.

♦   ♦   ♦

Three times within a period of two weeks seemed an ominous pattern to Dinah Reidelhuber, but to her co-worker, Elizabeth Brower, these "sightings" were harmless apparitions, the products of an overactive imagination. Elizabeth herself had not seen Edward Neal's shadowy figure in many months, and she convinced herself that the threat was past. Why was it that only Dinah ever happened to spot the gray Oldsmobile? Twice, she claimed, it was parked along Eleventh Street, once at a vacant lot on the west side and once at the A&P Food Store on the east. The other time it paused along the curb, engine running, near the intersection of Twelfth and Washington. How Dinah could hear the engine running at such a distance—almost to the Texas Fireproof Storage warehouse—was a mystery that argued against the veracity of her statements.

For better or worse, Elizabeth was inclined to dismiss such unsubstantiated reports out of hand, but she did promise to call one of her brothers for help, if and when the suspicions were corroborated or Neal was identified as the automobile's occupant. The problem was, there were lots of gray Oldsmobiles on the road.

It was unassuming Bradley Gann, of all people, who made a discovery that triggered a brutal succession of events, ultimately leading to the detention of two people and the permanent disfigurement of another. Young Bradley, whose taste in literature did not exceed the scholarly demands of fourth-grade comic books, found himself leafing through a like-new copy of Plato's *Republic* in the filling station office. Though, if pressed, he could have defined most of the individual words, when linked together in philosophical musings they made absolutely no sense to him. What, for instance, did he stand to gain from the experience of traversing such passages as this?

> Then what gives the objects of knowledge their truth and the mind the power of knowing is the Form of the Good. It is the cause of knowledge and truth, and you will be right to think of it as being itself known, and yet as being something other than, and even higher than, knowledge and truth. And just as it was right to think of light and sight as being like the sun, but wrong to think of them as being the sun itself, so here again it is right to think of knowledge and truth as being like the Good, but wrong to think of either of them as being the Good, which must be given a still higher place of honor ...

He recognized the writing as being very erudite, and that alone was enough to close his mental receptors. Even a primitive attempt to analyze the initial sentence led nowhere, already more than his cogitative stamina could endure. But he was a conscientious human being, trustworthy to a fault, and there were few people his age in whose hands this tome was safer from physical neglect or theft. When he found it, the book was lying facedown on the pavement, just inches away from a meandering rivulet of oily water. Thus rescued from certain destruction, Plato's thoughts resided for perhaps ten minutes upon a metal shelf, incongruously sharing space with a greasy, OPA-approved parts catalogue and an unwashed coffee cup labeled "Butch."

It was then that Bradley approached Dinah Reidelhuber for advice, and she told the boy, "I'll bet it belongs to that Baylor professor who came in—an 'A' sticker, older car with a dented fender. Louis said he'll fix it for him next week."

"D'ya know his name?"

Dinah shook her head. "Is it written inside the front cover?"

"Nope, nothin' there."

"Ask Elizabeth. She seemed to know who he was."

Bradley smiled, displaying his missing incisors. Funny, he seemed to have too few teeth, and Dinah seemed to have too many.

"Is she workin' today?"

Dinah pointed to the ladies' room.

Bradley was embarrassed. "I guess I'll just wait 'til she comes outta there."

"Yes," she said, "please do."

After a short while, Elizabeth emerged from the lavatory, and Bradley walked outside to intercept her. Showing her the book, he asked the professor's name.

"That Baylor teacher? I don't know, but I'm sure that our boarder has him for a class."

Bradley's face brightened. Now he was getting somewhere. "If I kin find out his name, I'll take the book back to him whenever I'm out on a service call."

Hannah Lane was not at home, so Elizabeth called the switchboard of Crawford-Austin Manufacturing Company. Once paged, it was just a matter of two minutes before Hannah came to the telephone.

"Hannah? This is Lizzie. Don't you take philosophy at Baylor?"

There was a great deal of noise on the other end of the line, but Elizabeth could hear Hannah say, "I did in the fall."

"What was your teacher's name? I think we found his book, and we'd like to return it to him."

"What?" A loud motor was making the conversation virtually impossible.

Elizabeth shouted, "What was your teacher's name?"

"Dr. Hall ... Arthur Jackson Hall. Why?"

"I think we found his book, here at the filling station."

"You did?" The motor stopped. "What's the book?"

Elizabeth consulted the cover. "*The Republic* by Plato. Translated by Francis MacDonald Cornford."

"Yep, that would be Dr. Hall's, all right," Hannah said with a laugh. "Pleasure reading."

"Thanks. Our boy'll drive it over to his house this afternoon."

"His wife should be home, if he's not. They live on Speight, near the Baylor Service Station. Same side of the street."

"Maybe Dr. Hall will give you an 'A' mark for this."

"Too late," Hannah said. "He already did."

Plato in hand, Bradley got into the tow truck and began driving down Eleventh Street. Just a block away, he saw an older automobile with a slightly dented front fender. It was parked at the Alexander Medical & Surgical Clinic, and someone was inside. The driver did not appear to be a Baylor professor, though. Clad in a brown leather jacket, he was a man in his upper twenties, and in front of his eyes he held a pair of binoculars. Strangely, he seemed to be looking at—or even spying on—the filling station. Why would anybody want to do that?

Bradley was not by nature a suspicious young man, but this was wartime, and one of the few principles that had captured his attention in school was that suspected enemy agents should be reported to the proper authorities. He turned the truck around and drove back to the SRC station.

Business was still slow, and Elizabeth and Dinah were both in the office, awaiting the next customer.

But it was Bradley who suddenly appeared, and Elizabeth said to him, "I thought you already left."

He was unsmiling, intent on saving the world from Nazi saboteurs. "Take a look at that car, but don't let him see you."

"Who?" Dinah asked.

"Someone's in that car—the gray Oldsmobile—and he's casin' the joint."

Elizabeth shivered and sat down. "A gray Oldsmobile?"

"Someone's in it," the boy told her. "He's lookin' this way with field glasses."

"Phone my brother," Elizabeth whispered, "and tell him to get right over here."

Bradley looked at her in surprise. "Shouldn't we call the police?" he asked.

"Please phone my brother. I'm too shaky to talk."

The Browers' telephone rang, and Nora answered it. She heard a familiar voice.

"Hello, Mrs. Brower. This is Bradley Gann. I work where Lizzie does, but I need to talk to her bother." His pinched intonation betrayed nervousness.

"Is there something wrong, Bradley? Is Lizzie all right?"

"Oh, yes, ma'am. She's just fine. Is your son at home?"

"Stephen's here," she told the boy, "but Wesley's still at school."

"Kin I talk to Stephen then, please?"

Bradley could hear the woman calling to her son, but he could not make out precisely what she said or the response. She must have covered up the mouthpiece with her hand.

Then Steve came on the line, and he was very abrupt and businesslike, perhaps taking a signal from his mother's distress. "Yes? This is Stephen."

Nora saw no change in his expression as he listened to Bradley's lengthy report, and she became even more worried. "About ten minutes—no more than that," Steve said. He nodded his head, though of course Bradley could not see him do that. "Act normal until I get there, understand?" Steve listened to the boy's concern about German spies and told him, "Stay out of the way, that's all. If he leaves before I get there, just let him go."

Though Nora tried to dissuade her son from taking this matter into his own hands, he would not be deterred. Steve had been waiting to confront Elizabeth's assailant for eight and a half months, biding his time while away, so he was not about to miss the opportunity for retribution now—if, indeed, the suspicious person did prove to be Edward Neal and not just an innocent bystander or harmless voyeur. The binoculars and gray Oldsmobile added up to just cause for further investigation.

Steve jumped into the family Chevrolet and backed out of the garage so fast that the automobile's tires threw gravel against the workbench thirty feet away. Hitting the pavement with a screech of rubber, he ignored the speed limit and raced southeast toward Eleventh and Washington, all the while formulating a sketchy plan of action. He discounted Bradley's theory that the suspect was a German saboteur, lurking until the time was right to strike. No premeditating espionage ring in Berlin was likely to target the lowly Service Refining Company of Waco, Texas, for tactical destruction.

Two things were in Steve's favor. Although Neal presumably recalled that Mrs. Brower had a son in the military—having applied for rental of his vacated bedroom—he almost certainly had no idea what that serviceman looked like. Too, Neal probably would not recognize the Brower automobile, so a bold approach could be made without excessive caution hampering the element of surprise.

Drawing attention to himself was the last thing Steve wanted to do, so when the Chevy approached the intersection of Twelfth and Barron, he braked to about twenty miles per hour and eased it into first gear. His automobile was just one of many that might stop at the SRC station for gasoline and motor oil that day, so that is what he chose to do. Bradley came out of the office to greet the customer, and Steve could see that Elizabeth and another female employee were still inside.

"I'm Lizzie's brother," Steve told the boy. "Open the hood ... but don't look around at the other car."

"Don't you think we should call the police?"

"They can't do anything until he's caught in the act. It's not against the law to sit in your car and look at someone through binoculars, so their hands would be tied."

"But if he blows up the station, it'll be too late."

Steve shook his head. "Check my oil, will you?"

"For real?"

"Yes, for real," he said. Steve leaned his head out the window, pretending to be adjusting his side-view mirror. "Just try to act natural. If Neal sees any funny business over here, he'll be gone. And then Lizzie will be in a fix the whole time I'm away."

Now Bradley was totally confused. "Who's Neal?"

"I don't have time to explain it all to you. Tell Lizzie and that other girl to come out here—but only when they see you leaving in the truck."

Bradley stared in disbelief. "You want me to leave? What about the Nazi?"

"That's no Nazi—not a German one anyway. Listen, you go run that errand you were telling me about, just like nothing happened, but first do me a favor."

"Yeah?"

"Flash your brake lights twice if that guy's still snooping. He's too far away for me to see him very clearly from here."

There was a dazed look on Bradley's face. "Well, if that's what you want." He shut the Chevrolet hood with a loud thud. "I still think we oughta call the police. There could be a whole ring of 'em out there."

"Remember—two flashes."

Bradley did as he was told, climbing into the tow truck after telling Elizabeth and Dinah to come out of the office. They arrived at the automobile about the time the truck was crossing over into the right lane of Eleventh Street. A few seconds later, Bradley tapped his brake pedal twice and drove off toward Baylor.

Steve asked his sister, "What's her name?"

"Dinah Reidelhuber."

"Okay, Sis, now check my tire's air pressure—the left rear, I guess."

Elizabeth turned to her right and bent down with her tire gauge. The other girl looked petrified.

"Listen, Dinah. This is important," Steve said. "Walk as far away from Lizzie as you can, understand? Rinse out some rags or something—maybe near those oil drums—and try to keep your head turned the other way. Wait on a customer if one comes in, but then return to where I sent you."

"Yes, sir." Her hands were shaking, and she looked as if she might collapse at any moment.

Steve leaned out the window and said to his sister, "Be strong now. I want you to do something way out there by the street. I'm going to drive away from his view, but I'll be right back on foot. Trust me."

"Don't go, Steve," she whispered. "I'm scared."

"It's the only way. We've got to catch him in the act."

"I can't do it."

"Yes, you can," he said. "Believe me, I won't let anything happen to you. It's now or never. You've lived with this fear long enough." Swallowing hard, she nodded her head. There were tears of fright in her eyes.

Steve started the engine and drove slowly onto Washington Avenue, heading east. Elizabeth, avoiding a glance toward the lurker, rotated the handle on the outdoor faucet and dragged the open end of a hundred-foot hose out to the far curb. Then she worked—methodically, terribly alone—and waited.

After a few minutes, the engine of the gray Oldsmobile started up, but too distant to forewarn those at the filling station. Then, just as suddenly, the engine became silent again, as something postponed the driver's action.

It was a customer. A teenager had driven his unsightly wreck of an automobile—a 1931 Model A that appeared to have been sandblasted by desert winds—onto the property of Service Refining Company. Dinah responded with assistance, in the form of water for the steaming radiator. And then, all too soon, the customer was gone from the premises, and Elizabeth resumed her lonely ordeal.

She did not have to wait for long. With rehearsed precision, Edward Neal drove forward, then cut his engine and coasted to a stop, wholly undetected by a trusting soul who had been asked to turn her back on impending danger. Out of the hush, he was upon her, pouncing like a cat. He knocked away the hose and, swift as a calf roper, bound both hands behind her back.

Elizabeth screamed in terror, but the attacker did not even bother to silence her, so intent was he on dragging the girl toward the open door of his automobile. Even struggling for her life, she was no match for Neal's muscular frame and athleticism, and he would have made it all the way inside the vehicle were it not for a strong hand that grasped his shoulder from behind. Aflame with pent-up fury, Stephen Brower spun the abductor around and landed a hard fist into Neal's face, fracturing the nose with a loud crack and splattering blood down the front of the leather jacket. Elizabeth broke free and ran.

Though injured, Neal reacted instinctively and with the fleetness of a predatory animal. He powered an elbow into Steve's abdomen, doubling his adversary over and giving himself just enough time to reach inside the jacket for his handgun. But Steve was ready for him, having brought a weapon of his own. Before Neal could aim the pistol, he was struck full-force on the side of the head with the pointed end of a tire iron, instantly losing his left eye and suffering a deep gash to the temple. His only shot was errant, the bullet passing over Steve's right shoulder and striking some underbrush across the street. Neal's knees buckled, and he fell facedown on the pavement. Even then he was not finished, squeezing off two more ineffectual shots until Steve could plant a foot on his wrist and dislodge the weapon from his grasp. With his foot, he skidded it across the pavement and far out of reach.

"Call an ambulance," Steve shouted to Dinah, who had come running. "And the police."

"Is Elizabeth hurt?" she asked.

"I hope not. I pray she's not," he said.

Dinah ran toward the office, and Steve, after tossing down the tire iron, hurried over to his sister. He untied the thin rope that bound her wrists and put an arm around her shoulders. "You're safe now. You're safe. He won't be bothering you anymore." He was surprised to feel a wetness on his hand and to discover that it was her blood.

"What happened to your arm?" he asked, but she did not answer. Evidently, Neal's fingernails had scratched her during the violent scuffle.

"You okay?" he asked.

She nodded her head but remained mute.

"Sure?"

Still she said nothing. Instead, Elizabeth closed her eyes and began to cry, shuddering uncontrollably. As if in a daze, she took a few steps toward the gruesome scene. She stared for a moment at Edward Neal's sprawled form, his head lying in a pool of blood. And then, without warning, she lunged forward and began to scream with rage at her vanquished aggressor. She seemed irrational, near the point of hysterics. Steve prevented her from advancing any closer to the body, or no doubt she would have tried to kick Neal repeatedly in the side.

"You're safe now," he told her again. "He won't be bothering you anymore."

Steve led her away, back to the office, but three police patrol cars had already arrived before she finally began to exhibit some signs of calming down.

Realizing what she had endured over the past several months—never knowing when the stalker might strike next—he could hardly blame her for that.

Within a few minutes, ambulance workers came to rush Edward Neil to the hospital, and only two of the six investigating policemen remained at Service Refining Company. "We're pretty well finished here, miss," one of them said to Dinah, "so you can get your business back to normal." Then, to the sailor he said, "We'll have to take you downtown for more statements."

Once the last police car drove off, transporting Elizabeth back home, the quietness reminded Dinah that water was still running at full volume. Prior to calling Mr. Harkins on the telephone, she walked outside and picked up the hose, which was lying right where Elizabeth had dropped it. She squirted the pavement clean of most of the residual blood, allowing it to run into the gutter and down the storm drain. No doubt a persistent stain would cling to that spot for years to come. Such a vile blemish was capable of withstanding every effort to wash it away.

◆　　◆　　◆

The desk sergeant swore audibly when his elbow brushed against the red ink pad and sent it tumbling onto the floor. So occupied was he with his bureaucratic chores that he was not even aware that anyone else had entered the room. Spotting a lady near the doorway, he softened his language to "Criminy!" as he inspected the fresh discoloration on his long-sleeved uniform top. He took a sip of coffee and irritably slammed his cup onto the wooden surface that was his workday domain.

"This is just one of those days," he told the woman. With a loud sigh, he hopped down from his stool to retrieve the ink pad, which had landed topsy-turvy against the scarred, plywood baseboard. "Pardon my French, by the way."

"That's quite all right," she said. "Are you the officer in charge?"

"No, ma'am, but maybe I can help you."

"My son is being held for questioning."

"The sailor?"

"Yes, sir."

The desk sergeant turned the page of his blotter for reference and was about to escort the lady to an interrogation room when two young policemen appeared. "Say, Mike," he said to one of them, "Mrs. Brower's here to see her son."

"I'm on my way to the courthouse, but Darren can take care of her."

The other officer, a clean-cut man of about thirty, tipped his cap and said, "Come right this way, ma'am." They entered an adjacent room, where he added, "I'll get your boy. You can wait here."

"Is he in jail?" Nora asked.

The officer looked at her but said nothing, silently closing the door behind him.

Nervously, she took a seat on a wooden chair, not too different from that found in public school classrooms. Ten minutes passed before the young officer returned. "Your son will be right here," he told the woman.

"Is he behind bars?" she asked, but again the officer did not reply. Smiling politely, he leaned against the wall and wound the mainspring of his wristwatch.

Almost at once, some approaching voices could be heard, and Nora recognized Steve's among them. When the door opened, a pair of men accompanied her son into the room. Neither was wearing a uniform, so she assumed that they were detectives of some sort.

"Hello, Mrs. Brower," the older of the two said to her. He was a rather thin, gray-haired man with a handlebar mustache. "Your son will be free to leave in just a few minutes. We appreciate your coming down here to take him home." He pointed Steve toward one of the remaining empty chairs. "Have a seat, Mr. Brower. This won't take long."

Nora studied Steve's appearance and decided that he seemed none the worse for wear from his clash with the hoodlum. There were no obvious bruises or lacerations to be seen. Nor was he wearing any shackles or handcuffs, so perhaps there would be no legal proceedings in the wake of the violence. Steve gave her a reassuring smile.

Now the younger plainclothesman, very muscular and athletic-looking, became the spokesperson. "We're sorry that we had to hold your son all this time," he said, "but when the case became a federal matter, of course we had to go through the proper channels."

Shock was evident on Nora's face. "Are you G-men?" Her question sounded more dramatic than she intended.

"I guess you could put it that way, ma'am," the younger agent said. "My name is Colley, and this is Samford. We were called in for two reasons. One, your son's in the military. Two, it turned out that the suspect is wanted on felony charges in another state."

Nora was visibly impressed, but not by the outstanding warrants. "You came here all the way from the FBI in Washington?" she asked.

Agent Colley contrived a modest grin. "No, we're local ... assigned to a field office at the Federal Building, right here in Waco."

Mrs. Brower looked more closely at her son, and she noticed that there were bloodstains on the right arm of his uniform.

Seeing her concern, Colley apologized. "We hope you understand that the police can't allow civil disturbances of any type to go uninvestigated, so they had to bring your son in for questioning. Turns out it was pretty routine."

Agent Samford nodded his head. "By all accounts, your son only resorted to using a weapon after the suspect pulled a gun on him. Clearly self-defense, no question."

"A *gun?*" Nora asked. She looked more closely at Steve's uniform.

"Don't worry, ma'am," Colley told her. "That's not your son's blood. The suspect's in a hospital, and he won't be getting out anytime soon."

Steve said, "I'm fine, Mom—really."

"Are you sure?"

He nodded his head. "Oh, I've got a couple of bruised ribs, and my right hand's a little bit sore, but ..."

That brought even more worries than before, so Steve kissed her on the cheek. "Look, Mom. I got banged up worse than this at football practice."

In obeisance to the feds, the Waco officer had been standing there in silence, but now, glancing at the wall clock, he asked the agents, "Where's the other fellow?"

"His stepmother picked him up a half-hour ago," Samford said. Then he turned to Nora and added, "Your son's free to go too, if you're ready. We just wanted to say a few words to you, to let you know everything's complete here."

"Thank you. That was very kind of you."

"Yes, thanks for helping to sort this out," Steve said. He stood up to leave.

Agent Samford grinned at him. "Looks like you got some good combat training, son."

"Yes, sir."

On the way home, with Nora driving, Steve filled her in on a few sordid details. The suspect, Edward Neal, was wanted by Nevada authorities on charges of attempted murder and rape. "And to think," she said, "that monster was inside our house—looking at your bedroom. Remembering that gives me the chills."

Steve stared out the passenger window. "I'm just glad Lizzie's all right," he said. "I swear to God, I would have killed that vermin if he'd hurt her."

When Nora looked at her son and his bloodstained uniform, tears came to her eyes. "That was a very brave thing you did today." She nearly choked on the words. "No two ways about it ... you're a genuine hero."

Steve shook his head. "No, I'm far from a hero. If we can't even face up to thugs like that, how can we fight the Germans and Japs?"

"Well, Lizzie will always think of you as a hero."

"Maybe so," he said, "but it's just not true. The Sullivans were heroes. And Doris Miller, he was a hero at Pearl Harbor. Jeez, all I did was protect my kid sister from a bully. People do that every day on the playground."

"You may have saved her life."

"Oh, I don't think—"

"He had a gun."

"Well, sure, but—"

"Did he or did he not have a loaded gun?"

Steve marveled at his mother's persistence. "Yes, counselor, he did."

As the automobile slowly made its way across Proctor Avenue, one thing still puzzled Nora Brower. "Who was the other person the police were talking to?" she asked.

"What other person?"

"The policeman said there was someone else being questioned with you."

Steve had to laugh. "Oh, that boy in the tow truck—what's his name?"

"Bradley?"

"Could be."

"Missing teeth in front?" she asked.

"Yep, kind of shallow thinking."

"That's Bradley Gann. Lizzie works with him sometimes."

"Well, this Bradley came back after all the excitement was over. The ambulance was already gone by then, but he parked his wrecker a few inches behind two of the squad cars."

"Oh, dear."

"Then he walked over to me and asked, at the top of his voice, 'Didja catch the German spy?' That really got the cops' attention."

"Poor Bradley. I'm sure he meant well."

Steve laughed. "They wanted to hustle him downtown, but those two cars were blocked by his truck. One of the cops was really mad, pacing back and forth like a caged lion. I think the boy thought they were going to stand him up against a wall and execute him right there at the filling station."

◆　　◆　　◆

Stephen Brower had a long-standing invitation from his younger brother to witness a performance of "Behold Tomorrow" sometime while he was on a furlough from military duty. Initially, this offer was extended in the form of a postscript that Wesley appended to a letter from his mother. Now, with Steve's embarkation leave drawing to a close, it became clear that Thursday afternoon would be his last opportunity to attend. Wesley scrambled to make the necessary arrangements.

It so happened that one of the show's production staff, technical director Sol Glickman, had a stepson named Wally Hirsch, who graduated with Steve from Waco High School. Like most of the males in the Class of 1943, Wally was away in uniform, but Steve had become acquainted with the boy's father as well, through two scrap drives in which they used Glickman's 1.5-ton Chevrolet flatbed to haul discarded major appliances to the Square. Wesley inquired whether it might be permissible for Steve to watch from the control room, and Glickman replied that he would be honored to welcome him as his personal guest, even promising to give him "the full fifty-cent tour" once the studio was vacated. After all, he said, his stepson, too, was a serviceman—and a fellow member of the United States Navy.

In point of fact, Steve had been to the radio station on two previous occasions. The first was way back when he was a boy of six, nearly seven, in the early summer of 1932. His father took him to KWXN's "Dog and Pony Show," an unabashedly silly audience-participation program for children that aired on Saturday mornings for about three years, until it was canceled soon after the resignation of its hyperkinetic master of ceremonies, Jiggs Rolland, who, under a pseudonym, went on to bigger and better things in the southeast. The second time was when Steve's entire eighth-grade class toured the studios on a field trip during the fall of 1938, only three weeks before Harold Brower's sudden and unexpected death. The "tour guide" on that day, teenager Richie Seegers, would later be killed in a flight-training exercise at Goodfellow Field in San Angelo.

On this current visit, the first thing that Steve noticed about live radio presentations was how frenetic everybody appeared to be prior to airtime. Cast and crew were running to and from the studio—shouting at the top of their lungs, grinding their teeth, even reduced to cursing—until just a few seconds before the broadcast began. He wondered why this should be. After all, it was not as though the three-o'clock "curtain" took anybody by surprise.

In common with most laymen, Steve was blissfully unaware of the innumerable minutiae that had to be resolved in order for a radio drama to succeed as an effectively mounted performance. A relatively innocent last-minute change of dialogue, for instance, might precipitate the altering of other characters' lines or the deletion of an entire thread of subplot material from the story narrative. Worse yet, any lost time would then have to be replaced "on the fly" by the writers or, if absolutely necessary, by the script girl, usually Monica Whaley.

Once the April 20 program began, and despite the fascinating process that unfolded before him in the studio, Steve found it increasingly difficult to look anywhere but at the attractive Monica, who stood, clipboard in hand, not more than twenty feet to his right. Though seven years his senior, she retained a youthful loveliness that endeared her to wolves, romantics, and schoolboys alike, virtually any male who found himself in the control room on a weekday afternoon. Perhaps she could sense Steve's interest, for she assiduously avoided glancing in his direction for whatever reason, even when it might have been deemed a normal response to Kenton's barking of orders. Noting the sailor's divided attention, Sol Glickman leaned over to him and whispered with an understanding smile, "Third Finger, Left Hand," the title of a recent motion picture starring Myrna Loy and Melvyn Douglas. Steve saw Monica's sparkling gemstone and nodded his thanks.

It occurred to the visiting serviceman that his brother's role in the radio play was, for the most part, to sit quietly in a chair behind those who actually stepped up to the microphones and articulated their lines. But this was an atypical episode of "Behold Tomorrow," for Kip Hanson did not appear on the scene until the final ninety seconds of airtime—and even then he only had four passages of dialogue to deliver:

"Where's Bud? I haven't seen him since the banquet."
"Don't talk about him like that! He's worth ten of you."
"Hank Carrigan must've done it."
"Okay, whatever you say, but he'll be coming back to check on the shipment ... and Trixie's gonna go through the roof if he tells her it's still here in the warehouse."

When the program was over, and the stentorian announcer began to intone his commercial adjacency, a handful of cast members—Wesley included—departed through the studio door, and a roughly equal number of performers appeared at the microphones for "West of the Brazos." One of the beauties of radio, of course, was that no costume changes were necessary for those actors who worked both shows. A fresh script in hand was all that was required for him or her to transport the audience from wartime Baltimore to the dusty streets of Old Waco.

Neither was it particularly troubling for the sound-effects man to tackle a double-duty assignment. On this particular day—the script calling for an unusually modest array of paraphernalia—Rodney DeBonaventura found enough spare time during the interim to pore over the *Daily Racing Form* while maneuvering his unschooled but robust baritone through two and a half verses of "Aura Lee."

With the second of KWXN's afternoon serials about to begin, Steve tapped Sol Glickman on the arm, nodded thanks to him, and then tiptoed out the control room door, meeting up with his brother, as planned, in the hallway to the offices.

He said, "Well done, Mr. Kip Hanson!" and offered his hand.

But Wesley did not acknowledge the compliment or return the handshake. "Did you see that ... that hussy?" was all the response he could manage. He was livid, barely able to restrain himself from punching the wall.

"Which one?" Steve asked. He thought a joke might take the edge off his brother's rage.

"Oh, you saw her. The one in the booth—with the announcer. That d—" He could not bring himself to finish the sentence.

"Nope, I didn't see any girl."

"She was there all right—sitting on the floor and smiling up at him, even holding his hand. And of course he goes on with his high-and-mighty announcing, as if nothing was happening." Wesley shook his head, taking a deep breath. "Very unprofessional. I hope Kenton lowers the boom on both of them."

"Well, maybe he will."

"I doubt it. The station can't seem to do enough for those two."

"Was that Marshall McFall in there?" Steve asked.

"How'd you guess?"

"I thought I recognized his voice."

"Oh, sure, the great and famous Marshall McFall—God's gift to microphones."

"Have they got something going?"

"Who knows? All I can say is that Sandy has really changed—as a person—since she started working here."

The name rang a bell in Steve's memory, and he gave his brother a look of surprise. "Is this the same Sandy you were chasing a few months ago?"

Wesley could hardly believe his ears. "What makes you say that? I never chased after her. In fact, if you ask me, it was the other way around."

Steve could not help but laugh. "You were pretty sweet on her, as I recall."

"Okay, maybe so," Wesley said, "but she's not the same person she used to be. We hardly speak anymore—unless she wants something from me."

Steve nodded his head. "I've known girls like that."

"I even got an autograph for her from that actor who plays Dagwood Bumstead in pictures."

"Yeah?"

"I met him on the train, coming home."

"No kidding? Was 'Blondie' with him?"

"Not that I saw. I think he was on personal business."

"Was Sandy excited to get it?"

"I don't know. I haven't given it to her because she's never even bothered to say a word about it." Wesley shook his head in disgust. "And after all I went through to get that autograph."

"I'd keep it for myself, if I were you."

"Don't worry. I plan to."

The receptionist, Myra Culp, had been away from her desk when Steve arrived at the radio station, but she was back at her post when the brothers walked toward the front of the building. Wesley introduced them to one another, and Myra said, "Always pleased to meet a boy in uniform—especially a good-looking one of marriageable age."

Wesley shook his head. "Don't mind her. She's all talk. Besides, she's old enough to be your—"

"Much older sister," Myra said, and she winked at the sailor. "How long are you in town?"

"Just today. I've been here all week."

Myra frowned at Wesley. "Why'd you keep him such a secret?"

"I didn't want you to get your hooks into him, that's all."

One of the station's salesmen, Calvin Trent, passed by, pausing just long enough to turn his card to "OUT." He was a sloppy dresser for someone in his line of work, habitually chewing on a cigar butt and tightening his sagging necktie. "See you later, sweetcakes," he said to the receptionist.

"Don't forget to write," she told him.

The studio door opened about that time, and a half-dozen or more "talent" made their way, laughing and joking, toward the employees' lounge. Sure enough, the overhead speakers confirmed that "West of the Brazos" had come to an end. After the ten-second station identification, a network announcer came on the air, presenting his opening remarks for "Time Views the News."

Oblivious to Wesley's presence in the lobby was Sandra Whittsel, who exited the studio with actress Beverly Jaynes and turned down the long corridor to follow the other performers. But something caught her eye just then, causing her to look at the front desk. She flashed a grin at the handsome sailor before noticing that Wesley, too, was standing right there, alongside him. Beverly proceeded on, but it seemed perfectly natural for Sandy to approach the young men. Indeed, it would have been discourteous to simply walk away without saying a word to them.

"Great show today," she told Wesley, but she was looking at Steve when she said it.

"I think it went pretty well," the boy said. "Doug messed up a couple of words, and of course Phyllis lost her place and missed that cue."

"She did?"

Wesley glared at her. "Maybe you weren't paying much attention."

"When was all this?"

"Right near the end—until Neddy pointed to her line in the script. I almost had to start ad-libbing, and I'm not very good at that."

She giggled. "How well I know."

Myra leaned forward to hand Sandy three or four envelopes. "Fan mail for Miss Sally Holt. Not much today."

"Thanks." She glanced again at Steve. "Well, Wes, aren't you even going to introduce me?"

Embarrassed, Wesley cleared his throat. "Sandy, I'd like for you to meet my older brother, Stephen. He's home on leave."

"Hello, Stephen," she said. "So you're the football player then?"

"I played, yes."

"And Steve," Wesley continued, "this is Sandra Whittsel. You've probably heard me mention her once or twice. She goes to school with me."

"How do you do?" Steve said. He studied her pretty face. "Do you go by Sandra or Sandy?"

She looked up and smiled. "That depends. Do you go by Stephen or Steve?"

Myra glanced knowingly at Wesley, whose face reddened.

"Steve is fine," the sailor said.

"How long will you be in town?" Sandy asked him.

"Only until tomorrow morning."

The corners of her mouth descended into a pout. "Gee, that's a shame. Then I won't get to see you again."

"No. I'll be going directly to the train station."

"Well, in that case," she said, "I'll just have to keep track of you through Wes. I'm sure he won't mind."

Wesley raised his eyebrows at this presumptuous notion, but he managed to hold his tongue.

Steve, though, detected nothing but kindness in her suggestion, and he granted consent without the slightest hesitation. "Oh, I'm sure it'll be all right with him," he told her. Sandy's dark brown eyes were lovely, and Steve—try though he might—was finding it more and more difficult to remain aloof. So this was the girl who had stolen his brother's heart those many months ago. Small wonder, he thought.

The pungent smell of tobacco smoke announced Hugh Kenton's arrival in the lobby even before Wesley was able to spot him behind soundman Dickie Waterhouse, college intern Brian Quaid, technical director Sol Glickman, and sponsor Anthony Potter.

"There he is," Kenton said. Cigar ashes floated to the floor as he walked toward the front desk. "Listen, Wes. Sol says this might be a good time for him to show your brother around, if you can spare him for a few minutes."

Wesley agreed, so Steve reluctantly followed Glickman from the lobby, turning to take one final look at his newest acquaintance.

When they finally disappeared from view behind the heavy studio door, Wesley could feel Sandy's gaze shift from Steve to himself, and he heard her say with practiced detachment, "When did your brother graduate? I don't ever remember seeing him at school." She was idly fingering the glass lid of an empty candy bowl that sat atop the desk.

"Last May," Wesley told her. There was absolutely no reaction, nothing to indicate that she even heard what he said. "It's pretty obvious you weren't here for football season."

"I sure remember him," Myra said. "He was a Big Man on Campus, wasn't he, Wes? Had his name in the paper every Saturday."

Wesley looked carefully at Sandy, trying to decide what her motives might have been in asking such a question, but she remained expressionless, ever the enigma.

That changed the instant she glanced at Myra Culp. Unaccountably, for reasons beyond male understanding, the pair of women began to smile at each other, then to giggle, and then to outright laugh with abandon. Wesley was at a loss for an explanation, and he suddenly felt quite out of place—like the only man at a baby shower. The best he could figure, their curious behavior had something to do with the recent presence of a well-built male athlete who made a striking appearance in his government-issue uniform.

Myra was laughing so hard that tears were in her eyes. So was Sandy—that is, until she quickly wiped them away with the back of her hand upon seeing McFall come into the lobby with Douglas Pierson. The announcer marched right up to the desk and asked the receptionist if he had any mail. He patted Pierson on the back. "You want a Dr. Pepper? I'm buying." They walked away, toward the soda pop dispenser, and Wesley could see that Sandy's eyes were following McFall's every step. She seemed to have lost all interest in everything else, even to the point of failing to hear a parcel post worker when he asked her to step aside for a moment so he could lay a package on the corner of Myra's desk.

Wesley felt betrayed, slapped in the face, and he sensed that it was high time to clear the air.

"I was surprised to see you there today," he said. "Evidently, you watch the show even when your character's not in the script."

The remark caught Sandy off guard. "Sure I do, silly. Don't you?"

"Not very often," he told her. "But then I don't have such a cozy place to view it from either." His face seemed flushed, even confrontational.

She sighed. "And what could you possibly mean by that?"

"I mean, it's awfully embarrassing to see you in the announcing booth, alone with a man. What were you supposed to be doing in there anyway, tapping the ashes off Marshall's cigarette?"

"I fail to see what concern it is of yours."

"What if a sponsor saw you ... or a class of school kids? Did you ever think of that?"

"Oh, so it's the station's reputation that you're worried about."

"Right."

That made her grin. "Wesley Brower, you're just too good to be true."

"Is that so?"

"Yes, and you know what else I think? I think you're jealous of Marshall McFall—that's what I think." She shrugged her shoulders. "Oh, well, I suppose I should be flattered."

"That's a conceited thing to say. Why should I be jealous of Marshall McFall? It would mean that I care something about you, and that's just not true."

She thought for a moment, smiled, and then lightly touched the tip of his nose with her index finger. "Poor Wesley," she whispered. "You can't even be honest with yourself. You know you care for me ... at least a smidgen." Now she seemed to be toying with him, relishing the verbal exchange as if acting out her part in some stage production. Even having the stunned Myra Culp sitting there as a captive audience did not seem to bother her in the least. With a playful look, Sandy asked, "You're in tomorrow's show, aren't you?"

"Just a few lines," Wesley said. "It's mostly Doug and Phyllis."

She yawned and stretched, elbows nearly touching behind her back. "I don't think we're in any scenes together, are we?"

"Not tomorrow."

"Too bad. I think Sally and Kip are sort of cute together, don't you?"

He laughed. "I guess so. We've only been on the same page about twice." There was always a chance that the writers were building up to a stronger relationship between them, though.

Sandy glanced at her wristwatch. "Will you walk with me to the lounge?" Again Wesley felt the delicious sensation of falling captive to her charm.

"We do have time, don't we?" he asked.

"Uh-huh. My script's in there."

A few people had emerged from the room, but most were still relaxing inside.

"Rehearsal starts in a couple of minutes," Hugh Kenton said as he passed by the lounge. In one hand was his cigar and in the other a freshly brewed cup of coffee—an inviolable routine for him at this particular juncture of the day. "Sandy, you're first up ... over some train noise," he told the girl, "so maybe you should work on your levels with Rodney ahead of time."

"Right away, Mr. Kenton," she said.

Kenton gave her a cheerful wink. "I'll have Dickie standing by."

Sandy started walking toward the studio. "Wes, be a dear and get my script for me, will you? Your legs are longer than mine."

He nodded his head and then rushed down the hallway, nearly colliding with Glickman and Pierson en route.

Sandy, too, was in a hurry. She entered the studio—just in time to exchange smiles with the attractive serviceman, whose backstage tour was coming to an end.

◆　　◆　　◆

Steve's last night at home was a restless one. He was in bed by eleven o'clock but slept spasmodically. Once—it must have been a couple of hours later—he thought he could hear his mother sobbing outside the bedroom, and the pitiful sound tore at his heart. She seemed to be whispering to someone, probably Elizabeth, and he was tempted to get up and give them both a hug of assurance. But his instinct told him that this would only make matters worse, so he rolled onto his side and placed the pillow over his ear, hoping to catch a few hours of slumber before daybreak.

When next he awoke, he felt physically and mentally drained. His subconscious had worked overtime during the interim, contriving worrisome dreams that awarded him precious little peace. Now, as he lay there, he could hear the rhythm of deep breathing from across the room, where Wesley slept on a sturdy but none-too-comfortable camping cot. Careful not to disturb him, Steve shined a flashlight on the alarm clock and saw that it was ten minutes to three.

A half-hour of wakefulness later, he finally decided that it was futile to struggle against this persistent form of insomnia. Too many weighty considerations crowded upon his mind—thoughts of the frigid sea, shipboard fires, the Japs, home, mother, family, death. Even when sitting up in bed, his body felt no inclination to relax and succumb to drowsiness. The troubling concepts swirled all about, stubbornly rejecting surcease, until finally he resolved to wander downstairs and have a smoke. He could make up for his lost hours of sleep once he was on the train.

Valentino accompanied him down the dark stairway, directly underfoot for much of the way, so Steve had to descend very gingerly in order to avoid stepping on him. No light shone through the living room curtains—it being almost a new moon—but his "seaman's eye" enabled him to switch on the floor lamp without mishap. He warmed up some leftover coffee in the kitchen, carried the steaming cup to his father's study, and then relaxed at the writing table with the first book he spotted on the shelves—*Babbitt* by Sinclair Lewis—one of the relatively few works of fiction to be found in the Harold Brower collection. "His name was George F. Babbitt," Steve read. "He was forty-six years old now, in April, 1920, and he made nothing in particular, neither butter nor shoes nor poetry, but he was nimble in the calling of selling houses for more than people could afford to pay." Steve lit up his pipe of nearly expended tobacco, found contentment in taking a few leisurely puffs, but then laid the pipe down to allow its fire to go out. He read on, for as long as he could abide, but the balm of sleepiness stubbornly refused to descend upon him.

He heard the clock chime four times, and that made him think of the radio news and his old habit of searching around the dial for clear-channel stations that reached Waco only in the wee hours of the morning. Overnight was an entirely different world of listening, with odd sounds and exotic call letters, many of which began with the letter "W" rather than "K." On this particular occasion—using his father's Emerson "Duo-Vox" table radio—he was able to pick up transmissions from as far away as WAPI in Birmingham, WHO in Des Moines, WTIC in Hartford, WCCO in Minneapolis, and KFI in Los Angeles. He was straining to hear yet another distant signal when a rattling, metallic noise caught his attention.

Evidence of a key in the front door surely would have alarmed him in ordinary times, but he was aware that the worker who boarded with them kept rather strange hours—to meet the insatiable demands of war production. In any case, Hannah was probably more surprised than Steve. Attracted by the unusual sight of light emanating from Mr. Brower's study so early in the morning, she peeked around the corner and saw the sailor, dressed in pajamas and bathrobe, draining the last drops of liquid from his coffee cup. His pipe and a book lay on the writing table in front of him, and the radio brought forth a dimly heard program that seemed to contain roughly equal measures of dance music and static.

"Couldn't sleep?" she asked.

"Nope. Last time at home for a while, you know. Are you just getting off the job?"

Hannah nodded her head. "I was only supposed to work the swing shift, but I took the first half of a graveyard too."

Steve picked up his dormant pipe, discarded its expired contents into an ashtray, and began the process of refilling. During his months in the service, he had discovered that this always seemed to help him unwind, whether he was alone or in the company of others. But that was not his only reason for choosing this particular moment to do so. In common with most pipe smokers, he just naturally assumed, whether accurately or not, that ladies had an instinctive attraction for its sweet aroma. He smiled at the boarder, not even bothering to ask if she minded.

"Are you still going to Baylor?" he said.

"Don't I look like it?" She laughed, apparently in reference to her present attire. Hannah was wearing an unflattering, one-piece jumpsuit that seemed to be tailored for the mobility of an overweight shade-tree mechanic. Her face was smudged with grease, her hair was a chaotic mess, and the ungainly work shoes were at least two sizes too large and discolored by toxic solvents of every description.

"How do you keep these hours and still pass your classes?" Steve asked.

"I have a 'walk' in my nine-o'clock today. Otherwise, I couldn't have done it."

"What do you mean, a 'walk'?"

"My psychology teacher's out of town, so my first class isn't until eleven."

He raised his eyebrows. "Psychology, huh? Is that your major?"

"Hardly," she said. "I'm a Bible student. In fact, that's the only reason I transferred to Baylor. You can take psych anywhere. My nine-o'clock is just an elective—Psychology 225, 'Mental Hygiene'."

He gave her a playful wink. "Well?"

"Well, what?"

"Are you mentally hygienic?"

She sighed, rolling her eyes. "Reasonably so—although I can think of at least one prof who might argue with that."

"Let me guess," Steve said. He took a shallow puff. "Your Bible professor?"

"How'd you know?"

"You just seem passionate about it, that's all, so I figured you might have had a run-in."

"It was just a friendly disagreement, but I don't think he's ever forgiven me for contradicting him in class."

Steve nodded his head. "Don't I recall that your daddy's a minister?" He already knew the answer, but he wanted to keep the conversation going a while longer, loath to return to his solitude.

"That's right," she said. "He's a Southern Baptist preacher." Her voice was beginning to sound hollow and tired.

"In North Carolina?" he asked.

"Yep." She stole a glance at the desk clock.

"Uh, Winston-Salem?"

"Close ... Mount Airy. You've got a good memory."

"Not really. My mother was talking about you to Lizzie a couple of days ago, and I just happened to overhear."

That aroused her curiosity. "Why would they be talking about me?"

"Oh, nothing very mysterious," he said. "I think you got a letter from back home or something."

Hannah nodded her head. The strain of working for twelve straight hours was taking its toll, and she seemed suddenly distant–anxious to be anywhere but leaning against a doorjamb, conducting small talk in the pre-dawn hours. "Well, it's been nice chatting, but I've really got to get some sleep."

"Wait!" Steve rose to his feet. "Don't go yet. It's nice having someone to talk to."

"Even if I'm half asleep?"

"Even so."

Hannah yawned, right on cue, which caused them both to laugh.

"Say, I'm going to get another cup of coffee," he said. "You want some?"

She shook her head. "It keeps me awake, and that's the last thing I need right now."

"Well, at least convoy me to the kitchen." He grinned at the girl. "I'm afraid of the dark ... and you never know what might be lurking."

Hannah shook her head but then clomped along behind him in her oversized shoes. "All I can say is there better not be a wolf in there."

"Nope. Wolves walk on all fours."

Steve lit the gas burner with a loud *poof* and then turned it high enough to boil the pot's contents in a matter of seconds.

"Sure you won't have any?" he asked when the beverage was piping hot.

"No, thanks. Honestly, I only drink coffee in the morning."

"It *is* the morning."

"You know what I mean."

He sat himself at the breakfast table, but Hannah declined to join him. "I'll be going up now," she said again, and this time she followed through. Taking a sip of scalding coffee, Steve caught a final glimpse of the boarder as she casually waved goodbye and then disappeared into the shadows of the entryway.

Surrendering to the comfort of the living room's easy chair, Steve slept fitfully for a half-hour or so, until he was awakened by the gentle noise of clinking glass. He figured it must be around five o'clock because that is when the milkman usually made his way to the Brower household on his daily rounds.

Steve walked toward the back door as the truck reversed itself down the gravel driveway, and he wondered for a moment whether the deliveryman was still Mr. Jackey. He opened the door just enough to see the bottles–three quarts of milk and a pint of cream–in their resting place on the porch, while adeptly using one foot to discourage Valentino from scampering outside so early in the morning. Then, by the handle of their metal rack, he carried the bottles inside and placed them, one-by-one, in the refrigerator. He laid the empty rack in its customary place by the door.

When he turned around, he was startled to see Hannah standing in the kitchen, no more than ten feet away. She was still dressed in her jumpsuit but now wore slippers instead of the heavy work shoes. That explained why he did not hear her come into the room. Her hair had been brushed, and her face was freshly scrubbed.

Puzzled by her presence, Steve said, "I thought you were sleepy."

"Your insomnia must be contagious," Hannah told him. "Usually I don't have any trouble falling asleep, but now I'm wide awake. Sorry."

"Don't apologize. I can use the company."

"Any coffee left?"

He shook the pot and offered to make a new batch.

With a loud sigh, Hannah said, "You know, I almost dropped off a few minutes ago, but then that milk truck woke me up again. I never even made it out of my work clothes."

"So I see."

She frowned. "Is it really that ugly?"

"Well ..."

"Tell me the truth."

"The truth? You look fine."

"Thanks for that—although I guess compliments don't mean much, coming from a sailor home on leave."

"I may be a sailor, but I'm a lot harder to please than most of them."

"That's very flattering, I guess—even if it *is* just a line."

Steve smiled but said nothing.

When they carried their coffee into the living room, Steve seated himself on the sofa instead of the easy chair, a maneuver that did not go unnoticed. Hannah sat about two feet away from him and cautiously laid her cup near his on the coffee table.

"What happened to your fingers?" she asked. Steve still wore a small bandage across the knuckles of his right hand.

"Oh, I got mixed up with a troublemaker a couple days ago. He was bothering my sister."

Hannah looked shocked. "He did that to your hand?"

"No, I did that to my own hand. I slugged him in the nose, and I guess one of his teeth must have cut me."

"Was that the same man who's been ...?" She thought back for a moment. "Your mother said someone's been following Lizzie around for months."

"Same guy," Steve said. "He'll be locked up now. The cops have plenty on him."

"Gosh. I just saw your sister yesterday, and she seemed perfectly normal—happy even. She was bringing in some beans from the victory garden."

"I think she's still in shock. Either that, or she's just relieved to get this animal off the streets." Steve took a sip of coffee, and there was a sparkle of pride in his eyes. "Lizzie's plenty tough inside. Not many girls would have put themselves in danger like that."

"What do you mean?" Hannah picked up her coffee and blew on its surface.

"We had to flush him out of his hiding place—to catch him in the act."

"That's scary." She took the tiniest of sips.

"We didn't find out he was armed until later."

"Good Lord," she said. "A gun?"

He nodded his head.

"Well, I'd say you were pretty courageous yourself."

Steve scoffed at the notion. "Don't give me too much credit," he said. "To tell you the truth, I really didn't think he had a gun when I slugged him. I'm not that crazy."

"Did he shoot at you?"

"Just once, but he didn't have time to aim. I guess he was more of a rodeo star than a marksman."

"Thank God."

"He shot a couple more times, but by then he was lying flat on his kisser."

Hannah studied Steve's face for a moment, even squinting as she took another sip of coffee. "You seem pretty calm about it. Weren't you afraid?"

"Not too much. I didn't have time to be scared."

"I would have been."

"No. Like I said, I didn't think he had a weapon. And besides, I had one of my own."

She was wide-eyed. "You had a gun too?"

"Nope, just an everyday tire iron. One of those things you use to change a flat."

Hannah grinned. "I always thought it was a jack. That's what my daddy called it."

"Not to lift up the car, silly—to pry off the hubcaps and loosen the lug nuts."

"And so, you hit him with that?"

"Had to. He wouldn't have missed again at such close range."

"But the police know it was self-defense, don't they? You're not in any kind of trouble."

"Sure they do." He leaned toward her and lowered his voice. "I probably shouldn't be telling you this, but one of those detectives offered to buy me a steak dinner for what I did. He said it'll look good for Waco PD to have caught this bum. Evidently, he's got a whole slew of convictions out west."

Hannah became very serious, staring at him with glistening eyes. "Well, you're just being modest. I still say it was a brave thing for you to do."

Steve laughed. "If I knew he was such a criminal, I might not have done anything. I'm no hero."

Quietly she said, "I think you would have ... just exactly the same. I really do."

♦   ♦   ♦

Late that morning—a few minutes before noon—the train on which Steve would be riding pulled into Waco's passenger depot for a short stay of a half-hour, to take on water and fuel before heading for Fort Worth and destinations to the west. It was drawn by a steam engine of the old-fashioned type, many of which were pressed into service during the national emergency. The Katy had several on its tracks.

Nora, in common with every war mother, was saddened by her son's impending departure for battle. But there was something else that appeared to cause her almost as much distress—the fact that she was the only person there to see him off. "It just doesn't seem right," she told a kindly porter who was leaning on the tall handle of his luggage cart. When he nodded his understanding, she said, "And it breaks my heart to see him leave like this."

Wesley and Elizabeth had wished Steve goodbye earlier in the day and were now in their respective classrooms at Waco High School. Nora's closest friend, Mabel Johns, was helping with gauze preparation at the Red Cross Surgical Dressing Center on Austin Avenue. Giulia Coletti was scheduled to work that afternoon at Rawley Flooring. Hannah Lane was in class at Baylor University. And Madeleine Givens, who had indicated she might be present—it being her day off from the Washington Avenue USO—was needed as a substitute at the newly opened Franklin Avenue facility near the river.

During the wait, Steve wore a cheerful face but at the cost of considerable emotional sinew, particularly in view of his lack of adequate sleep the night before. He wished the entire ordeal were over—not that he wanted to leave but because he dreaded those painful moments of farewell that were sure to come. Though a sentimental part of him was disappointed that the others were not there to say goodbye, his more pragmatic side, steeling itself for the spartan deprivations ahead, would have preferred that there be no one around at all.

Finally, the call came—"All 'board!"—and Nora began to cry profusely. Steve hugged her and kissed her on the cheek. "I'd better go," he whispered. "Don't want to miss the war, you know." His determinedly upbeat tone of voice masked the way he really felt.

"Goodbye, son," was all Nora managed to say through trembling lips, but her tearful eyes conveyed more sorrow than any words possibly could. She clutched one of his hands in her own and would not let go.

"I'll write as often as I can," he said. "Maybe it'll all be over in a few months." He tugged his hand from her grasp and took a step backward. Then, forcing a smile, he winked at her and began to turn around, hoisting the heavy seabag atop his shoulder.

From the periphery of his gaze appeared the slim figure of a girl, possibly of high school age or a bit older, who was running toward the boarding platform. He dismissed her from his mind because she did not seem familiar to him—that is, until a few seconds later when she removed her hat and slowed her approach to a walk.

"I was afraid I'd miss you," Giulia Coletti said to him. She was panting, out of breath from her dash across the parking lot. She nodded a greeting to Nora, who smiled back. Steve surmised that his mother must have told Giulia the time of his leaving, for certainly he himself had not done so. He figured that such information would have no positive effect anyway—only jeopardizing the girl's job status in the estimation of her punctilious boss.

"Mr. Sawyer drove me over," Giulia said. She motioned to a rotund businessman who waved at them from a hundred or more feet away. "He's on a sales call, so it wasn't very far out of his way. His name's Marlon, but everyone calls him 'Mutt'."

Steve laughed. "Well, tell 'Mutt' thanks for me."

"All 'board!" came the conductor's call, and this time it was more insistent than before.

"You'd better go, Steve," the girl said. "I just wanted to say goodbye."

The train's air brakes let off a cloud of steam, nearly concealing a little boy who was boarding ahead of his civilian father. Once those two were safely clear of the vestibule door, Steve tossed his bag onto the top step of the coach and turned to Giulia. "Goodbye," he said. "I'm glad you could come. It means a lot to me."

Giving one last glance at his mother, he stepped upon the bright yellow footstool and then, with a metallic clank, onto the bottom plate of the entrance. Before he could ascend any higher, however, Giulia had taken his hand and pulled him back to street level. With tears in her eyes, she kissed him warmly on the lips, in full view of every well-wisher on the platform—including, of course, Nora Brower, who was busy wiping away tears of her own. Without another word, Steve climbed aboard, retrieving his seabag and disappearing from view into the coach.

Mere moments later, the train lurched noisily and started to move forward, its wheels squeaking across the shiny rails. As it picked up speed, the more jaded onlookers quickly lost interest and returned, through the passenger depot, to their waiting vehicles. Some, though, stayed to watch the "rattler" snake its way toward the obscured horizon. Among them were Nora Brower and Giulia Coletti, who now stood next to each other, connected in a shared sense of loss.

"How often do you write to him, Mrs. Brower?" the girl asked when there was nothing more to see.

"At least three times a week, usually," the lady told her. "I'm sure he gets tired of reading the same old news over and over again."

"I hardly think so," Giulia said. She noticed that Mutt Sawyer was still leaning against the building, puffing contentedly on the final inch of his cigar. "I'd better get back to work. I didn't tell Steve this, but my ride had to concoct a story for me to leave."

"Oh?"

They began walking toward the loitering businessman, who seemed unaware even that the train had pulled out from the station. There he stood, patiently chomping his cigar stub and flipping through a small stack of tattered papers.

"My boss thinks Mr. Sawyer took me with him to visit a client," Giulia said. She did not appear to be overly concerned, nearly breaking into a smile.

"You don't think you'll get into trouble, do you?" Nora asked.

"As long as Mr. Sawyer lands an order from Hubby-Reese, everything will be fine. Butler Lindeman has been working on them for months."

Mutt Sawyer looked up when the women were about ten feet away, and he removed his hat.

"Mr. Sawyer," Giulia said, "I'd like for you to meet Mrs. Brower."

"How do you do?" He responded with a friendly grin and tossed the cigar onto the pavement with his free hand. "Giulia thinks very highly of your son."

"Well, she's very sweet to say so," Nora said. She smiled at the girl. "I can't begin to tell you how much I appreciate her helping me give Stephen a proper send-off."

"But it was Mr. Sawyer who gave me the ride," Giulia said. "Otherwise, I couldn't have been here at all."

Nora took his hand and patted it between her own. "That was a very Christian thing to do, and I'm sure the Lord will repay you for your thoughtfulness."

The salesman turned a little red in the face. "Chrissakes, it was the least I could do," he said. "I've got to be in this part of town anyway—only a few blocks down Mary."

"Well, thank you just the same, Mr. Sawyer. You needn't have done so."

"Glad to, ma'am." He put his hat back on, embarrassed at all the attention. He looked up to watch a flock of birds fly overhead. "Say, Mrs. Brower," he added, "do you need a lift anywhere? Anywhere at all. I've got time on my hands today—just two calls to make."

"No, sir, but thank you for the kind offer. My car's right over there in the lot."

A few minutes later, as Mutt was chauffeuring Giulia back to work, Nora experienced a sudden chill inside—not loneliness really, but a stabbing, empty feeling. Sitting in the automobile only made matters worse. In order to drive home safely, she had to adjust the mirrors, all three of which were set for the visibility of a much taller person behind the wheel. Steve had escorted her to the train depot, and she was reluctant to change a solitary thing that might be a physical reminder of his presence inside the vehicle—so recently, not even an hour ago.

It was then that she happened to notice the brown paper sack on the floorboard, and her heart sank even lower. So shattering was the discovery that she cried aloud, "No! No!" and burst into tears. She leaned over and tenderly picked up the sack, placing it beside her on the seat. That morning, she had prepared a lunch for her son to eat on the train, but somehow, in all the confusion and anxiety of the moment, both she and Steve had forgotten to take it from the automobile. It must have fallen to the floorboard between them when they came to a stop.

For a time, Nora could not bring herself to open the sack, but she finally willed herself to do so. She could not bear the thought of simply discarding its contents without proper respect, so she looked inside, even though she knew full well what she would find. Lovingly wrapped in wax paper were two bacon, lettuce, and tomato sandwiches and a thick slice of potato cake, along with a shiny red apple and a piece of peppermint candy. But what was that at the very bottom of the sack? Nestled below the food items was something that she had not seen before—a plain, white sheet of paper, folded neatly into eighths. Curious, she opened it and gazed upon a farewell note, carelessly scribbled in an untidy hand that seemed decidedly masculine: "Stephen, I pray that God will protect you in the days and months ahead. I'll never forget our brief time together on your last day at home. Please write to me—if and when you can. Hannah."

The boarder must have slipped her note into the sack while Nora was either upstairs getting dressed or next door, with Steve, at the Blooms. Eileen Bloom had made Nora promise to bring her sailor son by the house sometime before his leave ended, and this was the last opportunity. Steve disliked goodbyes, but he did enjoy playing with the dog, McGonnigle, for a few minutes while the ladies talked. A rolled-up strip of rubber tubing—"too small for the scrap drive"—made a dandy *faux-proie* for their improvised game of fetch, something of which the sprightly pooch never seemed to tire.

Nora wiped the tears from her eyes and, after a couple of deep breaths, judged herself competent enough to drive home. She also decided that the best thing to do with the note was to fold it back up and return it, with apologies, to Hannah Lane. The neglected lunch would go straight into the refrigerator, destined to be a late-afternoon snack for Elizabeth and Wesley. This was wartime, and nothing of an edible nature—be it a trifling olive or saltine cracker—would ever go to waste at the Brower household, not so long as Nora was in charge of the kitchen.

◆　　◆　　◆

Just how the ensuing maelstrom began is not clear, for the wronged woman in question never saw fit to divulge the identity of her informant. One may safely assume that it was either Lavinia Baldridge or Dottie Anderson, both of whom were present at Waco's passenger depot when the alleged impropriety occurred. Mrs. Baldridge was bidding her aged mother farewell on the return trip to Benbrook, and Mrs. Anderson was greeting the arrival of her youngest brother, a member of the United States Marine Corps. Whoever passed the accusations along surely did so not in vindictiveness but out of total innocence, for there was not a shred of personal gain to be had in disclosing the facts—unless, of course, the sheer pleasure of gossiping was considered satisfaction enough.

It was a Sunday evening, shortly after 6:30, and "The Jack Benny Program" had concluded on NBC. Paolina Coletti was in the living room, leaning on her walking stick as she rotated the radio dial to the Blue Network for "The Quiz Kids." Suddenly, the tuner's whistling sound was joined by an impatient series of taps on the front door, and she became frightened at once. This was not a friendly visitor—the emphatic knocking was too percussive for that—so she approached the entryway warily, with a sense of dread. Was it someone forwarding bad news from the War Department? Did a relative die? Had Father Kearns fallen ill again?

The pounding noise did not cease but instead grew even more insistent as Paolina hobbled toward the door. This seemed to her extremely impolite—so much so that, just for an instant, a wave of peevishness actually supplanted her fears. "I'm coming!" she shouted. "Hold your horses." Still the knocking continued, up to the very moment that she reached for the knob and unlocked the door. When it swung open, there stood Bess Clarke, scowling with hat in hand.

"May I come in?" she asked.

Paolina nodded her head and stepped aside. "What's wrong? It's not Archie, is it?"

"No, it's not Archie, but thank you for asking." While removing her gloves, she forged straight for the living room. "Actually, it does concern him, in a way."

"I don't understand," Paolina said. She pointed toward the sofa. "Please sit down."

Mrs. Clarke laid her hat and gloves on the end table and seated herself. "Would you switch that radio off? I'm fit to be tied."

Moderator Joe Kelly was beginning to introduce that week's panel of half-pint geniuses, but Paolina could tell that the sound was annoying Mrs. Clarke, who obviously wanted her undivided attention. She finally made her way over to the radio and clicked the dial off.

"I heard something today that I hope and pray is an untruth," Archie's mother said. "That's why I'm here—to give your daughter a chance to lay this terrible incident to rest."

Paolina sat down too, about a foot away from her. "Well, I'm sure she would be more than happy to do that—if she were here."

Mrs. Clarke's eyes widened.

"Giulia's over at her father's house," Paolina told her.

"When will she be home?"

"Not long. There's another streetcar about 6:50."

Mrs. Clarke emitted an angry sigh. "All I can say is that she had better be able to justify her actions. Everybody in town seems to know about this but you."

"Just exactly what did she do that was so horrible?" Paolina asked, and she could feel her heart racing.

"That's for me and her to discuss. I don't want to drag you into it. I've got nothing against you, really."

"Oh, but that's where you're wrong. If you've got something against my Giulia, then you've got something against me."

Mrs. Clarke consulted her wristwatch. "Nevertheless, I'll wait for Giulia, if you don't mind."

Paolina rested against the sofa back and tried to smile. "Listen, Bess, there's no reason for us to be locking horns over this. I'm sure we can act like civilized adults."

Mrs. Clarke's eyes flashed red. "It's your daughter who's been acting uncivilized, not I, Mrs. Coletti."

"Well, then we should let Giulia explain it to us. I'm sure it was only a misunderstanding."

"Hrmph!"

"Just sit there and relax, and I'll put on some coffee."

To her credit, Mrs. Clarke was willing to make the attempt. She took a deep breath to regain her composure. "I'm sorry. Maybe a cup of coffee would do me some good. I'm a nervous wreck over this."

Paolina struggled to her feet. "Cream and sugar?" she asked.

"No sugar, thanks. I cannot stomach sweet coffee—never could."

"That's probably just as well, the way things are these days." Paolina walked unsteadily to the kitchen. Once there, she turned to view the sofa, secretly wishing that Mrs. Clarke would grow tired of waiting and leave. Whatever seemed so appalling to her now might be considerably less so in the clear light of morning.

But that was not meant to be. While Paolina was preparing the coffee—which was not yet even lukewarm—she heard the rattling sound of a key in the front door. Instinctively, she tried to caution Giulia before Bess Clarke ambushed her point-blank. "Giulia, is that you?" she shouted. "Would you come into the kitchen for a minute, dear?"

Giulia, however, spotted the back of Mrs. Clarke's head and deemed it common courtesy to exchange a few friendly words before excusing herself to go elsewhere. "I'll be right there, Mamma," she said. "Hello, Mrs. Clarke."

Bess Clarke stood up and stared icily at the young lady. "How nice to see you, Miss Coletti." Her voice was devoid of warmth.

Giulia, taken aback by the chilly reception, could do no more than nod her head. She looked toward the kitchen for clarification and saw her mother limping back into the living room with a grave expression on her face.

"Is there something wrong?" Giulia asked. "It's not Archie, is it?" She glanced from one lady to the other, but both were mute.

Finally, it was Mrs. Clarke who spoke up. "Archie's fine, as far as I know. Not that his well-being would make much difference to you."

Giulia turned to her mother, who stammered an explanation. "Mrs. Clarke heard some gossip today, and she says it concerns you."

"What kind of gossip?" Giulia looked at her accuser.

Mrs. Clarke, though, addressed the girl's mother. "Excuse me, Mrs. Coletti, but my friend does not make up stories, and I will thank you for not calling her a gossip."

"I'm sorry, Mrs. Clarke. Then, perhaps if you would kindly tell my daughter what heinous crime she has committed."

Mrs. Clarke stared at the distant wall. "Oh, I think she knows what I'm talking about all right," she said. "At the train depot ...?"

Giulia sat down on the arm of the easy chair. "I was at the train station about a week ago, if that's what you mean."

"Were you saying goodbye to someone in particular?" Mrs. Clarke asked, and she sounded for all the world like a prosecuting attorney.

"Yes, I was. Is there a law against that?"

Paolina could see that her daughter was becoming angry, so she interjected a question of her own. "Who was it that were you seeing off, dear?"

"Just a friend."

"Someone from school?"

"Yes, as a matter of fact."

Mrs. Clarke glared at the girl. "Is your 'friend' aware that you are engaged to be married?"

"I don't know. Why?"

"Because you kissed this friend, that's why. Right there in broad daylight, in front of everyone."

Giulia said nothing, and tears were beginning to form.

"Is that true, Giulia?" her mother asked.

"Yes, I don't deny it."

"Who was he?"

"Stephen Brower."

"Nora Brower's boy?"

"Yes, ma'am. He's in the Navy." Giulia turned to the visitor and said, "He's going off to war."

At this, Mrs. Clarke's eyes flared with anger. "Oh, please, Miss Coletti! Don't go draping yourself with the American flag over this. You know good and well it was not your patriotic duty to kiss this boy on the lips."

"I never said I did it for patriotic reasons, Mrs. Clarke."

"Then why did you?"

Giulia thought for a moment. "Because I didn't think you would have your spies there, watching me."

Mrs. Clarke was aghast. "In other words, kissing this boy in public didn't bother you one bit—only the fact that you got caught."

Giulia smiled. "Yes, I feel terrible that you caught me, so from now on I won't go around kissing every sailor I happen to pass on the street."

"Well!" Mrs. Clarke stood up, fuming. "I have never been so insulted in all my life—and I shall never forget this. You are nothing but a common tramp."

Now it was Paolina's turn to arise. Pointing a finger at her guest, she shouted, "You will leave this house, Bess Clarke, and never be welcome here again."

"Gladly." The lady snatched up her hat and gloves from the end table and marched heavily toward the front door. "I'll let myself out."

"Yes, you will," Paolina said, "and good riddance."

Mrs. Clarke slammed the door so hard that a small mirror fell from the wall and came crashing down into pieces on the hardwood floor.

♦   ♦   ♦

He was not much of a dancer, but two of his buddies were going, so Danny Rignold decided to tag along. Norvis Pelham was a corporal too, a New Englander with a gift for making intractable engines really sing. Randall Box, though nearly a year their senior in military time, was only a private first class. Twice he had been busted for insubordination, and his basic-training AWOL blot—a typographical lapse that was never expunged from his service record—dogged him every step of the way.

Being that the other two men would not be released from duty until 1630 hours, Private Box somehow had to squander most of the afternoon before meeting up with them, which was perfectly fine with him. Randy possessed that most useful of all military knacks among enlisted personnel—ingratiating himself with the officer ranks—and he enjoyed nothing more than driving around Waco on Army gasoline while stretching inconsequential ten-minute errands into leisurely tours through the local environs. More often than not, this involved an unscheduled stop or two at a hotel lobby or coffee shop, where he would lounge while waiting for his supposed big-brass "passenger" to return to the vehicle.

On this particular Saturday morning, Major Peter Alberghetti asked his PFC orderly to deliver a package of misdirected instructional manuals to his analogous flight-training officer at Waco Army Air Field. Randy was only too happy to comply. Several of the Women Airforce Service Pilots there were quite pleasant to view, though it must be conceded that they paid him no reciprocal attention. Even more than the male pilots-in-training, the WASPs seemed to keep their minds strictly on business. But that did not stop Randall Box, who reasoned that it cost a shopper nothing to admire the merchandise.

No sooner had he passed beyond the Blackland gate than a pair of inhabitants in another jeep—brandishing a "Military Police" sign on either flank—pulled him over to the side of the road and demanded to see his identification.

"Box, huh?" one of them said. "What kind of name is that?"

"I don't know. English, I guess."

They also examined the back seat, presumably to see whether any contraband was stowed there. Then, after their suspicions were allayed, the MPs explained to Randy that a vehicle similar to the one he was driving was listed as missing from the WAAF motor pool, and they only wanted to make sure that he was not the culprit in question, simply out for a joy ride.

Randy could not help laughing. "Why would someone drive a stolen jeep over to another military base?" he asked. "That doesn't make any sense."

Both MPs remained serious. "We have reason to believe it's here," the older of them said.

"Well, maybe it's just a clerical snafu. That happens all the time around this place."

"Nope. Not according to the top sergeant."

Private Box gestured behind him. "What were you fellas looking for in back?"

At this, the younger MP nearly broke into a smile. "The colonel's case of scotch. I think he's more worried about that than the jeep."

"Yeah?"

"Harder to replace."

The older MP waved the BAAF jeep on. "Sorry for the delay, Private Box," he said. "Try not to look so guilty next time."

"You can count on it, sergeant." When Randy pulled away from the side of the road, he noticed, with a glimpse over his shoulder, that the MPs were continuing their search in a westerly direction, right onto the Blackland base itself. He wondered why in the world anyone would want to steal a jeep. They rode rough—loosening the teeth—and would be impossible to disguise as a civilian vehicle. Maybe it was for the whiskey at that.

The fly-girls at Waco Army Air Field were a disappointment that day. Randy drove by the WASP quarters, as he always did on such excursions, but the barracks were unlit inside and seemed to be deserted. His wolf whistle would have to wait for another trip.

Elsewhere, though, the base was bustling with activity. An unbroken procession of single-engine trainers was taking to the air, and what appeared to be a whole battalion of cadets was drilling on the asphalt parade grounds in front of him. Off in the distance, he could just make out the martial sounds of an enormous contingent of wind-band musicians—no doubt in rehearsal for the unforgiving ears of some high-ranking dignitary. Possibly two hundred strong, they appeared to be attired in their dress uniforms, which was quite extraordinary for this time of day.

Consulting Major Alberghetti's hastily scrawled note, Randy learned that he was to present the instructional manuals personally to an officer by the name of McDaniel—Major Gilbert McDaniel—at the BT-13 hangar. As luck would have it, Major McDaniel was not in the office, but a bespectacled corporal accepted the package in his absence and promised to let his superior know that the missing textbooks had been delivered. After all, he explained, classes had been postponed for two days while awaiting their arrival. The Vultee BT-13 (or "Valiant, as it was commonly known) was considerably more complex than the primary trainers—faster and heavier, with a two-position variable-pitch propeller. It also represented the student pilot's first exposure to the use of two-way radio communications with the ground. Clearly, a detailed instructional manual was essential.

"When will Major McDaniel be back?" the private asked. "My orders are to give it to him personally."

"Not until 1300 hours," the corporal said.

"Our HQ called to make sure he'd be here."

"Sorry, but the major had to attend a meeting, and then he'll be heading directly to the officers' mess. I'm fully authorized to sign for him."

Randy scratched his chin. "I guess that'll be okay."

"Got to be. The flight instructors need 'em today," the corporal told him. "How'd they wind up at Blackland anyhow?"

"Search me. Looks like an AAF screw-up, not the post office."

"Wouldn't be the first time." The corporal accepted the package and laid it on his well-ordered desktop. He was quite young, and his thick eyeglasses made him appear to be a college freshman, perhaps a pre-med student somewhere back east.

Randy was beginning to have second thoughts. "Say, let me write the major's name on the wrapping paper," he said.

Frowning, the corporal offered his fountain pen. "You really don't trust me, do you, private?"

"Nothing personal," Randy said. He wrote "MAJOR McDANIEL" in large block letters on the top surface of the package and returned the pen.

"I think he'll notice that," the corporal told him with a smirk.

A few minutes later, just as Randy was jumping into the jeep, an Army bus clattered past, and what he espied within its confines more than made up for his earlier letdown at the WASP barracks. Merrily waving at him through its smudged windows were some of the loveliest young ladies he had seen in a long while on a military post. There must have been two dozen or more of them on the bus. He threw the jeep into gear and followed closely behind, laughing at the funny faces two teenage gals were making at him through the rear glass. Steering with his knees, he lit a cigarette and then flicked the match out of his cupped hands to the pavement.

He wondered who they were, so many beauteous civilians riding in a military conveyance. The thought occurred to him that there was no school this morning, it being a Saturday, and that happy circumstance is what must have freed the girls for their present outing. Curious to see where their travels would take them, he followed along behind the bus as far as he could, all the way to downtown. He made it a point to take a mental picture of the brunette in the right rear window, hoping someday to see her again. She certainly did appear to be patriotic, he mused. Making eye contact with a man in uniform was not all that common from such a youngster, and he flattered himself that this pretty maiden had designs for him somewhere down the line.

Private Box was within ten feet of the girl as the bus pulled to a stop at the curb in front of Waco High School. He swerved to the left and waved jauntily to her, but she turned away, giggling with her friend at the GI she had teased from afar, safely insulated from him by their moving vehicles. No doubt she had forgotten all about him by the time the bus unloaded its passengers.

Randy's attention eventually wandered elsewhere too, only in his case not because he had grown tired of the subject matter. He parked the jeep down by the Burleson Realty Company and walked back to the southwest corner of Fourth and Austin, slipping into an imposing, twelve-story building by way of its side entrance. The Roosevelt Hotel had a swell Cadet Club that made it easy for him to hide among throngs of others in uniform, and Major Alberghetti, his mind occupied by more pressing concerns, would not expect him to return to battalion headquarters anytime soon.

Gus Marek was there, and so were Andy Dockery and the diminutive Bill Jones, so it promised to be a fun time. No brass was in sight, either, which rendered the atmosphere just that much more convivial. Randy made his way over to the mahogany table where the others sat, and he pulled up a chair. Bill offered him a smoke, and a shiny something caught his eye.

He took a puff and asked, "Is that your lighter?" It was a souvenir edition from the old Palace Theatre, Forty-seventh and Broadway, one of New York's great vaudeville houses.

"I stole it from a guy in the chow line," Bill said, and there was an angelic look of innocence about him. "Didn't mean to, really," he added. "Just forgot to give it back to him, and he was leaving. Tall guy with red hair. I'll give it back if I ever bump into him again."

"Oh, sure," Gus said. "You'd swallow it whole if he walked in here right now."

Randy grinned at the others. "What are you playing?"

Gus crushed his cigarette in the ashtray and immediately lit another. "High-low, split the pot. Are you in?"

"I've only got about an hour. Is that okay with you fellas?"

Andy and Gus nodded their heads.

"We don't care how much time you have," Bill said. "It's your money that we're interested in." He laughed, but everyone knew there was some truth to the comment. Bill was not at the table to be sociable, and the pile of chips in front of him attested to that.

When it was all over, Randall Box was $8.70 poorer, but he was proud to have stared down Corporal Jones in a one-on-one bidding frenzy that closed the final memorable hand. He stood to lose a cool $35.50, had the card shark bluffed him into submission. He reckoned this to be a successful day's wagering and hopped into the jeep with Bill's cigarette lighter safely buttoned inside his shirt pocket. Randy planned to honor noble Army tradition by hanging onto it until someone else pilfered it from him.

Things turned sour about halfway to the base. With little or no warning, the jeep's engine began to run rough, so he pulled over to investigate under the hood. His limited mechanical instincts led him to suspect that the problem lay within the fuel line, probably the fuel pump itself. Nothing to do but test his theory. Sure enough, he discovered that the jeep was drivable for a mile or so before the engine would die. Then, after a waiting period of fifteen or twenty minutes, for some reason he could start it right up again, and the jeep would be fine for nearly another mile. Unfortunately, each time this happened he was able to travel a slightly lesser distance. With any luck, even in the face of these diminishing returns, he could cajole the vehicle back onto the base for repairs—and still get there before he had to leave for the dance.

Randy was one of those people who take setbacks in full stride. After considering his predicament for a few minutes, he decided that the jeep's impending breakdown was really nothing more than an opportunity in disguise. A foolproof alibi had fallen into his lap, a plausible excuse to account for his dilatory return to the fold. Military life was actually rather simple—if you kept your eyes, ears, and options open.

A civilian motorist happened along, but Randy politely refused all assistance. "I'll make it back to base, even if it takes me the whole afternoon," he said. His new acquaintance, a muscular farmer in tattered overalls, laughed at what he assumed was empty bravado. Then, as he ambled back to his truck, the farmer spit tobacco juice in the general direction of the disabled vehicle, shaking his head with amusement.

No one was manning the motor pool except for an SFC, two buck privates, and a fresh-faced corporal who resembled Harold Lloyd. The jeep sputtered to a stop just a hundred feet away from its destination, and that is where Randy left it. He trudged ahead and pointed with his thumb. "There's one you can tow in. Who does the maintenance on these things anyhow?" The corporal nodded to one of the privates, who laid down his oil funnel and went to assess the damage. The sergeant, though, never troubled himself to look up from his stack of paperwork. Instead, he leaned back even farther in the squeaky desk chair, unbothered by a housefly treading across his half-eaten Hershey's bar.

◆   ◆   ◆

The Girls' Service Organization was bringing to a close the busiest week that any of its members could recall. Every night for the past six there had been entertainment activities, helping the boys in uniform to feel more at home in their unfamiliar Waco surroundings. But those other occasions all paled in comparison with the "extravaganza" that was planned for Saturday night at the downtown USO club. Many of the girls already had formal dresses, and those who were without made it a priority to beg, borrow, or buy one for this auspicious event. The male attendees, of course, faced no such conundrum. Uncle Sam made their clothing decisions for them.

Private Randall Box, Corporal Daniel Rignold, and Corporal Norvis Pelham hitchhiked to the dance, inasmuch as no government-issue vehicle was available to them in their off-duty hours. Even the normally cooperative Major Alberghetti was unwilling to bend the rules quite far enough to requisition a jeep in order for his subordinates to chase after women. That was the way he saw it anyway, and he knew the line had to be drawn somewhere.

The accommodating driver who picked them up, Marvin Finsterwald, was a fiftyish man who had no hair whatsoever on top of his head but an orchard of muttonchops adorning each jaw line. He made the boys feel as though they were doing him a favor by consenting to be transported downtown in his creaky 1936 Packard touring sedan. Once a praiseworthy machine, this five-passenger Model 120 set him back more than $1,100 when new. Now, though, it had grown a bit forlorn from wartime neglect, and Finsterwald apologized for its appearance and bumpy ride. He need not have wasted his breath, for the soldiers were more than happy to be conveyed anywhere by whatever means, and a non-stop leg of eleven miles with no "transfers" was as scarce as unrationed steak.

Not until the automobile was chugging its way through Bosqueville did Norvis Pelham, who was in the front seat, notice that their benefactor had only one arm. So smoothly did Finsterwald shift gears—bracing the steering wheel with his ample belly for the blink of an eye—that he could have been Barney Oldfield, for all the corporal knew. Norvis glanced back at his companions, but they were looking at what passed for local scenery, and Private Box appeared entirely lost in thought behind the thick cloud of his cigarette smoke.

"How'd you lose the arm?" Norvis asked.

The driver smiled. "The Boches did it to me—a grenade, I guess."

"In France?"

Finsterwald nodded his head. "I get by okay, though. Some days I hardly remember I ever had one on the port side."

Corporal Pelham felt self-conscious, and he slowly edged his right forearm away from the passenger-window ledge and onto his lap.

"Funny thing about it, my name is German. There's even a Finsterwald coat of arms that my family had. Southern folks, just north of the Austrian border. My grandmother used to call Grandpapa *Ein echter Bayer*, and all of us kids would laugh."

"Are you married?"

"Me? Of course I'm married. I've got two sons in the service—a marine and a sailor. They're both overseas. You?"

"No. That's why we're going to this dance," Norvis said. "You think my wife would approve of something like that?"

Finsterwald chuckled. "Not if she knew about it, huh?" He cleared his throat and spit out the driver window. "Me, I didn't meet my wife until 1922. I was already thirty at the time, so there's really no hurry."

"How'd you meet her?"

"At the Cotton Palace. She's from a little town called Rosebud."

"Where's that?"

"It's about forty miles south of here, down in Falls County. Her daddy ran a cottonseed mill there. Ripley's *Believe It or Not* said, 'There Is a Rose Bush in Every Yard in Rosebud, Texas.' That kind of made it famous for a while."

"Is that where the Cotton Palace is?"

Finsterwald looked at him in disbelief and then lowered his eyes. "It's not anywhere, son," he whispered. "There's no Cotton Palace anymore, and it's a crying shame. They tore it down about a dozen years ago. Waco just tore it down."

When they finally reached Washington Avenue, the sun was descending behind some treetops, making it difficult to see whether the intersection was clear from the west. Finsterwald very nearly pulled out in front of a fleet Cadillac Sedanette, whose driver, without slowing down a whit, honked its horn and made an obscene gesture as he passed.

"Go ahead, brother. Hell ain't half full!" Finsterwald shouted. The speeding automobile was shiny and new—well, as new as they came in 1944—and Finsterwald declared that it must have been driven by the spoiled son of a doctor or lawyer. "He'd better hope that I don't meet him again somewhere down the road," he added. "I'll stick that brave middle finger of his where it's not meant to go."

Norvis studied Finsterwald's profile—round head, pug nose, jutting jaw—and thought to himself that this man, handicap and all, would be a formidable opponent in a fistfight. The circumference of Finsterwald's one forearm would equal the sum total of most people's two. In that respect, he resembled the Cubs' Jimmie Foxx, whom Norvis had seen playing years earlier when the Athletics were on the road in Detroit. This Finsterwald might have given ol' Double X a good run for his money in arm wrestling—or even Hack Wilson, for that matter.

"Mister, I hope you're not goin' too far out of your way," Danny Rignold said from the back seat.

Finsterwald stared straight ahead. "Don't worry about it. I already told you— both of my sons are in the service, overseas. And if I can't give you fellas a half-hour of my precious time, then I'm not much of a war dad. You know what I mean?"

Eight girls, attired in white formals, were going in the front entrance of the USO, guided by an Army lieutenant in his dress uniform. Randy gave a quiet wolf whistle when he spotted the young ladies, and the other two soldiers craned their necks for a better look. Finsterwald shimmied his automobile to a halt at the curb and said, "Okay, boys, end of the line."

"Thanks, pal," Corporal Box told the driver, and he opened the door and climbed out. Norvis and Danny did the same.

Finsterwald shook his head. "Not at all. Thanks for the company."

"Hey, I'll dance with a gorgeous one for you," Norvis said.

"You do that."

When the Packard coughed and drove away, Danny felt a lump in his throat. That car would be lucky to get seven miles a gallon, he thought. Mr. Finsterwald had donated most of his weekly gasoline ration to the cause, and he did it cheerfully.

◆　　◆　　◆

Randy and Norvis went inside the USO, and Danny followed close behind. They were early for the affair, but dozens of soldiers were already there, lounging, smoking, and laughing in the library area. Evidently, the young ladies were in the back room, receiving last-minute instructions and not yet free to mingle. The place was very loud, with recorded music playing at full volume, and a live band was in the process of setting up its gear at the far end of the rec room. From the looks of it, this was going to be a large ensemble: the saxophone section alone numbered upwards of eight. Most of the reading tables had been pushed back, leaving enough space for a nice-sized dance floor.

Around 6:30, Madeleine Givens stepped forward and announced to the gathered soldiers, "Thanks for being patient, gentlemen. We're still waiting for most of the girls to arrive, and I'm sure you wouldn't want to get started without them." Her crimson skirt was tiny at the waist, accentuating the full bodice—much to the delight of several of the less sophisticated men, who made eyes at her while shouting familiar innuendos that she had long since learned to ignore.

Within ten minutes, two additional busloads of women in their teens and twenties had filed through the area, joining their predecessors in the back room. Again there were catcalls from the gallery of men and a few off-color whoops that made the more genteel among them laugh with embarrassment. A lady introducing herself as Claudine Wren ("... with a double-yoo") served as mistress of ceremonies, and she invited the boys to give a warm round of applause to Sergeant Dalton Rizzotti and his Waco Army Air Field Band. As the musicians struck up their first tune, the girls emerged from seclusion and lavished a generic friendliness on the soldiers, even the most brazen of whom were now on their best behavior. Something about close contact with those formal, chiffon dresses brought out a degree of refinement in the ranks that had been sorely wanting just moments ago.

Norvis Pelham began chatting with an ebullient redhead who smiled prettily enough but whose eyes wandered about the room without coming to rest on anyone in particular, least of all him. Near the refreshment table, Danny Rignold and Randall Box traded small talk with a pair of teenage sisters, neither of whom seemed at all willing to become separated from the other. The younger one seemed to be only about fifteen years of age, which may have accounted for her evident case of nerves in a room full of earthy warriors. In time, the dancing finally began, and the three soldier friends chose to sit out, presumably hoping for more satisfactory companions to come along.

Randy had emptied his coffee cup and was starting to cut into a small square of white cake—"wedding cake," the helper called it—when a faintly remembered face caught his attention from across the room. He sat up straight and tried to squint for a better look. But the girl now turned the other way, visiting with two blustery GIs who may have imbibed a few drinks before arriving at the alcohol-free dance. Motioning for Norvis to safeguard the cake, Randy laid down his fork and circled around for a better look. It had to be the same girl. That bobbed finger-wave hairstyle, once so very popular, was by now considered passé. How conceivable was it that more than one brunette teenager in Waco would be wearing her hair that outmoded way?

What really confirmed his suspicions, however, was the young lady's smile. "My aunt dances wilder than that at her lonely hearts club," a tipsy soldier said, and she laughed at the remark. Randy knew instantly that this was the very girl who had smiled down at him through the back window of the Army bus—the same dimpled cheeks and beautiful teeth. Unfortunately, he now saw that she could not have been more than about sixteen, so he refused to allow his imagination to stray very far from conventional decency.

His curiosity satisfied, Private Box suddenly lost interest, returning to his place at the card table with Norvis and Danny. Meanwhile, another of the GSO volunteers, this one a couple years older than his underage fantasy gal, had invited herself to sit down, and Norvis especially was engaged in a stream of shallow chatter. He laughed and leaned his upper arm against hers. "You don't eat peas with a knife, you know. So why wear a fancy dress like that to a dance?"

She looked genuinely hurt. "Don't you think it's pretty, then?"

"Oh, sure, it's pretty enough. Don't get me wrong. But it just doesn't make any sense to go dancing in a gown like that."

"Why not?"

"Well, your fella might step on the hem or something. That could be disastrous."

Randy looked directly at the girl. "Or maybe it would add some excitement—depending on how far it tore."

"Shaddup," Norvis said. "This isn't that kind of place."

"Is that your own dress?" Danny asked her.

"This one is my older sister's, but most of the girls just rent them."

"Is she here too?"

"Goodness no. She's been married for four years." The girl giggled at the notion and took a sip of punch. "My sister couldn't begin to fit into this dress anymore—two kids already, with another on the way. That's what happens, you know."

Norvis winked. "So I've heard."

That Brower girl caught Danny's attention when she walked by their table carrying a tray of napkins, sugar cubes, and stirring sticks, and he debated whether to stop her and say hello. He had not seen her for three or four months and was not even sure whether she would remember him. Ultimately, he thought better of the idea. He always had an eye for her, but it made little sense for him to pursue someone so young, particularly when he was unlikely to stay in Waco, Texas, very much longer anyway. He was due for reassignment, and he had a feeling that his next duty station would not be this remote from the actual shooting war. Murray Spink, his pal over in the parts depot, speculated that some of his flight wing were being assigned to air bases in Australia. But then it was also Murray who predicted that the Giants would win the National League flag, and they finished dead last. Elizabeth disappeared from view in the back of the room, and Danny did not give her another thought.

The evening's highlight—at least from the dispassionate, bureaucratic viewpoint of the USO—was a graceful waltz exhibition performed by eight members of the Girls' Service Organization, as accompanied by the WAAF Band. No doubt it was meant to be subtly elegant, an affirmation of the visual arts, but that virtue was entirely wasted on most in the audience, from whence came a smattering of suggestive whistles that seriously compromised the lofty intentions.

"Hey, Norv, some of them are real knockouts," Randall Box said. "I'll take the second one from the right."

"You can have her. Give me the third from the left." They both turned to Danny.

Corporal Rignold stood up to get a better look, but that was all for show. "Fourth from the left," he finally told them. In truth, he had noticed her first off, when Mrs. Wren made the introductions, even going so far as to scribble "Lois" on a napkin.

About three hundred service personnel were inside the building's street-level floor when the dance reached its height around 9:30. There was hardly enough room to move and inhale at the same time. That made it cozy, of course, and more than one lovely volunteer was heard to shout, "Fresh!" An unshaven private, whose hands wandered slightly off the wholesome path, received the full force of an angry slap to the face, leaving a clear, red image of four parallel fingers.

By and large, though, the civilian chaperones handled their responsibilities exceedingly well—a bit too exceedingly for Private Box's liking. It was his understanding that the girls were there to circulate freely among the soldier crowd, but tonight it was obvious that the USO matrons and Red Cross auxiliary were more interested in providing protection for their wards than entertainment for the boys in uniform. A dozen or more of the GSO volunteers were whisked away before ten o'clock. "Must be past their bedtime," one GI said. His smart-alecky quip put into words what many of the others were thinking to themselves.

To make matters even worse, those few females who stayed behind were unapproachable in both senses of the term. After Randy's waltzing cutie gave him an unceremonious brush off, having mistaken him for a masher she met at the Cadet Club, he resolved to throw caution to the wind and become friendly with the shapeliest girl in the room, a statuesque blonde who clearly was of Scandinavian descent. The problem was, this particular objective seemed invariably to be surrounded by a perimeter of khaki suitors. She was one of those charmed females of the species for whom attracting young men was no more strenuous than winding spaghetti around a fork.

Her name was Johanna. He could not help but gather that much information from the loud-mouthed braggarts who vied with each other for the vivacious lady's attention. Someone named Gordy seemed to have the upper hand. He sat next to her and wisecracked one ribald witticism after another. She, in turn—though only sporadically comprehending his oddball humor—made it a point to laugh at regular intervals, just to keep him interested. The pungent smell around this red-headed private made Randy wonder whether the punch had been spiked. Five minutes later, these suspicions were confirmed when he saw Gordy unscrew a tin flask and introduce an ounce or so of its potent contents into his half-filled cup.

By temperament, Norvis Pelham was less selective than Randy when it came to feminine companionship. He danced with five or six different girls, all of whom were interchangeable in his mind. Maybe his romantic apathy could be traced back to that quickie New Hampshire wedding-cum-annulment of two years ago, something about which he never spoke but which surely continued to affect his attitude toward investing in a lasting relationship.

As for Danny Rignold, he was perfectly content to watch from afar, sipping coffee and occasionally returning a smile to a pretty face. It was not that he shied away from mingling because he feared that these USO gals were of the same ilk as Nadine Cobb and Ann-Rae Jansek at the Colonial Hotel. On the contrary, his assumptions tended to gravitate toward the opposite extreme. Far from being cynical when it came to young women, he was more often guilty of being too idealistic for his own good. He saw them as altruistic virgins, a whole roomful of girls next door whose motives were purely to grant the servicemen a little relaxation from their dangerous jobs at the Waco bases. And, if the truth be known, in more cases than not he was probably correct.

The Waco Army Air Field Band was a polished outfit, with talented collegiate and high school musicians from all over the country, and Sergeant Rizzotti really knew how to make his men swing. Danny found himself entranced by the wind section, especially the clarinets in one of the Benny Goodman tunes, and he resolved to pick up his own licorice stick again whenever he went home on leave. He had not played it seriously since mid-April of his senior year, when the concert band—a scaled-down version of the famed Big Red—played a half-dozen selections in the high school gym. He remembered that lots of the old codgers from John Felder's Grocery were over in one corner, loudly discussing Whippet football as if the band were only there to provide background music for their gridiron debate.

Danny felt a gentle tap on the shoulder, and he turned to see the smiling face of Elizabeth Brower, the girl he had rescued from the clutches of that agile predator last summer.

"Do you mind if I sit down for a minute, soldier?" she said.

"Please do." Danny scrambled to his feet and slid out a chair for her. He noticed that she was casually dressed, possibly even in work clothes. One thing for certain—she did not measure up very well to the other young ladies, all regally bedecked in their formal gowns. "Are you here for the dance?" He asked this just to be on the safe side, for he had no idea how her fashion tastes ran.

"No, silly! Do I really look like it?" She slid her palms over the faded olive blouse. "I'm on duty tonight, but it's time for my ten-minute break. I get one every two hours. You knew I worked at the USO, didn't you?"

"Sure, I guess so. Wasn't that why you were here when—?" He pulled up short, embarrassed, sensing that he might provoke some unpleasant memories in the poor lass.

"Don't worry," she said. "I'm all over that. In fact, he's in some California prison by now. My older brother nearly killed him with a tire doo-dad. You know, one of those pointed tools you use to change a flat."

"Steve?"

"You've got a good memory."

"Well, that's my father's name," he told her.

"But the hoodlum's arrest doesn't diminish what you did for me last summer. That was very brave of you."

Danny gave a self-deprecating laugh. "All I did was catch his fist. I never was much of a boxer."

Elizabeth gazed at him with admiration. "I'll never forget what you did ... what you tried to do ... for me. It was sweet of you."

He could feel his face redden. "That's all right." Danny stared down at his folded hands. "I guess my only mistake was not havin' a tire iron with me."

She giggled and kissed him on the cheek. Then, as abruptly as she came, she was standing to leave. "I've got to get back to work, or they'll sack me."

"They can't sack a volunteer, can they?" he asked.

"Well, no, maybe not. But they sure could make life miserable for me around here." Elizabeth thought for a moment. "Why don't you find some pretty girl to dance with? I'd be happy to do it myself, except that I'm on the clock."

"You certainly do qualify," he said with a wink. She looked puzzled, so he added, "The pretty part."

Now it was her turn to blush. "You think so? Even in my work duds?" She batted her eyelashes in jest.

"Especially in your work duds."

"Oh, please," she said as she backed away. "Now I know you're just shooting me a line."

He shook his head. "I'm really not all that clever at pickin' up girls. Sometimes I wish I was."

Elizabeth smiled at him and said, "Goodbye, Danny." And then she was gone.

Danny glanced at the scrawled letters on his napkin and looked around the room, wondering which one of these young ladies was named Lois.

◆   ◆   ◆

The halls of Waco High School were rife with surplus energy these days, very much as they would be in mid-May of any year, global strife or not. Only a pair of weeks remained before the spring term would recess for summer vacation, so teachers had already begun shifting their curricula into what might best be termed holding patterns, invoking daily routines that were geared more toward busy work than the nuts and bolts of basic instruction. The signs of change were unmistakable. Callow freshmen, with nine months of experience under their belts, suddenly found themselves brimming with unaccustomed confidence, poised to position themselves on the next rung of the academic ladder. At the other end of the spectrum, uppermost classmen were afflicted with a euphoric condition called "senior fever," impatiently waiting for the final year of public schooling to conclude so they could get on with their lives.

But that is where any similarity to normal times came to a definite halt. During this wartime year, as in the past couple, there obtained one sobering departure from traditional graduation plans: senior boys were compelled to decide whether to join up posthaste or simply bide time until their numbers were called. For the able-bodied among them, it made little practical difference which path they chose to follow. Even college enrollment, marriage, and fatherhood were no guarantees of exemption. On federal orders, all customary loopholes had been revoked by the local draft boards, except for the drastic measures of self-mutilation and spiritually motivated pacifism. Admittedly, both of these courses of action required a certain fortitude to pursue, but that would not prevent the civilian public from branding such male non-combatants as agents of cowardice. After all, were not *their* sons, brothers, husbands, fathers, nephews, and school chums willing to fight on the front lines and die in defense of their country?

It so happened that one reluctant belligerent, an eighteen-year-old bookworm by the name of Peter Gerken, was an acquaintance of Wesley Brower. They were in the same mathematics class for two terms, and they both took part in a number of scrap-metal and rubber drives. Peter was the middle child of three, positioned between older and younger sisters—Katherine and Gladys, respectively. Kitty's husband was an Annapolis man through and through, at last report serving as a lieutenant junior grade in the Mediterranean, and his Gerken in-laws made no secret of the fact that they could not have been prouder of her "catch." Peter's Uncle Sully, his mother's brother, was also a lifer, having risen in the ranks to master sergeant, at one time seriously contemplating retirement until the Pearl Harbor attack scuttled his visions of a three-bedroom beach house in Pensacola.

A nominal Presbyterian at best, Peter rarely attended church except on Easter Sundays, but he was devout on his own terms, shepherding a Bible-study group that met at his kitchen table on alternate Wednesday nights. He was particularly strong in spreading the social gospel, seldom mentioning his Lord and Savior by name but passionately espousing the humanitarian teachings of His earthly ministry. On more than one occasion, he let it slip that, in his estimation, the living embodiment of those tenets was the man who currently occupied the White House, Franklin Delano Roosevelt. Peter Gerken spoke eloquently of the First and Second New Deals—allowing the alphabet-soup bureaucracies of NRA, CWA, PWA, WPA, and TVA to flow off his tongue with reverence befitting a genealogy of the Patriarchs.

Peter had once tried to recruit Wesley for his Bible class, but this came at a fortuitous point in Wesley's radio career when he was serving as a substitute newscaster in Grant Tollefson's absence—an alibi that Peter methodically verified by tuning in to KWXN no fewer than three times on alternate (non-class) Wednesdays. Much to Wesley's relief, the proselytizer never thought of renewing his invitation after the young man had become Kip Hanson, a transformation that presumably left his evenings free for intellectual pursuits.

If Peter Gerken was not ranked third in his graduating class, then he was not very far removed from that rarefied plateau. The first two spots were common knowledge, and surely no one could begrudge either of them. Unquestionably, Betty Bruck was the top student at Waco High School and thus would be delivering the valedictory address at commencement ceremonies in Municipal Stadium on June 1. Just below her in academic standing was Bobby Pillow, salutatorian for the Class of 1944.

Peter had earned a devastating "B" in speech class during his junior year, ostensibly because of a philosophical difference of opinion with his teacher, who was a royalist and outspoken proponent of the British Crown. Peter resented that viewpoint so fervently that he was utterly powerless to speak otherwise, even with his scholastic reputation on the line. He saw the world conflict in a different light entirely, using his four-minute classroom harangue to portray America's faithful ally as imperialistic war-mongers and disparaging the House of Windsor as illegitimate wielders of power. Simply put, the monarchy was a dinosaur that had outlived its time. Talking with his speech teacher about the matter did no good at all. In fact, their civilized discussion quickly degenerated into a shouting match, and Peter stomped from the room well before Mr. Haddox's office hour drew to a close.

Wesley Brower knew Peter to be a rather outspoken senior whose mouth usually ran well ahead of his better judgment, but otherwise he considered him to be a decent fellow and a friend. By and large, Peter did not flaunt his antiwar sentiment among his classmates, choosing to reserve that particular soapbox for his biweekly Bible study sessions. Neither did the nation's war footing suffer from his neglect. He did his bit by joining in conservation efforts, various projects that sometimes brought him into contact with Wesley away from the school setting.

When the third Saturday in May arrived, Wesley found himself as one of seven high school students, three boys and four girls, who were tying stacks of newspapers into bundles for shipment to the salvage center. Peter Gerken was there, and so were Harriette Hoover and Rhonda Finch from his civics class. Indeed, it was his civics teacher who arranged to have them participate in the project, which could earn up to ten extra-credit points apiece, depending upon how long they worked. The remaining teenagers—one slovenly boy and two very prim girls—Wesley had seen at school but did not know by name. The shorter of these girls, a sophomore with curly brown hair, was rather attractive. The other, a shy senior with long, black hair and a creamy complexion, was one of the most charming young ladies he had ever seen. He remembered beholding her from afar several times in the lunchroom, even as long ago as his freshman year.

On this seemingly fateful Saturday, if he did nothing else for the war effort, Wesley was determined to learn the dark-haired beauty's identity, for most likely never again would he stumble upon such favorable circumstances to do so. When the curly-headed girl went for more hemp twine, he turned to the other and, with as much nonchalance as he could effect on such short notice, asked her name.

"Giulia," she said. Her pleasant smile was surprisingly friendly and without a trace of conceit.

"I'm Wes," he told her, though she did not actually request the information. "Are you a senior?"

"Yes," was all she replied, and again the girl, though reserved, appeared to be quite amiable.

"I'm a junior," he said. A touch of nervousness was beginning to invest his otherwise well-modulated radio voice. "But I was born in November, so I'm almost a senior. What about you?"

"August ... August the twelfth."

"Of '26?" She nodded her head, so he made a quick calculation. "Then you're only about three months older than I am."

She laughed. "Well, I must say, you're very good at math."

"The way I figure, you just beat the cutoff date for attending school."

"Maybe so."

She was no longer looking at him, concentrating all her attention on tying a bundle of newspapers as tightly as possible. Watching her, Wesley could not help but smile, for she had an endearing habit of letting the very tip of her tongue show whenever she exerted force in securing a knot. Surely no one else was even aware of this little mannerism, and maybe not Giulia herself.

To Wesley's annoyance, it soon became apparent that Peter Gerken was on rather close terms with this lovely creature. That really should not have come as any great surprise. They were, after all, both members of the same graduating class at Waco High School. But Peter knew more about her than seemed proper. He knew her last name, he knew precisely where her house was located, he knew who lived next-door to her, and he knew where she worked part-time. He knew that her boss was a Mr. Lindeman. And he revealed to Wesley that "Miss Coletti," as he invariably referred to her, would not be taking part in commencement exercises with the rest of the class, due to her decision to drop out of school and care for her partially incapacitated mother. She hoped to enroll again at a later date—perhaps as soon as September—whenever her mother's condition had sufficiently improved.

All afternoon long, Wesley kept one eye and one ear on this beautiful girl, gathering tiny crumbs of information as they drifted his way in the course of ordinary conversations. Most were inconsequential, even trivial, but one statement felt like Joe Louis had landed a hard right to his stomach. It occurred as Peter was stacking heavy bundles of newsprint onto a wooden pallet. "Tell me," he said to her. "Is that fiancé of yours still stationed in Australia?"

So shaken was Wesley by the compelling question that he did not catch her reply, if indeed she ever made one. By the time he regained his mental equilibrium, either she or Peter had managed to change the subject to such an extent that eavesdropper Wesley lost track of their train of thought. Oddly, this bride-to-be was not wearing an engagement ring, for whatever that was worth.

Having taken no part in the discussions thus far was the other boy in this work detail, a grossly overweight goldbricker named Arnold Acker. Oblivious to all normal concerns of world affairs, he seemed perfectly content to sit on his immense derrière for hours on end, bestirring himself only to waddle forth to the gentlemen's rest room. True enough, to give credit where credit was due, Arnold did cooperate in ticking off some donors' names from the scrap-drive roster, even if this laudable burst of energy ceased the instant he broke the point on his lead pencil and did not bother to resharpen it.

Arnold finally found enough initiative to exercise his vocal chords. "Are you gonna join up next year, Wes?" he asked.

Wesley thought for a moment. "Probably so, if the war's still on."

"I didn't pass the physical," Arnold told him. Then he added with a grin, "The recruiting sergeant said I was too short for my weight."

"My brother's in the Navy," Wesley said. "Somewhere in the Atlantic, I gather."

Still smiling, Arnold yawned and stretched his arms overhead. "What about you, Pete? You gonna enlist or just let Uncle Whiskers grab you?"

Peter did not bother to look up from his work. "I really haven't given it much thought."

"Are you serious?" Arnold asked. "Graduation's in a week and a half."

"I know when graduation is."

"Well, you sure are awful calm about it."

Peter shrugged his shoulders and glanced at the girls, all of whom were now looking his way. "Whatever the draft board does won't make any difference to me," he said, "because I don't plan on going."

Arnold's jaw dropped. "Jeez, they can send you to jail for that."

"Let 'em try."

"Are you a ... conscientious objector, then?"

"That's me."

The room became quiet, and everyone but Peter was absolutely still, wondering what to do or say. Only he appeared unconcerned, swaying his head to the rhythm of an imaginary dance tune as he squared up the stack of newspapers in front of him and reached for some twine.

Curly-haired Carlotta Dingle broke the silence and for a moment actually sounded as if she were coming to Peter's defense. "Personally, I think each boy should do what he thinks is right," she said. "It's a free country."

Rhonda Finch was appalled at her ignorance. "It's not a free country during wartime. How can you even say that?"

Carlotta shook her head. "All I mean is that you should be free to do whatever you want—if you're willing to pay the price."

"Like going to prison?"

"Sure."

Rhonda was not buying her argument. "Well, that's easy for a girl to say. Talk is cheap when you're—"

"No, she's right," Peter said, and he leaned back in his chair. "I don't care what those war lobbyists in Washington say. Even during hostilities, there's something called the United States Constitution, and our government is obliged to follow it to the letter."

"I don't think the Constitution even mentions a draft," Rhonda said to him.

"Precisely. And that's why I don't think conscription is constitutional."

"Lincoln had a draft, didn't he?"

"Sure, good Republican that he was, but that doesn't make it legal. I wouldn't have gone then either." Comfortably ensconced within his element, Peter was becoming more animated by the second. He looked at the other two female volunteers, those who had not yet spoken up, and wondered where each of them stood on this seminal issue. Particularly, he was interested in what Giulia Coletti thought, although he would never be so foolhardy as to confront her with the question directly. Instead, he turned to the boy.

"You say your brother's in the Navy, Wes?" he asked.

A wave of anxiety swept over Wesley. He felt woefully unqualified to engage in an impromptu debate with such a savvy activist as Peter Gerken. All Wesley knew was what he read in the newspaper or heard on the news, whereas Peter lived and breathed the cynicism of political intrigue.

Wesley swallowed hard. "Yes, he is. He enlisted."

"You don't say. And how long has he been in the service?"

"Almost a year now. He joined right after graduation."

Peter walked over to him, stopping just five feet away. "How would you feel if his ship went down?" he asked.

Wesley laughed nervously. "Terrible, of course. What kind of question is that?"

"Only this. If your brother does not return from the present war, his blood will be on the hands of the Roosevelt administration." Wesley started to say something in response, but Peter held up his hand to stop him. "I know what you're thinking, Wes, but I'm only an FDR man when it comes to his domestic policies, not on foreign affairs. He led us down the primrose path with both eyes open, and I'm sure he'll be made to pay for his recklessness, come election time."

"You sound like a defeatist," Wesley said, and a couple of the girls nodded in agreement.

"Far from it, my dear fellow. In fact, I hope to see Hitler blown to kingdom come at least as much as you do." Taking a deep breath, he used his index finger to hammer the tabletop for dramatic effect. "But the point is, it's not our fight—it's England's. I don't intend to become cannon fodder for King and Country. I would rather have all four of my limbs than one Victoria Cross, thank you."

Peter Gerken was no coward, and Wesley knew instinctively that there was more to his professed pacifism than the saving of his own skin. Maybe he really was sincere about this CO business after all. Maybe he really did dissent on purely ethical or religious grounds. Wesley began to concede a grudging admiration for Peter's iconoclastic views, while at the same time acknowledging that the two of them would never see eye to eye on the morality of warfare.

But Wesley recoiled a bit when the very next words out of Peter's mouth suggested a darker motive beneath his idealism. "Listen, Wes, it's the Russians who got it right," he said. "Unlike us, they didn't fight the Germans until attacked. Unlike us, they were in the cross hairs of the Nazis, so they had no choice but to defend themselves. Stalin and the Red Army—Zhukov and Rokossovsky, in particular—they are the real heroes of this war."

Suddenly, a great rumble was heard, growing louder by the second upon approach. At first, Wesley thought a B-17 was flying far too close to the ground for safety, but he quickly learned that the sound did not come from an aircraft at all but a 1940 Mack EG truck, which backed up to the loading dock and came to a stop with its engine idling. Peter opened the warehouse's overhead door and waved to the driver, Hubie Watson, a spindly black man with neatly trimmed white hair and beard. Effortfully, Arnold struggled to his feet and motioned for Wesley to follow. Their job now was to help Hubie load the truck with the stacks of salvaged newspapers.

When Peter pointed to the cab with a puzzled look, Hubie said, "I'm just gonna leave the motor runnin'. County says it burns less diesel that way than startin' and stoppin' all the time."

"Well, just don't let the exhaust suffocate these girls," Peter told him. Happily, there was little chance of that, for the swirling breeze was carrying most of the fumes away from the service entrance.

Working together as a team, Hubie, Wesley, and Peter had the outgoing shipment loaded in less than fifteen minutes, with Arnold begging off due to his chronically sore back. Meanwhile, the quartet of girls remained inside, straightening up the workroom and piling unbound newspapers for a subsequent shift of volunteers to inherit for processing.

"Thank you for the help, fellas," Hubie said. He cast a contemptuous glance at Arnold, who by now was reclining on a pew bench and eating an apple.

Peter acknowledged the driver's thanks with a friendly nod and mock military salute. "See you next week."

The entire building shook to its foundations as Hubie revved the engine and then shuddered the truck into first gear beneath the heavy load and drove away.

That was a most welcome signal for impatient Arnold Acker, who reached for the clipboard and wrote "4:55" in the TIME OUT column next to his name. Peter Gerken did the same, and so did Wesley Brower. When it was Giulia's turn to log her time, she spotted a familiar surname among the others on the sheet, one that she had not noticed when she signed in at noon. The entry read, "W. Brower," which, by process of elimination, she knew must represent the Waco High junior whom she met that afternoon.

"Do you have a brother named Stephen?" Giulia asked him. She passed the clipboard to Harriette Hoover.

The query, seemingly originating from out of the blue, took Wesley by surprise. "How do you know Steve?" He smiled the moment his eyes met hers.

"I was at the train station when he left for the Navy. He told me he'd write, but he never has."

"Well, the postal system's kind of willy-nilly, now that he's overseas. My mom's only gotten a handful of letters."

"Am I still supposed to write him at 'FPO, New York'? That's not much of an address."

"That's all they need," he said. When she nodded her head, Wesley was dazzled by the perfectly proportioned features of her face. He felt as if he were back in Hollywood—only this time chatting informally with some photogenic starlet. He envisioned a bigwig producer interrupting their talk with a contract, whispering to Wesley, "She can't miss."

"What did he say?" Giulia asked, and it brought Wesley's brief reverie to an abrupt end.

He cleared his throat nervously. "In the letters?"

"Yes, the letters." She smiled, amused by his dazed look. "Does Steve say he's doing all right?"

Wesley fumbled for words. "I guess. Well, yeah, I think so." A deep breath restored some of his composure. "Steve can't give us very much news," he said. "You know, the censors and all that."

Giulia picked up a slip of paper and jotted something on it, speaking as she wrote. "Would you do me a favor? Seeing as how I never seem to hear from him."

He felt a rush of adrenalin. "Sure. Just name it."

She finished writing and handed Wesley the paper. "Would you keep me posted on what Steve's doing? I promised to keep in touch with him, but it looks like the war is getting in the way."

Wesley looked at her telephone number and address, taking care not to allow his eyes to linger improperly at first glance. He sighed at the beautifully rendered, feminine penmanship—just the way he expected someone like her to write—and yet he pointed to one of the numerals. "Is that a nine?"

Giulia leaned her head closer to his. "Yes, I make my nines funny," she told him. "I guess I always have."

Wesley knew very well that it was a nine, but her smile was so lovely, her perfume so intoxicating, that at the moment he did not feel above any pretext to keep her near. "Would you rather that I write to you or call on the telephone?" he asked.

"Either one. But you might have better luck catching me if you just drop me a note. My work hours are hard to predict."

What he was really thinking is that he could use her address not for note dropping but for paying an occasional visit. The mails were so impersonal.

◆　　◆　　◆

It seemed an odd quirk of planning that Baylor University should schedule the last day of the spring quarter for a Monday, but that was the only way for final examinations to conclude on Friday, in time for commencement activities to begin the following morning. Her last class now completed, junior transfer student Hannah Lane was strolling along the pathway between the tennis courts and the heating plant, and off in the distance loomed Brooks Hall, home to more than two hundred Baylor boys whose towns of origin were too far away from campus for commuting.

She knew that Delbert Roush would be waiting for her outside because he needed his commentary back in time to study for the imminent final exam in The General Epistles (Bible 232). He and Hannah were in the same class, and Hannah had borrowed his heavily annotated volume as a secondary source for a term paper she wrote on why the book of Hebrews, despite its uncertain authorship, should be included among the other non-Pauline epistles.

"I'm sorry, Mrs. Brower, but Hannah has already left. Class ended about ten minutes ago. ... No, ma'am, actually that's my husband, Woodson. My name is Sybil Armes, and I'm her teacher. ... Is it an emergency? Oh, dear. ... Yes, I certainly will, if she happens to come by my office."

Ever reliable, there was Delbert at the rear of the central archway, leaning against the bricked tunnel with a half-eaten banana in hand. Though ignorant of Baptist finesse—and thus an easy target for intellectuals from Southwestern Seminary to ridicule—this young man from Bluff Dale, just northeast of Stephenville, was called to the ministry with a dedication beyond that of anyone else Hannah had ever met in her Christian walk. He lived and breathed the pulpit, evangelizing on street corners when no rural church asked him to supply on a given Sunday. And yet he lacked any vestige of an ego and was never stuffy or patronizing in his preaching, convicted as he was that the words which sprang forth so effortlessly from his mouth were not his own but an inspiration of the indwelling Holy Spirit.

Delbert would be graduating in precisely one week's time, and it made Hannah rather sad. She would miss having him in her classes—his eccentricities, his naïveté, his wide-eyed, bucolic wonderment. Probably never in his life would this honest fisher of men deliver a sermon in any church of more than a hundred members—he had little use for what he termed "those silver-dollar words"—but his unassuming congregations, with callused hands and soil under their fingernails, would be blessed by immersion in the Living Water of scripture.

She thanked Delbert for the use of his commentary, surprised him with a sisterly peck on the cheek, and then began walking down Dutton Street toward Fifth. She decided that there was just enough time to eat a quick meal before she was due at work. Noon classes were in session, so the campus was relatively deserted, and she could make good time on foot. Hannah was not an athlete—in terms of participating in organized sports like tennis, golf, or swimming—but she did possess a muscular athleticism that enabled her to walk faster than the vast majority of boys she knew, a healthy stride and stamina that would probably reduce them to gasping for breath.

Across Fifth Street from the Rena Marrs McLean Physical Education Building, two squirrels were chasing each other around the trunk of a majestic oak tree, a mating ritual that seemed to occur most frequently about this time of year. "Even the squirrels have spring fever," she thought with a smile. Hannah remembered the days of her youth when she and her father would go fishing on the northern bank of the Yadkin River near Siloam, and the dragonflies and butterflies would be so thick you could catch a dozen of them in the air with a single swipe of the coffee can. Although steadfastly conscientious in tending to his pastoral flock, the Reverend Samuel Lane delighted in getting away from it all on those rare occasions when the duties of church administration and compassionate visitation would permit. Now that Hannah thought about it, those were the only times when she ever saw him truly relaxed, lying on his old AEF blanket with the warm sun baking his skin and not worrying what, if anything, was hooked on the end of his line.

The temperature was about the same today as on those idyllic excursions, but somehow Waco always seemed more humid than back home. Perhaps that was indeed the case, but there was at least some likelihood that her memory was being selective, reviving in her mind only the pleasantest of images from before the war. Nothing whatsoever did she recall of her mother's death, for instance, despite the fact that a five-year-old was well past the age of knowing and fully capable of carrying such traumatic sorrows deep into adulthood.

"No, ma'am, I don't see her. She's usually not here until sometime after one on Mondays because she needs to ride the streetcar from Baylor. ...Yes, ma'am, I'll give your message to the secretary when she gets back from lunch–I'm just subbing for her–and she'll make sure Hannah gets it. ...Would you give me that telephone number again please?"

Dodging traffic, Hannah jaywalked across Speight and entered the Campus Grill, right next to the post office. Though a fine jazz-band program, "The Captivators," was playing over WACO, it did not turn out to be a very enjoyable dining experience. The counter person this day was an argumentative woman with repugnant nicotine stains on the fingernails of her right hand, a self-satisfied widow of about sixty whom Hannah had never seen before and hoped to avoid in the future. When it came time to pay her tab, she laid a penny beside her plate instead of the more customary dime and walked over to the cash register with no sense of guilt, staring the waitress straight in the eye. She was one to tip on the basis of personality at least as much as service, and disagreeable attendants could expect no charity from her camp, not when it took such a negligible amount of effort to construct a modest smile or articulate a civil greeting. That really was very little to ask of a human being, and those who seemed unaware of such fundamental niceties were well advised to stay clear of Hannah Lane.

By the time she went back outside to wait for the streetcar, classes were in the process of changing, and students were scurrying in all directions. Most of them, of course, were women. Of the nearly sixteen hundred students enrolled in the spring quarter, not even five hundred were men—and a fair percentage of them were in uniform, soon to be leaving. She gazed up Fifth Street, far to the north, and could see the Amicable Life Insurance Building, Waco's only true skyscraper. Somehow, it made her feel important to be educated in a city with a building like that, more than twice as tall as Raleigh's Sir Walter Raleigh Hotel on Fayetteville Street.

The streetcar arrived, bell clanging and electrical sparks sputtering overhead, and Hannah climbed aboard, along with nine other Baylor students. Some doubtlessly had business to conduct downtown, paying bills and such, but two of the girls appeared to be going on a shopping spree, so giddy were they with the novel sensation of giving their brains a well-deserved rest. Final examinations would begin the next day, but that was hours away yet, and after all, could they not devote their entire evening to study? They had the best of intentions.

The streetcar stopped at Austin Avenue, and Hannah walked the few short blocks back to Crawford-Austin Manufacturing Company, now located in its roomier facility at Sixth and Jackson. She nodded a greeting to treasurer Oscar Tabb—and also to his wife, Ethel, who had brought him a sack lunch—and then made her way toward the larger of the two woodworking shops. Not too long ago, she had been "borrowed," temporarily but indefinitely, by the camp furniture division, and it made her none too pleased. Hannah was eager to help in any way that she could, but she always felt much less proficient with lathe, ban-saw, and finishing brush than she had been with the industrial-grade treadles, bobbin winders, and stitching needles that had filled her working hours before the move. She also missed having Mr. Hinckley as a supervisor, particularly when compared to her present foreman, a rather overbearing, former retiree named Mark Teller. Crawford-Austin Vice President Raymond Goddard had talked "Old Man" Teller into returning when Andy Lowe, despite being protected in an exempt position, suddenly resigned in favor of military service.

Hannah wrapped the heavy apron around herself and was tying it behind her back when—over the cacophony of drill presses and circular saws—she thought she heard someone calling out her name: "Hannah! Hannah Lane!" It was Mr. Teller's secretary, Candace Nixon, a dour, middle-aged woman who could not have weighed more than eighty-five pounds in a wet fur coat. Candace appeared to be beckoning her with the fingers of her cupped hand, so Hannah walked briskly over to the desk.

"Someone rang for you, about a half-hour ago while I was at lunch. Janie took the message. She said it was an emergency."

Candace handed a slip of paper to Hannah, who read, "Mon., 12:50, Hannah Lane. Mrs. Brower—Call home—Urgent."

"You can use the telephone in Mr. Teller's office," the lady told her. "He's gone for the afternoon."

Hannah shut the door of the foreman's windowless cubicle and dialed the number. Nora Brower must have been sitting next to the telephone because she answered on the first ring.

"Hello?"

"Mrs. B., this is Hannah. Can you hear me all right?"

"Yes, dear." Her voice sounded tense—pinched and nasal. "Your Aunt Winnie called from North Carolina. She says your father is back in the hospital."

There was a pause, as Hannah recalled the week before Thanksgiving. "Pneumonia?" she asked.

"No, she says it's his heart. Not a heart attack exactly, but your daddy had chest pains so severe that he was unconscious when they found him."

"Dear God."

"She doesn't think you need to come back immediately—well, the doctors don't think so anyway—but she did want you to know that he was ailing."

"Yes, of course." A hundred concerns raced through Hannah's mind. "I don't think I can get a train ticket on such short notice anyway, and final exams start tomorrow."

"Your aunt said don't worry about coming, not just now. She left a telephone number, somewhere you can reach her when you get off work, and she said you could reverse the charges."

"I'm pretty sure my boss would let me off now for an emergency like this."

"No, dear, I know your father would want you to stay on the job—especially with this war on. Besides, your aunt said he's getting the best of care and resting comfortably. His life doesn't seem to be in danger."

All afternoon long, Hannah worked as if she were in a trance, with ideas on how to return home to her father's side taking precedence over the task at hand, war production or not.

♦   ♦   ♦

Dear Mom,

How is everyone back home? I am fine, taking to the nautical life like a duckling does to water. I think I can tell you that I am aboard a destroyer, but I am not allowed to specify where I am sailing. Let's just say somewhere in the Atlantic. I don't think the censors will snip that out. If they did, then you wouldn't be reading it now.

Some of the men are seasick, but so far I have not experienced any of that. The trip has been uneventful, except for one evening, just after sunset, when we got to see a carrier launch around fifty planes into the prevailing winds. Pretty impressive, but it's hard to imagine those fly-boys landing on that same deck in the dark. That takes guts, let me tell you.

The weather has been fine for the most part, though we did hit one squall line just a couple of days out. It didn't feel as bad as it would have on terra firma because we're used to the sea spray and rocking motion anyhow. Sailors are taught to stand watch by looking above the horizon and viewing objects in our peripheral vision. Try it sometime—it really does work that way.

I had a surprise the other day when I walked over to the ship's store and came face-to-face with Howard Korbas. Do you remember him? He's a couple of years older than I am, played basketball for Coach Keithly, and used to work at the Karmelkorn Shop. He looks just the same as he did in high school, except for shedding a few pounds and adding a few strands of GRAY HAIR above his ears, and he's only about twenty-one. So that's what I've got to look forward to …

This ship is really like a small city, with everything you could need and plenty of room to move around. Usually the chow is not too bad—lots better than the Army and Marines are getting, at least from what I've heard. Sleeping quarters are a little cramped though, and you sure can't play catch with a football like we could on dry land. One of the guys in my outfit has a Yorkshire terrier named "Ashcan," which is what we call our depth charges (little packages of joy for the U-boats).

I got off duty about two hours ago and go on watch pretty soon for four hours, so it'll be a long night. Mostly what we seem to be doing is fire drills. We're experts at that by now.

I'll write again when I can find some spare time. They keep us plenty busy—whether there's something useful to do or not! I received your last letter, the one when you talked about Mrs. Howington's stray pig. She shouldn't worry about him getting hit by a car. He probably moves faster than the traffic does these days.

Goodbye for now.

Love, S—

Dear Hannah,

I hope all is well with you and that your Baylor studies are not too bad.

We're somewhere in the Atlantic, can't be more specific than that, and I'm pretty sure we'll be seeing some action soon. So far, my Navy career has been mostly drills, classes, K.P. duty, and saluting officers, but I suspect that is about to change.

It gets pretty chilly at night, but I can't complain because I missed the really cold time of year at sea. I guess I'll have to endure it the next time around, if this war is still on. When there is a new moon, it's almost total darkness out here, but we've got technical instruments to tell us if anything is approaching in any direction—friend or foe.

Has Lizzie heard anything more from the police about that human rat who attacked her? Something as scary as that can affect a person's whole life, and I sure don't want that for her. She's a pretty tough customer, though, so maybe she's already forgotten all about it by now. (Don't let Lizzie read this because I wouldn't want her to get sappy about it, thinking that I'm worried about my kid sister!)

The chow aboard ship is usually pretty good. Lots of Navy beans of course (ha ha) and meat and potatoes. There's even dessert because servicemen get all that sugar you landlubbers have so generously volunteered to give up. Sometimes there are little worms in the beans, but they are very much dead, so you can easily set them aside with your spoon. Our cook says they put iron in your diet, but then I'm sure he eats from cans that are not blessed with all that extra protein.

Please look after Mom while I'm gone—and say hi to Lizzie and Wes. Oh, and scratch Valentino's back for me the next time you see him. There aren't many pets to be seen around here, except for a few that have been smuggled aboard, including a Yorkshire terrier and a dachshund puppy. One fellow has a goldfish in a jar, and he's real careful with it. I don't think Goldy would last very long if he washed overboard into that saltwater.

Well, I need to go on watch in a little while, so I'd better stop scribbling this before I get thrown into the brig. Drop me a note whenever you can. Sorry I don't write more often.

Love, Steve

Dear Giulia,

I have a few minutes to spare, so I thought that I would write you a short note, to let you know what is happening in my life these days. I just heard eight bells, which meant that my four-hour evening watch was finally over. It was pretty boring, which is fine with me. The last thing you ever want is an eventful watch. I heard that there was a ship sighting on the first dog watch, just after 6:30, but it turned out to be friendly. I don't think I'm giving away any military secrets there, so maybe the censor will let this get through.

It's a few minutes past midnight as I write this, and I am snacking on an orange. They like for us to eat a lot of fruit—presumably to keep away the scurvy. I heard a dog bark a while ago, and I do know for a fact that there are a couple of canine stowaways aboard. I have seen (and petted) a little Yorkie. One mess attendant from Pennsylvania has trained a seagull to follow the ship, occasionally tossing the bird a piece of raw fish from the galley to keep it interested. I can't figure out where that gull spends its nights in mid-ocean, unless it perches on our stern after sundown.

It must be about graduation time at Waco High, huh? Golly, it seems a lot longer than just a year ago when I got my diploma. Do you think you will finish up your schooling whenever your mother's back gets better? My brother wrote me a letter (well, actually a couple of lines in my mom's letter) to say that Clarence Lyndon and Alice Ann Turk got married. Do you remember them? Alice Ann organized a war-bonds rally when I was there, and her daddy was on the school board.

Belated thanks for coming to the train station to wish me "bon voyage." It meant a lot to me and to my mother, and I hope you did not get into trouble with that Mr. Lindermann (spelling?) of yours. That swell send-off is one of the fondest memories of my entire leave, and your kiss has kept me warm for all these weeks at sea. Please mail me a picture of yourself, whenever you can. I have just the right place for it, between my locker and bunk. It will look very pretty there (or anywhere).

Love, Steve

◆　　◆　　◆

By the time Elizabeth came downstairs on Thursday morning, her brother was already seated at the table with their mother. He was eating a bowl of Rice Krispies and dressed for the day. Curious, she tiptoed a bit closer and watched him for a moment. After placing a spoonful of cereal in his mouth, Wesley would pick up a pencil and draw a line through some dialogue in a radio script that rested just to the left of his breakfast. Then he would repeat the process, occasionally looking up toward the ceiling, as if committing the typewritten words to memory.

Nora sat in her usual chair, diagonally from her son. She was enjoying a nearly burned slice of toast, spread with a miserly coating of orange marmalade. This fruity indulgence, rather scarce because of its high concentration of rationed sugar, was canned in a half-pint Mason jar by her good friend, Mabel Johns, who was known all over north Waco for her delectable preserves.

When Nora looked up, she happened to spot Elizabeth standing behind the floor lamp. "And about time you rolled out of bed, sleepy-head," she said. "Don't you know it's almost noon?" That was a slight exaggeration, as the kitchen clock clearly read 8:20.

Now that her observation post was uncovered, Elizabeth approached the others and seated herself across from Wesley. She leaned down to greet the family's spoiled cat, Valentino, when she felt him rubbing against her leg.

"Are you hungry, Lizzie?" Nora asked. "We're nearly finished, but I hated to wake you. What time did you go to bed last night?"

"Not until 11:30," the girl said. "I was talking to Christine McElroy on the telephone." She craned her neck to read Wesley's script, but it was upside-down to her.

"Why so late?"

"Oh, you know her. She's got some personal problems that we were trying to sort out."

"Shhhh ..." Wesley said.

Nora began whispering. "Did you solve everything?" She stood up to get her daughter a glass of apple juice.

"Hardly. It's a bigger mess now than when she called."

"Oh, dear." Chuckling quietly, Nora opened the refrigerator door and began pouring the juice.

"Chrissy's boyfriend is a senior, you know," Elizabeth said aloud. "He'll be moving away to Iowa for college—that is, if he doesn't enlist first."

Nora walked over and handed her daughter the glass. "Why Iowa?" she asked. That seemed an unusual choice for a local boy to make. Most of them—those not in the service—naturally gravitated toward Texas schools.

Elizabeth took a sip of the juice. "She says his daddy went to Drake too. It's in Des Moines, the capital."

"Shhhh ..." Wesley told his sister. "Can you gossip somewhere else, please?"

She glowered at him. "Who do you think you are, the kitchen police? All we're having is a normal conversation."

Nora scooted her chair back. "Maybe we should go into the living room, dear. Poor Wes has a lot of lines this afternoon. Bring your apple juice with you, but be careful not to spill it."

Elizabeth made a face at her brother. "Well, why didn't he study last night?" she asked. "That's what a real professional would have done."

"I *am* a professional, dopey," Wesley told her. "I get paid, don't I?"

"Oh, sure. Like Waco, Texas, is the big time."

Nora had one foot in the living room, and she was motioning for her daughter to follow. "Wes wasn't here last night—as you very well know," she said. "Now, stop bickering, you two."

"Is it true you were at a girl's house?" Elizabeth shouted from the other room.

Wesley did not reply because he could sense that his sister was aware of the answer already, and any kind of response—particularly a fumbling denial—would only encourage her to pursue the matter to its logical extremes of embarrassment. But he wondered how in the world she found out where he went. Those freshman girls seemed to have a communications network that rivaled the OSS. He had told his mother nothing beyond that he was going to Morton Wilson's house, and indeed he did visit there for fifteen minutes or so, just to validate his stretching of the truth.

All things considered, Wesley decided it was better to remain silent than incriminate himself, and besides, there was no changing his sister's suspicions anyway. Elizabeth would assume that he went over to Giulia's house for romantic intentions, and it was a futile proposition to try to convince her otherwise. His motive in seeing the young lady was nothing more sensational than letting her read his brother's most recent letter home, but he knew that Giulia Coletti was far too pretty for anyone to believe that. In all honesty, even he doubted it at times.

Wesley sighed and returned to the script. Though he had been studying his lines for nearly a half-hour now, it seemed to him that the farther along he progressed, the more unread pages there were to be learned. Worse yet, tomorrow's show would be a cliffhanger concerning Kip Hanson and Sally Holt, so he wanted to be at his best for that one as well. Much like what confronted him in the preparation for today's episode, this evening, too, was shaping up to be a difficult study opportunity for tomorrow's show, owing to a coincidental quirk of the calendar.

As misfortune would have it, the first of June happened to be the very evening of Waco High School's commencement exercises, which he normally would have skipped with pleasure but now felt compelled to attend. Wesley figured that Giulia would be there, it being her graduating class in the spotlight, and he certainly did not want to have to rely on another letter from Steve for a credible reason to see her again. This annual occasion, so cherished by parents and (especially) grandparents, had been moved indoors to Waco Hall a few days earlier because—with the spectators' comfort and safety at heart—school and city officials judged that the recent onslaught of inclement weather had rendered Municipal Stadium unfit to host such an event. Wesley did not yet know Giulia well enough to invite her to go with him, so his prospects were reduced to the off chance of spotting her among the twelve hundred or more people expected to be present.

At first, Wesley was annoyed when his sister and mother came back into the kitchen, but then it occurred to him that his concentration had been drifting far from the task at hand anyway, and there was no one to blame but himself. For the past ten minutes or so, though he was staring at words on paper, his thoughts were elsewhere, dealing with the less urgent but even more challenging issue of how to secure a seat near Giulia Coletti at commencement. Apparently, Elizabeth was not speaking to him, miffed at the way he had treated her. But this would not last. It never did.

That afternoon's "Behold Tomorrow" went very well, so well in fact that Wesley entertained the brash idea of abstaining from any read-through whatsoever prior to the Friday show. He would never attempt this figurative tightrope walk of his own accord, of course, but somehow it was reassuring to know that such a feat could be accomplished if dire necessity left no other choice. In actuality, even when the "On Air" light was glowing, his printed script was always right there in front of him, to guide him along, word by word. That was the beauty of performing on radio, as opposed to acting in the legitimate theater. Needless to say, stage actors would argue just as vehemently that this was a profound weakness of the medium, an utter lack of the spontaneity and characterization that a memorized and thus more fully assimilated role can impart to an audience.

In contrast to Thursday's performance, the cast rehearsal for Friday's show was an unmitigated fiasco, as everything that could possibly go wrong invariably did. Neddy Wright appeared to be either sleep-walking or sight-reading, Phyllis Sherry broke her eyeglasses and had to borrow a pair from hyperopic Patience Glover in bookkeeping, Monica Whaley was having only moderate success in coaxing the mimeograph machine to function long enough for a final revision, and Ray Leftwich became mildly ill and ultimately had to flee the premises. In this pitiable company, even Wesley's muted contribution positively shone, though Sandra Whittsel later found fault with his, as she put it, "monotone delivery" in the Ferris wheel scene. "You sounded like a trained parrot my cousin had ... taught by rote," she said, much to the amusement of Marshall McFall. She was correct, but that did not excuse her from at least making a token attempt at civility. The protruding cold sore on McFall's upper lip was all that made the moment bearable.

Wesley rode a streetcar to Baylor University, and he seemed to be the only person aboard who was dressed for commencement exercises. That could be explained by the fact that he arrived two hours early for the event, when most other attendees were still at home, probably just sitting down to dinner. He assumed that the start time would be around 7:00, when really it did not begin until 8:15. He spent the interim in the reading room of Carroll Library, which fortunately was accessible to the public because the summer quarter was already in progress, having opened the day before. He devoted his time to skimming through some back issues of *Life* magazine—those with Admiral Nimitz, Esther Williams, and Princess Elizabeth on the covers—but his eyes kept wandering across the room. The Baylor coeds always looked so much more sophisticated than high school girls.

Around 7:15, Wesley walked down the library stairs, through the doors, and into the balmy springtime air. Earlier, he heard on the radio that it was eighty-seven degrees that afternoon, and the humidity made it feel much hotter than that. He crossed Fifth Street for a chilled bottle of Coca-Cola at the Piggly Wiggly store, then headed west on Speight, only to discover that people were already streaming into the big auditorium. Ahead he could see Brandon Marks and his parents going up the front steps together, and Brandon's graduation gown was draped over his right arm. That was a sensible move, the sunlight being uncomfortably warm for donning the regalia outside.

Wesley trotted up the steps and into the marble vestibule, listening to the echoes of hushed voices as he passed through to the carpeted foyer. Lying there, next to each of the auditorium doors, was a stack of commencement programs for the ushers to distribute. It happened that the young lady at door "III-II" was preoccupied at the moment, a friend having engaged her in animated conversation, so Wesley took the opportunity to secure a three-inch stack of programs and enter the hall as if he were engaged to do so. This was his only chance.

To the front of the mammoth room he went, all the way down to the orchestra pit, and then he began handing programs to the relatively few individuals who had not received them upon entering the hall. It worked like a charm. Wesley was able to scan the audience as if on duty, without appearing too conspicuous to school administrators. Indeed, one of the unsuspecting people to whom he gave a program was Waco High School's dean of girls, Miss Annie Forsgard. He sustained this little charade for more than forty minutes, all the while searching the masses for one very pretty face in particular and refusing to admit to himself that the endeavor was hopeless. Only when the acting principal, Marian Butler, requested that the audience stand for the Pledge of Allegiance did Wesley finally concede defeat.

I pledge allegiance to the flag of the United States of America, and to the republic, for which it stands, one nation, indivisible, with liberty and justice for all.

He dared not continue to stand with his back to the stage any longer, calling attention to himself and arousing suspicion, so he carried the remaining programs with him up the aisle and out of the auditorium. Either Giulia Coletti was not present for her own class's graduation exercises or he had simply missed spotting her among the thousand or more onlookers on the main floor. But then he had another idea, and he made one last, desperate attempt. After laying the programs on their original stack, he trudged up the staircase, entered the second balcony from its rear, and proceeded straight to the front corner seat, from where he could view the scattered patrons. Perhaps the girl had chosen to sit in one of the two balconies.

The Senior Band played its opening music under Lyle Skinner's direction, and then two school officials delivered short speeches, followed by those of valedictorian Betty Bruck and salutatorian Bobby Pillow. Wesley searched faces for Giulia but finally surrendered all hope when Sam Darden, president of the Waco School Board, began presenting the diplomas. Each graduate's name was read—some 200 girls but only 122 boys, a disparity caused by the manpower needs of America's war effort. How could Wesley have sensed that Giulia was seated a mere thirty feet away, almost directly below him? A half-hour before, when his eyes scrutinized that particular section of the bottom floor, the girl happened to select just such an unlucky moment to bend forward and place her purse beneath the chair.

The evening ended quite late, but early enough for him to catch the last streetcar back to north Waco. Otherwise, he would have had to hitch a ride from one of the underclassmen, whom he saw congregating near the ceiling-to-floor bronze plaque that immortalized the late Samuel Palmer Brooks's final, poignant, undelivered speech. It was just as well, as Wesley was peeved and in no mood for company on the way home.

◆   ◆   ◆

A heavy-set but proportionally tall ("big boned") woman named Roberta Funk was in charge of commercial writing at the radio station—had been for ten years now—and she, perhaps more than anyone else at KWXN, was delighted that public school was out for the summer months. What it meant to her was that some of the station's part-time employees could be elevated to full-time status to fill in the gaps left by enlistments and the draft. Two of her small staff of four had left for military service, the most recent being Bill Ordway, who followed Henry Smith into the Navy by a mere month and a half. Mimi Mitchell, a bookish-looking Baylor dropout in the newsroom, was shifted to replace Henry, and Mrs. Funk recruited Wesley Brower to take over Bill's account list until the first of September. The position was not exactly what Wesley would have selected, had he a choice in the matter, but it still promised to bring in a considerable amount of money, and he was able to work alongside many people he knew. Besides that, the new assignment placed him right there at the radio station for his daily "Behold Tomorrow" rehearsals and performances.

It seemed odd to arrive with the other employees rather than simply joining them from school, as he had done for so many months. Early on his first day as a full-timer, he leaned his bicycle against the groundskeepers' tool shed and walked, lunch sack in hand, across the dewy grass to the station entrance. There he greeted a gloomy, Monday morning flock of office girls, five of whom car-pooled every dawn in Mary Sturgeon's 1939 Oldsmobile Series 60 Sedan. Already they seemed to be looking forward to the weekend.

Unaccustomed to such a long schedule, Wesley watched the day inch along in slow motion. Fortunately, about twenty-five minutes prior to "Behold Tomorrow," he was able to resume his regular routine in the studio with the rest of the cast, and from then on he felt so in tune with daily activities that it actually took him by surprise when he looked up at the clock and saw that it was past five. This would take some getting used to, he thought, but it made him proud to be considered an adult employee, just like all the others, instead of a glorified high school intern.

Normal times did not last for long. Only moments after he reported for his second full day of work, Wesley realized that this was not going to be a morning he would soon forget. Though he had heard a few sketchy accounts over breakfast, somehow he was unable to grasp the full significance of this pivotal occasion until he was surrounded by the news staff, the production staff, and management—all of whom were huddled near the wall-mounted radio in the newsroom and listening with bated breath to every word the CBS announcers spoke over the air. Work could wait on this day, except of course for essential, on-air personnel who took care of whatever preparations were necessary and then returned promptly to the newsroom for further reports on the Allied invasion of Hitler's Fortress Europe.

Douglas Edwards was on the network airwaves during that first hour of the KWXN workday, and at precisely 8:13 (Central War Time), he told of early reaction to the landings: "People kept on working overnight shifts in shipyards and other factories and went to work as usual this morning. But everyone seems to be more serious, and many stopped in their tasks long enough to offer prayers for the success of the Allied effort."

Wesley noticed that Monica Whaley was tearful, even though her husband was in the Marine Corps and on the other side of the globe from this, the largest seaborne military operation in history. She had no way of knowing it, but the 3rd Division of US Marines had embarked at Guadalcanal three days earlier and were now sailing for Kwajalein in the Marshall Islands, en route to the Marianas. Wesley wondered why she was crying, and then it occurred to him that, for her at least, the events of this day represented far more than a momentous juncture of world history. To her, the Allied attack of German-occupied France meant that Marine Corporal Herbert Whaley was one step closer to returning home. It spelled the beginning of the end for worry, separation, loneliness, a postponed family, and unfulfilled dreams.

At eleven o'clock that morning, as Wesley was busy hunting-and-pecking some Towne Jewelers copy on the battered Royal typewriter, he ran into confusion with a pendant description and was obliged to call the store manager, Charles Cole, for details. He, in turn, had to telephone the shop's owner in Dallas for final approval of the text. During the intervening time, which amounted to the better part of an hour, Wesley left his post to get an update on the war news. Most everyone else had heard the basic details of what was happening on the beaches of northwestern France, but he, for good reason, had been left unaware. With verbal creativity in mind, the copy room was the one place at KWXN where a radio broadcast was not piped over loudspeakers. Even the announcing booths had them—though in there, of course, the speakers became mute whenever microphones were opened.

Only about a dozen people were in the newsroom when Wesley entered. "Kate Smith Speaks" was being carried over the CBS network, but her folksy, fifteen-minute visit was anything but typical this day. General Foods—the makers of Sure Gel—had dispensed with their standard commercial messages. Instead, Kate Smith opened the hour with a three-and-a-half-minute commentary on the Allied offensive and then turned the show over to her regular announcer, Ted Collins. After a recap of the latest news from the European Theater, he relayed to his audience the dramatic words of an American correspondent who rode in a plane and witnessed the historic assault first-hand: "Peering down, you can see our troops scrambling ashore under a canopy of shells, hurled over their heads by warships in a harbor that dents the shoreline. In the half-light we can see the flashes from German shore batteries all along the coastline and inside the harbor."

When Wesley returned to the copy room, a note of instructions was lying next to his typewriter. It was a message from Tex Cole himself, owner of Towne Jewelers. The station's receptionist, Myra Culp, had transcribed his long-distance comments into her clearly legible hand, probably dispatching one of the continuity girls to deliver the memo to Wesley's desk. This pricing clarification enabled the young man to finish his sixty-second spot, read it over for timing—a bit long, so he deleted three superfluous words—and place it in the production tray for traffic to sort and distribute.

He wrote two more commercials, thirty- and sixty-second spots for Brazelton Appliance Company, and then ate his sack lunch in the employees' lounge. Yesterday it had worked well to do so because many of the staff went out to eat for salesman Rusty Hertel's fortieth birthday, but today was a different story. There was only a smattering of empty spaces at the tables, and none of the availabilities happened to be near people whom he knew well enough to feel comfortable chatting with over his peanut butter and jelly sandwich and green apple.

Wesley finally settled for a solitary chair near the opposite wall of the room. There was so much lively conversation in the lounge that it was virtually impossible to hear the war news unless one happened to be sitting close enough to either of the two wall speakers, mounted just below ceiling level. Funny, this morning the station had come to a virtual standstill for D-Day information, but now nobody seemed to be paying it any mind whatsoever. Later, when he happened to mention this phenomenon to his department head, Roberta Funk, she just laughed and attributed it to what she termed the "sanctity of the lunch hour." Interest revived as the afternoon wore on, so maybe there was some truth to her fanciful theory.

The typewriter slowly clattered under Wesley's untutored index fingers:

SPRING CLEANING IS NOT JUST FOR YOUR HOME. YOUR CLOTHING IS IN NEED OF A FRESH, SPRINGTIME LOOK AND SMELL TOO. AT MAJESTIC CLEANERS, LADIES' DRESSES ARE OUR SPECIALTY ... WITH EVERY GARMENT CAREFULLY MEASURED BEFORE AND AFTER CLEANING. MAJESTIC IS ALSO YOUR ONE-STOP SHOP FOR HAT CARE, WITH PROFESSIONAL CLEANING AND BLOCKING. AND DON'T FORGET OUR CLOTH REWEAVING SERVICES, WHICH MAKE MOTH HOLES AND CIGARETTE BURNS DISAPPEAR LIKE MAGIC. COME BY MAJESTIC CLEANERS AND EXPERT DYERS AT 1420 COLCORD, OR TELEPHONE 701. MAJESTIC ... YOUR SPRINGTIME CLEANERS.

After he placed this new, thirty-second spot in the production tray—a rush job for the 2:30 adjacency—he wandered back to the newsroom for the latest word on today's amphibious assault in northwestern France. Beyond the usual reporters and staff writers, there were several office girls present, presumably hoping to learn the latest war news as they took a break from their mundane clerical duties. Three young ladies from traffic were seated uncommonly close to newsman Johnny Clayton, however, so maybe there was more to it than high-principled intellectual curiosity.

It was at two o'clock that the Columbia Broadcasting System preempted "The Story of Mary Marlin" for a D-Day message from London by the English monarch. "At this historic moment," King George VI told his subjects, "surely not one of us is too busy, too young, or too old to play a part in a nationwide, a worldwide vigil of prayer, as the great crusade sets forth."

At fifteen minutes past the hour, commentator Alan Jackson went on the air, substituting for Robert Trout, who had been up all night with the continuous network coverage. According to Jackson, "The Allied invasion armies—landed in northwestern France this morning—have now driven at least nine and a half miles into the vaunted Nazi west wall to the town of Caen, and after twelve hours of fighting, they held beachheads on a broad front along the coast of Normandy."

Two of KWXN's cub reporters came into the room about this time, and one of them was Sandra Whittsel. Now that school was out, she was assisting in the news department, while sustaining her burgeoning role as Sally Holt in the afternoon serial. For the past several months, Wesley had perceived that Sandy blew hot and cold in her attitude toward him. Today was one of the cool days, for she hardly even looked his direction, choosing instead to doodle on a scrap of paper while listening apathetically to the latest information from the European Theater.

Sandy seemed to be in the doldrums, and Wesley wondered why. Maybe she and Marshall McFall had a squabble, he thought, and it was all he could do to hold back a smile. But this pleasant speculation was dashed five minutes later when the announcer himself came strolling into the newsroom and took a seat next to her, encountering no apparent resistance when he placed his hand upon hers. Wesley could not help noticing that Sandy's blouse seemed awfully snug, straining at the buttons as if a size too small. Of course, it was not inconceivable that she was still developing physically, as Sandy was only sixteen. Then again, there was always a chance that she selected one of her junior high school tops simply to attract attention. If so, it worked, and Wesley was a good thirty feet away.

He did his best to ignore Sandy from that moment on, but with only partial success. So undeniably attractive was she to the male eye that Wesley did not feel the slightest twinge of guilt about appreciating her charms whenever the opportunity presented itself. But he was intent upon maintaining some semblance of professionalism here, reminding himself that, after all, Sandra Whittsel was not the real reason he had come to the newsroom. What was happening on the coastline of France far overshadowed any romantic aspirations that he might retain. And besides that, he did not want to give her the satisfaction of seeing him stare.

At 2:30, CBS opened its microphones at the radio gallery of the House of Representatives, asking correspondent Bill Henry to gather opinions from the nation's lawmakers. Marshall McFall left the newsroom soon thereafter, and

Wesley stole a look at Sandy's profile as she began to compose a news story for four o'clock. Her face was the ideal of a silhouettist's dreams, with that pretty, turned-up nose, the long eyelashes, the sensuous mouth. She was enchanting from the neck down too, leaning forward over the typewriter keyboard to decipher the faintly readable wire copy. Wesley captured that image for bittersweet reference, taking it with him back to his desk and locking it into his memory for longer than he would care to admit.

That day's installments of "Behold Tomorrow" and "West of the Brazos" were preempted by continuing coverage of the great crusade.

♦   ♦   ♦

Hannah had read Steve's most recent letter several times, being careful not to let Elizabeth lay eyes upon it. Even Steve himself considered one sentimental passage a bit too "sappy" for sharing with his sister. Hannah refolded the letter, slipped it back in the envelope, and then laid it on the small stack of like correspondence that she concealed beneath her underwear in the chest of drawers. Steve was not a prolific writer, but then neither was she. Hannah had only written to him twice since his embarkation leave, which was over two months ago. Their latest efforts must have crossed in the mails, for his letter arrived just a couple of days after she posted hers.

Mindful of the dramatic conflicts that were transpiring overseas, she could not help wondering whether Steve's ship was one of the hundreds involved in the Allied invasion of France. But the more she thought about it, the more unlikely that seemed. Steve had been at home a mere six weeks before the assault, and surely there would have to be months of preparation beforehand. Reliant upon newspapers and radio as her only sources of war information, she—being an ordinary citizen—could not know that the men of DD-621, the destroyer USS *Jeffers*, had been training all along and sailed from New York City for the British Isles on the fifth of May.

This Monday was Hannah's only free evening of the week, and she had a date planned with a Baylor boy, Eddie Shaughnessy—her first social outing in more than three months. Why she ever accepted his invitation had grown unclear to her with the passage of the weekend. It seemed a pleasant enough diversion when he telephoned last Thursday, but now she regretted being so quick to say yes. Though Eddie had been in her fall-quarter American History class, there was little else in common between them, and they had not so much as said a word to each other since late November.

The telephone call had taken Hannah by surprise, catching her with no plausible excuse for refusing his kind gesture. How well she knew that her sole night of leisure could be put to much better use than sitting in a darkened movie theater, watching two wartime pictures with a casual acquaintance, trying to avoid an accidental bumping of elbows atop the armrest. Thinking back, it crossed Hannah's mind that Eddie Shaughnessy did appear awfully interested in her whenever they happened to speak to each other in class. Weeks ago, she had consented to give him the Browers' telephone number, so that he might compare notes with her on the Louisiana Purchase—a mutually productive conversation that probably helped her at least as much as it did him on the ensuing test. But when the telephone rang on Thursday, Hannah realized that Eddie had retained this number for future reference. Otherwise, he would have been unable to reach her, for there was no intuitive reason for him to search under "Brower" in the telephone directory, nor could an operator give him the number without a name.

The Fifth War Loan was in progress, and Monday night's admission to the Grand Theatre was restricted to customers who bought a bond, either at the box office or at one of the many outlets scattered about town. That morning, Eddie Shaughnessy purchased two of them—one for himself and one for his guest—at a local five-cent store, W. T. Grant Company, which was located just a block down from the theater on Austin Avenue. Hannah, though, would have none of that, doggedly refusing to accept the bond as a gift and insisting upon paying Eddie back in full, so as not to violate her stringent practice of going Dutch. Their demonstrative negotiations were completed, much to the amusement of others in line, on the sidewalk outside the Grand Theatre, directly across from Waco's Amicable skyscraper. No doubt young Mr. Shaughnessy could only wonder at the predicament he had gotten himself into, discovering too late that this particular stray kitten possessed claws sharp enough to draw blood.

But the evening settled down nicely, once Eddie knew where he stood with his spirited companion. A special war-bond screening opened the program, the musical comedy *So's Your Uncle*, starring Billie Burke and Donald Woods. Next on the double feature was a drama with Edward Arnold, Fay Bainter, and Van Johnson, *The War Against Mrs. Hadley*. Miss Bainter, as the title character, Stella Hadley, depicted a patrician widow in Washington, D.C., who fell out of touch with the war effort and suffered the consequences. For the film's captive audience, this message was rather like preaching to the choir, inasmuch as the price of admission was already a solid affirmation of patriotic sentiment. And yet manager Cleve Pullen took the opportunity, during the forty minutes between films, to impress upon his customers the urgent need to invest in further bond purchases, which—for the audience's convenience—could be made right there in the Grand Theatre lobby before the house lights dimmed once again.

To Eddie's credit, never once did he try to test the waters by extending his arm around the back of Hannah's chair. This was an old trick that, in theory at least, would allow the suitor to preview a girl's response while stopping short of venturing physical contact. It usually fooled no one and accomplished next to nothing, but many vacillating young men persisted in exercising the hackneyed technique, sometimes repeatedly in a single sitting. The sole untoward incident of the evening came when Eddie visited the rest room during the second feature and returned to find a soused interloper occupying his seat. The man became quite disorderly until an usher shined a flashlight into his glazed eyes and allowed him to misconstrue the snappy theater uniform as that of a Waco police officer.

Thereafter, he moved to an available spot near the rear of the auditorium and promptly fell asleep.

By sheer coincidence, it happened that this same Eddie Shaughnessy was the cousin of one of Hannah's closest friends at church, Belinda O'Rourke, who was at the movies too. Hannah spotted her first, as Belinda walked among a throng of people exiting the Grand Theater, and she called out her name, "Lindy!"

Eddie was surprised when none other than the daughter of his mother's sister turned around and nodded in recognition. He looked quizzically at Hannah. "How do you know her?"

"We both go to First Baptist," Hannah said, and she was similarly confused at him. "Why?"

"Eddie!" Belinda shouted as she came closer. "What are you doing here?" Then she stopped, glancing from one to the other. "Are you two together?" There was the tiniest hint of amusement in her voice.

"We just saw these pictures, that's all," Hannah said. "Doing our bit, you know."

"Eddie's my cousin," Belinda told her friend. "We live next door to each other in Goldthwaite—when school's not in."

"Small world."

"Not really. Both of my parents went to Baylor, and so did both of his. Mom says I should bleed green and gold."

Eddie looked at the departing crowd but saw no one lingering behind. "Are you here alone?" he asked.

Belinda nodded her head. "My date stood me up, actually. He was supposed to meet me at seven sharp, but he never did show."

"Anyone I know?"

"Nope. I hardly know him myself. We just worked on the same scrap drive a couple of weeks ago—over in Sanger Heights." Belinda flashed a shallow smile but could not hide her humiliation. She was a very plain-looking girl, and the social scars of past discouragements clouded her face. "Are you going straight back to Baylor?" she asked. "My roommate brought me here, but now I'm stranded."

Eddie hesitated, glancing at his date before answering. "Well, Hannah lives off-campus, but I thought I'd take her for a bite to eat over at the Elite."

This was news to Hannah, who had no burning desire to prolong the evening.

"Which one?" Belinda asked. A second Elite Café location had opened on the traffic circle.

Eddie motioned westward with his thumb. "This one's only a couple of blocks away. It wouldn't make any sense to drive all the way back to the circle, not when I have to bring Hannah home afterwards." He studied Belinda's face, wondering whether she was inviting herself along for the ride. She just stood there, apparently waiting for him to say the next word. But Eddie could be stubborn too, particularly in the middle of a meaningful date, so he made no concession to the kindly party crasher, blood relative or not.

It remained for Hannah to break the awkward silence, wondering whether it might be all right for her friend from church to tag along, seeing as how Belinda would be in need of a ride back to her dorm room anyway. The summer quarter was in full swing—entering the fourth of its eleven weeks—and this was, after all, a school night. Eddie, being a gentleman and seeing no other way out, consented to the request without verbal objection, though the grinding teeth and nasal sigh betrayed his true feelings. Meanwhile, if Hannah was crestfallen by this turn of events, she certainly did hide it well. Glumly resigned, poor Eddie Shaughnessy trudged his way down Austin Avenue, while the girls followed gleefully behind, chatting like magpies.

In the Elite Café, the three of them were shown to their booth at once, narrowly beating a contingent of a dozen or so moviegoers who had chosen to pause in front of the Amicable Building to observe an itinerant street-corner evangelist—one whose patter turned out to be far more keenly developed than his grasp of scripture. Hannah waited for Eddie to sit down, then positioned herself on the opposite side of the table, next to his cousin.

Two booths away, inciting the waitress's ire, sat a quartet of loitering soldiers. They had been ensconced for two hours now, purchasing a grand total of seven cups of coffee among them in all that while. They did not figure to give much of a tip either. Finally, the waitress could stand it no longer, and she asked the GIs to leave, nodding her head toward the waiting customers. To her relief, the four men did not cause any trouble. As docilely as lambs, they stood up and slowly made their way toward the cashier, allowing six other customers to squeeze into their vacated booth. From her vantage point, Hannah thought she recognized one of the withdrawing soldiers, so she began paying closer attention to their monetary transaction.

"You paying, Gus?" a private asked.

"Nope," came the answer. "Danny's turn."

"Not hardly. Cliff's got a fiver." It was Danny Rignold.

Grinning, Corporal Clifford Howser pulled out his wallet and paid the bill, whispering something to Danny, who walked back to the booth and left a quarter. He told its new occupants, "That's for the girl."

As Danny was turning to go, he noticed Hannah Lane sitting there, a couple of booths beyond, her face partially hidden by the menu. He walked over to her table, motioning to his pals that he would be joining them in a moment.

"Hey, got a piece of gum?" he asked, but her frosty reception suggested that Hannah did not know him from the Archbishop of Canterbury. Helpfully, he added, "Danny Rignold, your former Sunday school partner. Remember?"

"Vaguely," she said. "It's been a while. Did Lillie let you down or something?"

"I haven't even seen her since then."

"That's not what she says."

Danny looked embarrassed, wondering how much this girl knew. "I did get a ride from her once. Does that count?"

"A ride to a movie, if I'm not mistaken."

"Well, I was plannin' to see it anyway, and she was too, so I thought we might as well go in her Studebaker and sit together," he told her. "She was just bein' friendly."

"Oh? How friendly was she?"

"Not very, come to think of it, but you can't blame a guy for tryin'." Danny felt on the defensive, so he tried to joke his way out of it.

Hannah, however, remained serious, looking him squarely in the eye. "Anyway," she said, "now I know why you wanted that lift to Sunday school."

"And how could you know that? Are you a mind reader or somethin'?"

"I know when somebody's sincere—and when it's all just a big act. I'm surprised you didn't make a play for her in the church's parking lot."

Danny shook his head. "I think you're just jealous because I was more interested in Lillie than I was in you."

"Here, soldier," Hannah said. "Your friends are getting impatient." She tossed a piece of gum on the tabletop.

He picked up the spiteful gift, unwrapped its Wrigley's Spearmint stick, and put it in his mouth. Then he rolled the foil into a ball and gave it back to Hannah. "I believe you collect these."

"Gee, thanks."

By this time, Corporal Clifford Howser and Private Randall Box had sauntered over to the booth, leaving the congenial Gus Marek to chat with proprietor George Colias and his wife, Eugenia, both of whom had just arrived from the Chamber of Commerce banquet on Franklin and were lingering near the cash register to greet the patrons.

Randy was quite taken by Hannah, that much was clear. "Hi, sweetie," the private said to her. He smiled and tightened the necktie of his uniform.

But Hannah—still stung by what she saw as the hypocrisy of Danny Rignold—showed only disdain for the newcomer, sizing him up as a masher on the prowl. That she was at least partially correct in her assessment did not excuse the impudent way she dismissed him, with a contrived yawn and a glance at Eddie's wristwatch. Randy, however, thought nothing of the affront. "Hey," he said to Danny, "where you been hiding her?"

Across the table, Eddie Shaughnessy was too much in awe of the soldiers to speak up at all. There was something intimidating about those uniforms and the confident, worldly way in which the men acquitted themselves. He sat in silence, mentally distancing himself from the high-stakes badinage that went on around him, feeling contempt for his own shortcomings as a suitor and admiration for how effortlessly his date maintained her equilibrium in such fast company.

Meanwhile, only Corporal Howser bothered to acknowledge the other girl's very existence. He offered Belinda O'Rourke an impersonal nod of the head, much like an aristocrat might grant to his domestic servant, expecting and receiving nothing in return. Belinda began to smile but then looked down, content to draw figure eights through the salt that she had spilled in repeatedly unscrewing the shaker top. To her way of thinking, being seated on the inside of the booth certainly did have its advantages.

"Come on, let's get out of here," Danny said. "I've got early duty in the mornin'." He stomped away, with Clifford Howser not far behind.

Randall Box tarried just long enough to ask his new acquaintance, "What's your name, honey?" He wore a rakish grin, totally disregarding his competition in the booth.

"Ask your pal," Hannah said. "He's got a wonderful memory for names." She tucked Danny's tiny ball of foil in her purse.

The private grinned. "Hey, sort of testy, aren't you?"

"I'm just trying to enjoy a meal, if you have no objections," she told him. When he did not seem inclined to leave, she added, "Listen, there are plenty of girls who don't mind being picked up by strangers. Go to Second and Mary, and I'm sure you'll find somebody just your style."

"All right, all right. You don't have to get snotty about it." Randy backed away from the table. "You Baylor gals have an awful high opinion of yourselves."

Once the soldiers had gone out the door, Hannah turned to Belinda. "How'd he know I went to Baylor?" she asked.

But it was Eddie who answered with a question of his own. "Because you have an awfully high opinion of yourself?" Belinda looked startled at the comment, knowing that her cousin would never dream of saying something like that in jest.

◆　　◆　　◆

Among the duties of someone involved with commercial writing, in a small market like Waco anyway, was an occasional visit with clients about the wording of their advertising copy. Usually the consultation could be handled over the telephone, and—in view of gasoline restrictions—this method was encouraged whenever possible, but there were those few eccentrics in town who, for whatever reason, insisted upon hosting the radio staff at their various places of business. One of these, a contact from Bill Ordway's old account list, was Virgil Suchron, manager of the Liberty Hat Shop on Austin Avenue. Though he and his wife, Denise, had taken the plunge and invested in a telephone at work, they resorted to using it only in the case of an emergency. Their home was free of such a maddening device, and they proudly proclaimed that odd proclivity to anyone who would listen.

In all other respects, however, the gracious couple were considered to be quite normal—even commonplace—unless their twin daughters, confirmed nudists living on a commune in southern Oregon, could be counted against them. Wesley's summertime boss, Roberta Funk, cautioned him to avoid any reference to Karen and Katie, as this was thought to be a sore subject for the Suchrons. But the power of suggestion proved too much for Wesley, and he found his eyes drawn to that framed photograph on Virgil's orderly bookshelf. The girls in the photo were very pretty indeed and, there being snow plainly visible on the ground behind them, fully dressed.

Even more so than her husband, Denise Suchron treated Wesley Brower as a bona fide celebrity. She recognized his voice at once, right from the very instant they were introduced at the front of their store, and from then on, anything he happened to say was accepted with disproportionate gravity, as if it had been uttered by Bud Hanson's genial nephew, the crafty-for-his-age Kipper himself. At such moments—flattering and yet slightly eerie too—so complete was this middle-aged woman's identification with the daytime serial that Wesley wondered whether she was wholly mindful that the shop to be promoted over KWXN was situated in Waco, Texas, rather than in Baltimore, Maryland. It seemed, to Wesley's ears at least, that she would affect an eastern-seaboard accent, as if playing a minor role opposite some kingpin of the crime syndicate.

Not until the commercial possibilities touched upon headwear for the younger set, those in their teens and twenties, was Wesley aware that Mr. and Mrs. Suchron were also the parents of a son. At Virgil's mention of the boy's name, Denise's eyes welled up with tears, and she whispered, "Roddy," as if she were affirming her priest's heartfelt prayer with a devout "Amen." Only then did Wesley notice that there was another framed photograph at the far end of the bookshelf, and even from halfway across the shop's tidy office, he could tell that it depicted a naval officer, standing at attention in his dress blues. Details were sketchy for public consumption—not excluding parents of the deceased—but War Department files counted Roderick Suchron among fifty-four enlisted men and officers who were presumed to be lost in the disappearance of SS-177, the Porpoise-class submarine USS *Pickerel*, in Japanese waters on April 3, 1943. No survivors were reported, and the sub's captain, Lieutenant Commander Augustus Alston, Jr., went down with his ship.

Maybe the empty spot in their lives contributed to the Suchrons' attachment to Wesley Brower—that and, of course, his celebrity status as a radio actor. He could do no wrong in their eyes. Even his inexperienced creativity with words was greeted with acclaim well beyond its intrinsic merit. Soon he became embarrassed at their ready approval because he knew in his heart that his fumbling attempts at conversational scripting fell considerably short of what would be construed as acceptable copy back at the station. With all due respect, the modest hat—be it ever so humble—was not something that instilled much enthusiasm in his writing style, and to make things worse, his commercial vocabulary was not yet sufficiently developed to lend much "punch" to the announcements. No matter, for every one of his suggestions was just dandy with them, even the idea of extolling the virtues of an all-year hat, when a seasonal purchase was much more in line with profit theory and the management of a small-business concern.

Denise gave the visitor a wistful look. "You're such a fine young man," she said. "Our daughters and you would be so compatible—especially Karen, don't you think, honey?" She glanced at her husband but did not wait for him to reply. "They live in the northwest, but I would love to bring them back home, away from all of those un-Christian influences."

Wesley smiled and tried his best to change the subject, not wishing to go too deeply into the influences that were so troubling to this kind lady. "It rains a lot up there, doesn't it?" he asked.

"Ah, terrible. Just terrible," she told him. "Sometimes their shoes have green mold growing under them in the closet. Certainly not like Texas—

well, around here anyway. Maybe Houston is like that, but not central Texas. And it gets awfully cold up there too."

Wesley visualized the lovely Suchron twins outside, but in contrast to the photograph, his view of them happened to come on a warm, sunny day.

"Why did they go so far away from home?" he asked.

"Katie has a friend who lives in Oregon—a boyfriend—or should I say 'had'? She no longer sees him, and Karen never could stand him. Funny how our daughters are so unlike each another. They're identical twins, you know, but their personalities are as different as night and day."

Virgil frowned at his wife. "Dear, I'm quite sure Mr. Brower does not have all morning to listen to our family history. He probably needs to be getting back to the radio station."

"Oh, that's all right, Mr. Suchron," Wesley said. "We want you to be happy with your radio commercials. That's the most important thing." He was rather surprised at his own gift of gab with the company line, and his biggest fear was that it might sound too patronizing to these good-hearted people.

Contrived or not, the conversation went on for another thirty-five minutes, mostly dealing with business but occasionally touching upon Karen and Katie and once even upon the girls' late brother.

"Roddy cannot be a prisoner of war," Denise said. "That's what Lieutenant Commander Coffrey assured us when he brought the news. 'All hands were lost,' was the way he put it. He seemed quite certain of that."

Unaware, in her absentmindedness, that she was winding a ringlet of hair around her index finger, the pencil she was holding in that same hand fell to the floor, breaking its lead point before bounding out of sight. Her voice was not much stronger than a whisper when she added, "Men aboard a submarine are killed almost instantly—that's what he told us—and there was no suffering, none at all. We derive great comfort from this."

Mr. Suchron cleared his throat. "Now, dear, we must not monopolize any more of Mr. Brower's busy day. Isn't that right, young man?"

Wesley wanted to agree but felt that would not be very considerate. Instead, he responded with an equivocal "Well ..."

In any case, Virgil stood up and offered his hand to the radio station's emissary.

Wesley shook it cordially and smiled at Mrs. Suchron, whose distended lower lip made her appear to be pouting, even though she was not. Actually, she was deep in thought, wondering what was to become of her beloved Jeannie Gabriel. "I don't trust that Travis Earnshaw," she told Wesley, who promised to pass along her concerns to KWXN. "I think he's in cahoots with Odom Cashley, if you want my opinion. 'Course, I don't have much faith in lawyers anyway, as a general rule." Her eyes were tearful when she added, "I fear for her life."

Virgil Suchron walked Wesley to the door, tacitly shaken by his wife's grievous decline in stability over the past two months. His eyes apologized to the visitor more eloquently than his voice ever could, and a tinkling bell above the door sounded as he shut himself within his cloistered world for yet another day of coping with the sad, inevitable darkness that was gathering around him.

That young lad brought a ray of sunshine from the outside, a teasing reminder of what life had always been but never would be again.

As he relit his pipe, Virgil shrugged at the fragility of it all. He had become a desperate onlooker, reduced to appreciating the sunrise and sunset of each passing day. His wife's affable, fading smile would accompany him for a while longer, but the thought of her coming release already made him cry.

◆　　◆　　◆

Nora heard the sirens, but she thought nothing much about them at the time. More than a half-hour elapsed before Mabel Johns placed a frantic telephone call to her with the dreadful details. The vast majority of Moek Grocery had been destroyed by a two-alarm fire "of suspicious origin." The blaze swept through most of the store, engulfing the back half of the wooden structure and leaving only the front dairy case and part of a canned-goods aisle unscathed.

When Nora learned the news, she gasped at the sheer magnitude of this disaster. "That's just awful! Was anyone injured? Are Hermann and Trudy all right?"

"Everybody is in one piece," Mabel told her, "but their poor store is almost a total loss. The front wall is still standing, but that is about all."

Struggling to express herself, Nora was nearly at a loss for words. "How ... how ... utterly horrible!" she finally said. "Do they know what started the fire?"

"They're not saying anything. Blanche Lewin's husband is a Waco fireman, and she told me that it must've started in the kitchen area, way back where the lunch counter is."

"Oh, my heavens. And that was Hermann's pride and joy too. This will just devastate him, I'm afraid."

"He's taking it very well, so I've heard—according to Blanche—but Trudy was administered a sedative and sent to bed by her doctor."

"When do you suppose we can see her?" Nora asked. "She needs to know that we support her—all of her friends. Shall we arrange for some dinners through the church?"

"I don't know. I think she and Hermann go to the E and R church—or, at least they did until Conrad was killed. I'm not sure they go anywhere now. Trudy, especially, had her faith shaken. If the Moeks are still members, I presume that the church ladies there will get something together for them."

"I would hope so," Nora said. "And our church certainly could organize some meals—at the very least," she added. "So many of our congregation know the Moeks."

Mabel lowered her voice, as if reading aloud the contents of a classified dossier. "Did you know that their church held services in German until a few years ago? They may deny it, but it's a fact. That language always sounds so ugly to me, especially of course when Herr Schickelgruber is spewing it."

"I'm just glad they stopped preaching in German before this war started," Nora said. "That's not a very popular language nowadays, and some decent Americans might have been thought unpatriotic if they spoke it—even reading the scriptures. You could not hope to find two more loyal Americans than Hermann and Trudy."

Mabel did not comment, so her friend let the subject drop.

Though Nora did not feel up to visiting Gertrude that very day, she knew she must do so before too much time elapsed. All morning long—and, for that matter, a good portion of the previous evening—her spirits had been at a low ebb, the effect of a nagging melancholy that almost certainly could be traced back to the unhappy fact that her older son, for the first time in his nineteen years of life, had spent a birthday away from home. To her, birthdays were occasions for excessive celebration, a chance to spoil the honoree and smother him or her with motherly affection. And she liked to believe that Steve, despite his outward protestations whenever another July Fourth rolled around, secretly welcomed them as well.

In order to sidestep the knotty question of ecclesiastical protocol, the Columbus Avenue Baptist Church women decided it might be best to simply prepare a meal on their own, distinct from any organizational auspices. By Friday, just two days after the disastrous blaze, Gertrude Moek was resting comfortably at home, and the Germania Mutual Aid Association's office in Brenham—with whom the couple had been policyholders since their days in San Antonio before the Great War—had provided a more than equitable settlement.

Hermann seemed quite philosophical about the entire calamity when he answered the doorbell early that afternoon. "Come on in, ladies," he told them. "I'm sure Trudy will be thrilled to eat something that was not cooked by me. In point of fact, so will I." The two visitors took their boxes of food to the kitchen and placed the perishables in the refrigerator. There was even a pecan pie, baked by Mabel and utilizing confectionery ingredients that were purchased with the ration stamps of no fewer than five ladies, each of whose names was penciled on a small card taped to the pan lid. "Ah! That's her favorite," Hermann said when told what lay beneath the metal cover.

A radio could be heard playing softly in the far corner of the living room as he invited the two ladies to take a seat on the sofa. Nora was unsure what program was on the air at this time, but it sounded to her, ironically enough, like it might be the Blue Network's "Ladies Be Seated," an audience-participation show starring its new hosts, Johnny Olson and his wife, Penny. Nora was not well acquainted with it, as she usually listened to a rival show, NBC's "Portia Faces Life."

"I'll go get Trudy," Hermann told the women. "She'll be pleased to see you— a nice change from the fire marshal and sheriff's investigators."

"Now, don't wake her on our account," Mabel said. "She needs her rest."

"No. No, I won't. She's already awake." He picked up a wicker hamper of folded socks and carried it with him. "I was in there when you called earlier, and I told her you'd be coming. She'd be awfully disappointed if she missed you."

Mabel leaned over to Nora and whispered, "Let's not tire her out. This has been quite a trauma for poor Trudy." Nora nodded with a frown, miffed that her friend would think it necessary to tell her the self-evident.

When the Moeks came into the room, Hermann was supporting his wife with his strong right arm. Gertrude made a brave effort to smile, but the expression just would not appear. Instead, her mouth seemed to be contorted by a wince of pain. She did manage a shallow laugh, however, in response to the absurd collision that occurred when both visitors attempted to stand up at precisely the same instant and gently bumped heads.

"Hermann told me what you brought," Gertrude said. "If you're trying to make me fat, you're much too late for d'at." With her husband's assistance, she sat in the armchair.

Nora noticed that Hermann kept glancing at the mantel clock, as if he were due somewhere for an appointment. Actually, though, he was only attempting to protect his wife from becoming too fatigued. On doctor's advice, he had taken it upon himself to make certain that Gertrude went back to bed in a timely fashion, no matter how chatty the two other ladies happened to be and how much his wife was enjoying their visit. Dr. Mullins had cautioned him about letting Frau Moek's innate sociability tire her out, at least for another week or so, particularly if the obvious topic of conversation showed signs of dampening her spirits. Hermann intended to follow that prescription implicitly.

"Oh, not too bad, considering," Gertrude said in reply to Nora's obligatory inquiry about her health. "D'ere's not anyt'ing wrong wit' me d'at a million dollars wouldn't cure. I just worry so much about d'e money, you know—what we are to do for a living. D'is house ist paid for, t'ank d'e Lord, or I fear we would be standing on d'e corner, selling pencils right now."

"Mabel and I want you to know that we'll do anything we can to help out," Nora told her. "Either us or the other ladies of our church."

"How long do you think it will take for them to rebuild the store?" Mabel asked.

Gertrude deferred to her husband, and Hermann replied, with little conviction, "Most estimates are two months, minimum." For a man of such a cheery disposition, he sounded curiously skeptical. "So that probably means three or four," he added after a moment of reflection. "The lunch counter was a total loss."

"Is that what caused the fire?" Mabel asked.

Anger shot through Hermann, who was suddenly defensive about assigning cause without recourse to the facts. "Did I say that?" he said. "No, I never said that. I can tell you that the counter was not involved whatsoever, except indirectly— when the fire spread downward from the roof."

"I'm sorry, Hermann. I just meant ..."

His scowl became a contrite smile, and he stood at attention, drawing a deep breath. "No, Miz Johns, I am the one who is sorry, and I apologize to you. That was very discourteous of me. It's just that so many firemen and policemen—even a know-it-all newspaper reporter—have pointed their fingers at the grill area. And it infuriates me, especially because it isn't true." He stared at the clock and then at Gertrude, as if wondering whether to elaborate.

Mabel shrugged her shoulders. "Well, do they know what caused it?"

"Fire investigators sifted through the debris this morning," Hermann said. He avoided the gaze of his wife, who sat with an uncomprehending look on her face. "Trudy doesn't know this, but I guess it won't do any harm to say. It's what's going on the official report anyway, so it will be public knowledge by this time tomorrow."

But Hermann must have had second thoughts when he looked again at the mantel clock. "I think we'd better get you back to bed, Mutter," he said. "The doctor'll stand me in front of a firing squad for keeping you up so long." This remark surprised Nora, who did not consider the stay to have been of unreasonable duration. Indeed, to her it hardly seemed worth the effort for Gertrude to come to the living room for such a brief visit. What Nora did not know was that Gertrude had insisted upon thanking her friends in person for their generosity and compassion, and part of the stated agreement with her husband was that she consent to be back in bed by two o'clock sharp.

As the Moeks were leaving for their bedroom, Nora and Mabel exchanged glances and knew precisely what the other was thinking. It was a distressing thought but one that was too credible to be disregarded out of hand. Certainly Hermann's misfortune would not have been the first time during this war that someone with a Germanic surname was targeted with violence. Nora recalled one Saturday afternoon—it must have been in the spring of 1942—when two unidentified thugs beat up Karlheinz Berger outside his north Waco home, reputedly for snubbing the recent Flying Fortress Campaign. The assailants, never identified but thought to be two high school dropouts from the rural Hewitt area, took it upon themselves to donate Mr. Berger's bicycle, his only means of transportation, to the scrap-metal drive at Sixth and Mary.

And now this. Nora knew that much worse anti-German sentiment had been rampant during the last war, but that did not diminish her outrage over the damage sustained by her friends' humble wooden structure on Colcord.

Hermann returned to the living room a moment later and, true to his word, passed along the official statement. Though the physical destruction was of course irreversible, still it was with a sense of relief that Nora and Mabel heard him say that the blaze had not been set deliberately. It appeared that young people indeed were involved, but not with vengeance or even vandalism in their hearts. According to the fire marshal, Daniel Nicholson, all indications were that this conflagration was of an accidental nature, ignited when three youngsters launched an errant Roman candle—left over from the previous night's patriotic celebrations—and it landed upon the right rear segment of the roof atop Moek Grocery, soon engulfing the "matchbox" (as Nicholson called it) in flames. There was precious little his people could do, given the volatile materials that fueled the inferno, other than to prevent it from spreading to surrounding structures. As it was, a concomitant grass fire nearly made its way to the shoe repair shop behind Moek's, and only quick action by WFD personnel saved that business from joining the grocery store in burning to the ground. "It could have been much worse," Nicholson declared—but not from Hermann Moek's perspective. The young boys (ages seven, nine, and ten) were given stern reprimands, as were their parents, but no charges were filed.

"I don't know that we'll ever rebuild," Hermann told the two ladies. His manner of speech now sounded tired and defeated, and though standing, he relied upon the armchair to support most of his considerable weight. When he spoke, he looked not directly at Mabel and Nora but slightly above their heads, as if making eye contact might reduce him to tears—an unthinkable prospect for such proud Germanic stock. "The insurance settlement was more than fair, I must admit, but I am no longer a young man. I do not have the energy to begin again from scratch."

◆   ◆   ◆

Early one Thursday afternoon near the end of July, Wesley heard receptionist Myra Culp paging him over the intercom: "Wesley Brower, there's someone to see you in the lobby." The tone of her voice indicated that this was not to be yet another vanity call by a sponsor or a summer field trip by a troop of Boy Scouts. Thus forewarned, he approached the front desk stealthily, detouring through Studio B, so as to give himself as much advance notice as possible. But the guest must have heard his footsteps on the well-worn, carpeted surface because she turned her head toward him at a point where he still lacked about twenty feet from being able to recognize her with any certainty. Wesley had no choice but to slow his pace while the mysterious visitor's identity gradually made itself known.

There stood Giulia Coletti. She was breathtakingly lovely, and he became tongue-tied standing alongside her, just as he always did in her presence whenever a conversational prop, such as one of Steve's letters or a bundle of discarded newspapers, was not handy to rely upon for verbal support. "Giulia!" he said, almost choking on her name. "Gee, what are you doing here?"

She merely grinned, as if no clarification were necessary.

Glancing at Myra, Wesley coaxed Giulia away from the desk and over toward the newsroom door. "Are you here to see me?"

"No, of course not."

He was both disappointed and relieved at the same time.

"Well, I know you didn't come here to buy any commercial time," he told her. His nervousness made the wisecrack seem more desperate than funny.

"I'll let you guess," Giulia said with a relaxed smile. She was not going to make this any easier for him.

"I'm not sure—unless you just want somebody to show you around the place. I can do that."

"Exactly. You invited me to come see the radio station. Don't you remember?"

That explained it. About a month ago, when Wesley first suggested to her that she stop by the radio station, he had extended the invitation out of courtesy, more rhetorical than sincere. It was one of those improvised comments that leak out when words are beginning to falter but awkward silence is not an endurable option. Giulia had said yes at the time, but her tepid acceptance failed to alert him to the possibility that she might actually turn up at KWXN one day, all bright-eyed and star-struck, wishing to be guided through the premises by one of local broadcasting's reigning celebrities.

The timing could hardly have been worse. Her surprise visit happened to fall within a particularly unsettled span of adjustment, when production personnel were fundamentally modifying the station's daytime serials. From now until at least the end of August, the writers were called upon to revamp both dramas. For Wesley's show, "Behold Tomorrow," these weeks would be a transitional period, with the relatively youthful Ray Temple replacing curmudgeonly Harvey Samuelson on the writing staff of Ethel Coody. Samuelson was due to retire on August 10 and presumably devote his sunset years to farming cotton in the rural suburb of Rosenthal. Gerald Byrd, who was almost solely responsible for the emergence of Kip Hanson as a major character, would acquire Samuelson's corner office, while Temple, in turn, would inherit the windowless enclave that had been Jerry's. In the midst of all this administrative turmoil, Wesley had new lines to learn, three commercials to write, and a spec spot to deliver to Southland Ice Company, way over in East Waco.

Giulia frowned. "Is this a bad day? I can come back again later."

"No, this is a good day," Wesley said. He was determined not to chase her away with inhospitable talk. "In fact, it's a very good day." He walked backward toward his office. "Wait here for a minute while I get my script. We're on the air at three." Kip Hanson had almost a whole page in the Thursday show, so Wesley would be needed in the studio in precisely forty minutes. He ran down the hallway at top speed, narrowly avoiding a collision with Monica Whaley, who, it so happened, was looking for him.

"Insert," she said. "The green sheet. You've got to introduce Sally to her future sweetheart, so it's an important scene. Just six more lines, though, so not too bad."

"Will we rehearse it?"

"Just once, I'm afraid." Monica was already turning to walk away. "This was all Jerry's idea. I know it's awfully late, but I just got it myself."

"Why's he writing these things right before airtime? It's not fair to anyone."

Monica shrugged her shoulders. "He says it'll make tomorrow's show 'infinitely more comprehensible'—those were his precise words—and Jerry loves a Friday cliffhanger."

"How well I know. He did the same thing to us last week."

"Sorry, Kip Hanson," she said with mock, singsong cheerfulness. And then she added, "Sally will love you for it."

For a second, Wesley wondered if he had heard correctly. "What do you mean?" he asked. But the hesitation was just long enough for Monica to stride around the corner in search of other cast members. Not having the time to pursue her, he rushed into the office for his script and then headed back to the front desk.

Giulia was still in the lobby, all right, but she was not alone. Besides the receptionist, a salesman, too, had begun chatting with her—laughing heartily as he chewed on his unlit cigar butt—and he showed no signs of letting her go anytime soon. Calvin Trent always did have a pronounced weakness for a pretty face. Though in his early fifties, married, and the father of an AAF captain, he seemed to favor the younger crowd, girls of high school age or even younger. He was harmless enough, but his jokes were usually of the double-entendre type that would make any decent woman blush.

Wesley arrived just in time to hear the punch line, "And never again did he eat a pomegranate with the lights off." Giulia smiled politely, though stopping short of dignifying the crude witticism with an outright laugh. Myra, who had heard the same joke twice before and at this very spot, was not even listening. But that made little difference to the salesman. Like all good storytellers, he spoke to amuse himself at least as much as to entertain any perceived audience. His lusty guffaw was so loud that four birds on the front lawn were startled into flying to safety, with Trent's vocalized shock waves passing right through the closed glass door.

The instant Wesley saw the salesman's eyes beginning to venture down from Giulia's face to her figure, he cleared his throat and said, "Come on, Miss Coletti, I'll give you a quick tour before the show." He took the girl's hand and guided her toward the mundane array of business offices.

Trent took the setback in good humor. He remained by Myra's desk, an attentive observer, until the guest's curvaceous summer dress had disappeared from view.

◆   ◆   ◆

That afternoon's 2:35 rehearsal went splendidly, and Wesley was pleased with the additional lines that his role was assigned—well written, idiomatic, very much in character, and seamlessly flowing into the existing narrative. After one quick reading, he could almost recite the new material from memory, though no self-respecting radio actor would ever attempt such a stunt by choice. Too much was waiting to go wrong in those prideful circumstances. As this latest revision demonstrated anew, Gerald Byrd was truly a fine writer, his dialogue streaming so naturally that it was a joy to read, especially for male members of the cast. On the distaff side, Phyllis Sherry would lodge an occasional complaint that "Jeannie Gabriel would never say something like that," but by and large Jerry's imaginative scripting was beyond reproach, and station management was unanimous in feeling that he was worth every penny of his three-hundred-dollar monthly salary.

When the actors returned from their 2:50 "potty breaks," as director Hugh Kenton called them, confidence was running high that this would be one of the best shows of the year, possibly boosting the story line to a level not heard on "Behold Tomorrow" since the coerced suicide of philanthropist Konradin Nagy had jolted the audience two years earlier.

But it was not meant to be. Something intangible swept into the studio like an unseen fog, sapping energy from the Thursday performance and delivering a body of work that everyone agreed was dead on arrival. What had gone wrong? Kenton thought he knew, but no one else agreed with him, and later that afternoon he came to recant his contention that the fault lay entirely with Neddy Wright and his unfortunate head cold. After all, Bud Hanson only appeared in the opening moments—a deficient portrayal, by Neddy's lofty standards, but so was everything else that followed. Even the normally high-voltage chemistry between Sally and Kip was lacking, not to mention the laughably unconvincing "mad scene" of Jeannie Gabriel.

"Some days are just like that, gang," Kenton told the cast about a half-hour after the final curtain. "Who knows? Maybe that means dynamite for tomorrow."

By the time he uttered those hopeful words, a hastily arranged meeting among Ethel Coody, Gerald Byrd, and newcomer Ray Temple was already in progress in Jerry's corner office, and if their glum faces going into the fray were any indication, it promised to be a long and acrimonious night.

The inexplicable breakdown of that day's "Behold Tomorrow" caused Wesley some concern, but not so much that he neglected his lovely visitor. Giulia had witnessed the drama from the energetic setting of a control room, where conditions tended to present observers with an unrealistic concept of what listeners at home were hearing. A visual dimension was superimposed upon the audio production, and—for those inexperienced at judging such things— this could lead to a misrepresentation of what was actually transmitted. When Wesley approached her during the 3:14 adjacency, the girl's face was aglow with excitement, visibly impressed by what she had heard ... and seen.

Heretofore, Giulia had not been aware that actors wandered around the studio quite so much, making their way to and from the microphones at will. Both sibling toddlers, she learned, were played by one in the same person, a matronly adult named Beverly Jaynes. The sound effects amazed her, too, especially smacking a head of cabbage for a punch to the jaw and using a common roller skate to simulate the opening and closing of an elevator door. Perhaps most of all, Giulia was surprised by the calmness that prevailed when a script girl tiptoed in with some new pages for the performers to read—right in the middle of a lengthy stretch of dialogue. Only the director seemed to become outraged by this last-second revision, and he managed to swallow his diatribe of four-letter words in deference to the sweet, young guest who stood nearby, taking it all in with innocent wonder.

"Oh, I thought it was grand," Giulia said to Wesley. She was blissfully ignorant that the Thursday show would go down in KWXN annals as an unmitigated flop. "And you were swell too," she added, almost as an afterthought. Not more than twenty feet away, Marshall McFall was introducing the radio audience to that day's edition of "West of the Brazos," speaking with headphones so as to fully appreciate the bass frequencies of his mellifluous voice. Giulia glanced at the announcer and grinned, a response elicited by McFall's dashing wink of an eye while reading. He was adept at performing this task-juggling maneuver whenever a girl was attractive enough to warrant the effort and a script was familiar enough to him that he could recite it by rote.

Sandra Whittsel was in the lobby when it came time for Giulia to leave, and it crossed Wesley's mind that maybe she was lying in wait for him. According to Hugh Kenton, Sandy was not at all pleased with his portrayal of Kip Hanson that afternoon, and Wesley had learned the hard way—on three or four separate occasions—that she was not one to hide her resentment of sub-standard mike work opposite the character of Sally Holt.

Wesley tried to turn back, but it was too late. Sandy saw him and motioned for him to come over to Myra Culp's desk. She certainly did seem friendly, brandishing a vibrant smile, so he ventured forth with Giulia alongside. "We were just saying what a clever boy actor you are," Sandy said, much to Myra's surprise. Then, compelled by common courtesy, she gave the visitor a dismissive glance and added, "Hello there." Not to be outdone, Giulia nodded her head but said nothing, quickly looking away with the sure instinct of a teenage girl. Sandy's superior attitude rankled Wesley too, but he knew better than to unloose his tongue while standing between such contentious females.

"My mother would like for you to come over for a cast party on Saturday evening, if you can," Sandy told Wesley. She stepped closer to him and gazed up into his eyes. "This is something that she's been wanting to do for quite some time, and Daddy's off duty that night." Wesley had forgotten how short in stature Sandy was, barely coming up to Giulia's shoulders, and her dark eyes and hair were as beguiling as ever. "Oh, and your sweetheart is welcome to tag along too." He marveled at the girl's craftiness in ignoring Miss Coletti at such a moment, thus preserving the anonymity of her invitation.

"Is Marshall going to be there?" Wesley asked with an innocent look. "Or is this only for the cast?" Sometimes he surprised himself with his own impudence.

But Sandy was hardly flustered. "Well, maybe cast and crew would be a better way of putting it. I should have been more explicit." She smiled at two newsmen who came in the front door, each of them picking up a pack of matches from the glass bowl on Myra's desk. They smiled back.

"Say, sevenish?" Sandy asked.

Wesley tried to stay noncommittal. "Maybe so. How dressy will it be?"

"Just casual. Some people will be coming directly from work—three or four of the production crew. And I've invited a few of my newsroom friends too."

"Oh?"

"And their dates. You know, Grant Tollefson's getting married."

"So I've heard. Poor girl."

Sandy gave him a mischievous look. "Just remember that my parents will be there to chaperone, so no funny business. This won't be like those wild Hollywood parties you probably went to on the coast."

"Oh, sure," Wesley said. "Hugh Kenton, Clive Ramey, and I—we really showed those actors how to party all right." He smiled at Giulia, who sighed impatiently.

"You don't have to give me an answer right now," Sandy told him, "but I'll need your RSVP by tomorrow."

"To give me time to check with my 'sweetheart,' huh?"

"Well, that's up to you, Wes. Just come stag, if you prefer. I am."

Wesley looked puzzled. "I thought you said Marshall would be there."

"He will," she said. "But I don't need for him to take me to my own house, silly." There was a twinkle in her eye.

Sandy had a way of taking the upper hand in most any conversation—in terms of sophisticated repartee anyway—and Wesley wondered whether her beloved Marshall McFall ever experienced the same feelings of inadequacy when in her presence. Conceivably not, as they were two peas in a pod when it came to societal confidence, seemingly never at a loss for words. Indeed, perhaps the roles were reversed, and his dominance drove her otherwise forceful personality into willing submission.

"I think I see my ride out there," Giulia said, and she slowly walked toward the exit. "Thanks for the tour, Wesley. I enjoyed it."

He hurried to stop her at the door. "Wait a second, Giulia. Don't go away mad."

"I'm not mad. My ride's waiting in the parking lot, and I promised Mamma that I'd be back home by 3:30."

He lowered his voice. "Did you hear what Sandy was saying?"

"Yes, I heard her. Why?"

"Well, would you ..." Wesley felt himself beginning to stammer, so he took a deep breath. "Would you like to go with me to that party she was talking about?"

Giulia thought for an instant. "I don't think so, but thanks just the same. I don't imagine I would fit in with that crowd."

Wesley glanced at Sandy, who wore her best deadpan expression. "Sure you would," he whispered. "Besides, Sandy told me I could bring someone."

"She said to bring a sweetheart, as I recall."

"Or a friend. She's invited some of her news pals."

Giulia shook her head and pushed the door open. "Sorry, but let me know if you hear from your brother, okay?" She flashed a smile and walked away.

"Oh, sure. I'll do that," he said in a detached, guttural voice. Wesley once heard a station salesman say—without any hint of shame—that a client's rejection actually choked him up for a minute. Now he knew how the salesman must have felt.

When Saturday evening rolled around, Wesley could not bring himself to attend the party—nearly everyone there, including the lovely daughter of hostess Charlotte Whittsel, would have a date—so he stayed home, lying on his bed in the dark, listening to the radio. Nora answered the telephone at 7:40, and she relayed word to Sandy that Wesley was feeling unwell. That was not far from the truth.

◆　　◆　　◆

A new worker joined the ranks of Crawford-Austin Manufacturing Company in the third week of August when a seventeen-year-old Oklahoman punched her time card for the first time amidst little notice from the jaded regulars. She had gone through the formative years of her life with the graceless name of Galen Crotch, and it was as such that she proudly introduced herself to apathetic colleagues on the production line. She accepted their disinterest with the equanimity of one who did not expect to remain in these coarse environs for very long. Galen was far more concerned with upward mobility, allowing her eyes to indulge in roving toward ambitious young men in management strata, particularly those few military-age males whom, for whatever reason, the wide net of the draft had failed to ensnare. Though not conventionally pretty, in a wholesome sense, she had a seductive way of carrying herself that inspired those so attuned to feel reasonably certain that here was someone who might respond to sincere pursuit.

Her older brother, too, was newly hired, though his assignment took him to the other Crawford-Austin building, the warehouse and shipping depot, where he soon learned to plug his ears to counter the adverse din of heavy machinery. William Crotch was nineteen and a diabetic, which malady assured his exemption from the armed services. Family lore branded him the namesake of William Crotch of Norwich, an English organist, pianist, composer, and teacher whose life overlapped that of Mozart and whose musical precocity nearly equaled that of his illustrious Austrian contemporary. But William Crotch of Ardmore had no interest in the fine arts or anything else that smacked of gentility. Likely the only piece of classical music he knew was a piano arrangement of the celebrated "Ständchen" from Schubert's *Schwanengesang*, which Al Gabler used to play on an ill-tuned brothel upright whenever the mood struck.

Galen Crotch did not make friends easily, nor was that her intent. Those who tried to crack through her malevolent exterior did so on a unilateral basis, with little encouragement from her. Retired farmer Horton Stokes, solitary among all the men in tent production, seemed quite taken with the teenager's *hauteur*, perhaps sensing that a more receptive personality lay hidden beneath the surface. One time, when he brought her an unsolicited clean apron from the storeroom, she very nearly smiled. And yet, as the shift wore on, doubt began to creep in, and he could not quite decide whether her softening was provoked by gratitude or amusement. Her use of the derisive "gramps" and "hayseed"—right to his face— only made matters worse, and by nine o'clock, when Galen took it upon herself to divert his favorite shears and tracing wheel to her own work tray, Horton was among her most vengeful adversaries.

For nearly three months, Hannah Lane had been loaned to the camp furniture division—serving "like a good soldier," foreman Mark Teller said—but now she was back in the tentworks section, where she felt much better suited for the work at hand. Mr. Hinckley had no choice but to assign Miss Crotch to the day shift, virtually unheard of for a novice, whereas Hannah, being a college student who would soon be returning to her classes, was relegated to the swing shift, with an occasional graveyard stint thrown in for good measure. This adjusted schedule meant that Hannah, though employed full-time during the summer months, did not cross paths with the standoffish newcomer until more than a week after she joined the payroll. Still, she had heard something of Galen through the normal, embellished narratives of company scuttlebutt.

Hannah did not know which version of the story to believe. According to Rowena Downing, this "Gay Lynn Crutch" (as she invariably called her) was a she-dog that needed to be put in her place. Liv Saunders, the wife of a Methodist minister, described the young lady in more charitable terms, excusing her blatant disregard for others as a defense mechanism to obfuscate an inferiority complex— no doubt, she inferred, stemming from her lack of proper education. Meanwhile, the vaguely reptilian Thomas Bridges made it a point to disparage "that slut's" unfriendly countenance, but his lascivious grin suggested that he did not find her to be physically lacking in any other important respect.

"So, you're Galen," Hannah said when they finally met at the time clock. She had seen what appeared to be "A. G. Crotch" or "O. G. Crotch" scrawled along the top edge of the cardboard voucher.

Galen grunted and looked away, wiping her front teeth with a soiled sleeve to remove the remnants of lunch. "And you're ...?" She did not wait for a reply. Surely Hannah would have felt slighted, if only Hoyt Miner had not blocked Miss Crotch's brusque exit with his generous rump. Forcibly entrapped while the oblivious Hoyt chatted with Doyle Knorr from chemicals, Galen heard her co-worker introduce herself.

"What's your first name?" Hannah asked, just to see where the conversation might lead.

Galen seemed offended by this infringement of her privacy, so Hannah added, "I saw the initials." She nodded toward the rack of time cards.

"Opal," Miss Crotch said. "Granny's idea." Seeing that Hoyt Miner's backside still obstructed her escape route, she took a deep breath and elaborated, "Opal is Granny's name, see? Mama didn't give a rip what they called me—that's for sure." And that is where the conversation ended, for Galen proceeded to kneel down and blow her nose into a grease rag that lay on the floor, carelessly tossing it aside with no consideration whatever for the unsuspecting custodian who might pick it up later for transfer to the laundry basket.

This was the first complete day shift that Hannah had worked in over a month, and it felt strange to have Galen and so many other unfamiliar faces around her. To her left on the production line was the bespectacled, bird-like Estelle Evan ("singular," she said of her surname). Straight across the worktable was elderly Jacqueline Clemmons, a proud great-grandmother of six. Immediately to Hannah's right was Rose Quigley, who was as convivial as Galen was aloof. Jackie Hester lost an eye in the first war, but he could operate a steam press better than most anyone at the plant—and regale the other men with a marginally dirty joke while doing it. The bashful Marcia Venturi, a "floater" whose duty it was to fill any vacant post, spoke almost no English and pronounced her given name as "MAHR-chah." And Pansy Linkus, on the far side of Galen from where Hannah was stationed, possessed every bit as much arm hair as any man on the shipping docks.

The initial two hours passed uneventfully, but around twenty minutes past ten, Miss Crotch approached Hannah and asked for a stick of chewing gum, recalling that Hannah had offered her one early in the morning, even before the eight-o'clock whistle sounded. When Hannah complied with the request, Galen's eyes followed her left hand with rather more than routine interest, but not quite enough to arouse undue suspicion.

It was not until 11:45, after Hannah had walked down the long corridor to the commissary for her lunch hour, that she noticed the absence of two one-dollar bills, which she had folded and carefully tucked into the unbuttoned pocket of her coveralls. Fortunately, Bee Fetters owed her one dollar, so there would be no problem purchasing her meal that day. This, however, did not assuage the unsettling feeling that there was a thief in their midst, and she had a fair idea who the culprit might be.

She seated herself between Bee and a "bachelor gal" named Leona Mayes, who despite that self-proclaimed title could hardly have been over thirty. Across the room, eating contentedly by themselves at a table for six, sat Galen Crotch and someone Hannah took to be Galen's older brother. It was understood that Galen had a sibling who operated heavy equipment—forklifts and such—at the warehouse and loading platform.

"What do you know about the new girl?" Hannah asked. She gestured toward her with a nod of the head.

"Who? Galen?" Bee said. "Oh, she's all right, I guess. My husband would call her a ne'er-do-well, but then he's a lot more polite than I am." She chuckled and glanced again at Miss Crotch, searching for just the right words. "I'd say she was poor white trash."

"What about her brother?"

"Same, I'm sure. Anybody who'd have a tattoo like that." What appeared to be a slightly obscene depiction of a call girl decorated the boy's forearm. It would not have been out of place as nose art on a bomber.

Leona started to turn around, just out of curiosity, but Hannah stopped her by whispering, "Don't look now!" William was staring at them, but he quickly lost interest and returned his attention to an unbuttered yeast roll.

"I once knew a woman with a tattoo," Leona said. "Yep, she had it on the back of her neck, of all places." Bee gaped in disbelief.

"A tattoo of what?" Hannah asked.

"A pretty butterfly. It was very artistic, really, but of course it made her look like a whore. Maybe that's what she was because she lived well on no visible income."

Hannah leaned toward Bee and asked, "Is this Galen trustworthy? I think she may have taken a couple of dollars from me."

"Have you told Mr. Hinckley?"

"I can't until I'm sure. I'm just going to do a little investigative work."

"Well, you do what you want, but I'd tell him, if I were you. He doesn't put up with anything like that—dishonesty in his plant."

Hannah studied the siblings from afar. They neither talked to anyone else in the room nor to each other. Despite exacerbated health risks for a diabetic, William Crotch lit up a cigarette the instant he laid down his fork for the last time, and his first smoke was followed in rapid succession by another. Galen, it seemed, had not developed a nicotine habit, but apparently she did share with William a fondness for liquor. Each of them indulged in a swig of hooch from what appeared to be a camouflaged hip flask, which Galen then slipped inside her purse when she thought nobody was watching. Hannah viewed this entire shameful display, possibly undetected, and she resolved to approach Miss Crotch in private whenever her brother returned to work.

But William, exhibiting the natural instincts of a good accomplice, thwarted her plan by overstaying his welcome at the table, so Hannah was forced to delay her confrontation until later, by which time the unquestioned clout of immediacy would be forfeited. After all, it mattered little, in the scheme of human events, if a couple of dollars were taken a week or two ago. Marshaling her ire, Hannah was half tempted to have it out with Galen then and there, brother or no brother, but her better judgment wisely counseled her to do otherwise. She glanced again at the pair of siblings when she stood up to leave the commissary. Their faces remained expressionless. As she walked away, she had the distinct feeling that watchful eyes were following her every step.

The Crotches, in any case, were gone within a week—before the sun went down on their first payday.

◆　　　◆　　　◆

Bess Clarke had not visited the Coletti home in nearly four months, ever since a stormy dispute arose over the incident at Waco's passenger depot. It made little difference that Paolina's anger subsided within a few hours. Mrs. Clarke took the words of her hostess quite literally—"never be welcome here again"—and the resentment festered. Neither had she spoken to her son's avowed sweetheart, Miss Giulia Coletti, in that same length of time. Although Archie wrote letters to his mother with some regularity, not once did Mrs. Clarke make the effort to pass along his comments to Giulia, something that she used to do as a matter of course.

When Giulia answered the doorbell, Archie Clarke's mother was the last person she expected to see, and it was painfully clear that this somber woman, standing on the doorstep beneath her umbrella, had no intention of setting foot inside.

"Please do come in," Giulia said.

Mrs. Clarke shot back an embittered look that was almost violent in its intensity. "I certainly will not, young lady," she said, "and you can tell your mother for me that all the apologies in the world will not cure the injuries that she has caused."

It had been raining, off and on, for much of the day, and the front yard was pockmarked with reflective puddles.

"Mamma didn't mean what she said, Mrs. Clarke, and she would like for you to feel welcome in our house, I'm sure. Please try to understand."

"I have never been so humiliated in all my life. She might as well have spit in my eye—speaking to me like some dog that she was trying to shoo off your front lawn."

"She didn't mean it the way it sounded, honestly."

"A fine one you are to talk!" Mrs. Clarke nearly turned on her heels, forgetting why she had come. Then, as if counting silently to herself, she took a deep breath and regained her composure. "There's some news I need to give you—assuming, of course, that you would be interested."

Giulia tried to read the woman's face. "Some news about Archie?" She ventured forward and quietly shut the door behind her, so as not to disturb her mother. The visitor grudgingly came a bit closer to share her umbrella.

"What is it, Mrs. Clarke?" Giulia asked, as respectfully as she could.

This time, Mrs. Clarke actually did turn to leave, but she stopped short of stepping off the front porch. "No, I said I was going to tell you, and that is what I intend to do." She pivoted around, keeping the umbrella to herself, and said in a wavering voice, "I received a telegram, and it cannot be a good thing."

With rainwater now dripping from her nose, Giulia took the woman's free hand and noticed that she was crying. "What is it, Mrs. Clarke?"

The lady's lower lip was trembling, and she seemed unable to speak.

"Has something happened to Archie?" the girl asked, but there was no reply. Tears had begun to stream from Mrs. Clarke's eyes, so Giulia said, "Won't you come inside ... please? I'll fix you a nice glass of tea, and we can visit. Come on. Mamma's sleeping and won't even know you're here."

Most human beings are habitual in their actions, and Bess Clarke was no exception. After surrendering the umbrella and consenting to come inside, she seated herself on the sofa, right next to the end table, precisely where she had sat during that unpleasant altercation on the last day of April. She even laid her hat and gloves where she had placed them before. Though the temperature on this summer afternoon had climbed into the lower eighties, she insisted upon being properly accoutered whenever she went calling.

When Giulia entered the living room with two tall glasses of iced tea, Mrs. Clarke took a sip to calm her nerves and then reached over to her purse and produced a telegram, neatly folded into thirds. It was the sketchiest of communications, explaining that Sergeant Archibald Clarke had been wounded in action on 2 AUG during combat in New Guinea.

"When did you get this?" Giulia asked her.

Mrs. Clarke glanced at the postmark. "It came on the eleventh."

"But this is the twenty-eighth. Why did you wait so long to tell me?"

The lady could not reply. She shook her head and quietly wept.

Giulia persisted. "Have you found out where he is?"

"No."

"Do you think the Red Cross would be able to tell you?" Giulia asked.

Again Mrs. Clarke was unresponsive.

"I know someone who works there. Maybe she can get some information for us."

"No!" the lady shouted. Suddenly, she was wrathful and without a vestige of weariness in her voice. "If you are referring to Mrs. Nora Brower, mother of that boy you kissed in broad daylight at the train depot, the answer is no." She wiped the tears from her eyes and gave Giulia a cross look. "I forbid you from telling her about my Archie," she said. "I will not have his name dishonored by letting that woman make inquiries on his behalf."

A daily serial, "The Right to Happiness," had been playing softly on the radio all along. When the room went otherwise silent, the program became quite audible indeed, and Giulia became fearful that her mother would be coming into the room at any moment to hear "Backstage Wife," a show she seldom missed. Paolina Coletti was enamored with the Larry Noble character, and it would be fair to say that she identified fully with—and lived vicariously through—his young wife, Mary Noble, an Iowa girl who married a man whom NBC publicists called "the matinée idol of a million other women."

Giulia thought it only fair to warn her guest. "My mother will probably be here in a couple of minutes, Mrs. Clarke," she said. "I wish you would stay and tell her about Archie."

Mrs. Clarke stood, securing the strap of her purse in the process. "I really must be leaving," she told the girl. "I have no desire to remain where I am not welcome."

The sound of Paolina's voice echoed down the hallway. "Giulia, dear, is someone there with you?"

With hat and gloves in hand, Mrs. Clarke hurried toward the front door.

"Please stay," Giulia said. "I think I know how to contact Archie."

"A lot you care!" The lady knelt to retrieve her umbrella. "I don't know why I even bothered to tell you."

The summer shower could still be heard, pelting the rooftop harder than before, and a parlor window showed that the sky had turned an ominous shade of black. "Please, Mrs. Clarke," Giulia said again. "At least wait until the rain lets up." Just then, a bolt of lightning struck in the vicinity, followed a half-second later by a boom of thunder that sounded like a shotgun blast. Large raindrops began pounding against the front door, apparently at an angle that was almost horizontal. Surely the storm would not last for long, Giulia insisted, particularly at this time of the year, when precipitation was such a rare commodity.

"Who are you talking to?" Paolina asked from afar.

"It's Mrs. Clarke, Mamma," the girl shouted toward the living room. Again there came a bright flash and loud clap of thunder.

"Well, tell her to make herself comfortable, dear. I'm glad she made it safely through this terrible weather."

"Yes, Mamma." Giulia smiled compassionately at Mrs. Clarke, whose gaze was locked on the dangerous tempest outside. "Please," the girl told her, and the woman uttered a resigned sigh while leaning her umbrella against the hat rack.

"Bess, come in and sit down," Paolina said. She had finally made her way over to the others, having traversed the length of the living room with the aid of her walking cane. "Why are you standing in the entryway like that?" she asked. "Take off your hat and stay a while."

"I suppose I really have no choice," Mrs. Clarke said with an icy glare.

"Giulia, get Mrs. Clarke something cool to drink."

"I already have, Mamma—some tea. It's on the end table."

"Oh?" Paolina's look was an uncertain mixture of surprise and hurt.

"We've been having a chat," Giulia told her. Then, with a trembling voice, she continued. "She's received a telegram about Archie."

"A telegram?" Paolina's face turned pale, and the very word seemed to bring terror to her soul. She gave a searching glance at Mrs. Clarke, took her by the arm, and led her back into the living room.

Never before had Giulia seen her mother switch off the radio when "Backstage Wife" was on the air.

◆　　◆　　◆

Gertrude Moek was leaning heavily on her hoe when Nora Brower arrived with a sack full of edibles. The grocer's wife wiped her forehead and grinned. "Oh, you didn't need to do d'at, dear. We're managing just fine."

"Nonsense. You can always use a break from cooking. Russell Mimms tells me you're spending way too much time out here. He's real worried about you."

"D'at boy! Russell's d'e one who's got it rough now—not Hermann and me." Gertrude reached down with her tool and cultivated halfheartedly, her mind clearly on something other than gardening. "We hope to give him his old job back by November. You know, he's been working at Trautschold's while d'ey rebuild our store."

"That's what someone told me."

"Russell's hard of hearing and not too skilled, but he can help wit' deliveries— t'ings like d'at. Carl Trautschold was considerate enough to give him a job for a few weeks. I didn't ask Carl to do it. He just came up to me and offered."

"How nice."

"And he can eat right d'ere at d'e Club Café too. It's only a short walk."

Nora hesitated before making a confession. "You know, I've had to do my food shopping at Piggly Wiggly for the past couple of months. I hope you don't mind."

"Now, why would I mind? You have to eat, don't you?"

"Well, I just feel a bit disloyal, going over there after patronizing your store for so many years."

In spite of herself, Gertrude wanted to learn about the competition. "D'ey have shopping carts for you to push, don't d'ey?"

"Yes, they do."

"D'ey call it scientific shopping, but I like to t'ink d'at personalized service counts for somet'ing in d'is life."

"I do too."

"Which store, d'e one on Herring?"

"No, Fifteenth."

"Well, maybe we can reopen in seven or eight weeks."

"I hope so, Trudy. I do."

Gertrude's eyes were watery, but she did not put into words the unstated bond of friendship that existed between them. "D'at rain sure did keep d'ese vegetables alive. I t'ought d'ey were going to be burned up." She poked her hoe at some stubborn pebbles.

Nora smiled. "Our victory garden's not nearly as fine as yours is. Of course, I don't work it like I should, so I have no one to blame but myself. And Wes and Lizzie certainly were not blessed with green thumbs either."

This was the time of year when the Moeks were fully in the process of planting their fall vegetables. Squash was already making some headway in the ground, brussels sprouts had been transplanted, and now Gertrude was cultivating the soil for that season's crop of pinto beans, lettuce, English peas, and spinach. Hermann did the heavier work, but he readily acknowledged that it was his wife who possessed a knack for agriculture. "She could make a watermelon grow through a crack in the sidewalk," he would quip. With any luck, the local rainfall—so unreliable at this time of year—might cooperate with central Texas tillers of the soil better than in 1943. Certainly the recent showers boded well for the near future, if that was any indication.

The silhouettes of a half-dozen AAF trainers were discernible in the distance—flying in formation over East Waco—but what captured the ladies' awareness was the sound of an approaching automobile. A moment later, they saw Hermann's 1938 Packard sedan slowly pulling to a stop in the driveway, and there was someone with him. Both men climbed out and closed their doors nearly simultaneously. The stranger was carrying a briefcase.

"This is Mr. Robert Albright, Trudy," Hermann said. The sun made him squint as he and the other man—a dapper gent of about forty—walked toward the garden. "He's with the Red Cross."

Gertrude's draw dropped. "My goodness ..."

"Now, don't let his visit upset you, dear. Mr. Albright is in town to help us."

Albright gave her a reassuring smile. "That's right, Mrs. Moek."

Somewhat belatedly, Hermann resumed the introductions. "And this is our good friend, Nora Brower," he told the Red Cross agent, who tipped his hat. "Sorry to interrupt, Nora."

"Oh, Trudy and I were just visiting," she said. "I brought you some groceries."

Hermann snapped to attention and gave a shallow bow. "That was very kind of you. Are they heavy? Here, let me take them off your hands." Nora gave the sack to him with a nod of appreciation.

Then Albright turned to Gertrude with an explanation. "The Houston office has sent me to Waco. They wanted me to ... to return some things. Things we think you should have."

Nora glanced at the others and sensed that it might be best to withdraw, leaving the Moeks to their privacy. "I should really be going," she said. "They'll be wondering where I am."

Gertrude, though, would have none of it, and she insisted that her friend remain with them. "I don't t'ink d'ere's anyt'ing here d'at would be a secret, ist d'ere, Mr. Albright?" she asked.

The Red Cross agent shook his head. "No, ma'am, I don't suppose so. You're perfectly welcome to join us, if you'd like to, Mrs. Brower."

Hermann took a deep breath and said, "Well, let's all go in the house then, shall we?"

Again Nora tried her best to decline the offer—feeling like an intruder—but Gertrude begged her to stay.

Hermann held the screen door open until everyone was inside, and then he cushioned it from slamming too loudly behind him. He asked the ladies, "Do I need to put these things in the ice box, or will they keep?"

Gertrude looked at Nora, who replied, "Yes, please. I think everything needs to be chilled. All except the rolls in that little sack inside the big one."

"Right-o," he said.

A few minutes later, the four of them were seated around the breakfast table, an unopened briefcase lying in front of Robert Albright and an aluminum, stovetop percolator in operation across the room, brewing coffee. For some reason, the latter's aroma brought back to Hermann memories of a convention in San Antonio about three weeks before the stock market collapse. Conrad was there with him that time, just watching his father at work, and he could not have been more than fifteen or sixteen. The conference room in the twenty-year-old St. Anthony Hotel was crowded with grocery merchants from all over the southeast, and Conrad told his father that he wanted to be just like him when he finished his schooling—only his goal in life would be to own a whole chain of food stores in California. "Why there?" his bemused father asked, and Conrad answered that he loved palm trees, but they will not thrive so well in Texas.

When Albright opened the briefcase, he did so very solemnly, knowing that its contents represented a direct connection to the Moeks' deceased son. "This introductory statement has been translated from the German," he said, "but I guess that was not required in this instance, was it?"

"No, sir," Hermann told him. "I am not ashamed to say that Trudy and I both speak the German language—as did our son, of course."

Albright nodded without comment and then slowly began unfolding the yellow piece of paper. After taking a leisurely sip of coffee from the ceramic cup that Gertrude placed in front of him, he reached into his suit coat's inside pocket for a pair of reading glasses. Then, with a deep breath, he read the paragraph aloud.

Nora marveled at how detached the man suddenly became. He uttered the words in a droning voice, replete with all the practiced objectivity of someone who dealt in such emotional issues on a regular basis. She recalled what her late husband had told her about serving on a month-long burial detail while in the United States Army. At first, the daily ritual of a twenty-one-gun salute and flag-folding ceremony was heartrending to the point of tears, particularly when the bereaved widow was glimpsed. But just a day or two later, this duty at rural cemeteries somehow transformed itself into nothing more than a cold routine, shallow in substance and mechanical in its repetitive motions.

"These few belongings," Albright recited from the handwritten translation, "were the only effects found on the slain body of Corporal Conradin Philipp Moek on 28 April 1943, near the coastal town of Bizerta, Tunisia. It is with all due respect to this fallen hero of the Reich, and to the glory of its Führer, that they are hereby given over from the Deutsches Rotes Kreuz to the American

Red Cross. It may unequivocally be stated that Corporal Moek died bravely on the field of battle, and it is to his eternal memory that these artifacts are now entrusted to the custody of his parents. (signed) Carl-Eduard Herzog von Sachsen-Coburg und Gotha, President."

Gertrude listened quietly and wept, but Hermann became quite enraged. "How ... dare ... this *grausamer Unmensch* write such lies to us ... and have you proclaim them in our own home!"

"Now, Mr. Moek," Robert Albright said, "this is to be expected, believe me. The note is, in effect, nothing more than a form letter with your son's name inserted."

"Mr. Albright, I don't think you realize who this monster is," Hermann told him, "or you would not have read his words in our presence. I apologize for you to my dear Gertrude Sophie."

Suddenly bereft of his composure, the embarrassed Red Cross agent did well to mumble a garbled response in his own behalf. "No, sir. I'm ... I must confess that I don't. I'm terribly sorry if I ..." He glanced across the table at the two ladies. "I'm sorry if I offended you and your wife, which, I can assure you, is the last thing in the world that I intended to do."

Hermann stood up, his hands shaking. "Charles Edward is the grandson of Queen Victoria, for God's sake! His uncle was Edward VII. He was nobility until he stabbed his family in the back—in the last war and again in this one."

Albright shrugged his shoulders and sat up straight. "My charge is to present this correspondence to you, along with your son's effects. Nothing more and nothing less." With a frown, he handed the note to Hermann, who angrily snatched it from him.

"I accept this scrap of paper only to burn it, sir. My son, Mr. Albright, was not a Nazi, and no Goebbels lie is going to implicate him."

"I quite understand," Albright said, and he glanced at his wristwatch. "Shall we continue?" From the briefcase he took Conrad Moek's *Soldbuch*, traditional repository for a German soldier's vital statistics, parents' names, shot records, eye examinations, and list of military units. Hermann accepted the book with political disdain, but he soon acquiesced, upon acknowledging that this slim volume was carried throughout the war by his only son. From back to front, he flipped through some of the pages, pausing when he reached the inside front cover. There he saw a grim, unsmiling photograph of Conrad in uniform, as well as his signature. Slowly, he drew a fingertip across the dried ink, as if that simple act could somehow bring him closer to the departed.

Next, Albright produced from the briefcase a small packet, wrapped in discolored white paper and secured with a slipknot of twine. Only about a half-inch thick, the packet's lateral dimensions probably measured no more than four by five. He handed it to Gertrude, who, after taking a pensive breath, slowly removed the twine and unfolded the brittle paper. Within were some snapshots of various sizes, perhaps fifteen in number. Several were of Conrad and his army comrades, enjoying happy times in what appeared to be a major European city. There, too, was a picture of a terrier dog with a stick in his mouth, two of a very pretty girl shading her eyes from the sun, one of a circus clown standing near a Ferris wheel (the Prater?), an old photo of the Moeks' home in San Antonio, and a familiar shot from about 1930 of the boy's parents, who stood, arm in arm, near the Ford that was Hermann's first automobile. Seeing this likeness of herself brought tears to Gertrude's eyes. "See here, Liebling," she told her husband, "he kept us in his heart all d'is time."

Hermann looked through the photos next, and he could not help wondering who the young lady might be. He turned those two pictures over and saw, scribbled in ink on each of them, "Resi—März, 1943." To the best of his knowledge, Conrad had never married, so this beautiful woman, presumably named Theresia, must have been someone whom he met while assigned to military service. Viewing her lovely features again, he smiled at what a nice girl she seemed to be—not at all coarse, like so many tarts who made it their business to prey on soldiers. Behind her in one of the snapshots, visible in the distance, was a merchant's shop with a sign that read, "Jos. Grünewald, Hutmacher." That was the only clue.

Also in the briefcase, presented to the slain soldier's parents as a secondary bundle, were toiletries and other mundane artifacts that doubtlessly caused the Moeks to ask themselves, "Is this, then, all that remains of our little boy?" Even the manner of wrapping seemed rudely dispassionate and offensive to them, securing the contents within a rough-hewn onionskin that was scarcely less abrasive than an emery board. Albright explained that oftentimes military authorities would repackage such personal belongings, removing anything that might conceivably disclose geographic bearings, not to mention confiscating for their own enrichment what was judged to be of intrinsic value.

Throughout these melancholy proceedings, Nora remained a passive witness. She wished dearly to be somewhere else—far from this encroachment on the private lives of grieving parents—but whenever she began to scoot her chair away from the table, she would feel one of Gertrude's hands grasp her own, as if begging her to stay in emotional support.

A set of eyeglasses caused the Moeks some confusion, for neither parent could ever recall seeing Conrad wearing corrective lenses of any sort, and none of the present photos indicated that he relied upon them in casual activity. Hermann could guess what Gertrude was wondering because the same uneasy thought crossed his mind as well: "Were these effects indeed our son's?"

But any lingering doubt as to the proprietor and authenticity of this passel of meager holdings dissipated a moment later when Hermann picked up a round, well-worn medallion that lay partially concealed beneath a misshapen cake of shaving-mug soap. He choked on the words he was about to say, swallowed hard, and then silently handed the precious article to his wife. At once she was reduced to tears, for lovingly cradled in her palm was all that remained of a childhood souvenir that Conrad had cherished for most of his life.

It was a commemorative token from the Boy Scout Association's First World Jamboree, held in London during July of 1920. The red, white, and blue ribbon (emblematic of Britain's national colors) had long since torn away, but the copper medal was in surprisingly recognizable condition—what a numismatist might evaluate as "VG-F." Gertrude could no longer remember how her son came into possession of this keepsake memento. Conrad would never have been permitted to travel abroad at the tender age of seven, of course, so perhaps some adult among the American contingent later presented it to him as a gift. Whatever the origin may have been, he treasured it while a young boy, guarding the trinket as if it were a valuable coin.

Still crying, Gertrude thanked the Red Cross man for bringing home these few tangible reminders of their son. "You know, we still have all Conrad's toys in a chest in d'e attic," she said. "And his letters are in d'ere too."

Hermann extended his right hand and shook that of Robert Albright, all the while fighting back tears of his own. When he finally managed to speak, it was in a breathless monotone, his throat sounding oddly constricted by sorrow. "We have not seen our boy for ten years ... so I hope you can understand what ... how much ... this means to us."

Albright, well accustomed to fending off such unwarranted appreciation, deftly minimized his role by stating that this was merely his job. And yet, as professional and impersonal as he strove to maintain these dealings, it was clear to see that he did feel some sympathy for his bereaved clients. He blinked involuntarily and took care to avoid making direct eye contact until the Moeks' emotions had subsided somewhat. Taking a sip of coffee, he snapped shut the latches of his briefcase and then began stretching the elastic band of his wristwatch, complaining that it was pinching his skin. Tension broken, Hermann joked that he, too, knew the feeling, and both men were still more relieved when the topic reverted to victory gardens, a conversation in which Gertrude was pleased to join.

Nora Brower stood up with the others when Albright was about to leave, but immediately she walked across the kitchen and busied herself by pouring another cup of coffee. The hour-long session had been uncomfortably frank and intimate for someone outside the family, and she deemed it was not her place to converse with the Red Cross agent any more than need be during such a sensitive time as this. Only her loyalty to Gertrude, who seemed in need of close companionship during the ordeal, obliged her to stay as long as she did. Once Hermann went to drive Robert Albright back to the county Red Cross office—opposite Blanton's Flower Shop on Austin Avenue—Nora excused herself and told Gertrude, "If there's anything I can do to help, please call."

"May d'e good Lord bless you for being here today," the other woman said. She clasped both of Nora's hands between her own. "I believe everyt'ing happens for a reason, and He put you here to help me t'rough d'is time, I'm sure."

Nora thought so too, which caused her to feel all the more ashamed when she began walking down the driveway toward home. Being brutally honest with herself, she had to concede that her preoccupied mind, throughout this morning's proceedings, had been focused less upon the late Conrad Moek and more upon the precarious welfare of her own son, Seaman First Class Stephen Brower, who, despite the recent fusillade of letter-writing by his anxious mother, had not been heard from in nearly a month.

♦   ♦   ♦

It was a Tuesday, registration morning for the fall quarter. Two hours earlier, upon her arrival in Waco Hall at eight o'clock, Hannah dutifully walked from desk to desk on stage, collecting paperwork that had to be filled out even before she left the building. Then she returned to her seat with a packet of note cards and a handful of forms, each of which had to be completed for the Registrar's Office to process by Thursday morning, when classes would resume.

With that bureaucratic hurdle cleared for another term, she now relaxed on a swing beneath one of the venerable campus oaks, sighing heavily and allowing her thoughts to drift into dangerous territory. Perhaps the tedious regimen of nightly study had worn her down. Or maybe the war's fearsome impact simply relegated rival objectives—even those so estimable as a college degree—to lesser stature.

Yet another possible drain on her educational ambitions that day was the springlike weather, which was well-nigh ideal for inducing a dreamy state of apathy. The temperature hovered in the low seventies, and the maximum was expected to climb to no higher than eighty degrees. Bearing in mind that a hundred was not unheard-of for central Texas during the second week of September, Hannah felt blessed to sit back, close her eyes, and savor the comfort of a gentle, caressing breeze. Enjoy it while you can, she thought.

Directly above her, in the treetop, she saw a squirrel leap from branch to branch and envied the creature's freedom. Placing a stick of Juicy Fruit into her mouth, she turned her head toward Waco Hall and watched an assortment of her fellow students descend the steps and then go their various ways, no doubt planning activities to make the most of their last two days of the quarter system's abbreviated summer break.

"'Ten ... HUT!" someone shouted not five feet away from her ear, and so startled was Hannah that she very nearly fell when scrambling to her feet. "Hey! Who do you think you are?" she said.

"Who do *you* think I am?" came the cheerful reply. Grinning at her from behind the swing was Private Randall Box, whom she had encountered briefly at the Elite Café three months ago.

"I haven't the faintest," Hannah told him. She stood in a confrontational posture, with hands on hips.

"Some restaurant—a few weeks back. Me and my buddies were there." He waited an appropriate few seconds for her to recall, but she only glowered at him. "Randy Box," he added, still to no avail. "Come on now. Don't tell me I'm that easy to forget."

"'Fraid so, soldier," Hannah said. "Listen, I've really got some things to do." She began to walk away but stopped for a parting comment. "Why aren't you off somewhere, winning the war? Don't you have a job for the Army?"

"This *is* my job, just wandering around aimlessly on a GI expense account. Pretty cushy, huh?"

She popped her chewing gum and smirked. "I ought to turn you in. You're no better than any other slacker."

"It may not look like it to you, sweetie, but I'm working right now. Had to make a delivery to the first sergeant at ASTP." Then, before he even said it, Randy smiled at his forthcoming joke. "Seems the top needed some Army manuals to pass out to his teachers—so the pre-engineering students could play like they were really in the military."

"How long have *you* been playing?"

"Me? I'm a card-carrying member of Uncle Sam's air forces. Want to see my matching socks to prove it? Strictly olive drab—both of them."

"I really don't care what color your undergarments are, Mr. Box."

"Private Box."

She shrugged with disinterest. "Private."

"Randy."

In spite of herself, Hannah had to laugh, and the airman advanced two steps toward her, pleased with his progress thus far. He pointed with a thumb. "I was wondering if you wanted to go for a quick spin in that motor-pool Cadillac of mine. I've still got a little time to kill."

Hannah glanced at the vehicles parked along Seventh Street, and there indeed was a jeep, all dusty and dented from hard driving. She eyed him with suspicion. "I would think you'd get into trouble, letting a civilian ride with you."

"Some people might, but not me."

"I guess you don't pay much attention to Army regulations."

"Nope. Well, the big stuff I obey," he told her. "The nitpicking regs were made to be broken."

"In other words, you choose which rules you want to follow. How very patriotic of you."

"Say, don't get me wrong, missy. I'm as patriotic as the next guy. It's just that some of the brass take little things too seriously. You know what I mean?"

Randy paused to admire a pretty coed, who smiled at him as she passed.

"The Army's not a bad life if you learn how to roll with the punches," he added. "And know where to hide when they're looking for names to put on the duty list. That's important too. I haven't done any bubble dancing in over eight months."

"Bubble dancing?"

"Better known as KP."

The Westminster chimes in Pat Neff Hall tower tolled the top of the hour, an occasion Hannah saw as a good excuse to explain to the airman that she really needed to go. She was expecting an important letter and check from her father, Hannah informed him, and the postman usually delivered the morning mail by ten o'clock. If she was to deposit its contents at the bank before her work shift, she had to catch the next streetcar downtown.

Undeterred, Randy playfully blocked her exit. "I'll do you one better than that," he said. "I'll get you home in ten minutes flat—guaranteed—to any point in Waco."

"Haven't you heard the news? There's a thirty-five-miles-per-hour speed limit."

"Well ..."

"Another one of those nitpicking regs?"

"Yep."

Again Hannah began to walk away, only this time Randy willingly stepped aside. "You never did tell me your name," he called after her.

"Oh, I'm sure I did," Hannah told him. She glanced back over her shoulder. "At the Elite. You just forgot."

"Nope. I would have written it in my little black book," he said. "I'm well organized when it comes to keeping track of the women in my life."

"That I believe," she shouted straight ahead—but plenty loud enough for him to hear.

Hannah's friend, Margo Burke, caught up with her about midway between the Women's Hospital and the Studio Theater and wondered who her soldier boy might be. "He's rather nice looking, isn't he?" she asked.

"In a crass sort of way, I suppose. But he's just a gigolo, like most of the others."

"Really?" Margo said with a suggestive grin. "What's his name?"

Hannah just shook her head. "Don't get involved. Believe me, he's nothing but trouble."

They walked together toward the streetcar stop, unaware that a jeep was tailing them along Speight. The military vehicle and the two civilian pedestrians reached Fifth almost simultaneously, much to Hannah's embarrassment. All the while, she had been trying to convince Margo that she hardly knew the airman.

"You ladies want a ride?" came a shout. "Hop in."

Margo seemed willing, but Hannah ignored the offer.

"How about it?" Randy directed his smile at Hannah's friend. "We're here to serve."

"Which way are you going?" Margo asked.

"Whatever's your pleasure."

"To Barnard ... just past Columbus?"

"That's on my route."

Margo thought for a moment and then walked over to the jeep. "Why not? I've never ridden with the Army." She looked at her friend, who stared back in disbelief. "Come on, Hannah. It'll be fun. He can drop you off too."

"Come on ... *Hannah*," Randy said. "I won't even switch on the meter, if that's what's worrying you."

As Margo was climbing into the jeep, Hannah forced herself to turn away. She was shocked that someone of college age, a solid B+ student at that, could possibly be so naïve and gullible as to risk her life just for the sake of adventure.

"Farewell ... *Hannah*," Randall Box shouted, but Hannah did not deign to glance toward him. She could hear Margo laughing with glee as the driver slammed his vehicle into gear, wheeled left around the corner, and sped up Fifth Street by weaving in and out of the campus traffic.

Hannah felt sure that her name was now ineradicably filed in this smooth operator's memory, and soon it would be etched in his little black book, whenever he had a free moment from killing time on the government dole. Noisily smacking a fresh stick of chewing gum, she stood at the streetcar stop with three other young women, counting it a moral victory that only a tiny corner of her mind regretted the decision to take a proper conveyance home.

One of the waiting girls smiled at her and then resumed reading in her science textbook, no doubt trying to get a head start on the next term. The others appeared to be good friends, and their matching blouses attested that both were members of the same social club on campus. Had Hannah been more conscious of ladies' fashions, she might have noticed that their stylish footwear was nearly identical too. Although unmistakably clannish—as much a prevalent conceit in Baylor clubs as in national sororities—they were courteous enough to refrain from calling attention to the work shoes that Hannah wore, correctly assuming that she was on her way to a job in support of the war effort.

♦　　♦　　♦

As the final days of September slipped by, Wesley began to feel more and more like the high school senior that he was. There were no longer any upperclassmen to cast superior glances at him, so his self-assurance responded with a healthy upsurge, stopping just short of swagger. Accordingly, and in common with the majority of his fellow twelfth graders, he grew to shun the newly enrolled freshmen. Though in truth it had not been all that long since he himself was on the receiving end of interclass condescension, these neophytes, to his seasoned eyes, appeared to be as immature as little children.

His sister had turned sixteen two weeks earlier, and Giulia Coletti was now eighteen, an age he would not attain for another month and a half. Wesley had found no occasion to speak to Giulia since the day he gave her a tour of the radio station. He did see her from a distance one time, when she was purchasing some groceries at the Piggly Wiggly, but she averted her eyes and did not seem inclined to renew acquaintances. It was not until sometime later that he learned, from the trustworthy mouth of his mother, that Miss Coletti was believed to be anguished over the condition of her fiancé, who had been wounded in combat. This report, however, was fourth-hand and unsubstantiated.

Waiting outside Wesley's English class after the bell rang was Morton Wilson, who seemed excited to tell him something important. Wesley rightly assumed that his communiqué must be related to baseball, as this topic of discussion had grown to become almost an obsession with him in the past couple of years. The Cardinals were shoo-ins by now for the National League title, but over in the American League, the Tigers, Yankees, and Browns were embroiled in a pennant race that promised to go down to the wire.

Morton was a diehard Browns fan, if for no other reason than he could pick up some of their games on WEW Radio—when atmospheric conditions were just right—so he felt like they were his very own home team. The Cards and Browns not only shared a playing field, Sportsman's Park, but also announcers Johnny O'Hara and Dizzy Dean, who did the play-by-play for both teams, depending upon who was in town. Morton's favorite player was aging first baseman George McQuinn, and he was most afraid of the Tigers, who had won twenty-two of their last twenty-seven contests and were clinging to a one-game lead in the junior circuit.

"You think Newhouser can win thirty?" he asked. "Just three more to go, but time's running out." Wesley shrugged but did not feel qualified to answer. "Pinky Higgins drove in five yesterday," Morton told his friend. "He's from Red Oak, you know. I wonder if he comes back in the off-season."

"Probably."

"They had forty-eight thousand fans at Briggs Stadium," Morton said. Then, with a cynical smirk, he added, "The Browns are lucky to have that many in a home stand."

A steady stream of students was passing by, headed toward their next classes. Morton waved to Kenneth Dominick and his brother, Sal. They were new to Waco, transplants from back east.

"I think my Brownies can still take the pennant," he told Wesley. "The Red Sox are coming to town, and they've lost seven straight. The Tigers swept them."

With an eye on the hall clock, Wesley had managed to edge his way toward the crowded stairway when Morton stopped him with an afterthought, for once not about the national pastime. "Sandy says she wants to see you before you go to the radio station."

Wesley's heart pounded. "Sandy Whittsel?" he asked.

"Yeah."

"What for? Did she say?"

"Something about school, I think, but she wanted to talk to you ... alone." Morton seemed amused by Wesley's look of shock. "I think she likes you, Wes," he said.

"Nope. She's got a boyfriend. The only thing she likes about me is when I help her with homework." Morton gave him a knowing grin and walked away.

Wesley shared no afternoon classes with Sandy this term, so he figured that his only chance to catch her would be in the school cafeteria. But when lunchtime finally arrived, and he went down to the basement to survey the room, she was nowhere to be seen. Her good friend, Clarice Thurman, had no idea where she might be, except to say that Sandy only ate on campus about three days a week. On the other two days, someone usually picked her up for lunch—a much older boy who smoked cigarettes and, when not busy shifting gears, always drove with his right arm around her shoulders.

On this particular day, Wesley seated himself with a group of junior boys whom he hardly knew. It was a strategically located table, providing an unobstructed view of the lunchroom, but Sandy, true to form, never made an appearance. There was a time, of course, when Wesley would have moved mountains to honor the girl's desire for an audience, but those days were over for good. Upon depositing his lunch tray onto the stack near the kitchen, he was in no frame of mind to chase after anyone, least of all a fickle female who brought nothing but frustration to his life. If it was a favor she wanted, let her precious Marshall McFall do it for her. He could not care less.

Monday's broadcast went much more smoothly than Wesley had any right to expect. Sandra Whittsel performed well, particularly in a challenging sequence that involved laughing, screaming, and crying within a frantic span of ninety seconds of airtime. Wesley was not in that scene, but from his folding chair nearby, he could not help but admire her portrayal of Sally Holt, the ostensibly shallow box-office girl who rose to a dubious prominence within the Cashley syndicate. Small wonder that Sandy was a clear favorite in the public's estimation of radio stars. She brought an uncanny depth to her role that perhaps even the writers never suspected was there. Though admittedly envious, Wesley was also objective enough to recognize her natural prowess on the air.

"I'm warning you, Odom," Sandy shouted into the microphone. "Don't sell me short. If there's one thing that riles me to the point of ... to apoplexy ... it's when someone sells me short. My schooling is plenty good enough to match wits with the likes of you." As Rodney DeBonaventura rattled some silverware and plinked a glass or two, Sandy rose to her full height—nearly five foot on tiptoes—and flung a hateful scowl through the airwaves. "Cross me again, buster, and you'll think you've squashed an ant hill in your bare feet. That Bradford 'goon' (as you call him) has money to burn ... more than anyone named Cashley will ever hope to see ... so I sure don't need a preachy lecture from no petty thief like you. Shut your annoying trap ... and, while you're at it, pass the sugar, dear, if it's not too heavy for you to lift." She was at the top of her game.

Another unquestioned talent, relaxing at this same moment within the acoustical properties of his soundproof booth, was the acknowledged Dean of Central Texas Announcers. So experienced and supremely confident was Marshall McFall that he was fully capable of scrutinizing the entire studio, even while one eye remained firmly focused on the copy before him. Masterfully, he intoned the close to "Behold Tomorrow," read a thirty-second commercial for Bee Line Coaches, noted to himself that Sandra Whittsel was chatting with Phyllis Sherry, reminded members of his audience that they were listening to KWXN, read a thirty-second commercial for Levine's ("First in Fashion"), and watched as Sandy departed with that high school kid who plays Kip Hanson. Then, without so much as missing a beat, he articulated from memory the familiar opening: "Before the days of streetcars and automobiles and airplanes, Waco, Texas, was often referred to as 'Six-Shooter Junction.' Come with us now as we relive those exciting days of gunslingers and lawmen, when civilization pushed back the frontiers of Texas and established a settlement 'West of the Brazos'." His eyes were still peering at the studio door when it shut, just in time for the Old West to spring to life once again. He opened a fresh pack of Raleighs.

As Wesley followed Sandy through the lobby, both waved to receptionist Myra Culp, who was deeply involved in a telephone conversation at the moment. Wesley lagged a couple of steps behind the girl because he had a sneaking suspicion that Morton had played a prank on him, and he was not about to embarrass himself by becoming too friendly.

It was Sandy who made the first move. With an unsmiling urgency, she looked him directly in the eye. "Wes, I need to talk with you, and it can't be here at the station."

"Well, sure," he said. "What about?"

"Can't tell you now. Will you be at home tonight?"

Wesley thought for a moment. "I guess so." And he added, "My mother won't be there. Is that all right?"

"So much the better," Sandy told him. She did so without a trace of seductiveness, either in her attitude or tone of voice. Wesley studied the girl's face, hoping for some sort of a clue, but she was being far too mysterious for that. Never once did she bring up the name of Morton Wilson or demand to know why Wesley did not bother to see her at school that afternoon.

A further source of confusion was how much at ease Sandy had seemed in the studio, but surely that could be attributed to her instinctive professionalism as an actress. It was widely known that this young artist took great pride in not allowing external influences to affect her on-mike performance. Even Hugh Kenton commented on that, marveling at the integrity of her acting for someone so inexperienced. Often he would cite her as an example of how to prepare for a role—to assimilate a character into one's own psyche, as he liked to put it.

◆　　◆　　◆

That evening, Nora Brower left soon after dinner was finished, pitching in with her volunteer work at the Red Cross. This was just fine with Wesley because he could sense that Sandy had something important—and private—to tell him. A syndicated program called "10-2-4 Ranch" could be heard on the radio, so he surmised that the Philco console was tuned to WACO. He sat on the sofa, pretending to listen but actually watching his sister wash and dry the dishes, a chore that typically took her about twenty minutes to accomplish. "Energy sags in the long hours between meals," came the radio voice, "so drink a bite to eat, the icy cold Dr. Pepper. Keep time in mind, and drink Dr. Pepper daily at ten, two, four o'clock, or anytime you are hungry or tired."

Wesley calculated that his sister would be leaving for the filling station early enough to punch in at seven o'clock. She always had difficulty getting her homework done in a timely fashion on Mondays and Thursdays because of the way the schedule was arranged at Service Refining Company. Still, Mr. Harkins was kind enough to let her have Wednesdays off for church activities, so she could not complain. And only occasionally did she have to work a three-hour shift on Tuesday nights, whenever Dinah Reidelhuber or Bobbie Groves needed to be elsewhere. It was the weekends that accounted for most of the value of her modest paychecks.

While "The Lone Ranger" was on, Wesley came and went, dividing time between studying in his bedroom and keeping tabs on Elizabeth's whereabouts. Gradually, it began to worry him that perhaps she was not scheduled to work at all. Sure enough, she showed no signs of changing into her SRC coveralls and remained at home, diagramming sentences for English class, throughout

"Watch the World Go By" and "Lum and Abner." Worse yet, at 7:30—just when Sandy might appear on the Brower doorstep at any moment—Elizabeth raced downstairs to enjoy "Blind Date," a program that, as luck would have it, was a particular favorite among high school girls. It was a secret fantasy of hers that she might compete on the program in a year or two and win a romantic date with some proper GI or sailor. Little did Elizabeth know that emcee Arlene Francis and the Blue Network studios were in far-off New York City. She had always assumed that the show originated from either Dallas or Houston. Besides, the women in question were not contestants at all but beautiful models and starlets who were paid fifty dollars apiece to provide companionship for the servicemen as they enjoyed their chaperoned nights on the town.

It seemed hours before the doorbell finally rang, and paradoxically, the sound grated on him like the dissonant vibration of fingernails on a blackboard. A pretty visitor such as Sandra Whittsel should have been cause for joyful anticipation, but Wesley felt only dread. The evening was shaping up to be a bitter fiasco. Would Elizabeth stubbornly continue to lounge on the living room sofa while her brother entertained a guest of the opposite sex? How discomfiting this would be, not to mention that Sandy would never feel free to confide her problem to him with a third party lurking in the room.

Unsure what else to do in the circumstances, Wesley decided to affect surprise, trusting that his watchful sister would not suspect that this rendezvous was contrived several hours ago, across town, in a smoke-filled lobby. "Well, aren't you going to get it?" she asked with brooding impatience when the doorbell rang. It was ten minutes to eight, and six handsome (as she saw them) servicemen were in the final stages of vying for the affections of an enticing trio of prospective dates. This was no time to be interrupted by a thoughtless intruder, so she took the liberty of walking over to the radio and giving its volume dial a bold, clockwise nudge.

When Wesley accompanied his caller into the room, Elizabeth's attention was diverted from the game show just long enough to appraise the visitor's appearance. This was the same girl she spoke with after the Victory Concert. She was sure of it.

Wesley motioned with a hand. "Lizzie, this is Sandy. Sandy, my sister."

"How do you do?" Sandy said. She found it rather irksome that this Lizzie was by now looking toward the radio instead of at her.

"'Blind Date'," Elizabeth told the guest, as if to excuse her rude behavior.

"Oh, I *love* that show." Sandy hurried forward to seat herself on the nearest cushion of the sofa, and Elizabeth—sitting on the farthest cushion—smiled at her.

Wesley could hardly believe his eyes. Suddenly, the girls were kindred spirits, all because of a sappy radio program. At least the disagreeable chore ahead of him would be postponed for a while. He sat in the easy chair, admiring Sandy's half-forgotten profile, and again, in defiance of his better judgment, he fell hopelessly under her spell.

During the sponsor's closing commercial, advertising the manifold benefits of Lehn & Fink products for busy wartime housewives, Elizabeth stood up and returned to the Philco console. "Do you mind if I turn on 'Lux'?" she asked. "It's a Ginger Rogers movie I saw a few years ago ... with Ronald Colman."

Sandy giggled. "You saw it with Ronald Colman?"

"Don't I wish!" Elizabeth twisted the volume knob a bit louder.

Wesley was struck by how chummy the two girls were with one another, and he tried to recall if Sandy had ever met his sister before. He thought that unlikely. In any case, maybe it would not be so bad if Elizabeth did stay around to lend moral support. He was not looking forward to being all by himself with the enigmatic Miss Whittsel, unable to guess what in the world was on her mind and why she had suddenly promoted him to the status of long-lost confidant.

Hearing a deep-throated announcer deliver the station identification for KWXN instantly changed Sandy's mien for the worst, and Wesley began to wish that his sister had left the dial tuned to "Counterspy" instead of switching over to the prestige drama. Tonight's CBS offering was a comedy, but a deaf observer would have found that difficult to detect from the visitor's dour countenance. Wesley feared that she was on the verge of tears, and he hoped Elizabeth would pay her no notice, now that the program had started.

"Lux presents Hollywood," John Milton Kennedy intoned. "The 'Lux Radio Theatre' brings you Don Ameche and Lucille Ball in *Lucky Partners*. Ladies and gentlemen, your producer, Mr. Cecil B. DeMille." Sandy stared straight ahead, oblivious to her new friend's critical remark: "Well, they should be good too, but the picture's stars were a scream." Moments later, Elizabeth listened intently as the superstitious protagonists introduced themselves to one another.

JEAN:	*You must be new around here.*
DAVID:	*Yes. Yes, I am. My name is Grant ... David Grant.*
JEAN:	*Oh, I'm Jean Newton. I work right across the street there in my aunt's shop, the Book Nook.*

It was only five minutes into the program, but already Sandy had heard enough. She turned to Wesley and whispered, "I think we'd better talk." Her look was serious, all pretense of playfulness long since vanished.

With a glance toward his sister, Wesley slowly rose to his feet. "Listen, Sandy, why don't we go for a walk? It's awfully warm in here." Sandy stood up too, imperceptibly nodding her head, but she dared not let Elizabeth see her eyes.

"Please don't go running off on my account," the younger girl said. Her gaze went from one to the other, and she broke into a broad grin. "Honestly, I have lots more homework I need to do. Sit on the sofa—the both of you." As she was leaving the room, Wesley had a sheepish smile on his face, but the visitor persisted in looking away, evidently brought to shame by the awkwardness of this romantic setting. "Three's a crowd," were Elizabeth's final, teasing words as she disappeared up the stairs. Oh, well, she liked Ronald Colman and Ginger Rogers much better anyway.

| JEAN: | *I hope you don't think this is too silly, but I'm playing a hunch, and it has to do with you.* |
| DAVID: | *Oh?* |

JEAN:	*You see, it all began this morning when you wished me good luck.*
	Well, I ran smack into some good luck right away. And suddenly I
	began to feel lucky ... you know.
DAVID:	*Vaguely.*
JEAN:	*Well, all I want is for you to share a sweepstakes ticket with me.*

Sandy sat down again, but this time on the distant spot that Elizabeth had just vacated. Wesley walked a few feet to seat himself at the near end of the sofa, about a yardstick's length away from the girl, and waited for her to begin speaking. But the only voices he heard belonged to Don Ameche and Lucille Ball.

DAVID:	*What do you want money for?*
JEAN:	*I plan to get married.*
DAVID:	*Oh. To a fortune hunter?*
JEAN:	*He's nothing of the kind!*

Wesley watched as his guest stared at the floor, hands folded demurely in her lap. She cleared her throat once but said nothing. Not knowing how else to proceed, he broke the tension by offering her a glass of water. The temperature today had reached ninety degrees at five o'clock, and it was not much cooler than that now. "Yes, please," Sandy said in a hollow voice. She considered for a moment and added, "Unless you have something stronger."

The best he could find in the refrigerator was a pitcher of lemonade, almost certainly not what she had in mind. In the kitchen, as he poured two tall glasses of the summertime beverage, he observed that Sandy continued to sit perfectly still on the sofa, not even bothering to say a word to him during the interim. Her head hardly moved at all, except when she leaned forward to pet the cat, Valentino, who had rubbed against her leg to solicit attention.

JEAN:	*The money's here in this envelope, and half of it's yours.*
DAVID:	*Well, good ol' Freddy!*
JEAN:	*Yes.*
DAVID:	*Oh, but wait a minute. No. No, none of this is mine. He sold your*
	half.
JEAN:	*Oh, no. It's fifty-fifty. Uh, Freddy said so.*

"Do you mind if I turn that down?" Wesley asked. He handed her one of the glasses.

"No." She took a sip and nodded thanks.

Wesley reduced the volume until it was barely audible. "It's a little hard to talk with all that going on."

"Yes, it is."

He laid his glass on the coffee table and seated himself, grinning at her with as much confidence as he could muster. "Well?" he said, and she flashed her prettiest smile. That was a good sign, no doubt—and so positive that a reassuring thought crept into his mind. Maybe Sandy was making this impending conversation more dramatic than it really warranted. After all, she was a very good actress, and theater people sometimes are prone to histrionics. Wesley had noticed such a characteristic even in high school, and that must be about the lowest form of theater there is.

"Are we alone?" Sandy asked.

Wesley stood up again and quietly approached the stairway, peeking around the corner at the ascending steps. Then he came back and reported, "No one there, and I can hear the radio going in my mother's bedroom. I guess Lizzie's listening to 'Lux' in there."

Sandy looked down at her folded hands. "I've been trying to come up with a nice way of saying this, but I really can't think of anything."

Wesley sat on the sofa. "Well, what do you want to tell me?" he asked. "Is it something I've done?"

There was the merest token of a smile on Sandy's face, but it was gone in an instant, supplanted by gloom. "No, it's nothing you've done," she told him. "You're too innocent. You'd never get into a mess like this one." She took a tiny sip of lemonade, as if she hoped to make the glassful last throughout the evening.

Wesley viewed her profile for a moment, not knowing what to say. Her eyes were a bit redder now than they were before, but otherwise she remained as lovely as ever. He felt sorry for her and protective. He wished that he had the poise of some of his friends, the boldness to scoot closer and put his arm around her. This he felt quite unable to do.

"Wes," she said, "I'm ... expecting."

He stared at her in disbelief.

"I'm going to have a baby ... I'm pregnant." Her secret now divulged, Sandy bent forward and cradled her face in her hands. "I feel like I'm living in a nightmare." She did not cry, but her voice trembled.

Wesley swallowed hard and took a deep breath. "Are you sure ... about the baby?"

Sandy stared at him with watery eyes. "Oh, yes, I'm sure. There's no doubt about it." She leaned back and lightly patted her abdomen. "Can't you tell?" She did look fuller around the midsection than usual. "I'll be showing real soon, so I need to do something drastic right away."

That sounded ominous, and it frightened Wesley to hear her make such a comment. "Have you told Marshall?" he asked.

"No ..."

"Don't you think you should?"

"Why?"

Wesley said nothing in reply. He would have thought it was obvious.

Sandy glanced over her shoulder toward the stairway, making sure that Wesley's sister was not within earshot. "I haven't told Marshall because I hope he'll never know."

"How can you say that?"

Looking straight ahead, she whispered, "Because he's not the father."

Wesley sat in shock, trying to grasp the implications of what she just said. Although he found it embarrassing to discuss such intimate details with a girl, it was clear that Sandy felt the need to talk with someone about her condition. Had he more knowledge about the subject matter, no doubt he would have been flattered that she turned to him for advice.

Sandy again gazed nervously toward the stairway, and Wesley took her unease as a hint to walk over and make sure their discreet conversation remained private. Sure enough, no one was stirring above, and the radio still played loudly in his mother's bedroom. He knew that Elizabeth often studied to the accompaniment of the "Lux Radio Theatre." That being the case, there was little cause for worry, at least until nine o'clock.

When he returned to the sofa, he could not help but notice that the girl had positioned herself upon the center cushion, much closer to where he was sitting. Sandy looked up into his eyes. "You must think I'm a horrible person." She was serious, not at all coy or flirtatious, so Wesley accepted her statement at face value.

"No," he said. "I would never think that of you." The perfume she was wearing smelled sweet, the very essence of femininity.

"It happened at that party my parents threw," Sandy told him. "You didn't come."

So close together were they now that her leg was nearly touching his. He fought the urge to put his arm around her, though he could have done it quite naturally at this point, and she may very well have responded favorably to the comforting gesture. Wesley decided to listen and not interrupt because Elizabeth would soon be coming downstairs to join them.

"Most of the cast were there," Sandy said, "and Marshall of course, and Hugh Kenton and his wife, lots of others, the Glickmans. My daddy invited some of his Army boys too, about eight or nine of them, I guess. One of the GIs began to talk to me—all very respectable and harmless, you know—and I saw Marshall flirting with two pretty girls. I didn't know them, so I'm sure they came with their Army dates from the base. One of them was really gorgeous, wearing a low-cut dress, but I never did find out her name.

"Anyway, this sergeant and I struck up a conversation, and one thing led to another. He brought me a few drinks, and my daddy did not seem to mind. That surprised me, but maybe he just lost count. Daddy was awfully busy keeping the food coming and mingling like a good host is supposed to do. He wore his uniform, and everyone was saluting him—just for a lark, you know—and he was thoroughly enjoying himself. After an hour or so, the party was spilling over into three or four rooms, but you could still hear the combo from anywhere. I guess my dad recruited them from Blackland. Just six guys, but they put out a grand sound.

"I began feeling kind of light-headed, and this young sergeant of mine was *very* nice looking. Chuck, I think, was his name. I liked him quite a lot actually, and I even forgot that poor Marshall was there. I became giddy, and the room was spinning a little, and everything seemed funny to me. After a while, the boy and I were laughing so hard at any silly thing we said to each other that I nearly wet ... well, I needed to visit the rest room very badly. He escorted me there and afterwards took my arm, and I led him to one of the bedrooms ... where all the shades were pulled and it was nice and dark. I just wanted to kiss him, but I was too juiced up to stop. It was a miracle that no one came in on us because we didn't even bother to lock the door. They would have gotten quite an eyeful."

Wesley picked up his glass and took a sip of lemonade. Thus reminded, Sandy paused from her discourse long enough to do likewise, and Wesley watched in fascination as a drop of condensation splashed upon the base of her neck and slowly trickled its way down into the bodice of her dress. "Ooh," she said in response to the cold drop's journey below, and her leg involuntarily bumped against his, remaining there instead of reverting to where it had been before. She laid the glass in front of her.

By now, more than adequate time had passed for Wesley to work up the courage to inquire where he stood in all of this. He appreciated Sandy's candor with him in such a delicate matter, and he wished to be completely honest with her in return. "Don't get me wrong, but why are you telling me this?" he asked. "I'm glad to be your friend and give you all the support I can, but I really don't understand what I can do beyond that."

"I just need to talk to someone, that's all," she said. "When I missed my period again ... Sorry to be so gauche, Wes, but I don't see any reason to pussyfoot around it after all the secrets I've told you about myself. When I knew for sure what was happening inside of me, I was scared to death ... and all alone. I can't tell my mother about this, and my daddy would never forgive me if he knew, not to mention what he would do to Chuck ... I don't even know his last name, I'm ashamed to say."

"Your dad will know him."

"Of course he will, but he mustn't ever find out about this."

"Who? Your dad or Chuck?"

"Neither one of them."

Wesley let that sink in for a moment and then asked what he thought was a logical question. "How can you hide something like that for very long?"

"You can't. My time for hiding this is running out. In fact, it's really too late already, and I can't believe my parents haven't noticed the telltale signs."

"I wouldn't have noticed."

Sandy smiled. "But you're so pure of mind and body, Wes. I only wish I still had some of that in me."

"You do," he told her. "I remember when I first met you, and you haven't changed all that much." Wesley at once wished that he had not said such a foolish thing, having resolved, only moments earlier, to be totally honest with her. She had changed considerably, and not for the better either.

To Sandy's credit, she accepted her friend's patronizing remark, but a wistfulness crossed her face, as if she were trying somehow to visualize the past and recapture the person she used to be. Then, as Wesley waited in silence, she took a deep breath. "Wes, I need to ask you a big favor. My daddy will be in Wichita Falls for the next seven days, and that will be my only chance to have a medical procedure."

"You're going to do away with your baby?"

She sighed loudly and began to pout. "Please don't say it like that."

"Well, is that what you're going to do?"

"I don't have any other choice. Can't you see that? I did a foolish thing, and I admit it. But I can't let it ruin my life and scandalize my parents. Daddy's an officer, and he's supposed to be setting a high standard of morality. I never would have done this if I hadn't been drunk at the time. I haven't even allowed Marshall ..."

Wesley's eyes widened. "Then, it's the first time you've ever done anything like this?" He had no idea where this line of questioning might lead.

Sandy's grinning response took him by surprise. "Why, Wesley Brower. Are you asking me if I was a virgin?"

He was shocked by how blunt her language could sometimes be—and in mixed company too—and she seemed to enjoy making him blush. "Well, that's not what I said, exactly, but I guess that's what it amounts to."

"Then the answer to your nosy question is yes," she said. "Does that disappoint you?"

"Why would it do that?"

"I always thought you had a crush on me, right from the start, and I figured part of the attraction was because you saw me as a fast girl."

"That's not true! I never thought you were a fast girl."

The corners of her mouth curled up slightly. "But you admit you had a crush on me."

"Yes. I think everyone did, at least at first."

"Do you still?"

He paused before answering. "Yes."

"I'm glad." She smiled.

"Oh ... just to look at, not to touch."

"I don't mind if you touch me. Never did."

Even at a very low dynamic, familiar tunes have a way of catching one's ear, and Wesley turned his head in response to the closing music for the "Lux Radio Theatre." That meant it was nearly nine—actually, four minutes before the hour, according to the wall clock. Wesley walked over to the Philco console and dialed up the volume, knowing that his sister might make her appearance at any moment.

"Our music was directed by Louis Silvers. This program is broadcast to our fighting forces overseas through cooperation with the Armed Forces Radio Service. And this is your announcer, John M. Kennedy, reminding you to tune in again next Monday night to hear *Home in Indiana*, starring Walter Brennan, Charlotte Greenwood, June Haver, and Jeanne Crain."

No sooner had station identification given way to "The Lady Esther Screen Guild Theatre" than Elizabeth's footsteps were heard noisily traversing the steps. Perhaps she was louder than customary in order to give fair warning to the others, who now sat very chastely below, she on the sofa and he a respectable distance away in the easy chair.

"I just came down to get my civics book," the girl said. But her prying eyes as she hurried by argued otherwise. Being the observant type, she wondered why there were two glasses of lemonade on the coffee table and only one person sitting on the sofa to drink them. And Wesley's guilty expression did nothing to allay her suspicions. "I'll be going back up, so don't let me interrupt."

"For how long?" Wesley asked. His sister's pesky curiosity was annoying.

"About a half-hour," Elizabeth said with a smirk, "but Mom will be home long before that." She made another quick survey of the room as she skipped back to the stairway. Then, turning the corner with a giggle, she shouted, "Don't do anything I wouldn't do!"

Sandy laughed and patted the sofa cushion next to her. She was nothing if not bold. Wesley began to wish that a more secluded venue had been found for this frank discussion. Sensing that a meddlesome sibling might be eavesdropping from above, he tiptoed over to the stairway and saw Elizabeth sheepishly peering through the banister on the second floor. "I'm leaving," she said. "Don't worry. I'm not going to miss *It Happened Tomorrow* because of you—no matter how racy things become down there."

"And shut the door!" he shouted. She complied with a resounding slam.

What Elizabeth said was true, he soon discovered. "Screen Guild" was indeed presenting *It Happened Tomorrow*, the very story with which "Lux" had closed its ninth season just three months earlier. But instead of an hour, this new production had only thirty minutes at its disposal, a daunting challenge for any radio-play adapter. How much it might suffer in the abbreviated retelling would go unnoticed by Wesley because he marched straight over to the console and dialed the volume control until it clicked off.

He resumed his former position next to Sandy, listening attentively to her while trying to keep his ears subliminally attuned to the crackling sound of rubber tires upon gravel. After all, though his mother knew who Sandra Whittsel was, surely she would consider it inappropriate for such an attractive young lady to be sharing a sofa with her son without the inhibiting presence of an adult. And it goes without saying that she would have been mortified to discover the content of their conversation.

"The timing is what's critical," Sandy told the boy. She spoke as if issuing flight briefings to a squadron of fighter pilots, and it was evident that she had given her battle plan much careful thought. "My daddy will be in Wichita Falls until Monday night."

"What's there?"

"He's training some flight instructors at Shepperd Field."

Wesley nodded his acknowledgement, even though he had never heard of that particular air base.

"And my mother is going to a wedding—very high-class affair—down in San Antonio, but only from Thursday afternoon through Sunday afternoon. Daddy will be flying out of Waco, of course, and Mother will be taking the train to Randolph."

"Check."

"Wes, I need for you to take me out the Gholson Road, to a farmhouse where this doctor lives. He's retired after many years of practice just north of the Red River."

"Is this legal?" Wesley asked.

"Technically, no, but this doc gets more business than he can handle."

"That doesn't make it right."

Sandy was well prepared for this line of interrogation, and she countered with a rhetorical question. "Don't you think it's a little late for me to be worrying about that?"

Wesley shrugged his shoulders. "How did you find out about him?"

"A girlfriend of mine used him about a year ago—someone from school. She came through it fine."

He sensed that nothing would be learned by asking her name, so he settled for "Someone I know?"

Donning her most evasive poker face, "Could be ..." was all Sandy would say.

Wesley took a slow drink of lemonade, a none-too-convincing way of buying himself some time to think. So he was to be an accomplice in this sordid affair, he thought, but then would he not be breaking the law too? And just who was this other girl who aborted a pregnancy? It sure must have been awfully hush-hush around school. He laid his glass down and said, "If you really want to go through with ... with the procedure ... why not have this girlfriend of yours drive you out there instead of me?"

"Because she can't know I'm going to visit him."

"You asked her about the doctor, didn't you?"

"That was long before any of this happened to me. She doesn't suspect a thing."

He shook his head. "I don't mind telling you ... I don't want to have anything to do with this."

Tears came to Sandy's eyes. "Then I might as well go and kill myself."

"Don't say that." He put his hand on hers.

Sandy's cheeks were now becoming wet. "Wesley, you're the only one I can trust." She glanced over her shoulder, fearing that her voice could be heard upstairs. "That girl I was telling you about is a chatterbox," she whispered. "If she ever found out, the whole world would know."

Wesley stood up and paced the room. "But it's against my religion ... probably against all religions. Killing a baby is a mortal sin."

"Then it'll be my sin," she said.

He pondered that reasoning for a moment but found little comfort in it. "And mine too."

"I don't think God would want me to have this baby," Sandy told him. "It was conceived in ... There was no love involved, and I don't even know the soldier's name."

"Oh, I see. So abortion is God's will. Is that it?"

"Of course not. I didn't say that."

"Well?"

"My sin was getting pregnant in the first place, without being married."

"Two wrongs don't make a right."

"I've already sinned, and I admit that. But the way I figure it, bringing an unwanted baby into the world would only compound the problem."

"That's a different topic entirely."

"Don't you see, Wes? I've committed a mortal sin anyway, so another one—a *corrective* sin, you might call it—cannot condemn me more than I am already. Ending this pregnancy is my only choice."

"Then you'll have to find somebody else," he told her. "It's very unfair of you to ask me to do this. I'm not the father."

"I wish you were," she said, and Wesley's eyes looked directly into hers.

He sat back down, not knowing what to think, and heard himself say, "Okay, I'll take you to this doctor. When do you need me?"

"Saturday morning," Sandy said with a beaming face, and she kissed him on the lips. Smiling through her tears, she added in a voice choked with emotion, "I'll never forget you for this. Never!"

♦   ♦   ♦

Whenever she was not otherwise occupied by volunteer work at the Red Cross or USO, Thursday night meant one thing to Nora Brower: beginning at eight o'clock, she would spend a half-hour tuned to NBC for Bing Crosby and his "Kraft Music Hall." Like many another fickle listener, she abandoned "Major Bowes and the Original Amateur Hour" when it was trimmed to thirty minutes, and she never again made that venerable CBS show a part of her weekly routine. Bing was her favorite singer, and she owed her allegiance to him.

But when it came to afternoon listening, one weekday was pretty much like any other. Thus, on the final Thursday of September, she was preparing dinner to the sounds of children's fare on the new broadcasting network—less than a year old—the former NBC Blue, now enjoying a life of its own and rechristened the Blue Network. After school, this upstart service offered youngsters a steady stream of adventures like "Dick Tracy," "Terry and the Pirates," "Hap Harrigan," "Jack Armstrong, the All-American Boy," and "Captain Midnight," and was rewarded for its demographically targeted efforts by solid numbers in the Hooper ratings, at least by daytime standards.

Seemingly oblivious to the radio's modulating amplitude was Elizabeth, who was curled up on the sofa with her current English assignment, a Pulitzer Prize-winning novel from 1938 called *The Yearling* by Marjorie Kinnan Rawlings. What surprised her most about this particular book was that, unlike the majority of coerced literary projects in her experience, she actually enjoyed reading it. The sad but ultimately inspiring narrative of Jody Baxter and Flag succeeded in opening up a whole vista of imagination to her that other works of literature—and even motion pictures— somehow failed to do. She wept quietly during the more sentimental passages, a girly response that Wesley noted but graciously chose to overlook. He was sprawled on the living room floor, only a couple of feet away from the radio console.

Being more passively engaged than the distaff side of the family, it was he who consented to answer the front door when someone knocked at ten minutes past five.

Upon swinging the door open, Wesley was chilled to see a grim serviceman standing there before him, and his blood ran cold. Steve had not written in over a month now, causing intense disquietude about his health and well-being, and the sudden arrival of a stranger in uniform portended tragic news.

"Are you Wesley Brower?" the mysterious GI asked.

Wesley swallowed hard. "Yes, sir."

"I know your mother and your sister. Is either one of them home?"

"Both of them are."

"May I see Lizzie?"

That seemed an odd request, and Wesley relaxed his guard.

By now, Nora had overheard the hushed conversing and was sufficiently curious to abandon her cooking chores for the moment, wondering just who this unannounced visitor might be.

"Why, Daniel Rignold!" She rushed forward to greet the soldier.

"Hello, Mrs. Brower," Danny said with a broad grin. He removed his cap, and they shook hands.

Nora turned to her son. "Wes, this is the wonderful young man who saved Lizzie's life, Corporal Daniel Rignold."

Danny balked at that effusive description. "Well, not exactly ..." He shook Wesley's hand.

Nora led the way to the living room, motioning for the other two to follow. "Come on in and sit down, Danny. It's awfully good to see you again."

"Thank you, ma'am."

Elizabeth, aroused from deep concentration, looked up from her book to see a familiar face from her past. "Danny! What are you doing here?" She looked at her mother for clarification, but Nora appeared to be every bit as baffled as she was.

"Actually, it's you that I wanted to see," Danny told the girl.

"Me?" Elizabeth's face was reddening, and she hoped the soldier did not notice.

"Shall we leave, then?" Nora asked, but Danny shook his head.

"No, I just came to say goodbye to you folks. You've been swell to me, and I was wonderin' if Lizzie here might want to contribute to the war effort by showin' a lonely serviceman an evenin' on the town. It's my last night in Waco before shippin' out."

All eyes turned to Elizabeth, who was flustered with surprise. "Gee, I'm not sure," she finally said, not quite knowing what the GI had in mind.

"Will you be going overseas?" Nora asked him. This gave her daughter a few seconds to think.

"Yes, ma'am. I think it'll be England this time—but don't tell the Secretary of War that I said so."

"Danny's an airplane mechanic," Nora told her son.

Wesley nodded his head. "Keeping 'em flying, huh?"

"Tryin' to. I've just been workin' on trainers at Blackland, mainly. Now I'll get some of the bigger crates."

"Bombers?"

"Could be." He seemed to be excited about the prospect.

From afar, there came a soft, hissing sound, growing progressively louder.

"Oh, dear, my potatoes are boiling over," Nora said. Having identified the noise's source, she scurried back to the kitchen.

Danny smiled at the girl. "Well, Lizzie—what say you?" He was still standing, cap in hand.

"Tonight?" she asked. "You know, that's really not very much notice."

Wesley glanced at the pair for a second or two and then lay back down on the floor, feigning interest in his geometry textbook.

"Sorry to spring this on you," Danny whispered to her. "Nothin' fancy, just an informal jaunt."

"But why me?" She blushed. "How about one of your girlfriends? I'm sure you have plenty to choose from."

Danny laughed. "I just couldn't pick which one."

"Remember, soldier—she's only sixteen," came a kindly shout from the kitchen. "And barely that!"

Elizabeth rolled her eyes. "My birthday was a couple of weeks ago."

"How about joinin' me for a movie?" he asked. "I sure would hate to go alone."

That final remark hit her squarely in the heart—visualizing a homesick GI in some stale movie house, all by himself—and she decided right then and there to relent. "Well, I guess I owe you that much," she said with a cheerful wink.

"Swell!"

The girl stood up and walked toward the stairs. "I'll just be a few minutes," she told him. "Read a magazine or something."

He sat down on the sofa, but there were no magazines on the table in front of him.

Elizabeth peeked around the corner, as if struck by a sudden thought. "Incidentally, how'd you get here anyway?"

"I thumbed it," he said.

"And is that how you plan to get us downtown—hitchhiking?"

"I *said* it was informal."

"Golly, big spender!" She went up to change clothes.

Danny spotted some magazines over on the end table but decided to just bide his time instead, listening halfheartedly to "Jack Armstrong."

As it turned out, Nora was insistent that Corporal Rignold drive the family's Chevrolet—however depleted the gasoline ration—so the guest would have enough spare time to enjoy a bite of home cooking before leaving on what he jokingly called his "embarkation date." Danny and Elizabeth consulted the newspaper for movie listings and settled on a rereleased film from six years earlier, *Brother Rat*, starring Priscilla Lane, Wayne Morris, screen newcomer Eddie Albert, and real-life couple Ronald Reagan and Jane Wyman. It was playing at the Rivoli Theatre on Austin Avenue, right next door to Keton's Bakery.

After arriving downtown, the first of two brief showers, summerlike though technically a full week into fall, compelled the moviegoers to run for cover between their parking place on Eighth Street and the awning-sheltered box office window. Danny certainly was a good driver, Elizabeth thought, and she told him as much while he was fumbling for change to pay the lady inside the booth. But that was to be expected of airplane mechanics, wasn't it? Wouldn't they be good at such things? A car was mechanical too, and it made sense that he probably knew, inside and out, how various kinds of machines worked. He even stopped without skidding on the wet asphalt—and managed the feat with nearly bald tires.

Elizabeth was pleased that Danny Rignold resisted the temptation of putting "moves" on her in the darkened theater. This did not really surprise her all that much, as she considered him to be too proper for such high-schoolish antics. Mitigating her appreciation somewhat was the flattering suspicion that her mother's cautionary reminder still resonated within him and more or less tied his hands. In any case, what an odd sensation it was—feeling relief at not having to fend off physical advances when, scarcely an hour earlier, she had gone to such extremes to encourage that very behavior by the way she dressed. Elizabeth looked quite lovely in her favorite chiffon blouse, and the seductive perfume that she applied to strategic areas of her person must surely have been savored by anyone within a radius of thirty feet. Maybe she applied too much of it.

The promised "nightcap," to which her date referred three times during the course of the movie, proved to be nothing more than ice cream sodas in the Cozy Café at Eighth and Washington. The place was about to shut down for the night when they arrived, but she and Danny were served very courteously, and the workers' cleanup activities went largely unnoticed around them. Conversation became stilted, as it sometimes does between two people who realize that they hardly know one another, and while their time together wore on, Danny's innate cheerfulness slowly descended into a sort of bittersweet despair. When Elizabeth tried valiantly to break the awkward silence, her efforts fell flat. Stating that she saw an obituary in the paper for Aimee McPherson, the famous evangelist who died of a heart attack in Oakland the day before, Danny could only respond that he was not familiar with the name. Then he made things even worse by reporting the equally morose news that bandleader Benny Goodman's kid brother, Jerome, had been killed in the crash of an Army plane in Wyoming. What "something" mechanical, he wondered, had gone wrong? Elizabeth, of course, had not the faintest idea.

Taking her home after the much vaunted but ultimately subdued nightcap, Danny parked at the curb instead of noisily driving over the rain-soaked gravel toward the garage. When he reached down to switch off the ignition, Elizabeth thought she detected a glistening in his eyes. He said nothing for a moment, and she was content to sit quietly beside him. Puddles of standing water were on the lawn, and a distant street lamp shone through a prism of droplets on the windshield. She stole a glance at the house and noticed that a light was on in her mother's upstairs bedroom. Only a couple minutes past ten, it was too early for sleep, so the nightstand radio was probably tuned to either the news or "I Love a Mystery."

The corporal cleared his throat, as if commencing to speak, but then he changed his mind and flipped open a cigarette lighter instead, casting its flickering glow upon his wristwatch. "I'd better get you in, I s'pose," came his words, but he seemed loath to leave.

"How are you going to get back to base?" Elizabeth asked.

"Good question. Fortunately, I don't have any duty tomorrow mornin', so I could walk back if I had to." Clearly, that was meant in jest because Blackland lay more than six miles away—as the crow flies—and no one in his right mind would attempt such a foolish stunt at this hour. "I've got some twin-engine pilots to nurse along after lunch, but other than that, my workdays in Waco are finished."

"When do you leave for England?"

"I catch a train tomorrow at 1730 hours," he said. "That's 5:30 to you."

Elizabeth was in no mood to laugh or even smile, and she stared directly into his eyes. Then she reached over and placed her left hand on top of his right hand, giving it an affectionate squeeze. "I can't tell you how nice it's been to know you, Danny. I never seem to realize what I have until it's gone. That's just the way I am, I guess."

An automobile passed by, gently splashing rainwater to either side.

"You're awfully young. You were only fourteen when we met," Danny said, and he added with a grin, "Your mother would've killed me if I even tried to shake your hand."

To his surprise, this child of a girl, barely sixteen, leaned her head on his shoulder and began crying softly to herself. "You risked your life to save me," she told him, "and I never so much as said thanks. I'm terribly selfish. It's one of my biggest faults."

Almost as a reflex action, his arm went around her, and he patted her shoulder for comfort. Both of them sat for a minute or two without saying a word.

"You know," Danny finally said to the girl, "this scruffy little town has meant a great deal to me. I didn't think it would at the start, but it really does. Who knows? Maybe I'll settle down in Waco whenever I come out of the service."

Elizabeth looked up at him and smiled. "I thought you were from a littler town than this one."

Charmed by her juvenile choice of words, he could only laugh with glee. "Now that you mention it, I guess Kosciusko *is* littler than Waco."

She laughed too, but there were tears in her eyes. "I hope you do come back someday, Corporal Daniel Rignold. Waco is not such a bad place to live, you know."

Danny thought for a few seconds and had to agree. "Nope, it's really not. Of course, there's not much excitement for a GI, but that all depends on what you're tryin' to find. A couple of my pals got more than they bargained for—if you know what I mean."

Elizabeth had no frame of reference for what he had said, so she squeezed his hand again, simply enjoying the moment. And Danny smiled at her sweet naïveté, wishing everyone in the world could be as innocent as Lizzie Brower. He fought back a tear or two of his own, realizing that most likely he would never see this special young lady again.

♦   ♦   ♦

It was Ray Temple who revised the scripts to accommodate the two days that Sandra Whittsel would be away from the station. Initially, Gerald Byrd was to have done it, but his attitude was so irascible toward the girl—"Since when do we let our cast members off, to go to a wedding?"—that Ethel Coody assigned the task instead to Temple. Her reasoning was that he had not been there long enough to raise much of a fuss. She shuddered to think what old Harvey Samuelson would have said about it.

Prodigiously resourceful, Temple grafted on a brief scene from Wednesday's show to make up for Sandy's absence on Monday, and this slight of hand did surprisingly little violence to either script. Expediting matters was the stroke of luck that Sally Holt only had two thirds of a page of double-spaced presence in that one. But the gaping hole in Tuesday's show was not so easily filled, and a subplot of mostly original material burst forth from Temple's typewriter to redress that deficiency. He was quite proud of the way it flowed, smoothly bridging all five pages between the dramatic parking lot shooting at Pimlico Race Course and the suspicious fire that destroyed the stage and dance floor of The Blues Lagoon. Best of all, from a director's standpoint, it timed out to within eighteen seconds of the original.

When Sandy returned to school on Wednesday morning, one of her classmates, kindly Joanne Timmons, wondered where she had been for the past two days, concerned because the unexpected absence blemished an otherwise perfect attendance record. Sandy smiled and described for her, in imaginative detail, the most beautiful wedding she had ever seen in her entire life. It took place, she said, in an elegantly appointed drawing room of the so-called "Taj Mahal" building at Randolph Field. This towering edifice, she said, was constructed about fifteen years ago in a Spanish Colonial Revival Style of architecture, as were all of the hangars on base. The bride, she said, wore a lovely, antebellum dress that once belonged to her grandmother, who was a descendant of one of the heroes of the Alamo. The gown's magnificent, flowing train required three little-girl attendants to facilitate movement for Rebecca, and Major Carlton Hudspeth, she said, wore his Army dress uniform and saber, which nicely complemented the sword arch through which the happy couple departed. Being ceremonially under arms, the major also wore white dress gloves, though he discreetly handed them to his best man just prior to the exchange of rings. As in all of the better weddings, she said, Major Hudspeth cut the three-tiered cake with a saber, lending a solemn military bearing to the occasion.

As for Waco High School administrators, they knew nothing of Miss Whittsel's alleged trip to Randolph Field, nor would the young lady have acknowledged that spurious affair had she been interrogated on the subject. The official excuse for her truancy, while clouded in euphemism, was still much closer to fact than was the public version. In accordance with a note from the trusting Charlotte Whittsel, her daughter's two-day absence was attributed simply to "female complaint." That did seem to explain the pain pills and the trace of blood that stained a sheet found in the clothes hamper.

Wesley had not seen Sandy since he drove the girl back home for recovery after her two-hour medical process in the innocuous-looking farmhouse near Gholson. Sandy's acute discomfort during the return trip was apparent from the way she would continually shift her weight and bite her lower lip. She spoke very sparingly, the few words she uttered sounding breathless and strained. At one point, Wesley actually feared for her life, but he kept assuring himself that the doctor would not have released her in such a perilous condition as that. Feeling some sense of responsibility, he wanted to check on her during the next three days, but of course he dared not take that chance. Mrs. Whittsel was due home by Sunday afternoon and Colonel Whittsel the following night. Instead, he fervently prayed that she was getting better, a supplication that rang hollow when he saw within it the eerie reflection of his own complicity.

Despite her male friend's decidedly tainted entreaty for godly intervention, Sandy emerged from the elective procedure in satisfactory shape, suffering remarkably few ill effects, at least of a corporeal nature. Residual emotional scars are far less treatable than those symptoms that respond to tablets, ointments, and time. But Sandy was a strong-willed young woman, as anyone who crossed her soon discovered, and her confidence level seemed well suited to master whatever challenges lay ahead. In short, she was entirely capable of forgetting past indiscretions, carrying with her only the least burdensome of psychological baggage. And she was pretty too, which in itself is never an impediment to success.

Sandy had missed the rehearsal for Wednesday's show, but Wesley located her in the school cafeteria and let her study his copy of the script. Indeed, she was still reading over her lines as she drove herself to the radio station shortly after two. The lower speed limit made it easier—if not danger free—to do such a foolhardy thing, and the back streets generally were rather deserted at that hour of the afternoon. Her biggest driving difficulty that day was not keeping her eyes on the road but shifting gears. Not yet fully healed, she found it quite painful to depress the clutch pedal with any degree of proficiency. Ironically, that worked to her advantage, as a motorcycle cop hidden behind the trees on Gorman did not even bother to give her a second glance. In normal circumstances, Sandy was not one to adhere very closely to traffic regulations, and over the past year she had been stopped no fewer than five times for speeding violations. Four were dismissed at the scene, and she was impressed by how courteous—and even friendly—Waco's police officers were, particularly the young ones.

During the radio performance, her first since the preceding Friday, Sandy flubbed a line rather badly, the only time anyone in the cast could recall that happening. She covered it up well, remaining in character and making it seem that Sally Holt was flustered, peppering her subsequent dialogue with touches of stuttering. Surely no one in the listening audience suspected that anything had gone awry, but those in the studio—with scripts in hand—knew better. No one is perfect, of course, but Neddy Wright smirked and privately enjoyed the moment.

Here before him stood the much-touted actress who, according to the newspaper, was "personally responsible for a three-point rise in her show's Hooper ratings." Nice to know, he thought, that she too was fallible. Serves her right for missing rehearsal.

After the close, Sandy seemed tired and not at all herself. As the cast dispersed to make way for "West of the Brazos," she stumbled over an audio cable and grabbed Wesley's arm to keep from falling. Instinctively, Wesley looked toward the announcer's booth. There sat Marshall McFall, sipping a fresh cup of coffee and casually leafing through the pages of an old *Photoplay* that had a picture of Joan Fontaine on the cover. He seemed blissfully ignorant of Sandy's desperate, on-the-air improvisation, and for good reason. The Dean of Central Texas Announcers, so sure of his impeccable timing, rarely bothered to follow along with a script (except, of course, those of a commercial nature). No doubt he was, even at this moment, marveling to himself at Sandy's insightful portrayal of the hidden insecurities of Sally Holt.

It was in the parking lot that Wesley finally had a chance to talk with this troubled young lady, who now seemed to him so worldly for her age. She was, after all, only seventeen years old, and already she was a local radio celebrity, an honor student at Waco High School, and very nearly—had nature been allowed to take its proper course—an unwed mother.

"Are you on two wheels or four?" she asked him.

"Two," he said. "I'll be pedaling for the foreseeable future, I'm afraid."

Confused by such an odd statement, Sandy studied his face. "What do you mean?"

"My mother can't figure out where all the gasoline went."

She lowered her eyes and whispered, "Sorry."

"That's all right. We'll manage."

Michael Dill waddled by, on the way to his final sales call of the day. The wind had whipped his necktie over one lapel of his coat. "Good show. I caught part of it," he told the pair without pausing to chat.

Wesley smiled at him. "Thanks, Mickey."

When the salesman went around the corner of the building, the girl said, "I wonder which part."

Wesley did not comment, sensing that it would only make matters worse. "How are you feeling?"

"Not very well, actually, but thanks for asking."

"No better?"

Sandy shrugged. "A little, maybe. It's hard to say."

"Is there anything I can do?"

"You've already done more than I had any right to expect. I really don't know what I would have done without you."

He looked away, embarrassed, and saw a large truck chugging its way beneath a heavy load of scrap metal.

"Well, there is *one* thing," she added. "Can you drive me home? It still hurts quite a lot."

Though willing to help, Wesley did not quite know what to say. "What'll I do with my bike?" he asked. "I can't just leave it here, and how would I come back to get it?"

"Let's see if it'll fit in the trunk," she said.

It did, with not an inch to spare.

Once they were moving, Sandy cried quietly on the way home, and Wesley pretended not to notice. After a few minutes, she managed to say, "I feel terrible about what I did, Wes. I never should have done it." Her voice was shaky, scarcely under control.

He drove another block, saying nothing. But then, though it sounded cruel or even brazen, he blurted a single word. "Which?"

She was taken aback. "Getting rid of the baby, of course. How do you mean?" She acted as though he had slapped her hard across the face.

"And what about doing that with a soldier? Doesn't that bother you a little too?"

"Sure it does. I told you that before. What kind of girl do you think I am?"

"You don't even know his last name, for God's sake." Wesley felt himself getting angry, and he wondered why.

"I feel terrible about that too, Wes, although at the time I didn't know what I was doing."

"And why was that?" The question was phrased so sarcastically that Sandy could hardly believe her ears.

"Because I was drunk. I admit that." She sighed, and her voice acquired a caustic edge to it. "Listen, I hardly ever drink. Have you ever seen me drinking?"

"No," he said. "But then again, I don't hang around with the same people as you do."

"Oh, I see. So it's all Marshall's fault, is it?"

He raised his eyebrows, leaving her to guess, and in so doing, it suddenly became clear to him just why he had become so ill-tempered about something that did not concern him in any personal way. Marshall McFall was guilty of robbing this girl of her innocence, irrespective of the fact that—by Sandy's own admission— they had never consummated their affair. It was Marshall McFall who taught her, and encouraged her, to drink alcohol, and none of this would have happened, were it not for him.

They came to a stop sign, and a bus with thirty or more Army personnel turned the corner in front of them. Some of the GIs shouted and whistled at Sandy, and she smiled back in return, flattered by their attention. Wesley could only shake his head. In the context of their present discussion, one of utmost seriousness—of life and death itself—he was ashamed of her and disappointed too. Soon she was again sad and remorseful, but that did not prevent her from watching the soldier boys until they were out of sight.

A sudden jab of pain caused her to alter the position in which she was sitting, and this tiny shift of weight brought immediate relief. It also told her that she was getting better, almost well enough by now to resume her normal routine. Some things, of course, would have to change. She had learned valuable lessons from all of this, and she resolved to behave quite differently in the future. A part of her was genuinely penitent, something that could be seen from the look of determination in her eyes. And yet when she again gazed far down the street, toward where the military bus had disappeared from view, an impartial observer might have been forgiven for wondering whether this girl had sworn off casual indulgence or merely vowed to be more careful in its pursuit.

♦   ♦   ♦

By the fall of 1944, mail from abroad had become notoriously unreliable. That, at least, was the hopeful conclusion reached by Nora Brower as the weeks without a letter from Steve continued to pass by, and postman Bill Johnston apologized for arriving day after day "empty-handed." In common with all mothers of servicemen from time immemorial, anxiety was her constant companion, sometimes restrained but never entirely absent, and she expended a great deal of energy in trying to avoid falling prey to the dark imaginings of what may have happened.

So it was a profound relief to her—and, for that matter, to Mr. Johnston too—when no fewer than four pieces of overseas mail finally reached their destination on the very same Wednesday morning. Somehow, the FPO-NY mails had experienced a temporary clog in the system, and now delivery evidently was returning to more conventional norms.

After sending the postman on his way with a joyous hug, Nora hurried over to the kitchen table, sorted the letters into chronological order by postmark, and then tore into them in sequence to catch up on her older son's adventures aboard ship, "somewhere in the Atlantic." The most recent piece of correspondence was dated, in Steve's own handwriting, 9th OCT. '44, so she knew for certain that he was hale and hearty less than three weeks ago. The letters were quite breezy in tone, though sidestepping any mention of geographical and nautical minutiae that could be of any conceivable use to the enemy. Nora was pleased to read that Steve had gotten all but the latest couple of notes that she sent to him, and both of those, as she recalled, were mailed within the past week and a half.

On Friday morning, not long after Wesley and Elizabeth left for school, Giulia Coletti came by the Brower home to show Steve's mother yet another two letters from him, each of which Giulia had received the previous afternoon. One was penned in the middle of August, and the other in late September. Nora chuckled at how quickly things had turned around, from the uncertainty of prolonged silence to what was now fast becoming almost an embarrassment of riches.

"Coffee, dear?" she asked with a smile. "I'll have to reheat it, but it's what passes for fresh around here."

The girl nodded her head. "Yes, ma'am."

As Giulia seated herself on the sofa, casually removing her gloves and laying them on the end table, Nora studied her profile from where she stood in the kitchen, and she was stunned by how naturally beautiful the young lady was—all the more so in that she appeared to be wearing virtually no cosmetics whatsoever. Giulia, it appeared, was one of those exceedingly rare women who, the moment she awoke in the morning, probably could grace the cover of *Vogue* or *Cosmopolitan*. Small wonder that both Steve and Wesley seemed to be interested in her.

The coffee pot took ages to boil, so anxious was Nora to see what her son had to say. In the meantime, she spooned some cat food into Valentino's dish, all the while being affectionately rubbed about her arms and hands by the shedding feline. Hearing an insistent meowing as the food dish was placed back onto the mat, cat-lover Giulia was lured to the kitchen, where she stooped down and petted Valentino while he ate. She had not seen the Browers' cat before—or even been aware that they had one. Wesley never mentioned the existence of any pets to her, at least that she could remember.

Coffee cups in hand, the women went into the living room and sat next to each other on the sofa. The radio console was playing so softly that Nora had forgotten it was on, but now she could hear the familiar voice of Don McNeill. This was the very day before "The Breakfast Club" would introduce its long-running "Prayer Time" for American servicemen: "All over the nation, each in his own words, each in his own way, for a world united in peace, bow your heads, let us pray."

When Giulia handed her a pair of nearly identical envelopes, Nora said, "Would you rather read them to me, dear?" She asked this out of courtesy, as there was always a chance that they might contain some private words that were not intended for anyone but the addressee.

"No, not at all," Giulia said. "Please."

The first of the letters presented no information beyond what Nora had already seen, but the second one intimated—between the lines, at any rate—that there was some talk of combat ahead. "We've been doing mainly custodial chores and watches," Steve wrote, "but most of the guys think the time should pass pretty quickly around here once the action picks up." Perhaps she was reading into it more than was actually there. After all, the censor did not see fit to snip that sentence, so most likely it was innocent of divulging any tactical secrets.

While there, Giulia took the opportunity to read the four letters that Steve had sent to his own home. This, she reasoned, would save Wesley the trouble of bringing them over to her house. She declined a second cup of coffee, explaining that she had to see to her mother's needs and then go to work.

Nora was surprised when Giulia set out on foot, for she knew that the girl lived a considerable distance away. As best she could recall, the return trip would take her to the southern part of the city, in the general vicinity of the Baylor campus. "May I take you home, dear?" she asked.

"No, thank you, ma'am," Giulia said. "It's not far to the streetcar stop."

"I just assumed that you drove over here."

"No, ma'am. We don't even own a car. Never have."

A couple of hours later—after Giulia picked some vegetables from the Coletti victory garden, bathed, accomplished several household chores for her mother, and ate a sliced turkey sandwich—she arrived at the office just in time to hear from her boss that all plans for the workday would be turned upside-down. Instead of tackling some significant inventory discrepancies, a project of some urgency, she was being invited to join Butler Lindeman and salesman Mutt Sawyer as official representatives of Rawley Flooring at a flag-raising ceremony out of town. This was the day that the United States Government selected to honor Bluebonnet Ordnance Plant with the coveted Army-Navy "E" Award.

According to Lindeman, bus transportation from Waco to McGregor was to be provided by National Gypsum Company of Buffalo, New York, operators of the plant. Open house would run from 1:00 to 5:30, the award would be presented at 3:30, and tours of the facilities (hospital, cafeteria, and the munitions factory itself) would begin at 4:00. Not only would the distinctive banner be flying overhead thereafter, until the return of peace, but each employee of the plant would receive an "E" button in recognition of meritorious service to the country's war effort. Truly, this was a national honor, and Lindeman was insistent that Rawley Flooring, as suppliers of almost thirty thousand square feet of wooden surface for Bluebonnet office space, have a visible presence there on such an auspicious occasion. It would demonstrate his company's patriotic ideals—support for high productivity and low absenteeism—while, now that he thought of it, generating some additional sales in the process.

As a full-time employee, Tina Wolff was often in the midst of lunch hour whenever Giulia fetched her boss an afternoon cup of coffee. She saw Giulia enter the staff lounge at 12:35 and motioned for her to come over to the table. "Is it true that you're going to McGregor with Mr. Lindeman?" Tina asked. She seemed rather tense and short of breath.

"Yes—and Mutt. Why?"

"Aren't you afraid of what might happen?"

Giulia laughed. "Should I be? It's just a ceremony for one of our clients."

"Is Mr. Lindeman driving you there?"

"No, we'll be taking the bus."

"Will you sit next to each other?"

"I don't know. Maybe."

"I'd say there's a very good chance of that."

Bemused by her friend's dramatics, Giulia grinned. "Okay, what gives?"

"It's just that this bus of yours is not going to be quite as crowded as you originally thought." Tina took a bite of her cheese sandwich and glanced around the room, letting her friend stew for a moment. About a dozen women were in there, as well as three or four sweaty-looking installers from the shop. She swallowed and then took a sip of Dr. Pepper. "Bobby and Patrice were in here a few minutes ago," she finally added, "and I had a chance to confirm something very interesting that Francine told me earlier this morning."

"Oh ... Francine!" Giulia rolled her eyes, considering the source.

"Listen, she was right about this one, and Bobby Sawyer should know, if anyone does."

"What does Bobby have to do with any of this?"

"Well, he's Mutt's son, isn't he?"

"So?"

Tina leaned forward, for effect, and spoke just above a whisper. "It may interest you to know, sweetie, that Mutt is not coming to work today. He never even planned on being here today. He's in Lampasas, fixing the roof on his brother's house. So, it's just you, Mr. L., and the birds and the bees."

A worried look came to Giulia's face, and she stood up, not quite knowing what to do. "Does Mr. Lindeman know about this?"

"That Mutt's out of the picture? Sure, he does, and he's probably licking his chops right now. Bobby said his dad asked for a three-day weekend way back in July."

"Good Lord!" Giulia said, and her outburst drew stares from a few of the staff. "Well, I'm not going. That's all there is to it. I'm just not going!"

"It's not as simple as that."

"What do you mean?"

"Patrice says that Mr. Lindeman is thinking of canning all of his part-timers, including her."

"You're kidding."

"Nope."

"Bobby would never stand for that, and neither would his father."

Tina shrugged her shoulders. "Mutt's got the inside word, and he told her that sales are way down for the third quarter. According to him, people must have decided to live on dirt floors after all."

"Even Mr. Lindeman would never fire someone who's expecting. Bobby would quit too."

"Can't afford to. They're going to have three mouths to feed by New Year's at the latest, and Bobby can't just start over. No, he'll stay, and so will Mutt."

Noticing the time, Giulia took a step backward toward the door. "I'd better get this coffee to him before he goes apoplectic. Thanks for the warning."

"What are you planning to do?" Tina took another bite, eyeing her friend as she continued to chew.

"I guess I'll just have to go," Giulia said. "What other choice do I have? My mother doesn't get a paycheck anymore, and I sure can't work a forty-eight-hour week—not with her at home by herself."

"Well, good luck. You'll need it. Just tell the boss to keep his grubby little hands to himself."

"You really think he'll keep me on here—if I play ball?"

Tina chuckled. "*Play ball?* You've been watching too many gangster pictures."

"You know what I mean."

"I think the odds are pretty good, actually—with your looks."

Giulia thought of something and frowned. "There's a word for girls who do things like this, isn't there?"

"Things like what?"

"Compromise their values for money."

"Oh, sure. I can think of several."

◆　　◆　　◆

Just as Tina had predicted, Mutt Sawyer was not aboard the bus when it pulled out from Waco a few minutes before two o'clock. According to Butler Lindeman, the veteran salesman was struck by a twenty-four-hour virus that prevented him from accompanying them to McGregor or even reporting for a half-day of work. This was doubly unfortunate, of course, because Mutt was the company's sales rep for Bluebonnet. Giulia accepted this explanation with no visible sign of doubt.

Ever punctual at the wheel, Lindeman made certain that he and his young business associate arrived at the bus terminal well ahead of time, in fact early enough for them to grab a quick bite to eat. He gave Giulia a choice between the terminal's rather nondescript short-order kitchen and a more appetizing café, the Purple Cow, which stood across the street. The latter establishment was operated by John Anderson, who resided with his wife, Marie, right next door to their restaurant—just an elevator's ride up in the ten-story Raleigh Hotel.

Protesting that she had already eaten, Giulia declined to state a preference, so her boss grudgingly settled upon the bus depot's coffee shop, from where he could see when the next shuttle coach would be loading with passengers. If possible, Lindeman explained, he wanted to have adjacent seats, so they could discuss the new job-order form that management was considering for wholesale transactions.

Once the bus was rolling, Giulia feared the worst but instead was pleasantly surprised by how nicely Lindeman comported himself on the forty-minute westward excursion along US Highway 84. Surrounded by dozens of fellow travelers, he seemed to be the very model of a cultured gentleman throughout the journey, with the possible exception of one instance when she caught him glancing down her modest neckline as she bent forward to retrieve the cigarette lighter he dropped. That was not so very terrible, she reasoned. Most any red-blooded man would do the same.

A large crowd was already much in evidence at Bluebonnet Ordnance Plant by the time the two Rawley Flooring representatives arrived on the scene. Free bus service had begun at noon, with National Gypsum Company footing the bill, and reporters estimated that there were perhaps five thousand spectators on the grounds. Many of them simply milled about during open house, but others walked directly to the administration building, in front of which the large, red-and-blue "E" banner would soon be raised to assume its place beneath the Stars and Stripes.

"There's Clark Moyers," Lindeman said, not even one minute after stepping down from the bus. Moyers, a diminutive fifty-year-old who walked with a pronounced limp, wore an enormous black boot on his right foot, in an effort to compensate for the four-inch shortage of that leg. He was a competitor in name only, woefully introverted and more than willing to concede territorial privilege to anyone casting a net for prospective buyers. And yet somehow he maintained a client roster that was the envy of many a brash hotshot. If ever there was a doubt that amiability still counted for something in the business world, Clark Moyers was the perfect exemplar to lay such skepticism to rest. Cold calls approached him, rather than the other way around, and his record of repeat sales was almost gaudy.

"Hello, B. H.," Moyers said when he saw his friendly rival.

"Clark."

"Pretty day to be outdoors, huh?"

Lindeman nodded his head. "Yep, Bluebonnet lucked out with the weather. Could be chilly by now." Halloween was only four days away, but the McGregor temperature was already eighty-two, and it promised to peak another couple of degrees beyond that. "Have you ever met my executive assistant?" he asked.

"I don't believe I've had the pleasure." Moyers smiled at the lovely girl, who, at five foot nine, stood almost a half-foot taller than the sales manager of Schuyler Carpeting. What puzzled Giulia was why her boss selected that particular title over the other, more accurate choices—clerk, receptionist, acting secretary—all of which described her duties better than the grandiose term that he used.

With time on their hands, Lindeman escorted Giulia over to the plant hospital, the administrative sector of which utilized a durable composite material that was laid by Rawley Flooring workmen just eight months earlier. The cafeteria, too, boasted surfaces of Rawley products—ceramic tile, linoleum, and carpeting— that were color-coordinated to make a finer aesthetic impression than one would expect to encounter at a bomb factory.

The strains of a military march filled the air around three o'clock, so the two Rawley attendees hurried back to the administration building to claim a good vantage point. This was just the opening salvo of a thirty-minute program by the dress-uniformed Blackland Army Air Force Band, a contingent of crack musicians of professional caliber. Then, as 3:30 neared, an impressive array of Army brass and Navy braid began appearing on the elevated stage, which was draped in patriotic bunting. Plant employee Oma Owens led the crowd in the singing of "America."

Master of ceremonies for the day—all the way from Buffalo, New York— was Melvin Baker, president of National Gypsum Company, who introduced the military and civilian dignitaries seated behind him on the platform of honor. Field Director of Ammunition Plants, Colonel T. C. Gerber, was there, representing Undersecretary of War Robert Patterson and Secretary of the Navy James Forrestal, and it was he who presented the "E" (for Excellence) flag to the plant's general manager, L. R. Sanderson.

"Two years ago, on October 16," Sanderson said over the public-address system, "we produced the first ammunition here at Bluebonnet. Since then, thousands of pounds have gone out. Every pound has been of the highest quality. We are soldiers of production." The crowd was still applauding his remarks when a color guard from Blackland Army Air Field came forward, accepted the "E" banner from him, and slowly raised it up the flagpole.

Giulia noticed, from a distance, that her father was among the thousands in attendance. He stood about fifty feet away, but it may as well have been ten miles. Though she had not seen him for two months, there was scant possibility of approaching him now. Once the ceremonies were over, people would be scampering in a dozen directions all at the same time.

Returning to the microphone, moderator Melvin Baker had high words of praise for the plant's workers. "Without such internal good will, this record could not have been made. This award speaks for your record. I am proud of you."

Closing the half-hour ceremonies, which were broadcast live over radio stations WACO in Waco and KTEM in Temple, was the band's playing of "The Star-Spangled Banner."

Lindeman took Giulia by the arm, so as not to become separated in the throng of humanity. She allowed him to hold on rather tightly because there was a good bit of pushing and shoving taking place while the crowd dispersed. Against all odds, Giulia's father must have spotted her too, for he appeared to be intent upon heading in that direction. She shouted to her boss, "My father," and nodded toward an older man of about sixty who was being jostled by departing spectators. Laughing at the futility of "swimming upstream," Mr. Coletti finally decided to stand his ground, motionless, and simply wait for Giulia and her companion to approach him instead. More people were headed that way, where the public buses were parked, so it required less effort and produced better results.

"Hello, Papà," she shouted when they were within arm's reach of each other.

"Giulia, my child," he said with glistening eyes. "As pretty as a picture!" They embraced, and for a moment he buried his head against her shoulder. They were about the same height, though she may have exceeded him by a half-inch.

"I called you twice this week, but you weren't there," the girl said.

Francesco Coletti nodded his head sadly. "I've been going back and forth to Hearne—new job. Uncle Sam's paying for the gasoline, so I don't mind."

"War work?" she asked.

"As close to the war as I could get."

Lindeman cleared his throat, prompting Giulia to introduce him.

"Papà, this is Butler Lindeman, my boss at Rawley. Mr. Lindeman, my father, Frank Coletti."

"How do you do, Mr. Coletti?" Lindeman said.

"How do you do?" They shook hands, and Frank eyed the stranger suspiciously. Was that a wedding band on his left hand?

Giulia blushed, for no valid reason of guilt, and tried not to seem too defensive. "We sold quite a lot of flooring to the Bluebonnet plant, so we wanted to be here for the ceremony. The salesman couldn't make it, or he would be here with us too."

Lindeman changed the subject. "What's in Hearne?" he asked. "Some sort of governmental project?"

"A camp for POWs—Germans, mostly," Frank said. "I'm a clerk down there."

"I thought it was in Mexia."

"There is one there, but the Hearne unit had an opening for a pencil pusher."

"You work in an office?"

"That's right. The Army handles the prisoners. I rarely ever see them."

Giulia was surprised—even a little hurt—by how much she did not know about her own father. "How long have you been doing that? I never heard."

"Three weeks now."

"Interesting work?" Lindeman asked.

"Can be. I'll be moving down there whenever they'll let me."

Giulia's eyes widened. "Will you be living inside the prison?"

"Just outside, honey," he said with a chuckle. "Do I look like a Nazi to you?"

"When will you be leaving, Papà?"

"After my probationary period is up—thirty days." He turned to Lindeman and explained. "I used to have a drinking problem, so they hired me provisionally." Frank did not seem the slightest bit embarrassed about disclosing this sensitive matter in public. Maybe that meant he had his weakness licked for good.

He made his daughter promise to visit him during the next week, for he figured to be living seventy miles away soon thereafter.

◆　　◆　　◆

"Do you have any particular college in mind?" the man asked.

"No, sir," Wesley said. "I really don't know." He glanced at his mother.

"Baylor?"

"I haven't given it much thought, sir—not with the war on."

The man smiled amiably but pressed on with the questioning. "And you're perfectly right to be concerned about the war. The truth is, you may not be able to enroll for next year at all, if your number comes up."

Nora was uncomfortable with the bluntness of that statement, so she proffered her own version. "All we are telling you is to have a plan in place for your education, just in case the draft board does not call you to serve."

"Precisely," the visitor added. "That's what I really meant to say."

"But I don't see why they wouldn't take me," Wesley said.

Nora shook her head. "Well, you never know. Laurie Inglefield's son has never been called up, and he's twenty."

Turning away from his two inquisitors, Wesley stared at the floor for a moment. Then he said, very quietly, "Besides, I'd probably enlist if they didn't."

His mother frowned but did not argue the point. "Wes is interested in naval aviation," she told their guest.

"A fine idea, no doubt about it," Benjamin Reich said. "There's absolutely nothing wrong with that. But if the war ends, you don't want to be caught napping."

Nora gently patted her son on the back. "I think it's wonderful that Mr. Reich is offering to pay for your entire college education, Wes. It would be very difficult for us to make ends meet without him, especially with the way business is going." She smiled at the white-haired visitor. "Well, we just couldn't do it, that's all."

"We're blessed with some fine institutions in our own backyard," Reich said, "no more than a couple hundred miles away from where we're sitting right now. Besides Baylor, of course, there's A&M College, Texas Christian,

Southern Methodist in Dallas, the University of Texas—even Rice Institute, if you've got the grades." He added with a broad grin, "Just give it some thought."

Wesley appeared to be less than enthusiastic about this generous proposal, surely not the response Reich had expected to encounter. And yet the man made allowances for the boy's youthfulness, remembering how ill-defined his own outlook on life was in his teens. Another Roosevelt was in the White House back then, and it goes without saying that the early part of the century—before the Great War—was a different world entirely. It was the Age of Optimism, in America if nowhere else. Triumphs in the Spanish-American War were still fresh in people's minds, and the Great White Fleet flexed its muscles in circumnavigating the globe. The United States seemed invincible, with two broad oceans protecting the country from foreign invasion. Ironically, it was also the time when a fifty-one-mile canal was nearing completion in Panama, in a superhuman attempt to connect those very same oceans. Most Americans of the day had never seen an "aeroplane" in person, and the automobile was more curiosity than convenience.

Benjamin Abel Reich was a local lad, graduating among the Waco High School Class of 1909. This was when the old brick building at Fourth and Webster was still being used, more than a year before the modern facilities opened on Columbus Avenue. Rather than following his father's advice to secure a higher education, he set out on his own, burning bridges as he went. Admittedly cocksure of himself, he was determined, at all costs, to establish his name in the manufacturing centers, where easy money was said to be had. That, he found, was simply not the case. He had been sold a bill of goods, and his life very nearly came to ruin.

Turning to the bottle for consolation, he fell in with a dissolute crowd of penny-ante pool hustlers and petty thieves, landing himself a weeklong stay in the Freestone County Jail before the age of twenty. By the time he was twenty-three, Reich had become little more than a drifter, dissolving a marriage in Oklahoma by annulment after but two days and then stealing fruit from south Texas farmers for sustenance.

"It sounds funny to say, but the war probably saved my life," Reich said to Nora. "Having nowhere else to go, I joined up in May of 1917 and finally had some discipline pounded into me. I saw a little action with the AEF in France, but mostly I was not on the front lines. Then the downward spiral started all over again when I got out and tried to find work."

He fixed his gaze on the boy. "I'm sure it must seem awfully preachy to a young fellow such as yourself, but I submit to you that my aimless outlook on life effectively disqualified me for the choicer positions, even before anyone would give me a chance to prove what I could do for them. I had no sense of direction."

The ex-serviceman took menial jobs in southeast Texas and Louisiana and barely made enough to survive, bouncing around from one demeaning chore to another. He drank too much and gambled the rest of his pittance away. Back in Waco at last, disheveled and choking on his own pride, he approached his now-widowed father with hat in hand and received the shock of his life. Not only did Richard Reich welcome his prodigal son into the family home, but he saw to it that Benjie made himself presentable and worthy of being interviewed by prospective employers.

"Easier said than done," Reich told Wesley. "I tried for two solid months, but nobody would have me—except maybe as a dishwasher, and that's not what I wanted. Only your dad was willing to overlook my lazy speech and bad posture, and even he might not have done so if it were not for the ineptitude of a future felon named Buddy Beckham—may he rest in peace."

Reich laughed at his own anecdote, wiped his runny nose with a handkerchief, and confessed a long-buried transgression. "I don't think I've ever told you this, Mrs. Brower, but now's as good a time as any."

Not knowing what to think, she forced a smile.

"You see," he said, "I once robbed Superior Office Supply. Yes, I did."

Nora's eyes went wide in disbelief, and she shook her head. "No, I'm sure you're mistaken, Mr. Reich. To the best of my knowledge, we have never been robbed, thank God, not in our long history. And Wayne Espy can confirm that. He goes back to the early days with us."

"I know Wayne. I bought him lunch just yesterday at this time. But your Harold did not take Wayne into his confidence about everything."

"How do you mean?"

"You are looking at a man who stole sixty-three dollars from Superior Office Supply."

"Were you arrested?"

"Nope. My record is clean—except for a few earlier scrapes here and there."

"You don't seem like a thief to me," the lady said.

Reich glanced at Wesley to make sure he was listening, and he added a touch of drama to his voice. "Right when things seemed like a dead end," he told the boy, "that's where Buddy Beckham came into the picture. Mrs. Brower, do you remember a scoundrel named Ike Skelly?"

"I'm afraid so."

"Well, Ike and his older brother, Walter Skelly, talked me into going with them and Buddy Beckham to 'borrow' some spending money one Sunday night, just enough for booze and butts, they called it. There was this little café on Austin—I don't think it's still there—but the cash register had nothing in it besides a key to the washroom and maybe a cuff link that some customer lost. So we decided to try the shop across the street, which was dark too. It was eleven ... eleven thirty ... something like that, and nobody around. One of the Skelly boys had a flashlight."

Suddenly, Reich's expression changed from the boyish delight in telling a good story to the wistful sadness of nostalgia. He said nothing for a moment, just taking a deep breath, and his eyes became watery. Nora and her son exchanged glances with one another, wondering what to do.

Reich looked at them and shook his head slowly. "The plan was to make this heist, see? Then we'd split the take, never dreaming that it would amount to much. But that's not how it went. The Good Lord saw to that, I'm convinced." With a sigh, he reached into the breast pocket of his suit coat and offered Nora a cigarette.

She declined, but he lit up and inhaled the smoke deeply, holding it in his lungs for five seconds or more, something Wesley had never seen anyone do before.

"We made a haul of two hundred fifty-two dollars and fifty-eight cents—I remember it down to the penny—and, I mean to tell you, that was a small fortune back then."

"How did you get into the cash register?" Wesley asked, and Reich smiled at the lad's curiosity.

"Didn't have to, as it turned out. We found the money in a desk. Buddy had a crowbar with him, and he pried open the locked middle drawer, the one above where someone would sit. That released the three drawers on the right side, and we found Mr. Brower's Saturday deposit in the bottom one, wrapped up in a coin sack—just as neat as a pin—all the currency sorted and tied with a piece of string. There was even a deposit slip, made out and dated for Monday."

The doorbell rang, so Nora excused herself to see who was there. Wesley was left alone with Reich, who, noticeably impatient, engaged in small talk with the boy while occasionally glancing over his shoulder toward the front door. He seemed to have forgotten entirely about his cigarette, which lay smoldering in an ashtray atop the end table. Either that first long drag had satisfied his craving or, like many another storyteller, he merely used it as a prop and thus had no need for it while half of his audience was away.

When Nora returned to the living room, she was carrying her purse, which she laid beside her on the sofa. "I beg your pardon, Mr. Reich," she said. "The paperboy was here, collecting."

"Oh, that's quite all right. Commerce is what keeps the wheels turning." Reich picked up his cigarette again and puffed it back to life. "You know, I still get the Waco paper every day. But it's by mail, so the news I see is a couple of days old." He blew some smoke straight up into the air and laughed. "If it happened yesterday, I don't know a thing about it."

Nora smiled at him. "Well, it's nice to know that you still take an interest in our fair city, after so many years have passed."

"It's my fair city too, remember. A person doesn't change hometowns just by getting a new mailing address." He winked at Wesley and added, "This Waco Tiger still has his stripes."

"Is your wife from Waco too?" Nora asked.

"She was born in Austin, but yep, I met her right here. Her folks were big in the Waco Lawn Tennis Club. Sounds kind of snooty, but really it was more of an athletic club, with a swimming pool and all. Susan certainly wasn't high society, and I guess maybe that's what attracted me to her in the first place."

Nora's face turned quite serious. "How's Susie doing, Mr. Reich?"

He leaned forward, hands folded. "Not very well, I'm afraid. Thanks for asking. A nurse is with her now, and I rarely leave Stephenville these days. Just a quick business trip every now and again—usually to Dallas or Amarillo. And, of course, I was here in town for Edwin Drescher's funeral."

"If there's anything I can do to help, please let me know. I haven't seen her in—my goodness—more than twenty years now, I guess. But Susie was always someone very special to me. She once offered to teach me piano, picking up where I left off as a child, but somehow I never quite got around to it."

"I remember."

"You do?"

"Yes, indeed. You and Harold were still living over there near Katy Park."

"Uh-huh. That was our first house, on Clay."

This got Wesley's attention, and he asked his mother, "Could you hear the ball games?"

"Only if the wind was blowing just right, and the crowd was big enough."

"Could you see the lights?"

She thought for a moment. "I don't recall. Could have, I suppose."

"No, you wouldn't have," Reich said. "The first night game for the Cubs wasn't until 1930. The first for the Texas League too."

Nora was impressed. "How did you know that? You'd already left Waco by then."

"I came to see Ruth and Gehrig play here in '29, and I know for a fact that the lights weren't there yet. I think they were installed the very next year, which would have been 1930."

When Nora's purse toppled over beside her, spilling a hairbrush onto the carpet, this seemed to remind the visitor that he had not yet completed his story. In fact, the most important part still remained to be told. "Now, where was I?" he asked the boy.

"You were robbing our store," Wesley said.

Reich cleared his throat and looked uncomfortable. "So I was. Indeed I was. Let's call a spade a spade."

It was times like this that made Nora Brower cringe at being the mother of a teenager. She glared at Wesley, but he was looking at their guest and did not seem to notice.

"We split the pot," Reich said, "which meant that each of us walked away with sixty-three dollars and some odd change. Or would have, if the lights hadn't come on. It took us so long to divvy the cash—we didn't trust each other—that our luck ran out." He made a sweeping motion with his hand. "The other three ran out the door, where we had broken into the shop. But I was on the far side of the desk, and my foot caught on it as I tried to jump across. When I looked up from the floor, two men were standing over me—one who turned out to be the owner, and also some relative of his with a pistol. Why he didn't fire at the others before they got away, I don't know."

"Oh, dear. That would have been my brother. He's the only one in our family who owned a gun. But he never carried it with him."

"Well, he did this night," Reich told her. "I was looking right down the barrel."

"Someone outside probably saw the flashlight or heard a noise," Nora said. "Then, when they called Harold, he must have brought Matty along with him."

Reich nodded his head, grinning at how proud she seemed of her sleuthing.

"Were you arrested?" Wesley asked.

"Nope. Should have been—had every reason to be—but I wasn't."

"Why not?"

"After I handed back my portion of the money, your dad convinced the other man, your uncle, that I was not a violent sort. He told him to leave but not to say a word to anyone about what happened."

Wesley was puzzled. "Why did he do that?"

Reich shrugged his shoulders. "That was your dad. I'll never know why. Maybe he saw something in me that no one else did. I don't know."

"But what about your friends?" Wesley asked. "And the rest of the money."

Reich's nostrils flared, and he waved his index finger for emphasis. "They weren't my friends, son, and I don't want you to think that they were." Then, more calmly, he added, "I just got mixed up with the wrong crowd, that's all—and I'd probably have landed in prison by now if it weren't for your dad. Maybe even be dead."

The man leaned over to crush his cigarette in the ashtray.

"What happened to the rest of that money?" Wesley asked again.

"Gone," Reich said.

Nora was astonished. "Harold just let it go? Didn't even try to recover it?"

"Almost two hundred bucks. Your husband ate the loss—for the time being."

"Why would he do such a thing?" she asked. "Couldn't the police have gotten you to identify the others?"

"No doubt."

"Then why? Two hundred dollars is a lot of money."

Reich grinned. "He had his reasons."

"Why did he never tell me about any of this?"

"I'm sure he felt it would be wrong for him to talk about it, when he made your brother swear to keep mum. That's all I can figure."

Wesley looked astonished. "Two hundred dollars ..."

Again, Reich pulled out his handkerchief. "The bigger question," he said, "is why he chose to let me off the hook in the first place. He didn't know me from Adam, and there I was, caught red-handed."

He wiped his nose, but this time he did not bother folding the cloth before tucking it back into his coat pocket. With a contented sigh, he leaned back slightly and crossed his right leg over the left. The suit he wore was an expensive one and neatly tailored, dark charcoal in color, with a subdued pinstripe to lend a tasteful elegance. His shiny mane of white hair made him look like a citizen of some prominence, a senator perhaps, and the gemstones of the ring on his left hand formed a Texas star pattern that was nearly the size of a quarter.

"I've often wondered why Harold did not turn me in and press charges," he said. "Certainly that's what I deserved. But instead, he decided to invest in me. That was the very word he used—invest. He gave me a job at Superior and made it clear that I was not to pocket any of my wages until I had paid back every cent of the stolen money."

"I had no idea," Nora told him. "I just thought Harold hired a new boy to work at the counter. For all these years I thought that."

"How did he make you pay the money back?" Wesley asked. "Couldn't you have just cashed your paycheck and made a run for it?"

Reich laughed at the frank question. "And don't think I didn't consider that," he said. "No, your dad had the goods on me, and I knew it. I was like a parolee, and he could have turned me over to the cops the minute I broke my end of the bargain. He was well respected around town, and they would have believed him for sure."

Nora gave the man a puzzled look. "Your father must have wondered why there was no money coming in."

"Oh, did he ever. Sakes alive! After a couple of weeks, he had to be told—there was no way around it—and so Harold made a special trip over to our house to do just that. I came close to crying, right there in front of my own father. I felt terrible, thinking about all Daddy had done to set me straight, and then I go out and burglarize a business."

He paused, deep in thought, but then reached for his handkerchief to muffle an explosive sneeze. After blowing his nose with a honk, he told Wesley, "It's no picnic growing old, son. It can be a mighty lonely feeling—unless you've got your life in order."

When he turned to the boy's mother, there was sorrow in his eyes that took her by surprise. He had seemed so self-assured, right up until that moment.

"Would you care for some coffee, Mr. Reich?" Nora asked him. She was not sure if he heard the offer, so she waited.

An instant later, as if shaken from a daydream, he was able to focus upon her with more certainty. "No, ma'am, no. I really must be going. Time passes by much too quickly."

◆　　◆　　◆

When Madeleine Givens heard through the grapevine that she was to be transferred to the second USO facility on Monday, she let director Jefferson Isbell know how unhappy she was with his decision. No, he countered, actually it was not his idea at all but that of her new boss, John Wilson, who was in dire need of experienced workers to manage the fast-approaching holiday season. Madeleine had served at the Franklin Avenue club from time to time, but never did she have occasion to meet Mr. Wilson. Her natural fear of the unknown caused her to dislike the man already. Soon, today in fact, she would be meeting him face-to-face.

Parallel parking was not one of Madeleine's strongest suits as a driver, so it took her three or four back-and-forth motions before her 1939 Chevrolet was satisfactorily positioned at the curb on Franklin. Such a maneuver, in depressing the clutch pedal repeatedly, always caused her left leg to ache. Her husband, Harland, taught her to drive in this automobile when he learned that he would likely be leaving for overseas, and she very nearly stripped the gears in the process. Now, with three years of practice behind her, she was quite proud of her shifting ability. Rarely did the engine stall, and then only on rainy or excessively humid days. It was a Master DeLuxe sedan, blue in color, and Harland made her promise to wash it at least once a month, a commitment she was faithful to honor. That was saying something, too, because it collected copious amounts of road grit on her weekly trips to visit the twins in Riesel.

A sustained rumble in the air caught her attention after she slammed the Chevy's door. The noise seemed to emanate from directly in front of her or perhaps slightly to her left, toward the northwest, but nothing out of the ordinary was apparent to the eye. With twenty-five minutes to spare before she needed to clock in, Madeleine let curiosity get the better of her, so she proceeded on foot across Franklin and past the savory smells of Joyce's Café toward the corner. There, visible up Fourth Street, was a gathering of people, waiting expectantly at the intersection of Austin Avenue. Judging from all the craning necks, there seemed to be a parade or demonstration on the way, evidently progressing from west to east toward the river. Drawing closer, she could see a color guard from Waco Army Air Field and then, following about ten paces behind this quartet of soldiers, a banner that proclaimed, "The Third Army in the 6th War Loan, Retail Employees of the U.S.A." She recognized one of the two men carrying the banner—Bill Rook, a decorator for Montgomery Ward—but she felt it might seem frivolous or even unpatriotic to wave her hand at him as he carried out his civic duty.

"Mrs. Givens!" came a woman's voice.

Madeleine turned her head. "Yes ...?" She answered in tentative fashion, not quite certain who it was that called her name. The sidewalk was crowded with spectators at this particular juncture of the parade route, and the first of some nine hundred retail workers, marching down the middle of the street, were just now coming abreast with her. This large contingent of men and women was passing by in rows and columns that were surprisingly well defined for civilians. Just four blocks back, they had emerged from a motivational session at the Waco Theatre, where they were issued final instructions prior to launching the fund-raising campaign.

"Mrs. Givens!" the voice repeated, and Madeleine peered toward the sea of faces. A woman in her late twenties stepped forward, separating herself from the other bystanders. "I see you don't remember me. I'm Julie May Tuttle. We worked together two or three times."

"Oh, yes, hello ..." Madeleine told her, but she was still a bit confused. "I'm not very good with names, I'm afraid."

"Well, I was Julie May Steen back then. I got married three months ago."

"Congratulations."

"You were my supervisor a couple of times, whenever Mrs. Fowles was out sick."

Once it dawned on Madeleine that this young lady was referring to the Franklin Avenue club, what she was saying made sense. "Yes, now I remember you. I think you and I had a mishap with the bathrooms, didn't we?"

"That's me. Someone made the commodes overflow, and the custodian, Terrence, said it was not an accident." Julie May put her hands in her coat pocket and laughed. "Some of those soldiers are nothing but overgrown boys."

The weather on this Monday was not really chilly enough to justify the heavy coat, but the novelty of her wedding ring had not yet worn off, and Julie May did not want to expose it to the elements any more than was necessary. She had met an airman from Wichita, Kansas, in June, and by her birthday, August 19, they were married. Six weeks later, Gordon Tuttle was shipped overseas, and she was on her own again.

"Are you working today?" Madeleine asked. She hoped so, not wishing to be surrounded by total strangers in her new post.

"Yes, ma'am, at ten."

Madeleine bristled at the use of "ma'am"—a deference she thought worthy of being reserved for someone much older—but otherwise she was pleased by Julie May's answer. "Good," she said. "I'll walk over there with you."

Julie May was surprised. "Are you with us, then?"

"Permanently, from what little I've been told," Madeleine told her. "I guess Mr. Wilson must have talked with Mr. Isbell, and that was that." Although outwardly scowling, she tried to remain philosophical. "You know, ours is not to reason why ..."

"Well, you'll like it at this club," the younger woman said. "I've never worked on Washington except as an alternate, but it seems a lot busier there. This new one hasn't quite caught on yet, and of course we're much smaller."

"Oh, give it time, sister. Believe me, the joint will be jumping."

Waco's second United Service Organizations facility—located at 208 Franklin Avenue, almost directly across the street from the PDQ Coffee Shop—was installed in what was, until recently, a vacant string of retail spaces. For that matter, the store immediately to the east remained empty, at least until such time as the USO might choose to expand.

When the parade dispersed, Madeleine walked to her new post with Julie May. Though she felt some normal trepidation in setting out for what amounted to uncharted territory, the mere fact of having a sympathetic acquaintance alongside helped to ease the transition. Standing for the parade must have loosened her troublesome leg, for she scarcely limped at all, at least in her own mind. Julie May could not fail to notice, however, and she made a discreet allowance in her step to accommodate the slower gait.

Soon after punching in, Madeleine paid what she termed a "courtesy call" on the director, Mr. John L. Wilson, and to her relief, she found him to be quite affable and polite, certainly nothing like the hobgoblin her imagination had counseled her to resent. Introductions happily accomplished, she wandered over to the storage room and began sifting through the chaotic assortment of Christmas wreaths and ornaments. These mismatched decorations were donated to the cause by widespread USO clubs—of which there were more than three thousand—and by such other helpful sources as local schools and the public library. She knew from past experience that it would not be long before the men would expect to enjoy some colorful Yuletide cheer in their "home away from home."

During the next week or so, the two Army wives, Mrs. Givens and Mrs. Tuttle, established a close friendship, though one of them was almost six years the other's senior. Madeleine soon discovered that what Julie May had told her was indeed true: the new club was much less crowded than the original. That all changed dramatically with the arrival of Thanksgiving. Suddenly, the Franklin Avenue club's attendance swelled to capacity, and staff members were strained to their very limits of endurance. Food ran out, tables were full, unoccupied chairs in the lounging area were nowhere to be found, and dance-floor enthusiasts swayed elbow-to-elbow to the sounds of the jukebox. It was a nice problem to have, but the newfound popularity came with a price. Two of the forty-four-hour employees had to work overtime, and the director had no other choice but to borrow three inexperienced part-timers from the Washington Avenue location to cover the holiday rush.

While most of the country celebrated Thanksgiving on the fourth Thursday of November, Texas and seven other states still held to the old tradition—decreed by President Lincoln in 1863—that this sacred holiday should be observed on the last Thursday of the month. In most years, this would make no difference whatsoever, but the 1944 calendar had five Thursdays in the penultimate month, and so it was that the Lone Star State delayed its official celebration until November 30, a full week later than most of the nation. This, of course, meant that the majority of USO patrons that year experienced the odd sensation of a postponed Thanksgiving. Letters from home referred to turkey dinners in the past tense, and radio shows originating in California and New York had long since extended their holiday greetings to listeners.

It was on that "second" Thanksgiving that Nathan Reynolds, through no premeditated design of his own, entered Madeleine's life for the first time in a dozen years. They hardly recognized each other, he in his Army uniform and she ten pounds heavier and wearing her hair in the fashionable style of Patty Andrews.

The soldier snuffed out his cigarette in the ashtray, stood up, and smiled. "Maddy?" he whispered. Hitching up his trousers, he took two steps closer and noticed that she was smiling too.

"Hello, Nate," Madeleine said to him. It was all she could do to hide the embarrassment. "Funny what this war will turn up."

Nate Reynolds was very tall, and so long were his arms that, when standing, his fingertips almost touched the tops of his knees. At one time, he had intended to play basketball at Hamline University—his father's alma mater—but he quickly abandoned that notion upon discovering that high school competition, at which he excelled, was a pale reflection of what he could expect to encounter in the Minnesota Intercollegiate Athletic Conference. After one year, he transferred to Dakota Wesleyan and never again gave the lure of athletics more than a passing thought.

"So, what brings you to Waco?" Madeleine asked.

He looked down. "Don't these khakis sort of give me away?"

"But why did the Army decide to send you back here? I thought soldiers never got stationed where they really wanted to be."

"Who said I wanted to come back to Waco?"

She noticed the gold band on his left hand. "Don't your parents still live here?"

Nate nodded his head. "They do, but they're separated now. Have been for nearly ten years."

"I'm sorry to hear that. I always liked both of them very much."

"Pop was crazy about you. He once told me that you were the one who got away."

Madeleine grinned but said nothing. She was trying not to remember very much.

"Have you been working here all along?" Nate asked her. "I don't recall seeing you here before."

"A little over a week. They transferred me here from the other club."

He glanced at a table of rambunctious GIs. "The guys in my outfit like it over here better. Not as crowded." One of his pals caught Madeleine's eye and blew her a kiss from where he sat.

Nate chuckled. "Don't pay any attention to Graham. He does that to all the gals."

"I resent that!" the soldier shouted. "If the truth be known, I'm only in love with the gorgeous ones." He addressed the comment to Nate, but his eyes never left Madeleine.

Nate waved him off with the back of his hand. Then he turned to Madeleine and said, "He's from Massachusetts," as if that explained it all.

Madeleine did not sense any danger signs until about an hour later. That was when she brought coffee to the table, and Nate asked her if she would like to join them. She declined the offer, instinctively becoming a bit wary of her old admirer. By this stage of her USO employment, she was quite used to the idea of men in uniform asking her such things—no real harm in being friendly—but there was something unsettling in the way Nate began to look at her.

Graham, the most animated of his cohorts, said, "Come on, honey. We don't bite," but he spoke in a playful way that seemed innocent enough. Another NCO, Hennessy by name, pulled out a chair for her and winked at his friends, tapping the ashes off the end of his Chesterfield.

Madeleine deflected these advances with aplomb, invoking all the dispassion of a paid companion—which, in a sense, is precisely what she was. Her two and a half years of experience had trained her to put a soldier in his place while actually making him feel gratified by her rejection. It was an art form that came with all those months in the trenches, like a nightclub comedian fending off hecklers.

Adept or not, she had no desire to linger any longer than necessary among the wolves. Consequently, when a female volunteer passed by with what appeared to be a heavy box of donated books, Madeleine used that opportunity to take one end of it and accompany her to the workroom. There she intended to stay, showing the young woman—no more than a girl, really—how to process newly received reading material for the library shelves.

Nate Reynolds was undeterred. He had not seen his high school sweetheart for over a decade, and he was not about to be satisfied with any five-minute chat session—in public, no less, and with his own clique of soldier chums as the drooling audience. About an hour before he was due back at the base—assigned to inspect what amounted to an entire company of raw recruits ("On Thanksgiving?"

he asked top, who said, "That was last week, sergeant. You can't have it both ways.")—he made his move.

He eluded his seated comrades by the simple expedient of a trip to the USO latrine. But instead of returning to the table, he made a quick detour to the coffee pot for a refill and then to an open room at the rear, into which he had seen Madeleine disappear only moments before. Taking a sip from his cup, he gazed around the room with a confident smile, almost a smirk, and was dumbfounded to learn that no one was there but the young girl. She sat quietly working at a desk until, startled by the feeling that she was not alone, she turned her head and asked, "May I help you?"

Nate again surveyed the room, certain that he had overlooked his quarry the first time. She was not there. "Do you know where Miss Terry is?"

"Who?"

He realized that he had used her maiden name. "The lady who helped you carry the books back here."

"Mrs. Givens?"

"Yes. Do you know where she is?"

"No, sir. She was here, but then she left."

She was not in the lounge area either, nor was she serving refreshments to the clientele.

Now Nate was more determined than ever to find her, if only to satisfy his male ego that Madeleine did not vanish into thin air on his account. He entered John Wilson's office without knocking and earnestly informed the director that it was a matter of life and death that he locate "Mrs. Gibbons" posthaste. His mispronunciation of her name suggested to Wilson that this soldier was not a close, personal friend.

Being met by a frown, Nate put his hands on the desk and leaned forward, glancing down at a wooden nameplate. His voice became ingratiating. "Listen, Mr. ... Wilson ... I'll level with you. I'm an old friend of Madeleine's, and she just wanted to reminisce about Waco High, that's all." He forced a smile. "Give a guy a break. I've got to hurry back to base."

Even Nate's resorting to near honesty failed to convince the director, who stood up and led his guest to the door. "I'll have a look around, sergeant," he said. "That's all I can do. And if I find her, I'll let you know." He squinted at the intruder. "You *are* aware that Madeleine is married, aren't you?"

Nate evaded the question by asking one of his own. "What time does she get off work?"

"At five, I suppose," Wilson told him, "but this is a holiday, so I'd have to consult the schedule." He had encountered plenty of mashers in his day, and—protective of his girls—he was methodically vigilant about withholding information from strangers. "Why don't you just plan to see her the next time you're in town?"

Nate's buddies were growing restless, so when he approached the table, they took their caps and hurried toward the front door. "I'll have to do some fancy driving to get us there by 1630," Graham said. He zigzagged through the crowded room like a broken-field running back. Following his interference, the others were not far behind.

Hennessy asked Nate, "What's so great about that dame anyway? She's nothin' special."

"Well, I notice you about broke a blood vessel pulling that chair out for her."

"Naw. They're all the same to me."

In five seconds flat, they were out the door and hopping into the jeep. Nate glanced back at the USO as they lurched away from the curb, with Graham making a mockery of the national speed limit.

◆　　　◆　　　◆

The weather was a bit chilly but not abnormally cold for the third week of December. Radio forecasters were cautioning that temperatures could be expected to plunge any day now, a prognostication supported by decades of historical data and the *Farmer's Almanac*. None of that troubled Hannah Lane in the slightest. Indeed, she voiced a quiet prayer of thanks to her Lord for the fact that this day—of all days—was bearable for someone in his upper fifties who did not enjoy the most flourishing health.

A northwesterly wind flapped the lapels of her winter coat as she stood on the platform, awaiting the appearance of her father's train. She had not seen him for more than eighteen months, and she feared the worst. According to his letters, the lung malady from which he suffered refused to loosen its grip on him, despite the fact that he made regular visits across town to the doctor's office. Old Doc Tarkanian, long since retired until pressed into service by exigencies of the war, was loath to make house calls to those who had attained the age of driving and were able-bodied enough to do so.

Hannah was not alone at the passenger station. Wesley and his mother accompanied her there, though not venturing any farther than the parking lot, which is where they now sat in the family automobile. Nora insisted upon giving their boarder some privacy during this happy moment of reunion, but Wesley agreed only under protest. Like most American boys, he found it exciting to be in the presence of trains, to witness the power of their engines, to be jolted by the unpredictable emissions of steam, to watch people of all descriptions coming and going. On this day, sitting behind the steering wheel, Wesley said nothing but sulked conspicuously enough to register his displeasure. When a distant whistle blew, this provided him with ample time to catch a glimpse of the decelerating train's engine, just before the wooden depot obscured it, and then he heard quite clearly its noisy arrival. But this was a poor substitute for the thrill of standing within arm's length of the wondrous machine.

When the train finally inched to a stop, the expression on Hannah's face changed from glee to concern. Her father, now guardedly plodding down the metal steps of the Pullman, seemed to have aged twenty years since she kissed him goodbye at the bus station in Mount Airy. Was it really just the summer before last? The frame of his body appeared frail to the touch, his weight had dropped dangerously low, and his formerly graying hair was now totally white. Yet his smile remained as bright as ever, and Hannah's anxiety dissipated like magic when Reverend Samuel Lane took her in his strong arms and gave her the fatherly hug that she had coveted so often in his absence.

"You look quite the young lady," were the first words out of his mouth, and he was unable to say anything further for fully two minutes while his eyes watered and his throat contracted with emotion. Hannah cried too, and this, in turn, caused an elderly black woman standing nearby to have a tear or two running down her own cheeks. "God bless you," the onlooker said with a joyful nod, and then she went to greet her husband, who rode the rails as a Katy porter. For her, experiencing such trainside reunions had become a way of life and, even more, an affirmation of the good that resided in all people.

Nora Brower arranged for Hannah's father to sleep in the master bedroom, while she herself would share accommodations with daughter Elizabeth. The pair of widowed parents had never met previously, of course, but Nora had the odd sensation that she knew the pastor quite well, thanks to everything Hannah related to her in letters from back home.

As for Samuel, he could recall nothing of substance beyond each family member's Christian name. Hannah, he explained with a downcast shake of the head, was not an effusive writer. "But if that is a daughter's only failing," he said, "then so be it! Amen."

"Our older boy, Stephen, is just the same," Nora told him. "He rarely writes anymore. We used to receive two letters a week from him, but now we're lucky to get more than one a month." She turned to her daughter, who was carrying the smaller of Samuel's suitcases. "How long has it been?"

"Twenty-six days now, Mother." The girl's voice had an air of certainty to it, as if she had consulted a calendar that very morning. She laid the suitcase down and glanced at Hannah, wondering why the boarder's eyes were closed. "I'm sure we'll get another one soon," Elizabeth said. "The mail's pretty unreliable."

"Well, and that's understandable," Samuel added. "It's a miracle that we can communicate with our fighting men at all. One lady in our church—a very dear and faithful member—has three boys in uniform, and she places all of their letters in a scrapbook. Each boy has his own. You know Frieda Merck, honey?"

"Of course I do, Papa. Ralphie, Bill, and Hatch are good friends of mine."

"Two of them are in the Navy, Mrs. Brower, like your son," Samuel said. "The other is stateside in the Coast Guard."

The cat wandered near, and Reverend Lane was the first to bend down and stroke him under the chin. Though usually leery of strangers, Valentino made an exception in the present company, perhaps obeying his senses that this visitor was a cat lover. And indeed he was, with three of his own—named Surry, Hatteras, and Bragg. Samuel's knees creaked as he struggled back to his feet, and he promptly excused himself for a well-deserved nap after his long journey.

He had just arrived, but already Hannah found herself dreading the day when her father would leave Waco for the return trip to North Carolina. She was only too aware that it might be the last time she would see him in this life. Discouraging fares aside, the fearsome logistics of civilian transportation during wartime were daunting even to the most resolute of travelers, and her job and schooling did not present her with many opportunities for jumping aboard a train for a cross-country excursion. Samuel Lane himself, though possessed of a naturally sunny disposition, intimated that he would be disinclined to ever attempt such a westward passage again. Every mile of it was a grueling struggle, definitely not for the faint of heart.

On a more positive note, it did not take him long to feel right at home in what he gratefully accepted as his central Texas haven from the rigors of travel. The clean sheets smelled of lilac, and he felt quite pampered during his ten-day stay—almost to the point of embarrassment. "You really need to stop spoiling me like this," he shouted to Nora from the bathroom. He was standing at the washbasin, combing his hair, but there in the corner of the mirror was her image, leaning down to spread an extra blanket over the bed. Poor circulation sometimes caused his feet to become cold during the nights, and Nora evidently was determined to address that symptom with as much as a half-foot of weighty covers, if that was what it took.

Samuel Lane's journey to visit his daughter was timed to coincide with Christmas recess at Baylor University, which fell just a couple of weeks into the winter quarter. Hannah would be off until January 2, two days after his train was scheduled to depart from Waco. Wesley and Elizabeth, too, were enjoying a break from school, so the house was alive with more activity than Nora could remember encountering since the war began. Not that she was complaining, for to be useful to guests under her roof was a source of great satisfaction that often eluded her during the normal course of life. With a sense of shame, she acknowledged to herself that sometimes—like many another mother—she was guilty of taking her own children for granted in that respect.

A disparity of temperatures seemed to be just one of the old house's characteristics that was destined never to change. In contrast to the chilly second floor, the downstairs rooms were warm and inviting. Moreover, at this time of year they offered a composite fragrance of pine, apple cider, and cinnamon. No fewer than three of the rooms were filled with yuletide decorations, including a six-foot tree that Wesley transported home on the back seat of the Chevrolet, thereby depositing a profusion of needles that required over an hour to remove. Christmas cards from friends and relatives stood on the mantel above the fireplace, though Nora remarked that there appeared to be not quite as many of them as in years past. Adorning the front door was a holly wreath, hanging no more than ten feet away from Steve's blue star.

◆ ◆ ◆

The preacher's first couple of days in Texas were given over to much-needed relaxation, but by Saturday he felt strong enough to venture out of the house. Nora took this opportunity to share him with her friends and neighbors, introducing Samuel to one and all as the "Southern Baptist minister from North Carolina," and Hannah accompanied them on their rounds more often than not. Highlighting the day was a visit to Waco's Cameron Park, with its picturesque series of bluffs and gullies fronting the Brazos and Bosque Rivers. For a confirmed outdoorsman like Reverend Lane, the park's dense foliage, towering vistas (including the aptly named Lover's Leap), and circuitous bottomlands were something akin to communing with God.

Cordiality took a decided turn for the worse on the morning of Christmas Eve, when Hannah escorted her father to the regular eleven-o'clock worship service at First Baptist Church. She did so in all innocence, heedless that Pastor Joseph Martin Dawson would choose this particular occasion to hammer long and loudly on the Social Gospel instead of the Virgin Birth. Certainly his sermon title, "Jesus, the Realist: A Christmas Sermon," suggested to her no such departure from the traditional Nativity messages of Matthew, Mark, and Luke, so she did not think to issue an advisement of what to expect. Feeling a bit "moralized" (as he later put it), Samuel squirmed in his pew, fiddled with the collar of his starched dress shirt, and sighed just emphatically enough to capture his daughter's fearful look.

Now, it must be noted that the North Carolinian took a back seat to no one when it came to advocating progress on such divisive issues as child labor, the exploitation of immigrants, and women's rights, but he drew the line when he heard the Waco preacher use his sermon to advocate an organized response to racial prejudice and the Ku Klux Klan. It was not so much that Samuel supported movements like these—he most emphatically did not—but he felt strongly that, in time, tenets of the church would lead Christians away from bigotry without resorting to political invective to speed the process along. He was an unswerving proponent of religious autonomy, and he scrutinized the government's infringement upon affairs of the church with grave suspicion. In his opinion, this pastor, with whom he had enjoyed an acquaintanceship for many years, approached precariously close to espousing the party line. Being a staunch Democrat himself, Samuel voted for Franklin Delano Roosevelt all four times, but that did nothing to alter his conviction that political doctrine had no place in the pulpit.

Lillie Cockerham's 1942 Studebaker had a good heater, and that feature was much appreciated on the way home from church. So was the radio, which was playing a set of hits by Glenn Miller, one of Reverend Lane's favorite bandleaders. The two Baylor coeds were sitting in the front seat, talking, so Samuel only caught a portion of what the radio announcer was saying, something about "… lost over the English Channel." Following the song "Blue Orchids," the announcer solemnly repeated his wire report. Major Glenn Miller was presumed to have been killed nine days earlier, in "terrible weather conditions," when a single-engine aircraft crashed into the English Channel with him and two other officers aboard. He was en route from England to Paris, to join his band and perform for Allied troops.

"Isn't that just dreadful?" Lillie asked her friend. Hannah nodded her head.

"I saw him when he was just getting started—in Atlantic City," Samuel told the girls.

Eyes wide, Lillie glanced back at him. "You saw Glenn Miller perform, in person?"

"At Hamid's Million Dollar Pier," he said. "That would have been about 1939." But then, with furrowed brow, he looked at his daughter. "No, I know exactly when it was. It had to be August of '38, when I drove to Philadelphia for a conference, and you stayed with your Aunt Patty in Spring Lake."

"Did you get to meet him, Papa?" Hannah asked.

"No, honey, I'm afraid not." He sighed, allowing an index finger to fan the pages of the Bible on his lap. "But I did see him up close on the pier the next day—him and Tex Beneke and some of the other boys. A newspaper photographer lined them up for a publicity shot. Linda Keene was there too—beautiful girl and nice singer—and Ray Eberle. Later on, they all became pretty famous. Especially Glenn, of course." On the short trip back to the Brower house, little more was said by anyone in the automobile. Somber news from the war front had a way of reminding all people, ministers included, of their own mortality.

Though she was a thousand miles removed from her home in Mount Airy, North Carolina, this Christmas morning began for Hannah just as they always had, for as far back as she could remember. Her father stood in the middle of the living room, proclaiming verbatim the Nativity story to those who were seated around him, either cross-legged on the floor or in chairs. And yet this time, as a guest, the preacher was a bit reluctant to impose himself upon others in so public a manner. It was Hannah who virtually insisted, taking her father by surprise but not wholly unprepared. In a stentorian voice, quite different from his normal speaking delivery, Samuel intoned, by heart, the entire second chapter of the book of Luke. He never faltered for an instant, quoting aloud in a fluent stream of elocution that, Appalachian accent aside, may well have been worthy of the court of King James.

Wesley was duly impressed, having learned the hard way how difficult it is to articulate such a lengthy passage without stumbling—and doubly so without the benefit of a written script. When it was over, he felt like standing up and applauding, but he knew this would be an unwelcome intrusion into the air of reverence that had visited the room. Instead, he looked down at his folded hands, waiting until such time as one of the adults broke the mood by speaking first. His mother reached for her coffee cup but chose not to cheapen the moment by referring to the pastor's oratorical skills. She took a sip and then quietly invited Elizabeth to help her prepare breakfast in the kitchen. Hannah offered her assistance, too, but was denied. After all, Nora insisted, her father would only be in town for a few more days.

In common with most American radio listeners—as substantiated by a Hooper share of 24.5—Samuel Lane was an avid fan of the "Lux Radio Theatre," so he was only too pleased to join his daughter and the Brower family in listening to a Christmas night broadcast of *The Vagabond King*. This production of Rudolf

Friml's musical starred Dennis Morgan as François Villon and Kathryn Grayson as Lady Katherine, and it was inspired not so much by 1930's groundbreaking, two-strip Technicolor, all-talky film as it was by a recent Broadway revival at the Shubert Theatre, a modestly successful run of fifty-six performances during the summer of 1943.

Nora's best Christmas gift of 1944 did not arrive until Wednesday, the twenty-seventh, on an afternoon when she and Elizabeth were busy removing the festive decorations that had served to brighten up the house for the past two weeks. Wesley was at the radio station for the broadcast of "Behold Tomorrow," and Hannah borrowed the Browers' automobile to drive her father around Baylor University. The pastor had read much about it in her letters, but never before had he set foot on campus. With the late-December air now moderating, conditions were ideal for such a leisurely tour, particularly inasmuch as the grounds were largely deserted for Christmas break.

Elizabeth was not scheduled to report for work that day until five o'clock because her boss, Mr. Harkins, had neglected to recall that Waco High School was not in session. And that is why it was she who heard the telltale noise emanating from the front porch. As was her practice on those relatively rare occasions when she was home on a weekday afternoon, she ran to the source of the metallic rattling, in the process abandoning whatever she happened to be doing at the time. In this case, she was carrying a strand of tinsel in one hand and a wooden Santa Claus and reindeer ornaments in the other.

Meanwhile, across the room, Nora was oblivious to her daughter's brief absence. She continued to wrap glass figurines in old newspaper, hoping to protect them from accidental breakage during another year of storage. So long was it since Steve last wrote home that Nora lately had begun training herself not to presume that an additional letter might arrive on any given day. She did not even bother to look up in expectation, as she surely would have done back when that anticipation was materially rewarded two or three times a week. It was only when she heard the front door slam, followed by the sound of Elizabeth's scampering footsteps, that she finally diverted her attention from the project at hand.

"Mother! Steve wrote!" the girl shouted. She stopped, only a couple of paces inside the living room, and stood as if in a daze. "It's addressed in his own handwriting, so I know he's safe." There were tears in her eyes.

"Oh, praise the Lord!" Nora said. Kneeling near the denuded Christmas tree, she struggled to her feet and limped toward Elizabeth on stiff legs.

The girl seemed to be stunned with delight. She held the precious bit of correspondence at her side, savoring the happy moment and in no hurry to open the envelope. When her mother came near, the teenager impulsively decided to play keep-away. From past experience, Nora knew better than to try to snag it from her cat-quick daughter, so she contrived to sigh loudly and appear more annoyed than she really was. "Please, Lizzie. This is no time for games."

"I'll bet you can't get it," Elizabeth said. She held the envelope a tantalizing two feet from her mother's eyes.

In spite of herself, Nora smiled, just as the girl knew she would, and the match was won. Now Elizabeth was perfectly willing to surrender the envelope. That done, she rushed over to fetch the letter-opener from atop the breadbox, next to which the daily mail usually found its final resting place after migrating from the entry table.

"Do you think he's coming home on leave?" Nora asked. She posed the question in such a rhetorical tone of voice that Elizabeth did not even bother to answer. Then, upon receiving the letter opener from her daughter, she paused for several seconds with her eyes closed in silent prayer.

The letter was written on USO stationery, probably a surplus sheet that Steve borrowed from a club in San Diego during his basic-training days. It was dated November 17, which meant that over a month had gone by since the boy's thoughts were committed to paper. That made little difference. A piece of correspondence was accepted as clear evidence that its writer was safe from harm—at this very moment—despite the fact that several weeks may have elapsed in the meantime. Nora began quoting aloud from her son's letter, pausing here and there to decipher his handwriting.

"We have seen some action," she read, "but nothing we can't handle. Our skipper is a swell guy, and I can walk right up and speak to him as a friend. Formalities are pretty relaxed at sea—Navy protocol, they call it—and saluting is kept to a minimum. At least that's how it is on our ship.

"I can't recall if I told you that I was sick for five or six days a few months ago. Most of the men I know were laid up, so evidently it was contagious. Rumor has it that the problem was something we ate, but the official report said otherwise. Anyway, everyone seems to be fine now, so whatever it was has left us, thank God. I think it was some kind of flu because we were only about a day's journey away from [SNIPPED BY CENSOR] when we all started feeling poorly.

"The weather has been grand for the past week and a half, and at times it almost feels like we're on a pleasure cruise. But at other times ...

"Tell Wesley that one of my shipmates used to announce for a radio station in Dubuque, Iowa. He says he read the news and also hosted his own half-hour game program called 'How Smart Is Your Husband?' that was pretty popular every weekday at 12:30. Housewives loved the show, but then Howie got conscripted. He claims that he would have joined up anyway, but I've never met a draftee yet who didn't say that!"

Steve's letter concluded with the obligatory wishes of love for his mother, brother, and sister, but something in the way he phrased it—"Eternal love to you all"—made Nora uneasy and apprehensive about what the future might hold.

"It's just a figure of speech," Elizabeth said.

"But he's never written anything like that before. It seems so ... fatalistic. Almost like he's expecting something horrible to happen."

"He's only being affectionate, Mother. I would think you'd be pleased by it instead of resentful."

"I'm not resentful. I think what he said is very sweet." Nora walked over to the sofa and sat down. "Oh, I'm being a silly, old woman, dear. Don't even listen to me when I get like this."

"I don't think it's silly at all. You're just worried about your son, and that's perfectly normal in my book." Elizabeth sat beside her and held out her hand, palm up. When Nora gave her the letter, the girl reread it to herself, especially the concluding portion.

Hannah read it, too, when she and her father returned from their impromptu tour of Baylor. Steve had stopped writing directly to her long ago—not that he ever did it very regularly at best—so she was always pleased to glean whatever information she could from this secondary source.

♦   ♦   ♦

Despite what those in Waco, Texas, may have assumed from reading his forty-day-old letter, Stephen Collins Brower was not presently on the high seas, nor had he been for the past eleven and a half weeks. As with all military intelligence, the whereabouts of his ship was classified information that he was not at liberty to reveal, even in the most general of terms. Little did his mother and sister suspect that Steve was now only 1,450 miles to the northeast, awaiting departure aboard the newly configured *USS Jeffers* for duty in the Pacific. In precisely one week's time, she was due to sail out of New York Harbor, with her DD-621 classification revised to DMS-27. The *Jeffers* had been converted from a Gleaves-class destroyer to a high-speed, ocean-going minesweeper, one of twenty-four such hybrid vessels that would see action in the war.

It had been an eventful period. Following the summertime troop landings between Toulon and Cannes in southeastern France, the *Jeffers* had cruised along the Côte d'Azur in a support role until leaving the Mediterranean for the North Atlantic on September 28. She arrived in New York nine days later and immediately underwent a substantial conversion process that required six weeks of toil at the shipyards, ultimately acquiring her official reclassification as a destroyer-minesweeper on November 15. Steve and much of her crew, meantime, were assigned to the Naval Mine Warfare School at Yorktown, Virginia, where they were recipients of concentrated instruction on the York River. There, making full use of several school ships, the students engaged in minesweeping exercises that were designed to prepare them for most every eventuality they might encounter in actual combat situations.

This was a far cry from any training Steve had received in his nineteen months of military service. He and the other men were taught to detect, remove, destroy, or neutralize explosive marine mines. The Yorktown school, upon obtaining temporary authorization from Army engineers, periodically planted a representative supply of "enemy" mines in the lower river. These dummies were non-explosive, of course, but in all other respects they appeared and behaved much like the real things. Knowing that the lives of countless sailors, soldiers, and marines could very well depend upon the skills they learned at the NMWS, virtually every student there remained keenly attentive, even when ceaseless repetition might otherwise have led their minds to wander. Still, it would have been stretching the truth to deny that leaving their training behind them and returning to the excitement of the big city was anything but a welcome change. The men positively reveled in their new surroundings, and the coming twenty-four-hour pass, their last before putting to sea, beckoned like the proverbial lighthouse on a moonless night.

For Steve and three of his buddies, this free Thursday meant a trip to the shops, restaurants, and tourist attractions of Manhattan, to which only one of them had ever been before. That was Peter "Sparks" Roth, who hailed from Sault Sainte Marie, Michigan, just across the international border from Ontario. The carefree Sparks had been a truck driver in civilian life, but the United States Navy, in its bureaucratic wisdom, chose to train him instead as a radioman. Far from being disheartened, he rationalized this rate with the words, "Rubber tires don't do much good on the Atlantic."

Also tagging along on this seasonably frigid day were Freddie Lidge, a brooding mathematics whiz from Albuquerque, New Mexico, who seemed to live in his own world and was fond of puns to the point of eccentricity, and chubby Anthony Marino, a former carpenter's apprentice from De Kalb, Illinois, not far from Chicago. Anthony was a self-described womanizer, though his innate shyness rarely allowed him to set his desires into motion. He was said to have more pin-up photos below decks than anyone else aboard the *Jeffers*.

Sparks appointed himself as leader. Though his one and only trek to New York City came when he was eight years old, nonetheless he was quick to assume the role of tour guide for this motley foursome, soon demonstrating his ineptitude by losing their way at every turn of the mission. He protested, to unsympathetic ears, that the Borough of Manhattan had changed considerably since his earlier visit to the city, and thus he should not be held accountable for the geographical confusion from which he was suffering.

What a trip that earlier one had been, with the weather in stark contrast to the frozen present. It was in the summer of 1927 that paper distributor Alexander Roth traveled to New York for a business meeting, and seeing as how all expenses were paid by the parent company, he decided to bring his wife and little Petie along with him on the train. The incident that established itself most indelibly in the young boy's memory was a game at Yankee Stadium between the visiting Browns and Miller Huggins's stellar club. With the temperature quite sweltering in the upper eighties—and humidity to match—only about ten thousand fans were in attendance for the Thursday afternoon contest, but they went home happy with a 9 to 4 victory. For Petie, the moment that made it so memorable occurred in the eighth inning when Babe Ruth slugged a two-run homer off southpaw Walter Stewart. He saw it from afar, seated in the left-field grandstands, well down the line. The ball soared majestically, to the right of the scoreboard, easily cleared the 407-foot sign, and landed deep in the right-center field bleachers. This Herculean blast was the Babe's thirty-fourth round-tripper of the year, putting him one ahead of teammate Lou Gehrig, who went hitless in the game but did manage to score earlier after working Stewart for a walk. The Babe's image remained with Peter Roth from that day forward.

But so much had changed. Now, on a bone-chilling morning in late December of 1944, there were icy patches here and there, where water puddles had frozen overnight, and it seemed that the effects of war had blanketed the whole island. Newsboys shouted, "U.S. Tanks Smash into Bastogne," traffic proceeded at a federally mandated snail's pace, posters in shop windows proclaimed "Stay On The Job—To Finish The Job," and a large percentage of those who walked the city's streets were in military uniform. Radios, when overheard by pedestrians passing by the retail businesses, carried late-breaking bulletins of combat from overseas. And it was women who made many of the storefront deliveries, unloading goods from trucks that they themselves had driven from market. Even some of the omnipresent taxicabs had ladies at the wheel, darting through the congestion with the best of them and honking horns no less vehemently than their male counterparts.

After an early-morning elevator ride to the top of the Empire State Building, the four tourists from the *Jeffers* took subways to a pair of ballparks, which stood within a Bunyanesque fungo wallop of each other across the Harlem River—the Polo Grounds and Yankee Stadium. That left only one other jewel in the New York baseball crown, Ebbets Field, whose craggy exterior they saw during an afternoon trip to the deserted Coney Island. It was not a propitious time of year to visit such popular attractions because most were shuttered for the winter. Still, Steve, Freddie, and Anthony were unanimous in supporting Sparks's desire to see every last one of them in person—if only from the outside looking in—for there was no guarantee that they would ever again find themselves in the Empire City.

They took their lunchtime meal at a savory delicatessen not far from Bloomingdale's, where hot vegetable soup and Reuben sandwiches proved to be perfect antidotes for the wintry shivers. The eatery's music-loving proprietor was an Italian immigrant who insisted that no other radio station play over his speakers but WQXR, the newly acquired voice of the *New York Times*. Its noonday newscast reported that American composer Mrs. H. H. A. Beach—née Amy Marcy Cheney—had died the day before in her suite at the Hotel Barclay on Forty-eighth Street. She was seventy-seven. The announcer also related that a new musical called *On the Town* would open that night at the Adelphi Theatre. This caught Steve's attention, and he wondered whether his pals might want to be there for the excitement of a Broadway premiere, but all three seemed to prefer attending a picture instead. He pressed them no further, though secretly he was disappointed. After all, people could catch a screening of *Meet Me in St. Louis* in most any American town that was large enough to have a movie house.

At twilight, with their day of sightseeing nearly at an end, the sailors were returning to Manhattan aboard the Staten Island Ferry. On the port side, off in the distance, was the Statue of Liberty, and straight ahead was an awesome scene that took them very much by surprise. How strange it was to witness such a brilliantly illuminated skyline during a time of war. Most of the ports of call within their experience still observed at least a token nod to the theory of blackout, even with the once-invincible Germans in retreat and the Japanese beginning to lose hold of their early conquests. The tide of war may have turned, but—still prodded by a healthy instinct for survival—those nations that were not shielded from the hostilities by two massive oceans continued to practice their precautionary measures of civilian defense.

The temperature had dipped to below freezing, thirty-one degrees, after an afternoon high of thirty-six, but somehow—perhaps it was psychological—the men did not feel the cold so acutely when they were aboard ship. They were accustomed to enduring more severe weather conditions than this on the open seas.

"What'll it be, men?" Sparks asked in the ferry terminal. No one answered, so he told the others, "Remember where we'll meet—the automat at Forty-sixth."

Suddenly, Anthony arrived at a decision. "The Judy Garland picture, I s'pose." The cigarette between his lips waggled as he spoke. Freddie, aloof and ever scowling, nodded his assent.

"Well, I'm headed for that musical," Steve said. "How often do you get to see a world premiere?"

"Too late, ain't it?" Sparks asked. He glanced at a clock on the wall.

"Not if I hurry—8:30 curtain time." Beginning to walk away, Steve looked back at the others. "Anyone else game?"

Anthony wavered. "A premiere, huh?"

"Yep. Red carpet and all that."

Sparks shook his head. "It's probably sold out. What'll you do then?"

"I'll find you," Steve told him. "Where's the movie?"

Sparks looked at his closemouthed pal for help.

"Forty-fifth and Broadway," Freddie said. "The Astor."

Walking backward, Steve took a couple of steps. "'Tone?"

Anthony thought for an instant. "Okay, I'm in."

The two rushed away, with Anthony verbalizing his wishes: "Might be some beautiful blondes there—in mink coats."

◆　◆　◆

In trying to squeeze as many activities as possible into their one full day ashore, the four pals from the *Jeffers* found themselves scrambling across town when darkness fell. Sparks and Freddie had the shorter trek, up Broadway to Forty-fifth Street, not so very far from Times Square. Still, by the time they arrived at the movie theater, twenty minutes of *Meet Me in St. Louis* had elapsed, and they had no choice but to join the picture in progress. This saga of Alonzo Smith's family was rather long—113 minutes—so waiting for it to begin anew was out of the question, as the final showing would have a closing time that was prohibitively late. To make matters worse, a middle-aged lady in the box office informed the boys that they could have picked up free tickets at 99 Park Avenue, headquarters of the New York City Defense Recreation Committee. The Astor, she explained, was one of a dozen or so movie houses that honored such passes for men and women in the various services.

"*Now* you tell us," Sparks said.

"Well, keep it in mind for next time," she told them. Her lips continued to move as she counted their change.

Freddie snatched up the tickets. "Sure, we'll do that." He was an inveterate penny-pincher, and such a lost opportunity might very well prey on his mind for the entire length of a feature film.

Meanwhile, about a half-mile to the north, the other two sailors had problems of their own. They exited their subway near Carnegie Hall and continued on foot through the theater district in search of the Adelphi. As it turned out, they could not have easily missed it, for there was a teeming crowd outside the entrance, braving the cold for a last smoke before curtain time. With the temperature now hovering at twenty-nine, people's breath had become visible, mingling with the pungent smell of tobacco. Many of the women were in furs, and tuxedos seemed to be the conspicuous dress code for men—beneath their overcoats, of course.

What was most alarming to Steve was that everyone he saw already seemed to have a ticket. Certainly very few people were paying any notice whatsoever to the box office, where a chic lady in her late thirties sat with a look of jaded disinterest. There were no scalpers to be found, and Steve reasoned that perhaps such profiteering was only considered proper at sporting events. Turning high the collars of their pea coats to stymie the biting wind, he and Anthony approached the box office with fading hopes of being admitted to the theater. Nor was there any sign of encouragement from the sullen woman who sat behind the booth's smudged glass. It was obvious to see that she hardly regarded them as potential customers. Indeed, her eyes seemed to look slightly above them throughout their encounter, even when they were bold enough to engage her in dialogue.

"Sorry, fellas, but we're sold out," the woman said, and she reached for her next cigarette.

"Nothing at all?" Steve asked. She shook her head.

Anthony spoke next. "Any standing room?" He even tried winking at her, but it was a misplaced attempt. She was not one to be charmed.

"This is opening night," she said. Losing interest, her gaze wandered to a novel that lay facedown beside her. *Forever Amber* was displayed in gilt lettering on the cover and spine of its chartreuse dust jacket.

Leaning his arms upon the counter, Anthony could feel heated air gusting toward him from the window's semi-circle, the hole through which transactions were made. He warmed his hands for a minute or so, under the pretense of gathering information.

"Does anyone ever return unwanted tickets?" he asked.

"Not on opening night."

"How much are tickets?"

"Assuming that we had any to sell?"

He bristled. "Yes, ma'am."

"On a normal night, they're a dollar-twenty to twelve dollars, depending upon location."

Anthony blew into his hands. "What about on opening night? How much are they then?"

"Fifty dollars apiece for premium seating," she said.

"Assuming that you had any to sell ..."

"That's right." She looked at him defiantly.

"Too rich for my blood," the chubby sailor told her.

With a puff on her cigarette, the woman resumed *Forever Amber*. End of conversation.

"Don't catch cold, sweetie," Anthony said as he walked away.

Steve hurried after him. "Let's see if we can find Sparks and Freddie. I think it's the Astor."

But Anthony was preoccupied, and he glanced back at the box office. "You know, I didn't much care for her attitude. I have half a mind to ..."

"Give her a break, 'Tone," Steve said, and he moved in front of his friend. "Look, she's probably used to Lotharios trying to make time with her. She's okay."

Anthony relaxed. "Yeah, maybe you're right. I don't want to give her the satisfaction of turning me down."

Steve felt a tapping on his shoulder. "I beg your pardon," an elderly gentleman said. He was elegantly dressed, as was the woman standing next to him.

"Yes, sir?"

"My wife and I could not help overhearing your dilemma."

Steve was confused by the comment. "What dilemma?"

Anthony stepped closer, and the woman smiled at them both. Still quite attractive at an advanced age, she must have been a real beauty in her day.

"We have two tickets you can use," the man said. He offered them with outstretched hand. "Please."

Anthony gave him a sly grin. "How much are they? We're not Rockefellers, you know."

"Won't cost you a penny," the man said. "Take them. We can come anytime."

Steve and Anthony regarded the dignified couple with disbelief, and the tickets remained dangling before their eyes.

"Please. It will make us happy if you'll use them," the lady said.

Anthony accepted the gift and nodded his thanks. At the risk of seeming unappreciative, he tried his best to study the tickets in the poor lighting, but with little success.

"They're just the cheap seats, if it makes you feel any better," the man said. He wound the silk scarf a bit more tightly around his neck.

His wife nodded her head. "We want you servicemen to have a nice time in New York. We live here, so we can come to the theater whenever we want to."

Steve managed to say, "Well, thank you, but—"

"Enjoy the show," the man added with a smile. He took his wife by the arm, and they strolled away.

It was hard to believe this facility could accommodate fourteen hundred people, for it looked rather modest from the street. The interior, however, turned out to be very spacious, even resplendent, with elevated boxes and balcony adding considerably to the seating capacity. An usher consulted the sailors' tickets—raising his eyebrows in response—and promptly marched forward down the right aisle. He did not stop until he reached the third row and pointed to the center. "Seventeen and eighteen," the attendant said. With a respectful nod of the head, he handed the tickets back to the men and, much to their surprise, refrained from holding out his palm for a tip.

Once they were seated, Steve and Anthony looked around uneasily, sensing that there had been some mistake. And yet, by the time the orchestra was tuning, still no one had asked them to leave, so they felt more and more entitled to settle back in comfort. Evidently, their benefactor was a person of some means, for it would have been difficult to imagine a more advantageous line of sight to the stage. Far from being "the cheap seats," as the old gent professed, this particular vantage point must have required an outlay of one hundred dollars for the pair. "Jeez," Anthony said, "I don't think we thanked them enough."

Although Steve spent the remaining time flipping through a playbill, Anthony appeared more interested in appraising the female spectators in his vicinity, most of whom, he was sad to see, were old enough to be his mother. That was the trouble with seats in the front half of the orchestra, he decided. Toward the back of the house were several comely girls about his age. One of them was really quite stunning, and he resolved to mingle in her direction during intermission. But for the time being, he slipped away for just a few minutes of casual "dame hunting."

Meanwhile, Steve was content to stay seated. His eyes scanned down the listings of cast and crew, wondering whether any famous names might jump out at him.

ON THE TOWN, a musical comedy in two acts and seventeen scenes. Book by Betty Comden and Adolph Green, based on an idea by Jerome Robbins. Music by Leonard Bernstein. Lyrics by Miss Comden, Mr. Green, and Mr. Bernstein. Musical numbers and choreography staged by Mr. Robbins; scenery designed by Oliver Smith and costumes by Alvin Colt; entire production directed by George Abbott; musical director, Max Goberman; presented by Mr. Smith and Paul Feigay.

Workman	Marten Sameth
2d Workman	Frank Milton
3d Workman	Herbert Greene
Ozzie	Adolph Green
Chip	Cris Alexander
Sailor	Lyle Clark
Gabey	John Battles
Andy	Frank Westbrook
Tom	Richard D'Arcy
Flossie	Florence MacMichael
Flossie's Friend	Marion Kohler
Bill Poster	Larry Bolton
Little Old Lady	Maxine Arnold
Policeman	Lonny Jackson
S. Uperman	Milton Taubman
Hildy	Nancy Walker

Policeman ....Roger Treat
Figment.. Remo Bufano
Claire .... Betty Comden
High School Girl..Nellie Fisher
Sailor in Blue...Richard D'Arcy
Maude P. Dilly... Susan Steell
Ivy ....Sono Osato
Lucy Schmeeler.. Alice Pearce
Pitkin .... Robert Chisholm
Master of Ceremonies .... Frank Milton
Singer...Frances Cassard
Waiter ....Herbert Greene
Spanish Singer..Jeanne Gordon
The Great Lover .... Ray Harrison
Conductor...Herbert Greene
Bimmy .... Robert Lorenz

Nancy Walker seemed familiar, but he could not recall precisely where he might have heard of her. And, of course, the musical's composer had been in the news a year or so earlier for stepping in to conduct the New York Philharmonic when Bruno Walter was taken ill. Presumably, some in the cast were household names to the regular theater crowd, but Steve was a mere dilettante in that respect. An obviously more cultured gentleman sat directly to his left, loudly informing an ancient companion with white handlebar mustache, "George is—without question, I think—the finest director in legitimate theater today." He went on to convey, emphatically enough for people's heads to turn, that he conversed with "George" just this past Monday at lunch, and "George" was confident that they had a hit on their hands. The older man must have been awfully hard of hearing.

When Anthony returned to his seat, he elbowed Steve and nodded toward a very pretty young lady who was sitting two rows behind them and well over to the right. Steve acknowledged with a smile, but inwardly he found it difficult to get too excited about anyone—no matter how gorgeous—whom he never again was likely to see in his whole life. He looked down at his wristwatch and discovered that two minutes had elapsed beyond the scheduled curtain time of 8:30. That, he surmised, was nothing unusual for a Broadway musical—especially a first performance, with all the inherent pitfalls of opening night. Then he was taken by surprise by something he overheard a woman behind him contend: this was not, strictly speaking, a world premiere at all. *On the Town* had opened for a ten-day trial run in Boston before traveling here to New York, a normal practice for, as she put it, "working out the kinks." Moments later, with ushers still hurrying half a dozen stragglers from the coat-check room to their seats, the house lights dimmed, conductor Max Goberman gave the downbeat, and the show began.

Never had Steve seen and heard anything quite like it. In common with most high school graduates, he had attended two or three amateur musicals, but that in no way prepared him for the visceral impact of a fully professional production, particularly one just a city block removed from the Great White Way itself. Several of the numbers captured his fancy. "New York, New York" was a catchy tune, and he liked "Carried Away," "Lucky to Be Me," and Hildy's cleverly risqué "I Can Cook Too," replete with double entendres.

As for Anthony Marino, the inventive music was largely wasted on him. He squirmed restlessly in his seat during the opening sequences, probably wishing that he had gone to the movie house instead. At least he knew what to expect from Judy Garland. But his cool attitude changed, dramatically and with a vengeance, the instant Ozzie, played by one of the show's lyricists, arrived at the Museum of Natural History. That is when Anthony became enamored with the actress who portrayed Claire de Loon. Little did he suspect, or care, that this fetching twenty-five-year-old from Brooklyn happened to be the show's other lyricist. All that mattered to him was her pretty visage across the proscenium. From then on, much as Gabey, in the play, developed an irrational yearning for Ivy Smith ("Miss Turnstiles of the Month"), so did the pudgy sailor from De Kalb, in real life, set his sights on establishing a meaningful relationship with Betty Comden. Needless to say, this was a futile prospect, and it would have been downright pathetic, were it not for the mitigating urgency of a serviceman on shore leave. In any case, there was every reason to believe that such a stage-light infatuation would be forgotten by him with the appearance of the next pretty face.

Intermission presented just such a test. After he and Steve were swept willingly along with a mass of humanity toward the back of the theater, Anthony winked at his pal and ventured toward a rollicking group of young women who had congregated near (but not at) the wet bar. From a distance, he reckoned them to be no older than fifteen, but surely they were college age, judging from the company they kept. As Anthony neared the girls, one of them seemed to flash a smile at him, but he could not be certain of that without further investigation. Two others were smoking and, he thought, trying to look sophisticated beyond their years. Worst of all, the men in the group occupied their attention much more than he would have preferred, and with the exception of that initial glance, not a single one of these lovely girls paid any notice whatsoever to a sailor in uniform. Upon closer scrutiny, he found that all but one of them wore diamond rings on their left hands, and that particular lady was in the process of kissing her escort repeatedly, giggling as if playing a game. She was not lonely.

Steve spent the interval people-watching, gazing with envy at the civilian theatergoers who appeared to be so unaffected by the war. His eyes alighted on a very animated family of five—speaking Yiddish and enjoying themselves immensely—and Steve thought of how fortunate they were to be so far away from the conflagration in Europe. The mother was quite pretty indeed, but one of her sons had a facial discoloration that suggested he once was the victim of a fire. Then Steve noticed that three Army officers were there, one wearing a gold leaf, one a silver leaf, and the other a single star. The general was very serious and aloof, but the colonel and major joked with each other just like any enlisted men might do at a ball game. On the far side of a small souvenir table stood a tall, middle-aged man, beverage glass in hand and chattering incessantly to a lovely woman of about twenty-five who seemed thoroughly bored by whatever it was he had to say. For the entire ten minutes that Steve watched this beleaguered woman, not once did she so much as smile or say a word. She did blow her nose into a handkerchief on two occasions, but otherwise she displayed no sign of life.

"May I buy the Navy a drink?" came a well-modulated voice from behind Steve, and he turned to see an elderly gentleman leaning against a pillar beneath the balcony.

"No, sir. But thanks, just the same." Steve was not a drinker by any means, though he did enjoy an occasional beer with the boys during R & R.

"How do you like New York?"

"I like it fine, sir."

"Are you stationed here?"

Steve became cautious. "No, sir."

"I was fifty-one when the First War started for us, so I never did serve." He grinned, eyes blinking behind his thick glasses. "I would have been willing, though, if they wanted me."

"Yes, sir."

"My wife died last year, but I've kept coming to the musicals. We never did like straight drama, you know. Just musicals."

"Is that so?"

"Life is depressing enough without some playwright making it even gloomier."

Steve chuckled at the philosophy. "I suppose."

"When do you ship out, or are you here for the long haul?" The man's face was kindly and reassuring.

"All I can say is we're having a fine time here." Steve dared not say more, and yet, by the same token, he did not wish to be rude.

"Have you seen some action?"

"Yes, sir, we have."

"Killed some Japs?"

"No, sir."

"Krauts?"

"A few, maybe." Steve's eyes wandered, trying to spot his friend, but Anthony was nowhere to be found.

"My grandson is a sergeant in the Army," the man said. "So's his cousin, for that matter—and she's a *she*! Camellia is in the WACs, bless her heart." He pulled out his wallet and produced a tiny snapshot. "That's Aaron. He's my daughter's boy. Stationed somewhere in France, I gather."

Steve looked at the photo for a moment and then extended his hand. "Well, sir, I guess I'd better start getting back to my seat. I've enjoyed talking with you."

"Same here, my boy." They shook hands. "I hope you didn't mind talking to an old geezer like me."

"Of course not."

"What's your name?"

"Stephen Brower ... from Texas."

"All the way from Texas?" The playbill dropped from his hand, but he was spry enough to pick it up. "I always wanted to go there, but I never did."

"Well, I've always wanted to come to New York."

"But you made it. That's the difference."

"Yes, sir." The house lights began to flash, signaling the impending close of intermission.

"What unit are you in, son? Maybe I could write."

Steve held up his hands and smiled with a wink. "Loose lips ..."

The widower nodded his head, and his mouth appeared to tremble. "Best of luck to you, Stephen. Or, may I say ... shalom?"

"Yes, sir, that would be fine. Thank you." So this man was Jewish too. Steve decided then and there that they were a very friendly and warm people. As he walked back down the aisle toward his seat, he tried without success to recall if there were any of them in his circle of friends back home—something he had never thought about before. Surely he knew some Jews in Waco, he concluded, but they just blended into the population more inconspicuously than here in New York.

The house lights were growing dim by the time Anthony, out of breath, finally trampled across the row of people's feet and took his seat. "You see that girl over there?" he asked. "Well, it's too dark now, but there's a girl named Valery who gave me her telephone number."

Unimpressed, Steve told him, "She must be a quality gal."

"Why do you say that?" Anthony seemed hurt by his friend's remark.

"Because why would some girl want a strange sailor to pick her up after a sixty-second conversation?" Anthony did not reply, so Steve added, "Why don't you just copy down a number from a toilet stall?"

"Hey, you don't even know her!"

"I don't have to. Look, 'Tone, what good is a blessed telephone number going to do you now? It's not like you'll ever be able to see her again."

"How do you know? For Chrissakes, we don't ship out for another six days, and I can make a lot of—"

"Quiet, you idiot!" Steve whispered with fire in his eyes. "You want to get us all killed?"

Anthony looked around, embarrassed at the breach of security. He hoped nobody heard, but a dozen or so people around him could hardly have failed to learn this naval secret. As the curtain went up, Steve was glaring at his pal, and Anthony, angry with himself but powerless to reverse what had been done, stared straight ahead in silent misery. And thus, for two sailors at the Adelphi, the second act of *On the Town* began on a sour note.

Several numbers passed by before Steve finally began to relax again, reassuring himself by mentally calculating what the odds must be that an Axis spy would be seated in such close proximity. Most of those in the premium sector of the auditorium were sure to be New Yorkers, and they were not likely to be working for the enemy. Still, that did not excuse Anthony's carelessness, and Steve intended to impress upon him that the lives of 275 shipmates were at stake whenever he opened his big mouth in public. Combat aboard a destroyer—or minesweeper, for that matter—was plenty dangerous enough without the wagging tongue of some unthinking skirt-chaser telegraphing her every move.

Both of Steve's favorite numbers after intermission, the raucous "Ya Got Me" and the bittersweet "Some Other Time," brought Claire de Loon into the spotlight, but fickle Anthony Marino seemed to hardly notice that Miss Comden was on stage. His allegiance had drifted instead to a twenty-year-old named Valery Something, whose Yonkers telephone number was scrawled illegibly on the back of his ticket stub. Valery was sitting far to his right, toward the rear of the theater, and she would be out the exit door during curtain calls, long before Anthony could even make it over to the aisle.

It was windy and a stinging twenty-six degrees when he and Steve walked to the Horn & Hardart on the west side of Broadway, just north of Forty-sixth Street. Sparks and Freddie were already there, glumly drinking their third cups of hot, automated coffee.

◆   ◆   ◆

Even during the best of times, New Year's Eve was typically greeted with subdued enthusiasm in the Brower household, possibly because no one under that roof was animated by the artificial stimulation of strong drink. This year, too, was a noticeably muted affair. With the war still raging and ration books showing no signs of fading into the past, there seemed little to celebrate in the chronological passage of one calendar year to the next. If the impending arrival of 1945 was cause for hope, it was only in a theoretical sense—a contrived sort of optimism generated by nothing more tangible than the annual revolution of the Earth around the Sun.

A particularly somber day awaited Hannah, whose father was due to leave that afternoon on the 4:10 train. And who could say with certainty when, or if, she would ever see him again? Lying in bed that Sunday morning, her mind was heavy with regret, and she felt a twinge of guilt at having abandoned him for the selfish purpose of going west to further her education. Through the closed door of her room, she could hear Reverend Samuel Lane speaking quietly to someone in the hallway, and her heart was gripped by a sharp sense of loss. Tomorrow at this time, as she awakened to a new day, his voice would be long since departed—and perhaps forever silenced to her ears. She sighed and forced herself to slip from beneath the warm bed covers.

As it happened, the weather conspired to darken Hannah's spirit even further, and a quick look through the curtains of her second-story window told her not to expect any dramatic improvement in that regard. The onset of dawn had brought a cool and cloudy winter day, with drizzle falling and temperatures tending to do the same. It was a bearable fifty-two now, but that was predicted to drop another ten degrees by afternoon—one of those Texas days when the thermometer was topsy-turvy and the persistent humidity chilled a person to the bone. Her bare feet were cold, so she stood for a minute or two on the grating of her room's floor heating vent. Then she knelt by the bed and prayed, a practice her father had taught her many years ago.

Over a flavorful repast of hotcakes, maple syrup, and bacon—Nora's specialty for weekend guests—Wesley surprised nearly everybody at the table by announcing that he would soon become an apprentice "sales rep" for KWXN. It was for two practical reasons that he chose such an odd moment to inform his mother. For one thing, sales manager Lee Graffen stipulated that this part-time job would require written permission from Mrs. Brower by Monday morning at ten o'clock. For another, Wesley reckoned that it would be more difficult for her to squelch the idea outright in front of so many dispassionate witnesses.

"Would this be in addition to your regular duties at the station?" she asked him.

"Yes, ma'am. And more money too."

"But will you continue to be an actor?"

"Oh, sure. Kip Hanson is alive and well." He glanced at Reverend Lane, who winked and gave a slight nod of the head.

Nora, who could hardly fail to notice the collusion, wondered what possible motive this Baptist preacher might have in lending support to her son's cause. She smiled, looking from one schemer to the other. "What's going on here?"

Chuckling, Samuel wiped his mouth with a napkin. "You may as well know, Mrs. Brower, because I can see there's no keeping a secret from you anyway."

Hannah laughed at that remark and busied herself by passing the apricot marmalade to Elizabeth, who awaited it with a crisp slice of toast in hand.

Samuel became silent, idly stirring some cream into his coffee, and Wesley seemed to be watching his every move, almost in awe.

"Well? Do you care to explain?" Nora asked. She enjoyed the old man's gruff disposition and thought he must be an imposing figure in the pulpit.

Samuel looked up with a roguish grin. "When your boy here took me on a tour of the radio station yesterday, I broached the subject to Mr. Graffen. I mean, I came right out and asked him what it took to make some real money in the radio business. If Waco is anything like Mount Airy, the men in sales are the ones who bring home the biggest paychecks. Why should my young friend, Wesley, be left out? And Mr. Graffen agreed to try him out on weekends."

Puzzled, Nora turned to her son. "Is this something you want?"

"Yes, ma'am. I'd like to be station manager someday, and this is the only way to do that."

"Station manager? My goodness, that's quite a lofty ambition."

"Yes, ma'am." He stared straight at her, not at all embarrassed.

"But why selling? Don't you like announcing—being an actor?"

"Sure, I do, but this is a side of the business that I don't know anything about. According to what Hugh Kenton says, selling is 'the passport to management'." Wesley turned to Reverend Lane. "Mr. Kenton is our director—the older man with glasses and mustache."

"Smokes cigars ..."

"That's him."

Samuel was amused by what the boy considered to be "older," for this director of his could not have been much over forty-five.

Nora promised to take the matter under advisement, but she was resentful of the fact that the station's sales manager needed an answer so quickly. That seemed awfully pushy to her.

What startled Hannah most of all during breakfast was her father's impulsive decision to attend the Browers' church that day instead of First Baptist. Only once before had she failed to be in the J. M. Dawson congregation on Sunday morning—back in early October when silly Collette Myers begged her to visit Seventh and James Baptist Church, next to the Baylor campus, so she could meet a handsome sophomore from Westphalia named Grady Settles. As it turned out, this Grady was not there, nor did he ever again appear in Collette's French class. She figured he must have dropped out of college to join the Army.

No sooner had the dishes been cleared than Hannah was on the telephone, informing her friend, Lillie Cockerham, that there would be no need to stop by on the way to church. Wesley usually did the Sunday driving for the Browers, now that Steve was away at war, and of course today there would be two extra passengers. Reverend Lane sat up front, and the ladies occupied the back seat, all the while babbling about Dora Finn's divorced boyfriend, whose sweet daughter and delinquent son both transferred to Waco High School this past Tuesday. Willard had already been in the principal's office for fighting.

H. H. Hargrove's final sermon of 1944 was "Preparation for Prayer," and, much to Hannah's relief, her father found it to be more to his liking than was Dr. Dawson's the week before. Indeed, following the service, Samuel introduced himself to the CABC preacher and told him how much he appreciated such a practical and scripturally sound study of the Christian's most valuable tool. It was nearly a quarter to one by the time the two gentlemen finished talking, and Nora stood alongside, gracious but visibly impatient for their discussion to end. She considered it a privilege to cook Sunday dinner for five, but her guest of honor—so unconcerned with matters of the clock—had a train to catch in just three and a half hours. To the best of her knowledge, he had not even packed.

While the preachers were conversing in the sanctuary, Elizabeth and Wesley showed Hannah around the church property, exploring such outlying reaches as the educational wing, choir room, and children's department. Unlike Elizabeth, Hannah was profoundly unmusical, and she admitted as much without a touch of shame, almost taking a perverse pride in that shortcoming. And yet, for some reason, she became quite curious about the hand bells that were lying neatly in chromatic order on a table in the music suite, next to the choir risers. "Do you think they'd mind?" she asked. Without waiting for an answer, Hannah bonged two very loud notes on the largest bells.

"You're supposed to put gloves on before you handle them," Elizabeth told her. "Our music minister would kill you if he saw you do that."

"Well, he'd just have to kill me, then," Hannah said, "because I'm sure not going to put on a pair of those nasty things." She nodded toward a stack of white gloves that lay beside the bells. "People's hands sweat, you know."

Wesley wisecracked that boys sweat, and girls perspire. "Those are the proper terms, according to our gym coach."

"A rose by any other name ..." Hannah said. She looked up when a boy rushed into the room.

Lew Robbey came to retrieve his Bible, which he had left beneath one of the chairs. After locating the Good Book, which was still lying right where he had forgotten it, he smiled at Elizabeth, hardly noticing that anyone else was there with her.

"Hi, Beth," he said. "Happy New Year."

"Hi, Lew."

"Are you going to stay up until midnight?"

"I guess so. We always do."

He glanced down at what he was carrying. "I forgot my Bible, and my parents had to drive me all the way back to get it. Pop's plenty sore because we don't have much gas in the tank."

"Did you have a nice Christmas?" Elizabeth asked. She seemed a little taken with the boy, who was rather handsome—in a gangly, fifteen-year-old sort of way.

"Sure did. No school! What about you?"

"Yes." She cleared her throat, nervously.

During the awkward silence that ensued, Wesley and Hannah grinned at each other and waited.

Lew observed the onlookers for a moment. "My older brother's still in the service," he told Elizabeth. "Army."

"Same here—Navy," Elizabeth said. She nodded her head, failing to think of anything else to say.

"Well, I've got to go. Pop's already mad enough at me."

"'Bye, Lew. See you at school." The boy hurried from the room, and she could hear him running down the hallway.

Wesley tried to keep a straight face. "Is that your boyfriend, Lizzie?"

"Don't be ridiculous. I've only just met him." Elizabeth wanted to make certain that everyone knew where she stood. "His family moved here from Hamilton last summer, for the war work." She looked at Hannah and asked, "Do you know his father?"

Hannah was confused. "Why would I know his father?"

"I think he works where you do."

"Crawford-Austin?"

"I think so. Is there a Mr. Robbey?"

"Not that I'm aware of, but it's a big place." Hannah decided to tease the girl. "Hey, at least your boyfriend's a Baptist, though. That's something in his favor." She was only halfway joking.

"Actually, his mother is a Catholic," Elizabeth told her. "The parents go to different churches, but they're right next to each other." Saint Mary's Church of the Assumption stood at Fourteenth and Washington.

"That couldn't be very healthy for a marriage," Hannah said. "I've always held that couples should share the same faith."

Elizabeth shrugged her shoulders over the theological implications, but all she muttered was, "And he's *not* my boyfriend."

Though served a half-hour later than Nora had planned, Sunday dinner was plentiful and, except for some lumpy potatoes, quite palatable as well. She discovered, too late, that the butter ration was depleted, so she was forced to substitute margarine at the last possible moment. This the good reverend could not abide, and he apologized to the hostess for his inability to digest the vegetable-oil concoction. Winking, she responded that he must eat two desserts instead, a demand with which he was only too happy to comply. Angel food cake and peach cobbler were among his favorites, and he proceeded to combine the two in a large bowl and leave not a morsel behind. For an elderly man of wiry constitution, he certainly did have a robust appetite, and Nora remarked that it blessed her soul to see him enjoy himself so much at the table.

♦   ♦   ♦

The passenger depot was not as crowded as usual for a Sunday afternoon. Most people probably chose not to travel on New Year's Eve, seeing it as a time better spent celebrating with family and friends. But Reverend Lane had no flexibility in the matter, for he needed to be in Mount Airy by Thursday evening at the very latest. Jim Ray Wilburn had supplied for the past two Sundays, but he was not available for services on January 7, when he would be preaching at his home church in Fayetteville. The friendship of these two ordained ministers dated back some eighteen years. Wilburn, in fact, had served under Samuel Lane for nearly a full decade before being called to begin a missionary church about 150 miles to the southeast. Now, ironically, the proximity of Fort Bragg insured that the burgeoning Fayetteville pastorate would have a much larger congregation than Mount Airy could ever hope to achieve with its static population. Such were the vicissitudes of life as a Baptist preacher, but Reverend Lane would have it no other way.

Though Hannah managed to keep a brave smile, her eyes were a telltale red when Nora, Wesley, and Elizabeth bade their visitor goodbye and returned to the parking lot—thereby granting father and daughter a final few minutes of privacy. The pair stood in silence for a long while, she absentmindedly fingering the handle of the larger of his two suitcases. This one was a rather sizable and shabby specimen, well worn by years of BSCNC travel on behalf of the Surry Baptist Association. The other one was much smaller and almost new, a gift from the parents of a lovely bride, at whose wedding ceremony he recently co-officiated down in Lumberton.

Time was running short. The shrill whistle of an approaching train could be heard from afar, as clanging, controlled roadways were traversed in the western outskirts of town. "I'm going to miss you something awful, sweetie," the old man said. He kissed his daughter on the forehead.

Hannah nodded silently, too choked up to speak. There were only six other people waiting on the platform, and that included a dour workman with his pushcart. It was he who would be taking care of whatever baggage was destined for Waco.

Squinting into the sun, Samuel looked down the tracks toward the sound of a growing rumble, but the train was not yet in view. "Tell the Browers again how much I appreciate their hospitality," he said.

"One way or another, we'll see each other this summer," Hannah told him. Both of them knew that it was just an empty claim, designed to soften the pain of parting, but they hugged to seal the pact. Somehow this mental game made what followed a bit easier to endure.

Another person chose that very moment to wander onto the scene unannounced—apparently there at the depot to greet an arriving passenger, as he brought with him no luggage. Hannah did not recognize him at first, but it was indeed the selfsame Eddie Shaughnessy who was in her American History class the year before. She dated him once, to the motion pictures at the end of June, but their evening together failed to produce any discernible effect whatsoever— much less of a romantic nature—and there was no contact between them since that solitary outing. It was Eddie's misfortune now to blunder into the hope that today's encounter was no chance meeting at all, but rather the handiwork of fate. He walked toward her with the confident step of one guided by destiny. Alas for him, such was not the case.

As Hannah saw it, this was no occasion for renewing old acquaintances, not with her father about to depart from her, perhaps forever, and she resented the boy's intrusion into her personal life. The incontrovertible words of James, brother of Jesus, rang in her mind with a vengeance: "Ye know not what shall be on the morrow. For what is your life? It is even a vapour, that appeareth for a little time, and then vanisheth away." The future was a great, densely veiled unknown, elevating these last, precious moments with her father to a stature far above the presumed pleasures of common socializing.

She had no intention of letting a virtual stranger come between them, and she put poor Eddie in his place with a curt "Hello" that sent him reeling, left to wonder what had just transpired. In truth, he had committed no infraction beyond finding himself in the wrong place at the wrong time. Nonetheless, her dismissive word stung him like a slap in the face, and thereafter he stood submissively, hands folded behind his back and staring straight ahead, awaiting his cousin's arrival from Goldthwaite. But the affront rankled, and he swore vengefully that it would be a snowy day in hell before he would speak to this minx again. She was too tomboyish for his tastes anyhow. The face was cute in a vaguely athletic sort of way—he gave her that much—but the body was without curves, hardly feminine at all. Who needed her?

The train appeared. What to Hannah had been a joyous sight just ten days earlier was now a bleak apparition, and her heart cried out in anguish. But there was of course no stopping the approach, as screeching metal against metal struck her through like a knife. When the Pullman cars came to rest, only five feet away from where she and her father were waiting on the platform, Hannah wept openly. She felt like a helpless infant, unable to shield her emotions with an adult veneer. "Oh, Papa!" she said. "I can't bear to have you so far away again!" This was more than homesickness. This was sensing that life, as she knew it, was veering beyond any hope of return.

Samuel held her in his protective arms for one last time, much as he had done so often before when she was just a girl. "There is no other way, child," he whispered in her ear. "It grieves me too, but we must accept this as being an instrument of God's will." His voice may have wavered the tiniest bit, but when he stood tall and smiled down at her, she noticed that his eyes remained perfectly clear and dry. Somehow, this remarkable human being seemed propped up by a powerful knowledge that far eclipsed the scope of her tender years, and Hannah could only gaze at him in wonder, through her tears, feeling the bittersweet pangs of love and imminent loss.

"'Board!" came the conductor's call, and Samuel obediently climbed up the hinged iron steps and made his way toward a window seat, from which he could watch her waving goodbye. She looked so lonely and bewildered, standing on the platform with the wind blowing through her scruffy blonde hair. Suddenly, the train lurched forward, and he mouthed the words "I love you" while she was still close enough to read his lips. He had no way of knowing it, but Hannah would persist in waving long after his angle of vision afforded any view of the passenger depot. She watched the train disappear around a curve as it headed toward the railway bridge across the Brazos, and only then did the raised right hand drop to her side. She stood there, still as a statue, until the rumble and plaintive whistle finally ebbed from her hearing, and he was gone.

Awaiting Hannah—at a respectful distance and undetected—was her friend from church, Belinda O'Rourke, who had arrived back in Waco from a visit home for the holidays. She patiently chatted with her cousin near the exterior door of the ticket agent's office, but Eddie was not pleasant company today. Still miffed, he was seated upon Belinda's upright suitcase, casting only the most grudging of glances toward Hannah. The preacher's daughter, for her part, continued to pay him no mind, despite the fact that she had regained a fair degree of her composure after just a moment to herself. As she began making her way toward the parking lot, Belinda called out her name.

When Hannah turned, she spotted her friend at once and cried out, "Lindy!" The two hugged, as coeds are wont to do after even the briefest of separations. "So that's why Eddie is here," she added.

Belinda nodded her head. "My mother asked him to pick me up, and he was kind enough to do it."

Still Hannah did not acknowledge the young man. She wiped away the last vestiges of tears from her eyes and asked, "How was your Christmas?"

"Fine," Belinda said. "We had a swell time, and I got some new shoes and a pretty blouse to wear to class." She was, to be charitable about it, homely of face, but there was no denying the attractiveness of her present attire, and invariably she was well groomed.

Eddie took a couple of steps in Hannah's direction. "*Of course* that's why I'm here."

Hannah acted as though his sudden reappearance took her by surprise. "I beg your pardon ..." Full of scorn, she emphasized each word in turn.

"Of course that's why I'm here," he said again. "What did you expect? That I came here to the passenger depot to see you?"

"And why would I think that?"

His face flushed red. "I don't appreciate the way you acted to me before the train came."

She glared at him and fired back. "Oh, you poor baby! Look, Eddie, I just happened to be saying goodbye to my one and only father—maybe for the last time ever—and I did not particularly want to have an audience looking over my shoulder at that very private moment. If that offended you, then so be it."

Eddie stood his ground. "And how was I to know that? He wasn't wearing a sign or anything."

"Well, you might have given it some thought, instead of just barging in like it was a fraternity mixer."

"What are you talking—?"

"I could see you circling around, making your play, and I don't like that stunt. I'm not anybody's fool."

Belinda stepped between them and reminded Eddie that she was due back at the dorm by five. Would he please drive her there now, so her roommate would not worry? "You know Carline. She'd probably turn me in to the Missing Persons Bureau."

Hannah pivoted on one foot like a soldier on the parade grounds and began marching away. "'Bye, Lindy. 'Bye, Lindy's cousin. Sorry for the misunderstanding." The apology did not sound very heartfelt.

Eddie stared at her for a moment and then shook his head in awe. It was difficult to stay angry with her for very long. All he could think of was how perky Hannah was when she lost her temper.

◆　　　◆　　　◆

If Wesley Brower had assumed that landing a job in radio sales was tantamount to instant success in the broadcast industry, he was either cruelly misinformed or the willing victim of his own wishful thinking. Whichever the case, he reported for duty on the first Saturday morning of 1945 with shoes freshly polished, necktie painstakingly knotted, and attitude keenly attuned to the challenge of joining KWXN's cadre of sales associates. Ever since his first day on the station payroll, Wesley had envied this gregarious brotherhood of advertising reps, who seemed to come and go as they pleased, unshackled by management and virtually unlimited in their earning power.

Sales manager Lee Graffen was there at the radio station to greet him, having valiantly given up a tee time at the golf course to show his young protégé the ropes. Winter, in any case, was never a felicitous season to play this maddening game, and that went a long way toward alleviating his sense of regret. The temperature hovered around forty degrees, a harsh condition that numbed the hands of all sportsmen and often proved ruinous to weekend hackers such as himself. Also conspiring against a golfer these days was the governmentally imposed War Time, an hour-long contrivance that deferred sunrise on January 6 until 8:31. As one of the men in his regular foursome said, "It's awfully hard to swing a golf club with a flashlight clamped between your teeth."

The novice's orientation session began with Graffen extolling the virtues of his esteemed profession. Salesmen, he attested with all due humility, were the true backbone of any business venture, generating the profits that kept the entire operation afloat. "There would be no KWXN without its sales team," he said. "Just ask the ladies in bookkeeping." Hearing Graffen tell it, a young intern might conclude that salesmen pursued their daily rounds for the sole purpose of making certain that payroll had plenty of cash to spread around to everyone else. Words such as "integrity," "ethical," and "selfless" were bandied about, not to mention "modern-day knights." Left unsaid, for obvious reasons, were the derisive monikers that more candid salespeople were fond of using among themselves, terms like "time peddler," "glad-hander," and even "commercial pickpocket."

Little did Wesley suspect that the business of radio sales was so ruthlessly competitive—and not only against the various rivals across town either. Within the station's own sales office, there was quite enough throat-cutting and backbiting to test the survival instincts of pugnacious veterans, men who chewed up rejection and call reluctance and spit them out like buckshot pellets. Clearly, Wesley was not in their class at this stage of his training, and before the day was out, he began to wonder whether he would ever be able to live up to the field exploits of someone like Calvin Trent or Bob Ed Moffett, let alone the justly celebrated Brian Sexton, who once closed seven productive sales within the span of two hours.

For one thing, the call sheet that Wesley inherited, and of which he was initially so very proud, consisted entirely of castoffs from the full-timers. Graffen referred to this ragtag assemblage of company names as the "Encore List," and it was so described at the top of the tattered, ink-smeared paper. No one had bothered to retype the names in more presentable fashion, which perhaps should have been some indication of the low esteem that these forty-two clients enjoyed in the eyes of men who should know. One former prospect was stricken from the list so vehemently that the pencil lead almost ground a three-inch-long slit through the paper. That, too, was not a promising sign. Neither was the cardboard folder that lay open on Graffen's chair. In an unsupervised moment, Wesley turned it over to reveal the handwritten label, "Junk Accounts."

Wesley was assigned a desk, but it was not a piece of furniture that he could rightfully call his own. During the week, this same space was occupied by a newcomer named Darrell Nimmer, who had migrated over from WACO just two weeks back. Graffen gave Wesley explicit instructions not to disturb anything on top of or within the desk, as regular members of the sales staff were entitled to expect their personal belongings and office supplies to be left intact over the weekend. No exceptions.

"May I use his telephone?" Wesley asked.

Graffen frowned. "Of course you may use the telephone. That's what it's there for."

The working arrangement for a weekend intern was a half-day shift, from eight o'clock until noon, the identical hours during which many companies were open on Saturdays. Wesley was instructed to record his sales activity on a separate time card from the usual one, as bookkeeping needed to be aware of the lower pay scale involved. Should any airtime be sold, he would receive a fifteen-percent commission, over and above the modest hourly wages. As Wesley saw it, this was just an extra source of income, and that was precisely how Lee Graffen portrayed it as well. "Nothing ventured, nothing gained," the sales manager told him. "Take your rate books home to study because there are few people in life more pathetic than the salesman who is not familiar with his product."

"Yes, sir."

"And another thing, Brower. You'll need to acquire a good, sturdy valise for transporting your papers to and from sales calls. Bring that with you next week. Whenever you're in the field, that briefcase will become your office."

"Do I get to drive a company car?"

Graffen was so stunned by this question that he laughed aloud. "A company car? Come now, son, be reasonable. I don't even get to drive a company car, and I'm in charge of the whole sales department. Do you think this station is made of money?"

"No, sir."

"And forget about a gasoline allowance too. I've lobbied for that since rationing came in, but no dice. The secret is just to make more money than you're spending."

Wesley swallowed hard, but Graffen plowed ahead.

"Most of our boys make a comfortable living—and, you know, every one of us had to start somewhere. Oh, and be sure to make all of your telephone calls in the first half-hour or so. We don't like for our salesmen to be lounging around the station when they could be out making personal contact with clients. No one's ever found a better way to sell than the old face-to-face."

When Wesley again looked down at his list of potential buyers, this time the names—numbered from one to forty-three, with number seventeen crossed out—did not seem as approachable as before. In fact, they had become downright intimidating. Graffen, being sales manager, sensed at once that the lad's confidence was shaken, and he endeavored to fortify it with a few kind words of encouragement. "I'll go out with you at first, just for a couple of courtesy calls, and you'll see how simple it really is. 'Servicing the account,' we say. Of course, these will be my regular customers, but the principle is the same."

And Graffen did make it seem awfully easy. Both clients he contacted actually walked to the front of their stores to shake his hand and offer a cup of coffee. One slapped him on the back, wondering how the wife was. The other was surprised to see him on a Saturday, assuming that he would be out on the links. "Too chilly, Vance. Besides, I've got to keep an eye on our new, hotshot salesman here—so he doesn't fill up all the good airtimes and leave nothing for me." Wesley gave a friendly smile, but client Vance did not even deign to introduce himself. Respect in the business world, it appeared, had to be earned the hard way.

Wesley Brower returned home that day feeling a bit shell-shocked. There was more to this selling than your average man on the street might suppose. Still, he was determined to have a fair go at it, so he issued a sacred promise to himself. By next Saturday, when he was making cold calls of his own, he would have the entire rate book committed to memory. At the very minimum, he did not want to look pathetic.

◆　　◆　　◆

Fatigue-clad GIs, having scoured the worst of that day's grease and grime from their hands, were lounging around the enlisted men's game room, awaiting chow. The lucky ones among them spent this half-hour of leisure time reading through letters received from family and friends back in the States. There was no envelope postmarked Kosciusko, but that was to be expected. The airman from that Mississippi town—a stopping point between Jackson and Columbus—had gotten two letters from his parents in just the past five days. What puzzled him was when the orderly called out "Rignold" and then proceeded to toss him a piece of mail that was postmarked "Waco, Tex."

It was the first correspondence that he had received from his final stateside duty station since leaving there three and a half months earlier. The envelope bore a pretty, stylized address that brought back unpleasant memories of a note that Nadine Cobb had sent to him long ago—prompting him and his buddy, Michael Tobin, into a mystifying encounter with Nadine and the sullen Ann-Rae Jansek. But when he tore open this envelope, Danny was relieved to see that the letter inside was not on Colonial Hotel stationery. It was from Elizabeth Brower.

He retreated to the relative privacy of his barracks hut, an odious, prefabricated structure that he now called home. It measured twenty feet by forty-eight feet of corrugated steel, with a ten-foot radius that served as a ceiling. But that was only along the very middle of this quasi half-cylinder, a generous height that served as an axis for what might be termed the hut's "fuselage." Elsewhere across the width, headroom diminished steadily until there was hardly any at all at the two sides, providing the men with scant clearance when they arose at reveille from their ramshackle cots. Even while stationed here in England, most of the men called them Quonset huts, which is what they were used to saying in the USA, but the more proper term was Nissen huts, for they were based on the 1916 design of an American-born Canadian engineer, Major Peter Norman Nissen. Whichever name applied, the fact remained that they were miserably cold affairs, and the three-foot-tall, coke-burning stove did little to help.

Danny sat upon his meticulously tucked blanket—so tight that a quarter could bounce off it—and pulled from the envelope a neatly trifolded sheet of paper that had presumably traveled by naval vessel all the way from the central reaches of America. Truth be told, he never suspected that he would hear from anyone in Texas, life being what it was and humanity moving about the world as never before. It stood to reason that people would lose contact with one another and turn their attention to present, more pressing matters. And yet here was a note from "Lizzie," daughter of that nice USO lady who taught him how to send a voice-letter to the folks back home. It was odd, the way relationships could begin by sheer coincidence and then carry over into the next chapter of one's life. Grafton Underwood had nothing whatever to do with Waco, but a tenuous connection was established between the two by the mere act of jotting down a few words and dropping a stamped envelope into the mail slot of the local post office.

"Sweet kid!" Will Gott said. "Is this the way they grow 'em in Mississippi?" The corporal appeared to be examining a small snapshot, and it was obvious that he liked what he saw.

Danny looked up. "What about Mississippi?"

"Ain't that where you're from, Rignold?"

"What about it?" Suddenly curious, he reached for the picture, but he was not quick enough.

Will pulled it away and gave a vulgar laugh. "Who's the Mississippi miss?"

"The what?"

Will kissed the photo. "The lass from back home?"

"Let me see that!"

"Not until you give me her address, pal."

It dawned on Danny that this picture must have fallen from the letter when he removed it from the envelope, and Will Gott had picked it up off the floor. "Okay, you've had your fun," he said. "Now hand it over!" And he meant business.

"All right, all right. You don't have to get hostile about it." (Will pronounced it "hoss-TILE.") Grinning with glee, he handed the snapshot over, but ever so slowly.

Danny glanced at the pert face and slipped the photo back into its envelope. "Nope, sorry. Not Mississippi." He showed no change of expression.

"Well, then who's the gal?" Will asked.

Chris Lakey was also standing there, still shirtless after washing up. "Hey, let me see, Danny boy!"

"Well, you bums won't relax until I tell you, so she's my ... niece."

"Aw, no one's niece looks like that," Will said. "Have a look, Chris."

Danny relented and held the photograph out, at arm's length, for both of them to see. Chris was impressed too, nodding his head and even giving a whistle of approval. "How's she related to you?" he asked.

"She's my father's sister's daughter from Iowa. The name's Ruth."

Will was not convinced. "Then why does it say 'Love, Lizzie' on the back? Lizzie's not short for Ruth, is it?" He grinned, proud of his airtight case.

Danny turned the snapshot over and saw that Will was correct. "No," he told him, "Lizzie's my aunt—well, it's really Elizabeth—and her daughter, like I said, is Ruth. Ruth Smith."

Chris chuckled. "Ruth Smith, huh? That doesn't sound much like the name of a niece."

"Why not? Everyone in the world named Ruth Smith is probably somebody's niece."

The men accepted that reasoning, but Will wanted one small favor. "Give me her address, Dan."

"Not a chance. I sure don't want someone like you in my family."

When his pals walked away, Danny sat back down on the cot. He wondered why this girl would have bothered writing to him. After all, Elizabeth was much too young to be considered an actual girlfriend. Or was she? Try as he might, he could not remember exactly, except for the fact that her mother seemed to object to his perceived interest. Was she sixteen or seventeen? Sixteen, he thought, but she seemed a little older than that. No doubt about it: this war made young people grow up much faster than in peacetime, and that was not necessarily a bad thing. Even at her age, Elizabeth already had two jobs, working at a filling station for pay and volunteering at the servicemen's club for free. And that did not count her full-time studies at school. She was also active in scrap drives and household conservation, not to mention writing morale-boosting letters to soldiers and sailors abroad, most of whom she did not know beyond their names on a list. Maybe that was it—he was just a name on her list. But then why would she sign the picture "Love, Lizzie"?

The off-duty men from his platoon, about twelve or thirteen of them, had started making their way to the mess hall, so Danny hurriedly unfolded the letter and began to read. First, though, he studied the photograph that Elizabeth mailed. She looked a lot more mature than her years might suggest, especially in the glamorous pose that she decided to send to him in England. It was a very attractive shot of her—any man would agree with that—but he could not shake the sensation that she looked quite different here than she did in person. The innocence was missing, the charming remnants of girlhood that still resided within most young ladies who had barely attained the age of sixteen.

> Hello, Danny. You don't mind if I call you by your first name, do you, Mr. Rignold? (ha ha) This tiny note is just to let you know that I have not dismissed you from my mind completely. No, not completely, although the passage of time does make one forget. For instance, I sometimes cannot remember what you even look like. Will you please send me a photograph of yourself? I have sent mine to you, in advance, as an even exchange. But what I do remember is that sad "nightcap" and of course the final minutes we spent together in my mom's car. As a matter of fact, I'll never forget that time, which seemed to me as beautiful as a romantic movie, and we were the stars. Do you remember me? I hope maybe the snapshot I sent will help. My friend, Olive, and I took some pictures at a photo booth in the dime store. She's in half of them, but I thought you would rather see only me! Sorry the edges are not perfectly straight, but she cut the very next frame to it (I guess she's not too good with scissors), and this one was my favorite of me alone. I hope you like it and will carry it with you. I pray that you are safe and that sometime in the near future you will decide to come back and see us (ME) in Texas.
>
> Love, Lizzie

He laid the letter down for a moment and reexamined the girl's photograph. Clearly, too many years separated them in age for any serious involvement, but that did not lessen the genuine pain he felt in missing her. Someday, perhaps, he would return to Waco with his wife and kids and say hello once again to this lovely Elizabeth Brower. Maybe she, too, would be married by then and have children of her own. Without warning, a chill went up his spine, and he felt sure that he knew the reason why. Then and there, the last person in a lonely Nissen hut in Northamptonshire, he thanked God that he had been chosen for the privilege of rescuing her from the clutches of that thug. Danny folded up the letter and inserted it back inside the envelope, all the while admiring the soft, pleasing penmanship that spelled out his APO address. Then he carefully placed the precious snapshot inside his wallet, where only he would be aware of its very existence. As she requested, he would indeed carry it with him.

◆　　　◆　　　◆

Four and a half months had elapsed since that day the American Red Cross agent delivered to Hermann and Gertrude a parcel containing their son's effects, retrieved from a battlefield on the Mediterranean coast of Tunisia. Little did the Moeks suspect that their lives would ever again be touched so profoundly by that same charitable organization—only this time in a much happier context than when Robert Albright paid his solemn visit.

An unexpected letter from the agency's Waco-McLennan County chapter provided the first inkling of what was in store for this bereaved German-American couple. When Gertrude saw the sender's familiar address, 1020 Austin Avenue, she recoiled in dread, perhaps subconsciously reliving the emotions of that terrible day—back in the spring of 1943—when the initial notification of Conrad's death came in the mail. This time, however, the correspondent was the executive secretary of the local chapter, Paul T. Darwin, and he personalized the message by including mention of his own wife in an introductory paragraph that read, "The Red Cross is in need of help, with regard to a local placement problem that requires a fluent knowledge of the German language. Mrs. Darwin and I have been informed by our Houston chapter that you may be able to provide us with the requisite assistance." This was something out of the ordinary.

The letter arrived at the Moek home on Friday, January 19, the final full day of Franklin Delano Roosevelt's third term. It would be an easy date to remember because when Hermann drove Gertrude and himself to Darwin's office late the next morning, all of the networks were broadcasting the President's fourth inaugural speech, live, from the portico of the White House. So concise was it that the Moeks heard the entire address—only 573 words long—between their house and the Red Cross headquarters downtown. "And so today," the Commander in Chief proclaimed, "in this year of war, 1945, we have learned lessons, at a fearful cost, and we shall profit by them."

Darwin, too, had been listening to the speech, but he switched off his table radio in the midst of NBC's subsequent commentary when the front door opened and shut. His guests, understandably baffled by the strange request, made their way very warily toward where he was standing to greet them, but his broad smile carried swift assurance that they had nothing to fear from this meeting. He said, "Mr. Moek, Mrs. Moek, so good of you to come," and ushered them to his office, where two utilitarian chairs had been arranged on the opposite side of the desk from where he would be sitting. "Please," Darwin told them. He motioned with his hand, and the couple seated themselves in silence, awaiting whatever news was to follow. "Coffee?" Gertrude accepted a cup, but Hermann declined. "Cigar?" Hermann shook his head.

"You must be confused by all of this, so I'll get right to the point," Darwin said. "There is a young man named Klaus-Peter Schang, and the boy—he's around nine or ten, I think—is on his way to the United States to meet his aunt. Both of his parents were killed in an air raid on Düren, Germany, a couple of months ago, and the International Red Cross has recommended that he be sent to live with his next of kin. Klaus-Peter is aboard a returning Liberty ship that has linked up with a convoy to cross the Atlantic. And that's really all I know about the boy, except to say that his late mother's sister has been judged to be unfit to take custody."

Hermann squirmed in his chair. "Why wasn't this established before the boy left his home?"

Darwin looked a little embarrassed. "The aunt's background was okayed without her knowledge—just a cursory check—but is no longer acceptable to authorities. The lady and her boyfriend were involved in some petty thefts where he works in Deer Park, and now, of course, she has a jail record."

"So that's where we come in," Hermann said.

Darwin smiled. "So that's where you come in. The boy could be sent to an orphanage in the Houston area, or he could be delivered into the care of foster parents. The problem is, Klaus-Peter speaks no English at all, so Mr. Albright suggested that I contact you to inquire whether you might be interested. I do know that you lost your son in the war."

Gertrude grasped Hermann's hand. "Goodness!"

"You don't need to give me an answer right away," Darwin said, "but the boy will be arriving in Texas by the middle of next week, so if you could decide by then, that would make for a much smoother transition for him. He has gone through some pretty harrowing times, as you might well imagine, and he needs as stable a life as possible."

Gertrude, who was taken by more intense surprise than her husband, could only say, "Dear me!"

Hermann remained outwardly calm throughout, but he did tell the Red Cross officer, "Maybe I will have that coffee after all."

Darwin chuckled at the belated request and said, "I perfectly understand. This is a life-changing decision, and it is not to be taken lightly." He poured the coffee. "Cream and sugar, Mr. Moek?"

"Just black will be fine, please."

Darwin handed the cup to Hermann, who nodded his thanks and blew a stream of air into the hot coffee.

Smiling at the couple, Darwin took his seat and leaned back slightly. "The fact that you have not already said 'no' tells me that you are at least considering the proposal. But we at the Red Cross want for you to be entirely comfortable with your part in this matter."

"Thank you, sir," Hermann said.

"Please sleep on it. In fact, take a few days to think it over."

Gertrude stared at her husband.

"Then," the Red Cross agent continued, "whenever you reach a decision, give me a call here at 521, and we'll take care of all the arrangements. Or, if you prefer, Mayme and I will be pleased to have you ring us at home anytime, day or night." Gertrude seemed bewildered, so he added, "My wife, you see, is also our chapter secretary." Darwin began to give Hermann a black-and-white business card, which prominently displayed (in black ink) the organization's traditional cross insignia. But, as only his office number was printed upon it, he took an extra moment to write down in pencil his home telephone number, 4178, for further reference.

"Would this be a temporary situation?" Hermann asked.

"Raising the boy?"

"Yes, sir."

"Oh, no, Mr. Moek. You would have full, legal custody of Klaus-Peter, entitling you and Mrs. Moek to raise him as your own son. Our lawyers are quite proficient in this area, I can assure you."

"When would all of this come about?"

"Well, of course, this being a bureaucracy, there still remains a lot of red tape to cut through—paperwork, in-processing, medical testing, maybe even a short period of quarantine. And, as you can appreciate, there are some international regulations involved, and those must be followed explicitly. I would venture to guess that you could assume custody of the child in two weeks—three at most."

"What if the boy's aunt tries to gain custody from us?"

Darwin shook his head. "Her name has been stricken from consideration. She's out of the picture for good." Hermann seemed unconvinced, so Darwin leaned forward, as one might do in divulging classified information. "To be honest with you folks, the boy's aunt never did actively seek custody, so the field is clear. All we need from you is a simple yes or no, and we'll proceed accordingly."

The Moeks looked at each other with the unspoken clarity that only a long and close marriage can achieve.

Hermann swallowed a sip of coffee, thought for a moment, and stated with profound certainty, "Just show us any papers that we need to sign."

And Gertrude added, "We don't need to t'ink it over, Mr. Darwin. D'is boy is d'e answer to our prayers."

Now it was Paul T. Darwin who was surprised. "So you both are sure this is what you want?"

"Yes, sir," Hermann told him. "We are sure."

Darwin opened the file folder of Klaus-Peter Schang and withdrew an application form for the couple to read over and sign. "Rarely is a case as complex as this one resolved so quickly," he said, and there was a sense of relief in his voice. "I really don't know what we would have done, had you not been willing to accept this offer. Klaus-Peter will be on American soil in less than a week, and it would have been a frightening experience for him to be housed with total strangers—none of whom could communicate with the boy."

"We will provide him with a loving home, Mr. Darwin," Hermann said. "And we will teach him to speak English."

Wiping away a tear, Gertrude told the Red Cross agent, "We will raise him to be an American."

◆   ◆   ◆

After the introductory week, Wesley's first two Saturdays in radio sales came and went without conspicuous success, and he quickly lowered his sights to recouping the cost of the new briefcase. So far, he had invested more than he earned, an unhealthy situation that violated Lee Graffen's First Commandment: "The secret is just to make more money than you're spending." Wesley's black leather satchel—serviceable but hardly extravagant—had set him back six dollars, wholesale, and this despite the fact that it came from Superior Office Supply. Being a son of the proprietor did not mean that merchandise was simply his for the asking. Inventory on the shelves had a direct correlation with money in the bank.

One thing working in Wesley's favor was knowledge of his product. Even before his second day as a salesman, January 20, the KWXN rate book was ingrained in his memory, enabling him to quote prices for run-of-station or designated dayparts with the fluency of an auctioneer. He was ready to let the ratings service of C. E. Hooper, Incorporated, guide him to the promised land, providing ironclad statistics that would render his sales pitch virtually irresistible.

Ever since the 1935-1936 season, Hooper numbers had been the primary gauge of audience size, charting telephone calls made to random listeners in from twenty-eight to thirty-six major cities where the programs were carried. For network offerings, they comprised the Bible of broadcast sales, and many a local contract was written by demonstrating that, for instance, CBS's "Take It or Leave It" comfortably bettered both NBC's "Hour of Charm" and the Blue Network's "The Life of Riley" in the Sunday evening slot that they shared.

With the passage of time, Wesley gradually came to accept as fact the suspected notion that all forty-two businesses that appeared on his list were nothing more than jettisoned accounts from other sales representatives on the staff. Little wonder, then, that the firms' owners, managers, and shopkeepers were less than hospitable when they saw this naïve high schooler make an unsolicited call with his briefcase and uneasy smile. Far from enjoying an established rapport with his clients, Wesley Brower was confronted with the disconsolate challenge of overcoming months or even years of rejection, distrust, and animosity. His expectations deflated, he began to consider it a moral victory to be leaving empty-handed so long as his host did not instruct him never to show his face again.

Among the least unfriendly of his Saturday morning acquaintances was Rob Glynn, a mustached gentleman of about forty who ran The Smoker's Den on weekends for owner Donnie Lee Satterfield. Perhaps a bit shy himself, Mr. Glynn appeared to feel some sympathy for the neophyte salesman, engaging him in conversation when there was no customer around to occupy his attention. Wesley, in turn, appreciated the store manager's civil attitude and, even more shocking, the offer of coffee, which was extended on just his second visit. No advertising was likely to come of such hospitality—Rob Glynn was a farmer by trade, and only Mr. Satterfield could purchase airtime—but for Wesley this respite proved to be a safe harbor where he could relax for fifteen minutes or so before heading back to the streets to complete his rounds like a glorified Fuller Brush man. Accordingly, he decided right away to make this stop a weekly routine. After all, not even the legendary Brian Sexton worked every minute of his waking hours.

On his third Saturday as a salesman, when he entered The Smoker's Den and timidly waved to Rob Glynn, Wesley's heart skipped a beat, and he had difficulty drawing his next breath. Sitting on a tall, wooden stool behind the counter, affixing price tags to pouches of pipe tobacco, was a lovely girl whose straight, honey-brown hair glimmered in the morning light. She had not seen him as yet, but he could not take his eyes off her charming profile. As casually as possible, he walked over to the life-sized cigar store Indian—garrisoned indoors to cheat the effects of weather— and managed to use it as cover to steal a more intimate peek, now from a vantage point of less than twenty feet. Still she did not look up, so Wesley decided to peer around the other side of the Indian, hoping against hope that ...

"Hello, Mr. Bower," came Rob's cheerful greeting.

Wesley turned with a guilty smile and, improvising, patted the Indian's stomach. "There must not be too many of these around anymore."

"I don't guess," Rob said. "You know, Mr. Satterfield bought Tecumseh in Davenport, Iowa, of all places."

"Oh?" Wesley glanced at the girl, who kept to her work.

"Yessiree. Brought him down here standing in the flatbed of his delivery truck, along with some of the furniture you see in here. That table and fringed lamp came from there too."

"Are they for sale?"

"Nope. Only coffee and tobacco."

Just then, the girl looked up from her labors, and Wesley was finally able to catch a glimpse of her sweet face. He took a deep breath.

"Poor Tecumseh," Rob said. "He was nearly decapitated by a low bridge in Little Rock. You can feel where the gash is."

"Huh?"

"Go ahead. Feel the back of his head."

Wesley reached up, and sure enough, a small chunk of the Indian's cranium was missing—about the size of a plum.

"It was nighttime, so Mr. Satterfield never could find the missing piece, though he got down on his hands and knees to try. Must've splintered into a zillion pieces." Rob chuckled. "He said when that Indian hit the bridge, going sixty miles an hour, it made such a God-awful noise that they must've heard it all the way to Missouri."

Rob laughed so hard at his own storytelling that he had to wipe away the tears, and this made Wesley laugh out loud too. He watched the girl roll her eyes and stifle a smile.

"Anyways," Rob added, "I just painted over the gouge, and no one's the wiser." He paused for a moment to admire the statue. "You know, whatever else you might think of Mr. Satterfield, he's got a nose for a bargain."

Wesley noticed that the young lady now had her hand raised high in the air, as if wishing to answer a question at school. He whispered to Rob, "Uh ... I think that girl over there wants you for something."

When Rob turned to her, she asked him, "How much is the Bond Street?"

"Fifteen."

"What about the Revelation pocket package?"

"Same price, honey—fifteen cents."

The perplexed look on Wesley's face induced Rob to explain. "She's my daughter, Pippa."

"Pippa," Wesley repeated.

Rob remembered another instruction. "Oh, and those two brands need to be grouped next to each other on the shelf. That's the way Philip Morris wants them displayed."

"Yes, Daddy."

He proudly whispered to Wesley, "She's a very good worker—for someone just earning a little extra spending money like this."

The boy nodded his head.

Then, without warning, Rob told the girl. "Honey, come over here for just a minute."

Wesley had mixed emotions. He wanted to meet her, of course, but no one could possibly live up to that enchanting first impression.

"Pippa, this is Wesley Bower, a salesman at one of the radio stations."

"Nice to meet you, Mr. Bower," she said with a bashful smile.

"Same here." Wesley did not quite know what else to add by way of pleasant conversation. "Uh ... but it's Brower, with two 'r's. Wesley Brower."

"Oops, sorry," Rob said. "My mistake."

Wesley shrugged. "That's okay. You must see hundreds of people every day."

"No, not hundreds. Tobacco's a little scarce these days—most of it's being shipped overseas to the fighting men—and we all know about coffee rationing."

"Yes, sir."

"Pippa here is a senior in high school."

"Really? So am I." Wesley smiled at the girl, but then a puzzling thought occurred to him. "How come I've never seen you at school? I thought I knew just about everybody at Waco High—especially the seniors. And I'm sure I would have noticed *you*." He hoped that last remark did not sound too much like a gigolo.

"We live over in Axtell," her father said, "and we think Pippa has a chance of being valedictorian there."

She giggled. "Well, a slim chance."

Wesley grinned at her. "No worry that I'll have to deliver a commencement speech."

"Ah, but you're a big tycoon," Rob said. He patted him on the shoulder. "Lots of the kids aren't, and that makes a difference in study time."

"Don't you use a lot of gas, driving back and forth from Axtell?" the boy asked.

"It would, but I only come in on Saturdays—just to give the owner a day off. Mr. Satterfield's my brother-in-law, you know. He married my older sister."

"I thought you'd have a 'C' sticker, since you're a farmer."

"Nope, just an 'A.' Driving the family car to town isn't considered to be farm use."

Pippa interrupted. "Excuse me, Daddy, but I have to get back to work."

"Certainly, dear."

"Nice to meet you, Mr. Brower," the girl said. She dipped slightly at the knees, the modern equivalent of a curtsy.

Wesley nodded politely but could think of no words to convey his true feelings. And perhaps that was just as well.

A few minutes later, as he was about to leave The Smoker's Den, he called out to her. "Maybe I'll see you again sometime."

"Yes, maybe," she shouted back from the other side of the room. But he could hardly hear what she said because an elderly gentleman had entered the store, causing the overhead bell to jingle.

"Pippa only comes with me to work about once a month," Rob said. He turned his head for a moment to give the white-haired customer a smile. "She's a country girl, you know, and has her animals to look after. She certainly does love those horses." He watched the old man head toward the tobacco counter. "Pippa does a bang-up job for us too, even if I do say so myself. And it helps out Della Ryman—lets her do some occasional volunteering for the Salvation Army."

As Wesley walked out the front door, he could not resist looking back one more time, only to be confronted by the disappointment that Pippa Glynn was not so easily distracted from her chores.

◆　　◆　　◆

"Hannah! There's someone down here to see you." Her landlady's voice disturbed a peaceful evening at home.

"Coming, Mrs. B. I'll be right there."

Margo Burke and her current boyfriend, Timmy Royster, were standing just inside the house when Hannah reached the bottom of the stairs. "Grab a coat," Margo told her. "We're going to the concert."

"What concert?" Hannah asked. She was in no mood to leave the comfort of her bedroom at such an hour on a Thursday night.

Margo laughed. "The *centennial* concert, of course."

"Oh, my goodness! If I never hear that word again ..."

The Republic of Texas chartered Baylor University precisely one hundred years earlier, on February 1, 1845, and President Pat Neff and his administration were pulling out all stops to mark the occasion. Already it had been a long day of campus celebrations.

"Come with us. It'll be fun," Timmy told her, "and I'll even take y'all for a bite to eat afterwards."

"Thanks for the invitation, but no." Hannah chewed her gum loudly, trying to think of a believable excuse. "You two go. I'm about ready to take a bath."

Timmy was becoming impatient, so he pulled Margo aside. "Look, it's already 7:40. Go ahead and tell her."

Margo forced a smile. "All right, Hannah, here's the real story," she said. "Timmy's roommate is going too, and–"

"And he needs a date," Timmy added.

"Well, I don't go out on blind dates," Hannah told them. "What's his name? Do I know him?"

"Bob ... and I don't think so."

"Just Bob?"

"Bob Madsen."

"He's a junior, majoring in journalism–a swell guy," Margo said. "Works for the *Lariat*."

By now, Timmy was not above begging. "Please, Hannah. I promised him you'd go with us. Don't let me down."

Hannah shook her head. "Sorry."

"He's dropping out of Baylor to enlist," Margo added.

"And so ... you're appealing to my sense of patriotism."

"If that's what you want to call it, yes."

Out of desperation, Timmy spoke from the heart. "Come on, Hannah. It's not a real date–just someone for Bob to sit next to at the concert."

"Let Margo sit between you two boys."

"That's not the same thing, and you know it."

"But why me?"

"Because you're the only attractive girl I know who's unattached." He looked at her for a couple of seconds and then gave a sheepish grin. "Well, the only one I could think of on such short notice."

"At least you're honest about it."

"Yep, that's us. Honest through and through." He winked at Margo, who giggled.

"What time would I be back? I have to work a swing shift tomorrow, so I'll need a good night's sleep."

"You'll be back by 10:30, guaranteed. And to show my good faith, I'll even drop you off here before we go eat."

Hannah hesitated but then, with a frown, agreed. "Okay, you've talked me into it. I must be a real sucker."

Margo and her boyfriend both smiled. "You won't regret it," Timmy said.

Unconvinced, Hannah glared at him. "I'll be down in five minutes." She took a couple of steps up the stairs and then, turning back toward them, pointed a finger. "I'm just doing this as a favor to you two—and Uncle Sam."

"Understood," Margo told her, and Timmy added, "We won't forget this."

The wooden double doors were already shut by the time Timmy and Margo arrived at Waco Hall with their reluctant guest. The first thing Timmy did was try to spot his roommate in the lobby, but Bob was nowhere to be found. Three student ushers were gathering up their supply of undistributed programs, and they were the only people there.

"Has it started yet?" Timmy asked one of them. She was a tall, very thin girl who seemed none too interested in her job.

"I don't think so," she told him. "We just closed the doors a few seconds ago."

That was when a student with wire eyeglasses came running up to the others, a winter coat draped over his shoulder. "Where have you been?" the young man asked. "I went around the corner to see if you were there. It's after eight." He spoke much too loudly, and the ushers were concerned that his voice might be heard inside the auditorium.

"I'll tell you later," Timmy said. He snatched four programs from the nearest usher and scampered toward the central door. "Bob ... meet Hannah. Hannah ... Bob." He gave a program to each.

No music could be heard, so they assumed it was permissible to enter. Timmy opened the door, and the four of them hurried inside. What worked to their disadvantage was the fact that the auditorium was darkened by now, except of course for the orchestral lighting, and the broad doorway through which they passed briefly emitted enough illumination to attract the glances of many dozens of concertgoers at the rear of the hall. Worse yet for Timmy, Margo, Hannah, and Bob, their graceless incursion was rather noticeable from the podium area. As they searched in vain for four seats together—not an easy task in such a dimly lit section—they sensed a tension in the air and heard a low murmuring among the audience. Hannah was the first to look up, and she was mortified by what she saw.

In many social settings, it is quite acceptable—even fashionable—to be a little late. Evidently, a Baylor Symphony Orchestra concert in 1945 was not one of them. There on stage, defiantly staring at them, stood the authoritarian figure of conductor Daniel Sternberg: hands on hips, towering a good nine feet tall, as motionless as some cruel predator ready to strike. This grisly phantasm seemed like a bad dream to Hannah, and her escape from it was every bit as ineffectual as in a nightmare. Urgently she tapped Bob on the back, and he in turn relayed the alarm to the other two. All knew at once that they were responsible for a serious breach of concert etiquette. Margo and Timmy sat down in the first two adjacent vacancies they came to in the row, and Bob settled upon an empty seat all by his lonesome. That left Hannah to scurry for the aisle—carelessly stepping on toes as she went—before retreating another three rows and finally landing wherever a chair was not already accommodating somebody else's hindquarters. Her new neighbors glowered at her, but at least she no longer was a vulnerable target for the conductor's remorseless eyes. The hall grew quiet.

Finally satisfied that this pocket of rebellion had been quashed, Maestro Sternberg turned briskly to his players, smiled at the concertmaster, raised his baton, and gave the downbeat. Six minutes late, this culmination of Baylor's opening salvo of centennial observances had begun. To Hannah, it felt like it was at least ten o'clock.

The performance itself was just a blur to this unmusical North Carolinian, but early the next day she noticed the printed program, still lying unread on top of her dresser. From it, she learned that the concert had opened with a world premiere by Daniel Sternberg himself, his *Centennial Overture*. Maybe that was why he was so annoyed by the disruption, she reasoned. It was his own piece, and it had never been played before. Then two members of the Baylor faculty, Lino Bartoli and Mary Ellen Proudfit, joined the orchestra's string players for Johann Sebastian Bach's Concerto in D minor for Two Violins. Following intermission, the Baylor Symphony played the *Academic Festival Overture* of Johannes Brahms, the "Unfinished" Symphony of Franz Schubert, and then the conductor's own setting for orchestra of the university alma mater, "That Good Old Baylor Line."

As for her "date," Hannah never did see Bob again, except to watch him walk past at intermission. That was at the very instant when four fellow Bible majors had surrounded her and were frantically discussing Dr. Benjamin Oscar Herring's forthcoming test in Comparative Religion (Bible 220). A rendezvous was destined not to be, for after the second half of the concert was over, Hannah—still, of course, seated at the extreme rear of Waco Hall—was one of the very first to exit. Seemingly hundreds of people passed by her in the lobby before she finally espied Margo strolling hand-in-hand with her boyfriend. She offered them some chewing gum. When they declined, she put two sticks in her own mouth. Hannah looked around, but Bob was conspicuous in his absence.

"We said goodbye to him for you in there," Margo told her. "Too bad you never got to know him very well. I think you would have liked him a lot."

"I thought you were going to take him out to eat with you," Hannah said. "I hope I didn't ruin your plans—but, you know, I've got a full day of classes tomorrow, plus eight hours of war work."

Margo glanced at Timmy, who confided that Bob was not even aware that they were going out to eat afterwards. "That was just our way of getting you to come to the concert. We thought a romantic evening—with a free meal on top of it—might do the trick. Everything was for your own good."

"How so?"

Margo lowered her voice. "You need to get out more often. We both think you're far too pretty to be an old maid, don't we, Tim?" He nodded his head.

Hannah chuckled. "I'm only twenty."

"But you never date," Margo said. "How do you expect to find a husband like that?"

She shrugged her shoulders. "If it's God's will, I'll marry. If not, I won't." She blew a small bubble with her gum.

So much for her unavailing date with Bob Madsen, who would leave Baylor a week later for the military. Hannah felt sure that Uncle Sam would forgive her.

◆　◆▸　◆

On the evening of Tuesday, February 13, Americans began hearing reports over the various radio networks that British bombers were laying waste to the ancient German city of Dresden, unleashing a merciless fire storm, the likes of which the world had never seen. Newspapers carried graphic descriptions the next day, indicating that two successive waves of Lancasters from RAF Bomber Command—244 of them at 2213 hours, local time, and 529 at 0130 hours— dropped 1,478 tons of high explosives and 1,182 tons of incendiaries. So intense was the rising column of heat that it burned oxygen from the sky and generated winds of hurricane strength, with temperatures climbing above one thousand degrees Fahrenheit.

At 1212 hours on Wednesday, a torrent of 316 B-17s from the US 8th Air Force scored hits with 771 tons of bombs on the flaming city, and a Thursday raid by another 210 American B-17s dropped 461 tons of explosives. In all, the hellish immolation lasted for four days and could be seen from as far away as two hundred miles. Of the city's 700,000 inhabitants, plus a half-million refugees who were fleeing Soviet troops from the east, some 135,000 were killed, many of them suffocating in oxygen-starved bomb shelters or baked alive in the superheated atmosphere that engulfed Dresden.

The extent of devastation was shocking, even by modern standards in warfare, but the terrible statistics took on a much more human dimension for readers and listeners who had family members in the targeted area. One such emigrant of Germany— now living in Waco, Texas, with her husband—was Gertrude Moek, whose father, mother, and two sisters were all residents of Dresden. When she heard mention of her beautiful city on the Elbe River, she wept openly for her immediate family and for the many other relatives and friends she had left behind, probably never to see again. But it was only sadness that she felt, never hatred for the American and British airmen. That emotion she reserved especially for the tyrannical Herr Hitler, without whose brutal assault on humankind the city of her birth would still be standing, and her loved ones would not have been displaced, maimed for life, or suffered an agonizing death.

And yet, as quite often happens in this earthly existence, one's personal tragedy can soon be countervailed by a personal blessing of equal or even greater magnitude. Believers would call it the hand of God.

At the very time that American crews were returning to base after their first of two bombing missions over Dresden, Hermann Moek was conversing on the telephone with Paul T. Darwin, Executive Secretary of the Waco-McLennan

County chapter of the American Red Cross. The purpose of Darwin's early-morning call was to notify the German-American couple that their nine-year-old charge, Klaus-Peter Schang, had been cleared by doctors and US immigration officials. He was now perfectly free to begin living under their guardianship, with the full force of law.

Just a moment later, Hermann—electing to speak in English—told his wife the good news. "Trudy," he said. "Our boy, young Klaus-Peter, will be arriving here on Friday. We must have the house ready for him, so he will feel welcome."

Overcome with joy, Gertrude burst into tears. "Oh, dear God! I cannot believe our dreams are coming true." Following his lead, she too spoke in their adopted language.

The automobile that pulled into the Moeks' driveway just before eleven o'clock on Friday morning was not a Red Cross vehicle, as they had envisioned, but rather a black, governmental Oldsmobile with no distinguishing features whatsoever, save for the federal EXEMPT license plate. Gertrude pulled back the curtain from the front window and watched two men in dark suits emerge from the driver and passenger sides. This passenger, whom she recognized to be Mr. Albright, slammed his door and then reached out to open the rear door for a brown-haired youngster who carried a battered suitcase that was nearly as long as he was tall. Hermann thought it more civil to remain seated until a knocking was heard, but his wife could not suppress her excitement, and he certainly did not feel it appropriate to scold her for being so happy. Indeed, his tolerant smile could easily have been construed as a sign of approval.

After Hermann greeted the men at the door and invited them in, Albright removed his hat and told him, "Hello, Mr. Moek. Nice to see you again." Klaus-Peter did not move until the other man turned and said to him, "KO-men zee hair-INE." He spoke haltingly and with a thick American accent, which suggested that his phonetic rendering may have been one of just a few basic expressions he had committed to memory for the occasion. Still, the boy understood and did as he was instructed. Once inside, rather stiff greetings and introductions were exchanged, and with a handshake, the G-man formally identified himself as "Roy Brown, Immigration Bureau, Labor Department." He was curt and businesslike but not unfriendly. In fact, he grinned broadly when Gertrude knelt down to kiss the boy on his cheek.

Robert Albright thanked the Moeks for being willing to assume responsibility for young Klaus-Peter. In turn, Hermann expressed his appreciation to the Red Cross agent for his crucial role in placing the German lad in their foster home. "Without your kind suggestion—and remembering the loss of our son—none of this would have happened."

"My pleasure," Albright said. "You know, sir, difficult placements such as this do not always end so happily—but it sure is nice when they do."

Not until the men had left did Gertrude and Hermann come to realize that the boy was yet to utter a single word in their presence. During the brief proceedings, he stood by silently, watching with interest but comprehending nothing of what was being discussed about his future in America. At first encounter, he seemed a surprisingly well-adjusted boy, not at all sullen like a typical war orphan whose young soul was tortured by horrific memories of pain and death.

Hermann walked over to the lad and leaned forward, hands on knees. He began conversing with him in his native tongue. *"Are you hungry, my boy?"* he asked.

"No, sir," the youngster said in German. He fidgeted, looking down at his shoes.

"Mrs. Moek would be delighted to fix something for you to eat."

"No, thank you, sir. We stopped to eat."

"Are you sure?"

"Yes, sir."

Gertrude could see that Klaus-Peter was a little intimidated by the man of the house, so she took the lad by his hand and led him over to the sofa. She said in German, *"Let's sit next to each other here and have a nice talk. Would you like that?"*

Klaus-Peter shrugged his shoulders.

"Do you like dogs?" she asked.

His face lit up with interest. *"Yes."*

"We used to have a German shepherd by the name of Maximilian. Would you like to see a picture of Max?"

"Yes, ma'am."

She turned to her husband. "Hermann, will you get me d'e photo album, please?" They had vowed to speak to each other only in English when the boy was present—and as soon as possible in conversing with the youngster too.

Dutifully, Hermann opened the book cabinet—eager to be of service—but then his eyes caught sight of eleven nearly identical photograph albums, standing upright, side by side. "Which one do you want, dear?"

"D'e one wit' Maxie in it, of course." She smiled and asked the boy, *"Do you like music?"*

Without waiting for his response, she stood up and lumbered over to the radio console. Dialing its frequency knob, she found a station that was playing dance tunes. *"Do you like American music, Klaus-Peter?"*

"Yes, ma'am."

Having sat back down, she listened for a moment with her eyes closed, swaying to the rhythm. *"That's Jo Stafford."*

"Jo Stafford."

"Yes!" She was delighted to hear him repeat the name. *"Have you heard of her?"*

"No."

"Well, don't worry about it. Pretty soon, you'll know all of the big hits ... just like the other American kids." A minute or two later, she pointed to the radio. *"That one's called 'It Could Happen to You.' Dorothy Lamour performed it first, in the movie* And the Angels Sing."

Klaus-Peter was so impressed that his eyes grew wide. *"You sure know music!"* he told her.

"*And movies,*" Hermann added from across the room. "*She reads the movie magazines too.*"

Gertrude was annoyed to see that her husband was still staring helplessly at the photograph albums, totally out of his element and unable to assist. "Oh, good gracious," she said. "D'is poor boy will be in high school by d'e time you find d'e photo book."

Though not comprehending what was said, Klaus-Peter grinned in amusement, rocking back and forth on the sofa cushion.

Gertrude quickly located the proper album and told the boy, "*If you want something done right, you have to do it yourself.*"

Klaus-Peter enjoyed looking at the pictures of Maximilian, a spoiled pooch that appeared to be treated as just another member of the family. Gertrude also showed him one later album, which included progressive pictures, roughly at week-to-week intervals, of the remodeling of Moek Grocery. She was astonished to see how fascinated the lad seemed to be with the process of construction.

After the pair had spent about forty-five minutes browsing through snapshots, Hermann finally interrupted. "*Young man, bring your suitcase, and I'll show you to your room. Come along now. You can look at those later.*"

Gertrude smiled at her husband and closed the photograph album. Then she stood and, reaching down, playfully rubbed Klaus-Peter's head. "*Yes, and I think you'll be wanting a nice, warm bath too.*"

"*Welcome, my boy,*" Hermann said. "*And please, we hope that you will feel like a member of our family now.*"

"*Thank you, sir.*"

It was a euphoric feeling for Gertrude, having a son in the house again. She felt on top of the world as she made her way over to the book cabinet to place the two albums back on the shelf. Meanwhile, as books are wont to do when no one is watching, the other albums had leaned over to occupy the empty space to their right, and Gertrude had to straighten them up to make room for reshelving the later volumes. In so doing, she caught sight of the older sets, those she had avoided showing to Klaus-Peter. With the boy sitting alongside her, she feared that images of Conrad would be too painful for her to endure.

She also had not pulled from the shelf the very first album she ever assembled after her marriage to Hermann. Viewing its tattered spine now, a cold emptiness suddenly crept over her, as she recalled the news reports of recent days. She remained heartsick over the fate of her parents, her sisters, and her sisters' families, and it could be weeks before word was received. In her present state of mind, she was not at all sure whether she could ever bear to see that volume's idyllic images again, a nostalgic time of long ago when the ill-fated city of Dresden was still untouched by this frightful war—architecturally resplendent, hauntingly beautiful, and home.

◆   ◆   ◆

"Some girl was looking for you, and she said it was awfully important," Dinah Reidelhuber said to Elizabeth. They passed one another in the grease-stenched office, Dinah relinquishing her post just as Elizabeth reported for duty after school. The younger of the two had rushed into the room and, turning her hand backward, hurriedly let the nail of her index finger flick through the neatly arrayed time cards in the rack.

"What girl?" she asked, still breathless from running.

"How should I know?"

Elizabeth shook her head. Sometimes Dinah could be so exasperating, almost as if she were doing it on purpose. "Well, didn't she even tell you her name?"

"Not that I recall. Maybe Bobbie remembers."

Having found her card, Elizabeth popped it into the machine and sighed with relief. Only now did she bother to remove her sweater, for every minute of wages counted in such difficult times as these. Besides, 4:01 seemed awfully late when she was scheduled to punch in at four o'clock sharp.

"Well, what did the girl look like?"

"Brown hair, maybe—I don't know." Dinah reached into the desk drawer to retrieve her purse. "It was an odd name, more than one beat."

"Like Reidelhuber?"

"Well, you don't need to get sarcastic about it," Dinah said. "I was only trying to help."

"I didn't mean Reidelhuber is odd," Elizabeth told her. "I meant it's more than one syllable."

Personally affronted, Dinah stomped away in a huff. She was like that sometimes, and Elizabeth could not figure out why. Maybe she was having man problems again. Elizabeth knew for a fact that Dinah was now on her third boyfriend since Sheldon left her—and that was not counting the anonymous ensign who dropped anchor for a single night and then vanished forever with thirty-four dollars of her rent money. But Elizabeth had to admit that Dinah possessed many good qualities as well. Following one of her snits, more often than not, she was perfectly fine the next time they met.

Bobbie Groves was scheduled to work that night too, matching Elizabeth's three-hour shift in its entirety and continuing until closing time. Though she had a mere two months of seniority over Elizabeth, owner Hoyle Harkins recently promoted Bobbie to an assistant manager of Service Refining Company, and nobody begrudged her the title. Apart from a modest widow's pension, this was her only source of income, and she was known to contribute a generous portion of each paycheck to war bonds. She possessed a deep faith, and others admired her for showing such great resilience in the face of personal tragedy. Not long after Pearl Harbor, on the final day of February in 1942, Bobbie's husband was aboard a destroyer, the USS *Jacob Jones*, when the ship was sunk, with heavy loss of life, by a German U-boat off Delaware Bay. Earl Groves was not among the eleven survivors. Bobbie was the only war widow whom Elizabeth knew so well, and although this gracious woman rarely made mention of her loss, the grim reality of it caused the teenager to feel sad whenever the two talked.

While she was in the process of searching for Bobbie in the most likely places, Elizabeth finally came across her in the garage bay—down on all fours, retrieving a dozen valve-stem caps that had spilled onto the pavement when the box slipped out of her hand. "Help me, will you?" the assistant manager asked. "Two of the little caps are missing. They rolled everywhere."

"I see one of them way over there," Elizabeth said. She ran over to scoop it up, as if it might flee the scene if not instantly recaptured.

"I guess all it takes is a fresh set of eyes. I've been looking for ten minutes."

"Why all the fuss over a couple of silly stem caps? They only cost a fraction of a cent."

"That doesn't matter, Lizzie. They're still on the inventory, and everything has to be accounted for."

"Here's a penny," Elizabeth said with coin in hand. "Put it in the cash drawer, if it will make you feel better."

"That's not the point. I'm entrusted with everything of Mr. Harkins, and I intend to find it."

Elizabeth shrugged. "You're the boss."

Suddenly, the diligent woman sat on the floor and shook her pants legs. Out flipped a black cap, dislodged from its hiding place. "Ah-hah!" Bobbie shouted. You would have thought she found a hundred-dollar bill in her cuff. "What are the odds it would land there? Not one in a thousand."

"Those must be prewar slacks."

Curious, Bobbie stared at them. "How come?"

"They still have cuffs. Look at mine."

Amused at the girl's shrewd observation, Bobbie stood up and dusted herself off. "Say, did Dinah already leave?"

"Yep, and thank goodness. She certainly was in a state."

"That girl was driving me crazy today," Bobbie said. "In fact, I almost sent her home early, so I could get some work done."

"What's her problem now?"

"Beats me. Sometimes she turns into Dr. Jekyll on you—without any warning at all. Just poof!"

"You mean Mr. Hyde."

Bobbie frowned. "Okay ... Frankenstein, then. Is that better?"

Elizabeth giggled at her. "You mean Frankenstein's monster."

They were walking back toward the office when the bell dinged. An automobile of old vintage—an early Model A, it was—pulled up to the pump, and its driver got out. "Soda pop?" he asked. Elizabeth pointed him to the beverage case and followed Bobbie inside.

"Was there some girl here earlier, wanting to see me?"

"Yes, there was. Dinah promised to tell you."

Elizabeth grinned. "Well, she told me, all right, but she couldn't recall the girl's name, so it really didn't do much good."

"I swear—that Dinah!"

"Do you remember who it was? Dinah said it was very important."

"It must have been. She told me the girl was crying."

"My goodness!"

"I heard her mention the name," Bobbie said, "so I'm pretty sure it'll come back to me. Just let me think about it for a minute."

Looking down at the floor, she took a couple of steps away from Elizabeth, who persisted in asking, "Well, what did the girl look like?"

Bobbie shook her head. "I never saw her, so I can't say. Dinah just told me her name, in case she forgot to tell you."

Through the window, Elizabeth watched the man outside take a swig from his bottle of Pepsi-Cola and wave thanks to her before climbing back into the Ford and driving off.

"Not much business today," she said. "A nickel an hour won't keep this company afloat."

"Louis said we had a good morning. He fixed a carburetor, did two lube jobs, and patched a couple of flats. And he said the bell had Dinah jumping up from her movie magazine every few minutes."

Elizabeth frowned. "Maybe *that's* why she was in such a bad mood—all those interruptions."

Meanwhile, Bobbie's mind had shifted in another direction entirely. "Was it Peggy ... Peg ...?"

"Well, there is a Peggy Sue Bryant, but she's older than I am, about my brother Wes's age."

"No, that doesn't sound familiar at all. I just wish Dinah had written it down."

Elizabeth became alert. "I know a Meg."

"Maybe that was it."

"Meg Oliphant?"

"Yes, that's it. I'm positive that's the name."

Elizabeth felt a sudden chill. "Oh, my gosh, I hope nothing has happened. Meg's brother and boyfriend are both in the service. And so is her uncle, who's almost ten years younger than her dad."

"Do you want to call her on the telephone? I'll cover for you."

Though Elizabeth was tempted to take Bobbie up on her offer, she quickly thought better of the idea. "No. I'll wait until seven. If it's as important as Meg says it is, I'd rather see her in person anyway. You can't really tell what someone is thinking on the telephone."

◆　　　◆　　　◆

Their meeting that night never took place. Elizabeth asked her mother to drive her to Meg's house on Lasker Avenue instead of back home, but no one was there when they arrived at 7:20, just as the sun was setting. The curtained windows were dark, the doorbell drew no response, and the garage door was closed and locked. Behind a chain-link fence, the Oliphants' dog, Buster, growled and barked like an animal possessed—a territorial stance he did not adopt whenever family members were around.

Determined to speak with her friend face-to-face, Elizabeth had no choice but to wait until the next day, when she would attempt to track Meg down at school. For obvious reasons, their mutual English class in the afternoon would not be an appropriate venue, but they did share the same lunch period, and that seemed to be a much better time—and place—to talk.

Elizabeth was already there and waiting as Meg came into the basement cafeteria, all alone and looking quite forlorn. When Meg reached the end of the serving line, Elizabeth waved to attract her attention, and Meg, unsmiling, made her way over to the table and laid the lunch tray down across from her friend's.

Meg's face was deathly pale, besieged with distress. She was hardly recognizable in such a pitiable state, her hair disheveled and without so much as a touch of make-up. Elizabeth walked around the table and sat next to her. "Someone said you came by to see me yesterday—at the filling station," she said, scarcely above a whisper. "I'm sorry I wasn't there yet, but I did stop by your house last night."

Meg looked at her with desperately sad eyes and broke down at once. Tears flowed freely, and she laid her head upon her folded arms and cried. She sobbed so loudly that many of the students in the lunchroom were staring at her, not quite knowing how to react. For two or three minutes, she was inconsolable, despite Elizabeth's attempts to comfort her with an arm around the shoulders and gentle words of affirmation. When her crying subsided a bit, and she started wiping her eyes and apologizing for causing such an embarrassing commotion in public, the attention of others in the room gradually drifted elsewhere, and Elizabeth sat down in her own chair to hear what it was that had so badly shaken her friend.

Meg took a deep breath. "It's my ..." She started to cry again but, with great effort, managed to regain her composure. "Oh, Lizzie!"

"Take your time—there's no hurry. I'm right here for you, so just talk when you feel ready."

Meg shook her head and valiantly tried to speak. "It's my boyfriend ... He's ..."

Elizabeth swallowed hard. "Yes? Phillip ... What's happened? You can tell me."

Her friend did not respond. She sat wide-eyed, as if in a daze, and her lips were trembling.

"Don't be afraid. Go ahead and tell me about Phillip."

Meg closed her eyes. "Phil is ..." She shook her head and started over. "The War Department says Phil is ... missing in action." Tears returned to her eyes, and she cried quietly. "Oh, I just can't believe it, Lizzie. They say Phillip is presumed ... dead!" A few others in the room glanced her way again but were considerate enough to avert their eyes. By this advanced point in the war, virtually all were accustomed to such outbreaks of bereavement and shattered emotions.

But then a strange thing occurred. Once Meg had shared her sadness with Elizabeth and experienced a long, soothing cry, she seemed far better able to cope with the terrible news, which had come to her home the day before in a telegram. It was not an original wire from the War Department, of course, but an enveloped copy of a telegram that Phillip's father and mother, Mr. and Mrs. Colbert Gunnison, had received a couple of days earlier in Altadena, California. The grief-stricken parents, devastated by this harsh reality, could not bring themselves to tell her by telephone. They never would have made it through the conversation. Phillip was an only child, and now the Gunnisons had lost everything to the war. In time, even their prospective daughter-in-law, whom they loved like a member of the family, would become little more than a bittersweet memory.

"Let me know what I can do to help," Elizabeth said when the girls finished lunch, after no more than picking at their food. Few words had been exchanged between them as they went through the motions of eating, so Elizabeth was now anxious to gather enough information to be of assistance during this difficult time.

"I don't know what any of us can do at this point, Lizzie. Just pray, I guess."

"How serious were you?"

"With Phil? The two of us?"

Elizabeth nodded her head and stared into Meg's eyes.

"Serious enough, I think," the girl said. "He mentioned marriage ..." Meg looked down at the food on their plates. "He talked about getting married someday ... in his last letter to me, he did."

"Gee, I didn't have any idea." Elizabeth gave a deep sigh. "Do you think there's a chance that the War Department could be wrong?"

"There's always that chance, I'm sure."

"Well, I would hold onto that hope as long as possible—until you hear one way or another. That and prayer can work miracles."

"Thanks, Lizzie. I'll try."

"I'm not telling you anything you don't already know—I'm certainly no expert or psychologist—but it just seems like you ... that you should keep your hopes up for as long ..." She was grasping for how to finish her thought.

"I know what you mean, Lizzie. You're a good friend, and I felt that you were the one person in this entire world I could talk to about Phil."

Elizabeth was puzzled by that statement. "Because my brother's in the Navy?"

"Not just that. Lots of people have friends and relatives in the service—most people do."

"Then why?"

"I don't know why. I just do." She thought for a moment. "Maybe it's because you're a good listener."

"That's sweet of you to say, and I appreciate it—but I don't think I deserve any special praise for just knowing when to shut up."

The impish way she phrased it made Meg smile, and that was just the reaction Elizabeth was hoping to see. "Oh, there's a lot more to listening than that," Meg said, "and you know it very well."

Although most of the students had disappeared from the lunchroom by now, Meg Oliphant and Elizabeth Brower continued to talk for another few minutes. Meg's eyes were still red from crying, but she had made it over some painfully rugged terrain on her path to healing. And Elizabeth, whose older brother faced many of the same dangers as Phillip Gunnison, had learned the valuable lesson of what it meant to share one's hurt with a caring friend.

◆   ◆   ◆

One of the most successful fund-raising efforts of Saint Mary's—even more lucrative than the Saturday bazaars—was the occasional fried-fish supper, held three times a year, always on a Friday night. Seldom did Paolina Coletti and her daughter miss the popular feast, which often seemed as well attended by parishioners as Sunday morning mass. Not only was this activity consecrated by the holy church, but the meal tasted wonderful and brought upstanding Christian people together for a time of fellowship. Back at October's event, even Father Kearns had to smile when old Mrs. McDevitt, widowed for some sixty years, loudly assured him that it was "sinfully delicious." His rejoinder, "Then I'll expect all of you at confession, I suppose," drew hearty laughs from those seated around him at the long table.

The March renewal of the supper was slated to begin at 4:30 (a half-hour earlier than usual) and continue until seven o'clock (a half-hour later), and this expanded duration fit into the Colettis' plans very well. Giulia worked that morning at Rawley Flooring, so she had the entire afternoon to take care of her mother and to handle any errands that needed to be accomplished. Lorna Shannon agreed to pick them up at six o'clock, shortly after her husband, Lou, returned home from work with the automobile. Lou was not a sociable person, to say the least, and the church rolls had long since declared him to be a "non-practicing Catholic," which disclaimer consigned him to a sort of membership purgatory, somewhere between worthy of redemption and outright excommunication. But this cautionary stigma did not disturb Louis Shannon, who, in any case, had not darkened the door of a church more than a dozen times since his marriage to Lorna in Jersey City some twenty-eight years ago. That worked out to less than one appearance before the altar every biennial. And yet Big Lou was not exactly an agnostic either. He crossed himself countless times a day, whenever he felt the need for absolution, mental acuity, or simply a run of luck.

While Giulia was away, delivering a small basket of oatmeal muffins to Ike and Bella Sturdevant—both of whom were legally blind and living on a subsistence pension—Bess Clarke came to call. She had patched up her rift with Paolina and was now quite willing to visit the Coletti home, whether invited or not. Fortunately, Giulia's mother was in the living room when the doorbell rang, or no one would have answered within a reasonable period of time, and this perceived slight may very well have derailed their uneasy friendship all over again.

Bess Clarke glanced around the room. "She's not here, then?"

"No, ma'am."

The woman assumed a look of disappointment. "Not in the kitchen?"

"No."

"You're sure?"

Paolina chuckled. "Yes, I'm very sure."

"Well, then I suppose I could tell you, if you'll promise to tell Giulia."

"Of course."

"I have some good news from Archie."

It had been six months since Sergeant Clarke was wounded while fighting at Aitape in Dutch New Guinea. The injury was not considered to be life threatening, so he was evacuated to a field hospital for stabilization and then transported back to Australia for a minor operation and recovery. By the middle of October, his leg showed no ill effects, and he was reunited with his outfit. A ligament tear to that same leg, possibly traceable to his earlier surgery, took him out of action for good during the first week of February.

"He's coming home, Paolina!" Now all restraint was gone, and Mrs. Clarke was beaming with joy. "My Archie is coming home."

Paolina put her hand on the other woman's and told her, "Oh, that is wonderful news, Bess! I'm happy for you."

"He'll be home within a couple of weeks, I'm sure."

"Did Archie write to you?"

"No, this wasn't from Archie." Mrs. Clarke looked at her friend proudly. "This was an official communication from the War Department."

"A telegram?"

"That's right, a cable from the US Government. You know, it's terrifying to receive one of those during wartime, so you can imagine my relief when I saw what it said."

"Yes, I would be the same way," Paolina told her. "Did it give a date for his arrival?"

Mrs. Clarke seemed to be taken aback by this simple question. "Well, no, it didn't say. I'm just guessing that it would be about two weeks or so."

Paolina sighed. "So ... you really don't know when your son will be back home."

"Not exactly, no. The telegram just said Archie was injured in action and would be relieved from combat duty."

"But the telegram did indicate that he would be coming home?"

"Oh, yes, it did say that. It just didn't give an exact date."

"I see."

"But the important thing is, he'll be here soon. You see why I said it was good news?" Then her face darkened suddenly. "When will Giulia be here?"

"Maybe an hour, no more than that."

"Well, where did she go? She doesn't usually leave like this during the day, does she?" Obviously, Mrs. Clarke was impatient to spread the word about Archie.

"She's just paying a visit to Bella Sturdevant and her husband, down the street. Do you know Bella?"

"No, I don't. And why did she have to visit them today, of all days?"

Paolina chose not to answer, certain that ministering to the blind needed no justification from her. "Is Archie's leg going to be all right?" she asked. "Can he walk on it yet, or does he need crutches?"

Apparently, such a thought had never occurred to Mrs. Clarke, for she looked at Paolina with terror in her eyes. "I don't know. Oh, Lord, do you suppose he'll never walk again without crutches? The telegram didn't say."

"Now, that's certainly not what I meant, so please don't go worrying yourself into a frazzle. I was only wondering if the doctors were satisfied with the pace of his rehabilitation, that's all."

Bess Clarke just sat there, mute and wringing her hands.

Across town, the Sturdevants could not thank Giulia enough for her thoughtfulness in bringing the muffins, particularly with sugar in such short supply. "Well, I skimped a little in that department," she told them. "I hope they were sweet enough."

"Plenty sweet," Ike said. He was a man of few words.

Bella grinned and patted her husband's tummy. "I've had to buy him a longer belt, now that he's sitting around so much." Ike Sturdevant was laid off from his job on the first of December, but he did receive a nice retirement party from the management at Texas Power & Light. After three decades of faithful service, surely he deserved nothing less.

"Those few extra pounds won't hurt you, Mr. Sturdevant," Giulia said, "and you still look fine to me." Her honeyed words made him tongue-tied all the more.

"Now, don't encourage him," his wife told the girl. "You might not guess it from his drab exterior, but Ike's quite the lady's man ... once you get to know him."

"That's me," he said with a twinkle in the eye.

Her visitation concluded, Giulia set out on foot for home, pleased to have brought some joy into a lonely couple's lives, but she stopped dead in her tracks when she spotted Mrs. Clarke's 1935 Nash parked in the driveway. There were, after all, limits to how much giving one person could be expected to perform in a single day. She decided to pace around the block until the coast was clear, unaware that Bess Clarke, too, was prepared to invest as much time as it took to wait for her. Giulia, of course, had the distinct advantage in this test of wills, for she could monitor the automobile's movement and thus know for a fact when it was safe to make an appearance. What she did not anticipate, however, was for an hour and twenty minutes to elapse, causing this waiting game to be something of a pyrrhic victory. It was ten minutes past three before the front door finally opened, and Archie's mother vacated the premises in her "Advanced Six" sedan, the very same automobile in which Archie learned to drive. An objective spectator would have noted one thing from the lady's departure: for someone with such joyous news to share, she did not look very cheerful.

Once inside, Giulia went directly to her bedroom, as she knew that her mother would grill her on where she had been and why she was so late in returning. Closing the door behind her did little good. "Giulia, is that you, dear?" came the call.

"Yes, it is, Mamma. I'm here."

To her surprise, no inquisition was forthcoming. In fact, her mother made no reference whatsoever to the lateness of the hour. "You missed Mrs. Clarke by just a few minutes. She wanted to tell you that Archie will be coming home pretty soon. She doesn't know exactly when."

"How come?" Giulia asked, and she seemed devoid of emotion.

"'How come?' Is that the best you can do? You could at least act happy about it."

"I am happy. I'm very happy that he's alive, if that's what you mean."

"Now, 'Bina, I know things are not right between you and Archie, but he is a human being, after all."

"I'm sorry to seem so ... insensitive. I do thank God that he'll be coming back safely from the war. I really do."

"But ...?"

"It's just that I have no intention of getting serious with Archie Clarke ever again."

"Aren't you still engaged to be married?"

"Engaged!" she shouted.

"Aren't you and Archie still engaged? I would think that is a fair question for your own mother to ask."

Giulia shook her head in exasperation. "Listen, Mamma, I ..." She took a deep breath, closed her eyes, and tried to remain calm. "To the best of my knowledge—and wouldn't I know?—Archie and I have never been engaged to be married. Never." She stared intently at her mother. "That trumped-up detail of our relationship was a fantasy of his, based on something I may or may not have said when his train was leaving, and Mrs. Clarke, for whatever reason, has decided to perpetuate the myth. Please, Mamma ..." Giulia could feel her temper slipping away, and she enunciated each word separately. "I will thank you not to add any more ammunition to her side of the argument."

"Well, you don't have to bite my head off," Paolina said in her own defense. "I'm on your side. You know I am. And let's not forget who had to sit here and listen to Bess Clarke rant and rave for two hours while you enjoyed the afternoon at Ike and Bella's house—and God only knows where else."

Stung by the veiled accusation, Giulia's jaw dropped in shock. "What do you mean by that?"

Paolina glanced at the clock. "I know for a fact that it didn't take any two and a half hours to deliver muffins to the Sturdevants. Maybe you should tell me where you've been for all this time."

"Don't you trust me?"

"Of course I do, but you're not totally innocent in this affair."

"What affair? I haven't done anything wrong."

"Well, you must admit that you have been acting very strange lately, and I think I have the right to know why."

Giulia's eyes began to fill with tears. "I'm a good girl. You know that."

Paolina threw her hands in the air. "I don't know what to think anymore. All I know is that you have mysteriously disappeared for most of the afternoon, that you receive letters from servicemen overseas—"

"Mamma!"

"And that you kiss sailors in public at the train station, not caring that the whole world is there to see."

Giulia bristled. "Did she bring that up again?"

"Yes, she did. It bothers her terribly ... and, honestly, I can't say that I blame her."

Furious, Giulia picked up that morning's refolded newspaper and threw it across the room as hard as she could, knocking a lampshade sideways and nearly causing a vase to fall to the floor. "Well, that witch!" she shouted. "That witch! So help me, I'm going to settle this thing once and for all. Even if I did love Archie Clarke, and ours was a match made in heaven—which I don't, and which it isn't—I would not marry him and move into the same family with that ... that ..."

"Witch ...?" Paolina asked.

"That witch!"

"... with a capital 'B'?"

Giulia thought for a moment, confused, but then nodded her head with conviction.

They both laughed, and Paolina put an arm around her daughter's shoulders. "My baby, my baby. Everything will work out fine. You'll see."

Giulia nodded her head, hoping more than trusting that she was right.

◆   ◆   ◆

Around 5:40 that afternoon, already dressed for the church supper, Paolina placed a hurried telephone call to Lorna Shannon, telling her not to pick them up after all. "There's been a change of plans. We found an injured boy on our doorstep."

"A what?" Lorna asked.

"An injured boy who needs our help."

"Who is it? What happened to him?"

"Never mind. It's nothing serious, really. Just give Father John our regrets."

The "boy" in question was actually a young man of nineteen, one of Giulia's former schoolmates at Waco High. Peter Gerken also happened to be one of the very few able-bodied male graduates of the Class of '44 who was not in uniform. He achieved conscientious objector status by pleading his case to the local draft board, whom he convinced that his religious ideals forbade participation in the armed services. Giulia had not laid eyes upon him since spring commencement, when she was in Waco Hall to watch her fellow seniors walk across the stage and receive their diplomas. She hoped to be doing the same thing someday, once her mother recovered enough of her ambulatory skills to be self-sufficient.

But Giulia certainly did not recognize him earlier that day, as he lay on the bloodstained Coletti welcome mat, having gained her attention by desperately kicking at the front door. "Mamma!" she cried, upon discovering that a human being, now lying in a fetal position, was in urgent need of medical assistance. Giulia knelt by the man's body and leaned over to see his contorted face. He was alive and breathing, even to the extent of attempting to speak.

"Just relax," she whispered to him. "Don't try to talk." Over her shoulder, she shouted again, "Mamma!"

Together, with some effort, mother and daughter rolled the injured man onto his back. Then, when this seemed to assist his respiratory system somewhat, they dragged him by the shoulders into the house, positioning a soft bag of discarded clothing beneath his head on the hardwood surface.

"We should call for an ambulance," Paolina said, and Giulia hurried toward the telephone.

"No!" the man shouted. "Don't call!"

Giulia rushed back and knelt down again. "Why shouldn't we call? You need to go to the hospital. You're badly hurt."

Meantime, Giulia's mother had gone for a clean, wet rag to gently pat the man's bloody face, and this too brought him some comfort. "Thank you," he struggled to say. "That feels better, thanks." His lips were bleeding profusely, and he might have lost a tooth or two as well. Also, his nose was set at an odd angle to his mouth, and there was a deep gash beneath his right eye.

Only then did Giulia finally put the voice and appearance together. "Peter?" she asked.

"Hello, Giulia." He seemed embarrassed that they should meet this way. The girl went to the kitchen to fetch him a glass of water.

Paolina saw just the practical side of the matter, making certain that the injured person's life was not in danger. "Are you sure you don't want us to send for an ambulance, young man?"

"No, ma'am. Please don't."

"And why not? Are you wanted by the law or something?" She had heard many a radio program that included such scenes.

"I think Giulia can tell you why it might be better for me if you didn't bring the authorities into this."

Giulia returned from the kitchen. "Sit up, if you can," she told him. "Here, drink."

That, too, seemed to help, and only ten minutes later, Peter felt strong enough— with assistance at each elbow from the ladies—to limp over to the living room sofa. There he sat for a few minutes of relief, nursing his split lip with another clean cloth, wrapped around some ice cubes.

"Do you feel well enough to tell us what happened to you?" Giulia asked.

"Not until after I've met this kind lady," the young man said.

"I'm sorry. Peter, this is my mother. Mamma, this is Peter Gerken. He graduated last year in my class."

"Hello, Mrs. Coletti."

"Nice to meet you, Peter, though I wish it were under more pleasant circumstances."

"*You* do ... ouch!" He chuckled. "Actually, I've been to your house before— twice, as a matter of fact."

"You have?" Paolina glanced at her daughter.

"Yes, ma'am," Peter said, "but you were in your bedroom both times. It's a pleasure to finally meet you in person."

"Did you have an accident?" Giulia asked.

He tried to smile. "Yeah, I guess you could put it that way. I met with an unfortunate accident."

"Mamma, Peter here is a conscientious objector. He opposes the war on philosophical grounds."

"Theological, really," he said. The distinction seemed to be important to him. Paolina's face turned grim, but she made no comment.

"Please tell us what happened, Peter," Giulia said. "We want to know. Maybe we can do something to help."

He scoffed at the notion. "Not likely."

But she persisted. "Well, try us anyway." Her lovely smile may have had some influence upon his decision to talk.

"I was just minding my own business, killing some time at The Nook, over on Washington, when these four thugs came in and started picking a fight. I know what you're thinking, but I wasn't spouting off. They were looking for trouble."

"For no reason?" she asked.

"Well, I knew a couple of them from high school—they're both seniors now. Jerry Maple was one of them, and his older brother was with them too. He just got discharged from the Army, so they said."

"So, Jerry was there, and Rick Maple ..."

"And Fisher ... what's-his-name, the basketball player."

"Fisher Selmon?"

"Yeah, and some other goon—real ugly, weighed about two hundred." Peter sat up straight and rubbed his aching back.

"Are you all right?" Paolina leaned closer with a concerned look. "I've got every kind of ointment there is for back pain."

"No, thanks. I'll be okay. I guess one of them kicked me in the ribs."

Giulia was shocked. "They beat you up in a bookstore?"

"Actually, they were waiting for me outside."

"What started it all?"

"They must've seen me go into the shop. Maybe they were eating at Mamie's, across the street—I don't know." He sighed, and that caused him to wince in pain.

"You might have a broken rib," Giulia said.

Peter shook his head. "I know what a broken bone feels like, and this is just a bad bruise." He spit some blood into one of the rags. "Oh, I've had a couple of run-ins with Jerry Maple before. We don't see eye to eye politically, and I'm pretty sure he was out to get me. Anyhow, they kind of surrounded me in the aisle, calling me a few names, and that Fisher kid took exception to the book I was holding."

"What was it?"

"A collection of essays by Bertrand Russell."

"What about?"

"He's a British philosopher—and a leading pacifist and progressive thinker. But what's ironic is that he's for the war against Hitler."

"These were pro-war essays, then?" Paolina asked.

"No, I can't say that. They were some pacifist tracts from around the First War, brilliantly argued moral tenets that people like Fisher—and certainly those Maple dunces—couldn't begin to comprehend."

Giulia noticed that the left knee of Peter's pants leg was torn, and so was the left shoulder section of his sweater. "Did they confront you right there in the shop?"

"Only verbally. The owner, James Ballard, heard the commotion and told them to leave. His wife was there too, and he sure didn't appreciate the way soldier boy was talking to me—the language he used. Mr. Ballard and I may be on opposite sides of the fence on most issues, but he's open-minded and always lets me browse to my heart's content."

"What did they call you?"

Peter laughed. "Mostly 'slacker,' with a few four-letter words thrown it for good measure. Anyway, they were waiting for me behind The Nook when I walked out to my car. No one else was around, so they beat me up all they wanted and then kicked the living daylights out of me when I went down. Four against one, it was. They were really brave heroes, weren't they?"

"How in the world did you make it over to this neighborhood?" Giulia's mother asked. "This is a long way from downtown."

"I tried to drive to my aunt's, but then I felt like I was going to pass out, so I stopped. I don't know—maybe I did pass out because one of my car's tires ended up over the curb." He looked at Giulia. "I just got out and started walking, and then I remembered that you live on Gurley, so I came here for help."

"Where's your car now?"

"Somewhere on Fourteenth Street or maybe Fifteenth. It's not blocking traffic. I do know that much."

Paolina walked toward the entry. "I'm going to call Theresa," she said. "Maybe Dirk can give this boy a ride home."

"What if he can't?"

She stopped. "Well, then I'll try Marvel Foiles and her husband. Or even Robbie across the street. He's sixteen now."

While her mother was away from the living room, Giulia asked Peter, "Aren't you going to report this to the police?"

"Hardly! I wouldn't get a fair hearing on the Square. They've got it in for conchies like me, but at least I have my principles to keep me warm at night. That's more than those murderers in uniform can say for themselves."

Giulia resented that remark, and she frowned accordingly.

"Don't you see?" he told her. "There would be no war if our soldiers refused to kill. It's really that simple. They've compromised their humanity for the god of capitalism."

"You consider our servicemen to be murderers?"

"In a sense, yes. They do nothing to protest against such insanity. They do not take a stand. They just obey orders like model soldiers are taught to do—mindless killing machines who sacrifice their beliefs on the altar of national conceit."

"And all that the Germans and Japs have done is perfectly fine?"

"I didn't say that. I despise Hitler at least as much as you do, maybe more. The Krauts invaded the Soviet Union without provocation, and now it's Stalin's men who are fighting for their country's very existence—certainly not Roosevelt and Churchill."

Giulia squinched her eyes at him. "I seem to recall that you admire Russia quite a lot."

"I do indeed," Peter said. He was flattered that she would remember such an arcane detail. "When did I ever tell you that?"

"You told Wesley Brower, and I just happened to be listening."

"When was that?"

"We worked together on a paper salvage drive, remember? You said this war is not our fight—it's Europe's."

He smiled. "Well said! You have a good memory."

"You also implied that Wesley's brother was a sucker to enlist in the Navy."

Peter's eyes widened, stung by the allegation. "I never said such a thing."

"Not in so many words, maybe, but that's what you meant. We were talking about either answering the call of your government or declaring yourself a CO, and you strongly suggested that Wesley's brother made the wrong choice by going."

"To my way of thinking, he did. I'm a pacifist. But that's a long way from saying that all servicemen are suckers. Please don't put words into my mouth."

"But they are murderers?"

"In a sense, yes."

"So, Stephen Brower is a murderer because he's patriotic enough to fight for his country."

Peter Gerken was tongue-tied, weighing whether to affirm his principles or preserve a friendship that was dear to him. It was a decision he found himself making quite often these days, usually at the cost of another friend.

"I don't think you're a pacifist at all, deep down," Giulia told him. "I'll bet you tried to fight back today."

"I was attacked."

"Well, so was the United States."

"That's debatable."

"Tell that to the parents of the men killed at Pearl Harbor."

"Jesus told us to turn the other cheek. He told us to love our enemies as we love ourselves."

"There's a war on, Peter. We can't love our enemies during a war, or they would kill us without giving it a second thought."

"I'm just telling you what the Bible says. I base my whole life on it, not just when it's convenient—like in peacetime. Do you think I enjoy being a conscientious objector?"

She thought for a moment and said, "You know, in a perverse sort of way, I think you really do."

That was when Giulia's mother returned to tell her, "Stan Foiles is going to drive Peter home. He'll be over here in ten minutes or so." Almost at once, she could sense an uneasiness in the air, as if an argument had taken place while she was gone. Giulia was tight-lipped and brooding, while Peter ministered to his wounds in glum silence.

Paolina just shook her head, suddenly too tired to be concerned about such matters. Instead, she started wondering what she could fix for the evening meal, now that plans for the fried-fish supper had fallen through.

   ◆   ◆   ◆

"Just your luck, Jakey. It so happens that Anson Gabriel is the one person in this town that you're not going to be able to bribe."

"Everyone has a price. All you have to do is find how much it is."

"Ten grand is a nice, round figure, don't you think?"

"Ten G's! That'll change anyone from a saint to a sinner."

"Don't be a sap, Bruno. That kind of money don't mean nothin' to someone with Gabriel's dough."

And so it went: five characters, voiced by three actors. Such was the economy of radio.

Customarily, the Friday show was a cliffhanger, and this one concerned two city councilmen bringing to light the deeds of a reputed crime syndicate, the first time they had ever done so in the civic arena of a town hall meeting. By show's end, one of the muckrakers would be dead, found floating facedown in a tidal basin, with the audience kept in suspense as to the victim's identity. Trouble was, no definitive way could be found to pin the murder—if indeed foul play was involved—on anyone answering to the name of Cashley. Stranger yet, the police detective assigned to the case seemed doggedly determined to prove otherwise.

Though inhabiting a relatively minor subplot for this particular episode, the character of Sally Holt, as always, spoke some of the best lines in the show—or maybe it was just that Sandra Whittsel made them sound that way. She brought accolades to Ethel Coody, Gerald Byrd, and Ray Temple, and they expressed their appreciation, like good writers will do, by turning out their finest work with her in mind. And thus, success bred success, and the program's "gun moll" (as loyal listeners perceived her) rose to a prominence that was far out of proportion to her supportive role.

"Oh, no, she's much more than that," Sandy would insist at her public appearances. "Gun molls belong to a gang, but on 'Behold Tomorrow' it's more like the gang belongs to her." That invariably drew applause and vigorous nods of the head from her legion of fans, most of whom, by now, belonged to The Sally Club of Waco. In contrast, Kip Hanson had no such organized following, though he also was a very popular character. Probably, the role was too juvenile for the general public to champion with equal fervor. By the same token, few of the locals would recognize Wesley Brower on the street because he did not have his photograph in the newspaper on a regular basis, as did the comely Miss Whittsel.

Neither character had any lines in the third act of Friday's episode, so Sandy and Wesley sat quietly, in the secondary chairs that were positioned farthest away from the microphones. It was common courtesy for actors to utilize these remote chairs whenever the script did not call for active participation before the next commercial break. Hugh Kenton referred to them as the "catbird seats," but others, especially the actors themselves, favored the baseball term of "bullpen."

Whatever the nomenclature, Wesley enjoyed being there today. Throughout the whole act, the side of Sandy's leg was pressed against his, so close were the chairs together. He was unobtrusive in his attempts to steal peeks at her lovely profile, though once or twice his eyes may have lingered a bit longer than a casual observer might do. Her perfume, in such proximity, had a powerful effect upon him as well—not that there was anything coarse or manipulative about it, for the fragrance had been applied sparingly and with good taste. It was just that she was so very near to him.

When the program concluded, and the "West of the Brazos" cast was dashing in to assume their places, Sandy walked alongside Wesley to the lobby. Kenton had alerted everyone that there would be no rehearsal at 3:30 but to be ready to "hit the ground running" at 2:20 on Monday afternoon to make up for it.

"How would you like to take me to the picture show tonight, Wes?" Sandy looked around the lobby, anywhere but at Wesley, while she awaited his reply. The girl did this out of consideration for him—so he would not feel put on the spot— but of course she would have resorted to a more coercive tactic in a heartbeat, had it come down to that.

Though Wesley could think of few things in life that he would rather do tonight than be with Sandra Whittsel, he felt that he owed it to his own sense of pride not to appear too anxious. And so he asked her, "Why me? What about your boyfriend?" Just then, the sound of Marshall McFall's voice could be heard over the loudspeakers: "Before the days of streetcars and automobiles and airplanes, Waco, Texas, was often referred to as 'Six-Shooter Junction.' Come with us now as we ..."

"Marshall and I are on the skids," she told him. "He's going out with some flat-chested reporter from WACO." Wesley knew at once who it must be. He had spotted a very pretty girl at the last county commissioners' meeting, which newsman Lonnie Thomson asked him to cover while Lonnie was in Hico.

"I felt like slapping him when I found out, but I never did do it," she said. "We haven't spoken for two weeks."

Myra Culp, the receptionist, was finding this deskside drama of more interest than answering the pesky telephone, so Sandy motioned for Wesley to accompany her around the corner and into the hallway, where they could plan their evening in relative seclusion.

"This doesn't have to be a real date," she told him. "Not if you don't want it to be." Then she smiled. "You won't even have to kiss me good night if you don't want to. It's entirely up to you."

Standing so close to her, he could feel himself quickly losing his hard edge, his determination to be in control of the situation. "No, it's all right for it to be a real date," he said. "I don't have anything against that." So much for pride.

"Then you'll go?"

"I guess so."

"It's a Van Johnson picture, and you know how much I adore Van Johnson."

Wesley was aware of no such thing, but he nodded his head anyway, dutifully acting like it was common knowledge.

The Orpheum Theatre stood on North Sixth Street, between Austin and Washington. As per Sandy's request, they arrived there a little early. Wesley parked the automobile at the curb, allowing them plenty of time to stroll along the sidewalk with no thought of being in a hurry. A beggar on the street requested spare change, and Wesley gave him a nickel for a cup of coffee. When they neared the movie house, a street photographer stepped forward and snapped a few pictures. Wesley could not help but notice how very affectionate Sandy was, quite willing to pose cheek-to-cheek for the camera.

Once they were inside the Orpheum, a newsreel—including some very graphic footage of the Dresden raids—opened the program, and that was followed by a Woody Woodpecker cartoon. Someone in the audience gave a creditable imitation of Ben Hardaway's famous laugh for the anthropomorphic bird, but the general approbation began wearing a bit thin after the fifth or sixth outburst.

The feature presentation was *Between Two Women*, starring screen sensation Van Johnson as Dr. Red Adams, with the ever-dependable Lionel Barrymore reprising his role as Dr. Leonard Gillespie, and as the pair of title characters, Gloria De Haven and Marilyn Maxwell. This was Mr. Johnson's first solo lead, after attracting notice for supporting roles in *Thirty Seconds Over Tokyo*, *A Guy Named Joe*, and *Two Girls and a Sailor*. Wesley had to admit that Johnson was likable, but he was also man enough to reject Sandy's appraisal of the actor as "dreamy."

The story itself was a light drama that did not require much cerebral energy, and this was just fine with Sandy, who spent much of the time whispering to Wesley—to the annoyance of those sitting behind—and also snuggling his right arm whenever the convoluted plot might conceivably cause passionate desires to surface. Not that Wesley was complaining. What normal high school male would object to the undivided attention of such a strikingly attractive young lady in a darkened theater? Moreover, whenever Sandy whispered, she had the habit of exhaling substantially more air than was necessary and directing it in a stream that tickled his outer ear. Suffice it to say that there were some sizable gaps in his appreciation of the film's implausible narrative.

"I can't ask you in," Sandy told him when the Brower Chevrolet squeaked to a stop in her driveway. "My daddy does not allow boys in the house. He's a colonel in the Army."

"I remember."

"That's right. You went with Daddy and me to that air show at Blackland—with all the tactical aerial bombing." When she talked like that, Sandy sounded every bit the Army brat she was.

"So, you've never snuck a boy into your house?"

She flashed a playful smile. "Well, not when Daddy was home anyway."

"What about your mother?"

"Oh, she just goes into the other part of the house and stays there. She respects my privacy much more than he does. I guess she's just a trusting person."

Wesley saw some irony there, knowing of the girl's recent medical procedure, but he ventured no comment that might ruin the evening. Instead, he just stated the obvious: "I take it, then, that your father is home tonight."

Sandy frowned. "Oh, yes. I'm afraid so."

He began to fumble for the door handle.

"But that doesn't mean we can't say our goodbyes in the car," she said. "I mean, it wasn't a terribly long movie." With a look of mischief, she scooted across the seat, giggling all the while. When she could slide no further, she reached forward to turn off the engine. Wesley let go of the metal handle and settled back against the seat.

"Thank you for being so swell," Sandy whispered to him with her prettiest smile. "I just didn't want to be left all alone tonight." She looked so grateful, staring up at him like that, almost tearfully. Then, without any further preliminaries, she leaned toward him, closed her eyes, and kissed him gently on the mouth. It developed into a long, lingering kiss, a transporting experience that was unlike anything he had ever known before. Her lips were soft and wet, and her tongue touched his own and explored around it without even once surrendering contact. But as exciting as this was to a novice lover like Wesley Brower, it could not compare to the sensation of feeling her left breast tightly pressing against his upper arm while they kissed. She displayed no embarrassment by such intimate touching and did nothing to hasten its premature end.

Through it all, it was quite clear to Wesley that this young girl was out of his league when it came to the physicality of love. She had some worldly moves in her repertoire that were beyond his ken, but to her credit, she used them judiciously and knew precisely how far to go without crossing the line into blatant sensuality. For instance, as they kissed, she found his left hand and placed it upon her right shoulder, turning ever so slightly toward him to allow his right arm ample room to envelope her left shoulder. Then it was a simple matter to slowly lie back on the seat and bring him on top of her for a warm and full embrace. Her accomplished hands, now free from the critical job of guiding his arms around her, began to massage his back, skillfully moving about and applying just enough downward pressure to show him that she sincerely wished to give him pleasure.

It was when Wesley's hands began to implement an agenda of their own, seeking to wander across areas where they should not properly be, that Sandy—confident this would happen—promptly heard a noise that caused her to sit up and look toward the house. "Was that light on before?" she asked. "I'm sure it wasn't. Do you remember seeing it?"

As if suddenly awakened from a beautiful dream, Wesley was confused and uncomprehending. He reached out to pull her closer, but Sandy heard another noise and turned her back to him, frightened that their romancing had been discovered by one of her parents.

"There's no one there," Wesley told her, but of course she knew that his opinion was based more upon self-gratification than self-preservation. Still staring toward the house, she smiled at the immense satisfaction it gave her to be so desperately desired by a boy, and she sensed that this, without question, was the most exquisite feeling to be had in life. The fact that this young man may have been left so unfulfilled by the brief encounter meant relatively little to her. After all, had he not been treated to many of the same delectable sensations that stirred her heart and body? By every indication, he seemed to be having a wonderful time throughout the "necking" session—as she termed it in her mind—and anyhow, it was not her fault that mysterious noises interrupted their love play just when it was heating up to a level of passion that might well have proven rather interesting.

On his way home, Wesley consoled himself with the knowledge that tomorrow was Saturday, and surely he would see that lovely vision who was Rob Glynn's daughter, Pippa. He had only laid his eyes upon her that one time, and six full weeks had elapsed since then. Rob said the girl usually came to Waco about once a month, so she was overdue.

♦   ♦   ♦

But reality does not often live up to the promises of one's wishful imagination. Soon after entering The Smoker's Den, Wesley was disappointed to observe that the shop was no different than it had been for the past five Saturdays, devoid of the ethereal glow that Miss Glynn brought to the place back on the morning of January 27.

Rob Glynn shared coffee with him but noticed that the young salesman appeared to be fidgety, anxious to be on his way again. "I think Pippa is planning to be here two weeks from today," Rob told him in passing. "She has to show a sheep next Saturday in Kosse, but she'll come to town with me on the twenty-fourth. If you have a few minutes, pop in and say hello."

"Yes, sir. I'll try to do that."

"You know, she doesn't have many close friends at school, and I'm sure she'd like to see you again."

Wesley actually made two sales that day, neither of which originated from his "Junk Accounts" list. The S. M. Kirkpatrick Furniture Company purchased an ROS package of fifteen thirty-second spots, and Waco Grain & Seed Company bought a package of six sixty-second adjacencies leading into the "Farm and Ranch Hour." His commission would not amount to much, but at least he felt like he was learning the craft of selling. And, of course, sales manager Lee Graffen presumably would be pleased with this tangible sign of progress. After dropping his sales orders into Graffen's metal in-basket, he drove home shortly past noon, listening to "Casa Loma Time" on the radio and feeling very pleased with himself.

That would all change in just over twenty-four hours. During the Sunday morning service at Columbus Avenue Baptist Church, his attention strayed several times from H. H. Hargrove's sermon, "Investing in the Future." Mostly, his flights of fancy were on girls. Wesley thought back to the date with Sandra Whittsel and forward to the prospect of seeing Pippa Glynn again. For some reason, the title of the motion picture that he and Sandy saw, *Between Two Women*, came to mind, and he flattered himself that this could also apply to his own state of affairs. It was a nice problem to have.

The sound of rumbling thunder could be heard as he, his sister, and his mother were preparing to leave from church. Nora was about to open her umbrella when Wesley's friend, Morton Wilson, came up to him and wondered if he had seen the morning newspaper.

"Not yet."

"Well, you ought to take a look at it."

"Why? What's up?"

"You'll see, lover boy." Morton laughed and then ran off, through the rain, to catch up with his parents.

"What was that all about?" Wesley's mother asked.

"Beats me."

A similar thing happened in the parking lot across the street, only this time the messenger was Rosetta Patrick, a fellow member of the Class of '45. "Saw you in the paper, Wes!" she called from the rear seat of her parents' automobile. Wesley thought he could hear Rosetta laughing as she rolled up the passenger window to keep the rain out.

Fearing the worst, the first thing Wesley did upon arriving home was to search through the *Waco Sunday Tribune-Herald*, scanning every article and photo until he reached page three of the local section. And there they were, two side-by-side photographs above a caption that read ...

> Are Sally Holt and Kip Hanson lovebirds in real life? Our intrepid photographer caught up with classmates Sandra Whittsel and Wesley Brower, stars of KWXN's daily serial "Behold Tomorrow," as they attended the premiere showing of Metro-Goldwyn-Mayer's new comedy "Between Two Women" at the Orpheum Theatre on Friday night. At left, Miss Whittsel and Mr. Brower are all lovey-dovey for the camera as they wait to enter the movie house, where, we suspect, they will find two cozy perches in the balcony. At right, they are seen holding hands as they make their way inside. We presume that Mr. Brower paid for both tickets, or did they go Dutch? Either way, it's clear to see that life is imitating art when these two youngsters come together beyond the soundproof walls of the broadcast studio. Can wedding bells be far away for the thespians who play Sally and Kip? Both graduate from Waco High School this May.

He fought for breath. Should he be angry, amused, or humiliated by these photographs? Most everyone in Waco would view them before the day was out, and Wesley did not know what to think. In a way, he was delighted to see himself in such sweet poses with the photogenic Sandy, to whom the camera was every bit as kind as the microphone. On the other hand, he was sure to receive a week or so of ruthless ribbing from everyone who knew him—at school, at work, and at church.

Then a wave of unsettling questions swept over him, and he started to resent the pictures, no matter how lighthearted was their intent. Exactly who was this cameraman? He identified himself as a street photographer, but it turned out that he was employed by the local newspaper [PHOTO CREDITS: TRIBUNE-HERALD STAFF].

Did Sandy know this beforehand and possibly arrange for him to be there at that location and at that precise time? Was the entire date with Miss Whittsel just an opportunity for Sally Holt to capture some cheap publicity at his expense? And how extensive was this elaborate charade anyway? Did it encompass their time together in the theater? Their romantic stroll after the movie? Their delicious moments of intimacy when they kissed each other good night? In short, was his date with Sandy one big sham, from beginning to end? He would demand some answers from her tomorrow, though of course any such allegations were likely to be denied by someone as clever as she.

Then, soon before bedtime and without any conscious effort on his part, the painful truth blindsided him. No matter how hard he tried to push the troubling thought from his mind, it remained the most plausible explanation. Sandy did indeed arrange for those provocative photographs to appear in the newspaper, but not only as a publicity stunt. She was scheming to make Marshall McFall insanely jealous, thereby driving the announcer back to her waiting arms—the same arms that, just two days earlier, had held Wesley so tightly to her bosom in a warm, loving embrace. He was nothing but a pawn.

♦   ♦   ♦

"Fancy a pint, mate?"

Danny Rignold looked up and saw a British airman standing there, cap in hand. Two of his pals were alongside, and this seemed to be their polite way of inviting themselves to sit down at the sole mostly available table in The Red Lion.

"Sure. Why not?"

One of the sergeants and a corporal took their seats, while the other sergeant went after the drinks.

"Need some help, Geoff?" the corporal called, but the sergeant shook his head and kept walking toward the bar.

The corporal turned to Danny. "I'm Albert Driscoll, and this is Charles Windham."

"Pleased to meet you. My name's Rignold—Danny Rignold." He was sporting a new stripe, having been promoted to sergeant a month earlier.

"What brings an American all the way to Kettering?" Driscoll asked.

Danny laughed. "It's only four miles from base."

"But we don't see a lot of you chaps over here. Most head over to Brigstock these days, where the beer's not so watered down."

"I like to travel around whenever I can—pretty countryside."

"Aye, it'd be a nice place to live, if it wasn't for this lot. Where you from?"

"The south—Mississippi."

The sergeant returned, grumbling as he carried a tray with four glasses of dark beer. "One sloshed over, so that'll be mine." He seated himself in the only remaining chair and slid the glasses to each of the others.

"That's Geoffrey Hoak," Driscoll said with a grin. "And he's steadier with a waist gun."

Danny shook hands with him and, belatedly, with the other two Raffies as well.

"Danny's from the south—*Gone With the Wind* territory."

Windham spoke up at last. "Well, I'd sure like a piece of Scarlett."

Hoak swatted him on the chest with the back of his hand. "She's from Blighty, you dimwitted sot!" They all laughed.

"Well, Miss Leigh may be," Sergeant Windham said, "but Scarlett's a Yank through and through. Isn't that right, Rignold?"

Danny shook his head and smiled. "Point well taken. But she'd probably scratch your eyes out if you called her that." Hoak chuckled, but Windham was confused.

"Besides that," Driscoll added, "I don't think Larry Olivier would appreciate it much if you tried to move in on her." After taking a deep swig of the brew, he pulled out a pack of cigarettes and offered them around.

"Put those away, corporal," Danny said, and he reached into his shirt pocket. "Have mine, boys. We get 'em by the hundreds, and I don't smoke." He tossed the pack of twenty cigarettes onto the table, and each of the men took one.

"We've found Jolly Saint Nick!" Windham said. He used his own match to light up. The others, in turn, lit their cigarettes from his.

"Ta," Hoak said, and Driscoll nodded his thanks.

"Where are you fellas from?" Danny asked.

"London," Driscoll said. Then, glancing around, he amended that. "Well, Bayswater, actually."

"Oh, Christ!" Sergeant Windham said with a laugh. Driscoll glared at him.

"Liverpool," Hoak said. He picked up the remaining cigarettes and slipped them into his own pocket.

Windham was still chuckling. "Weymouth," he said, "so I'm a southerner too."

Some RAF airmen were playing snooker nearby, and they howled at an impossible shot by one of them. There was also a lively game of darts against the back wall, and being a place of modest dimensions, every last table in the pub was full of customers, save for a few vacant chairs here and there. Everybody, except for about a half-dozen assorted civilian girls, was in uniform. All along, Danny had been watching one of the young ladies from afar. Her hair was golden, and she walked—and even sat—with a confident grace that was quite beguiling to a country boy.

"Hey, there's Simpkins!" Driscoll and Hoak shouted almost simultaneously, and a new arrival in the pub sauntered over to their table. Passing through the room, he spotted an unused chair and dragged it along as he approached. Hoak and Windham made some space for him. "Who's the Yank?" he wanted to know.

"Rignold," Sergeant Hoak told him. "And this would be the famous Sammy Simpkins."

Leaning over the table, they shook hands.

"Hi, corporal," Danny said.

"You keeping 'em flying at Grafton, Rignold?"

"Tryin' to. Just call me Danny." Then he asked, "How'd you know?"

"The nails. You can tell a lot from somebody's nails."

"Sammy here's our procurer," Windham said, but Danny did not know whether to smile or be impressed. A twinkle in the sergeant's eye told him the statement was in jest.

"He's the one who gets us pretty women and gorgeous bottles of scotch."

Simpkins grinned with pride. "And you should know that, Chuckie. Better than anyone, you should." Noticing the glasses of beer, he asked, "Who's buying?"

Driscoll frowned and stood up. "I'll get it this time."

"Be a prince, Albie, and get me two," Simpkins called after him.

"Not bloody likely!" Driscoll shouted from the bar.

Simpkins looked at the American. "Oh, Albie Driscoll's a good bloke, if you don't expect to get paid for services rendered."

"Hah! That's a laugh, coming from the likes of you," Hoak said.

"Uh-oh ... Complaint Department."

"Listen, Sammy, I've flown seven ops without a judy to show for them."

"Then I've probably saved your life many times over," Simpkins told him. "Keep your mind on business, I always say. I don't want to be the one to pick the flak out of your pants."

"Some friend you are."

"Hey, for me, *this* is business! Can I help it if it takes up most of my duty time?"

Danny could not resist telling the entrepreneur, "I need a date for Thursday. Can you help?"

In the blink of an eye, Simpkins rushed over to the recently vacated chair next to Danny and moved Driscoll's half-empty beer glass to where he himself had been sitting.

"What's the occasion, sergeant—dance, romantic meal, cinema, seeing the many tourist attractions of Northamptonshire? You name it."

"All of that, I guess," Danny said, but he quickly added, "if it's the right girl."

When Driscoll came back with the pint, he saw that his chair had been expropriated for business dealings, so he laid the glass in front of Simpkins and took a seat between Windham and Hoak.

"My clients are among the most satisfied in the entire RAF," Simpkins told the American. Sergeant Hoak begged to differ with that unsubstantiated claim, but Simpkins held up his hand and stopped him in mid-sentence. "Yours was a special case, Geoff. My sister's roommate in Bedworth was not on my roster at the time, and you know it." He turned back to Danny. "She sent a substitute—on her own, mind you—who fell far short of my high standards. Well, didn't she, Geoff?"

"She looked like a bull terrier," Hoak said, and Windham broke out laughing at the comment.

"Did I charge you for the escort?"

Hoak glowered at him. "Well, no, but there was mental distress involved, and you should have paid me."

Simpkins shook his head. "These things happen," he told the Yank. "When do you need this lady?"

"Like I said, next Thursday—a week from tonight. There's a dance for enlisted men at the Aeroclub."

Simpkins nodded his head. "The American Red Cross."

"That's right."

"What sort of girl do you have in mind?"

Danny thought for a moment. "See that baby doll over there?" They all turned around to have a look. "Someone like her would be swell."

"And I'd like King George to come to my next birthday party," Windham said.

Corporal Simpkins ignored the remark. "You want me to ask her for you?"

That was too sudden for comfort. "N—No," Danny said in a panic. "Just some ... Just somebody like her. She seems to have plenty of attention already, and I don't want to have to fight my way out of here."

"I'll get to work on it right away," the corporal told him, "but it'll cost you a fiver." Simpkins knew that the typical Yank had plenty of money, so he adjusted his asking price to what the market would bear. "Five quid, sargeant."

"Is that five *pounds*? Just for you to get started?"

"Up front." He tapped his fingertip very forcefully. "Money on the table."

"I don't carry around that kind of cash."

"How much do you have?"

Danny pulled out his wallet. "Just two pounds and ... some change. Nearly three, I'd say."

"That'll do for a first-time customer. Call it an introductory offer." Reluctantly, Danny handed over the cash.

"No, just keep the coins," Simpkins told him. "That will show my good faith." He returned all but the two blue-pink bank notes.

"What if you take my money, and I never see you again?"

"Oh, you'll see me again all right," he said, "because I'll expect to collect the other three when I deliver the girl."

Knowing that he had no other choice, Danny acceded to the offer. "If you don't mind my askin', when will all this happen?"

"No, indeed, that's a fair question. I'll have the girl here for you on Thursday at six, and she's yours for the evening. But bring her back by midnight, mind, or it'll cost you another quid."

"Listen, corporal, this won't be some whore, will it? I only want a nice English girl to dance with and maybe take to the movies."

"What a coincidence," Simpkins said. "I only traffic in nice girls."

Danny slowly nodded his head. "Deal."

Sammy Simpkins quaffed the remainder of his beer and stood up. "Well, always a pleasure doing business with an ally." He shook hands with Danny and took one last look at the golden-haired girl, as if locking her splendid appearance in his memory. She would be hard to match.

◆   ◆   ◆

As he waited for the Salome brothers to open for business, Wesley idly drummed his left hand on the steering wheel and browsed through his scribbled list of the day's calls. By now, he knew that Saturday morning meant frustration and rejection, mitigated only by the odd sale of a few bucks' worth of airtime. He was beginning to tire of the futility of part-time sales, though manager Lee Graffen's encouragement continually dangled a carrot just out of reach. "Be patient, son. Once it clicks, you'll be running on all eight cylinders. Art Clem went through this very same thing, and now he's pulling in three thousand a year—not gross but net."

Wesley yawned and then felt the need to shut his eyes for a minute or two. He had slept a total of four hours at best, fitfully tossing and turning as he anticipated what the morning would bring. An intentionally cool shower helped awaken him, as did a second cup of coffee, which he downed while reading the newspaper. "Patton's Men Swarm over Rhine and Head for Berlin Against Weak German Defenses" screamed its headline—yet another indication that the die was cast in Europe, and the Third Reich was now in its death throes. How shallow it seemed, with all the cataclysmic events around the world, for him to be so worried about saying a few inconsequential words to some farm girl from Axtell. He felt a little ashamed to place his selfish yearning on such an exalted plateau, particularly with Steve still far away, risking his life and playing a role of true significance on the global stage. Well, he thought, maybe he too would enlist, come the summer.

At one minute past nine, his peaceful reverie drew to a sudden finish when a dark-complexioned man unlocked the door and flipped the hanging sign around to read OPEN. Wesley sized him up from a distance and surmised that this must be Tom Salome, for he closely resembled Constantine, whom he met several weeks before. Constantine Salome was by no means a believer in the power of advertising, but maybe his brother would be more receptive to the idea. Their general merchandise store was located on Speight Avenue, not far from where Thirteenth Street intersected it and came to an abrupt and inexplicable dead-end.

Though Wesley wore a jaunty smile as he entered the establishment, in truth he did not hold out much hope that he would be writing a contract before he left. And he was right. Tom advised him to "see my brother, who handles whatever little advertising is done. We do not have a budget for that." Constantine was unloading crates in the stock room at the rear, and—while polite enough in his refusal—he was not noticeably more interested in radio commercials than he had been the first time he was contacted.

Being in the vicinity of Baylor University anyway, Wesley decided to visit Daniel Pharmacy, at the corner of Twelfth and Speight, as well as the furniture repair shop of Frank Votaw—both of which turned out to be closed on Saturdays. A more promising stop would have been the Safeway grocery store at Eleventh Street, but such a lucrative account invariably was to be found on another salesman's list of clients. Besides, Safeway advertising was managed by an agency, and Lee Graffen had never bothered to explain to Wesley how that mysterious process might work.

One more cold call remained before he would head downtown for his weekly cup of dark-roasted coffee at The Smoker's Den. All morning long, he kept reminding himself that this was just another Saturday morning. He tried not to dwell on his prospects of ever seeing the girl again, for otherwise he would be courting disappointment. Sure, a couple of weeks ago Rob Glynn did mention that his daughter might ride into town with him on the twenty-fourth, but by now her plans may have vacillated several times over. In any case, her animal husbandry endeavors undoubtedly were much more important to her than puttering around the retail shop for meager pay. Probably she would not be there, he decided, and that was final.

Among the commercial names that he had scrawled on his call list while preparing for the day's rounds was Potts-Moore Gravel Company. Upon closer inspection of the firm's locale, he now saw that the numerals 1610-1612 referred not to a street address but to an office suite number, high up in the Amicable Life Insurance Building at Fifth and Austin. Never in his entire eighteen years had Wesley set foot inside Waco's venerable skyscraper, but today that would change. He parallel parked along Fifth Street and, briefcase in hand, made his way into the art-deco lobby. This being a Saturday, the premises were not crowded with businessmen plying their various trades. The First National Bank was there on the street level, but it was closed for the weekend.

"Sixteen, please," he told the lethargic elevator operator, and up they went. It was a swiftly moving car, reaching its desired elevation in but a few seconds.

"Sixteen," the man said. The doors opened onto a floor that might have been found within an office building anywhere in America. There was no sensation of being almost two hundred feet in the air.

Wesley walked down a long corridor and viewed the stately titles on the doors: "Fred W. Pfaeffle & Company, Insurance," "Cleveland H. Brooks, Physician," "F. Glassell Elliott & Charles J. Eubank, Investments," "John B. McNamara, John B. Atkinson, & C. S. Farmer, Attorneys at Law," and finally, "Potts-Moore Gravel Company, Incorporated." Clearly, this was a sanctuary for the rich and powerful, and it felt bracing to be among them.

He knocked on the door marked 1610, but no one answered. As he was turning to walk away, Wesley tried the knob and was surprised to discover that it was unlocked. He peeked his head inside and called, "Hello?"

A distinguished-looking gentleman came forward from a rear office and identified himself as William H. Prentice, vice president of the firm. Obviously, he was not accustomed to having visitors on a Saturday morning, for Mr. Prentice was not wearing a necktie in public. Hanging on the wall behind the executive was an artistically rendered sign that read, "Washed and Screened Gravel and Sand, Road Gravel and Railroad Ballast, Largest and Best Equipped Pits in Central Texas, Wholesale and Retail, Thirty-One Years of Satisfactory Service, Phone 5176."

When the gentleman learned what Wesley's mission was in scaling the Amicable Building this particular day, he suggested that he come back at some more propitious time and present his credentials to C. W. Crisler, the manager and secretary-treasurer. "If anyone can help you, Mr. Crisler can," the vice president said. "He manages our advertising and has done so for many years now." Wesley excused himself and exited from the luxurious, high-rise amenities. Rarely before, if ever, had he been in close proximity to a company official of true stature, and it made him feel proud to be accorded such sympathetic attention.

Skies were overcast, and there was an uncomfortable mugginess in the air as he drove toward his next stop. Though it was only a quarter past ten, the temperature had already climbed into the upper sixties, unusually warm for one of the first days of spring. Some darkish patches of moisture were scattered in the cloud cover, but so far no rain had fallen. This he considered to be a fortunate development, all in all, for early that morning he had leaned his umbrella against the hat rack at home and then—still half asleep—promptly walked off without it. He would have felt awfully embarrassed to appear at The Smoker's Den with rain-drenched hair and rumpled shirt.

◆　　◆　　◆

Wesley pulled into a parking space with none of the difficulty that he might have encountered on a busy weekday, were he a member of the regular sales staff. With the engine idling, he switched on the radio for a moment to hear what KWXN was carrying. The voice of "Uncle" Bill Adams told him at once that it was "Let's Pretend," a nationwide children's program that utilized pre-teen actors in the major roles, and very convincingly too. Creator Nila Mack was still in charge after fifteen years on the air, seeing to it that a high standard of quality was maintained, and the sponsor, Cream of Wheat, took a proprietary interest in the show. His curiosity satisfied, Wesley silenced the radio and reached down to switch off the engine. Then he took a deep breath, grabbed his briefcase, and marched straight to the front door of The Smoker's Den.

At first glance, he saw no one inside, except for a woman customer with two small children. Both tots, a boy of about four and his younger sister, were gathered around the life-sized Indian statue—not quite afraid of it, but not fully trusting either. Rob Glynn must have heard the overhead bell tinkle when Wesley entered the store, for he came from the back room with his daughter and walked forward to greet him. As for Pippa, she returned to her customer with a canister of Colombian coffee, explaining to the woman and her children, as best she could, the story of how Tecumseh happened to make Waco, Texas, his permanent home. Naturally, Wesley would have preferred to devote his attention to her alone, but he could hardly ignore the friendly handshake, so he smiled at Rob and said, "Sure," when the manager offered him a freshly brewed cup of something called "Aromatique d'Amazon."

While they were walking toward one of the tables near the rear of the shop, Wesley could hear from the back room the sound of "Let's Pretend," and of course it grew louder as they came closer. Rob pulled out a chair for the boy and then continued over to the long line of commercial drip brewers.

"You have good taste in radio stations," Wesley said after seating himself.

"What did you say?" Rob asked with a smile. He was busy pouring two cups of that week's featured flavor.

"I hear KWXN," Wesley told him. "The radio."

"Oh, that. I think Pippa was listening to some cooking show before we opened up."

"That would have been Mary Lee Taylor," Wesley said. "She's been on the air for a dozen years. Her sponsor is Pet Milk." Obviously, he was proud of his product knowledge.

Rob, who did not seem to be listening very intently, brought two steaming cups over to the table. "I think you'll really like this blend."

The shop smelled wonderful. Owner Donnie Lee Satterfield specialized in the imported varieties, and his South American blends were especially enticing. This particular Brazilian coffee was dark and rich but rather too bitter for Wesley's relatively inexperienced taste buds. He was used to the tamer store-bought brands, while Rob, by the very nature of his job, was more of an adventurous cognoscente. Not two Saturdays in a row had he served the same coffee, and he exulted in being able to assess the quality of each, putting into descriptive words their strengths and shortcomings.

As for "Aromatique d'Amazon," Wesley drank half a cup, without complaint, before truthfully reporting that the previous flavor-of-the-week, also from Brazil, was marginally better. "Well, that's what Mr. Satterfield wants to know," Rob said. "It's the only way he can find out what people might like to buy." Consulting a descriptive brochure that was distributed with the pair of Brazilian blends, he read to Wesley that "the two are grown only about 350 miles apart, and yet their flavors and aromas are quite distinct, a paradox attributable to variances in rainfall and soil composition."

All of this was quite fascinating, Wesley felt sure, but he was much more interested in learning details about the girl who stood at the counter behind him—totally removed from his field of vision—and he was squandering precious time in conversation about coffee beans of the Amazon Basin. He was sorely tempted to pivot around anyway, under some pretext or other, but he feared that this maneuver might be too transparent, inasmuch as his genial host was the girl's own father, who no doubt was somewhat protective of her privacy. Wesley lowered his left forearm slightly below the level of the tabletop, so as to peek at his wristwatch without being detected. Ten forty, he saw, time to leave on his last couple of calls before returning to the station. It was now or never, he knew, and he steeled up his courage to change the subject.

"Daddy, can you help this customer find something?"

Wesley turned his head and saw that Pippa was standing no more than five feet away. He smiled at her, blushing slightly, and she smiled back, but only for a brief second.

"I'm sorry. Did I interrupt?" she asked her father.

"Yes, but that's quite all right, honey," Rob said. He rose to his feet.

"Excuse us," Pippa told Wesley. Then she accompanied her father back toward the tobacco counter. She was slight of build and rather short, certainly no taller than five foot three. Her dress swayed as she walked, for she had never been to the equivalent of charm school, and admittedly her gait was more suitable for feeding chickens than traversing a stage with a book balanced on top of her head.

With Rob Glynn's departure, Wesley was now free to swivel his chair around, and he gazed longingly at Pippa as she worked. She was pretty in a natural way, make-up or not, and her unaffected ways—some might say provincial or rustic—were very endearing to Wesley. He noticed that Pippa paid strict attention to her father while he explained the finer points of Cuban cigars to a white-haired man in his sixties. She appeared to be genuinely concerned about learning the business, occasionally nodding in response, never letting her eyes wander as if bored by what was being discussed. The negative side of this conscientiousness was that not even once did she glance back at Wesley, and he began to suspect that perhaps she was not the sort of girl who would be interested in him. For one thing, they might have very little in common. That fear, unsubstantiated though it was, felt like a knife cutting through his heart, for this Pippa Glynn enchanted him like nobody else ever had—and she did so without any artifice at all, just by being herself.

A purchase was made, and the white-haired man went away, satisfied with his replenished supply of premium cigars. Rob, meanwhile, had returned to the stock room momentarily, leaving his daughter out front, standing on the business side of the tobacco display case. Wesley knew that there was no time to lose. Swallowing hard, he stood up and grasped the handle of his briefcase. If he went back to the radio station, he might not see the girl for at least another month. And who could say for sure? She might stop coming to town altogether, and then he would very likely never see her again. He was not about to let that happen.

"Do you mind if I buy something from you?" he asked.

Pippa giggled. "Of course not. That's what we're here for."

"Swell." He smiled and walked over to her, laying his professional-looking briefcase by the counter.

"I'll bet you want some Aromatique d'Amazon, right?" she said. There was a twinkle in her eye that made him wonder if she was serious.

"No, thanks. I don't need any coffee today."

She frowned. "Do you smoke, then?"

"Oh, no." He was flattered that she would even ask such a worldly thing of him. "Not yet, anyway."

Pippa leaned her arms on the countertop and grinned. "Well, that's all we have—just coffee and tobacco. You'll have to choose between those two."

"Actually, it's for my brother, Steve. He's in the Navy, and I think he'd like for me to send him some pipe tobacco."

"What brand does he use?"

"I have no idea. What can you recommend?"

"Search me. That's a matter of personal taste." She surveyed the shelves. "Want to come over here and have a look?"

He walked around the end of the counter and did not stop until he was standing right next to her, only about a foot apart. But he seemed to be staring more at her than at the pouches of tobacco. She placed her hand on his back and gently turned him toward the shelves. "I thought you wanted some pipe tobacco."

"Yes, for my brother."

"Steve."

He looked at her, a little puzzled, but then recalled that he had told her the name just a minute earlier. Wesley dragged his index finger across several of the package ends and settled upon a brand that boasted its name in ornate script. "What about this one?" he asked.

Unsure of that product's reputation, Pippa shook her head. "No, I want you to be satisfied with your purchase, 'Mr. Customer,' and I think Steve would much prefer to smoke one of the major brands. How about something from Philip Morris here?" She reached for a package of Bond Street and handed it to Wesley. "It's fifteen cents. I put the price tag on it myself."

"I remember."

"You do?" She smiled up at him.

"It was exactly eight weeks ago today. You were wearing a lime green dress with little white ruffles around the collar."

"I do have a dress like that," she said.

Wesley examined the package of tobacco and then held it up to his nose. "Go ahead and give me two more. They won't be expensive to mail."

"Would you like to try a sample, just to make sure?" she asked. "We have some trial pipes, and we steam clean them after every use."

"No, thanks, Pippa. My brother's the smoker, not me."

"I don't even remember your name. Isn't that rude of me?"

"Wesley Brower. Most people call me Wes."

"Okay, Wes."

"Pippa is a pretty name. It suits you."

She rolled her eyes. "It's from a poem by Browning, but I'm not very fond of it. I don't know what my parents were thinking."

"Then why don't you go by your middle name instead?"

"Herndon?" They both laughed. "I do know where that came from. It's a family name."

"I still like Pippa."

"Thank you. That's very sweet—even if you are just saying it to be nice. Mama heard the name in English class and always liked it. Pippa is the character who sings, 'God's in His heaven - All's right with the world'."

"So, you're named after somebody famous."

"Well, sort of, but she wasn't a real person."

Rob Glynn appeared once again and was surprised to see his daughter and the young salesman standing together behind the tobacco counter. Wesley hurried around to the customer side, three packages in hand. "I've decided on this kind, Mr. Glynn—for my brother."

"His brother's in the Navy, Daddy," Pippa said, unfazed by the seemingly embarrassing situation. "His name is Steve."

Rob looked at both of them and then smiled. "That'll be forty-five cents, Wes. It's about time we got some money out of you." He walked over to the cash register and pressed down heavily on the key. "She's a good salesgirl, isn't she?"

"I'll say," Wesley said. He paid the store manager with a shiny, new Walking Liberty half-dollar, and Rob gave him a wartime copper/silver/manganese five-cent piece in change. As was his habit, Wesley glanced at the nickel before sliding it into his pocket. A large "P" was above Monticello, so he knew the coin had traveled all the way from Philadelphia—probably in a sack aboard an Army train, for reasons of security.

Wesley had stayed much longer than planned. The radio in the back room could be heard just loudly enough to tell him that it was nearly eleven o'clock. "A Pretty Girl Is Like a Melody" was playing after a Listerine commercial, so he knew "The Billie Burke Show" was coming to an end.

After shaking hands again, he said goodbye and was about to walk out the door when Rob thought of the briefcase. "Say, aren't you forgetting something?"

Wesley remembered at once. "I might be needing that. It's got my list of junk accounts." He realized, too late, what he had blurted and trusted that Rob would not take the capricious remark personally.

"I'll get it!" Pippa said. She ran across the room to fetch the briefcase. "Here, Wes," she said and then turned to her father. "Daddy, maybe sometime he would like to see my horses."

"You're invited," Rob told the young man. He looked down at his daughter and added, "Maybe Mommy can fix him a Sunday dinner." She nodded her head slightly but otherwise betrayed no emotion.

"Do you like fried chicken, son?" Rob asked.

"Oh, yes, sir," Wesley said. In fact, one of his very favorite meals was fried chicken. He only hoped that the main dish would be of the Piggly Wiggly variety and not former pets of Pippa.

♦   ♦   ♦

At first glance, Corporal Samuel Simpkins appeared to be a man of his word. He showed up at the appointed time and place, rather than skipping away with Danny Rignold's down payment of two pounds sterling. When the American sergeant arrived at The Red Lion on Thursday at six, he spotted the procurer at once—sitting by himself at a table, not far from where four airmen were engaged in a game of ninepins on the pub's skittle alley. It was still a bit early for many soldiers to be around, so Danny had an unobstructed view of him from far across the room. What unsettled the Yank was his observation that all Simpkins had to keep him company was a partially consumed pint of lager. There was no female hireling to be seen.

"Where is she?" Danny demanded to know, and he did so with none of the normal preliminaries of polite society.

"Hello, Rignold, old boy. You're here to pay me my three quid, aren't you?"

Danny was not amused. "Well, there are certain conditions to be met before I do that."

"I know, I know. And I suppose you're wondering where Vickie is." He took a swallow of beer. "Want some?"

"All I want, corporal—"

"Call me Sammy."

"All I want, corporal, is my date for tonight, and I don't detect anyone who fits that description. I'm gonna look awfully silly dancin' with a broom."

"Don't worry. I'll give your money back—double—if she doesn't show. That's how much I trust her."

This was a bold statement to make, and Danny accepted it at face value. He pulled back a chair and sat down at the table. "You say her name's Vickie?"

"Victoria Forrest."

"And she's on her way now?"

"She'd be here already, but you see, she's not a Kettering girl. She's from Rothwell, out toward the uplands."

"How far is that?"

"Rothwell? Oh, I'd say about five miles, maybe less. One of my men is bringing her."

Danny laughed. "Since when does a corporal have men workin' for him?"

"A private named Imbrie offered to drive the lady here, in lieu of a debt he owes me."

Feeling better about the situation, Danny informed the airman that perhaps he would have that pint after all.

"That's right, relax," Simpkins told him. "She'll be here any minute now—you'll see." He walked over to the bar and returned with a glass of beer for his client.

"Thanks," Danny said, and he took a sip of the dark brew.

"Listen, mate, there's something I need to tell you about Vickie."

"Uh-oh, here it comes." Danny frowned, certain that the entire plan was about to fall apart. To fortify himself for bad news, he swallowed a mouthful of the lager. "Okay—shoot. What about her?"

"You don't trust me very much, do you?"

"It's not that, corporal. Only—"

"Sammy."

"Okay, then ... Sammy."

Simpkins savored some more of his pint, and then, as he was thinking about how to phrase what he had to say, his eyes suddenly widened. He made a gesture with his head.

Danny turned around and saw a fair-skinned girl coming toward them. The first thing he noticed about her was how slender she was—rather too thin for good health. But she also had a charming face, pretty enough to appear in one of those magazine ads for facial cream.

"Hello, Vickie," the corporal said with an easy smile. "I'd like for you to meet Sergeant Rignold. He's a member of the USAAF."

"Just Danny ..." the American told his date.

Simpkins beckoned her with his free, non-beer hand. "Come over here and have a seat for a minute, won't you, love?"

Vickie did as she was told, sitting between the two servicemen. Danny immediately liked what he saw, at least in terms of attractiveness. But at the same time, he felt sorry for the girl, who seemed timid and not at all comfortable being a date of convenience. He could already see that this might not be a pleasant experience for either of them, so he was about to call the whole thing off, figuring that Simpkins would be entitled to the two-pound deposit, nothing more. And yet something in the sadness of her face made him think twice about rejecting her so cruelly. She might assume that he had done so on the basis of looks alone, and that would be a crushing blow to any young lady such as this. Besides, she really was quite lovely, despite her sylphlike figure, and her green eyes stared at him with a loneliness that touched his heart.

No sooner had she joined them at the table than Simpkins took a swig of beer and was on his feet. "Excuse us, Vickie, but the sarge here would like to settle up, and then you two can be on your way." She answered their polite smiles with a nervous one of her own, granting the men a few minutes to converse about her in private. They walked across the pub and stopped outside the room marked TOILET.

Danny spoke first. "Can she talk? I mean, she hasn't said a single word."

"But you must admit, she's a very pretty girl."

"Okay, sure, but does she say anythin'? Does she even speak English?"

Simpkins shook his head in frustration. "Of course she speaks English. I told you she's from Rothwell. It's just that she's a very quiet person, and she's been through an awful lot."

"Listen, I'm not a psychiatrist, and I don't want to be responsible for anyone who's on the verge of a nervous breakdown. All I want is somebody nice to dance with for a couple of hours. That's what I paid you for."

"Which reminds me, sarge. You've only given me two of the five pounds I'm due."

Danny tried to detect what Simpkins was thinking, but the British corporal wore the impenetrable face of a con artist. "First, tell me what you wanted to say earlier."

"About what?"

"Don't, Simpkins. I'm not in the mood to play guessin' games. What we're doin' now is wastin' time—on my money. You said there was somethin' you needed to tell me about my date."

Simpkins suddenly recalled. "Oh, that. Well, there's not much to it. All I wanted to say was that Vickie has been through hell in the past year, and she might not be the friendliest company in the world—until you get to know her better."

"What's the story?"

Simpkins looked toward the girl, and even from this distance, he could see that she was not exactly illuminating the pub with her effervescence. Indeed, she was sitting with her head down, arms folded across her chest, the very epitome of clinical depression. He would not tell the Yank that, of course.

"Well?"

"Vickie's married, for one thing."

"Oh? Any other little details you should mention?"

"Her husband's American, a P-51 pilot. He's missing, believed killed."

Danny nodded his head. "Well, that's awfully sad—and I'm just as sorry as I can be—but the fact remains that I don't think she'll be a bundle of laughs tonight, which is what I'm payin' you for."

Simpkins could see his five pounds flying away. "Is it really? Is that all you're paying me for? What about intelligent conversation? What about a very pretty face? What about boosting her spirit a little?" He leaned closer and lowered his voice. "What about giving her a squeeze when she hasn't had any for a year, hey?"

"That's not what I'm after, and you know it," Danny said.

That made the corporal smirk. "You mean to tell me that if a girl like this invited you back to her flat, all you'd do is have tea and cake?"

"I don't expect much more excitement than that for my lousy five pounds," Danny told him. "But I also don't expect her to sit in silence for half the night, like a wallflower. Can you guarantee me that she'll talk?"

"She talks to me, mate."

"Is she gettin' paid for this?"

"You mean, am I paying her to be your date?" Simpkins chuckled and held up his hands. "That I'm not at liberty to say. I can't violate the sacred trust between a client and her agent."

Danny pulled out the money. "You say she likes Americans, huh?"

"She married one, didn't she?"

Corporal Simpkins was three pounds richer when they returned to the table, and he was in a fine mood. "Well, you two children have fun, won't you? Danny, just have her back here by midnight is all I ask, and I'll see to it that she gets home safely."

♦   ♦   ♦

The Army jeep that Danny borrowed for the evening was fun to maneuver through traffic, but driving on the left side of the road took considerable practice and a few near misses before it really could be mastered. Strictly speaking, he had no prerogative to be driving this unauthorized vehicle, but few MPs were known to patrol the country roads that far west of Grafton Underwood, so he was safe for the time being.

The only reason the jeep was at his disposal this night was because Mike Hibbett owed him a small favor for the surplus Mae West that Danny gave him. Hibbett was a mechanic in the motor pool, and a clever one at that, but it was unclear what possible use he could make of an inflatable life vest from the quartermaster. Maybe he just planned to generate some money from it down the line, for he was forever covetous of other people's discretionary income. And he made a nifty deal on the payback arrangement with Sergeant Rignold too. The loan of this vehicle cost him nothing whatsoever—except, of course, his bleeding hide if the jeep happened to return to camp with more dents on it than when it left.

As for Vickie Forrest, she did not mind riding in an American jeep at all. In fact, she seemed to enjoy the experience again. She and her husband, Jimmy, used to zip around Raydon in one of them not so very long ago. Jimmy was one of those fly-boys who simply liked speed—of whatever description—whether he was on flat terrain in a four-wheeler or kissing the stratosphere in his four-hundred-fifty-miles-per-hour Mustang.

"You have a pretty smile," Danny said to her as they neared Grafton. He had told Vickie a funny story about his mother's cow, which possessed the same name as her sister-in-law.

"Thank you, sergeant, but you really don't have to pass out the compliments. I'm past that stage of my life." She was back to being serious again.

"How old are you, if you don't mind my askin'."

"Actually, I do mind. Let's just say I'm almost thirty."

"Fair enough." He liked the way the wind blew through her short brown hair but did not seem to displace it. "You do this often?"

"Ride around in jeeps with strange Americans?"

He shook his head. "Go to dances with strange Americans."

"This is the first time I've been to a dance since ... since Jimmy. I never went to Grafton Underwood without him. It just happens to be near my home."

"You live with your parents?"

"Yes, and my younger sister."

No MPs were anywhere to be seen, so Danny did not have to go to the extreme of asking his date to hide under Hibbett's blanket in back. That was only a last resort, and besides, it was a well-known fact that snowdrops usually looked the other way whenever a pretty date was involved. Same thing with the native redcaps, for that matter.

The Aeroclub was decorated to the hilt, and British girls were there in splendid profusion. It was plain to see that the American fliers were making the most of this opportunity, for all but a few were on the dance floor at a given time. Just a handful of their introverted counterparts chose to sit out the musical action, occupying themselves by leafing through magazines or writing letters home. No alcohol was permitted inside, but a few of the men brought their own—on the sly of course. And then, for the less enterprising drinkers, there were three varieties of punch to complement the tasty assortment of cake and cookies arrayed on the back table. A sugar shortage in the military was not in evidence.

Danny eyed the jitterbuggers. "Care to?" he asked, and Vickie nodded yes. She was an excellent dancer, fleet and nimble in the wilder numbers, more athletic than her tiny frame might have suggested. In contrast, Danny was passable at best. It was all he could do to just keep up with the beat and not appear so ungainly that he attracted attention.

While they were dancing to a slow tune—about one of every four in the chart rotation—he asked Vickie why she had been so quiet at The Red Lion. This puzzled him because it was like she had a split personality. "I don't trust Corporal Simpkins," she said, "and I don't want to give that spiv any wrong ideas."

"What has he ever done to you?"

"Nothing, to me personally. I hardly know the man. But he deals in all kinds of trade—anything that's worth money, and that includes women."

Danny was shocked. "You mean ...?"

"He knows every woman east of Birmingham, and some of them make money the hard way."

"Are you afraid of him?"

"A little, perhaps. He has a friend who knew Jimmy, and that's how he happened to ring me about this occasion tonight."

Danny escorted her over to a table and then went for two cups of strawberry-coconut punch. Immediately, the young lady lit up a cigarette.

Upon returning, he asked her point-blank, "Did the corporal pay you to come with me?" He scooted out his chair to sit down, awaiting her answer.

Vickie rested her burning cigarette in an ashtray and drank the punch instead. "He made me promise not to tell you. He said it might make you feel bad." Then, with a sarcastic laugh, she added, "As if he cares for a minute how you feel."

"I will have to give him some credit, though," Danny said. "He found me a swell date."

"Thank you, but just don't get too interested in me, sergeant. Remember, I'm still a married woman." She reached down for her cigarette and took a puff. "The only reason I'm here is to entertain an American soldier for a few hours. I don't think Jimmy would mind that. In fact, I think he'd be proud of me."

"How long ago did he ...?"

"Six months." She answered him like this was a recurring question, which it probably was.

"Have you heard anythin'?"

"Just that first telegram, 'The Department of War regrets to inform you,' but nothing more. Oh, they claim to be making some sort of investigation, you know, through official channels. 'But these things take time,' they say. I don't believe them. I know Jimmy, and he would have found a way to contact me—if he was still alive. I know in my heart that he's not." Her eyes were turning red with emotion. "He was shot down over Germany. You know, Mustangs can fly with bombers all the way to Berlin and back without even refueling."

"Shhhh. I know," Danny whispered. "But don't tell everyone else our little secret."

She lowered her voice. "I guess you would know that, wouldn't you? I mean, in your line of business."

"Well, I don't work on P-51s, but I do have a pretty good idea of their range."

Vickie took a deep breath and sighed. "Jimmy's plane didn't make it. He never returned from the raids of September 27. The newspaper said Americans bombed Cologne, Mainz, Kassel, and Ludwigshafen that day, so I suppose it happened over one of those cities. Now he's either dead or a prisoner of war."

"I'm sorry. I shouldn't have asked," Danny said. "You didn't come here to be reminded of ..." He could not think of how to finish the sentence in a way that would not be hurtful. "You didn't come here to be reminded."

"That's quite all right. I don't mind thinking about Jimmy. I do it all the time." She wiped her eyes. "But I'm not doing tonight's job very well, am I?"

"Better than you think ... Mrs. Forrest."

"Oh, please! That sounds dreadfully rigid. Tonight I'm just plain Vickie."

"Okay, Vickie. And I'm Danny to you. No more of that 'sergeant' stuff."

"That's a deal, Danny."

He drank some punch and watched her take another drag of the cigarette. "But your real name's Victoria. Are you named after the Queen?"

"Naturally—being a good subject of the Crown." She turned her head and exhaled the smoke through rounded lips. "My grandparents once saw the Queen in London, near the very end of her life. I think she was about eighty at the time. They're the ones who wanted to name me after her, not my parents."

"Were these your father's folks or your mother's?"

She thought for a minute. "I honestly don't know. I never did think to ask. Isn't that daft?"

"Well, either way you have the prestige of a royal name."

"My husband says he was named after General Doolittle, but I'm pretty certain he was just kidding me."

"That's a safe assumption," Danny said.

She giggled, recalling her own gullibility. "Jimmy always had a good sense of humor, and maybe that's what first drew me to him. He was a little older than his pals, so he was kind of their leader, I think." Then her face turned serious, and she added, "Most of them are gone now too."

"Do you hold out any hope at all?"

"There's always that, isn't there? But as time goes by, you begin to lose some of it, day by day. After six months, mine's all but disappeared."

"And of course there's prayer," he said.

She was not keen on the idea. "I'm not very strong when it comes to that, I'm afraid."

Danny smiled. "You should try it sometime. It can work wonders." For some reason, he thought of Elizabeth Brower, that sweet teenager in Texas. Maybe it was because of the deep faith he sensed in her. He also remembered attending church one time with a college coed who rented a room at the Brower house. That girl was very religious. And her friend drove a beautiful 1942 Studebaker President—a Skyway Land Cruiser, it was. Funny, he could picture it but not the driver.

After the dance was over, on the road back to Kettering, Vickie posed the startling appeal that Danny take her directly to her home instead of returning to The Red Lion.

"We can't do that," the American sergeant told her. "Simpkins will think I kidnapped you—or worse—and he'd probably have the MPs hot on my trail. Besides, he'd charge me extra for keepin' you overtime."

"If it's the money, don't worry about that. I just don't want to meet with Sammy Simpkins again—and I have my reasons."

"But won't you need to be there to get paid?"

She grinned. "Who said I'm getting paid? Maybe I'm just doing this to help our American cousins in khaki."

Danny smiled but kept his eyes on the road. "Is that how you think of me—as your cousin?"

"No. More like my brother, if I had one. My slightly younger brother, whom I love."

"Good answer."

Sammy Simpkins was sitting at a table alongside Geoffrey Hoak when Danny entered the pub with his date. A lieutenant was playing the upright piano, and many of the airmen in The Red Lion were singing "Kiss Me Goodnight, Sergeant Major," an Art Noel/Don Pelosi hit from the earliest days of the war. The corporal and sergeant were not indulging in song, but they had participated most heartily in downing drafts of beer, empty pint glasses of which now stood in silent tribute to their prowess. Hoak had three in front of him, and his pal did him one better.

Simpkins glanced up and saw Sergeant Rignold approaching. "Can't be! Is it that time already?" A glance at Hoak's wristwatch confirmed to him that it was indeed ten minutes before midnight. Danny walked right up to the table, but Vickie hardly came into the pub at all, remaining a good distance away, still quite near the front door. "Hey, did you show our Yank a good time, love?" Simpkins shouted. The girl did not answer.

"She's asked me to take her home, rather than troublin' you," Danny said. "She's grown quite fond of that jeep."

"Oh, no trouble at all, I can assure you," Simpkins told him. "Her late husband and I had a mutual friend, so I feel very close to her."

"That may be the case, Sammy—and I'm sure it is—but still she's asked me to take her home, and I feel honor-bound to do so, just to finish off a pleasant evenin'. How about it?"

The British corporal's attitude changed in a flash to one of resentment, almost like a scorned lover, and he glared at the girl who stood in the shadows. "I should remind Mrs. Forrest that we have a business deal, and *she* should feel honor-bound to do precisely as it stipulates."

"All right. I'll go tell her that," Danny said. He turned away from the corporal but then paused and asked him, "What's the name of your friend?"

"What's it to you?"

"Just idle curiosity, I guess. Well, if you don't want to tell me, I can ask her." He took a step toward the girl, but Simpkins jumped to his feet and grabbed the American's shoulder. "Hold it. Don't bother her with that. It just brings back sad memories to her."

"Then you'll let me take her?"

"It'll cost you another pound—for keeping her out past midnight. That's what our agreement says, and Geoff was right here with me when the deal was struck. He'll bear me out."

Danny looked at Sergeant Hoak, who obviously had no idea what was being discussed, much less that he was a material witness.

"Okay, Simpkins," Danny said. "Fair enough."

"And another quid for denying me the pleasure of her company. After all, you are, in essence, abrogating the entire deal."

None too happy, Danny pulled out two pounds and extended the money for Simpkins to take, which he refused to do. "No, you give that to the lass," he told him. "It'll be much simpler that way, and she'll know why."

"All right, then," Danny said with a frown. The way he figured it, this date had cost him the princely sum of seven pounds—five to Simpkins and two to Vickie Forrest. "But I will say somethin' for you, Sammy."

"Huh?"

"You have very good taste in women, and I appreciate that much anyway. See you around maybe."

"Yeah, maybe."

"Goodbye, Hoak."

"Tara."

◆   ◆   ◆

It was only about five miles to Rothwell, but it seemed much farther than that—at least when driving through unfamiliar territory in the dead of night. If Kettering was considered to be a small town, then its sister settlement to the northwest was hardly more than a village or even a hamlet. Rothwell lay on the road to Leicester, but it was nestled in a farmland stretch of Northamptonshire, and Sergeant Rignold encountered no other vehicular traffic the entire way. His passenger, Vickie Forrest, told him there was an ancient church in Rothwell, an impressive structure that dated from the thirteenth century and was well worth seeing in the daylight.

Danny grinned. "I guess that'll have to wait for some other time."

"Yes, I should think so." She knew that Jimmy's hypothetical consent for her date with the American would not extend very far into the morning hours.

"Will your folks be up at this time of night?" Danny asked.

Vickie laughed softly. "Well, don't be surprised if they are—especially Mum, who thinks I've just climbed out of the pram. Dad needs to rise early, so I'm not so sure about him."

"Is he a farmer?"

"No. He's employed at a metal factory in Burton Latimer now—over on the other side of Kettering. He used to be at a shoe factory in Rowell, but they needed him for war work, so he changed jobs."

"Were you born in Rothwell?"

"Oh, yes. I've come back to the house I was born in."

"You were born at home?"

"So I've been told—with a midwife and all."

"Do you like it better than where your husband was stationed?"

"It's hard to compare the two because Raydon's just outside Ipswich, which is a rather large city. Rowell's a market town, and it used to be bigger than Kettering—

until the railroad came, and it hasn't grown much since then. Have you ever heard of the Rowell Fair?"

"No."

"The fair's been going for over seven hundred years, on the day after Trinity Sunday—eight weeks past Easter. Our parish church is named Holy Trinity for that reason."

Danny smiled at her. "You sound like a history teacher."

"As a matter of fact, history was one of my weakest subjects in school. It's just that I've heard this kind of talk all my life."

"You could have fooled me."

Vickie acknowledged the compliment with a smile. "Besides the annual fair, Rowell has a market every Monday, so that brings lots of folks to town—or it did before the war."

"Why do you call it Rowell?"

"I don't know. That's just what we say around here. I do know that Rothwell means 'red well.' The springs in the area have reddish water, and local residents used to claim they had healing powers. It's a friendly town, you know—full of good people, if I do say so myself—but I doubt that I would have chosen to spend my whole life there."

An animal ran across the road, narrowly escaping the jeep. It scampered so fast that—in the dim and bouncing headlight beams—Danny could not determine if it was a small dog or a large rabbit. It certainly was not a nocturnal animal like an opossum, for they were too slow afoot to make it to the other side in one piece, and anyhow, he did not suspect that they had many "possums" in England.

"Was your husband gonna take you back to the States with him after the war?"

"We never really discussed it. I suppose so, but I can't say for certain. He was from New Jersey."

"Do you know his parents?"

"No. We wrote to each other after the wedding, but only twice. I have a picture of them, but I'm not exactly sure where it is."

Vickie's house was a very modest structure, not much more than four rooms, or so it seemed from the outside. The front window was lit from within, so either someone in her family had waited up for her, or they had left a lamp on for her return. "Oh, before I forget," Danny said. He reached into his coat pocket for the two pounds. "This is from Sammy Simpkins."

"Just give me one," she told him, "for services rendered. You had to bring me all the way home, and surely that's worth something, isn't it?"

He hesitated for a moment before finally agreeing. "Well, maybe so. I did get soaked pretty badly by that shyster. I'm not complainin', though. I had a swell time."

"I did too, but remember what I told you. Nothing personal." She leaned over and kissed him on the cheek. "You know, I'm rather partial to Americans in uniform."

He switched off the engine. "What's gonna happen now?"

"For me?"

He nodded his head. "How long do you think it'll be?"

"If I don't hear anything in seven years' time, then Jimmy will be declared officially dead, and so of course I'll become an instant widow." She uttered this statement with an emotionless detachment that took Danny by surprise, and she could see it in his eyes. "I shouldn't be so churlish about this, I know, but I've just about given up all hope of ever receiving a definite answer. I can be rather a cold fish when it comes to Army protocol and the governmental manner of doing things." She tapped her chest. "But in here ... Believe me, not a day goes by that I don't cry for my husband."

"Well, no matter what some people say, the War Department is awfully skillful at notifyin' relatives. We've got Jerry on the run now, so it can't last much longer." He patted her hand in brotherly fashion. "I think you'll hear soon enough. I pray to God that you do—and you can take that to the bank, comin' from a good Catholic boy like me."

"Do you want to come inside for a few minutes? I'd like to show my mum that I didn't go out with an oversexed Yank." She saw him blush at her frank comment. "Sorry, Danny, but that's what she was sure I was getting myself into."

"That's all right. I understand."

"Our boys say you Yanks are 'overpaid, overfed, oversexed, and over here'."

"I know. And we say the Brits are 'underpaid, underfed, undersexed, and under Eisenhower'."

The girl laughed. "I'm sure we deserved that, in a way." She gestured toward the house. "Shall we?"

The front door was unlocked, so Vickie walked right in, stepping aside to let Danny pass. A gray-haired lady in a faded, floral dress stood up, smiling uneasily.

"Mum, I'd like for you to meet Sergeant Rignold. Danny's in the USAAF, an airplane mechanic who services the heavy bombers. Who knows? Jimmy may have escorted some of his planes."

"Pleased to make your acquaintance, sergeant. I'm Olivia Coulter." She extended her hand very daintily, as women often do, and Danny shook it as gently as he could. "Would you like some tea? I'll go put on the kettle." Not waiting for an answer, she disappeared into the kitchen, and Vickie giggled.

"Mum can't do anything these days without a cup of tea within reach. I think it steadies her nerves, now that she's stopped smoking."

A tall, imposing man of about sixty entered the room, followed by a bashful girl who was probably still in her teens—or very early twenties at most.

"I hope I didn't wake you, Dad," Vickie said. "This is Sergeant Danny Rignold."

"Well, I'm up, aren't I, Chick?" He was gruff and showed no signs of smiling.

"I did too wake him, Danny, because I can tell that he's not his usual sweet self."

The man brushed off the comment and held out his hand. "I'm Jack Coulter, sergeant. What outfit are you with?"

"Grafton Underwood. I'm a mechanic." They shook hands.

"The 384th Bombardment Group—Heavy ... B-17Gs, right?"

Danny was so astonished that he could not answer, and this caused his host to nearly crack a smile.

"Don't forget," Jack told him, "we're an Army family—and the American Army at that—so we do hear things."

"It's very reassurin' to know that our security is so tight," the Yank said, and Jack Coulter had to laugh.

"Well, we do see the odd Flying Fortress go over, so Grafton's really not much of a mystery to us."

Vickie continued the introductions. "And that's my younger sister. Margery, this is Sergeant Danny Rignold."

"Nice to meet you," she said with a shallow bow. Margery was not as pretty in the face as her sister, but neither was she so very thin.

"So, Danny, it's 'Keep the Show on the Road,' hey?" Jack said. He was proud of himself for knowing all of these state secrets.

"Yes, sir, that's our motto."

Vickie giggled. "Oh, don't humor him, Danny. He just likes to show off in front of strangers, and some day it will land him in jail if he starts doing it to a German spy."

"Tommyrot!" Jack told her. "If I can't trust a GI who takes my own daughter to a dance, then what is this world coming to? Did you know Jimmy Forrest?"

"No, sir. I've only been here since October, and that was after ... Anyway, I understand he was over at Raydon, and I've never been east of London."

"Well, he came to Grafton many times, of course, when he was here on leave with Vickie. I suppose some of your mates know him, don't you think?"

"I don't know, sir. That's possible, I guess."

"Ah, he's a fine-looking boy, tall as a tree and always smiling. Vickie showed you his pictures, didn't she?"

"No, sir."

Jack bellowed, "Mother!" toward the kitchen.

Olivia Coulter, carrying a serving tray, came back into the room and confronted her husband. "Why is it that you are so loud at this hour of the morning?" She looked at her daughters. "Girls?" They took the tray from her and laid it on the dinner table. Vickie motioned for Danny to join them, which he did.

Across the room, Jack was telling Olivia that their guest wished to see a photo album. "Some fellows in the sergeant's unit may have seen Jimmy when he was at Grafton Underwood."

"Oh?" She hurried over to the bookcase and found Vickie's wedding album. Then, as she carried it over to the table, she told Danny, "I'm sure Jimmy will be safe. We'll hear something from the War Department soon."

"That's right," her husband said. "The bloody Jerries will be whipped before we know it, and Jimmy will come marching home—hey, Chick?" Vickie just looked at him, saying nothing.

Olivia, however, glared at him. "Don't swear, Father—with a guest in the house."

"It's not swearing when it's the bloody Jerries!" he said.

"Milk, sergeant?" Mrs. Coulter asked. She was about ready to pour.

"Wait, Mum," Vickie said. "Americans don't like it that way. At least Jimmy didn't." With a wistful smile, she looked at the Yank.

Embarrassed, Danny informed his hostess that he was not fond of milk or sugar in his tea.

"How can you drink it like that, lad?" Mr. Coulter asked. He and the others added milk liberally and also stirred in two or three spoonfuls of saccharine apiece.

"Now, there's Jimmy," Olivia said. She indicated two pages of his flying photos, all neatly mounted and captioned, as if in a scrapbook. There were some newspaper clippings too.

Danny surveyed the pages but had to be truthful. "I really don't think there's much of a chance my pals saw him. Grafton has thousands of personnel, and if Jimmy only came to the PX ..."

Jack nodded his head, with more disappointment than surprise. "Well, I suppose it's just too big of a place, is this Grafton Underwood."

"Let me show you the wedding pictures," Vickie's mother said. She presented Danny with six crowded pages of photos, all snapped, he was told, inside the Church of the Holy Trinity.

"Jimmy's a handsome boy, isn't he?" Olivia asked.

"Oh, yes, ma'am," Danny said, but mostly he was admiring the lovely bride who stood beside him.

The hour was growing quite late when the two sisters cleared away the cups, saucers, pitchers, and teapot. Vickie's parents relaxed on the sofa for a moment, and Danny sat in an adjacent chair.

"It's not every day that we get an American soldier out here in Rowell," Olivia said. "We miss having Jimmy around."

"I'm sure you do, and I'm sorry." He glanced across the room, making certain that Vickie was not within earshot. "Do you think there's much hope that he'll be found alive?"

Jack sighed. "Every day that goes by makes it less likely, to my thinking. Olivia's more optimistic than I am, aren't you, love?"

"Sometimes. Other days, I'm as hopeless as can be. Right now, for some reason, I do think we'll see Jimmy again, but I don't know how to explain it—just a feeling I have."

Danny nodded his head. "If he was able to hit the silk in time, there's always a chance. No eyewitnesses, huh?"

"None," Jack told him, but he qualified the statement by adding a more positive note. "Several crewmen in the lost bombers, so I've heard, are known to have been taken into enemy hands ... and a few fighter pilots too. Then word came just three days ago that another airman is a prisoner as well ... a navigator/bombardier. I don't think bookkeeping is Germany's highest priority right now."

Consulting his wristwatch, Danny announced that he had to be going. "It's a workday tomorrow, and I've got a borrowed jeep to return to the motor pool."

"Past my bedtime too," Jack Coulter said, "but it's been grand meeting you, lad. I think tonight has done Chick a world of good. She mopes about quite a lot lately, as you might imagine."

"Vickie says you do war work, sir."

"I'm employed at Sterling Metals in Burton Latimer these days—melting ingots into liquid to mold the bomb casings, you know. I used to work at the Groococks Shoe Factory, right here in Rowell, but Sterling pays better, and I feel like I'm helping more. Maybe even avenging Jimmy, if it comes to that."

When the girls returned, their parents stood up and bid a warm farewell to the visiting soldier. Margery walked over to him and kissed him on the cheek, just as her sister had done about an hour earlier in the jeep. Then the three of them retired to their respective beds, leaving Vickie and Danny alone in the front room.

"Thank you for a marvelous evening, Sergeant Danny Rignold," Vickie said. She took both of his hands in her own.

Danny smiled. "Thank you ... Mrs. Victoria Forrest. I had a swell time."

She stared at him for a moment, tears forming in her eyes, and then she threw her arms around Danny and kissed him on the lips. Releasing him a moment later, Vickie stepped backward and again grasped both of his hands. She was visibly trembling as she whispered, "I miss my husband desperately, Danny, and I will do anything to get him back. Tomorrow I even plan to try your praying idea."

"So will I," he said. "I promise to do the same."

As he turned to go, Vickie stopped him for a moment and did a strange thing—at least it seemed strange to him. She kissed the palm of her hand and touched Danny's forehead with it. Tears were streaming down her cheeks by now, but he could not hear her crying. Her lips were quivering slightly, but otherwise she appeared to be quite composed, at peace with herself, perhaps even hopeful.

He walked out the door, but just before Vickie shut it behind him, she whispered, "Goodbye, dear Danny. Please think good thoughts of me here in Rowell."

◆　　　◆　　　◆

It had been five months since Giulia last saw her father—on the day the Bluebonnet Ordnance Plant received its "E" flag for excellence in war work. Merely a week later, in early November, Francesco "Frank" Coletti packed up his belongings and moved southeast about sixty miles to Robertson County. That was when his new job's thirty-day probationary period ended, qualifying him as a civilian office clerk for the United States Army. His duty station was a compound for war prisoners called Camp Hearne.

Giulia boarded the Waco-to-Houston bus at 7:10 in the morning, with hopes of greeting her father in Hearne shortly after nine o'clock. Two wild-eyed high school boys ogled the attractive passenger when she entered the bus. They seemed to have been drinking, even at that early hour and that early age, so she hurried up the aisle toward the rear, finding an available seat next to an elderly Mexican man whose two companions sat directly in front of them. From the way the men dressed and talked, Giulia guessed that they were migrant workers of some sort.

They spoke not a word of English during the entire trip but kept up a steady conversation with one another through the small opening between the chair backs.

As Giulia occupied an aisle seat, she could not follow her progress as closely as she liked, so instead she relied upon the infrequent announcements from the driver—Riesel, Perry, Marlin, Reagan, Calvert, and finally Hearne. When the bus came to a stop, Giulia stood up and began making her way forward. A young soldier several rows in front of her exited first, and she saw him pass by the high school boys, who were still aboard. As she neared them, one happened to look back and notice her, and he of course elbowed his friend. Each of them proceeded to give a wolf whistle and make some ribald commentary until the driver glowered them into silence. Standing to his full height, he spoke softly but left little doubt that he meant business. "As long as I'm at the wheel, scamps, the ladies on this coach will not be treated with disrespect. If it happens again, I'll be more than happy to let you off at the next town, and you can walk to Houston."

As Giulia stepped down from the bus, her suspense did not last for long, for the very first person she saw in Hearne was her father, who was waiting on the sidewalk, not ten feet away. At once, he put his arm around her, and she hugged him back.

"Hi, Daddy," she said. "Are we on time?"

"Hello, sweetie girl. Yes, indeed. In fact, you're five minutes early." He smiled at her and declared his usual "As pretty as a picture!"

The driver set foot outside briefly to retrieve the passengers' bags from the storage compartment. Having placed to one side the soldier's duffle bag and the girl's suitcase, he slammed the luggage door shut and secured the latch. Then he stood the duffle bag on its closed end for the GI and carried the suitcase over to Giulia. "Sorry for the way those young bucks acted, miss. I'll not tolerate such conduct."

"That's all right, mister. Thank you." She smiled at him, and he seemed pleased.

While the bus was pulling away in a cloud of fumes, Frank asked her, "Is that your only grip, honey?

"Well, sure. How many do you think I need for one night?"

Her fellow departing passenger, the young soldier, was a red-headed lad who was not far removed from his teen years himself. He had paused to light a cigarette and was now walking past the Colettis, duffle bag slung over his left shoulder.

"Going to the camp, son?" Frank asked.

"Nope." He beamed at the strangers. "Home on leave."

"Swell. For how long?"

"Two weeks with the folks, sir—and am I looking forward to it!"

"Been overseas, then?"

His smile utterly vanished. "Yep," he said, and his face went pale. The soldier tipped his cap to Giulia, nodded to her father, and walked on, offering no elaboration. Noting the boy's odd behavior, Frank wondered whether he had been furloughed on medical leave, perhaps for shell shock or some similar psychological disorder. Presumably, he hoped to use this time with family to rid his mind of the combat horrors that were burned into his memory. If so, it would be the best medicine of all.

Giulia's sojourn in Hearne was to be much more abbreviated than the GI's. She planned to stay overnight and then ride to Waco with her father for the morning service on Easter Sunday. He would drive back to Hearne late in the afternoon. This, of course, meant that Frank and Paolina Coletti would both be at Saint Mary's Church of the Assumption at the same time, but that would be nothing new. Such had been the case ever since their separation, and neither spouse would so much as recognize the existence of the other. Trapped in the middle of this schism, Giulia would always sit by her mother, for it was she who had assumed *de facto* custody through all these years of estrangement.

In view of the acute housing shortage, Frank considered himself very fortunate to have found a rental property in Hearne that was so conveniently located—just a mile and a half from where he worked. It was a modest, cockroach-ridden duplex that contained a bedroom, living room, den, bathroom, and small kitchen. The place reeked of cigarettes, though the only tobacco Frank used was the chewable variety. Contributing to the unfavorable first impression of his dwelling was the kitchen wallpaper, which did not begin to approximate the color of the ceiling paint and, worse yet, was peeling in a number of conspicuous patches.

"I'll just be here until the war ends or I get canned, whichever comes first," he told his daughter.

"But you passed your probationary time, didn't you? Why should they fire you?"

"I'm just a little gun-shy, I guess. Still haven't gotten over the last time."

"You're not drinking, are you?" she asked. "If you start that up again, you're a … Well, your …"

"My goose is cooked?"

"Close enough," Giulia said with a wry smile. "Anyway, I hereby order you to stay away from the bottle. Waco is two hours from here, so I can't be checking up on you like I used to do. I've got to trust you, so don't let me down."

Frank motioned with his head. "Come here for a minute. I want to show you something." He walked to the kitchen, and she followed. From a top drawer, he produced a fifth of bourbon whiskey. The bottle was unopened. "For some people, this would be the kiss of death, but for me, it has a positive effect. Each time I bypass this bottle, I consider it a victory, and it makes me stronger all the time."

Giulia, however, did not have much faith in that wisdom. "You be careful, Papà. I really wish you would pour that down the drain and be done with it."

"I can handle it, honey. Honest, it's been eight months since my last drink."

She put her suitcase in the tiny den, where there was a rollaway bed that would suffice quite nicely. Although Frank insisted that she take the bedroom, Giulia refused just as firmly, claiming that, if anything, he probably needed a good night's sleep more than she did. The next-door neighbors had a baby girl, only two months old, and the infant usually managed to keep him awake for hours at a time. Now that the Morans were away for Easter weekend, this was his one chance to catch up.

◆　　◆　　◆

Camp Hearne was a major complex, the third largest of the seventy prisoner-of-war units in the state of Texas. Most of the other sixty-seven were quite small, with just a few hundred POWs apiece, but the Hearne facility housed upwards of forty-seven hundred men. Eighty percent of the Hearne detainees were NCOs, who were not obligated to do any work whatsoever, so that left only a fifth of the prison population to do all the manual labor in and around the camp. Though it was Saturday morning, a contingent of eight hundred or so inmates, each with a large "PW" on his back, was already in the fields around town and at the Brazos Bottoms, digging onions and picking cotton for the regulated wage of eighty cents apiece per diem. This was payable in canteen scrip, negotiable at the camp store—ample purchasing power for a daily allotment of cigarettes, with the balance designated toward saving for that future day of repatriation.

In contrast to the manual laborers, non-commissioned officers were paid three dollars a week for doing next to nothing beyond cultivating their various hobbies and educational pursuits. A group of them, for instance, constructed a series of four-foot-high stonework scale models of German castles, complete with moats, drawbridges, and waterfalls. They also built shallow-water ponds with goldfish and turtles, and for entertainment there was an orchestra and a theater troupe. Quite naturally, the American public felt that these prisoners were being coddled, but such were the provisions of the Geneva Convention of 1929, which served as a virtual Bible of prisoner administration for camp commanders. Once the NCOs' leisurely way of life became known to outsiders, people in Hearne started calling their hometown facility the "Fritz Ritz."

Giulia's father was anxious to show her where he worked, but he explained to her that only military personnel were permitted to enter the secure perimeter of Camp Hearne. This came as something of a letdown, for she had expected to get an insider's look at the prison, naïvely assuming that civilian employees and their guests would be accorded the same privileges as those extended to men in uniform. "But we'll get close enough to smell the sauerkraut," he said.

Frank Coletti parked his gray 1937 Ford coupe in the regular spot, fifth space over in a lot adjacent to the camp's administrative offices. He himself was not scheduled to serve on weekends, but that in no way suggested that the entire operation ceased activity. Indeed, a full compliment of staff was on duty at the garrison this day, and a half-crew would be manning the office on Easter Sunday. As he led his daughter toward the front door of the utilitarian, clapboard building, Giulia gazed with fascination upon an eerie sight. Off in the distance, beyond a barbed-wire fence, stood the stark expanse of the prisoners' compound of Camp Hearne, situated just to the northwest of town.

Bounded on the north by State Highway 190, on the east by Vaughan Lane, on the south by Sandy Creek, and on the west by the Little Brazos River, Camp Hearne encompassed 720 acres of land. Construction of the site was accomplished at a torrid pace, between September of 1942 and March of 1943, and completed just in time to welcome the first group of captured German soldiers, members of General Erwin Rommel's elite Afrika Korps. Arriving aboard heavily guarded cars of the Southern Pacific Railroad, near the point where State Highway 6 intersected State Highway 190, the captives were paraded along the latter road to camp, as a couple hundred or more onlookers stood by in awe. For many of the locals, no doubt, it seemed that a movie-house newsreel had miraculously sprung to life in color. The war had come home to Hearne.

Frank's immediate boss was Lieutenant Dodds, who saw to it that the captives' records were maintained in proper order. Food and other supplies also passed through the administrative unit, as did the valuable inventory of canteen scrip, and in case of dispute, a well-worn copy of the Geneva Convention lay on a dictionary stand for ready reference. About three out of every five workers seemed to be servicemen and WACs, and the remaining two-fifths were either civilians or cooperative—that is to say, anti-Nazi—prisoners of war. For the past several months, another building was commandeered to house the postal distribution center for all German POWs in the entire United States, a massive (and notoriously infiltrated) mail-processing unit that really put Camp Hearne on the national map for a time.

One of the German orderlies in Frank's office this day was Hans Steuer, whom "Herr Coletti" had gotten to know quite well in the weeks after Christmas. Hans and Sergeant Jürgen Lindheimer, that rarest of non-commissioned officers who actually chose to work for extra pay, were probably Frank's two closest acquaintances among the detainees. Jürgen would not get to meet Giulia, as he was under medical supervision for a malady that was at first thought to be meningitis, a fearful diagnosis that later proved to be groundless. But Hans Steuer did see Frank's daughter, and to say the least, he was enamored to the point of distraction. He could get nothing done through most of the morning, as his eyes were always upon her. Hans was only twenty-two years old, a conscripted violinist from Stettin who survived desert warfare but then was nearly killed in Hearne, Texas, where a relatively small but fanatical gang of Nazis was struggling to gain control through a campaign of intimidation, coerced suicide, and brute force. By all rights, this German private should have been out in the cotton, onion, or peanut fields with the other enlisted men, but Hans was able to convince the prison staff—and justifiably so—that his life was in peril. The fact that he sometimes performed impromptu recitals for the Americans may have softened their hearts just a bit.

Shortly before lunchtime, Frank walked his daughter over to the barbed-wire confines of Camp Hearne and let her observe the installation from up close. The compound was divided into three distinct sections, each with mess hall, latrine, company office, and six barracks that measured twenty feet by one hundred feet. These sleeping quarters, Frank said, were known in characteristic Army parlance as "war mobilization structures." They were unsightly dwellings, constructed of wood and covered with black tar paper for protection against the elements. From where she was standing, Giulia could see the elevated guard towers, each of which was equipped with a searchlight and machine gun. If nothing else, this showed that American compassion had its limits.

"A German prisoner was beaten to death here at the camp," Frank said.

Giulia's jaw dropped. "By the guards?"

He chuckled. "No, of course not. By the Nazis."

"There are Nazis in the camp?"

"Hundreds of them. Don't kid yourself."

"Were you here when it happened?"

"No, this was in the winter of '43, just before Christmas. The boy's name was Krauss—Hugo Krauss—a corporal with strong American ties. Seems he'd lived in the United States for a dozen years as a young man, and both of his parents were naturalized citizens."

"They killed him for that?"

"Well, he was fluent in English, so the camp commander used him as an interpreter. The Nazi bunch saw that as treasonous, I guess. He spoke openly against the Third Reich, too, and that made him a marked man. Anyhow, late one night seven of the Krauts cut their way through the wire fence into the anti-Nazi section of the camp, where Krauss was, and they dragged him out of the barracks, screaming. Then they pounded him with clubs, a lead pipe, and boards with nails in them. His pals were afraid to come to his aid because the Hitlerites had scared the anti-Nazis into submission and even threatened harm to their families back in Germany."

"How awful!"

"They beat poor Krauss to a pulp—fractured skull, two broken arms—and he died six days later in the camp hospital. He was twenty-four."

Giulia was aghast. "Right here in Hearne?"

"Yep, over there," Frank said. He pointed toward a group of barracks.

"How come we've never heard of this?"

"Well, it's not exactly the sort of thing you publicize, is it?"

The Colettis went back inside for a few minutes, so Frank could go through his mail. Meantime, Hans Steuer approached Giulia and introduced himself, clicking his heels together in proper Germanic fashion. He spoke fairly good English, which of course made him suspect with the Nazi element of detainees.

"May I sometime play for you on my violin, Fräulein Coletti?" he asked.

"I'm afraid not, Mr. Shto—"

"Just call me Hans," he said with a friendly smile.

"I'm only here for the day, Hans, and then I go back to Waco, where I live."

"That is the home of the University of Baylor," Hans told her.

Giulia chuckled. "Yes, that's right." Clearly, he was proud of his geographical knowledge.

"When you return here with your father another day, I shall play for you some of the Bach Sonatas and Partitas. There are six in all, you know, three of each."

"Is that so?"

"Are you musical, Fräulein Coletti?"

"I play the piano a little—not very well."

"You must accompany me in the two Beethoven *Romances*. I have an excellent piano reduction of the orchestral parts, so we can make beautiful music together."

"That sounds nice, Hans, but I'm sure I don't play anywhere near well enough to master that. I can play a few Grainger pieces, and 'The Girl with Flaxen Hair' by Debussy, and parts of *Rhapsody in Blue*."

"Gershwin! I have the Paul Whiteman recording at home."

"Where is home, Hans?"

Giulia's father walked over and stood next to her. "So you've met?" he asked.

"Yes, I have met your charming daughter," Hans told him, and he became quite serious.

Giulia smiled at her new friend. "I was wondering where Hans was from."

"Oh," Frank said. He glanced from one to the other.

"My home is in Stettin, far up on the Baltic Sea, at the mouth of the Oder River. It is a seaport city, much shipbuilding, very important in the German economy since the fourteenth century. You have heard of the Hanseatic League?"

"Yes, I think so," Giulia said.

"We have a fine orchestra—or did have, until the war—of which I was assistant concertmaster. The city has been bombed many times now, and of course musical life has been suspended."

"Are your parents still there?"

"Yes. Our house is outside the city proper, so they have not been fire bombed like the central district and the docks. Thank God, they are still alive."

Frank began walking away—for the prisoner's own good—because he knew that Hans could get into trouble for socializing on such familiar terms with a civilian visitor. "We really have to go," he told the German orderly.

Hans snapped to attention and formally nodded his head in acknowledgment. "Most pleasant indeed to meet you, Fräulein."

"Same here, Hans. Good luck, and I hope you are allowed to go back home soon."

Hans watched the girl with great care as she left, noting every movement, capturing her graceful beauty for all time in his memory. And then he closed his eyes for a moment, sighed, and went back to his assigned duties. In the absence of Lieutenant Dodds, the officer in charge this day was Lieutenant Baldwyn, who chose to overlook Prisoner Steuer's inactivity, seeing as how his fraternization with that lovely civilian girl also included one of the clerical staff. For all he knew, they were talking about official business. Steuer was normally a very good worker.

◆ ◆ ◆

During the week after Easter, on Wednesday, April 4, 1945, Susan McVey Reich died at the age of fifty-three in Stephenville, Texas, after a long battle with cancer. She was the wife of Benjamin Abel Reich, a businessman, formerly of Waco. Nora Brower heard the news from Wayne Espy, who called her on the telephone when one of his regular customers informed him during the course of a sale. Details appeared in the *Waco News-Tribune*, though the obituary failed to mention the fact that they were wed in Waco and lived their first few years of married life there as well.

That weekend, as Nora was washing dishes after Sunday dinner, the telephone rang, and Wesley answered it. He told his mother that an associate of Mr. Ben Reich wished to speak with her. Nora handed the dishrag to Elizabeth, who had been drying, and hurried to take the call. A man identifying himself as Wallace Hopper informed her that a major delivery would be made to the Brower address the very next day, and he wished to know whether someone would be there to receive it. Nora assured him that she would be home throughout the afternoon, which would be a much more convenient span of time than the morning hours, when she would be doing laundry and shopping for the week's groceries.

"That's fine, Mrs. Brower," the caller said. "Our delivery truck could not possibly arrive there before one." Nora thanked him and returned to the kitchen.

"Lizzie, dear, I have a surprise to show you after we finish with the dishes."

"A good surprise?" Elizabeth asked.

"I think you'll be pleased." Nora wore an inscrutable grin, and no amount of begging could convince her to reveal the secret. Of course, she drew the suspense out even further once she knew that her daughter was beside herself to learn the true nature of this puzzle. After Elizabeth dried the last saucer and placed it back in the cupboard, she tossed the towel aside and went directly to the living room, where her mother had already made herself comfortable on the sofa.

"Well?" Elizabeth said.

"Well, would you rather listen to 'The Andrews Sisters' or 'Nelson Eddy'?"

"Mother!"

"I'm giving you the choice, honey."

"You promised!"

Nora giggled. "I'm just teasing you." She turned to Wesley, who was an interested bystander, and whispered something to him. Glancing at his sister, he immediately left the room and went upstairs.

"What's with all these secrets?" Elizabeth asked.

"You'll see soon enough, dear."

About two minutes later, as Nora was tuning in to the final stunt on "Darts for Dough"—which preceded LaVerne, Maxene, and Patty Andrews on the Blue Network—Wesley came down the stairway, burdened with a heavy box that had been securely sealed with tape and then tied with twine. He struggled mightily with the rectangular, cardboard container and proceeded to deposit it in the middle of the living room floor.

"There it is, Lizzie—part of the surprise," her mother said. "This will be a pretty obvious hint that will give the rest of it away."

Elizabeth was bursting with curiosity. "May I open it?"

"You may. Wes, please get me a pocket knife or a pair of scissors."

Wesley was almost as anxious as Elizabeth to know the contents of the box, so he ran to his father's roll-top desk to fetch the scissors. Walking back, he handed them to Nora, who asked, "Lizzie, do you remember when that nice Mr. Reich introduced himself to you at the filling station?"

She nodded her head. "He left something here for me."

"That was almost two years ago, and I said you couldn't have it until the time was right. I've kept it hidden away in your father's closet until now."

Elizabeth looked at the box. "That's the gift?"

"Well, that's a small portion of it. I guess you could say it's just something to go along with the big gift. What's inside the box belonged to Mr. Reich's wife, but she was no longer able to use it, and she wanted to give it a good home."

Elizabeth examined the container more closely, even pushing it as hard as she could. The box did not even budge. "What is it, a box of anvils?"

"Why don't you see for yourself?" Nora offered her daughter the scissors.

Elizabeth snipped the twine with no trouble, but the box was so tightly sealed with cellulose tape that she nearly gave up trying to cut her way into it. Finally, though, she managed to open the top flaps just far enough to discover that the mystery gift seemed to be a large collection of books. "Gosh! Are all of these for me?" She continued slicing through tape until the box lay open to view.

"Yes, they are. Mr. Reich told me that there are two complete sets." Seeing that her daughter was so excited made Nora smile. "Mr. Reich said his wife had an entire room full of sheet music, from ceiling to floor, and they distributed it to music lovers all over the state—as well as to some of the college libraries. He thought you would particularly enjoy having these two sets because they were more general in scope than most of her collection."

Elizabeth read on the spines, *The International Library of Music: Pianoforte Compositions*, and she saw that the volumes were numbered from one to eight, each attractively housed in a hard, red binding. Leafing through the top book at random, she noticed works by Beethoven, Schumann, Scharwenka, Chopin, Moszkowski, and Grieg, among countless others.

"Not many people can afford to buy a collection like that unless they're professional musicians," Nora said. "Susan Reich was a well-known piano teacher for thirty years. She taught lots of the John Tarleton students."

Delving more deeply into the box, Elizabeth discovered that, sure enough, the bottom half of the books comprised a different set entirely. The binding, though, was surprisingly similar, almost as if one product had been modeled on the other for marketing purposes. As she flipped through the first of nine volumes in *The Scribner Radio Music Library*, her eyes caught such composer names as Schubert, Liszt, Gluck, Rubinstein, Weber, Mendelssohn, Mozart, and Field.

Both were splendid anthologies, of course, but the more she browsed, the more the girl's elation deserted her. "Don't you think these are too difficult for me?"

"Right now they are, dear, but with lots of practice ..."

"See? There's always a catch," Wesley told her.

Elizabeth frowned. "I wonder if I'll ever be able to play most of these pieces." She was discouraged by the sheer profusion of black notes on the staves and—worse yet—ledger lines, causing some of the pieces to resemble a piano student's surrealistic nightmare of Hanon exercises.

"Well, you've always said you wanted to devote your free time to piano, now that your job forced you to give up the flute at school."

Suddenly, she looked more confident. "Yes, ma'am, and I meant it too."

"Well, now's your chance."

With the suspense vanished, Wesley's concentration strayed away from the gift books and toward the radio broadcast. The Andrews Sisters had just performed a song, and Gabby Hayes was engaged in a comedy sketch with them. Over on WFAA, Arturo Toscanini and the NBC Symphony Orchestra would be coming on at four.

"Will you tell Mr. Reich thank you for the music?" Elizabeth asked. "Or do you think I should send him a note?"

Her mother chose to answer this query with an instructive question. "Which do you think would be more personal?"

"Well, since you put it that way ..."

"That really would be better, dear. First, though, you need to wait for the rest of the gift to arrive."

Elizabeth's eyes widened, but she dared not let herself imagine what the other portion of it might be.

Nora felt that it was time to explain. "The Reichs wanted you to have these music books ... and also something to play them on."

"Oh, Mother!"

"Mr. Reich is going to have their grand piano delivered here. We'll be giving our old piano to the USO—the one on Franklin Avenue, where Madeleine works now."

That news captured Wesley's attention. "A concert grand?"

Nora grinned. "A nine-foot Steinway. It'll be a tight squeeze in our small parlor, but I measured the floor space to make sure it will fit. And Mr. Reich says he'll pay for a thorough tuning too. Poor Susie hasn't been able to play it for almost three years."

"I want to be here when it arrives!" Elizabeth told her.

"No, they'll bring it during the early afternoon, so you'll still be at school. But it'll be waiting for you when you get home."

"I don't care whether the piano is tuned or not. I'm going to play every one of those books, from beginning to end, all seventeen volumes!"

Nora chuckled at her daughter's giddy enthusiasm, but there was also an underlying sense of remorse. She felt a little guilty for being so happy at a time like this, right after the death of a very special person. And yet she knew in her heart that such delight over the gift of music is precisely what Susie would have wanted. "May God bless Mrs. Reich," Nora said. "She was a dear lady."

This remarkable Sunday was not quite finished for Elizabeth Brower. Late that same afternoon, as she and her mother were listening to a CBS comedy called "The Adventures of Ozzie and Harriet" (starring bandleader Oswald George Nelson and his real-life singing wife, the former Harriet Hilliard), there came a frantic-sounding knock on the front door.

Wesley bounded down the stairs to answer it, and in skipped Meg Oliphant. "Where's Beth?" she shouted, and Wesley pointed to the living room. Elizabeth was already standing when her friend ran into the room. Meg threw her arms around her and began whirling the two of them in a frenzied dance of jubilation. "He's safe!" the girl screamed, and tears were flowing down her cheeks.

"Phillip is?" Elizabeth asked. She, too, was now crying with delight, and so was Nora, as if the emotion were contagious.

Meg stopped their spinning and grasped both of her friend's hands. "Phil is safe! His parents called me from California to say that he's been found!"

"Oh, thank God," Nora said. "That's the answer to prayer."

The girl smiled through her tears. "The War Department notified them that his platoon—or squad, or whatever it was—got separated from the others near the Agno River on Luzon, but now they've all turned up, hungry and filthy but none the worse for wear. He's back with his unit now, and only one or two had to go to the hospital for dehydration. They lived off the land."

"Gee, that's wonderful, Meg," Elizabeth said. She wiped away some tears with a sleeve of her blouse. "I told you not to give up hope."

Meg beamed. "You did tell me that, Beth, and you're a true friend." She ran toward the door, departing just as buoyantly as she arrived. "I wanted you to be the first to know! My mother's in the car, and we're going to tell everyone the good news."

Elizabeth sat down on the sofa, next to her mother. "And if I know her," she said, "Meg will write a note to him every day this week. He'll probably get them all in one fat packet, tied with string. I wonder how long it takes for mail to get to the Philippines."

"Too long," Nora said with a giggle. "Far too long, I'm sure, to satisfy your Meg."

♦   ♦   ♦

Julie May Tuttle rolled her eyes. "Gordon is from Wichita, Kansas," she said, "and that is hardly out in the country."

"But he's not exactly from Dallas or Houston, either, and that's my point," Madeleine Givens told her. She and her friend were both off from work on the same day, a rarity now that the Franklin USO had begun rivaling the Washington club for business. "He'd love it out here, where it's not so congested."

Julie May knew better. "He's a city boy at heart. He wants to settle someplace where he can buy a T-bone steak at three in the morning, if that's what he's in the mood for. Nope, those years in Saint Louis spoiled him, Maddy. He'd get cabin fever living in Waco—let alone out here in the ..." She stopped, embarrassed.

"Sticks?"

"Nothing personal."

"Well, he can have the big city," Madeleine said. "Harland and I will take the open road anytime."

And that is just where the two women were at the moment: traveling east on State Highway 6, only about a mile from reaching the community of Hallsburg. The rain had let up a bit, but it was still drizzling enough to make the windshield wipers necessary. Madeleine's weekly trip from Waco to her in-laws' home outside of Riesel took a half-hour even in dry conditions, what with the reduced speed limit, but having a friend along certainly did make the time go faster. It was nice to get away and leave her problems behind. Her old high school sweetheart, Nathan Reynolds, tried to reestablish contact with her about five months back, but after two weeks of steady rejection—at first quite polite but then progressively harsher—he finally took the hint and gave up. She figured Nate was transferred elsewhere by now, maybe even overseas.

Madeleine's two children, Cindy and Ronny, were waiting at the gate when they spotted a blue sedan approaching the turnoff. They ran up to the house at top speed, shouting, "She's here, Grandpa," and a man who had been rocking in a chair on the front porch arose and went inside to tell his wife. Mr. and Mrs. Givens did not expect their daughter-in-law to arrive until at least ten o'clock, but the twins insisted upon becoming "car spotters" not long after 8:30. Their grandfather had taught them to identify silhouettes of German and Japanese airplanes when the children were only five years old, and the present earthbound game was a logical extension of those early days of the war. Even before the pair were halfway back down to the wooden gate, their mother had already swung it open and was climbing into the automobile. The kids noticed that there was someone else alongside her, so they beat a hasty retreat.

"Hello, rascals!" Madeleine said to her fleet-footed youngsters when the 1939 Chevrolet finally caught up with them at the farmhouse and came to a stop. She stepped out, and Harland's parents were surprised to see a guest emerge from the passenger side. Their daughter-in-law put her arms around the twins and hugged them so hard that they squealed with glee. "Mom and Dad, this is Julie May Tuttle from the USO. I thought she might enjoy a drive in the country. Sorry for the extra mouth to feed."

"We'll have more than ample," Eunice Givens said. "Nice to meet you, Miss Tuttle."

"It's actually *Mrs.* Tuttle," Madeleine told her. "Julie May's husband is in the Army."

"Well, it's swell having you here, Mrs. Tuttle," Spencer Givens said, and he motioned for everyone to head toward the house. "We hardly ever hear from Harl anymore. I guess he's plenty busy with the push through Italy. Say, ladies, did you hear the Russkies are on the outskirts of Berlin? I'll wager Adolf's burrowing like a yellow gopher by now."

Madeleine paused long enough to allow her friend to step onto the porch ahead of her. "Julie May's not exactly sure where her Gordon is," she said, "but she thinks it must be somewhere in western Germany."

The younger woman nodded her head. "Maybe in the Ruhr Valley, which I spotted on a map. Of course, he can't say very much in his letters, so that's just a guess. He wrote a couple of words in German."

Spencer held the screen door open for the others and then let it slam shut behind him when they were all inside. "Dang!" he said, "I only wish Roosevelt could have lived to see it."

Purely out of curiosity, Cindy and Ronny hurried over to the stranger when she sat down in a straight-back chair near the fireplace. They wanted to get a good look at her, especially since her husband was fighting in Germany. "And how old are you two?" she asked them.

"Seven," the girl said, "but we'll be eight in June."

"June seventeenth," the boy added.

Julie May smiled at them. "Really? I have a sister whose birthday is June the sixteenth."

"Then she's a day older that we are," Cindy said with a laugh, and the visitor giggled at her little joke.

"Excuse me, ladies, but I've got some hungry cows to feed," Spencer said. "For some reason, they don't seem to understand the concept of weekends." He leaned over to pick up his work gloves.

"Oh, honey, why don't you stay and talk for a while?" Eunice told him. "Surely they don't need hay in April."

"No, but I want to move them to the other pasture. They're overgrazing like crazy, and they seem to like it wet." He went out the front door, leaving his wife to see after the guests.

Eunice walked over to the children. "Now, you moppets give poor Mrs. Tuttle some peace. She's been working hard all week, and I'm sure she wants to relax on a Saturday."

"That's all right," Julie May said. "It feels nice just to be away from the USO for a change. I don't know why I'm not scheduled to work today—just the luck of the draw. I certainly don't have much seniority."

"Run along, children," their grandmother told them. "Go upstairs and draw a picture for Mrs. Tuttle."

Finding that idea to their liking, the twins raced each other to the stairway and disappeared around the corner. Far off in the distance, rolling thunder could be heard, but it was probably part of the same storm system that had already pushed through the area.

"Do you have children, Mrs. Tuttle?" Eunice asked.

The young lady blushed. "Just call me Julie May, if that's all right with you. The other seems so formal."

"Fair enough, and my name's Eunice. We're Eunice and Spencer."

"To answer your question, no, we don't have any children yet. Gordon and I were only married for six weeks before he was drafted, but we do hope to start a family whenever he comes back home."

"We have three," Eunice told her. "Harland has two older sisters, and each of them moved away right after high school. One's in Minnesota, and the other's in Shreveport, Louisiana. They're both happily married, thank God."

Madeleine chuckled. "Harl says he was always tormented by his sisters, so when I married him, he was already used to being henpecked."

"Are you and your husband both from Riesel?" Julie May asked Eunice.

"Oh, no," she said. "Spencer is, but I'm from a town called Leroy, which is only about half as big. When I was a little girl, Riesel seemed like a city to me, and of course Waco seemed like a great metropolis. I didn't think anywhere could be much larger."

"Harland's father inherited this land from *his* father," Madeleine told her friend, "and it's been in the family for a lot longer than that. Even before the Civil War, I guess." She looked at Eunice.

"I don't know about that, dear, but it has been an awfully long time. That's why Spencer is so determined to keep it and to make sure it stays productive. We have our own burial plots in the family cemetery. Harland and Madeleine will inherit all of this from us when we're gone."

"Well, we trust that will be a good, long time from now," her daughter-in-law said, but before Eunice could thank her for the kind sentiment, Madeleine added, "Because I don't know the first thing about farming and ranching."

"Don't get over-emotional about it," the older woman said, and Julie May laughed at the good-natured ribbing. Madeleine certainly did seem to get along well with her mother-in-law, and that was something not altogether common in such relationships, whether in war or peace. Gordon's mother, for one, exasperated Julie May to no end, although in their case the daughter-in-law had been able to rein in her resentment and—so far, at least—forestall any open confrontation.

◆　　◆　　◆

With the sole exception of Sundays, it was a long-standing tradition at the Givens home that dinner would be served at noon or whenever Spencer returned home from the feedlot or fields. Accordingly, Eunice excused herself and went to the kitchen shortly before eleven, politely rejecting all offers of assistance from Madeleine and Julie May. When the twins returned downstairs, they had their artwork with them. Cindy's was a picture of a lady labeled "Mrs. Tuddle," standing between what appeared to be a cow and a horse (or perhaps a sheep). The sun was yellow, the sky was blue, and the grass was green. Ronny's depicted an airplane taking off from a carrier. Clearly, it was an American plane because there were stars on its wings. The sun was yellow, the sky was blue, and the sea was green.

Julie May told them how much she liked the crayon drawings, and she wondered whether she might take them with her to put on the refrigerator, a request that made the children beam with satisfaction. Just then, the familiar sound of an airplane was heard overhead, though much louder than normal for being so distant from the Waco bases' landing strips. AAF training continued on a massive scale, despite the bold advances in Europe. The subjugation of Japan still called for untold thousands of new pilots.

"Did you see that your dress is brown?" Cindy asked. She was pointing to "Mrs. Tuddle."

"I did," Julie May said, "and I like the white gloves too." She had since removed those and laid them next to her hat on the bookcase.

Ronny placed his own picture on top of Cindy's. "See? The American plane's chasing a Zero, and there's a torpedo that's going to sink a Jap battleship."

"Aircraft carriers don't shoot torpedoes, dopey," his sister told him.

"This one does."

"I think they're both fine pictures," the twins' mother said with pride, "and I'm sure Mrs. Tuttle will enjoy looking at them."

Spencer had not yet come home at 12:10, so Madeleine switched on the radio for herself and Julie May as they waited for dinner to be served. KRLD in Dallas was carrying "Hometown Editor" and then fifteen minutes of news. CBS had moved its half-hour docudrama "Report to the Nation" from Tuesday night to Saturday afternoon at 12:30, so they listened to that next, and Eunice joined them while her food simmered atop the stove. A third of the way into the program, still with no sign of her husband, she finally spoke up. "Where could he be? He's never this late."

Madeleine shrugged her shoulders and turned to the twins, who were playing checkers on the floor. "Children," she said, "would you please go see what's taking your grandpa so long? Dinner's going to spoil."

Ronny and Cindy ran out the front door and then raced each other toward the cattle pastures that their grandfather was known to be using these days. With concern on her face, Eunice looked at the other ladies and whispered, "I hope nothing's wrong."

Not ten minutes later, the sound of the children could be heard, their chatter growing louder as they approached the house. Madeleine scurried to the door and opened it for them to enter. Directly behind the twins walked Spencer in his overalls, now stained with streaks of black soot or grease. Eunice, who had been in the kitchen to check on dinner, hurried into the living room and was startled by her husband's appearance.

"Good heavens! What happened to you?"

"There's been an accident," Spencer said, quite calmly. He did not appear to be injured.

His wife walked over to him. "A car accident?"

"Worse than that—an airplane. Two men are dead."

"An Army plane?" Madeleine asked. One hand partially covered her mouth in shock.

Spencer nodded his head. "It was a trainer. I heard the engine sputtering and saw the plane disappear over the tree line." He pulled off his filthy work gloves and tossed them onto a tool chest that lay next to the writing desk. "There was no smoke or anything, so I figured the pilot was stalling on purpose—some sort of training maneuver. It was so far away by then that I couldn't hear anything but a dull thud. And then I could see black smoke coming up from behind the trees."

Feeling a bit wobbly, Madeleine sat on the arm of a chair. "It crashed?"

"Yes, ma'am. It crashed beyond our property, just over into Falls County. I jumped onto the tractor and headed that direction because I knew I wouldn't be any help if I came all the way back to the house to get the truck."

"Good Lord!" Eunice said. "And you could see the smoke?"

"By the time I got near, Pat Hungerford was already there with four of his laborers. It was literally out his back door. Betsy called the fire department and police, so they were on the way. Evidently, the plane narrowly missed their house. It struck a tree or power line or something and crashed in the field. There was nothing anyone could do because the plane exploded on impact and went up in flames. We all tried to see if anyone was still alive, but I'm sure they were both killed instantly."

"Two Army men?" Madeleine asked.

"A cadet from Waco Field and an officer, probably a captain. That's what the police said when they got there."

"Will they be able to identify them?"

"I wouldn't think so, not until they check the flight records. It was a big blaze, and it didn't leave much to see. The volunteer fire department put it out. All that aviation fuel was burning until they got there. A grass fire started too, but it didn't amount to much because everything was still pretty wet from the rain."

Ronny was standing by his sister behind the sofa. "What kind of plane was it?" he asked.

"A two-seater, son—maybe an AT-6, if they're still flying those. You remember the 'Texan'?"

The boy nodded his head, recalling pictures of training aircraft that he clipped from the Waco newspaper.

His grandfather added, "It definitely had two seats under a single canopy. You could tell that much."

"How horrible!" Eunice said. "Two of our boys ..."

Just then, a chilling thought struck Madeleine. "That must have been the airplane we heard fly over."

Spencer turned toward her. "You heard it?"

"Uh-huh," she said. "It sounded like it was going to land on the house, didn't it?" Julie May nodded her head in agreement.

"Then it must have been coming from the southwest," Spencer said. "At the time I spotted it, the plane was flying from northwest to southeast. That's a pretty drastic turn, so something was wrong. Did the engine sound normal to you?"

Julie May answered. "Yes, sir—but very loud. Closer to the rooftop than it should have been."

"Too close for comfort," Madeleine told him.

His wife asked, "So, what comes next, Spence?"

"Well, an official investigation. These things happen in training, of course, but the Army always tries to determine the cause."

"Do you think they'll ask you?"

"I wouldn't be surprised. I gave my name to the police, in case they need me as an eyewitness."

For the first time, Eunice noticed that Spencer's forearm was bleeding. "Oh! You cut your arm, dear." She stepped forward for a better look.

"No, it's not a cut. It's a burn. Like I say, we tried to get as near as we could, and I guess I underestimated how hot it was, even at what I thought was a safe distance."

"Does it hurt a lot?"

Spencer stared at the arm. "Not really," he said. "No worse than when I bump it against a hot engine."

"At least let me clean it up for you and maybe wrap some ice around it—or spread some cream."

He glanced at the ladies. "Okay, whatever you say, dear. But then let's have dinner. I've made you all wait long enough as it is."

"I'm proud of you, honey. You tried to help." Eunice kissed him on the cheek and hurried to the kitchen.

"Yes, we all are," Madeleine said. "That was very brave of you—getting so close to a burning airplane, for goodness sake. Who knows? There could have been another explosion."

He shook his head. "I didn't do anything but watch what was happening and get in everyone else's way."

Like the most conscientious of nurses, Eunice was already hurrying back to treat her injured patient. "The fact remains, Spencer Givens, that you tried to help—and at the risk of your own safety. Here, hold still." Using a wet cloth, she gently patted his arm with soap and cold water. Then she spread onto the affected area some ointment from her first-aid kit, which she always kept handy in the kitchen for emergencies.

A minute later, while their grandfather was upstairs, washing his face and hands and changing out of his smoke-stained overalls, Ronny and Cindy were bringing Mrs. Tuttle to a place of honor at the table—that is, a spot right between them. "Grand Central Station" was coming on the air, and much to Julie May's amazement, both youngsters proceeded to quote the opening sequence, word for word.

"As a bullet seeks its target," they recited, "shining rails in every part of our great country are aimed at GRAND CENTRAL STATION, heart of the nation's greatest city. Drawn by the magnetic force of the fantastic metropolis, day and night great trains rush toward the Hudson River, sweep down its eastern bank for one hundred forty miles, flash briefly by the long, red row of tenement houses south of One Hundred Twenty-fifth Street, dive with a roar into the two-and-one-half-mile tunnel which burrows beneath the glitter and swank of Park Avenue, and then EEEESSSSHHHHhhsssssss, GRAND CENTRAL STATION! Crossroads of a million private lives! Gigantic stage on which are played a thousand dramas daily!"

Genuinely impressed, Julie May applauded the children's flawless effort, and little Cindy bowed deeply, lost in her dreams of becoming an actress on Broadway. The other youngster, however, only scoffed. "Gosh, we hear it every Saturday." Ronny may have been his sister's fraternal twin, but he was much less of a theatrical ham.

"Help me and Gran bring the food in, little darlings," Madeleine said. "Your Grandpa will be here any second." To their credit, Cindy and Ronny did just that, although certainly a part of their cooperation must have stemmed from a desire to show off in front of company.

It was 1:10 before dinner was served. Spencer, now wearing a clean, plaid shirt, seated himself at the traditional head of the table and pronounced grace, taking a moment to remember the two fallen airmen and to raise up their families in time of grief. He also prayed—in behalf of soldiers Harland Givens and Gordon Tuttle—for the Lord's guidance and protection in the campaign against their Axis foe. As for the meal itself, though the lima beans were a bit mushy and the stewed tomatoes almost liquefied from simmering for over an hour, the pork roast turned out to be far juicier than anyone had a right to expect.

Madeleine washed the dishes, and her USO friend dried them, leaving Eunice with the leisurely assignment of putting them away. She felt inhospitable to see a guest roll up her sleeves like this, but Julie May simply would not take no for an answer. The two young women spent part of the afternoon feeding the chickens, a bucolic chore that was interrupted when the twins arrived on the scene to tell their mother that the Chevy had a flat tire. Spencer was not far behind them, and he greeted the ladies with an apologetic look, as if somehow it were his fault that Madeleine drove over a nail or screw or roofing staple on the road to her in-laws.

"Don't worry," Spencer told them. "I can fix a puncture in no time at all. Believe me, I've had more than my share of them on my tractors." He said to his grandson, "Ron, I can use your help," and the boy seemed thrilled to be considered for such a grown-up task.

Sure enough, the automobile was ready to roll within fifteen minutes. The tire had precious little tread, but of course there was no thought of replacement, not with rubber in such short supply. Instead, Spencer patched it as well as any professional could do, just another unassuming skill that came with the experience of running one's own farm. Although Ronny's main contribution was to collect and count the lug nuts, his grandfather was quick to give him half the credit.

At dusk, on the road back to Waco, Madeleine glanced at Julie May, wondering how her friend must feel about this day in the country. What was intended to be an escape from the war—a few hours of enjoying the simple life—had instead brought the horror of war closer to them than ever before. Throughout the return trip, the women said little to each another, for this tragedy had touched them personally, unlike something they might read in the newspaper or hear on the news. Moreover, it would remain with them as a sad reminder. Never again would they be able to hear a low-flying airplane without recalling the fiery crash. They would think of those anonymous servicemen at the controls, that pair of aviators who were still very much alive when they flew over the house. Cadet trainee and seasoned instructor, these men had put their lives on the line for the benefit of the nation. Though their names would never be found in annals of the war, they too were heroes.

◆　　◆　　◆

"Did you know Sandy Whittsel is moving away?" Rollie Barnes was speaking to Wesley as they passed each other in the hallway.

"No!"

"Yep, she is."

Wesley looked at his friend in disbelief. "How can she do that? She's on 'Behold Tomorrow'—one of the regulars. She's Sally Holt!"

Rollie shrugged his shoulders. "That's what I heard from Mort Wilson."

"There's got to be some mistake. Sandy would've told me, if it's true."

"He says her old man's being transferred to the Pacific, now that Hitler's nearly licked."

"Aw, what does Mort know? He's a Browns fan."

Wesley felt queasy for the rest of the school day, almost as if a close relative or the family cat had died. Sandra Whittsel was an important part of his life, though perhaps more fantasy than actual flesh and blood. Despite this ethereal quality—or maybe because of it—she had long since been the central feature of his adolescent dreams. She was his ideal beauty of a girl, just out of reach, just beyond his ability to touch in any meaningful way. To him, infatuation felt a lot like love.

When he arrived at the radio station that afternoon, the first thing Wesley did was ask Myra Culp if the rumor was true.

"Not that I'm aware of," she said. "At least, not anytime soon."

"Are you sure?"

"No, I'm not sure, but if anyone would know, it would probably be me." She claimed this not in any conceited way but merely as a statement of fact. The front desk was where office talk reached its most sophisticated stage of development. It was the crossroads of interpersonal communication, from mundane business all the way up to smutty gossip.

"A pal of mine said her father was being sent to the Pacific," Wesley told her.

"Well, my goodness, then that's not a very well kept Army secret, is it?"

"Not very. Is Sandy here yet?"

"In the little girls' room, sport." Myra knew that Wesley carried a torch for KWXN's frisky brunette, and she enjoyed watching him blush whenever some slightly unwholesome wordage presented itself.

He decided to go into the studio rather than let Sandy catch him waiting for her in the lobby. After two years, he had finally come to the conclusion that she showed more interest in him when he was decidedly cool towards her. Now, why that should be was forever beyond his grasp—being of the opposite sex—but he noticed this attitudinal fluctuation too often for it to be pure coincidence. Maybe someday Myra could explain it to him, though conceivably there was some unwritten code of female conduct that would prohibit her from doing so.

Hugh Kenton's voice came over the loudspeaker in Studio A: "Rehearsal in three minutes." Wesley looked toward the control room and saw the mustached director puff a huge cloud of cigar smoke as he wiped his eyeglasses with a handkerchief. Sandy was yet to arrive in the studio, but that was not unusual for her. What was unusual for her was to be even a second later than the appointed time. In that sense, she was a consummate professional, not overanxious to impress the boss but not dilatory enough to incite his rancor. Just as Kenton was calling for quiet, in she walked with script in hand, wearing a pretty smile and a close-fitting blouse that was very becoming to her figure. Her waistline, she once blurted to

Wesley in an unguarded moment, was a petite twenty-three inches, which made her other measurements all the more alluring.

The rehearsal went reasonably well, with the exception of a serious blunder by Douglas Pierson. Kenton was spitting nails until it was determined that Pierson, through clerical mismanagement, did not have a page seven in his script package, and he could hardly be expected to possess psychic abilities. "Monica!" the director shouted into his intercom microphone. "Make sure Mr. Pierson has a page seven in five minutes!" Monica Whaley rushed away to make a copy of the missing sheet of dialogue. In her thankless job, even the tiniest of mistakes would always surface.

During the "West of the Brazos" run-through, many of the "Behold Tomorrow" cast relaxed in the staff lounge, individually flipping through their scripts to brush up on tricky passages. Wesley sat next to Sandy and informed the girl that a rumor about her was circulating at school.

"So, what's new?" she said with a twinkle in her eye.

Wesley lowered his voice, barely above a whisper. "Is your father being transferred?"

"That's the ugly rumor?"

"Who said the rumor was ugly?"

"Well, I just assumed."

"Someone told me that Colonel Whittsel was being transferred to the Pacific Theater."

"I thought you said the rumor was about me."

Wesley sighed, sensing that Sandy was not being as forthcoming as she could be. "The person said that you would be moving, too, and I presumed he meant back to Georgia."

"He? So it's a boy who's spreading this rumor."

Wesley stood up, exasperated, and glared at her. "Listen, if you don't want to tell me, why not just say so? I was worried that you were leaving Waco, that's all."

"Oh, Wes, I'm sorry. Please sit down." She said it with a sincere tone and look of concern. "Please."

Her lovely face captured his heart, as always, and he sat back down.

"Were you really worried about me?"

"Yes, I ..." Wesley felt a sharp sadness come over him, and his throat tightened with emotion. "Yes, strange as it may seem, I ..." He glanced away, staring at the wall. "I would miss you something terrible."

"Oh, Wesley." Sandy took his hand and rubbed the back of it against the soft skin of her cheek. "I'm going to miss you too."

He swallowed hard. "Then it's true ..."

"That I'll be moving away?"

Wesley nodded his head. For one of the few times in their acquaintance, he looked directly at her on equal terms, in total honesty.

"But you see, I have no other choice in the matter," she said. "My father is going overseas, as you say, and my mother will be moving back to Savannah."

"Do you have to go with her?"

"Yes, but not until school's out. Not before commencement."

He managed a brave smile. "So, you'll graduate as a Waco High Tiger?"

"GGGRRR!" Sandy smiled, too, and took a deep breath. Her eyes were a little teary, which came as a shock to Wesley, so completely out of character did it seem.

"How long will you be here, then?" he asked.

"Well, commencement's on the thirty-first ..."

"Uh-huh."

"... so about five weeks."

"What about your boyfriend?"

She gave a self-deprecating laugh. "I don't seem to have one of those at the present time."

"Marshall McFall?"

"He's found somebody else," she said. "I thought you knew about that girl reporter from WACO."

"He's still going with her? I thought she was just a flash in the pan."

"As far as I know, she is—for about two months now, I guess."

Wesley shook his head. "Well, all I can say is, he must be nuts."

"Thank you. That's very sweet." Sandy squeezed his hand. "I must be nuts too."

◆　　　◆　　　◆

The minesweeper *USS Jeffers* (DMS-27) was now a Pacific vessel. Having set sail from New York Harbor on the third day of the new year, she passed through the Panama Canal en route to California. After precisely two weeks at sea, the ship arrived in San Diego for further training of her crew. And thus it was that the naval life of Stephen Collins Brower had gone full circle, returning to the site of his boot camp, way back in June of 1943. His days of combat action were soon to come.

In February, following a stopover at Pearl Harbor, the *Jeffers* steamed to the atoll group of islands known as Ulithi, which had been transformed, with a sense of urgency, into a major advance fleet base after being taken by American forces in late September. Here the ship and her crew were readied for the impending invasion of Okinawa. Code-named "Iceberg," this assault would prove to be the largest amphibious operation in the Pacific War, with some fifteen hundred vessels and a half-million men (US Army, US Navy, US Marines, and British Royal Navy) taking part.

By the time Iceberg commenced at 0406 hours on Easter morning, April 1, the *Jeffers* had already been busy for a full week with the preliminary work of clearing mines and marking boat lanes. During the invasion itself, her support mission turned to air defense and antisubmarine screening. The powerful Japanese counterattack of April 6 brought a confirmed "kill" for the *Jeffers*, as her gunners managed to down a twin-engine bomber in the raid.

Less than a week later, she again came under heavy enemy fire. This occurred on April 12, when the *Jeffers* was on radar picket duty, and 185 kamikazes and two hundred conventional fighters attacked her battle group. One of the Yokosuka

MXY-7 Ohka flying bombs, guided by human pilots, had the *Jeffers* in its sights, but the Baka narrowly missed its target. A destroyer, *Mannert L. Abele* (DD-733), was not so fortunate. She suffered a deadly blow from a Jap A6M Zero, and then a Baka finished her off, sinking the ship in five minutes with the loss of seventy-nine crewmen. Manned by a suicidal pilot, the Baka—when released from its "mother" aircraft—became a formidable weapon, powered by three rockets that could generate enough force to thrust the winged bomb at speeds in excess of four hundred miles per hour. During this engagement, the *Jeffers* shot down at least one of the attackers and helped to rescue survivors from the sunken destroyer.

That same afternoon, the ship sailed to Kerama Retto—just fifteen miles west of Okinawa—where she underwent repairs for battle damage. This small group of islands, hammered by the 77th Infantry Division on March 26 and secured five days later, was vital to the massive assault. It became a staging area, providing relatively stable conditions for combat craft to refuel and replenish ammunition—still dangerous but clearly preferable to doing so on the high seas. Though sixty or more ships were awaiting repair, the *Jeffers* went to the front of the line because priority was given to vessels that could most quickly be made ready to fight again. Indeed, repair of the *Jeffers* required only four days of work, indicative of her relatively good fortune during the heated opening attacks of Iceberg. The three nights at Kerama Retto were anything but restful, as the Japanese launched kamikaze air raids to destroy the defenseless ships, whose only protection was afforded by smoke screens from the Navy's LCVPs. Then it was back to Okinawa for operations amidst a carrier group, in support of the invading ground forces.

On Thursday, May 3, the *USS Jeffers* departed Japanese waters and headed far to the southeast for further repairs. These would be effected on the largest of the Mariana Islands, that of Guam, liberated by American forces in August and, since January 28, serving as headquarters for the US Navy in the Pacific. It was to be a journey of some fourteen hundred miles, giving the *Jeffers* crew some welcome relief from the rigors of battle.

Stephen Brower put some of his leisure hours to good use, writing long-overdue letters to loved ones in the States. Not only did he set down individual missives to his mother, brother, and sister, but also chatty epistles to a couple of girls he knew—Giulia Coletti and Hannah Lane—as well as to his aunt and uncle in Harlingen. So many lengthy notes did Steve compose in one sitting that he was beginning to experience writer's cramp, surely not the sort of disability one associates with wartime duty in the armed services. At one point, he had the letters and their corresponding envelopes arrayed in sequential order, rather like an assembly line, and it was impressive to see. But his shipboard pal, Mel Zelinsky, saw in them only a chance for mischief, splashing a little *eau de toilette* on the envelopes in the hopes that the girl back home, whoever she may be, would get the idea that her sailor was quite a bit more serious than he really was. Snatching the envelopes away, Steve stuffed the letters inside and sealed them before Mel could get his pesky hands on them again. They did smell nice, though.

♦　　♦　　♦

Whatever the future might hold, Giulia would never forget the precise day when Archie Clarke returned home from the war. It was burned into her mind—not so much for any romantic association as for the vast historical significance. It was Tuesday, May 8, 1945, and the occasion was the unconditional surrender of the German armed forces. Actually, Generaloberst Alfred Jodl had signed the papers at a schoolroom in Reims the day before that, on May 7, but the surrender was not ratified by Soviet authorities in Berlin until shortly before midnight on the eighth. And it was on May 8 that President Truman made the official announcement of V-E Day to the American people.

Jubilant war news notwithstanding, Giulia looked distraught upon being told that Bess Clarke was on the phone—and what it was that she had called to arrange. "Mamma, I don't want to see Archie yet. I'm just not up to it. Let him get used to civilian life again. Please call Mrs. Clarke back, and tell her I'm not home."

But Paolina would have none of it, a shirking of responsibility that was not only fainthearted but unpatriotic. "You need to show him respect for being an American soldier, if nothing else. You owe him that much, as we all do."

That drew ire from Giulia, and her Italian blood began to boil. "Well, that would be just as dandy as candy, if all he wanted from me was a pat on the back," she said. "But Archie seems to think it's only a matter of time before we announce the date, and I have no intention of doing that—not in this lifetime."

Paolina held out her hands, as if to say "simmer down, child," and she admonished her daughter to behave like any decent human being should. "Listen, all I ask is that you act civil to him, a returning serviceman."

"I can do that much, but he'll be sadly disappointed if he expects anything more."

"Fine. He'll be here at four."

"Four!"

"That gives you two hours to grow up and be mature about this."

Giulia rolled her eyes and sighed. "Will it only be Archie, or is that mother of his coming too?"

"I'm not sure. She never said."

"Didn't you even think to ask?"

Paolina frowned. "Now, just how would I phrase that little gem? 'Can you give my daughter some advance warning if you'll be coming with him?' I don't imagine Mrs. Clarke would take too kindly to that."

"I really don't care what that dragon thinks."

"Giulia!"

"Well, I mean it. Not after the way she's treated me—spreading gossip and trying to ruin my reputation, all in the name of finding a suitable mate for her precious sonny boy. Mark my words, Mamma, one of these days, I'm going to tell her off, and I'll do it right to her face."

"Lord help anyone who does finally succeed in tying the knot with you," Paolina told her. "My goodness but you have a hot streak!"

"Then I must have gotten it from you."

She squinted at her daughter. "Oh, you would be surprised. I could tell you stories about your daddy."

Giulia's eyes flared with anger, and she shouted, not two feet away from her mother's face, "Don't say that about Papà! He's a dear man, and I love him."

"He can be a dear man, that's true," Paolina said, "but there's another side of him that you don't know. Why do you think I left him in the first place? We would have been divorced long ago if we weren't of the Catholic faith. As it is, separation is as good as divorce. They're one in the same."

"How can you live with somebody for twenty-five years and not feel anything for him?"

"Oh, I feel plenty for him—resentment, anger, pity. Your father is a sick man, but he does nothing to help himself. He's probably got a bottle stashed away right now, and it changes him. He goes out of control after the liquor starts flowing through his veins. I've been struck one too many times. Nobody should have to put up with that."

Giulia looked stunned. "He hit you?"

"Yes, he did."

"You mean he slapped you ..."

"I mean he hit me."

"With his fist?"

"On more than one occasion, I'm ashamed to say—ashamed because I stayed with him for so long when I should have turned him in to the police for battery and domestic violence."

"But he didn't know what he was doing."

"Oh, he felt remorse in the morning, I'll grant you that much. But no one held a gun to his head and forced him to drink. He was responsible for that part of his downfall, and his weakness for booze was responsible for the dissolution of our marriage. Personally, I have nothing but contempt for the man."

"But he's trying to change, Mamma. I really think he is."

"I don't believe it for a minute."

"He has an unopened bottle in a kitchen drawer, and it's full of whiskey of some sort."

Paolina laughed out loud. "Well, isn't that cute? Next thing you know, he'll be dressing like Little Lord Fauntleroy."

"He says he uses it to give him strength," Giulia told her. "That bottle is for his will power, and he feels better about himself every time he sees it."

"Oh, please! That's a new one on me—a bottle of will power. You just wait until the first time he happens to get thirsty. Then there'll be no will power left in that bottle, and he'll be a foulmouthed bully until he sleeps it off. Don't be so gullible, sweetie. He's no prince. The poor man is only trying to court your sympathy, maybe as a way to get back at me."

At that, Giulia stomped away in a huff. "I think it's terrible of you to speak about Papà like that," she said. "Anyway, how did he come into the conversation? I seem to recall that we were discussing Sergeant Archibald Clarke." Even the way she said the soldier's name was sarcastic, and Paolina could only shake her head. Giulia slammed the bedroom door shut behind her. "I'm going to lie down for a while, if you don't mind," she shouted. "With any luck, the ceiling will fall on top of me before he gets here."

But the ceiling did not fall, nor did the girl persist in viewing her predicament in an entirely negative light. Lying on her back, analyzing her options, it suddenly crystallized in her mind that this dreaded reunion might prove to be a blessing in disguise—just the opportunity she needed to bring the whole lopsided love affair to a swift and lasting conclusion. She also became convinced, beyond any reasonable doubt, that Mrs. Clarke would be there too. Giulia could feel it in her head, like a nagging migraine.

Paolina, meanwhile, had spent much of her time in the kitchen, percolating some coffee and brewing a batch of tea. She was not certain which hot beverage the Clarkes preferred, so she thought it best to make both available. This was no occasion for playing fast and loose with precarious sensitivities. Should Bess go on a vindictive rant, any pleasurable amenity would be to the good. And there were six Coca-Colas in the refrigerator, just in case.

Giulia left her room a few minutes prior to four o'clock and went purposefully to the kitchen. Even at a glance, Paolina was gladdened by the improvement in her daughter's attitude. She seemed quite chipper, all things considered, and that could only help matters, regardless of what direction this meeting might go. "Do you think Archie's mother will come with him?" the girl asked.

"It wouldn't surprise me in the slightest," Paolina said. "You know Bess Clarke."

A slight grin animated Giulia's face. "I was kind of hoping you'd say that."

"Oh?" Paolina cocked her head to one side, staring at her daughter with suspicion.

"Yep. I'm ready to get this whole thing out in the open, so everyone knows exactly where everyone else stands."

Turning her back to the girl, Paolina took a deep breath and sighed. If anything, she now felt more nervous about the meeting than Giulia did, and that was a distinct surprise. As much out of anxiety as actual need, she continued to putter with the coffee pot and teakettle, though both were ready and waiting.

An eternity passed before the doorbell finally rang at 4:20, and the instant it did, all of Giulia's confidence threatened to melt away like snow in a spring thaw. She looked pleadingly at her mother, who reassured her with a wink and smile. "Just show respect for a boy in uniform," she told the girl. "That's all you really need to do."

Giulia opened the door and, just as she had imagined, there was Bess Clarke standing right next to her son. But it was Archie who stepped forward, unsmiling, probably more fearful than he ever was in combat. Somehow, this made it easier, for Giulia could sense that he too was afflicted with common human frailty.

"Welcome home, soldier," the girl said. She had heard someone speak that line in a "B" movie, and it sounded impersonal enough for her to borrow as an official greeting.

"Thanks. It's nice to be here," came the equally stilted reply. Archie gave a boyish grin, and the two young people shook hands.

"Well, don't just stand there. Come on in," Paolina said, and there were polite smiles all around.

Already Giulia felt a little less decisive. One thing she had failed to consider in formulating her master plan for sabotaging the relationship was how very handsome Sergeant Archie Clarke would look in his Army green.

♦   ♦   ♦

A tense stillness permeated the room until Mrs. Clarke took it upon herself to utter a self-evident question. "Isn't it wonderful that Hitler's thrown in the towel?"

Paolina nodded her head. "We've been praying for this a long time."

Archie grinned at his mother. "Aw, he's done us a bigger favor than that. He's cashed in his chips!" The soldier gave a shallow laugh. "You know, if he was going to kill himself anyway, I would have been glad to pull the trigger. All he had to do was ask."

Giulia was not so sure. "How do we know he's really dead?"

"Oh, now, it's been on all the newscasts for a week," her mother said. "I don't think there's much chance that every network got it wrong." No one could argue with that.

Archie and Mrs. Clarke were side-by-side on the sofa, and Mrs. Coletti and her daughter were sitting in chairs nearby, Giulia closer to the sergeant and Paolina closer to his mother. The young people were drinking Coca-Colas, Bess Clarke a cup of coffee, and Giulia's mother some hot tea.

"How is your leg, Archie?" Paolina asked. "You don't seem to be limping much."

"No, ma'am, not anymore, but just a week ago I was a regular Hopalong Cassidy." He rubbed his left knee. "It still hurts a lot, but I think it'll get back to normal in another month or so. I'm hopeful."

Bess Clarke patted him on his good leg. "The Army doesn't want him anymore, and that's the most important thing. He did his duty, and he's back from the war— all in one piece."

"Amen," Paolina said. "We're proud of you, Archie."

He accepted the comment graciously and looked at the girl, who added, "Yes, we are. You certainly did your bit."

The conversation did not shake loose of its mannerly façade until ten minutes later when, to her son's evident surprise, Mrs. Clarke abruptly took it upon herself to invite Giulia over for dinner "one night next week."

"Well, Mother, maybe she'd rather wait until I'm back in my civvies. There's no real hurry, now that I'm stateside and—as the Aussies say—about to demob."

"Maybe that would be best," Giulia said, and she took a cold sip from her glass. Despite the fact that it was his own suggestion, Archie seemed hurt that she was so quick to concur.

Undaunted, Bess Clarke pressed forward with her grand design. "Then perhaps you two could go to the movies or something, just to get reacquainted. You know, it's been nearly three years since Archie went away—July of '42, it was. That doesn't seem possible, does it, Paolina?"

"No, it doesn't," her friend said. To disagree with such an innocent question would have been interpreted as rude, if not downright provocative.

"Well, I'm game," Archie said. "How about it? Maybe Friday night?"

"I don't think that would be such a good idea," Giulia told him.

He smiled nervously. "Saturday?"

There was a pause. "Not at all," she said.

Mrs. Clarke gasped audibly, and Paolina looked at her daughter, stupefied.

"You won't even go to the picture show with me?" Archie asked. He was more embarrassed than angry.

"I'm sorry, but no. I see no point in it." She stared at the floor in front of her.

"You see no point ..." He stood up and took a step toward her. "Well, what did I say? What did I do wrong? I don't understand, and I think you owe me an explanation."

Giulia arose too, and they both glanced at their mothers.

Mrs. Clarke, in particular, seemed badly shaken, so Paolina offered to help her up. "I think we should let them discuss this in private, Bess, don't you?"

"Yes ... Yes, of course." The woman's voice sounded rattled by this turn of events.

"Wait, Mother," Archie said. "You two stay right here. Giulia and I will go somewhere, and we won't be long. Let me take the car, and I'll have her back here in an hour."

"Yes, dear. All right."

He drove her to the Williams Drug Store, at the corner of Ninth and Austin, and bought each of them a scoop of ice cream, vanilla for himself, strawberry for her. The soda fountain's counter was not crowded at this time of day, so its attendant—a pimply faced teenager whom Giulia recognized from school but did not know by name—was grateful for any business he could get. Throughout their stay, the boy persisted in calling Archie "sir," a mistaken identity that made the sergeant grin a time or two. He did not bother to inform the lad that he "worked for a living," an NCO quip that was probably generations old, if not centuries.

After finishing his ice cream, Archie took a deep breath and sighed slowly, allowing the exhaling air to fill his cheeks like a ship's sails. All the while, he gazed at the empty dish in front of him, and his face become so earnest that Giulia knew he must be struggling with how to phrase what he had to say. "Look, Giulia ..." he began, but the next words would not come. He observed her for an instant but then turned away, resting his chin upon a fist. Giulia waited patiently, for even in her determined state, she possessed enough sense of fair play to give him the right to speak first.

Clearing his throat, he started anew, only this time Archie looked her straight in the eye. "Listen, Giulia, I'm not going to give a fancy speech here, but I do want to express a couple of thoughts that I've been kicking around. First, I don't think we should see each other for a while. No dates, no plans—no nothing."

Though surprised, Giulia made an effort to hide her personal sentiments from view, not wishing to inhibit the candor of his own. She felt it best to get this over with now, so she just waited for him to express what was on his mind.

"If we ever get back together again, fine," he said, "but forcing someone into a relationship is a sure way to doom it. And that, I think, is what I've been doing to you—cornering you and making you feel trapped." He reached for a cigarette and asked, "Do you mind if I ...?"

"No, of course not."

Archie lit up the cigarette, puffed thoughtfully for a second or two, and then told her, "In my own defense, I think I'll just blame everything on the war." Giulia smiled at his little joke but said nothing. "Really, though, being so far away did make me too possessive. I guess I thought it was my only chance to keep you for myself, and that's not how it works. We didn't have a strong enough foundation— by a long shot—to build an engagement upon, and it scared you out of your wits, rightly so. I apologize for that, and I'm willing to go back to square one, if need be, or just call it quits entirely, if that's what you want."

He flicked his ashes onto a saucer, there being no ashtray on the counter that was within arm's length. "The second thing I want to say is that I do not intend to live permanently in Waco. I love my mother, but I can see that she ... Let's just say that she tries to run my life a little more than she probably should. She means well, she honestly does, but that doesn't alter the fact that I feel stifled whenever I'm around her for very long. What I'm trying to tell you is that I'll be moving on pretty soon—within the next year or so, if the Japs surrender by then. That'll be good news to you, if you just can't wait to see the last of me."

Giulia shook her head. "Now, did I ever say that? I just wasn't ready to become—"

He interrupted her. "And, of course, this move of mine also means that you would not have to put up with Mother's overbearing ways, should the two of us ever actually get serious. I've got big plans for the future. Being away at war changed me in many ways, and I think you'll be surprised to learn that I'm not the same person you used to know."

"You do seem different," she said, "but I just supposed it was because we hadn't seen each other for so long."

"You've changed too, whether you realize it or not," he told her. "You've grown up. When I left to join Uncle Sam, you were still a schoolgirl."

She blushed. "I was kind of silly back then, I'm sure."

"Weren't we all?" Archie said. He took a drag and blew the smoke to one side.

Giulia stared at his cigarette, as if noticing it for the first time. "Did you always smoke? I don't remember."

Archie frowned. "No. That's a bad habit I picked up in the Army. All the Yanks in Australia smoke—or at least ninety percent of them anyway. I lasted longer than most before I finally gave in. It was just something you did in your leisure time, something to take your mind off the war for a few minutes." He studied her face. "Have you ever tried it?"

"No!" the girl said. "And I don't have any desire to stick a burning weed in my mouth."

"Good for you."

Giulia giggled, looking at him with a new appreciation. "You know what?"

"What?"

"We act like we're on a first date."

Archie laughed but had to nod his head in agreement. "I do believe you're right. Maybe that's a good thing."

"Maybe so." She smiled up at him. "Tell me your name again, soldier."

"Archibald Leland Clarke ... Sergeant ... 3-8-7-3-1-8-4-2."

"Pleased to meet you, I'm sure." Then she chuckled. "Leland ...?"

"That's right. Is there something wrong with it? What's your middle name anyhow?"

"Marcellina," she said. "I'm very Italian."

"Do you always go around picking up stray GIs?"

"No, of course not. Only the good-looking ones who aren't married."

"That leaves quite a few."

"But I'm very picky."

Archie sat upright on his stool and swiveled toward her. "We'll have to do this again some time."

"Maybe so, Sergeant Clarke. I like it better when we're not engaged."

"Same here." He grinned at her and loosened his necktie. "A lot less pressure."

Giulia extended her arm, shook his hand like a casual acquaintance, and said, "Won't our mothers be shocked?"

"And how."

During the drive back to Giulia's house, Archie asked her whether she dated much while he was overseas.

"What kind of question is that?"

"I'm just being nosy, that's all."

Giulia grinned. "I wouldn't tell you if I did."

"That's the attitude! Remember, tonight was our first date, and we've got no claims on each other. Whatever happens, happens."

"Agreed."

"I may be going away soon, and I don't want any entangling alliances."

"Understood."

He gave her a mischievous look. "Well?"

"Well, what?"

"Did you date much while I was gone?"

Giulia sighed, playfully loud. "My goodness. You're a regular Jimmie Fidler, aren't you?"

"I've got a healthy case of curiosity, that's all. I'm just a red-blooded American male."

"So I've noticed."

A small cattle truck met them at an intersection, both vehicles reaching the four-way stop at the same time, and Archie waved at its driver to proceed. The rancher nodded his thanks and drove past. "Mmm, burgers," the sergeant said. "He's got the right of way, in my book." Meat was a rationed commodity, and military consumption did not leave much for the civilians.

Finally, Giulia blurted her answer. "I saw one boy, if that's the scoop you're after." She awaited his reaction but detected none. "I'm not much of a dater."

Archie may have been holding back a smile. "Did he kiss you?"

"Yes, as if it's any of your concern, he did kiss me—and furthermore, I kissed him right back too."

"Good. Practice makes perfect." He turned the Nash sedan into the Colettis' driveway. "Anything else happen?"

"Absolutely not. The date ended with a kiss." She flashed a smile, coy rather than seductive. "What sort of girl do you think I am?"

"I've really never given it much thought."

Giulia giggled. "Oh, sure. I believe that!"

"Well, it seemed like the right thing to say."

Suddenly serious, they looked at one another in silence for a moment. Then Archie pointed to the passenger door. "Out, Miss Coletti, if you please. It's time to tell my dear mother to mind her own blankety-blank business—in a nice, roundabout way, of course."

◆　　◆　　◆

"Would it be all right if my son comes with me instead?" Hermann asked. "My wife has to stay home and mind the store."

"You have two tickets to use however you want, Mr. Moek. It's really up to you."

"Thank you, Mr. Chandler. I just wanted to make sure."

"Enjoy the trip," the chamber officer said. He handed Hermann an envelope, and the two men shook hands.

This Monday morning transaction took place at the Waco Chamber of Commerce Building, 416 Franklin Avenue. Hermann paid Boyd Chandler, who in turn would forward the money—less a small commission—to the Independent Retail Grocers Association's national headquarters in Cincinnati, Ohio.

The offer was too attractive for Hermann to pass up—receiving rail transportation for two, merely for the price of booking three nights at a luxury hotel in Saint Louis. It was a promotional deal, fashioned by IRGA as a way to boost attendance at their annual convention.

Taking Klaus-Peter along would provide a wonderful learning experience for the boy. Though he had been on American soil for less than four months, he was already becoming quite conversant in the English language. Right from the outset,

Hermann and Gertrude made a pact with each other to speak nothing but English at home, in an effort to encourage the youngster to assimilate the foreign tongue as rapidly as possible. As Hermann jokingly put it, learning by this immersion method was "like drinking water from a fire hose." The process was accelerated, almost to the point of mental cruelty, but there was no denying the effectiveness. Besides, it was for the lad's own good. He would be starting school in the fall term, and it was absolutely essential that he be fluent in English by then.

The two-day railroad journey was an eye-opener for Klaus-Peter Schang, a German orphan who, until his evacuation to the New World, had never been more than fifty miles from his hometown of Düren, in the old Prussian province of Westphalia. Neither the immense ocean voyage nor the five-hour automobile trip from Houston to Waco could begin to approximate, in his imagination, the magnificent vastness of America's heartland. The locomotive chugged for mile after mile after unending mile, and the panoramic view through his coach window transformed itself alternately from grassy prairie to arid plains to rolling hills to teeming forest to fertile plateau. One thing struck him for certain: Missouri, judging from what he had seen, appeared to be much more like the Fatherland than Texas did.

On Wednesday, when the train finally arrived at Union Station in Missouri's largest city, Hermann and the boy went by taxicab to 822 Washington Avenue. Klaus-Peter stood on the sidewalk and, squinting through the rain, looked up at the top of the Statler Hotel.

"Have you ever seen anything like it?" Hermann asked.

"No, sir. Except for one or two buildings in Houston and, of course, the Amicable Building." He wiped raindrops from his forehead. "We'll be dwelling in a skyscraper."

Smiling at Klaus-Peter's choice of words, Hermann patted him on the back. "Yes, that's where we'll be dwelling, all right. Come on, son." They went inside the resplendent lobby and checked in, discovering that their reservation directed them to a room on the twelfth floor of the twenty-story structure. Under normal conditions, that room—one of 650 in the Statler—would have afforded them a marvelous view of the city, but on this day, clouds and steady rainfall significantly restricted the visibility. "I sure do hope the rain lets up," Hermann told the boy. "I thought we could take in the Browns game tomorrow."

"The Brauns?"

"The Saint Louis Browns—like the color brown. They're a professional baseball team, and I mean the major leagues!"

Klaus-Peter grinned. "I have heard of baseball. It's the national pastime."

"It is, indeed," Hermann said. He rubbed his chin in thought. "Now, I don't know very much about the Browns, except to say that they are the defending American League Champions. They lost to the Saint Louis Cardinals in last year's World Series, four games to two."

"Why do they call it the World Series, if only teams from Saint Louis play?"

Hermann chuckled. "Well, that was what you call a fluke, son. It just so happened that both Saint Louis teams won their respective league pennants."

"Is Saint Louis the only city allowed to have two teams?"

"Oh, no. Several other large cities do—New York, Chicago, Philadelphia, and Boston, to be exact. In fact, New York has three major league teams, if you count Brooklyn."

"Three!"

"Have you ever heard of the New York Yankees?"

"No, sir."

"Do you know who Babe Ruth is?"

"No, sir."

Hermann Moek shook his head sadly but then issued a bold proclamation. "We've got a lot of baseball to learn, and this trip is as good a time as any to begin."

The following morning, a Thursday, conventioneers congregated in the sumptuous, two-story ballroom at the very top of the Statler, and a pair of engaging speakers opened the proceedings with humorous talks on the follies of wartime strategy for profit-making. Klaus-Peter stayed in the hotel room, for he had nowhere else to go. He did have a radio to keep him company, not to mention plenty of juvenile books on American history and government.

By noon, when Hermann returned to the room to take the boy to lunch, the weather still had not improved to any appreciable extent, and it was a foregone conclusion that the game at Sportsman's Park against Boston would not be played, due to wet grounds. It was discouraging to know that a Saint Louis rainy spell could last for so long, washing away an entire four-game series with the Red Sox, and Hermann began to worry that young Klaus-Peter might not be attending a baseball game after all. One more opportunity remained before they would be leaving for home—a night game against those very New York Yankees whom Hermann had mentioned to the lad—and local weathermen were optimistic that conditions would be more satisfactory by late morning on Friday, giving the saturated outfield grass several hours to dry before game time.

Klaus-Peter awoke at dawn and tiptoed over to the curtain to have a look. Persistent clouds darkened the skies, but at least the rain had abated. This promised to be a long day for him, anxious to see his first ball game and with little to keep him occupied beyond the serials that seemed to air for hours on end over the radio. By now, he had read all of the books he brought from Waco, including one about the Alamo that particularly captured his fancy. He wondered if it might be possible to purchase a coonskin cap in Saint Louis, but his foster father was doubtful of the prospects and suggested instead that he plan to wait until they were back in Texas. Maybe he could find one at Cox's or Sears.

The last thing Hermann said to Klaus-Peter before attending his final full day of IRGA sessions was, "We'll ride over to the baseball field when I get back. There's a streetcar that goes straight to Sportsman's Park."

The boy's eyes lit up, and his face was aglow. "Can we eat there? I'd like to watch the teams prepare to play."

"I never miss batting practice, son," Hermann said with a wink.

As the hours crept by, Klaus-Peter often looked outside at the sky. Though still overcast, the cloud cover was indeed beginning to thin in several places, and this allowed the sun to break through, however fleetingly. Seeing the sun at all was a welcome sight after the dreariness of the past couple of days, and it boded well for an evening free of any additional precipitation.

Klaus-Peter wanted to listen to a game on the radio, to better acquaint himself with what to expect at the ballpark. He did not know the first thing about baseball, and any exposure to the specialist jargon involved would certainly help him to learn about this uniquely American sport. Despite dialing the tuning knob from left to right and back again, no baseball game was to be heard. Shouldn't the other Saint Louis team be playing? Then he thought to consult the *Post-Dispatch*, which his father had tossed onto the bed after breakfast. This authoritative source explained today's absence of baseball on the radio. The second Saint Louis team, known as the Cardinals, was playing at Philadelphia, but it too was scheduled to be a night game.

When Hermann returned to the hotel room that afternoon, his arms were full of promotional materials that wholesalers distributed among the IRGA crowd, planting seeds for future innovations in merchandising. Most of it was of negligible value, but a few pieces were quite interesting indeed. And yet Hermann laid the stack on a table, realizing that he would have plenty of time to go through it all on the train. He did not wish to dawdle now, as Klaus-Peter was excited beyond words. All Hermann needed to say was, "Are you ready for a ball game?" and the boy was at his side in a flash.

◆　　◆　　◆

The streetcar ride was not a long one, just to the northwest of downtown, and it stopped on Grand Boulevard, right next to the pavilion entrance to Sportsman's Park. Like the boy, Hermann had not seen a major league ballpark in person before, and he was astonished by the sheer size of the facility. The many minor league parks he had visited were nothing like this. As for the impressionable youth himself, Klaus-Peter beamed with delight. Never in his fondest dreams had he hoped to see such a magnificent building. It was like something out of a fairy tale—a castle, perhaps, or an impregnable fortress.

Before they went to the ticket office, which was not yet open in any case, Hermann and the boy decided to walk around the entire structure. They set forth in a northerly direction, up Grand Boulevard. When they reached Sullivan Avenue, in deepest center field, they viewed the impressive YMCA building across the intersection. Going west on Sullivan, they passed by the back side of the mammoth scoreboard that towered above the left-field bleachers. In traversing Spring Avenue to the south, they savored the tempting smells of a sausage stand on wheels that was just about to open for business. A white-haired man who stood within the metal contraption waved at them and cheered, "Go, Brownies!" Soon they had reached Dodier Street, directly behind home plate, and they walked past the ballfield's main entrance, glancing up to read the sign SPORTSMAN'S PARK.

Heading east on Dodier, the double-decked stands loomed overhead, ranging all the way to the right-field foul pole. At Grand, the pair turned left once again and finished up their trek right where it began. They felt that they knew the massive structure pretty well by now, and they had not yet even been inside.

The Browns' ticket office opened its windows fifteen minutes later, and there did not seem to be a rush to secure seating. Hermann asked the man who was standing in front of him in line, "Do you think there will be any seats left?"

The man gave him an incredulous look. "There's always plenty of seats for the Brownies, Mack."

Once within the ballpark's perimeter, Hermann bought the boy a five-cent scorecard, and they headed toward a concession stand for hot dogs and soft drinks. Some vendors were hawking their goods below the stands, and Klaus-Peter enjoyed listening to the way their voices echoed. Strolling past a tunnel, the boy and his foster father glimpsed the infield grass, and it was a remarkable color and texture—resembling a thick, bright green carpet. A few minutes later, with food and drinks in hand, they came to their own tunnel and entered the grandstands. It was awe-inspiring to see that emerald blanket and those bold, white lines stretching all the way to the distant fences. The skin part of the infield was being watered, which seemed extravagant after all these days of steady rain. Hermann explained that this part of the playing surface had been covered with a tarpaulin during the inclement weather, so it was now being watered to keep the dust to a minimum.

Their tickets led them to seats on the third-base side, four rows behind the home dugout. Right in front of them, warming up in foul territory, were members of the Saint Louis Browns. They sported their white uniforms, of course, with brown and orange trim, brown socks with three orange stripes, and the nickname BROWNS emblazoned in a convex arch across the chest. In support of the war effort, they wore patriotic emblems, sewn onto their left sleeves. Each of these patches had thirteen vertical stripes, alternating red and white, set below a horizontal, blue field arrayed with thirteen white stars.

The Yankees—loosening up their arms beyond the first-base line—wore the same red, white, and blue patches on their left sleeves. Being on the road, they donned their slightly gray, off-white uniforms, not pin-striped away from the Bronx, with dark blue (almost black) socks and the city name NEW YORK arching across the chest.

"These are the New York Yankees that you were telling me about?" Klaus-Peter asked.

"Well, it's the same team, son, but most of the best players are wearing a different uniform now, in the military. These aren't the famous Yankees anymore. They're still plenty good—right behind the White Sox in the standings—but not like they would be in peacetime. Bill Dickey's gone ... and Joe Gordon, Phil Rizzuto, Tommy Henrich, and of course the greatest of them all, Joe DiMaggio."

"Do the White Sox really wear white socks?"

Hermann punched the boy playfully on the leg. "Sure they do. How do you think they got that name?"

He tried to think of who the Browns' top player was, but he could not recall. "Let me see that list for a minute, will you, champ?" A quick perusal of the roster reminded him that it was shortstop Vern Stephens, and he handed the scorecard back to the boy. "Look for number five, son. That's the best player for Saint Louis."

Klaus-Peter spotted him in no time. "There he is," he said, "throwing the ball to number four ..." He consulted the roster. "... Don Gutteridge."

"That Stephens fellow has a lot of power for a shortstop. He's leading the league in homers with six." Klaus-Peter had no idea what his foster father was talking about, but he gazed with new respect at the man who wore number five. Stephens was not very tall, only about five-ten, but he was muscular. His face was round, with wide-set eyes and large forehead. He seemed like he would be a kindly person with a good sense of humor.

Batting practice was a treat, as first the Yankees and then the Browns swung from the heels, and rather often their prodigious drives found the bleacher seats. Even with the wartime depletion of talent, these residual players could still perform quite well. After all, most would have been competing at the Class-A level in normal times, and that was just one step below the major leagues.

The dimensions of Sportsman's Park were decidedly favorable to left-handed batters, enticing hitters with a cozy 310-foot poke down the right-field line and only 322 to straightaway right. In contrast, the left-field foul pole stood a distant 351 feet from home plate, and the left-field power alley measured a demanding 379. To compensate somewhat, Browns management had installed a 33-foot-tall screen in front of the right-field pavilion, and any ball that struck it was considered to be in play. The screen stretched for 156 feet, all the way from the foul pole to right-center field.

"That man just has one arm!" Klaus-Peter shouted, and this drew some smiling stares from fans nearby.

"That's Pete Gray. He's been in all the newspapers since coming up to the big leagues this year." They watched with admiration as Gray, a left-handed hitter, stroked several solid line drives in batting practice.

"How can he play baseball with one arm?"

"Well, it's a very inspirational story. As I understand it—"

"Did he lose it in the war?"

"No, son, he lost his right arm in a truck accident when he was a child. He developed into a very good minor league baseball player, so the Browns brought him up this spring. I can't remember where I read that, but it must have been in the *News-Tribune*."

Klaus-Peter enjoyed looking at the colorful advertising signs on the outfield fence. Straight in front of him, far out in right field, were ads for Griesedieck Brothers Premium Light Lager Beer ("Naturally Smoother") and Lifebuoy Soap ("Gets Skin Cleaner ... Stops B.O."). To his left, beyond the warning track, the fence promoted City Ice Cubes ("They're Crystal Clear") and Winthrop Shoes ("For Men and Boys ... Styles for Every Occasion"). High above those, the scoreboard proclaimed sales messages from Falstaff Beer ("Premium Quality") and Gem Razor Blades ("Once Over ... You're Clean!").

When the Browns took the field, and the game finally started, the arc lights were just beginning to take effect, so Hermann wondered how the Yankee hitters could possibly see Jack Kramer's pitches in such dim conditions. It hardly seemed better than playing in the dusk with no artificial lighting at all. Other than Pete Gray's single off Yankee starter Hank Borowy's very first pitch, the opening inning was uneventful, but then New York's Nick Etten led off the second with a home run to put the Bronx Bombers in front. In the bottom of the third inning, Saint Louis rallied. After left fielder Gray drew a walk, he stole second base. Borowy then issued free passes to the next two batters, third baseman Len Schulte and center fielder Mike Kreevich, thereby loading the bases.

With two out, Vern Stephens stepped into the box and, after fouling off a couple of pitches, he tagged a one-two offering for a long home run into the left-field bleachers. The fans—what few of them there were—went wild as their slugging shortstop rounded the bases. There were 7,918 spectators in the stands that day, swallowed up by a cavernous park that boasted a seating capacity of 34,000. The Stephens grand-slam homer gave the Browns a four-to-one lead that they would never relinquish, for the rest of the game went scoreless, and the hometown team chalked up a victory in their first western encounter against the Yankees. If nothing else, the defending champs were efficient at the plate, eking out four runs on a total of only four hits off Borowy and reliever Jim Turner, who was on the mound for the seventh and eighth innings.

For a displaced orphan from war-ravaged Germany, this night was the thrill of his young life, and Klaus-Peter talked about nothing but baseball during the return streetcar trip to the Statler Hotel, over Saturday morning breakfast, throughout the cab ride back to Union Station, and for nearly every waking moment of the pair's two-day journey by train to central Texas.

"Can we hear the Browns' games on our radio in Waco?" he asked. They were nearly home, crossing the Washington Street Bridge over the Brazos River.

"No, I'm afraid not," Hermann told him, "unless the weather conditions are just right." His face brightened. "But there will be box scores in the Waco paper, and you can follow the team that way."

"Vern Stephens is my favorite player," the boy said, and the Americanization of Klaus-Peter brought tears to his foster father's eyes.

Hermann and Gertrude Moek missed their son Conrad terribly, but the arrival of this nine-year-old descendant of the late Ludwig and Ulrike Schang of Düren, Westphalia, was—as Hermann never tired of testifying to anyone who would listen—"truly a god-send and all the evidence we need for belief in the Almighty."

♦   ♦   ♦

It was the third Saturday in May when Wesley, from out of the blue, informed his mother that he was planning a Sunday excursion to Axtell.

"Axtell?"

"It's a little town about fifteen miles from here."

"Yes, I know where Axtell is, but why in the world do you want to go there?"

"One of my radio clients invited me for Sunday dinner. Haven't I mentioned Rob Glynn to you before?"

"Not that I remember."

"He works at a tobacco shop on Saturdays, and he's been wanting me to come see his farm. His wife's specialty is fried chicken."

"Do you mean tomorrow?"

"No, a week from tomorrow. It'll be my last chance to go before graduation." Wesley glanced at his sister, who was sitting with them at the dinner table.

Nora frowned and said, "Gee, I don't know." She made a quick calculation. With their three gallons of fuel a week, this trip to Axtell—thirteen or fourteen miles, one way—would use about one fourth of the monthly allotment. "I'm sorry, Wes, but I really don't think we can spare the gas."

"Yes, ma'am, I've thought of that. I'll ride my bicycle to school and the radio station every day this week, and that'll more than make up the difference."

That appeared to mollify her, at least for now, so Wesley did not feel compelled to enumerate his intentions any further. Indeed, the true reason for this purported "sales call" may have gone undiscovered, were it not for his perceptive sister, who suspected an ulterior motive right from the start. There was something in the way his eyes brightened when he mentioned the name of this rural town. Elizabeth deduced that a mere business appointment would not generate quite the degree of emotional involvement that seemed to be inhabiting his rationale for the visit.

She gave him a smug smile. "It's a girl, isn't it?"

"Why do you say that?" Wesley asked. He glanced at his mother, doing a poor job of masking his feelings. She stared right back, suddenly all ears.

"Because I know how nutty you get whenever a pretty girl is around," Elizabeth told him.

To the young man's credit—or maybe because he saw how futile it would be to argue otherwise—Wesley readily conceded that Elizabeth's suspicions were well founded. With a sheepish grin, he even went so far as to volunteer the girl's name. "All right, I'll come clean about her. She's Pippa Glynn, and she's a senior at Axtell High School." Much to his own surprise, he found that talking about Pippa in front of others was actually enjoyable, something that he never recalled happening before.

"And where did you meet this girl?" Nora asked.

"On a sales call, like I said."

"Pippa advertises on the radio?" That was Elizabeth, feigning innocence. Sometimes she enjoyed acting befuddled, particularly when it might agitate her brother.

Wesley heaved a sigh. "No, goofy, Pippa is not a client. She's only eighteen years old." He tried to picture the lovely girl in his memory, but with only faint success. It was now eight weeks since he had seen her.

"Well, if that was such a stupid question," his sister said, "then who is this so-called client you're talking about?"

"You don't believe me!" He chuckled softly to himself. "Listen, Pippa's dad really does work at a tobacco shop on Saturdays, and she comes with him to Waco every once in a while. I try to sell radio time to her dad."

"So, he's the owner?" Nora asked.

"No, Mr. Glynn just works there once a week, to give the owner a day off. He's really a farmer, with a plot of land somewhere out near Axtell."

"Then, that makes your Pippa a farmer's daughter," Elizabeth told him.

"Lizzie!" her mother said. She was too amused to be truly angry at the indiscretion.

"Well, I thought it was funny," the girl said.

The Big Day finally arrived, and Wesley could not decide whether he was more excited or nervous about it. While at church, whenever his mind wandered momentarily to Dr. Hargrove's sermon, a return to thoughts of Pippa would bring a jolt of adrenaline that made his heart pound faster but was not unpleasant in the least. If she had that much effect on him after just two brief meetings, he reasoned, then maybe this was the real thing. What he chose to ignore, of course, was that every attractive girl he had ever known produced this very same effect. If only he could remember what Pippa looked like. His mental conception of her was growing dimmer by the day, and attempts at sharpening the image only made it that much fuzzier.

Just the day before, over a terribly bitter cup of coffee that refused to be tamed by any amount of cream, Rob Glynn had told him which roads to take and where the turnoff was for the Rocking H Ranch. Perhaps it was called that because Mrs. Glynn's maiden name was Herndon. That, at least, is what Wesley presumed, but probably he would never know for sure. Asking such a question might prove awkward or even embarrassing for the man of the house, though why that should be the case was not entirely clear. After all, it was Mr. Glynn, more than anyone else, who worked the land and cared for the animals, so certainly he too had a vested interest in the property, regardless of from which side of the family the inheritance happened to come.

Wesley followed US Highway 84 until it split off to State Highway 31, and it seemed to him that he was already far out in the country. The temperature was becoming quite hot, almost summery, the forecasters' anticipated high of eighty-five having been eclipsed and still climbing. He rolled down the window all the way, so that more air could circulate, but that made his hair blow as if it were in the wind tunnel of a carnival midway. He feared resembling a rodeo clown when he next came face-to-face with the girl. Sacrificing comfort for vanity, he rolled the glass back up a bit, a compromise that helped the coiffure but stimulated the sweat glands more than was desirable. And there she was, no doubt, sipping iced tea in front of an electric fan, thus positioning herself at a distinct advantage in terms of appearance.

He arrived at the cutoff, where a small "Axtell" sign pointed to an indifferently maintained two-lane road that was hardly wide enough for opposing vehicles to pass one another without exchanging coats of paint. Now all he had to do was spot the entryway to the Glynns' farm, which was not such an easy task way out here in the middle of nowhere. Grasping the steering wheel with Rob's notes held at eye level should hit the target, Wesley figured, and that indeed was the case. A rutted trail, with buffalo grass staking its claim to the center, looked promising, and it did match up quite well with the handwritten instructions. Yes, there it was—a farmhouse far down the circuitous road, so Wesley maneuvered his 1938 coupe along the worn path, raising a cloud of dust that did not hover for long in the hot winds.

Rob Glynn was outside when the automobile approached, and he waved frantically for Wesley to pull around to the side of the house, rather than block the most direct tractor route from field to barn. The farmer smiled and tipped his hat in thanks, then ambled over to the dark green Chevrolet to welcome his guest.

"A real scorcher today, huh, Wes?"

"Yes, sir. I'll bet you wouldn't mind some rain either."

"Isn't that the truth!" Rob slammed the door for him when Wesley got out. "Have any trouble finding the place, son?"

"No, sir. I thought I would, but I just drove up like I was the county sheriff."

Rob motioned for Wesley to follow him, and they walked toward the house. "Incidentally, he's a good friend of mine, in case you ever need a lawman."

"The sheriff is?"

"Yep. And his wife, Margaret, worked on a couple of scrap-metal drives with my wife."

"Way out here in the country?"

Rob grinned. "We are fighting on the same side, you know."

A mother cat and her four kittens, probably feral, trotted by about twenty feet in front of them, leery of human companionship. "Watch this," Rob said. He waited for a moment and then gave one clap of the hands. The five cats ran, full-tilt, through a rotted opening in one of the planks at the corner of the barn. "They keep well fed on mice and lizards and what-not, I guess, because we never give them anything to eat."

The farmer and the young man continued their walk toward the house, over yellowish-brown grass that clung to life despite being parched by the hot Texas sun and beaten down by the movement of heavy equipment.

"I don't even know who the sheriff is," Wesley said, and it was clear to see that the confession made him a little embarrassed.

"Homer Casey," Rob told him with a wry smile. "I would've thought a newsman like yourself would be pals with all the county bigwigs." He winked at the boy, just to show that he was not serious.

"Oh, I haven't announced the news for a long time. I used to, though. Now I'm just doing a drama show. "

"And selling advertising."

"Well, sort of."

"Pippa said she heard you on the air one time."

"Reading the news?"

"I don't know. Maybe it was that program."

"Probably, if it wasn't too long ago."

"Just a couple of months, I'd say."

The mere mention of her name made Wesley's heart race, and he found it difficult to believe that he would be seeing her again at any minute. He barely remembered what the girl looked like, except that she was cute enough to take his breath away. That much he did recall. "I hope I wasn't too bad that day. Some shows are better than others."

Rob shrugged his shoulders. "She seemed to think it was fine. At least, she didn't say it wasn't."

Wesley chuckled. "I'll take that as a positive review."

His host stepped onto the front porch and reached for the screen door. "After you, son."

Entering the house, Wesley could smell the savory aroma of Sunday dinner. He had not eaten since 8:30, and he feared that his stomach might start to growl at any moment.

"Come on and meet the missus," Rob said, and he led the way to the kitchen. "Jill, this is that radio salesman from Waco, Wesley Brower. He drove all the way out here to have some of your fried chicken."

Mrs. Glynn laid down the hot pad she was holding. "How do you do, Wesley? Rob has said some nice things about you." They shook hands.

"Things like you're not a very pushy salesman," Rob said. "And that you'll drink just about any exotic coffee I put in front of you."

"I guess that's true."

Rob looked around. "Where has our daughter disappeared to, hon?"

"Last I saw, she was changing out of her good clothes."

"Now, doesn't that make you feel honored, Wes? She sure wouldn't want to look too nice, would she?"

He patted Wesley on the back, and the boy laughed. "That's fine with me, sir."

"What Rob means," Jillian told the boy, "is that we've been to church, and she's not going to stay in her Sunday dress all day long."

"It was a special baccalaureate service," Rob added, "killing two birds with one stone."

Wesley seemed surprised. "Waco's is tonight."

"Ours is usually in the afternoon," Jillian said, "but this year—what with the hard times and all—the high school couldn't afford to hire a guest preacher for baccalaureate. Pastor Magness agreed to have the ceremony during Axtell Baptist Church's regular eleven-o'clock service."

"When is Axtell's commencement?"

"Friday night at eight in the high school gym," Rob told him. "You're invited, if you'd like to see Pippa graduate."

"Gee, I wish I could, but we just don't have the gasoline to spare."

Rob nodded his head. "I understand, believe you me."

Wesley seemed about to ask something but then stopped.

"Well, go ahead, son."

"I was just wondering if Pippa is valedictorian."

"No, I'm afraid not. Who is it, hon?"

"Pauline Logan. And a girl named Patsy Ruth Robertson is salutatorian."

"Is Pippa disappointed?"

"Hah! She's thrilled to death," Rob said. "Not to have to make a speech, that is. She's a good student, all right, but just not a genius like her mother."

Jillian pretended to swat her husband with a dish towel.

"How many Axtell kids are graduating?" Wesley asked. He watched Pippa's mother roll some chicken pieces in breading.

"Four girls and two boys," Jillian said as she worked. "Some of the other boys have gone to war, of course."

Wesley could hardly believe his ears. "Are you saying that only six people are graduating from Axtell High School—in all?"

Rob smiled at the boy, amused by his reaction. "We're a very small community."

"Gosh. I think we have more than two hundred graduating from Waco High."

"Well, that's what you get for living in the big city."

"Six people in all?"

"Just six."

◆   ◆   ◆

When Pippa finally did appear, Rob and Wesley were looking at the handcrafted radio receiver that the farmer had built many years ago, back when he was just a boy himself. It still worked, though earphones were necessary, and only a few stations were audible.

Rob turned toward his daughter and smiled. "Hello, sugar. We thought maybe you'd gone back to bed or something."

"Oh, Daddy!" There was laughter in her voice, but her face remained serious.

"You remember Wes, don't you?"

"Yes, sir." She nodded to the boy. "Hello, Wes."

"Hello." Wesley desperately wanted to say more than a single word, but all he did was look. What struck him most was the girl's unaffected prettiness. Why in the world had he been so powerless to picture her in his thoughts for the past few weeks? The answer, he supposed, was that Pippa possessed such classic features that she was almost plain, at least in terms of how a Hollywood talent scout might see her. There were no outstanding characteristics that would qualify her for instant stardom on the big screen. But her face had a girlish innocence about it, an unsophisticated sweetness. The mere fact that she seemed totally unaware of her attractiveness made her that much more enchanting, and this intangible quality was something the so-called beauty queens would never be able to simulate with their cosmetics and professional coaching. All of this raced through his mind in perhaps three seconds' time, as he continued to stare at her, his heart pounding.

Meanwhile, the girl's mother had come into the living room, and she said, "Why don't you show him around outside, dear? It'll be a good half-hour before dinner is ready."

"Yes, ma'am." Dutifully, Pippa walked toward the front door, trusting that her visitor would not be too far behind. She heard Wesley's chair scoot back and her father say, "Don't be long, you two. I'm starting to get hungry."

Wesley must have run, for he reached for the doorknob before Pippa could, and he seemed to chuckle at himself—at the silly way he was falling head over heels like this, and with other people there to see. Somehow, he did not even care.

Pippa took him to their large pond, which she called a "tank," and demonstrated how fish would swim near its surface when she dipped a piece of straw into the water.

"How did they get in there?" Wesley asked.

She stared at him as if he were kidding. "A man stocked the tank for us. What do you think, that they fell from the sky during a heavy rain?"

"I don't know very much about farms," he told her.

"Actually, I think of this as a ranch, not a farm. A ranch has livestock that earn a substantial portion of the income."

"Then why does your dad call it his farm?"

She thought for a moment and laughed. "I'm not sure. Maybe he's more interested in the crops than I am."

"He says you love the animals."

Serious again, she said, "Oh, I do, Wes. They're my babies."

While they were strolling toward the grain silos, Wesley made it a point to stay half a step behind, savoring the way she moved, the gracefulness of her petite body, and even the clothes that she wore, rippling in the high winds. Her unassuming togs were a green and white checkered shirt under what amounted to blue denim coveralls. Most girls would probably deck themselves out with more pretentious attire than this for the benefit of company.

In the middle of the northwest field rested one of Rob's three tractors. The young lady hopped upon its seat with aplomb, as if she had been doing so all of her life, which indeed maybe she had. Unlike the city girls he knew, Pippa looked right at home up there, not as if she were posing for a funny snapshot in some high school yearbook. "Want to see what it feels like?" She jumped off the metal seat, lightly breaking her descent by touching the foot platform on her way down.

Wesley swallowed hard, then climbed aboard with utmost exertion, curious to understand why there were so few convenient handles to grasp for something as tall as this. Once secure on his precipitous throne, he smiled proudly and even pretended to manipulate the array of levers, shifts, and pedals that surrounded his feet. "Go for a ride, if you want," the girl shouted to him. She was only teasing, of course, and Wesley accepted it in the proper spirit, awkwardly dismounting the behemoth contraption before he embarrassed himself any further. Pippa giggled with delight and then, impulsively, she set his world aflame by kissing him on the cheek. Wesley tried to maintain some semblance of equanimity, but he wondered why the dry grass was crackling under his shoes when he was walking five feet above the ground.

Inside the barn stood two of her prized horses—not prized in the sense of thorough breeding, but because of the high estimation they elicited in the girl's heart. "This is Rocco," she said, patting the sorrel gelding on his white nose.

None too sure, Wesley asked, "Rock-o?"

"R-O-C-C-O. It's an Italian name. It stands for ... I don't know, something. Maybe strength, but I forget."

Across the way, pawing the straw beneath her front left hoof, was a silver-colored mare. As Pippa approached, the horse extended her nose for an affectionate stroke. "She's Betty. We would call her the old gray mare ... but she's only eight."

"Do you ride them, or are they just pets?"

"Well, sure, I ride them. I take both of them out every day, unless the weather is bad. They're very pampered. My mother says they're spoiled, but I don't think so. Do you, Wes?"

He squinted at her, suspecting a trick. "How do you know if a horse is spoiled?"

Her eyes sparkled. "You just take my word for it, if you know what's good for you. I don't like for people to call my horses names!"

Wesley chuckled for an instant, but then the smile faded, and he just gazed at the girl. Breathing deeply, he wanted to take Pippa Glynn in his arms and smother her with kisses. Fool! That only happens in the movies, he thought, so he let the magical opportunity escape. If Pippa sensed his temptation, she did not betray any outward emotion to that effect. Instead, she turned away and cheerfully began brushing Betty's flank. "She loves this," Pippa said. "Watch her lean towards me when I move the brush." It was true, and Wesley nodded his head. Cautiously, he patted the mare's nose, as he had seen the girl do, and Betty did seem to enjoy the attention. "See, she likes you," Pippa added.

Suddenly, a loud, clanging noise was heard, apparently originating far off in the distance. Pippa gave an annoyed sigh and told Wesley, "Oh, that's Mama. She only does that to embarrass me."

"What is it, the dinner bell?"

Shocked at his rural acuity, she said, "We'll have you plowing and harvesting in no time!"

That pleased Wesley, who certainly took no offense, but Pippa quickly blushed, appearing to disown the remark the moment it left her mouth. She hoped it did not sound too presumptuous, as if she were staking proprietary claim on her young visitor. That was not her intent.

The dinner table presented quite a spread for a Sunday during wartime. There was fried chicken galore, mashed potatoes with real butter, steaming cobs of corn, deep-fried breaded okra, and made-from-scratch yeast rolls that were larger than a man's fist and soft as a ball of cotton.

Rob said a prayer, and then the four of them enjoyed this feast.

"In case you're wondering," he said, "we grow most of our own vegetables."

The boy smiled. "So I guessed."

"In a way," Rob added, "our farm is one big victory garden."

"Not the potatoes, of course," Jillian said.

"What, dear?"

"We don't produce our own potatoes."

"Well, no, we've never had much luck with potatoes in this climate. Those came from town—by way of Idaho, I suppose."

Wesley laid down the chicken thigh that he was devouring and took a drink of iced tea. He did not know how many fowl the Glynns raised, but he suspected that there were about three fewer of them today.

"For dessert, there's apple pie with homemade ice cream on top," Jillian said. "How does that sound, Wes?"

The boy gave a pat to his abdomen. "Maybe I can find just enough room for that, Mrs. Glynn. You know, I'd have to grow a second stomach if I lived here. Do you always eat like this?"

Rob chuckled. "Not quite. We were putting on some airs for our guest from the city." But then he shook his head. "Seriously, though, we do our share for the war effort too."

"Yes, sir."

"In fact, I'm bond chairman for the northeastern quadrant of McLennan County, and Jill contributes cans of fat to the butcher shop, not to mention saving our surplus food for the Salvation Army. She also has a list of soldiers that she writes to overseas." He looked at his daughter. "And Pippa here uses the majority of her contest winnings and livestock sales to buy war bonds. She'll be a rich little girl a few years after this war ends."

Pippa rolled her eyes. "Daddy! I'm eighteen. I'm not your little girl any longer." She smiled at her friend from Waco.

"You'll always be my little girl, honey. Age has nothing to do with it."

Wesley surveyed the dinner table. "I can't remember when I've eaten this much. You all must think I'm part pig."

Rob smiled, but then something crossed his mind, and he became thoughtful. "Son, the reason I brought all that up—about what we're doing for the war effort—wasn't to brag about how swell this particular family is. I didn't want you to think that we're a bunch of gluttons out here, living off the fat of the land. We just do our part, like every other American. We're nothing special."

"Yes, sir. I knew what you meant."

Before dessert was served, Jillian began clearing the table of dinner plates, bowls, silverware, and glasses. "Care for some coffee, Wes?" Rob asked him with a grin. How many times had he posed that same question to him at The Smoker's Den?

"That depends, sir. Is it from the Amazon Basin? As you know, I only like a tropical blend from the Amazon Basin."

Rob laughed heartily at that comment, but Jillian—never having set foot inside The Smoker's Den—did not catch the humor, so her smile was only out of courtesy.

"Actually, son, it's Maxwell House from the Safeway store on Eighteenth Street. Donnie Lee Satterfield doesn't give anything away—even to his own brother-in-law."

Jillian punctuated her husband's comment with a smirk. "You can say that again. And we're not about to pay him two dollars a pound for some exotic import."

"Well, Maxwell House sounds fine to me," Wesley said. "That's what we always drink at home."

Pippa did not care for coffee. She liked the smell of it, but not the flavor. Ever since she was old enough to sit at the table, she would have hot cocoa with her parents instead of coffee, but in an identical cup. During the warmer months of the year, she would substitute chocolate milk, and that is what she had in her cup today, sitting next to a generous slice of her mother's apple pie.

Out of the corner of his eye, Wesley watched her eating and noticed that she was more enthusiastic about dessert than the meal itself. She had a reasonably hearty appetite—for a girl—but it was clear to see that apple pie *à la mode* was her favorite course. Her mother whispered to Wesley, "She eats like a truck driver and never puts on a pound." That was not entirely surprising, for Jillian too possessed an attractive figure. The trait must have been hereditary.

"May Wes and I go back outside?" Pippa asked when she finished her last bite of dessert. "There's more that I need to show him."

But Jillian told her, "Aren't you forgetting about your job?"

Pippa looked apologetically at Wesley. "Do you mind if I dry the dishes first?"

Before the boy could open his mouth to answer, Rob volunteered his own services. "I'll do them for you. Go run along."

♦   ♦   ♦

One thing for sure: ninety-degree weather seemed much hotter in May than it did in July or August, when such temperatures were below the norm. The parching winds felt like a furnace to them when Pippa led Wesley outside and across the dry creek to the old windmill. "Let's climb it," she said. "On a perfect day, you can see the Amicable Building."

Up they went, she first and he following as closely behind as he dared. She climbed like a monkey, never stopping to plant a foot or secure a hand. Consequently, when she arrived at the top, her hand had three splinters, and she begged for Wesley to remove the tiny slivers of wood.

"Now?" he screamed over the sound of the rushing air. Wesley was hanging on for dear life, as the top seemed much higher now than it did when he was standing safely on the ground. Moreover, in these strong winds, the structure creaked back and forth, and having the weight of two people near its summit caused the center of gravity to shift dangerously upwards.

"Can you see it?" Pippa shouted.

"The splinter?"

"No, silly, the Amicable Building! Can you see Waco?"

He looked toward his best guess of where west-southwest might be, but resting upon this insecure perch, he could not focus his vision for long. Worse yet, too swift an eye movement at such a height brought instant vertigo, and he finally gave up trying.

"There it is!" the girl yelled, and she pointed excitedly while leaning an arm's length away from the tower. Wesley thought he felt the windmill lunge a bit when she did so, and he leaned as best he could in the opposite direction to counterbalance her shifting weight.

"Well, do you see it?" Pippa asked him again. She was still beaming with elation at her discovery.

Squinching his eyelids together while looking directly into the teeth of a forty-miles-per-hour wind, Wesley valiantly scanned the horizon again, trying to follow where Pippa was pointing. Just as she had promised, there indeed was the distinctive skyline of Waco—one building—as seen from a distance of fifteen miles.

"I see it!" he announced with a shout, and she vigorously nodded her head. The windmill seemed to be swaying more unsteadily now, so he suggested that they begin their descent.

"Ouch!" she said. "Can you get this one out at least?"

"Up here?"

"Yes, please. It hurts, and going down will only make things worse."

"It's like a hurricane at this altitude."

"What?" she screamed.

"Never mind." Very slowly, he stepped around the tower to where Pippa was standing, still casually holding on with a single hand. She reached toward him with her free hand and yelled, "It's at the tip of my pointer finger. See it?"

Wesley could hardly see her hand, much less her finger, much less her splinter. "The wind is drying out my eyes. I can't keep them open for very long." The windmill emitted another creaking sound, more loudly now. "Did you hear that?" he asked.

She had not. "Come over here, so you'll be facing the other direction," she said. Both of them moved in circular fashion around the central axis of the tower. "Is that better?"

"Oh, yeah, a whole lot better," Wesley yelled, now with sarcasm. He thought he might be getting sick, whether from the excitement of being with Pippa or, more likely, from the anxiety of approaching so perilously near to sudden death.

The girl extended the index finger of her right hand, and Wesley examined it as best he could while holding on to a suspiciously rickety wooden plank. Above them, the vanes of the rotor were turning furiously, and the fantail responded to every variation in the drafts of air by constantly shifting this spinning wheel into the prevailing wind.

Wesley managed to pry loose the grip of one of his hands and then proceeded to pick with a fingernail at the approximate location of her virtually invisible splinter. "I think you hit it," she told him.

"Is it out?" he shouted.

"Nope!"

He glanced at her face and could see that Pippa was enjoying every minute of this adventure. "Here. Use your teeth," she said.

Wesley complied and, within four or five attempts—whether by the grace of God or blind luck—somehow clamped down in the precise spot that dislodged the offending sliver of wood. He spit it out of his mouth, and the tiny particle probably blew all the way to Ellis County before finally drifting to earth.

"Take one last look at Waco," she told him, and Wesley hoped she meant that figuratively. He gazed in the vague direction of his home city and acknowledged success with a nod of the head. "Weeeee! Isn't this exhilarating?" she shouted. Still holding on with one hand, the girl's hair was blowing wildly, and her eyes were nearly closed as she tried to look directly into the gale-force winds. Though Wesley did not quite hear what Pippa said, he could now smile at her, for he realized that his next step would be taking him that much closer to solid ground.

Pippa set foot upon *terra firma* well before her friend did, and she shouted up to him, "What's taking you so long?"

By the time he finally hopped down from the last plank, a height of about three feet, Wesley was laughing. "You're crazy! You know that? You could've killed both of us."

"Naw, there's nothing to worry about. I go up there pretty often, only usually it's not quite that blustery. That's where I go to get away."

The girl's hair was in her eyes, and Wesley reached out to brush it back. She allowed him to do so, smiling up at him, squinting from the sun.

"I appreciate your going up there with me, Wes, because I know you really didn't want to at all. It was brave, and you are someone very special."

He shook his head and chuckled. "If you want to know the absolute truth, my legs were shaking the whole time."

"But you still did it, and that means the world to me."

Wesley studied her pretty face, and he took a deep breath and then another, not saying a word. Just to be together with her, alone like this, seemed heavenly to him, almost beyond belief.

"Let's go cat hunting!" Pippa said. Not waiting for Wesley, she ran at full speed toward an old, forsaken barn and turned around when she came to its weather-beaten door, the red coat of paint so badly worn that it no longer afforded any protection from the elements. The door sagged at both hinges, such that the edge of its bottom rail was cutting a deep groove into the dirt whenever someone wished to enter or leave. Once inside, it took two of them to drag the door closed.

"What did you say?" Wesley asked, a little out of breath from sprinting after her.

"I didn't say anything," she whispered. "Shhhh. We need to be perfectly quiet."

He lowered his voice. "Did I hear you say, 'cat hunting'?"

"Oh, that. Yes, I did say that."

"Well, I'm not going to kill a cat. I'm a cat lover, and we have one of our own."

She smiled with delight. "What's her name?"

"*His* name is Valentino."

"That's a strange name for a cat."

"He used to be the neighborhood lover, until a vet took away his passion."

She giggled. "Aw, that's no fun."

Wesley glanced around the barn. A decrepit, nineteenth-century mule yoke was propped against one wall, the hay loft was in disrepair—tilted at a hazardous angle—and part of the drooping roof at the far end appeared to be in danger of collapse.

Pippa leaned closer to Wesley. "It just so happens that I'm a cat lover too," she whispered, "and that's the reason we're here now."

"To hunt cats?"

"We have a mama cat with a brood of kittens, and we're going to hunt for them."

"In here?"

"I think this is where they usually stay."

"Four kittens?"

Pippa looked shocked. "How did you know that?"

"Your dad and I saw them when I got here."

"Oh." She nodded her head. "They don't trust human beings—at all—but I'm determined to make friends with them one of these days." She looked around the dimly lit interior of the barn. "Shhhh. Come with me."

Wesley followed Pippa as she peeked into all of the likely hiding spaces. Finally, she spotted the cats, cowering in fright near the back of the barn, partially concealed by a rotting shelf that once served as a workbench. Pippa motioned for Wesley to stay put, but she herself slowly advanced forward, one very deliberate step at a time, until she sat down only ten feet away from the cats' cozy lair.

Seeing this, Wesley sat down too, prepared to wait it out with his friend. Several minutes later, Pippa began to scoot forward on the rear of her coveralls, almost imperceptibly, until she came to rest just four feet away from the felines. Wesley grinned at her progress, but then an abrupt movement caught his eye. Some straw beneath the broken window seemed to stir in an undulating wave, moving a few inches to the left at a time. He got a glimpse of the creature and, trying to remain calm, loudly whispered to the girl, "Pippa! There's a snake."

Pippa turned her head to the right and detected that same mysterious motion. She lay on her side and watched intently. Then, satisfied as to its identity, she sat up again and whispered to her friend, "It's just a garter snake—nonpoisonous." She resumed her vigil.

Wesley, though, was not so well versed in herpetology. Garter snake or not, when the reptile slithered blindly toward him under the straw, he stood up and retreated out of its meandering path. However "nonpoisonous" it might be, he did not much relish the thought of a snake crawling up the inside of his pants leg.

The drama of the furry mammals ended happily. Less than fifteen minutes after Wesley backtracked toward the door, he could hear a soothing female voice, no longer reduced to a whisper. Stalking forward a few paces, he witnessed a heartwarming vision. Pippa was on her hands and knees, petting the mother cat, which rubbed affectionately against her legs. The kittens, of course, would not venture very close, but neither did they flee. Pippa looked back and smiled at Wesley, who vigorously nodded his head in admiration. For some unaccountable reason, his throat choked up at what he had seen, causing his voice to become so constricted that Pippa did not even hear him say, "You are something else."

A short while later, as they were about to leave the barn and return to the farmhouse, the girl paused for a couple of minutes to brush several bits of straw from her clothing and hair, something the boy had already done for himself. When the two friends finally began walking toward the sagging door, Wesley took Pippa's hand, and she turned and stopped, offering the other one as well. Without smiling, she looked up at him and said, "I love you, Wesley Brower." He stared at her for a moment—hardly believing what had just happened—and then, feeling a calm certainty within himself, he told her, "And I love you, Pippa Glynn." At that, the girl threw herself into his arms, and the pair embraced and kissed in what seemed like an impossibly rapturous dream. Being uninitiated in the rituals of romance, neither of them had ever experienced anything remotely like it before.

Upon their eventual arrival at the house, Jillian could not help but notice that her daughter was unusually quiet and subdued. And yet there was also a sense of joy about her, bubbling just beneath the surface, as if she were fighting very hard to restrain a powerful smile that, once released, would never go away. "Did you two have a good time?" the mother asked.

"Oh, yes, ma'am," Wesley told her, "I would have to say that this was a perfect day." He, too, looked a bit dazed by their afternoon together, and Jillian no doubt wondered just what it was that happened between the two of them. She trusted her daughter implicitly, so she felt confident that nothing improper had taken place while they were gone.

"Well, I've really got to be getting back home," the boy said. "Baccalaureate's tonight, and I need to get ready for that." He glanced around the room. "Where is Mr. Glynn?"

"He's having to fix a tractor that stalled in one of the fields."

Pippa looked at Wesley and giggled. "See, Wes? It wouldn't have gone anywhere, even if you tried."

Shaking her head in confusion, Jillian said, "Well, I'm sure you two know what you're talking about."

"Would you please tell him goodbye for me, Mrs. Glynn? And thanks to you both for a swell day. It was ... well, it was just swell, that's all."

"You're entirely welcome, Wes. We've enjoyed having you, and you'll have to come back again soon."

Wesley grinned and slowly walked toward the door. Pippa followed him, a step behind, and they stopped to shake hands. The girl's smile had disappeared, and she seemed on the verge of tears.

Jillian Glynn waved to the boy, saying, "Goodbye, Wes." He waved back to her, and then the two young people went out the door. A few minutes later, Jillian heard the automobile's tires crackle down the gravel road, and Pippa came back inside.

"He's a nice boy, isn't he, dear?" the mother said. "So polite and considerate. I think your father likes to have him visit the shop on Saturdays."

"Mama, I'm going to marry Wesley Brower someday."

♦   ♦   ♦

By the time Monday arrived, Hannah Lane already had more than her fill of graduation activities. The problem was that nearly every waking hour of Saturday—her solitary day off from Crawford-Austin that week—was devoted specifically to honoring the Centennial Class, and Hannah could not very well excuse herself from these events, inasmuch as her supervisor, Mr. Hinckley, moved mountains to enable her to attend. Saturday had opened with a breakfast at nine o'clock in the dining room of Brooks Hall, followed two hours later by a band concert in Waco Hall. Then, at 3:30 in Waco Hall, her class played a role in preparation of the centennial monument—containing relics of every conceivable kind from the institution's first hundred years—and class president James Leo Garrett entrusted this time capsule to Baylor President Pat Neff, on behalf of the university. An hour-long reception for the Centennial Class began at five o'clock on the south side of Burleson Quadrangle, and that in turn gave way to a traditional floral and musical observance known as Ring-Out, symbolizing a transition from one class (and, in this case, one academic century) to another. Capping off the busy day was an 8:15 concert, performed by alumni from the School of Music.

Sunday's agenda was almost as crowded, but Hannah was scheduled to work the swing shift, so she felt justified in bypassing everything but the morning baccalaureate service at eleven o'clock. The guest speaker on this occasion was Southern Theological Seminary's president, Ellis Fuller, whose sermon topic was "Hearing Ears and Seeing Eyes." The new poet laureate of Texas, Southern Methodist University's David Russell, read his prize-winning ode, which commemorated Baylor University's first hundred years of operation and ministry.

With baccalaureate behind her, all that remained for Hannah—in terms of her college life—was the commencement program itself. But commencement of what? Owing to the vicissitudes of war, her future was anything but definite. Whatever plans she once had were either scrapped entirely or put on hold for the duration. Even that most fundamental issue of all, whether she would return home to the Tar Heel State, was uncertain at this point. For the present, she would continue working in behalf of industrial production, most likely expanding her hours at Crawford-Austin to full-time status. Beyond that, she was unable to say.

Baylor administrators, through the bully pulpit of Pat Neff, instructed members of the graduating class to report in front of Carroll Science Building by 9:20 on Monday morning. There, they would line up in proper order for the procession to Waco Hall. Bearing this arrival time in mind, Hannah suggested that her ride for the day, Timmy Royster, show up no later than nine o'clock. He would be driving his girlfriend, Margo Burke, back to campus anyway—after eating breakfast at a gathering of both of their families—so the additional stop was scarcely eight blocks out of his way. Hannah planned to carry her cap and gown to Baylor, rather than wearing them in the automobile, but that idea changed when there was still no sign of her source of transportation at ten minutes after nine. Concerned that she might be missing her own graduation, Hannah telephoned Timmy's home. The call went unanswered, and her alarm grew to desperation.

When Timmy and Margo finally knocked on the door at 9:15, exhibiting absolutely no sense of urgency, it was all Hannah could do to hold her anger in check. "So nice of you to come," she said with a glower.

The unmistakably surly welcome put Timmy on defense. "I thought this big rendezvous was supposed to be at 9:30." He glanced at Margo for confirmation.

"That's what it said in the newspaper," she told him.

"Nope. They changed the time. Didn't you get a form letter from President Neff?"

Timmy shrugged. "Not that I recall."

Visibly annoyed with both of them, Hannah stepped outside, locked the door, and fairly pushed them toward the car—anything to give their inert bodies some positive momentum. "Besides, you said you'd be here at nine."

Margo and her boyfriend looked at each other with equal parts of guilt (for being so late) and resentment (for being criticized by someone who was essentially bumming a ride). Hannah Lane certainly could get testy at times, they noted—and with scant provocation too.

Timmy double-parked momentarily on Fifth Street, so he could drop his two passengers off at the Science Hall. They ran across the busy roadway in their caps and gowns and, enduring no little embarrassment, slipped into line in proper sequence, having recognized their alphabetical "neighbors" from rehearsal. A surprising number of parents were still on the Quadrangle, presumably trusting other relatives to reserve seats for them inside the auditorium. This was a rather gloomy prospect for Hannah, for it brought to mind the fact that no one in Waco Hall today would be there for the purpose of seeing her walk across the stage. Her father, Reverend Samuel Lane, was in no physical condition to traverse half a continent again, something that he had done, with great difficulty, as recently as Christmastime. Nor would anyone from the Brower family be able to attend. Wesley and Elizabeth were at school for their next-to-last day of final examinations, and skipping those was out of the question. Nora probably could have begged out of a four-hour stint at the Red Cross, but Hannah insisted that her landlady honor this commitment to the war effort, which was infinitely more important than any academic ceremony.

"Hey, beautiful!" came a raspy voice from among the crowd of onlookers in front of Old Main Hall. The procession had not yet begun, so there were still a couple of minutes to say hello to one's family and friends. For that reason, Hannah thought nothing of the boisterous greeting—until, that is, she spotted a vaguely familiar soldier approaching the Centennial Class. It was Randall Box, now a corporal again—for the third time—and he marched straight up to Miss Lane and kissed her on the cheek. Hannah immediately flushed with anger and very nearly slapped the well-meaning serviceman. Randy then found Margo Burke and also kissed her, much to the shock of her boyfriend. Timmy had just arrived on the scene, after finally locating a parking spot on the crowded campus.

"Who's that guy?" he asked, as the GI ambled away.

"I don't remember his name," Margo said. "Someone I used to know."

"He kisses you, and you don't even know his name?"

All she could do was offer a red-faced giggle.

Randy returned to Hannah just when the line was starting to move. Being Randall Box, he saw nothing wrong with moving right along with it. "I seem to recall that you're all alone here in Waco—no family—so I thought I'd be your cheering section for the day."

Hannah still had not forgiven him. "That was very fresh, you know, kissing me in front of the entire Centennial Class. You ought to be ashamed of yourself."

"Oh, I am!" he told her, but his grin argued otherwise.

Tight-lipped, she whispered loudly, "And what right do you have to yell 'Hey, beautiful' in a solemn setting like this? Aren't you aware that this is graduation?"

"How do you know I was yelling at *you?*"

She shook her head, fighting back a smile.

"Honest, Hannah, I just had an hour to kill," he said, "so I thought I'd come over here and lend you some moral support."

"Don't you ever work?"

"Not if I can help it." He blew her a kiss and then melted back into the crowd, stepping on a lady's foot in the process.

The commencement ceremony began precisely at ten o'clock, and the guest speaker was noted Baptist layman Francis P. Gaines, who also happened to be president of Washington and Lee University in Lexington, Kentucky, as well as president of the American Association of Colleges. In keeping with this unique setting and the challenging times, Dr. Gaines delivered a message on "Religion and Citizenship." The heart of that morning's session, conferment of academic degrees, progressed more quickly than usual, and for an obvious reason: there were so very few recipients. Only 232 women and men were awarded diplomas, principally due to the fact that most of the university's male population was away, serving in the armed forces.

One by one, the names of the Centennial Class were announced, and as the youthful scholars strode from the west side of the stage to the east, pursuant to receiving their coveted certificates, occasionally some raucous cheers from family members were heard. Margo was one of those with the dubious honor of being so recognized. Her parents and brother were there from Yoakum—or more precisely, the tiny burg of Sweet Home, Texas—and they were not about to let this opportunity pass without a robust stab at vocalizing. Many other students were subjected to scattered shouts of acclamation too, and this was one time that Hannah was pleased to be on her own, far away from home. Still, when the public address system announced "Hannah Deborah Lane," and she started to march across the Waco Hall stage, there echoed from the balcony a comically anachronistic "Huzzah for Hannah!" and now she knew what Corporal Box had meant by lending his moral support. Happily, the audience was, by this point in the alphabet, somewhat inured to the idea and appeared to take the soldier's unsolicited commentary in the proper spirit. Miss Lane's vexing concern was that people might presume that he was her sweetheart, returned from battle and eager to tie the conjugal knot.

As was customary within the confines of Waco Hall, whenever commencement exercises ended, graduates who so chose would congregate in the general seating area, where they were free to mingle with their families, accepting hugs, kisses, and accolades. Many were the tears, as friends bade farewell to friends, some of whom they might never see again. Hannah, in contrast, presented a solitary figure, and that was fine with her, for she was anything but sentimental. Feeling disdain for the hubbub of greetings, her fondest wish was to locate Margo and Timmy for the ride home and, once there, to remove the oppressively hot gown. And yet, as she scanned the hall in search of those two friends, whom did she see coming toward her instead but a khaki-clad soldier?

"Hey, beautiful!" Randy shouted.

Hannah looked aside, but there was no escape. She smirked at him. "Hello, corporal."

Skipping any preliminaries, he got right to the point. "My question for you is, have you ever ridden in an open-aired military vehicle while wearing a cap and gown?"

"To tell you the truth, I've never had that burning desire."

"No matter. I'm here to inform you that this is your lucky day, little lady."

She rolled her eyes. "What's up, Randy?"

"Your friends deserted you, that's what."

"Oh?"

"I asked Margo if I could take you home, and she agreed. Didn't even put up a squawk."

"Some friend."

"In fact, she said it would do you good. What do you think she meant by that?"

"I can only guess." Hannah pulled out a pack of chewing gum from her purse. She put a stick in her mouth and offered one to the soldier.

"No, thanks. I'm on duty." He laughed. "You know, I don't think Margo's boyfriend likes me very much. It's not as if I was trying to move in on his territory. She's not even my type."

"And what is your type, pray tell?"

He smiled suggestively at her, pretending to twist his nonexistent handlebar mustaches. "That's for me to know and you to find out."

Feeling insulted, Hannah gave him a sneer. "No, thanks, soldier boy." She turned to walk away.

Randy jumped in front of her. "Listen, I'm sorry, Hannah. Really, my bark is worse than my bite, and I think you'd find me to be a pretty decent chap, given half a chance. I'm not interested in anything serious. I'm just a soldier on the prowl, out for some good times."

"Some good times!" She glared at him. "Are you on a secret mission or something? Because if you're not, I think it's shameful the way you shirk your duty—when millions of brave men are overseas, risking their lives to defend our freedom. Some of them come back in caskets or with arms and legs missing, and here you are, just out for some good times."

"Hey, that's what soldiers do when they're stateside. Can I help it if I landed in an outfit that lets me get away with murder?"

"I have half a mind to turn you in to the authorities, Corporal Box."

He appeared to be genuinely hurt by that remark, and his voice grew quiet. "Well, that's gratitude for you. And here I was, extending to you a free trip back home. All I wanted was a little companionship. For Chrissakes, just forget I ever mentioned it."

She slapped him hard across the face. "Don't you ever use my Lord's name in vain ... not in my presence."

The blow did not draw blood, but it came close. The inside of his cheek was slightly cut by his molars. Seeing the act of violence, three men standing nearby came to the girl's aid. "Is he getting fresh with you, miss?" one of them asked.

"No, sir. He just needs to wash his mouth out with soap."

"Are you sure?"

"Yes, sir, I'm sure."

As the men returned to their startled wives, Randy picked up his cap, which had fallen to the floor. "You Baylor girls are nothing but trouble," he told her. "Maybe this is a good thing. Maybe now I've finally learned my lesson." He rubbed his reddened cheek.

Hannah did not show much sympathy. "Goodbye, corporal. I'm sorry our blossoming relationship had to end this way."

"Yeah, me too," the soldier said. After taking about three steps, he stopped, now completely serious. "My offer still holds. I don't want to leave you stranded here. I feel responsible."

"That's quite all right. I'll find a ride with somebody else—anybody."

Randy thought for a minute. "Say, if it makes you feel any better, I'm awfully sorry."

"Goodbye, corporal," she told him again.

Frowning, the soldier shook his head and gave her one last questioning look. Then he slowly departed from the auditorium, no doubt wondering what went wrong. Usually, he was so successful with the ladies. This coed, while certainly eye-catching enough, had a mean streak that could erupt at any moment. Some might call it spunk, others gumption, but to him it was just plain orneriness. Not until he was outside the building—and away from her view—did Randy again reach up to massage his throbbing cheek. To give Miss Lane her due, she packed quite a wallop for a female.

"Corporal, wait!" Hannah shouted from the steps of Waco Hall. "I will accept your apology—if it was sincere."

He turned around. "It was."

When she caught up to him, Randy offered his arm, and—to his great astonishment—she actually took it.

"I'm a real louse sometimes," he said with a grin.

"No, you're just ... enterprising."

"Is that a polite way to say I'm a con artist?"

"Maybe so." She smiled at him. "A nice one, though, all in all."

There was no hint of romance between them—just a hard-earned friendship, and somehow that seemed enough.

"You're a funny kid," the soldier told her as they walked across Founder's Mall. "Funny, in both senses of the word."

"Yes, that's me, all right." She squeezed his arm. "And you're really a swell guy, way down deep—way, way down deep."

"That's quite a compliment, coming from a spitfire like you."

They strolled along in silence for a minute or so until Hannah suddenly giggled. "You know, I'm glad we made up."

"Same here," Randy said, but his cheerful look darkened when he gazed at the unfamiliar buildings around him. "Now, if only I could remember where I parked the jeep."

♦   ♦   ♦

With a population estimated at eighty thousand people in 1945, Waco, Texas, was considered a medium-sized city. As such, it was large enough to possess a commodious auditorium for civic events and yet too small to offer more than one from which to choose. Consequently, just three days after the Baylor University commencement ceremony, the same facility, Waco Hall, would be pressed into service again for the city's high school graduation. The war's direct impact on the lives of young men was evident in a statistical comparison of the two events. Though the graduating seniors of Waco High School numbered a mere 225 boys and girls—less than half of the record 501 just four years earlier—that modest total was only seven fewer than Baylor University's entire Centennial Class.

Even with the cessation of classwork, the last week of May had been a busy time for the Waco High seniors, beginning with Pastor J. M. Dawson delivering a baccalaureate address ("The Centuries Against the Hours") at First Baptist Church on Sunday night. Final exams at the school continued through Tuesday afternoon, and caps and gowns were distributed the following day. Wesley Brower, whose surname fell between A and L in the alphabet, received his regalia at nine o'clock in the morning. Seniors such as Sandra Whittsel, whose last names were alphabetized between the letters M and Z, had to wait until two o'clock in the afternoon to receive theirs.

There were several among the graduating class who had no need for the finery of caps and gowns. A half-dozen young men felt obliged to take a more active role in the war effort than stamps, bonds, and scrap drives could provide. To these six—Charles Van Cleave, Bert Surber, Fred Bostwick, Clark Mitchell, Murray Thaxton, and Bob Joe Curry—the school extended full academic credit, despite the fact that they left school early to enlist in the armed forces. Their diplomas would be mailed home.

Although final report cards could not be issued until examinations concluded, it was already a matter of public knowledge who the two highest achievers at Waco High School were. Valedictorian was Annette Levy of 1816 Colonial, with a grade point average of 97.13. She was the only child of Abe Levy, manager of the Rivoli Theatre, and his wife, Selma. In addition to being a gifted student, Miss Levy was quite musical, having performed as one of the two pianists on the recent baccalaureate program. Salutatorian was Douglas King of 400 North Twenty-sixth Street, with a mark of 97.08. He was the son of Loula King, a teacher at South Junior High School, and her late husband, B. L. King.

A vast majority of the graduating seniors probably endured some degree of butterflies over participating in such a public display as commencement exercises—and that was understandable. No fewer than a thousand spectators filled Waco Hall's main-floor seating, and all but the outer sections of the balconies were packed to the rafters. Wesley Brower would have been just as nervous as anyone else, but tonight his mind was occupied by concerns far more exalted than the straightforward act of parading across a perfectly flat, wooden stage and accepting a prosaic sheepskin from Mr. Darden. Four days earlier, on an idyllic stroll from barn to farmhouse, Wesley invited a pretty girl from Axtell to attend his graduation. With sadness in her eyes, she shook her head. Barring a miracle, she could not be there with him, except in spirit. Her parents had made it quite clear that they did not like for such an inexperienced motorist as she to drive on two-lane country roads, particularly in the dark. She would ask them for permission, of course, but the final word would belong to Rob and Jillian Glynn, and Pippa fully expected it to be an emphatic "No."

At 8:15 on Thursday night, May 31, while Wesley and the other capped and gowned students were gathering in the lobby of Waco Hall, band director Lyle Skinner conducted the likely members of next year's Waco High School Senior Orchestra in a brief concert inside the auditorium itself. Then, when the first strain of Charles Roberts's "Pomp and Chivalry" march was heard, the Class of 1945 began filing into the hall to take their assigned seats, just as they had rehearsed that morning at ten o'clock. Tommy Hanna led the class in singing "The Star-Spangled Banner," and Reverend Charles T. Caldwell delivered the invocation.

It was time for Annette Levy to step from her seat of honor to the podium microphone and present the valedictory address, "Waco High School in the Future." The most pressing need, she declared, was "a more adequately equipped building than the present one, constructed in 1910." Salutatorian Douglas King's ensuing speech dealt with "Waco High School Yesterday." He traced the development of Waco's private, denominational, and public schools over the course of the past hundred years. "From the early days," he said, "Waco was noted for the excellence of its schools and held the distinction of being the first city in the state to utilize and perfect her public school system."

While his two classmates were speaking, Wesley attempted—as unobtrusively as he could—to locate his mother and sister in the audience, but he was never able to do so with any certainty. The seniors' vantage point did not lend itself to such a pursuit because they were seated in the first sixteen rows of the middle section, facing forward. If Wesley's family members were sitting anywhere behind him, rather than to a side, there would be no conceivable way to pick them out from the crowd. He knew full well that Hannah Lane would not be present, having been dealt a swing shift at Crawford-Austin, so he did not expend any effort in trying to spot her among the multitude.

After Superintendent of Public Schools Irby Carruth briefly addressed the class, he turned the microphone over to Sam Darden, president of the Waco Board of Education, who began conferring the diplomas in strict alphabetical sequence. Less than seven minutes into his presentations, an amplified voice read, "Shirley Ann Brockseker," and the girl in front of Wesley walked across the stage. Then came "Wesley Franklin Brower," and it was Wesley's turn to approach Mr. Darden, shake the superintendent's hand, and receive his diploma. The process was as simple and tidy as that, and suddenly his participation in the event had concluded. While returning to his seat—third row, second chair from the right aisle—he again searched in vain for his mother and sister, finally conceding that it was a lost cause.

To help pass the remaining time, Wesley did some quick counting and computation. He was twenty-fifth in line, which meant that there were exactly two hundred students behind him. At roughly five names per minute, this suggested that another forty minutes of diploma presentations were yet to occur. He yawned, momentarily forgetting that he was in a public arena, where such a display of drowsiness might be construed as apathy or even boredom. Soon, immediately behind him, the inhabitants of Row D would be rising to make their way to the stage. He stifled another yawn.

Sitting almost directly behind Wesley—third seat from the right aisle, but way back in Row P—was Sandra Whittsel. In fact, so deeply buried in the alphabet was her surname that only ten graduating seniors would come after her in the roll call. It was a tedious wait, but finally her row's turn to stand up and file forward came as well. Wesley watched with mixed feelings as this lovely girl passed him in the aisle. Though diminutive, she presented a striking figure in her gown. Only the barest outline of her sable-colored hair was visible beneath the cap, but it nicely framed her dark brown eyes, turned-up nose, and winsome lips.

Wesley breathed deeply when he saw her climb the steps and wait on stage for her name, Sandra Jean Whittsel, to be called. Whatever else he may have felt for her, there was an undeniable affection that refused to go away—perhaps never would leave him entirely. Being a Georgian, past and probably future too, none of her relatives were in attendance, with the sole exception of her mother, Charlotte. Her father, Lieutenant Colonel Duncan Whittsel, was halfway around the world, training Air Corps pilots for eventual invasion of the Japanese Empire's home islands. It was a little sad, really, Wesley thought. A beautiful girl like that—with no boyfriend. But if Sandy was lonely, she certainly did hide it well. And anyway, such a state of affairs could not last for long, not for someone with her looks and lively personality. He remembered that kiss ...

Doris Ladene York accepted her diploma from Mr. Darden and followed the path of George Forrest Wortham, Jr., back to her seat. The school board president nodded to Miss Grace Hamilton, who signaled the class of honor to stand, as one, for the singing of Floyd Kymes Russell's "Spirit of Waco High." Then it remained for James Leo Garrett to give the benediction, and the commencement exercises were at an end.

The first thing Wesley did was walk straight up to Sandra Whittsel and congratulate her. In return, she gave him a winning smile and gentle hug.

"Thanks, Wes. The same to you." Then, in public or not, she rose on her tiptoes and kissed his cheek. Mere seconds later, a handsome young man in uniform approached her, and the two disappeared together into the crowd, hand-in-hand. Maybe she was not so lonesome after all.

When Nora and Elizabeth arrived where Wesley was waiting, they each hugged the boy and offered their best wishes on his academic achievement. "Where were you sitting?" he asked. "I looked all over the place for you."

Elizabeth pointed a thumb behind her. "Section two, about eighteen or twenty rows back."

"Row R," his mother told him.

"I guess Uncle Matt and Aunt Barbara couldn't make it, huh?"

"No, son, they have another graduation tomorrow in Harlingen. It's that time of year, you know. They did send their regrets—and a ten-dollar bill."

That more than consoled Wesley. "Oh!" he said with a beaming face.

Then his eyes wandered slightly to the right, and he nearly gasped in surprise. She was there! Pippa was standing between her parents, Rob and Jillian Glynn.

Wesley smiled at the girl, and she stepped forward until she was just an arm's length away. "Hello, you," Pippa said. She looked up at him with bashful eyes.

"Mom, Lizzie, I'd like for you to meet Pippa Glynn—the girl I was telling you about."

Nora smiled at her. "From Axtell?"

"Yes, ma'am."

Wesley stared in wonder at the girl. She was so pretty, so natural, so unaffected, so ... It was the first time he had seen her in a stylish dress, and it looked very smart on her, soft and feminine. Belatedly, he remembered his social graces. "Oh, and these are her parents, Rob Glynn and his wife, uh ..."

"Jill," the girl's mother said with a smile. The two women shook hands, chuckling when they noticed that their gloves were almost identical.

"How does it feel to be a man of the world, Wes?" Rob asked.

"It feels fine, sir."

"What are your plans?"

Wesley looked at his mother. "Well, she'd like for me to go to college—probably Baylor, of course—but I really want to join the Navy."

"Like your brother."

"No, sir, Naval aviation."

Nora played devil's advocate. "Do you think the war will still be on by the time you're trained to fly?"

"I sure hope so!" Wesley said, but then, realizing how heartless that sounded, he quickly added, "I mean, it would be a shame to put in so much work at flight school—and then have it all be for nothing."

"Then maybe you should plan on continuing your education," his mother told him.

Elizabeth changed the subject. "Are you a senior too, Pippa?"

"Yes, I am. Our graduation is tomorrow night."

"She was almost salutatorian," her father said. "She should have been, too, except for the way her teacher graded the—"

"Oh, Daddy, please. They don't want to hear about that. I had no desire to give a speech anyway, so everything turned out for the best." Pippa smiled at Wesley, who grinned back.

"I didn't address the crowd, either," he told the girl, "so don't feel too disappointed."

"I'm not disappointed. It's my daddy who's disappointed."

"Only a little," Rob said, "but I'll get over it."

"Would you like to join us for cake and coffee?" Nora asked the Glynns.

Jillian shook her head. "That's kind of you, Mrs. Brower, but we really need to be heading home. You know, Rob gets up at four in the morning."

"My goodness."

"Farmers' hours," he told the boy's mother.

"Well, it was very thoughtful of you to come to Wesley's graduation, and it's been a pleasure to meet you all."

"Same here, Mrs. Brower," Jillian said. "And Lizzie too, of course."

Rob added, "Most of all, congratulations to you, Wes. Well done!" His wife nodded in agreement.

Nora smiled at the Axtell girl. "And early congratulations to you, dear—for tomorrow night. It sounds like you are an excellent student."

Pippa giggled at the compliment. "I don't know about that, but thank you, ma'am."

As the Glynns said goodbye and turned to leave, Wesley steered his friend aside. "When can I see you again?" he asked in a hushed voice.

"I don't know. Soon."

"When?"

Pippa glanced at her father. "Saturday," she whispered. "I'll see you on Saturday."

Wesley was confused. "Doesn't Della work this week?"

"Yes, she does, but I'll be there anyway. I need to talk to you."

◆　　　◆　　　◆

Danny was beginning to wonder when, if ever, he would be embarking for the States. After all, of the quarter-million GIs still in the British Isles when Germany capitulated, fully five thousand each day were climbing aboard vessels bound for New York, Boston, and Hampton Roads. Not until five weeks after V-E Day did he finally receive word that his passage was booked. Then, after all this time had elapsed, the Army, in typical fashion, granted him just four hours to prepare for the trip home.

"Fifteen hundred?"

The master sergeant remained engrossed in paperwork. "Fifteen hundred hours," he said.

"Today?"

The sergeant looked up and scowled. "No, three months from today, Rignold." He shook his head and tossed a broken pencil into the wastebasket. "Of course I mean today."

Danny would have to act quickly. His first priority was, of necessity, readying his military kit and few personal belongings. He raced to the barracks and spent the next twenty-five minutes folding clothes and packing all of his possessions into the duffle bag. But foremost in his mind throughout this task was the unsettling fact that he had not heard from Vickie Forrest in about two and a half weeks. He certainly did not want to leave England without wishing her a proper goodbye.

In response to the female "emergency," Dave Raitt at the motor pool willingly loaned his pal a jeep, so this time there was no bartering attached, as there had been in the case of Mike Hibbett a couple of months earlier. Off Danny went, raising a cloud of dust between Grafton and Kettering. He was unsure how to get to Burton Latimer directly, so he drove to Kettering first and then turned southeast for a few miles, easily spotting Sterling Metals, the foundry where Vickie's father was employed. Once he inquired at the plant's mucky office, however, Danny had no choice but to wait for the secretary to find Jack Coulter, an ineffectual search that consumed nearly fifteen minutes. It finally fell to the foreman to track him down.

"Hello, lad," Jack said. "Sorry, but I was in my gear, and Miss Pence must have walked by me four times before she finally thought to ask Mr. Gorman."

"Hi, Mr. Coulter. Can you tell me where Vickie might be?"

Jack's face darkened. "You do know what happened, don't you, son?"

"What do you mean?" Danny swallowed hard, anticipating bad news.

"The US War Department ... they sent word about Vickie's husband." Jack looked the Yank directly in the eye. "Jimmy is now confirmed dead."

Danny sighed. "Oh, Lord. I'm sorry to hear that, sir." He went over to a dingy window and stared out at the brick wall of an adjoining structure. "How is she takin' it?"

"Vickie is shattered, of course. All this time, she never did give up hope, though she may have pretended to do so. Troops of occupation recovered the body near Ludwigshafen, and it was identified as James Forrest. Badly burned in the wreckage ... but not beyond recognition."

"Gosh, that's rough. Do you think she's up to receivin' a visitor?"

"I'm sure she'd like to see an American just now. It might be the best thing for her."

"Do you know if she's home?"

"Should be. She hasn't worked since she got that telegram."

Danny extended his arm. "I'll say goodbye now, Mr. Coulter." They shook hands, and the soldier added, "I'm due to leave Grafton this afternoon at three."

"Going for good, then, are you?"

"Yes, sir. How's the quickest way to get to Rothwell from here?"

"It couldn't be simpler." He pointed north. "Go back out the same way you came into town, turn left to the Kettering Road, and that'll take you all the way to Rowell."

"Thank you, sir," Danny said. He began to walk away but then stopped. "Oh, all the best to you—and to your wife and other daughter too, in case I don't see them."

"Good luck, sergeant. You've meant a lot to Vickie through all this, and we wish you well." Danny liked Vickie's father quite a bit. There was an inner strength about him that—common laborer or not—brought a dignity that money could never buy.

Back to Kettering the Yank motored, and thence west-northwestward to Rothwell, where, despite the broad daylight, he encountered no little difficulty locating Vickie's home. In the dark of night, it had appeared to be quite isolated—out in the countryside—but now, after a process of elimination, he discovered that it actually lay well within the environs of this sparsely populated town. A low stone wall's embedded sign identified the domicile by family surname. He knocked on the door, and Olivia Coulter invited him inside. Vickie's younger sister, Margery, was listening to the radio while folding the family's laundry. A cup of tea was nearby. She gazed bashfully at the American soldier and seemed hopeful that he would offer a few words to her.

"Hello, Margery," Danny said with a wink. "Nice to see you again." He glanced at the girl's mother. "I'll bet Margery here has so many boyfriends you have to chase them away."

Margery beamed at him. "I wish that's how it was." She gave him her most seductive look and added, "Do you know of anyone who might be interested?"

"Margery!" Olivia meant this to scold, but her suggestion of a smile softened the effect. "You'll have to excuse her, Danny. The poor lass is quite boy crazy these days."

Margery giggled. "Don't listen to her, sergeant. Sometimes Mum treats me like a child."

Danny grinned for a second, but then a sense of urgency came to his eyes. "Can you tell me where Vickie is?" he asked the girl's mother. "I really need to see her right away."

"Is there anything wrong?"

"Yes, ma'am. I'll be leavin' Grafton later today, and then England too."

"Aw!" Margery rushed over and took him by the hand. "And we were just getting to know each other."

Olivia glared at her. "Margery, please. This is a serious matter." The girl took a couple of steps back and pouted.

"Try the church, Danny," the older woman said. She pointed back over her shoulder. "It's within walking distance. Vickie's been going there most days around noontime—since she got the news, you know." A thought came over her, and she gulped. "Oh, dear! You do know about poor Jimmy ..."

"Yes, ma'am. I saw your husband earlier, and he told me about him." He nodded at the ladies. "Goodbye to both of you. It's been swell knowin' you."

"And you, Danny. Are you sure you won't stop for a cup of tea?"

"No, ma'am, but thank you."

Margery, clearly love-struck, watched him leave with tears in her eyes.

Danny hurried out the front door of the house, and then—uniform cap clutched in hand—broke into a loping run down the road, his destination constantly in view above the treetops.

The Church of the Holy Trinity was a majestic house of God, half a millennium old and, except for the fair, Rothwell's only claim to fame that reached beyond the county lines. Inside its sanctuary, for just an instant, Vickie Forrest thought she had seen a ghost. "Oh, dear! You gave me such a start!" she said. "Hello, Danny."

"Hi, Vickie." He was out of breath from his dash across town. "Your mother said I'd find you here."

"Oh, yes. The vicar must think I'm haunting this place."

An elderly parishioner, a man of about eighty, crossed himself and stepped backward, away from the chancel. Vickie and Danny watched him hobble down the center aisle and leave the sanctuary.

"I suppose you know all about Jimmy by now," she said.

Danny nodded. "Your father told me."

"You've been to Burton Latimer?"

"I wanted to say goodbye to all of you."

Vickie crossed herself before the altar and took Danny by the hand, pulling him toward the corner of the nave. "We can talk here," she told him.

They sat together in a wooden pew. "I'm leavin' Grafton today, and then I'll be shippin' out soon," Danny said. "I just found out a couple of hours ago."

She frowned. "They don't give you much time, do they?"

"That's the Army—as you well know."

Almost imperceptibly, she nodded her head, and her eyes filled with tears. "I remember complaining about it at the time, but now I would give anything to have those days back."

"I'm sorry. I was sad to hear the news. This was official word, then, I take it?"

"Yes, I'm afraid so. No more 'presumed dead' for my husband." She turned aside and began to cry softly. "What did I call myself, an 'instant widow'? Well, that's what I am, all right. I think I may have cursed myself with such a flippant remark as that. It was almost like I was mocking God or something."

"Now, don't be so hard on yourself." Danny reached out and patted her hand with his own. "I'm sure God doesn't operate like that."

Her voice became bitter. "Then, can you please tell me what He does do? I mean, apparently one thing He does *not* do is answer prayers, Danny, because I have been praying several times a day since you and I first met. Do you remember when you suggested that prayer might bring my husband back? I sincerely believed that God would intervene and save Jimmy from death. He would restore him to me. But He did nothing of the kind. He did nothing at all." Suddenly, her outrage turned to fright, and again she crossed herself. "Oh, may God forgive me for saying such things. I am truly a horrendous person sometimes, and I shall go straight to hell." She shuddered, as if overcome by chill.

Danny shook his head. "On the contrary, you are about the most wonderful person I have ever known, and I'm sure God understands exactly how you feel at a time like this. It wasn't that your prayers went unanswered. Jimmy was already gone ... only we had no way of knowin' that. God will not permit Himself to alter the natural laws that He has established, so He could not very well reverse the process after your husband had died."

She smiled bravely through her tears. "I know that, deep down inside. I'm being foolish ... and terribly selfish too."

Danny's throat tightened, and he struggled to say, "No, you're just bein' human. You'll see, Vickie. God will help you through this rough time."

The girl gazed into his eyes. "I think you're right. In fact ... I know in my heart that you're right." She touched the tip of his nose with her index finger. "And can you guess how I know that?"

He shrugged his shoulders, not venturing an answer.

"Because God sent you to me at just the right moment. He used you—an American soldier, just like Jimmy—to comfort me in the loss of my husband. He brought you and me together. Even that horrid Sammy Simpkins was part of His plan."

Danny laughed, to think that the shady corporal was involved in such a divine scheme. But then he told her, "You know, maybe he was at that."

A quietness settled upon both of them, and for a few minutes they said nothing, simply thinking their private thoughts. It was Vickie who spoke first. "Where will you be going now?" she asked the soldier.

"To some stagin' camp called Tidworth—at least for a while."

She nodded her head, and he seemed surprised by that.

"You've heard of it?"

"Of course. It's near Southampton."

"Rumor is that we'll be on either the *Queen Mary* or the *Queen Elizabeth*. Goin' in style."

Her lower lip trembled a bit. "I'll miss you, Danny."

"I'll miss you too. Funny how people meet and then part."

"Never to meet again."

"Say, I could always take you back as my war bride," he said with a giggle. "How long does it take you to pack?"

This time, Vickie found it impossible to smile through her sorrow. "You'll make somebody a smashing husband."

Danny brushed aside the compliment and glanced at his wristwatch. "May I walk you back home?"

"Please do, sergeant."

They took the long route, a leisurely stroll, arm-in-arm, that left him with barely enough time to hightail it to Grafton Underwood by three o'clock. Behind a sprawling ash tree, out of the view of gossiping neighbors, they experienced a lingering kiss that was more like lovers than brother and sister. Then they exchanged a sad farewell, knowing that they would not see each other again.

Vickie wept into a pillow in the privacy of her bedroom, and Danny, choked with emotion, drove away without even looking back at the market town of Rothwell. For many days thereafter, he thought of little else but the young woman from Northamptonshire, just as one might, upon awakening, struggle in vain to hold onto a beautiful dream that was slipping away forever.

❖   ❖   ❖

Butler Lindeman was in the process of telling Mutt Sawyer a raunchy joke when Giulia popped into the boss's office. The men became silent.

"Go ahead," she said. "Don't stop on my account." Giulia was carrying a small stack of papers that needed signatures.

"Give us sixty seconds, Miss Coletti," Lindeman told her. He waited for Giulia to shut the door before delivering his punch line. A gale of laughter signaled that it was permissible to reenter.

"It must have been a good one," she said to Mutt.

The salesman was still chuckling. "You have no idea! It was not for tender ears, though—and that's for sure."

"Oh, it wasn't all that bad," Lindeman told the girl. "In fact, maybe someday I'll repeat it for you."

Mutt's face reddened at the thought. "You wouldn't!"

"No, I'm only kidding."

Giulia gave a loud sigh and laid the papers on the corner of Lindeman's desk. "Well, if there's nothing else you need from me ..."

Instantly, both men were doubled over with laughter, and Giulia knew she had said something indelicate. Probably, it reminded them of the joke they just shared, but that was hard to say.

"No, miss ... nothing at the ... moment," Lindeman told the girl in between snorts of tittering. Then, when he glanced at Mutt, both men started laughing anew.

Giulia smiled at them and turned to leave. "I'll be going now. You children behave yourselves, you hear?"

Mutt was finally regaining control. "We're sorry, Miss Coletti," he said. "You just came in at the wrong time, that's all."

"Evidently." She shook her head and grinned. "Honestly, just like two little boys on the playground. 'Bye, fellas."

The men watched their shapely co-worker walk from the office, bend over her desk to retrieve gloves and purse, and then head toward the metal exit door.

"Have a nice weekend," Lindeman shouted.

And Mutt added, "See you Monday."

Giulia thought she could hear them laughing again before the door slammed shut behind her.

Right on time, Lauren Fite was waiting for her in the parking lot. Lauren was Miss Reliable, always good for transportation in either direction, for she went home every day on her lunch hour to take care of her four dogs. That meant that whether Giulia was scheduled for a morning shift, like today, or an afternoon shift, she could depend upon riding both ways with Lauren. The only problem was that dog hair would collect on her dress. Evidently, Lauren's canine pets were frequent passengers, and they were prone to shed in various colors that clung to fabric.

Having arrived home, Giulia waved goodbye to Lauren, brushed off some of the dog hair, unlocked the front door, and as usual, went directly to her mother's bedroom. Paolina had the radio on—the 12:15 newscast—and she was sitting up in bed, testing her skill with a crossword puzzle. "Hello, sweetie," she said. "Did you see there was some mail for you?"

"No. Who from?"

"I think it's a letter from your sailor friend."

Her face lit up. "Really? He hasn't written in weeks!"

"Maybe that's just as well," Paolina said, "now that things are patched up with Archie."

"Mamma, Archie and I are just pals. I keep telling you that."

"And this Steve ...?"

Giulia shook her head. "Same thing. Just pals." She changed the subject. "How are you feeling today? Do you need anything?"

"Would you bring me my reading glasses, honey? I left them on the back of the sofa, I think, and this puzzle is starting to give me a headache." She rubbed her temples. "Whenever you can. No hurry."

"Yes, ma'am."

Giulia walked back to the entryway and sifted through some pieces of morning mail that her mother had placed on the telephone table. Finding the envelope addressed to her, she opened it and was pleased to smell an enchanting fragrance of perfume. Smiling, she began to read ... but then stopped, almost at once. "Dear Hannah," it said, and she laid the letter down, as if it were burning her hands. She peered at the salutation again: "Dear Hannah." Hurt and offended—betrayed even—Giulia forced herself to read the entire letter, from beginning to end.

Dear Hannah,

Greetings from the beautiful Pacific Theater! That sounds nice, doesn't it? Makes it seem like a play or musical, instead of a combat zone. Actually, it really would be pretty here, "somewhere in the Pacific," if it were not for this war. (Looking on the positive side, I certainly will be well-traveled when I return home to the States.) I think the censor will permit me to say that we have seen some action, but now we have a little leisure time, so I will take this opportunity to drop you a note.

I hope all goes well with Baylor University graduation. If memory serves, the Baylor Bears usually graduate toward the end of May, so you might be reading this letter before that illustrious event, depending upon how prompt the mails are. Or maybe considerably after.

I still carry your New Testament with me wherever I go, and sometimes I actually have the time to read a few lines. It means a lot to me that you would think enough of your "roommate" to give him such a gift.

Glad to read that Lizzie is doing fine after her ordeal with that worthless sewer rat of humanity. She is very resilient, mature for her years, isn't she? I am proud of her, though you don't need to tell her I said so. I would not want her to get too conceited about being my sister. (ha ha)

What do you plan to do with your life after college? I trust that you will not leave immediately for NC because I would like to see you again, if at all possible. I have very pleasant memories of our "intimate" time together in the wee hours of the morning—me in my pajamas, and you in your beekeeper's outfit or whatever that was. To say that you looked lovely even in that garb must be the highest of compliments.

As a way to seal our friendship, I have kissed the top of this letter, where your name appears, and all you have to do in order to collect this sincere offer of affection is to kiss there yourself. That is rather romantic, don't you think? I know what you're saying: "Oh, sure, from the safe distance of halfway around the world." Well, it's the thought that counts.

I must stop writing now, as it is nearly time for our skipper to tuck us into bed and sing a lullaby. Seriously, though, he does treat us with kindness and respect, as do all of the officers. On the other hand, the non-coms—well, that's a different story. Write to me when you can.

Love, Steve

Giulia could hardly believe what she had seen. Yes, it was a note from her "sailor friend," all right, but to a perfect stranger, and she began to cry—quietly, to herself. How could Steve do such a thing to her? It was humiliating, having to read his innuendo-laden flirtation with someone else—Hannah, whoever she might be—and she felt violated. Sniffling, Giulia wiped her eyes and thought for a moment. Should she burn this misdirected letter or somehow try to forward it to the rightful owner? Maybe she should ask her mother for advice.

That afternoon, across town at Sixth and Jackson, Hannah Lane clocked out from Crawford-Austin precisely at four and, as arranged, hitched a ride home with Bee Fetters. Upon entering the Browers' house, she paused to check the mail before going upstairs. A note from Steve! He had not written to her in a month and a half, and she nearly shouted for joy. Racing up to her bedroom, she tore the envelope open, unfolded the sheet of paper, and began reading.

"Dear Giulia." Her jaw dropped.

Giulia! What was this, someone's idea of a depraved joke? She read those two words again, "Dear Giulia." Growing angrier by the second, she plunged into the letter with defiance, fully aware that it was not for her to see, almost challenging the artful words to hit her with their best shot.

Dear Giulia,

There is a lull in the action right now, so I am taking a few minutes to write to you, something I have not been very good at accomplishing with any regularity, it seems. I am doing fine, and so is my ship, which we always refer to as a female because she is a real beauty! The food is pretty good for being at sea—much better than you would expect under these conditions, and far preferable, I'd guess, to what the doughboys and leathernecks are having for chow these days. You couldn't really say that we're getting spoiled, but things could be worse. Just ask the Japs!

Sometimes we can pick up the broadcasts of Tokyo Rose, and we all get a kick out of that. Her commentary is all wet, of course, but the dance music she plays is some of the best you'll hear anywhere. Bernie Pope, a chum of mine aboard ship, swears that he recognizes Tokyo Rose's voice as a girl he once knew in Los Angeles. He's going to try to look her up after the war—and ask her where she spent the past few years! By the way, despite his name, Bernie is Jewish, so we kid him a lot with those "Is the Pope Catholic?" jokes.

We just heard of the German surrender—our skipper announced it on the loudspeakers—and boy, was there ever a great cheer all over the ship. But he stressed that the Pacific War is far from finished, and we can testify to that from first-hand experience. How did you celebrate the victory over Jerry? Were there big demonstrations in downtown Waco, or was it more subdued than that? I'll bet there were plenty of Hitlers burning in effigy, huh? Serves him right, I say, and good riddance!

The photo of yourself (at Galveston) that you sent to me is propped up in my metal locker. Ooooo, nice swimsuit. I hope that you don't mind if I scissored your cousins out of it because they are not the ones I'm interested in. Besides, one of them happens to be a boy, and the other only looks to be around ten years old. The person in the middle of the snapshot certainly is no boy, and she's the one that caught my eye!!! Several of my fellow swabbies have commented about you too, complete with wolf whistles, so be very careful if we're ever in port and you come down to visit me at the dock.

I'd better close now, as I'm due to go on watch pretty soon. I still think back upon our fond farewell at the train station, and memories of it make me determined to get back to Waco as soon as possible. Your sweet goodbye kiss keeps me awake at night sometimes, but that is the kind of sleeplessness I do not mind at all!

Love, Steve

Any objective reader would agree that this was quite a nice letter from a lonely sailor overseas, but for an unintended recipient it presented the wrong kind of warmth entirely, that of a slap in the face. Incensed, Hannah snatched up the envelope and reread its address, the handwriting of which most assuredly specified her own name. Who, then, was this Giulia?

Hannah resolved to share her dilemma with someone in whom she could confide, and now was none too soon. After changing out of her work clothes, she went downstairs and found her landlady sitting on the sofa, reattaching a button to one of Wesley's dress shirts.

"Mrs. B?" she asked.

"Yes, dear."

"I got a letter from Steve today—at least, it was addressed to me." Hannah was holding the envelope.

"Yes, I know. I saw it in the stack of mail."

"Would you mind telling me if you notice anything unusual about it?"

Nora had a worried look. "Unusual? How do you mean?"

"Here." Hannah unfolded the letter and handed it to her confidante. "See if you can detect anything peculiar."

"It smells like perfume."

"No, I mean something that Steve wrote."

Nora started to read but then stopped almost immediately. "Oh, dear! Was this sent to you?"

"Yes, ma'am. Here's the envelope."

Nora turned it around and read the address. "What do you make of it?"

The girl shrugged her shoulders. "You know Steve a lot better than I do."

"Well, it's obviously a mistake of some sort. Either he wrote down the wrong name, or he sent someone else's letter to you. Can you tell which?"

"I'm afraid so."

"What do you propose to do?"

"I'd like for you to read it, and then tell me whose letter it really is."

"You want me to read someone else's mail?"

"Technically, it's not someone else's mail," Hannah said. "He addressed it to me."

Nora balked at the idea. Beyond the purely ethical matter of privacy, it seemed inadvisable for a mother to pry into her son's correspondence with the opposite sex.

"Blame me, if it makes you feel any better," Hannah told her. "But I need your advice."

"Yes, all right, then—if you really think it's necessary."

"I do."

Steve's mother proceeded to read through the entire letter, from "Dear Giulia" to "Love, Steve," and was relieved to see that there was nothing very unseemly in it. "Well?" she asked her boarder.

"Well, who is this Giulia person? Can you tell from what he wrote?"

Nora was reluctant to answer. "I ... I can't ... say for sure," she told her. But then she thought of that "fond farewell at the train station" and decided it was of no use to hold back the girl's identity. "I only know one Giulia—who spells her name like that, I mean."

"Tell me her address, and I'll deliver the letter to her personally," Hannah said.

"I don't think that would be a very wise idea, do you?"

"I don't see why not." The corners of Hannah's mouth hinted at a smile. "Actually, the more I think about it, this might prove to be very interesting."

"Oh, dear."

"I'll go now, if you don't mind."

"Now? But I'll be starting dinner in a few minutes."

"Please. I want to get this mess cleaned up." Hannah reached out, and Nora placed the letter in her hand. "Would you please call this Giulia and let her know I'm coming?"

"Wes has the car. He's still at the radio station."

"I'll walk."

Nora giggled. "No. It's much too far, dear. The Colettis live—"

"I once walked from our home, in the western part of Mount Airy, all the way to Bannertown—and that was three or four miles in the snow. I can walk forever, Mrs. B., really. Write down her address for me, will you, please?"

"It's way over by Baylor. Take the streetcar instead."

"I've walked from here to class before—several times."

Clearly, there was no talking her out of it, and so, while Hannah was putting on her "hiking togs," as she referred to them, Nora jotted down the street address and then telephoned the Colettis. She spoke with Paolina, whom she knew from some war-bond functions, and was in the process of explaining the embarrassing situation to her when Hannah reappeared, just in time to accept the slip of paper.

"Tell her I'll be there in sixty minutes," the girl said as she rushed past, with the address now in hand and the letter securely hidden away in a back pocket.

◆　　◆　　◆

Hannah located the doorbell but decided it might be more forceful to knock instead. Paolina answered and invited the "lovely Baylor coed" (as Nora described her on the telephone) to come inside. Giulia was sitting glumly on the sofa, but she stood up when the visitor entered the living room.

"Giulia, this is Hannah Lane—and, Hannah, this is my daughter, Giulia."

They both said, "How do you do?" or something to that effect, and then they stared, for just an instant, as if sizing each other up for a confrontation.

"Hannah walked all the way over here," Paolina said, putting on a cheerful face. She glanced at her wristwatch. "And right on time too."

Hannah nodded her head. "I would have been here sooner, but a dog cornered me on Primrose."

"Goodness! What did you do?"

"I ran until he gave up the chase—whenever I finally got out of his territory, I guess. Then I went around the block and never saw him again."

"Well, we're glad you're safe, aren't we, Giulia?"

"Oh, sure."

"Please make yourself comfortable, dear," Paolina told Hannah. "Would you like something to drink after your long walk?"

"Water would be fine." She sat, as did Giulia, but at opposite ends of the sofa.

"How about a Dr. Pepper?" Paolina called from the kitchen.

"Yes, please." Hannah surveyed the room, noting particularly the upright piano, its rack covered by scattered sheet music. A piece called "The Rosary" was front and center. "Oh? Do you play?" she asked the other girl. There was something in her voice that sounded condescending.

"Play what?" Giulia said, refusing to be had.

Hannah sighed. "Never mind. It's not important."

"I can't find one," Paolina shouted. She was standing before the open refrigerator. "Would a Coca-Cola be all right instead?"

"Yes, please. But just a little."

Giulia cleared her throat. "I see that you graduated from Baylor University recently. Congratulations." It seemed a normal enough comment, on the surface, but Hannah had cause to suspect there was more to it than that.

"How did you know?" she asked. "I'm not wearing my cap and gown."

Giulia grinned. "Thank you for pointing that out to me. No, actually, I read it in a letter."

Paolina returned with the drink, and that gave Hannah a few valuable seconds to weigh what she had just heard.

"Uh, Mrs. Coletti ... Giulia here was saying that she read about my graduation in a letter. Whatever do you think she means?" Hannah was indignant, almost fighting mad.

Giulia's mother seated herself in a chair, looking from one girl to the other. "Listen, I think there's been a silly mix-up by the post office."

Hannah frowned at that notion. "No, ma'am, we can't blame the post office for this." She took a sip of her Coca-Cola.

"Well, whoever was at fault, I still see no reason why you two should be cross with each other."

"All right," Hannah said with a smirk, and she turned to Giulia. "Would you please tell me who in the world might have written a letter to you that just happened to mention that I—someone you don't even know—graduated from Baylor University?"

"I guess you could say he's a mutual friend," Giulia told her.

"A mutual friend named Steve?"

Giulia did not answer. She just smiled at her rival.

In her role as peacemaker, Paolina said to their guest, "Mrs. Brower tells me that you brought something for my daughter to have."

"Yes, ma'am, that's true." Hannah shifted her weight to the left a bit, to enable her to slide the envelope out of the right, rear pocket of her denim slacks. "I'm sorry, but I seem to have slightly crushed it." She handed it to the other girl. "You see how it's addressed?"

Without so much as even glancing at the gift, Giulia laid it beside her on the sofa. Then she arose and walked over to the sewing table, upon which was lying a similar envelope. She offered it to Hannah, saying, "I believe this is yours," and took her seat.

"Well, is everyone satisfied?" Paolina asked. "That was not so bad, was it?"

Hannah drank some more of the cold beverage, casually looking down at her correspondence from Steve, and something very annoying caught her eye. It was the wrong addressee, so she said, "I think we need to swap envelopes too, if you don't mind."

Giulia scowled, as if this were a major imposition, but the exchange was made.

Taking a last swallow, Hannah gazed again at "The Rosary." She began to say something to Giulia but held her tongue.

"Now, why don't you read your real letters, girls?" Paolina told them. "It might help to clear the air, especially since, as it turns out, neither of you has anything to be angry about."

"I really need to be going, Mrs. Coletti," Hannah said. She stood up, laying her empty glass on the end table.

"Please, Miss Lane. I don't want you to go away mad. Read the letter. It'll only take a couple of minutes, and I'll be most appreciative." She turned to her daughter. "You too, 'Bina. Do me that favor."

Hannah sat down, and she and Giulia opened their respective envelopes, seeing for the first time what Steve had actually written to them.

Paolina, meanwhile, deemed it prudent to leave them alone with their thoughts, so she chose that opportunity to carry Hannah's glass back to the kitchen and then stir the broccoli and boiled new potatoes that she was preparing for dinner. When she returned to the other room, she was disappointed to sense that there was every bit as much hostility in the air as before—perhaps even more. Had fate not intervened, surely both young women would have been well pleased by the endearing words they read. But as it was, these letters would remain fatally tainted by the realization that someone else's eyes had viewed them first. Worse yet, the insidious specter of divided affections now infiltrated their thoughts, compromising whatever naïve trust they once had in a sailor's loyalty to the girl back home.

As Hannah was about to leave, Paolina took her hand and said, "I feel awful that it's such a long walk for you. I want you to know that we'd be happy to give you a ride, but we don't have a car."

"That's all right, Mrs. Coletti. I can use the time to think." The way Hannah felt at the moment, that neighborhood dog had better keep its distance.

"And thank you for helping us straighten out this mess," Paolina added. "I'm sure Giulia appreciates it too, don't you, dear?"

Her daughter said, "Yes, ma'am," without the slightest conviction.

Hannah looked directly at her adversary. "At least now we know where we stand."

Giulia feigned a smile. "Don't forget to kiss the top of your *roommate's* letter."

Not to be outdone, Hannah quickly shot back with "Ooooo, nice swimsuit!"

Paolina could only stand by, watching helplessly and shaking her head.

◆　　◆　　◆

The nation's 6,443 local draft boards did not suddenly close up shop the moment Germany surrendered. Their unpaid staffs remained hard at work, aware that a tenacious enemy was yet to be defeated and that substantial manpower quotas still had to be met. By the middle of 1945, twelve million Americans were under arms, either in training or combat, charged with the daunting task of pacifying the Empire of Japan.

In compliance with federal law, Wesley Brower had registered with Selective Service on his eighteenth birthday, in November of 1944. Six and a half months later, he had graduated from high school. Once those two probable grounds for deferment—minimum age and state-mandated academics—were no longer applicable to him, it seemed only a matter of time before his number would be called. But two other factors, as if on cue, now emerged to take their places. Although college and marriage could not be said to figure prominently in his immediate future, both were more distinct prospects than he would have thought possible just a few short weeks earlier.

The boy's pipe dream of a career in naval aviation had come to naught when a preliminary physical for the benefit of recruiters determined that his eyesight was not acute enough to enter that visually demanding field of service. This disappointing medical report blunted his enthusiasm for enlisting in the armed forces, and he felt compelled to step back and take his chances with the draft, along with the majority of able-bodied eighteen-year-old males. As a consequence, enrolling at Baylor University became a much more viable option, at least until summoned for military duty.

Wesley's pretty girlfriend from Axtell, Pippa Glynn, was making it a practice to accompany her father to town each and every Saturday, without fail, thus giving Della Ryman more time away from The Smoker's Den for her volunteer work. This required no additional gasoline consumption for the Glynns, of course, as Rob would be coming to Waco anyway. Pippa contended that she needed the extra hours to earn money for eventual purchase of either a new bull or a used automobile—she did not yet know which. Whatever the rationale, it goes without saying that the arrangement was perfectly fine with Wesley, for now he was able to see her on a weekly basis instead of just once a month. A subtlety of her behavior that told him their relationship was warming was Pippa's budding desire to kiss him hello and goodbye, even in plain sight of her father, something she never would have considered doing in the recent past. The first time she did so, Wesley turned red, glancing at Rob, who quickly averted his eyes. But Pippa was not at all embarrassed by this open show of affection, and the girl's utter lack of self-consciousness made it much easier for Wesley to feel comfortable with her in public.

Pippa was not the only one earning higher wages than ever before. Now that Wesley was out of school for the summer, it became possible for him to work a normal, forty-four-hour week at the radio station. Moreover, the wartime labor shortage virtually guaranteed that such a position would be there for the asking. At first, he assisted with the publicity campaigns of KWXN, writing promotional announcements, sending programming logs to the newspapers, designing print advertising, and even making two personal appearances as Kip Hanson. Then, in early July, soundman Dickie Waterhouse received a "Greeting" from President Truman, and he notified director Hugh Kenton that he would be heading off to war. During his remaining few days on the job, those which overlapped Wesley's improvised apprenticeship, he trained the young man in how to adjust and properly monitor the array of potentiometers, VU meters, and switches that translated into good audio performance.

One obvious question was bothering Wesley. Who would run the board when "Behold Tomorrow" was on the air? Certainly he could not be expected to handle the audio chores while also acting in the daytime serial.

Dickie turned to Hugh Kenton, who told the protégé, "Why not? You're a pretty fast runner, aren't you?"

Wesley naturally supposed that the director was kidding, and yet Kenton said it so matter-of-factly that, for an uneasy moment, Wesley actually thought he was serious. "Do you mean that I ...?"

Kenton retained his straight face for another instant but finally did explain. "Relax, Wes. That little problem surfaced in our meeting with Dickie, and I think we have a viable solution."

Dickie grinned, amused by the boy's look of relief.

"We had a Baylor intern—about a year ago—named Brian Quaid," the director added, "and he can sit in for you during that quarter-hour, Monday through Friday. He'll do 'West of the Brazos' too, while he's at it, and of course the rehearsals for both shows. We've got him working in traffic and part-time telephone sales anyway, so he'll be here at the station." Kenton looked at Dickie. "Brian was your understudy for a couple of months, as I recall."

"For a whole term."

"Better yet!" Kenton said. He puffed cheerfully on his cigar.

Wesley's first two days to solo as soundman went quite well indeed, considering his inexperience, and could even be described as routine or uneventful. The next day, however, was anything but that, for it coincided with Sandra Whittsel's very last appearance on the air. Her character, Sally Holt, was by now so popular in Waco that sacks full of fan mail poured in when word reached the public that she would soon be leaving.

"Is Sally going to get bumped off?" was a common concern that they raised.

So troubled were Sally's many admirers that chief writer Ethel Coody felt obliged to "leak" an official statement to the Waco newspapers, intimating that Sally Holt's life was not in imminent danger. She would be moving to Cincinnati, where her brother owned a nightclub that was in need of a thick-skinned manager who would take no guff from disruptive customers.

Sandra Whittsel's final line of dialogue as an actress for KWXN was true to her character: "Sure, Kip, I may come back to Baltimore someday ... but only if I hop aboard the wrong freight train." The fact that she spoke it to him, sharing the same microphone, pleased Wesley in a professional sense, but her actual real-life departure from his world made him very sad indeed.

Late that afternoon, a studio cast party was given in her honor by station manager Clive Ramey and owner Brantley B. Wollach. There, among his colleagues and friends, Wesley had one last chance to talk to this charming, maddening, delightful, frustrating enigma of a girl who once brought so much spirit and desire to his life—and probably could do so again at a moment's notice, were she so inclined. "Oh, my dear, sweet Sandy," he thought, gazing at her now, and he knew that his heart would always ache from her absence.

But he and she only conversed briefly at the party—and in a very public, stilted fashion—for Sandy was the star attraction, always surrounded by a dozen or more well-wishers. Conspicuously missing from the bittersweet send-off was announcer Marshall McFall, who had another engagement, to which he sped immediately after the conclusion of "West of the Brazos." He did not even say goodbye.

Mr. Wollach delivered a few well-chosen words to bring the occasion to a close, and people began drifting away from Studio A—waving farewell to Sandy and quickly forgetting that they ever knew her. Wesley watched her pick up the gifts and carry them under her arm toward the exit, but she did not see him standing there in the shadows. Either that, or she did not wish to speak any further. He hesitated but then let her go. The door, seemingly in slow motion, swung shut behind her.

Wesley had an empty feeling inside that caused him to shudder, and he knew that he could not let it end like this. He raced to catch her and did so at the front curb, just as she was about to walk to her automobile in the parking lot. "Sandy!" he shouted, but then, realizing that he was much too loud, he repeated quietly, "Sandy."

She smiled at him, but it was not a happy smile. "Do you want a lift home?" she asked.

He pointed to the green Chevrolet and frowned. "I drove to work today."

"Care to sit in my car for five minutes and just talk?"

Wesley nodded his head. "Yes, I would like that very much."

They walked together in silence, and when Wesley offered to carry the gifts, he could see that the girl was crying. He opened the door for her and then went around to the passenger side, sliding the gifts in before him.

Once she was seated, Sandy took a deep breath and appeared to regain her composure. "Do you remember the first time we ever spoke?" she asked him.

"I sure do." There was no sense in denying it, no time for games. Besides, he could see that scene as clearly now as on the day it happened. Every detail was burned into his memory.

"You were riding your bicycle down Sanger," she said, "and I drove up behind you."

"I know."

A couple of her gifts seemed determined to topple onto the floorboard, so she gathered them up and asked Wesley to lay the unwieldy stack on the back seat. In so doing, he took a moment to admire one of the most thoughtful among them—a wooden picture frame that encased a publicity photo of her costumed radio persona, along with the signatures of 119 members of The Sally Club of Waco.

She smiled at Wesley. "We've had some good times, haven't we?"

He nodded, biting his lip with a sudden rush of emotion. "Yes, we have."

But her smile vanished when she added, "I've been rotten to you—more than once."

"No ..." He shook his head, unable to continue, to say what was in his heart.

"Yes, I have, and somehow I want to make it up to you—or at least explain."

Wesley had never felt so sad in his life, and he wanted to reach out and take Sandy in his arms, to tell her everything was all right, that he forgave her, that he loved her and always would. But he did not know how she would respond to such an admission, and he sensed that it would be the wrong thing to do. It was too late for that. If only he could turn the clock around and start all over again with her. Everything might be different this time.

"Mother and I are leaving for Savannah tomorrow morning. She's already packed. She wants to go."

"Do you?"

She sighed. "No, I don't ever want to leave. I feel like I belong here."

Wesley grasped desperately at that hope. "Can't you stay? You're out of school now. You're on your own. You could make enough money to live on."

"There's more to it than that, Wes."

He swallowed hard, his throat so tight that he almost choked.

"I plan to be married soon," she told him. Her tone of voice was nonchalant, as if this were the most casual statement imaginable.

"Married?" His mouth fell open. "You're going to be married?"

"As soon as possible."

"What's the rush?"

For a moment, Sandy tried to think of some way to phrase it to him that would not be painful, but then she decided just to be honest about it instead. "Rick thinks he'll be sent overseas soon. He's my fiancé."

The word crushed Wesley. Though he had no claim on her, the realization still shattered his spirit, and he felt out of breath, as if he had sustained a hard blow to the stomach. So it was all over. His dream, unspoken for all these months and years, had been snuffed out by a single word.

"Was he the soldier at graduation?" he managed to say.

"Yes, he was."

With sudden fascination, Sandy watched a bird swoop down, circle around, and land on the hood of the automobile next to hers. She tapped on her windshield, and the bird flew away. "That's Neddy Wright's car, and he doesn't like bird poop." She grinned for just an instant but then became serious again.

"Listen, I'm sorry I didn't introduce you to Rick," Sandy said, "but he was in a big hurry. I think you'd like each other."

"And you want to marry him before he leaves?"

"Wes, I have to marry him."

Despite himself, an angry tone crept into Wesley's voice. The more he thought, the more outraged he became. Finally, he nearly shouted at her, "What are you saying to me, Sandy? Haven't you learned anything? What kind of a girl are you anyway?" So bitter was he that he actually reached for the door handle and was about to leave her sitting there alone. But then he stopped. Maybe he had misunderstood what she meant. Wesley looked directly at her, and very quietly he asked, "Are you trying to tell me that you're pregnant again? Please don't say that. Dear God, Sandy, please don't tell me that."

To his immense relief, she shook her head, indicating that she was not.

"Then why do you have to get hitched? No one's holding a gun to your head."

"Because if he doesn't marry me before he goes overseas, I don't think he ever will."

"You think he'll be killed?"

"It's not that," she said. "I think he'll forget all about me."

He gazed at her pretty face. "Somehow, I find that hard to believe."

"Really, Wes. Out of sight, out of mind."

"Then good riddance—if he doesn't love you any more than that."

She glowered at him. "You don't even know Rick, so you have no right to say that."

"Maybe not, but I know how I would feel if—" Wesley stopped.

Sandy did not hear him, or so she pretended. "I'm afraid he'll find someone else—unless I do something drastic."

"I don't follow."

"That's where my getting pregnant comes into it."

For a moment, he just stared at her in disbelief. "You use it as a weapon, don't you?"

She chuckled. "What?"

"Can't you try keeping your legs together?"

Now she laughed out loud. "Why, Wesley Brower! Are you calling me a whore?" He blushed, and her eyes twinkled with mirth. "It may seem that way to you, but I'll have you know that I'm not a pleasure machine for others. I'm doing this purely for selfish motives."

"And so you're going to trap this poor, unsuspecting soldier."

"I need to—and the sooner, the better. Maybe even on the train. Maybe even with my mother asleep in the same compartment. Who knows?"

"Are you serious?"

"Whatever it takes."

He stared at her in awe. "You are so wild."

"Oh, I'm not all that wild, just pragmatic. Yep, that's me—Miss Practical."

"What if you become pregnant, and he still refuses to marry you? Have you ever thought of that?"

"I promise you, that won't happen. My daddy would have the entire 13th Air Force on him."

"You have it all figured it out, don't you?"

She smiled, almost proudly.

"Why is this Rick fellow traveling back to Georgia with you and your mother? I take it, you haven't let him in on your harmless little scheme."

"Hardly! No, it just so happens that he has a week's leave coming."

"And you've planned exactly how he can enjoy it."

"I don't think he'll complain much."

Wesley looked out the side window. "Why are you telling me all this?"

Sandy did not answer.

"You know what I think? I think you like talking to boys about sex. It gives you some sort of perverse excitement." He turned toward her again, awaiting her reaction.

"Oh, I would much rather do it than talk about it," she said. Then, noticing his discomfort, she added, "How about you?"

"What do you mean?"

"What is your opinion of sex?"

"Well, I think it's fine."

"I don't mean just in principle, Wes. I mean ..."

Wesley took a deep breath. "I don't know. I ... I've never done it."

"That's a shame ... because I would have taught you, if you had only said the word."

That may have been her idea of flattery, but it was the last thing Wesley wanted to hear from her. Instantly, he knew it would haunt him for years to come, and he tried in vain to forget that she ever said it.

"I really need to go now," she told him.

"Sandy, please don't do this. Please don't go through with it. Don't leave. I'll do anything for you. You can have part of my paycheck every week, if that'll help you afford to stay. Tell your mother you've changed your mind. Tell Rick that you'll write to him every day. We need you here. I need you here. I love you."

Tears came to her eyes, and she whispered, "That's very sweet of you, Wes. I love you too, in a very special way."

"But not as a lover?"

"No, not as a lover. You're much too nice for that. You're different than the boys I seem to attract. And I go after boys who are a little older and—"

"More experienced?"

"Yes." She smiled at him, not without sympathy. "Someday you'll probably top them all, just wait and see. I have great faith in you."

"But not enough faith to make you forget about Rick."

"No, of course not. I love Rick. I really do. Please don't think that all I want is to take a tumble with him and have his child. I want to live with him as husband and wife, and I'm sure we can make each other happy."

He remained unconvinced. "Pardon my saying so, but that seems like the wrong way to begin a trusting relationship, don't you think?"

"Maybe so. Probably so. But he has wandering eyes—his pick of girls—and I need to do something to set myself apart from the others. Oh, you wouldn't understand."

Wesley thought for a minute and, for some reason unknown even to him, he said, "You know what your problem is? You're just too pretty for you own good."

She laughed. "And what is that supposed to mean? Should I accept it as a compliment?"

"Maybe so. That's up to you."

She took a deep breath, and her lovely face was apologetic. "I'm sorry, Wes, but I really have to go now. It's been much longer than five minutes."

A single teardrop rolled down Wesley's left cheek. Embarrassed, he quickly wiped it away. When he swallowed, his throat felt like it was on fire. "Goodbye, Sandy," he whispered. "I can't begin to tell you how much I'm going to miss you. I love you now, and I always will."

Sandy managed a little smile through her tears, but then she began sobbing. "Goodbye, Wesley Brower. I love you, honey."

She slid across the seat and threw her arms around him, crying profusely. When she buried her face in his neck, he could feel her tears flowing down inside his shirt collar. Wesley hugged her very tightly, and he sensed the warmth and softness of her breasts as they pressed hard against his chest. He did not want to let go of this adorable girl whom, in all likelihood, he would never see again.

She began kissing him very rapidly over every inch of his face, and all the while her delicately smooth skin rubbed across his. In due time, the sensuality of their embrace relaxed, and the passion of their kisses gradually subsided, becoming more tender and deliberate, until they ceased altogether, and the young woman and young man merely looked at one another, lost in their thoughts.

Sandy sat up straight, now staring ahead over the steering wheel, and her lower lip quivered with emotion. She said not another word. Wesley patted her gently on the leg, said, "Goodbye, sweetie," and opened the passenger door. As he walked over to his Chevy coupe, he heard the girl's automobile start up. He watched with a sense of profound loss as she turned the corner and then, ever so slowly, passed forever from his life.

Wesley sat alone in his automobile and wept for a good ten minutes, perhaps even longer. Then, when someone happened to drive into the parking lot, he lay supine on the seat and continued to weep. He felt silly and immature, like an eighteen-year-old baby, but he simply could not stop crying.

Goodbye, my dear Sandy.

♦   ♦   ♦

The next morning, after a restless night of tossing and turning in bed, Wesley was half asleep as he showered, dressed, and pecked at a breakfast of rationed scrambled eggs and toast.

"You're very quiet today. Are you feeling okay?" his mother asked. She had a worried expression on her face as she pressed the back of her hand against his forehead. "You feel a little feverish. Why don't you stay home? Mr. Graffen will understand."

"No, ma'am, I'm fine," he said. How could you tell your own mother that you were suffering from a broken heart?

Wesley looked at the clock and realized that Sandy, her mother, and the soldier named Rick were already on their way east. There was a 7:25 train, and he felt sure that they were on it. Then a troubling thought crossed his mind. He wondered what time the girl planned to become romantic with her fiancé— maybe more than once on such a long journey. In all his life, he had never heard of anyone being so frivolous about sexual intercourse, an act he always assumed was meant to be a momentous affair. Miss Whittsel, though, seemed to treat it with about as much gravity as choosing which shoes to wear to the prom. And, of course, that made her even more exciting.

With the grief of Sandy's absence weighing heavily upon him, Wesley was far from being his normal self that morning. He found it impossible to concentrate on his work, and the sales calls were unanimously counterproductive. Many of his clients were uncharacteristically aloof, no doubt a function of his own personal detachment. Even the weather seemed to conspire against him. The summer heat was oppressive, already climbing into the upper eighties.

Through it all, Sandy was almost always in his thoughts, usually in a platonic sense, with genuine concern over the girl's well-being. Sometimes, though, in less guarded moments, Wesley would allow himself to fantasize that he, not Soldier Rick, was her traveling companion, and it had become his solemn duty to perform as the chosen recipient of her ambrosial favors. Those were the moments when his mind paid little attention to banal pursuits like salesmanship and the fine art of conversation, let alone the speed limit. One traffic cop, seemingly out of the goodness of his heart, overlooked the hightailing Chevrolet: forty-five miles per hour in a thirty-five zone. The automobile may have been on Franklin Avenue, but Wesley's brain was somewhere between Texas and Georgia, trying to locate a private compartment, an inviting place where the deed could be done.

Such thoughts did not prepare him well for his customary "sales call" at The Smoker's Den. He might just as well have taken Sandy in there with him, for all the regard he gave to Pippa Glynn. She accepted it in stride, being a girl of great equanimity, but that did not necessarily mean she would be panting to see the young man the next time he deigned to pay her a visit.

The following week, when Wesley again made his rounds to the tobacconist, Pippa had been replaced by the regular Saturday worker, Della Ryman. This dealt a major blow to the boy, who by now had regained his capacity for reasoning. No longer was he fixated on visions of Sandra Whittsel, at least not when in the actual flesh-and-blood presence of another attractive female of suitable age. Pippa certainly fit that description—except for the part about being present. Sadly, she was elsewhere today, and Della Ryman made an unacceptable substitute, not least of all because she was gaunt, married, and the mother of two children.

"Hi, Wes," Rob Glynn said. He seemed as cheerful as ever, apparently unaware that the earth had stopped rotating on its celestial axis.

Wesley got right to the point. "Where's Pippa? I see Della over there."

"Oh, Pippa begged off today. Something about a friend of hers."

"A ... girlfriend?"

"I suppose so. She didn't say."

"Probably a girlfriend from Axtell." Wesley spoke as if merely stringing those words together would make it so. "Pippa said three other girls graduated with her, so I'm sure it was one of them."

Rob laughed. "Could be."

"Do you know when she'll be back?" Now he could feel himself starting to obsess about Pippa instead of Sandy.

"Maybe next Saturday. She said to tell you hello."

So Wesley had to be content with waiting another whole week for a chance to see her again, and there was no guarantee that she would be at The Smoker's Den on that day either. As it happened, Pippa did report to work the following Saturday, but Wesley soon noticed that things were not right between them. She was very reserved, hardly replying in multiple syllables whenever he asked her a question. He suspected that this was her manner of retaliation for the way he behaved two weeks earlier, back when the devastating loss of Sandy was still torturing his mind and adversely affecting his every move.

Finally, after unsuccessfully trying to tease the resentment out of Pippa, he decided to throw caution to the wind and confront the girl about her current disposition. He was shocked to learn that the basis for her coolness ran far deeper than he ever could have imagined.

"All right, I'll tell you," she said. "It's because of something I heard about you." She looked him directly in the eye, as if studying how he might react to that assertion.

Wesley glanced at Rob, across the room, and he hoped that the girl's father could not hear what they were saying. "What have I done?" he asked her, barely above a whisper.

Pippa began whispering too. "Someone told a friend of mine that you were necking with a girl."

His jaw dropped. "Necking? That's a lie!"

"This person saw you with her own eyes."

"Then it must have been someone who looks like me."

"Wes, it happened in front of the radio station where you work, which leads me to believe that it was not a case of mistaken identity."

So that was it. A spy or troublemaker must have spotted him in the parking lot.

"All right," he said. "Now I know where that story came from, but I was just kissing a girl goodbye. There's no law against that." Pippa seemed unswayed, so he elaborated. "Look, the girl played Sally Holt on a daytime serial, but she was leaving Waco—going back home to Savannah. I'll probably never see her again."

"According to this person, it was much more than a goodbye kiss."

Wesley thought for a moment. "Do you know who 'this person' might be?"

"No, I don't, but my friend says she is a very reliable source."

"Who would your friend know that has anything to do with the radio station?"

"I can't tell you that. All I know is that the person said it was much more than just a simple goodbye kiss."

"Well, yes, we were very close. Sandy and I were school friends, and we acted on the same radio serial."

"Were you lovers?"

This remark knocked him off balance. "No, of course not. She had a boyfriend at the station. We never ..." Exasperated, Wesley took a deep breath and let the air out slowly. "Look, it was all perfectly innocent. We kissed, and then she broke down and cried in my arms. Please believe me. I don't want you to think that I did anything ... uh ... that I shouldn't have."

"Like groping?"

Again, Wesley was stunned. "Why do you say that?"

"Because that's the rumor. This person says you were groping the girl's ... chest."

"That's a dirty lie!" Wesley shouted, and the outcry drew Rob's attention and that of two customers, a husband and wife.

"Oh, is it?" Pippa asked.

"Don't you think I would remember that?"

"I'm not sure of anything anymore."

Rob walked over to assist the couple, who seemed interested in a gift box of cigars.

Pippa approached him with a stern face. "Daddy, could Wes and I discuss something in the back room for a few minutes?" She motioned for Wesley to follow her.

By the time the girl and boy reached their designated meeting place, Pippa was fuming mad. She closed the door. "But that's not the worst of it," she told Wesley, "not by a long shot. I think you know what I'm referring to."

"I don't have the vaguest idea. Why don't you illuminate me?" Two could play the anger game.

"Well, you don't have to be sarcastic!"

"And you don't have to repeat false accusations."

"Are you calling my friend a liar?"

"Are you calling *me* a liar?"

Pippa marched right over to the desk and produced a sheet of paper, folded in half. She opened it. "Does the name Dr. Schuller mean anything to you?"

He nearly coughed on a mouthful of air, the very antithesis of a poker face. "Why? Should it?" he struggled to reply, just to buy a few seconds of time.

"I think so. It's not likely you'd forget something such as that."

Wesley turned a chair around and sat down. Were those tears forming in Pippa's lovely, green eyes? She was very upset—clearly beyond the capacity of any silly piece of gossip about necking. He sighed, fearing that the girl knew everything, and he saw no way out but to come clean. On the other hand, it seemed awfully risky to do too much talking, so he decided to just sit tight and listen.

"There's a rumor going around ..." Pippa said. She refolded the sheet of paper. "There's a rumor that Sandra Whittsel was expecting a baby, that you were the father, and that she had an abortion."

Wesley remained tight-lipped, but his eyes gave him away.

"Well?" she asked.

"I promised not to tell anyone about Sandy's ... problem."

"Her abortion."

"Yeah."

Pippa waited. "Is that all you have to say? Because if it is, I never want to see you again. Please leave, and don't come back."

Wesley studied her face. She looked more betrayed than sad, and she was not crying.

"At least hear my side of it," he said.

"That's why we're here."

He rubbed his chin, wondering where to start. "Well, first of all, I was not the father." He glanced at Pippa.

"Go on."

"Sandy was pregnant, that's true. She made a mistake at some party—an Army guy. They were drunk. Then, when she found out, she had nowhere to turn. The GI was long gone, of course. I don't even think she knew his name. Anyway, she asked me to help her."

"Which you did ..."

"Yes. She was desperate."

"You killed the baby."

He rolled his eyes. "I drove Sandy to Dr. Schuller's."

"And he killed the baby."

Wesley looked down. "Yes."

"Anything else?"

He frowned at the girl. "I feel like I'm on the witness stand."

"I'm sorry, Wes, but I need to know these things."

Sighing, he slowly shook his head. "No, I'm the one who's sorry. I guess I made a mess of everything."

"Do you believe in abortion?"

He glared. "Of course not. What kind of a monster do you think I am?"

"You didn't refuse."

"Look, Sandy was at the end of her rope. She even said she might kill herself."

"Do you think she meant it?"

"Maybe. I don't know. She was pretty hysterical by then. I think she was afraid that her father would find out."

Pippa stared at him for a long time, and the anger in her face eventually gave way to a gentle nod of the head that told Wesley she was willing to forgive, if not entirely forget. "This whole thing was her own fault," she said. "No one made her do it. She was not exactly an innocent victim of circumstances."

"I know that. Sandy knew it too, and she even admitted it to me."

There was a pause. "Was she wild?"

Wesley looked shocked by the question. "What?" he said with a shallow laugh.

"Was she a wild girl?"

"Who ... Sandy? No, I don't think so. At least, not that I ever saw."

No longer was Pippa the criminal prosecutor. Her tone had changed to one of benevolent curiosity, a teenager's need to satisfy her inquiring mind, to somehow sort out the sexual confusion of adult life. "Did you ever ... I mean ...?"

Wesley watched her grasping for the right word, and this was one instance when he was not about to offer any help.

"You know, Wes ... Did you ever go beyond just kissing her?"

Now, as if spurred on by the hormones of male ego, Wesley suddenly became the fount of all wisdom on that compelling topic, of which he knew precious little. Pippa's expression was friendly, almost deferential, so he felt free to be as candid as common decency might allow.

"I didn't ever go all the way, if that's what you're wondering."

She nodded acknowledgment.

"But we came pretty close."

Smiling, she probed further. "Did both of you take off your clothes?"

Unfortunately, the limits of being candid did not extend all the way to outright lying. "Not exactly. But we might as well have."

"What do you mean?"

"I mean there was a lot of hand movement going on, and not much was left to the imagination." That sounded adult.

While all of this was playing out, it struck Wesley as odd that Pippa now seemed to be quite pleased with his racy answers, whereas only a few minutes before, she was terribly upset because she suspected him of plain old necking. No doubt about it—the female mind was an *enigma*. That was a term he learned in English class.

"Did you ever want to ... do more with her?" the girl asked.

That was a silly question. Is the sky blue? Can birds fly? Does Audie Murphy wear combat boots?

Wesley was walking a tightrope here. He wanted to sound suitably lustful, but at the same time, he did not want his speech to come across as that of a raving sex maniac. One brief glimpse confirmed that Pippa was still friendly, curious, and inquisitive enough, so that gave him plenty of latitude.

"Pippa!" Rob shouted from the tobacco counter. "Would you please bring me the scissors?"

She looked at Wesley and mouthed, "Sorry." Smiling, she called back to her father, "Why do you need the scissors?"

"Just bring me the scissors, please," came the reply.

She searched through the desk drawer and quickly located the implement, carrying it by the closed blades, as she had been instructed in first grade. "Coming," she shouted and disappeared from the room.

Wesley made good use of the girl's absence by stealing a look at the mysterious paper that Pippa was using as court's evidence. It was some sort of invoice, or a copy thereof, and at the top, serving as a printed letterhead, was the name "Maurice Schuller, M.D." In a column marked "Charges and Fees" was the ambiguous descriptive, "Services rendered for patient Sandra Whittsel." To the right was another column with the numerals "75.00." How in the world did such an incriminating piece of correspondence fall into the hands of an ostensibly upstanding teenage girl from Axtell? Sandy had bitter enemies, of course—like every attractive female with talent and ambition—but who at the radio station would have been so vindictive as to snatch a medical record from her purse? He refolded the paper and placed it precisely where his friend had laid it just a moment before.

Pippa returned and shut the door. "Daddy needed for me to snip the price off a cigar box wrapper. A wedding gift."

Wesley laughed. "That seems like a strange gift for a wedding."

"How come?"

"Well, what does the bride get?"

"Search me," Pippa said. "Maybe they have to get married, and those cigars are for the groom to pass around whenever the baby is born."

Wesley cocked his head. "You're just kidding, aren't you?"

"Of course!" she told him with a grin. "First things first, I always say."

Her little joke made Wesley think of Sandy, and he wondered if she was "with child" yet. It was hard to feel too sorry for Rick, though. That was good duty.

"So, where were we?" the girl asked.

Wesley shrugged his shoulders, playing dumb.

"Come on, silly. You know very well what we were about to discuss."

"Remind me."

"Did you ever want to ... become intimate with that girl?"

"Whatever do you mean?"

"Wes! Are you going to make me come right out and say it?"

"Only if you want me to answer."

Pippa ran over to the door, opened it slightly, and peeked into the other room. When she walked back to where Wesley was sitting, she whispered to him, "Did you ever want to *screw* Sandy?"

That was a pretty advanced term for a country lass to be brandishing, and Wesley looked surprised. As if reading his mind, Pippa said, "Girls talk about such things too, you know."

He smiled. "I guess so."

"Well?" She waited. "Did you ever want to do that with her?"

Wesley tried to come up with some clever turns of phrase, but instead, in the interest of full disclosure, he settled for honesty. "I thought about it all the time."

"Then why didn't you do it?"

"I wasn't planning to rape her!"

"No, but wouldn't she have cooperated?"

He cleared his throat, for this was not the type of question to be taken lightly. "I didn't think so at the time, but later on she told–" He stopped in mid-sentence.

Pippa leaned forward. "Go on."

"Later on—too late, because I was already kissing her goodbye—Sandy told me that she would have taught me all she knew about sex. Which is quite a lot, believe you me." That last part was just for embellishment, but no doubt true.

The girl smiled. "And then you could have shared what you learned with me." She said it ever so quietly and did not seem at all embarrassed.

It was to be another sleepless night for Wesley Brower.

♦   ♦   ♦

Nora considered herself to be an orderly homemaker. The normal routine called for grocery shopping on Thursday morning, with an additional stop on Monday for the acquisition of a few perishable items—usually not more than a small box full. But on Monday, August 6, 1945, she was needed as a substitute worker for the aging and ailing Florence Kipp at the USO. And so it happened that Nora was not at Moek Grocery until the morning of Tuesday, August 7, the day after the atom bomb was dropped.

The city of Hiroshima virtually ceased to exist at eight seconds past 8:16 A.M., Japanese time, on August 6. Colonel Paul Tibbets piloted the *Enola Gay*, a B-29 Superfortress, on a five-and-a-half-hour flight from the Mariana Island of Tinian. A 9,000-pound bomb, "Little Boy," was dropped from an altitude of 31,600 feet and detonated in the air at 1,900 feet. The explosion obliterated three-fifths of the city and instantly killed about 75,000 people.

The official announcement was broadcast from the White House on Monday night, when President Truman told a nationwide radio audience, "My fellow Americans, the British, Chinese, and United States governments have given the Japanese people adequate warning of what is in store for them. The world will note that the first atomic bomb was dropped on Hiroshima, a military base. If Japan does not surrender, bombs will have to be dropped on her war industries, and unfortunately thousands of civilian lives will be lost. I urge Japanese civilians to leave industrial cities immediately and save themselves."

But Nora, having retired to bed at her usual time, heard only the sketchiest of reports and remained oblivious to the epochal magnitude of the event until the following morning, when she was gripped by the 7:30 radio news as she was washing dishes after breakfast. Both Elizabeth and Wesley had already left for work—she to pump gasoline at Service Refining Company and he to man the audio board at KWXN.

The personal significance of that cataclysmic blast was not lost upon grocer Hermann Moek. Upon seeing Nora enter the store, the first words out of his mouth were, "Did you hear the news? It looks like this war will be over in no time at all, and I'll wager a guess that your Steve will be coming home in a matter of months."

"Hi, Hermann. Yes, I heard. It can't last much longer now, can it?"

"A week—tops. That's what I would give it. Rumor is, there won't even be an invasion."

"Wouldn't that be wonderful? There's been far too much bloodshed already." Her son's ship, the minesweeper *USS Jeffers* remained anchored off Okinawa, at least for the time being, but any attack order would no doubt place Steve in the thick of the action again.

The screen door opened, and in came Hermann's wife, Gertrude, along with their foster son. "Well, look who's here," the lady said when she spotted Nora. "Have you heard d'e news?"

"Yes, Trudy, I did. Hermann thinks Steve will be home soon."

"Well, I didn't put it quite that way." Hermann grinned, a little amused at Nora's wishful thinking. "Actually, what I said was that the war should be over in no time. I hear that they'll be keeping our boys in uniform for six months after that."

"Still, praise the Lord. I certainly cannot complain. Lots of mothers have lost their sons." The moment Nora uttered these words, she regretted them.

Taking Gertrude's hand in her own, she said, "Oh, I'm sorry, Trudy. You know what I meant." Nora had been thinking of American sons, and the Moeks' loss of their Conrad did not even cross her mind in that context.

Gertrude smiled. "D'at's all right, dear. I knew what you were trying to say."

Nora stepped over to Klaus-Peter and leaned down. "And how's this handsome young man doing today?"

The boy looked at his foster mother, who told him, "Well, go ahead and tell Mrs. Brower how you are, Klaus. You can speak English."

"I'm fine, Mrs. Brower," the lad said. Her name sounded German to him—Brauer—so it was easily learned and repeated.

Hermann smiled proudly. "He'll be starting school next month, and I think he'll do very well with the language."

"I would hate to think that I had to learn German in such a short time," Nora said. She turned to Hermann and asked him, "How long has he been with you now?"

"Six months and some change, that's all. He's made remarkable progress, and I think the reason is we forbid the speaking of German at home. That's our rule: not a word of German, especially if young Klaus is around." Hermann chuckled. "Sometimes I tease him that, at this rate, he will undoubtedly wind up as an English professor at some college."

Modesty impelled Klaus-Peter to turn away, but his smile indicated that the adulation pleased him.

Suddenly, Gertrude thought of something that could not wait. "I forgot to tell you, Hermann," she said. "We got a letter from Liesel!" That was their daughter, who lived in Boerne, about 175 miles to the southwest. Due to the war and its travel difficulties, they had not seen Anneliese and her family—husband Ross and their four children—since Thanksgiving of 1943, more than twenty months ago. "She says if d'e war ends soon, d'ey'll be coming for Christmas."

Hermann nodded his head but felt compelled to interject a disclaimer. "Problem is, even after the war ends, I don't think gasoline rationing will be lifted overnight. We might be getting our miserable allotment of gallons per week for a long time to come."

Gertrude frowned at him. "Well, Ross is an engineer, so I'm sure he knows more about it d'an we do."

"Maybe you're right, Mutter. I do hope you're right." Hermann looked at Nora and shook his head, as if to say, "See what I have to put up with?"

Once Hermann finished gathering all the groceries from Nora's list, she paid him, and he packed the goods in a tidy cardboard box. "Would you like to have Russell deliver these for you?" he asked.

"If you don't mind. I have another errand to run this morning."

Gertrude laughed. "D'at'll suit Russell just fine. He always mentions d'e tip you give him."

"It's only a half-dollar."

"Most folks just give him a dime or fifteen cents," Hermann told her. "And sometimes nothing at all."

"I think that's just shameful—for a hard-working boy like that."

Hermann shrugged his shoulders, philosophically, and said, "Well, that just goes to show you." Exactly what, he never divulged, but Nora nodded her head in agreement just the same.

As for Russell Mimms, he knew to find the Browers' key in its usual hiding spot. He would let himself in, place the chilled items in the refrigerator, and lock back up before leaving. Four bits was a hefty tip, to be sure, but Nora appreciated the reliable service. She also felt a little sorry for Russell, who was simple-minded and nearly deaf. He could use the extra spending money. Few merchants besides the Moeks would hire him, though he did work for Trautschold's while the grocery store was being rebuilt after the fire.

Nora was particularly grateful for young Russell on days like this, when she was planning to go directly from her grocery shopping to another engagement on the opposite side of town. She drove the automobile today after accepting an invitation from Paolina Coletti to please drop by and have a talk with Giulia. The topic of conversation was not specified, but Nora could guess easily enough.

◆ ◆ ◆

The Colettis lived a good distance away, southwest of the Baylor campus, and Nora Brower had not been to their house before. All she had to direct her there was a street address, so she was careful to check the mailbox before knocking. It read "Francesco Coletti." That was the correct family name, all right, and she knew that Paolina and her husband had been estranged for years but unable to seek divorce.

Giulia must have heard the automobile drive up and park because she opened the front door even before the visitor had a chance to ring the doorbell or knock. "Hello, Mrs. Brower," she said. "Won't you come in?" She was friendly but unsmiling. She was also very pretty, as attractive as any starlet a movie producer could hope to discover. Nora had not seen Giulia in almost two years, so she had forgotten how truly beautiful the girl was. One quick glance was sufficient time to remind her.

Standing in the entryway to greet her was Paolina, who asked at once whether she had heard the news. Nora replied that yes, indeed she had, adding that her fondest hope was that this terrible new weapon would shorten the war dramatically and hasten the homecoming.

"Amen to that," Paolina said. Then, with the assistance of her walking cane, she showed their caller to the living room. "Would you like for me to bring you some coffee, Mrs. Brower?" she asked.

"Oh, yes, please. I usually have another cup about now. That would be nice."

But Giulia had a different idea. "Mamma, do you think we could drink it at the kitchen table instead of in here?"

"Whatever for, child?"

"I have my reasons—that is, if it's okay with you." The girl seemed oddly listless or withdrawn.

"Well, I suppose so. Is that all right with you, Mrs. Brower?"

"Certainly."

"Oh, and get out the cinnamon muffins too, 'Bina. They're in the breadbox."

Nora held up her hand. "None for me, thanks."

The three ladies seated themselves at the square kitchen table, Nora and Giulia across from each other, and Paolina at a side between them. Very soon, less than a minute after the hot coffee arrived, so did the name of Stephen Brower. It came from the uncharacteristically pouting lips of Giulia, who wished to know how the sailor was doing.

"Oh, Steve's quite well," Nora told her, "as far as I can gather from his letters. They don't go into great detail, you know. Just a little of this and a little of that."

"Especially a little of that," Giulia said. The sharp edge to her voice took both of the other women by surprise, as did the vigorous manner in which she stirred the coffee.

Paolina sensed that it might be best to get right to the point. "As you know," she told Nora, "your boarder came to see us a few weeks ago."

"Yes. Hannah was determined to come, and I couldn't talk her out of it."

"We do want to thank you for telephoning ahead, to say she was on her way."

"I can't take credit for that. Hannah asked me to call you. Whatever you may think of her, she's not the sort who would ambush you without fair warning."

Giulia flashed an ironic grin. "We exchanged letters."

"Yes, I know, dear," Nora said. "I'm truly sorry all of this happened."

"Have you ever told Steve about the mix-up?" Paolina asked.

"No, ma'am, I'm afraid I haven't. I thought it would mortify him."

"There seems to be a lot of that going around these days," the girl added. "I've had a bad case of it myself."

Fearing that her daughter's Italian spirit was on the rise, Paolina sought to dampen it. "Now, 'Bina, please let's be civil about this. After all, it was nobody's fault."

Tears of humiliation began forming in Giulia's eyes. "Well, if nothing else," she told Nora, "it certainly has been a golden opportunity to see what your Stephen really thinks of us. That is one thing Hannah and I have in common."

Nora smiled kindly at the girl. "I can understand why you might say such a thing, dear, but it was an honest mistake. Don't you see that?" She glanced at Giulia's mother. "As a matter of fact, I happen to think that both of the letters were very sweet."

Giulia jumped to her feet. "You read them? You saw the letters?" Her mouth was trembling.

"Hannah wanted my advice," Nora told her, "so she showed me the one intended for you. No one else ever saw it, I promise you."

"So much for privacy," the girl said. She sat back down in a huff, arms folded.

"And then, of course, Hannah read me her own letter the night she got it back from you."

"Of course! I'm surprised she didn't hire someone to read them on the radio."

Nora took a sip of coffee and turned to Paolina. "If you don't mind my asking, just why is it that you wanted me to come over here?"

The woman blushed with embarrassment. "Giulia has been very hurt by this whole episode, and I thought it might be a good thing to talk it over and clear the air." She stirred some cream into her cup. "By the way, how is your Hannah taking it?"

Nora had to laugh. "Oh, nothing much bothers that girl for very long. She's a pretty tough cookie—too tough really. I think she's forgotten all about it. In fact, Hannah wrote him another letter within a couple of days, although I'm sure she didn't mention the mishap."

Giulia was expressionless, unimpressed by this recitation of Hannah's sterling traits. "So, does Steve prefer tough girls or sensitive ones?" she asked.

"Giulia!" her mother said. "What an unladylike thing to say."

But Nora took no offense. "That's all right, Mrs. Coletti. I really can't blame her for being so upset. I would be too. It cannot be very pleasant to have your personal correspondence become public property."

By now, Giulia's attitude had softened quite noticeably, to such an extent that she felt confident enough to pose an even more intimate question. She asked their guest, "What could I do to make Steve go absolutely head-over-heels crazy over me?"

Nora's eyes widened, and she leaned back in her chair to think for a moment. "Goodness, that's the sixty-four-dollar question, isn't it?" Now she understood why Giulia wanted to sit face-to-face instead of on the sofa.

"I hate to put you on the spot like this," the girl added, "but I do want to give myself a fighting chance."

Nora chuckled. "That's pretty sneaky, trying to collect classified information from the boy's own mother."

"Well, I'm sure you and Hannah talk about him sometimes."

"Yes, sometimes we do—I must admit."

"What do you tell her?"

"To be perfectly frank, she's never really come right out and asked such a thing."

Paolina smiled with a mother's indulgence and said, "Few people would."

That brought a giggle from Nora, who decided to be open in her response. "I suppose I would advise you, above all else, to be honest and to just be yourself. Steve is very adept at detecting phoniness, particularly in a girl. He can spot it a mile away. Thousands of miles away if he's 'somewhere in the Pacific'."

Giulia nodded her head. "How often should I write to him, so I don't become a pest?"

"I don't know. Maybe once a week would be about right. He probably has more time to write to you now, with the war winding down and all."

"One more thing, Mrs. Brower. Do you happen to have any old letters that Steve has written to you? I would like to know as much about him as I can. Your other son used to bring some of them to me, but he stopped doing that a long time ago."

Nora squinted at the girl. "First, please tell me why it's an invasion of privacy for me to see your letter but perfectly fine for you to have a look at mine."

"Simple. A letter from a boy to a girl obviously would have more juicy stuff in it than a letter from a boy to his mother. They're two completely different things."

Nora could hardly argue with that line of reasoning, so she relented. "Okay, I'll see what I can find. Hannah has read most of the letters anyway, second-hand, so I suppose it would be the decent thing to do. I'll have Wes drop them by in a few days."

"Thank you, Mrs. Brower. I really do appreciate this, and I hope it isn't too much of an imposition."

A darkness crept over Nora's face, something between sadness and guilt. "To tell you the truth, dear, I do feel like I'm betraying Hannah, who's almost like a daughter to me. I'm sure she would resent my helping you, in any form or fashion. That's just human nature."

"But if she's seen the letters ..."

"I know, I know. I'm just trying to be as impartial as I can, but good intentions do not change the fact that Hannah would consider it an act of disloyalty on my part—like going over to the enemy camp." Nora swallowed her last drop of coffee and scooted her chair away from the table. "Still, I said I'd do it, and I will. I think both you and Hannah are lovely young ladies, and Steve should feel very fortunate to have either one of you as a friend."

Paolina reached over and patted the visitor's hand. "Well, we really do appreciate your thoughtfulness in this whole affair. You've been more than kind."

"That's quite all right," Nora said, and she stood up to leave. But then another thought crossed her mind. "And what about the sergeant?" she asked.

"Archie? Oh, he's back from the Far East," Giulia told her. "He was injured and won a Purple Heart."

"You were engaged to be married at one time, weren't you?"

"Never officially. In his mind, mostly."

"Do you have any plans for the future?"

"Just to *not* see each other for a while," the girl said. "Isn't that romantic?"

When Nora looked puzzled, Paolina offered an explanation. "They've decided to go their separate ways and let the future take care of itself."

Giulia nodded her head. "Archie wants to leave Waco as soon as he can, once the war is over."

"Why?"

"I don't know how he would answer that, but if you ask me, it's to get away from his mother."

"Will you be staying in touch with him?"

"Not seriously—just as good friends. Otherwise, I wouldn't be writing to Steve. Archie is in my past, although I'm not really sure he accepts that."

A little bewildered, Nora turned to Paolina. "Was our generation this confusing?"

"Probably, but that was so long ago I can't recall."

◆　　　◆　　　◆

Dear Lizzie,

Just a quick note to tell you that I am back on American soil. Lots of my buddies went to Istres, France, but for some reason I was sent west instead of east. This man's Army works in mysterious ways, but I'm not complaining. The passage from Southampton to New York was very boring, but I must say that is better than dodging U-boats like we did earlier in the war. Our ship was kind of cramped—definitely not as luxurious as the Queen Elizabeth or Queen Mary would have been. The Atlantic is like a big lake now, though I wouldn't be surprised if there were still a few German subs hanging around, just for old time's sake. Drop me a line whenever you have a minute or two. Now that I am stateside again, mail delivery should be a lot faster—almost like a regular conversation. I hope you are enjoying the summer. Loafing around sure does beat schoolwork, doesn't it? As I recall, your birthday is coming up pretty soon. Wow, seventeen! I still have your pretty snapshot in my wallet, and it has kept me company for all these months. Write when you can—that is, if you haven't forgotten all about your Army pal.

Love, Danny

Hello, Danny!

How nice it was to receive your letter. That is swell that you are back in the States. Did you have fun in Jolly Old England? Did you drive on the left side of the road like a good Tommy? Could your brand of English be understood by the natives? Even Americans can hardly converse with Mississippians! (ha ha) You are right—my seventeenth birthday is next month, September 11th. By then I will be a junior at Waco High School. The younger of my brothers graduated in May and is waiting for Uncle Sam to call him for duty. Although the war is nearly over, I'm pretty sure they're still drafting men for military service. Wes is thinking about going to Baylor, if he's not already wearing an Army uniform when classes start. Glad you're still carrying my picture. I sent you a small one so you would not be tempted to put it on a dartboard. I hope to see you again one of these days—or months—or years. Have fun in New York City. There's even more to do there than in Waco!!!

Love, Lizzie

Hi, Lizzie.

Thanks for writing! It looks like military life is winding down for yours truly, now that Hitler is burning in hell and the Japs are about to throw in the towel (thanks to the Atom Bomb). It sure will seem strange to take off this olive-drab costume for the last time. Word is that we may have to stay in the service for several months after the war ends. I may be assigned to a unit in occupied Europe, as part of the reconstruction effort. (Normally, such "classified" information would have been snipped by the censor, but he has been much more relaxed since V-E Day. If there is not a hole cut in this paper, I guess it got through all right!) My grandmother died in Indianola, but I was not able to attend the funeral because of a training session—just to keep us busy. She was 76. One of our guys brought back a golden retriever from England. "Pep" is no longer a puppy but almost full-grown. Send me another picture of yourself, if you can. The one in my wallet has seen better days, and I would like to "retire" it from active duty before it disintegrates completely. Something in a bathing suit would be nice... "Woo-wooooo" (wolf whistle).

 Love, Danny

Dear Danny,

 Your two letters in rapid succession are spoiling me—almost like talking with each other in person, heh? You will notice that the requested photograph was not in this envelope. All that was in it (besides this paper) was one warm kiss. Did you catch it, or did it escape? I could not locate a decent swimsuit picture of me. All of them were too daring to pass through the U.S. Mails. I'll try to find something else, not quite as explosive! My brother, Wes, is still a civilian. He thought his number would be called by now, but so far that has not happened. I suppose he will become a Baylor Bear instead. Registration for B.U. freshmen will be two days after my birthday. I'm sure he will major in Radio, while continuing to work at the local station. His classes should not conflict with the daytime serial that he is in. I am getting quite good at the piano these days, so maybe there is something to be said for this novel idea of practicing. Yesterday I played a Brahms intermezzo all the way through without a flub. If ever you are within a thousand miles of Waco, Tex., be sure to stop at the Brower household. I promise to accompany you to the picture show. (Aren't I rude—inviting myself on a date like this?) I am still working at the filling station, but my closest friend there has quit to get married. Her husband-to-be is a sergeant at (guess!) Blackland Army Air Field. Remember that place? Write soon. This is fun.

 Love, Lizzie
 (p.s., a second Atom Bomb today.)

Hi, Lizzie.

 I am still in a holding unit "somewhere in the northeast" (i.e., N.Y. City). Not sure how long we'll remain here, as they are running out of busy work to keep us occupied. My pal Zolly and I went sightseeing this past weekend, staying overnight in a very cheap hotel. Saw the usual tourist spots: Empire State Building, Statue of Liberty, Times Square, Grant's Tomb, Central Park, Macy's, etc. We went to a Broadway show at the Cort Theatre on Saturday—Fredric March in "A Bell for Adano." Also a doubleheader at the Polo Grounds on Sunday—Giants over Cincinnati, 3-2 and 6-5, with Mel Ott hitting a homer in both. (He's the Giants' player-manager, in case you're interested.) There are lots of military uniforms to be seen in the city, so we felt right at home. Interesting to read that your brother will be going to Baylor. Doesn't that girl who lives with you go there too? Is that what you plan to do after you leave WHS? It looks like the Japs are about down for the count, and then it'll be the first peacetime for us in nearly four years. That kiss you mailed to me must have flown out of the envelope, so you still owe me one (with interest). About the photograph—an explosive one will be just fine, thanks!

    Love, Danny

Dearest Danny. (That has a nice ring to it!)

    There was no "explosive" snapshot to send, so I have enclosed my sophomore class photograph instead. I'm afraid it's not very _ _ _ _ because I appear to be about 8 years old! (It looks like I should be holding a doll or maybe licking a lollipop.) Sorry, but that is the best I could do on quick notice. I guess you'll just have to show up in person and get the real thing instead. Awwww! Now that the Japs have surrendered, will you be getting out of the service soon, or does that 6-month rule still apply? Your trip to New York City sounds exciting. The tallest structure I've ever been inside is the Amicable Life Insurance Building, right here in Waco. I'm scared of heights, though, so probably the Empire State Building would cause me to scream until I was rescued by a handsome soldier. (Any takers?) I don't care too much for baseball, but attending a Broadway show seems like it would be fun. Speaking of entertainment, Tuesday night I went with a girlfriend to see a picture called "Best Foot Forward." We both thought it was very good and think you would like it too. Did you catch the kiss I put in this envelope? No again? Well, then I owe you two of them. Keep counting!

    Love, Lizzie

Hi, Lizzie!

    It looks like I may be assigned to a base in either Louisiana or South Dakota. If it turns out to be Barksdale Field, I may just swing over to central Texas and see you. On the other hand, if it's Rapid City A.A.B., I think you'll agree that is too far for a weekend pass! Even though the Japs are finished now, it looks like we men in uniform will stay dressed like this for the foreseeable future—maybe about six months. If nothing else, at least that will give me some time to decide what's next for my life. Pearl Harbor seems ages ago, but it was only 44 months. Hard to believe! So you're scared of heights, huh? That's too bad because I was planning to carry you up the side of the Empire State Building like King Kong did with Fay Wray. The photo you sent of yourself is a cute one, but you're right, it's not as _ _ _ _ as it could be. You can do better than that!!! I haven't seen "Best Foot Forward," but I'll keep an eye out for it. Say hello to your mom and brother for me. I keep forgetting to ask you to do that.

Love, Danny

Dearest Danny!

It is SO hard to believe that the war is finally over. Lots of civilians, including me, will not know how to act anymore. I wonder how long the rationing will continue, and the slow speed limit, and the bond drives, and the Central War Time, and the draft. Speaking of the draft, I think we have figured out why my brother was not taken. Don't quote me on this, but it could be that he has a "friend in high places." We found out that the man who gave us the piano just happens to be very close to not one but two people on the McLennan County Draft Board! Wes was willing to go, but he just never got the call. That being the case, it looks like Baylor University is almost a certainty for him now. Freshman registration is on September 13. As for your situation, on a purely selfish basis I hope you're stationed in Louisiana because wouldn't a trip to Waco, Texas, be a nice way to spend your weekend leave? Not so incidentally, by the time you come here, I will have turned seventeen years old. Maybe my mother would accept our age difference better than when I was fourteen! Oh, and when you arrive in Waco, be sure to drive on over to the northeast corner of Eleventh and Washington for your gasoline needs. I hear that a gorgeous attendant works there, and she would be delighted to wait on you. It will be VERY friendly service!

All My Love, Lizzie

◆　　◆　　◆

It seemed the only sensible thing to do. That was what Hannah kept telling herself, and sometimes she almost believed it.

She had informed no one of her decision, and for good reason—even she did not know about it until Tuesday night, when the unsettling thought began to take root as she closed her eyes for bed. She bolted upright and was unable to fall asleep for another two hours. Fervent prayer did nothing to change her mind.

If anything, it seemed to encourage her leap of faith. Clearly, this was the right choice. Yes, now she was quite sure of it.

Accorded the dubious honor of becoming the very first person to know was Mr. Hinckley, her immediate supervisor at Crawford-Austin Manufacturing Company. She approached him on her morning break, wondering whether he had a minute or two to discuss something of importance. "Certainly, Miss Lane," he said.

Mr. Hinkley ushered her back to his office, where the noise of heavy machinery was not so pronounced as to drown out all attempts at normal conversation. With a wan smile, he motioned for her to sit down. "Let me guess. You're going to be leaving us."

Hannah was only mildly surprised at his prescience, for he always did seem to have a firm grasp of what she was thinking.

"Coffee?" he asked.

"No, thanks." She sat in the chair opposite his cluttered desk.

"I could see it coming for months, Miss Lane. Anyone with half a brain could honestly say that."

"Really?" Hannah grinned at him. "Then what does that make me? I wasn't aware of it until Tuesday night."

Mr. Hinckley chuckled. "Well, with the war over and your college education in the bag, I suppose there's nothing much to hold you here in Waco. You're an easterner, after all."

"A southerner, if you please!" she said.

"Oh, sorry. Still saluting the Stars and Bars, huh?"

She nodded her head with conviction. "Yes, sir. I was born in Dixie, and I suppose that's where I'll die."

"Waco, Texas, was part of Dixie too, you know. Several Confederate generals came from right here in McLennan County, or so I've been told. This isn't such a bad place for a southerner to live."

"No, that's true enough—but it's not where I'm from." She looked down at her folded hands. "I don't know. Maybe I just feel the need to go home. I've been away for over two years."

All trace of levity now gone, Mr. Hinckley stared at the girl with admiration. "You've been a model employee, and we'll be sorry to see you go. Most important of all, of course, you've performed a great service for your country. If they passed out medals to civilians, you would be one of the first people to get one, I think."

"Thank you, sir. I was just doing my job, and I got paid for it."

"Now, don't sell yourself short. Lots of able-bodied people chose to sit out this war. Not only did you hold down a rather demanding job, but you also went full-time to a major university and came out with a degree." His voice quavered ever so slightly as he told her, "You are quite an extraordinary young woman."

That was the closest Hannah had ever seen her boss come to displaying genuine emotion. Usually he was so stiff, formal, and impersonal in his dealings with other people.

"I appreciate your understanding," she said. "You know ... allowing me to work around my Baylor schedule."

A little embarrassed, Mr. Hinckley cleared his throat. "Maybe this would be a good chance for me to own up to something I've never told you. Those flexible hours of yours were not my idea at all. As a matter of fact, they went against everything I ever stood for as a shop foreman. It was Pat Neff and Dr. Tidwell who helped me see the error of my ways." Then he added, "And they were right, of course."

Hannah glanced at her wristwatch and said, "I guess it's about time I got back to work, don't you think?"

"Yes, I do, miss. Short-timer or not, the fact remains that you are on the clock." He grinned to let her know he was only teasing. And that, in Hannah's recollection, was about the nearest he ever came to telling a joke. "How much longer will you be with us, then?" he asked.

"I was planning to catch a train on September 8, which would be one more full week. Is that too little notice?"

"No, no, not at all," Mr. Hinckley said. He rose to escort her to the door. "As you might imagine, we'll be cutting our work force down considerably, now that war contracts are a thing of the past."

"In other words, I'm just one less person you'll have to terminate."

He smiled at her forthright attitude. "I suppose you could put it that way, Miss Lane. But I don't think your neck would ever land on the Crawford-Austin chopping block. You're one employee I will hate to see leave—and I mean that sincerely."

"Thank you, sir."

"If you ever change your mind ..."

"Thank you." She walked out his door and stopped. "You're a tough boss, but also a very fair one, and I respect you for showing such integrity. All the workers feel that way, although they might not come right out and say it."

"I consider that to be the highest of compliments," he told her, and they shook hands. "How did your landlady take the news?"

"I haven't told her yet," Hannah said, "and I dread the thought of doing it. That's what I have to look forward to tonight."

◆　　◆　　◆

Now that the family's insistent feline was fed, Nora was finally able to turn her attention to human food. She was standing in the kitchen, preparing dinner, when her daughter appeared with a question that seemed awfully important to her. "Which would you pick, Mother? We can't make up our minds." She had that morning's newspaper opened to the movie page. "Corky doesn't know or won't say, and I want to get your opinion before giving him an answer."

Laying down her stirring spoon, Nora had to cock her head to see the choices, so Elizabeth handed her the paper. "Well, *Topper* is an older movie that's been around for several years. It's very funny. *The Navy Way* ... hmm, Corky would probably like that better than you. It's a war picture, of course. *The Great John L* is supposed to be a very good biography of the famous boxer, so that might be fine. What else, uh ...?" She let her eyes scan to the right, across the page. "*Incendiary Blonde*. Now, there's a good picture to see. You'd both like that. It's the story of Texas Guinan—and she was from Waco."

Elizabeth had a doubtful look on her face. "Why would they make a movie about somebody from Waco?"

"Well, that's a nice thing to say!" Nora stifled a laugh. "Actually, she was born in Waco, but then she led a very colorful life in New York City during the Roaring Twenties. I've heard that Betty Hutton is excellent in it."

Elizabeth was not impressed. "What about the others?"

"*Dangerous Passage* and *The Singing Sheriff*. That's a double feature at the Crystal. I've never heard of anybody in that first one. Oh, Bob Crosby's in the western. That's Bing's younger brother, you know. I doubt if you and Corky want to sit through two movies, do you? And watch a singing cowboy picture?"

"No, I don't think so." The girl coaxed the newspaper down a bit, so she could see it too. "All right. I'll tell him either *The Great John L* at the Orpheum or *Incendiary Blonde* at the Waco. Knowing him, he'll probably choose the boxing picture."

"Don't be so sure. The other one probably has lots of beautiful dancing girls in it."

"Hah! Corky's only interested in football—and, of course, tank warfare. Honestly, do you know of any other kid in the world who has a picture of General George S. Patton tacked to the inside of his bedroom door?"

Nora was surprised, but for an entirely different reason than her daughter expected. "And what, may I ask, were you doing inside Corky's bedroom?"

"Oh, Mother, please! He was just showing me his hamsters. Don't worry. His mom was right there with us."

Elizabeth did not go out on dates as often as one might imagine, given her attractiveness. She was just not very interested in any of the high school boys she knew. Perhaps it was her years of volunteering at the USO, associating with older men, that ruined her appreciation for youngsters her own age. Her peers seemed so childish and immature, compared to the soldiers, sailors, and airmen with whom she was acquainted. And these servicemen came from all over the country too—exciting places sometimes, much more intriguing than her oh-so-familiar hometown.

Elizabeth's companion for the night was Lukas "Corky" Yarbrough, an undersized but scrappy offensive and defensive tackle on the football team. Though only a C+ student, he certainly did not act unintelligent, so maybe his disappointing grades were merely a consequence of failing to apply himself in the classroom—not so unusual for a football player, she figured. Corky was a rather nice boy, and Elizabeth was flattered to be asked out, but somehow she could not get very enthused. She wanted more. She wanted her escort to be in uniform—someone like the man who saved her life, for instance.

The Browers were eating a little earlier than usual, in order to allow Elizabeth ample time to get fixed up before Corky came knocking at the door. Wesley and

Hannah, in fact, had just arrived home from their respective jobs. Wesley, after kissing his mother, went directly into the living room, plopped down on the floor, and began listening to "Terry and the Pirates" on KGKO. Nora noticed that he was a bit blue these days, now that his pretty friend from school was no longer on the radio show with him. From what she could gather, the young lady's father—a high ranking officer in the AAF—had been transferred to Australia, so she and her mother went back to Georgia. She seemed like a sweet girl.

When the boarder, Hannah Lane, arrived home, she waved cheerfully to Nora and then went up to change out of her dirty work clothes. Crawford-Austin supplied her with four sets of coveralls, which was a fortunate thing because she definitely could not wear them more than one time apiece without a thorough washing. She sometimes quipped that they could walk by themselves.

Upon returning downstairs, Hannah kept her landlady company for a while, but she was not quite her normal, chipper self. Nora attributed this to the fact that another day had gone by without a letter from her father in Mount Airy. No doubt she was worried about him, for his health was none too stable in recent years.

Throughout the meal, Hannah smiled and was pleasant enough, nodding when appropriate and laughing when something humorous was said, but clearly her thoughts were elsewhere. She could not answer the simplest question without having the person repeat it. Normally such a hearty eater, she only picked at her food. Once, she began to say something but then thought better of it and mumbled, "Never mind."

Ever the watchful amateur nurse, Nora turned to her and asked, "Are you feeling all right, dear?" She would have reached over and felt the girl's forehead, were she not all the way across the table from her.

"Oh, yes, ma'am," Hannah said. She looked at the three of them. "Only ..."

Just then, Elizabeth drank the last of her iced tea, daintily wiped her mouth with a napkin, and requested to be excused from the table.

"Certainly, dear," her mother said. "That new blouse is lying on the bed."

"Me too, Mom?" Wesley scooted his chair back.

Nora nodded her head. "Yes, you too."

"May I say something before you two go?" Hannah asked. Brother and sister turned around, staring at her. She cleared her throat.

"Sit down for just a minute," Nora told them. "The both of you." She laid her fork on the plate and looked at the boarder.

"I'm afraid I have an unpleasant announcement to make," Hannah said, "and I thought it might be easier if I had you all together like this." She tried to smile. "Seems I was wrong. It's still not very easy at all."

Wesley and Elizabeth returned to their chairs, glancing at each other in confusion.

"I've been a guest in your home for more than two years," Hannah said, "much longer than any of us probably expected when I suddenly showed up on your doorstep. You've made me feel welcome and treated me swell, and I appreciate that more than you'll ever know or that I could ever express." Her voice was becoming more emotional than she intended, so she paused and took a deep breath. "But the war is over now, my job will be cut back, and I've finished my studies at Baylor." Again, she cleared her throat. "You can probably guess what I'm going to say. It's just that the time has come for me to leave you and go back to North Carolina, where I really belong."

The Browers sat in stunned silence for a moment, not knowing quite how to react.

Then Elizabeth stood up, circled the table, and put her arm around Hannah's shoulders. "No! You absolutely cannot go," she said. "You're one of our family."

Nora agreed. "That *is* how we feel about you, dear. You're just like my daughter—and their sister."

"This is where you belong," Wesley added. "It wouldn't be the same around here without you."

Genuinely touched by their sentiment, Hannah could only respond, "You're not making this any easier for me, you know."

From the boarder, Nora's gaze turned instead to her children, and she told them, "Wes and Lizzie, you run along now, so I can talk to Hannah."

As they reluctantly left the room, all the while staring back at their "sister," Nora stepped around the table and sat next to Hannah, squeezing her hand. "Are you absolutely sure this is what you want?"

"Oh, I know this is awful of me, springing my surprise on you without any warning, but I only recently made up my mind."

"Have you thought it over carefully ... every possible effect that this decision could have on your life?"

"How do you mean?"

Nora frowned. "Well, for example ..."

"Stephen Collins Brower, for example?" Hannah asked.

"Maybe."

"Sure, I've thought about him a lot."

"If you leave, you may never see him again. Have you considered that?"

"Yes, I have."

"And yet you're still determined to go?"

Hannah thought for a moment. "Don't take this wrong, Mrs. B., but I guess you could say that Steve is just a dream of mine. He's not even a real person to me. I hardly know him. We talked for a while one morning when he couldn't sleep, that's all."

"Well, you're very real to him."

"I am?" She studied Nora's face.

"Whatever you did that morning, it certainly made a favorable impression on him."

Hannah laughed. "We didn't do anything but talk—and I was half asleep most of the time. It's a wonder he even remembers my name."

"Oh, he remembers much more than just your name."

The girl's smile faded. "He also remembers other people's names, of course—and swimsuits. And goodbye kisses."

"Now, Hannah ... Don't make too much of that."

"Why shouldn't I? If you ask me, Steve seems to be spellbound by that Giulia Coletti." She frowned. "And, you know, I really can't say as I blame him. She's a gorgeous girl. Anyone can see that, and it sure didn't escape Steve's notice."

"Well, he's only human, after all." When Hannah gave her a questioning look, Nora smiled, very kindly. "Isn't a lonely sailor entitled to be interested in more than one girl at a time? I wouldn't be too hard on him, not just now. Not while he's overseas, sowing those wild oats in his mind. Who knows what goes through a young man's head?"

"Look, Mrs. B., I guess what it comes down to is that I'm just not interested in becoming serious with Steve or anyone else at the present time. I like him, sure, but ..." She pulled out a pack of chewing gum. "Want some?"

"No, thank you."

Hannah unwrapped a stick of Wrigley's Spearmint and put it in her mouth, enjoying the initial surge of flavor. The foil now went for trash instead of salvage.

"I've prayed long and hard for the past few days," she said, "and I'm firmly convinced that going back to Mount Airy is what the Lord would have me to do."

"Then, by all means, you should do it."

"I mean, isn't it kind of strange? College ended, and the war ended—almost simultaneously—and now there's nothing to keep me here any longer. On the other hand, my father needs me, and his church needs me. That's the difference. Despite his age and delicate health, he pastors a growing congregation, and that is the work which means so much to me."

"Have you written to him about your plans?"

"I sent him a note on Wednesday."

"He'll be delighted that you're coming back."

She grinned, nodding her head.

"But we'll miss you, Hannah. Like Wes said, it just won't be the same around here anymore."

"Oh, you'll get another boarder."

"You're much more than that to us."

♦   ♦   ♦

Up and down the dial, every radio station was carrying news reports of the formal Japanese surrender. There were even some "actualities," brief audio recordings from the ceremony itself, that were distributed to the worldwide press by a communication ship, *USS Ancon*. Wesley listened, as he drove northeast along State Highway 31.

USS Missouri was anchored in Tokyo Bay, and among the thousands aboard the battleship was an eleven-man Japanese delegation, headed by foreign minister Mamoru Shigemitsu and General Yoshijiro Umezu, the army chief of staff. This pair stepped forward—the top-hatted foreign minister limping on his prosthetic leg—and signed the Instrument of Surrender. Soon thereafter, representatives of the nine Allied navies affixed their signatures as well. General Douglas MacArthur represented the combatant nations that had been at war against Japan. Altogether, the ceremony lasted a mere twenty-three minutes, and it concluded when General MacArthur solemnly proclaimed, "Let us pray that peace will now be restored to the world, and that God will preserve it always. These proceedings are closed."

So a car radio, passing through desolate countryside, informed Wesley that the horrific war had come to an end. He was on his second trip to Axtell, more confident than before that he knew where the Glynns' house was located, and he navigated the Brower automobile as if he had resided in the hinterland all his life. No one was there to greet him, but he could see a cloud of dust in the distance, the telltale sign of a heavy piece of farm equipment at work. He parked at the side of the house, rather than in front of it, careful not to block Rob's preferred tractor route from field to barn. As he walked toward the residence, he could hear cows mooing and chickens clucking, and two or three noisy mockingbirds screamed at him from overhead. Mounting the weather-beaten steps of the wooden porch, he knocked on the screen door and waited ... and waited ... and waited some more.

It was Jillian Glynn who finally answered and invited him to come inside. "Sorry to make you wait all that time." She was smiling brightly, despite her apologetic tone. "I was pouring some corn bread batter in a couple of pans and could not stop in midstream."

Wesley felt that a judicious fib was in order. "That's all right. It wasn't long," he told her.

Jillian explained to him that her daughter was still in the process of getting ready. "Pippa is slower than anyone I know to change her clothes. You'd think she was competing for Miss America."

As usual, there was an apron tied around the woman's waist. In fact, Wesley was unable to recall ever seeing Mrs. Glynn when she was not wearing that kitchen accouterment, except when she sat down to eat and, obviously, at his graduation in Waco Hall. Whether she was cooking the food or washing the dishes, that apron was her constant companion, and she seemed to wear it as a badge of honor, perfectly adjusted to her role as farm wife.

Pointing toward a comfortable-looking chair, Jillian invited the young man to have a seat. "I'll bring you a glass of iced tea. Pippa should be here shortly."

"Thanks, Mrs. Glynn." He sat down and began flipping through an issue of *The Saturday Evening Post*, the current one, with illustrator Albert Staehle's whimsical cover art of a dog weighing itself on scales. The tea Jillian offered him tasted wonderful, suspiciously reminiscent of honest-to-goodness real sugar. That commodity was difficult to come by these days, with strict rationing controls still very much in place.

Every minute or two, Wesley looked up from the magazine to see whether Pippa had come into the room, but so far she had not. Her mother was right—she did take a substantial while to get ready. Perhaps he should feel flattered that she wanted to get everything just right for him. To hear her mother talk, however, it did not sound as if this delay was necessarily attributable to his presence. Maybe Pippa liked to make a grand entry for dramatic effect.

Wesley was enjoying another leisurely sip of tea when, suddenly and without warning, two hands shot over his eyes from behind, and a voice shouted, "Guess who!" It so startled the guest that a generous portion of iced tea spilled down his shirtfront, the resulting chill of which caused him to yell, "AAAEEE!" And that, in turn, took the girl by such surprise that she screamed like a child on the playground.

"Oh, Wes, honey, I'm so sorry," Pippa said when she saw what had happened. "I couldn't tell that you had anything in your hand."

He laid the now half-empty glass on the coaster and forced a grin. What else could he do? She looked like an angel standing there in her blouse and slacks, so natural and pretty, and he instantly forgot about the cold shower and stained shirt. Forgotten, too, were her hasty words of regret—all but one sweet term of endearment that still resonated in his ear: "honey."

"Mother! Please bring a couple of towels in here," the girl shouted. "We've had an accident."

Jillian took charge of the situation immediately. In no time whatsoever, the mess was tidied up, she produced one of Rob's clean shirts for the visitor to wear, and Wesley's own shirt was soaking in a pan of soapy water.

When Wesley returned to the living room after changing, he was decked out in a red, checkered garment that resembled something Smiley Burnette might wear while eating beans from a tin plate around Gene Autry's campfire. Meanwhile, Jillian confronted Pippa with a perfectly sensible admonition: "Let that teach you a lesson, young lady. In the future, kindly think before you do such a foolish thing."

Pippa giggled. "Aw, but that makes life so dull."

Jillian turned away, probably smiling, and she shook her head as she walked back to the kitchen. "What are we going to do with this girl of ours?"

That day, much to Pippa's chagrin, Wesley was accorded the great honor of ringing the dinner bell—summoning her father in from the fields. The tenderfoot must have handled his assignment properly, for not even five minutes after his ear-splitting racket, an approaching tractor could be discerned from afar. "I hate that noisy triangle," Pippa said. "It makes us sound like Ma and Pa Kettle." To Wesley, though, the iron alarm seemed like a very practical instrument for long-distance communication. Much less demeaning than calling the hogs, for instance.

Sunday dinner proved to be another sumptuous repast, and again Wesley could not help wondering how the Glynns managed to offer such a generous spread while grappling with the economic challenges that—despite the arrival of peace—continued to prevail unchecked. Good household management was the key, he decided, coupled with the advantageous fact that so much of a farm family's produce was homegrown. Then again, perhaps Sunday was their only such feast of the week, or to carry the argument one step further, maybe just those Sundays with an invited guest. Whatever the explanation, Wesley savored the plentiful fried chicken, corn on the cob (with real butter), black-eyed peas, fried and breaded okra, sweet potatoes, hot corn bread (with real butter), and pecan pie.

Allowing his mind to drift back fourteen weeks, Wesley recalled the first time he shared Sunday dinner with the Glynns. Then it was Jillian herself who washed the dishes, and Rob dried. Today, however, Pippa volunteered her services as washer, and she deputized Wesley for the drying duties. This unselfish gesture gave Jillian a well-deserved period of rest, after having spent more than two laborious hours in the hot kitchen. In gratitude, she loaned Pippa her precious apron, and the girl looked cute in it, almost like a genuine housewife.

♦　　♦　　♦

In central Texas, unlike more moderate climes to the north, early September was not so far removed from the height of summer. Accordingly, the four-o'clock temperature in Axtell had risen to a parching ninety-seven degrees. And yet, whether by design or blind architectural good luck, the Glynns' horse barn was quite tolerable inside—warm but not brutally hot—so Pippa allowed Wesley to observe as she invested a half-hour in washing down the shiny coats of Rocco and Betty. "I rode each of them in the cool of the morning, before church," she told him, "but they could stand some more exercise. See how fat she's getting?" Pippa patted the ample flank of Betty, and Wesley nodded his head in faithful support of her diagnosis. In truth, of course, he would not have been able to distinguish a fat horse from a trim one, were it not for the girl's prompting. But she did not necessarily have to know that.

"Well, shall we?" she asked.

"Shall we what?"

"Go for a short ride. What about it?"

"Gee, I don't know. I'm not an *equestrian*, by any stretch of the imagination." He had learned that word just for this occasion, never dreaming that he could actually work it into a conversation. "I'd probably set horsemanship back a century."

"How do you expect to master animal husbandry if you don't give it a try?"

"What's that supposed to mean?"

"A rancher. Someone who works with livestock."

"Who ever said I wanted to become a rancher? I'm a city boy, remember?"

"Pleeeeaaaase." She flashed a pretty smile that made Wesley's heart quicken, and instantly he was powerless to resist. It was as if her beauty cast a paralyzing spell over his better senses. With great reluctance, not to mention profound trepidation, he consented to, as she said, "give it a try." Only Wesley chose to call it "risk his life." First, though, he demanded that Pippa identify for him the more placid of the two beasts. It was Rocco, just the opposite of what he would have guessed. Naturally, Wesley suspected a trick, but being a complete novice in the field of equestrian sport, he was in no position to call her bluff. Okay then, Rocco it was. He certainly hoped the horse's name did not mean "maniacal" or "bloodthirsty" in Italian.

Wesley watched in awe as this slightly built wisp of a young girl tossed a hefty saddle atop each of the wild broncos and pulled tight the girth straps with such practiced skill that his eyes could hardly follow along. Then, after affectionately stroking the horses' forelocks and noses, she secured the headgear, calling out a whole litany of esoteric terminology as she went: crownpiece, throat latch, browband, cheek strap, snaffle strap, noseband, curb bit, curb chain, snaffle bit, curb rein, snaffle rein. This innocent-looking contraption had more moving parts than the Mighty Wurlitzer.

Now that the steeds were standing in noble readiness, Pippa hopped aboard Betty, and Wesley hopped aboard Rocco. Actually, Wesley crawled up Rocco's side wall, grabbed the saddle horn like a drowning man might latch onto a lifesaver, and swung his right leg over a reddish-brown mountain of potentially violent muscular energy. Regardless of how he arrived there, Wesley was poised for some recreational sportsmanship—a graceful bonding, as horse and rider become as one. Off they went, with Pippa and Betty leading their counterpart males in a slow walk, out of the paddock and into the starting gate.

In contrast to the foreboding instructive preparation, the ride itself was something of an anticlimax, and that was just fine with Wesley. Soon it became all too clear that his horse, the fearsome Rocco, would rather walk than trot, and he obviously preferred grazing to either of those more strenuous forms of activity. No question about it—Rocco was definitely a spoiled, lazy horse, though Wesley would never think of suggesting this irreverent possibility to Pippa. Ironically, it was she who later described the gelding as such. As they were returning to the barn, a mere three furlongs out, she said, "He's really quite docile—just a big, overgrown colt. But he does need to get some proper exercise, and I suppose now's as good a time as any."

Suddenly, a mischievous gleam came to her eyes. "I'll race you back to the stable," she shouted. That is when Pippa leaned over and swatted Rocco on the rump, inspiring the surprised animal to break into a gallop. Although Wesley would not have been mistaken for Gary Cooper in the saddle, somehow he secured the reins well enough to stay relatively upright, and that satisfied his first and only objective—to survive. Pippa, aboard Betty, overtook him almost at once, of course, and was waiting for Wesley at the barn when Rocco finally came trotting up to the finish line.

Pippa dismounted, swinging her right leg high and jumping to the ground in a single, fluid motion. Wesley tried to follow suit, but in so doing, he nearly got his left foot caught in the stirrup, and the girl had to cushion his fall.

"Sorry," he told her, ashamed to appear so clumsy. But it surely did feel nice to be cradled in her arms, even if for only as long as it took the girl to save him from breaking his neck.

"Thank you for going riding with me," Pippa said, and she kissed him on the cheek. "If that was your first time ever on a horse, I think you did very well."

Wesley could not, in good conscience, accept such unmerited praise without admitting that he had ridden a horse one other time. "But that was at a carnival," he told her, "and all that horse did was go around in a circle. Or maybe it was a burro."

Pippa laughed. "Well, I think you did fine, and as a token of my appreciation, I'm going to take you to my favorite spot."

He gulped. "The windmill?"

"No, the stock tank."

"I thought the windmill was your favorite spot."

"Well ... it is."

"You can't have more than one favorite spot."

"Why not?"

Wesley could not think of a valid answer.

♦   ♦   ♦

After Pippa saw to her animals' needs, she and Wesley set out for the tank, a hike of nearly two miles in the sweltering heat. By the time they finally arrived, Wesley had worked up a noticeable sweat, and he hoped his clothes were not too disheveled looking. Pippa, on the other hand, seemed as fetching as ever. How do girls manage to stay so fresh?

The two of them spent about a quarter-hour skipping stones. Her best toss was four skips, and his, due to a stronger throwing arm, was five skips. That was quite an achievement in these conditions, considering that the available stones were irregularly shaped, not the smooth projectiles that one might typically encounter at the seashore.

"Gee, you're pretty good," Pippa told him at the completion of their contest. "Did you play baseball?"

"Not in high school. I could field and throw okay but not hit." Perspiration was dripping from his brow, so he wiped it onto the sleeve of his shirt. Too late, he remembered that it was actually Rob Glynn's shirt, not his own.

"You know, I wish they let girls play baseball at school," Pippa said. "I could have made Axtell's team."

Wesley responded with a smirk.

"You don't believe me!" She playfully punched him on the shoulder. "It may interest you to know that I'm very athletic."

"Well, maybe so, but ... a girl playing baseball!"

"There's a whole league of girls who play professional baseball—six teams. Girls can do a lot more things than you give us credit for."

"Such as?"

"Shooting, for instance. My dad's a skeet marksman, and I'm nearly as good."

That appeared to impress the boy, so she continued. "And what about horseback riding?"

Wesley nodded his head. "You seem pretty good to me."

"And running. I could probably beat you in a sprint."

"I don't think so."

"And swimming. I'm very good at that too."

"Same here. Swimming is one of my strongest sports. That and basketball."

Her eyes widened. "Really?"

"Yes, I'm very good at it."

"So, prove it."

"What?"

"Did you bring a swimsuit?" she asked.

Wesley was taken off guard. "No, of course not. Why?"

"Then we'll just have to swim in the nude."

He gaped at her, unable to hide the look of shock on his face. Pippa had issued this bold comment without even the slightest hint of embarrassment, and already she was out of her shoes and socks.

"Are you serious?" he asked.

She grinned at him, unbuttoning her blouse.

Wesley was astonished by her casual attitude. "Have you done this before?"

"Sure, silly. Lots of times." She removed her blouse and laid it neatly upon a rock.

"With other people around?"

"Not usually. A couple of times there was another girl with me." She slipped off her slacks and was now standing before him in nothing but her panties and brassiere. She had an enchanting figure, slight of build but curvaceous too.

"Maybe I could just swim in my underwear," he said.

"Nope. We don't want to get our clothes wet."

"Have you ever done this with a boy?"

She smiled. "Gotten naked?"

"Uh-huh."

"No, but I guess there's a first time for everything."

Very tentatively, Wesley kicked off his shoes and laid them to one side. When he sat down to remove his socks, he noticed that Pippa seemed amused.

"Now, you have to close your eyes while I get in the water," she said. "Promise?"

He stared at her, enjoying the view and in no hurry to answer.

"Do you promise or not?" She was reaching behind her back.

"Okay, I promise," he told her, and he was as good as his word. He did not even sneak a peek, though the temptation was almost unbearable.

A few seconds later, Wesley could hear the sound of splashing water, so he knew that it would be permissible to open his eyes again. The girl was about forty feet away, and only her head was visible above the water's surface.

"All right, Wes, your turn," she shouted.

"Is it cold?"

"Not bad. Actually, quite comfortable."

"Are you treading water or standing on the bottom?"

"It's about ten feet deep out here. There's a very steep drop-off, so be careful." Then she laughed. "And quit stalling too. Don't be so shy."

The boy removed his borrowed shirt and carefully laid it atop the shoes. As he began to unfasten his trousers, he glanced at Pippa again and noticed that she was giggling at him.

"Turn around, please," he shouted to her, and she complied.

Soon, Wesley too had slipped out of his clothes and into the cool water, and it felt very refreshing on a hot summer's day. He trudged along until the tank's bottom descended away from the shore at such a precipitous slope that he was compelled to tread water. Stealthily, he floated toward the girl.

"Is this a man-made lake?" Wesley asked. He figured that a scientific topic was always safe.

She nodded. "It was built as a reservoir, to hold water for the livestock."

"That doesn't sound like it would be very clean." He was now only about fifteen feet away and closing.

"Well, I sure wouldn't drink it, if that's what you mean," she said. "But I think it's fine for wading. I've certainly never gotten sick from it."

Wesley nodded, as clinically as a census taker. "The water feels nice," was all he could think to add, for other things were on his mind. He noticed, for example, that such close proximity tended to do a relatively poor job of concealing whatever was slightly below the surface. When the angles of refracted light were just right, the girl's breasts became quite visible indeed—not that he allowed his eyes to take unfair advantage of the situation. Either Pippa was blissfully unaware of the physics involved, or she did not really care how much he gazed upon her. Whichever the case, it was plain to see that she was not overly self-conscious about her body.

Just then, an odd expression crossed Wesley's face, and he looked down at his side. "Say, do fish ever bump into you? I mean ... I thought I felt something brush against me."

"Yes, they do, pretty often. They're just hungry, I think, searching for something to eat."

He laughed nervously. "Oh, swell! What do they eat?"

"I don't know—worms and other wiggly things, I suppose. That's what people use for bait."

Wesley looked down again, even more concerned.

Pippa added, "I would say that you have more to worry about than I do."

When it finally dawned on him that she was teasing, he splashed water at her face, and she shrieked with laughter before diving beneath the surface. She came up again and scored a direct hit, causing him to cough and blink the water from his eyes. Feigning anger, he lunged after her, and she fled, swimming as fast as she could toward the far side of the tank.

Wesley truly was a strong swimmer, for he caught up with the girl well before she neared the shoreline. He grabbed at her foot, but she kicked free. When she eventually attained that point where her feet could touch bottom, she tried to exploit this temporary advantage by fleeing around the curved perimeter. But Wesley pounced, making a nifty flying tackle, and both of them tumbled into the murky depths. Flailing blindly beneath the water, he captured the struggling girl in his arms and lifted her up, so that both of their heads were now visible above the surface. All the while, Pippa was giggling and squirming to break loose, but that only caused him to hold her more tightly still. They both were laughing hysterically in locked embrace until something—perhaps the smoothness of skin on skin—brought them to their senses, and they peered into one another's eyes, trembling a little but not saying a word.

They kissed, fervently holding each other and letting their hands wander up and down the other's back. Kiss followed passionate kiss until Wesley's lips gradually strayed from hers and began kissing her chin, her neck, and even the delicate skin that began to suggest the contours of her breasts. She threw her head back and held him close, savoring the thrill of his exploring lips and tongue. This could not continue. She knew it, and he knew it. Both of them were losing control, indulging in fleshly desires that were more enticing than either had dreamed possible.

It was Pippa who took it upon herself to whisper, "Not now, Wes. We need to go back." Wesley simply could not believe his ears. His mind comprehended all too well, but his aroused body did not. He gently guided her a couple of steps closer to shore, and for a moment she seemed willing to consent, or at least unprepared to offer any meaningful resistance. She smiled at him, but there was a touch of sadness too, an awareness that this would be the wrong act at the wrong time. Wesley saw the fear in her eyes, respected it, and relented. He looked contrite, perhaps ashamed of being too forceful with her, but Pippa said to him, "That's okay. I'm glad you feel that way about me. And I wasn't exactly trying very hard to get away, as you recall."

They dropped into the deep water and swam alongside one another to the opposite shore, where their discarded clothes lay baking in the hot sun. "You go first, Wes," Pippa told him, and she added with a grin, "I'll try my best not to look."

Obediently, Wesley took a few steps onto the yellowed grass, glancing back to make sure she was facing the other direction. Then he lay down, legs modestly together, and allowed the breeze to evaporate the moisture that still clung to his skin. "It won't take long in this heat," Pippa shouted away from him. Meantime, she amused herself by softly splashing the water's surface while eyeing the darting movements of the fish below.

Once Wesley was dry and fully dressed, he sat down on the same smooth rock where he had earlier spread his clothes. "Okay, your turn," he called.

Wesley turned his back toward the girl, to afford her some privacy, but he could hear the faint sound of churning water as she swam toward the shore. He tried to occupy his mind with something—anything—that might distract him from the thoughts of what he would be missing. When his eyes happened upon the wood rot of an abandoned ox cart just the other side of the dry ravine, he spoke up. "Whose old wagon is that—over by the gully?"

"I don't know," Pippa said. "It's always been there—for as long as I can remember. I suppose it was my grandfather's, but I can't say for sure." Judging from her voice, she could not have been more than twenty feet away.

"Can I turn around yet?" Wesley asked.

"No, you certainly may not," the girl said. "I'm extremely indecent at the moment, and I'm counting on you to behave like a gentleman."

Wesley laughed, but there was an emptiness inside, a longing that assailed him for being so proper. Behind him, the girl was humming softly to herself, either standing up or lying down as she dried—he could not tell which. A pair of mockingbirds squawked overhead, and he could also hear the rustling of wind through the tall summer grass. As the minutes passed, he sensed that a sweet opportunity was drifting away forever.

Against every cell and fiber of who he was, Wesley twisted slightly and ventured a peek, without calling undue attention to himself. When he opened the slits of his eyes a bit wider, he could see that Pippa had closed hers and was lying on her back, unconcerned and trustful, allowing the hot breezes to evaporate what few droplets of water still remained. Her female form was an entrancing sight, but his better judgment counseled him not to linger for long. And so, with determined effort, he forced himself to turn away, half expecting to feel the onslaught of guilty remorse. Instead, he found himself warmed by the lovely vision that persisted in his mind.

Considerable time elapsed before Pippa proclaimed herself to be dry and fully clothed. Wesley stood up, walked over to her, and proceeded to straighten the collar of her blouse, one corner of which had become folded under.

"Did you like what you saw?" she asked.

Wesley's eyes widened. "What do you mean?"

"I noticed that you were staring at me earlier."

"Oh." He looked down in shame.

"I don't mind—really. I'm glad you looked."

"You are?"

"Yes."

"Why?"

"Because now you'll know what you're getting."

Wesley smiled at her frankness, what nearly amounted to a declaration of love. Choosing his words carefully, he told her, "I've always known that your face is beautiful, and now I know that the rest of you is too."

Pippa grinned. "That's very nice of you to say. Almost poetic."

"Well, I mean it."

Suddenly, her face clouded. "You don't think they're too small, do you?"

He glanced at her blouse. "No," he said. "I think they're perfect."

She looked away from him, surveying the large expanse of water. "I have a confession to make."

"You do?"

"Uh-huh. They say it's good for the soul."

"I've heard that." Wesley stood still, as if frozen in place, wondering what would come next.

Pippa turned to him, took a deep breath, and said, "I peeked at you too. When you were drying off and had your eyes closed."

"You did?"

"Yes, and I got a good look."

"Oh." He tried to smile, but nerves would not let him.

"I'm very sorry for being so dishonest, Wes."

"That's all right. Why did you do it?"

"I don't know. Curiosity, I guess."

Holding hands, the two young people strolled back toward the farmhouse. A story would have to be concocted, of course—and her parents would believe it, of course. Somehow, that did not matter anymore. In that one transforming moment as they walked along, Wesley Franklin Brower and Pippa Herndon Glynn knew that there would be no one else in their lives. Both felt sure that they were made for each other.

But teenage love rarely proves itself to be quite that simple.

◆　　◆　　◆

An ancient train—well past traditional retirement age—rattled across east Texas, and through one of its grease-stained windows a sailor smiled at the familiar sights that welcomed him back to his native state. There were pine trees and pick-up trucks, cattle grazing on a hill, farm-to-market roads, country churches, and even a couple of red barns with garish advertising painted on them. What an odd sensation it was to observe, first-hand, that so little of the Texas landscape had changed while he was away. Here in the heartland of America, it was almost as if the war had never occurred. American civilians, by all outward appearances, had gone about their daily existence wholly isolated from the devastation and atrocities that the rest of the world had come to accept as grim reality. But of course that was only half the story. He also knew that workers in the United States were second to none, among the most dynamic on the face of the earth and, on their own home-front battlefield, as heroic as the soldiers and sailors in uniform. In the final analysis, it was production that won the war.

Stephen Brower had plenty of time to contemplate such lofty thoughts on this three-day journey from Norfolk, Virginia. Although he revered his ship, no tears were shed when he bid her farewell for the final time. He recalled the near misses of the kamikaze pilots, the rescuing of survivors at sea, the downing of an enemy plane, and that dramatic scene in Tokyo Bay when the Japanese ceremonially surrendered to the Allied Forces. Even thereafter, the *Jeffers* had remained active and very much in harm's way for some time to come, conducting minesweeping efforts in the coastal waters of Japan, notably in the perilous Tsushima Strait, a strategic channel that connected the Sea of Japan with the East China Sea. From the ship's base of operations at Sasebo on Kyushu's Omura Bay, she spent the month of November sweeping the Yellow Sea. Then, on December 5, she finally set sail for the United States, arriving at San Diego eighteen days later. Passage through the Panama Canal led her to the North Atlantic Ocean, where she steamed up to Norfolk, making landfall on the ninth of January.

Less than two years had elapsed since Steve last visited his Waco home on leave, but somehow that idyllic sojourn had become just a distant memory to him. Back then, he was essentially still a kid, a high school graduate trying to act a lot more mature than he really was. In many ways, it proved to be the end of his age of innocence—before he drank beer among his pals, smoked cigarettes, lived away from home for any appreciable time, dallied with the ladies, tasted combat, and ultimately became an eyewitness to world history in the making. But now, on this train in mid-April of 1946, he felt much more like a man, more serious, more ambitious perhaps, more certain of what he wanted out of life. Though still nearly three months shy of his twenty-first birthday, his exemplary conduct in the cauldron of fire had long since earned him the right to be considered an adult.

Steve reached into his wallet and removed a tiny key that was his father's. This slim, unremarkable piece of metal once permitted entrance to a secret desk drawer that contained what Harold Brower apparently considered to be a cherished treasure, a crudely drawn birthday card from a little child named Stevie. That same key had accompanied a grown-up Stephen wherever the war took him to fight in the service of his country. Steve grinned warmly at the key, kissed it again, as he had done so often during the past several months, and returned it to its accustomed place of honor in his wallet. Then he tried to catch some sleep, not an easy thing to do on a lurching train that had, by a wide margin, exceeded its useful years of providing comfort for its passengers.

Little did the sailor realize that activities were much more frantic about a hundred miles to the west, where preparations were being made for a coming-home party at the Brower house. Initially, Nora wanted to stage the celebration elsewhere, at a meeting hall or hotel ballroom, but then she and her daughter both reached the same conclusion, independently—that Steve would probably desire nothing more than simply being at home.

It was Elizabeth's further idea to refine their plans by converting the festivities into a surprise party, for otherwise she felt certain that Steve would object. She could hear him now: "Please don't make a fuss over me. I'm just glad to be home." But she was not about to let her older brother be neglected. A hero's return called for something special in the way of recognition, and a house full of familiar faces was just the thing. Elizabeth was in charge of the invitations, and she sent them far and wide. Unfortunately, Steve had not given early enough notice to allow for RSVPs to be implemented, so this organizational committee of one was, as she put it, "flying blind." She was anticipating perhaps forty attendees, but there could turn out to be half that number or even twice that number. Who could say?

For the umpteenth time, Elizabeth checked her guest list. Beyond her immediate family, the only people who she knew would be there, for certain, were Uncle Matt and Aunt Barbara from Harlingen, Hermann and Gertrude Moek of Waco, Madeleine Givens of Waco, Benjamin Reich of Stephenville, Mabel Johns of Waco, Wayne Espy of Waco, Teddy Gaunce of Cleburne, and about a dozen others, including many of her mother's closest friends.

The Moeks were generous enough to donate all of the food, but Elizabeth's invitations were so scattershot that it was really anybody's guess how many respondents there would be and, consequently, how many mouths to feed. Though the city's two USO facilities had closed their doors with the deactivation of Blackland Army Air Field and Waco Army Air Field, that did not stop Madeleine from enlisting the assistance of several of her former volunteers to convert the Brower house into a reception hall and to serve light refreshments throughout the evening.

Nora and her daughter were so busy with the myriad details of preparation that it fell to Wesley alone to pick up his older brother at the train station. The boy arrived home from KWXN just in time to leave once again on this important mission. The surprise party was not due to begin until seven o'clock, so there would be almost two full hours for the family to welcome Steve home in private before the general public would have him in their midst.

◆   ◆   ◆

A mother's physical senses can become extraordinarily acute when need be, and this was just such a time. The volunteer ladies were setting up tables and decorations in the living room—and generating a steady tumult in the process. That did not prevent Nora from being the first to hear the Chevrolet rolling its way up the driveway and coming to a squeaky stop in front of the garage. She hurried out the back door and made a beeline for the passenger side of the automobile. Out stepped Steve with a broad smile, and they embraced. Meanwhile, Wesley had unlatched the turtleback and removed its two articles of content, his brother's seabag and a large suitcase that Steve had bought while at his final duty station in Norfolk, Virginia.

As the three of them walked toward the house—Wesley carrying the suitcase and Steve his oversized bag—Elizabeth came bounding out the back door and threw her arms around big brother. "Oh, I can't believe you're really here!" she said.

"Nope, neither can I, Lizzie girl." He kissed her cheek. "I've been trying to picture this exact moment for a couple of years now."

Nora wiped away some tears. "And it's finally come true ... for all of us."

What the sailor saw when he arrived inside took him by complete surprise. It was not an everyday happening to encounter eight ladies arranging tablecloths, punch bowls, silverware, streamers, and a banner in the Brower living room.

He gave his mother a questioning look. "Say, what gives?"

"Oh, yes," she told him, "we're going to have a small get-together to properly welcome you home. It was Lizzie's idea to make it a surprise, and that's why we didn't say anything in our letters."

Steve gently punched the girl's arm. "Thanks a lot, traitor. And here I thought you were my pal."

"Well, it was either this or a big soirée at the Waco Lawn Tennis Club," Elizabeth said.

"Point well taken. On second thought, this is just fine." He reached down and petted the spoiled cat, Valentino, who had made his appearance out of idle curiosity. "He looks a little fatter than before."

"No wonder," Nora said. "He eats like a horse, and his food—unlike ours—doesn't need ration points."

They all went directly upstairs. Now that the family's boarder had graduated from Baylor and moved back to North Carolina, Steve would be reclaiming his old bedroom, and his mother had taken the liberty of "de-feminizing" it after the girl's occupancy. She removed the flower vases and frilly curtains, for instance, doing her best to return the room to a condition that Steve might remember as being his own. He pretended to be pleased, but something about the change made him feel a little sad. He recalled viewing it as the living space for Hannah Lane, and she had put some very personal touches on it that could not easily be erased from his memory. Nor could the time they spent together on his last night of leave.

"Do you want me to stay in this Popeye costume?" he asked. "I mean, for the party."

"Please, if you don't mind," Nora told him. "I think the guests will enjoy seeing you in uniform, and I would like to show you off to them."

"My friends will think you're a dreamboat," Elizabeth added.

Steve laughed. "The things I must do for public relations."

"By the way, are you hungry, or did you eat on the train?" Nora asked.

"Starving. I only had a peanut butter sandwich on stale bread."

"I'll fix you a nice meal, which you can eat *after* you take a shower."

"Uh-oh. Do I really smell that bad?"

"No, but let's not risk it, shall we? You must have picked up a lot of railroad grit along the way."

"Okay, but that means I'll have to wear my dress uniform."

"Ooh. Better yet!" his sister said. "Bonnie Thompson will propose to you on the spot."

He feigned interest. "No kidding? What does she look like?"

"Ugliest girl in the eleventh grade."

♦　　♦　　♦

The early arrivals showed up at 6:40, and the crowd continued to grow steadily after that. Soon it became uncomfortably clear that Elizabeth had done her job a bit too well. She was expecting perhaps forty guests, but slightly more than ninety were actually there to greet the returning serviceman, and automobiles lined both sides of the street for the better part of two blocks in either direction.

With Hermann's blessings, Madeleine Givens twice drove back and forth to Moek Grocery to acquire additional foodstuffs for the refreshment tables. Gertrude went with her—to unlock the store, which closed for business at 5:30, and to help her gather the needed provisions. Even on their first trip, the sun had already gone down, for War Time was a thing of the distant past, having been rescinded by federal edict on September 30. For that matter, Texas would be among twenty-three states to remain on Standard Time even after it again became permissible to turn clocks ahead by one hour on April 28.

As the guest of honor in his own house, it was Steve's duty to mingle with the well-wishers, which meant conversing with hordes of his mother's friends, almost all of whom proclaimed, "And how handsome you look!" He kept moving among the crowd, like a good host will do, trying to make certain that everyone there felt significant and worthy of his acknowledgment. Whenever a few partygoers happened to leave for various reasons, others would appear on the scene to take their places, thus sustaining the average attendance at over the seventy-five mark for nearly three hours. Sometimes it reached as high as a hundred.

Entertainment was supplied by Bryce Pidcock, a senior at Waco High School, whom Elizabeth inveigled into playing popular melodies on the parlor's nine-foot Steinway. She suggested to him that Clarice Thurman might be there, and that was all it took. He had a crush on Clarice, though she was two years older than he and probably not even aware of his existence. She really was a very attractive girl, one of Sandra Whittsel's closest friends until they graduated and went their separate ways. Clarice was now training to be a dental assistant, with the hope of joining her father's practice in Waco. Dr. Thurman chose to send her to Baylor for her pre-dental studies—including such "solids" as inorganic chemistry, organic chemistry, biology, and physics—and then she would transfer to Baylor University's College of Dentistry in Dallas for her Bachelor of Science degree.

"Hey, there she is," Bryce whispered to Elizabeth during the refrain of "It Might As Well Be Spring." After letting Elizabeth turn the page for him, he completed the piece and said, "Play something while I go talk to her. She might get away."

Bryce took a break, Elizabeth quickly snatched "All the Things You Are" and "Deep Purple" from the piano bench, and the music resumed. He still had not reported back to the piano when she finished her two pieces, so she thumbed through her sheet music and produced "I'll Be Seeing You," "The Trolley Song," and "Swinging on a Star" to fill some more time. When he finally made a reappearance, his spirit was low, and Elizabeth wondered why.

"Clarice is engaged—to that guy wearing the Princeton sweater." The man in question looked as if he were thirty years old. Bryce spent the rest of the evening playing maudlin tunes that brought tears to the eyes—especially his own—all the while trying to drown his sorrows in cup after cup of (non-alcoholic) raspberry punch.

Freed from piano servitude, Elizabeth went in search of her older brother, to whom she had some interesting news to impart. She located him in the living room, surrounded by "a gaggle of gray-haired guinea hens," as her Uncle Matt would put it, and Steve was only too delighted to be rescued from this onerous burden.

"Thanks, Lizzie. You're a swell sis," he told her, but she seemed too preoccupied to accept the compliment.

"Giulia's here, Steve—the Coletti girl—and does she ever look grand!"

He smiled. "Where?"

She saluted him, in military fashion. "In the parlor, sir, last time I reconnoitered."

"Thank you, Ensign Brower. As you were." He returned a snappy salute and went in search of his honest-to-goodness pin-up girl—the central inch and a half of a fading four-by-six snapshot from Galveston, minus her two superfluous cousins.

Steve found her in the parlor, standing alongside her mother, and even from a distance it was plain to see that Giulia was a knockout. He approached with a confidence that surprised even himself, and she nearly dropped her plate of snacks when she spotted him coming.

"Hello, Steve," she said. "Well, how does it feel to be back home?"

"It's feeling pretty wonderful right about now."

He glanced at Paolina, who told him, "I'm sure your mother must be brimming with pride."

"Oh, I don't know about that, Mrs. Coletti. Mostly, she's just thankful to God that I survived the war and somehow managed to come back in one piece. Lots of the boys didn't."

Paolina had the good sense to know when to disappear from a room. "I think I'll go try to find her, Steve. Can you tell me where she might be?"

He was staring at Giulia when he answered. "Living room, ma'am—by the sewing table."

The moment Paolina left, Steve stepped over to the girl and kissed her on the mouth, not caring what others in the parlor might think. That sweet kiss brought back memories of their goodbye scene at the train depot two years earlier, a dreamlike moment that warmed many a night for him on the high seas.

Steve smiled involuntarily at the sheer beauty of her face. "Hello, there," he said. She was lovely enough to be a cover girl for *Coronet* or one of the other national magazines.

And Giulia tried to smile back. Nervous at meeting him again, she was uncertain how to break the ice. "You look very nice in your uniform," she told him.

"Thanks. I feel like an imposter, though, now that I'm on civvy street. This will be the last time anyone sees me as a war hero, I can promise you that." He grinned at his own little joke.

But Giulia, badly smitten, accepted his self-deprecating humor verbatim. He did seem like a hero to her. "Did you shoot down any Jap planes?" she asked. "You said you aimed the guns."

"Nope. Didn't aim them well enough, I guess. Anyway, we still won the war— no thanks to me."

She remained serious. "You poke fun at yourself, but I think you're swell. And I'll bet you did lots of things that helped us to win."

"Well, I never shot down one of our own, if that's what you mean."

"Steve!" She chuckled, finally relaxing a bit. Only twenty feet away, Bryce Pidcock was playing "When the Lights Go On Again." Giulia brushed some stray hair from her eyes and said to the sailor, "Oh, I loved hearing that song, didn't you? It was so sad. The version I remember best was by Vaughn Monroe."

"Vera Lynn sang it in England. She's 'The Forces' Sweetheart,' you know."

"So I've heard."

"And there were plenty of American swabbies who loved her too. That tiny sob in her voice made her seem vulnerable, like the girl next door. We all wanted to protect her from the dirty Hun."

An elderly gentleman surprised Steve by patting him on the back. "Good to have you home, son—safe and sound," he said. They shook hands.

"Thank you, sir. It's great to be back."

"And the piano sounds absolutely first-rate in here, doesn't it?" he asked as he walked past.

"Yes, sir."

The plaintive strains of "I'll Never Smile Again" could be heard.

Steve leaned closer to Giulia and whispered, "Who was that man? I feel like I've been talking for an hour and a half to a houseful of total strangers."

She watched the white-haired gentleman go into the living room. "I don't recognize him, but he seemed to know you."

Steve glanced at the front window, where the blue service star still hung in his honor, and suddenly he wanted to get away. "Would you care to go for a walk?"

"No, thank you, Steve. You belong in here. It's your party."

He laughed. "I guess you're right. For some reason, I keep forgetting that I'm the center of the universe."

Giulia giggled.

"Actually, you know, the real heroes of this war are those who never came back," Steve said. "Guys like Davey Scott. He was one of my best pals while I was in San Diego." He sighed. "We bummed around together for six weeks. Our fates could have been reversed, just as easily."

"I'll take a rain check, though," Giulia added.

Steve looked confused.

"The walk." She gave a bashful smile.

"Oh, sure, the walk. There'll be lots of time for that."

"I hope so." Looking around at the crowded parlor, she told him, "You'd better circulate now. I don't want to monopolize you. Mamma and I need to be going anyway, to catch our ride."

"Aye aye, sir," Steve said with a wink. Giving her hand a warm squeeze, he returned to his social obligations.

◆   ◆   ◆

While chatting at one of the refreshment tables with Lurline Papke, a charmingly dignified veteran of the defunct Franklin Avenue USO, Elizabeth happened to overhear her mother say that the people who traveled the farthest to welcome Steve home were Mr. Ben Reich of Stephenville and Dr. Raeford "Ray" Muldoon, Nora's old friend who now served on the faculty of Southwestern University in Georgetown. But then, at a quarter to nine—roughly two hours behind schedule—in walked Matthew Coleman and his wife, Barbara. They had driven all the way up from Harlingen, an arduous journey of 425 miles, and—due to a series of mishaps—very nearly missed the celebration entirely.

"Well, look what the cat dragged in!" Nora shouted when she noticed them. She scampered across the living room to give big hugs to her brother and sister-in-law. "I was afraid you decided not to come. Did you have car trouble?"

"Yep, tires," Matthew told her. "Two blowouts—one in Kingsville and one just south of Giddings."

"Oh, dear. That's what we all get for riding around on bald tires," Nora said.

"And I thought Babs would *never* get them changed," he added with a straight face.

"Well, at least you made it. Steve would have been awfully disappointed."

Barbara frowned, exhausted from their fourteen-hour ordeal. "Brilliant Matty here—he left the jack in our pastor's car, playing Good Samaritan a few weeks ago."

Nora chuckled at her brother. "That'll earn a star for your crown in heaven."

"Thanks for the kind sentiment," Barbara said, "but I'm sure the language he used disqualified him for that."

Ignoring the snide comment, Matthew smiled at his niece and younger nephew, who had walked over to greet their south Texas relations. "Hello, Lizzie. How's high school treating you?"

The girl hugged her Uncle Matt's neck. "Fine."

"And, by golly, there's Wes." They shook hands. "You're a man of the world now, huh? A real, live Baylor Bear."

"Yes, sir."

"Are you in your second semester now, son?"

"No, sir. Baylor's on the quarter system. I've already gone to the fall and winter quarters, and this is the spring. Best of all, I'll have three weeks off after the summer quarter ends."

"Summer recess was always my favorite semester."

Nora clasped her sister-in-law's hands in her own. "How long can you stay with us, Babs? A good, restful while, I hope."

"Actually, we've booked a hotel room," Barbara told her. "We knew you'd be too tired to put up with out-of-towners on top of all this."

"We'll be going back early on Sunday, Sis," Matthew said. He was eyeing the chicken salad sandwiches. "Say, where's the man of the hour?" He picked up a sandwich and took a bite.

Nora gestured toward the other room. "In the parlor. You can't miss him. He'll be the good-looking fellow in uniform—with a two-hour smile frozen onto his face."

"Aw, poor kid. And he thought boot camp was rough!"

Barbara took a sandwich, too, and tagged along after her husband.

Meanwhile, Wesley was getting bored with the whole affair. He knew very few people besides relatives, Giulia Coletti, Mr. Reich, and the Moeks—and Valentino showed no interest in playing with a shoelace snake, not with so many intruders disrupting his normal routine. The boy could not seek refuge upstairs, either, for both bathrooms seemed to be in constant use, what with the number of guests and the amount of fruit punch being consumed. In desperation, he switched on the radio, collapsed to the floor in front of the console, and listened to "The Danny Kaye Show." Two children eventually joined him there, a lad of about ten and a girl half that age. In addition to the star's lively patter, no doubt Eve Arden was heard, as well as the music of Harry James and the distinctive voice of Frank Nelson as Mr. Pabst. But Wesley could not have said for sure because his thoughts were many miles away. He had a dilemma to resolve—involving girls, of course—a decision to make that was almost certain to change his life. In a way, he wished the breezy letter from Atlanta had never reached him at all. One excerpt, "Poor Rick! Seems I was more talk than action," kept running through his mind.

It was 9:35 when the last person to arrive at Steve's party finally made a belated appearance. When this guest opened the front door and stepped inside, Elizabeth squealed with delight and ran at top speed to greet her. They embraced, and both began sobbing in each other's arms. "Mother!" Elizabeth shouted. "Come quick!"

Nora was in the kitchen when she heard her daughter's plea for help. Laying her knife on the cutting board, she hurried through the living room to the entryway. About ten feet from the visitor, she stopped in disbelief, as if she were gazing upon the ghost of a loved one. "Hannah! Oh, my dear Hannah!" she cried, and she rushed forward and threw her arms around the young woman. She burst into tears at once and simply would not let go of her former boarder, lest she disappear from their lives forever.

Elizabeth went in search of her older brother, and she located him in the parlor, chatting with his old football chum, Teddy Gaunce, who was now married to a Cleburne girl and in business for himself. Steve could see from Elizabeth's tears and dazed expression that something was amiss. She motioned for him to follow her. "Excuse me," he told his friend, and he dashed after his sister.

And there stood Hannah Lane, only a step or two from the door. She looked frightened and lonesome. Her cheeks were wet from crying, and her wayward blonde hair was even more of a mess than usual. She was chewing some gum, and her unflattering, boyish clothes appeared to have been slept in for at least a night or two. To Steve, she looked beautiful and very much herself.

"Why is it, you always see me at my worst?" were the first words she said to him.

"You look fine, Hannah. Better than that."

Nora motioned for Elizabeth to come with her to the kitchen, but then she stopped, remembering to express her condolences. "We were so sorry to hear about your father."

"Thank you," the girl said, and she looked down at the floor.

Steve stared at his mother, who explained. "Hannah's father passed away in January. He was a wonderful Christian, a true man of God. I wish you could have met him."

"He had a heart ailment," Hannah told the sailor, and her voice sounded very tired. "We knew he wasn't healthy—and hadn't been, for quite some time—so when the Lord took him ... well, it really did not come as much of a surprise."

Nora tugged on the sleeve of her daughter's blouse. "Come along, Lizzie. There's a stack of cups and plates that need to be washed, or we'll be running out." They departed for the kitchen.

That left Steve and Hannah alone—except for about sixty other people, each of whom suddenly seemed to be scrutinizing them, even those guests who had already congratulated the returning serviceman and welcomed him back from the war.

Grinning at the onlookers, Steve turned Hannah by the shoulder and opened the front door. "Let's get out of here for a while," he whispered. Then, once outside, he said, "I think I've done more than my fair share of mingling tonight. No one can say I wasn't a social butterfly."

◆　　◆　　◆

Steve and Hannah strolled leisurely down the sidewalk, not arm-in-arm as lovers might do but simply talking to each other like any typical pair of good friends. The evening air was quite agreeable, with the temperature poised in the middle sixties after an afternoon high of seventy-four.

"Look how popular you are," Hannah said. She gestured toward the automobiles that were parked on both sides of the street for as far as the eye could see.

Steve laughed. "It seems like most of them were my mother's friends. They were nice, though, I've got to admit."

"What about your football chums?"

"Yeah, four or five of them. It was good seeing those men again—especially Teddy and Billy, of course. They were my closest buddies at school."

"Is Giulia there?"

Steve stopped dead in his tracks. "Giulia?"

"Giulia Coletti."

"Do you know her?"

"Well, sure. Giulia and I are the best of pals. Is she there?"

"She *was* there—but just briefly." He tried to study her face under the street lamp. "How do you two happen to know each other?"

"We met by accident, not very long after I graduated."

"Oh?"

"It was on June 22, 1945, to be exact."

He eyed her with suspicion. "Why do you remember the date?"

"I don't know. It just stuck in my mind. Here, want a piece of gum?" She opened a new pack and offered him a stick.

"I guess." Steve unwrapped it and put the gum in his mouth. "Thanks, kid."

They began walking again, and Hannah asked him, "Why did you call me that?"

"I don't know. It just seemed like something Humphrey Bogart would say in that situation."

She giggled. "What situation is that?"

"Walking along with Lauren Bacall, in the moonlight."

Hannah glanced up. "But it's cloudy—and I'm sure not Lauren Bacall."

Steve adopted his best Bogart voice. "This could be the start of a beautiful friendship."

She shook her head. "You sailors really do have the smooth lines, don't you?"

"Not me. Despite this clever disguise, I'm a civilian now, remember?"

"You could've fooled me."

Steve laughed quietly but did not respond. They walked along in silence until he asked her, "How long will you be in Texas?"

"That all depends."

"Did you come all this way just to go to a party?"

"Partly. Lizzie sent me an invitation, you know, but I'm sure she never expected me to be here. Frankly, neither did I."

"When did you decide to come?"

"Three days ago—while I was sitting at home in the dark, feeling sorry for myself. I prayed long and hard about it, and ... well, here I am."

"So I see," he said with a smile. "Was it a rough trip?"

"It wasn't very pleasant. I can't sleep well on trains—not in those uncomfortable chairs. And I probably smell like a skunk."

He pretended to look around. "Gee, I thought that *was* a skunk."

"Nope. Just me. I haven't had a proper bath since I left Mount Airy."

"Well, we can fix that."

"Oh, yeah? What are we going to do, run through the sprinklers?"

"You're coming home with me. I'll spend the night with Wes, and you can have your old room back. You can stay as long as you want, no strings attached."

She stopped walking. "No, Steve. That's awfully sweet of you, but I wouldn't think of it. Besides, I've got a hotel room booked."

"Which one?"

"The State House. It's at Sixth and Franklin, not too far from the newspaper building." She popped her chewing gum.

"How did you get from there to here?"

"On foot, of course. After I dropped off my luggage." She used the back of her hand to sweep the blonde bangs from her eyes.

"That's quite a trek," the sailor said. He grinned, leaning back to have a better look at her. "No wonder you're such a mess." Steve seemed to be tickled by her untidy appearance, but Hannah did not see anything funny about it.

"Thank you so much for that kind compliment," she told him. "Instead of throwing insults at me, I think you should feel very honored."

"Well, I am. I'm—"

"Sure, I could have taken the time to wash up—like that precious Giulia probably did—but then I would have missed your party."

"Say, Hannah, don't—"

"I hope you know that I came all the way from North Carolina just to see you."

"I do. I—"

"You don't have any right to talk that way about me—not after all I've been through to get here on a train that—"

Steve put his hand over her mouth, trying to get a word in edgewise. "Listen, I'm sorry, sweetie," he said, "and I do appreciate it, more than you'll ever know. I was only teasing—and you really look fine, just fine."

In a heartbeat, Hannah's anger became a mischievous smile. "No, I don't, you lying weasel. I *am* a mess!" They both laughed.

Gently, Steve placed a hand on each of her shoulders, and the amused expression left his face. "There aren't many people who would have pulled a stunt as crazy as yours—going halfway across the country to a silly party—and you did it for me." For a moment, he simply stood there, lost in her blue eyes and saying nothing. Finally he added, "You're really something, you know that?"

Hannah laughed quietly, staring up at him with a questioning look. "I just had a special feeling about you, and I thought I'd take the chance, that's all."

He stepped closer and tossed his gum aside. "You said you haven't had a proper bath since you left Mount Airy. Well, there's something else you probably haven't had a proper one of, either." He leaned toward her, and they kissed, very softly. He took her in his arms, and they kissed again—over and over, with rising passion—each holding the other so tightly that they felt as one.

At that most inopportune moment, a neighborhood gentleman passed by them on the sidewalk, and the lovers reluctantly parted, a little embarrassed. "Go, Navy," the man said with a good-natured laugh, and he continued on his way.

Steve and Hannah both giggled too, in spite of themselves. Then he took both of her hands in his own and asked, "Now, where were we?"

She blocked his embrace. "You were going to take me back to your house. Don't you remember?"

"But what about your luggage? I thought you preferred to spend the night at that hotel."

"Would you mind driving me over there to retrieve my suitcase? Like you said, it's a long walk."

Steve kissed her on the forehead. "Hannah, my dear, I would be delighted. You know, my mother always said that you were one of the family."

Hannah's smile was radiant. "Mmm, that sounds nice!"

"I think so too," Steve said.

He put his arm around her, and they walked home together.

◆　　　◆　　　◆

Milestone events in her life always made Nora Brower think of the past, to take stock of where she was now and how she had arrived at that particular point. Weddings affected her like that, even those of mere acquaintances, perhaps the daughter of a friend of a friend at church or the nephew of the USO director's former roommate at Texas Christian University. It made little difference. She would pause over a cup of coffee and reflect. And how much more so when it was her own son who was getting married.

Inevitably, Nora pondered her age. That, sad to say, was part and parcel of the remembering process. Try as she might to skirt such an unpalatable issue, the fact remained that she was not getting any younger. Her husband had been gone for nearly a decade, and on this very afternoon their eldest child was entering into the sacred bond of matrimony. It hardly seemed possible that their "Stevie" would be turning twenty-one in less than two weeks. He was already a war veteran, and in just a few short hours he would have a wife of his own. Nora could almost hear it now, the booming voice of announcer Westbrook Van Voorhis: "Time Marches On!"

She took a sip of coffee, heartening herself with the firm knowledge that two Brower children were still in the nest. But even that was a precarious supposition. Wesley, too, appeared to be getting quite serious about someone—that darling Axtell girl who came to his graduation—so who could say for certain how long it would be before he joined the ranks of the married? Only the youngest, Elizabeth, was sure to be living at home for some time to come. She had no steady boyfriend, and her infatuation with the airman from Mississippi offered little chance of enduring success. The last Nora heard, he was stationed in South Dakota, which did not portend well for the future. Yes, he was to be in the wedding party—at Lizzie's behest—but their mutual affection was unlikely to progress much past the friendship stage. Clearly, he was much too old for her ... wasn't he?

In her musings, one agent of pairing that struck Nora as nothing short of miraculous was the unseen force that led Steve to meet his bride-to-be. Until June of 1943, Hannah Lane lived half a continent away in North Carolina. Higher education drew her to Texas, but it was the prospect of war work that inspired her to petition for off-campus lodging rather than staying in a dormitory like most Baylor coeds were compelled to do. Were it not for both of these factors in tandem—college and the war—the engaged couple undoubtedly never would have met.

She poured another cup of hot coffee and switched on the radio to divert her overwrought mind. KWXN was carrying the Columbia Broadcasting System's weekly cooking program, "Mary Lee Taylor," and she figured that might serve the purpose. Competing in the time slot was a Mutual children's show called "Rainbow House," but Nora did not wish to be reminded of youngsters just now. The last thing she needed was a reason to feel even more nostalgic than she already did, and the medium of radio possessed an emotive power that sometimes touched her in that very way. She still suffered pangs of sorrow whenever she recalled the shattering death of twenty-eight-year-old actress Donna Damerel, who for many years performed alongside her real-life mother, Myrtle Vail, on radio's popular "Myrt and Marge." Pretty Miss Damerel, wife of former Olympic swimmer Peter Fick, died tragically, in childbirth, at a hospital in Englewood, New Jersey, at one o'clock on the morning of February 15, 1941. Only half a day earlier, she was reading her lines as Marge Spear in New York's CBS Studios.

Culinary radio distractions or not, Nora's thoughts still wandered to Wesley and Elizabeth—and particularly the manner in which they were responding to their older brother's impending marriage. Beyond the normal fraternal approbation, Wesley had a more self-serving reason for looking forward to Steve's wedding. On this glorious day, June 22, 1946, he again would have a bedroom sanctuary to call his very own. For the past ten weeks, Steve had been the recipient of his kid brother's grudging hospitality as sibling roommates, while Hannah was living as a boarder in the Brower household, just like she had done during the war.

Nora glanced at the clock—8:40—only five hours away. It was to be a two-o'clock wedding, and everything was in readiness, as far as she or anyone else could tell. Elizabeth had been a true blessing in that respect, for she saw to the details far better than Nora ever could. Maybe it was the girl's youth or maybe just a certain proclivity for taking large projects and boiling them down to their essential elements, tackling each facet in turn before proceeding to the next. In any case, nothing remained to be done but the waiting, which was plenty difficult enough.

First Baptist Church, rather than Columbus Avenue, would be the site of Steve's nuptials, a decision that he himself made in deference to his fiancée's admiration for Reverend J. M. Dawson while she was a Bible student at Baylor. Although her Uncle Vernon had preceded her father in death, Hannah was fortunate that the men's sister, Mrs. Patty Lemaster of Spring Lake (near Fayetteville), and younger brother, Pastor Hudson Lane of Asheville, were both still alive and able to manage every aspect of Samuel's modest estate. Thus, Hannah could stay in central Texas throughout her engagement period, having all of her belongings shipped to her from Mount Airy in three oversized cases. The freight charges were exorbitant, she thought, but worth the investment. This arrangement allowed her to become gainfully employed for six weeks, earning a steady paycheck from her alma mater as secretary to Sara Lowrey, Paul Baker, and Glenn Capp in Baylor University's Speech Department. Hannah filled the job vacancy quite well, stepping in for a young woman who required time off for pregnancy leave. The position closed on Friday, May 31, four days after spring commencement, which satisfied Hannah's needs perfectly, granting her three full weeks to devote to wedding plans.

About fifteen minutes into the cooking show, just as Nora was beginning to relax a bit, she heard the sound of a toilet flushing upstairs, so she knew that somebody was finally stirring. Wesley was already at work, doing his weekly stint in radio sales, so it had to be Steve or Elizabeth, each of whom had vowed to sleep in after staying up so late the night before. Elizabeth did not come home until 12:30, and Steve's bachelor party persisted for an hour after that. Nora knew of their return times probably better than they did, for she hardly slept at all, intent upon verifying that the two made it back safely. Having a bridal shower on the night before a wedding was unusual, to say the least, but so many of Hannah's people from Mount Airy High School and Wake Forest College were unable to reach Waco before Friday that there was really no other choice. The affair was hosted by her best friend from Baylor, Margo Burke Royster, who was a newlywed herself, having married Timmy Royster on December 14, the birthday of Margo's mother.

From the light tread of footsteps on the stairway, Nora surmised that it was Elizabeth who was coming down for breakfast, and she was right. The first thing the teenager did upon entering the kitchen was yawn. This elicited very little sympathy from her mother, for an eight-hour snooze did not exactly fall into the category of sleep deprivation. The girl wore a robe in addition to her nightgown, but that outer garment was strictly for modesty's sake, as the overnight low temperature was a warm seventy-three degrees. After all, summer had officially arrived the day before.

Elizabeth took a slice of bread and put it in the toaster. "I wish you had come to keep me company, Mother. I was the only single girl there, besides Hannah."

"I'm sorry, dear, but I was too tired—with all these last-minute preparations." Nora handed her daughter the dish of strawberry jam.

"You'll be happy to know that Hannah got a lot of good loot," Elizabeth said. "She even received a gift from Mrs. Coletti."

"No!"

"Yes, she did. A set of dinner glasses."

"Was she there?"

"No, and neither was her daughter, of course, but I thought it was nice of them to give something—especially after the way Steve treated Giulia."

Nora frowned. "What do you mean by that?"

"Well, he did sort of cast her overboard."

"Now, I wouldn't go so far as to say that. He was in love with Hannah. He just thought Giulia was beautiful. There's a big difference."

Elizabeth pondered that for a moment. "Do you think he would have married Giulia, if Hannah hadn't come back from North Carolina?"

"Could be ... in time." She shook her head. "But we'll never know, and it serves no purpose to speculate about such things."

"I think he would have, I really do. Giulia is nuts about him, you know, and I sort of feel sorry for her."

"My goodness! Someone with her looks? Believe me, she'll do fine. She'll probably marry some famous doctor or lawyer. She's pretty enough to be in pictures."

"Who is?" Steve asked. He entered the room with the exaggerated swagger of someone trying to compensate for a bad case of nerves.

Nora thought it best to improvise. "Hannah, of course," she said. "Did you forget who it is that you're marrying?"

"Hardly. She's a peach. 'Hannah Brower' sounds pretty good, doesn't it?"

"I thought you'd be in bed 'til ten," Elizabeth told him. "You sure won't be getting much sleep tonight."

Steve scoffed at her. "What would you know about it, little girl?"

"I know plenty." She glanced at her mother, who appeared anxious to hear more. "But I can't go into detail right at the present time."

"Oh, I see."

"How was the bachelor party?" Nora asked.

"It was pretty tame, if you ask me," he said. "Teddy thought of hiring a hootchy-kootchy girl, but then he chickened out at the last minute."

"Well, thank goodness for that."

Elizabeth grinned. "Anyway, where would you find one of them in Waco?"

"You'd be surprised what you can find in Waco, if you look the right places."

Nora decided to probe a bit further. "So, what did you do at the party?"

"Oh, just things, Mom. You know, just the things young men do."

His sister giggled at the evasive comment. "Like putting on fur coats and singing college songs?"

"Yeah, something like that. And climbing into telephone booths."

Nora was less interested in joking than interrogating. "Was there any alcohol involved? I don't think I trust Teddy all that much."

"Only beer, Mom. Nothing stronger than that."

She was surprised. "When did you start to drink beer?"

"Well, I *was* in the Navy, you know."

"I know, but ..."

"Don't worry. I was just sowing some wild oats. To be honest with you, I don't even like the flavor of it."

"That's good to hear."

Elizabeth was eating a piece of toast, topped with a thin layer of strawberry jam, but such light fare did not look very appetizing to Steve. He requested a fried-egg sandwich instead, and his mother soon was busy preparing it for him.

Meanwhile, his sister went fishing for information. "Was Danny there ... at your party?"

Steve turned to her and asked, "Danny who?" He would not make this easy.

"Rignold, of course. Was he there?"

"Yes, he was there."

"Well?"

"Well, what?"

She cleared her throat. "Did he say anything about me?"

"Why would he do that?"

"I think he liked me, at one time."

"Didn't you see him yesterday?"

"Only for about two minutes. Not enough time to really—"

"To answer your question, no, he didn't say anything about you. The subject never came up."

Elizabeth looked away, trying to appear unconcerned, but her brother could see that this hurt her badly. "Look, Sis, he's one of my groomsmen, so I can boss him around today. I'll order him to talk to you. How's that?"

She smiled. "Thanks."

Nora stared at her son. "Are you very nervous?"

"Like a condemned man," he said.

"But you don't have cold feet."

"Oh, no, nothing like that. I'll go through with it all right." He pursed his lips, deep in thought. "Being with Hannah doesn't worry me. It's the blasted ceremony. To tell you the truth, I wish we were already on our honeymoon."

"You're all packed, aren't you?"

"Our suitcases are standing in my bedroom right now ... well, *her* bedroom. Where's Hannah camping out?"

"At Margo and Timmy Royster's," Nora said.

Steve nodded his head. "Where they had that hen party last night."

"Hey!" Elizabeth shouted. "Who are you calling a hen?"

"All right, I'm sorry. Don't lay an egg." He grinned and retreated a step, an instant too late.

Elizabeth slapped him on the upper arm, harder than she intended, and he winced.

"My gosh," Steve said. "I pity the poor soul who ever marries you."

He rubbed away the pain, stopping just long enough to chase his ticklish sister from the kitchen.

◆   ◆   ◆

"Dearly beloved, we are gathered here today, in the sight of God and in the presence of this company, to join together this man, Stephen Collins Brower, and this woman, Hannah Deborah Lane, in holy matrimony—which is instituted of God, regulated in His Word, and to be held in honor among all men."

Steve watched J. M. Dawson intently, impressed by the pastor's evident sincerity, his forceful delivery of lines that no doubt he had proclaimed in public many hundreds of times before.

"Let us therefore remember that God has established and sanctified marriage for the welfare and happiness of mankind. Jesus Himself declared that a man should leave his father and mother and be united to his wife."

By now, Steve, Hannah, and probably most of those in attendance were aware that this was to be one of Dr. Dawson's last marriage ceremonies as head of the Waco congregation. Only six days prior to the Brower-Lane wedding, the venerable pastor announced his impending retirement from the pulpit after thirty-one years of spiritual leadership. He planned to deliver his final sermon in five weeks' time, on July 28, and then, at the end of August, move with his wife to Washington, D.C., where he would assume his new position as Executive Director of the Joint Committee on Public Relations for the Baptists of the United States. As the minister himself described it to the press, this new agency "would seek to maintain the historic Baptist contention for complete separation of church and state, with full religious liberty for every human being."

Standing at the altar, alongside the other bridesmaids, Elizabeth appraised her older brother as objectively as possible and found him to be extremely handsome in his black tuxedo. And so, for that matter, was the groomsman from Mississippi, whom she practically insisted be accepted as an additional member of the wedding party. Danny was careful to focus his concentration on the groom, for the most part, so as not to give Steve's kid sister the idea that he was making eyes at her. But occasionally, when his vigilance waned, he did happen to glance in her direction, and each time she was staring at him with a slight grin on her face. It made him a little uncomfortable but also rather pleased, for there was no denying that she was very attractive indeed—for a teenager. If only Lizzie were more his age, he thought, there might be some future to this relationship. As it was, he could only look but not touch, and he was not much of a window shopper.

The groom was smiling at his bride when he heard the minister say, "It is your duty, Stephen, to be for Hannah a considerate, tender, faithful, and loving husband—to support, guide, and cherish her through prosperity and trouble ..." Steve caught her eye, through the diaphanous veil, and she smiled back. "... to thoughtfully and carefully enlarge the place she holds in your life—to constantly show to her the tokens of your affection—to shelter her from danger—and to reserve for her your undivided attention and affection. It is commanded in God's Word that husbands should love their wives, even as Christ loved the Church and gave His own life for her."

Wesley had begged out of serving as a groomsman, which was really no problem for Steve because he had more than enough likely candidates to fill the six spots. Although none of Steve's Navy buddies could be there, having been scattered far and wide after their discharges, eight tenths of his fellow offensive starters from the 1942 Waco High School football team were available to assist, in addition to Danny Rignold. As a reasonably credible excuse for his absenteeism from the altar, Wesley explained that he was expected to work that morning, which, strictly speaking, was the honest truth. Had Steve been facing the audience rather than the minister, he would have noticed at once the actual motive behind his brother's decision. Sitting right next to Wesley, with her mother and father on the other side of her, was an exceedingly pretty girl. Steve had never met Pippa Glynn, but presumably he would do so at the reception, and Wesley felt sure that this worldly-wise sailor would approve of his taste in women.

"It is your duty, Hannah, to be for Stephen a considerate, tender, faithful, and loving wife—to counsel, comfort, and cherish him in prosperity and trouble—to give to him the unfailing evidences of your affection—and, as time passes, to make the place he holds in your heart broader and deeper. God's Word commands that wives should respect and honor their husbands, even as the Church respects and honors Christ."

Nora thought Hannah looked stunningly beautiful in her wedding dress. This was the same gown that the girl's late mother had worn when she wedded Samuel Lane, a fledgling Baptist preacher in Sharpsburg, near Rocky Mount. Hannah was not the most feminine of young ladies, but her lissome, tomboyish figure was as trim and muscular as that of a female athlete. She carried herself well, with a genteel pride, and that in turn lent an air of refinement, something the unpretentious bride probably never suspected she had. From her vantage point in the front pew, Nora stared at Hannah Lane in wonder. What were the odds, she mused, that this North Carolinian would cross the country, secure a place in her home, and capture the heart of her firstborn son? Nora was always more apt to cry at weddings than at funerals, and the tears did come when the pastor said to bride and groom, "Please unite your hands and face each other." She cried from sorrow for losing a son, and she cried from joy for gaining a daughter.

"Do you, Stephen, solemnly pledge your faith to Hannah? Do you promise to live with her according to God's plan in the holy estate of matrimony? Do you promise to love her, comfort her, honor and keep her, in sickness and in health, and forsaking all others, keep yourself only for her? Do you promise, through God's grace, to be a faithful and devoted husband, as long as you both shall live?"

"I do," Steve said, and he gave his bride a reassuring smile.

"Do you, Hannah, solemnly pledge your faith to Stephen? Do you promise to live with him according to God's plan in the holy estate of matrimony? Do you promise to love him, comfort him, respect and honor him, in sickness and in health, and forsaking all others, keep yourself only for him? Do you promise, through God's grace, to be a faithful and devoted wife, as long as you both shall live?"

Hannah said, "I do." She gently squeezed his hands.

When Elizabeth again went in search of Danny's attention, he seemed determined to look anywhere but at her, and this was a bitter disappointment that brought her nearly to tears. Maybe he did not hold much affection for her after all, despite what he had espoused in his letters, both during the war and after. It made her angry, and she was tempted to give him the cold shoulder from here on out.

"The rings which you are about to exchange will serve as a reminder to you of the vows which you have shared today. The gold in these rings reminds you of the purity of your marriage covenant, and the circle reminds you of the unbroken love that you will forever share."

Steve placed the ring on Hannah's finger and repeated the minister's words. "With this ring, I pledge my faith and trust. Receive it as a symbol of our endless union and our unbroken love." Then Hannah placed the groom's ring on his finger and repeated the same vow.

Dr. Dawson said, "Let these rings continue to be, to you both, a symbol of the value, the purity, and the constancy of true wedded love, and the seal of the vows which you have both made today."

There followed a pastoral prayer, which the minister requested be heard with heads bowed and eyes closed. But scarcely a minute into the voiced meditation, Elizabeth could not resist peeking, and what she saw made her heart skip a beat. While glancing at Danny, he returned a slight grin and then playfully blew her a kiss. Though surely a little irreverent, it was also one of the most exciting moments she had ever experienced, to see Danny place himself at risk of being caught by others in such a frivolous act. Instantly, he was forgiven, the cold shoulder was forgotten, and she could not wait to engage him in flirtatious small talk at the reception.

"Now that you, Stephen and Hannah, have consented together in holy matrimony and pledged your faith to each other by giving and receiving rings, before God and these witnesses, in the name of the Father, the Son, and the Holy Spirit, I now pronounce you man and wife. What God has joined together, let no man put asunder." With a kindly, almost fatherly grin, J. M. Dawson addressed the groom with six words Steve was waiting to hear: "You may now kiss the bride."

Steve lifted Hannah's veil, and the young couple kissed, drawing some amiable titters from the audience when the show of affection persevered a little beyond "respectable" duration for a church wedding. Then, as prompted by Dr. Dawson, the pair turned to face those gathered in the sanctuary, and the pastor announced, "It is my privilege to present to you, for the first time, Mr. and Mrs. Stephen Brower."

Onlookers arose to express their approbation with a warm round of applause for the newlyweds, and the organist played the "Wedding March" from Felix Mendelssohn's incidental music to *A Midsummer Night's Dream.*

That was when Steve and Hannah Brower made their way up the aisle, arm-in-arm, taking their first steps together as husband and wife. Hidden away in the interior pocket of his tuxedo coat was a tiny book with the handwritten inscription, "Dear Stephen, please keep this NT with you at all times. It will protect you and bring you back to us safely."

◆   ◆   ◆

Still driving the prewar Chevrolet coupe, Wesley picked up Pippa shortly after breakfast, and they were on the road by 8:20. Rob was out in the fields—had been for two and a half hours already—but Jillian waved goodbye to the young people as they traveled down the long driveway and then turned left beyond her line of sight. Wesley promised to have their daughter back home by seven o'clock.

What made this last Monday in August so special was the fact that Wesley Brower and Pippa Glynn would actually be together for an appreciable length of time on a weekday. Except for public gatherings like his high school graduation, very seldom since they met had Wesley ever been with his girlfriend when it was neither a Saturday at The Smoker's Den nor a Sunday at the farmhouse. He thought this might prove to be an interesting excursion for a country girl who had been to a radio station only once in her life, on a school field trip to WACO when she was in the third grade. That was way back in the spring of 1936, so long ago that Wesley's father was still alive.

The boy was now in a position to preside over her visit to KWXN with the authority of a true insider. Baylor's summer quarter had ended on Friday, and the fall quarter would not begin until September 18, so that meant he had more than three weeks off, plenty of opportunity to make some extra money by working full-time. Hugh Kenton assured Wesley that he could find ample hours for him on the audio board, besides which there were promotional assignments to be had, salesmanship by telephone, and of course the three-o'clock performances of "Behold Tomorrow" with their attendant rehearsals. He would show her around the place in grand style.

"What program is your station carrying?" Pippa asked as they drove along.

Wesley had to think for a few seconds. "I'm not sure." He extended his right hand toward the dashboard.

Playfully, she pushed his hand away from the radio dial. "That's cheating. Just tell me what's on KWXN—from memory."

"I don't listen much on weekday mornings."

"But you do sell advertising, don't you?" She stared at him. "So shouldn't you know the broadcast schedule?"

Wesley could not quite decide whether Pippa was serious about learning the answers or just bedeviling him to make mischief. Her expressionless face offered no clue.

"Well, it's either 'Valiant Lady' or 'The Light of the World,' one or the other," Wesley said, but he was none too sure.

"I thought 'Valiant Lady' was going off the air," Pippa told him. "That's what it said in the paper."

Wesley frowned. "You're right. I'd forgotten about that."

"And 'The Light of the World' is moving over to NBC, isn't it?"

He grinned at her, a bit suspicious. "How did you become such a radio buff, all of a sudden?"

"My mother reads *Photoplay* and lots of those other magazines. I guess I caught it from her."

He nodded his head, not entirely convinced by her response, which sounded extemporized on the spot.

"Maybe that's why I'm so interested in your career," she added.

"My what?" He smiled at her, flattered by the choice of words. It was a job, yes, but never had Wesley considered his employment at KWXN to be a career. Perhaps she was right, and it boosted his confidence to know that she had such faith in him.

"Have you ever seen anyone famous—in person?" the girl asked.

"I met Arthur Lake on a train trip."

"Who?"

"Dagwood Bumstead—in the *Blondie* pictures. He signed an autograph for me."

Pippa was not impressed. "I mean someone who's a household name."

"Well ... I watched some people waiting in line to see Frank Sinatra."

She giggled. "That doesn't count."

"I saw William Bendix and Preston Foster on the 'Lux Radio Theatre.' What about them?"

Pippa shook her head. "Sorry."

"And Cecil B. DeMille too. He's very famous."

"The director?"

"Uh-huh."

"Okay. He'll have to do."

"Gee, thanks," Wesley said with a sigh. He wanted nothing more than to be alone with Pippa, but here she was, evidently determined to squander their precious time together with her very own version of Mutual's "Twenty Questions." The idea occurred to him that she might not be as interested as he was in allowing their relationship to develop more fully. Was it conceivable that this inconsequential banter of hers was just a polite way to keep him at arm's length? Still, she certainly did seem cheerful enough, at one point even softly humming while she gazed upon the farmland that extended along Highway 31.

As their day together at KWXN progressed through the morning hours, Wesley hoped his girlfriend would not find it too boring to watch him grapple with such mundane chores as monitoring network audio and typing up promotional spots for staff announcers to read on the air. He need not have worried, for Pippa appeared to be fascinated by every miniscule task that he performed. This came as a welcome relief, and all he could figure was that her mother's show-biz magazines somehow made commercial radio seem more glamorous to the layman than it really was.

One problem, not totally unexpected, was that the prowling Marshall McFall found himself quite enamored with this eye-catching lass from Axtell. She was a new female for him to conquer, and he was simply powerless to refrain from making a play for her. Wesley marveled at how skillfully Pippa was able to parry the announcer's bold advances, leaving him disappointed, frustrated, chagrined, and defeated at every turn. In the end, McFall retreated to his lair, the soundproof booth, to lie in wait for a more responsive temptress to pass his way.

But what gave Wesley more pleasure than anything else was McFall's empty, pining countenance when he left the booth just long enough to ask, "So, where is Sandy these days, Wes?" The question took him by complete surprise, for this was the first time the two had spoken, with a civil tongue anyhow, in almost three years.

Wesley dug in his heels. "Who?"

"Sandy Whittsel. You know ... Sally Holt."

"Oh, her." The shameful way McFall had treated her made Wesley feel justified in stretching the truth a little. "The last I heard, she was married—with one child and another on the way. Her husband is some big executive, as I recall."

The announcer's devastated look was priceless. "Do you think she'll ever come this way again, now that they've written Sally out of the story line for good?"

"Nope. I think you missed your chance. Sandy's long gone—and I doubt that you're on her Christmas card list."

When lunchtime arrived, Wesley and Pippa spent it with his older brother, who had inherited the reins of Superior Office Supply upon the retirement of Wayne Espy in the middle of July. This meant that day-to-day operations of the shop were headed by a Brower once again, for the first time in fifteen years. Nora had nothing but positive things to say about Espy and the dependable stewardship he demonstrated throughout that long period of transition. Elizabeth, too, was now employed by the family firm, though only on a part-time basis. Her job at Service Refining Company had come to an inglorious end when discharged soldiers and sailors returned to the civilian work force in overwhelming numbers. Pretty faces at filling stations could not compete with knowledgeable professionals who sported grease under their fingernails.

The trio ate at the Lone Star Café, on the north side of Austin Avenue, right next door to the Rex Theatre. This was not the first time for Pippa to see Wesley's brother. She was introduced to him and his bride at the wedding reception, where they indulged in the superficial chatter of a receiving line. Two months of marital adjustment were now behind Steve and Hannah, as they experienced the usual ups and downs of young couples who were new to the challenge of coexisting under one roof as husband and wife. Despite the occasional spat or minor annoyance,

somehow they managed to live through it all, and even to fall more deeply in love for their efforts. The scene of this small triumph was a cozy, four-room rental house in north Waco, virtually in the shadow of Providence Hospital.

Steve was waiting for them just inside the restaurant's entrance. After a hostess escorted the three to a table, he proudly announced to Wesley and Pippa that he had driven there in his "new" automobile, which was actually a used 1940 Dodge business coupe with abundant tire tread and very low mileage for a six-year-old vehicle. He bought it for four hundred dollars from an elderly widow in far northwest Waco, an honest-looking woman who maintained that she only drove it to church on Sundays. Steve had no compelling reason to doubt the veracity of her clichéd story, so he blithely accepted it as the gospel truth. And, if the first ten days were any indication, his trusting spirit stood to be rewarded many times over. Steve always was a perceptive judge of character.

"So, how's married life treating you, big brother?" Wesley asked.

"Swell. I recommend it highly," came the reply.

"Is Hannah still working at Baylor?"

"In the Bible office—Dr. Humphrey—but I'm trying to get her to quit. We'd like to have a family, of course. Four or five kids would be nice, at least for starters."

That remark struck Wesley as rather suggestive for mixed company, but he could see that Pippa was not offended.

Steve chuckled to himself. "I get the feeling Hannah's trying to reform me. We're at church every time the door's unlocked—twice on Sundays and even on Wednesday nights."

"Do you go to that same church where you were married?" Pippa asked.

"Yep, First Baptist." Steve thought for a moment. "I keep forgetting you're not a Waco girl. Where are you from?"

"Axtell."

"I've heard of it."

Wesley laughed. "Golly, it's just down the road. She's not from another planet, you know."

Steve studied the girl. "No, she definitely looks like an earthling to me. And a very pretty one at that. I approve of your keen eye for gals, Wes."

"Thanks. I think so too." The boy winked at his girlfriend.

"Oh, and on top of everything else, I start teaching a Bible study class this coming Sunday—when the new church year opens. Like I say, she's putting me on the straight and narrow."

"Nothing wrong with that," Pippa told him. "In fact, I think it's wonderful."

"I do too, really," Steve said. "I tease Hannah a lot, but she's a positive influence on me, and I guess the Good Lord brought us together for a reason."

Pippa smiled at him. "That's a sweet thing to say, and I'm sure it's true."

"I've even given up a couple of my Navy vices—drinking beer and smoking cigarettes," he told the girl. "But I'm still working on tossing away the pipe."

"Ooh, I love the smell of a pipe!" she said. "My daddy is a pipe smoker."

"Is that so?"

"In fact, he works at my uncle's tobacco shop on Saturdays."

Wesley added, "Where do you think those three packages came from that I mailed to you?"

"Ah, yes—the Philip Morris Bond Street. Nice choice."

"I can't take all the credit," Wesley said. "That cute saleslady helped a little."

Steve nodded his thanks to Pippa, who offered a suggestion to him. "Maybe someday you can teach Wes to smoke a pipe."

"Could be," he said, "although I'm certainly not what you would call a connoisseur. Your dad is probably twice the expert I am."

When the soup and sandwiches arrived, Wesley mouthed to the waitress, "One check," and pointed to himself. Steve initially balked at the idea, but his younger brother insisted. "I'm drawing a full-time paycheck for the next few weeks, so I can afford to bankroll your eighty-five cents."

Steve grinned and gave Wesley a salute. "Aye aye, sir, since you put it that way. I wasn't aware of your newfound wealth."

About that time, a commonplace piece of tableware attracted Pippa's eye, an accessory she had seldom encountered in recent years. There, next to the usual salt and pepper shakers, rested a bowl of real sugar—despite the fact that the Second War Powers Act mandated rationing through March 31, 1947, and the OPA was advocating an additional year on top of that. Feeling extravagant, she stirred two heaping spoonfuls into her tall glass of iced tea and sampled the tempting beverage. It tasted deliciously postwar.

The girl turned to Steve. "Do I remember Wes telling me that you spent your honeymoon in North Carolina?"

"We did, yes. It wasn't exactly Niagara Falls, but we had a swell time just the same. Hannah's from there, and her relatives were grand—treated us like royalty. There were lots of loose ends to tie up after her father's death."

"That's a long train trip," Pippa said.

"Sure was—too long for comfort—and I can tell you, those upper berths aren't designed for two people."

She smiled. "Sounds romantic, though."

"Can be—especially for newlyweds, of course." Steve laughed, but then he noticed that the girl was blushing a little, so he directed the conversation elsewhere.

"Say, Wes, your Bears will be back on the gridiron this season, won't they?"

"That's what I hear. But not one of them has played a single down of college football yet, so they'll be plenty rusty."

"Are you a football fan, Miss Glynn?" Steve asked.

"No, not really. Except for the Longhorns."

"Texas is always strong."

Wesley shook his head. "I think she means the Axtell Longhorns. Pippa is kind of provincial when it comes to sports."

"I've never been to a college game," she said, "but I'm hoping that Wes will take me to one this season."

"Well, don't expect too much from Baylor's team this year," Steve told her. "The war saw to that."

After the meal was finished, Steve showed them his newly acquired automobile. Then he bid them goodbye with a pointed comment. "Listen, why don't Hannah and I have you two over for dinner sometime? Give you a glimpse of married life."

His younger brother eyed him suspiciously. Was it really that obvious?

◆   ◆   ◆

Part-time receptionist Naomi Hardesty had relinquished her post by the time Wesley and Pippa returned to the radio station from their meal with Steve. Myra Culp was back on duty after her lunch break, and she extended her arm like a traffic cop to stop the two young people, who were rushing by her desk. "Aren't you going to introduce me to your friend?" she asked. Somehow, Myra had failed to catch sight of the pair both times that they passed through the lobby that morning.

"Oh, sorry," Wesley told her. "Myra, this is Pippa Glynn. Pippa ... Myra Culp, the receptionist."

Myra smiled at the girl. "How do you do? My, you're a very sweet thing. Do you go to Waco High?"

"No, ma'am. I graduated from Axtell. Wesley's giving me a tour."

"Gee, you don't look old enough to be out of high school," the receptionist said. Then she added with a giggle, "Maybe you can take over as Sally Holt, now that Sandy Whittsel is gone. Our Hoopers are sinking fast without her. You know, Wes brought Sandy to the station too, and sometimes lightning will strike twice."

Wesley pulled Pippa after him. "We've got to hurry, Myra. Sorry, but I think Mr. Kenton is expecting us." The girl nearly stumbled, so urgent was Wesley's tug on her arm.

Rather than going to the control room, however, he escorted Pippa to that bastion of creative writing, the copy room, where he normally shared desk space with an intern named Betty Coats. Betty was a college student from Hobbs, New Mexico—just beyond the state border—but she would be gone for the remainder of the interim period, until Baylor classes resumed in the fall. Wesley sat at the typewriter, and Pippa took a chair beside him, admiring his every hunt and peck. He wrote three commercials, two promos, and one public service announcement in scarcely more than an hour. All the while, fortyish Edgar Wilkins, seated across the room, kept glancing at the delightful stranger, but he never did intrude.

Now it was time to shift mental gears and become Kip Hanson in the flesh. Wesley took Pippa on a roundabout, indirect passage to Studio A, so as to avoid the receptionist's unsolicited advice for casting "Behold Tomorrow." En route, they crossed paths with Douglas Pierson and Phyllis Sherry, who played the roles of Anson and Jeannie Gabriel in the serial.

"Did you get the rewrite?" Phyllis asked the boy. "Nothing specifically for Kip, but there's three quarters of a page that might make you lose your place."

Wesley frowned. "Nope. When did this happen?"

Pierson slapped his script with the backs of his fingers. "Oh, that numskull Monica's asleep at the switch again." Out of respect for the charming visitor in their presence, Pierson tempered his language considerably. Not known for his meek tolerance of slapdash workmanship, he ordinarily would have tracked the perpetrator down and upbraided her in no uncertain terms. Douglas Pierson and Monica Whaley were anything but the best of friends. Indeed, they rarely had a polite word to say to one another, unless the inhibiting factor of a studio audience left them with no other choice.

"Well, thanks for the warning," Wesley said. He gestured for his girlfriend to move along, not deeming it a wise idea for the station's dirty laundry to be on display like this. Pippa, though, was not at all disturbed by the lack of decorum, and she followed Wesley away with some reluctance, even trying to eavesdrop on the receding conversation behind her.

Quite by accident, Dave Flint flicked on the studio lights just as the two young people were entering, and it took the girl by surprise. She patted her chest in shock. "That gave me the scare of my life! I thought it was something I did."

Hugh Kenton noticed her stunned reaction all the way from the control room, so he kidded her over the intercom. "Your friend really lights up a room, Wes."

A few minutes later, with all of the actors in place, the director decreed that it was perfectly fine for Pippa to be in the studio during rehearsal, though of course she would need to vacate the area prior to airtime. While the run-through was in progress, Monica slipped Wesley his page 7-A, copies of which everyone else already had in their possession.

"And kindly inform Doug that he can go to hell, for all I care," Monica told the boy. "Feel free to quote me on that." Those were strong words, coming from a lady as proper as Monica Whaley, and she pronounced them loudly enough for the intended recipient to hear her suggestion with minimal effort. Then, having delivered the missing page, she strutted out of the studio, stomping both feet as she went. Apparently, Monica wished to disrupt the rehearsal to the utmost extreme while not quite losing her job in the process.

"Sorry you had to hear such language, miss," Pierson said to the guest, "but that's what goes on backstage around here." The other cast members grinned slightly—all but Wesley, that is.

"What gives?" Kenton shouted over the speakers. He was in no mood to brook dissension, not with the performance only twenty-five minutes away.

Neddy Wright improvised into the closest microphone. "Oh, just Monica, letting off some steam."

Kenton knew better. "Don't bother covering for him, Neddy. I know Doug was involved in this somehow. His fingerprints are all over it."

"Now listen, Hugh—" Pierson said, only to be stopped short by the director.

"Believe me, I'll clear the studio, if I have to go that far. We're all on the same team, folks, so simmer down and pay attention to your lines. Monica does her best, and more often than not it's the writers who instigate those last-minute changes. Don't use her as a whipping girl."

At five minutes before three, Pippa was ushered into the control room by soundman Brian Quaid, who then returned to his audio console in time to meet the network break. Marshall McFall showed up about then too, and he sauntered to his announcer's booth, winking at the pert young lady as he passed.

"You may want to watch from in here," he said. "It affords a great view of Studio A."

"No, thank you," Pippa told him, and she looked aside.

"I promise to be on my best behavior."

"No, thanks ... really," the girl said again, this time with a smile. In spite of herself, she was amused by his overzealous ego.

McFall shrugged his shoulders. "Well, if you change your mind ..."

The show went swimmingly—indeed, to such a splendid degree that even the fastidious Hugh Kenton was ecstatic. He puffed on his cigar and had to chuckle at Neddy's final lines in the concluding scene. "Well done, Raymond Temple!" he declared, a testament to the newest writer on the staff.

But there was little time to wallow in self-congratulation. "West of the Brazos" would begin right after the commercial break, and as Kenton knew only too well from personal experience, many a triumph paved the way to a calamitous train wreck. A director was merely as good as his last production, which is what made live radio so exhilarating—and so intimidating. Cast and crew could scale the heights and plunge the depths in the course of a single daredevilish, tightrope-walking minute of airtime.

The young man who portrayed Kip Hanson greeted Pippa in the hushed control room, just as the next serial was about to begin. She beamed with joy and squeezed his hand. Never had she been more proud of anyone whom she knew to be a friend. Though Wesley Brower spoke just ten expendable lines in that day's radio play, he was solely responsible for its success. He was a genius, a brilliant star, an actor of the first magnitude. In her eyes, he could do no wrong.

♦   ♦   ♦

Following a two-hour stint on the audio board—during which time Wesley rode the gain for, among other shows, the network broadcasts of two kids' adventures, "Cimarron Tavern" and "The Sparrow and the Hawk"—he took his lovely companion to the front of the station. Pippa was in the most buoyant of moods, exploiting Wesley's ticklish midriff to delirious effect. Then she interlocked her arm with his, and they marched step for step, laughing as they whistled and sang Johnny Mercer's current hit, "Personality," popularized by Dorothy Lamour in the Crosby-Hope picture, *The Road to Utopia*.

Myra Culp was smiling when they arrived at her desk. "Hey, you two sound pretty good as a duet—considering that Wes can't sing a lick."

"That says something for Pippa then," he said.

It was just after six o'clock, so the receptionist, too, was about to leave for the day. "Here's your mail. You never did pick it up."

"Nope, I forgot." Wesley grinned at his friend. "I was kind of distracted today." He flipped through the paltry total of four envelopes and handed them to Pippa, who seemed impressed.

"Gosh, do you always get this many fan letters?" the girl asked. She looked more closely at them, one by one.

"That's hard to say. It just depends on how much airtime I'm getting. Sometimes there's not a single piece."

Surely with no ill intent, Myra placed his latest haul in historical perspective. "I remember when Sandy Whittsel used to get two dozen or more almost every day. We had to toss them in a basket for her—heaps of letters from the Sally Club of Waco."

Wesley frowned at the comment but tried to be philosophical about it. "Well, at least the ratings haven't quite sunk our ship yet. That's all that really matters." He stepped aside to let the receptionist pass by. "See you tomorrow, Myra."

Walking toward the door, purse in hand, Myra smiled back at both of them. "Good night, Wes. Nice meeting you, Miss Glynn."

"Thank you, Miz Culp," the girl said. "All of the people here have been so kind."

Myra laughed. "Then you must have caught us on a good day!" She exited the building and turned left, where her automobile was parked in the shade of a tree. The 1936 Dodge had a windshield crack that resembled a huge spider web, causing it to be very difficult to maneuver whenever she was heading west after work. She would drive home slowly.

Wesley and his girlfriend went to the main parking lot, the one on the right. As they strolled along, it could not escape his attention that Pippa appeared to be much more subdued than she had been only moments before. Once inside the automobile, she said not a word, and as Wesley started the engine, he had a distinct feeling that the girl was staring at him. He turned and saw that there were tears forming in her eyes.

"We need to have an understanding," she told him. "Can we go somewhere and talk?"

Indeed, the same thought had occurred to him, many times over, during the course of their day together, and he was hoping that she would be receptive to the idea of making their intentions known to each other. "Sure, we can," he said, "and I know just the place."

Wesley drove them out to Cameron Park, where he positioned the Chevrolet in a scenic clearing, about a hundred feet from the banks of the lazily flowing Brazos River. He turned off the engine and, rubbing his chin nervously, gazed at the panorama before him.

After a minute or so had passed, Pippa began to say something, but Wesley, being the man, felt it was his duty and responsibility to speak first. "I've been wanting to ask you an important question—for a long time," he said. Surely her face would brighten.

But it was sadness, not glee, that swept over her. "I wish it were that simple, Wes," she said. "I really do."

His mouth fell open. "I don't understand."

"I mean, I wish life were just a matter of popping the question and then living happily ever after. Call me overly cautious, but I don't plan to get married more than once. That's just how I'm made."

A third A-bomb, detonated in McLennan County, could hardly have shaken Wesley any more than this forthright statement did. He tried to grasp the full significance of what she avowed, for it was very likely that their entire future together depended upon how he handled the next few minutes.

"Tell me what's bothering you," he said. "I think you owe me that much."

In response, Pippa simply handed him one of the four envelopes. It had been sent to the radio station, in care of "Mr. Wesley Brower," and in the upper left corner was a florid set of initials, "S. J. W.," but no return address.

Wesley gulped nervously, avoiding the girl's eyes. "Why did you give this to me?"

"Maybe you should open it now, while I'm here with you," she told him.

"I'd rather not waste time reading fan mail. We need to get you home by seven."

The girl gazed at the envelope. "Do you believe in fate?" she asked.

"Not really. Why?"

"Do you think God can bring things into our lives that keep us from making terrible, impulsive mistakes?"

"That's not fate. It's called divine intervention."

"Fine. Whatever the term is, do you believe in it?"

Wesley stared at her, dreading some unforeseen snag that might lay ruin to their whole relationship. "Are you talking about this mail?"

"It's from Sandra Whittsel, isn't it?"

"How should I know? Those initials could belong to a lot of people."

"Why don't you open it and find out?"

"Right now?"

"If you don't mind."

Fearing the worst, Wesley used the ignition key to slice open the envelope. Then, after unfolding the letter, he began reading to himself. Pippa gave him enough time to finish.

"So it was from her," she said when he looked up.

"Yes." He laid the sheet of paper on his lap. "I hope you don't think getting letters from Sandy is an everyday thing for me. This is only the second one I've ever received."

"How long ago was the first one?"

"In April, just before my brother came home from the war."

"Did you ever write her back?"

"No. I couldn't have, even if I wanted to. As you can see, she doesn't bother to show her address."

"*Did* you want to write her back?"

"I guess so, sure. Why not?"

Pippa glanced down at the unfolded letter. "So, how is she doing?"

"Oh, Sandy always lands on her feet," he said. "It says she worked at a Savannah radio station for a few months, hosting a children's show mostly, but now she's back to acting again—in the big city."

"Atlanta?"

"Yep."

"I suppose that means she won't be returning here."

"I guess she never will. Waco must seem like small potatoes to her now, and she wants to latch on with one of the networks."

There was a pause before Pippa asked, "Is she married?"

"She doesn't mention anything about that, but I'm sure she's not."

"How do you know?"

"Because it's the first thing she would have told me." Wesley nodded his head and smirked. "Yessiree, that Sandy had the world by the tail—or so she thought."

"Wasn't Sandra Whittsel the one I saw kissing you at graduation?"

"Did she? I don't recall."

"Oh, sure!"

"It's possible that she kissed me. I really can't say."

"Well, if she didn't, then someone else certainly did. I was walking toward you with my parents, and I couldn't have missed something like that."

"Okay," he said upon further reflection, "I guess maybe it was Sandy after all. But her kiss wasn't a romantic one—just on the cheek."

"She's a pretty girl, don't you think?"

Wesley did not answer, sensing that any response whatsoever could only make matters worse.

"Well, isn't she? Be honest."

He shrugged his shoulders. "Sure, I can't deny that. I find her to be extremely attractive. Is that what you want me to say?"

"Say whatever you want, but if you're serious about me, I think you ought to forget about your old flame."

"She's not an old flame. My gosh, Sandy wouldn't even give me the time of day when she was running with her beloved Marshall McFall."

"Then why did they break up?"

"I think he found somebody else. He likes to chase the ladies, you know."

"No fooling ..."

Wesley chuckled. "He does that to all the girls, so don't feel too flattered."

"Why did you tell him that Sandy's married, with two kids?"

"I just said that to make Marshall squirm. He treated her like dirt."

"And you felt a sense of duty to defend her honor?"

"Sandy was a good friend, that's all."

Pippa looked out the passenger window. "Is she still available?"

"I suppose so—theoretically. Like I say, I don't think she's ever gotten married."

The girl turned to him and glared. "You know what I mean. Is she still available to *you?*"

Wesley sighed. "Why do you keep talking about Sandy?"

"Because she still means a lot to you. I can tell. Call it woman's intuition."

"She's a thousand miles away."

"She's as close as a three-cent stamp!"

The sudden fire in Pippa's eyes took him off guard. "Gee, whiz ..."

"It's true, Wes. Like it or not, Sandra Whittsel could write to you tomorrow, and it might start all over again. And where would that leave me?" Her eyes were filling with tears again. "If we're ever going to make plans for the future, then I have to know that your heart will remain faithful to one special person. I'm very traditional in that way."

Wesley shook his head. "There was nothing to it—honest. Sandy was a fantasy, a figment of my imagination. She was just a tease."

"Did she tease *you*?"

He paused, reminding himself to be careful. "I'm sure she did, in a certain way. But nothing physical. Like I told you before, I never saw her naked."

"Would you like to have seen her that way, with no clothes on?"

"Of course! That's a silly question. I would like to see any girl naked—and particularly her."

"But you never did."

"No."

"And that's one of your life's biggest disappointments."

"Yes."

Pippa sulked for a few seconds, but then the iciness thawed somewhat, and she actually began to smile. "Well, I guess that's one advantage I have over Sandra Whittsel, huh?"

He grinned back. "A beautiful advantage."

"Why, thank you."

"But it's not just a matter of how pretty I think you are. There's so much more about you ... things that I can't even begin to ... things I ..." Unable to find the right words, Wesley took the girl's hand and held it tightly in his own. "Pippa Glynn, I love you, and I want to be with you forever—more than anything else in the world." He hated how formal that sounded, but it was too late now to retrieve the words and start over.

Pippa, though, appeared to accept them in the proper spirit. She looked up at him and said, "I love you too, Wes. I have loved you from the very beginning, and I told you that the first time you came to visit me."

He nodded his head and smiled. "I remember."

She smiled too, but then, mere seconds later, she started to cry very softly to herself.

"I hope those are tears of happiness," Wesley said.

Sniffling, she giggled at him. "I think so."

"You *think* so?"

"I don't seem to be very sure of anything right now."

"You can be sure of me. I promise."

The calm way he stated it gave her the strength to study Wesley's face, searching for—and finding—the truth in his eyes. "I believe you," she said. "I really and truly do."

He reached out and brushed the hair from her forehead, and they gently kissed. Her upper lip was wet from the tears. A moment later, Wesley took a deep breath, and he heard himself say—in an unfamiliar, shaky voice—"Pippa, will you marry me?"

There was no hesitation. "Of course I'll marry you, Wes."

The boy leaned toward the girl, and they kissed again, only this time with a confident embrace that affirmed their nascent bond. Neither of them would ever forget the pristine setting that surrounded them, nor the soft sounds of nature that filled the air.

"My heart is pounding so hard!" Pippa said.

Wesley grinned. "Mine too."

And yet it all proved a bit too much for people so young. Feeling stunned, both of them fell silent for a moment, trying to fully appreciate the monumental import of what they had decided.

Finally, Wesley spoke. "I remember the first day we ever met. It was exactly a year and seven months ago—well, it will be tomorrow—and that's longer than most engagements are these days."

"Yes, it is."

"So no one can say we're barging into this," he added, perhaps trying to convince himself.

"No, they can't." She gazed into his eyes. "I don't feel that way, do you?"

"No, of course not." And that was when Wesley suggested one small proviso. "It can't be until after this school year."

"I understand. My daddy probably wouldn't let me go before then anyway. I'm an extra hired hand right now."

"Maybe next summer?"

"That sounds fine," she said.

A few unwelcome mosquitoes were beginning to circle around them, but the summer air was much too warm for rolling up the windows to keep such nuisances out. Wesley clapped in their general direction a couple of times, and that aggressive show of force was just enough to chase the insects away for good.

"When should we tell your parents?" he asked.

"I don't know. What do you think?"

"How about tonight?"

Pippa shivered at the notion. "Gee, that seems so sudden."

"Well, whatever you say. They're your parents, not mine."

The girl considered for a minute, and in just that brief time, her courage came rushing back like a torrent. "We'll tell them tonight," she said. With a determined look, she nodded her head and repeated, "Yes, we'll tell them tonight."

"And I'll let my mother know right when I get home."

They smiled at each another and then sat back, staring straight ahead until it was time to leave the beauty of Cameron Park. This was an exciting stage in their youthful lives, but more than a little frightening too.

Overwhelmed by the day's events, Pippa said next to nothing on the way to Axtell, so Wesley's mind was free to wander. He thought back through the convoluted history of how this happy moment had come about—so inexplicable, unlikely, and wondrous did it seem, as if an unseen hand had guided him to this point in his life. He remembered his newspaper route … his first day at KWXN … meeting Sandra Whittsel … the new boarder … his fractured arm … the trip west … the soldier boy who rescued his sister … becoming radio's Kip Hanson … his crush on Giulia Coletti … The Smoker's Den … Rob Glynn … high school graduation … Sandy's goodbye … Pippa … her horses … the windmill … the swim … their vows of love. This pleasant reverie continued for a long while, with hardly a word from the young lady at his side.

As they neared the Axtell turnoff from State Highway 31, the sun was just beginning to dip below the horizon. It was about then that Pippa spoke up once again. "We'll have a wonderful life together. I'm sure of it."

"Same here," Wesley said. He gave her a roguish grin. "Do you mind if I stay in radio?"

"Of course not. Do you mind if I have a couple of horses, so we can go riding in the evenings?"

"I'd like that very much—as long as you let mine walk and don't go swatting him on the rear."

She laughed. "Agreed. But that's no way to become a horseman."

By this time, the farmhouse had come into view, and its porch light was shining brightly through the dusk. Rob Glynn was sitting there in a rocking chair, contentedly smoking a pipe, and he did not trouble himself to look up as the automobile approached. Somehow, he seemed different to Wesley's eyes now—more like a father-in-law than a business client or even a friend—and surely that was a good sign.

"I only hope I can think of the right things to say," the boy whispered to his fiancée.

Pippa squeezed his arm and said, "Don't worry about him too much. Daddy just wants me to be happy—and he knows how crazy I am about you."

After parking at the side of the house, Wesley trotted around the rear of the automobile to open the girl's door. He said a silent prayer as he went, more certain than ever before that it would be answered.

www.ingramcontent.com/pod-product-compliance
Lightning Source LLC
Chambersburg PA
CBHW031923110726

47902CB00001B/18